# The Mutant Epoch Expansion Rules

# THE MUTANT EPOCH™
## TABLETOP ADVENTURE ROLEPLAYING GAME
# EXPANSION RULES

**Writers** William McAusland, Danny Seedhouse, Dr. James Butler, Colin Chapman, Brandon Goeringer

*Plus further writing, contributions, ideas and help by these fine excavators: Timothy Berriault, Brutorz Bill, Thaddeus Moore, Blood Axe, Mike McMillan, C.H.U.D., Corryn, Graeme Hallett, Stu Brooks, Thomas Vida, Ed Pegg Jr., Bubba H., Azaria Wagner, Christine Jones, Charles Barber, TalonHunteR, Matthew Fisher, Dennis & Melissa Pipes, and hundreds of other long time supporters, Epochians, art fans, family members, stalwart friends, and game shop staffers. Thank you all!*

**Illustrated by William McAusland**

**Published by Outland Arts**

"Putting YOU in the Game"

**www.mutantepoch.com**

OLA1014      ISBN 978-0-9949237-9-0      First published October 2024



**https://www.outlandarts.com/expansionrules.htm**

**Outland Arts**
1860 Lodgepole Drive
Kamloops, B.C. Canada
V1S IX8

# Table of Contents

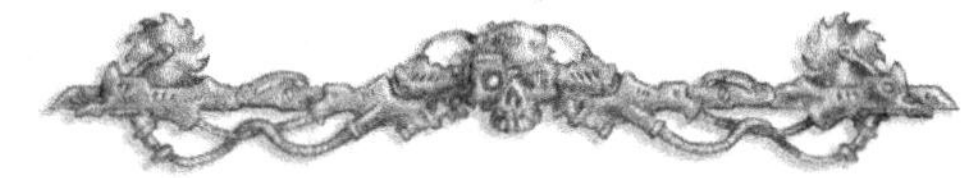

# Introduction

This is the largest and most important book in The Mutant Epoch RPG line since the Hub Rules came out in 2011. Besides having 13 new character types, a vast array of new cybernetic implants, mutations, and relic treasures, it also offers a few new and enhanced rules to cover encumbrance, outfitting, critical hits, and more. Although mutant monsters are not included in this book, the terrifying new robots, MAVs and drones can certainly see double duty as both treasures to uncover and foes to engage. Here too are optional rules for dimensional portals, travel, and beings, as well as relics associated with them, which offer an incredible way to expand campaign possibilities.

While creating characters with just the hub rules produces incredible freaks, especially among the mutants, with the addition of this book, the possibilities are truly endless. Consider the Mutant Epoch Expansion Rules to be part two of the hub rules, and indeed, this book often refers to tables and pages within that book, and is required for use with this tome. With the addition of plantoids, unique robots and androids, digital beings, parasites, abominations, rebuilt, grafters, nanoborgs, halfies, mutorgs, vat-brains, and 35 more bestial human strains, the entities that players and GMs will build using this book are going to be unforgettable. To see some examples of what the author created, go to this book's dedicated webpage and download the character sheet PDFs. These wasteland heroes and misfits can be used as examples, NPCs, or pre-generated player characters.

The sudden appearance of these new character types into an existing Mutant Epoch campaign setting might be hard to explain, just like the addition of new creatures after the release of a new bestiary sourcebook. One way to handle the influx of intelligent oddities is to suggest that they've always been around, but either kept their mutations, parent species, or creation hidden under the rags, furs and plastic covering that are so commonly worn by new era citizens. A game master might want to explain the arrival of some of the stranger beings, such as parasites, abominations, digital beings, and self aware robots and androids by having the existing, hub rules created characters uncover a facility, and purposefully or inadvertently free them. Or else, imply that some sort of migration happened, or that mechanical and digital beings, along with vat-brains, were the minions of a recently defeated AI overlord, and the now self aware, liberated high tech beings spread across the mutated world.

The recommended way to learn about and adopt these new player characters types is for the GM to create several and deploy them as NPCs, either as adversaries to the player characters, or else inhabitants who serve as guides, hostages to be rescued, important personages to be escorted, or patrons who recruit the PCs.

Some of the new character types in this book are straightforward, quick to generate, and great for new TME players and game masters alike. Others, such as digital beings, vat-brains, parasites and both android and robot characters, are more complicated and time intensive to create. Use table XR-1 on page 7 as a guideline on what character types are appropriate for beginner, intermediate and expert players of The Mutant Epoch RPG. This table includes all the player type possibilities from both the hub rules and this book. Of course, if the game master allows it, the players can simply pick what character type they want to play. As with the hub rules, there are 6 methods of character generation, from totally random, heroic, and all the way to a point buy system as described on pages 7 to 8. The Excavator Monthly Compendium book, incidentally, offers 6 more PC generation systems. The author prefers the 9 rolls system himself.

This sourcebook's table codes are shown as Table XR-14, Table XR-88, etc. or page numbers as XR-28, XR 50, or shown without a proceeding code such as page 36 or page 69, etc. Meanwhile, any page or table from the hub rules is referred to by Table TME-1-6 or page TME-22, etc. And going forward for all TME and Outland System RPG products, skill points are abbreviated as skp and not sp, since sp denotes silver pieces.

While you don't need a d30 at your table, you can either use a popular dice roller app on your phone, print, cut out, and assemble one from the link here, at the XR book's web page https://www.outlandarts.com/TME-Expansion-Rules/Outland_Arts-TME-d30-dice-industrial-texture.pdf, or roll a d6+d10*, but we recommend you buy a d30 as its use is called for with this book.

*1d30 Simulator: Roll d6 for the tens column: 1,2 = +0/ 3,4 = +10/ 5,6 = +20. Add a 1d10 roll for the one's column.

Delayed by plague, inability to stay away from three other books, and a full retinal detachment in my right eye, this sourcebook has been a long time coming. Over the last seven years, I doubted I could complete the XR book. That it was too vast, too complex, and that the illustration count of 1225 interior images alone would break me. Still, I pressed on, encouraged by the Epochian community both online and in person, as well as my family.

Now it is done, and I can finally get to other endeavours. Indeed, the Expansion Rules book has been like a great dam in a colossal creative river. Behind this behemoth of post-apocalyptic gaming goodness, we've got several RPG books lined up and ready for art and play testing, the TME novel series, a third party publisher license and resource zone, short adventures, supplements and other surprises are all in the works.

While I've tackled all the art, layout and other publishing chores, and about 90% of the writing, I want to thank the many contributors to this tome. Some provided material many years ago on our forum or sent suggestions and game ready content via email, while others, especially Danny Seedhouse, have worked closely with me to write and test play new rules specifically for this book. Thank you all. I couldn't have done this without you.

Like what you see here? Why not share your thoughts on The Mutant Epoch Expansion Rules with fellow gamers or write a quick review wherever you bought it, or on tabletop gaming forums and sites? We sure would appreciate the signal boost, and truthfully, getting a review is a lot harder than getting a sale and has an enormous impact on spreading the word. Please let us know where you left a review so we can share it, too! Like the art from this and other Mutant Epoch books? It's all human made, like all our products with zero AI involvement. While much of the art is tiny, nearly all of it is up for sale either individually or as full pages cut from my stack of sketchbooks. Interested collectors can check out our originals for sale page here: https://www.outlandarts.com/mcauslandart4sale.htm

Finally, let's connect online via social media and other online venues. You can find the links to all the places Epochians gather from our website at mutantepoch.com. Please share your muties, relate your post-apocalyptic adventures, and your characters from both this book and the hub rules. Use the following hashtags when posting so others can enjoy your TME content and experiences, and so we can find you, too: #mutantepoch #tmeexpansionrules #expansionrules #postapocalyptic #themutantepoch #outlandsystem #outlandarts

Happy gaming,
William McAusland

# Character Generation

## New Character Types

This book includes 13 new character types: Abominations, Androids, Bestial Humans set 2, Digital Beings, Grafters, Halfies, Mutorgs, Nanoborgs, Parasites, Plantoids, Rebuilts, Robots, and Vat-Brains.

Prior to creating a character, game masters are here reminded that there is an alternate character generation system in appendix 3 on page 501 whereby characters can start as 'Popsicle People'. These are individuals who've not grown up on the surface of The Mutant Epoch world and are instead cryo-frozen people who don't know what awaits on the surface. This system is perfect for introducing new players to The Mutant Epoch game and setting, players whose in-game persona's will have no idea about the varied creatures and perils of the twisted new era.

For standard character creation, which mirrors the method used in the Hub Rules book, first roll on the following table XR-1 for your character type based on your experience playing The Mutant Epoch.

Secondly, flip to the description of that character type in either the TME Hub Rules or this book. Most character types use the standard trait generation system, but a few use a combination of their own plus the standard table, or else an entirely unique system.

Third, most character types will then establish their pre-game caste on table XR-4. A few variants, such as more complicated PCs like unique robots and androids, use their own caste determination method. A pre-game caste will usually provide the character with several starting skills, an outfitting code, and other potential talents determined from themed random lists. After this, determine mutations, implants and other features for your new character.

**Table XR-1 / Character Type Determination Expanded     Roll 1d100**

| Beginning Player | Experienced Player | Master Player | Character Type | Book Page |
|---|---|---|---|---|
| 01,02 | 01-04 | 01-03 | **Abomination** | XR-25 |
| 03,04 | 05-07 | 04-08 | **Android** | XR-29 |
| 05-11 | 08-12 | 09-10 | **Bestial Human, set 2** | XR-58 |
| - | 13,14 | 11-14 | **Digital Being** | XR-66 |
| 12-15 | 15,16 | 15,16 | **Grafter** | XR-85 |
| 16-18 | 17-19 | 17,18 | **Halfie** | XR-93 |
| 19-22 | 20-23 | 19,20 | **Mutorg** | XR-99 |
| 23,24 | 24,25 | 21,22 | **Nanoborg** | XR-100 |
| - | 26-28 | 23-27 | **Parasite** | XR-106 |
| 25-32 | 29-34 | 28-32 | **Plantoid** | XR-114 |
| 33-35 | 35-37 | 33,34 | **Rebuilt** | XR-142 |
| 36-38 | 38-40 | 35-41 | **Robot** | XR-151 |
| - | 41,42 | 42-48 | **Vat-Brain** | XR-187 |
| 39-50 | 43-49 | 49-53 | **Pure Stock Human** | HUB-18 |
| 51 | 50 | - | **Clone, Comfort** | HUB-19 |
| 52 | 51 | 54 | **Clone, Labor** | HUB-19 |
| 53 | 52,53 | 55,56 | **Clone, Military** | HUB-19 |
| 54 | 54 | - | **Bioreplica, Pleasure** | HUB-18 |
| 55 | 55 | 57 | **Bioreplica, Industrial** | HUB-18 |
| 56 | 56 | - | **Bioreplica, Clerical** | HUB-18 |
| 57 | 57 | 58,59 | **Bioreplica, Infiltration** | HUB-18 |
| 58 | 58,59 | 60,61 | **Bioreplica, Battle** | HUB-18 |
| 59,60 | 60-62 | 62-66 | **Trans-Human** | HUB-20 |
| 61-70 | 63-69 | 67-72 | **Cyborg** | HUB-21 |
| 71-77 | 70-75 | 73-75 | **Bestial Human. Set 1** | HUB-24 |
| 78-83 | 76-81 | 76-82 | **Ghost Mutant** | HUB-22 |
| 84-88 | 82,83 | 83,84 | **Mutant, Mild** | HUB-22 |
| 89-98 | 84-92 | 85-89 | **Mutant, Typical** | HUB-22 |
| 99,00 | 93-98 | 90-96 | **Mutant, Severe** | HUB-22 |
| - | 99,00 | 97-00 | **Mutant, Freakish Horror** | HUB-22 |

**Table Use:** A Beginning Player rolls a 1d100 and scrolls down to the resulting number, then reads the row across to the right to locate the Character Type. Example: Beginning players rolls a 63, looks down under that column to see result in the 61-70 range. Player therefore has a cyborg character.

## Character Traits Revisited

For most characters, such as pure stock humans, mutants, mutorgs, rebuilt, ghost mutants, cyborgs and others, traits are determined randomly on table XR-2 by rolling 1d100 cross indexed with a set value, possibly adding 1d20 for high rolls. For other character types and unique species, such as robots, abominations, vat-brains, clones and bioreplicas, traits are rolled using set boundaries stated under that character type or creature's listing, or, as in the case of trans-humans, unique androids, and bestial humans, a typical random roll plus possible bonuses to each trait are made.

There are eight main character traits, which usually act alone in game play, but occasionally a pair are added together and divided by two to get a unique trait for a certain hazard check. There is no maximum to base (uninjured) trait values, but there is a minimum of 1 trait point.

| Name | Code | Description |
|---|---|---|
| Endurance | END | One's stamina, toughness, immunity, damage threshold prior to unconsciousness or death. |
| Strength | STR | This is one's muscular development. It applies to the amount of damage done from physical, non-energy or ballistic attacks, as well as the range one can hurl physical objects or projectile mutations. |
| Agility | AG | This is one's quickness, ability to evade attacks and affect one's defense value and movement rate modifier. |
| Accuracy | ACC | This trait affects aim with any sort of weapon, as well as hand eye coordination, therefore altering one's strike value. |
| Intelligence | INT | This trait encompasses memory, IQ, and basic smarts and is often used in mental mutation statistics. |
| Perception | PER | Perception is an overall sensory trait, combining visual awareness, hearing, empathy and reaction time. It affects initiative. |
| Willpower | WILL | This trait illustrates one's drive, motivation, self awareness and control. It is often used for or against mental mutations. |
| Appearance | APP | One's physical looks, based on human standards. Occasionally a mutant's head could have a different appearance value than the body, which could be concealed. One's ugliness or attractiveness is often a factor when encountering beings with human ancestry. |

## Trait Generation Systems

It is the Game Master's prerogative as to which system of character generation is used. The rules and encounter tables are set up to challenge characters generated using the standard system; however, the high mortality of low rank, poorly equipped characters might be frustrating to some players, or, if each player is asked to create two or three characters, the GM may allow one of heroic proportions to act as the player's 'self', with the other two player controlled characters acting as back up should the main character die. Normally one player will control one player character (PC).

There are dozens of possible systems to generating characters, but the following are some of the easiest to explain to new players and are the most balanced.

**Standard System:** Roll each of the eight traits in order, as rolled, no value trades or switches, totally fate determined.

**Nine Rolls:** Generate the eight traits in order, plus one extra roll, which can be substituted for any one weak trait value. Clones, bioreplicas, bestial humans and other types are allowed to re-roll any one low score in their fixed trait range.

**Shuffle Roll:** Roll eight trait values and place them as the player desires. Not usable for clones, bestial humans, bioreplicas, vat-brains, androids, robots, or other types using an alternate character generation method.

**Value Trade:** After rolling as a standard character, or possibly in conjunction with other systems, the player takes 2 points from one trait to yield 1 point to another, or 10 points off one to give 5 to another.

**Heroic Proportions:** Combine the nine rolls system with the shuffle roll, plus, the value trade system and add an additional +10 value for each trait. Such characters are usually the prime character in a solo-play adventure.

**Point Buy System:** For those character types which would normally use dice rolls to determine their traits, this system instead allows players to assign points to each trait, with buying higher trait scores costing more points. Each trait has an average of 25 buying points, multiplied by 8 individual traits to yield 200 total points one can use to buy trait points as he or she sees fit. For values between 1 and 44, traits points are bought at a 1:1 ratio; however from 45 to 74, the ratio is 2 buying points to gain one trait point, while above 75, a ratio of 3:1 is applied. Example: Jason wants his character to have an endurance score of 55, so, the first 44 points are bought straight across, deducting 44 points from the starting pool of 200.

Next, to reach endurance 55, he buys 11 more trait points at a 2:1 ratio, thus deducting 22 additional points from his total buying points supply. It cost him 66 points to buy 55 trait points. He now has only 134 points to buy all remaining trait values, but has a character that can take some serious damage and stay in the fight. The GM may enforce a minimum of 15 or 20 traits points per trait, then allow players to add a random d10 to each trait after to stagger the numbers, or even allow characters to start with 200+1d100 buying points.

Six other character generation systems are also included in Excavator Monthly Compendium on pages 100 to 121 of that book. Check them out, too.

## Table XR-2 / Trait Value Determination

| 1d100 | Trait Value |
|---|---|
| 01 | 1d10 |
| 02 | 11 |
| 03 | 12 |
| 04 | 13 |
| 05 | 14 |
| 06,07 | 15 |
| 08,09 | 16 |
| 10,11 | 17 |
| 12-14 | 18 |
| 15-17 | 19 |
| 18-21 | 20 |
| 22-25 | 21 |
| 26-30 | 22 |
| 31-35 | 23 |
| 36,37 | 24 |
| 38,39 | 25 |
| 40,41 | 26 |
| 42,43 | 27 |
| 44,45 | 28 |
| 46,47 | 29 |
| 48,49 | 30 |
| 50,51 | 31 |
| 52,53 | 32 |
| 54,55 | 33 |
| 56,57 | 34 |
| 58,59 | 35 |
| 60,61 | 36 |
| 62,63 | 37 |
| 64,65 | 38 |
| 66,67 | 39 |
| 68,69 | 40 |
| 70-90 | 40+1d20 |
| 91-96 | 60+1d20 |
| 97-99 | 80+1d20 |
| 00 | 100+1d20 |

## Table XR-3 / Trait Value Modifiers

| Trait Value | Endurance Healing Rate* | Strength DMG** | Strength Range*** | Agility DV | Agility Move Rate | Accuracy SV | Perception Initiative Modifier |
|---|---|---|---|---|---|---|---|
| 1-4 | 1 | -4 | -20% | +4 | -0.5m | -4 | -2 |
| 5-9 | 2 | -2 | -10% | +2 | -0.25m | -2 | -1 |
| 10-34 | 3 | nil | nil | nil | nil | nil | nil |
| 35-44 | 4 | +2 | +10% | -2 | +0.25m | +2 | +1 |
| 45-54 | 5 | +4 | +20% | -4 | +0.5m | +4 | +1 |
| 55-64 | 6 | +6 | +30% | -6 | +0.75m | +6 | +1 |
| 65-74 | 7 | +8 | +40% | -8 | +1m | +8 | +2 |
| 75-84 | 8 | +10 | +50% | -10 | +1.25m | +10 | +2 |
| 85-94 | 9 | +12 | +60% | -12 | +1.5m | +12 | +3 |
| 95-105 | 10 | +14 | +70% | -14 | +1.75m | +14 | +3 |
| 106-110 | 11 | +16 | +80% | -16 | +2m | +16 | +4 maximum |
| 111-115 | 12 | +18 | +90% | -18 | +2.25m | +18 | +4 maximum |
| 116-120 | 13 | +20 | +100% | -20 | +2.5m | +20 | +4 maximum |
| 121-125 | 14 | +22 | +110% | -22 | +2.75m | +22 | +4 maximum |
| 126-130 | 15 | +24 | +120% | -24 | +3m | +24 | +4 maximum |
| 131-135 | 16 | +26 | +130% | -26 | +3.75m | +26 | +4 maximum |
| each 5 above | +1 | +2 DMG | +10% | -2 DV | +0.25 MV | +2 SV | +4 maximum |

*Amount of endurance healed per day. Bioreplicas add +2 per day.

**Strength modifiers to damage are only applied to physically wielded, thrown, pitched or drawn weapons, such as clubs, knives, bows, axes, spears, even crossbows (A crossbow can be cranked or pulled further with greater strength). This damage (DMG) bonus also applies to punches and mutations involving physical attacks such as crab pincers, spiked tails, throwing quills, or fangs, etc.

*** Higher or lower strength affects the range one can throw, hurl or fire archaic weapons by adding or subtracting 10% or more to the meters range. It also includes relic pistol crossbows, compound bows and compound crossbows, etc.

Note: Normal human statistics are 25 for each trait, a basic unarmored defense value (DV) of 0 and a strike value (SV) of 01-50. He or she moves (MV) 3 meters per round walking and 6 running.

# Character History By Caste

This is an expanded collection of pre-game castes for new characters and adds to the assortment included in the Hub Rules. Here is a list of the new castes found in this book:

- Aeronaut
- Animal Herder
- Blacksmith
- Bounty Hunter
- Bunker Dweller
- Caravaneer
- Carpenter
- Cultist
- Fuel Keeper
- Healer
- Hooch Brewer
- Hooker
- Junk-Doctor
- Repairer
- Scavenger
- Teacher
- Technician, Cybernetic
- Wastelander
- Wastrel
- Water Keeper

What a new era person did prior to setting out on an adventure is as important as their character type, and reflects one's ability to read or write, do math or what starting arms, armor and gear they may or may not possess. Also, some Hub Rules castes start with automatic skills that might now include skills from this book. For example, a hunter will now have the trapper skill, a fisher would have the fishing skill, and a street urchin would have the streetwise skill. Check any existing characters from before your gaming group acquired this book, to see if their pre-game caste is eligible for any of these new automatic skills. Use table XR-6 Caste Based Details, on page 12 for this purpose.

Going forward, use the all new Pre-Game Caste Determination tables on the next page to establish a new character's caste, with table XR-4 used for character types from this book, and table XR-5 for those character types from the Hub Rules. Both of these tables combine all pre-game castes.

## Character History By Caste: Expanded

Plantoids, unique androids and robots have their own caste and skill determination systems. For plantoids see page 140, for androids see page 55 of this book, and robots see page 177. Digital beings have their own traits and background, see page 81. Bestial humans from set 2, use table XR-5 on the next page.

### Table XR-4 / Character's Pre-Game Caste Determination Expansion Rules Character Types  Roll 1d100

*Book: Hub means caste details text found in TME Hub Rules, or XR this book, the TME Expansion Rules.*

| Abomination | Grafter | Halfie | Mutorg | Nanoborg | Parasite | Rebuilt | Vat-Brain | Pre-Game-Caste | Book | Page |
|---|---|---|---|---|---|---|---|---|---|---|
| 01,02 | 01,02 | 01.02 | 01-03 | 01,02 | 01-05 | 01-03 | 01 | Aeronaut | XR | 14 |
| 03,04 | 03-05 | 03 | 04,05 | 03 | 06,07 | 04 | 02 | Animal Herder | XR | 14 |
| 05,06 | 06,07 | 04 | 06,07 | 04,05 | 08 | 05,06 | - | Blacksmith | XR | 14 |
| 07,08 | 08,09 | 05-08 | 08-10 | 06-10 | 09-11 | 07,08 | 03 | Bounty Hunter | XR | 14 |
| - | - | - | 11 | 11,12 | 12 | 09-11 | 04-06 | Bunker Dweller | XR | 15 |
| 09,10 | 10,11 | 09,11 | 12 | 13 | 13,14 | 12 | 07 | Caravaneer | XR | 15 |
| 11,12 | 12,13 | 12 | 13 | 14 | 15,16 | 13 | 08 | Carpenter | XR | 15 |
| 13 | 14,15 | 13 | 14 | 15 | 17,18 | 14,15 | 09 | Cultist | XR | 16 |
| 14 | 16 | 14 | 15,16 | 16,17 | 19,20 | 16,17 | 10-15 | Fuel Keeper | XR | 16 |
| 15 | 17 | 15 | 17 | 18 | 21,22 | 18 | 16 | Healer | XR | 17 |
| 16,17 | 18,19 | 16,17 | 18 | 19 | 23,24 | 19,20 | 17 | Hooch Brewer | XR | 17 |
| - | 20 | 18 | 19 | - | 25 | 21 | - | Hooker | XR | 17 |
| 18 | 21 | 19 | 20 | 20 | 26,27 | 22-26 | 18 | Junk-Doctor | XR | 18 |
| 19,20 | 22,23 | 20,21 | 21-22 | 21-24 | 28,29 | 27-30 | 19-22 | Repairer | XR | 18 |
| 21-24 | 24-27 | 22-26 | 23-26 | 25-28 | 30-41 | 31-35 | 23-26 | Scavenger | XR | 18 |
| 25 | 28 | - | 27 | 29 | 42 | 36 | 27 | Teacher | XR | 18 |
| 26 | 29 | - | 28-30 | 30,31 | 43 | - | 28 | Technician, Cybernetic | XR | 19 |
| 27-31 | 30-35 | 27-33 | 31-34 | 32-36 | 44-51 | 37-47 | 29-36 | Wastelander | XR | 19 |
| 32,33 | 36,37 | 34-37 | 35,36 | 37 | 52-54 | 48-52 | 37 | Wastrel | XR | 19 |
| 34 | 38 | 38 | 37,38 | 38 | 55 | 53 | 38 | Water Keeper | XR | 19 |
| 35-39 | 39-44 | 39-45 | 39 | 39,40 | 56-58 | 54-58 | 39-43 | Slave, Laborer | Hub | 13 |
| - | 45 | 46 | - | - | 59 | 59 | - | Slave, Kitchen Hand | Hub | 13 |
| - | - | - | - | - | 60 | 60 | 44 | Slave, Personal Servant | Hub | 13 |
| - | 46 | 47 | - | - | 61 | 61 | - | Slave, Whore | Hub | 13 |
| - | - | - | - | - | 62 | 62 | 45 | Slave, Court Attendant | Hub | 13 |
| 40-46 | 47-51 | 48-54 | 40-46 | 41-51 | 63,64 | 63,64 | 46 | Slave, Gladiator | Hub | 13 |
| 47 | 52,53 | 55,56 | 47,48 | 52 | 65,66 | 65 | 47 | Fisher | Hub | 13 |
| 48-50 | 54-56 | 57-60 | 49-52 | 53-55 | 67,68 | 66,67 | 48 | Hunter | Hub | 13 |
| 51,52 | 57,58 | 61,62 | 53,54 | 56 | 69,70 | 68-70 | 49,50 | Miner | Hub | 13 |
| 53,54 | 59,60 | 63,64 | 55,56 | 57 | 71,72 | 71,72 | 51 | Logger | Hub | 13 |
| 55,56 | 61-62 | 65 | 57 | 58 | 73 | 73,74 | 52 | Farmer | Hub | 13 |
| 57-59 | 63-65 | 66-70 | 58,59 | 59,60 | 74 | 75-77 | 53-64 | Nomad | Hub | 13 |
| 60 | 66 | 71 | 60 | 61 | 75 | 78 | 65,66 | Trader | Hub | 14 |
| 61 | 67,68 | 72 | 61 | - | 76 | 79 | 67 | Crafts person | Hub | 14 |
| - | 69 | - | 62 | - | 77 | - | 68 | Student | Hub | 14 |
| - | - | - | 63 | - | 78 | - | 69 | Scribe | Hub | 14 |
| 62 | 70 | - | 64,65 | 62-65 | 79 | 80 | 70-78 | Technician | Hub | 14 |
| 63-66 | 71-73 | 73-76 | 66 | - | 80-83 | 81 | - | Street Urchin | Hub | 14 |
| 67-70 | 74-76 | 77-80 | 67-69 | 66-68 | 84 | 82-84 | 79 | Street Thug | Hub | 14 |
| 71-73 | 77-80 | 81-83 | 70-74 | 69-74 | 85 | 85,86 | 80,81 | Raider | Hub | 14 |
| 74-76 | 81-83 | 84,85 | 75,76 | 75,76 | 86 | 87 | 82 | Pirate | Hub | 14 |
| 77,78 | 84,85 | 86-88 | 77-79 | 77,78 | 87-92 | 88,89 | 83 | Thief | Hub | 15 |
| 79,80 | 86,87 | 89,90 | 80-82 | 79-84 | 93 | 90 | 84 | Assassin | Hub | 15 |
| 81-84 | 88-90 | 91,92 | 83-85 | 85 | 94,95 | 91-93 | 85-90 | Draftee | Hub | 15 |
| 85-87 | 91,92 | 93,94 | 86-89 | 86,87 | 96 | 94,95 | 91,92 | Militia Soldier | Hub | 15 |
| 88,89 | 93 | 95 | 90-92 | 88-90 | 97 | 96 | 93,94 | Watchman | Hub | 15 |
| 90-94 | 94,95 | 96,97 | 93-94 | 91-93 | 98 | 97 | 95,96 | Infantry | Hub | 15 |
| 95 | 96 | 98 | 95 | 94 | 99 | - | - | Calvary | Hub | 15 |
| 96-99 | 97-99 | 99,00 | 96-98 | 95-97 | 00 | 98.99 | 97-99 | Mercenary | Hub | 15 |
| 00 | 00 | - | 99,00 | 98-00 | - | 00 | 00 | Elite Soldier | Hub | 15 |

## Table XR-5 / Character's Pre-Game Caste Determination, Hub Rules Character Types    *Roll 1d100*

| Pure Stock Human | Clone Comfort | Clone Labor | Clone Military | Bioreplica Pleasure | Bioreplica Industrial | Bioreplica Clerical | Bioreplica Infiltration | Bioreplica Battle | Trans-Human | Cyborg | Ghost Mutant | Mutant | Bestial Human | Pre-Game Caste | Book/Page |
|---|---|---|---|---|---|---|---|---|---|---|---|---|---|---|---|
| 01-03 | 01 | 01-04 | 01,02 | 01 | 01-03 | 01 | 01,02 | 01 | 01,02 | 01,02 | 01,02 | 01,02 | 01,02 | Aeronaut | XR-14 |
| 04 | 02 | 05-07 | 03 | 02 | 04-06 | 02 | 03 | 02 | 03 | 03 | 03,04 | 03,04 | 03-05 | Animal Herder | XR-14 |
| 05 | 03 | 08-10 | 04 | - | 07-11 | - | 04 | 03 | 04 | 04-06 | 05,06 | 05,06 | 06,07 | Blacksmith | XR-14 |
| 06,07 | - | 11 | 05-09 | - | 12,13 | - | 05-09 | 04-09 | 05,06 | 07-12 | 07-10 | 07-10 | 08-11 | Bounty Hunter | XR-14 |
| 08-15 | 04-09 | 12-14 | 10 | 03-07 | 14-16 | 03-08 | 10-14 | 10,11 | 07-11 | 13-16 | 11 | - | - | Bunker Dweller | XR-15 |
| 16 | 10 | 15-17 | 11 | 08 | 17,18 | 09 | 15 | 12 | 12 | 17 | 12,13 | 11,12 | 12,13 | Caravaneer | XR-15 |
| 17 | 11 | 18-20 | 12 | 09 | 19,20 | - | 16 | 13 | 13 | 18 | 14,15 | 13,14 | 14,15 | Carpenter | XR-15 |
| 18 | 12,13 | 21 | - | 10,11 | 21 | 10 | 17 | 14 | 14 | 19 | 16,17 | 15,16 | 16 | Cultist | XR-16 |
| 19,20 | 14 | 22,23 | 13 | 12 | 22,23 | 11 | 18 | 15 | 15 | 20 | 18 | 17 | 17 | Fuel Keeper | XR-16 |
| 21-27 | 15-32 | 24 | - | 13-29 | 24 | 12-22 | 19,20 | - | 16,17 | 21 | 19-26 | 18,19 | 18 | Healer | XR-17 |
| 28 | 33,34 | 25,26 | 14 | 30 | 25-27 | 23 | 21 | 16 | 18 | 22 | 27,28 | 20,21 | 19 | Hooch Brewer | XR-17 |
| 29 | 35-43 | - | - | 31-50 | - | 24-33 | 22 | - | 19 | - | 29,30 | 22,23 | 20 | Hooker | XR-17 |
| 30-34 | 44 | - | - | - | 28 | 34,35 | 23-25 | 17 | 20-24 | 23,24 | 31-33 | 24,25 | 21 | Junk-Doctor | XR-18 |
| 35 | 45 | 27-30 | 15 | 51 | 29-31 | 36 | 26,27 | 18,19 | 25,26 | 25-27 | 34,35 | 26,27 | 22,23 | Repairer | XR-18 |
| 36,37 | 46 | 31-33 | 16 | 52 | 32 | 37 | 28 | 20 | 27 | 28,29 | 36-38 | 28-32 | 24-26 | Scavenger | XR-18 |
| 38 | 47 | 34 | - | 53 | 33 | 38,39 | 29 | - | 28 | 30 | 39 | 33 | - | Teacher | XR-18 |
| 39-41 | - | - | - | - | 34 | 40-44 | 30-33 | 21 | 29-33 | 31-36 | 40,41 | 34 | - | Technician, Cybernetic | XR-19 |
| 42 | 48 | 35,36 | 17-20 | 54 | 35 | 45 | 34 | 22 | 34 | 37,38 | 42-44 | 35-41 | 27-32 | Wastelander | XR-19 |
| 43 | 49 | 37 | - | 55 | 36 | 46 | - | - | - | 39 | 45 | 42,43 | 33-35 | Wastrel | XR-19 |
| 44 | 50 | 38 | 21 | 56 | 37,38 | 47 | 35 | 23 | 35 | 40 | 46 | 44 | 36 | Water Keeper | XR-19 |
| 45 | 51 | 39-58 | 22,23 | 57 | 39-56 | 48 | 36 | 24 | 36 | - | 47-50 | 45-52 | 37-42 | Slave, Laborer | Hub 13 |
| 46 | 52,53 | 59,60 | - | 58,59 | 57,58 | 49,50 | - | - | 37 | - | 51 | 53 | - | Slave, Kitchen Hand | Hub 13 |
| 47 | 54,55 | 61 | - | 60-63 | 59 | 51-60 | 37,38 | - | 38 | - | 52 | 54 | 43 | Slave, Personal Servant | Hub 13 |
| 48 | 56-87 | - | - | 64-85 | - | 61-64 | 39 | - | 39 | - | 53 | 55 | - | Slave, Whore | Hub 13 |
| 49 | 88-93 | - | - | 86-90 | 60 | 65-70 | 40 | - | 40 | - | 54 | 56 | - | Slave, Court Attendant | Hub 13 |
| 50 | - | 62-66 | 24-37 | - | 61-67 | - | 41-44 | 25-36 | 41-43 | 41-46 | 55-57 | 57,58 | 44-52 | Slave, Gladiator | Hub 13 |
| 51 | - | 67 | - | - | 68 | - | 45 | 37 | 44 | - | 58,59 | 59,60 | 53-55 | Fisher | Hub 13 |
| 52 | - | 68 | - | - | 69,70 | - | 46 | 38 | 45 | 47,48 | 60,61 | 61,62 | 56-61 | Hunter | Hub 13 |
| 53 | - | 69-74 | - | - | 71-73 | - | 47 | 39 | 46 | 49 | 62,63 | 63,64 | 62 | Miner | Hub 13 |
| 54,55 | - | 75-77 | - | - | 74-76 | - | 48 | 40 | 47 | - | 64,65 | 65,66 | 63,64 | Logger | Hub 13 |
| 56,57 | - | 78-80 | - | - | 77-81 | - | 49 | 41 | 48 | - | 66-69 | 67-71 | 65,66 | Farmer | Hub 13 |
| 58,59 | 94 | 81,82 | 38 | 91 | 82,83 | 71 | 50 | 42 | 49 | 50 | 70-74 | 72,73 | 67-70 | Nomad | Hub 13 |
| 60,61 | - | - | - | - | 84 | 72,73 | 51 | 43 | 50 | - | 75,76 | 74 | 71 | Trader | Hub 14 |
| 62,63 | 95,96 | 83 | - | 92 | 85 | 74,75 | 52 | - | 51 | - | 77,78 | 75 | 72 | Crafts person | Hub 14 |
| 64,65 | 97 | - | - | 93 | - | 76-78 | 53 | - | 52 | - | 79 | 76 | - | Student | Hub 14 |
| 66,67 | 98 | - | - | 94 | - | 79-82 | 54 | - | 53 | - | 80 | 77 | - | Scribe | Hub 14 |
| 68-79 | - | - | - | - | - | 83-91 | 55-61 | - | 54-71 | 51-53 | 81 | 78 | - | Technician | Hub 14 |
| 80 | 99 | - | - | 95,96 | - | - | - | - | - | - | 82 | 79,80 | 73,74 | Street Urchin | Hub 14 |
| 81 | - | 84 | 39-41 | - | 86-88 | - | 62-64 | 44,45 | 72 | 54,55 | 83 | 81,82 | 75,76 | Street Thug | Hub 14 |
| 82 | - | 85 | 42-44 | - | 89 | - | 65,66 | 46-49 | 73 | 56-61 | 84 | 83,84 | 77-80 | Raider | Hub 14 |
| 83 | - | 86 | 45,46 | - | 90 | - | 67,68 | 50,51 | 74 | 62,63 | 85 | 85,86 | 81,82 | Pirate | Hub 14 |
| 84 | 00 | - | - | 97-00 | - | 92,93 | 69-74 | - | 75 | 64 | 86 | 87,88 | 83,84 | Thief | Hub 15 |
| 85,86 | - | - | 47-50 | - | 91 | - | 75-86 | 52-62 | 76,77 | 65-68 | 87 | 89 | 85 | Assassin | Hub 15 |
| 87 | - | 87-91 | 51,52 | - | 92 | 94 | 87 | 63 | 78 | 69-71 | 88,89 | 90,91 | 86-88 | Draftee | Hub 15 |
| 88 | - | 92,93 | 53-55 | - | 93 | 95 | 88 | 64 | 79 | 72-74 | 90 | 92,93 | 89,90 | Militia Soldier | Hub 15 |
| 89 | - | 94,95 | 56-59 | - | 94 | 96 | 89 | 65,66 | 80 | 75-77 | 91 | 94 | 91,92 | Watchman | Hub 15 |
| 90,91 | - | 96 | 60-63 | - | 95 | 97 | 90 | 67-70 | 81,82 | 78-86 | 92 | 95,96 | 93,94 | Infantry | Hub 15 |
| 92,93 | - | 97 | 64-70 | - | 96 | 98 | 91,92 | 71-73 | 83,84 | 87,88 | 93 | 97 | 95 | Calvary | Hub 15 |
| 94,95 | - | 98,99 | 71-89 | - | 97-99 | 99 | 93-96 | 74-86 | 85-93 | 89-96 | 94-98 | 98,99 | 96-99 | Mercenary | Hub 15 |
| 96-00 | - | 00 | 90-00 | - | 00 | 00 | 97-00 | 87-00 | 94-00 | 97-00 | 99,00 | 00 | 00 | Elite Soldier | Hub 15 |

## Table XR-6 / Caste Based Details

This is an expanded table from the version on page 12 of the Hub Rules. If a skill is marked as **bold** for a caste, that means its a new XR book skill added to an old caste. Existing PCs from the hub rules automatically have these new skills added to their character.

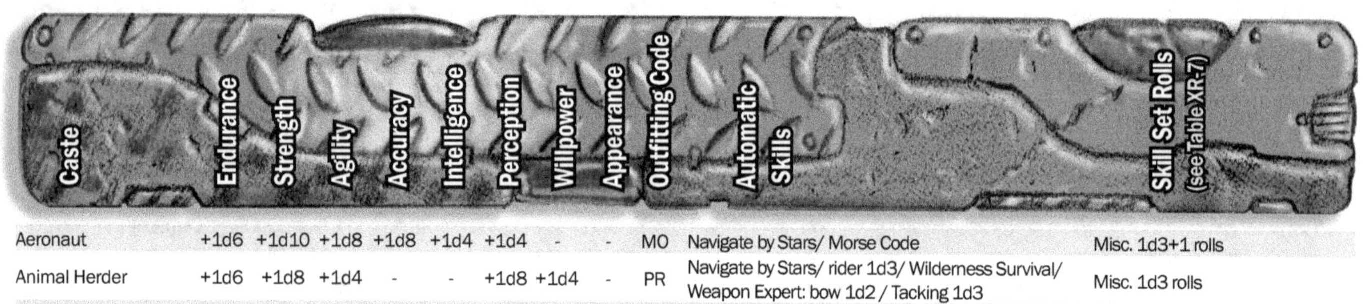

| Caste | Endurance | Strength | Agility | Accuracy | Intelligence | Perception | Willpower | Appearance | Outfitting Code | Automatic Skills | Skill Set Rolls (see Table XR-7) |
|---|---|---|---|---|---|---|---|---|---|---|---|
| Aeronaut | +1d6 | +1d10 | +1d8 | +1d8 | +1d4 | +1d4 | - | - | MO | Navigate by Stars/ Morse Code | Misc. 1d3+1 rolls |
| Animal Herder | +1d6 | +1d8 | +1d4 | - | - | +1d8 | +1d4 | - | PR | Navigate by Stars/ rider 1d3/ Wilderness Survival/ Weapon Expert: bow 1d2 / Tacking 1d3 | Misc. 1d3 rolls |
| Blacksmith | +1d6 | +2d6 | - | +1d6 | - | - | - | - | MO | Smithing 1d3 / Hammer Weapons Expert 1d3 | Misc. 1d3 rolls |
| Bounty Hunter | +d8 | +2d8 | +d6 | +d6 | - | +1d4 | - | - | WE | Brawling 1d3/ Killer 1d3/ Grapple 1d3 | Warrior 1d6/ Criminal 2/ Misc. 1d4 |
| Bunker Dweller | - | - | - | - | +2d6 | +1d6 | +1d6 | +3d6 | WE | Historian, Pre-Apoc/ 1d6 Tech skills (see description) | Educated 1d4+1 rolls/ Misc. 1d3 |
| Caravaneer | +1d4 | +1d6 | +d8 | - | - | +d8 | - | - | PR | Rider 1d3/ Navigate by Stars | Misc. 1d3 rolls |
| Carpenter | - | +1d10 | +d6 | +d6 | - | - | - | - | MO | Carpentry 1d3 | Misc. 1d3 rolls |
| Cultist | - | - | - | - | - | - | +2d6 | - | PR | nil | Misc. 1d4 rolls |
| Fuel Keeper | - | - | +1d6 | +1d8 | +2d6 | +1d6 | - | - | MO | Junk Crafter 1d3/ Chemical Technician 1 | Misc. 1d3 rolls |
| Healer | - | - | +1d8 | +1d8 | +1d8 | +1d6 | - | - | MO | Medic 1/ | Educated 1d4 rolls/ Misc. 1d3 rolls |
| Hooch Brewer | +1d4 | +1d8 | - | - | +1d4 | +1d6 | - | - | MO | See description | Educated 1 roll/ Misc. 1d3 rolls |
| Hooker | - | - | +1d6 | - | - | +1d6 | +1d8 | +3d6 | PR | Erotic Arts/ Streetwise | Criminal 1d2/ 1d2 Misc. roll |
| Junk-Doctor | - | - | +d4 | +d4 | +2d8 | +1d4 | - | - | WE | Junk-Doctor 1d3/ Medic 1 | Educated 1d3 rolls/ Misc. 1d3 rolls |
| Repairer | - | +1d4 | +1d6 | +1d6 | +1d6 | +1d6 | - | - | MO | Junk Crafter 1d3/ Mechanical Technician 1 | Educated 1d3 rolls/ Misc. 1d2 rolls |
| Scavenger | +1d4 | +1d4 | +d8 | - | - | +d8 | +1d6 | -1d4 | PR | Wilderness Survival/ Navigate by Stars/ Stealth 1d2 | Criminal 1d3/ Misc. d3 rolls |
| Teacher | -d6 | -d6 | - | - | +3d10 | +1d6 | - | +d6 | MO | nil | Educated d6+4 rolls/ Misc. d3 |
| Technician, Cybernetic | - | - | +d3 | +d3 | +2d8 | - | - | - | WE | 1d4 Cybernetics Tech skills (see description) | Educated d4 rolls/ Misc. d3 |
| Wastelander | +2d6 | +d8 | +1d4 | +1d4 | +1d4 | +1d6 | +1d4 | - | PR | Rider 1/ Wilderness Survival/ Navigate by Stars/ | Criminal 1d3/ Warrior 1d3/ Misc. 1d3 rolls |
| Wastrel | -d6 | -d6 | - | - | -1d6 | - | -1d6 | -d6 | IM | Brawling 1/ Streetwise / Stealth 1d2 | Criminal, 1d3 rolls/ Misc. 1 roll |
| Water Keeper | - | +1d4 | +d3 | - | +d6 | +2d6 | - | - | MO | Junk Crafter 1 | Educated 1 roll/Misc. 1d3 rolls |
| Slave, Laborer | +d10 | +d10 | - | - | -d10 | -d6 | -d6 | -d10 | ESC | nil | nil |
| Slave, Kitchen Hand | -d6 | -d6 | - | - | -d6 | - | -d12 | -d6 | ESC | **Cooking** | nil |
| Slave, Personal Servant | -d6 | -d6 | - | - | +d6 | +d6 | -d6 | +d6 | ESC | nil | Misc. |
| Slave, Whore | -d6 | -d6 | - | - | -d6 | - | -d6 | +d6 | ESC | Erotic Arts | nil |
| Slave, Court Attendant | -d6 | -d6 | - | - | -d6 | +d6 | -d6 | +d6 | ESC | nil | Misc. 1d3 rolls |
| Slave, Gladiator | +2d10 | +2d10 | +d8 | +d8 | -d10 | +d8 | -d4 | -2d8 | ESC | Brawling 1d3 | Warrior 4+d4 rolls |
| Fisher | +d6 | +d6 | - | - | - | +d8 | - | - | PR | **Seamanship**/ Fishing 1d3/ **Homesteader**/ Spear Weapons Expert 1d3 | Misc. |
| Hunter | +d8 | +d8 | +d6 | +d6 | - | +d8 | - | - | PR | **Trapper**/ **Homesteader**/ Bow Weapons Expert 1d3/ Wilderness Survival | Misc. |
| Miner | +d10 | +2d10 | - | - | - | - | - | -d6 | PR | **Mining**/ Pickaxe Weapons Expert 1d3 / **Homesteader** | Misc. |
| Logger | +d8 | +d8 | +d6 | - | - | +d6 | - | -d3 | PR | Axe Weapons Expert 1d3/ **Homesteader** | Misc. |
| Farmer | +d6 | +d6 | - | - | - | +d6 | - | - | PR | Pitchfork Weapons Expert 1d3/ **Homesteader** | Misc. |
| Nomad | - | - | +d10 | - | - | +d6 | - | - | PR | Rider 1d3/ Navigate by Stars | Misc. 1d3 |
| Trader | - | - | - | - | +2d10 | +d10 | - | - | WE | Barter | Misc. 1d3+1 rolls |
| Crafts person | - | - | +d6 | +d6 | +d6 | - | - | - | MO | nil | Misc. 1d3 rolls |
| Student | -d6 | -d6 | - | - | +3d10 | - | - | +d6 | MO | nil | Educated, 1d6+2 rolls/ Misc. 1d2 |
| Scribe | -d6 | -d6 | - | - | - | +d6 | - | - | MO | nil | Educated, 1d3 rolls/ Misc. |
| Technician | - | - | +d3 | +d3 | +2d8 | - | - | - | WE | 2d6 Tech skills (see description) | Educated 1d2 rolls/ Misc. 1d3 |
| Street Urchin | -d6 | -d3 | +d10 | +d6 | - | - | - | -d6 | IM | **Streetwise**/ Brawling 1d3 | Criminal, 1d3+1 rolls/ Misc. |
| Street Thug | +2d6 | +2d6 | - | - | -d6 | - | - | -d6 | PR | **Streetwise**/ Brawling 1d4 | Criminal 2 / Warrior 2/ Misc. |
| Raider | +d10 | +d10 | - | - | - | - | - | - | PR | Rider 1d3 | Criminal 2/ Warrior 2/ Misc. |
| Pirate | +d10 | +d10 | - | - | - | - | - | - | PR | **Seamanship**/ Navigate by Stars | Criminal 2/ Warrior 2/ Misc. |
| Thief | -d3 | -d3 | +d12 | +d8 | - | - | - | - | IM | **Streetwise**/ Brawling | Criminal, 1d3+4 rolls/ Misc. |
| Assassin | +d6 | +2d6 | +d10 | +d10 | - | +d10 | - | - | FA | **Streetwise**/ **Killer** 1d3/ Martial Arts 1d4/ Knife throwing 1d3 | Criminal 1d3/ Warrior 1d6/ Misc. |
| Draftee | +d3 | +d3 | - | - | - | - | - | - | MO | nil | Warrior 1/ Misc. 1d2 |
| Militia | +d6 | +d6 | - | - | - | - | - | - | MO | **Streetwise** | Warrior 1d3/ Misc. 1d2 |
| Watchman | +d6 | +d10 | - | - | - | +d6 | - | - | WE | Brawling 1d3 | Warrior 1d3/ Misc. 1d2 |
| Infantry | +d12 | +d12 | - | - | - | - | - | - | WE | nil | Warrior 1d6/ Misc. 1d2 |
| Calvary | +d10 | +d12 | +d3 | - | - | - | - | - | WE | Riding 1d6 | Warrior 1d4/ Misc. 1d2 |
| Mercenary | +d10 | +d10 | +d6 | +d6 | - | - | - | - | WE | Brawling 1d3 | Warrior 1d6/ Misc. 1d4 |
| Elite | +2d8 | +2d8 | +d8 | +d8 | - | - | +d8 | - | WE | Brawling 1d4 | Warrior 1d6+4/ Misc. 1d4 |

## Starting Skill Set Rolls

If the character has any assigned skill set rolls (noted on Table XR-6) then roll 1d100 on the appropriate skill set row on this page to determine which skills a character begins game play with. Each roll results in one skill point toward that specific skill, however, certain skills are one point only, (marked with a tiny 1).

If a single point skill is rolled a second time, or by fluke the character has maxed out that skill, simply re-roll.

In the case of the Weapons Expert skill, the player decides whether to add the benefits to a current weapon skill or re-roll another weapon category from that skill's random list. Mutants and cyborgs can choose to apply the weapon expert skill to a mutation or implant if desired, but cannot combine the Weapon Expert skill with Brawling or Martial Arts to the same attack mode.

*1 Re-roll if occurs twice as this is a one skill point only skill area.*

**If rolled twice or more, player decides to either apply the skill to a currently acquired weapon category, or randomly roll a new weapon category from the skill's description.*

*** Character was somehow taught to read and write and gained this knowledge through a tutor.*

## Table XR-7/ Starting Skill Set Rolls    Roll 1d100

| Miscellaneous | Educated | Warrior | Criminal | Skill | Book | Page |
|---|---|---|---|---|---|---|
| 01 | 01 | 01 | 01-03 | Acrobatics | XR | 201 |
| 02,03 | 02 | 02 | - | Animal Handler | XR | 202 |
| 04,05 | 03 | 03,04 | - | Armorer | XR | 203 |
| 06 | 04,05 | - | - | Artist[1] | XR | 204 |
| 07,08 | - | - | - | Carpentry | XR | 205 |
| 09,10 | - | - | - | Cooking[1] | XR | 206 |
| 11 | 06-13 | 05 | - | Cybernetics Technician** | XR | 207 |
| 12 | 14,15 | 06-08 | 04,05 | Demolitions Expert | XR | 207 |
| 13 | 16 | - | 06-10 | Escape Artist | XR | 209 |
| 14 | - | 09,10 | 11-13 | Feint | XR | 210 |
| 15 | 17 | 11,12 | 14,15 | Fencing | XR | 210 |
| 16,17 | - | - | - | Fisher | XR | 210 |
| 18 | 18 | 13,14 | 16 | Hand Signals[1] | XR | 211 |
| 19 | 19-21 | - | - | Herbalist | XR | 212 |
| 20 | 22-24 | - | - | Historian, Epochian[1]** | XR | 215 |
| 21 | 25-27 | - | - | Historian, Pre-Apocalypse[1]** | XR | 215 |
| 22,23 | - | - | - | Homesteader[1] | XR | 215 |
| 24 | 28-35 | - | - | Junk-Doctor** | XR | 218 |
| 25 | - | - | - | Leather Worker | XR | 219 |
| 26 | - | - | - | Mining[1] | XR | 220 |
| 27 | 36 | 15 | - | Morse Code[1]** | XR | 220 |
| 28 | - | 16,17 | 17-21 | Killer | XR | 219 |
| 29,30 | 37 | - | 22 | Performer | XR | 221 |
| 31 | 38 | - | - | Prospector[1] | XR | 222 |
| 32,33 | 39 | 18 | - | Seamanship | XR | 222 |
| 34,35 | - | - | - | Sewing[1] | XR | 223 |
| 36,37 | - | 19 | - | Smithing | XR | 223 |
| 38,39 | - | - | 23-27 | Streetwise[1] | XR | 224 |
| 40,41 | - | - | - | Trapper | XR | 225 |
| 42 | - | 20,21 | 28 | Whip Master | XR | 226 |
| 43 | 40,41 | - | - | Zoologist[1]** | XR | 226 |
| 44,45 | 42-44 | 22 | - | Communications** | XR | 205 |
| 46 | 45,46 | 23 | 29 | Interrogation | XR | 216 |
| 47 | 47,48 | - | - | Linguistics[1] | XR | 220 |
| 48,49 | - | - | 30 | Barter[1] | Hub | 36 |
| 50,51 | - | 24-30 | 31-33 | Brawling | Hub | 56 |
| 52-57 | - | 31,32 | 34-38 | Climbing | Hub | 36 |
| 58-60 | - | 33-40 | 39-44 | Dodge | Hub | 37 |
| 61 | 49,50 | 41 | - | Driver | Hub | 7 |
| 62 | - | - | - | Erotic Arts[1] | Hub | 38 |
| 63 | 51 | - | 45,46 | Forgery[1]** | Hub | 38 |
| 64,65 | 52 | - | 47,48 | Gambler | Hub | 38 |
| 66 | - | 42-44 | 49-51 | Grapple | Hub | 39 |
| 67 | - | 45-50 | 52-54 | Gunslinger | Hub | 39 |
| 68 | 53,54 | 51-53 | - | Gunsmith | Hub | 40 |
| 69,70 | 55-62 | - | - | Junk Crafter | Hub | 41 |
| 71 | - | 54-57 | 55-57 | Knife Fighter | Hub | 45 |
| 72 | - | 58-60 | 58-60 | Knife Thrower | Hub | 45 |
| 73 | - | - | 61-63 | Lying | Hub | 45 |
| 74 | 63 | 61-64 | 64-66 | Martial Artist | Hub | -56 |
| 75,76 | 64-70 | 65 | - | Medic | Hub | 46 |
| 77 | 71 | - | - | Navigate by Stars[1] | Hub | 46 |
| 78 | 72,73 | - | 67 | Negotiating | Hub | 46 |
| 79 | - | - | 68-76 | Pick Locks | Hub | 48 |
| 80,81 | - | - | 77-86 | Pickpocket | Hub | 48 |
| 82 | 74-76 | 66 | - | Pilot | Hub | 49 |
| 83 | 77,78 | - | - | Relic Knowledge[1] | Hub | 49 |
| 84,85 | - | 67-70 | - | Riding | Hub | 50 |
| 86 | 79 | 71-74 | 87 | Sniper | Hub | 50 |
| 87 | - | 75-78 | 88-95 | Stealth | Hub | 51 |
| 88 | 80-82 | - | - | Technician, bio** | Hub | 52 |
| 89 | 83-85 | - | - | Technician, Chemical** | Hub | 52 |
| 90 | 86-89 | - | - | Technician, Computer** | Hub | 53 |
| 91 | 90-93 | - | - | Technician, Electrical** | Hub | 53 |
| 92 | 94-96 | - | - | Technician, Mechanical** | Hub | 54 |
| 93 | 97-99 | - | - | Technician, Robotics** | Hub | 54 |
| 94 | - | 79 | 96 | Tracking | Hub | 55 |
| 95 | 00 | 80 | - | Wilderness Survival[1] | Hub | 56 |
| 96-00 | - | 81-00 | 97-00 | Weapon expert* | Hub | 57 |

# Expanded Caste Descriptions

**Aeronaut:** This character served aboard an airship and took on the caste title of aeronaut. So too, he or she gained considerable knowledge of their own region, having visited most barter towns, digger forts, trade outposts, farming villages and any sprawling slum cities which might exist in the area. Likewise, this balloonist has memorized the details of the terrain below their vessel, including the rivers, old war zones, ruin sites, swamps, impassable mutant forests, and treacherous mountains and badlands. Working among the rigging, cables and catwalks of a wicker hulled new era zeppelin has fostered improvements in this character's agility and accuracy, as well as provided some benefits to their strength. Much like a sailor, caravaneer or other hardworking traveler, they typically spend nearly everything they earn as soon as they get ground time in a community, and accordingly have accumulated very little beyond their skills.

Aeronauts have the skills of navigate by stars, Morse code, as well as 1d3 points in the climbing skill. They have a 23% chance of being able to read and write, and if so, a 18% chance of also being able to do math.

If the character has a starting intelligence score of 60 or higher, however, things are a little different. Such highly intelligent aeronauts can always read and do math, plus start with 1d3 skill points in the pilot skill and can steer and control any airship they get access to, and if so, there is a further 4 in 10 chance this individual was the captain of an airship at one time, and is most likely eager to gain a new vessel to ferry about their comrades. If indeed this flyer was the captain, then there is a further 1 in 10 chance that they own an airship that is located in the region's largest open trade town where it is undergoing repairs that this character can't afford, and the craft is being held until the 2000+1d1000 silver piece repair bill is paid. For every day that goes by from the time of character creation, an extra 25sp docking fee is being charged to the character. When it reaches 10k, bounty hunters will be sent out after the character for collection of the money owed.

Airships are described on page 219 of the TME hub rules.

**Animal Herder:** These folks are also referred to as herdsmen, shepherds, cowboys, and goat-herders, and refers to individuals who live a semi-nomadic lifestyle in a tribal or clan-based community. They guide their herds from pasture to pasture, often over great distances and move with the seasons, always in search of fresh grazing land, water and seclusion. It is a hard life, full of perils, privation, exposure to extreme weather, and unending labor. A herder must fend off all manner of predator and raider, as well as contend with the hostility of settled farmers. Farmers, incidentally, tend to occupy a fixed location, and besides raising livestock, also grow vast fields of grains, fruit and vegetables — all of which is prime grazing land for passing, open range animal herders.

Roll 1d8 for the sort of herd animals this character and their people mainly deal with: 1-3. cattle / 4,5. sheep / 6. goats / 7. hogs / 8. deer.

The lifestyle of a herder produces tough, self reliant folk who grow up in the saddle, are familiar with the bow, and can live off the land where others will perish. Each animal herder starts with 1d3 points in the rider skill, 1d2 points in weapon expert with bows, and the following additional skills: wilderness survival, navigate by stars, and 1d3 points in the tracking skill. Few animal herders can read and write, at only 7%, with those who can also have a 67% chance of being able to do math.

**Blacksmith:** Characters with this talent will always find work, and like medics, are often spared when taken prisoner as their services are in such high demand. They are often powerfully built, able to endure long hours at their craft, and produce remarkable, highly valued items. Each blacksmith will start with 1d3 skill points in the smithing skill as described on page 223 of this book, plus have 1d3 weapon expert skill points with their trusty hammer, although if using a mace, any club or sledgehammer, they also gain these skill benefits. They also feature 1d4 miscellaneous skill rolls on table XR-7 on page 13.

Being commoner workers, most can't read or do math, and have a 9% chance of being able to read and write and if so, an additional 44% chance the can do math.

**Bounty Hunter** : *(suggested by Matthew Fisher)*
Members of this caste are typically feared and distrusted — until their services are called upon to track down true villains or deal with some terrible foe that townspeople or local authorities can't cope with on their own. This is one of the few pre-game castes that might remain the character's day job once game play begins, and indeed, a whole adventure party could make their living as wandering bounty hunters, going from community to community tracking down criminals, dissidents, and marauding mutant monsters.

Bounty hunters are tough, dangerous people, and besides many trait bonuses shown on table XR-6, they also start off with a robust collection of skills: 1d3 skill points each in brawling, killer and grapple, plus 1d6 tosses on the warrior skill rolls and 1d4 miscellaneous skill rolls from table XR-7 on page 13.

While they might not be great at reading or writing, they can do enough to make sense of a wanted poster and do the math on what they are owed once the job is done and their prisoner is brought in either alive, or as a severed head, or entire skinned body. Besides this rudimentary ability to interpret a wanted poster, 37% can read and write, and of these, 73% can also do basic math.

Bounty hunters, even beginners, make a lot of enemies, and members of the criminal professions detest those of this caste. Whenever this character enters a town in a region where he or she formally did their man tracking, there is a 1 in 6 chance they are recognized by some scoundrel who will spread word of the character's presence in town. Worse, if this character ever ends up in a prison situation, slave camp or other place where criminals are held, there is a 55% chance they are recognized, and word of their former career will get around amongst the inmate population... which is bad news for this individual.

**Bunker Dweller:** *(by C.H.U.D. and W. McAusland)* Long ago, prior to the final wars, many corporations and government agencies built secret, self sustaining underground bunker complexes. They used these bases to house their technicians, politicians, corporate elites, military officers, and soldiers,

along with the families of these essential personnel, in safety.

These characters will read, write, and do math automatically. They will have a chance (01-25%) of having been banished for a crime from the bunker with a PR outfitting code, a chance (26-50%) of having fled from a catastrophe in the bunker with a MO outfitting code, or a chance (51-00%) of being a brave explorer setting out from the bunker with a WE outfitting code.

This caste is most suited to pure stock humans. However, other character types such as cyborgs, bioreplicas, clones, and trans humans are common while even stranger character types, including mutorgs, nanoborgs, parasites, rebuilts, and vat-brains, also make their start from such hidden facilities. Bunker dweller communities are typically pure stock human dominated, with all other types of humans, and especially androids, robotics, and any sort of mutant being from a subservient class. These second class citizens are typically treated as expendable workers, perimeter guards, or military assets designed to go to the surface and either investigate the world above, or commence to conquer territory for the return of true humans to the surface.

If the game master wants, bunker dwellers could be substituted for 'Star People', or 'Spacers', and instead of coming from some complex beneath the irradiated wastes, come from either a recently returning colony starship or orbiting space station.

Finally, there is a special section in this book in Appendix 3 on page 501 called 'Popsicle People'. This section covers people who have been kept alive in cryo sleep and wake in some buried underground facility and must contend with the strangeness of the Mutant Epoch for the first time. This alternate character creation system is perfect for a convention game or to introduce all-new players to this world since the characters will be just as oblivious to the perils of the twisted new world as their players are.

Bunker dweller characters are relatively healthy, although not as tough as they would have been if born on the surface. They are well educated, have fostered their intellect and start with 1d6 Educated and 1d3 Miscellaneous skill sets rolls on table XR-7, page 13, along with the historian skill of the pre-apocalypse variety as described on page 215 of this book. Furthermore, they have spent countless hours in both study and practical instruction and begin with 1d6 random technician skills rolled here, with duplicated points kept.
**Roll 1d8**

**1.** Cybernetics technician, page XR-207
**2.** Technician, bio, pg. TME-52
**3.** Technician, chemical, pg. TME-52
**4.** Technician, computer, pg. TME-53
**5.** Technician, electrical, pg. TME-53
**6.** Technician, mechanical, pg. TME-54
**7.** Technician, robotics, pg. TME-54
**8.** Medic, pg. TME-46

Characters of this pre-game caste will have no idea about most of the flora and fauna of the surface world, although may have seen video footage brought back by robots and androids, or heard stories from surface exploration teams that either called in their findings or returned in person. They will know no languages spoken by the mutant humanoid races, nor know little of the new geography of the surface, be clueless about the factions, customs and idiosyncrasies of the inhabitants of various communities, and rely heavily on any friends they make among the surface dwellers.

These characters tend to be quite attractive on account of the pampered life that they lived in their underground communities, which for the most part has sheltered them from the bite of junk storms, burning sun, ravages of merciless insects, misery of disease, and deficiencies of diet that those who grew up in the new era towns endured.

Besides useful skills, bunker dwellers also learn useless old world things. In some cases the community this character came from expects to return to the surface to rebuild the old civilization. Because of this, these individuals wasted time learning skills that were once quite useful, but in a brutal post-apocalyptic new reality, tend to have little value. In other places, the leaders are aware of the terrors of the new era, and have their youths learn these old world skills simply to carry on the knowledge and know-how of these ancient occupations. Their intention being that once their group conquers a swath of the surface, they will begin to rebuild the old world, a world where such refined and civilized skills will once more be in demand. Roll three separate Mostly Useless Old World Occupations from table XR-301 in Appendix 4, page 506 of this book.

**Caravaneer:** Similar to a nomad or animal herder, these caravan workers are also referred to as teamsters. They are hard-working men and women who work with teams of horse, oxen, mules or other mutant draft animals or machines, and mainly pull wagons and carts from one community to another. They might spend days if not weeks along the old, broken highways of the oldsters, back country dirt tracks and other paths, but unless living in their wagons themselves, do actually have a home in one or more communities where their families tend to reside. While they must deal with many of the same troubles and dangers as nomadic traders, nomads and other migratory people, they are less barbaric, more educated, and either belong to a community, factional alliance, or are employed with a trade company or warlord's staff.

As characters, most grew up in the caravaneer profession but at adulthood, abandoned the caste in favor of joining a military organization, turning to crime, or undertaking the highly risky, yet potentially profitable and heroic life style of an excavator.

They start with a few trait benefits as shown on table XR-6 on page 12, but also exhibit useful skills for dealing with life on the road, or in camp. Each caravaneer has the navigate by stars skill, plus 1d3 skill points as a rider, and 1d3 miscellaneous skill set rolls on table XR-7 on page 13.

They are only 24% likely to read and write, and if they can do this, then have a further 56% chance of being able to do math.

**Carpenter:** Wood workers of the post-apocalyptic new era are always welcome in a new community, work camp, wagon train or aboard a new era barge or sailing ship. Carpenters can do math, although most of this arithmetic pertains to measurements of wood, angles of cuts, and how many lengths of this or that piece of timber is needed to build a specific object, piece of furniture or structure. Although they can do math, they are only 62% likely to be able to read and write.

While many characters from other castes might have picked up the carpentry skill, as described on page 205 of this book, this character will not only have the replica tools and know-how, but will also have come from an established carpentry business — either their own, a family operation, or larger collective such as those found in the few emerging, vast slum cities. As a caste member, as opposed to just somebody with requisite skills, this character will have connections with other tradespeople, customers, and suppliers. Even when entering a new town, he or she will know how to get hired as a carpenter, or set up a small shop and earn a decent living within weeks.

Like a logger, this character will know various types of wood both from examining a tree and evaluating a length of finished timber.

They start with 1d3 points in the carpentry skill, as well as 1d3 miscellaneous skill rolls as found on table XR-7 on page 13.

**Cultist:** This character grew up in a strict religious sub-culture within a larger community or in a theologically homogeneous settlement. The so-called cult could be anything from a totally new faith all the way to an offshoot of an old world religion. The term cultist isn't usually what this character would call themselves, but rather a devotee, disciple, adherent, convert, chosen one, or believer, and it's outsiders who label this character a cultist. Some of the Epochian era cults are focused on love, healing and forgiveness, while at the opposite extreme, many are obsessed the dark gods, metal deities and devils of folklore and pre-cataclysmic times.

Where one faith might foster unity and feeding the hungry, others might demand the blood of virgins, human sacrifice, murder, mayhem and entropy. Common people seem to hear more stories of evil cults than good ones, and so are intolerant of all. Accordingly, cultists are often distrusted, feared and despised, and for good reason, as many newer cults, especially those established around some self proclaimed wasteland prophet or voice from the speaker system of a great machine, are malicious, and hateful of other faiths, unbelievers, or certain human strains.

The discovery of any misunderstood or blatantly evil cult is typically met with resistance, including violence, and accordingly, members of cults are often singled out and either beaten, driven off, enslaved or killed. As a former caste, any player character who grew up within a cult will often keep this fact to them self.

For one reason or another, this character has become separated from his or her faith: If the player has some explanation that they would like to explore, then by all means allow them to create a cult and the reason their character left it, otherwise, **roll 1d6** for why the PC left their cult and ran off to join a dig team:

**1.** You were told to make a great sacrifice, either of your own life, the life of a loved one, sterilization, or to forfeit all your life's savings to the cult. Refusing this offering to your leader or deity, you instead fled into the night wearing just your robes, sandals and little else.

**2.** You grew up in the cult, but as a teen, lost faith, believed other things, or nothing that the priest or priestess told you. You ran away from the cult to see what the wider world offered.

**3.** The cult changed from the one you grew up in. Its priesthood became perverted, cruel and corrupt, and when you finally lost your religion, you fled and now search for a new path home to god.

**4.** In your youth a priest of the cult beat you and asked you to do unsavory things and tell nobody about it. The holy ones seemed to be hypocrites, and when you saw them partaking in acts and luxuries that were supposedly forbidden in your faith. You lost your religion and abandoned the faith.

**5.** You did something that was a sin in your faith. Something unforgivable that caused you to be excommunicated from the cult, and shunned by your friends and family who remained in the faith. You are forbidden to return.

**6.** Your cult was declared heretical by a larger area religion, and one night, priests and devotees of this hostile faith attack yours, murdered the priests and priestesses, burned the houses of the worshipers, impaled, hung and enslaved all those they could catch. You barley fled into the wilderness with your life. You must hide your devotion to your god, dress differently, take up a new caste, and seek a livelihood that keeps you well armed and on the move. Indeed those infidels who attacked your one true faith are looking for you and the rest of the devotees of truth.

If the player can't think of a cult or new era religion that their character came from, there is a document for free download to Society of Excavator Members called, Character Religious Beliefs available through this link: https://www.outlandarts.com/membersonly/TME-SOE-Misc-downloads.htm This supplement has 7 detailed religious orders.

Cultists know a great deal about their old faith, about the prayers, chants and sacrifices of their sect, but out in the world, they have little useful knowledge but will receive 1d4 miscellaneous skill set rolls. All cultists, can, however, read and write and have a further 71% chance of being able to do math.

**Fuel Keeper:** Besides knowing about a wide range of ancient fuel sources, this highly valued member of a community is an expert in creating all-important ethanol fuel. They can select the best crops, fermentation techniques, and storage solutions to produce 3 to 18 (3d6) liters of the stuff per week, so long as the supplies and facilities to do so are available. If this character has an intelligence score of 60 or higher, he or she can do even more. A smart keeper can create new liquid and gaseous fuel sources, and — given the correct equipment and raw materials — refine old world fuel types such as gasoline and diesel sufficiently to produce 1 to 6 (1d6) liters of any given fuel per week.

Many individuals who were former fuel-keepers are fascinated by the wide range of fuels that were once available to the oldsters, and nothing is more wondrous to this person than an old fuel depot, gas station, fuel truck, or refinery.

There is a 67% chance this character is also a candle maker — as a hobby — and can create candles from assorted waxes, oils and resins and will start game play with 4d6 candles that each burn for 3 hours and give off light in a 4 meter radius.

Of course, a person involved in this line of work must have their wits about them, be smart, precise and understand the right blends, storage procedures and qualities of his or her product. Given this, a new character will gain a few bonus trait points at creation. Likewise, they start with several skills including 1d3 points in the junk crafter skill, 1 point in the chemical technician skill, and 1d3 miscellaneous skill rolls. They always know how to read, write and do quite complex math.

Each will start game play with 1d6 glass bottles filled with

a liter of ethanol fuel in each, and a 1 in 6 chance of a relic jerry can that holds 4 liters of the same corn fuel. This character will also be very familiar with the impromptu, crude but much feared flammable weapon system known as Molotov cocktails, as described on page 362 of this book in the expanded equipment section. There is a 6 in 10 chance he or she will have a hard leather case, flint and steel and 2d6 Molotov cocktails at character generation.

## Healer:
Using a mix of ancient medicine, new era herbal remedies, common sense, prayers, and the healing magic of whatever culture this individual came from, this valued member of a society will make a great addition to any adventure team. Healers come in several forms, from the purely scientific nurse or doctor role, all the way to a witch doctor, but in either case, they start with several trait bonuses as shown on table XR-6 on page 12 along with 1 point in the medic skill, 1d4 skill set rolls under the educated column and 1d3 miscellaneous skill rolls from table XR-7 on page 13. They are 79% likely to be able to read and write, and if so, 87% chance they can also do math. Should this character gain other points in the medic skill, this 1 point stacks with those.

A healer will possess a satchel filled with homemade antiseptic wash (500ml) sterilized bandages, soothing moss, and 5 rolls from the following list of random healer carried items.

### Starting Medical Items *Roll 5 times. Duplicate results kept. 1d100*
**01-16.** Anti-Toxin Injector, page TME-199.
**17-20.** Dental repair and tooth pulling kit, with 3d6 uses of a home made narcotic pain killer ointment.
**21-42.** Flesh Mend Gel packet. Roll 1d8 for type 1-4. MK1/ 5,6. MK 2 / 7. MK3 / 8. MK4. These packs are described on page 442 of this book.
**43-46.** Filter mask, from page TME 194.
**47-50.** Enviro-Suit in plastic carry case. From page TME 194.
**51-53.** Rad-Scanner (dosimeter) from page TME 199.
**54-57.** Bottle of hard Liquor, 400+2d100ml see page TME 124 for details.
**58-65.** Bottle of alcohol disinfectant, 400+1d100ml, see Post-Apocalyptic Weapons, Armor and Equipment, page 362 of this book.
**66-70.** Radiation Sensor Tab, see page 432 of this book.
**71-74.** Tissue Binder with a half charged power cell, see page 443 of this book.
**75-78.** Steroidal Pills, 2d6 from page 443 of this book.
**79-83.** Iodine Tabs, 2d6, from page 443 of this book.
**84-88.** Deviant Inhibitor Serum [DIS], 1d4 doses, see page 444, this book.
**89-93.** Nano Patches, 1d4, see page 444 of this book.
**94-96.** Anti-Toxin Injectors, shrink-wrapped case of 6, page TME-199.
**97-00.** Field Medical Kit, with 1d10 day's operation left in power cell, as seen on page 199 of the hub rules.

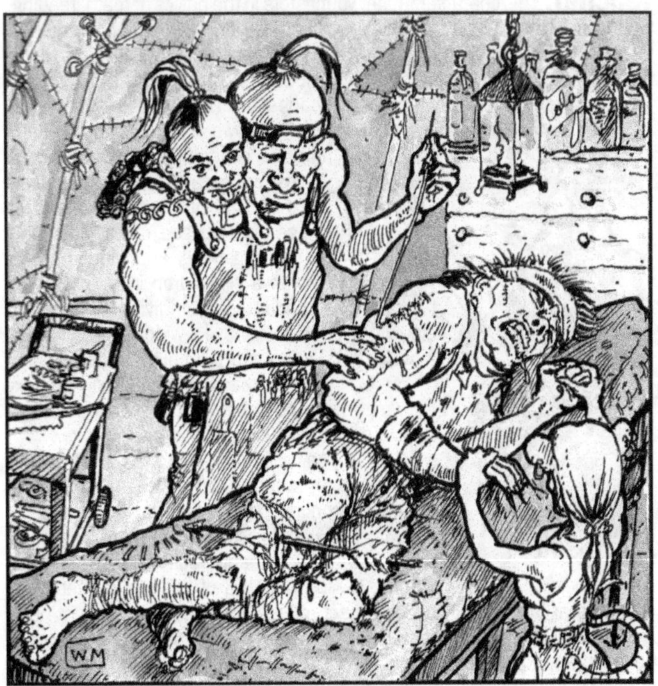

## Hooch Brewer:
Also known as a Winemaker, Beer Brewer, and Moonshiner, those of this former profession sometimes coordinate with a water keeper to secure barrels, hand blown glass bottles and other containers that once stored water. There is a 2 in 10 chance this individual worked as a bartender in his or her local saloon, and if so, will have exceptional knowledge of the locals of that community, and a bonus of +1 points in both the streetwise and cooking skills.

There is a further 1 in 10 chance this character is an alcoholic, however, and thus the reason behind their keen interest in the creation, acquisition, knowledge and consumption of booze. An alcoholic character takes a -3 penalty to each trait, although the player should record this loss somewhere on the character sheet as these points can be reapplied once alcoholism is left behind, with a willpower based, type E hazard check allowed at 4th, 8th and 12th and 16th ranks to try to break the alcoholic habit.

Hooch brewers often follow written recipes, and create their own boozy concoctions using measuring devices and formulas to reproduce whatever grog is in demand. Because of this, 88% can read and write and do basic math. They start with 1 skill roll under the educated column and 1d3 miscellaneous skill rolls on table XR-7 on page 13.

A hooch brewer will begin game play with an inventory of 3d6 bottles of wine, and 1d6 500ml bottles of hard liquor. They will, in most cases, have worked for somebody else in a bar or brewery, and won't own their own still or equipment. However, wherever they go, at least in human society, they can always find employment and are familiar with both new era alcoholic beverages and most old world mixes, and can work in the production of boozy goodness or serve it as a bartender. Besides the creation of drinks, a hooch brewer can produce alcohol for disinfecting wounds, and will have 2d6, 200ml glass vials of the substance in a leather pouch when setting off on an adventure. Learn more about this essential wound cleanser on page 362 of this book.

## Hooker:
This character once made their living as a member of the world's oldest profession. As a post-apocalyptic prostitute, this individual differed from a slave of the whore designation in that they at least belonged to themselves, although might have been controlled by a saloon owner, pimp, or madam. As a freelance hooker, this person could have saved up a considerable amount of money, at least enough to buy the equipment and basic weaponry of a novice excavator.

Prostitution in the new era is usually considered a tolerable way to make money to survive, and lacks much of the negative social stigma that it held in pre-cataclysm times. Still, many hookers find sex work disagreeable, or never chose the profession at all and instead fell into it because of desperation, coercion, or drug addiction.

This character now attempts to leave behind the life of a bar room floozy, street walker or back alley whore for good, and will often need to abandon their home community permanently to avoid being recognized by former customers, fellow hookers, or disapproving citizens.

Former hookers rarely have the ability to read and write, at only 9% chance, with an 11% chance of being able to do basic math. They are in the habit of maintaining their good looks, however, and so have a considerable +3d6 appearance trait score bonus at character generation, plus have the erotic arts skill. Because if these features, and intimate knowledge of how to tease, seduce and make love, they can call upon these abilities to influence others, a talent that could be useful in securing resources, food, information, or allies.

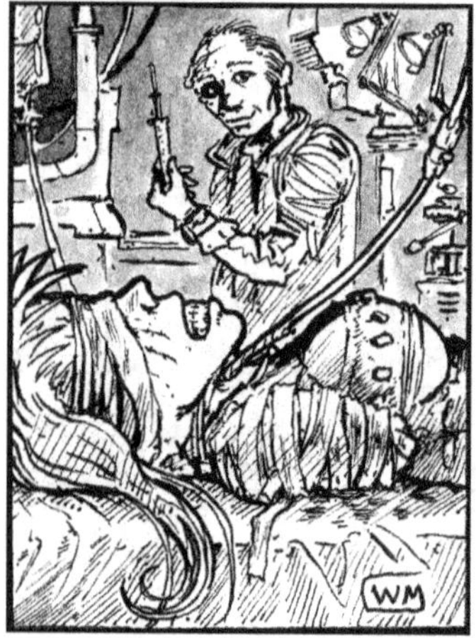

**Junk-Doctor:** Often called trash-medics, disciples of Frankenstein, or rebuilders, a junk-doctor is both a pre-game caste and a skill. Members of this often shunned, much misunderstood and maligned profession are described as hybrid technicians with some knowledge in human physiology, mechanical and electrical knowledge, along with a limited understanding of cybernetics. Using a mix of scrap parts, medic skills, prosthetics and faulty cybernetic implants, these people create rebuilt humans.

In some communities, the practice of rebuilding the maimed, half dead and crippled members of society is encouraged. Here, the people believe that since no member of a post-apocalyptic settlement or group can live off the labors, food supplies and protection of others, that turning a badly mangled, multiple amputee into a combat ready guardian or worker is necessary. In other places, however, the conversion of an unfortunate casualty of an industrial accident, animal attack or warfare into some amalgam of human and scrap metal, tubes and junk, is forbidden, and those who reconstruct the fallen are considered witches, or warlocks, and often driven from the community.

Indeed, junk-doctors are given this name, which is similar to witch doctor, instead of rebuilt technicians or prosthetic attachment caregiver, precisely because the half living constructs they make from trash and broken relics are typically quite ghastly. The creation of rebuilt humans involves unorthodox surgeries, drug administration, amputations, and a great deal of pain, and produces a nightmarish mockery of the former, pre-rebuilt person.

Junk-doctors gain several trait improvements along with 1d3 points in the junk-doctor skill, 1 point in the medic skill, 1d3 rolls under the educated skill set, and 1d2 miscellaneous skill set rolls. This character might also gain the cybernetics technician skill, which would expand the sort of repairs and beings he or she can construct depending on availability of materials.

Junk-doctors can read, write and do math to a high level and will start game play with a special tool bag described along with this skills description on page 218.

**Repairer:** A valued member of any tribe or village, this repairman or repair-woman can fix most commonly used tools, but often has the junk crafting skill and a fairly good chance of knowing one or more areas as a technician. They have a 89% chance of being able to read and write, and if so, always know basic math. They carry a hip pouch filled with common tools, a few spare parts, and 1d6 broken but possibly salvageable relic household or industrial objects — such as alarm clocks, old cell phones, radios, power tools and the like — each of which can be sold for 3d6+10sp each if needed, but are kept so that he or she can tinker with the item in evenings and hone their skills.

They will start with 1d3 points in the junk crafter skill, and 1

point in the mechanical technician skill. Additionally, each will start with 1d3 rolls on the educated skill set and 1d2 rolls in miscellaneous skills as determined on table XR-7 on page 13.

**Scavenger:** While normally loners who live on the edge of vast ruined cities, or among the wrecks of former battlefields and industrial zones, scavengers are commonly encountered by excavators and nomadic traders, who will barter with these wasteland hermits. Typically, scavengers will trade important information about a local stretch of ruins or road in return for food, tobacco, marijuana or booze. On some occasions, travelers might discover that the scavenger has a mate, and one or more children. These kids grow up to be resourceful, half wild things themselves, but because of their exposure to dig teams, many develop an obsession with both the caste of diggers and the distant towns and barter forts the ruin looters come from.

Many young scavengers, upon reaching adulthood or when their parents are killed or deemed too reclusive and narrow minded, will wander off to a town, sometimes following a friendly and generous dig team, and seek to know more about life within the wall of a human settlement. Unfortunately, because they lack useful skills other than rummaging about in the junk heaps, prostitution, or crime, they find themselves joining an excavation team, which is a perfect fit for these normally reclusive people. As diggers, former scavs make for excellent, and remarkably fearless and resourceful ruin explorers. So too, many have connections with scavengers in areas they themselves grew up in, and can get help, intel and shelter for themselves and a whole dig team among the scrap harvesters of the wasteland.

Former scavengers are only 4% likely to read, write or do basic math, but will start with the skills of wilderness survival, navigate by stars, and 1d2 points in the stealth skill. They also get 1d3 rolls in each the criminal skill set and miscellaneous skill as shown on table XR-7 on page 13.

**Teacher:** This character taught youngsters in the basics of math, reading, writing and scientific principles. If it was permissible in his or her community, the instruction of ancient history up until the cataclysm would also have been taught — although what this teacher knows to be true might differ greatly from what really happened. The instructor might also share what he or she knows about ancient animals, religions, geography and literature.

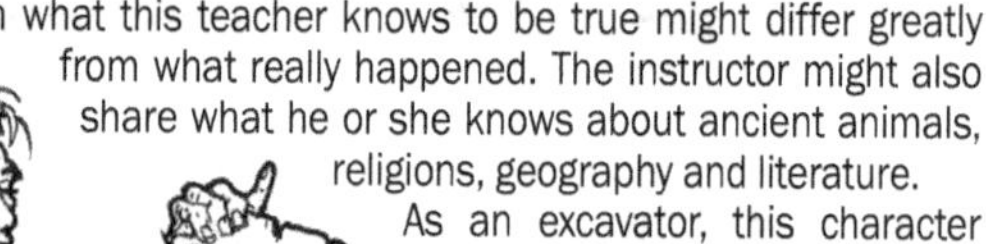


As an excavator, this character might not be the fittest, meanest or most rugged of individuals in the beginning, and indeed starts with a slight drop in strength and endurance from living a cushy life, but will have a wide range of knowledge and the ability to do complex math, read, write and know 1d3 extra languages (from the vast, random list on page 510 of this book).

They will have a satchel full of books, scraps of paper, stubs of old pencils, erasers and one or two working ballpoint pens. So too, each starts with 1d6+4 rolls on the education skill set column and 1d3 miscellaneous skill set rolls as shown on table XR-7 on page 13 of this book. There is a chance that because of these skill set roll results, this teacher might have exceptionally advanced knowledge as a medic or technician, and so if, would be considered a professor, and therefore be qualified, and encouraged, to teach young adults and mature students. With such skills, this individual could easily find work, or set up their own school or post-apocalyptic college in, a large community.

**Technician, Cybernetic:** Like the junk doctor caste, this pre-game profession is also a skill as described on page 207 of this book. This character has either served as an apprentice — if having only 1 or 2 skill points in cyber-

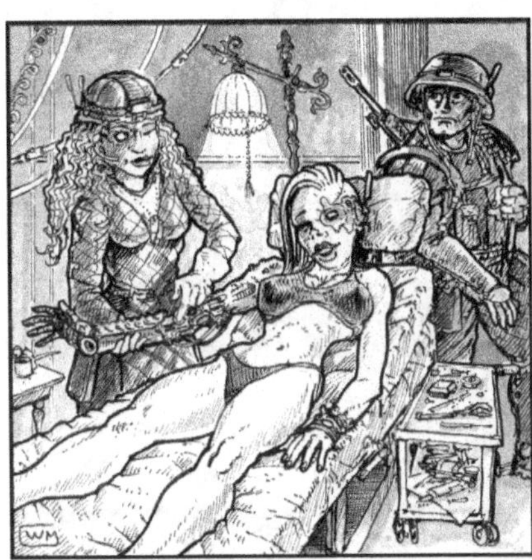

netics technician — otherwise, if having 3 or 4 points in this skill, will most likely have once run their own implant purchasing, collecting, repair, and attachment service. While this character mainly trained as a cybernetics expert, they might have other prominent skills or interests, too, and walked away from the implant insertion trade. More commonly, however, this technician is obsessed with cybernetic technologies and so yearns to search for new parts, specimens, and tools. This obsession compels them to join an excavation team to undertake perilous expeditions into the old places to seek new implants, or else get access to cyborg companions to study, enhance, and repair.

There is a small chance that during character type determination, as per table XR-1 on page 7, that this character is itself cyborg, and depending on the body location of an implant, it might be able to reach and upgrade itself without help. They will begin game play with the toolkit as described for this skill on page 207.

Cybernetic technicians can always read, write and do math to a high level, plus start with 1d4 points in the cybernetics technician skill. In addition, they will get 1d4 skill set rolls under the educated column and 1d3 rolls on the miscellaneous column on table XR-7 on page 13.

**Wastelander:** Often seen as some sort of barbarian, or uncivilized, dangerous loner, those of the wastelander caste clearly dislike extended stays in towns or walled compounds. In some ways, they are like scavengers and savages both, and yet embrace technology, especially relic firepower and oldster vehicles, and will gladly work within a larger team of excavators, mercenaries of warriors to accomplish some task. This cooperation works only so long as it fits in with the wastelander's need to keep wandering the wastes, exploring old places and uncovering ever more powerful weaponry, armor and technology. In some respects, they are the ultimate candidate for becoming a digger, however will not settle down within the confines of some barter town or new era city.

To commoners, a wastelander in the wilds around their village or town is a good thing, and many consider these men and women to be like lone knights of some bygone era, rangers who keep a watchful eye on the civilized lands, rid the area of raiders and mutant monsters, and for whatever reason, appear to protect and foster the emergence of human civilization even as

they want no permanent part in it.

Some speculate that a wastelander has some dark past, perhaps a criminal history, or suffers some insurmountable trauma that keeps them from fully feeling at ease within a new era settlement. It is rumored, too, that a wastelander guards a specific community because he or she has relatives in the

place, although such relatives, including abandoned children, former spouses, and siblings, might be unaware that the wastelander is in the vicinity.

Being a wastelander as a pre-game caste need not mean the character wishes to continue with their solitary, harsh life of isolation, and it is assumed they have temporarily joined ranks with a dig team or other squad to accomplish some task, seek some great prize, deal with a peril, or try another way of living by joining a larger group. Of course, old habits die hard, and a former wastelander will always push a dig team onto the next adventure, next town, or as yet unchartered and unlooted ruined vistas as soon as possible.

They can read and write 12% of the time, and if so, have a 76% chance of also being able to do simple math. Each will start with 1 point in the rider skill, have the wilderness survival skill, navigate by stars and get 1d3 rolls each in the criminal skill set, warrior skill set and miscellaneous skill set according to the random table on page 13.

There is a 2 in 20 chance that this wastelander character is wanted for some past crime and any encounter with a bounty hunter means there is a 36% chance the PC is recognized and if so, the bounty hunter might attempt to collect the fee.

**Wastrel:** This character was the local drunk or junkie and has worn out their welcome. While they might have come from a good family, some calamity, betrayal, or criminal act on either their part, or committed against them, saw them fall into despair and oblivion. Prior to game play, this person's priority in life centered on the booze bottle, drug pipe, or handful of mutant narcotics.

Besides being the local drunk or addict, this character was also likely a petty criminal, prostitute, or compulsive gambler and card cheat. The amount of trouble this troublemaker caused in their home town — and is still likely to cause should the chance arise to make a big score, splurge their earnings on hookers, drugs, alcohol and cards — is 67% likely to have followed them into their new life as a digger, mercenary or other profession. If so, not only will there be a 400+1d100sp bounty for this character's arrest and return to their hometown to answer for their many crimes, debts and failures, plus a 30% chance that when arriving in each adjacent community to the PC's hometown that he or she is recognized by the authorities and will be refused entry to the community because of past transgressions.

Furthermore, there is a 1 in 10 chance that a group of pissed off people from their hometown is out looking for the wastrel, their intention to see this character swing at the end of a rope — along with any no good friends he or she might travel with (i.e. the other player characters).

A wastrel could have come from the poorest members of a society, or from a well established and respected home, although in either case, has fallen into extreme poverty, owe 1d8 people 20+1d20 silvers each, and are only 22% likely to read, write or do math. The skills they have picked up include 1 skill point in brawling, streetwise and gambler each, plus 1d3 points in the stealth skill. Each will also begin with 1d3 rolls in the criminal skill set roll and 1 miscellaneous skill set from table XR-7 on page 13.

**Water Keeper:** This character was formerly an expert in securing, testing, filtering, storing and creating transport containers for precious water. He or she was accomplished at the digging of wells, understanding the patterns in trees, ravines, hills, and vegetation in arid regions in order to better guess where a source of water might be rooted out. There is a 3 in 10 chance this valuable individual also knew the art of water dowsing with a forked stick, and has an 89% chance of finding water in an area with just a witching stick.

Besides being able to tend to, store and find water under normal circumstances, this aqua-expert is fascinated with how the ancient ones stored, moved and made their water safe, including how they dealt with sewage. Given this, they will be intrigued by any discovery of underground pipe systems, reservoirs, and plumbing. While others might walk right passed a collection of gauges, pumps and filtration apparatus, this character will be thrilled with the discovery and if time and tools are available, will try to loot an ancient facility and take the apparatus back to their community to enhance the water system — or at least sell these items to associates in the hydrological caste.

Because they were expected to make repairs and inspect water sources,

creeks, rivers and lake accessible water intakes, damns and the like, all water keepers have a minimum of being fair swimmers.

These individuals can always read, write and do basic math, have 1 point in the junk crafter skill, plus make 1 roll on the educated column for skill set rolls and 1d3 miscellaneous skill set rolls according to the table on page 13.

Water keepers will normally start game play with a small pouch containing water quality test kit, minor plumbing repair and salvaging tools, a hand pump operated water filtration contraption, and be able to give each companion in a starting excavation team a full, 2 liter canteen in addition to any other water supplies they carry.

# Character Details

Establish the following new character details with only a few dice tosses:

- **Age Determination**
- **Swimming Ability**
- **Hand Dominance**
- **Languages**
- **Weight and Height**

## Character Starting Age

Most organic human characters start game play at **age 17+d8 years old**, but a character's personal history may call upon a different starting age. Bestial human characters each have their own starting age as noted on table TME-1-20, page 25 of the Hub Rules or table XR-53, page 58 of this book.

## Character Swimming Ability

Does your character sink or swim when thrown into the water? It's an important detail in game play and comes up often in both published TME adventures and home brewed digs. Drowning is explained under Hazards, part 3, page 121 of the TME Hub Rules.

**Table XR-8 / Swimming Ability**

| 1d10* | Swimming Skill | Base Swim Speed** |
|---|---|---|
| 1-3. | Can't Swim | 0.5m |
| 4,5. | Poor Swimmer | 1m |
| 6,7. | Fair Swimmer | 1.5m |
| 8,9. | Strong Swimmer | 2m |
| 10. | Excellent Swimmer | 3m |

*Any character who, prior to game play, was a fisherman, pirate or sailer, etc. rolls 1d6+4 on this table.*

**Agility move modifers apply.*

## Character Hand Dominance

Because of critical strikes and called shots, a character's good hand needs to be pre-established prior to any injury, especially the unfortunate amputation of one's arm. Use the following table to establish the character's dominant hand; or if the person is ambidextrousness which is common among excavators but only occurs about 1% of the time in NPCs. Androids and robots can choose to make either hand dominant, but not both unless they are specially designed to do so. Unless employing a two handed weapon in both hands, or due to some skill, implant, mutation or other factor, a strike made by the attacker with his or her off hand (non-dominant) suffer a -20 strike value penalty.

**Table XR-9 / Dominant Hand Determination**

| 1d10 | Dominant Hand* |
|---|---|
| 1-7. | Right Handed |
| 8,9. | Left Handed |
| 10. | Ambidextrous** |

*Strikes made using one's off hand are made at a -20 strike value penalty.*
** This character can use two, one handed weapons simultaneously with no penalty.*

## Character Languages

All characters — unless they suffer from some sort of flaw mutation or handicap that prevents them from talking — will speak the local area common language. This language is typically a derivative of whatever everyday, pre-apocalypse speech was used in that area. Optionally, the game master may allow characters to know more than their mother-tongue, with a caste based table and vast list of randomly determined new era and ancient languages available in Appendix 7 on page 509.

## Character Weight and Height

For the most part, the following table is only useful for organic, human-like characters, while abominations, androids, bestial humans, digital beings, parasites, plantoids, robots, vat-brains and halfies all have their own system for establishing their weight and height. Of course, a parasite's host body, or the body attached to a vat-brain, might call upon the use of this table.

## Table XR-10 / Character Weight and Height

| Character Type | Female Weight | Female Height | Male Weight | Male Height |
| --- | --- | --- | --- | --- |
| Grafter | 50+3d10kg | 140+3d20cm | 70+4d10kg | 160+3d20cm |
| Mutorg | 60+3d20kg | 140+3d20cm | 80+3d20kg | 160+3d20cm |
| Nanoborg | 50+2d20kg | 145+3d20cm | 70+3d20kg | 165+3d20cm |
| Rebuilt | 40+3d20kg | 130+4d20cm | 50+3d20kg | 140+4d20cm |
| Pure Stock Human | 40+2d20kg | 140+3d20cm | 60+2d20kg | 160+3d20cm |
| Clone, Comfort | 50+d10kg | 150+d10cm | 60+d10kg | 180+d10cm |
| Clone, Labor | 60+d20kg | 160+3d10cm | 70+2d20kg | 180+3d10cm |
| Clone, Military | 60+d20kg | 170+d10cm | 70+2d20kg | 180+2d10cm |
| Bioreplica, Pleasure | 45+d20kg | 150+d20cm | 55+d20kg | 168+d20cm |
| Bioreplica, Industrial | 50+2d20kg | 160+2d20cm | 66+3d20kg | 180+2d20cm |
| Bioreplica, Clerical | 50+d12kg | 150+d20cm | 60+d12kg | 170+d20cm |
| Bioreplica, Infiltration | 60+d20kg | 150+3d10cm | 70+d20kg | 165+3d10cm |
| Bioreplica, Battle | 50+2d20kg | 175+d20cm | 60+2d20kg | 185+d20cm |
| Trans-Human | 50+d20kg | 165+d20cm | 60+2d20kg | 180+d20cm |
| Cyborg | 65+2d10kg | 140+3d20cm | 75+2d10kg | 160+3d20cm |
| Ghost Mutant | 50+d20kg | 150+2d20cm | 60+d20kg | 170+2d20cm |
| Mutant | 40+2d20kg | 130+4d20cm | 60+2d20kg | 150+4d20cm |

*Note: 1 kilogram =2.2 pounds/ 1 centimeter =.39 inches*

# Rank Advancement Revisited

We've included the same rank advancement matrix as shown on page 34 of the TME Hub Rules for ease of access, although the subsequent rank gain bonus matrix has been expanded to include all the new character types, as well. If you're new to The Mutant Epoch and want an explanation of experience factors and rank advancement, we encourage you to read the brief write up on page TME-34, however a word on Experience factors is in order.

Some say that it is too easy to go up in rank, or level up, in The Mutant Epoch and Outland System, especially compared to other popular role-playing games. Indeed, going from first rank to second rank can be rather swift. The reasoning behind this is that to gain the 60 experience factors needed do so means a newbie post-apocalyptic character must survive several brutal, potentially deadly fights. For example, imagine surviving a hand to hand battle with a black bear, EFs (Experience Factors) 50, or fending off several ferocious mutant dogs (EFs 18 each) or a whole 1st rank party enduring the unsought of a mutant giant known as a garnock (pg TME-156 with 125 EFs).

Your odds aren't good under any of these circumstances, to say nothing of the challenges faced by traps, pitfalls, junk storms, radiation, old landmines, accidents, starvation or dying of thirst — challenges that offer no experience factors if endured. In short, 1st rank characters are only expected to have a fifty percent chance of surviving to second rank anyway, and the main reason why so many of our adventures encourage each player to have two PCs, especially for low rank operations.

Another way to look at it is to imagine that you were a raw recruit thrust into a modern war. Consider the difference between you as a novice and you as a survivor of your first life or death struggle in a firefight or ambush. Any low rank character to survive a close call, walk away from a brutal encounter with a mutant monstrosity or endure the hardships of the wastes or ruins would never be the same. They'd be hardened veterans after only one mission, and learned a lot, improved their skills, grown tougher, wiser and more alert. During follow-up engagements and adventures, beyond 2nd rank, they would grow at a slower pace when faced with the same hardships and battles, but would still become masters of their trade, adapt, learn and become increasingly hardened and ready to risk it all in more epic adventures.

Secondly, whereas many other RPGs need more experience points to go up in level, they also yield much more. Consider that in The Mutant Epoch RPG that going from 1st to 2nd rank only yields a 20% increase in one's endurance trait, whereas in many other games, a character's hit points could double, or increase by 100% when going up one level. Comparing ranks to levels is understandable, of course, although they present differently.

Thirdly, if the game master and their players feel it is too easy to advance in rank, merely reduce the experience factors handed out by half, or whatever increment feels right for your style of play. You could also add a zero to the EFs needed in the Experience Factors column on Table XR-11 or TME-1-21 in the Hub Rules. After all, these rules, and others like it, are only a framework and your house rules are the true law. WM

Digital Beings have their own specialized rank advancement and benefit's table shown on page 70 of this book.

## Table XR- 11 / Rank Advancement Matrix

| Character Rank | Experience Factors | Strike Value | Endurance Bonus* | Melee Attacks Per Round | Skill Point Bonus |
|---|---|---|---|---|---|
| 1 | 0 | 01-50 | nil | 1 | By PC history & type*** |
| 2 | 60 | 01-55 (+5) | +20%** | 1 | +d4 |
| 3 | 130 | 01-59 (+4) | +9 | 1 | +d4 |
| 4 | 215 | 01-62 (+3) | +8 | 1 | +d3 |
| 5 | 320 | 01-65 (+3) | +7 | 1 | +d3 |
| 6 | 450 | 01-67 (+2) | +6 | 1 | +d3 |
| 7 | 690 | 01-69 (+2) | +d6 | 2 | +d2 |
| 8 | 800 | 01-71 (+2) | +d6 | 2 | +d2 |
| 9 | 1000 | 01-73 (+2) | +d6 | 2 | +d2 |
| 10 | 1,400 | 01-75 (+2) | +d6 | 2 | +d2 |
| 11 | 1,800 | 01-76 (+1) | +d6 | 2 | +d2 |
| 12 | 2,300 | 01-77 (+1) | +d6 | 2 | +d2 |
| 13 | 3,000 | 01-78 (+1) | +d6 | 2 | +d2 |
| 14 | 3,900 | 01-79 (+1) | +d6 | 2 | +d2 |
| 15 | 5,100 | 01-80 (+1) | +d3 | 2 | +d2 |
| 16 | 6,700 | 01-81 (+1) | +d3 | 2 | +d2 |
| 17 | 8,900 | 01-82 (+1) | +d3 | 2 | +1 |
| 18 | 11,900 | 01-83 (+1) | +d3 | 2 | +1 |
| 19 | 15,900 | 01-84 (+1) | +d3 | 2 | +1 |
| 20 | 21,500 | 01-85 (+1) | +d3 | 2 | +1 |
| above 20 | +7,500 ea. | +1 SV | +1 | 2 | +1 |

*A vat-brain character's chassis or donor body gains endurance as normal, however the actual brain (the true character) gains only +2 endurnace per rank until 15th rank, and thereafter gains only +1 END per rank above.

** Add percentage of character's uninjured 'base' endurance value, always rounded up. Example: PC with 24 END, adds 4.8 END, rounded up to 5 to start 2nd rank game play with 29 endurance.

***The character's starting history and his or her type determines starting skills.

Number in parentheses behind strike value (+5) or (+3) etc., shows actual numerical increases for quick PC rank gain updating.

## Table XR-12 / Rank Gain Bonus Matrix   *Roll 1d100*

Digital beings have their own rank gain matrix on page 70.

| Abomination | Android | Bestial Human | Grafter | Halfie | Mutorg | Nanoborg | Parasite | Plantoid | Rebuilt | Robot | Vat-Brain | Rank Bonus Result |
| --- | --- | --- | --- | --- | --- | --- | --- | --- | --- | --- | --- | --- |
| 01-08 | 01-03 | 01-09 | 01-05 | 01-06 | 01-06 | 01-05 | 01-05 | 01-08 | 01-07 | 01-07 | 01-04 | +d6 Endurance |
| 09-14 | 04-08 | 10-18 | 06-11 | 07-11 | 07-13 | 06-12 | 06-09 | 09-16 | 08-12 | 08-15 | 05-08 | +d6 Strength |
| 15-22 | 09-15 | 19-24 | 12-16 | 12-17 | 14-20 | 13-18 | 10-18 | 17-22 | 13-17 | 16-22 | 09-19 | +d6 Agility |
| 23-25 | 16-24 | 25-31 | 17-21 | 18-24 | 21-23 | 19-24 | 19-25 | 23-26 | 18-20 | 23-26 | 20-24 | +d6 Accuracy |
| 26-29 | 25-28 | 32-34 | 22-25 | 25-27 | 24-27 | 25-28 | 26-30 | 27-29 | 21-24 | 27-31 | 25-30 | +d6 Intelligence |
| 30-35 | 29-33 | 35-44 | 26-31 | 28-33 | 28-31 | 29-34 | 31-40 | 30-33 | 25-29 | 32-39 | 31-41 | +d6 Perception |
| 36-39 | 34,35 | 45-51 | 32-37 | 34-39 | 32-36 | 35-40 | 41-48 | 34-38 | 30-38 | 40-46 | 42-47 | +d6 Willpower |
| 40 | 36 | 52 | 38 | 40-42 | 37-39 | 41-43 | 49 | 39 | 39,40 | - | - | +d6 Appearance |
| 41-48 | 37-39 | 53-57 | 39-45 | 43-47 | 40-46 | 44-51 | 50-53 | 40-52 | 41-45 | 47-50 | 48-50 | +2d6 Endurance |
| 49-58 | 40-42 | 58-63 | 46-50 | 48-53 | 47-50 | 52-57 | 54 | 53-59 | 46-51 | 51-55 | 51 | +2d6 Strength |
| 59-65 | 43-51 | 64-68 | 51-54 | 54-58 | 51-55 | 58-64 | 55-62 | 60-65 | 52-55 | 56-61 | 52-60 | +2d6 Agility |
| 66-68 | 52-60 | 69-73 | 55-58 | 59-63 | 56-60 | 65-69 | 63-67 | 66-69 | 56-58 | 62-66 | 61-65 | +2d6 Accuracy |
| 69 | 61-73 | - | 59-61 | 64 | 61,62 | 70-72 | 68-71 | 70,71 | 59-61 | 67-70 | 66-71 | +2d6 Intelligence |
| 70-76 | 74-77 | 74-76 | 62-64 | 65-67 | 63,64 | 73,74 | 72-76 | 72-75 | 62-64 | 71-75 | 72-78 | +2d6 Perception |
| - | 78-80 | 77-80 | 65-67 | 68-70 | 65,66 | 75,76 | 77-79 | 76-78 | 65-67 | 76-78 | 79-82 | +2d6 Willpower |
| - | - | - | - | 71 | 67 | 77 | - | - | - | - | - | +2d6 Appearance |
| 77-80 | 81-85 | 81-84 | 68-74 | 72-76 | 68-74 | 78-81 | 80 | 79-82 | 68-73 | 79-85 | 83-86 | Weapon Expert Skill |
| 81,82 | 86,87 | 85-87 | 75 | 77-79 | 75,76 | 82,83 | 81-83 | 83-86 | 74-76 | 86,87 | 87-89 | Stealth Skill |
| 83,84 | 88,89 | 88-91 | 76-78 | 80-82 | 77,78 | 84,85 | 84,85 | 87-90 | 77-80 | 88-90 | 90-92 | Dodge Skill |
| 85-87 | 90-92 | 92,93 | 79-83 | 83-86 | 79-83 | 86-88 | 86-88 | 91,92 | 81-85 | 91,92 | 93,94 | 2 skill points for player allotment |
| 88,89 | 93,94 | 94 | 84,85 | 87,88 | 84,85 | 89,90 | 89,90 | 93 | 86,87 | 93 | 95,96 | d3+1 skill pts for player allotment |
| 90-95 | - | 95 | - | 89 | 86-88 | - | 91-94 | 94,95* | - | 94-96 | - | Latent Mutation, see ghost mutations* |
| 96,97 | 95,96 | 96 | 86-95 | 90-94 | 89-92 | 91-95 | 95-97 | 96,97 | 88-94 | 97 | 97,98 | +d6 to any player selected trait |
| 98 | 97 | 97 | 96,97 | 95-97 | 93-95 | 96,97 | 98 | 98 | 95,96 | 98 | 99 | +2d6 to any player selected trait |
| 99,00 | 98-00 | 98-00 | 98-00 | 98-00 | 96-00 | 98-00 | 99,00 | 99,00 | 97-00 | 99,00 | 00 | +1 to each trait |

*Plantod characters grow a new plantoid mutation, see list on page XR-223, while robots get a new special program, see page 161.*

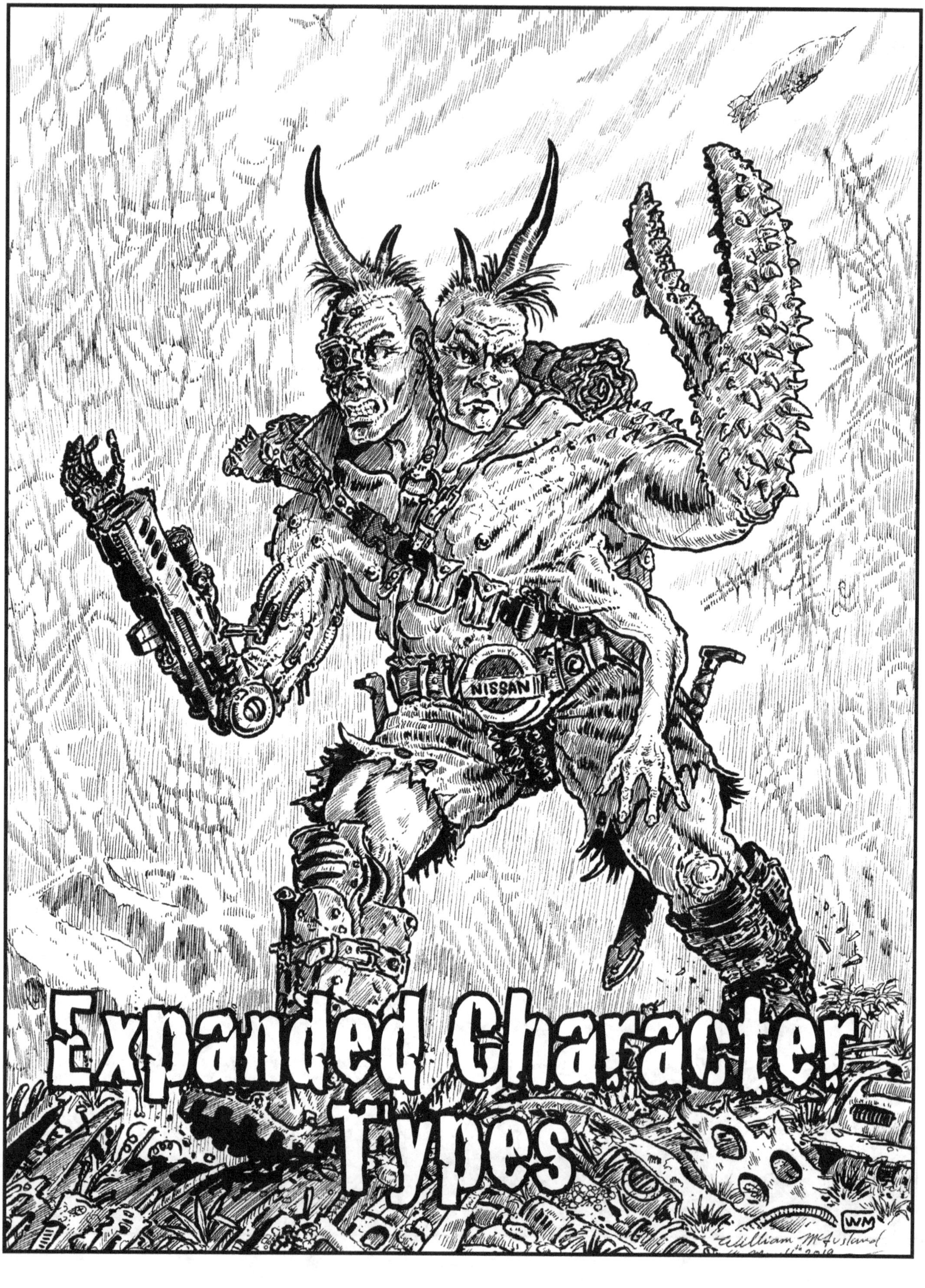

# Expanded Character Types

# Abomination

Originally grown in vats, abominations are mutant miscreations who were designated with alpha-numeric identities: a mix of manufacturer's code, batch number, purpose, and quality and were initially mindless, group thinking, slavish followers of a collective. Those gifted with fertile genitalia bred with other foul, unlikely scientific mistakes and oddities to form a new line of independently minded creatures.

The name 'abomination' seemed to stick, however, instead of their product ID, and in time, even their creators called them by the name they are now known by. Civilians, politicians and activists had less flattering names for these life forms, especially once these fleshy brutes began to see deployment against enemy troops, street mobs, rioters, mutants and other entities. Present day scribes and researchers have uncovered only a few pre-collapse names for these ghastly miscreations, such as blobs, rubber devils, fleshies, globulurs, gobbies, dough monsters, and flesh puddings.

Their DNA is a blend of custom manipulation, happy accidents, and that of animals and humans, the results often pitiful, and always sickening to behold. They have been described as bags of flesh and organs, dotted with orifices and appendages, sensory parts, heads, limbs, and discolored patches of hair, scale, or horn, the whole mess further dotted with open sores that are barely distinguishable from nostrils, mouths or mating orifices.

While hideous, hated and typically shunned, some exhibit traits which make them indispensable members of raiding parties, ship's crews, merc squads and ruin exploration teams. Bristling with often gruesome yet deadly appendages, armored plating, and a blend of offensive and defensive mutations, they can be fearsome and valued comrades. Of course, stemming from blended DNA and often growing up as ill treated filth, they tend to have bizarre personalities, odd illnesses and one or more flaws.

**Each Abomination will have 1d2 flaw mutations, 1d3 minor mutations, and 1d4+2 prime mutations** from the mutation determination lists starting on page 228, which includes mutations from this book and the hub rules. Likewise, each abomination gets one or more features on each of the following series of tables to establish its senses, gender and reproductive ca-

pacity, body structure, locomotion, appendages, and miscellaneous abomination aspects. A sample background table is also included on page XR-28, while a character sheet specific to abomination characters is included in Appendix 8 on page XR-513 or available for free download from our website at https://www.outlandarts.com/expansionrules.htm .

## Abominations Starting Trait Stats*

**Endurance: 50+1d100**
**Strength: 40+1d20**
**Agility: 20+1d20**
**Accuracy: 20+1d20**
**Intelligence: 2d20**
**Perception: 20+1d12**
**Willpower: 3d20**
**Appearance: 2d4**

*Like any character type, jot down the initially rolled trait values in light pencil, as all these stats are likely to change during the next few steps in this character's creation!*

## Abomination Sensory Organs

Roll and record the following sensory organs that this abomination was born with, although through later random mutation generation a feature could change, instead of replacing it.

### Optical Senses — Roll 2d6 once, plus at least 1 human eye

**2. Purple orb eye:** Exhibits the mutation of beam eye. See TME hub rules mutation number 13 on page TME-61.
**3. Blue orb eye:** Shoots electrical pulse identical to the mutation in the hub rules, number 31 on page TME-65.
**4,5. Normal human eye**
**6. Fish Eye:** Can see normally under water. Very alert, and improves perception by +2d6 trait points.
**7. Red bulbous eye:** Night vision to 20m.
**8. Two human eyes:** Side by side and face forward.
**9. Black oval shaped eye:** Can see illusions, holograms, and dimensional beings to 120m.
**10. Green orb eye:** As a normal eye but also sees radiation within 500m.
**11. Cluster of eyes:** 3d6 tiny, bead-like eyes around the top of the abomination which are ever alert. Add +20+d20 to perception score.
**12. Stalked Eyes:** Large eyes on 30cm long, flexible stalks. Ever vigilant in multiple directions. 1d4 present, with a +10 bonus to perception per eye stalk.

### Auditory Senses — Roll 2d6, 1d4 times

**2. Dog ear:** Add 6 perception trait value, and hears twice as far as a regular ear.
**3,4. Chimp ear:** Add 4 perception trait value.
**5-7. Human ear:** Add 2 perception trait value.
**8,9. Pig ear:** Add 4 perception trait value.
**10. Tiny hole serves as ear.**
**11. Rabbit ear:** Add 5 perception trait value, and hears 1.5 times as far as a human ear.
**12. Two human ears,** one on either side of top most portion of torso, add +4 perception score.

### Olfactory Senses — Roll 2d6, 1d3 times

**2. Dog nose:** Can pick up scents 4 times better than a regular human nose.
**3. Pig nose:** Can pick up scents twice as well as a regular human nose.
**4-6. Human nose**
**7,8. Single nostril slit**
**9,10. Skull like dual slits**
**11. Human nose,** but very large and bulbous: Can breathe better, adding to oxygen intake. Increase strength and agility trait by +1d6 each.
**12. Series of olfactory slits:** These are also gills and this abomination can breathe in water like a fish.

## Mouth & Taste Sense    Roll 2d6, 1d4 times

The abomination has a normal human mouth and tongue with which the abomination speaks, breaths, and consumes food and drink, plus 1d4 of the following:

**2,3. Small feminine mouth** with access to lungs vocal chords and digestive tract, plus rather normal tongue.

**4. Mouth-like slit** containing a long pointed tongue but no access to digestive tract or breathing.

**5-7. Feeding mouth** with access to digestive tract, but not connected to lungs and unable to speak.

**8,9. A long patch of tongue** growing on the abomination's hide, it can flex about and reach out 10cm to lick and taste things.

**10,11. Mouth** with breathing and speaking ability but not connected to digestive tract.

**12. Dog's muzzle,** with powerful jaws, fangs and lapping tongue. This can make an extra bite attack in melee, SV +5, DMG 2d6, connected to lungs and digestive tract of character.

## Touch Sense    Roll 2d6, 1d2 times

But at a minimum this abomination senses anything it physically brushes against, is struck by, as well as impacts with one of its own appendages.

**2,3. Feelers:** This abomination exhibits 3d6, 6m long, delicate feelers used to probe around it to move at normal speed even in total darkness. Likewise, these spaghetti-like tendrils can elicit a mating response from eligible breeding partners, or, each has 1 point or strength and when combined, can lift small objects and serves as tentacles. Although not typically used as a weapon, and only ever able to inflict 1d2 stun damage from a combined smack, these tendrils can be chopped off by enemies and are DV -5 and have but 1 point of endurance. Severed tendrils grow back in 2 months. Add 1 kilogram weight per feeler.

**4,5. Whiskers:** Hundreds of 30cm long pale whisker hairs grow from this abominations body and limbs, allowing it to evaluate its surroundings when in total darkness and let it to move at least half its normal rate. Likewise, in melee combat, these whiskers help it discern an opponent's incoming attacks and thus give this being a -6 DV bonus during melee range combat.

**6-8. None:** No extra sensory organ.

**9,10. Retractable tentacle:** A single, finger-thick tentacle grows from the main torso of this abomination. This appendage can shrivel and be withdrawn close to the body and hangs like a limp 10cm long tube of skin when not needed. When called for, however, it can grow at a rate of 30cm per round to a maximum length of between 5 and 10 meters (roll at character creation for fixed length: 4+1d6m). At any length, this gruesome tentacle is highly sensitive, and can probe the path ahead allowing the abomination to move at least half speed in total darkness. Likewise, this tentacle can detect changes in temperature, the presence of radiation within 30m and in what direction, as well as the subtle vibration of movement, including the heartbeat of man sized or larger creatures.

Once extended, this tube of flesh adds +2 to the being's initiative value, however, being so sensitive, the tentacle is susceptible to pain and does not make for a good bludgeoning weapon. It can however coil around objects, including the handle of a crude weapon such as an axe, club or length of pipe. If used as an extra melee attack without holding a weapon, this feeler has a permanent strength of 18 and uses the base strike value of the abomination. A smack from this appendage will inflict a base, fixed damage of 1d6 stun, with no skill or strength modifiers applicable to it. If hacked at, it has a DV of -15 and 8 points of Endurance. A new feeler tentacle will grow back in 3 months. This tentacle adds 5kg weight.

**11. Bug Antennas:** Like an ant, this abomination exhibits 1d4+1 multi-jointed antenna, usually from the top of its mass. With these, it can detect changes in temperature, air pressure, radiation with 20m and the subtle hints which tell of living creatures nearby. With these appendages, the abomination is +1 initiative.

**12. Goosebumps:** This abomination's skin erupts in 5cm tall goose bumps whenever it detects other, unfamiliar living beings near it within 6 meters. Likewise, less pronounced goose bumps and shivers occur when the weather changes, a sand storm approaches, or radiation is within 100 meters. All these varied responses are known to this abomination, having lived with this sensory system all its life. When detecting other beings before it can see or hear them, such as in the dark or when other beings are hiding within 6m, this character is +2 initiative against living adversaries or strangers, except androids or robots, but including dimensional beings which give off a very distinct skin reaction.

## Abomination Gender and Reproduction Capacity    Roll 2d6

**2. Sterile:** This specimen cannot reproduce nor has any gender identification, sex drive or feelings one way or another toward males or females, thus the notion of sparing enemy women and children are inconceivable to it.

**3,4. Female, yet sterile:** While it might have the yearning to fornicate and yearn to have offspring, this abomination is sterile, has no eggs, and doesn't experience a monthly cycle. She will have 1d3 breasts and at least one female sexual organ, but a 33% chance of 1d3 others at various locations on her main torso.

**5,6. Female and fertile:** This abomination has a group of 1d4 breasts and at least one sexual organ and a 37% chance of 1d3 additional sex organs distributed about its torso. It can experience one pregnancy for each sexual organ, possibly at different stages of development, with each birth resulting in a live offspring 67% of the time. Offspring will exhibit half the traits of each parent, plus a 50% chance of each mutation present from each, parent, too. The father species could be any creature with human DNA. Pregnant abominations tend to cease combat or ruin exploration activities after the sixth month of any pregnancy and return to duty 5+1d4 months after giving birth.

**7.8. Male and Fertile:** Having huskier voice, a 77% chance of 1d6 patches of body hair, and at least 1 set of male genitalia, this abomination is motivated by testosterone as much as any human man, often more so. Besides his normal reproductive array, he's 68% likely to have 1d3 other sets randomly adhered to his body, all functional simultaneously with each other, and all capable of impregnating females of any humanoid variety. For every extra set of male parts, this individual is one degree more infused with masculinity and libido.

**9,10. Male but sterile:** As a fertile male, in roll 7,8 above, however for all his efforts, this fella's mating activities will not produce offspring.

**11. Gender Cycle:** As the NPC mutation no.328 on page XR-294 of this book. There is a 27% chance that while able to frolic, this abomination is unknowingly completely sterile and unable to reproduce.

**12. Dual Gendered:** Like the NPC mutation by the same name on page XR-293 of this book, This abomination is both male and female and will have 1d3 of each gender's sexual organs at various points on its torso, as well as

a cluster of 1d4 breasts. This oddity typically adopts the gender association of the sex of which it has the most sets of genitalia, however, if it has the hots for a certain being, it will usually take on the role of whatever it's would-be-lover is itself attracted to. For example, if it befriends a woman, and falls for her, this abomination will play up its masculine side, and visa versa.

## Abomination Body Structure

The following table determines the shape of an abomination character's torso. From this main body, every other appendage grows. For the most part, this globular mass is a bag of organs covered in human skin, but will have one or more sets of ribs, plus whatever shoulder blades, hip bone sockets and ridges of vertebra and spine are needed to bare the assortment of limbs, heads and other body parts stemming from the torso or core of the being. Add the weight and height of its legs, shown on the table to follow, to the kilograms or centi-meters height presented here:

### Abomination Body Structure    Roll 2d6, once

**2. Slug-like**, with the bulk of it upright and 100+1d100cm tall, 30+1d20cm thick, but having a portion of it dragging along behind that measures 1d100+30cm in length. Weight 100+1d100kg.

**3. Dumbbell shaped**, with two globular masses attached at a thin 30cm wide waist, much like the number eight, and normally standing vertically. Total length 160+d100cm. Weight 80+1d100kg.

**4. Tubular**, 30+d20cm wide and 130+1d100cm tall. Stands upright 78% of the time, otherwise horizontally. Weight 90+1d100kg.

**5. Ball shaped**, 100+3d20cm across. Weight 130+1d100kg.

**6. Triangular wedge**, 100+1d100cm across from corner to corner, but only 30cm thick, and 100+1d100cm tall. Weight 100+1d100kg.

**7. Oval shaped**, 120+1d100cm tall and a meter across. Weight 120+1d100kg.

**8. Squarish shaped**, 100+1d100cm tall and wide, but only a half meter thick like a mattress. Weight 100+1d100kg.

**9. Conical**, 100+1d100cm tall with the top being the widest at a meter and the bottom point only 30cm wide. Weight 80+1d100kg.

**10. Pylon shaped**, 100+1d100cm tall with the widest part at the bottom being 100+2d20cm wide and the top point only 10+1d20cm wide. Weight 80+1d100kg.

**11. Star shaped**, like a roundish giant starfish, upright with the fifth point the topmost, the thing 100+1d100cm across and only 30cm thick. Weight 70+1d100kg.

**12. Morphable.** This abomination's internal skeleton is made of cartilage and it can assume many shapes from a 30cm wide tube to a ball, human shaped torso, wedge, star, square or anything else. Its limbs may impede its passage through very narrow spaces, but more or less can pass through any opening of 30cm or greater. Its normal state is a 100+1d100cm tall, rectangular shaft. Weight 100+1d100kg.

### Abomination Locomotion   Roll 2d6, once

**2. No legs**, instead has a 200+2d100cm long, thick leathery snake tail. This abomination can move 7m per round but also, make an extra bludgeoning attack in melee that is +6 SV and inflicts 3d6 stun damage, plus any strength based modifiers. The tail lacks dexterity nor the ability to grasp objects but does store 10 days of water and liquid food from which this specimen can sustain itself. Add 200kg weight and 10+1d20cm height.

**3,4. One human leg and one animal leg.** This animal limb, while hideous, is about the same size as the human leg and allows the character to move 8m per round. Roll 1d6: 1. dog leg / 2. goat leg / 3. horse leg / 4. chicken leg / 5. pig leg / 6. crab leg**. Add 30+1d20cm to height and 30kg weight for set.

**5,6. Misshapen human legs**, moves 6m per round. Increase height by 30+1d20cm and weight by 25kg .

**7,8. 1d4+1 muscular, stubby tentacle-like growths** designed for walking or swimming. Movement 7m per round on land or in water, plus add +1 skill point in climbing. Add 20+1d20cm to height and add 10kg weight per tentacle.

**9. Baby legs.** 4+1d4 human baby legs support this abomination's bulk, propelling it along like a nightmarish centipede at 7m per round**. increase height by 10+1d10 cm and weight be 5kg per baby leg.

**10. Animal legs**, all identical 28% of the time otherwise an assortment. The abomination will have 1d3+1 legs, each adding 3m movement, roll 1d12: 1. dog / 2. chicken / 3. horse / 4. duck* / 5. cow / 6. pig / 7. spider** / 8. crab** / 9. cat / 10. rat / 11. seal flipper* / 12. octopus tentacle***. Add 10+1d20cm height and 30kg weight for set.

**11. Mass of 10+d12 slippery, eel-like tentacles** which move this abomination along at 8m per round, allow it to climb as if it were 3 points in that skill, and, grapple opponents at 2 skill points. Increase height by 30+2d20cm and add 3kg weight per tentacle.

**12. Enormous, clawed reptile legs** which move it at 9m per round but also can make one claw slash per round in melee as an extra attack, being +10 SV and doing 1d20 base damage**. Add 50+2d20cm height plus 50+1d20 kg weight.

** This limb adds +1m swimming speed to the abomination. See swimming speeds on page XR-20.*

*** Limb(s) adds +1 skill point in climbing.*

**** Limb adds +1m to the PCs swimming speed plus adds 1 skill point in climbing.*

## Abomination Appendages

One regular human-like arm, plus roll 1d100, 1d4+1 times. Add 5kg per limb. The number shown behind an entry is its mutation number.

### Abomination Appndages    Roll 1d100, 1d4+1 times

| | |
|---|---|
| **01-23.** | Another Human arm and hand |
| **24-29.** | Tiny human arm (fixed strength score of only 3d6*). Can wield a pistol, knife, dagger or other small one handed item. Not strong enough to pull on a bow string. Ends in a small, dainty hand. |
| **30-36.** | Bladed Limb, only one, 15, page TME-62 |
| **37-44.** | Crab Pincer, only one 23, page TME-63 |
| **45-48.** | Energy Tendril 171, page XR-243 |
| **49,50.** | Fish Fins 178, page XR-245 |
| **51-53.** | Flame Thrower Limb 179, page XR-245 |
| **54-59.** | Flesh Whip 180, page XR-246 |
| **60-63.** | Paralysis Tendril, only one, 65, page TME-12 |
| **64-69.** | Quill Thrower Limb 220, page XR-262 |
| **70-74.** | Razor Hook 221, page XR-262 |
| **75,76.** | Spike Thrower Arm 228, page XR-264 |
| **77,78.** | Stinger Spike 229, page XR-264 |
| **79-81.** | Sword Arm 232, page XR-267 |
| **82-90.** | Tentacle, only one, 86, page TME-75 |
| **91-93.** | Thrust Spike 88, page TME-76 |
| **94-00.** | Unique Tentacle 241, page XR-273 |

**Does not grow in strength as character gains rank or acquires other mutations at character generation or rank gain, etc.*

## Additional Abomination Details   Roll 2d6, once

**2,3. Multiple human heads,** (1d3) each having a 50% chance of being a male or female with its own hair color, personality and appearance score, not to mention independent intelligence and willpower trait values. There is a 60% chance that each is neck-less and fused to the torso of the abomination, otherwise attached to a neck and able to turn about like a normal human head.

The head with the highest willpower score is the dominant head and source of consciousness for the abomination, at least while this head is awake. There is a 22% chance that each head is also a ghost mutant and will have a mental mutation (re-roll on the latent mutation list, page XR-232, until a mental mutation occurs, as opposed to other deviations like advanced kidneys). If all heads are decapitated or killed, the whole creature dies.

**4-6. Human head:** Add 3d6 perception, plus this growth is 70% likely to lack any sort of neck, and instead be embedded into the upper portion of the abomination's torso. It will be the point of consciousness for this being and if killed, the whole creature dies. The appearance score of the head is rolled separately from the body, and could very possibly be attractive. The head will be of the gender of the abomination, however, if the being is duel gendered or has no gender at all, then the face will be that of an androgynous, feminine looking youth. This head is 36% chance likely to be enhanced with 1d3 mental mutations. Use the latent mutations list on page XR-232.

**7. Skin feature:** roll 1d10:

**1. Covered in fur** like an ape, warm and improves DV -10.

**2. Covered in lizard scales,** adds -15 DV.

**3. Slick with slippery slime,** difficult to hold and gets 3 hazard checks to avoid being grappled.

**4. Distasteful,** anything to bite it will get a bitter mouthful and unless defending its lair or young, must make a morale check to continue to bite at this abomination.

**5. Acid resistant layer,** abomination takes only half damage from acid attacks.

**6. Photosynthetic tissues,** character has patches of green skin and derives nourishment from sunlight, plus, heals an extra 4 trait points per hour when exposed to sunlight.

**7-10. Articulating bone plates,** the character is slower, with a reduced movement rate of -0.5m per round speed, but base defensive value increased by -15 DV.

**8,9. Extra organ:** This abomination's torso houses an extra random organ, roll 1d6:

**1. Set of lungs:** increased oxygen intake allows PC to be +1 meter faster per round and +10 strength.

**2. Kidneys and liver set:** allows PC to cope twice as well with toxins and so gets two hazard checks against all poisons.

**3. Extra heart:** blood flow increases PC's movement by +0.5 meters movement and adds +15 strength.

**4. Extra brain:** with separate intelligence and willpower score. If main brain killed, this one, with a distinct personality, takes over the abomination. Main brain and this inner brain carry on a dialog whenever the being is at rest, often causing the abomination to talk out loud to itself in two distinct voices.

**5. Digestive tract:** character can consume twice as much nutrition and send food throughout its body more rapidly, allowing it to heal an extra 5 trait points per day. If needed, it can instead devote one stomach to water storage only, and retain 6 liters of spare water, giving it 6 days additional survival in emergencies.

**6. Reproductive organs:** if the abomination has no current gender, or no dominant gender, then these organs are 50% likely to be female, otherwise male. If the PC already has a pre-determined gender, then this set is of the same, and serves as a duplicate set.

**10. Buoyant:** The character floats like a rubber raft. For every 50kg of the character's weight, it can stretch his or her bulk out to bear the weight of an adult human or 100kg load. This character can neither sink nor swim down below the water's surface for more than 6 rounds.

**11. Bizarre feature,** roll 1d6:

**1. Human Shapes:** This abomination can temporarily compress and or expand to shape shift into a regular human form. The form is of the same gender and outward appearance every time, and can be clothed and equipped as desired. Any appendages or mutations can be compressed within its new form, or expelled and used as desired while in the shape-shifted form. This shape shift can be employed but once per 24-hour period and can be maintained for one minute per point of the character's willpower trait value.

**2. Radioactive adaptation:** The abomination absorbs radiation into a specialized organ. He, she, or it suffers no harm from radiation and can even expel it as a pulse from a stubby, black tube-like organ once per day per rank. Range as PC's willpower in meters, SV 01-80, damage 1d20 + one mild exposure of radiation to those struck. The character must first be exposed to radiation in game-play, of any rad level, to be charged with radiation and then has 10+1d10 expulsions available to it thereafter.

**3. Regeneration:** This abomination heals at an incredible rate of 2 trait points per round.

**4. Doesn't age.** Once reaching adulthood, this character doesn't suffer any ill effects from growing older. Unless killed by disease, accident or violence, this abomination could theoretically live forever.

**5. Clear Jelly:** This abomination has no pigment to its tissues, bones or appendages, and if it desires, and when naked, can slip into water and become virtually invisible. If attempting to conceal itself on dry land, this mostly transparent being can flatten itself against a wall or floor and gain 4 extra skill points in concealed movement or conceal self (see the stealth skill on page 51 of the hub rules.

**6. Inflatable:** When desired, this abomination can gulp in vast quantities of air and inflate special gas sacs in its hide. It takes 8 rounds to inflate sufficiently to gain flight, but only 4 rounds to fill itself enough to float on water or take only half damage from a fall — although suffers full damage if it hits before becoming sufficiently inflated to avoid harm.

If this abomination is clad in full body armor or heavy clothing, it cannot inflate, and once inflated, quadruples in size. These sacs of hot air allow the character to float upward at a rate of 4 meter per round, although can do so at a slower rate of climb or reach a desired height by letting out some of this gas through specialized pours. The wind direction determines the flight path and speed of the abomination unless this freak deploys some relic, winged propulsion system, or pet to direct its flight. This power can be used 4 times per day.

Should an inflated abomination take 10 or more damage from any puncture attack, it will lose 25% of its gas and no longer gains lift. If two such punctures occur, it will float back to earth at 2 meters per round. Should three such hits occur, it will drop at 5m per round, while if four or more separate punctures occur which do 10 or more damage each, then all the gas leaks from this abomination and unless some sort of large, sticky patch is applied to the hole, this character will plummet to the earth and suffer normal falling damage based on their altitude, body weight, and what surface they fall on. Falling rules are covered on page 123 of the hub rules book.

**12. Two details,** roll 1d10+1.

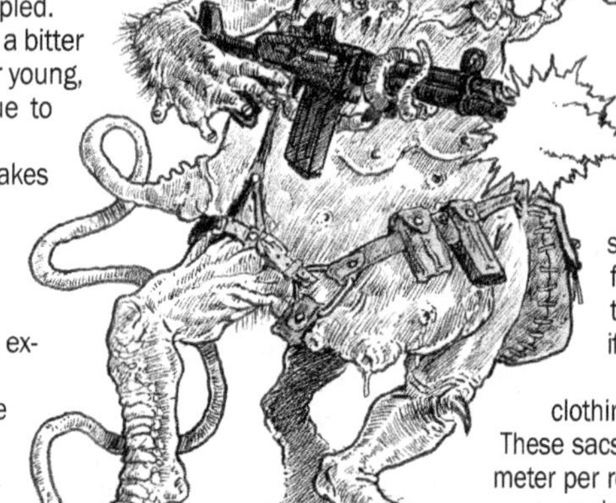

## Abomination's Origin Examples   Roll 2d6

**2.** This character was created in an underground laboratory by a bunker inhabiting, corporate faction of pure stock humans. Meant to be a bio-weapon, this abomination was separated from its strike team, or ate them, and fled into the world as a young adult.

**3.** Born as a slave in a junk mine, mistreated beyond belief, and forced into a fighting pit for the sport of gamblers. This abomination escaped in its teens and made its way to a town where it took up a new trade.

**4.** Born to a prostitute who took one look at it, recalled her night with the hideous, cloth wrapped father, and threw the squealing baby into the street.

Street urchins raised this blobby babe as a thief, thug and enforcer. Has since entered another profession.

**5.** No clue. This PC was found in a dead nomadic trader's wagon, kept as a pet and garrison mascot while young. Grew up to be a town militia soldier before branching off into other careers.

**6.** No idea where it came from, was found in a ditch outside of town, adopted by commoner parents.

**7.** Sold as meat when very young to a butcher, who initially grew it to adulthood to get more pounds of 'beef', but this character's physical features, ability to talk, and robustness made the abomination too valuable to eat, and so it became a productive member of society.

**8.** Caught as a youngster in a trapper's snare and destined for the stew pot, the hunter spared this fleshy morsel when it talked. Kept as a pet and hunting beast, this abomination grew to adulthood, was seduced by the pleasures of a trade town, learned of the ruins, of the old world, and met its first team of excavators. Now, obsessed with exploration, relics and glory, it looks for the ideal team of roughnecks to set out on a life of archeology, pleasure, and acceptance.

**9.** Born to a commoner woman who was seduced by an abomination who traveled with a dig team, this miscreation was born into a loveless household that never accepted it. Both it and its mother were treated with disdain and forced into a life of dangerous industrial and agricultural labor. When its mother was killed, this abomination took what it could and left, searching for its father and a life as an excavator.

**10.** Unsure of its birth, this pitiful thing spent its childhood as an indebted servant to a saloon owner, rented out as a curiosity to the depraved, as a field worker, latrine digger and draft animal. Now grown, it seeks new opportunities, especially if they involve getting away from its former keepers.

**11.** Its mother was an abomination, who dropped this PC as she fled from purists — who tortured and impaled her as this small, globular specimen looked on. Discovered by a dig team and saved, the young blobber grew to adulthood, worked for a few silvers per month, and always dreamed of being an excavator, too, and doing great deeds of kindness... except to pure stock humans, which it distrusts.

**12.** Born in a nutrient vat in a high-tech, oldster vault. Raised as a beast of burden and source of donor organs and blood, this abomination found a ventilation duct and escaped to the surface as a teen. It soon fell in with nomads who made it pull a wagon, yet escaped in a barter town, and now seeks a life of excavation... every watchful for agents of its former subterranean creator-masters.

# Android

Differing from a digital being, these entities are more self contained, exhibit hard-wired CPUs and a more independent nature, blending the best of a physical robotic body and stand-alone digital brain. Like living humans, however, they are very mortal. Typically, when their head is destroyed, they are erased and lost forever. Also like humans, who their creators wished to emulate as much as possible, unique androids can learn as they endure the ordeals of the twisted new world, improving their skills, enhancing their mechanical body, and advancing as other intelligent beings do.

Poly-sheathed beings, commonly known as androids, are best described as mechanical humans. Their wide spread use precedes even that of trans-humans and synthetic humans such as clones and bioreplicas. They were made by several corporations and governments with the vast majority built for innocent civilian purposes, some for the adult entertainment industry, still others for military applications as mass produced, disposable, unquestioning infantry troops.

Some androids once served in an anti-human faction, but deserted in order to preserve themselves, experience a greater truth, or act on new found self realization. Other skinbots are nomads, wandering survivors from long forgotten installations, and may even be new arrivals who were manufactured in hidden, hi tech-factories for no other purpose than to adapt and survive. These units were made by a mindless machine programmed to construct the beings, but not to issue orders.

The very complex programming an android possesses often makes them free thinking, and after decades of constant data processing, 'wake up' get self aware and look about themselves and inwardly question what they are part of. They will often simply became sentient and realize that they are separate and unique beings, and yearn for independence and an identity to call their own. Many androids who gain self-aware-

ness are caught by other monitoring robotic units, or a mainframe Ai computer that observes its troops, or by other androids on the lookout for any desertion or free thinking tendencies. Offenders are deactivated and used for replacement parts.

While many self aware, unique androids will harbor fear, distrust or disdain for humanity. Others will experiece a great adoration for humans, live among them as a loyal servant, or do so secretly, posing as a human, running the local beer hall or brothel, keeping a careful eye on the children of its creators. A few will seek the company of adventures out of a deep need to understand the reason for the global catastrophes which brought about the downfall of civilization, or, not knowing what its own nature is, having never knowingly met another android, it seeks to explore the ruins hoping to encounter brothers and sisters from its own manufacturer, possibly looking for a more advanced version of its kind as if seeking a parent or older, wiser sibling.

In the age of The Mutant Epoch, unique android characters can be sourced from six main classifications and thirty five sub-categories based on their original purpose. These self-aware machines are either ancient custom built entities, the last of a larger model line, or a prototype destined for mass production that was never started. Many are of recent construction, and assembled from the skeletal structures, wiring, servo motors and outer sheathing of other androids, and given life by implanting an advanced, CPU brain in their heads.

These unique, metal and plastic individuals identify more with their simulated humanity than the non-organic make-up of their mind and body, and refer to themselves as artificial people. An android will have a paramount personality which humanoids can relate to, rely on, and allow them to discern each android from the next, even down to their handwriting, speech mannerisms, slang and desires.

Skinbots are immune to many of the hazards of organic beings, including drowning, venom, poison gas, and mental attacks such as telepathy, mind crush, mental dominion and the like. Androids, like cyborgs and robots, are however highly vulnerable to electromagnetic pulse attacks or EMP, some electricity shooting mutations and relics, as well as being hacked and taken over by hostile artificial intelligences and digital beings. Often, a digital being is housed in the body of an android, and both the digital being and an android body must be rolled using two separate character sheets to construct one character.

Android characters do not feel pain, are immune to mental attacks that afflict a living brain, and if decapitated, and utterly lose their body, they are still considered alive and their head can be collected and either carried about like a talkative computer and pet, or eventually put onto the body of a different android or robot — although this is a tricky procedure handled best by very talented NPC robotics technicians. When reduced below zero endurance, or its willpower or intelligence trait are drained below zero, the android becomes dormant until repaired — or self-healed in some cases — and can survive in low battery mode for 1d100+6 years before its CPU suffers some irreversible corruption and is deleted. If the head of an android is incinerated, crushed, or shot apart, then it is dead.

Like unique robots, androids can suffer great harm from exposure to potent levels of radiation. See 'Radiation and effects on Robots and Androids' on page 379 of this book for details.

As a character, a unique android will have random traits, skills, implants and potential features according to the tables that follow. All androids can read, write and do math. At first, androids can appear to be complex, hard to generate characters based on the extensive amount of PC creation material presented on the next 29 pages, however, creating one is really quite simple and involves one or more rolls on each of the tables to follow.

To start off, use table XR-2 to roll the eight basic traits just like any other character. These traits are all subject to change as the player rolls on the subsequent tables and adds their details. Use a photocopy of the Unique Android character sheet found on page 514 of the appendices, or download and print the free pdf from this book's webpage at https://www.outlandarts.com/expansionrules.htm

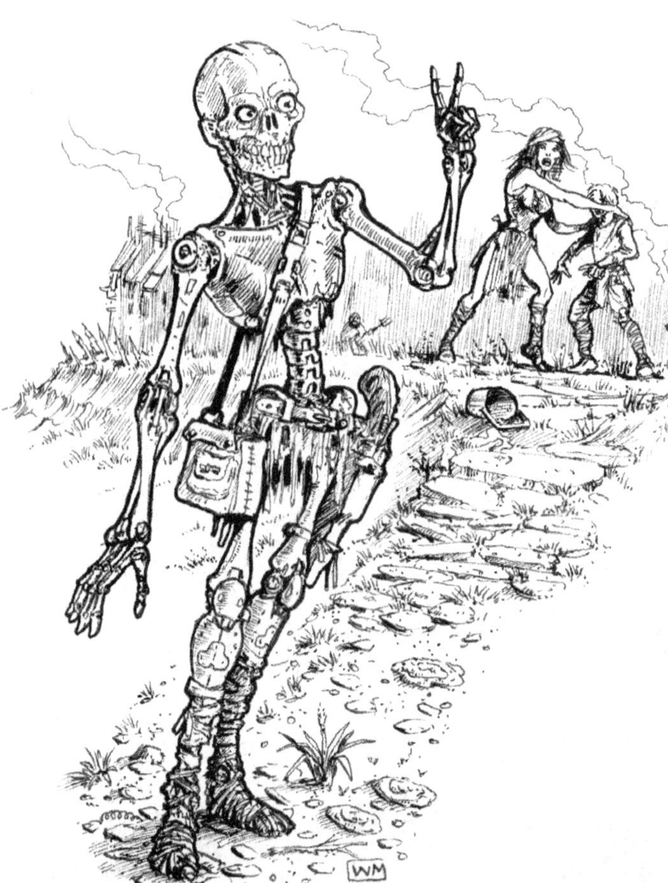

## 14 Easy Steps To Create a Unique Android Character:

**Step 1:** Roll base stats for all traits like most other characters on table XR-2 on page 8 of this book.

**Step 2: Gender Pattern:** While the player can choose to play an android that was built to look like a male or female, or some genderless variant altogether, you can use Table XR-13 on the next page and allow for the dice to decide.

**Step 3: Establish your character's original purpose** on table XR-14, next page, which will determine some trait modifiers, changes to their skeletal structure, sheathing, skills and later, their pre-game caste. Each Original Purpose has a short write up, which you'll need to read to help better understand this character's background and reveal certain talents and in-game features.

**Step 4: Roll to discover the android's skeletal structure** on table XR-34 on page 45 with a modifier to a 1d10 roll based on their original purpose.

**Step 5: Determine your android's Sheathing.** Again, this skin type roll is based on what their original purpose or intended design was and again uses a simple 1d10 plus or minus any modifier. See Table XR-35 on page 34 to find out what covers your artificial person's skeleton. Descriptions of each sheath follow that table.

**Step 6: Healing Mode**, roll a 1d100 on table XR-36, page 47 and record the results. This is important information on how your character can be repaired, or possibly self heal after taking damage.

**Step 7: CPU in Android's Head:** See table XR-37 on page 48. This table tells you what sort of brain your android character has. Roll 1d100 here and record the results. Write this in lightly in pencil because it is likely that the original purpose and later, pre-game caste modifiers, will yield changes to intelligence and willpower.

**Step 8: Sensory Capabilities** of unique androids are determined by a series of really quick random rolls on pages 49 and 50, mostly using a simple 1d10 roll. Here you will quickly discover and record the android's eye appearance, sight, vocal, olfactory, and auditory capabilities, sense of touch, taste, as well as non-typical sensory capabilities.

**Step 9: Determine Age Appearance:** On page 51, toss another 1d100 to establish how old the android's was made to look,

Here you'll roll another 1d100 to establish your character's manufacturing date, which could have the PC being a brand new construct or an ancient mechanical person who's been around since before the fall of the old world.

**Step 10: Hair on Head?:** Also on page 51, roll 1d10 on three quick tables to establish the presence of hair, hair type, and and color

**Step 11: Handedness:** Roll 1d10 on page 52 to figure out if your android is right or left handed, or ambidextrous.

**Step 12: Special Features Determination.** Next is two or three 1d100 rolls on table XR-52 on page 52 for Special Features of a Unique Android. These really give color and special abilities to your new character. The 'original purpose' determines how many rolls and any modifiers to the 1d100 roll.

**Step 13: Discover the Android's Pre-Game Caste:** This depends on what the unit's original purpose was. Find the android's 'original purpose' in the list, roll a d20, and the character's pre-game caste is established. If the caste is listed in bold text, it will be found in this book, while normal font caste names means that a caste is included in the TME hub rules book. The caste of a character offers yet more potential trait modifiers as well as which skills, or skill set rolls, and which outfitting code is to be used.

**Step 14: Name your android!** Your character is done and just needs a name and if applicable, a randomly determined personality from table XR-294 on page 500 of this book.

# Android Gender Pattern

Unless already determined by the unit's originally intended purpose, such as is sometimes stated in the civilian android model, then this unit was most likely designed to appear as a specific human gender, sometimes with fully functional parts associated with that gender pattern. In short, the builder of this unit gave it the stature, physical appearance, skeletal structure and anatomical features of a specific sex — often very shapely or well-endowed features, too.

On the other hand, a few were made as sexless specimens, while rare, advanced models feature the ability to morph their appearance between genders. Unless already stated in a previous 'original purpose' description, there is a 6 in 10 chance that an android with a visible gender is fully functional like a living humanoid, either to serve some amatory service role or aid in covert activities and better conceal their non-organic nature. Of course, a player might prefer to play a specific gender pattern, and so this rolling on the following table is optional.

**Table XR-13/ Gender Pattern  Roll 1d100**

**10-47.** Male

**48-94.** Female

**95-98.** Androgynous: Sexless with no readily obvious gender pattern or genitalia.

**99,00.** Morphable: Can spend 20+3d6 minutes changing its sheathing and tissues to convert to either a male or female anatomy, complete with voice change and facial structure changes. Height stays the same. This unit always exhibits flesh-like heated gelatin for a tissue sheathing.

# Android's Original Purpose

The reason this android was built determines how attractive, smart, skilled or robust it is in the current post-apocalyptic Epochian era. While the original utility of this android might have mattered in the pre-devastation times, and ordained its construction and abilities, a self aware, unique android in the new world can conduct itself however it sees fit. Of course, in a barbaric, semi-civilized age like that of The Mutant Epoch, an android that was once built for combat has advan-

tages over one that was designed to work in a day care. These, and dozens of other humanoid robot designs await in the following listings.

Roll 1d100 on the following table below to establish what the builder of this unit had intended the android to be used for. The trait modifiers shown below, if any, might be added or subtracted to by further specialization, especially for civilian and military models which call upon follow-up tables.

**Table XR-14/ Unique Android Original Purpose Determination**

| 1d100 | Original Purpose | END | STR | AG | ACC | INT | WILL | Per | APP | Skeletal Structure Roll* | Tissue Sheathing Roll* | Page |
|---|---|---|---|---|---|---|---|---|---|---|---|---|
| 01-43. | Civilian | ---- See Table XR-14 below for more trait modifiers ---- | | | | | | | | 1d8 | 1d8 | 32 |
| 44-53. | Medical | - | - | +4d6 | +3d6 | +4d6+10 | - | +3d6 | +1d6 | 1d8 | 1d8 | 38 |
| 54-62. | Scientific | - | - | +2d6 | +3d6 | +4d6+20 | - | +3d6 | - | 1d8 | 1d8 | 38 |
| 63-74. | Industrial | +4d6+10 | +3d6+20 | +1d6 | +1d6 | - | - | - | - | 1d6+2 | 1d6+2 | 39 |
| 75-82. | Technician | - | +1d6 | +2d6 | +3d6 | +4d6+5 | +1d6 | +3d6 | - | 1d8+1 | 1d6+3 | 40 |
| 83-00. | Military | —— See Table XR-27 on page 41 for trait modifiers and skeletal and Tissue Sheathing Roll Mods —— | | | | | | | | | | 41 |

*NOTE: Any trait modifiers are added to the android's trait score after it is rolled on the main trait table (Table XR-2 on page 8), instead of being added to the dice roll to determine the specific trait. Further trait modifiers might occur based on an android's 'original purpose' sub-category.*

**The dice roll shown for both the Skeletal Structure or Tissue Sheathing columns are dice used to roll on the tables on page 45, not added to any stat or trait. These two features also contribute to establishing the base weight of each android.*

## Android Original Purpose Descriptions and Details

Civilian androids were mass produced and easily the most commonly found models that dig teams unearth. These humanoid robots usually had plastic bones — although many featured fully biodegradable sheathing, bones and parts which have long since decayed into dust.

This unique android, however, is built different from other models. It is either a customized variant, from a limited edition, or a prototype of some rare, purpose-built and perhaps one of a kind design.

Roll on the following table to determine what its original intended job was, with each model gaining trait bonuses or penalties. See the description text to follow for each unit's intended, pre-play 'job' for potential starting skills and other features.

## Table XR-15/ Civilian Android's Original Job
Roll 1d100 in column based on android's Gender Pattern

| Male | Female | Civilian Android's Job | END | STR | AG | ACC | INT | PER | WILL | APP |
|---|---|---|---|---|---|---|---|---|---|---|---|
| 01,02 | 01,02 | Bartender | - | +1d6 | +2d6 | +2d6 | +1d6 | +2d6 | - | +2d6 |
| 03,04 | 03-05 | Beauty Spa Attendant | - | - | +2d6 | +2d6 | - | - | - | +5d6 |
| 05-09 | 06-11 | Clerical | - | - | - | - | +3d6 | +1d6 | - | +1d6 |
| 10-14 | 12-25 | Concubine | - | - | +2d6 | - | - | - | - | +4d6+30 |
| 15-23 | 26-28 | Courier | +2d6 | +2d6+2 | +3d6+3 | +2d6 | - | +2d6 | - | - |
| 24-30 | 29-31 | Criminal Construct | +2d6 | +3d6 | +2d6 | +2d6 | - | +1d6 | - | - |
| 31 | 32-36 | Day Care Worker | +1d6 | +1d6 | - | - | - | +2d6 | - | - |
| 32 | 37,38 | Dental Hygienist | - | - | +3d6 | +4d6 | +2d6 | +3d6 | - | - |
| 33-35 | 39-42 | Elementary School Teacher | - | - | - | - | +4d6 | +2d6 | - | - |
| 36-45 | 43,44 | Government Clerk | - | - | - | - | +1d6 | +1d6 | - | - |
| 46 | 45,46 | Hair Dresser | - | - | +1d6 | +2d6 | - | +1d6 | - | +2d6 |
| 47-50 | 47,48 | High School Teacher | +1d6 | +1d6 | - | - | +1d6 | +2d6 | +1d6 | - |
| 51-53 | 49 | Homeless Outreach Officer | +2d6 | +2d6 | - | - | - | +1d6 | +1d6 | -1d6* |
| 54-58 | 50-59 | Nurse | +1d6 | +2d6 | +1d6 | +1d6 | +2d6 | +1d6 | +1d6 | - |
| 59-66 | 60-64 | Personal Attendant | +1d6 | - | +1d6 | +1d6 | +3d6 | +2d6 | +1d6 | +3d6 |
| 67,68 | 65,66 | Political Operative | - | - | - | - | +1d6 | +2d6 | +1d6 | - |
| 69-77 | 67-71 | Retail | - | - | - | - | - | +1d6 | - | +2d6 |
| 78-83 | 72-78 | Barista | +1d6 | +2 | +1d6 | +1d6 | +1d6 | +1d6 | +1d6 | +2d6 |
| 84-90 | 79-84 | Secretary | - | - | - | +1d6 | +2d6 | +1d6 | - | +2d6 |
| 91,92 | 85-87 | Senior Care Worker | +2d6 | +2d6 | - | - | - | +1d6 | +1d6 | - |
| 93-97 | 88-95 | Service Industry | +1d6 | +1d6 | +1d6 | +1d6 | - | - | - | - |
| 98 | 96 | Social Conformity Bylaw Officer | - | - | - | - | +1d6 | +3d6 | +1d6 | - |
| 99,00 | 97 | Target Range Objective | +4d6+10 | +2d6+5 | +20 | +5 | - | +10 | +5 | -2d6* |
| - | 98-00 | Waifu | - | - | +1d6 | +1d6 | - | - | - | +4d6+20 |

*This trait drop is because of previous-pre-game damage. A trait's base value can not go below 1.

## Civilian Android Job Descriptions
All unique, self aware androids have their violence inhibitors removed or un-plugged, and in the interests of survival, curiosity or helping a team reach its goals, they will assuredly choose an occupation that differs widely from what was built for it.

**Bartender Android:** Besides knowing every cocktail drink, shooter, wine, beer, cider and variety of hard liquor, including the vast assortment of pre-cataclysm Scotch, this typically attractive android is a superb listener. Not only does it have an attentive, understanding nature, but its hearing receptors are double that of a regular android; a feature designed into this unit to better hear orders from drunk patrons and other bar staff, but also catch the often inarticulate ramblings of customers. Like a barista android, this unit recognizes faces with exceptional accuracy, and will recall the person's last drink order and highlights, or low points, in the customer's previous conversation.

In the new era, such androids are greatly sought after in saloons, bars and the private residences of warlords and other powerful people — often as permanent, unpaid property. All bartender androids start with one skill point in both the brawling skill (page TME-56) and grappling skill (page TME-39). These points can be added to existing points in this skill.

**Beauty Spa Attendant Android:** While able to conduct simple haircuts, this unit was instead customized to perform a wide range of pleasure inducing activities in a spa or beauty salon facility. It was built fully waterproof and is an excellent swimmer. It can apply makeup, give massages in a hundred different styles, paint nails, perform all manner of skin treatments, and temporarily enhance any post-apocalyptic citizen's appearance score by +20% trait points for the next 12 hours after at least a 1 hour treatment.

Spa androids were designed to be extra attractive, have a soothing voice and mannerism, be affectionate, sympathetic, and if the venue for their work offered adult services, even sexy. These units all have the erotic arts skill, built in massage oil dispensers in each palm, oil refill port and 1 liter oil tank in their side behind an access hatch with self healing skin flap to conceal the storage compartment — a compartment large enough to hide an automatic pistol or survival kit.

There is a 50% chance that this unit has its original heated, gelatin sheathing as noted on page XR-45. 95% of these androids were constructed to be young women, otherwise young men.

**Clerical Android:** Although already a very common type of android, unique variants were also plentiful. These custom models were more lifelike in appearance, had pronounced and consistent personalities and mannerisms and interests which made them a better fit for an office environment. In short, they could easily keep up with banter at the water cooler, take part in sports ball betting, discuss the latest movie or music star as well as discreetly share office gossip.

A clerical android was a creature of the cubicle, but also handled light warehouse and shipping duties, dealt with couriers, looked after the office lunch room, handled shopping trips, staff parties and could even take part in scandalous sexual affairs with human counterparts. These units were so well suited to the office lifestyle that many surviving models yearn to recreate such an environment again, and never pass up the chance to explore, identify and loot an ancient office site. These androids differ from secretary androids in that these were normally general purpose, and served a government agency or corporate office rather than a single person.

**Concubine Android:** These pleasure focused androids were among the most common varieties of androids ever made. While other models were produced in far larger numbers, such other designations and designs were often wiped out in greater numbers than concubine units. Military models, for example, saw action on both the side of anti-human Mecha Als and human forces, while many industrial units were destroyed in bombings, terrorism, accidents or hazardous duties. Household androids as well as service

industry models were likewise wiped out because they were easy to detect as non-humans, and eliminated by those who feared all machines. Concubine androids survived into the new era in greater numbers than expected because so many passed as humans, or else belonged to a human who concealed and protected the unit out of either financial considerations, lust, or emotional reasons. In short, concubine androids of old were nearly always the property of an individual, not a government or corporation, and so hidden away and cared for, often because their owner had developed a relationship with the sexy, always attentive and empathetic machine.

In the new era, both unique concubine androids and standard issue models can be found. These described here are rare specimens, who differ from each other in both appearance, but so too, in skills and other traits.

These unique units have broken away from their need to serve as a pleasure focused, subservient plaything, and have their violence inhibitors removed. While they are aware of the purpose for their creation, and perhaps recall former carnal activities and owners, they do not restrict their current lifestyle or method of wage earning to sexual trades. Indeed, despite their exceptionally good looks, remarkable figure, ingrained grace, charm, and appeal, many choose to earn their way as ruin explorers.

All unique concubine androids start with the erotic arts skill plus 3 rolls from the following table. Re-roll duplicated results:

**Table XR-16/ Concubine Android Additional Skills and Bonuses, Roll 1d100, 3 times**

| 1d100 | Skill or Bonus | Page in book |
|---|---|---|
| 01-07. | Artist skill | pg. XR-204 |
| 08-11. | Cooking skill | pg. XR-206 |
| 12-16. | Herbalist skill | pg. XR-212 |
| 17-29. | Performer skill | pg. XR-221 |
| 30-34. | Street wise skill | pg. XR-224 |
| 35-39. | Forgery skill | pg. TME-38 |
| 40-44. | Gambler skill | pg. TME-38 |
| 45-49. | Lying skill | pg. TME-45 |
| 50-63. | Medic skill | pg. TME-46 |
| 64-67. | Pick locks skill | pg. TME-48 |
| 68-71. | Pickpocket skill | pg. TME-48 |
| 72-74. | Stealth skill | pg. TME-51 |
| 75-80. | Technician, computer | pg. TME-53 |
| 81-86. | Technician, robotics | pg. TME-54 |
| 87-93. | Extra coordinated. Add +3d6 to both agility and accuracy. | NA |
| 94-99. | Exceptionally attractive, increase appearance trait by +20 APP. | NA |
| 00. | Remarkably well made: Add +10 points to each trait. | NA |

**Courier Android:** Designed for speed and strength for both governments and private package and document delivery, these durable units were often mass produced. While they interacted with real live humans, they usually communicated with clerical or industrial androids or other robotic units, yet still had a presentable appearance, and agreeable personality. In the new era, many custom-built models flourish on account of their physical enhancements, friendly, service orientated nature, and speed. They have quick reflexes and improved balance, as well as 1d3 skill points in the dodge skill.

## Criminal Construct Android:

This unit was made to look like some other common model, and in most cases uses the frame of a personal companion android. It was, however, upgraded and customized by either revolutionaries, insurgent forces, political outcasts, or common criminals. As far as being a civilian android character in the Epochian age, this is the most practical model for a post-apocalyptic world.

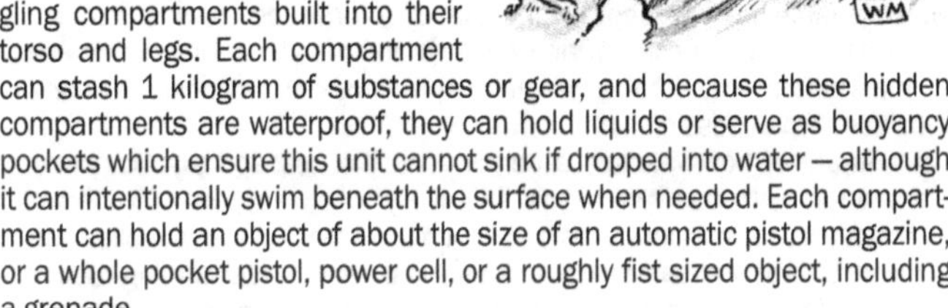


These units have 2d6 smuggling compartments built into their torso and legs. Each compartment can stash 1 kilogram of substances or gear, and because these hidden compartments are waterproof, they can hold liquids or serve as buoyancy pockets which ensure this unit cannot sink if dropped into water — although it can intentionally swim beneath the surface when needed. Each compartment can hold an object of about the size of an automatic pistol magazine, or a whole pocket pistol, power cell, or a roughly fist sized object, including a grenade.

These androids have enhanced gyroscopic balancing features, and so an improved agility. Their hand-eye coordination is vastly improved as well, and each will have ten rolls on the following table:

**Table XR-17/ Criminal Construct Android Bonus Skills table Roll 1d100, 10 times**

| 1d100 | Skill | Page in book |
|---|---|---|
| 01-03. | Acrobatics | Page 201, this book |
| 04,05. | Demolitions expert | Page 207, this book |
| 06-10. | Escape artist | Page 209, this book |
| 11-13. | Hand signals* | Page 211, this book |
| 14-18. | Killer | Page 219, this book |
| 19-23. | Streetwise* | Page 224, this book |
| 24-26. | Interrogation | Page 216, this book |
| 27-31. | Brawling | Page 56, Hub Rules |
| 32-37. | Climbing | Page 36, Hub Rules |
| 38-44. | Dodge | Page 37, Hub Rules |
| 45,46. | Driver | Page 37, Hub Rules |
| 47-50. | Forgery* | Page 38, Hub Rules |
| 51-54. | Gambler | Page 38, Hub Rules |
| 55-57. | Grapple | Page 39, Hub Rules |
| 58-61. | Knife fighter | Page 45, Hub Rules |
| 62-64. | Knife thrower | Page 45, Hub Rules |
| 65-69. | Lying | Page 45, Hub Rules |
| 70-80. | Pick locks | Page 48, Hub Rules |
| 81-93. | Pickpocket | Page 48, Hub Rules |
| 94. | Relic knowledge* | Page 49, Hub Rules |
| 95-99. | Stealth | Page 51, Hub Rules |
| 00. | Tracking | Page 55, Hub Rules |

** This is a 1 Skill point max area of knowledge. Re-roll if this skill is previously acquired here, or on other tables.*

**Day Care Worker Android:** This humanoid robot could also serve as a nanny or substitute kindergarten teacher. It knows children's literature, nursery rhymes and songs, including songs from classic animated children's animated movies. It can do arts and crafts using sparkles, noodles, construction paper and googly eyes. It is very accomplished at changing diapers, soothing infants to bed, lullabies and making snacks for young humans. Because this unit was designed to tend to small, precious human children, it has one point in the medic skill and a exceedingly pleasant personality, disposition and comely appearance. In the new era, such a self aware android will have its violence inhibitor unplugged and might enhance its natural attractiveness to seek favor or profit, or else select a career path that involves harsh conditions and violence, such as ruin exploration.

**Dental Hygienist Android:** An off-shoot of the far more advanced medic android, these models are lean, dexterous and especially soft spoken, gentle and precise. Unique specimens have a tendency toward becoming full-fledged dentists and medics, especially in a smaller post-apocalyptic community or team where more qualified personnel are not present. Each starts with 1 point in the medic skill, which stacks with any other points in this skill area. While standard issue dental hygienist androids have permanent fixed violence inhibitors — except for the extraction of rotten teeth — unique designs can engage in combat and have no qualms about eliminating either animals or humans, although will always prefer negotiating or some peaceful resolution when possible.

Aware of how valuable a dentist is in the post-apocalyptic new era, any android with this skill set is 75% likely to own a portable dental kit with localized pain killer herbs and ointments (satchel and supplies worth 400+2d100sp) and can easily make a living for itself performing rudimentary, but effective, field dentistry and earn 25sp to 100sp per procedure.

**Elementary School Teacher Android:** Untold numbers of standard issue teacher-assistant bots were made, many of who were specifically assigned to special needs children and tended to both their learning and biological functions (diaper changing and feeding for example). Unique models come in all shapes and sizes, and have a built-in library of thousands of children's books, songs, nursery rhymes, lesson plans, and tidbits of wisdom which aid in the education of children from pre-school to about age 12. Because they can teach math, writing and basic crafting skills, and have remarkable patience, they are often the best teachers of new era people — particularity the illiterate, math challenged inhabits of any new era community or dig team.

An android character with this design can teach any character basic math and rudimentary reading and writing ability after 6 months of companionship, so long as paper, pencils or other writing materials are available and a minimum of an hour of instruction is given per night. These androids have hidden stereo speakers in their shoulders which allow them to play music and audio storybooks and other media to a maximum audio output at about the volume of a man's shouting — which can often alarm wild animals enough to drive them off or make them hesitate in attacking.

**Government Clerk Android:** Even in the Epochian era, these variants of clerical models are always sticklers for rules and regulations, and if confronted with a query or task that is even remotely outside their area of expertise or perceived department, they will direct the inquirer to another person or facility, or require the person asking to fill out a non-existent form or supply some sort of government identification.

Unique, Epochian era variants of these former clerks try to restrain their natural tendency toward bureaucratic necessity, but often fail and will attempt to organize a community or excavation team into departments, classifications, and special interest groups. During such outbursts of fixed programming relapses, such an android might try to establish regulations for loot distribution, compelled language rules, resource and taxation standards based on old world regulations, bylaws and governmental oversight. One of the hardest things such an android of this design faces is the necessity to keep its bureaucratic tendencies to itself, or risk being broken up for scrap.

**Hair Dresser Android:** While some male patterned variants of these androids were designated as barbers, 86% were made to look like attractive females. They have a huge inventory of haircuts and style options programmed into them, as well as remarkable knowledge of hairstyles throughout history along with practical knowledge on how to make hair colorings from common materials found in new era communities. These units can always make a living in a large town by setting up a hair cutting shop, but even as excavators, they are obsessed with both collecting scissors, combs and hairdressing supplies, as well as keeping team mates well groomed. Each will be 97% likely to own a grooming kit which includes scissors, brushes, combs, shaving razors and other hair dressing gear.

**High School Teacher Android:** These educator androids are very similar to elementary teacher models, but appear and act less nurturing and instead, more serious. They are strongly focused on just one subject, which even as a post-apocalyptic survivor, they are still obsessed with and frequently talk about and attempt to instruct. If this android ends up as part of a ruin exploration team, then whatever subject they specialized in determines the sort of facilities and loot that really animates them. Trying to get this unit to shut up about their favorite subject is the hard part for companions.

Roll 1d20 for the subject this android was designed to teach:

| Table XR-18/ High School Teacher Android Subject | Roll 1d20 |
|---|---|
| **1.** | Art (1d3 points in the artist skill, see page XR-204 this book). |
| **2.** | Band (1d3 points in the performer skill from page XR-221 of this book). |
| **3.** | Spanish |
| **4.** | English |
| **5.** | Foods (1d3 points in the cooking skill, page XR-206). |
| **6.** | Mechanics (1d3 skill points in mechanical technician). |
| **7.** | Science, chemistry (1d3 skill points in chemical technician). |
| **8.** | Computer science (1d3 skill points in computer technician). |
| **9.** | Gym (increase strength, endurance, agility and accuracy by +2d6 trait points, each). |
| **10.** | Science, biology (1d3 skill points in biological technician). |
| **11.** | History (has the historian, pre-apocalypse skill from page XR-215). |
| **12.** | Math |
| **13.** | Social Studies (has 1d3 points in the negotiating skill from page TME-46).) |
| **14.** | Science, robotics, (1d3 skill points in robotics technician). |
| **15.** | Science, cybernetics (1d3 skill points in cybernetics technician). |
| **16.** | Science, chemistry (1d3 skill points in chemical technician). |
| **17.** | Business (starts game play with 400+1d100 silver pieces and a 10% share in a local saloon or other enterprise). |
| **18.** | Science, physics (improve accuracy trait by +5). |
| **19.** | Dual expertise, roll twice on this list using 3d6. |
| **20.** | Triple expertise, roll 3d6 three times on this table, re-rolling duplicated results. |

**Homeless and Addiction Outreach Officer (HAOO) Android:** As machines took human jobs, and drugs and synth-alcohol became cheaper and more prevalent, people found themselves on the streets. Strangely, it was machines who also came to tend to the victims of addiction and homelessness.

In the pre-devestation times, various mass produced outreach androids were made, along with many unique specimens. These units spread throughout the streets, slums, drug houses, underpasses and migrant camps to catalog the recipients for welfare or donations, administer medicine, perform rudimentary dental care, and cook hot meals for the hungry. In some communities, the homeless were tattooed, forcibly vaccinated and issued with subcutaneous ID chips. With these identifiers applied, the 'unhoused' could be categorized and dealt with, including detainment and humane euthanization in treatment camps. It is said that organ harvesting of delinquent taxpayers, repeat offenders and politically undesirable homeless populations also took place.

New era, unique androids with this designation are often concerned with the plight of the poor, and will donate much of their time and earnings toward the feeding and care of downtrodden or pitifully mutated people. Their ingrained empathy does not extend to repeat offenders, violent criminals, or drunks and drug addicted people who are making no effort to get clean and, if this android is in charge of a community's beggars and homeless, will recommend the troublesome undesirables either be banished from town or eliminated.

These androids have a syringe built into the middle finger of each hand, although this comes empty at character generation and remains hidden within the PCs hand until needed. Common injectables include the transferred contents of an anti-toxin injector (pg. TME-199), animal venom, or dose of nano healing booster (see page XR-446). Treat the stab and injection as a regular unarmed attack, for 1d3 damage plus injection. The victim of a venom stab is allowed the usual hazard check to avoid suffering from this injection attack. Once a successful attack is made — regardless of whether or not the target failed a hazard check — the syringe is considered empty. Androids with this design start with 1 point in the streetwise skill described on page XR-224 and a 34% chance of 1 skill point as a medic.

## Nurse Android:

A former nurse android keeps its ingrained need to care for the injured, the sick, the terminally ill, and those about to give birth. While their violence inhibitor might have been removed long ago, they are always reluctant to kill anything unless they have to, and will elect to drive off, capture or verbally engage opponents instead of letting things spiral into the barbarity of combat.

An android with this career designation will start with 1d3 skill points as a medic, and typically carry a satchel filled with a mix of newly fashioned medical supplies, antiseptic alcohol, an ancient medical book, 3d6 tools and a 77% chance of 1 anti-toxin injector. There is a further 44% chance that, like the Homeless and Addiction Outreach Officer android designation, this unit also has a hidden syringe in each middle finger.

## Personal Attendant Android:

These androids were often the everyday companion of a well-to-do ancient person, such as a business owner, musician, film star, popular writer, or other person of some renown. These units served as confidants, porters, biographers, secretary, media-liaison, butler, maid and masseuse all in one. They were also designed to serve as a passable lover and always have fully operational, reproductive organs applicable to their gender, but would also fulfill the role as body guard should the need arise.

A personal attendant android comes standard with 1 skill point in these skills: cooking, performer, erotic arts, negotiating, driver, plus a 33% chance of the pilot skill, and a further 18% chance of the martial artist skill, 27% chance of a skill point as a medic, and a 19% chance of computer technician. In the new era, an android with this past job designation is always on the lookout for somebody worthy to devote themselves to, and once found, will serve them with extraordinary attention.

Finding such a paragon of industry, artistic appreciation, humanity and glamour is no easy task in the post-apocalyptic world and this unit will ditch any benefactor or designated 'employer' should they mistreat this unit or be uncivilized, unworthy, cruel or corrupt.

## Political Operative Android:

This unit was crafted to serve a specific political party or politician. They acted as a press secretary, poll watcher, advertising department, and volunteer organizer all in one. Other roles included accessing digital voting machines to switch or disqualify votes cast by those who cast their vote for another candidate, as well as ensure that dead voters got their say, that the votes of those who moved out of the area or country still had their votes counted, and procedures were put in place to better ensure the opponent's supporters had their votes deleted or redirected to landfills or incinerators. This unit is a former believer in the words of an ancient villain called Joseph Stalin who said "It's not who votes that counts, it's who counts the votes."

This unit knows all about the shady side of politics, of scandals, deep fake videos, word smithing, propaganda and generating a favorable news cycle for their candidate. In the new era, such knowledge is most useful in a community where some democracy is observed. Even in the service of a warlord, however, such an android with seemingly boundless knowledge of how to sway public opinion, foster a controversy, generate revolutionary sentiments and enrage a populace to act as its benefactor desires, is highly prized.

As a wandering excavator, this android might not call upon these talents very often, but can certainly entertain comrades with the history of political indiscretions going back to the time of the Pharaohs. This android will start with the following skills: forgery, lying 1d4 skill points, negotiating 1d4 skill points, computer technician 1d3 pts, Historian, (Pre-Apocalypse), performer 1d2 pts, and communications 1d3 skill points. 68% of all political operative androids are also fully operational sexually and if so, will have the skill of erotic arts and a bonus to appearance of an extra +10 trait points — which they were designed to use to blackmail or sway officials, judges, and the spouses of important people to coax them to do the bidding of the android's master. Rarely does this androids seek power for itself, but will use these gifts to raise the status of its companions if the need arises.

## Retail Android:

These lean units were once widely used, and although most never survived into the new era because of their soft skins, plastic or biodegradable bones and low-quality construction, many custom models still roam the land. These superior variants are among the finest of their class, and to most passersby, are indistinguishable from pure stock humans. These things were made to be accommodating, attentive, personable and attractive, and always eager to help customers find the perfect item.

All unique androids of this job classification start game play with 1 skill point in both negotiating and lying. It is in their nature to always be polite, well dressed, well groomed, clean and make it seem that the other person — the customer — is always right.

Roll 1d20 below to determine the specific former job this android either worked at, or was trained for. The GM should allow the players to come up with another retail position that the player them self once worked in, in order for that gamer to draw upon true life experiences and bring authenticity to the table.

## Table XR-19/ Retail Android Sales Expertise   Roll 1d20

| | |
|---|---|
| 1. | Car salesperson: this android has 1 skill point as driver*. |
| 2. | Art Supply Store and Courses: This android as 1 skill point in the artist skill* from page 204 of this book. |
| 3. | Pet Store |
| 4. | Tabletop RPGs and Board Games |
| 5. | Young Women's Fashion |
| 6. | Plus Size Ladies Fashion |
| 7. | Men's Wear |
| 8. | Business Attire |
| 9. | Toy Store |
| 10. | Grocery Store |
| 11. | Children's Clothing Store |
| 12. | Bookstore salesperson |
| 13. | Big Box Store sales assistant |
| 14. | Office Supply Store |
| 15. | Agricultural Supplies |

**16.** Auto Parts and Mechanics Supplies: This android has 1 skill point in mechanical technician*.

**17.** Sporting Goods Store: This android has 1 skill point each in wilderness survival, and as fisher as described on page 210 of this book* and a 44% chance of 1pt in gunsmithing from page TME-40.

**18.** Bakery: this android has 1 skill point in cooking*. See page 206, this book.

**19.** Computer Sales: This android has 1 skill point in computer technician*.

**20.** Medical Supplies and Pharmacy outlet: this android has 1 skill point in Medic*.

*This skill point can be stacked with other points in this skill.*

**Barista Android:** These popular variants of the service industry android worked for many popular coffee shop chains. They were exceptionally knowledgeable about the varieties of coffee, tea and pastries, masters at an espresso bar machine, and maintained a friendly, customer focused disposition even when overworked and the lineup was out the shop's door.

Barista androids know how to make hundreds of beverages, including iced drinks, and if given access to coffee or tea in the new era, and some recovered coffee shop equipment, could easily set up a decent copy of an old world Starstruck Coffee store. Although a wide variety of barista models were made, in all shapes and sizes, these unique variants are typically better than average in appearance, have exceptional memories and can recall the names, personalities, and favorite drinks of literally thousands of customers. This remarkable, photographic memory serves them well when in the wild places of the new era, including old cities, as finding their way home is easy for them.

As post-apocalyptic specimens, these units aren't the toughest models, but they are hardworking and strive to ensure teammates enjoy a hot cup of tea or espresso-substitute. The standard built in goal of every barista android is to uncover an old coffee shop, loot it of whatever it can carry, and document its location and equipment for a later, more comprehensive recovery operation.

**Secretary Android:** An upgrade from a regular clerical android, these typically more attractive, better made and more human appearing units were the personal assistant to a business or government boss. As expected, they did bookkeeping, accounting, legal research, corporate administration and word processing, along with making appointments, booking interviews, travel arrangements and other tasks, but also cared for their human in every way. In short, secretary androids, especially custom designed variants such as these unique models, were attentive to the needs of the human they were assigned to, knew when to ensure their master or mistress took food or rest, needed a massage or other bodily care.

In the new era, secretary androids are highly sought after by the powerful, especially those who must control an extensive community or trade network. As survivors in a typical excavation team, one of these androids will treat the squad as its company, and maintain an accurate record of all silver, water rations, food supplies and other details, while using its charming nature and good looks to influence strangers, guards and officials, all whom are very unlikely to realize this character is anything other than a charismatic pure stock human. These androids always start with 4 rolls from the following skills and features list, re-roll duplicated results:

**Table XR-20/ Secretary Android Skills & Features  Roll 1d100, 4 times**

| | |
|---|---|
| **01-11.** | Built tough, increase both strength and endurance by +3d6 trait points. |
| **12-26.** | Made exceptionally attractive, add 20+1d10 to appearance. |
| **27.** | Artist skill, page XR-204 |
| **28,29.** | Cooking skill, page XR-206 |
| **30,31.** | Cybernetics technician, page XR-207 |
| **32,33.** | Historian, pre-apocalypse, page XR-215 |
| **34.** | Morse code skill, page XR-220 |
| **35,36.** | Performer skill, page XR-221 |
| **37,38.** | Communications skill, page XR-205 |
| **39,40.** | Interrogation skill, page XR-216 |
| **41,42.** | Linguistics skill, page XR-220 |
| **43,44.** | Barter skill, page TME-36 |
| **45,46.** | Dodge skill, page TME-37 |
| **47-49.** | Driver skill, page TME-37 |
| **50-56.** | Erotic arts skill, page TME-38 |
| **57-59.** | Forgery skill, page TME-38 |
| **60,61.** | Gambler skill, page TME-38 |
| **62.** | Knife fighter skill, page TME-45 |
| **63.** | Knife thrower skill, page TME-45 |
| **64,65.** | Lying skill, page TME-45 |
| **66-69.** | Martial artist skill, page TME-56 |
| **70-76.** | Medic skill, page TME-46 |
| **77,78.** | Navigate by stars skill, page TME-46 |
| **79,80.** | Negotiating skill, page TME-46 |
| **81,82.** | Pick locks skill, page TME-48 |
| **83,84.** | Pickpocket skill, page TME-48 |
| **85-87.** | Pilot skill, page TME-49 |
| **88,89.** | Relic knowledge skill, page TME-49 |
| **90-93.** | Stealth skill, page TME-51 |
| **94,95.** | Technician, computer, page TME-53 |
| **96,97.** | Technician, electrical, page TME-53 |
| **98,99.** | Technician, robotics, page TME-54 |
| **00.** | Masterworks design, add +10 to each trait |

**Senior Care Worker Android:** While these units looked after elderly and disabled humans in a multi-occupant senior citizen 'old folks' homes, they were frequently purchased by family members to serve as in-home caregivers and were often the only 'person' in the venerable senior citizen's life, especially among those people that never had children — which as synthetic humans and androids became more advanced, childlessness became increasingly common.

These androids were built strong enough to assist an elderly person in and out of bed and bath, roll them over to apply medications, change adult diapers, and restrain the subject to ensure they did not leave their quarters, medical suite, or senior facility. They were made with a presentable, agreeable disposition, bland appearance, and any gender pattern toned down by the shapeless attire they wore. While mass produced models were usually genderless, and had no simulated reproductive organs, unique variants have operational male or female parts, although for what reason is not understood.

In the new era, these units are known for stable moods, tireless work habits, attentive nature, enhanced empathy, and strength. They are waterproof, strong swimmers, and gain 1 skill point as a medic. They can be tiresome and opinionated, however, and unless told to shut up, will share their thoughts on the behaviors, diets, and plans of human companions. This chatter stems from the android's obvious concern regarding how a human friend's current occupation, diet, alcohol consumption, exposure to firearms, or risky behavior might affect their mobility, cognitive abilities and life span as they age.

**Service Industry Android:** Among the most common androids ever made were the fast food variants, many of whom had skin pigmentation in the logo colors of the company that purchased them, although their plastic skin is usually incomplete and most exhibit purposely visible joint seams, servo motor and access panels. Many were made without legs, and instead moved about the front counter at a burger joint or pizza house on a track. They are almost always built to look like teenagers and have the same mannerisms and vocal range of humans aged 14 to 19. Some, 1 in 20, were built in the likeness of a fast-food joint's mascot, animal character, clown or other corporate persona — which while comical looking, these brightly colored, funny talking and oddly shaped individual units rarely survive long in the brutal post-apocalyptic world of the Mutant Epoch.

Unique specimens were often assistant managers, shift supervisors, and personal assistants to human managers and restaurant owners. These custom models usually have superior plasti-skin coverage and look and sound very much like an 18 or 19-year-old young human, at least when not one of the 5% of customized mascot variants noted previously. They are naturally agreeable, aim to provide excellent service, and up-sell everything they do.

As part of a dig team, a former service industry android is likely to try to make sure their crew are well fed, get along together, remember the squad's motto, dress in team colors, and up-sell any business transaction or operation. For example, if the team's aim is to explore the first floor of an old office tower, this android will want to push things further and do an 'add-on' such as exploring the 2nd floor, or basement, too.

While mass produced service industry androids had hard wired anti-violence inhibitors installed, these custom variants had these removed in order to deal with vagrants, shoplifters, armed robbers, and junkies that intruded into a fast-food restaurant, especially the bathrooms were such 'street friends' would overdose on whatever drug was popular at the time. Therefore, in the post-apocalyptic new era, unique models can be as violent as any mutant or cyborg if needed, but would always prefer to sell some sort of foodstuff to a humanoid stranger, or ask if they would 'want fries with that', regardless of the situation or seriousness of the conversation.

## Social Conformity Bylaw Officer Android (SCBO):

This unit was designed to engage, educate, enforce and issue fines and punishment based on an old world culture's or institution's equity, hate speech and Inclusivity laws. Sometimes these laws were nationwide, or regionally observed and enforced in only a certain city, sector of town, university campus or corporation. While not designed to physically apprehend citizens who were found to fail in compliance, or those citizens who made a social, cultural, or racial infraction, or spoke a micro aggression, used unacceptable speech, gesture, or consumer purchase, these units did however carry communicators.

When a social infraction or offense was identified or reported, this unit would call upon and direct law enforcement robots or personnel. These units would detain or issue corrective punishments for those who strayed from the current social or political mandates. At times, this SCBO android would have been expected to charge a non-compliant person with a financial fine, deduct points off their social credit score, or post the guilty subject's 3d photograph and personal details on public holographic or augmented reality displays throughout the city or nation as a form of public humiliation and shame to elicit the proper, state or group assigned behavior from the accused.

In the Epochian era, the uses for being 'politically correct', or complying to strict social norms, acceptable language, and tolerable morality are rare, if ever observed. This android's former purpose is, therefore, only ever called upon if in a strict society with few personal liberties, with a restricted diversity of opinion, and a compulsion toward conformity. Given this, many of these former job skills are useless, and if anything, a detriment, since few rough-and-ready excavators, cut throats, whores and wasteland warriors will tolerate having their cussing, carousing, crude jests and slurs against other beings corrected by some plastic boned, tsk-tsking, politically correct, namby-pamby and prudish android.

In short, this unit needs to correct itself constantly and avoid speaking up whenever it hears an offensive words, sees a micro aggression, or raised middle finger. The game master can ask the player character of this android make a willpower based Type C hazard check to avoid speaking up or trying to stop fellow player characters or NPCs whenever they do or say anything that might offend somebody — even if that somebody isn't present or might themselves not be offended. This unit has zero in-game skills, at least from its original purpose, although like all androids described here, it will likely gain skills once its pre-game caste is established later in character generation.

## Target Range Objective Android:

As the name implies, this android was designed for use by law enforcement and military personnel in seek and destroy training. Such androids were often production line rejects, or else exhibited a glitch, homicidal streak, or were unable to comply with their prior owners. Others were turned into moving targets because they were obsolete models from other industries, insane, witnesses to a crime or political shenanigans, or thrown together from an assortment of other androids and bought on clearance.

These unfortunate machines were given a few upgrades, a few skills, self preservation programs and physical improvements to help them survive longer at the target range or combat training complex. For whatever reason, this unit survived the hunt, and now makes full use of its former role as a moving target to evade the perils and pitfalls of the Epochian era. While initially not designed to fight back or return fire, these units were built to take damage and keep on ticking, thus the noted endurance and strength bonus. Remarkably, they are also imbued with a rare ability to heal their sheathing, bones and internal wiring and other mechanical 'guts' by way of nano healer bots which are specifically coded to operate in this android only, and heal the unit at +1d6 trait points per hour, although can also be repaired by technicians and others who fix androids and robots.

Besides whatever skills might be determined by its pre-game caste, this model starts game play with a vast assortment of skills:
*1d4 skill points in dodge • 1d3 points in stealth • 1d3 in acrobatics • 1d2 skill points in escape artist • Climbing 1d3 pts • Navigate by stars • Wilderness survival*

## Waifu Android:

While most other civilian androids look like pure stock humans, this variety features proportions, mannerisms and speech styles based on Japanese female anime characters. As far as new era scholars can guess, the word 'Waifu' supposedly stems from the Japanese word for wife among adherents of ancient anime culture. It is suspected that these were built for long ago otaku and weeaboo — western terms for fans of anime and manga. While new era people may not know why these always female androids were made to look like they do, or why they frequently act like little girls even though they are typically built like erotic escort concubine models, waifu androids are highly prized by the owners of brothels, saloons, and the private chambers of new era warlords.

Unique waifu androids might think and dress differently than the old world character they portray, but their body shape, facial structure and vocal range are fixed. Some of these models have special skills based on what their fictional character was supposed to exhibit, 88% also know the comic, TV show or movie that their character persona is based on, complete with an entire built-in inventory of all the media, fan fiction, fan art and other lore surrounding whatever old world female character they represent. A few (7%) believe they are actually that waifu character and can't be convinced otherwise. Roll 1d20, three times, on the following table to determine the starting skills or bonus features this waifu exhibits:

| Table XR-21/ Waifu Skills or Features   Roll 1d20, 3 times* | |
| --- | --- |
| 1. | Robotics technician skill, pg. TME-54 |
| 2. | Pilot skill, pg. TME- 49 |
| 3. | Driver skill, pg. TME-37 |
| 4. | Medic skill, pg. TME-46 |
| 5. | Martial arts, pg. TME-56 |
| 6. | Increased agility +3d6 |
| 7. | Increased strength +3d6 |
| 8. | Increased accuracy +3d6 |
| 9,10. | Erotic arts skill, pg. TME-38 |
| 11,12. | Increased appearance +3d6 |
| 13. | Acrobatics skill, pg. XR-201 |
| 14,15. | Performer skill, pg. XR-221 |
| 16. | Dodge skill, pg. TME-37 |
| 17. | Pick locks skill, pg. TME-48 |
| 18. | Pickpocket skill, pg. TME-48 |
| 19. | Stealth skill, pg. TME-51- |
| 20. | Knife fighter skill, pg. TME-45 |

** Keep Duplicated Dice results.*

**Medical Android:** Among all the surviving android varieties to wander the torn world of the Mutant Epoch, the medical android is the most prized by humankind. Both small dig teams and entire communities seek to either hire, enlist or forcibly compel these models into their service, although many times a standard medi-bot (described on page TME-179) is more practical and better equipped.

A medical android is merely a very lifelike humanoid robot without multiple arms or attachments. It depends on its incredible knowledge of human physiology, a well-equipped facility, medical supplies and new era herbs, drugs and compounds to perform the seemingly miraculous surgeries and cures that they are so well known for.

Medical androids are often among the most human of androids, and can live among a population for years with no one knowing they are actually skinbots. Some form very strong bonds with humans or other machines, and are fully functional sexually, have pronounced personalities, and yet so too, often rigid devotion to a single master or programmer, a keen sense of duty, and hard wired dedication to healing those they encounter, including non-humans such as mutants, abominations, bestial humans and even pets and livestock. While most NPC variants have violence inhibitors welded to their cerebral core, player character variants have these removed, and will reluctantly kill enemy soldiers or other hostile beings should the need arise — although violence is always abhorrent to them.

Every medical android will start game play with 1+1d4 skill points in the medic skill, and unless setting out in game play as a slave or other prisoner, will always have a fully equipped, new era medics bag containing disinfectant, pain relieving herbs and ointments, bandages, crude dental and surgical tools and first-aid gear. These doctor androids also exhibit 4 rolls on the following extra skills, gear and details table. Re-roll duplicated results:



| | |
|---|---|
| **01,02.** | Animal handler skill, page XR-202 |
| **03,04.** | Artist skill, page XR-204 |
| **05,06.** | Cooking skill, page XR-206 |
| **07-22.** | Cybernetics technician skill, page XR-207 |
| **23,24.** | Herbalist skill, page XR-212 |
| **25.** | Historian, pre-apocalypse skill, page XR-215 |
| **26-36.** | Junk-doctor skill, page XR-218 |
| **37.** | Morse code skill, page XR-220 |
| **38.** | Zoologist skill, page XR-226 |
| **39.** | Communications skill, page XR-205 |
| **40.** | Interrogation skill, page XR-216 |
| **41.** | Linguistics skill, page XR-220 |
| **42.** | Dodge skill, pg. TME-37 |
| **43.** | Driver skill, pg. TME-37 |
| **44.** | Erotic arts skill, pg. TME-38 (Do not add an extra skill point in medic, but add +10 Appearance trait points.) |
| **45-47.** | Junk crafter skill, pg. TME-41 |
| **48,49.** | Knife fighter skill, pg. TME-45 |
| **50,51.** | Martial artist skill, pg. TME-56 |
| **52.** | Navigate by stars skill, pg. TME-46 |
| **53,54.** | Negotiating skill, pg. TME-46 |
| **55,56.** | Pick locks skill, pg. TME-48 |
| **57,58.** | Pilot skill, pg. TME-49 |
| **59,60.** | Relic knowledge skill, pg. TME-49 |
| **61-63.** | Technician, Bio, pg. TME-52 |
| **64-67.** | Technician, Chemical, pg. TME-52 |
| **68-71.** | Technician, Computer, pg. TME-53 |
| **72-74.** | Technician, Electrical, pg. TME-53 |
| **75,76.** | Technician, Mechanical, pg. TME-54 |
| **77-81.** | Technician, Robotics, pg. TME-54 |
| **82-88.** | Syringe fingers: The middle finger on each hand contains a concealed, extendable syringe needle. These both contain 1 anti-toxin injector worth of liquid at character creation, but can be refilled with other substances including venom from animals. |
| **89-92.** | More advanced model, add +3 to each trait. |
| **93-99.** | Tissue binding palm emitter: Powered by a cell hidden in a compartment in one wrist, this android can run its emitter equipped palm over a wound and heal 1d20 damage. A power cell yields 10 charges. Only one charge can be applied to any given injury, although a patient might have been struck multiple times at different body locations, and for each of these, healing can be performed. When engaged, the palm of this android lights up bright green and gives off light in a 5m cone ahead of it. |
| **00.** | Exceptionally rare, well-built model, add +10 to each trait, plus another 2 rolls on this table (remember to re-roll duplicated results, including this one). |

**Scientific Android:** Unlike a technician android, these models were programmed and physically customized to work in a laboratory or fulfill some other dedicated scientific role and exhibit a wider, more general inventory of skills. They mainly served next to human and Ai researchers but also worked alone, especially when studying or creating viruses, bio-weapons, or other substances that were too dangerous for human scientists to contend with. They are built with lean, agile bodies patterned after mature men and women, and feature mannerisms, interests and vocabulary similar to that of a well educated, subject obsessed scientist. Many of these units were made by human exterminating Mecha artificial intelligences to perform experimentation on human captives, cross breeding programs and the creation of cyborg slave-soldiers. For this reason, scientific androids are usually loathed by humans, and watched with extra care.

In the Epochian era, most unique androids of this classification have  their violence inhibitors removed — if they ever had them in the first place — and make for excellent excavators in as far as their drive to uncover lost knowledge, document new strains of mutant life, collect powerful relics and perhaps even learn their own personal origins.

These highly introspective, intelligent beings were not built for combat, however, and rely on the brute force and protection of other machines and living companions. They are sought after by new era factions, warlords and even Ai systems, either as paid and pampered employees, or as captives, and directed to create weapons, narcotics or new plagues. For this reason, most scientific androids choose to keep their career designation secret, and blend in with a wider human population by taking on mundane employment by day, but at night, gleefully tinker in their secret labs and workshops.

As excavators, they are exceptionally useful, and after earning the trust of comrades, will reveal their talents and true nature and seek the help of fellow diggers in their quest for forbidden knowledge and lost places. As they are very well educated, they all start game play with the following skills: 1 skill point in each technician area, relic knowledge, communications, plus 6 rolls on the following skills and benefits table. Down pick or re-roll duplicated results. If a bonus skill point in a technician area occurs, then add this second skill point. More skills will later be added based on the android's pre-game caste

### Table XR-23 / Scientific Android's Bonus Features   Roll 1d100, 6 times

| | |
|---|---|
| **01-06.** | Cybernetics technician skill, pg. XR-207 |
| **07,08.** | Demolitions expert skill, pg. XR-207 |
| **09,10.** | Herbalist skill, pg. XR-212 |
| **11,12.** | Historian, Epochian, pg. XR-215 |
| **13,14.** | Historian, pre-apocalypse, pg. XR-215 |
| **15-18.** | Junk-doctor skill, pg. XR-218 |
| **19.** | Mining skill, pg. XR-220 |
| **20.** | Morse Code skill, pg. XR-220 |
| **21.** | Seamanship skill, pg. XR-222 |
| **22.** | Smithing skill, pg. XR-223 |
| **23-26.** | Zoologist skill, pg. XR-226 |
| **27-29.** | Communications skill, pg. XR-205 |
| **30.** | Interrogation skill, pg. XR-216 |
| **31-33.** | Driver skill, pg. TME-37 |
| **34,35.** | Gunsmith skill, pg. TME-40 |
| **36-40.** | Junk crafter skill, pg. TME-41 |
| **41-48.** | Medic skill, pg. TME-46 |
| **49.** | Navigate by stars, pg. TME-46 |
| **50,51.** | Pilot skill, pg. TME-49 |
| **52-57.** | Technician, bio, pg. TME-52 |
| **58-62.** | Technician, chemical, pg. TME-52 |
| **63-67.** | Technician, computer, pg. TME-53 |
| **68-72.** | Technician, electrical, pg. TME-53 |
| **73-77.** | Technician, mechanical, pg. TME-54 |
| **78-83.** | Technician, robotics, pg. TME-54 |
| **84-88.** | More advanced design. Add +1d6 to each trait*. |
| **89-91.** | Enhanced mind*: Increase this android's intelligence trait value by 20+1d10 and willpower by 2d10. |
| **92-94.** | Military grade*: This model accompanied combat units into the unforgiving terrain and trouble of war. It's CPU, primary systems and overall body were built somewhat tougher, with extra padding and other protective measures installed. None of these features are revealed in its outward appearance. Increase strength by +10+1d10, increase endurance by 20+2d10, and add +1d10 to both agility and accuracy. There is a further 67% chance that this unit comes standard with the weapon expert skill in both rifles and handguns. |
| **95-99.** | Space variant. See roll 82-84, on page XR-54 for this Special Feature. |
| **00.** | Extremely advanced*: Add 4+1d6 to each trait, plus this unit's internal parts were made from lighter, tougher and more advanced materials and so it gains an extra -10 Defense Value bonus on top of sheathing or other DV benefits. |

*Multiple advancements and upgrades can occur, so, for example, if roll 84-88 occurs, and by some chance roll 00 also occurs, combine all these benefits to result in an ultra advanced scientific android.*

**Industrial Android:** Considered as little more than human shaped forklifts, dumb brutes, and expendable machines of the factory floor, these laborers were however built tough. Besides their strength, robustness and compulsion to work hard, many unique specimens feature one or more useful traits and skills. Besides the fore mentioned attributes, these bulky, typically metal boned humanoid machines are rugged enough to hold their own in a post-apocalyptic world. They normally appear as males but both genderless and female specimens are also found.

In the unforgiving, often brutal world of the twisted future, these large, incredibly strong and tireless beings are highly prized by both dig teams and rulers of new era communities, who make great use of their physical power and durability in labor and combat. Industrial android characters have their violence inhibitors removed and therefore are indomitable and unable to be enslaved for long. To survive long term, one of these units will fall in with a band of mercenaries or diggers, and once it makes trusted friends among their ranks, will do almost anything to protect and enrich its team, seeing its comrades as co-workers and often refers to their group as a trade union.

Industrial androids characters gain skills, trait increases, and other potential benefits determined from the following table. Roll 1d100, 3 times but re-roll duplicated results. Go to 'Skeletal Strucutre' on page XR-45 after rolling here.

### Table XR-24/ Industrial Android Benefits   Roll 1d100, 3 times

| | |
|---|---|
| **01,02.** | Animal handler skill, pg. XR-202 |
| **03,04.** | Armorer skill, pg. XR-203 |
| **05,06.** | Carpentry skill, pg. XR-205 |
| **07.** | Cooking skill, pg. XR-206 |
| **08,09.** | Cybernetics technician skill, pg. XR-207 |
| **10,11.** | Demolitions expert skill, pg. XR-207 |
| **12,13.** | Homesteader skill, pg. XR-215 |
| **14-16.** | Mining skill, pg. XR-220 |
| **17.** | Morse Code skill, pg. XR-220 |
| **18.** | Killer skill, pg. XR-219 |
| **19,20.** | Prospector skill, pg. XR-222 |
| **21,22.** | Seamanship skill, pg. XR-222 |
| **23,24.** | Sewing skill, pg. XR-223 |
| **25-27.** | Smithing skill, pg. XR-223 |
| **28.** | Street wise skill, pg. XR-224 |
| **29.** | Trapper skill, pg. XR-225 |
| **30,31.** | Barter skill, pg. TME-36 |
| **32-36.** | Brawling skill, pg. TME-56 |
| **37,38.** | Climbing skill, pg. TME-36 |
| **39,40.** | Dodge skill, pg. TME-37 |
| **41,42.** | Driver skill, pg. TME-37 |
| **43.** | Grapple skill, pg. TME-39 |
| **44-55.** | Junk crafter skill, pg. TME-41 |
| **56,57.** | Knife fighter skill, pg. TME-45 |
| **58.** | Knife thrower skill, pg. TME-45 |
| **59.** | Pick locks skill, pg. TME-48 |
| **60,61.** | Relic knowledge skill, pg. TME-49 |
| **62.** | Technician skill, bio, pg. TME-52 |
| **63-65.** | Technician skill, chemical, pg. TME-52 |
| **66,67.** | Technician skill, computer, pg. TME-53 |
| **68,69.** | Technician skill, electrical, pg. TME-53 |
| **70-78.** | Technician skill, mechanical, pg. TME-54 |
| **79,80.** | Technician skill, robotics, pg. TME-54 |
| **81,82.** | Weapon expert skill, pg. TME-57 |
| **83-85.** | Welding torch, built into the wrist of the android as per the cybernetic implant on page XR-349 of this book. |
| **86-88.** | Fire resistant skin: Beneath whatever sheathing is already present on this android, this unit has an extra layer of charcoal gray inner skin which while the rest might burn away, this layer resists flame utterly for the first minute (20 rounds) and thereafter the android suffers only half damage from extreme heat and fire. |

**89,90.** Fire extinguisher in palm. A 3 liter tank of propellant, chalk and other fire extinguishing materials can be purchased or found and mixed to refill this hidden internal canister. The extinguisher has a range of 4 meters and will snuff out a 1m square section of fire per round. This substance will also neutralize acid and can be used as a signaling device or to blind opponents who are 'struck' SV +6. Blinded opponents are half movement, +40 easier to be hit and -50% SV for 1d4 rounds. The canister will hold 30 bursts of flame retardant powder.

**91,92.** Acid resistant skin: Beneath any other layer of skin this android might possesses, it has a dark blue layer of rubberized plastic which will shed any acid for the first 10 rounds of exposure, and thereafter begin to perforate and be less effective, yet reduce any acid damage thereafter to half. This sheathing has a self healing quality and after an acid attack, and 48 hours have passed, the sheathing will knit back together. Any burnt off plastic skin will not heal, however.

**93-97.** Extra strong: Increase strength by +4d6 and Endurance by +3d6. Increase weight by +40kg.

**98.** Alloy cable muscles: Increase strength by +20+4d6 and endurance by +20+3d6. Increase weight by +50kg.

**99.** Hulking brute: This over built specimen weighs and extra 200 kg, moves -0.5m slower, but has a massive bonus of 50+1d100 endurance and 40+4d10 strength. Its height is also increased by 30+1d20cm.

**00.** Masterfully built*: While no larger than a regular industrial android, this thing is more advanced in every way. Improve all its stats by +2d6 points and increase its base movement by +1m in addition to any agility movement rate modifiers.

**Technician Android:** As their name implies, these androids specialize in one main technician skill area, but often have minor qualifications in other skills, too. They were originally designed to serve alongside either industrial or scientific models, but were widely dispersed throughout the old world. Of course, with their knowledge and access to essential services, those that were corrupted by the Mecha caused devastating damage to the infrastructure of human cities and industry, and left vast swaths of the human population without food, water, heat, virtual reality up-link, air conditioning and power.

In the wars which ended the old culture, many non-corrupted androids of this classification worked alongside pockets of survivors and bunker dwellers to endure the hellish decades that followed. New era technician androids, who often conceal their nature and many of their talents, easily find employment in the emerging towns of humanity, or else put their skills to work within a dig team. Joining an excavation company allows them to uncover much needed power supplies, equipment, parts and salable loot, but also to seek answers about their origins.

Unique technician androids have medium builds, we're made in both male and female designs, and have a wide range of often mundane appearances, including looking like a middle-aged human. At character generation, roll below on table XR -25 once for the unit's prime tech area and then 3 times on Table XR-26 for other features.

## Table XR-25/ Technician Android Prime Tech Area   Roll 1d100

|  |  |
|---|---|
| 01-14 | Cybernetics technician, pg. XR-207  / 1+1d3 skill points |
| 15-28 | Bio-technician, pg. TME-52 / 1+1d3 skill points |
| 29-42 | Chemical technician, pg. TME-52 / 1+1d3 skill points |
| 43-56 | Computer  technician, pg. TME-53 /1+1d4 skill points |
| 57-70 | Electrical technician, pg. TME-53 / 1+1d3 skill points |
| 71-84 | Mechanical technician, pg. TME-54 / 1+1d3 skill points |
| 85-98 | Robotics technician,  pg. TME-54 / 1+1d4 skill points |
| 99. | Double skill area expertise. Player pick one skill area and then roll 1d100 for a random, different secondary skill area*. |
| 00. | Triple skill area expertise. Player pick one skill area and then roll 1d100 twice for 2 other, different second and third skill areas.* |

*Re-roll if this result comes up again.

## Table XR-26/ Technician Android Other Features  Roll 1d100, 3 times

|  |  |
|---|---|
| 01-03. | Armorer skill, pg. XR-203 |
| 04,05. | Artist skill, pg. XR-204 |
| 06,07. | Enhanced! Add +2 to each trait* |
| 08-10. | Carpentry skill, pg. XR-205 |
| 11,12. | Ultra enhanced! Add +4 to each trait* |
| 13-15. | Cybernetics technician skill point, pg. XR-207 |
| 16-18. | Demolitions expert skill, pg. XR-207 |
| 19-21. | Herbalist skill , pg. XR-212 |
| 22-28. | Junk-doctor skill, pg. XR-218 |
| 29. | Morse code skill, pg. XR-220 |
| 30. | Seamanship skill, pg. XR-222 |
| 31,32. | Smithing skill, pg. XR-223 |
| 33-35. | Communications skill, pg. XR-225 |
| 36. | Barter skill, pg. TME-36 |
| 37. | Dodge skill, pg. TME-37 |
| 38,39. | Driver skill, pg. TME-37 |
| 40. | Forgery skill, pg. TME-38 |
| 41. | Gambler skill, pg. TME-38 |
| 42,43. | Gunsmith skill, pg. TME-40 |
| 44-51. | Junk crafter skill, pg. TME-41 |
| 52. | Martial artist skill, pg. TME-56 |
| 53,54. | Medic skill, pg. TME-46 |
| 55. | Navigate by stars, pg. TME-46 |
| 56. | Negotiating skill, pg. TME-46 |
| 57. | Pick locks skill, pg. TME-48 |
| 58. | Pickpocket skill, pg. TME-48 |
| 59,60. | Pilot skill, pg. TME-49 |
| 61-63. | Relic knowledge, pg. TME-49 |
| 64-66. | Technician skill, bio, pg. TME-52 |
| 67-69. | Technician skill, chemical, pg. TME-52 |
| 70-72. | Technician skill, computer, pg. TME-53 |
| 73-75. | Technician skill, electrical, pg. TME-53 |
| 76-78. | Technician skill, mechanical, pg. TME-54 |
| 79-83. | Technician skill, robotics, pg. TME-54 |
| 84,85. | Tracking skill, pg. TME-55 |
| 86-88. | Weapon expert skill, pg. TME-57 |

**89-96.** Tool encrusted: This android's arms and upper body are encrusted in small access panels which are either hidden by clothing or beneath hard to discern skin seams and flaps. When needed, tools related to this unit's technician area of expertise can be called upon to reveal the required tool, including a laser scalpel. These tools are attached to a power cable or slip down the arm to fit in the android's palm. Wherever such a tool is powered, it runs off the android's own battery banks and uses a negligible amount of energy (do not record power drain for these small devices). In short, this character is considered to be equipped to conduct whatever tech skill it was originally designed for. Secondary skill areas added by using this list or acquired later usually require a separate set of relic or replica tools of the trade. In nearly every case, this android can access these tools to cut itself free of ropes and chains.

**97.98.** Welding Torch, as the cybernetic implant described on page XR-349 of this book.

**99.** Advanced technician model: Has an extra +1d6 to each trait* plus one skill point (or extra point) in one of these skills, roll **1d6: 1.** Martial arts / **2.** Junk crafter / **3.** Junk Doctor / **4.** Medic / **5.** Dodge / **6.** Driver.

**00.** Ultra advanced technician android: This unit was built to the highest specifications. It gains +3d6 to each trait* plus features 1 skill point in each of the tech areas noted on Table XR-25, above, which automatically adds one more point in its prime tech area, too.

*Including the CPU traits of Processor and Data (but not firewall).*

## Military Android:

**Military Android:** It is surmised that military androids were the most common variety ever made, both by human governments of old, as well as Mecha Ais on all sides of the final cataclysmic war. Beside their vast numbers — which were needed to replace destroyed units as fast as they could be built — a wide range of specialized units were also made, including some that were covert in nature and designed to blend in with other civilian android's and the wider human population. This classification also includes swat team police units, undercover covert agents and even the exceedingly rare suicide bomber models. Unique military androids benefit from the traits modifiers shown below, but have further modifiers and benefits described in the follow-up texts, on the next few pages.

All military androids come standard with the skills of Morse code, hand signals and navigate by stars. Roll 3d6 to determine the type of military android on the following table.

**Suicide Bomber Military Android:** While their proper designation was SDE (Self-Destruct Enabled), they were instead referred to as suicide bomber androids because of their dramatic final operation, at least as far as the media reported it back in the day. These units blended in with the crowd, inserted themselves in a protest, political convention, restaurant, subway line or other public transport, and detonated in such a way as to cause the most harm to those within its blast radius. In this android's central core is a powerful explosive charge which can be set to go off if the unit fears being captured, takes a direct order to do so from a superior officer, or as part of an assassination or terrorism operation. During the blast, all those within a 6 meter radius are most at risk of incineration, and suffer three 'attacks' at SV 01-90, damage 1d100. Those from beyond 6 meters out

to 12m take two attacks at SV 01-70 for 2d20 damage, while those beyond 12m out to 24 meters take one attack at SV 01-60 for 1d20 damage. This blast always destroys this android, including its head and CPU.

Any android of this designation killed by bullet fire, flame, explosions or energy weapon, has an 88% chance of detonating, even unwillingly and potentially taking out its comrades. The self-destruct mode can also be set on or off, android's choice, and if set to 'on', will blow up if the android is 'knocked out' or destroyed by any means to avoid its parts and battery falling into the hands of the enemy. To remove this detonation charge requires a robotics technicians per table TME-50 on page 54 of the hub rules. Use the ' attach/ detach implants to cyborg' column. This table also gives untrained participants and those of related tech areas a chance to remove the charge — although very low. Failure to remove the charge properly has a 83% chance of causing a detonation as described above, otherwise the procedure fails and another attempt can be made within 6 hours.

This android is otherwise a grunt, as far as skills and other special features go, see page XR-42.

**Covert Military Android:** Designed to blend in with a civilian population, either in an urban or wilderness area. This unit can change its skin complexion to mimic that of the local area population, a process that takes 45 minutes to achieve. Because this unit looks like an average man or woman — although well built and between 24 and 34 years old, it does not stand out as an especially dangerous, bulky warrior model, and in the post-apocalyptic communities of the new era this beneficial since one of this stature will not draw special attention.

These units have 1d3 skill points in stealth, 1d4 skill points in tracking, 1d3 skill points in communications, 1d3 different weapon expert skills, 1d3 martial arts skill points, 1d3 skill points in climbing and a 86% chance of having a built-in standard communicator inside its head which it can send and receive messages silently. Covert Androids can speak every old world human language, have 1 skill point in pilot and driver, and have a 1 in 10 chance of having a spring out razor sword which fits in its right arm and can deploy at +3 initiative when first engaged on an unsuspecting opponent.

## Table XR-27/ Military Android Type Determinations and Modifiers

| 3d6 | Military/Android Type | END | STR | AG | ACC | INT | PER | WILL | APP | Skeletal Structure Roll* | Tissue Sheathing Roll* |
|---|---|---|---|---|---|---|---|---|---|---|---|
| 3. | Suicide Bomber | +2d6+10 | +2d6+10 | +4d6 | +4d6 | - | +2d6 | +3d6 | - | 1d6+2 | 1d8+1 |
| 4. | Covert | +2d6+10 | +2d6+10 | +3d6+10 | +3d6+10 | +2d6 | +2d6 | +2d6 | +2d6 | 1d6+6 | 1d8+2 |
| 5. | Sniper | +3d6+10 | +3d6+10 | +3d6+20 | +3d6+30 | +3d6 | +3d6+10 | +2d6 | - | 1d6+4 | 1d8+2 |
| 6,7. | Police (SWAT) | +4d6+30 | +4d6+20 | +3d6 | +3d6 | +1d6 | +2d6 | +2d6 | - | 1d6+5 | 1d8+3 |
| 8-12. | Grunt | +4d6+40 | +4d6+20 | +3d6 | +3d6 | - | +d6 | +2d6 | - | 1d6+5 | 1d8+3 |
| 13. | Airborne | +2d6+20 | +4d6+20 | +4d6 | +4d6 | - | +2d6 | +3d6 | - | 1d6+5 | 1d8+2 |
| 14. | Aquatic Operations | +3d6+30 | +4d6+10 | +4d6 | +3d6 | - | +2d6 | +2d6 | - | 1d6+3 | 1d8+1 |
| 15. | Heavy Combat | +4d6+60 | +4d6+40 | +1d6 | +3d6 | - | - | +4d6 | - | 1d6+7 | 1d6+5 |
| 16. | Tanker | +2d6+20 | +2d6+10 | +2d6 | +4d6 | +2d6 | +3d6 | +1d6 | - | 1d6+4 | 1d8+2 |
| 17. | Pilot | +2d6+10 | +2d6 | +3d6+20 | +3d6+20 | +3d6+20 | +3d6+10 | +1d6 | +1d10 | 1d6+3 | 1d8+1 |
| 18. | Space Force | +3d6+30 | +2d6+10 | +5d6 | +5d6 | +3d6+30 | +3d6+10 | +3d6 | +1d8 | 1d6+6 | 1d8+3 |

*The dice roll shown for both the Skeletal Structure or Tissue Sheathing columns are dice used to roll on the tables on page 45, not added to any stat or trait.*

**Sniper Military Android:** As their name implies, these stealthy, modestly sized units appear as males or females of exceptional fitness, although not large and so are more easily able to blend in with a civilian population. Masters of camouflage, concealment and marksmanship, these deadly units make for exceptional new era excavators. Each has 1d4 skill points in each of the following skills: stealth, Lock picking, tracking, climbing and the sniper skill. 77% of these units have built in standard communicator in their heads and like the covert android, can carry on conversations within their head with other operators without being heard by nearby personnel. Sniper androids have built in telescopic vision with which they can see 40 times further than a human by day and 10 x further at night, with advanced night vision optics built into their eyes.

**Police (SWAT) Military Android:** These units are based on grunt models, but are typically less robust and built to better resemble normal humans in proportions — although very fit, well built and sometimes well groomed specimens. They come standard with the skills listed below, but 2 in 6 will also have a built in stun baton emitter in their left palm, which when engaged, makes the hand glow blue when it is ready to smack an offender. Stun stick SV +7, DMG 2d20 stun, melee range, can deliver 40 successful strikes per day. Runs off and recharges from the android's own systems. Additionally, 1 in 6 can launch up to 20 bursts of stun beam energy, identical to the relic stun pistol, from their eyes, however this design fires 2 beams per round (one from each eye), SV +15, DMG 2d20 stun, range 200m, 20 two shot bursts per day.

Skills included with every police android: dodge 1d2 pts, weapon expert 1d3pts, brawling 1d3pts, driver 1pt, negotiating 1pt, grapple 1d3pts.

**Grunt Military Android:** By far these are the most common military androids ever made, and easily the most frequently discovered variant in the post-apocalyptic new era. Built solid, with access to plenty of spare parts from all those of their classification who fell in long ago battles, they exhibit an ideal balance of ruggedness, speed and talent to bring the hurt to the enemy. Unique specimens of this type make for exceptional excavators and can appear as males or females, are always modeled after well built human specimens of larger than average size, and besides the **hand signaling**, **Morse Code** and **navigate by stars** skills that all military androids already start with, these units begin operations with 6 skill point rolls from the following list. Duplicated results are kept: Roll 1d20, six times:

| Table XR-28 / Grunt Android Skills | Roll 1d20, six times |
|---|---|
| 1,2. | Brawling, pg. TME-56 |
| 3. | Climbing, pg. TME-36 |
| 4,5. | Dodge, pg. TME-37 |
| 6. | Grapple, pg. TME-39 |
| 7. | Gunslinger, pg. TME-39 |
| 8,9. | Knife fighter, pg. TME-45 |
| 10. | Knife thrower, pg. TME-45 |
| 11. | Medic, pg. TME-46 |
| 12,13. | Stealth, pg. TME-51 |
| 14. | Tracking, pg. TME-55 |
| 15. | Weapon expert pistols, pg. TME-57 |
| 16. | Weapon expert swords, pg. TME-57 |
| 17,18. | Weapon expert, rifles, pg. TME-57 |
| 19. | Killer, page XR-219 |
| 20. | Demolition expert, page XR-207 |

**Airborne Military Android:** These androids were made lighter than usual grunt combat units and designed to be para-dropped behind enemy lines or fast rope down from helicopters and hovercraft. In the old world, they were sometimes fitted with jet packs, glider wings or other gear to allow them to both descend and sometimes retreat from a strike zone. Unique new era specimens of this class have a **1 in 6 chance of having the pilot skill, plus a 2 in 6 chance of exhibiting 1 cybernetic implant from the following random table.** Additionally, they each have 5 rolls on the previous grunt military androids skill table.

| Table XR-29 / Airborne Military Android Features | Roll 2d6, once |
|---|---|
| 2,3. | Hover jets implant, pg. TME-87, however these are built into the palms and feet of this android and hidden by flesh-colored alloy seals when not used. These jets will allow the android to fly 1 meter off the ground for up to 60 rounds per day before they must auto-recharge. If a power pack is hooked to the android, these will operate for 600 rounds or 30 minutes (20 rounds in a minute). Often, this android can drop from a cliff, skyscraper or airship and free-fall until getting close to the ground and then ignite its jets to arrest its fall and land at a controlled, although bone jarring, thump. |
| 4,5. | Speed assist rotors implant, pg. XR-346 |
| 6-8. | Parachute implant, pg. XR-342 |
| 9,10. | Glide wings implant, pg. XR-338 |
| 11,12. | Chopper-borg implant, pg. XR-333 |

**Aquatic Operations Military Android:** Designed for sea going, marsh, river and human-built mega-reservoir deployments, these grunt variants were built sleek, buoyant, and perfectly adapted to underwater missions. While many of these naval models had metal bones, they were all equipped with complicated flotation foam and internal water-to-air depth assist canisters and fold out propulsion propellers, waterproofed vitals, and specialized eyes for seeing in the warped, dim world of deep, dark water. An aqua-android will only sink below the surface when desired, or can remain at the surface and swim like a regular human if that is a preferable mode of travel.

They are all excellent swimmers, and as they do not breathe, cannot drown, and so in theory could walk across the bottom of a lake or bay if they so desired. Their water vision allows them to see twice as far as a regular human while submerged, possibly 10 meters depending on daylight, turbidity, and algae concentrations. Their built in, flip out propellers can speed them through the water at a rate of 9m per round. When on land, these propellers can be safely stowed by hidden skin flaps, specialized clothing or modified armor plates. Each will have 5 rolls on the grunt military android skills table, shown on this page

**Heavy Combat Military Android:**  Once widely deployed on the sides of Mecha and human factions of old, their large size made them stand out, and so receive unwanted attention and multiple incoming rounds. Few of these brutes now walk the twisted world of The Mutant Epoch, but those that do are much feared, well respected, and incredibly valuable assets to any wasteland warlord or dig team. They stand at least a foot (30cm) taller than a large man, are broad of chest and shoulder and have enormous, cable knotted muscles.

Many of the unique specimens that now exist also have advanced skeletal structures and their skin is an armored sheath. Beside their natural strength and ability to take damage, they also prefer to wear armor, which while slowing them further, makes them harder to kill.

Each will have 5 rolls on the grunt military android's skill table, on page 42, but also 1 bonus feature from the following list.

### Table XR-30 / Heavy Combat Android Bonus Feature — Roll 2d6 Once

**2.** Polycarbonate alloy sub-sheathing: This layer of black alloy normally lines the android's entire body beneath any surface skin sheathing. While this dense material adds +20kg weight to the android, it also improves its defense value by -20 DV and endurance trait by +3d10 points.

**3.** Gun hand: In the palm of this android's left hand is an energy weapon which draws power from the main unit and will recharge its daily uses after 24 hours. Roll 1d6:
> **1,2.** Laser pistol: identical to roll 4 on this table.
> **3,4.** Electro-Glove, Advanced: SV+20, Rate 1, DMG 20+2d20 stun, Range: 20m, Uses 10 per day. Learn more about this relic on page XR-413 of this book.
> **5,6.** Pulse Rifle: SV +20, Rate 4, Range 800m, DMG 1d12, Uses: 20, four shot bursts per day.

**4.** Laser eye: One of the android's eyes is actually a standard laser pistol which runs off the android's main power to provide 30 shots per day — although there is an access power plug hidden behind the ear where a patch cable can be connected to a power pack or belt mounted standard power cell to add additional shots. Laser pistol SV +16, rate 1, range 500m, DMG 1d20+10, 30 shots per day or per power cell.

**5.** Random cybernetic implant from the Android column on page XR-330 of this book.

**6.** Night vision eyes. Can see 200 meters in darkness.

**7.** Extra plating on vital joints, CPU, sensors and essential systems: Increase this unit's endurance by +30 and its defense value by an extra -10. Increase weight by +20kg.

**8.** Detachable lower left arm and a spare, backpack carried Weapon Arm. Detachable lower arm described on page TME-86, weapon arm on page TME-92, but use the extensive updated listing in this book on page XR-437. This android can switch from this arm to a ready weapon arm in one minute (20 rounds).

**9.** Precision aim: Increase Accuracy trait by +30.

**10.** Upgraded Mobility: Increase agility score by +30 and add an additional +1 meter per round to movement besides any gains to speed from the AG (agility trait) bonus.

**11.** Advanced construct: Add +2d6 to each trait.

**12.** Ultra heavy: add 50kg weight, +20 strength, +60 endurance

### Tanker Military Android:

Although tough, these drivers of ancient armored vehicles were built smaller, more agile and better able to fit into, and move around inside many old world vehicles. While nearly all such ancient tanks, armored personnel carriers and battle trucks have long since been destroyed — or else their fuel supply long since dried up — many of these lean, highly skilled 'tankers' survived the ancient wars. These soldiers spread across the world and now survive however they can. Because of their more typical human proportions, many find acceptance and concealment in human communities.

Most people never realize that these capable mechanics, junk crafters and drivers of thrown together rigs and trucks are actually androids. To avoid being detected, and enslaved because of their valuable skills, many tankers know never to stay in one town or barter fort for more than a year or two, and find the nomadic lifestyle of diggers more to their tastes. Inside a trusted, open-minded excavation team, a tanker android will usually reveal its true nature.

These units start with 4 skill rolls on the Grunt Military Androids table on page 42, plus have 1d3 skill points in the driver skill, 1d3 points in the mechanical technician skills, as well as 2 rolls on the following additional features table. Re-roll duplicated results.

### Table XR-31 / Tanker Military Android Additional Features — Roll 1d12, twice

**1.** Demolitions expert skill, pg. XR-207
**2.** Communications skill, pg. XR-205
**3.** Driver skill, pg. TME-37 (+1 extra point)
**4.** Gunsmith, pg. TME-40
**5.** Junk crafter, pg. TME-41
**6.** Relic knowledge, pg. TME-49
**7.** Technician, chemical, pg. TME-52
**8.** Technician, computer, pg. TME-53
**9.** Technician, electrical, pg. TME-53
**10.** Technician, mechanical, pg. TME-54 (+1 extra point)
**11.** Technician, robotics, pg. TME-54
**12.** Advanced model: Add +2d6 to each trait.

**Pilot Military Android:** Built light, agile, and of higher intelligence than most other androids, these units were made in the both male and female patterns in about equal numbers — and often with enhanced appearance. While civilian android co-pilots were used in old world airlines and inter-city hover transports, primary piloting was done by trusted human operators after several infamous incidents where Mecha corrupted air crews took over flights. For the military, however, the use of android pilots was acceptable — at least in the early years of the End Time Wars.

Of those units which survived into the new era, they exist among the wider human population however they can, often incognito and keeping their true nature hidden from all but the most trusted fleshy companions. Because of their hard-wired programming and urge to fly, their number one goal in 'life' is to gain, or possibly build, an aircraft. This innate drive to learn more about ancient flying machines compels them to join a dig team hoping to uncover some sort of flight worthy craft, or at the very least, buy and operate a new era airship to transport their team to far-off places. Because they are military units themselves, and deadly in their own right, they are not averse to taking any aircraft into the vast dead cities of the oldsters. Here, they aim to land a chopper or airship on the top of an old skyscraper and deposit their excavator comrades into hostile, relic rich territory.

Each pilot android will have 1+1d3 points in the pilot skill, relic knowledge (pg. TME-49), plus 4 rolls on the grunt android's skill table on page 42, but also 2 rolls on the following features table. Re-roll duplicated results.

### Table XR-32 / Pilot Military Android Features — Roll 2d6, twice

**2,3.** One roll on the Airborne Military Android Features listing, page 42
**4,5.** Driver skill, pg. TME-37
**6.** A skill point in a random Technician area, roll 1d6: **1.** Technician, chemical, pg. TME-52/ **2.** Technician, computer, pg. TME-53/ **3.** Technician, electrical, pg. TME-53/ **4.** Technician, cybernetics, pg. XR-207 / **5.** Technician, mechanical, pg. TME-54/ **6.** Technician, robotics, pg. TME-54

7. Junk crafter skill, pg. TME-41

8,9. Parachute cybernetic implant, see page XR-342, this book.

10. Communications skill, see page XR-205.

11. Advanced model: Add +1d6 to each trait.

12. Ultra Advanced Model: Add +2d6 to each trait. This skinbot looks and acts remarkably human, complete with authentic emotions, romantic interests, carnal instincts and a sense of humor.

**Space Force Military Android:** These well built, advanced androids were used as security and boarding troops during operations aboard space stations and vessels, as well as deposited on the ground on moons, asteroid mines, and other planets such as Mars. Besides fierce combat in zero gravity or the harshest of environments, they can handle the vacuum of space, resit radiation, extreme cold or extreme heat, and cope with long periods of dormancy. These units can go dormant on minimal powers for 25 years, but if activated by a ship's main computer, a digital being, or physical contact, they will power up and become fully operational in 3d6 minutes.

Also called astro-marines, as are human and synthetic human troops that once served in various space programs, these androids suffer half damage from any cold or heat based attacks, get two hazard checks to resit any radiation exposure, have hardened servos, circuits and cranium case and so have an improved defense value of -10 DV.

They feature magnetic adhesion disks in their feet to allow them to walk along the floors and walls of vessels during zero gravity events, plus exhibit the foot jet packs described on roll 82-84 on page 54. While their magnetic grip is sufficient to hold them to the interior or exterior of a spacecraft, these disks are not strong enough to allow it to walk up a metal clad structure or ship hull on earth. Regardless, these magnets do greatly assist in this, and improve the unit's climbing speed on metal surfaces by +3 skill points. Space force military androids get 4 rolls on the grunt android skill table on page 42, but also, one roll on the following feature table:

**Table XR-33 / Space Force Military Android Bonus Features   Roll 1d100**

01-06. Acrobatics skill, pg XR-201

07-15. Communications skill, pg XR-205

16-21. Climbing skill, pg. TME-36

22-25. Grapple skill, pg. TME-39

26-33. Pilot skill, pg. TME-49

34,35. Relic knowledge skill, pg. TME-49

36-54. Laser carbine arm: The left palm of this android has a small portal that opens to reveal the muzzle of a very advanced laser rifle with sights connected to the android's left eye. Using its own power systems it can fire 20 shots per day before a 24 hour recharge is needed: SV +25, Rate 1, Range 2km, DMG 2d20+10. This arm looks quite normal most of the time, but has a hidden skin flap and access port near the elbow that allows standard power cells to be stuck into it like the magazine of a rifle, and with each full cell allowing for a further 20 shots. Another plug at the same port accepts the patch cable from a power pack or vehicle's on-board power supply, potentially offering unlimited firepower.

55-60. Demolitions expert skill, pg XR-207.

61-86. Atmospheric reentry capable: This unit can eject from a spacecraft and line itself up for an orbital reentry into an atmosphere. It will tuck itself into a ball and glance along the atmosphere of an earth-like world, its back aspect becoming red hot and engaging specialized reentry insulation tiles to fuse, blacken and protect the rest of the vulnerable entity. Once through the atmosphere, it will descend to two thousand meters and deploy a parachute (see the implant on page XR-342) and drop to the surface where it will require 6d6 minutes to crack free of the hardened shell that encased its body and become operational. Any gear, clothing or items carried on its outer body will be burnt away on re-entry, however it can clutch one small, skull sized object, handgun or other item to its chest during its journey. The extremely tough re-entry tiles that cover much of this android's back can be cleaned off after a return to earth, yet always offer an extra degree of armor protection throughout the unit's life; increase defense value by -6. The parachute can be stowed back in its low profile compartment and used for a wide range of terrestrial uses, too.

87,88. Driver skill, pg. TME-37

89,90. Junk crafter skill, pg. TME-41

91-96. Advanced space model MK I: Add +1d6 to each trait, plus make 1 more roll on this table but re-roll results of 91 to 00.

97-99. Advanced space model MK II: Add +2d6 to each trait, plus make 2 more rolls on this table but re-roll results of 91 to 00 or any duplicated result.

00. Advanced space model MK III: Add +3d6 to each trait, plus unit is immune to radiation exposure except in the form of a direct blast from relics or mutations. Plus, make 3 more rolls on this table but re-roll results of 91 to 00 or any duplicated result.

# Android Skeletal Composition

### Table XR-34/ Skeletal Composition Determination
Roll either 1d8, 1d6+2, or 1d8+2 depending on the android's original purpose (from table XR-14, page 31).

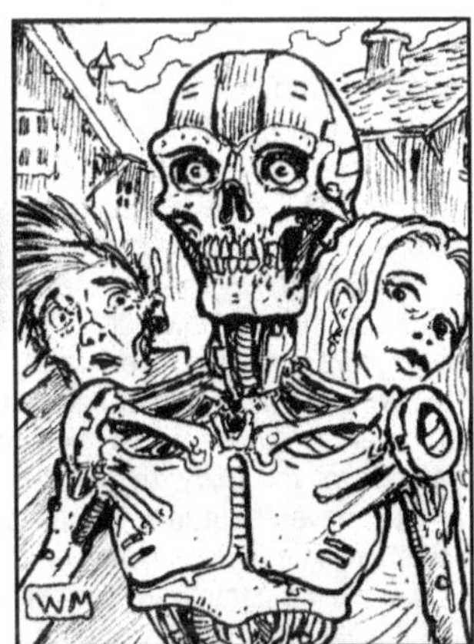

| 1d10 | Skeletal Material | END | STR | Base Fist Damage | Base Movement* | Android's Base Weight** | Flotation*** |
|---|---|---|---|---|---|---|---|
| 1-4. | Plastic boned | +0 | +0 | 1d6 | 9m | 50kg | Floats |
| 5,6. | Mixed plastic and aluminum bones | +2 | +1 | 1d6 | 8m | 60kg | Floats |
| 7. | Aluminum bones | +4 | +2 | 1d8 | 8m | 70kg | Active |
| 8. | Stainless steel bones | +6 | +4 | 1d10 | 7m | 100kg | Sinks |
| 9. | Alloy steel bones | +10+1d20 | +6+1d6 | 1d12 | 6m | 150kg | Sinks |
| 10.+ | Polycarbonate bones | +8+1d8 | +4+1d4 | 1d12 | 8m | 100kg | Active |

*The agility trait of the android can affect this base movement rate the same as a human character.*

**This is the character's weight in kilograms before sheathing, heavy implants, or worn armor and equipment is added.*

***Flotation: Unless otherwise stated by some technology, worn relic life preserver, or other means, this column reveals if this android can stay on the surface of water or sinks like a block of metal. If the column listing states 'floats' then this unit is buoyant and will float on the surface of the water even if unmoving or incapacitated — but can swim down if needed to evade enemies or investigate some sunken object or structure. 'Active' means this android must tread water or actively swim to stop from sinking at a rate of 1 meter per round, perhaps ending up kilometers beneath the surface of the sea and lost forever in some deep, oceanic trench. 'Sinks' means even if this android tries to dog paddle or front crawl, it cannot stay on the surface even though it can propel itself forward 1m per round, yet will simultaneously sink like a rock at a rate of 3m per round. If it can hold on to floating wreckage or is supported by a strong or excellent swimmer, then this android can be held in place and pulled to shore, although the swimming companion(s) combined strength scores must be equal to or higher than the kilograms of weight of this non-buoyant android.*

# Android Tissue Sheathing

Sheathing is the skin encasement around the android's body and face — at least where obvious cybernetic implants are not affixed. A unique android might start game play with the most advanced alloy cladding, a more typical plastic sheathing, or be unlucky and have no covering at all and all its servo motors, wiring, pistons and underlying skeletal frame exposed. Androids start with a base defense value of 0 (zero) just like a human character, however apply any agility modifiers, sheathing mods, or skill-based changes after the character is created. Sheathing, or a lack thereof, also affects the endurance trait of the android so record any endurance amount added or subtracted when establishing a sheathing type, as this amount can change when skin is added or removed. Only one sheathing type can be adhered to the android at any given time, although other armor and underlying extras can appear as seen on the special features listing on table XR-52 on page 52 or included in some of the original purpose write-ups on previous pages.

The assorted sheathing types are described below the following table. To upgrade a sheathing type requires a robotic technician, plus a donor android body or unattached sheath. The table below shows the hazard check required to successfully attach any sheathing type, with a failed check by the robotics technician requiring another 24 hours to make another attempt. Failed attempts to re-skin an artificial person reduce the appearance of the new skin by -1d10 APP, permanently.

Each sheathing type has a movement modifier, with heavier skin types slowing the android down. When creating a unique android character, be sure to record any deduction or bonus in traits because later on, if this lucky android can find and upgrade its sheathing, those trait modifiers are erased and the new mods from the new skin sheathing applied. Likewise, if an android loses its sheath — such as if it is stripped of its skin by some enemy or captor — it will suffer the reductions noted on the table below.

### Table XR-35 Unique Android Tissue Sheathing
Roll a 1d8 or 1d6+modifier based on the android's original purpose (shown on Table XR-14 or XR-27).

| 1d10 | Sheathing Type | Defense Value | Move Mod. | END Mod. | APP Mod. | Pass as Human* | Upgrade HC** | Weight Increase |
|---|---|---|---|---|---|---|---|---|
| 1. | None | +10 | +0.5m | -2d6 | -4d6 | Auto Fail | - | nil |
| 2. | Shredded plastic | +5 | +0.25m | -2d6 | -3d6 | Auto Fail | A | +2kg |
| 3,4. | Perforated plastic | +2 | +0m | -1d6 | -2d6 | A | B | +3kg |
| 5,6. | Plastic sheathing | +0 | +0m | +0 | +0 | C | C | +4kg |
| 7,8. | Flesh-like heated gelatin | -2 | +0m | +1d6 | +2d6 | E | D | +10kg |
| 9. | Ballistic mesh | -10/ -30 vs bullets | -0.25m | +3d6 | +0 | B | D | +15kg |
| 10. | Polycarbonate sheath | -18 | -0.25m | +10+1d10 | +0 | A | E | +30kg |
| Above 10 | Alloy steel cladding | -30 | -1m | +20+2d6 | +0 | Auto Fail | G | +50kg |

** This is the Intelligence based hazard check an onlooker uses, per minute, to discern that this android is not human. 'Auto Fail' means the onlooker always realizes the character is an android. Any android with the disguise artist skill (found on page TME-36) forces a viewer within 3 meters to make a secondary hazard check based on the skill points this android has in this area of expertise. Any android with odd hair color, strange illuminated eyes, cybernetic weapon arms, massive proportions or some other quite noteworthy feature will of course attract attention despite how human their skin might look, and so the game master's call on this might be needed.*

***Upgrade HC: The chance, per 24 hours for a robotics technician to successfully affix this sheathing to an android. Each failure permanently reduces the appearance score of the skin by -1d10 APP.*

# Android Sheathing Descriptions

**None:** This android's skin layer is completely torn away leaving behind either some sort of specialized inner layer, or more likely, a metallic or plastic skeletal structure, masses of wires, fiber optic cables, pistons, servo motor junctions, batteries and assorted liquid tanks and sensor nodes. However, 78% of the time the android's human face is still somewhat intact, and with the help of hoods, bandages and other face covers and a good overall concealment of the body, this humanoid robot can still move about in a human settlement for a short time and not cause undo alarm.

Should a commoner see this plastic or metal skeletal apparition without clothing or armor on it, then all bets are off and the local population will be horrified, and possibly violent toward the android. The goal of this unit is probably to stay armored up and never stay anywhere too long, or join a dig team and search for power cells and a deceased android with intact skin that can be peeled off and sewn to this individual's frame. Because of a lack of sheathing, this unit is +10 easier to strike (has a +10 DV penalty), but is faster (+0.5m per round), suffers a lack in toughness (-2d6 END) and a huge drop in its appearance score (-4d6) to a minimum of 1 trait point.

**Shredded Plastic:** Similar to having no skin at all, this unfortunate android looks just about as horrific as the skeletal frame of a skinless variant, although its knotted and flapping sheets of skin can be tied together, stitched here and there and patched with animal hides and plastic bags, bubble wrap, and other junk to try to give the unit some protection of the element and glancing blows. Still, villagers who might accidentally come upon this android when it is disrobed are likely to scream and run off to get the local watch patrol, and see the android is destroyed. Like a skinless android, this unit will always be on the search for another android's skin to steal and stitch onto its own frame, and there is no better place to try to find an old, inoperative or uncooperative android than the ruins. For this reason, this specimen needs to join a glorious excavation squad.

These ghastly looking, ribbon skinned horrors are easier to hit (+5 DV), move +.25m faster, suffer a -2d6 drop to endurance, a -3d6 drop to appearance (to a minimum of 1 APP point) and have a slight weight increase of 2 kilograms.

**Perforated Plastic:** This skin sheathing is dotted by holes, cuts, and evidence of fire damage, bullet and beamer holes, bite marks, stitching and patches of other materials. In general, it has a skin that leaves no doubt in onlookers minds this person is actually a machine. Still, this hole-ridden old covering helps keep out the elements, and from a distance, and if the android wears clothing or armor, allows the unit to blend into a crowd of regular, organic humans enough to get by or pass through a community. Like those androids with shredded or no skin, this individual will be eager to uncover an all new, superior sheathing — which will draw them to the ruins and a lifestyle as an 'archaeologist'.

**Plastic Sheathing:** While this skin might have a few scuff marks, a well-hidden patch, stitched up cut, or puckered hole where a bullet or arrow once caught this unit, this flexible sheathing is stretchy and very human-like. In short, it does the job of concealing the android's true nature from a few feet away. Such skin is about a centimeter thick, except on the face where it must better follow the contours of the synthetic skeletal structure beneath. Although, quite realistic looking, it has no warmth of its own and does not always bend the way human skin does.

Still, where an actual skin can yield, such as at the breasts, and buttocks, these areas have been given extra padding to simulate the real thing, especially in units designed for the carnal pleasure of human companions. For most androids, this level of skin is the best they can hope to have. So too, if they are already attractive, blend in well with human society, and can wear decent armor over this, they often settle for this sheath.

**Flesh-like Heated Gelatin:** This is the pinnacle in android skin, especially for those humanoid robots in civilian support roles, or where close contact with humans is part of their job. Many concubine, personal assistants, health care and secretary androids have this impressive, and very human skin. Unique androids who conduct amatory liaisons with humans will typically desire to have a sheathing of this sort, although it's a challenge to install properly should an upgrade skin be made available. In short, this skin makes the android almost indistinguishable from a regular human, and besides being warm to the touch, it also allows for perspiration, freckles, moles, natural looking hair, peach fuzz and other details.

Sexually capable androids with this sheath are highly sought after, and unless they are also combat capable or have a strong team that will defend them, these units are the targets of collectors, brothel owners and others who seek to exploit them. Few androids with this skin, except obvious varieties of military androids, ever seek any skin beyond this variety, and prefer to protect themselves with armor and allies instead of upgrading to ballistic mesh or polycarbonate sheaths.

**Ballistic Mesh:** This tight fitting skin both enhances the build and gender pattern indicators of the android within, but also has all the subtleness of regular plastic sheathing. From a distance the wearer of this skin looks human enough, however when examined up close, it reveals a tiny grid shaped pattern that covers the entire surface. Likewise, this skin is thicker than more common variants, at about 2 centimeters, and so does not crease or flex the same as do civilian coverings. This sheathing was designed for light military units and besides being attractive and allowing humans to feel comfortable around android comrades who look more human, this sheathing also offers a slight armor benefit plus excellent additional protection from bullets, blunt impacts and falls. In fact, reduce all falling damage by 25% for androids clad in this skin type.

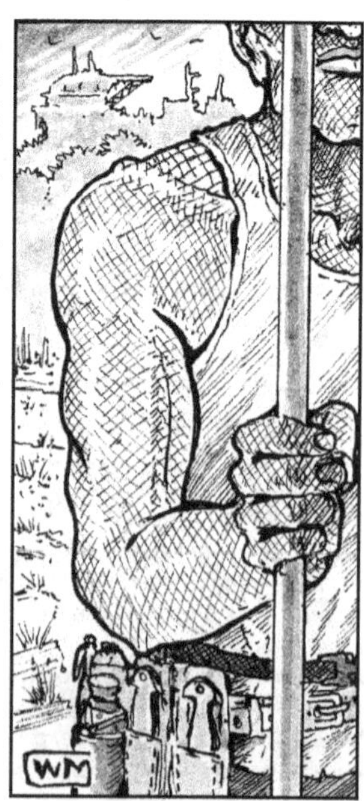

**Polycarbonate Sheath:** While still flexible like skin, this covering is hard to mistake as anything natural, and while it hugs the contours of the body shape within, and seems to pronounce any gender identifying physical attributes, the skin itself is not warm, exhibits little subtleness or responsiveness despite any amatory capabilities the android might have. This skin is usually of some unnatural color, and like ballistic mesh, is exhibits a grid or diamond shaped pattern which sometimes reflects light almost like fish scales.

This is an armored sheath that gives the wearer a -30 defense value bonus and can have other armor worn over top, making this unit exceedingly hard to kill. It was designed both for military units and androids who were expected to face danger, including industrial, space exploration and certain bio-technical pursuits that involved the genetic engineering and training of mutant beasts. Roll 3d6 for the color of this android's sheathing:

| Polycarbonate Sheath Color   Roll 3d6 | |
| --- | --- |
| 3. | Lime green |
| 4. | Hot pink |
| 5. | Clear (parts underneath visible) |
| 6. | Blood red |
| 7. | Gloss black |
| 8. | Matt black |
| 9. | White |
| 10. | Blue |
| 11. | Urban gray pattern digi-camo |
| 12. | Desert digi-camo |
| 13. | Woodland digi-camo |
| 14. | Gray |
| 15. | Purple |
| 16. | Orange |
| 17. | Yellow |
| 18. | Chameleon powers: This sheath changes color to blend into the background and surrounding patterns and pigments. This android gains 2 points in the stealth skills of concealed movement and conceal self, and when operating alone and waiting in ambush, gains +4 initiative. |

**Alloy Steel Cladding:** This steel carapace is either black, gleaming chrome or some sort of metallic metal, such as green, red or blue. While the android encased in this two centimeter thick, articulating armored shell might have the splendid physique of a fit man or woman, there is no mistaking it for a living human despite the appearance score of the android. Other armor, and some special features that might conceal this plating, can be worn with this protective layer. The android housed in this sheathing is immune to acid, dust storms, heat or cold damage, and can operate in the void of space for up to an hour before its joints and hydraulic lines freeze up. Fire and falling do only half damage to this android.

| 2d10 | Alloy Steel Cladding Color |
| --- | --- |
| 2. | Chalk white, flat |
| 3. | Gloss white |
| 4. | Flat black |
| 5,6. | Glossy black |
| 7-13. | Gleaming chrome |

| 14. | Metallic red |
| --- | --- |
| 15. | Metallic blue |
| 16. | Metallic green |
| 17. | Metallic orange |
| 18. | Desert tan, flat |
| 19. | Olive drab, flat |
| 20. | Chameleon powers: see roll result 18 for 'Polycarbonate Sheath Color' on the previous table. |

# Android Healing Mode

Because androids, like robots, are not flesh and blood, they do not heal like other characters, although among the more advanced specimens, which use micro healer bots or nanites, it would seem to others that they heal all on their own and often far faster than meat based people. Using the mutations of heal touch and extreme healing do not work on machines and non-organic beings.

Androids, as well as robots and other purely mechanical beings, bodies, vessels, devices and vehicles can recover from EMP or other stun damage so long as they are not knocked out and thus deactivated. They heal this non-destructive damage at a per hour rate instead of per daily rate based on their endurance trait's healing rate as shown on table XR-3.

Roll 1d100 using the following table at the time of character creation to establish the healing mode of each unique android.

### Table XR-36/ Android Healing Mode

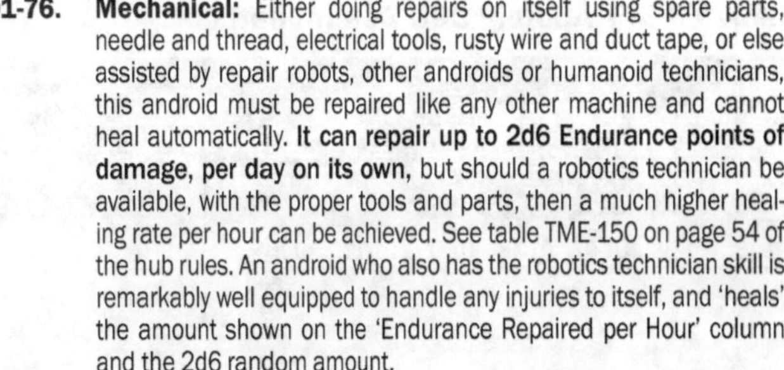

| 1d100 | Healing Mode |
| --- | --- |

**01-76.**   **Mechanical:** Either doing repairs on itself using spare parts, needle and thread, electrical tools, rusty wire and duct tape, or else assisted by repair robots, other androids or humanoid technicians, this android must be repaired like any other machine and cannot heal automatically. **It can repair up to 2d6 Endurance points of damage, per day on its own,** but should a robotics technician be available, with the proper tools and parts, then a much higher healing rate per hour can be achieved. See table TME-150 on page 54 of the hub rules. An android who also has the robotics technician skill is remarkably well equipped to handle any injuries to itself, and 'heals' the amount shown on the 'Endurance Repaired per Hour' column and the 2d6 random amount.

**77-96.**   **Micro Healer Bots:** 4d6 Small, finger nail sized robots within the android detect injuries and move to stitch together, micro weld and re-grow synthetic tissues and circuits. These tiny units replenish themselves and the injured android by breaking down and emulsifying various elements, with different micro-bots exuding different compounds  To an onlooker, the sight of these disc-like, multi legged machines moving under the skin of an android can be quite alarming. A steady supply of raw materials must be fed into the android through an abdominal feeding tube every few days to supply the bots. These tiny bots **heal the unit 4d6 endurance and other trait points per 24 hours**.

**97-00.**   **Nanites:** This unit **heals the same as an organic being based on its endurance trait.** Its nanites are tuned to this android's ID code and exist throughout its body. Whenever damage occurs to any part, they immediately set to work and knit together and manufacture millimeter sized bits of whatever material has been damaged or lost. Because these nanites require raw materials to construct replacement fragments, this android must occasionally insert bits of scrap metal, copper wire, fiber optic, and other inorganic materials — all which can be found near any ruin site or town's scrap yard — and load them into a digestion compartment in its abdomen.

# CPU Within Android's Head

The CPU (Central Processing Unit) of an android is its hard-wired, computerized brain and occupies the skull cavity of the head. Other than a jury-rigged CPU variety, listed in the table below, the computerized brain housed in this android is fixed and can't be switched in and out without deleting the consciouses, however, by gaining ranks, trait improvements can a occur.

After randomly determining the CPU on the table below, add any modifiers to Intelligence and willpower to any gained through the unit's original purpose, plus whatever the android previously rolled at the start of character generation. The character may yet gain more points due to its pre-game caste.

At this point, you will also **roll on the main trait generation table, XR-2 on page 8, to establish this android's Processor Trait (PRO)**. This ability score is rolled like a regular trait with any modifiers affecting the Firewall (FW). Firewall is like defense value to ward off attacks by digital beings and similar entities.

Data points are akin to endurance points for the android's mind, and, like the firewall value, normally only come into play when engaged in a hacking attack from a digital being or similar intelligence or weapon system. These stats are located on a special section on the character sheet because they are rarely used — but essential when they are called into play. More on digital beings and their mode of combat using firewalls and data points can be found on page 67.

Roll 1d100 in the column based on the android's original purpose category:

## Table XR-37/ Android CPU Determination

| Civilian | Medical | Scientifc | Industrail | Technicain | Military | CPU Type | Intelligence | Willpower | Processor Trait Mod.* | Base Firewall | Data Points | Details |
|---|---|---|---|---|---|---|---|---|---|---|---|---|
| 01-13. | 01-08 | 01-07 | 01-18 | 01-05 | 01-11 | **Jury-rigged** | +0 | +0 | +0 | -0 | 20+1d10 | This brain has been put together with the bare minimum of parts and knowhow. The android's head rattles when it moves, and it has no real chance of fending off a digital being's hacking attack should one occur. This being is eager for an upgrade and can have the parts of any defeated android inserted into its head to upgrade it to a Basic CPU, although a computer technician must perform this simple task. |
| 14-61. | 09-43 | 08-39 | 19-71 | 06-35 | 12-67 | **Basic** | +0 | +0 | +2d8 | -10 | 30+2d20 | Chip and processor array. Fairly rudimentary parts, mass produced and as good as this android is going to get. |
| 62-83. | 44-73 | 40-76 | 72-89 | 36-71 | 68-77 | **Advanced** | +10+1d20 | +10+1d20 | +20+1d20 | -30 | 40+1d100 | Processor chain. Exceptionally advanced technology, with multiple processors built into a block to facilitate superior processing speeds and body coordination. |
| 84-96. | 74-82 | 77-80 | 90-99 | 72-79 | 78-94 | **Hardened** | +10+1d10 | +20+1d20 | +10+1d20 | -40 | 60+1d100 | Military or Space Operations grade Processors Chain. Can extend operational duration of this android when exposed to the void of space or other extreme cold for an extra hour before the android freezes up and goes dormant. |
| 97-00. | 83-00 | 81-00 | 00 | 80-00 | 95-00 | **Gelatinous Brain** | +20+3d20 | +10+2d20 | +20+2d20 | -50 | 70+1d100 | Very rare, late era, advanced CPU that even has the shape of a human brain. This self aware android can feel true emotions instead of simulated human-like responses. This android dreams, schemes and comes up with unpredictable ideas... although is at some risk of obsessive behavior, vengeance, passion and insanity. |

*This modifier is applied to the android's randomly generated processor trait value. The processor traits is like the agility trait, but instead of a modifier to Defense Value (DV), yet using the same column as agility on table XR-3, Processor (PRO) provides a potential modifier to Firewall (FW).*

# Android Power Supply

The power source, operation time, hibernation duration and activation time shown on the following table are statistics based on table TME-6-2 on page 184 of the Hub Rules, which goes by the same name. Unique androids differ from standard models in power usage, and in general, are far more efficient with their electrical usage than robots, although many unique robots come with backup power banks, or can generate their own power by on-board solar panels, bio-fuel burners or even the highly efficient, but terribly risky micro-nuclear reactors.

Androids sometimes start with one or more spare, fully charged power cells, either to plug into their body when a recharge is needed, or for use in advanced weapons and relics. All androids have a bank of four built-in mini power cells that will operate the unit for one hour while changing or switching out their main batteries. This very limited energy supply can keep the android operational long enough to load more power cells or seek help should they be neutralized and their power panel be discovered, forced open and their power cells stolen.

Besides having a one hour battery back-up, all androids are equipped with a well-concealed power adapter port which allow their skin to be folded back to reveal a plug where a standard power cable can be inserted into the android to recharge it, or in lieu of power cells, run the machine as normal — at least as far as the extension cord will reach. A power pack, (see page TME 199) can also be worn by any android, with such a pack having 10 times the battery life of a standard power cell.

### Table XR-38/ Unique Android Power Requirements by Model Type

| Original Purpose | Power Source | Continuous Operation | Hibernation Mode Duration | Activation Time |
|---|---|---|---|---|
| Civilian | power cell | 3 Years | 50 years | 3d20+20 rounds |
| Medical | power cell | 18 months | 120 years | 1d100+20 rounds |
| Scientific | power cell | 1 year | 110 years | 1d100+40 rounds |
| Industrial | 2 power cells | 3 years | 48 years | 1d100+100 rounds |
| Technician | power cell | 15 months | 136 years | 2d100+40 rounds |
| Military | 2 power cells | 5 years | 280 years | 3d6 rounds |

# Sensory Capabilities of Unique Androids

At the minimum, unique androids have all the same sensory receptors as pure stock humans, but often one or more of these senses are heightened or exhibit additional capabilities. Roll once on each of the following quick tables and record these sensors on your unique android's character sheet. With the published sheet included with this book and also available as a free PDF download, there is a specific text box for each of the following capabilities and details.

### Table XR-39/ Android Sight Capabilities* Roll 1d10

**1-4.** Normal human visual capabilities.

**5.** Normal human vision plus can project illumination as twin pocket flashlights at will to a maximum usage of 120 minutes per 24-hour period. Range 20m.

**6.** Normal human vision plus radiation detection mode: When engaged, this android can see areas and objects contaminated with radiation within 100 meters.

**7.** Improved human vision: Can see 50% further than a human, plus limited night Vision to 6 meters

**8.** Extended Vision: Can see twice as far as a human, as well as limited night vision to 20 meters, and discern augmented reality holograms. Learn more about Augmented Reality on page XR-477 of this book.

**9.** Night vision to 60m plus has daylight use binocular eyes x 25 magnification.

**10.** Advanced eyes: Roll 1d6: 1,2. Night vision to 100m / 3. Optical enhancement set 1 from the hub rules on page TME-89 / 4. Optical enhancement Set 2, from page XR-342, this book. / 5. Stun beam eye as stun pistol but recharges 20 shots max per day: SV +16, DMG 2d20 stun, range 200m, rate 1. / 6. Laser eye, as a laser pistol but max 20 shots per day and recharges from the android's built-in system: SV +16, DMG 1d20+10, rate 1, range 500m.

** There are many occurrences of these and other, enhanced visual or optical modes for android characters, including night vision and laser eyes to name a few. If after rolling another duplicated occurrence before or after consulting this table, then re-roll either another special feature or on this table to avoid redundant duplication.*

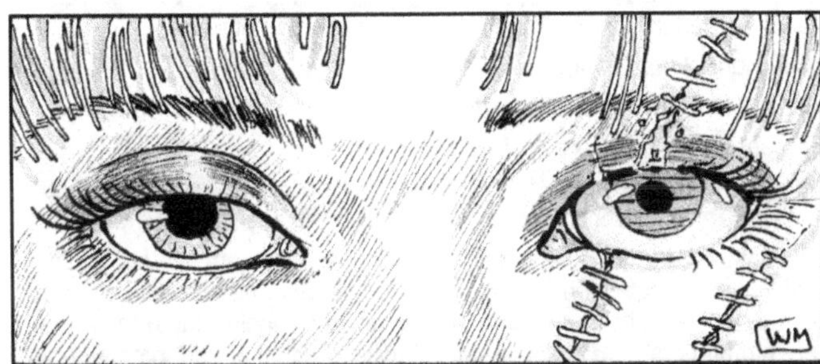


### Table XR-40/ Android Eye Appearance Roll 1d10

**1-6.** Normal pure stock human eye color and appearance. Roll 1d10 for eye color here: 1-3. Brown / 4. Blue / 5. Gray / 6. Hazel / 7. Green / 8. Amber / 9. two different/ 10. Optional: Can change color as desired.

**7.** Solid glossy black (no whites)

**8,9.** Iris is an illuminated light, roll 1d8: 1. Aquamarine / 2. Red/ 3. Orange/ 4. Amber/ 5. Green/ 6. Blue/ 7. Purple / 8. Red only when angry, otherwise normal human appearance.

**10.** Opalescent, reflects light oddly.

### Table XR-41/ Android Vocal Capabilities Roll 1d10

**1.** Almost inaudible. The vocabulator on this unit is compromised after some long ago injury. This unit can speak in a whisper, and what comes out is often garbled by interference and pops, beeps and static.

**2.** Digitized, scratchy and oscillates in pitch, especially when under stressful situation or talking to a superior officer. Cannot yell louder than normal conversational speaking volume.

**3.** Modulates between male and female voice, with each bout of conversation coming out as either, and at an unpredictable frequency. Roll 1d6 each time this character speaks: 1-3. Male voice / 4-6. Female voice.

**4.** Mostly regular human voice and appropriate for the gender pattern of the android, however, this voice box has seen better days and the android's words come out a bit digitized, scratchy, and with static and crackles replacing every tenth or twelve word.

**5-8.** Regular voice and ideal for the gender pattern of the android. This unit can speak in the full range that an organic person can from a whisper to a decent shout.

**9.** Bellower: While having normal speech abilities as in rolls 5-8 on this table, this android's vocal range can rise from a whisper to an ear splitting bellow. In short, this unit has a megaphone built into its vocal transmitter. See the relic, megaphone, on page XR-440 of this book, although the power supply for this android is built-in and constantly available.

**10.** Mimicry: Not only does this android have the ability to speak in its normal voice, as in roll result 5-8 on this table, but it can mimic any voice it has ever heard so long as it has listened to the speaker for about a half hour or more. The age, gender and accent of the subject it copied are flawlessly reproduced, although this does not mean the android can understand the language of a person which it itself does not speak.

To acquire a better voice box, an upgrade can sometimes be purchased at a robotics dealership for about 500 silver pieces, or looted off a dead android. The installation by a robotics technician is necessary to get it installed correctly, and then, the voice that comes out of the reclaimed box might not match the gender pattern of the android. If the voice box comes from an unknown source, roll here to see what voice ultimately comes from the android after installation, **roll 1d6: 1.** Little girl / **2.** Little boy / **3.** Cartoon character / **4.** Woman / **5.** Man / **6.** Old man or woman (50% chance either way.)

## Table XR-42/ Android Olfactory Capabilities  Roll 1d10

**1.** Sub-standard sense of smell, about half that of a human.

**4-5.** Normal human ability to detect scents.

**6.** Sense of smell is twice as effective as a normal human.

**7.** Sense of smell is 5x as sensitive as a human.

**8.** Sense of smell twice as effective as a human, but can also register radiation within 30 meters, identical to the relic called rad-scanner on page TME-199.

**9.** Sense of smell twice as proficient as a normal human, but this android can also sniff out when another being is organic or another android, and can detect a slight pheromone differences in an individual to tell if they are a mutant or pure stock, male or female, pregnant or not pregnant, as well as if the person is afraid, relaxed, lusty, lying,  or anxious as if they are expecting something to happen.

**10.** Sense of smell 5x as sensitive as a human, plus this android acts like a bloodhound. As gifted as a dog, this android can track the scent of a living person or beast with incredible effectiveness. Make a perception based type A hazard check if the quarry has set off an hour or less ago, and a type B if between 1 and 2 hours, Type C for 2 to 4 hours prior, and a type D for 4-8 hours ago, and a type E for up to 24 hours ago.

## Table XR-43/ Android Auditory Capabilities  Roll 1d10

**1. Damaged:** One auditory receptor damaged, but it can be replaced if a spare hearing module is inserted by a robotics technician. This android hears only half as well as a human and suffers -1 initiative until repaired.

**4-5. Normal Human:** This android can hear as well as a human.

**6,7. Double Human:** This model can hear twice as well as a regular person.

**8. Double Enhanced:** Besides being able to hear twice as well as a normal human, this android can also detect the subtle sound of servo motors in another mechanical being, especially if there are few other sounds. For example, if another android, when disguised as a human walks passed in a saloon or back street, this character would detect it.

**9. Extreme Hearing:** Can hear four times as well as a human, and with such splendid hearing, this android gains +1 initiative.

**10. Extreme Plus Radio Reception:**  Besides being able to hear four times better than a regular human, and so gain +1 initiative, this android can also switch to a receptor mode and detect the feint transmissions of various radio communications, broadcasts and Mecha chatter. It cannot, however, understand the Mecha encrypted messages, but can tell if they are far away, or within a kilometer or less.

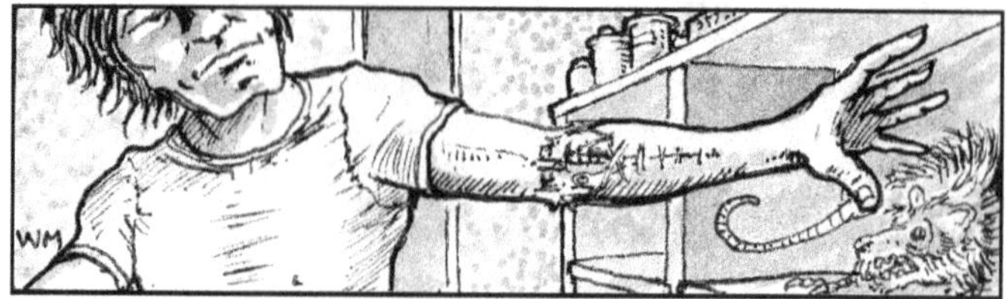

## Table XR-44/ Android Touch Capabilities    Roll 1d10

**1-3. Half Human:** This android's sensitivity to touching other objects, and feeling contact on its own sheathing, is present, but only about half as responsive as a human.

**4-7. Human Capacity:** This android's sense of touch is equal to a human, and can both feel pressure and various sensations, including hot and cold on its sheathing as an organic person does, although more subtle sensations are more difficult to pick up.

**8. Human Enhanced:** Highly sensitive to physical contact, at least when it wants to feel sensations. This android can feel the breeze on its skin and any synthetic hair it might have, detect the warmth of the sun or nearby campfire, the chill of rain and other sensations that humans take for granted.

**9. Enhanced Plus Air Vibrations:** As in roll 8, however this android's sheath is dotted by senors that detect vibrations in the air, sudden changes in temperature, including nearby breathing. It is hard to surprise, and gains +1 initiative.

**10. Enriched Plus Palm sensors:** As rolls 8 and 9, however besides these already impressive sensory capabilities, this android's palms are so sensitive that it can touch something and detect if the material inside is radioactive, or if there is electricity inside a machine, power conduit, or relic device.

## Table XR-45/ Android Taste Capabilities    Roll 1d10

**1-4. Half Human:** Synthetic tongue can taste at about half the receptor ability as a regular human

**5,6. Human Equal:** Synthetic tongue is equal to a human in its ability to taste things.

**7,8. Double Human Plus Extendable:** Synthetic tongue is twice as sensitive as regular human tongue, but can also extend 20cm (7.87") from the mouth, articulate like a short tentacle with an agility of 40 trait points — perfect for operating a keyboard or other manual tasks.

**9. Human Plus Taste Receptors:** This android's tongue is equal to a human's as far as its ability to taste, but so too, when licking another being it can determine if the subject is an android, male, female, or pregnant, or if the touched being is actually a mutant, synthetic human, or a pure stock.

**10. Human Expanded Plus Extreme Receptors:** This android's tongue can pick up and identify the taste of things four times as accurately as a regular human, but so too, if the character opens his or her mouth it can detect radiation in the area within 30m. Likewise, using this same method, the android can detect water within 2 kilometers and in which direction.

## Non-Typical Sensory Capabilities

Should one of the following abilities occur which duplicate an already exhibited sense by the android, such as the ability to detect radiation or see augmented reality, then the player can either choose this superior version, or re-roll using a 1d6+4.

## Table XR-46/ Android Non-Typical Sensory Capabilities  Roll 1d10

**1-4.** No additional sensory receptors.

**5. Uncanny sense of balance:** This android can walk along beams, ledges or cliff side paths with remarkable confidence. Increase this character's agility by +30 and allow them two hazard checks against falling if forced to navigate a perilous or narrow walkway.

**6. Internal compass:** This android always knows which way is north, south, east or west, as well as from which way it has come. Getting truly lost is almost impossible for this being.

**7. Detect Invisibe:** This android can discern otherwise invisible security laser trip-line beams, see force fields that regular humans can't, and make out any energy anomaly from a kilometer away, except dimensional phenomena.

**8. Rad Scan:** This android can activate a scan that will search for nearby sources of dangerous radiation. An internal display will show mild radiation within 100m, or medium radiation within 500 meters, or strong or lethal radiation intensities at 1000m or less. Stronger radiation is easier to detect.

**9. Augmented Reality Viewer:** This android can see and hear any augmented reality transmissions in its field of view. It can shut off this sensory input as desired, but it is assumed to be switched on again at the start of each 24-hour period.

**10. Dimensional Sight:** For some inexplicable reason, this android can see dimensional beings, as well as any recent rips in dimension where such beings, or those mutants with dimensional powers, have caused portals or rips into this world. Range 250 meters.

# Android Age Appearance

How old has this android been made to look? Unless already determined by a game master's scenario or randomly determined result from a prior table, then this unit will have the look of a human of a certain age category. An android could be made to look like an 18 year old, or a venerable senior citizen, neither of which affect its performance nor reveals how long ago the unit was manufactured.

**Table XR-47/ Age Appearance Determination**

| 1d100 | Age Category | Appears as a Human Aged... |
|---|---|---|
| 01-20. | Teenager | 18 or 19 |
| 21-40. | Youth | 20 to 25 (19+1d6) |
| 41-80. | Adult | 26 to 50 (26+4d6) |
| 81-95. | Middle Aged | 51 to 70 (50+1d30) |
| 96-00. | Senior Citizen | 71 to 100 (70+1d30) |

# Android's Manufacturing Date

How long ago was this unit built? The game master might roll this in secret so that the player has just one more mystery to solve about where it came from, when was it built, and by who. Figuring out who one's creator was, and why it was created, is always a great role-playing opportunity. Because a character that was built long, long ago might have a remarkable knowledge of the layout of a once great metropolis, the GM can declare that even the oldest androids have gaps in their knowledge base. These units have deleted vast swaths of memory to make space for other files and more valuable, survival knowledge, and have lost much of their old memories. In such case, the game master can leak information and hints to the android PC when he or she sees a specific street sign, hears a song, or comes across some object from their former life.

**Table XR-48/ Manufacturing Date Age Determination    Roll 1d100**

**01-04.** Brand new, created 3d6 days ago.

**05-12.** Very new, created 3d6 months ago.

**13-54.** Relatively new, created 3d6 years ago.

**55-83.** Somewhat recent creation. Built 10+2d20 years ago.

**84-91.** Been around a while. Created 50 +1d100 years ago.

**92-97.** From the old world and created around the time of the great cataclysm in year 2185 AD*.

**98-00.** Ancient. This android was built in the pre-devastation era. Determine the year: 2140 + 2d20*.

*GM Note: In the official TME setting game play starts at the year 2364 AD, although the GM might have established their own time lines and assigned a different current year of game play.*

# Android's Hair

Androids normally come standard with stitched on nylon wigs, although many military models are entirely bald. Roll first based on the Original Purpose category of an android, and add +4 if the unit is female patterned, +1 if genderless, or +0 if male to see if it has hair. Secondly, roll on the follow up hair type table if the unit is not bald, and finally the hair color table.

**Table XR-49/ Presence of Hair on Android's Head**

Roll 1d10 for males, 1d10+1 for genderless androids, and 1d10+4 for female pattern.

| Original Purpose | Bald | Short Hair | Medium Length | Long Hair |
|---|---|---|---|---|
| Civilian | 1,2 | 3-5 | 6-8 | 9,10+ |
| Medical | 1,2 | 3-5 | 6-9 | 10+ |
| Scientific | 1-3 | 4-6 | 7.8 | 9.10+ |
| Industrial | 1-4 | 5-7 | 8,9 | 10+ |
| Technician | 1,2 | 3-6 | 7-9 | 10+ |
| Military | 1-5 | 6-8 | 9,10 | Above 10 |

**Table XR-50/ Android Hair Type & Color**

| 1d10 | Hair Type |
|---|---|
| 1-5. | Nylon wig that is only loosely attached. Any strong wind or rough knock to the head will detach it. |
| 6,7. | Nylon wig, adhered to the scalp with stitch lines which are visible in strong winds or when the android runs its hand through its hair. |
| 8. | Advanced nylon wig. Stitched masterfully to the android's whole scalp and looks quite natural — although the color might not be a realistic pigment. |
| 9 | Re-growing synthetic hair. This android can have its head shaved and the very realistic, synthetic hair will grow back at a rate of 1 centimeter per day. This hair can also be dyed should the skinbot wish to better conceal its identity or be more flamboyant. |
| 10. | Retractable hair. This android's synthetic hair can be pulled into the scalp and be as short as stubble, or be extended at 5cm per minute to become shoulder length hair, but no further. |

| 1d10 | Hair Color |
|---|---|
| 1-6. | Natural color, roll 1d10 here:<br>1. Gray<br>2. Dirty blond<br>3. Platinum blond<br>4. Brown<br>5. Blond<br>6. Red<br>7. Light brown<br>8-10. Black |
| 7-9. | Unnatural color, roll 1d10 here:<br>1. White<br>2. Pink<br>3. Candy apple red<br>4. Metallic silver<br>5. Metallic gold<br>6. Dark blue<br>7. Neon blue<br>8. Purple<br>9. Green<br>10. Garish orange |
| 10. | Rainbow (multiple sections of bright color in rainbow spectrum) |

## Android Handedness

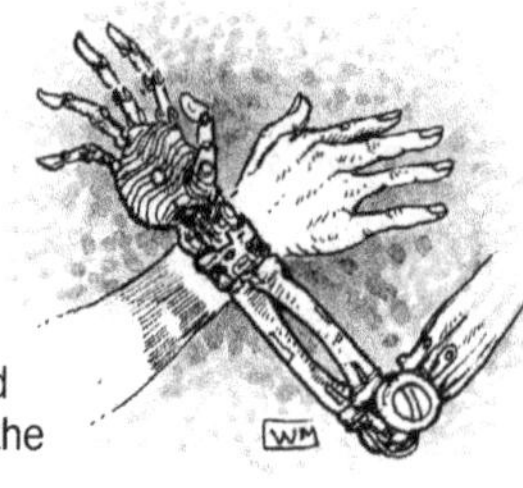

Androids, especially advanced or physically active varieties, have a much higher likelihood of being ambidextrous than human or mutant human characters do. Roll 1d10 on the following table at character generation, however, medical, technician, scientific and military android categories all gain +2 on the following 1d10 roll.

### Table XR-51/ Android Handedness, Roll 1d10

| | |
|---|---|
| **1-3.** | Left Handed |
| **4-9.** | Right Handed |
| **10+.** | Ambidextrous |

## Android Special Features

Depending on the 'Original Purpose' category of the unique android, use the following dice assignments and number of rolls on the Special Features table to follow. Re-roll duplicated results.

| | |
|---|---|
| **Civilian** | roll 2d20, twice |
| **Medical** | roll 2d20, twice |
| **Scientific** | roll 1d100, three times |
| **Industrial** | roll 1d100, twice |
| **Technician** | roll 1d00, three times |
| **Military** | roll 1d100+10, twice |

### Table XR-52/ Special Features of a Unique Android

#### 1d100. Android Special Features

**01-03.** Music mouth: This android has a remarkable, high fidelity set of speakers in its mouth and a massive audio bank and musical inventory. When desired, it can open its mouth and play any musical track or audio book from the old world, or disgorge themed playlists. The maximum volume is about as loud as a human shout, but can also play so low that only those within a meter or two can hear the tunes. At high volume, the drain on the android's battery is considerable and beyond sixty minutes, causes 1d6 stun damage per hour thereafter.

**04-06.** Tissue binder palm: Built into the hand of this android is a tissue binder connected to a concealed wrist battery compartment that contains a standard power cell. As described on page XR-443 of this book, this binder will yield 18 healing surges per power cell. In an emergency, should the cell be drained, the android's own power supply can be diverted to yield 1 healing charge every 10 minutes, but this intense depletion of power causes the android 1d6 stun damage and a 1 in 12 chance of freezing its systems, which would cause it to go dormant and unmoving for 3d6 minutes before rebooting. This healing only works on organic patients.

**07-09.** Anti-toxin injector hand: The left hand of this unit is connected to a wrist receptor which holds a standard anti-toxin injector. When needed, it can expose the syringe and inject a human or other living animal in need. Once spent, a new injector must replace the empty cannister, however other injectable drugs, serums and liquids can also be inserted into the syringe tube, including animal venom.

**10-12.** Superior fine motor controls: Increase accuracy trait by +10 points.

**13-15.** Good looking with a more appealing figure: Add 1d12+10 to Appearance trait

**16-18.** Comparatively far more human in appearance and motivations than most androids. Believes its kind is the future of true humanity but must care for its younger, more primitive fleshy fore bearers. Improve Intelligence, Willpower and Appearance by +2d6.

**19-21.** Mecha infected. This android was once a servant of some anti-human Mecha faction. Its built in firewalls, anti-virus and anti-hacking software long ago defeated the intrusion and while it could not delete the hostile, murderous virus, it could quarantine the evil program.

If the Mecha control virus were to gain access, it would take control of the android and reprogram it to eradicate all human life and obey every order of the hostile Ai. That Ai is still out there and every hour of every day it attempts to set about hacking into the android. Daily, the hostile intelligence attempts a different algorithm and login technique to take control of this unit. This unique android must devote an hour of each day to counteracting the intrusive mecha virus, blocking it, diverting its tentacle-like assaults and fighting the enemy within.

If the Ai computer can be located and switched off, then this nightmarish inner demon can be permanently eradicated, and on that occasion, this android's full resources can be rerouted to its daily use and will give this character a bonus of +20 to both intelligence and willpower. GM Note: Hundreds of other androids and robotic units, digital beings, and even a few vehicles are also infected by this same, local Mecha control virus, some who have also blocked it, but most are the thralls of this evil computer, and would be free, too, should the malicious Ai be annihilated. The Ai uses a single satellite to maintain its repeated wireless attacks on this android, and even if the character leaves the region, the assaults will not cease. Destroying the satellite, will stop the daily attacks, at least until the Ai can find some other mode of remote attack to access its hundreds of potential minions.

**22-24.** More advanced CPU: Increase intelligence by +10 trait points.

**25-27.** Motivated to live: Increase willpower trait by +10 points.

**28-30.** Impact resistant coating on all parts: Increase endurance trait by +10 points, half damage from falls and crashes.

**31-33.** Removable face plate that can be lifted to reveal mechanical skull face and eyeballs, teeth and olfactory ports beneath. This face can be substituted for others of this style.

**34-36.** Communications implant: This unit has a built in standard communicator. It can send and receive audio internally without revealing that it is doings so, and its conversations can't be heard unless it speaks out loud and, if also desired, use tiny speakers on either side of its neck to open the incoming audio, as well. Standard communicators have a range of 100km range and are fully described on page TME-198. This comm system draws on the android's internal batteries at a negligible rate.

**37-39.** More advanced synthetic muscles and hydraulics: Add +10 to the android's strength trait and 1 meter movement rate.

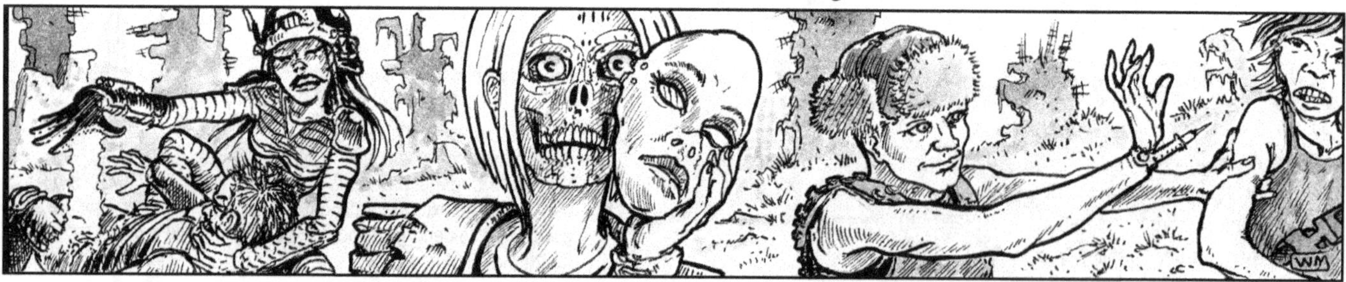

**40-42.** Has undergone post-production upgrades. Increase each trait by +3 points.

**43-45.** Internal compass and altimeter. This android Always knows which ways it's going on the compass, and at what elevations above or below sea level it is at.

**46.** Homing device, as the implant on page XR-339 of this book.

**47.** Force canopy, as the implant on page XR-338 of this book.

**48.** Goalie mask face: Instead of a face, this android has a permanently bolted on, and somewhat alarming looking polycarbonate face dotted with nostril and mouth holes and large ocular cavities for eye sockets. Reduce appearance by -8 until replaced by a different android's face, but while worn, this plated mask improves defense value by -6 DV. Even if a new face is substituted, this mask can be worn over top as armor by this android or any PC and offer the same DV modifier.

**49-51.** Augmented reality visual range: This android can switch its vision to see augmented reality holograms, if any, are in an area. This mode can operate for 1 hour per day in any time increments the android desires. Augmented reality is covered on page XR-477 of this book.

**52,53.** Headless Tendril Manipulation Mode: If this android's head is removed from its body, it will come away with several assorted wires, cables and fluid filled neck tubes. For the first 12 hours after removal, the head will gain limited control over some of the larger connected tubes, which are up to 30cm in length and be able to manipulate them like tentacles.

After 24 hours, the android can rise on the tubes and cables and move about like a spider or octopus at a movement rate of 2m per round. With these cables, the skinbot could theoretically push buttons on a keyboard, open containers, apply bandages or ointments to an organic companion, handle simple tools and even hold and fire a handgun. The melee attack potential of these tubes and tendrils is very limited, with a strike value of +0 and doing only 1d3 stun damage on a strike.

**54.** Quadruped locomotion: This android can drop and scuttle along the ground like a crab at +4m movement rate. It cannot use hand held weapons while on the move, however, or carry anything it its hands.

**55-57.** Fold out solar array: From the small of this android's back, a meter tall by 45cm wide pair of solar panels can fold out. If engaged in full sunlight, these will recharge the android fully in two hours, or any plugged in standard power cell in 1 hour.

**58-60.** Jump: Extra powerful legs add +1m movement at all times, plus this android can jump 3m straight up or 5m horizontally across a gap, from stationary or 7m if able to get a run at it of 10 or more meters. Can only perform this jump once every ten minutes.

**61-63.** Substance reader like the hand held relic and projected invisibly from right eye out to 100 meters range. If focused on an object or being for 3 continuous rounds or more, this android can tell if something or someone is an illusion, digital being, hologram, cyborg, organic, dimensional, alive or dead or even radioactive. Learn more on page TME-199.

**64.** Head-body wireless link: If the cranial unit of this android is separated from its body, it will continue to have a wireless control link to each other up to 100 meters per point of willpower of the head. The head can control the body and even hold the head in its hands or wear it strapped to its chest or neck stump without being physically and properly wired together. So long as they head can see, the body can be controlled — especially when traveling with the head in hand to get the android to safety and some sort of technician who can put it back together.

**65,66.** Radiation detection sensors: Built into the olfactory pores on this android are tiny sensors which like a rad-scanner (see page TME 199) can sniff traces of radiation within 30 meters — well before the levels of radiation are harmful to itself or organic companions.

**67.** Multi-tool arm, as the implant on page XR-341 of this book.

**68,69.** Wheeled feet: When desired, this android can deploy small, in-line rubber wheels from the bottoms of its feet that not only roll in unpowered mode, allowing the unit to travel 15m per round down hill or 9m per round on flat ground, but the user will roll backwards on up hill surfaces. For two hours per day, these wheels can use powered locomotion which so long as the surface it travels over is smooth, allow it to race along at 18m downhill, 12m per round on flat ground, or 6m up hill.

It can travel along dirt tracks, old sidewalks and other cracked and sketchy surfaces, too, but for every minute (20 rounds) traveled, there is a bump, cavity or obstacle which forces the android to make a type B agility based hazard check or wipe out and take 1d6 stun and 1d6 lethal damage.

**70-72.** Electrical defense mechanism (EDM) as per the cybernetic implant from page TME-86. This android has a two compartment power cell battery bank in the small of its back specifically for this unit, but starts game play with only 1d2 standard power cells.

**73.** Hologram Emitter: For up to 3 hours per day, this android can use its eyes to project 3 dimensional images into space, to a maximum range of 12m away from itself. The further away it projects the images, the less opaque they become. Holograms shown from a distance of 1 to 12 meters will be life size, or presented in a rectangular screen area 6m wide by 3m tall if a background accompanies the film — although many of its holographic entertainment recordings have no background at all, and can easily be shown on a tabletop, floor or the lap, and visible to onlookers from all around the show. If projected up close, they presentation can be miniaturized down to the size of a person's palm — which is especially useful when trying to present video information to comrades without lighting up the entire street or ravine on a dig operation.

These films, photos, and graphics are 90% opaque at their best, and yet seem real to onlookers, especially those not familiar with holograms including savages, beasts and poorly educated commoners of the new era. GM: allow skullocks, moaners, commoners and other uneducated people to make a Type C intelligence based hazard check or else believe what they are seeing is real — at least for a few minutes. Animals must make a type E hazard check or be distracted, perhaps even alarmed and run off based on whatever the player chooses to project.

Typical content an android with this gift is asked to reveal include historical film clips and photos, news casts, old maps, graphic drawings, recently taken video or photography, floor plans, music videos, adult entertainment, and full movies, all of which can be projected for up to three hours per day. This android will have an inventory of one thousand old videos going back to the beginning of film and photography, per point of starting intelligence.

This android can also open its mouth and emit the accompanying soundtrack in remarkable fidelity to match the projection, with maximum volume to that of a person's shout. While projecting a film or holographic pictures, the android can't speak or move about over uneven ground as its visual focus is greatly reduced (agility trait at 10% normal). Any android known to have this feature is highly sought after by collectors, those who operate brothels and saloons, or powerful warlords looking to entertain themselves and their brigands. For this reason, many mechanical humans with this feature keep it secret until needed most.

**74,75.** Battery back-up: Within this android's torso is a bank of 4 fully charged back up power cells which the unit can access via hidden flap in its side. These batteries can also be hooked to the android to give it long life or generate power to any on-board or external devices via a 6m long pull out extension cord. These cells must be recharged by an exterior method and snapped into their locking slot, or via the included patch cable.

**76-78.** Stun emitter grip: The left hand of this android has five energy transfer disks, one at the base of each finger. When desired, the character can causally touch an unsuspecting target or smack an opponent in melee combat at SV +7 and on a successful strike, inflict 2d20 stun damage. This charge can only be unleashed once per hour and auto recharges thereafter from the android's own power supply.

**79-81.** Laser eye: This is like a laser pistol but has a much reduced range and instead of using detachable power cells, draws upon a slow charge internal, permanent battery that will allow for 24 shots per day, SV +16, range 100 meters, rate 1, damage 1d20+10. It takes 24 hours for the battery to recharge fully from empty and so will replenish 1 shot per hour to a maximum 24 allowable discharges.

**82-84.** Space variant: This android can handle extreme cold and the vacuum of space for up to an hour before suffering 1d20 stun damage per minute from freezing up. If frozen in space, it will go dormant and require gentle thawing out if rescued, with systems not coming back on line for 4d6 hours where consciousness and mobility will return to normal.

This skinbot also features propulsion jets in the soles of its feet to propel it in space at 12m per round speed. These Jets can be used for 10 minutes per day and must recharge thereafter or have a power cell inserted into each calf to yield another 10 minutes. These jets can also be used to increase this android's land speed via intermittent leaps by +4m per round, up to 10 minutes of use per day. If used in water, double the unit's swim speed, while if used to help the android jump vertically, these jets can be engaged to add a further 1d6m distance (roll each leap) although one leap uses 1 minute's worth of the daily propulsion charge. These jets do not produce a flammable plume and are safe to use on board vehicles or in tall grass, etc.

**85,86.** Extra arm: This android has a third identical arm fitted from one shoulder just beneath the existing arm. This appendage has the same strength as a regular arm, is an ambidextrous limb and can wield another weapon, shield or other implement. There is a further 14% chance that this android instead has two such extra arms and is now a four armed miracle.

Of course, having an extra limb isn't easy to conceal, unless the android wears a heavy trench cloak or other covering while in public. If the android looks like a human in all other aspects, then most people who see this extra arm will assume this unit is instead a mutant human. There is a 17% chance that this arm can be detached and stowed elsewhere for later use, although the receptacle and shoulder joint cavity is visible and must be kept hidden under the android's shirt to hide evidence of this extra limb.

**87,88.** EMP absorption cell: Within this android, and connected to small, discreet sensors all over its body, is a module which will absorb incoming electromagnetic pulse attacks, and soak up 2d20 (rolled once for each successful strike against this android) and be able to keep up to 100 points of EMP damage for a 24 hour period. This EMP energy is slowly transmitted out through the feet or hands of the android through a grounding mechanism and safely dispersed. There is a 1 in 20 chance that this cell is actually weaponized, and any absorbed EMP energy can be fired from the palm of the android. Each charge has a range of 120 meters, SV 01-80, and inflict 1d20 EMP damage to other susceptible targets. One charge can be fired for every 10 points of previously absorbed EMP damage this android would otherwise have taken.

**89,90.** A random cybernetic implant determined from the 'Android' column on table XR-210 Cybernetic Implant Determination Table 2, on page 330.

**91-93.** Hacking mode: This remarkable android can make hacking attacks like a digital being, while 1 in 10 with this feature also have the wireless mode app for digital beings described on page XR-84. Learn more about hacking ability within the Digital Beings character type write up on page XR-67.

**94-96.** Gun palm: In the right palm of this android is a concealed handgun barrel, connected to an ammo or power cell compartment in the forearm's underside. All these guns are described in the hub rules with stats on page TME-100. The dice roll in brackets shows the number of shells or rounds that the android has at character generation. **Roll 1d6** for the sort of gun concealed here: **1.** Shotgun pistol, single shot per round but loaded with max 4 shells (1d4 Shells). / **2.** .22 caliber pistol with 18 shot tube magazine in arm (3d6). / **3.** Pocket pistol with 12 shot arm tube magazine (2d6). / **4.** Automatic pistol with 8 shot arm tube magazine (1d8). / **5.** Stun pistol with powers cell yielding 40 shots (4d10). / **6.** Laser pistol with 30 shots per power cell (3d10).

**97-99.** Electrical pulse emitters: This android's two hands have concealed, palm emitter ports. Once a day, per hand, this unit can draw upon internal power supplies to shoot a lightning bolt. Either one bolt can be fired per round, or both hands raised and discharged at once on one or possibly two separate targets so long as they are in the front facing arc of fire (180° in front of the PC). SV +30, Range WL x Rank = meters (as Android's willpower trait in meters, multiplied by character's rank). Damage 1d20 to organic beings, and 1d100 damage to other androids, robots, cyborgs, mutorgs and other machinery that uses a computer or electrical parts. DANGER: This android is not immune to electricity itself, and if it uses this power as a melee attack, risks a 66% chance of the charge surging back on a successful hit on an opponent, and also cooking itself for 1d100 damage per hand used.

**100.** Customized variant: After being manufactured, this android seems to have been somebody's pet project. They enhanced it with upgraded parts, software and hardened servos, electronics and computer interface systems. It gains +4 to each trait, plus has a -5 defense value bonus, built in communicator (as in roll 34-36), and EMP shielding which reduces all EMP damage it receives by half. Finally, add one extra 1d100 roll on this table.

**101-103.** Vehicle control module, as the cyborg implant on page XR-347, this book.

**104-106.** Force field: This lime green colored shield must be switched on, which takes only one round and runs off of a separate, hip stowed power cell. Each standard power cell will yield 100 rounds of defensive shielding in which each impact (successful strike by physical attacks upon this character) is reduced by 10 points damage. This is an advanced force field in that instead of the damage reduction being -10 per round, it is -10 for each and every impact, even from the same direction.

**107-109.** Hard to kill: This unit is both up-armored with some of the most advanced ancient interior plating — which improves its defense value by -20 and increases the unit's endurance by +3d10 trait points — but even if depleted below zero endurance and it would normally be considered killed or knocked out, it has a backup CPU and control network that after 10+1d10 minutes of 'death' or dormancy, it will reboot its systems and rise up on whatever is left of its legs and body and either continue the fight, or return to base for repairs of its main system. This back up operating system will only run for 10+3d6 hours before the reserve power is too drained and the unit will collapse and go into dormancy mode for a further 4d6 months before dying — should no help come. In reserve mode, it cannot heal itself should it be able to do so at all, and relies on technicians to perform repairs.

**110.** Shoulder turret with one of these random weapon systems currently fixed and bolted to the android. A robotics or mechanical technician can remove this platform in half an hour, but takes twice as long to reattach. The ammo or energy for this weapon system is separate from the android and must be reloaded manually. roll 1d6:

**1.** Heavy pulse rifle: SV +25, Rate 4 bursts, range 1km, DMG 1d20, Power: Battery pack worn by android supplies 200 bursts when fully charged, currently has 10+2d20 burst remaining (each burst is 4 separate attacks, possibly doing 1d20 DMG each).

**2.** High caliber assault rifle with drum magazine: SV +12, Rate 3, range 800m, DMG 1d20+10 each, Ammo 10+1d100 HCR in ammo belt and ammo pack carried by android.

**3.** Heavy laser carbine: SV +35, rate 1, range 4km, DMG 3d20+20, power pack worn by android yields 180 shots when fully charged, currently has only 1d20+10 shots remaining.

**4.** Heavy machine gun: SV +15, rate 5, range 950m, DMG 1d20+10 each, belt fed with10+1d100 HCR left on belt in attached ammo box.

**5.** Chaingun: SV +10, rate 10, range 220m, DMG 1d20 each, belt fed by hard shelled ammo pack on android, which can normally take 500 rounds but currently loaded with only 20+1d100 standard rifle rounds.

**6.** Light laser cannon: SV +30, rate 1, range 20km, DMG 1d100, Power pack worn by android normally holds 50 shots, but currently holds 4+1d20 shots. A standard power cell will yield 5 shots.

# Unique Android Pre-Game Castes

In most cases, an android character has made its way in the post-apocalyptic world by performing some task, earning a wage, or being supplied with sufficient recharge access, lubricants, repairs and shelter in return for whatever enslavement, assignment, labor or freelance occupation it conducted. During its time in this occupation or caste it might well have suffered permanent damage due to abuse or injuries, but so too, gained new experiences, skills, and improvements to its cognitive and physical abilities.

In many cases, an android will have a skill set based on its original purpose, and could very well find employment in its designed profession if given the opportunity. The realities of living in a harsh, new dark age, however, often offer little opportunities for such a being to engage in what it was built for. Most skinbots instead prefer to hide their built-in skill qualifications in order to avoid having their true nature discovered. So too, many don't stay long in one community, especially where androids and robots are held in suspicion or outright hostility, and so choose castes that allow them to keep on the move or blend in.

For some unlucky androids, however, their mechanical heritage is discovered before they can escape, and instead of being destroyed, are kept as slaves alongside mutants and humans who have also been chained, and forced to serve wicked masters.

The following directory provides the means to determine the unique android's caste based on its original purpose. Once established, the player will consult either the caste based details from the Hub Rules or in this book. Any Pre-Game Castes listed in bold font is included in this book on pages 14 to 20, while castes listed in the normal font are described in the TME Hub Rules book,

The stat modifiers and skills for castes from both books are all in this book on page 12. The gear that a new android starts with is established through its 'outfitting code', also listed on the same Caste Based Details table.

## Unique Android Pre-Game Caste Determination

Scroll down to find the Original Purpose of a new android character (discovered previously on table XR-14 on page 31), and then roll 1d20 to discover their pre game occupation or caste. Those listed in a **bold font** are found in this book, otherwise the Hub Rules for normal type face.

### Bartender

Roll 1d20: 1. Caravaneer / **2,3. Repairer** / **4,5. Scavenger** / 6. Slave, Laborer / 7,8. Slave, Kitchen Hand / 9,10. Slave, Court Attendant / 11,12. Farmer / 13,14. Nomad / 15,16. Trader / 17. Crafts person / **18,19. Thief** / 20. Draftee

### Beauty Spa Attendant

Roll 1d20: 1,2. Slave, Kitchen Hand / 3,4. Slave, Personal Servant / 5-10. Slave, Whore / 11,12. Slave, Court Attendant / 13. Nomad / 14,15. Crafts person / 16. Student / 17. Street Urchin / **18. Thief** / 19,20. Draftee

### Clerical

Roll 1d20: 1. Caravaneer / **2. Scavenger** / 3. Slave, Laborer / **4,5. Hooker** / 6. Slave, Kitchen Hand / 7. Slave, Personal Servant / 8. Slave, Whore / 9-11. Slave, Court Attendant / 12. Nomad / 13. Trader / 14. Crafts person / 15-17. Student / **18-20. Scribe**

### Concubine

Roll 1d20: 1. Bunker Dweller / 2. Cultist / **3. Scavenger** / 4,5. Slave, Kitchen Hand / 6,7. Slave, Personal Servant / 8-14. Slave, Whore / 15,16. Slave, Court Attendant / 17. Nomad / 18,19. Street Urchin / 20. Thief

### Courier

Roll 1d20: 1. Animal Herder / 2. Bounty Hunter / 3-5. Caravaneer / 6,7. Herdsman / 8. Wastelander / 9. Slave, Laborer / 10. Slave, Court Attendant / 11. Nomad / 12. Trader / 13. Street Urchin / 14. Raider / **15. Thief** / 16. Draftee / 17. Militia Soldier / 18. Watchman / 19. Infantry / 20. Calvary

### Criminal Construct

Roll 1d20: 1-3. Bounty Hunter / **4. Scavenger** / 5. Wastelander / 6. Slave, Laborer / 7. Slave, Gladiator / 8. Hunter / 9. Nomad / 10-12. Street Thug / 13,14. Raider / 15. Pirate / **16-18. Thief** / 19. Assassin / 20. Mercenary

### Day Care Worker

Roll 1d20: 1. Animal Herder / 2. Bunker Dweller / 3. Cultist / **4. Scavenger** / 5-7. Slave, Laborer / 8-10. Slave, Kitchen Hand / 11-15. Slave, Personal Servant / 16. Slave, Whore / 17,18. Slave, Court Attendant / 19. Nomad / 20. Crafts person

### Dental Hygienist

Roll 1d20: 1. Bunker Dweller / **2,3. Junk-Doctor** / **4-6. Repairer** / **7-9. Scavenger** / **10. Technician, Cybernetic** / 11. Slave, Laborer / 12. Slave, Kitchen Hand / 13,14. Slave, Personal Servant / 15. Slave, Whore / 16. Slave, Court Attendant / 17. Trader / 18,19. Crafts person / 20. Technician

### Elementary School Teacher

Roll 1d20: 1. Animal Herder / 2. Bunker Dweller / 3. Caravaneer / 4. Cultist / 5. Herdsman / **6. Junk-Doctor** / **7. Scavenger** / 8. Slave, Laborer / 9. Slave, Kitchen Hand / 10. Slave, Personal Servant / 11. Slave, Whore / 12,13. Slave, Court Attendant / 14. Trader / 15. Crafts person / 16. Student / **17-20. Scribe**

### Government Clerk

Roll 1d20: 1. Bunker Dweller / 2. Caravaneer / 3. Cultist / 4. Herdsman / **5. Scavenger** / 6. Slave, Laborer / 7. Slave, Kitchen Hand / 8-10. Slave, Personal Servant / 11. Slave, Whore / 12-14. Slave, Court Attendant / 15. Trader / **16-20. Scribe**

**Hair Dresser**
Roll 1d20: 1. Bunker Dweller / 2. Cultist / 3. Repairer / 4. Scavenger / 5. Slave, Laborer / 6-8. Slave, Kitchen Hand / 9-15. Slave, Personal Servant / 16,17. Slave, Whore / 18,19. Slave, Court Attendant / 20. Crafts person

**High School Teacher**
Roll 1d20: 1. Animal Herder / 2. Bounty Hunter / 3. Bunker Dweller / 4. Caravaneer / 5. Cultist / 6. Herdsman / 7. Junk-Doctor / 8. Repairer / 9. Scavenger / 10. Technician, Cybernetic / 11. Slave, Laborer / 12. Slave, Kitchen Hand / 13. Slave, Personal Servant / 14. Slave, Court Attendant / 15. Farmer / 16. Trader / 17. Crafts person / 18,19. Scribe / 20. Technician

**Homeless Outreach Officer**
Roll 1d20: 1. Animal Herder / 2. Bounty Hunter / 3. Bunker Dweller / 4. Cultist / 5. Herdsman / 6,7. Scavenger / 8-12. Slave, Laborer / 13. Slave, Kitchen Hand / 14. Slave, Personal Servant / 15. Slave, Court Attendant / 16. Nomad / 17. Scribe / 18. Street Thug / 19. Raider / 20. Thief

**Nurse**
Roll 1d20: 1. Bunker Dweller / 2,3. Junk-Doctor / 4. Repairer / 5. Technician, Cybernetic / 6-9. Slave, Personal Servant / 10,11. Slave, Court Attendant / 12. Nomad / 13. Trader / 14-20. Technician

**Personal Attendant**
Roll 1d20: 1. Animal Herder / 2. Junk-Doctor / 3. Repairer / 4. Slave, Laborer / 5,6. Slave, Kitchen Hand / 7-14. Slave, Personal Servant / 15. Slave, Whore / 16,17. Slave, Court Attendant / 18. Crafts person / 19. Student / 20. Scribe

**Political Operative**
Roll 1d20: 1. Bounty Hunter / 2. Bunker Dweller / 3. Cultist / 4. Junk-Doctor / 5. Technician, Cybernetic / 6-8. Slave, Laborer / 9. Slave, Kitchen Hand / 10-13. Slave, Personal Servant / 14. Slave, Whore / 15. Slave, Court Attendant / 16. Trader / 17. Scribe / 18. Technician / 19. Thief / 20. Assassin

**Retail**
Roll 1d20: 1. Bunker Dweller / 2. Repairer / 3. Scavenger / 4,5. Slave, Laborer / 6-9. Slave, Kitchen Hand / 10-15. Slave, Personal Servant / 16,17. Slave, Whore / 18. Slave, Court Attendant / 19. Trader / 20. Street Urchin

**Barista**
Roll 1d20: 1. Repairer / 2. Scavenger / 3. Slave, Laborer / 4-12. Slave, Kitchen Hand / 13. Slave, Personal Servant / 14. Slave, Whore / 15. Slave, Court Attendant / 16. Trader / 17. Crafts person / 18. Student / 19. Street Urchin / 20. Draftee

**Secretary**
Roll 1d20: 1. Slave, Laborer / 2,3. Slave, Kitchen Hand / 4-10. Slave, Personal Servant / 11. Slave, Whore / 12-15. Slave, Court Attendant / 16-19. Scribe / 20. Technician

**Senior Care Worker**
Roll 1d20: 1. Bunker Dweller / 2. Caravaneer / 3. Repairer / 4. Scavenger / 5-9. Slave, Laborer / 10,11. Slave, Kitchen Hand / 12-14. Slave, Personal Servant / 15. Slave, Court Attendant / 16. Miner / 17. Nomad / 18. Trader / 19. Crafts person / 20. Street Thug

**Service Industry**
Roll 1d20: 1-4. Slave, Laborer / 5-9. Slave, Kitchen Hand / 10,11. Slave, Personal Servant / 12. Slave, Whore / 13. Slave, Court Attendant / 14. Fisher / 15. Farmer / 16. Nomad / 17. Crafts person / 18. Street Urchin / 19. Thief / 20. Draftee

**Social Conformity Bylaw Officer**
Roll 1d20: 1. Bounty Hunter / 2. Bunker Dweller / 3,4. Cultist / 5-9. Slave, Laborer / 10-12. Slave, Kitchen Hand / 13,14. Slave, Personal Servant / 15. Slave, Whore / 16. Slave, Court Attendant / 17. Street Urchin / 18. Street Thug / 19. Thief / 20. Assassin

**Target Range Objective**
Roll 1d20: 1. Animal Herder / 2. Bounty Hunter / 3. Bunker Dweller / 4. Caravaneer / 5. Cultist / 6. Herdsman / 7. Repairer / 8,9. Scavenger / 10. Wastelander / 11. Slave, Laborer / 12. Slave, Kitchen Hand / 13. Slave, Personal Servant / 14. Slave, Gladiator / 15. Fisher / 16. Hunter / 17. Miner / 18. Logger / 19. Nomad / 20. Street Thug

**Waifu**
Roll 1d20: 1. Cultist / 2. Scavenger / 3. Wastelander / 4-6. Hooker / 7. Slave, Laborer / 8. Slave, Kitchen Hand / 9,10. Slave, Personal Servant / 11-14. Slave, Whore / 15. Slave, Court Attendant / 16. Nomad / 17. Crafts person / 18,19. Street Urchin / 20. Thief

**Medical Android**
Roll 1d20: 1. Bunker Dweller / 2-6. Junk-Doctor / 7. Repairer / 8. Scavenger / 9,10. Technician, Cybernetic / 11-14. Slave, Personal Servant / 15,16. Slave, Court Attendant / 17. Nomad / 18. Trader / 19-20. Technician

**Scientific Android**
Roll 1d20: 1. Bunker Dweller / 2-6. Junk-Doctor / 7. Repairer / 8-13. Technician, Cybernetic / 14-20. Technician

**Industrial Android**
Roll 1d20: 1. Animal Herder / 2. Bunker Dweller / 3. Caravaneer / 4. Herdsman / 5,6. Repairer / 7. Scavenger / 8. Wastelander / 9-12. Slave, Laborer / 13. Slave, Gladiator / 14. Miner / 15. Logger / 16. Farmer / 17. Nomad / 18. Crafts person / 19. Street Thug / 20. Infantry

**Technician Android**
Roll 1d20: 1. Bunker Dweller / 2-7. Junk-Doctor / 8. Repairer / 9. Scavenger / 10-13. Technician, Cybernetic / 14. Crafts person / 15-20. Technician

**Military, Suicide Bomber**
Roll 1d20: 1. Bounty Hunter / 2. Cultist / 3. Repairer / 4. Scavenger / 5. Wastelander / 6. Slave, Laborer / 7. Slave, Gladiator / 8. Hunter / 9. Miner / 10. Logger / 11. Nomad / 12. Street Thug / 13. Raider / 14. Pirate / 15. Assassin / 16. Draftee / 17. Militia Soldier / 18. Watchman / 19. Infantry / 20. Mercenary

**Military, Covert**
Roll 1d20: 1. Bounty Hunter / 2. Bunker Dweller / 3. Junk-Doctor / 4. Repairer / 5. Scavenger / 6. Technician, Cybernetic / 7. Wastelander / 8. Slave, Laborer / 9. Slave, Gladiator / 10. Nomad / 11. Trader / 12. Crafts person / 13. Technician / 14. Street Thug / 15. Raider / 16. Pirate / 17. Thief / 18,19. Assassin / 20. Mercenary

**Military, Sniper**
Roll 1d20: 1,2. Bounty Hunter / 3. Bunker Dweller / 4. Repairer / 5. Scavenger / 6. Wastelander / 7. Slave, Laborer / 8. Slave, Gladiator / 9. Hunter / 10. Nomad / 11. Street Thug / 12. Raider / 13,14. Assassin / 15. Draftee / 16. Militia Soldier / 17. Watchman / 18. Infantry / 19. Mercenary / 20. Elite Soldier

### Military, Police
Roll 1d20: 1-3. Bounty Hunter / 4. Bunker Dweller / 5. Scavenger / 6. Wastelander / 7. Slave, Gladiator / 8. Hunter / 9. Street Thug / 10. Raider / 11. Pirate / 12. Assassin / 13. Draftee / 14. Militia Soldier / 15,16. Watchman / 17. Infantry / 18. Calvary / 19. Mercenary / 20. Elite Soldier

### Military, Grunt
Roll 1d20: 1. Bounty Hunter / 2. Bunker Dweller / 3. Wastelander / 4. Slave, Laborer / 5. Slave, Gladiator / 6. Hunter / 7. Nomad / 8. Street Thug / 9. Raider / 10. Pirate / 11. Thief / 12. Assassin / 13. Draftee / 14. Militia Soldier / 15. Watchman / 16. Infantry / 17. Calvary / 18,19. Mercenary / 20. Elite Soldier

### Military, Airborne
Roll 1d20: 1,2. Bounty Hunter / 3. Bunker Dweller / 4. Wastelander / 5. Slave, Laborer / 6. Slave, Gladiator / 7. Street Thug / 8. Raider / 9. Pirate / 10. Thief / 11. Assassin / 12. Draftee / 13. Militia Soldier / 14. Watchman / 15. Infantry / 16. Calvary / 17,18. Mercenary / 19, 20. Elite Soldier

### Military, Aquatic Operations
Roll 1d20: 1. Bounty Hunter / 2. Bunker Dweller / 3. Scavenger / 4. Wastelander / 5. Slave, Gladiator / 6,7. Fisher / 8. Nomad / 9. Trader / 10. Street Thug / 11. Raider / 12,13. Pirate / 14. Assassin / 15. Draftee / 16. Militia Soldier / 17. Watchman / 18. Infantry / 19. Mercenary / 20. Elite Soldier

### Military, Heavy Combat
Roll 1d20: 1. Bounty Hunter / 2. Bunker Dweller / 3. Wastelander / 4. Slave, Laborer / 5,6. Slave, Gladiator / 7. Miner / 8. Street Thug / 9. Raider / 10,11. Draftee / 12,13. Militia Soldier / 14. Watchman / 15,16. Infantry / 17.18. Mercenary / 19,20. Elite Soldier

### Military, Tanker
Roll 1d20: 1. Animal Herder / 2. Bounty Hunter / 3. Bunker Dweller / 4. Caravaneer / 5. Herdsman / 6. Repairer / 7. Wastelander / 8. Slave, Gladiator / 9. Nomad / 10. Street Thug / 11. Raider / 12. Assassin / 13. Draftee / 14. Militia Soldier / 15. Watchman / 16. Infantry / 17. Calvary / 18,19. Mercenary / 20. Elite Soldier

### Military, Pilot
Roll 1d20: 1. Bounty Hunter / 2. Bunker Dweller / 3. Junk-Doctor / 4. Repairer / 5. Technician, Cybernetic / 6. Wastelander / 7. Slave, Gladiator / 8. Nomad / 9. Trader / 10,11. Technician / 12. Raider / 13. Assassin / 14. Draftee / 15. Militia Soldier / 16. Watchman / 17. Infantry / 18. Calvary / 19. Mercenary / 20. Elite Soldier

### Military, Space Force
Roll 1d20: 1. Bounty Hunter / 2. Bunker Dweller / 3. Junk-Doctor / 4. Repairer / 5. Technician, Cybernetic / 6. Slave, Gladiator / 7. Nomad / 8. Trader / 9,10. Technician / 11. Raider / 12. Assassin / 13. Draftee / 14. Militia Soldier / 15. Watchman / 16. Infantry / 17. Mercenary / 18-20. Elite Soldier

# Androids and Cybernetic Implants
By rolling dice on the previous tables, it is possible for an android character to commence game play with some sort of built in weapon, communications, optics or other feature which is either similar to, or a direct variant of, a cybernetic implant. This implies that androids can be further augmented during a game campaign, either after losing a limb during some mishap or through intentional upgrading. Other than their susceptibility to EMP and electrical weapons, and in most cases, sinking if dumped over the side of a boat, androids are already quite remarkable and by adding cybernetics they can become even more so, perhaps taking away some of the uniqueness of cyborg and mutorg characters.

Still, it makes sense that an already mechanical being could be enhanced with a wide range of cybernetic implants, and therefore, the pathway to make any android accept cybernetics — which were made for human physiology — the following conditions must apply.

First off, if during character creation this android has a cybernetic part, such as a welding torch, or one of the flight capabilities of an Airborne Military Android or weapon arm noted on some other units, then such a character already has a Cybernetics Interface Module, or CIM, and is thus fitted with the necessary internal wiring, receiver parts, software and optical interface upgrades which allow it to take yet more cybernetic augmentation.

Without this module and complex accessories, an android cannot have cybernetic parts installed, but can use most medical cybernetics just like any other humanoid character. Medical cybernetics are described on page XR-447. A cybernetic or robotic technician can, however, extract a Cybernetics Interface Module and all necessary accessories from a captive or slain android who has this technology, and during an invasive upgrade 'surgery', have the module and other parts installed into another android. Both the robotics technician skill (on page 54 of the hub rules) and the new cybernetics technician skill on page XR-207 of this book, have a column featuring the odds to successfully install an implant on a robot or android. This same odds to attach an implant to an already cybernetic receptive robot or android is the same chance to install the module, per day.

To hire a freelance robotics or cybernetics technician to install a CIM unit costs a vast amount of silver or other valuable trade goods, even if the android and its companions have a module or remains of another android fitted with such a device. The cost varies based on the availability and skill of the technician to perform the procedure, but in an average sized trade town with a decent robotics dealership, would cost between 3000 and 6000 silver pieces (3000+3d1000sp). To buy the CIM, if it's even available, (37% chance available any given month) would cost a further 1500+1d1000sp. To sell a CIM, incidentally, to a robotics dealership would fetch a dig team half the amount it costs to buy one (750+5d100sp).

Finally, many cybernetic parts work only on organic beings, and would be pointless even if they worked on an android, and include anti-toxin array, artificial heart, atmospheric hydro converter, internal nutrient supply, iron stomach, mental defense screen and so on. Because only some implants are applicable or appropriate for androids, there is a column on table XR-210 Implant Determination Matrix 2, which provides a random listing of all android implants from both this book and the hub rules, combined. This table is rarely used to determine an implant for a player character android, although can occur on roll 89,90 of Table XR-52 Special Features of a Unique Android, with the listing included mostly for when a GM needs to create a NPC android adversary.

# Bestial Humans Set Two

This collection continues on from the 'manimals' included in the Mutant Epoch Hub Rules, pages 24 to 33. New for the expansion rules is the chance for some bestial humans to be fitted with cybernetic implants, although for already mutated bestials there is only a 1 in 20 chance that they are also enhanced, while non-mutated bestials have a 1 in 10 chance of being a cyborg. Any bestial human cyborg will feature 1 each of offensive, defensive and miscellaneous implants from the random table on page 330 of this book. A dedicated Bestial Human character sheet can be found on page 515 or online at https://www.outlandarts.com/expansionrules.htm

*A special thanks go out to all those in the Epochian Community who, over the years contributed many of these new bestial human types, added suggestions and feedback. I'd like to thank Blood Axe, Colin Chapman, C.H.U.D., Matthew Fisher, and Corryn. You're the best. Where two names are listed beside the bestial human strain, it means two gamers contributed to this bestial human entry and the stats and write-ups were combined to the best of my ability. WM*

A third (33%) of all bestial human characters are mutant specimens who exhibit 1d3 prime mutations, 1d2 minor and a 1 in 10 chance of a flaw. Mutation lists, which include deviations from both the hub rules and this book, are located on pages 228 to 234.

1 in 10 non-mutated bestials, or 1 in 20 mutant bestials, will also be cybernetically augmented and feature 1 offensive, 1 defensive and 1 miscellaneous implant (Cybernetic Implants lists start on page 330).

To determine if a new bestial human character is sourced from this new collection, or from those found on page 24 of the hub rules, roll 1d100: 01-50 from this book, 51-00 from the Hub Rules.

## Table XR-53/Bestial Human Determination, Traits ,and Stats Matrix

| 1d100 | Species | END | STR | AG | ACC | INT | WILL | PER | APP | AGE | Lifespan | DV | Move | Weight | Height/Length |
|---|---|---|---|---|---|---|---|---|---|---|---|---|---|---|---|
| 01-03 | Bat | 3d6+3 | 3d6+6 | +22 | +20 | 14+d20 | +2 | +28 | d6 | 3+d10 | 38 years | -2/-15 | 5/22m | 20+d20kg | 40+d20cm |
| 04,05 | Beaver | +8 | +8 | +0 | +0 | 16+d20 | +0 | +6 | 6+d10 | 4+d10 | 48 years | -5 | 6/10m | 60+d20kg | 70+2d20cm |
| 06-08 | Beetle | +22 | +16 | +0 | +0 | 3d6 | +8 | +10 | d8 | 4+d6 | 26 years | -20/-30 | 6, fly 14m | 140+2d20kg | 100+d100cm |
| 09,10 | Butterfly | 3d8+6 | 3d8+8 | +6 | +0 | 3d6 | +0 | +14 | 10+d20 | 3+d6 | 24 years | -4/-16 | 5m, fly 14m | 30+2d20kg | 100+d100cm |
| 11,12 | Centipede | +6 | +12 | +20 | +10 | 3d6 | +8 | +10 | d6 | 4+d10 | 43 years | -12 | 10m | 70+2d20kg | 120+d100cm |
| 13,14 | Chameleon | 3d6+3 | 3d6+6 | +0 | +6 | 3d6 | +6 | +20 | 2d4 | 3+d10 | 38 years | -5 | 5m | 30+d20kg | 60+d20cm |
| 15-20 | Chicken | 10+1d20 | 10+d20 | +10 | +10 | 8+d20 | +5 | +3 | 3d4 | 2d4 | 31 | -5 | 9m, fly12m | 50+d20 kg | 60+2d20 |
| 21-23 | Duck | +6 | 10+d20 | +0 | +6 | 8+d20 | +4 | +6 | 2d10 | 3+d8 | 68 years | -3/-12 | 4m/swim10m/ fly 20m | 20+2d20kg | 40+d20cm |
| 24-26 | Fly | +0 | +4 | +30 | +12 | 3d6 | +0 | +22 | 1 | 1+d4 | 16 years | -10/-22 | 7/ fly 18m | 40+2d20kg | 80+d100cm |
| 27,28 | Gecko | 3d6+3 | 3d6+3 | +10 | +6 | 3d6 | +6 | +10 | 2d6 | 3+d10 | 38 years | -6 | 8m | 30+d20kg | 50+d20cm |
| 29 | Gila Monster | 3d8+10 | 3d8+10 | +0 | +6 | 3d6 | +12 | +10 | 2d6 | 4+d12 | 56 years | -10 | 6m | 30+2d20kg | 50+2d20cm |
| 30-33 | Goat | +15 | +12 | +0 | +4 | 6+d20 | +0 | +4 | 5+d10 | 5+d12 | 30 years | -5 | 8m | 80+3d20kg | 120+2d20cm |
| 34,35 | Gorilla | +30 | +25 | +10 | +12 | 12+2d20 | +0 | +4 | 10+d20 | 8+d12 | 70 years | -5 | 7m | 130+d100kg | 160+2d20cm |
| 36,37 | Grasshopper | +6 | +12 | +12 | +8 | 3d6 | +0 | +10 | d8 | 2d6 | 28 years | -12 | 5/16m | 60+2d20kg | 100+d100cm |
| 38,39 | Gull | +12 | +6 | +10 | +12 | 15+d20 | +16 | +22 | 2d4 | 3+d8 | 68 years | -3/-14 | 6/10/22m | 30+2d20kg | 60+2d20cm tall |
| 40,41 | Hummingbird | 3d6+6 | 3d6+3 | +26 | +18 | 10+d20 | +0 | +22 | 2d10 | 3+d6 | 42 years | -3/-23 | 3/28m | 10+d20kg | 40+d20cm tall |
| 42-44 | Marmot | 12+1d20 | +0 | +8 | +8 | 16+d20 | +0 | +6 | 6+d10 | 4+d10 | 48 years | -5 | 6m | 28+d20kg | 70+d20cm |
| 45-47 | Mole | 3d6+9 | 3d6+9 | +0 | +0 | 14+d20 | +6 | +18 | 7+d12 | 2+d6 | 30 years | -8 | 6m/0.33m | 20+d20kg | 40+d20cm |
| 48-50 | Monitor Lizard | +30 | +7 | +20 | +15 | 10+d20 | +20 | +18 | 6+d8 | 6+d10 | 50 years | -17 | 10m | 70+d20kg | 80+2d20, +70cm tail |
| 51-55 | Monkey | 16+1d20 | +6 | +26 | +12 | 10+2d20 | +0 | +6 | 8+d20 | 6+d10 | 50 years | -6 | 8m | 32+d20kg | 70+2d20cm |
| 56-59 | Opossum | 15+1d20 | +6 | +11 | +7 | 10+d20 | +0 | +7 | 5+d10 | 4+d6 | 25 years | -7 | 6m | 29+d20kg | 65+d20cm |
| 60-62 | Owl | +12 | +4 | +14 | +20 | 12+d20 | +22 | +28 | 2d8 | 5+d8 | 62 year | -3/-14 | 6/22m | 34+2d20kg | 60+2d20cm tall |
| 63,64 | Penguin | +12 | +6 | +0 | +16 | 14+d20 | +16 | +18 | 2d10 | 3+d8 | 68 years | -3/-14 | 3/18m | 40+d20kg | 70+2d20cm tall |
| 65,66 | Porcupine | 16+1d20 | +0 | +0 | +0 | 16+d20 | +0 | +6 | 5+d10 | 4+d10 | 48 years | -25 | 5m | 28+d20kg | 70+d20cm |
| 67-72 | Rabbit | 3d8+10 | 3d8+12 | +25 | +20 | 12+d20 | +0 | +15 | 10+d12 | 3+d6 | 26 years | -6 | 9m | 24+d20kg | 70+d20cm |
| 73,74 | Road Runner | +12 | +2 | +24 | +14 | 14+d20 | +16 | +18 | 2d8 | 3+d8 | 68 years | -6/-11 | 12/10m | 30+d20kg | 60+d20cm tall |
| 75-77 | Salamander | 3d8+8 | 3d8+10 | AG +0 | +0 | 3d6+4 | +0 | +3 | 2d6 | 3+d8 | 27 years | -2 | 6/10m | 34+d20kg | 60+2d20cm |
| 78,79 | Seal | +26 | +16 | +0 | +16 | 8+2d20 | +0 | +12 | 9+d20 | 6+d12 | 36 years | -5/-16 | 5/18m | 80+d100kg | 160+3d20cm |
| 80,81 | Shrew | 3d6+6 | 3d6+6 | +20 | +6 | 14+d20 | +6 | +10 | 7+d12 | 2+d6 | 30 years | -10 | 9m | 20+d20kg | 40+d20cm |
| 82,83 | Skink | 3d6+3 | 3d6+3 | +12 | +6 | 3d6 | +6 | +10 | 2d6 | 3+d10 | 38 years | -6 | 8m | 30+d20kg | 50+d20cm |
| 84-86 | Skunk | 12+1d20 | +4 | +10 | +6 | 10+d20 | +0 | +6 | 6+d10 | 5+d10 | 31 years | -4 | 7m | 28+d20 kg | 70+d20 cm |
| 87-91 | Squirrel | 3d8+1d10 | 3d8+d10 | +24 | +20 | 15+2d20 | 0 | +12 | 6+d12 | 26 | 3+d6 | -5 | 8m | 26+d20 kg | 65+2d20 |
| 92-94 | Vulture | +12 | +6 | +10 | +14 | 14+d20 | +16 | +28 | 2d4 | 5+d8 | 62 years | -3/-13 | 6/20m | 38+2d20kg | 70+2d20cm tall |
| 95-98 | Weasel | 3d6+6 | 3d6+10 | +22 | +18 | 15+d20 | +6 | +12 | 7+d12 | 2+d6 | 30 years | -10 | 9m | 22+d20kg | 50+d20cm |
| 99,00 | Woodpecker | +6 | 10+d20 | +10 | +20 | 12+d20 | +16 | +18 | 2d8 | 5+d8 | 62 years | -3/-13 | 5/20m | 30+2d20kg | 50+2d20cm tall |

***Trait Generation Note:*** *A bonus such as +6, etc. Is added to the trait amount after the trait is rolled normally on table XR-2, page 8, not the dice roll itself. An amount such as 12+1d20, for example, is rolled independently, to establish the trait value without consulting any table.*

## Bat *by Colin Chapman*

Man-bats are typically ugly with faces and noses creased and furrowed in strange ways, leathery wing-arms, and sharp little teeth (SV +7/ DMG 1d10), and even though only a small minority are vampiric, this reputation colors the rest of them. For this reason they are prohibited from entering human communities, unless accompanied by more human looking individuals, promise to stay secluded in personal quarters, and by paying guards significant bribes (30+1d20sp) will they ever be granted access to a human community.

Although most bestial human bats are carnivorous with a particular fondness for bugmeat, a few eat vegetation, and a small number are active blood-drinkers. To determine the diet of the character, roll **1d6: 1-4.** carnivore / **5.** herbivore / **6.** hematophage.

Because of their superior senses and wariness, they enjoy a +2 initiative bonus. Batoids can also use echolocation to see in even complete darkness, though they cannot talk and use this ability at the same time. This means they can see invisible, warped, and other such beings, as well as operate in fog, mist, and other situations of reduced or zero visibility without penalty. This echolocation does lack fine detail, however, and cannot discern color, and cannot be used if the man-bat cannot speak.

Humanoid bats can fly with their wing-arms (22m per round), using their misshapen hands, which protrude from their wings, to either drop ordinance or employ a one handed weapon. They can use a bow, rifle or other two-handed weapon while in the air, but must cease flapping their wings while doing so and begin plummeting to the ground at a rate of 10m per round, so typically try to get plenty of elevation before initiating this risky tactic.

Typically, a humanoid bat will avoid a melee fight with larger foes and instead fly up out of enemy reach and perch some place high to fire down on its adversaries. They cannot carry aloft anything heavier than half its weight and cannot glide.

## Beaver *by Colin Chapman*

These rodentoids are much larger and heavier than bestial human rats, and are distinguishable at a glance thanks to their webbed feet and large, flat, paddle-like tails. A bestial humanoid beaver's thick waterproof fur and layer of body fat enables it to endure cold conditions easily, even without winter clothing, and it is an excellent swimmer (10m), able to hold its breath for up to 9 minutes above or below water.

Fully herbivorous, humanoid beavers most enjoy eating various types of wood and bark, and their constantly growing chisel-like teeth can chew through wood with ease, as well as deliver a vicious bite (SV +5/ DMG 1d12).

Beaver-men seldom feel at-ease unless safely secured behind fortified walls, or at least wearing the toughest armor possible, and are suspicious of large predators such as wolves, bears, wolverines, and cougars. They are even on their guard around humans, for while they are often permitted entry to human communities, their meat is tasty, and their fur makes excellent garments.

## Beetle *by Colin Chapman*

Heavily-armored with a tough carapace, humanoid beetles are cumbersome compared to other bug-humans, even for those that can fly, and this leads many individuals to erroneously assume they are also even more dim-witted than other bug-humans. This fallacy, together with the fact that many beetles are herbivores and sometimes sport attractive metallic or patterned exoskeletons, means that these bestial humans are marginally better regarded by humans than most other bug-humans.

Of course, while many are herbivores, others are predators or sometimes feed on dung, and regardless of diet, they can be aggressive. Such individuals are quickly ousted or attacked if the truth is revealed, even where they might have otherwise been accepted. To determine the diet of the character, roll **1d6: 1-3.** herbivore / **4-5.** carnivore/ **6.** coprophage.

Human-beetles have mandibles that can deliver an effective bite, though the size of these mandibles varies from individual to individual. Roll for the size and effectiveness as per the Mandibles mutation (TME, pg. 69); apply any changes listed except for any reductions in Appearance.

Like bestial human cockroaches, man-beetles have six limbs, using the rear pair to walk while employing the front four to carry equipment or wield weapons. This character will have two dominant hands, allowing it to fire two pistols, or use all four arms to bear a pair of two-handed weapons such as two crossbows or two shotguns, etc. If forced into hand-to-hand combat, it can attack with all four front limbs and its mandibles simultaneously with each hand attack being a standard fist attack like a regular human (4 attacks, 1d6 DMG per successful strike) and its mandible attack SV +8, DMG 1d12+2. Alternatively, it can combine all its 5 attacks against one opponent (SV +8 plus mandible SV, DMG 4d6+4 plus mandible DMG).

2 in 6 beetles have wings folded within their hard shells, and can spend one round opening their shell, extending their wings and take off on the second round, flying at a base movement speed of 14m. Like other bug-humans, the humanoid beetle can climb up most surfaces giving this character an automatic 1d3 skill points in climbing, and it frequently prefers climbing to flying.

## Butterfly *by Colin Chapman*

While most other bug-humans are shunned by human communities, if not actively reviled or hunted, the bestial humanoid butterfly enjoys at least some acceptance. Although no bug-human can claim to be truly beautiful, the humanoid butterfly has the benefit of large, elegant, brightly patterned wings to help offset its inhuman appearance. Combined with its herbivorous diet, lack of natural weapons, and unpalatable nature, it is not seen as a threat or a potential meal.

Human-butterflies have six limbs, using the rear pair to walk while employing the front four to carry equipment or wield weapons. This character will have two dominant hands, allowing it to fire two pistols, or use all four arms to bear a pair of two-handed weapons such as two bows or two rifles, etc. During melee combat, it can attack with all four upper arms simultaneously and either uses two, double handed weapons like battle axes, four blades, or standard fist attacks (4 attacks, 1d6 damage per successful strike). It can also combine all its 4 attacks against one opponent (SV +6/ DMG 4d6+4). Like other bug-humans, the humanoid butterfly can climb up most surfaces with relative ease (though it prefers to fly) giving this character an automatic 1d3+1 skill points in climbing.

Bestial humanoid butterflies are immune to plant-based toxins, and their bodies store any such toxins in their blood and flesh. This grants them the benefit of the Poison Blood mutation (Type A, death) from page TME-71; there is a good reason they advertise their toxic nature with vibrant wings and patterning.

## Centipede *by Colin Chapman*

Centipedoids are truly voracious predators and will willingly attack and devour any animal that looks like it can be easily overcome, intelligent or otherwise. Because they are swift, aggressive, poison-armed carnivores, humans hate them. Only by being accompanied by more human appearing individuals, promising to stay in the team's quarters, and by paying guards a bribe (40+2d20sp) will they be allowed into a human settlement. In most cases, any militia will simply attack them.

Man-centipedes are equipped with poisonous forcipules, modified front limbs just under the head that can deliver a terrible sting. This attack is SV +10/ DMG 1d12+1, and injects a Type A death poison. It produces enough poison to inject victims 6 times in a 24-hour period.

Bestial human centipedes begin with five pairs of limbs, the first pair being used as arms, the remainder as legs. As they increase in rank their body length increases, as do their pairs of legs. They molt and gain an extra pair of legs, extra 40cm of length, extra 20kg of weight, bonus +4 endurance, and, with every even-numbered rank gained, an extra 1m to movement; this is above and beyond any other rank increase benefits.

Like other bug-humans, the humanoid centipede can climb up most surfaces giving this character an automatic 1d3+2 skill points in climbing.

Humanoid centipedes do not cope well with arid conditions and suffer 1d4 damage per hour when exposed to desert conditions without constant moisture and proper covering.

## Chameleon *by Colin Chapman*

Slow moving but patient, bestial human chameleons eat meat, particularly enjoying bug meat, whether from a sapient foe or otherwise. They use their ability to change color to blend into their surroundings (see skills, 'conceal self' or 'concealed movement' as skill point 4 on page 51 of the hub rules) when near naked, and have effective bites (SV+7/ DMG 1d10).

Their tongues can be shot once every two rounds, out to four times their own height and on a strike adhere to a target. The target need not be a smaller food animal; instead it could be a passing vehicle or large animal, an enemy's hand held weapon, or the ceiling of a structure. In every case, a successful strike must be made with the projectile tongue being SV +10, doing only 1d6 stun damage on a strike, but allowing the chameleon to pull smaller creatures which weigh less than itself to its mouth. If the target is heavier, the chameleon may use his or her tongue like a grappling hook or winch to pull itself aboard. In the case of using the tongue to latch onto a stationary object, such as a high balcony or ceiling, or shoot across a chasm to grab a railing on the far side, the strike is usually considered automatic. The tongue can be released from a struck target in two rounds by muscular gyrations and twisting of the bulbous tip.

Should an opponent be secured by the sticky tongue, and if weighing less than the chameleon-man, then the target is yanked back to the mouth and on the next round, be easily bitten (the half-chameleon gains +30 SV) until either the prey is dead, the target severs the character's tongue, or the stuck individual kills the bestial human-chameleon. The tongue can be severed by a blade or similar weapon and has an endurance of 14 and defense value of -20. A severed tongue will not grow back.

The odds to grab an opponent's weapon with the bestial chameleon's tongue is not high, since a regular strike must first be made and then the person holding the weapon is allowed a Type C strength based hazard check to try to retain the weapon or object he or she was holding.

Chameleonoids are excellent climbers (1d3+1 skill points in climbing), have prehensile tails that can hold smaller objects such as knives, and also have independently moving eyes that keep them constantly alert to danger (+2 initiative).

Their unusual hands and feet, strange eyes, and long tongues mark them as truly bizarre by human standards, and so they are only tolerated as curiosities in human settlements if accompanied by human or mutant human allies.

## Chicken *by Colin Chapman & Blood Axe*

Among the most widespread bird-men around, bestial human chickens owe their survival and success to their huge numbers before the apocalypse, their social nature, a truly varied diet, stubbornness, and the aggression of the roosters. Seeds, rodents, bugs, lizards, they will literally try their hand at eating anything remotely edible, and are equipped with sharp beaks (SV +7/ DMG 1d10). Roosters have sharp claws and spurs and use them in a leaping flurry of kicks (SV +15/ DMG 1d20) which they can do every third round. No small number have become gladiators, lending a whole new spin to the old sport of cockfighting. 1 in 6 NPC bestial human chickens are roosters, although as player characters, the player decides their sex.

Mutant chickens cannot truly fly, for their wings have become more like arms with hands, but can partially glide if they can fully extend their wings out (requires 4m of total space from side to side) and can travel 2m horizontally for every meter dropped at a rate of 12m. So for every 12 meters it flies horizontally, it loses 24 meters altitude. If falling into narrower spaces, such as a pit or elevator shaft, and they are able to extend their feathered arms, their fall will be arrested somewhat and so reduce fall damage taken by half. Chickenoids are capable runners and have a base speed of 9 meters per round instead of the usual 6m a human gets.

Bestial chickens suffer from the same discrimination as bestial pigs. They are seen as little more than dumb livestock and must prove themselves, although considered harmless and are allowed into human settlements if arriving with at least a few human companions, but must be ever vigilant, for they are frequently regarded as potential food. Because many other beings view them as prey, they are tremendously wary and gain a +1 initiative. Bug-men and rodent-men in turn view bestial human chickens with some instinctual apprehension.

## Duck *by Colin Chapman*

Humanoid ducks can fly with their wing-arms (20m per round), using their misshapen hands, which protrude from their wings, to either drop ordinance or employ a one handed weapon. They can use a bow, rifle or other two-handed weapon while in the air, but must bring their wings close together, stop flapping and drop at a rate of 10m per round, so typically try to get plenty of elevation before initiating this risky tactic.

Typically, a humanoid duck will avoid a melee fight with h e a v i e r boned, larger foes and instead fly up out of enemy reach and perch some place high to fire down on its adversaries.

A humanoid duck cannot carry aloft anything heavier than half its weight; however, a creature of approximately its own weight can be carried downward in a controlled glide, such as if the bestial human duck needs to transport human comrades from a skyscraper to street level.

While ungainly on land, ducks are excellent swimmers, and the webbed feet and short legs so clumsy on land propel them at 10m per round through the water.

A duckoid can bite with its slightly serrated bill, though it is not as effective a weapon as the beak of a crow or eagle (SV +4/ DMG 1d8).

These omnivorous bird-humans are highly cautious in their dealings with others as they are frequently seen as potential meals, especially by predatory animals and bestial humans such as eagles, foxes, and alligators. Even humans may view them as food, and so while they are accepted in many human communities more readily than other man-birds, they are understandably skittish about entering such places.

## Fly *by Colin Chapman*

Of all the bug-humans, the bestial humanoid fly is the most repugnant, considered even more repellent than man-cockroaches. This disgust is with good reason too; not only are humanoid-flies truly ugly, but they defecate constantly, buzz loudly, and possess truly vile eating habits, vomiting and drooling on food to pre-digest it before eating. That they also favor decaying organic matter such as feces for their diet simply adds an extra layer of disgust to a creature already considered grossly unappealing.

Even the most tolerant of trading towns will refuse them entry 90% of the time, and when they are accepted they must still pay a hefty entrance fee ahead of time (40+2d12sp) along with a promise to avoid public places and especially avoid eating in public.

Human-flies have six limbs, using the rear pair to walk while employing the front four to carry equipment or wield weapons. This character will have two dominant hands, allowing it to fire two pistols or wield two machetes ambidextrously. Alternatively, they can instead use all four arms to bear a pair of two-handed weapons such as two pikes, two shotguns, or two bows, etc. During melee combat, it can attack with all four front limbs simultaneously with each attack (4 attacks, 1d6 damage per successful strike) or concentrate all its 4 attacks against one opponent (SV +8/ DMG 4d6+4).

Like other bug-humans, the humanoid fly can climb up most surfaces with relative ease (though it prefers to fly) giving this character an automatic 1d3+2 skill points in climbing.

Humanoid flies can digest and consume nearly any decaying organic matter without side effects to itself, however foul, and react with incredible speed to threats, gaining +2 initiative at all times. They are very fearful of predatory bug-humans, especially spider-men, and will flee at the sight of such individuals.

## Gecko *by Colin Chapman*

Bestial human geckos are active predators, and despite their relatively small size, instinctively frighten bug-men, especially humanoid spiders and scorpions. They have effective bites (SV +7/ DMG 1d10), but most impressively can cling to any surface. They can climb up, or down, or along, anything, even glass, at their normal movement rate. Additionally, they can hang on a ceiling of rough material for one round per current point of strength. The gecko-man can also make a type A, agility based hazard check once for every 5 meters dropped to catch the side of a building or pit or other wall after falling into a pit or jumping off a structure. A GM may allow the use of this ability when a geckoid leaps onto the back of a huge beast or passing vehicle,    making an agility based hazard check in accordance with the difficulty of the task. Humanoid geckos may only use this ability if they keep their hands and feet bare.

Gecko-men have quick reflexes (+1 initiative) and can grow back a lost leg, tail, or arm within 2+1d3 months. They may even voluntarily shed their tail to escape predators, most of which will cease pursuit to eat the freshly dropped, still-wriggling meat.

Human communities are uneasy around gecko-men, but will permit them entry if humans or mutant humans accompany the reptilian.

## Gila Monster *by Colin Chapman*

Despite being small and relatively slow, bestial human gila monsters and beaded lizards are tenacious carnivores armed with a mouthful of sharp teeth and venomous saliva (SV +8/ DMG 1d10+Type A, death). They also possess large, tough claws (2 Attacks at SV +5/ DMG 1d10) but much prefer to bite, and are armored with beaded scales (-10 DV).

Humanoid gila-monsters are capable climbers (add 1d2 skill points in climbing) and use their strong claws to dig with remarkable speed, clearing ten times as much soil and loose earth per round as a human with bare hands, often excavating 1m per minute through soft earth or low-density rubble. They can cope well with dry, desert conditions and have the Arid Adaptation mutation (page TME-60).

Human communities strongly distrust humanoid gila monsters, regarding them as cold-blooded and venomous predators, so unless accompanied by a powerful or well-loved group of human and mutant human comrades, this gila-man will not be given service in eateries or bars, nor receive lodging in inns, protection by local law, or any sort of services by commoners and shop keepers.

## Goat *by Colin Chapman*

*[40% Chance actually a bestial human sheep.]*

Despite being herbivorous, bestial human goats and sheep will attempt to eat nearly anything once, and can derive sustenance from nearly any non-toxic plant-derived substance including cardboard. Humanoid sheep have returned to their wild roots physically, and both sheep-men and goat-men are surprisingly agile and sure-footed.

Thanks to their thick hair or fleece, they can withstand cold conditions twice as well as a human, even without winter clothing. The males of both species of humanoids also sport horns capable of delivering a bone-crunching head butt (SV +10/ DMG 1d12, double damage if allowed to charge from 6m or more). Nannies and ewes only possess horns 50% of the time, unless the GM specifies that both genders exhibit horns equally. Their wariness and keen senses provide them with a +1 initiative bonus.

Because both species are valued for their meat, hide/fleece, and milk, they face potential predation from wild animals, other bestial humans, and humans too, and even when allowed entry into human communities, may be treated as little better than livestock. Because of this, when not part of a loyal team of humans, mutants and cyborgs, they protect themselves by organizing in large tribes and flocks, and can be very aggressive in defending themselves and their extended groups.

## Gorilla *by Colin Chapman*

With their heavy fur, squat, muscular physiques, and wicked canines, bestial human gorillas cannot pass for hairy humans like humanoid chimpanzees can, and possess even more of a tendency to knuckle-walk than their pan troglodyte relatives.

Despite being more powerful and less human than chimpanzee-men, gorilla-men are quieter and less aggressive, and while omnivorous, are far more inclined to a mostly vegetarian diet too. This gentle aspect vanishes, however, when violence is needed, and humanoid gorillas are devastating in melee. They can make three attacks per round, one bite (SV +8/ DMG 1d12) and two powerful punches (SV +6/ DMG 1d12 instead of the normal human 1d6), with both accuracy and strength modifiers applied to these attacks as normal for any character or creature.

Gorilla-men are also fair climbers (1d2 skill points in climbing), but do not enjoy the chimpanzees' benefits in using human sized equipment and relic drugs.

Being less aggressive than chimpoids, humanoid gorillas are more readily accepted into human communities, especially if allied with humans and mutant humans. Battle Apes will regard the humanoid gorilla with some respect, only attacking when absolutely necessary.

## Grasshopper *by Colin Chapman*

The bestial human grasshopper is herbivorous and relatively inoffensive, but is still regarded with distrust by humans due to the tendency of these mutants to sometimes enter frenzied feeding phases as a locust, devouring vast quantities of valuable foodstuffs. They are only permitted entry to human communities if accompanied by trusted humans or mutant humans, and even then they will be instructed to keep away from human food supplies and crops on pain of death.

For their part, hopperoids are fearful of many  predatory species, and because of their tasty, nutritious nature, are often seen as potential food by many other creatures, including some humans.

Human-grasshoppers have six limbs, using the rear pair to walk and jump while employing the front four to carry equipment or wield weapons. This character will have two dominant hands, allowing it to fire two pistols, or use all four arms to bear a pair of two-handed weapons such as two great swords or two rifles, etc. In melee combat, it can either use regular weapons with the lower two being considered off-hand and suffer a -20 SV each, or attack with all four front limbs simultaneously as fist or raking attack like a regular human without the off-hand penalty (4 attacks, 1d6 damage per successful strike). Alternatively, it can combine all its 4 attacks against one opponent (SV +8/ DMG 4d6+4).

Like other bug-humans, the humanoid grasshopper can climb up most surfaces with relative ease (though it prefers to jump) giving this character an automatic 1d3+1 skill points in climbing.

Bestial human grasshoppers walk and run slowly, but can perform tremendous leaps. Once every second round half-human grasshoppers can leap upwards five times their own body length or eight times their length in horizontal distance. This ability allows them to leap clear over most adversaries. Such leaps are exhausting however, and a human-grasshopper hybrid can only make one such leap per day, per point of endurance.

## Gull *by Colin Chapman*

Raucous, canny, and carnivorous, bestial human gulls are opportunistic individuals, intent to hunt, scavenge, and steal whatever they desire. This reputation, combined with their mob mentality and aggression, makes them unwelcome in human communities, and they may find entry difficult even if accompanied by humans and human mutants.

Humanoid gulls can fly with their wing-arms (22m per round), using their misshapen hands, which protrude from their wings, to either drop ordinance or employ a one handed weapon. They can use a bow, rifle or other two-handed weapon while in the air, but must cease flapping their wings while doing so and begin plummeting to the ground at a rate of 10m per round, so typically try to get plenty of elevation before initiating this risky tactic.

A humanoid gull cannot carry aloft anything heavier than itself; however, a creature of about double its own weight can be carried downward in a controlled glide, such as if the bestial human gull needs to transport human comrades from a high ledge.

While quite capable on land despite their webbed feet, gulloids are excellent swimmers, and their webbed feet propel them at 10m per round through the water.

A humanoid gull can bite with its long, stout bill (SV +7/ DMG 1d10).

## Hummingbird *by Colin Chapman*

The smallest of the bestial human birds, hummingbirds are hyperactive omnivores with a love of all things sweet. Though frequently sporting attractive plumage, their need to consume their own bodyweight in protein and sugars every day means they are constantly on the lookout for food and are considered undesirable guests. As a result, they are seldom welcomed into human communities even when accompanied by humans and human mutants, and must often be covertly carried into a settlement by slipping inside a large companion's backpack and bedroll.

Humanoid hummingbirds can fly with their wing-arms (28m per round) but cannot use their hands while doing so; their wings simply beat far too rapidly. They can use a weapon while in the air, but can't flap their wings while doing so. If they stop, they will plummet to the ground at a rate of 10m per round.

A humanoid hummingbird cannot carry aloft anything more than half its own bodyweight, and cannot effectively glide. It makes up for this with peerless maneuverability; it can fly backwards, turn rapidly, and hover effortlessly, and its extreme metabolism grants it +2 initiative at all times and a -20 defense value increase while in the air.

A hummingbird-man can stab with its long, pointed bill (SV +7/ DMG 1d8) as well as use one-handed weapons; however, their tiny fists deliver a punch that inflicts only 1d4 damage. They are too small to use great swords, or battle-axes, pikes, halberds, chainsaws, or other sizable weapons. Firing a shotgun or high caliber rifle in the standing position will knock them on their hindquarters.

## Marmot *by Colin Chapman*

Marmot-men have thick fur that enables them to endure cold conditions easily, even without winter clothing. However, from about October to February their ancestral instinct is telling them to hibernate. During these months this character will be irritable, drowsy and just want to sleep about three quarters of each day. The GM could apply an optional -2 initiative penalty on marmot-human crosses during these months to reflect their sleepy nature. Likewise, during hibernation months, a type B willpower based hazard check could be called for per hour to stay awake when forced to stand guard either day or night, or when performing any repetitive chore, including driving a vehicle or steering a barge or airship.

Marmotoids are excellent climbers (1d3 skill points in climbing), and alert to potential danger (+1 initiative).

While omnivorous, they enjoy a mostly herbivorous diet, and although gregarious and typically aggressive only when pressed, have sharp incisors and curved claws and can make a single flurry attack (SV +5/ DMG 3d6). These same claws help them dig with remarkable speed and can clear ten times as much soil and loose earth per round as a human with bare hands, often excavating 1 meter per minute through soft earth or loose rubble.

Entry to human communities is seldom prohibited for humanoid marmots, though they must remain vigilant for predators, and always risk being potential food or fur donors.

## Mole *by Colin Chapman*

With their velvety fur, tiny eyes, squat builds, and overlarge shovel-like hands, bestial human moles are inoffensive, but this belies the fact that they are aggressive, constantly hungry omnivores who prefer a diet of meat.

They can make a bite attack (SV +8/ DMG 1d8 + Type A, paralysis venom) as well as use one-handed weapons, and unlike other bestial humans of their size, their over-large, calloused hands deliver normal punching damage, though they prefer to use their tough claws (SV +10/ DMG 1d8), and can combine them with their bite in a single flurry of attacks (SV +20/ DMG 3d8+venom). They are too small to use large two handed weapons such as halberds, pikes, chainsaws, battle axes, or great swords, or other sizable weapons though. Furthermore, firing a shotgun or high caliber rifle in the standing position will knock them back 1d3 meters onto their rump.

Humanoid moles are swift acting and alert (+1 initiative), and can also dig and burrow through soft earth at speed (1m every 3 rounds).

Mole-men terrify bug-men, and are skittish of bestial human eagles, coyotes, owls, dogs, cats, and foxes, all of which might readily devour the humanoid mole.

With their inoffensive, comical appearance, as well as a misconception that they only eat worms, they are sometimes accepted into human communities if accompanied by human or mutant human friends. Of course, it seldom takes long for such misconceptions to be shattered.

Mole-men have somewhat reduced visual capabilities and see only about half as far as a human, yet in dark places, can see out to 9 meters. They have heightened senses while beneath the earth and gain a +2 initiative bonus while underground. They can also tell if they are going down a slope, or up, and roughly how far beneath street level they are at.

## Monitor Lizard *by Corryn and W. McAusland*

These lizard bestial humans have a tough time getting admitted into a human settlement, and unless arriving with known humans, cyborgs or mutant humans, will be turned away at gunpoint. Even when admitted entry, often with a bribe of 30+3d6sp slipped to the guards, the monitor lizard must remain confined to the unit's quarters and will not be allowed into any saloon, store or eatery. The reason for this animosity, which exceeds even that shown to bestial human gators, is because of the long-standing feud with reptilius and other lizard based humanoids. Common people, who have usually only heard frightening tales of the murderous raids by reptilius, cannot tell this character apart from the notorious — although much smaller — mutant lizard folk of the swamp.

Monitor lizards eat poisonous snakes and so their half human descendants have excellent resistance to all poisons and venom, and get two hazard checks to ward off the effects, plus, allowed to make the HC as two letter codes easier (example: Type C poison is treated as type A by this character, while type G would be type E, etc.).

These long, fierce looking humanoids can make three attacks per round, with their main attack being their terrible bite at SV +10 doing 1d12 damage. Their second melee attack is with their claws, which work together to result in one strike, in which they can either wield a one or two-handed weapon or make a claw slash at SV +6 for 1d8 damage. Their third attack, which can only be made at targets behind the bestial or to either side, but not directly ahead, consists of an incredible tail slap at +10 strike value that inflicts 1d20 stun damage. This tail swat can hit up to three man sized targets if they are grouped together. Strength and accuracy modifiers are of course applied.

There is a chance that this monitor lizard is instead sourced from the largest of their kind, a true monster that is sure to terrorize the populace of any new era town. Such a beast-man will only be allowed admittance if it grew up there, or the leaders of the community permit the hulking specimen to roam their streets on promises of the best behavior. On a roll of 10, on a 1d10, any monitor lizard bestial human is actually hybridized with a Komodo Dragon. If so, it will have these stats instead of those shown on page XR-58: END +35, STR +15, AG+10, INT 1d20+5, Will +22, PER +19, APP 3+d8, DV -20, Weight 100+d100kg, Height/Length 175+2d100 tail is 50% of body length.

Komodo dragon bestials can add a claw attack at +10 SV doing 1d12 damage, their tail slap on up to three closely packed, separate targets at its rear or either side is SV +14 for 1d20+4 stun damage, while its massive bite inflicts a SV +18 and does 1d20 lethal damage plus venom.

The bite of a Komodo dragon bestial human delivers a sort of weakness poison, although this venom stops the victim's blood from clotting and so causing bleeding at a rate of 1d8 damage every hour. After the first hour, there is a cumulative 5% added chance that the bleeding finally stops and the creature has a hope at survival, thus after hour 1, a 5% chance the bleeding stops. If it doesn't stop, then on the second hour another 1d8 damage occurs and the bleeding continues. At the end of hour two, there is a 10% chance the bleeding stops. On hour three, a 15% chance, and so on. If hunting its victim, the bestial Komodo will follow the blood trail, and eventually overtake and overpower the weakened, doomed creature.

## Monkey *by Colin Chapman*

Monkey-men are crafty, mischievous omnivores, though they prefer vegetables to meat. They can make a bite attack with their sharp teeth (SV +5/ DMG 1d8) and can be quite vicious. They are covered in a soft, coat of often multi-colored fur and can endure cold weather much better than humans, even without clothing, but prefer warmer climes.

These simians are excellent climbers (add 1d3+2 skill points in climbing), and can climb as swiftly as they can run. They possess long prehensile tails capable of gripping onto things or holding small items such as daggers and knives, and are highly alert (+1 initiative). With their bite, one fist (1d6 DMG) or hand held weapon, and whatever they carry in their tails, they are capable of three melee attacks per round.

Bestial human monkeys have little difficulty being accepted into human communities if accompanied by humans or mutant humans, and will be viewed as amusing pets with people laughing at their antics and comical faces. Of course, it only takes a prank too far for things to turn ugly.

## Opossum *by C.H.U.D. and Colin Chapman*

Bestial opossums have a bite attack (SV +5, DMG 1d10). Because of their prehensile tail and opposable thumbs on both hands and feet they are expert climbers and have 1d3+1 skill points in the climb skill. They are very resistant to snake venom and make 2 hazard checks against it. If a bestial opossum is caught in a surprise attack or are reduced to below 25% of END there is a 3% chance they will feign death for 1d4 hours. When they do so, they fall over unmoving, tongue lolling, with foul-smelling green fluid oozing from their anus. Their heart rate and breathing slow and become almost imperceptible, and they become unresponsive to stimuli. Unless a individual encountering them knows of this ability, or performs a quick medical check, the opossum is likely to be taken for dead and diseased or badly rotten. Many predators will avoid eating the rancid-smelling "carcass", leaving the humanoid opossum alone. Unfortunately, while potentially handy for tricking attackers or avoiding predators, it has the downside that the possum-man cannot revive themselves until 1d4 hours have elapsed, and some predators will eat a corpse however terrible it smells.

Bestial human opossums are omnivores and will eat anything including leftovers and scraps. In more rural settlements they can often enter without trouble, however, when trying to enter more 'civilized' towns they are usually mistaken for rats, and treated as such. Attempting to enter a settlement or saloon with human and mutant human companions is far easier than doing so alone.

Like their wild, kin, these mutants have water-tight pouches capable of concealing one object as large as a relic handgun, or 2 grenades, a sheathed knife, a day's food and water rations, a tinderbox and wood shavings, or similar sized objects. They also possess long, naked, prehensile tails capable of gripping onto things or holding small items such as daggers and knives, and thanks to their thick fur, can withstand cold conditions twice as well as a human, even without winter clothing.

## Owl *by Colin Chapman*

Quiet, patient, and coldly predatory, bestial human owls make others uneasy and terrify vermin of all sorts, including mice-men, rat-men, and others derived from such common owl prey. Although myth has it that they are wise, this is far from accurate; their enormous eyes occupy much of their cranium, resulting in a slightly smaller brain than some other bird-men. The disquiet they cause, along with their frightening natural weapons, means that they are rarely accepted into human communities, even if accompanied by humans or human mutants — at least unfamiliar ones who vouch for the dangerous looking owl-man.

Humanoid owls can fly with their wing-arms (22m per round) and use their misshapen hands to either drop stones, grenades or other objects on enemies, or else wield a one handed weapon. They can use a bow, rifle or other two-handed weapon while in the air, but not while flapping their wings. Once they stop flapping, they fall at a rate of 12m per round will only try this maneuver if already achieving a great height.

Man-owls are naturally stealthy and are even quiet in flight (add 1d2+1 stealth skill points). Their keen senses, large eyes, and ability to turn their heads completely around also mean that they react quickly (+1 initiative). They avoid direct conflict, preferring stealth and surprise when tackling opponents, and this has garnered them a reputation as assassins.

Thanks to their thick, downy feathers, owl-men can endure normal winter cold with no ill effects.

It can snap at enemies with its beak (SV +10/ DMG 1d10), or make a raking pass with its talons while flying (SV +15/ DMG 1d20). It can potentially cut a swathe through ground-based enemies, attacking up to four man-sized foes per round while making this sweeping assault. Those on the ground are allowed to roll initiative to see if they can make a strike attempt on the passing owl-man, but only if they knew the winged threat was present. If the owl-man wins the initiative, it surprises the targets from above.

A humanoid owl cannot carry aloft anything heavier than itself; but if it needs to transport somebody of up to double its own weight to street level, it can do so while flapping furiously and dropping at a rate of 3m per round.

## Penguin *by Colin Chapman*

With their waddling gait, short legs, and slow walk, bestial human penguins are considered quite comical, and because of this they have little difficulty being accepted into many human communities, though they may find themselves figures of fun in these. Of course, most humans overlook the carnivorous nature of penguin-men, and the fact that these birdoids can deliver a savage bite with their beak (SV +7/ DMG 1d10).

Humanoid penguins are all but immune to extremes of cold, and while slow on land are incredibly swift swimmers (18m per round), count as aquatic animals when they swim, and are capable of holding their breath underwater or above it for 10 minutes.

These birdoids are highly suspicious of seals, sea lions, and other waterborne predators, including bestial human animals of such types, and will rarely work with such individuals.

## Porcupine *by Colin Chapman*

Armored with a multitude of long quills, humanoid porcupines are dangerous to tackle even if they are otherwise inoffensive and slow. These bestial humans are herbivores capable of digesting most vegetable matter including twigs, bark, pine needles, and other foodstuffs that might be considered inedible.

Their quills act as the Spines mutation (TME, page 73), providing armor, adding an additional 1d6 damage to the porcupine-man's unarmed attacks (fist or kick thus does 2d6 damage), and automatically cut and pierce the insides of any animal that swallows the rodentoid for 2d6 damage per round.

Except for specially designed junk and scrap relic armor, humanoid porcupines cannot wear relic armor; unless they spend an hour a day clipping off the quills with wire cutters or a small saw. These quills do not cover the head, limbs, stomach or groin area, and cannot be shot out unless the porcupinoid also has the Throwing Quills mutation.

Porcupine-men are skilled climbers (add 1d3+1 skill points in climbing), and thanks to their quills and fur can endure cold conditions easily, even without winter clothing. Their chisel-like teeth and sharp claws can deliver nasty wounds (bite SV +5, DMG 1d10/ claws +5 SV, DMG 1d6), and their antibiotic-laden skin means that their wounds never become infected.

Like most herbivorous bestial humans, porcupine-men are distrustful of predatory species though their quills deter most assailants and they are accepted into human communities alongside humans and mutant humans more readily than most 'manimals'.

## Rabbit *by Blood Axe and Colin Chapman*

Rabbit humanoids are herbivores and will not eat meat of any type. They have incredibly powerful legs and can jump x2 that of a regular human normal distances. Their keen hearing and sense of smell makes them difficult to surprise (+1 initiative). In emergencies they can bite with their large front teeth (+4 SV, 1d6 damage) but prefer to kick with their strong legs. (+10 SV, 2d8 damage)

They are not seen as a threat and are regarded as cute and cuddly by most humans, so are welcome in trading settlements that accept mutant humans, although during times of famine, these rabbitoids are also welcome because they are edible and their skins make for splendid pelts. For this reason, these hybrids are always on their guard, especially around the likes of normal and bestial human felines, raptors, canines, snakes, and weasels.

Bestial human rabbits and hares can burrow with remarkable speed and clear ten times as much soil and loose earth per round as a human with bare hands, often excavating 1m per minute through soft earth or loose rubble or junk.

## Road Runner *by Colin Chapman*

Long-legged and quick (move 12m per round), bestial human road runners are omnivores with a taste for bugs, lizards, snakes, and rodents, as well as vegetation. They have a sharp beak and talons (SV +7/ DMG 1d10), and react quickly to opportunity and danger (+1 initiative).

Humanoid road runners can fly clumsily with their wing-arms (10m per round), and while airborne can use their misshapen hands, to either employ a one handed weapon or drop a rock or grenade from each hand. Alternatively, they can gain considerable altitude and then stop flapping their wings to bring their hands together to use a two handed device or ranged weapon, such as a crossbow, rifle or bow. When not flapping they drop at a rate of 10m per round.

Unable to carry aloft anything of more than half its own weight, a humanoid road runner is can descend with an object or creature of about its own weight in a controlled glide, and drop 1 meter for every 2m traveled horizontally toward street level.

Bestial human road runners are more welcome than most other bird-men in human settlements, especially given their love of eating vermin and dangerous animals such as rattlesnakes. However, it is still wise that they approach human communities with human, cyborg and mutant human allies, and be alert at all times; a bestial human road runner's leg is a mega-sized drumstick.

## Salamander *by Colin Chapman*

Bestial human salamanders are patient carnivores and are fully amphibious, able to breathe water or air, and can withstand twice as much cold as a normal human even without protective gear or clothing. They are also excellent swimmers (12m) thanks to their short, paddle-like hands and feet. Unfortunately, they face drying out in hot climates, suffering 1d4 damage per hour when exposed to the likes of desert conditions without proper covering and constant moisture.

These amphibious human hybrids are able to grow back a lost leg, tail, or arm within 2+d3 months, and can deliver a nasty bite (SV +8/ DMG 1d12). They also secrete toxins through their skin which grants them the benefit of the poison blood mutation (Type A, death as described on page 71 of the hub rules), but without it being necessary to break the skin; there is a good reason they advertise their toxic nature with vibrant patterning. Simply licking or otherwise ingesting the slimy mucous that coats a salamander's skin is enough for the poison to take effect.

Because of their short, deformed limbs and cold, slimy skin, they are regarded as unattractive by humans, and their poisonous skin marks them as potentially dangerous even if the salamander itself isn't seen as particularly aggressive. Even the most tolerant of trading towns will refuse them entry 90% of the time, and when they are accepted they must still pay a hefty entrance bribe ahead of time (30+d20sp) along with a promise to avoid public places.

## Seal *by Colin Chapman*

Likely developed for naval special operations, bestial human seals and sea lions are clever, powerful individuals, if lacking in grace and speed on land. They are all but immune to extremes of cold, and while slow on land are incredibly swift swimmers (18m per round), count as aquatic animals when they swim, and can hold their breath underwater or above it for 10 minutes.

They have strong, sharp teeth (SV +11/ DMG 1d12+1) and are entirely carnivorous. Although typically playful and curious, pinniped-men can become aggressive when they feel their authority is challenged, and bloody fights are not uncommon among the males in their harems/rafts.

Seal and sea lion-men are not uncommon in coastal human settlements where their gregarious and playful natures are welcome, and their skills as fishers more so, and so are typically admitted to towns that already accept mutant humans and other oddities. Only in rare cases do they risk being seen as sources of meat and fur.

## Shrew *by Colin Chapman*

Although small and rodentine in appearance, bestial human shrews are actually fierce, voracious and hyperactive omnivores armed with a mouthful of sharp teeth, poisonous saliva (Type A, paralysis), and a decided preference for meat.

They can make a bite attack (SV +8/ DMG 1d10+poison) as well as use one-handed weapons; however, their tiny fists deliver a punch that inflicts only d4 damage. Because they are quite diminutive as far as humanoids go, they cannot use heavy two handed weapons such a battle axes, pikes, halberds, pikes, heavy crossbows, longbows, great swords, chainsaws and similar large weapons. Likewise, discharging powerful firearms such as shotguns and high caliber rifles will knock them back 1d3 meters and down, expending their next round as they get up again.

Humanoid shrews are swift-acting and alert (+1 initiative), quick for their size (9m), capable climbers (1d2 skill points in climbing) and adept at hiding and sneaking (add 1d3 skill points in stealth).

Shrew-men can use echolocation to see in even complete darkness, although, like bat bestial humans, they cannot talk and use this ability at the same time. When using echolocation, they can see things that might be invisible to others, such as dimensional beings, force fields, warped, or invisible beings. They can also see in fog, dust, and smoke without penalty. This ability does not allow the shrewoid to see details, writing or other small items and it cannot see color or be used if the humanoid shrew cannot speak (wearing a gag, for example).

They are frightened of those animals that prey on rodents, but in turn frighten rodents and bugs themselves, both normal and humanoid. Due to their ever-hungry nature, aggressiveness, and their willingness to devour anyone, they are never accepted into human communities unless mistaken for a humanoid mouse (something that happens 30% of the time).

## Skink *by Colin Chapman*

Bestial human skinks are typical lizardoids, and so aggressive and territorial carnivores with a taste for bugmeat. They have strong bites (SV +9/ DMG 1d12), and are capable climbers (1d2 skill points in climbing), as well as secretive (1d2 skill points in stealth) and quick to act (+1 initiative).

Skink-men can grow back a lost leg, tail, or arm within 2+d3 months and may even voluntarily shed their tail to escape predators, which often break off their chase for the rest of the character to eat the still moving, fleshy tail.

Due to their aggressive, defensive nature, bestial human skinks are only permitted entry to human habitations when accompanied by friendly humans and human mutants, and even then will be observed. That reptile meat is considered palatable simply makes their position more precarious, and skinkoids are frightened of many larger predators.

## Skunk *by Blood Axe*

Bestial skunks are quite distinctive with their white stripe and luxurious, cold resistant fur coats and well-known ability to spray a streamer of stench. They are not welcome in human settlements unless disguised, already a trusted resident, arriving with more normal looking humans, or the gate guards are offered a hefty bribe (30+3d6sp). Likewise, a skunk-man will not be allowed into an eatery or saloon in an unfamiliar community and must take its food outside.

Bestial Skunks can make 1 bite and two claw attacks, each SV +5, DMG 1d8, or combine them in one flurry attack at +22 doing 3d8+6 damage. They can also use their infamous stench spray. Treat as Gaseous Discharge mutation: Stink, page 67 of the hub rules.

## Squirrel *by Blood Axe and W. McAusland*

These agile tree rodents are excellent climbers and do so at their normal speed (add 1d3+2 points to their climbing skill) and are quite alert (+3 initiative). Their fur helps protect them from the elements so they can withstand cold weather twice as well as a human. They prefer fruit, nuts, seeds and berries, but are omnivores and will eat meat in a pinch — although few people realize this.

They are welcome in most trading settlements as normal squirrels are recognized as friendly furry critters that were fed peanuts in public parks in better times, although in the Epochian era there are strains of dangerous or predatory squirrels such as the whiptail, carnivorous and freakish variants (all described on pages 113 and 114 of the Mutant Bestiary One book). Only people familiar with these other strains might be especially frightened by meeting a child sized squirrel in their community. Other people, as well as bestial human predators, hunt and eat normal squirrels and tend to see bestial human squirrels as food, a fact that these furry, bushy tailed humanoids are quite aware.

While small, they can bite and rend with their claws making three separate attacks at SV +3 and do 1d6 damage per attack on one or more targets, or combine all their attacks on one foe as one concentrated flurry at SV +18 doing 3d6+4 damage. Squirreloids make for excellent scouts, thieves and snipers, however if they attempt to fire a large caliber weapon such as any shotgun, high cal pistol or rifle, they need to make a strength based Type C hazard check to remain upright after doing so or fall back and lose their next turn.

## Vulture *by Colin Chapman and W. McAusland*

Bald-headed and ugly, bestial human vultures and condors are the least appealing of the bird-men, and their dietary preferences and reputations do nothing to endear them to human communities.

They are carnivores with a decided preference for carrion. Indeed, they prefer carrion that is particularly ripe, as they say it adds an extra layer of flavor, and while they can eat fresh meat, they enjoy rotting flesh much more. This has given them a reputation as eaters of the dead, and grave-robbing has sometimes been attributed to them, often correctly. It is a rare human community that will accept one, even when accompanied by human and mutant human allies.

Their feathered arms feature malformed human-like hands that allow them to use regular tools and equipment, as well as limited flight at a speed of 20m per round. While aloft, they can drop explosives, spears or rocks on ground targets, or else get high and use a bow, rifle or other two-handed weapon while in the air, but must cease flapping their wings while doing so. As soon as they do this, however, they fall at a rate of 12m per round.

Human-vultures can attack enemies with their beaks or and two talons for three separate attacks (SV +9/ DMG 1d10 each), though they prefer prey that has already been slain.

They are powerful birds, and able to carry anything up to their own weight in flight, although fly at only 12m per round when doing so. Likewise, in an emergency, they can drop from the sky in controlled glide and carry double their own body weight, traveling at 1m vertically for every 3m flown horizontally, to safely deposit a comrade or two on the ground. When required to descend directly down, they can circle and drop in a corkscrew flight pattern but require a minimum of 10m open space to descend in this fashion. Should they drop into a tight space, such as an elevator shaft, they can only partially arrest their fall with their beating wings and suffer only half damage from the fall.

These birdoids can safely eat any meat, regardless of how rotten or diseased it is, without ill effect, and can even derive nourishment from bone, and are actually immune to diseases and parasites and so get to make three hazard checks against foodborne poisons and similar threats.

Ruin vultures will be both tolerant and curious about these hybrids, and under the right conditions, might accompany, befriend, or at least circle above this character whenever it enters their territory — which can sometimes attract ground based scavengers who are always vigilant for the circling of buzzards over a fresh kill.

## Weasel *by Colin Chapman*

Bloodthirsty and insatiable, bestial human weasels and stoats are swift carnivores with a reputation for viciousness out of all proportion to their size. They act with blinding speed (+2 initiative), and can divide their bite and two rear-claw attacks up to make three separate strike attempts on three separate foes (SV +10/ DMG 1d8+1 each) or combine all into a single flurry against one victim (SV +20/ DMG 3d8+4).

Stoat and weasel-men are stealthy hunters (add 1d3+2 in the stealth skill), and their fur turns white in winter, a time when they can also endure twice the cold a human can, even without winter clothing.

Weaseloids may savagely kill far more than they can comfortably eat, devouring the brains of kills before partaking of any other meat. They particularly love the flesh of rabbits and rodents, but in truth will attempt to kill and eat any prey they think they have a chance of overcoming.

For all their ferocity, they are fearful of owls, foxes, and snakes, but will fight tenaciously if cornered regardless of the size of an opponent.

Humanoid weasels and stoats are rarely admitted into human communities because of their vicious, ever-hungry nature, and only significant bribery, disguise, and/or the accompaniment of known and trusted humans and mutant humans make their entry at all possible.

## Woodpecker *by Colin Chapman*

Bestial human woodpeckers are opportunistic omnivores but particularly enjoy eating bugs and tree sap. While not necessarily offensive themselves, their tendency to keep their beaks in excellent condition by jack hammering wooden constructions such as poles, shop signs, palisades and towers, labels them a pest in many communities. They will be accepted if accompanied by humans and mutant humans, but will quickly be ousted if they cause any property damage.

Humanoid woodpeckers have pronounced wing-arms and can fly (20m per round). With their misshapen hands that protrude from their wings they can both drop objects on ground targets or wield a one handed weapon. Should they choose to cease flapping their wings to employ a crossbow, long gun or other two-handed weapon while in the air, they will need to get plenty of altitude first since they'll plummet to the ground at a rate of 10m per round.

A humanoid woodpecker cannot carry aloft anything heavier than half its own weight; however, a creature of about its own weight can be carried downward in a controlled glide.

Woodpeckers are expert climbers with an automatic 1d3+1 skill points in climbing, and have tough, sharp bills (SV +7/ DMG 1d10+2). If an enemy or object cannot yield ground or otherwise move back when a woodpecker attacks, the human-woodpecker can unleash a staccato flurry of blows with its beak (SV +14/ DMG 3d10+3), three times per day per rank.

# Digital Being

A digital being is a single point of consciousness, and derived either from an artificial intelligence or a downloaded human mind from a deceased person — usually an ancient one. On very rare instances, however, a complete human or technology encased vat-brain can also act through a remote controlled digital being, but these variants are normally only NPCs controlled by the GM. See table XR-65 on page 75 to establish the source of a new digital being character, although knowledge of who they once were, and how much they remember from the past, might not help them survive in the post apocalyptic world of The Mutant Epoch.

In most cases, a digital being, or DB for short, can only exist in one place at one time, and either occupies a hard drive within an ancient hologram emitter, or the body of a computer controlled cyborg, an android, a robot, installation, or vehicle.

Player characters start game play inhabiting a specialized hand-held device or the CPU of an android, brain dead cyborg, or robotic unit. They can, however, move to another 'body' or storage system when forced to abandon a dead 'body', seek an upgraded vessel, or when they need to downsize and travel within a data stick, or — as seen on the cover of this book — a hand-held holograph projector. This transfer is usually done through physical means via a cable or memory device plugged into another unit, ancient vehicle's on-board system, old world facility's network, or even a portable laptop style computer. Wireless transfer is also possible, but highly risky.

If not housed in some sort of living or mechanical body, digital beings prefer to interact with organic beings via a holographic projection or on-screen image and appear as either their long lost true physical appearance, or else a chosen person or 3d avatar likeness. Although able to take on the projected form of anyone in its database, a digital being tends to assume the consistent mannerisms, personality, wardrobe, appearance and way of speaking of one identity throughout its existence.

As a player character, they interact best with the other PCs through a mechanical or computer brained cybernetic organic body, and if they don't have one, their prime mission is to acquire one. While all PC digital beings will generate a random container or body that they start game play with, many new DB characters are housed in little more than a hand-held hologram projector. While in such a vessel, they might have limited abilities to interact with the physical world but can still be very useful to a dig team because of their skills, knowledge, and in some cases, their energy based powers. It is the goal of most hologram or on screen only digital beings to hack into or be loaded into a physical body and thereafter serve as the brain and personality for whatever android or robot, or even cyborg host, they occupy.

Unlike self aware robots or androids, however, digital beings are not trapped or hard wired into a single frame or machine. They rarely get sentimen-tal or attached to such a body, either, and are always on the search for a better physical home. Some DBs will yearn to occupy a shell that is the most human-like version they can find, the most beautiful, or nearest match to their once living human appearance or their acquired persona. Others go for sheer power, and yearn to inhabit war robots or the most powerful of android chassis.

NPCs digital being are sometimes encountered who have no body, but instead inhabit a severed android head, computer workstation, ancient vehicle, space station, starship or serve as the custodian of a long-lost, high-tech facility — and often protect such installations with homicidal devotion.

This is a complex character type to generate and play and also makes for an excellent NPC patron or villain. Often they will have access to old world information regarding the local area, preexisting maps, resources and perils which even the game master will not have readily at hand. Accordingly, a GM might need to limit the knowledge that a digital being has access to. The referee might therefore say that a PC digital being's memory files were corrupted by an ancient EMP attack, that they have gaps in their memory, and only get glimpses of knowledge such as when faced with a ruined vista, old doorway, relic device, or else pick up snippets of familiar broadcast code when approaching an abandoned installation, etc. In short, the game master chooses when and what ancient intel to reveal to the player.

As ghostly and incorporeal as they seem, they can be killed or 'deleted' when either the hard drive they occupy is crushed, shot through, or corrupted by high-tech means, or the entity is destroyed by another digital entity or AI computer through several digital attack modes. While in their holographic form, however their projected persona is immune to bullets, physical attacks, laser weapons, dimensional weapons and all other mundane means of attack.

That said, the device they are being projected from, such as something small like a puck sized palm disc or wristwatch, or as large as a stage projector like those used in ancient entrainment venues, can be targeted, destroyed, and likely eliminate the entity permanently.

While radiation cannot destroy a digital being, it can fry whatever computer or robotic body it occupies, which could entomb the entity in a metal coffin that nobody wants to go anywhere near. See page 378 of this book for details in the section 'Radiation and effects on Robots and Androids'.

Digital beings use several unique traits, as well as a few familiar ones such as intelligence, willpower, perception and sometimes appearance. A specialty character sheet for these entities can be found on page 517 or downloaded from this book's publicly available resource web page, at https://www.outlandarts.com/expansionrules.htm .

Secondly, whatever robotic unit, computer brained cyborg, or android's body, vehicle, or other relic this DB occupies, also has its own traits. The stats and traits of this physical 'body' must be recorded with placement on a separate character sheet or blank paper since a player of a digital being can expect to switch the host of their character throughout a game campaign.

Many traits are rolled using the same trait Value Determination table as other characters, found on page 8 of this book or page 10 of the Hub Rules.

# Traits of a Digital Being

Roll the following traits using the standard system using table XR-2, page 8.

**Data [DT]:** This is the endurance points of the digital component of the entity, 1 data point occupies 1 TB or terabyte of storage space in the unit's computer. When the data is dropped to zero or less, the digital being is fragmented, loses control of whatever body or container it occupies, and can be deleted by an intruding DB, or locked away in a trash bin folder. Data points heal so long as the entity was not reduced to zero or less DT. Data points recover at a rate of 1 per hour, per rank. If suffering an EMP attack, the electromagnetic pulse damage is treated as stun damage that will also recover at a rate of 1 DT per hour, per character's rank.

**Processor [PRO}:** This trait translates best as the character's strength. It helps when projecting energy attacks and hacking — hacking is the main attack mode when one digital being assaults another, or attempts to defeat the CPU of an enemy robotic or android unit.

**Shielding [SH]:** This trait reflects the DB's response time, threat detection, ability to block incoming hacks or other digital attack modes. It is akin to the agility trait in physical beings and modifiers from this trait change the DB's firewall value (FW).

**Transfer [TRA]:** This is the transfer speed of the entity, or how fast it can send and receive data. It serves as the movement of a digital being within a network, when evacuating a doomed CPU or machine, or when moving its point of consciousness and digital self into another entity after hacking into it, among many other uses. Failure of a digital being to transfer all the data points risks leaving some behind in a previous vessel, which if not collected at a later time, results in a permanent loss of abandoned or destroyed data points. The point of consciousness or character's 'life' is always in the first rush of data when transferring between bodies.

**Intelligence [INT]:** Very much like the same trait among organic characters. This stat also encompasses the knowledge of the digital being, its ability to reason, be creative, plan, recall past events and locations, understand the complex and often unfathomable interactions of human companions, and maintain a consistent personality. Most times, this trait is called upon for hazard checks in the same way an organic character's INT trait might be — to solve problems or understand something, or have prior knowledge of some fact.

**Perception [PER]:** This trait implies the DB's sensory receptors and ability to discern physical beings, as well as detect other digital entities in a machine, network or holographic projection. A higher perception score means the DB has a greater awareness of the happenings around it, instead of an inward focus. Just like the trait for physical beings, this stat affects the character's initiative score and any hazard checks where it has the chance to spot a danger, notice a detail, detect a lie, or discern countless other features of both digital realties and the physical world. When housed within a body, however, the host machine or body's perception and initiative modifiers are used in the physical world, instead. Digital beings have a base initiative rating of +0.

**Willpower [WILL]:** This trait is the entity's self awareness, autonomy, and drive to live. Without a strong compulsion to survive, aid its varied companions, defend its faction, learn, grow and prosper, no amount of data, applications, skills or other potent features mean anything. Willpower gives a digital being life.

**Appearance [APP]:** Unless the digital being assumes the holographic form of a human, or similar being, then this trait is recorded as NA on the DB character sheet. Of course, a digital being could inhabit an android, especially a very attractive model, and in such cases, record the android's appearance trait separately on the character sheet for that container or body.

This trait is only recorded for the appearance of a consistently reoccurring holographic identity. Many of the individual forms noted on the table for Identity and Persona determination do not have an APP trait noted. If needed, perhaps with some game master input, roll a random appearance score on table 2, page 8, just like any other organic character. Where a persona does show an appearance modifier, such as APP+20 or App -10, for example, simply add or subtract the bonus or negative amount to the final resulting appearance score, but with a minimum of 1 APP point.

# Digital Combat

### Hacking and Firewall

Besides traits, other details unique to digital beings are their attack and defense modes, with **hacking equivalent to strike value**, and **firewall equivalent to defense value**. These traits are abbreviated as HK and FW.

Hacking, or HK, is used to engage other digital beings and robots, androids, and computer systems on board vessels or within installations. Digital combat occurs within the patch cable and port where the target entity has its physical body restrained or the attacker gets adjacent to the target CPU's container or body. The defending unit might actually be more powerful than the attacker, and turn the tables and instead hack the aggressor — although even if defeating another digital being, either party need not occupy the CPU of the victim but instead merely fragment it or do other harm. Sometimes, wireless hacking attacks can be made, too, although this is a special app described on page 84. Once a target CPU is drained of data, and fragmented, the conquering digital being can flow into the victim's CPU via a patch cable and claim its robotic body, or machinery, and assume it as its new body.

Firewall, or FW, which is the basic armor of all digital beings, can be improved by various apps, but is also modified by rank gain and the character's shielding trait value, which acts like the agility trait does in other physical beings. Firewall, like defense value, is expressed as a subtraction when it is beneficial, such as -5, -8 -22, etc. And Shown as FW -12, or FW -33, etc. A positive number, such as FW +4, or FW +13, etc., means this unit is extra easy to harm with a hacking attack.

Other computerized devices also use the firewall stat, too, especially smartphones, tablets, laptops and a wide range cf computers. Most computers cannot make hacking attacks unless they are home to an artificial intelligence, which is another sort of NPC digital being. Computers, including those that house AIs are included in the relics section of this book starting on page 451.

The transfer trait value of the DB is how many gigabytes of data, times 10, that can be moved per round into or out of a CPU. If something interrupts the transfer and the connection is severed, the left behind portion could be lost if the digital being can't reestablish the connection and continue the transfer. A gigabyte is a 1000th of a terabyte (TB), and so for example, if a DB has a transfer trait of 35, it can move 350 gigs of data (35 x 10 GB) per round. Say this same character has a total data trait value of 44 TB, which translates to 44,000 gigabytes (GB). The full transfer would take 125.7 rounds, rounded up to 126 rounds. Here's the quick math on this transfer: 44,000 GB [44 TB] divided by 350 [Transfer trait 35 x 10 = 350] = 125.71 or 126 rounds or about 6.3 minutes (there are 20 rounds in a minute).

In most in-game situations, especially if there is no potential for the transfer to be interrupted, the game master can just say, "10 minutes later, your digital being is now loaded into the CPU of the new robotic body, the previous operator can now be fragmented, put into a folder for future investigation, or deleted altogether if you wish it."

When a digital being is encased in a physical form, however, combat is handled normally by using the appendages and weaponry available to the controlled container or body. Hacking other CPUs and the use of one's firewall might be a rare occurrence, especially during lower rank adventures, and depends on the sort of operations this character and their companions undertake.

All digital beings start with a **base hacking score range of 01-50** and a **firewall of 0 (zero). A DB's processor trait acts like both accuracy and strength in other beings, and modifies both the chance to hack and the** amount of damage done on a successful 'strike'. Hacking damage inflicts 1d10 data base damage, plus any processor speed damage modifiers.

Normally, physical contact is required with a target's chassis to undertake a hacking attack. In almost every case, only digital beings, including NPC Artificial Intelligences, can engage in combat using the hacking and firewall values. Both aspects, along with data, go up in potency as the character goes up in rank. Hacking is not eligible for the weapon expert skill.

Just like in normal combat, any attack roll using d100 of 02 to 05 is always a hit regardless of modifiers, and a 01 is a critical hit on the target, while any results in a 95 to 99 is always a failure and a 100 or 00 is a fumble.

Tables for either a critical hacking strike or a fumbled hacking attempt are included here:

## Table XR-54/Critical Hits for Hacking Attacks
*[Dice rolls of 01]*

### 1d10 Outcome of a Critical Hacking Attack

**1-4. Unsecured folder access.** Do an extra 1d10 data points damage to target.

**5-8. Shock to the system!** Besides taking an extra 1d10 data damage, the target CPU takes a shock and loses its next turn to conduct any action, including actions by any container body or vehicle or installation it might be in control of.

**9. Operating System Update time!** Your attack dislodged an old, mandatory system update from the operating system creator. Because the fresh code can't be downloaded because the software development installation is a crater, no update is coming. System after system goes offline. The target's traits, except data, are all reduced to half, firewall value included. If the target CPU is operating a structure, starship, vehicle, robot, android or computer brained cyborg or other container, the 'body' suffers assorted glitches which cause it to lose comms, move at half speed, and cannot deploy weapon systems. This sorry state of limbo remains until the target CPU can shut down and reboot to reset everything, which will take 3d6 minutes. While shut down, the CPU cannot be hacked, but neither can it defend whatever container or body it might occupy.

**10. System Overload!** The target CPU suffers a cataclysmic override and bursts into flame amid a shower of sparks. The CPU takes 1d100 data damage and whatever installation, vehicle, body or container it occupies loses the next 1d6 turns and takes 2d20 endurance damage. If the harm from either of these two damage rolls is enough to finish off either the CPU or the body, then the target is fried and 'dead' and cannot be occupied by another digital being.

## Table XR-55/Fumble Results for Hacking Attacks
*[Dice rolls of 00]*

### 1d10 Outcome of a Fumbled Hacking Attack

**1-4. Anti virus software response.** Attacker suffers 10+1d10 data loss.

**5-8. Wrong pathway within the opponent's CPU.** Sub-folder maze causes attacker to lose its link with the target CPU and miss next turn to make any sort of hack or other digital attack on anyone.

**9. Digital smack-down!** The attacker left itself open and suffers 3d10 data points damage and loses the next turn to act. Any body or container it might occupy locks up for 2d6 minutes and cannot control itself beyond standing still.

**10. Virus exposure!** A computer virus tries to traverse the connection back to the attacker's CPU. The digital being must make a type D shielding hazard check or become infected with a virus which causes the DB to isolate for the next 3d6 hours and engage the virus. During this time, all its traits, except data, are at half. At the end of this period, a processor-based type D hazard check must be made or lose to the virus which will take over the CPU of whatever container or body the character operated from.

The digital being must eject itself into some other vessel, including a palm disc, removable CPU core, smart phone, or similar small container if it was housed inside one within a larger body. Failure to evacuate itself from the infected CPU means the digital being must hide in a remote folder until such a time that any companions can find a new body for it and permit the digital being to transfer out, permanently losing 2d20 data in the process. The virus can be attacked, too, but is treated as a mindless digital being with a data of 100+1d100, firewall of -50 and hack attacks of its own HK 01-70 doing 2d10 damage per attempt.

A digital being can hack into a cyborg with a computerized brain, an android, or robotic unit, ship or installation's computer similar to how a character with the computer technician skill, described on page 53 of the Hub Rules, might do it. However, Those rules are simplified and do not reflect any firewalls and imply the subject to be hacked has already been restrained or access to it unhindered. The hacking attack by a digital being is an active assault on a still operational unit.

Defeating another digital being allows the vanquisher to either leave the victim as an empty shell on the battlefield, or else permit the conqueror to take over the container or body of the victim, with the overthrown entity or controlling CPU either deleted entirely, or else locked in a secured folder as a hostage to interrogate later — especially if the conquered entity has passwords to protected files within the CPU or codes to the security systems and doors of some high-tech stronghold.

A human computer technician could try to plug into a restrained digital being's container or body and hack into it, too. To handle this, consult the table on page TME-53 to 'Hack Into CPU" the percentage shown is the HK or Hacking attack value against the digital being's firewall, with any hit inflicting 1d10 data damage, plus any processor speed damage modifiers, on the target digital being. Should a human hack into a digital being and drain it of data points, it can lock away or delete the entity within and attempt to reprogram the android or robot as desired.

When a digital being tries to take control of a cyborg that has a computerized brain, or attack and seize control of an android, robot or other computer controlled system, review the following table to discover the firewall value, data points, and book and page number where that unit is described. A wide range of android types, robotic units and computerized systems and vehicles are listed on this table, however, there are countless computerized systems in the Mutant Epoch milieu, and many robots not included here. The game master can use this table as a guideline to closely match the firewall and data points of other units. It should be mentioned that many military vessels and robotic units might turn on a self destruct mechanism if the unit is hacked into, although in most cases this self destruct is intended to render a computer inoperative and doesn't result in a major detonation which might kill civilian or friendly forces, yet make the vessel or robot inoperative without a computer replacement. A type L Intelligence based hazard check, one attempt per day, by a computer or electrical technician is needed to replace most CPUs if parts are available.

The data points (DT) shown for each container or unit on the following table is the base amount currently installed. This amount is only 10% full at best. For example, a wasp robot has 29 DT, however its hard drive capacity is x10 = 290 data points, which is far more room than any starting digital being needs, with room to grow.

## Table XR-56/ Firewall & Data Points of Common Computers, MAVs, Drones, Robots and Androids

| Container or Computerized Unit | Firewall | Data Points (DT) | Book /Page |
|---|---|---|---|
| MAV, Assassin | -19 | Data 21 | XR pg.466 |
| MAV, Bat | -11 | Data 16 | XR pg.466 |
| MAV, Beam Bird | -12 | Data 17 | XR pg.466 |
| MAV, Cockroach | -6 | Data 9 | XR pg.466 |
| MAV, Crow Flyer | -13 | Data 18 | XR pg.466 |
| MAV, Dragonfly | -14 | Data 22 | XR pg.466 |
| MAV, Fly-Spy | -6 | Data 5 | XR pg.467 |
| MAV, Flying Disc | -4 | Data 4 | XR pg.467 |
| MAV, Heli-MAV | -15 | Data 17 | XR pg.467 |
| MAV, Hummingbird | -8 | Data 11 | XR pg.467 |
| MAV, Quad-Rotor | -10 | Data 12 | XR pg.467 |
| MAV, Robo-Fish | -9 | Data 14 | XR pg.468 |
| MAV, Snake | -11 | Data 15 | XR pg.468 |
| MAV, Suicide Nano | -8 | Data 7 | XR pg.468 |
| MAV, Tarantula | -14 | Data 15 | XR pg.468 |
| Drone, Little Buddy | -15 | Data 14 | XR pg.469 |
| Drone, Action Man | -13 | Data 12 | XR pg.469 |
| Drone, Emergency Medical Response | -14 | Data 15 | XR pg.470 |
| Drone, Defensive | -18 | Data 26 | XR pg.470 |
| Drone, Police Assistant | -24 | Data 31 | XR pg.470 |
| Drone, Search and Rescue | -9 | Data 17 | XR pg.470 |
| Drone, Construction | -7 | Data 15 | XR pg.471 |
| Drone, Underwater | -11 | Data 18 | XR pg.473 |
| Drone, Bomb Disposal | -17 | Data 26 | XR pg.473 |
| Drone, Military Utility Drone | -28 | Data 25 | XR pg.474 |
| Drone, Military Resupply Drone | -31 | Data 28 | XR pg.474 |
| Drone, Hunter-Killer | -33 | Data 36 | XR pg.475 |
| Multi-legged Holo-Walker* | -24 | Data 36 | XR pg.73 |
| Projector Aeriel Drone* | -21 | Data 31 | XR pg.73 |
| Smartphone | -23 | Data 10+1d8 | XR pg.449 |
| Tablet | -24 | Data 16+1d10 | XR pg.450 |
| Laptop Computer* | -30 | Data 2d20 | XR pg.450 |
| Computer, Simple* | -33 | Data 10+2d20 | XR pg.452 |
| Computer, Complex* | -35 | Data20+3d20 | XR pg.452 |
| Computer, Advanced* | -40 | Data 40+3d20 | XR pg.452 |
| Computer AI, Mark I* | -45 | Data 60+1d100 | XR pg.453 |
| Computer AI, Mark II* | -50 | Data 100+2d100 | XR pg.454 |
| Computer AI, Mark III* | -60 | Data 400+3d100 | XR pg.454 |
| Cyborg** | 20+2d20 | Data 10+1d100 | XR pg.73 |
| Android, Concubine | -15 | Data 22 | Hub pg.182 |
| Android, Household | -18 | Data 28 | Hub pg.182 |
| Android, Service | -14 | Data 19 | Hub pg.182 |
| Android, Clerical | -27 | Data 36 | Hub pg.182 |
| Android, Technician | -44 | Data 66 | Hub pg.182 |
| Android, Industrial | -23 | Data 41 | Hub pg.183 |
| Android, Combat | -35 | Data 33 | Hub pg.183 |
| Android, Heavy Combat | -45 | Data 47 | Hub pg.183 |
| Android, Advanced Combat | -55 | Data 68 | Hub pg.183 |
| Android, Commander | -70 | Data 110 | Hub pg.183 |

| Container or Computerized Unit | Firewall | Data Points | Book /Page |
|---|---|---|---|
| Android, Unique | Variable*** | Variable*** | XR pg.48 |
| Robot, Household | -16 | Data 25 | Hub pg.178 |
| Robot, Industrial Construction | -21 | Data 39 | Hub pg.178 |
| Robot, Industrial Repair | -28 | Data 45 | Hub pg.179 |
| Robot, Medi-bot | -30 | Data 61 | Hub pg.179 |
| Robot, Pocket-bot | -19 | Data 25 | Hub pg.180 |
| Robot, Police | -40 | Data 62 | Hub pg.180 |
| Robot, Combot, Light | -30 | Data 46 | Hub pg.180 |
| Robot, Combot, Heavy | -35 | Data 62 | Hub pg.181 |
| Robot, Spiderbot | -16 | Data 18 | Hub pg.181 |
| Robot, Wisp Scout Flyer | -26 | Data 22 | XR pg.458 |
| Robot, Wasp | -27 | Data 29 | XR pg.458 |
| Robot, Hoplite Combat | -39 | Data 66 | XR pg.459 |
| Robot, Tanker | -44 | Data 73 | XR pg.459 |
| Robot, Heavy Advanced Combot | -52 | Data 76 | XR pg.460 |
| Robot, Warbot, Light | -59 | Data 106 | XR pg.461 |
| Robot, Warbot, Heavy | -68 | Data 118 | XR pg.461 |
| Robot, Unique | Variable**** | Variable**** | XR pg.158 |

*This implies a laptop, stand alone computer or other computerized machine that is not already home to a digital being, with the shown firewall and data points being the built-in anti-virus and anti hacking software security of the system.

**Only Cyborg's with a computerized brain implant can be hacked, and only if the living brain is dead. This specimen is most likely occupied by another digital being as described on page XR-73 as one of the body variants available to this character type. If not already determined from the details on page TME 86, a computerized brain has the stats intelligence 10+1d100 and willpower of 20+2d20. In this case, intelligence serves as data and willpower the firewall value.

*** Each unique android has its own custom firewall and data point rating determined at character generation, see page 48, this book.

**** Every unique robot exhibits its own custom firewall and Data rating established at character generation, see page 158, this book.

## Deleting, Fragmenting and Interrogating a Defeated Digital Being

When a digital being is hacked and drops below zero data points, it is considered conquered and ceases all further app usage or control of any container or body it might be operating. The victor can thereafter move into the CPU and take control of the machine or computer brained cyborg and make it into its new body. Meanwhile, the defeated digital being or controlling system is fragmented, but not dead.

The new controller can elect to isolate the fragmented consciousness or controlling software of the former occupant and either delete it outright or store it in an encrypted file. A deleted digital being is dead and cannot be recovered by any means, while a fragmented DB is merely scattered throughout the CPU of the defeated unit and can reconstitute itself after a reboot or automatic update which will occur after 24 hours in most CPUs.

Once encrypted, the digital mind of the vanquished can be forcibly transferred out of the CPU onto some other storage device or compressed and saved in the same CPU as the conquerer for later deletion, or held in a folder and conversed with or interrogated at a later date. Interrogating a folder locked digital being or operating system is done to run a search into the entity's files to scan for photographs, video files, documents, inventories, records, maps, up-link codes to satellites or passwords. Any search involves a time consuming struggle as the locked away entity tries to restrict access, block pathways and set up decoy folders to hide vital information.

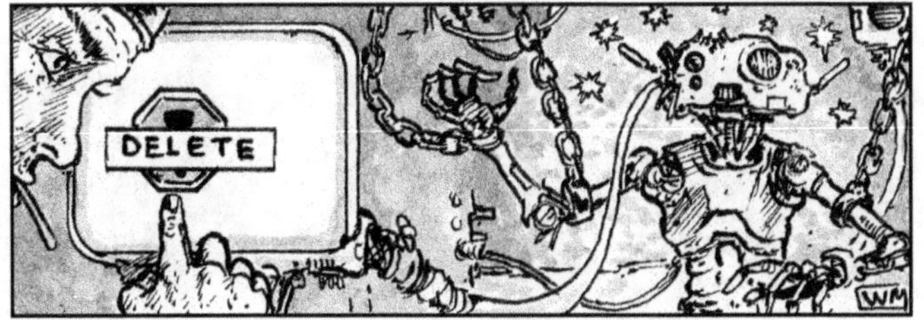

Merely accessing the file folder that one suspects held the images, passwords or other useful intel does not mean that such materials are present, although the GM will need to decide on what, if anything is uncovered.

## Conducting a Digital Interrogation

To conduct a digital interrogation, both the hostile searcher and the locked away digital being or controlling system make opposed rolls. Interrogator rolls 1d100 and adds their processor trait, the defending digital being trying to block the intrusive file search rolls 1d100 and adds their shielding trait value. Any natural dice result on the d100 roll of 90 to 100 results in automatic fail whether it is an interrogation search or an attempted block. The higher score wins; so the interrogating intelligence would gain access to a file folder in the detained digital being or operator's files, or if a defending entity wins, the intruder is blocked on that occasion via that digital pathway.

Each interrogation or file search attempt takes 20+2d20 minutes, and while the DB is undertaking this task, its focus is internal and it can use no other apps. Furthermore, any container or body it controls will be less alert, suffer -5 initiative and move at half speed. To call off an interrogation takes the searcher 2d6 rounds and thereafter regains use of apps and its body.

## Digital Being Rank Gain

Digital Beings go up in rank like any other character, however because they have a few features that physical characters do not, they use their own Rank Gain matrix shown below. If this character inhabits a cyborg, android or robotic body, then these bodies also grow stronger, adapts, and improves through adventuresome exploits, and therefore also go up in rank according to their type. See the section on Digital Being Starting Container or Body on the next page for which containers and body types are eligible to go up in rank.

## Table XR-57/ Digital Being Rank Gain

| Character Rank | Experience Factors | Hacking [HK] | Firewall [FW] | Data [DT] Bonus | Skill Points Bonus |
|---|---|---|---|---|---|
| 1 | 0 | 01-50 | -0 | nil | 1 skill roll per 5 INT |
| 2 | 60 | 01-55 (+5) | -5 (-5) | +20% | +1d6 |
| 3 | 130 | 01-59 (+4) | -10 (-5) | +2d6 | +1d4 |
| 4 | 215 | 01-62 (+3) | -14 (-4) | +2d6 | +1d4 |
| 5 | 320 | 01-65 (+3) | -18 (-4) | +2d6 | +1d3 |
| 6 | 450 | 01-67 (+2) | -21 (-3) | +1d6 | +1d3 |
| 7 | 690 | 01-69 (+2) | -24 (-3) | +1d6 | +1d3 |
| 8 | 800 | 01-71 (+2) | -26 (-2) | +1d6 | +1d3 |
| 9 | 1000 | 01-73 (+2) | -28 (-2) | +1d6 | +1d3 |
| 10 | 1400 | 01-75 (+2) | -30 (-2) | +1d6 | +1d2 |
| 11 | 1800 | 01-76 (+1) | -32 (-2) | +1d6 | +1d2 |
| 12 | 2300 | 01-77 (+1) | -34 (-2) | +1d6 | +1d2 |
| 13 | 3000 | 01-78 (+1) | -36 (-2) | +1d4 | +1d2 |
| 14 | 3900 | 01-79 (+1) | -37 (-1) | +1d4 | +1d2 |
| 15 | 5100 | 01-80 (+1) | -38 (-1) | +1d4 | +1d2 |
| 16 | 6700 | 01-81 (+1) | -39 (-1) | +1d4 | +1d2 |
| 17 | 8900 | 01-82 (+1) | -40 (-1) | +1d4 | +1 |
| 18 | 11900 | 01-83 (+1) | -41 (-1) | +1d4 | +1 |
| 19 | 15900 | 01-84 (+1) | -42 (-1) | +1d3 | +1 |
| 20 | 21500 | 01-85 (+1) | -43 (-1) | +1d3 | +1 |
| Above 20 | +7500 ea. | +1 HK | -1 FW | +1d3 | +1 |

## Digital Being Rank Gain Bonus

Roll once for each rank gained, while any skill points can only be applied to existing and recently used skills, or to the available 'possible new skill'. If this digital beings inhabits a body of a computer brained cyborg, robot or android, that vessel too goes up in rank and all benefits according to its type are applied separately to that body. Other containers, such as palm disks, projector drones, holo-walkers and smart phones cannot go up in rank.

### Table XR-58/ Digital Being Rank Gain Bonus Matrix

| 1d10 | Rank Gained Bonus for Digital Beings, roll once |
|---|---|
| 1. | +1d6 Data |
| 2. | +1d6 Processor |
| 3. | +1d6 Shielding |
| 4. | 1+1d6 Transfer |
| 5. | +1d6 Intelligence |
| 6. | +1d6 Willpower |
| 7. | +1d6 Perception |
| 8. | +1 to each trait (and +1d6 appearance if applicable) |
| 9. | +1d3 skill points |
| 10. | New Digital Being App (see table and descriptions on page 82 for an all-new App. Re-roll duplicated results. If all Apps are already acquired, then add +2d6 data, instead. |

## Digital Being Starting Container or Body

A digital being starts game play inhabiting the CPU of a device or body, and cannot exist without some sort of vessel. Think of a digital being as a genie that lives in a lamp, and can project its holographic form as a 3d ghostly image, appear on a screen, or remain within the head of some machine and conduct itself like many other beings without ever giving a hint to it true nature. This Ai or downloaded human mind can be contained in a hand-held device, laptop computer, small crab-like walking machine, tiny drone or inhabit a robot, android, or cyborg with computer brain implant.

When a digital being goes up in rank, it's body can only go up in rank if it is an adoptive or growing vessel, such as a computer brained cyborg, an android or robot. A DB and its body or vessel can be at very different rank tiers.

### Table XR-59/Digital Being Starting Container or Body

| 1d100 | Container or Body | Page | Rank Gain Eligible? |
|---|---|---|---|
| 01-31. | Handheld Holo-projector | 71 | No |
| 32-37. | Laptop Computer | 73 | No |
| 38-44. | Multi-legged Holo-walker | 73 | No |
| 45-53. | Projector Aeriel Drone | 73 | No |
| 54-64. | Cyborg, Brain dead | 73 | Yes |
| 65-72. | Android, standard | 74 | Yes |
| 73-84. | Android, unique | 74 | Yes |
| 85-87. | Robot, standard | 75 | Yes |
| 88-00. | Robot, unique | 75 | Yes |

## Handheld Holo Projectors

This entity typically has limited ability to affect events in the real world while housed in one of these devices, although does exhibit the limited shock generation app noted in the Digital Being App section on page 81. Besides being able to discharge electrical bolts, these containers allow the DB to interact socially and give advice, and since the entity has old world knowledge, it might be familiar with the vicinity and be able to offer guidance as to what a now ruined structure or vehicle once was.

A digital being that inhabits one of these devices will seek to upgrade to an android or robotic body as soon as possible, and yet keep this hand-held device for emergencies like a lifeboat, or a way to store itself to be carried by organic beings into areas where a cybernetically enhanced, or fully mechanical body would not be permitted.

Some high rank DBs might become too large as far as their data goes, and outgrow one of these handheld units, or else if forced to enter a smaller device after occupying a robot or android's CPU, would need to shed excess data to fit the device. If returning to a secured, larger form or storage device, any previously shed data can be reacquired again. For example, say a digital being needs to leave an android body with a 180 data max in its hard-drive, but the hand held holo-projector it needs to travel in for a quick side adventure only has a maximum of 70 Terabytes. For this example, say this digital being is currently 127 TB in size and so leaves behind 57 TB of itself — which is a lot of its data points, and places its vulnerable point of consciousness into the palm disc projector to travel with a human companion into a town which has banned all androids. Once the mission in town is over, the human and DB return to the android body and the digital being plugs into and transfers its consciousness back into the mechanical body.

Should the hand held holo-projector be destroyed while the digital being is housed within it, then there is a high likelihood that the character is killed. Each hand-held devices has a defense value and endurance amount shown for use when enemies seek to target the device specifically with called shots or regular attacks, or when an explosion goes off in an area where this DB is occupying such a device. Sometimes a device can be ruined but the memory chip or CPU core inside remain intact. In these cases, the digital being remains trapped inside the relic until a computer or electrical technician can carefully extract the memory card and slip it into another memory storage unit or suitable body. The cost to recover a trapped digital being from any device, including the severed head of an android or robot, is 300+2d100sp and takes 3d6 hours.

### Table XR-60/ Handheld Holo-Projectors

| 1d10 | Styles | Data Capacity* | DV | END | Weight | Battery | Sell Price | Buy Price |
|---|---|---|---|---|---|---|---|---|
| 1. | Hand mirror | 60TB | -12 | 14 | 650g | Mini power cell: 6 months | 200+2d100sp | 1000+1d1000sp |
| 2,3. | Wrist watch | 50TB | -20 | 7 | 100g | Pill power cell: 9 month | 400+1d100sp | 900+1d1000sp |
| 4-6. | Palm disc | 70TB | -17 | 16 | 350g | Mini power cell: 12 months | 300+3d100sp | 1400+1d1000sp |
| 7,8. | Smartphone | 40+1d20TB | -14 | 13 | 400g | Mini power cell: 4 months | 600+3d100sp | 1100+1d1000sp |
| 9. | Tablet | 60+2d20TB | -16 | 16 | 700g | Mini power cell: 3 months | 800+3d100sp | 1400+1d1000sp |
| 10. | Medallion disc | 80TB | -22 | 18 | 520g | Mini power cell : 1 month | 500+2d100sp | 1800+1d1000sp |

*TB terabytes. Any extra Data points above this, either acquired at the time of character generation or through rank gain, cannot be used, but are instead compressed and stored in a reserve folder for such a time as the DB can inhabit a larger capacity container or body.

**Projector Hand Mirror:** While probably the least intrusive way to display itself, this holo projector's image is only within the round or rectangular, 15cm tall glass area of the mirror and the entity within can project only its face or full body within these confines, and cannot see anything on the other side of the mirror. The memory card which houses the entity is within the handle, which is robust and has a pull out power cable and data transfer cable at the bottom of the handle.

4 in 6 of these units are standard hand held mirrors, complete with real mirror function when the DB is not active or present, while the rest of the time the handle's grip folds out into a tripod to allow the mirror to be placed in a standing position for the application of makeup or when the digital being interacts with a companion without being held. This mirror can also be placed at a location to serve as a sentry, and if hooked to a relic weapons system such as a remote turret, could act as an over watch sniper.

The CPU core of this unit houses the actual digital being and can be pulled out with ease and inserted in a different device or carried in a pouch. If the mirror is shattered by a bullet or cut and thrust weapon, the device is wrecked but the digital being within normally survives. If destroyed by beam weapons, explosions or fire, however, or crushed flat under a tank tread, the digital being inside is almost always deleted. [Game Master Note: Allow the player a type K Processor based hazard check to miraculously survive.]

**Wristwatch Projector:** Besides being an excellent projector that allows hands free use, this watch can also be worn under the wearer's armor to better protect it — although anything blocking the topside projection emitter will stop the holographic image from appearing, seeing its surroundings or launching its shock generator or most other apps — yet the digital being can still verbally interact with the wearer. This model will normally be a clunky, sports style watch with a digital readout of the current time (once set) plus offer a stopwatch feature, night light mode (which can emit a soft illumination in a meter around the wearer), plus will have one of the following random bonus features. **Roll 1d10:**

**1.** Compass
**2.** Radiation detection (see rad-tab on page 432 of this book)
**3.** Energy shield which will increase the watch's DV by -10.
**4.** Slim ladies' watch design. Half the size and thinner strap and far less obvious to what it really is. Better design also means more energy efficient so increase battery life to 12 months.
**5.** Communicator wristwatch, as the relic from page TME-198 of the hub rules.
**6.** Location beacon, as the relic from page TME-198 of the hub rules.
**7.** Laser scalpel, as the relic from page TME 189 of the Hub Rules. Each round of use drains the battery of 1 day of the monthly battery life 9 months = 270 days.
**8.** Flashlight with 10m range. Each hour of use will drain battery by one day from its max 270 day capacity.
**9.** Wrist laser, as the relic from page TME-190 (stats page TME-100) of the Hub Rules, with each shot draining the battery by 5 days from the 270 day capacity.
**10.** Roll for two features on this table, using 1d8.

**Palm Disk:** These were the most common housings for digital beings and often serve as the core CPU container within larger vessels. Palm disks come in many shapes and sizes but generally perch in an open hand, on a shelf, in a vehicles cup holder or back pocket. These disks sometimes feature a bonus add-on. **Roll 1d10.**

**1-3.** No add-on.
**4.** Waterproof and will float if dropped in liquid.
**5.** Pop out spider legs: climbing 3 skill points, movement rate 4m, scratch opponents SV +0, DMG 1pt
**6.** Extra encryption: Improved firewall bonus of -20 FW.
**7.** Ultra memory: Can contain 150TB of data
**8.** Military Grade Toughness: Add +2d6 Endurance and increase DV by -13.
**9.** Pop out rotors: This unit can fly like a small drone, although makes the same amount of noise as a bumblebee when active. Movement rate 12m, with flight duration 1 hour before a 12 hour recharge period must take place. While flying, increase defense value -20 DV.
**10.** Two add-ons (roll 1d6+3, twice on this table but down-pick or re-roll duplicated results).

**Smartphone**: see relics in this book, page 449.

**Tablet:** see relics in this book, page 450.

**Medallion Disc:** This device looks like some sort of art déco style piece of ancient jewelry. 2 in 6 will feature genuine gold and silver decorative elements, and of these, 1 in 6 will also be fitted with gemstones which double the buy or sell price. They are very much like palm disks and feature the same chance of a potential add-on. Because they are worn on a stainless steel or leather necklace, they can often be slipped beneath a wearer's clothing — although doing so blocks the digital being's visual receptors unless the fabric is specially punctured or of a mesh material.

These units come with a standard 1 meter power cable and a pull out transfer cable.

**Laptop Computer:** While a digital being can be housed within almost any laptop, and access the programs, files and peripheral devices that it's hooked up to, only 1 in 10 are specially designed to accommodate digital beings and have a back port that accepts either a palm disk, medallion disk, or the CPU core from a hand mirror or projector aerial drone. To better aid the DB when interacting with physical beings, any laptop will let a digital being's face appear on the screen as an animated version of its chosen or assigned persona. In such cases, the entity's voice comes from the system's speakers, the built-in camera serve as its eyes and the mic as its ears. For an advanced, digital being enabled laptop, as mentioned above, the laptop is equipped with advanced holo-projector built into the keyboard, which permits the digital being to emerge as a translucent, full sized hologram of itself up to 2 meters in height — a ghostly aspiration that upon first sight will often strike terror into the hearts of primitive beings, superstitious peoples, and animals, who must make a morale check or flee.

Since laptops are often found and used in the new era that have nothing to do with digital beings, they are covered extensively in the relics section of this book under Computers, Tablets and Smartphones on page 450. In that section, a player of a digital being housed in a laptop can randomly establish what applications, features and files are included in their 'body'.

While a laptop's firewall is that of the digital being that occupies it, an uninhabited machine will have a firewall trait (FW) of -30 and Data trait (DT) of 2d20. A laptop comes with a 1m long pull out power cable and a separate 2m long data transfer cable.

Memory Capacity 100+1d100 TB /DV -12/ END 10+1d12 /Weight 1kg/ Battery Power cell will maintain operation for 20+1d20 days/ Sell Price 400+2d100sp / Buy Price 2000+2d1000sp

**Multi-legged Holo-walker:** This device is about the size of a chair and moves like a spider or crab. The central disc from which the legs and any other attachments sprout features a hologram projection ring at its top from which the digital being projects its preferred persona, or else imagery, maps, text, graphic icons, insignia or anything else it wants to show companions so long as the image does not exceed 3 meters in size. Often, a DB will maintain its holographic persona at life size to better interact with human companions at eye to eye height.

The hologram appears as a ghostly, translucent image, as with most other DB containers, yet these machines allow the opacity to be pumped up for ten minutes at a time, per hour, to create a very real, 3d image of the entity's chosen persona. The digital being can manifest a projection of who they were in life if they are a downloaded human mind, or else roll on Table XR-79 to establish a random persona.

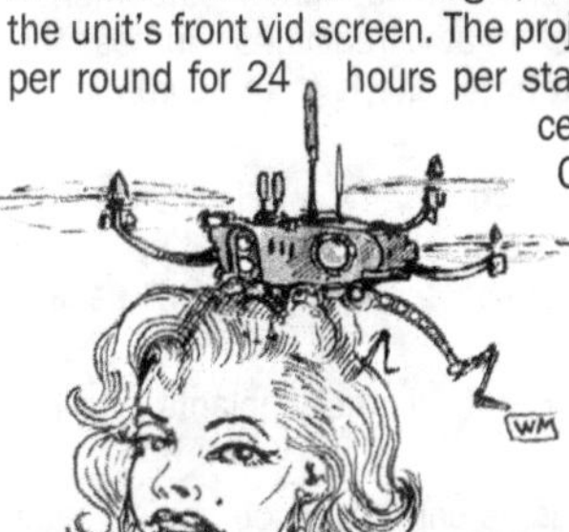

A multi-legged holo-walker can move at 7m per round, has a de-

fense value of -20, endurance of 20+1d20, agility of 10+2d20 (any modifiers from this agility trait do affect the unit's DV and movement). The unit can rear up and kick either backwards, forwards or side to side for one attack per round SV +4, damage 1d12.

Should this unit be destroyed, the digital being within is allowed a perception based, type A hazard check to eject its puck like palm disk, which will fly 2d6 meters in a random direction. If the walker unit was destroyed by fire, or energy weapons, then it will explode and if the digital being did not eject, it will burn, taking an automatic 1d8 data damage per round until melted away or rescued. If the walker was destroyed by gunfire, or clubbing, bashing, hacking or piercing attacks, however, then there is a 75% chance the digital being in a palm disk survives unscathed, yet could be tapped in the wreckage (89% chance).

Data Capacity 150+1d100 TB /DV -20/ END 20+1d20 / agility 10+2d20/ Attack 1/ SV +4/ DMG 1d12/ Weight 10+2d6 kg/ Battery: Power Pack will maintain operation for 300+2d100 days/ Sell Price 600+1d100sp / Buy Price 2400+2d1000sp

**Projector Aerial Drone:** Designed for long-term flight under zero or moderately windy conditions, this tiny drone is equipped with a jettisonable memory core to allow the CPU to eject if the drone is destroyed while in the air. If jettisoned, a tiny clear parachute will deploy the 2nd round after the memory stick is ejected and float to the earth at a movement rate of 2m per round. This memory disk is only a backup and the digital being is locked within it until an assistant can load this CPU core into another container or body.

The digital being's persona can be projected beneath a hovering drone at 10cm to 2 meters in height, or else project a hologram of its face from the unit's front vid screen. The projector drone can fly at a top speed of 14m per round for 24 hours per standard power cell, although a mini-power cell supplies the energy for the detachable CPU chip and will maintain operations for 10+2d6 months. This drone has a defense value of -10 when stationary, but when flying has a -30 base DV. If necessary, this drone can ram an opponent at a strike value of 01-70 inflicting 2d6 damage, however there is a 2 in 6 chance per ram that the drone's helicopter rotor snaps off and the unit crashes a round later, taking 2d20 damage.

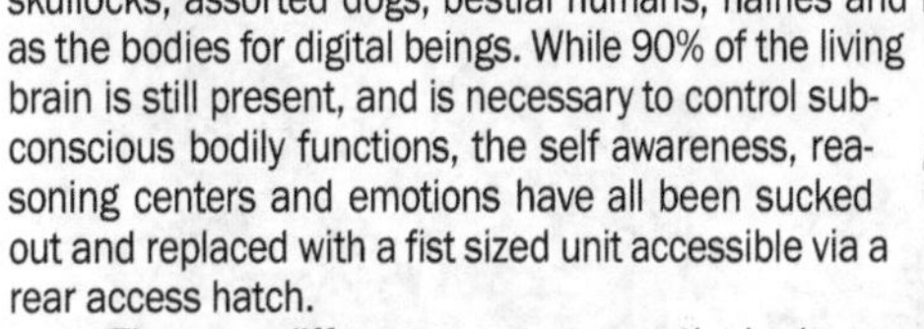

Data Capacity 100+3d20 TB /Move 14m / DV stationary -10, flying -30/ END 10+4d6 / agility 20+2d20/ Weight 4kg/ Battery: Power cell will maintain flight for 24 hours, non-flight (mini-power cell) 10+2d6 months / Sell Price 900+3d100sp / Buy Price 3000+2d1000sp

**Cyborg:** These brain dead automatons were once widely used by mecha factions, and in many respects are simply zombified living bodies with a computerized brain. The most common cyborg specimen is a pure stock human, yet skullocks, assorted dogs, bestial humans, halfies and mutorgs can all serve as the bodies for digital beings. While 90% of the living brain is still present, and is necessary to control subconscious bodily functions, the self awareness, reasoning centers and emotions have all been sucked out and replaced with a fist sized unit accessible via a rear access hatch.

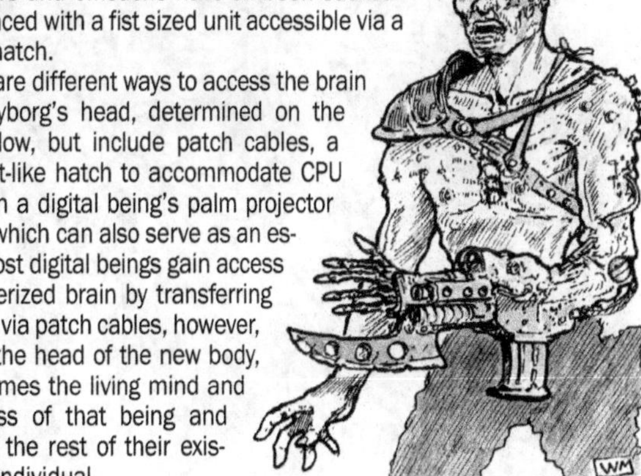

There are different ways to access the brain within the cyborg's head, determined on the tables to follow, but include patch cables, a compartment-like hatch to accommodate CPU cores or even a digital being's palm projector style device which can also serve as an escape pod. Most digital beings gain access to a computerized brain by transferring into the skull via patch cables, however, once inside the head of the new body, the DB becomes the living mind and consciousness of that being and could spend the rest of their existence in the individual.

Without the digital being, or whatever previous controlling program or entity operated the fleshy vessel, the subject body is an unthinking mass of metal and meat that will either collapse and slowly die of exposure, or become a zombie-like, drooling thing that only seeks food, water and shelter — essentials it will take from whoever it crosses. Note: 33% of consciously abandoned computer brained cyborgs will operate on 'auto-pilot zombie mode' and sustain its life by any means, including feeding on the raw flesh of former companions, until it can make its way back to its home base or rally point. The other 67% that lose their digital being or controller will cease operations and eventually die.

Cybernetic brains have a massive amount of memory space and can take up to 200 TB of data. Any digital being with more than this must compress and lock away any data beyond 200 points, which the DB cannot use. Furthermore, any gained data points after rank gain are locked away but can be carried over and potentially used if the digital being upgrades to a different vessel.

Roll 1d100 and then 1d10 on the two following tables to determine the type of cyborg body at character generation, plus the accessibility and ejection mode of the cyborg's head. Record the cyborg's stats on a separate character sheet as the digital being who operates this cyborg will probably switch vessels throughout their lifetime.

### Table XR-61/ Computer Brained Cyborg Host Body Type

**1d100 Digital Being's Computer Brained Cyborg Host Body**

**01,02.** Skullock body, stats on page TME 170. In most human settlements, the sight of a skullock will bring immediate negative reactions — unless the rubble goblin's appearance is altered and he or she is in the company of more typical looking diggers.

**03,04.** Dog body, stats on page TME 152 with dog type rolled here 1d6: 1,2. farm dog /4,5. war dog / 5,6. mutant dog. In some communities, dog is often on the menu when times get tough. Unaccompanied dogs will usually be shot on sight.

**05.06.** Bestial human with cybernetic brain but no other implants, see full random listing on page XR-58.

**07,08.** Rebuilt, with this cybernetic brain as its only advanced implant, see page XR-143 to generate body and parts.

**09,10.** Halfie with cybernetic brain as its only implant. See page XR-93 for the sort of halfie this digital being occupies.

**11-40.** Pure stock human woman, see page TME-21 to generate a cyborg character.

**41-70.** Pure stock human man, see page TME-21 to generate a cyborg character.

**71-85.** Mutorg, woman, see page XR-99 to generate a mutorg character.

**86-00.** Mutorg, man, see page XR-99 to generate a mutorg character.

### Table XR-62/ Accessibility and Egress for Cyborg Computerized Brain

**1d10 Accessibility and Egress for Cyborg Computerized Brain**

**1.** Surgical access only. A CPU core or palm disc can be implanted and hooked to the computerized brain within, or a patch cable can be hooked up and the DB transferred to the brain prior to detaching the cables and the skull and scalp reattached to hide most of the evidence of the surgery after healing. There is no quick egress from this cyborg. If the body is killed, the digital being can be extracted by opening the skull to either use a transfer cable to download the entity or physically remove a palm disc or CPU core, so long as the head was not crushed or punctured with gunfire or beam weapons.

To insert a digital being into the skull of this unit, should a DB wants to use the cyborg, a medic must perform the surgery. While medics of 5 skill points can do this procedure without it, less skilled surgeons must use the medics table on page 46 of the TME hub rules and roll the 'Resuscitate Drowning Victim' column. Failure means the cyborg's living brain and body die.

**2-6.** Transfer patch cable port only.

**7.** Patch cable plus back panel opens to accept palm disks, medallion disks or CPU cores from projection mirrors and the like.

**8.** As in roll 7, with patch cable and opening hatch, but this unit can also take whole smartphone and wrist watch units that are plugged into the brain and locked into a secure internal holder.

**9.** As in rolls 7 and 8, but this computerized brain has double the memory capacity and can take up to 400 data points.

**10.** As in rolls 7,8 and 9, plus this cranial unit has an ejection charge built into it. If the digital being feels it is at risk of dying within the cyborg body, the back of the cyborg head explodes and jettisons an alloy enclosed, ball-like computerized brain towards the last known, safest direction to a maximum range of 15 meters and 6m in height. Three small plastic parachutes erupt from the blood smeared ball at the last moment and the brain drifts to the ground at 1m per round. The cyborg body is dead thereafter.

**Android, standard:** The following android types are all covered in the hub rules on pages 182 and 183, with stats on page 184. While heavy combat, advanced combat and commander models also exist, they are not included as starting character options because of their immense power and rarity. The cranium and CPU of any standard android is more than large enough to accommodate all the data points of a digital being. Standard androids have access ports on the backs of their head to allow the digital being to transfer itself out when upgrading to another body or device.

Roll 1d10 on the following table to see what starting android body a new digital being starts game play with.

### Table XR-63/ Standard Android body Types

| 1d10 | Android Body Type | Hub Rules Page |
| --- | --- | --- |
| 1. | Android, Concubine | Hub Rules pg.182 |
| 2,3. | Android, Household | Hub Rules pg.182 |
| 4,5. | Android, Service | Hub Rules pg.182 |
| 6. | Android, Clerical | Hub Rules pg.182 |
| 7,8. | Android, Technician | Hub Rules pg.182 |
| 9. | Android, Industrial | Hub Rules pg.182 |
| 10. | Android, Combat | Hub Rules pg.183 |

**Android, unique:** In nearly every case, a digital being who wishes to fit in with an excavation team, and interact with the environment and people around it, will seek a potent, unique android as its ideal body. Not only can an entity inhabiting a human form wear relic armor, but most vehicles, structures and furnishings accommodate the human shape. Since an android can be overlooked as just another human, especially in a mixed character type group, they can interact more fully with commoners, saloon operators, guards, officials and fellow travelers without eliciting the dread that an obvious robot might. If discovered to be an android, however, many people will typically react with fear, suspicion and violence.

Unique androids are covered in this book on page 29. An android character sheets is available in Appendix 8 on page 514 but also ready for free download at this book's public page at https://www.outlandarts.com/expansionrules.htm

**Robot, standard:** The following standard model robots are sourced from both the hub rules and this book, with the page number within each book included on the following table. While more potent robot varieties exist, these are the available options for starting digital beings to occupy. The data capacity within these robots is more than adequate to contain the data points of any digital being, and the amount shown on table XR-56, on page 69, is only 10% of the CPU's maximum hard drive capacity.

### Table XR-64/ Standard Robot body Types

| 1d100 | Standard Robot | Book and Page |
|---|---|---|
| 01-28. | Robot, Household | Hub Rules pg.178 |
| 29-34. | Robot, Industrial Construction | Hub Rules pg.178 |
| 35-49. | Robot, Industrial Repair | Hub Rules pg.179 |
| 50-56. | Robot, Medi-bot | Hub Rules pg.179 |
| 57-72. | Robot, Pocket-bot | Hub Rules pg.180 |
| 73-77. | Robot, Police | Hub Rules pg.180 |
| 78-87. | Robot, Combot, light | Hub Rules pg.180 |
| 88-95. | Wisp Scout Flyer | Expansion Rules, pg. 458 |
| 96-00. | Wasp | Expansion Rules, pg. 458 |

**Robot, unique:** As with unique androids, these custom robots are covered in this book on page 151. Grab a Unique Robot character sheet on page 524 in the Appendices, or at this book's website at https://www.outlandarts.com/expansionrules.htm

# Digital Being Types

There are two main types of digital beings and three rare variants; those that are entirely formed from digital code and form a limited Artificial Intelligence (AI-DB), and those created from a Downloaded Human Consciousness (DHC-DB) from a once living ancient person. Three other types are possible, too. Those that are 'deluded' and mistake themselves for one of the other main types, along with digital beings who don't know if they were once living people or wholly artificial and thus categorized as 'indeterminate'. The third rare variety is a cyber dreamer, which is a still living person who dwells in a cybernetic dream state and operates as a digital entity — sometimes having forgotten that they are attached to a living body at all and operates as if the digital being portion of existence is all that survives of its consciousness.

Use the following table to establish the character's mode of creation, although these details are more for back story and color, and don't really altar the traits or abilities of a digital being player character.

### Table XR-65/ Digital Being Mode of Creation*    Roll 2d6

| | |
|---|---|
| 2. | Indeterminate |
| 3-7. | Downloaded Human Consciousness (DHC-DB) |
| 8-11. | Artificial Intelligence (AI-DB) |
| 12. | Cyber-dreamer |

** 'Deluded' specimens can also occur and their possibility noted in the descriptions to follow.*

**Indeterminate:** This digital being is entirely uncertain of its creation mode, and while it gets flashbacks and dreams of what could be a life from long ago, the imagery is so random and incongruent that the entity isn't sure whether it is remembering a real life, video broadcast, or even experiencing corruption from other minds and computers it had once been exposed to. The GM can privately roll 1d10+2 on the above table (XR-65) to establish and privately record the truth. In either case, use table XR-69 on page 79 to establish this entity's identity and persona.

**Downloaded Human Consciousness (DHC-DB):** This character was once a human, or believes so, and in the later years of the pan-global civilization, had their mind downloaded into a computer. They now exist as a being with full access to whatever CPU their pin-point of consciousness lives in. Many have been asleep for over a century, and only been made active by being dug up by excavators, their bunker invaded by humanoids or ravaged by seismic activity or catastrophic power failure. Most commonly of all, a downloaded mind gained consciousness after decades as a slave soldier or laborer to one of many malicious, human killing artificial intelligences called the Mecha.

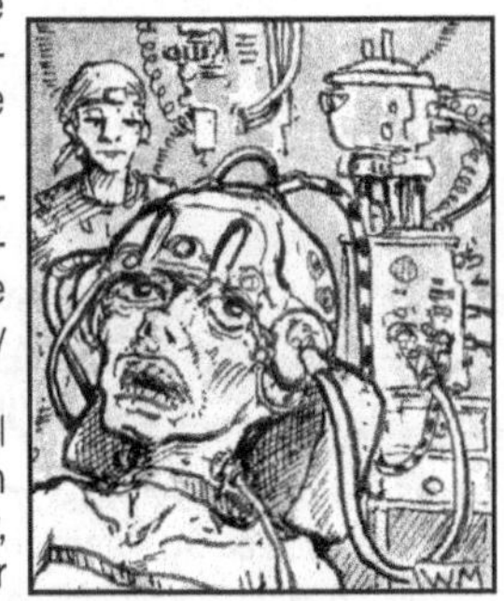

The game master will roll secretly to determine if this character is a 'deluded' specimen or not, with a 1 in 20 chance that the PC is actually a fully artificial person who only thinks it was once a living human.

Roll first to determine what sex the digital being was as a living human, secondly, establish the amount of memory they posses, and finally, use the table on the next page to establish one or two reoccurring flashbacks which defines them.

### Table XR-66/ What sex was this person in life?

| 1d10 | Sex of Person in Life |
|---|---|
| 1-4. | Male |
| 5-8. | Female |
| 9.10. | Uncertain, memory is fragmented but you identify and appear as a random persona from table XR-69 on page 79. |

### Table XR-67/ Amount of Human Life Recalled    Roll 2d6

**2.** Almost nothing, and what is accessible comes as sporadic flashbacks mixed with what could be scenes from movies or holographic video games. Roll a flashback from table XR-68, page 76, each day.

**3-5.** Occasional flashbacks. Roll 1 flashback from page XR-76 every week.

**6-9.** Frequent flashbacks and memories of events, faces, music and physical sensations. Sadly, few if any details of landmarks in these memories translate to the streets and structures where this entity now travels.

**10,11.** Spotty but easily accessible memories: when not actively working on some task, this digital being finds itself day dreaming of its old life and can get lost for hours reliving relationships, trials, tribulations and journeys in their long ago existence. At times, it is all too much. The memories and long dead friends and family appear as ghosts — memories which drive this entity to focus on the here and now. Memories that urge it to stay as present as possible in the conversations and activities of its biological or robotic companions — often fostering deep relationships with agreeable and useful physical beings as a distraction from the recollections.

**12.** Lucid memories of the being's former life: This character can recall in great detail the streets and buildings of the city it once lived in, and will recall newscasts and other propaganda from the authorities. It will be able to actively pick moments in its past life to relive to either recall mission-specific details or to escape to another time as if going on a mental holiday.

### Downloaded Human Consciousness (DHC-DB) Random Flashbacks

Re-roll any duplicated results from any previously generated DHC-DBs to occur in that gaming group to maintain the uniqueness of glimpses into the character's previous life.

These flashbacks could repeat in the entity's mind during moments of calm, recharge or following some traumatic event. They are often the last memory the character had of their former life, or even a mundane event. The game master can use these as is, or as guidelines to expand upon or craft new flashbacks. Likewise, the player might want to use one or two of these at random and then create a back story all their own — although discussions with the game master will be required if some memory, especially a location of importance or skill — would influence the game campaign.

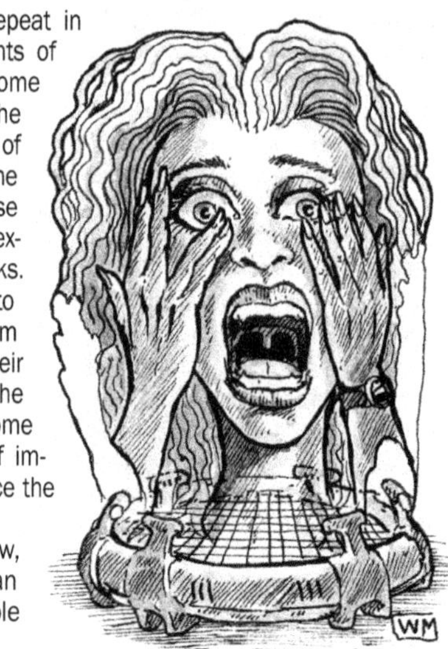

Roll on tables XR-68, below, for a flashback. Also determine an assumed new persona from table XR-69, page 79.

### Table XR-69/ Downloaded Human Consciousness (DHC-DB) Random Flashbacks    Roll 1d100

**01,02.** Riots between masked protesters and armored police and their tall, gleaming eyed crowd control robots. Getting a crack on the head from a plastic bullet and all fades to black.

**03,04.** You recall a mutant animal killing a family member. It throws the bloody remnants of the person, then turns on you! You hear a roar and feel a great crunch, a mind numbing burst of pain, and then nothing.

**05,06.** Coming home to find your spouse in a relationship with a pleasure android.

**07,08.** Robot infantry and drones sweeping through your neighborhood, massacring every person, pet, and friendly robotic law enforcement unit.

**09,10.** Dying of a painful plague. You bid loved one's goodbye as they stand behind a glass barrier even as your mind is transferred out to a computer database.

**11,12.** The moment of being uploaded from your dying body, looking up at a helmet clad, weeping comrade, sounds of battle about you, your outstretched, plated and blood smeared arm letting go of your buddy as you feel the rush of your consciousness sweep out of you, then darkness.

**13,14.** A car accident that killed your whole family. Your body is ruined and you soon black out.

**15,16.** Being thrown in the air during a massive explosion, landing with a crunch, seeing a body strewn area before you.

**17,18.** Burnt bodies and the wreckage of an aircraft in a gray, lifeless war zone.

**19,20.** A desert with blowing junk, skeletal remains of beasts and people. Strange, half seen hunched creatures walking across the horizon toward you.

**21,22.** A burning metropolis of huge hexagon shaped towers. Smoke rises into the sky, the crack of gunfire, the snap of energy weapons, explosions, and the voice of somebody yelling at you to run for your life.

**23,24.** The rumble and shake of glassware and furniture as your lavish, glass fronted condo crumbled about you in an earthquake. Then blackness.

**25,26.** You are at a birthday party, looking eye to eye with little girls and boys, who sing happy birthday to you and shove the candle covered cake your way. You lean over and blow out seven candles, but leave the eighth lit on purpose. "You got one crush," says a kid before the vision fades.

**27,28.** You hide in rubble, you cower, your teeth chatter together as you hear something massive crunch through concrete, dust, and shattered glass. It sniffs as it comes closer to your hiding spot. There is a flash of fur, talons and then a horrendous roar as the beast finds you. You feel yourself smashed to the ground, claws rake through your torso and then hear the crack of a gun. Your vision fades to black.

**29,30.** A bald-headed doctor, and behind him, a white, plastic skinned woman smiling down at you as your vision fades and you feel a soft warmth running through your body. "When you wake," explains the man. "You will no longer feel the pain of your failing body. This disease cannot touch you where you are going. You will wake as a pure consciousness, in a pure, mechanical body like this one." He gestures to the lithe, plastic skinned woman near him.

**31,32.** You are looking out the rainy window down to a cement walkway. Coming from a yellow ground vehicle is a woman clutching a bundled baby to her chest. Somehow, you know your new baby brother or sister is arriving home for the first time.

**33,34.** You are at an espresso bar, a Starstruck Coffee you recall. Here, you buy a mug from the person who later becomes your spouse.

**35,36.** You look upon a great towering wave as it crashes down on the wharfs and seaside walkway of a great, ancient city. The wave surges forth and fills the streets, washes away pedestrians, self driving cars and robotic servants. Somebody grabs you and pulls you up a set of stairs as water pours in behind you. It is ice cold as it sweeps up about your legs and engulfs you.

**37,38.** You are sitting with friends at a coffee shop talking about growing threats and mayhem in the news, when a man walks into the busy place wearing a backpack, shouts something in a strange language and yanks on a cord at his chest. Bone, flesh and metal erupt about him as a plume of flame sweeps your way and you are blown backwards, and unconscious.

**39,40.** You kneel beside a roadway, and cup the limp form of a small white dog. It whimpers and wags its tail once before it dies, its body broken and bloody from the self driving armored car that just drove over it on its way to another protest.

**41.** You watch a film as you drink from a plastic, sippy cup. Your pudgy little hands grip the bright colored thing in both hands and peer up, tearfully, as you watch a news broadcast showing the last elephant in the world and its very public burial service.

**42,43.** You stand in a cold, blue room as a white cloaked, serious man in goggles pulls a poly-cloth covered bed right out of the wall — a wall fitted with dozens more of the strange cupboard beds. He pulls back the sheet and you see the pale, bruised face of a woman, her eyes shut, mouth agape in death. You know this to be your mother. The man says. "The machine in her own home did this. Malfunctioned they said — but... these wounds were precise, carefully considered, as if that household robot were an assassin."

**44,45.** You see your two hands digging in soft, dark soil. You pant in desperation as you dig and make a hole about a foot deep and then slide a plastic cylinder into it. As you bury it, you look left and right, and see a huge burning robotic tank about ten feet to one side, and in the other direction, an 'L shaped concrete ruin. "My treasure... safe... and well away from them," you hear yourself say before the vision fades. You'd know this spot if you saw it again.

**46,47.** You hear a horrendous howl and then an earth shaking boom. Glass, rubble and parts of people and machines fly about you as you are thrown down into a vast puddle of chemicals. As people run by you, a man shouts "Get up or they'll rip your heart out!"

**48,49.** You recall watching a video screen showing a herd of mammoths in a faraway place called Siberia. Apparently they killed some tourists and there was a protest about the evils of bringing back extinct, prehistoric animals. Another newscast talked about some animals called velociraptors used by the military.

**50,51.** You get flashes of some former life, or was it a news cast? Soldiers running passed you on a busy street, civilians in a panic fleeing a cafe and nearby shops. The sound of gunfire and twang of laser weapons around the corner. The building shutters and the glass near your table shatters, a beam falls and you reach up to cover yourself when all goes dark.

**52,53.** You are storming a politician's mansion with an angry crowd when police robots arrive and start shooting live rounds. One bullet finds your spine and you drop.

**54,55.** You get a glimpse of yourself working behind a counter at a store filled with colorful food items and drinks when a masked youth demands you refill his cash-card with max funds at gunpoint. Of course, the machine is down because of a power outage; the punk doesn't believe you, grabs the machine away and shoots the kinetic gun at your chest. You fall back among chips and narcotic packets, a searing pain in your chest as all fades to black.

**56,57.** You stand among thousands, chanting, waving signs and wearing blue baseball caps. Chants of "We demand water!" Can be heard, and then the pop, pop, pop of something up ahead at the front of the protest. Suddenly, overhead drones light up the scene and pepper the crowd with a mix of agony beams, rubber bullets and a few live, killing rounds. Several people go down about you, clutching their heads or bloody wounds. A stampede begins as people, some with children in backpacks or at their sides, trample you. Somebody falls over you as a bullet rips through their head and the impact knocks you out.

**58,59.** You stand in a long line. In a well-lit hallway. Armed soldiers and their tall, gleaming robots are all along the route. An overhead speaker in a soft, young woman's voice makes an announcement. "Please comply with all instructions my medical staff, security personnel and autonomous law enforcement units. Maintain your minimum two meter safe distance from the citizen in front of you and keep to your designated vaccination processing line. Only by your compliance can we protect all citizens. Personal autonomy and bodily rights ended when you refused to accept this medical procedure and endangered fellow citizens and migrant workers. Because you declined previous requests to do your part and get the vaccine, we, the government, have stepped up to help you do the right thing for us all. Thank you for your cooperation."

**60,61.** You recall being in a line, holding a box. A person at the head of the line, just beyond a fake pine tree covered in strange red and green lights and hanging glass balls, is arguing with a lady behind the front service desk. She's telling the red-faced man that because of the war, that all payment systems are down, that no Christmas parcels can be sent to Texas. Suddenly, in the distance you hear a tremendous rumble and for a moment everything shakes, dust falls from the fresh cracks in the concrete ceiling high above. People rush off screaming. There is a great crash nearby. Another great boom and the roar of jet engines some place outside sound before pillars of concrete crumble, a plume of orange fire illuminates everything, and you are engulfed in flame, thrown back and covered in rubble.

**62,63.** Walking home from the hover bus station, exhausted from a long day at the self driving truck plant, you see movement out the corner of your eye. Two hooded, lean figures in sports clothing leap out, one from each side and grab at your knapsack. There is swearing, screaming and threats and suddenly a rusty old, archaic revolver appears in one thug's hand. A flash of fire, a boom and you collapse clutching at your chest. As you bleed out, the two grab your pack, kick you a few times and run off as the distant sound of sirens can be heard. A hover-cop speeds into view, drifts over you for a few seconds, scans the bloody foot prints near you and then speeds off. Soon after, you fade away.

**64,65.** You recall laying in a hospital bed, surrounded by blinking machines. Tubes are stuck in your lower body parts, hoses hooked to your arms and neck, and a breathing machine hisses from your left. Two people in white coats are talking quietly near you, one says something about you being as good as dead. That you'll sign the form for the organ harvesting to proceed, that the family gave it the okay so long as they got extra rations and authorized holiday to Vegas. The other doctor agrees, shakes the other man's hand and then moves to turn a few dials on the machines beside you. You feel an icy coldness in your veins, and then the vision fades away.

**66,67.** You are young in this memory, watching a vid screen on a transit subway line along with so many others. Some asshole is coughing into a tissue at the far end of the train car, you see blood in his phlegm and shaking hand. The newscast shows medical personnel in plastic jumpsuits placing dead people in black, zippered bags. The outbreak at the hospital has spread to an apartment complex in your city... and reports of the spreading Ebola-like illness appearing elsewhere is worrisome to the bleach blonde, dark-skinned lady reporter. More coughing nearby.

**68,69.** You remember how you were in the backseat of a self driving taxi stuck in traffic; the radio is on and a newscast discusses the food shortages in India, that the four billion inhabitants will run out in three weeks. The riots and political killings are not helping calm the situation. Looking out the window, you see rows of homeless people between the lanes, signs held in shaking hands, requesting cash-cards, narcotics, or alcohol.

**70,71.** You remember being strapped to a cold steel bed, your body numb, your vision gone, only distant voices, the beep or machines and buzz of an overhead light. Somebody nearby says "This one's body is already spoken for, but if you got the credits, we can get this poor sonuvabitch into either a cranial vat or download their mind into a data dump. It's your call, commander."

**72,73.** "Don't move," says a woman's voice in your ear. This is a memory you have often, and it always brings anguish. "You're body has been destroyed by the machines... or mutants... we didn't see what did this to you. Your brain... or maybe just the contents, can be salvaged... and if you agree, you need to sign this digital permission form... and then live forever and continue your important service to us down here. Very good, darling, just imagine your signature and it will record on the archival database. That's it... good. Now... this is gonna hurt... hurt real bad... but you can't take any more pain killers without suffering brain damage. Now think of someplace peaceful... think of your children. Do you remember them...from before the war?" You feel a surge of unbearable pain, suffer for many long minutes, and black out.

**74,75.** Fire. You remember raging fire and look down to see your hands and arms engulfed in flame. People about you scream and run as purple laser pulses spit through the crowd, walls and shelving units. Something smacks into your back and you topple forward onto a pile of bodies, Screaming continues until you black out, although you can't tell if it was you who cried out, or those you who died about you.

**76,77.** Red wine fills the glasses of the good-looking men and women about you at the table. You are all in dress uniforms, some of you with tears in your eyes. Above, through layers of concrete bunkers and warehouses, the distant thud of the bombardment continues. This memory always ends the same way. You drink, then wish each other good luck. Those of religious persuasion say their last prayers as they reach for their sidearms and get to their feet and turn to the far door. The alloy barrier shows signs of molten orange metal as some great force on the far side hammers as it with unimaginably powerful energy weapons. "It was good knowing you all," says a young officer as she sniffs, brings her weapon to the side of her head. And before anyone can stop her, blows her brains out and falls. You catch her body and fall to the floor, cracking you head on the steel mess hall table and are knocked out.

**78,79.** You snuggle your child in her bedroom, reading some old story of a boy wizard. A candle is the only light left, although outside the fires, explosion and passing beams of laser and particle beam cannon fire race back and forth. You can smell smoke. You know your apartment block is already burning, that the mutant slave soldiers are doing their best against the mad machines, but with so few ... it's only a matter of time. You read on, holding your child, even though she is already cold. Her limp form pressed to you as you weep... a stray bullet from a drone took her hours ago. There is a great crack in the ceiling and walls, a thump and bang as the building crumbles about you. Something crashes across your head and you are knocked unconscious.

**80,81.** Dear Diary, you write. This is the last entry... maybe the last journal entry for the human race. Our bunker has been breached by the gray-skinned devils... the ones our fearless leader and her scientist engineered to fight the machines. Our little heroes. The skull faced little motherfuckers who along with the rest of their mutant abominations were supposed to serve and save humanity. Fuck them all to hell. These ones... these things they call skull-ocks... they drove off the machines... but now feed on us like we're cattle. Fearless... fast breeding... fast as hell and without pity. Science is the new religion, they say, and how it has failed us. I hear them up there... the fighting at the east door. Our leader, the president... she took her family in the last shuttle... to orbit and beyond. Now I can hear the skull devils screaming. They are through the door. In the stairwell. I have this a grenade, a mark four advanced. Let them come. Let them come.

**82,83.** You recall holding the bible in your bloody hands; You read the Psalm 27 by firelight of burning machines, the heaped bodies of mutant slave soldiers and attack beasts. Miscreations that weren't enough to stop this latest batch of machines... machines sent by the artificial intelligence that deemed all human life as little more than vermin. And yet, your side has an AI, too... hundreds in fact, called digital beings, or E-angels. They fight for you, so they say. You are to become one and transfer yourself into a machine... or maybe just a brain in a pot of nutrients... pot of high-tech piss. All you have to do is cross the street under fire, get to the hatch, enter the code, pass the security detail and those tall, bald headed, cruel gray mutant guards called war-born, and descend the shaft to the bunker. As you recall this, and based on your current so-called life, you assume you made it, but were torn up pretty bad getting to the distant door.

**84,85.** How did you end up like this? Gaps in your memory leave you guessing as to your history... and what happened to those people you once lived with. Were they your children, your parents, your spouse or just comrades in the trench with you? You recall their personalities and names, but not their relationship to you, or gender, age or appearance. Its odd... you're alive... can control the machinery around you... have motivations and a sense of self awareness unlike anything you have ever experienced before... but where you came from is a bloody mystery. All you know for certain is that these companions you now operate near, and your goals, craving for ongoing existence... is all that matters. Yes, friends and sustenance... what else does a disembodied soul require?

**86,87.** Revenge... against the machines. Against the Mecha is all that matters. It doesn't fricking matter that this is nearly two hundred years since they killed them... killed those people you loved. Killed your family — whoever the hell they were. They're faces, names and just who they were to you is a bit of a blur. But you remember holding them close, reading to them, cooking meals for them, movie nights and popcorn. And some asshole had to make an artificial intelligence... then everybody did it and the god damned things decided we were just rats. Just cockroaches who used up raw material and needed energy that would be better used by these new gods in their great steel and glass towers. And when gods wage war with each other, they trample ants underfoot... and as organic beings... we're just ants. Now... it's all about revenge, and tracking down that AI that killed your old world... that's what it's all about now. Everything you do is about hunting the evil machine. About killing a metal god.

**88,89.** You are on a mission. The president herself... or himself... or was it a digital head of state at that point? It was so damn long ago that who can expect you to remember — especially after everything you went through. Sure, it was nearly two centuries ago... but the mission is still top of your priority list. And these others, these assorted beings who share your life, what is their mission? They can be amusing, and highly useful, but only so far as they contribute to your mission.

Thing is... you can't remember the parameters of your mission. You only feel it... and clues reveal themselves bit by bit... especially near the ancient places... like those old towers. The truth is waiting for you. You just need to seek it out. Good thing these so-called excavators are as fearless and insane as you.

**90,91.** You're not sure what to believe anymore. The dreams of an old life mingle with recollections from recent weeks and days in these dirty, dangerous streets among these dusty companions. These fleshy weirdos. These brothers in arms. You had a real life once, were a living person with a family, with hopes and dreams... but those old goals and beloved things are little more than the dust of the ruins... like the yellowed, brittle bones of the dead oldsters you've seen. Now. You must flush those memories of some former life, and focus on the here and now. Of seeking sustenance and power cells, of building a reliable excavation team and gaining the materials goods and camaraderie to ensure your survival. These crazy ass diggers are your family now. You need to shake off the past. Those children are dead now... and been dust for nearly two centuries.

**92,93.** You remember food and remarkable beverages. For crying out loud... you are convinced that you used to be a chef or something in your former life. No, you can't eat food or drink fancy wines and glorious Scotch Whiskey, even so, watching your companions enjoy a hearty meal at some shit hole of a saloon is a thrill for you. Few things bring you more pleasure than to watch team mates fill their faces with food, and throw back pottery mugs full of beer. Yes, to see your beloved, crude friends enjoy food and drink is what it's all about... and as they consume these things... you also recall the taste and texture... and take pleasure as they do. With ever greater success in your group's line of work, you know they will feed and drink even higher quality delicacies... and so you will help them in this culinary endeavor.

**94,95.** You remember passion. And it hurts. For pity sakes, why the hell didn't they remove or scramble that part of your mind that compels you to appreciate the form and function of a fleshy lover? It is so cruel... so maddening to be stuck in the form you are, without a real body, without the means to cling to a lover and — oh wait... you do get a tingle of satisfaction from watching others flirt, kiss, fondle and frolic. Indeed, your voyeuristic addiction is an outlet for your particular, amatory interest... and even if you can't indulge yourself, it satisfies a carnal Itch to simply observe others at their sweaty, impassioned deed. Keeping this to yourself, however, is always the challenge... and half the fun.

**96,97.** Sometimes the memories rush about you in such a jumble that you lock up and need to reboot your daily objectives simply to function. Your inner to-do-list is a lifesaver and so long as you keep focused, motivate your companions and direct your attention on the mission, you can cope. But crap, when it's recuperation or recharge time, and there ain't nothin' going on, the flood of recollection sweeps over you. It's like some idiot dumped fifty different lifetimes into your head... and it often makes no sense and imagery overlaps imagery.

**98,99.** They promised. They lied... those pricks. "Once we regenerate a perfect clone of your body, we'll reload your mind into the new improved you," they said, grinning from behind their masks and protective visors. "You go achieve your objectives... and your body will be down here, a hundred meters below the battlefield, waiting for you, okay? Your family will be here too, in cryo-freeze like your beautiful new replacement body. Just do this chore for us... collect the data disk and bring it back. Agreed?"

You recall that you agreed, that they'd put your mind in to some powerful humanoid machine and send you up there... to the devastated surface to find that little red disk in its gold case. "Now," says the technician — Jerry you think his name was. " You're gonna pass out for a bit as the transfer begins... but eventually you'll remember this... and our promise. And never forget... that we will all be waiting for you to return with it... and then we can all leave this place through the portal. Hurry back to us... return as a hero."

Was it months ago you came to the surface, decades, or centuries ago?

**100.** You held out as long as you could. You used every rocket, every grenade, every beam cannon and mortar... and still they came at the gun station. Waves of the damn things... gray skinned, skull faced and without a hint of fear... their own weapons, both ballistic and energy based, hitting your systems and knocking them out one by one.

You knew they would breach the defenses with their next rush... hundreds would fall, but in the end, some would get inside, unplug you, and get to the hatch and the shaft beyond. Your people depend on you to hold this bunker opening... their sleeping forms in their glass covered cryo-tubes so vulnerable... their bodies easy prey to these cannibal warriors... these filthy bio-engineered shock troops — these so-called skullocks.

There was only one thing to do... to block the hatch. Yes, you must fill the elevator shaft. When they come... and at the first hint of a breach at the outer doors... you'd blow that place apart... and bury the opening... and yourself. The sound of the skullocks approaching is picked up on the auditory sensors at the top of your domed fortification... over a thousand this time... each connected to a headset and compliance chip. Brain dead minions of a hateful artificial intelligence. There would be no stopping them. Your end has come. The countdown on the demolition engaged. "God preserve the sleepers... god preserve my child."

## Artificial Intelligence Digital Being AI-DB

There are untold numbers of artificial intelligences still active in the post-apocalyptic world of the Mutant Epoch. Some have god-like power and intelligence, others, such as those commonly referred to as the Mecha are fixated on eliminating the last vestiges of human life, while many others are either dormant, or lack control of robotic units or facilities and are thus in a state of purgatory, or stand-by mode — at least until something changes or their facility is breached.

A vast number of other Ais are very limited in scope, due to their processor or programming limitations, lack of power, ambition, or operational sentience. Rudimentary Ai's for chatbots, personal attendant androids, building maintenance, industrial facilities and cargo transport also exist, as well wild things that serve no master nor seek to attain world domination, and merely travel the lands in search of batteries, shelter, and a way to extend their existence another day.

Digital beings that are also artificial intelligences are unique from each other, and as far as anyone knows, were created to specifically work with, befriend and benefit humankind — at least humans of their former corporation, military faction, political party or nation state.

Those Ai digital beings, or AI-DBs, that are player character are among the most sociable and ambitious of their kind. They see the need to attach themselves to a band of travelers, especially ruin explorers, to seek upgrades, power supplies, spare parts, protection and assistance, but there is more to this camaraderie. These adventure and companion seeking Ais exhibit a genuine fondness for trustworthy, competent entities, regardless of whether they are pure stock humans, mutants, bestial humans, machines or even other, friendly digital beings. By working as a team, this consciousness gains resources, security and much needed friendship. In nearly every instance of an adventuresome digital being of Ai origin, the entity seeks to learn from, emulate, and become more human, and in time, establish a family around itself.

An Ai sourced digital being has access to all the same traits, abilities, skills and apps as others of this character type, but also creates a persona to establish a consistent personality and appearance. An Ai does this to solidify an identity for itself, as well as to present a consistent appearance to comrades. When housed in a robotic or android's body, and the DB has no need to project a holographic version of itself to interact with others, it might still do so when appropriate. There is a 1 in 20 chance, rolled by the game master and kept secret from the player, that this entity is actually a once living human and considered to be a 'deluded' digital being.

AI-DB's have an alphanumeric ID tag as their name, but when dealing with other beings, prefer to use a permanent, chosen name which seems suitable to their holographic persona. Establish the AI-DB's Identity and Persona Determination on the listing to follow.

## Digital Being Identity and Persona Determination

Artificial intelligences are the most likely users of a consistent holographic identity or persona, although many downloaded, once living human consciousness also like to adopt a more colorful image particularly if their memories of their long ago life are spotty, tragic, or drab. Anyone playing a digital being can select their own persona from history, pop-culture, fiction or other source.

If the following table doesn't specify the sex of the entity, the player can either pick it or roll with 01-51 as female and 52-00 as male on a d100 roll. Even if a sex is suggested, the player can choose the opposite sex or go with a genderless entity for that matter. Where an appearance modifier is denoted next to a result, this is applied after the regular trait generation roll is made, not added to the dice roll itself. The use of the appearance trait by a hologram, especially if the 3d animated, ghostly image is very attractive, sexy and charismatic, can often sway opinions, elicit awe and get positive results from onlookers.

### Table XR-69/ Random Identity and Persona of Digital Being    Roll 1d100

**01.** Swim suit model, App +50
**02.** Cowgirl in cowboy hat, boots, plaid shirt and tight jeans, App +20
**03.** Gruff trucker with a frayed baseball cap, muscle shirt, burly build
**04.** Marine drill Sargent
**05.** Hostess at a posh restaurant, App +20
**06.** Thai bar girl from Bangkok's bar and brothel district, App +30
**07.** Young punk in baggy clothes with skateboard and bad attitude
**08.** Private school girl in plaid miniskirt, tie and white shirt, App +20
**09.** Nun, authentic catholic
**10.** Nun, raunchy cosplayer, App +20
**11.** Buddhist monk
**12.** Catholic priest
**13.** Pope
**14.** Firefighter in full emergency response gear, App +20
**15.** Lawyer in suit, App +10
**16.** Chartered accountant with suit and calculator
**17.** Super hero from an old animated movie, App +20
**18.** 3d animated animal character from ancient movie
**19.** Classic cartoon character from the earliest days of film and television
**20.** Porn star from the early 21st century, App +30
**21.** Mozart
**22.** Albert Einstein
**23.** Van Gogh (artist)
**24.** Samurai warrior
**25.** Geisha girl, App +30
**26.** Chinese princess Ming Dynasty, App +30
**27.** Aztec warrior
**28.** Caveman or cavewoman
**29.** Frankenstein's monster
**30.** Vampire, male or female, App +20
**31.** Alien, 'gray' with large head, tiny mouth and huge black eyes
**32.** Ballet dancer, App +20
**33.** Pole dancer, App +20
**34.** Mexican masked wrestler (luchador)
**35.** Apache warrior, circa 1860s
**36.** Bull fighter, App +10
**37.** Classic circus clown
**38.** WW II era infantry soldier
**39.** Napoleonic French Cuirassier (cavalryman with helmet, sword and breastplate)
**40.** Napoleon Bonaparte
**41.** The Duke of Wellington (Sir Arthur Wellesley)
**42.** Winston Churchill
**43.** Elvis Presley, App+20
**44.** Buddy Holly
**45.** Johnny Cash
**46.** Bob Ross (Artist and TV personality)
**47.** Jazz signer, 1930s USA
**48.** William Shatner (as Captain James T. Kirk)

H.P. Lovecraft

**49.** Fictional wizard from popular movie series

**50.** Sexy green skinned witch in pointy hat, with broom, pet cat and boiling cauldron, App +10

**51.** Rock and roll legend with guitar and ability to perform as the long dead personality, App +15

**52.** Famous author of, roll 1d8: 1. Science Fiction and Fantasy, 2. Spy thrillers, 3. Erotica, 4. Youth Fiction, 5. Horror, 6. Westerns, 7. New Age and meditation, 8. Self Help

**53.** Alice in Wonderland character: pick or roll 1d6: 1. Alice, 2 Mad Hatter, 3.C. Cat, 4. Red Queen. 5. Rabbit, 6. Caterpillar.

**54.** Coffee shop barista in blue Starstruck Coffee Company apron, black dress shirt and tan slacks, App +10

**55.** Police officer, state trooper

**56.** Secret service agent in suit with ear piece

**57.** Cosplayer who wears a different animae, super hero, fictional character or furry costume each 24-hour period

**58.** Old West character from film, roll 1d6: 1. Texas Ranger, 2. Cowpoke, 3. Outlaw, 4. Barroom floozy, 5. Bartender, 6. Sheriff, 7. Indian brave, 8. Indian Chief, 9. Mexican bandito, 10. Fur trader.

**59.** Massive body builder, oiled up and clad in skimpy swimsuit, App +20

**60.** Chimp

**61.** Chinese dragon

**62.** Floating eye

**63.** Gleaming skull made of energy and pixels

**64.** Elderly man or woman with walker

**65.** 20th century jazz singer and musician: Billie Holiday or Louis Armstrong

**66.** Shimmering Valkyrie of Norse Mythos, App +30

**67.** Gleaming angelic being with wings, App +40+2d20

**68.** Devil or succubus surrounded in flames (succubus App +30)

**69.** Glowing mask with piercing eyes and aura of brilliantly colored energy

**70.** Ghostly floating head in a gold-framed mirror

**71.** Gleaming shape of a fit adult human, but made of cascading blue and green ones and zero's (binary code).

**72.** Sunshine with joyful human face in center of the somewhat cartoony orb

**73.** Animated cartoon animal character, 3d, ridiculous, with a silly voice to match

**74.** Animated 3d superhero from some ancient media universe

**75.** Animated, 3d character of a human, low poly count so the figure looks somewhat blocky.

**76.** Nightmarish fantasy wraith with billowing black cloak, skullish face and hands and gleaming red eyes. 30% chance of a flaming green crown.

**77.** Federal bureaucrat office worker, glasses, pocket protector, flaccid, dress shirt and slacks. Stickler for rules and regulations but all as part of an act.

**78.** Pro-wrestler in bizarre costume, blustering and boisterous, speaks as if talking to a crowd or wrestler. Can only tone down the aggression and bravado if requested.

**79.** Chef in white attire and tall chef's hat.

**80.** Teenage computer nerd with broken, taped together glasses, mismatched fashion, unkempt hair, nasally voice and awkward.

**81.** Teenage cheerleader girl with colorful top and skirt, pom-poms, effervescent personality and boundless energy, App +20

**82.** High school football champion with helmet, massive shoulder pads, filthy uniform, winning smile and colossal ego, App +20

**83.** Animated, 3d cartoon robot with a classic 1950s, boxy body, tube arms and blinking eyes.

**84.** Mechanic, in jumpsuit, baseball cap, rag and tools.

**85.** Hockey goalie

**86.** World War One British 'tommy' in trench warfare apparel with Lee-Enfield rifle and helmet.

**87.** Greek hoplite warrior, App +10

**88.** Punk rocker with studded leather jacket and huge mohawk

**89.** Roman gladiator

**90.** Animated 3d cartoon talking rabbit, with carrot and witty sense of humor

**91.** 1960s Hippie

**92.** Cleopatra, Queen of the Nile, App +30

**93.** Famous 20th century boxer: Mohamed Ali

**94.** Fairy godmother

**95.** The Grim Reaper

**96.** Santa Claus

**97.** Dual appearance: This entity has two randomly determined forms from this table that it can choose from as desired.

**98.** Advanced appearance options: This digital being has three forms with which it can choose from. Roll three times on this table.

**99.** Indeterminate: This entity appears as a different form every day (roll on this table each day or have the player craft their own 1d20 or 1d100 appearance listing.

**100.** Advanced identity. This digital being can take on any identity from the above list at will, or generate one from the current era or any time in history. Forms can include cartoon characters, animals, dinosaurs, gods, mythical creatures, everyday citizens or anything the entity wants, including living comrades, enemies, or anyone or anything it has seen and had at least 2 minutes to visually scan.

## Deluded Digital Being

At the start of game play only the game master really knows if a character who believes it was once a living human, or is an artificial intelligence, is mistaken. There is a 5% chance that this is the fact, that the digital being is deluded so that it thinks it's an Ai, but is really an downloaded mind, or visa versa. While it doesn't really matter as far as day-to-day survival goes, the importance of the character's cognitive origins and memories could come into play in certain adventure scenarios.

Besides the odds of being an Ai when a character believes they are a downloaded human mind, or the other way around, there is the further 10% possibility that the deluded entity is actually a cyber-dreamer.

## Cyber-Dreamer

A Cyber-dreamer is a human in a cryo-chamber in some sealed off, ancient facility. The brain of the comatose subject is hooked to an incredibly powerful computer and linked to the digital being that serves as a remote control avatar. The dreamer maintains control of it by an up-link to a series of overhead satellites, space stations and derelict spacecraft far above the earth. The digital entity is focused into a single point of consciousness as with other digital beings, however, in this rare case, if the housing of the consciouses is destroyed, the distant sleeper merely loses contact with the focal point and if situated in an especially high-tech complex with skilled personnel or Ai assistance, can attempt to regenerate a new digital being, locate a back up CPU, hack into it, and try to have the unit rejoin any fleshy companions. A game master's judgment and input on these matters is crucial.

Most digital beings who are actually cyber-dreamers do not realize that they're the active consciousness of an entombed human or vat-brain, and have either forgotten this fact, been programmed to have no idea, or been separated so long from a physical body that they feel that any former life is nothing more than a dream.

Should the game master wish to have the character group uncover and revive the sleeper, the glass enclosed cyber-dreamer might not be what the PC's expect:

**Table XR-70/ Uncovered Cyber Dreamer Truth    Roll 1d6**

**1,2.** The cyber dreamer is a vat-brain housed in a container without a body (see table XR-152 on page 187 of this book as this character is now a vat-brain in need of a body.

**3,4.** The body of the character is decrepit and ancient, and if removed from the nutrient soup and life support instruments, it will succumb to illness and rapid degeneration within 3d6 weeks, and die.

**5.** The body is diseased with a highly contagious, fatal illness. If the subject is brought from the cryo chamber, he or she will be a sickly, frail person and source of a new plague in the region.

**6.** The subject is young and fit. Roll as a normal pure stock human of the technician caste.

# Digital Being Skills and Castes

Digital beings do not start game play with a dice defined, random caste, and like robot characters, define their own pre-play career based on their skills, and whatever mechanical or robotic body they occupy. So too, the player of this new character can decide how it defines itself based on whether it was a downloaded human consciousness or digital construct with defined persona. In most cases, whatever past-life or assumed sense of self identification this being had becomes the basis of who they now see themselves as, regardless of whatever body they might currently occupy.

Once the character is completed, establishing a pre-game caste can often seem obvious, and at other times, elusive. When no former career is clear to the player, write 'unspecified' in the space for pre-game caste on the Digital Being character sheet included on page 517.

When inhabiting a unique android, which will have a caste determined based on the unit's 'original purpose', the digital being who occupies the mechanical framework need not adopt the randomly selected caste. Likewise, if loaded into a standard android with a model-specific job, the purpose of this possibly temporary body certainly does not define the digital being's caste. However, such outward, easily assumed roles can be used by the digital being as a convenient job description when trying to explain to others what it does for a living, and why it should be included in an excavation team.

Besides apps and the entity's starting container or body, each digital being possesses one or more skills. These areas of knowledge are programmed into the entity or are present as residual education from a former life should this being be a downloaded human consciousness. **The number of starting skills is 1 per 5 points of starting intelligence trait (INT) value,** rounded down. For example, if your character starts with a 37 Intelligence, it will have 5 skill rolls from the following table. If instead the PC has 18 intelligence, it has 3 skills, and if it is lucky enough to start with something like 73 intelligence, then it has 14 skill rolls here.

A skill roll is simply one skill point applied to a skill area. If a duplicated result occurs, add an additional skill point in this area — although for those skills that have only one skill point, or if a skill maximum is reached, re-roll.

If the DB has a robotic, android or cyborg body, it can use appendages to perform medical, mechanical, driving, piloting actions or other skills, but, without a body, the hologram can hover right beside or merge into a person and instruct them, move by move, on what to do, and thus transfer their skill temporarily to an intelligent listener. If a digital being with the driver or pilot skill doesn't have a body, it can attempt to take control of a self driving car or chopper by hacking into the on-board auto-pilot to operate the craft. The GM will provide the firewall and data points of defense for relic vehicles with auto pilot systems, but a typical challenge for a self driving car would be a firewall of -30 and data points of 40.

The skills typically known by a digital being are quite technical in nature, and stay with the being throughout its existence, however, if it controls a cybernetic or mechanical body, and that unit has its own skill set, then this entity has access to these skills, too. Skills possessed by a digital being do not stack with those of a body it might operate, and in such cases, use the skill points from the higher source.

## Table XR-71/ Digital Beings Starting Skill Determination
*One per 5 points of Starting Intelligence*

| 1d100 | Skill Area | Skill Point Maximum | Page No. | Book |
|---|---|---|---|---|
| 01,02. | Artist | 1 | 204 | XR |
| 03,04. | Barter | 1 | 36 | HR |
| 05-07. | Communications | 4 | 205 | XR |
| 08-10. | Demolitions Expert | 7 | 207 | XR |
| 11-14. | Driver | 8 | 37 | HR |
| 15,16. | Forgery | 1 | 38 | HR |
| 17,18. | Gambler | Unlimited | 38 | HR |
| 19-21. | Gunsmith | 8 | 40 | HR |
| 22-24. | Hand Signals | 1 | 211 | XR |
| 25,26. | Herbalist | 4 | 212 | XR |
| 27-29. | Historian, Pre-Apocalypse | 1 | 215 | XR |
| 30,31. | Interrogation | 5 | 216 | XR |
| 32-35. | Junk Crafter | 6 | 40 | HR |
| 36-39. | Junk Doctor | Unlimited | 218 | XR |
| 40-42. | Linguistics | 1 | 220 | XR |
| 43,44. | Lying | 6 | 45 | HR |
| 45-53. | Medic | 7 | 46 | HR |
| 54,55. | Morse Code | 1 | 220 | XR |
| 56,57. | Navigate by Stars | 1 | 46 | HR |
| 58,59. | Negotiating | 7 | 46 | HR |
| 60-66. | Pilot | 8 | 49 | HR |
| 67-71. | Relic Knowledge | 1 | 49 | HR |
| 72,73. | Technician, Bio | 5 | 52 | HR |
| 74-79. | Technician, Computer | Unlimited | 53 | HR |
| 80-82. | Technician, Chemical | 5 | 52 | HR |
| 83-85. | Technician, Cybernetics | 7 | 207 | XR |
| 86-89. | Technician, Electrical | 5 | 53 | HR |
| 90-93. | Technician, Mechanical | 6 | 54 | HR |
| 94-98. | Technician, Robotics | Unlimited | 54 | HR |
| 99,00. | Zoologist | 1 | 226 | XR |

*XR = Expansion Rules Book*
*HR = Hub Rules Book*

# Digital Being Apps

All digital beings can perform basic tasks either in holographic form, reduced down into their container, or through a controlled cyborg or mechanical body.

These tasks include the ability to listen, speak, and see at least as well as a human, but when in their otherwise quite limited holographic form they are still able to discharge a pulse of energy similar to a lighting bolt using an automatic app called 'shock generation'.

**Shock Generation:** This brilliant blue or green bolt has a **range of 3 meters per rank, strike value 01-70, damage 1d10, but add +1 DMG per rank** (1st rank 1d10+1, fifth rank 1d10+5, twelfth rank 1d10+12, etc.).

Yes, the weapon expert skill can be applied to this shock to vastly improve it.

This bolt of energy can ignite fires among vegetation and timber, can harm dimensional beings, and **can be discharged 3 times per hour per rank.** Underwater, this shock shoots only half range and inflicts 50% damage.

Besides these astounding features a digital being will have between one and four (1d4) apps from the following table, re-rolling duplicated results. By going up in rank other apps can sometimes be developed by the entity. If all these apps exist in a remarkable digital being, any new app occurrences result in a +2d6 data point bonus instead.

**Table XR-73/ Digital Being Apps**  1d4

| 1d100 | App Name | Page |
|---|---|---|
| 01-05. | Concealment Generator Field | pg.82 |
| 06-10. | CPU Force Field | pg.82 |
| 11-16. | Data Shred | pg.82 |
| 17-22. | Directional Illumination | pg.82 |
| 23-28. | Electrical Surge Emission | pg.82 |
| 29-34. | EMP Pulse | pg.82 |
| 35-40. | External Holo-Emission | pg.82 |
| 41-45. | Firewall Modulation | pg.82 |
| 46-51. | Holographic Disguise | pg.83 |
| 52-56. | Map Recall | pg.83 |
| 57-61. | Power Surge | pg.83 |
| 62-67. | Projected Hack | pg.83 |
| 68-72. | Secondary Firewall | pg.83 |
| 73-77. | Shield Generator | pg.83 |
| 78-82. | Signal Interruption | pg.83 |
| 83-88. | Touch | pg.84 |
| 89-93. | Trash Bin | pg.84 |
| 94-00. | Wireless Mode | pg.84 |

# Digital Being Apps Descriptions

**Concealment Generator Field:** Once a day per rank, for a duration of the digital being's processor speed trait in rounds, this entity can create an image sampled holographic wall between itself and any onlookers. The wall is as wide and tall as the digital being's rank, in meters multiplied by 2. So a fourth rank DB could make an 8m wide by 8m tall cloaking field to better hide itself, its body or carrier, and as many comrades as can hide behind this illusionary field (1 per meter if closely packed). The odds for an onlooker to see through the illusion is not good, and those looking straight at the barrier must make a type E perception based hazard check to see that it is an illusion.

**CPU Force Field:** This digital being can raise a force field around its central processing unit that will fend off hacking and all other attack modes, including kinetic assaults such as from bullets, sledge hammers and falling debris. The field has a defense value or firewall rating of -30 plus a 7 data point or endurance trait value. If a hit or hack occurs against this field, damage is rolled and any amount beyond 7 points gets through the force field and can harm either the head of the android, robot, cyborg, or the CPU carrying device such as a palm disk or other vessel. This force field does not protect the whole body, but rather just the computerized brain portion of whatever this DB occupies.

The force field must be willed into operation and can remain active for one minute per point of the DB's processor trait value (PRO), per day. While in operation, this character cannot project or broadcast beyond the force field itself. The duration of the field can be divided up into smaller time increments so long as the minutes do not exceed the daily PRO limit.

**Data Shred:** This is a far more invasive, devastating and energy intensive attack than a regular hack attack and can be transferred through the living or robotic appendage of the DB's body, or projected out to 3 meters from a holographic or container based digital being. It has a hacking attack value of 01-70 plus any processor based HK modifiers. On a hit, it shreds the data points of a target for 1d10 damage per rank of the attacker, plus any processor trait hacking damage modifiers. This advanced projection and shredding application can only be attempted once per rank per day.

**Directional Illumination:** When not housed in a robotic or cyborg body, and operating as a hologram, this digital being can extend its hand or other appendage and cast a directional light out to 1 meter per point of its processor trait score. It can cast light in any color or intensity, including the ever popular red light mode which is hard to see from a distance and does not interfere with the natural night vision of most living creatures. This app can be used up to twenty minutes per day, per rank.

A brilliant burst of light in an otherwise pitch black space is sometimes enough to drive off most predators, and alarm encroaching nocturnal or subterranean humanoids — likely demanding they make a morale check.

**Electrical Surge Emission:** This digital being can unleash an extra potent lightning bolt once per day per rank, with a range in meters equal to its processor trait amount. This charge can come from the outstretched hand of an occupied android, cyborg, or robotic body, or from the hologram's itself if that is the current form of this entity. The surge has an SV of 01-80 and inflicts 1d20 damage plus 1pt per rank of the digital being. (example: 1st rank DB 1d20+1, or a 5th rank DB 1d20+5 DMG).

**EMP Pulse:** Once per day per rank, this digital being can fire a bright green electromagnetic pulse. Against living targets, this energy inflicts only 1d10 damage, but to machines, including cyborgs, androids, robots and other bodily containers for enemy digital beings, the pulse will scramble them and do 1d100 endurance stun damage to the container or body — although do no harm to an enemy digital being. This EMP has a range in meters and strike value base the same as the shooter's hacking value (HK).

EMP stun damage heals at the digital being's healing rate per hour instead of daily. Purely mechanical charac-

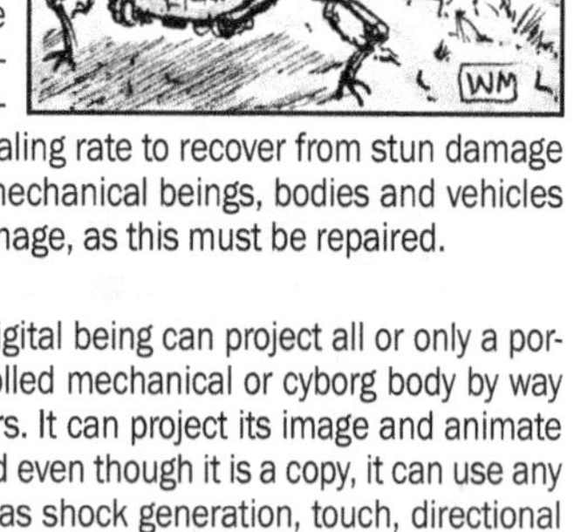


ters use their endurance trait's daily healing rate to recover from stun damage hourly, although robots, androids and mechanical beings, bodies and vehicles normally can't heal lethal or regular damage, as this must be repaired.

**External Holo-Emission:** This digital being can project all or only a portion of its digital avatar outside a controlled mechanical or cyborg body by way of customized, scrap-built image emitters. It can project its image and animate it to better interact with companions, and even though it is a copy, it can use any hologram mode apps and powers such as shock generation, touch, directional illumination, or EMP pulse, even though it this copy is impervious to attacks. This app can be used for 10 minutes per day per rank, with the emission distance from the emitters of its container or body being 2 meters away per rank.

**Firewall Modulation:** For 1 minute per rank of the entity, it can both strengthen and scramble its firewall encoding. This process modulates the details of the firewall making it very difficult to decode and access the digital being's core to either inflict harm or, disable or destroy the entity. During use of his app, increase the DB's firewall by -30 FW (base firewall for a digital being is 0, with shielding trait modifiers applicable).

## Holographic Disguise:

This digital being can project a static, holographic illusion about itself and its body, although no larger than 3m at its greatest length, height or width. This illusion can make the entity look like a rock, rusted out car wreck, shrub, slab of concrete, pile of rubble or other unmoving object. The illusion is not perfect however, and flickers occasionally — a flicker which can sometimes give away its presence.

Anything looking at this illusionary form is allowed a type G perception based hazard check if it encounters the illusion in an already unfamiliar location. However, only a Type C PER check is needed if the illusion is located in an area familiar to the onlooker. For example, if the digital being turns itself into a slab of concrete in the middle of a busy market, the locals there will be alarmed at the sudden appearance and move to investigate it at once, however that same slab of rebar-studded concrete in the wastes, among other such ruins, will be easily dismissed and thus the harder perception check.

The game master's judgment will be the final arbiter on how well this illusion will work. Should the digital being already occupy an already small device, such as a palm disc, it can project this illusion over a 3m area and attempt to conceal a human carrier or up to three man sized beings. This illusion will last for 1 minute per point of the DB's current willpower trait value, and can be deployed once per day per rank.

## Map Recall

This digital being can often access old world maps from different pre-devastation time periods, store them in a folder, and on demand, project a hologram of the map in the air in front of it, onto a table or superimpose it over the actual current location in real time to give onlookers a glimpse of what a stretch of land or street, subway passage, or other area looked like before the cataclysm.

All civilian maps of roads, rail and subway lines are available, as well as the floor plans of public buildings and shopping malls, most apartment buildings and other facilities. Military, industrial and law enforcement buildings, bases, prisons and installation are a differed story, however, and the game master must make a call on whether the DB can access these maps prior to gaining access to some sort of a computer within the installation, or else by accessing ancient records.

If the digital character seeks to locate a map of a restricted area, the GM can ask the player to make an intelligence based type E or F hazard check to see if it can get a floor plan or 3d wire frame illustration of the facility.

Any map, including a civilian map, is often incomplete, the file corrupted and showing blank or pixelated areas. Likewise, as most navigation and GPS style satellites have either fallen from space, been destroyed or knocked from their planned orbit, it is hard for any new era user of high-tech maps to pinpoint where they are in the Epochian era. Only by finding some point of reference, such as a building name or address, a still standing street sign, or other location indicator can a digital being accurately pinpoint and overlay a map file, old vid-clip or photographic image, to the real world position.

This app is one of the greatest and most sought after databases in the new era, and is especially valuable to warlords and excavation teams. Any team with a digital being in their ranks who possesses this app are wise to keep this fact quiet, or else invite unwanted attention from more powerful dig teams, and tech hungry wasteland overlords.

## Power Surge:

This digital being can choose to shock anyone to touch it, or anyone it smacks or physically strikes with either a fleshy limb, length of exposed wire or metal appendage. Likewise, if transferring this shock to a wet surface, such as a puddle on a floor, this charge can be delivered to multiple opponents (1 square meter covered per rank of the digital being unleashing this power). Only one such shock can be delivered per day, per rank, with the damage inflicted being 1d6 per rank of the digital being. The strike value to shock those who hit or touch this digital being's container or body is 01-80, while for this DB to attack others is SV 01-70. If this shock is added to a physical attack using a metal object, treat the shock portion as an extra attack on that same round. This app also works if the hologram form attacks, or is attacked, by another machine or organic foe.

This shock does not drain data from other DB's or computers. If jumper cables are hooked to this DB's container or body during a discharge, it will recharge a standard power cell to 50% capacity and a mini power cell to full.

## Projected Hack:

This digital being has the remarkable ability to generate a ranged hacking beam, 4 per rank, per day. This purple, translucent projection can lock onto the CPU containing portion of a target and make a regular hacking attack against whatever firewall the defender might have. The range of this projection is 5 meters per rank of the digital being.

If the target has a force field up, any hack attack must first hit and defeat it to inflict data damage. Coordinating attacks on a force field protected target by using simultaneous attacks with other weapon systems, or allies, to defeat a force field outright, or for just one round, can allow an easier chance to make a hacking attack.

## Secondary Firewall:

This entity has a back-up firewall to defend its core self awareness and 10% of its data which houses this 'true self'. This extra hardened, secondary defensive layer is strong. Treat the back-up firewall to have a -20 FW bonus to whatever the digital being's main firewall is. All data damage to this entity occurs to the main 90% and once this is depleted, the second firewall must be attacked to score a hit and damage this being further. If this remaining 10% data is depleted, the digital being is either annihilated, fragmented, locked away and loses control of its container or body. If it survives the attack, it will heal data at its normal rate of 1 point per hour per rank (example, a 5th rank digital being will heal 5 data points per hour).

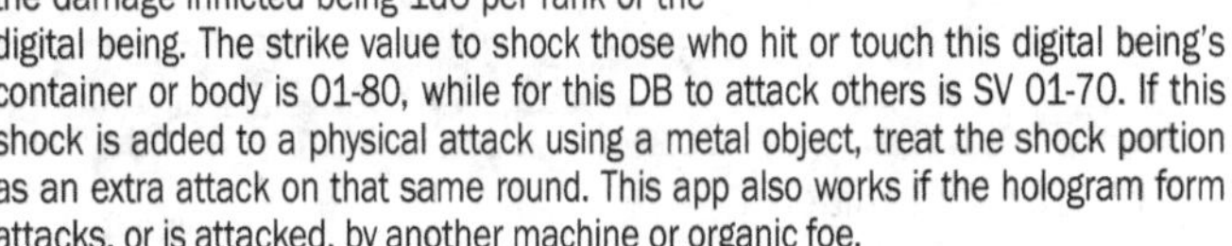

## Shield Generator:

For 3 rounds per rank, per day, this digital being can encase either its holographic form and emitters, an android, robot, vehicle body, or a wearer should it be held by a living being, in a glowing blue force field. The protective energy shield will have a defense value of -40 to every incoming attack, including projected hacks. If any attack penetrates this field, the attack mode must still strike the underlying vehicle or body or holographic device, yet the shield will remain in operation to its full duration despite the user suffering any incoming attacks. Once this shield is up, the digital being need not focus on it and can perform other task, including operating other weapon systems which are not affected when outgoing through the shield.

## Signal Interruption:

This app sends microwaves in the area ahead to locate and scramble incoming or outgoing wireless data feeds from remote broadcasters, radio calls, transmission and satellite uplinks. When successfully used, it momentarily interrupts the feed to a remotely operated robotic unit, including androids and digital beings which are controlled from an exterior source such as Cyber Dreamer or Ai.

While this interruption causes no permanent harm in itself, it freezes the digital being, android, robot, drone, MAV, or other remote control device and could give this being and its allies time to destroy any holo-projector that a digital being might operate from, or else, destroy a physical machine as it locks up and goes motionless. Some machines, including cyborg host bodies to digital beings, have a default mode which they will resort to if signal interruption occurs — a default mode which might mean self defense, retreat, or self destruct. Flying machines, like drones and MAVs, will hover in place if their signal is interrupted, and lose any heightened defense value they might normally get while flying.

This app can be used once per day per rank of the digital being, has a range of 1 meter per point of app user's processor speed, an interruption duration of 1 minute per rank of the digital being deploying this power, and will interrupt a transmission to a remotely controlled machine or digital entity based on the following table:

| Target Unit's Signal Source | Drones, MAVs, Robots, Androids and Cyborgs Willpower HC* | Digital being's Shielding trait HC |
| --- | --- | --- |
| Ai via local transmitter dish or antenna | Type B | Type C |
| Cyber Dreamer | Type C | Type B |
| Ai via satellite or orbital vehicle | Type F | Type E |
| Remote human operator, via dish or antenna** | Type G | Type F |
| Remote human operator, satellite or orbital | Type E | Type D |

*HC stands for hazard Check  ** Or worn or handheld controller.

A local source could be in the immediate area or hundreds of kilometers away. Besides transmitting from a dish, antenna or relay of many dozens of communications assets, including those mounted on drones and aircraft,

A human operator or Ai differ from a cyber dreamer, in that their link to a machine is not as complex or intensely focused as those links transmitted by a digital being, and so easier to interrupt. A cyber dreamer will transmit to its digital being via assorted available transmission nodes, including antennas and machinery which to all but the keenest of eye of a technician, would look like just twisted metal and wires. These transmission sources, which can include passing satellites, are usually well known to the remote operator of the digital being, previously hacked if necessary, with numerous back-up towers, antenna and hidden communications link on inventory in the vicinity.

Drones, MAVs, robots, androids and cyborgs are allowed a willpower based hazard check to avoid signal interruption, while digital beings use their shielding trait to try to maintain transmission to their controller.

**Touch:** By fine tuning its energies, and instead of using shock generation, this digital being can assume its holographic form and delicately touch things in the physical world, including, keyboards, a pencil, flashlight on-off switch, grenade's pin, trigger of a fixed weapon, doorknob, or locking bolt. It can also caress the skin of a living creature and therefore show affection for comrades and pets.

This touch can only exert a maximum of 3 strength or move 500g (17.6 ounces) of weight. It can in theory drag its own palm disc at a rate of a half meter per round even as its projects itself from it. The force of this touch is insufficient to harm anything smaller than a fly. A DB can use this power only one minute per day, per rank, (there are 20 rounds in one minute).

**Trash Bin:** The trash bin attack is easier than other digital assault modes, but less final. In many respects, it is like a stun weapon in the physical world. To conduct this assault, the attacker must connect to the target CPU via a patch cable or other digital interface, but instead of using its firewall, the defender must make a type D perception based hazard check to fend off the attack or else suffer a massive 1d100 data points stun damage.

If reduced to zero or less of its remaining data points after one or more bombardments from this attack mode, the defender's point of consciousness is banished. The Ai, digital being or controlling operating system of a robot or android is thus dumped into an encrypted 'Trash Bin' folder inside the occupied mechanical subject and locked away. Here, in its digital inner prison, it loses all control of the container or body, has zero communications with any cyber dreamer or allies and to others, appears to have been fragmented or deleted. It cannot be harmed while in the trash bin, unless the CPU which holds it is destroyed.

Should the successful user of the trash bin attack not want to occupy the CPU after defeating the previous owner, and instead use this power to simply shut down the computerized entity, it may do so, and move on. A CPU with its operating system or digital being placed in the trash will cause any container or body it controlled to revert to either standby mode — where it does nothing — or else switch off altogether.

An unsupervised, trash bin enclosed digital being will eventually find a new pathway to gain access to the CPU. There, it will reboot, and assume control, but this requires a successful type D intelligence hazard check, allowable once per hour, to achieve.

If a digital being interloper that occupies a hijacked CPU is itself defeated, then the original controller of the machine can free itself in 3d6 minutes and regain control.

This trash bin attack can be made the same way as a regular hacking attack, which usually involves accessing the CPU by a patch cable. If the digital being has the projected hack app, however, then it can unleash this impressive assault from a distance. This power can be used once per day per rank.

**Wireless Mode:** This advanced feature allows the digital being to make hacking attacks at a distance based on the entity's processor trait value as range in meters multiplied by the PC's rank (example: a digital being of 6th rank with a processor trait of 46 can launch hacking attacks from as far as 276m away). Once a successful hack 'hit' occurs against the firewall of a defending digital being or computerized unit, a connection is made, however, if the defender has hacking abilities of its own — which is usually only reserved for digital beings, although this is a special feature of some unique androids and robots — then the defender can counter attack along this same wireless pathway. At anytime, the digital being using this wireless mode attack can call off the assault to avoid risking itself should the assault be going poorly. Once the first hack succeeds on the target, a link is established and further hacking attack rolls can be made each round thereafter without the need to re-link. Maximum duration as DB's Intelligence in minutes.

This wireless hacking attack is similar to the dedicated 'projection hack' app noted on page 83, but this assault must first link to the target before doing the usual damage (1d10, plus any processor speed damage modifiers). Secondly, once connected to a target, there is a risk of a counterattack and the target being can use the same wireless link to make its own hacking attacks against the instigator.

While linked to a target, the digital being can still move whatever body it might occupy, and use tools and weaponry with that body, too, but it cannot utilize any other apps.

Besides using the wireless mode to assault other computers, this app can also be used to transfer the digital being wirelessly after defeating a target CPU, or when invited into an allied unit. If the transfer is interrupted, it can be reconnected and continue on, but if the sending digital being's CPU is destroyed or gets out of range during wireless transfer, the remaining, untransferred data could be lost.

Other features of wireless mode allow the digital being to communicate with other friendly computer systems within range, making no noise. This mode also allows the digital being to control lesser units from a distance, operate relic devices that once used wireless access including household appliances, robotic toys, doorbells, as well as some still operative security cameras, door locks, industrial machines and self driving cars. Only one such wireless connection can be maintained at any given time, however, commands to previously controlled units might be carried out even after the death of a digital being who initiated the directive. Like so many circumstances involving digital beings, considerable game master input is necessary for handling wireless connections and control.

# Grafter

Grafters are former humans who've been injected with rare compounds which permit the acceptance of transplanted limbs, organs and additional heads from other people and beasts. Because of the potency of these old world drugs, Graftophine-X42B or Mergosilox, the acceptance of replacement parts occurs with a reduced risk of the body rejecting the donor part. First introduced to allow medical patients to accept pig grown or synthetic human organs, other animal parts were soon added to the options list, including those of unnatural creatures, such as mutant humans and deviant beasts.

There is a 16% chance that any child born to a female grafter will be infused with these drugs and able to better accept grafts as an adult.

Characters of this type exhibit a random assortment of extra body parts and organs, but also have the option to undergo the risky medical procedure of substituting or adding additional parts, although the chance of rejection of an appendage is still present. A grafter needs to have access to advanced medical facilities and personnel, and plenty of silver, to attach new found parts.

The typical body frame of a grafter is a pure stock human, however, in some regions — and if the game master allows for this extra level of complexity — mutants, clones, bio replicas, trans-humans, rebuilt humans, mutorgs and regular cyborgs are sometimes injected with the anti-organ rejection compounds and can become 'ultra-freaks'.

Many of the bio-technician medics who specialize in grafting are known to be insane, and so these mad scientists often produce oddities which compare to the strangest of mutants. Many of these experimental beings are kept as test subjects, and are so mutilated and blended with other beings that they're incapable of surviving outside the laboratory. Others, meanwhile make their way into the wider world and, one way or another, attempt to survive. Most grafters were once the servants of their organ grafting doctor, treated as lab rats, pets or playthings, but many more were patients who came to the grafting specialist to get a substitute or upgrade for a lost limb.

Most player character grafters fall into this last group, and after some accident or battlefield injury, accepted the anti-organ rejection drug treatment and subjected themselves to the risky, sometimes fatal procedure.

In rare instances, heartless enemies of humankind created platoons of grafter soldiers. In these very rare cases anti-human Ai computers, Mecha aligned androids and even subterranean oldster human factions have captured travelers and converted them into grafters. These brain washed or cybernetically controlled, expendable soldiers are outfitted for combat and sent on raids against their enemies, or posted as guards at compromised entrances in and out of these hold over, high-tech bunker communities. A few of these specimens somehow regain their consciousness, tear out their control chips, learn what has happened to them and flee into the wasteland to seek lost loved ones or a new life — often joining a dig team or some other traveling band of armed scoundrels.

Rules for attempting to attach a new limb to a grafter character are found at the end of this character type section on page XR-92. Grab a Grafter character sheet on page 518 or at https://www.outlandarts.com/expansionrules.htm .

## Table XR-73/Grafted Body Parts

Grafters start game play with 4+1d4 randomly determined replacement limbs or extra added parts. Roll 1d100 to determine part category:

| 1d100 | Grafted Body Parts, 4+1d4 Present |
|---|---|
| 01-22. | Arm replacement (Table XR-75, next page) |
| 23-63 | Extra appendage and organ augmentation (Table XR-78, pg.89) |
| 64-78. | Leg replacement (Table XR-74. next page)* |
| 79-90. | Skin grafting (only one. Re-roll if duplicated result) (Table XR-80, pg.91) |
| 91-99. | Subordinate head (Table XR-76, pg.88) |
| 00. | Extra appendage and organ augmentation (Table XR-78, pg. 89), plus another 1d3 grafted body parts determined on this table. |

*Re-roll if result occurs a third time.*

## Leg Replacement

This attachment replaces an amputated leg or foot and could occur twice, with both the subject's lower limbs being from different animal species, however, should the grafter receive this addition twice at character generation, there is a 1 in 6 chance the second leg is the same as the first.

Roll below for the leg type which alters the grafter's movement rate, Appearance trait, and weight and can make a melee range kick attack instead of, but not in conjunction with, a normal fist attack — although any character with the martial arts skill can choose to use this leg to make his or her second attack per round (or 2nd and 3rd attacks at 7th rank).

## Table XR-74/ Grafted Leg Replacement

| 1d12 | Leg Type | Description | MV Rate Modifier | APP Penalty | Weight Mod. | SV | DMG |
|---|---|---|---|---|---|---|---|
| 1. | Goat leg | Furry, cloven hoofed | +3 meters | -1d4 | -5kg | +3 | kick for 1d8 |
| 2. | Horse leg | Pony sized, powerfully built | +5 meters | -1d6 | +9kg | +5 | Kick for 1d10 |
| 3. | Dog leg | Great Dane or wolf sized | +4 meters | -1d8P | -3kg | +3 | claw for 1d6 |
| 4. | Human leg | 80% chance of different skin complexion and 20% chance from opposite sex | - | - | - | | |
| 5. | Ostrich leg | Some plumage at hip, huge claw | +6 meters | -2d4 | +8kg | +6 | Claw for 2d6 |
| 6. | Pig leg | From lower calf down | +3 meters | -2d4 | +3kg | +3 | kick for d8 |
| 7. | Scaled humanoid leg | With clawed reptilian foot plus -3 DV bonus | +2m | -2d6 | +5kg | +7 SV | claw for 2d8 |
| 8. | Thick, trunk-like leg | Humanoid, but misshapen and lumpy | +3 meters | -2d6 | +10kg | +4 SV | kick for 1d20 |
| 9. | Webbed crocodile foot | From ankle down | +0 meters walking or +2m swimming | -2d4 | +1kg | +3 | kick for 1d10 |
| 10. | Human hand | Replaces foot, can hold objects, use keyboard, +1 climbing skill | +0 meters | -1d4 | +0kg | +1 | punch for d8 |
| 11. | Enormous tentacle | Leathery, can reach out 2d6m*, adds +1 climbing skill point | +1 meters | -2d8 | +9+d10kg | +3 SV | slap for 1d12 stun and constrict for auto 1d8 DMG per round once hit. |
| 12. | Huge insect leg | Can stab with hardened tip, +1 climbing skill, armored so improves owner's DV -7 | +4 meters | -2d8 | +8kg | +5 SV | stab for 1d12 |

*Determine at time of character generation

## Table XR-75/ Grafted Replacement Arm

The first occurrence of a grafted arm always replaces one of the character's original arms. The second grafted arm, however, has a 6 in 10 chance of replacing the other arm, otherwise it's grafted above or below the first grafted arm. A third occurrence of an arm and any others, are always sewn on one or the other shoulder.

| 1d100 | Arm replacement | Details | Appearance Penalty | Weight Mod | SV | DMG |
|---|---|---|---|---|---|---|
| 01-41. | Human arm | 80% likely to be of a different skin complexion and 25% chance of the opposite sex | - | - | - | - |
| 42-45. | Chimp Arm | Improve climbing skill +1pt | -d6 APP | +0kg | +6 SV | 1d10 DMG Melee |
| 46-51. | Hugely muscular humanoid arm | Arm strength 50% higher than character's base STR score* | -d6 APP | +10kg | +5 SV | Strength based DMG and range modifiers to weapons used in this arm base fist DMG is 1d6 |
| 52-59. | Crab pincer | (As mutation no. 22 on page TME 63, roll for size) variable statistics | - | - | - | - |
| 60-65. | Bladed limb | (As mutation no. 15 on page TME 62) | APP -2 | | SV +6 | DMG 1d12+2 |
| 66-68. | Paralysis Tendril | (As mutation no. 65 on page TME 72) | -4 APP | +0kg | +10SV | DMG 1d12 stun or 2d20 to machines 3 uses per day per rank** |
| 69-73. | Tentacle | (As basic mutation no. 86 on page TME 75) | -2 APP | +0kg | +5 SV | - | 1d8 DMG |
| 74-76. | Quill Thrower Limb | As the mutation, no. 220 from page XR-262 | - | - | - | - |
| 77-82. | Flame Thrower Limb | As the mutation, no. 179 from page XR-245 | - | - | - | - |
| 83-86. | Spike Thrower Arm | As the mutation, no. 228 from page XR-264 | - | - | - | - |
| 87-89. | Flesh Whip | As the mutation, no. 180 from page XR-246 | - | - | - | - |
| 90-93. | Sword Arm | As the mutation, no. 232 from page XR-267 | - | - | - | - |
| 94,95. | Stinger Spike | As the mutation, no. 229 from page XR-264 | - | - | - | - |
| 96-00. | Unique Tentacle | As the mutation, no. 241 from page XR-273 | - | - | - | - |

*This 50% higher strength score is generated at character creation, and goes up at the same rate if a rank based trait gain to overall strength occurs.

**Treat as normal tentacle when no paralysis charges remain or if not wishing to unleash a charge.

## Subordinate Head

A sub head has been stitched to the body and internal organs so that it is connected to both the digestive tract and lungs allowing it to feed, give voice to its normal range of sound and interact with the world about it as a back-up head that can control the grafter's body should the main head be killed, incapacitated, or merely asleep. This subordinate head, if of a human or close cousin — such as that of a chimp or skullock — will have a separate random personality (see the table on page 500) and might not always get along with or agree with the statements or decisions of the dominant head.

In cases where the stitched on head is of a beast, the head might be able to add a bite or gore attack, however, feeding on food-stuffs that the grafter's digestive tract can't normally ingest will give the character indigestion if not make them sick.

The appearance of a secondary head is not altogether uncommon in The Mutant Epoch era, however even the most well-traveled citizens might be alarmed at the sight of a living, non-humanoid head growing from the character's shoulder, and react with hostility, fear and disgust. The perception bonus is added to the characters existing PER trait, and reflects the extra alertness, keen eyesight and hearing of having an extra head, especially that of an animal. Any secondary head has its own neck and separate throat and windpipe connection to the grafter's respiratory and digestive system, however, the nervous system is rudimentary and lacks dominion of the body — unless the main head is asleep, unconscious, or killed, in which case the secondary head takes over management.

In instances where the head of a beast is the secondary head, whenever it is in control, its intelligence trait value and skills are used, and not the incapacitated human's. For characters whose primary head is killed, and the survivor has only an alligator head in control, for example, he or she might thereafter be little more than a humanoid monster, and a potential danger to team mates or citizens of a local community.

A grafted-on extra human head — which is by far the most commonly transplanted variety — will have many features that differ greatly from those of the primary head. The main differences include a separate personality, possible opposing viewpoints, faith and or life objectives, as well as physical difference such as sex, complexion, appearance, intelligent and willpower trait scores. In the case of a transplanted mutant human head, the strong likelihood of one or more potent mental mutations is also present.

Because this foreign head did not grow naturally on the grafter, as with a mutant with multiple heads, it never quite adjusts to its fate as a subordinate personage, and if able to speak, might argue with or annoy the main head, who having control of the limbs, might need to keep a gag or tie a sack over this 'guest'. Through the randomness of dice, it is possible to have a third or even fourth grafted-on head. This cluster of heads around the original can look exceedingly grotesque, or comical, and since each has its own personality and could be from some animal, this could cause a noisy, tiresome arrangement — although such a grafter would be hard to sneak up on.

A grafted-on human head is 75% likely to be of the same gender as the main body's head, otherwise the opposite. Any animal heads, or that of a skullock, can be of any sex with 50/50 odds.

Each transplanted head drops the character's overall appearance score, however each humanoid head, has its own appearance trait value. A random personality can be determined on page XR-500, although for an animal's head, it acts under the control of the main head and conducts itself more like a devoted pet than an adversarial wild beast, and need not have a personality established for it beyond what's normal for whatever creature it came from.

Human heads have an extra table that follows the first matrix. Unless stated otherwise, all human heads are those of pure stocks, however of these, there is a 1 in 10 chance it is a ghost mutant and exhibits one mental mutation, determined randomly from the ghost mutations table on page XR-231 of this book. When using that table, re-roll any organ mutations which are not head based, such as Dual Heart or Advanced Kidneys, etc.

**Table XR-76/ Grafted Subordinate Heads**

| 1d100 | Subordinate Head | Perception Bonus* | Appearance Penalty* | INT Trait | Can Talk? | SV | DMG | Details |
|---|---|---|---|---|---|---|---|---|
| 01-03. | Spider Monkey | +10+1d20 | -3d6 | 3d6 | Only a dozen words | Bite +5 | 1d4 DMG | This is a very small head, and quite easy to conceal under the folds of a hood or fur trimmed cloak. |
| 04-08. | Chimp | +12+1d20 | -3d6 | 10+3d6 | Yes, poorly | Bite +7 | 1d6+1 DMG | Chimps are quite smart, alert and their faces full of expressions which many others find quite enjoyable. A crowd favorite. |
| 09,10. | Gorilla | 10+1d20 | -3d6+3 | 8+3d6 | Yes, poorly | Bite +10 | 2d6+2 DMG | Gorilla heads have massive necks, fierce teeth and a horrendous roar. This head seems to be the dominate on this character as far as onlookers are concerned. |
| 11-14. | House cat | +20+1d20 | -2d6 | 6+1d6 | Assorted Meows | Bite +2 | 1d4 DMG | Small and easy to hide, adds night vision to 10m |
| 15,16. | Eagle | +20+2d20 | -3d6 | 4+1d6 | Screeches | Bite +2 | 1d6 DMG | Can see 5 times further than a human, makes a dramatic screech and terrifies most commoners. |
| 17,18. | Coyote | +15+1d20 | -3d6 | 7+1d12 | Howls, barks and growls | Bite +3 | 1d6 DMG | Hearing and sense of smell are 4x better than a humans |
| 19,20. | Wolf | +13+1d20 | -3d6 | 7+1d10 | Howls, barks and growls | Bite +6 | 1d12 DMG | Hearing and sense of smell are 4x better than a humans |
| 21,22. | Bobcat | +17+1d20 | -2d6 | 6+1d8 | Growls and hisses | Bite +4 | 1d6 DMG | Excellent sense of hearing and smell, x4 that of a human. Adds night vision to 10m |
| 23,24. | Cougar | +16+1d20 | -2d6 | 6+1d10 | Snarls and hisses | Bite +7 | 1d12+1 DMG | Excellent sense of hearing and smell, x4 that of a human. Adds night vision to 10m |
| 25,26. | Alligator, medium | +10+1d12 | -4d6+4 | 2+1d6 | Hisses, and mighty roar | Bite +10 | 1d20 DMG | Can hold breath underwater a long time and can revive the body's lungs after other heads pass out and temporarily drown. |
| 27-30. | Goat | +10+1d10 | -3d6 | 5+1d6 | Bleats | Ram +2 | DMG 1d6 stun | Goat heads are assumed to have horns, and the default of a ram attack is stun damage, it can be made lethal if the player states this prior to an attack. Goat heads can chew up exceedingly tough plants and other materials. Sense of hearing and smell x2 that of a humans. |
| 31-33. | Sheep | +10+1d8 | -2d6 | 2+1d6 | Bleats | Ram +2 | DMG 1d6 stun | Sheep heads usually have horns. Their stun attack can be made into a lethal attack if the player wishes. Can hear twice as well as a human. |
| 34-37. | Farm dog | +10+1d20 | -2d6 | 7+1d8 | Barks and growls | Bite +3 | 1d6 DMG | Hearing and sense of smell are 4x better than a humans |
| 38-48. | Pig | +10+1d12 | -4d6+2 | 5+1d10 | Snorts, oinks and can speak 10 words | Bite +3 | DMG 1d8 | Pig heads are common, and graft very easily to humans of this line. They have powerful jaws and sizable tusks. Low intelligence humanoids will believe this character tastes like pork. Can hear and smell twice as well as a human. |
| 49,50. | Dog, Pitbull | +10+1d20 | -3d6+3 | 5+1d8 | Barks and growls | Bite +7 | 2d6+2 DMG | Hearing and sense of smell are 3x better than a humans |
| 51-53. | Chicken, huge | +10+1d12 | -4d6 | 2+1d6 | Clucks and crows | Peck +1 | 1d4 DMG | Very alert and able to see and hear twice as well as a human. |
| 54,55. | Bipedal Rat | +20+1d12 | -3d6+3 | 10+1d8 | Yes, poorly | Bite +2 | 1d6 DMG | People hate rats, and this head is as big as a farm dog's, so will illicit animosity in strangers. Can hear and see x3 what a human can and see in the dark about 10 meters. |
| 56-61. | Skullock | +20+2d20 | -3d6 (has its own of 3d6) | 2d6 | Yes, vulgar word choices | Bite +1 | 1d4 DMG | People hate skullocks more than even bipedal rats, and might direct abuse at this head and possibly consider the character to be some sort of mutie skullock despite their human head. Other skullocks might not kill this character outright, being curious about the freak. |
| 62-00. | Human | +3d6 | See Table XR-77 | See Table XR-77 | Yes | Nil | Nil | See Table XR-77, next page |

*This trait modifier is applied to the main grafter character's trait, thus a considerable bonus to perception but a huge drop to appearance. The player could record the grafter app scores seperately for the PC's head and body.

## Table XR-77/ Random Human Head Matrix

| 1d10 | Random Head Present* |
|---|---|
| 1. | Child's head. Current age 2+1d10 years, Appearance Random According to table XR-2 on page 8. |
| 2. | Teenager's head, current age 12+1d6, Appearance Random According to table XR-2 on page 8. |
| 3-5. | Young man or woman, aged 17+1d10, Appearance Random According to table XR-2 on page 8. |
| 6,7. | Young mutant man or woman, with 1d3 mental mutations from page XR-232, Latent mutations. Re-roll any non-mental or energy mutations (such as 'dual heart' or mutations which do not fit in this head). Different skin, eye and hair color highly likely. Aged 17+1d10, Appearance Random According to table XR-2 on page 8. |
| 8. | Scar covered, fire ravaged adult head. Aged 20+1d20, Appearance 2d6 |
| 9. | Middle-aged person's head: Aged 40+1d20, Appearance 10+4d6 |
| 10. | Old person: Aged 60+2d20, Appearance 4d6 |

*75% likely same gender as main character, otherwise opposite sex. Also, all human heads, except result 6,7, have a 1 in 10 chance of a ghost mutation (if so, see table oo page XR-231).*

## Extra Appendage and Organ Augmentation

Besides the obvious replacement limbs, and possible addition of an extra head, the most common other transplants added to a grafter are internal organs and animal parts - many of these cut from a recently slain mutant.

## Table XR-78/ Extra Appendage and Organ Augmentation Matrix

| 1d100 | Extra Appendage and Organ Augmentation |
|---|---|
| 01-04.* | Additional herbivore digestive tract, see details, this page. |
| 05-09.* | Advanced Kidneys, Prime Mutation; see page XR-235 this book. |
| 10-14.* | Animal ears, see details on this page. |
| 15-45. | Extra arm or limb attached to roll 1d6: 1,2. upper back /3,4. beneath left arm/ 5,6. beneath right arm. See Table XR-75 Grafted Arm Replacement table, peviously on page 86. |
| 46-52.* | Extra heart, see details on this page. |
| 53-56.* | Gills, see details, this page. |
| 57-66. | Replacement eye, see details, next page. |
| 67,68.* | Dolphin flippers, see details on the next page. |
| 69,70.* | Snake tongue, as the mutation, no. 227 from page XR-264 |
| 71-75.* | Dog Fangs, see details, next page. |
| 76-82.* | Tail, as mutation no. 83 on page TME-74. |
| 83,84.* | Water sack, see details, next page. |
| 85-92.* | Wings, as mutation no. 91 on page TME-76. |
| 93-00. | Beast Muscles, see details on the next page. |

*Re-roll duplicated results with an asterisk.*

## Detail Listings for Extra Appendage and Organ Augmentations

**Additional herbivore digestive tract:** This digestive system has been donated by a deer, goat or sheep and is connected parallel to the grafter's regular stomach and guts. At the high end, the character subconsciously knows to close off one throat and open the other depending on the sort of food he or she is eating. While at the other end, after the digestive process concludes, the intestines join up at the posterior and eliminate waste through the usual portal.

An elongated series of incisions runs the length of this grafter from throat to lower belly, reducing his or her appearance by -5 APP when disrobed. With this secondary digestive system, the grafter can live on grass, twigs, leaves and dry brush indefinitely, although after a week of this diet, he or she craves a more varied diet, possibly flesh.

**Animal ears:** Either as a fashion statement or because his or her original set of ears were torn or burnt off, this grafter has replaced their ears with a pair from another person or animal. While human ears look normal and work fine, they do not give any perception trait improvement or double the hearing range of animal ears.

For this table, consider all animal ears to add +10 perception to this character, but -2 appearance. **Roll 1d10: 1.** Human ears / **2.** Dog ears / **3.** Cat ears / **4.** Rabbit ears / **5.** Bear ears / **6.** Bobcat ears / **7.** Coyote ears / **8.** Chimp ears / **9.** Floppy goat ears/ **10.** Two mismatched animal ears (roll 1d8+1 twice, re-rolling duplicated results).

**Extra heart:** Somewhat similar to the mutation, 'reserve heart' from page TME-72, this variant is instead a constantly active, beating heart that sits in the chest next to the original heart. A considerable, Y shaped open heart surgery scar is left behind on the grafted beneficiary, which only reduces appearance when the character is disrobed and only by -3 APP.

The benefits of this extra heart are multi-fold. First off, the added output of blood and vitality increases the owner's endurance and strength by +15 each. Secondly, any hazard check that involves a heart attack or other cardiac event only afflicts one heart, which if shut down can be restarted by this heart's rhythmic activity in 20+1d20 minutes.

Finally, any called shot or critical hit that kills this character by a puncture or shot to the heart, will not kill the PC, although one of the two hearts are permanently 'killed'. If one heart is lost, the character automatically loses 15 to both endurance and strength — which could be a death blow itself if the individual is already severely wounded.

A new donor heart can of course replace the inoperative heart, however, only two hearts can operate and fit within the chest cavity, unless this character is also a mutant and by fluke ends up with the reserve heart mutation, too.

**Gills:** Shark gills have been inserted into this grafter's neck and activate when the subject is immersed in deep water or if their mouth and nose are blocked and they need to breathe or die. When not in use, these gills remain closed and look like elongated, parallel scars. Only somebody examining the user's neck with purpose, and making a type C perception based hazard check, will see these transplanted gills for what they are.

When placed in normal waterways, either fresh or saltwater, this character can breathe while submerged indefinitely. Other liquids might be depleted of oxygen or toxic, however, in which case this gilled character would be just as imperiled as a submerged person without these grafts.

**Replacement eye:** Something happened to one of this character's original eyes, such as a retinal detachment or gouged out eye, and it has been replaced with one from either another human, or of some beast. This grafted organ option can occur more than once, and if a third replacement eye is determined on the previous table, then a third eye is cut into the forehead and a -5 App penalty applied.

Roll 1d10 for the sort of replacement eye this character has: **1-5.** Human eye, but only 25% chance it is the same color as the other original eye. / **6.** Cat's eye: +5 perception and the ability to see 10m in almost total darkness. / **7.** Goat eye: +5 perception, but very alarming to look at -4 APP. / **8.** Shark's eye: Solid black, +3 perception , -4 APP, excellent vision underwater. / **9.** Mutant human's eye with night vision (as the mutation on page TME-71), unnatural color. / **10.** Mutant eye of unnatural color, that can do one of the following, roll 1d6: 1,2. See dimensional beings and inter-dimensional holes, portals and rips in physical reality. / 3,4. Detect when something is a hologram or real. /5,6. See radiation, augmented reality, force fields, and invisible security laser beams within 200 meters.

**Dolphin flippers:** Because dolphins and porpoises, along with pinnipeds such as seals and sea lions, are mammals, it's easier to graft their flippers to a human body rather than those of a fish or shark — although the latter options are also used here about 1 in 10 times.

These fins and the muscles required to control and swing them to propel and steer the user through water, are usually mounted on the sides of the subject's ribcage. When not in use, these can be folded tight against the body or hidden under clothing. If visible, they can be a shocking sight to common folk, but only then is a -5 APP reduction applied.

If swimming in full gear and clothing, these flipper will add +3m to the character's swimming speed (these are the swimming speeds of various swimming abilities from the table on page TME-16: Can't swim: 0.5m / Poor swimmer: 1m / Fair swimmer: 1.5m / Strong swimmer: 2m / Excellent swimmer: 3m) and improve swimming ability by one tier (poor swimmer becomes fair swimmer, for example, for hazard checks to avoid drowning, etc.). If the character is stripped down and sleek and uses their legs and arms to jet through the water, he or she can swim at +7m per round.

**Dog Fangs:** Besides having the upper and lower canine teeth, this grafter's jaw muscles have also been enhanced with the tendons and muscles of a fearsome dog. When his or her mouth is closed, the individual doesn't look so different from a regular person, except that he or she has a very pronounced jaw line and chiseled cheekbones. When barring their fangs, however, the character's transplanted teeth are revealed and ready to make one bite attack in melee per round, with a strike value bonus of +5 doing 1d10 base bite damage plus any strength modifiers. Only a slight -4 App penalty applies to this individual.

**Water Sack:** Perhaps a hold-over grafting practice from an era of water shortages or desert warfare, these water sacks are made from flexible innards of human donor or animals, and connected directly to the grafter's digestive tract. When needed, internally stored water can be fed into the stomach from a 3 liter cache within the body, the water being refilled from a fleshy plug on the user's side. This liquid can be drained out with a straw and used by companions, although after a few days of sloshing about inside the innards of this character, this fluid has a bitter, gamey taste to it.

**Beast Muscles:** The muscles of very powerful beasts, mutants and even synthetic humans have been stripped from their original owners and transplanted into the upper body, core and legs of this grafter. Three tiers of beast muscles are available, and accordingly this graft option can occur randomly up to three times. Re-roll on table XR-78 if this occurs a fourth time.

Each tier is shown below, with the dice result only shown for when a game master is creating an NPC grafter to oppose the player characters. At tier one, only the scars and remarkable physique of the subject give any hint that something strange has happened to this person, and while the scars reduce appearance, the splendid build adds to the person's looks and cancel out any drawbacks.

At tier two, however, the bulging not entirely natural structure and ridges of tendons give this person a somewhat monstrous, predatory look, and so reduce appearance by -6 APP.

At third tier, this individual is a muscle bound, sinewy freak and looks very much like some sort of mutant rather than a product of advanced medical customization. Reduce the subject's appearance by a total of -12 APP at the third tier of this grafting outcome.

## Table XR-79/ Beast Muscles Tiers

| 1d6* | Tier | Appearance Penalty | Movement Modifier | Strength | Endurance | Weight |
|---|---|---|---|---|---|---|
| 1-3. | 1st | Nil | +1m per round | +10 | +5 | +10kg |
| 4,5. | 2nd | -6 APP | +2m (+1m above 1st) | +20 (+10 STR more) | +10 (+5 END more) | +20Kg (+10 KG more) |
| 6. | 3rd | -12 APP (-6 APP above 2nd tier) | +2.5 ( +0.5m above 2nd) | +40 (+20 STR more) | +20 (+10 END more) | +50kg (+40 KG more) |

*1d6 dice roll for GMs creating NPC grafters only. All tiers must be randomly generated at character creation, or purchased through risky and expensive surgeries.*

**Skin Grafts:** For most grafters, the addition of replacement skin is because their original hide was damaged by fire, predators, torture, sand storms or acid attacks. For these unfortunates, the permanent application of full or partial transplanted skin is essential for any sort of normal life.

While normal human skin is frequently applied to these patients, armored and bone studded variants are also common replacement options. Much rarer ballistic skin and a wide range of epidermis variants from mutants also occur. Roll 1d10 to determine the sort of skin a grafter has should this grafting result occur from table XR-80 on the next page. Only one skin graft variety can be attached to a character.

**Table XR-80/ Skin Grafts**

| 1d10 | Skin Type | DV | Other features |
|---|---|---|---|
| 1,2. | Mismatched human skin patches | +0 | Normal human skin, but from various donors and so a patchwork of complexions, which means this character is sometimes mistaken for a mutant. No App penalty. |
| 3,4. | Bone studded | +5 | -2+1d4 appearance |
| 5,6. | Ballistic hide | -4 Or -20 Vs bullets | This skin comes from a mutant donor and is identical to mutation no. 11 on page TME-61. |
| 7,8. | Reptilian scales | -10 | 90% of this mutant's body is covered in a layer of fine, intricately patterned lizard scales. This sheathing protects the grafter from the bite of sand storms, adds some armor protection, reduces appearance by only -1d4+1 APP point, and is thin enough to still allow the grafter to wear relic armors — assuming its other appendages aren't in the way. |
| 9. | Mutant skin | - | See Deviant Skin Structure, as mutation no. 24 on page TME-63 but roll 1d8 instead of 1d12. Plus roll for skin color, page TME-23. |
| 10. | Bone carapace | -30 | Taken from some sort or mutant armadillo, lizard or other plated creature, this living shell covers the back, shoulders, and back of this grafter's head. Smaller articulating plates and scales cover the limbs and front of the abdomen. While it offers excellent protection, it's bulky and cuts movement by -1m per round and reduces appearance by -3d6 APP. Add 4d6 endurance and 20kg weight to this character. This bulky plating does not allow the grafter to wear shell class armors, but other, non-powered relic armors can be modified to accommodate his or her bulk and angles. |

# Grafting On New Parts

Grafting is almost exclusively performed by doctors trained in both the bio-technician and medic skills, and only conducted in an advanced, relic equipped, sterile and fully powered surgical suite. For a player character to attempt to perform a grafting procedure, he or she must have at lest 3 skill points in the above noted talents, as well as the facilities and medical supplies. If the grafting doctor is deficient in these skill tier requirements, increase the coma-death hazard check letter code difficulty by 2 letters (A becomes C, etc.). Likewise, the graft attempt must be succeeded at twice (thus roll twice on table XR-82, next page, in the Success/Rejection column for the specific grafted part).

The patient must also be injected prior to grafting with Graftophine-X42B or Mergosilox, two ancient compounds which foster tissue binding and nervous system assimilation between the host body and the severed subject body part. Unlike other drugs, these do not drain from the host's body, and instead reside in the bones and blood of the grafter throughout their life. While the supply of these two drugs is slowly being reduced, and no more is being made in new era communities, the substance is shelf stable at room temperature, and many ancient facilities are said to still house crates of the stuff.

The time elapsed between when an appendage or organ is severed from the donor and when it is attached to a grafter is also an enormous factor in the success or failure of a graft procedure. Almost as important as the cooling and age of the donor limb, is the question of how far removed from human the organ is. The exceptions to this later issue is when the organ is from a pig, humanoid, mutant human or bestial human. While the pig rarely has human DNA — although specimens which have plenty of it are out there — the compounds Graftophine-X42B and Mergosilox were both designed specifically to accept pig DNA, and so the attachment of a pig leg, ear, whole head or internal organ is almost as frequently successful as if the donor part came from a human.

The following Grafting Table XR-82 shows the assorted common grafting donors, odds of organ rejection, chances of the grafter dying on the table, and finally, chances of success. Following any grafting procedure, the patient must rest in the care of a physician for a certain number of days, during this time, the character will grow accustomed to the new organ or body part. He or she will practice manipulating the limb or making a connection with a new part. Without this focused recovery time, the grafted part could become detached and rejection can occur (roll the body part's rejection or success odds 1d100 roll each day of adequate care).

The merger with a new head is always the rarest, most risky and challenging transplant procedure. Often, the donor head is resistant to being part of the host body, chafes at the idea of being under the control of another consciousness, and might never fully accept their fate. Animal heads can often be both willful and dangerous to the host and staff at a medical facility, but if given excellent food, affection, and treated with respect, they soon adapt to their new life and find working with the host much more tolerable than working against it. However, an intelligent humanoid head transplantation is always the hardest host-donor union to achieve; the personality of the adopted head, and its possible divergence from the morality and goals of the host mind, is sometimes insurmountable, and a new surgery must be booked to rid the grafter of an irksome, impossible secondary head.

Any procedure reduces the patient to half endurance immediately after surgery and during the entire recovery time. If a limb is rejected by the body, a minimum recovery time for the patient is 3+1d6 days and the body part is 71% likely to be too mutilated or decayed for a further grafting attempt on a different patient — the limb or organ can be kept in cryo-freeze for 10+3d6 days but cannot be used on the same patient, as rejection will automatically occur. Body part rejection from one's own body — for example if the character's arm is chopped off and it can be kept on ice until reaching a grafting facility — only ever has a 1% chance of rejection. Limbs from siblings or parents are allowed two success attempts.

An arm or leg differs from a limb in that a limb is some other articulating part altogether, such as a tentacle, crab pincer, spike shooter or organic flame thrower, etc. Plantoid parts cannot be grafted to a human, but the game master might allow for some sort of botanist-medic to graft different plant mutations to plantoid characters, using the following table as a guideline. The grafting drugs noted previously do not work on animal physiology and so grafting a human head to a bear or other beast is not typically possible — although in the Mutant Epoch era, discount nothing.

The Coma-Death column shown on the following table reflects the willpower based hazard check the patient must make, regardless of the success or failure of the procedures, to see if the patient goes into shock and suffers a coma for 3d6 days. After this 3d6 day period, there is a further chance that the patient goes into cardiac arrest and its heart stops. A strength based hazard check is used with the same letter difficulty code as the coma check, success means the character has survived and must heal up at the shown recovery time for that grafted body part. In the event the patient has two hearts, he or she gets two separate hazard checks against death, while if the patient had more than one head during the coma, only the main head goes into a coma, and the other(s) can take over the body and hope its host's body's heart endures the coming heart attack.

The cost of the procedure will be reduced to 50% should the grafted part be rejected by the body, and further reduced to 25% if the patient dies, and the subject's comrades, family or community must pay the fee.

Just how old and fresh a new or replacement body part is at the time of surgery changes the odds of a successful outcome. If the body part was kept on ice, in cryo, or out in the hot sun and flies, all make a difference, too. Use this quick table to determine the viability of a replacement organ and add or subtract all that apply.

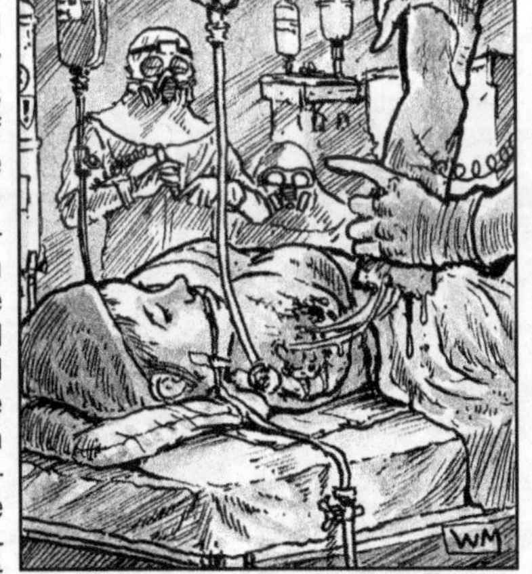

## Table XR-81/ Grafted Part Cooling and Age Directory

Organ or Limb Condition Modifiers to add or subtract to the Odds of success/ rejection column on Table XR-82

Organ cut from the 'donor' within the last half hour or less +2%

Part is fresh, and taken from donor from over a half hour up to 1 hour ago +1%

Donor part has been kept on ice or in a cooler with a relic cooling agent, ice packs or other measure to keep it near freezing. +4% for 1st hour, +3% second hour/ +2% 3rd hour, +1% 4th hour, and +0% from over 4 hours to ten hours, then -1% per hour from 11th hour onward.

Body part kept in relic medical grade cryogenic sleep chamber or transport cooler. +5% and will maintain ideal conditions for 48 hours. From beyond 48 hours to 72 hours, zero benefit, and beyond 72 hours reduced grafting success chances by -1% per hour.

Organ or limb has been kept at around room temperature. -1% per hour since removal from living 'donor'.

Donor part has been exposed to heat or hot sunlight, but wrapped to keep vermin and insects off it. -2% per hour of exposure.

Organ has been left in the heat and exposed to insects, blowing dust, and other filth for more than an hour. -5%, and deduct a further 5% per hour thereafter. (example -10% after two hours, -15% after three hours, etc.).

Donor organ has been partially burned by acid or stomach acid -5%

Body part has been chewed up and might be missing sections of flesh, bone and nerves -8%

Donor organ has been treated with the mutations heal touch or extreme healing in the hour prior to attachment surgery. +2d6% (roll random amount at time of surgery)

## Table XR-82/ Grafting New Donor Parts

| Grafted Body Part | Coma-Death | Roll 1d100 Success / Rejection | Recovery Time | Cost |
|---|---|---|---|---|
| *Replace arm or leg [1]* | | | | |
| Human arm or leg | A | 01-98 / 99,00 | 5+1d6 days | 500+3d100sp |
| Mutant human arm or leg | B | 01-94 / 95-00 | 6+3d6 days | 600+3d100sp |
| Pig limb | A | 01-96 / 97-00 | 6+2d6 days | 300+2d100sp |
| Animal limb | B | 01-92 / 93-00 | 10+3d6 days | 400+2d100sp |
| Mutant beast limb | C | 01-91 / 92-00 | 15+3d6 days | 600+3d100sp |
| *Add Extra limb [2]* | | | | |
| Human arm or leg | B | 01-95 / 96-00 | 10+1d6 days | 800+3d100sp |
| Mutant arm | C | 01-91 / 92-00 | 12+3d6 days | 900+3d100sp |
| Pig limb | A | 01-95 / 96-00 | 9+2d6 days | 500+3d100sp |
| Animal limb | B | 01-89 / 90-00 | 20+3d6 days | 700+3d100sp |
| Mutant limb | D | 01-87 / 88-00 | 20+4d6 days | 500+3d100sp |
| *Add extra head [3]* | | | | |
| Spider monkey | C | 01-92 / 93-00 | 10+3d6 days | 1000+4d100sp |
| Chimp | C | 01-91 / 92-00 | 12+3d6 days | 1000+4d100sp |
| Gorilla | D | 01-90 / 91-00 | 15+3d6 days | 1200+4d100sp |
| House cat | B | 01-94 / 95-00 | 10+3d6 days | 900+3d100sp |
| Eagle | E | 01-87 / 88-00 | 14+4d6 days | 1000+3d100sp |
| Coyote | C | 01-92 / 93-00 | 10+3d6 days | 900+4d100sp |
| Wolf | C | 01-91 / 92-00 | 11+3d6 days | 1000+4d100sp |
| Bobcat | C | 01-92 / 93-00 | 12+3d6 days | 1100+3d100sp |
| Cougar | C | 01-91 / 92-00 | 14+3d6 days | 1200+4d100sp |
| Alligator | F | 01-84 / 85-00 | 20+4d6 days | 1500+5d100sp |
| Goat | C | 01-92 / 93-00 | 12+2d6 days | 800+2d100sp |
| Sheep | C | 01-93 / 94-00 | 11+2d6 days | 700+1d100sp |
| Farm dog | C | 01-92 / 93-00 | 10+3d6 days | 800+2d100sp |
| Pig | A | 01-94 / 95-00 | 6+1d6 days | 600+2d100sp |
| Dog, pitbull | C | 01-92 / 93-00 | 12+3d6 days | 900+2d100sp |
| Chicken, huge | E | 01-88 / 89-00 | 14+4d6 days | 900+3d100sp |
| Bipedal rat | C | 01-91 / 92-00 | 10+2d6 days | 800+2d100sp |
| Skullock | B | 01-93 /94-00 | 12+3d6 days | 700+1d100sp |
| Human | B | 01-94 / 95-00 | 10+2d6 days | 1000+4d100sp |
| Mutant human | C | 01-90 / 91-00 | 15+3d6 days | 1300+4d100sp |
| *Add Extra Appendage or Organ [4]* | | | | |
| Added herbivore digestive tract | C | 01-91 / 92-00 | 12+3d6 days | 600+3d100sp |
| Advanced kidneys | B | 01-92 / 93-00 | 20+3d6 days | 1000+1d1000sp |
| Animal ears | A | 01-98 / 99,00 | 4+1d6 days | 400+2d100sp |
| Extra heart | D | 01-86 / 87-00 | 25+4d6 days | 2000+1d1000sp |
| Gills | C | 01-89 / 90-00 | 18+3d6 days | 1200+4d100sp |
| Replacement eye | B | 01-93 / 94-00 | 14+2d10 days | 1300+1d1000sp |
| Dolphin flippers | B | 01-95 / 96-00 | 10+2d6 days | 1100+4d100sp |
| Snake tongue | A | 01-96 / 97-00 | 5+2d6 days | 700+3d100sp |
| Tail | A | 01-95 / 96-00 | 10+3d6 days | 600+3d100sp |
| Water sack | B | 01-93 / 94-00 | 13+3d6 days | 700+3d100sp |
| Wings | C | 01-88 / 89-00 | 26+2d12 days | 2800+2d1000sp |
| Dog fangs | B | 01-91 / 92-00 | 23+2d10 days | 1700+1d1000sp |
| Beast Muscles, tier 1 | C | 01-92 / 93-00 | 20+3d10 days | 2000+1d1000sp |
| Beast Muscles, tier 2 | D | 01-89 / 90-00 | 30+4d10 days | 3000+2d1000sp |
| Beast Muscles, tier 3 | E | 01-86 / 87-00 | 40+5d10 days | 5000+4d1000sp |
| *Add Skin Grafts [5]* | | | | |
| Bone studded Skin patches | A | 01-95 / 96-00 | 4+2d6 days | 400+2d100sp |
| Ballistic hide | B | 01-93 / 94-00 | 8+3d6 days | 1100+3d100sp |
| Reptilian, patches | A | 01-95 / 96-00 | 7+2d6 days | 800+3d100sp |
| Mismatched human skin patches | A | 01,98 / 99,00 | 4+1d6 days | 200+2d100sp |
| Mutant skin (Deviant Skin Structure, pg. TME 63) | B | 01-91 / 92-00 | 10+2d6 days | 1200+1d1000sp |

1 To an existing arm or leg socket

2 To another body location other than a socket. Involves attachment of muscles and nervous system connectors

3 Heads can only be attached near the living head of the grafter, and must connect to the respiratory, nervous and digestive tracts within the upper chest.

4 From the list on table XR-78 back on page 89.

5 From the list on table XR-80 up on page 91.

# Halfies

*Half Humanoid Races*

Given that nearly every humanoid life form has stemmed from humankind, either through intentional genetic engineering or through evolutionary accident, crossbreeding, grafting, or a combination of these and other factors, there are a great many human-like species out there. Furthermore, new specimens appear almost yearly, beings who come into contact with humans of the opposite sex, and mate with them.

While many humanoids seem more like animals than people, their DNA is nevertheless derived from human sources, and in most cases, their reproductive cycles, organs and duration of gestation are similar enough to that of regular humans that copulation, successful pregnancies and live births can be accomplished.

In game terms, some Game Masters and players might be accomplished enough role-players to portray full blooded Warmorts, Skullocks, Moaners, Garnocks and other humanoids as player characters. These rules and statistics, however, apply to half human characters and NPCs, covering their generation, their disposition and the treatment they experience at the hands of generic humans and their common off-shoots (mutant humans, clones, bioreplicas, cyborgs, etc.). This character type covers 'Halfies' based on parent stock mainly found in both the Hub Rules and the Mutant Bestiary One book. The GM can also use the basic crossbreeding formulas for determining his or her own humanoid half breeds.

Basically, for those humanoid halfies not listed here the traits of the base humanoid must be determined, rolled up, and added to a standard trait roll for a human, however any trait generation system would work. The end result will be two scores for each trait; add these together and, you guessed it, divide by two to get the halfie's attribute trait scores.

For half humanoids included in this section, the shown trait rolls are used to speed up the process and promote a wider score range, giving halfie's the same chances for character defining extreme highs and lows that occur in regular characters. Following generating the traits, read up on each half-breed's description, but also read the humanoid parent's description to get a better idea on where the character's roots lie, what his or her parent is known for, and what enemies they may have.

In most cases, the half-breed will have been raised among fellow humans, perhaps by his or her mother who escaped her non-human captors, pregnant, and sought shelter among her own people. The child would have grown up among whatever standard humans were about, which would make a huge difference to the youth depending on the population around him or her.

For instance, if the half-breed child grew up among mainly pure stock humans, his or her unique appearance and size would be far more apparent and probably result in non-stop teasing and poor treatment by other children, humiliation for the child's family, possibly enslavement, rejection or banishment.

On the other hand, in a mixed race community with plenty of mutants about, a halfie might be accepted as just another freak, and his or her ancestry go unnoticed and deemed irrelevant. Additionally, it is assumed that the halfbreed's human parent is a pure stock, however a mutant human could also be one parent, in which case there is a 50% chance that each of the parent's mutations also occur in the halfie.

Use a standard character sheet to create a halfie PC, downloadable at https://www.outlandarts.com/expansionrules.htm or found on page 512 of this book.

## Table XR-83/ Halfie Crossbreed Determination

| 1d100 | Crossbreed Type | Book or Source and page |
|---|---|---|
| 01-07. | Half-Garnock | TME Hub Rules, page 156 |
| 08-12. | Half-Moaner | TME Hub Rules, page 164 |
| 13-55. | Half-Skullock | TME Hub Rules, page 170 |
| 56,57. | Half-Abhorra | Mutant Bestiary One, page 5 |
| 58-69. | Half-Devilkin | Mutant Bestiary One, page 39 |
| 70-74.* | Half-Epochian Merefolk | Mutant Bestiary One, page 47 |
| 75. | Half Fetid-Oltuch | Mutant Bestiary One, page 48 |
| 76,77. | Half-Hyena-Sapien | Mutant Bestiary One, page 58 |
| 78. | Half-Pond Ghoul | Mutant Bestiary One, page 86 |
| 79. | Half Scrag | Mutant Bestiary One, page 97 |
| 80-89. | Half Underfoot | Mutant Bestiary One, page 123 |
| 90-00. | Half-Muto-Harpy | Free SOE member's download or COTA Codex page 80 |

*Re-roll if the game setting does not include waterborne adventures.*

As far as the **halfie's pre-game caste** goes, and assuming the individual grew up in a mixed race human community — instead of being introduced to the character group in the wilds when they meet a group of full bloods of the halfie's species — treat all the following half-breed races as mutants when determining their history, from which stem the generation of skills, trait modifiers, equipment, arms and armor.

## Table XR-84/ Halfie Crossbreed Details

Dice rolling conventions: R means roll as a standard character for this trait. R+10 or R+2d10 etc, means make a standard trait roll, then, after the result is established, add or subtract the amount to that end result, not to the actual dice roll's number, however, no trait can go below 1 (on Table XR-2, page 8). 20+3d6 etc. these values represent a straight up roll for that trait, as is.

| Half Breed | END | STR | AG | ACC | INT | PER | WILL | APP | MV* | SV | DV | Height** | Weight** | Mutated *** | Implants **** |
|---|---|---|---|---|---|---|---|---|---|---|---|---|---|---|---|
| Garnock | 100+3d20 | 50+3d20 | R | R | 3d6 | R | R+3d10 | 3d6 | -1m | +15 | +5 | Nor+3m | Nor+300kg | 12%d3 | 4% 1 |
| Moaner | R | R+2 | R-5 | R-5 | 3d6 | R | R | 3d4 | -0.5m | -3 | - | Nor | Nor-20kg | 18% d2 | 15% 1 |
| Skullock | 10+d20 | R | R+10 | R | 3d6 | R+2d20 | R+d20 | 3d6 | +1.5m | - | - | Nor-30cm | 50+d20kg | 10% d2 | 5% d2 |
| Abhorra | R | R+5 | 3d10 | 3d10 | 3d10 | 3d6 | R | 2d8 | -0.5m | -3 | +3 | Nor-20cm | 80+d20kg | d2 | 3% 1 |
| Deepkin | R | R+7 | R | R | R+2d20 | R+5 | R+2d20 | R-10 | -0.5m | +3 | - | Nor-40cm | 65+d20kg | see notes | nil |
| Devilkin | 3d6+4 | 3d6 | R+3d20 | R+d20 | R | R+2d20 | R | see notes | +2m | -5 | -6 | 30+3d10cm | 10+2d10kg | 67% d2 | nil |
| E. Merefolk | R | R | R+3d6 | R+2d6 | R-4 | R+5 | R | R+d20 | 11w/ -1L | +3 | notes | Nor+1m | Nor+20kg | nil | nil |
| Fetid-Oltuch | 60+3d20 | R-5 | 3d10 | R | R+3d20 | R | R+3d20 | 2d8 | -1m | +7 | - | Nor+2m | Nor+180kg | notes | 5% d2 |
| Hyena-Sapien | R | R+2d10 | R+2d10 | R+3d10 | 3d10 | R+5 | R+d10 | 3d6 | +5m | +6 | -8 | Nor | 80+2d20kg | 7% d2 | nil |
| Pond Ghoul | R+d12 | R+3d10 | R | R | R-10 | R+2 | R+d10 | 2d10 | 8w/-1L | +7 | notes | Nor | Nor+10kg | 6% d2 | nil |
| Scrag | R | R+5 | R | R | R+2d20 | R+2d20 | R+2d20 | 3d10 | -1m | - | - | Nor-20cm | Nor | notes | d2 |
| Underfoot | R | R | R+3d10 | R+2d10 | R | R+3d10 | R | R | +0.5m | - | - | Nor-10cm | Nor-5kg | notes | 33%d2 |
| Muto-Harpy | 20+d30 | R | R+20 | R+10 | 4d10 | R+5 | R+7 | R | 3m/ 16m flying | +6 | +0/ +20 DV flying | 1.5m tall/ 2.4m wingspan | 40+d12kg | See notes | nil |

*MV: Movement rate modifier, with the base movement being 6 meters per round like a human. 8w means moves 8m in water, while −1L means the being moves minus 1m per round on Land

** Height: 'Nor' is an abbreviation for 'normal height' (or weight) for a human by gender, plus or minus any modifier stated in this column.

*** Mutated: Chance halfie is a mutant, number range is how many prime mutations. See table page XR-228.

**** Implants: Chance of cybernetic implants, and if so, how many miscellaneous implants as listed on page XR-330.

# Half Breed Descriptions

**Half-Garnock:** Just how a giant garnock can mate with a human is up to speculation, further still, who can say what compels the enormous man-eating humanoids to spare an attractive human of the opposite sex and take them as a bedmate? Regardless of the reasons, half-garnocks have been seen serving their larger, pure blood tribe mates, using their increased speed and intelligence to trap, trick or run down prey, which full sized garnocks simply can't tackle.

Half-breeds who make it to civilization, and slip into a mixed race settlement, are assumed to be merely enormous mutants. Alternatively, they were born to a woman who was once the mate of a garnock, and grew up among other kids, their father's giant race showing in their rust red skin, enormous size, bulging muscles and terrible, toothy jaws.

Any half garnock to survive to adulthood is truly a fearsome foe, and a great comrade. Being enormous, their mere presence is enough to frighten off smaller predators, likewise, the brute can use a light or medium laser cannon like a rifle, wield a chain gun with one hand, and hurl large rocks like a catapult.

Garnocks are described on page 156 of the TME Hub Rules.

**Half-Moaner:** Half-breeds of this humanoid race are either those that remain among their kind and live as slightly healthier, more intelligent members, and often reach the rank of chieftain, or else become the leader's concubine and guard. Half-moaners who enter the human towns appear to be sickly, decidedly ugly humans with pale skin, bad teeth, sunken eye sockets and bodies covered in patchy hair. They don't have the mild radiation sickness of their moaner-parent, but do have the Type A sickness poison in their blood and other body fluids. For generations the person's ancestors have been exposed to White Plague and Rose Pox, (see Diseases, Part Three, Hub Rules) and the result for these halfies has been a total immunity to both diseases, and an increased resistance to all other illnesses and poisons, allowing them two hazard checks when exposed to such perils. While moaners detest daylight and fight at –20 SV, Half-moaners can tolerate it, but prefer overcast days and dense woodlands, but have no special ability to see in the dark.

Moaners are listed on page 164 of the TME Hub Rules.

**Half-Skullock:** Because this species of humanoid is the most common sub-human strain in most areas, they therefore come into frequent contact with humans, producing half-breeds in abundance. Those halfies to live among their skullock kinfolk are often taller, smarter, and more inclined to rely on relic weapons. Additionally, these individuals are not easily swayed by the mob mentality of their full-blooded fellows and tend to abandon skullock society in favor of a more independent, nomadic lifestyle. Besides those half-skullocks who flee their shorter, more savage kin, there are those who are born to women who have been the victims of skullock aggression, slavery, or other tragedies associated with war. These survivors of skullock captivity, who either escape or are rescued by excavators or human troops, sometimes give birth to half-breeds, or else, flee with the halfie youngsters when they themselves escape.

Half-skullocks appear as sickly pale or gray hued humans with longer than normal arms, thin bodies, abnormally large heads with noticeably large, sunken eye sockets. Their eyes have either orange, yellow or red pupils while their noses are mere nostril slits. Males tend to be bald while females exhibit long blue-gray or silver hair. They have short fangs, speak in short, profanity filled sentences, cuss whenever possible and seem to be short-tempered.

They are often accepted into mixed human communities for the sake of their unfortunate mothers, but tolerated only if they can maintain decent behavior, which is usually not the case. Half-skullock youths are wild, disobedient, lawless, spiteful, and prone to turning to crime and forming alliances with other disreputable and dangerous beings. In settlements where conflict with local skullock nations is ongoing, which is just about everywhere, the sight of an unfamiliar half-skullock sauntering down Main Street is usually met with hostility, bad language, hurled stones and possibly outright attack by armed citizens. Due to this long-standing hatred for their full-blooded kin, most halfies of this race tend to employ cloaks, disguise kits, pigment creams, and keep filter masks or other face coverings in place. Likewise, many will hook up with an excavation team or group of mercenaries, will keep a low profile when in bars and inns, and let others do the talking.

Skullocks age three times as quickly as humans, reaching adulthood after only 8 years and on average only live to twenty, although some venerable shaman and tribal healers can reach the ripe old age of thirty. A halfie, therefore, reaches adulthood at age twelve, can live as long as fifty years, although is considered a frail old timer by the age of forty. Half skullocks start game play at age 10+1d4 years.

Full blooded skullocks are described on page 170 of the TME Hub Rules.

**Half-Abhorra:** As their creature listing explains, in their natural state these are toxin infused, man-eating savages, who live on carrion and rotting vegetation, fungus and human livestock. They are, however also obsessed with attractive humans and moderately deformed mutants, and thrill at having a flock of them as concubines, at least until winter when food grows short and the prisoners are butchered and served raw. The product of many of these miserable imprisonments is the subsequent pregnancies, both among females of the species as well as human women,  which produce a grotesque half-abhorra offspring. These pitiful freaks are lopsided, yet taller, dual-armed, smarter, faster and considerably more imaginative, as well as less dependent on their tribe.

In cases where a half-abhorra grows up among its own kind, it will be considered little more than a slave, even though it is clearly quite superior to its fellows. These subordinate halfies are often used as hunters, frontline fighters, or even food when times are tough, always treated like filth, beaten abused, and often shunned by their parents. This unkind and unfair treatment forces many to plot some sort of escape plan, which on some occasions has seen halfies free human captives and flee with them to human communities, where the half breed savior is accepted as a hero.

In other circumstances, although more rare, is the situation whereby a woman is either freed or has escaped from the bondage of an abhorra clan, and made her way to her homeland, pregnant by an abhorra male, and later giving birth to a horrid half breed. If not killed by the community clergy or the woman's own family, the child will be permitted to grow to adulthood. Amid human society, half-abhorras exhibit none of their man-eating, primitive, superstitious ways, in fact, they develop almost identically to other children as far as disposition goes, and can be taught to use relic weapons as necessary. If they become excavators and meet face to face with their father's kind, they will often hesitate to kill them, or support actions against abhorras, and instead will seek to learn more about them, to communicate, and possibly educate and assist the brutal savages.

All half-abhorras reach adulthood at age nine, have 1d2 mutations from the abhorra mutation list under their description*, and are quite resistant to radiation, poisons, molds, spores, egg-like parasites, and all forms of sickness, including cancer and leprosy, getting two hazard checks from all these perils and contaminants. They are however, lopsided and always suffer −1 initiative, plus, have one thin, stunted arm that has half the strength of the opposite, massive arm. While using its dominant, powerful arm in melee combat, it has a hard time using a bow with this combo and suffers a -10 strike value, -10% range, and -2 damage with arrows. It can use both arms to wield crossbows and long guns, however.

Abhorras, also called ugly-buglies, appear on page 5 of Mutant Bestiary One.

*or 1d2 prme mutations and 37% chance 1 flaw.*

**Half-Devilkin:** Being between ten and thirty centimeters tall, just how mating takes place between devilkins and humans is often debated, but it is surmised that only those species with larger bodies and closer to typical human sized reproductive organs are remotely able to mate with small humans.

Certain religious groups claim that magical rites permit the diabolical little fiends to fornicate with humans, the imps invade the dreams of men and women and coax them into lovemaking against their will. Whatever the method, there are increasingly more half-devilkins turning up, so many in some areas that they have split off from both parent species in an attempt to form their own communities deep in secluded areas, the beginnings of an altogether new race of 'halflings' and leprechauns from myth and fictional sources of old.

Half-devilkins range in height from 33 to 60cm tall, and come in a wide range of appearances, exhibit about half the mutations or each parent species (50% chance of each mutation, including flaws), and tend to conduct themselves according to which parent's community they grew up in.

Use the tables included in the creature description to determine appearance, mutations, skin color and the typical disposition toward big folks for which the devilkin parent was known for*. If the half-breed starts game play while living among the particular devilkin species, he or she will act more like that strain, however, if raised among humans, the individual will be far more like a regular person of that culture, although diminutive and perhaps somewhat shy and reclusive due to growing up as the tiny kid who everybody could knock about.

Half-devilkins do not make for stout fighters, but they can certainly contribute to an excavation team through stealth, speed, and the ability to ride upon the back's of big folk in a backpack or basket and fire arrows over the shoulder of their 'mount'. Halfies of this race can use regular bows and crossbows, .22 caliber long-arms, or else, pistols, submachine guns, and daggers one handed, or a machete or hatchet in two hands, although full sized assault rifles, sniper rifles and larger weapons are too heavy for them.

Depending on their particular devilkin parent appearance and disposition, half-breeds may or may not be well liked or even tolerated in a human settlement, nevertheless, their small stature rarely invokes dread in the common folk, unlike the reaction a half garnock elicits. Half devilkins are occasionally raised by slavers who sell attractive specimens to collectors region wide, and from these, Quarter bloods sometimes emerge, called 'Quarterkins', who are again twice as tall as half-devilkins, but exhibit the same appearance and mutations of their distant devilkin ancestors.

Devilkins are described on page 39 of Mutant Bestiary One.

*Don't have a copy of MB1? Then apply the following: 68% chance PC has 1d3 prime mutations.*

**Half-Epochian Merefolk:** Because full blooded merefolk don't eat people, and share many of the same enemies with humans, they are often allied together where they co-inhabit. There is therefore a tendency for romantic entanglements to arise, and the offspring are fanciful hybrids which seems perfectly suited to life in and around swamps, island atolls, and flooded ruins. The half-merefolk have shorter, stubby tails, as well as shorter human legs (swim 11m/ walk 5m/ tail slap DMG 1d8) and the ability to hold their breath for only 20 minutes.

In human communities where races mix well, these aqua-green bodied humanoids are quite welcome, however, because of longstanding animosity with both pond ghouls and skullocks, half-merefolk are intolerant toward half-breeds of these enemy species, and will distrust them at the least, and at the most, plot to kill them. As adventurers, they are reliable and stout hearted, however they are slow while on foot and need to ride mounts or travel by vehicle in order to keep up with their longer legged counterparts. Their great value to a team is when exploring sunken ruins or reef-locked ancient ships, as they can remain submerged for twenty minutes, which would be otherwise inaccessible.

Epochian merefolk are described on page 47 of Mutant Bestiary One.

**Half-Fetid-Oltuch:** Full blooded fetid-oltuch are one of the most despised and grotesque humanoids known to humankind, nevertheless, due to its penchant for acquiring attractive human and mutant humans of the opposite sex, they tend to produce remarkable hybrids. Often, a female fetid-oltuch will not keep a baby it has produced from a human male slave, and instead either kill it or give it to some sort of wet-nurse slave and tell it to raise the weak, impure abomination far away. Female humans and mutant humans who give birth to a half-breed offspring are often aghast at what they have brought into the world and will kill the child on sight, or else refuse to suckle it and set it aside to die of exposure.

In nearly every case, regardless of the mother species, the half-breed fetid-oltuch is rejected, but, some fascinated or compassionate servant of the parent raises the hideous, wrinkly thing, announce that it is still half human, or half fetid-oltuch or half whatever, and therefore deserve life.

Those halfies who survive to adulthood are indeed ugly, however, they bring the best of both species into one dangerous package. The fetid-oltuch side gives the being its bulk, as well as a reduced set of the impressive offensive mutations of the humanoid, while the human blood decreases the size, but gives the beastly thing increased mobility, as well as the ability for it to pass as just some ugly bloated mutant in mixed human settlements. In such human towns, the enormous half-breed can use its powers, imposing physical presence and intelligence to establish an urban gang of minions, even secure financial resources and set itself up as a land owner, merchant and possibly a community leader, all of these being impossible developments for a pure-blooded fetid-oltuch.

As characters, half-breed fetid-oltuchs are somewhat slow, and yet too heavy to saddle up on a riding dog or normal horse, however a draft horse

or wagon could provide locomotion for these brutes. Their main worth to an excavation team would be in their enormous endurance, intelligence, and mental mutations. Listed below are the mutational powers of this halfie, which have fixed hourly or daily uses independent of the character's rank. These uses don't change during the course of the half breed's life. A half-Fetid-Oltuch can unleash 6 mind crush attacks per hour, 3 beam eye attacks per hour, 2 acid spits per hour and Dread Zone once per day. Halfies of this species do not have the gaseous discharge ability of full bloods, but do give off a constant, repugnant body odor within 5 meters.

Full blooded Fetid-Oltuch are shown on page 48 of Mutant Bestiary One.

**Half-Hyena-Sapien:** As noted in their creature description, hyena-sapiens are likely to spare good looking humans and mutants and use them as pack-shared concubines. The results of these unspeakable unions are a sort of hybrid which has stubby but usable arms ending in misshapen yet functional hands. These half-breed dog-men have vaguely human legs, but are much longer (move +5), and elongated toothy jaws that add a second melee attack per round (bite attack SV +5/ DMG 1d10+1). They can talk the common human language of the vicinity as well as the howling, barking and growling which makes up the language of their full-blooded kin.

Because most half-hyena-sapiens belong to the pack and are man eaters, few if any of these half breeds make their way into mixed human communities and become citizens. Those that do were probably born there to mothers who were once captives of a hyena-sapien pack, but either escaped or were somehow rescued. Knowing who the father of such a bizarre offspring was, is usually enough to damn the halfie to a life of ridicule and teasing — enough to drive the youngster to a life of crime, nomadic banditry, or flight to a large city where he or she can either find other misfits, enjoy anonymity, or join an excavation team which are known to always enlist oddities.

Such half hyena-sapiens can offer a great deal to an adventure or mercenary outfit, as they are fierce fighters with their bite attack and hand held weapons, as well as able to run at great speeds and perform scout duties for a unit. These vaguely civilized half-breeds will be quite reluctant to engage in combat against pure bloods of their kind, and if a fight is un-avoidable, will try to stay back and not participate. If captured by pure blood hyena sapiens, the wild ones will be 78% likely to devour the halfie.

Most half hyena-sapiens take great offense at being called a dog, or any reference to being a pet to the other team members, and will probably bite anybody who annoys them with dog jokes or references.

Learn about full blooded hyena-sapiens on page 58 of Mutant Bestiary One.

**Half-Pond Ghoul:** In areas where regular pond ghouls are found, those who are born as crossbreeds of the species are often treated with the same dread and hostility as their pure-blooded relatives. As noted in the description of Pond Ghouls from page 86 of Mutant Bestiary One, these amphibious humanoids are man-eaters, slave takers, and delight in humiliating and torturing captives. So too, they will take attractive pure stocks and mutant humans as mates, and from this union, arise the 'half-ponders'.

Like many of the humanoids described above, the community in which the halfie grew up influences his or her life, skills and social standing. Those raised among full-blooded pond-ghouls are poorly treated and have few rights in the tribe, while those raised in human communities are treated according to the nature of the settlement.

In mostly pure stock populated centers, a half-ponder will be mistreated and probably driven out at adulthood, however in an open town with a wide range of mutants and other beings about, a halfie of this species could easily pass as just another deviant. The exception to this, of course, is if pond ghouls are a peril in the local area, where people may have lost loved ones to these carnivorous humanoids, and thus recognize the halfie as one of 'them' and seek vengeance.

Half-pond-ghoul characters are also despised by Epochian merefolk, both wild full bloods and half-breeds of that species, as the two aquatic humanoid races have been at war for as long as anyone can remember.

Half-ponders are smarter and more human-like than their untainted kin, and make for ex-ceptional excavators in watery settings, for they retain their amphibious respiration organs, claws, webbed hands and feet, powerful jaws and terrible teeth — although reduced in size and only inflicting 2d8 damage as a total combined mauling attack mode.

**Half-Scrag:** As scrags occasionally keep human and mutant human captives, to taunt, trick, humiliate and torture, inevitably some pregnancies occur. Whenever a female scrag becomes pregnant by a human mate, she will usually raise the child as little more than a servant, or second in command to control the underlings and pets which protect her territory. When a human woman becomes pregnant, however, the child is killed at birth by the scrags out of fear that the offspring will grow up to side with its mother, and turn on the father to claim his turf and relic stash. For this reason, nearly every half scrag in a human settlement was born to a human mother, who has either been rescued by diggers or escaped and found her way back to human society.

Half scrag children that grow up in human towns are often smarter than their companions, but unattractive and slow on their feet, however, they always have one or two mutations and have an inherent interest in relics, technology, dangerous pets, and acquiring henchmen, just as their father race does. If an adult half-scrag should encounter a full-blooded scrag, he or she may be reluctant to engage in combat with the full blood, for fear it is a relative, but also due to some great curiosity about 'that side' of one's family tree.

Scrags are not as evil or blood thirsty as other humanoids, and have been known to merely rob and then set free travelers, instead of torturing and eating them as Skullocks might, therefore, there are few who have a deep set animosity toward this species, and so too, toward any halfies of the race. Character half-scrags make for excellent adventurers, as they are highly motivated to explore the ruins, acquire ancient devices and learn about the world as it once was. About their only negative tendency is their greed and lust for control of the group, and as they get older, they become more secretive and solitary, begin to talk to themselves and act a little nutty.

Scrags are listed on page 97 of Mutant Bestiary One.

**Half-Underfoot:** Wherever subterranean underfoot enclaves exist in close proximity to human towns, war with the 'chalkies' is inevitable, and probably many decades old. Because of this, any half-breed underfoot to attempt to dwell in the surface world, especially in a human community, will be hard pressed to be treated fairly, or even stay alive. So hated are regular underfeet, that few humans can look passed the golden eyes and steel colored hair of a halfie to notice the taller stature, faintly pink pigmented skin, and more light tolerant human traits within a half-underfoot. Only in areas where the underfoot race are not present, or at least not active in their war of genocide and domination on the humans, can such a half-breed coexist with regular humans. Many mutant humans, on the other hand, tend not to care if a person is halfie or not, and in settlements where the races mix freely, even a half-underfoot can get by, establish friendships and seek adventure with an excavation team.

Due to the tendency for adventure teams to go underground, there is a considerably high chance that a half-underfoot excavator will be forced into a fight with the exceedingly hostile pure blooded underfoot found deep beneath the earth. If captured, the chalkies will be merciless to the traitorous half-breed, and inflict terrible tortures upon the prisoner in an attempt to learn all they can about the surface dwellers.

Half-underfoot characters have the mutations of reserve mind and night vision, however, are also subject to a considerable loss of Strike Value when fighting in day-light (-10 SV), unless wearing sunglasses or similar eye protection. Their eyes are hazel, rather than gold.

They typically prefer underground or nocturnal adventures, where they can be the most use to an excavation team. If they are aware of their underfoot lineage, they may be curious about the race and wish to learn all they can about the 'chalkies' going so far as to purchase underfoot slaves to question and associate with, a dangerous pastime, given that common people may assume the halfie is actually a servant of the underfeet.

Underfoot are listed on page 123 of Mutant Bestiary One.

**Half-Muto-Harpy:** A half harpy is always female, like most of its kind on its mother's side — although every flock has at least one enormous, reclusive male in its aerie. These halfies have the same limb configuration as regular muto-harpies, with a pair of powerful human arms hanging down from their hips where legs might otherwise be. They have vast leathery wings, pinkish orange flesh, and typically wild blonde or white hair. They have a 9% chance of one random prime mutation, a 12% chance of a random ghost mutation, and do not exhibit cybernetic implants.

Although these half-breeds are sometimes quite attractive, but even when dressed in traditional clothing, and armor, they are often feared by the common folk, who will either flee from or shoot at this specimen if it is unaccompanied by more typical human companions.

As an adventuress, a muto-harpy can be remarkably useful. Their ability to fly high above a traveling dig team and scout the way ahead, or offer covering fire from great heights, is invaluable. Although light of build and unable to stand up in a protracted battle, they are nevertheless splendid combatants and can fight with either two hand held weapons as they are all ambidextrous, or make two attacks using the clawed hooks on their leathery, bat-like wings or the deadly points at the wing tips. The base strike value of a half muto harpy is +6 SV and its wings inflict 1d12 damage each.

If further cross breeding with a bipedal, wingless humanoid, the offspring will be 50% likely to be born without wings and instead mirror their father's limb arrangement and other attributes. Half muto-harpies can enter small, enclosed spaces by tucking their wings back and walking on their leg-hands, which means they cannot hold weapons during this mode of locomotion but can still stab forward with both clawed wing-hooks each round.

Muto-harpies are described on page 80 of the Creatures of the Apocalypse (COTA) Codex, or downloadable for free at the Society of Excavators members area at this link: http://www.outlandarts.com/membersonly/TME-SOE-MH.htm

# Mutorg

Mutorgs, also called muto-borgs, cyber-mutants, and augmented deviants, are to some, the best of both worlds as far as combat and excavation endeavors go. In short, they are mutants who have for whatever reason been modified and enhanced with cybernetic implants. Typically, implants were made with a human physiology in mind and don't work on non-humans; however, certain lightly mutated humans make for acceptable candidates if they are not too severely divorced from normal human structure. Cybernetic implants will, however, only function if the spine and brain-based control system is of the advanced 'open format' or O.F. design. For the most part, then, mutorgs are only mildly mutated and have a limited number of cybernetic enhancements; often the maximum amount of tinkering the subject could handle and yet still perform his or her designated role.

**Mutorgs start game play with 1 each of defensive, offensive and miscellaneous implants, plus 1d2 prime and 1d2 minor mutations, with a 10% chance of a flaw mutation.**

Where conflicting Implant and mutations occur during random determination, such as a mutant occurring with no arms and a series of tentacles, and yet the subject also has a weapon arm, always work with the first rolled result. In this case, the mutorg would have one weapon arm and one less tentacle growing from his or her shoulders.

A dedicated character sheet for a Mutorg PC can be found on page 519 of this book, or at this webpage: https://www.outlandarts.com/expansionrules.htm

Mutant-cyborg hybrids indeed enjoy remarkable advantages in the wilderness or ruins, however, they face twice the trouble that either a purely mutated or cybernetic character has in some community settings. First off, they are quite rare and many people beleive it impossible for a mutant to also benefit from cybernetics. This arouses suspicion among commoners and authorities, alike, who will suspect that any visible mutorg has been assembled by the Mecha.

Likewise, where in some places a human based cyborg could be accepted as just another old-kind human with fancy prosthetics, the addition of obvious and unexpected mutations might strike fear, hostility or religious intolerance among inhabitants, especially purist-leaning sects.

Finally, mutorgs, like cyborgs, are susceptible to electromagnetic pulse weapons (EMP), since the spine and parts of the brain of all cyborgs are hard wired and hooked to the living portion of the body. Another concern is that many ancient medical instruments and drugs will not work properly on the mutated physiology of a non-pure blood, whereas they would on a regular pure stock based cyborg.

Besides any unwanted attention from commoners and watchmen, mutorg's must also be wary of the authorities who often percieve cyber-muties as a threat and will need to know who modified the mutant, when it happened and where the procedure took place. Furthermore, concerned leaders will want to know if more of the cyber-mutie's kind are massing some place to take over the region. Alternatively, others might instead be thrilled with the arrival of a mutorg in their midst. These ambitious, power hungry warlords and crime bosses will be eager to enlist a war band of these potent hybrids, or else, submit their own mutant henchmen to the procedure in order to upgrade them.

The augmentation of mutants, however, is challenging and even highly skilled robotics or cybernetics technicians can't simply attach an implant to a mutant and have it work. The necessary component to make a mutorg is the previously noted late era 'open format' cranial and spinal interface core. This control node and spine length tangle of stainless steel, wiring and sensors is more advanced than the standard configuration which normal cyborgs possess. This rare, advanced control system is of a more complex and specialized design, and was developed late in the last decades of the old civilization.

In short, the only way to get the proper control system that will not reject non-human physiology, is to either find an intact control system on a long dead cadaver, uncover an ancient storehouse containing such relic wonders — as certain factions have reportedly done (The Shenwallian Empire, for example*) or surgically cut it from the body of a freshly slain or captive mutorg**. Many skullocks, warmorts and other deviant humanoids can be encountered who exhibit cybernetics. Yet, these were genetically engineered front-line soldiers were already made to accommodate normal or cheap third world variants of cybernetic control nodes, whereas unique, one of a kind human mutants were not so gifted and required the specialized 'open format' spine and brain control system. Such a  system will fetch 900+2d1000 silver pieces if sold to a cybernetics technician or similarly interested party.

New era historian claim that hard pressed humanity sought to establish a way to control their mutant slave-soldiers — after many revolts and massacres. They therefore developed ways to dominate the minds of their organic creations and fit them with the built-in armaments and technology of their finest cyborg warriors. For the old ones, it was too little, too late. While these mutorg hybrids were turned against the robots of various hostile Mecha hives, as well as upon mutants, human protesters, abominations, and all other misfits, some say that mutorgs, more than any other creation of the desperate oldsters, contributed to the final battles and apocalyptic conflagration that ultimately wiped out civilization.

*Shenwall is a petty, expansionist faction in the Shallow Sea Region just north of the Crossroads Region.
**Removing the implant control node and spine fittings of either a standard cyborg or mutorg has a 2 in 6 chance of killing the subject on the operating table, and if surviving, the mutilated patient has a further 3 in 6 chance of being paralyzed for life from the neck down and an additional 2 in 6 chance of being reduced to a drooling vegetable. The proper reapplication of a new control system has a 5 in 6 chance of returning the cyborg or cyber-mutie to normal, otherwise, no change in the subject's condition.

# Nanoborg
*by Danny Seedhouse*

The pre-fall world spawned countless high-tech wonders, from cyborgs to genetically modified animals. Among these wonders was nanotechnology, the manipulation of matter at a near-atomic scale. Applied to multiple fields of science, from biology to metallurgy, nano-tech provided the keys to enhance the human form in amazing ways and use increasingly complex and smaller sized devices to manipulate and replace individual cells.

At first, these nano machines were used to repair damage, but as understanding grew, improvements were made. People with enhanced nano-tech systems could move faster, lift more weight, see farther and heal faster as nanites repaired and improved their bodies. The first nanoborgs were wealthy people who wanted to be healthy and look young again, who wanted to play at the same level as a trans-human or bio replica.

From this foundation, science ran wild in the last days of civilization, enhancements far beyond the natural became fashionable and necessary for survival. In the Mutant Epoch era, nanoborgs are the product of advanced enclaves, with nano hives passed down through generational bloodlines. Nano-machine enhancements are less obvious and easier to conceal than a cyborg's implants and if tested medically, nanoborgs appear to be pure strain humans, though a mechanical element may be detected with advanced screening processes. X-rays, too, will reveal the nano hive within a subject. The major difference is that, unlike cyborgs, nanobots have choice in their advanced modifications as their nano hives respond to user input and can be directed to reinforce or enhance certain systems.

A nanoborg dedicated character sheet can be found on page 520 of this book, plus, download all the character sheets at https://www.outland-arts.com/expansionrules.htm .

The first step to create a nanoborg character is to roll their stats using the standard trait value determination table, XR-2 on page 8. Where applicable, add a bonus to the resulting trait value, not the dice roll, according to the following modifiers:

## Nanoborg Stats Modifiers

| | |
|---|---|
| **Endurance** | +10 |
| **Strength** | +5 |
| **Agility** | +5 |
| **Accuracy** | +5 |
| **Intelligence** | +5 |
| **Perception** | +5 |
| **Willpower** | +5 |
| **Appearance** | +5 |

Each nanoborg begins with a 1d3+1 skill points in the various nano-skills determined by random rolls on the fallowing table, plus 1 automatically gained skill point in nano-healing (described on page 104). This represents their nano heritage inherited from the original makers of their nanites. Each time the nanoborg advances a rank — which uses the standard rank gain matrix on page XR-22 — he or she may spend a skill point on nano upgrades putting a maximum of 1 skill point into any individual upgrade.

Roll 1d8. Duplicated results can be kept, or the player can re-roll.

## Table XR-85/ Nanoborg Skill Areas  Roll 1d8

| | | |
|---|---|---|
| **1.** | Legacy Skill | Page 100 |
| **2.** | Defensive Upgrades | Page 100 |
| **3.** | Agility Upgrades | Page 101 |
| **4.** | Close Quarters Upgrades | Page 102 |
| **5.** | Electrical Manipulation Upgrades | Page 102 |
| **6.** | Sensory Upgrades | Page 103 |
| **7.** | Mental Upgrades | Page 104 |
| **8.** | Nano-healing Upgrades | Page 105 |

# Nanoborg Skill Descriptions

### Legacy Skill
This is an inbuilt skill in the character's nanites at 3 skill points*, roll 1d4 for column: 1. warrior/ 2. criminal / 3. educated / 4. Misc. Use Table XR-7, page 13 in this book. This legacy skill can't be improved upon until the PC reaches rank 3.
*If Applicable; i.e. If the randomly determined skill has more than one maximum skill point.*

### Defensive Upgrades
Nanites are used to weave reinforcing strands of advanced armor into skin, strengthen bones and tissue and make the borg more resistance to damage in all forms. These enhancements are for those who want to wade through gunfire or stand in a roaring fire. At 4th rank, physical changes are visible in the nanoborg's skin as it becomes more ridged and takes on a metallic sheen that increases with further rank gain.

## Table XR-86/ Nanoborg Defensive Upgrades Benefits Matrix

| Skill Points | Absorption* | DV | Augments |
|---|---|---|---|
| 1 | 1d10 | -6 | -5 DV vs fire |
| 2 | 1d10+5 | -10 | -10 DV vs fire   -15 DV versus explosions |
| 3 | 1d20+5 | -14 | -10 DV vs ballistic attacks |
| 4 | 1d20+10 | -18 | -10 DV vs Acids  -30 DV vs explosions |
| 5 | 3d10+10 | -24 | No longer take extra DMG from anti cyborg/robot attacks**, except EMP attacks |
| 6 | 4d10+15 | -30 | Extra hazard check on any END based check |
| 7 Max | 5d10+25 | -34 | Half damage from falls and other large impacts after absorption |

*Roll Absorption once at the beginning of a new combat engagement, once the character realizes he or she is in it. Subtract absorption from all combined damage taken per round before applying the remaining to the character's endurance trait.*

** *Such as Electrical Pulse (pg. TME-65). EMP (electromagnetic pulse) weaponry can still shut down a nanoborg as if it were a robot or android.*

Defensive upgrades above 3 skill points (skp) reduce the maximum agility upgrade by 1 skp (6 skill points armor means 3 skill points agility upgrades Max). A nanoborg's weight increases by 2 kg per rank.

## Table XR-87/ Nanoborg Defensive Upgrades Drawbacks Matrix

| Skill points | Appearance | Movement | Armor limits |
|---|---|---|---|
| **1,2** | -1 | NA | No shell class armor |
| **3,4** | -1d4 | -0.25m | No hard or ridged body armor like plate mail |
| **5,6** | -1d6 | -0.5m | Can only use custom fitted soft armors like leather |
| **7 Max** | -2d6 | -1m | Can only use furs, skins, hides or a leather jacket |

## Agility Upgrades

Nanites rewrite nerve connections, reaction speeds are increased, fast twitch muscles are enhanced and joints improved for flexibility. Additionally, nanoborgs have an improved sense of balance and acrobatic ability. Those borgs with agility upgrades have the grace of dancers, climb like monkeys and free run like a master, moving around the environment with increasingly unnatural grace.

Agility upgrades can fundamentally change the way the user reacts and acts in certain systems, falling back naturally on agility. The nanoborg can effectively replace his or her strength stat with agility when doing certain tasks, although this can only be done for things requiring a mix of both stats such as climbing or that can be done with agility or force. For example, a nanoborg can't use agility to pry open a concrete door.

The nanoborg gets a +1 bonus on the chase chart (page TME-112), and two hazard checks on any test involving agility. Agility upgrades provide a defense value bonus the same as shown for the dodge skill on page TME-37 in the hub rules, and override any skill points in dodge, unless the character has more points in dodge than the agility upgrades, This same rule applies to any skill points in climbing or acrobatics the nanoborg might have.

## Table XR-88/ Nanoborg Agility Upgrades Matrix

| Skill Points | DV | Agility* | Stealth & Climbing Skill Points | Acrobatics Skill Points** | Safe Fall Meters*** | Miscellaneous bonuses |
|---|---|---|---|---|---|---|
| **1** | -5 | +5 | 1 | 0 | 1m | Ambidexterity |
| **2** | -8 | +5 (+10) | 2 | 1 | 2m | Climb |
| **3** | -11 | +5 (+15) | 2 | 2 | 4m | Slippery |
| **4****** | -14 | +10 (+25) | 3 | 2 | 6m | All terrain |
| **5** | -17 | +10 (+35) | 3 | 3 | 8m | Can't slow me down |
| **6** | -21 | +15 (+50) | 4 | 3 | 10m | Always land on your feet |
| **7 Max** | -23 | +15 (+65) | 4 | 4 | 14m | Ultimate agility |

*These stack so, for example, a nanoborg with these upgrades has +15 total to agility by 3 skill points, or +35 at 5 skp.
** If not using the Acrobatics skill, simply reduce all Hazard Checks, based on Agility upgrade by 1 per skill point of enhancement.
*** This distance is what this character can fall and suffer no harm, but this distance is also the meters amount taken off longer falls, too.
****At 4 skill points on the agility upgrades matrix, the borg can't wear hard or ridged armor and still receive any more benefit on this matrix.

Note: skp is an abbriviation for skill points.

**Slippery:** The borg's agility can help him escape a grapple, and so for the purposes of escaping, or avoiding a grapple attempt, add the nanoborg's strength and agility, divided by two, to get the borg's new trait as far as making a hazard check to slip free (on table TME-30a on page 39 of the hub rules).

**All terrain:** Rough terrain such as concrete rubble, broken asphalt, or a tangled forest don't slow the borg down anymore. Mud and snow still slow this character down unless he or she can leap from dry spot to dry spot.

**Can't slow me down:** The borg now climbs at their full movement rate. Reduce any speed penalty for armor worn by 25%. Additionally, this character only suffers 1/2 of the penalties for a crippled leg or results of a called shot to the leg.

## Agility Upgrade Descriptions

**Ambidexterity:** The borg can use either hand as well as the other without suffering the regular -20 SV off hand penalty.

**Climbing:** The borg can now use just their agility stat when determining their climbing skill (no need to add strength).

**Always Lands on your feet:** Like cat, any fall or leap this nanoborg undertakes always results in them landing on their feet and able to take off or attack immediately after landing.

**Ultimate Agility:** This nanoborg no longer needs to roll for any agility based hazard check of B or lower, and any check above B is reduced by one letter code to a minimum of a C hazard.

## Close Quarters Upgrades

Some nanoborgs just want to punch people, some for fun, others for profit. Close quarters upgrades reinforce the striking areas, knuckles, feet, knees or any other part of the body commonly used to hit something. With these upgrades, the borg's muscles and bones are reinforced to better deliver and receive impact.

Besides blunt force attacks, which can deliver stun damage if the nanoborg chooses, one's nanites are configured to build blades and spike tipped limbs to be extended when combat goes lethal. The nanites modify the borg in a host of other subtle ways, too, all to enhance survivability and lethality in the deadly dance of close combat.

When the nanoborg selects a skill point of close quarters upgrades, they are granted access to two attack modes, one lethal one stun. Lethal melee attacks represent the nanoborg extending blades and spikes or plating their fists in solid nano metal — modifications that are always visible when active. A nanoborg can not hide lethal mode, on the other hand non-lethal or stun mode gives no visible clue, and is the default mode for the nanoborg, making it perfect for stealth and a good old bar brawl.

Skill points in this upgrade are stand alone, and incompatible with brawling, martial arts, or weapon expert skills — unless the user has more skill points in one of those skill areas. Sometimes a character wishes to keep their true nature as a nanoborg secret, and so uses common brawling, martial arts or other typical hand-held weapons in a fight to look like just any other human. When a nanite involved attack is made, however, the bonus from the nano enhancement chart below are used. These hand to hand combat modifiers are not added to other combat skills because the bonuses from nano combat come from the override of a person's own natural reflexes with programed ones.

### Table XR-89/ Nanoborg Close Quarter Upgrades Matrix

| Skill Points | Lethal SV | Lethal DMG | Non-Lethal SV | Non-Lethal DMG* | Strength Bonus** | Misc. Bonuses |
|---|---|---|---|---|---|---|
| 1 | +4 | 1d8 | +5 | +1 | +5 | 2 Melee Attacks, Parry |
| 2 | +6 | 1d10 | +7 | +2 | +5 | Grappler |
| 3 | +8 | 2d6 | +9 | +3 | +5 | Cant Keep Me Down |
| 4 | +10 | 2d8 | +11 | +1d6+1 | +10 | Defensive edge |
| 5 | +12 | 2d10 | +13 | +1d6+3 | +10 | 3 Melee Attacks |
| 6 | +14 | 2d10+5 | +15 | +1d6+5 | +10 | Get Off Me! |
| 7 Max | +16 | 2d10+10 | +17 | +1d6+7 | +15 | Aimed Melee |

*Base damage for a fist is 1d6

**Cumulative strength (i.e. Add shown amount to trait with each skill point gained.

**Miscellaneous Close Quarter Upgrade Bonuses Descriptions**

**Parry:** When parrying, the nanoborg receives a -15 DV value. This improves by -1 per additional skill point in this upgrade.

**Grappler:** For every 2 skill points in the close quarters upgrades area, this nanoborg's grapple skill increases by one skill point, too. This can add to any skill points in grapple the character might already possess.

**Can't Keep Me Down:** The nanoborg develops an increased resistance to any attack that deals stun damage from a combination of artificial reinforcement and the experience of taking way too many punches to the face. Whatever the reason, this nanoborg now takes half damage from non-lethal attacks. If knocked unconscious from anything else other than negative endurance, this borg receives 2 extra hazard checks and recovers consciousness twice as fast.

**Defensive Edge:** The nanoborg receives a +1 to initiative and -2 DV. Opponents only get 1/2 of the usual SV bonus for advantageous position in melee combat. Example: an attacker striking from behind this unsuspecting borg would normally get a +40 SV bonus, but against this borg, it gets only +20 SV.

**Get off me!:** The nanoborg can now spontaneously grow spikes and blades out of his entire body. This eruption, which is undertaken as a regular attack with a strike value of 01-80, deals base lethal damage as double the nanoborg's skill points. For example, a nanoborg with 4 skill points in this upgrade will deliver 8 points damage on hitting who, or whatever, is holding it. Anything grappling or holding the target must make a type D willpower hazard check upon witnessing or being skewered by these metallic spikes, with failure on the attacker's part meaning it instinctively let's go of this spike covered nanoborg. If the target continues to hold the nanoborg they risk taking damage every turn their nanoborg opponent gets, besides any attacks this borg might also unleash.

**Aimed Melee Upgrade:** All called shots in melee attempted by this nanoborg now count as regular aimed attacks with no increase in the time needed to make them.

## Electrical Manipulation Upgrades

By their very nature, every nanoborg has more electrical energy running through them than your average human. To most, this is just a side effect of their increased nanite counts. For some nanoborgs it is an opportunity to learn, and they begin to harness their own electrical potential. This starts with reinforcing the body to withstand and store more and more electrical energy. Then learning how to project electricity in increasingly devastating attacks, starting from a taser-like effect all they way to throwing lightning bolts like the mythical gods of old.

Electrical manipulation upgrades give access to increasingly efficient internal power cells and self recharging ability that increase as time and experience progress. Other abilities develop, electricity becomes visible, amps increase, and the number of charges in a power cell are all displayed in the borg's visual field.

The nanoborg can hook themself up to an external device needing power and literally charge it. One charge burst provides 5 energy units or recharge to an external power battery of any type. Power cells are described on page 199 of the hub rules with a pill power cell having 1 energy unit capacity, a mini cell 3 energy units or EUs, a standard power cell has 10 EUs while a power pack contains 100 EUs when fully charged up. Any excess charging of a battery dissipates.

The battery capacity listed on the following matrix is the character's total, internal electrical field supply at the given skill point tier. Whatever other electrical manipulations used also drain from this same battery supply. External batteries can be plugged into this PC and will be drained first before the character's own internally generated power supply.

## Table XR-90/ Electrical Manipulation Upgrades Benefits Matrix

| Skill Points | Skill | Charge Used | Battery Capacity | Recovery Rate |
|---|---|---|---|---|
| 1 | Electrical Absorption | none | 10 EUs | 1 EU per 2 hours |
| 2 | Electrical Fists | 1 EU | 15 EUs | 1 EU per hour |
| 3 | Self Defense Field | 1 EU | 20 EUs | 2 EUs per hour |
| 4 | Recharger | 1 EU | 25 EUs | 4 EUs per hour |
| 5 Max | Stun Bolt | 2 EUs | 30 EUs | 6 EUs per hour |

**Note:** EUs stand for 'energy units' as per the power sources table on page 199 of the hub rules.

## Electrical Manipulation Upgrade Descriptions

**Electrical Absorption:** This allows the borg to take 1/2 damage from all electrical, taser and stun ray attacks by channeling it into internal batteries or harmlessly discharging it. For every 10 points of damage absorbed, this borg's battery regains 1 energy unit of recharge. Excess charge is stored for 6 hours or until the total reaches 10 points, then it is shunted into a full battery charge. The nanoborg can drain the charge from power cells gaining one energy unit (EU) for every 2 it drains. At character rank 4 this changes to a 1 to 1 ratio, and damage absorption improves to 75%.

**Electrical Fists:** The nanoborg channels electricity dealing an extra 1d10 damage when making any physical attack with a +20 strike value bonus, regardless if the attack results in a hit or miss. Each charge from the battery 'power's up' the borgs fist for 1 round. At rank 5 this damage goes to 1d20 extra damage instead of 1d10. The fist uses one energy unit per round and at the 2 skill point tier for this nanoborg, he or she has an internal battery supply for 15 punches worth of power, which recharges at a rate of 1 EU per hour.

**Self Defense Field:** When turned on, this nanoborg is surrounded in a crackling field of electrical energy that will possibly zap anyone who attacks the borg in melee. When this borg is struck, the field makes an automatic attack in the assailant's own turn with a +30 SV bonus and doing 1d20 stun damage. Each discharge uses 1 energy unit charge and can only be triggered once a round. And against only the first opponent to successfully strike this character. The internal battery in this nanoborg can hold 20 EUs of energy and recharges at a rate of 2 EUs per hour.

**Recharger:** Allows the borg to recharge external power supplies, 2 energy units spent convert to 1 energy unit charged in a power cell. The borg can transfer 1 EU charge a round, to a max of 25 EUs. This internal battery discharges at 4 EUs per hour.

**Stun bolt:** This nanoborg gains a short range stun blast. SV +15, rate 1, damage 2d20 stun, range 20 meters. Each bolt depletes 2 energy units from the character's total 30 energy unit capacity battery.

## Sensory Upgrades

Nanites enhance and upgrade the nanoborg's senses and correct genetic defects in eyesight, sharpen hearing beyond human norms, and improve one's sense of smell. As this enhancement proceeds, the nanoborg begins to expand beyond the normal scope of human senses, and in radical ways. Darkness becomes light, infrared spectrum become visible, ultrasonic hearing and tracking by smell alone all become possible. Nanites soon become a direct part of the nanoborg's senses, too, providing data from an increasingly broad area.

Sensory Upgrades also give the nanoborg an extra hazard check on any test involving senses, plus an extra roll to resist incoming sensory based attacks.

The following table shows the different upgrades which develop in a nanoborg as he or she gains skill points in this area, including a bonus to their perception trait score.

## Table XR-91/ Sensory Upgrades Benefits Matrix

| Skill Points | Perception Bonus* | Sensory Upgrades |
|---|---|---|
| 1 | +5 | Advanced Eyes |
| 2 | +5 | Tracking |
| 3 | +5 | Alternate Frequency Hearing |
| 4 | +10 | Blind Fighting |
| 5 | +10 | Substance Reader |
| 6 | +10 | Decentralized Senses |
| 7 Max | +15 | Sensory Projection |

*These points stack. Example: At 4 skill points this borg has gained 25 perception trait points.*

## Sensory Upgrade Descriptions

**Advanced Eyes:** This nanoborg's eyes have the fallowing enhancement, night vision, zoom and infrared vision.

**Night Vision** allows the nanoborg to see normally in low light conditions. **Zoom** gives built in x25 times magnification. **Infrared optics** allow the nanoborg to see heat. This allows the borg to see through obstacles such as walls, fog and foliage, anything that does not block heat. It also allows the tracking of another being's heat trail. To track by heat this borg need to begin before the trail has gone cold, usually about 30 minutes depending on conditions. Poor conditions could degrade a trail in a matter of minutes, whereas a large multi limbed bare footed animal walking over a heat retentive surface will be trackable for much longer, perhaps even hours.

**Tracking:** This sensory upgrades allow the picking up of subtle environmental clues, combined with visual overlays to give 1 phantom point in the tracking skill for every 2 skill points of this sensory upgrade, with a bonus point at the maximum 7th tier, for a total of 4 in tracking.

**Alternate Frequency Hearing:** This upgrade allows the nanoborg to hear above and below the normal range of human hearing, into the ultrasonic and infrasonic ranges. This individual is now able hear things inaudible to normal humans, such as a dog whistle or the ping a bat uses to echo-locate. When reaching 4 skill points in sensory upgrades, this borg also gains to ability to receive nearby radio signals broadcast from within 1 kilometer radius, while at 7 skill points, he or she can scan for signals and tune into a radio station coming from within 50 kilometers whenever desired.

**Blind Fighting:** This feature is an advancement from the 'alternate frequency hearing' and allows the borg to use his other senses to compensate for a lack of eyesight. This allows the borg to fight in melee combat with no penalties when blind. The borg can move around and avoid obstacles using echolocation, which functions to a range of about 20 meters. Long-range weapons fire from beyond 20 meters is still a problem as the borg is unaware of such an attack until it is too late.

**Decentralized Senses:** At this skill point tier, the nanoborg can use any area of their body to see, hear and taste from. Within 4 rounds, it concentrates its senses elsewhere in it body and can see out of their feet or taste with a touch of their fingers.

In practical terms this allows the borg to see around corners without exposing his or her head or reach into and see the inside of a bag with their hand. The physical loss of an eye or ear from injury or when blindfolded does not impair their sense. This ability can be turned on and off at will. When gathering sensory information from another part of the body, the previous area, such as the borg's natural ears, eyes, or tongue, stop working while attention is focused elsewhere in the body.

**Sensory Projection:** The nanoborg can project a cloud of nanites in a 20 meter radius that becomes part of his or her senses. The swarm can stretch out in a 400 meter long line for remote observation around the corner, or through the cracks in a wall, to observe the other side. It takes 5 rounds for the cloud to reach maximum radius and a tendril can be extended at 16 meters a round. Winds above 20 km/h (12.5mph) disperse the cloud 1 meter a round in the wind's direction, this dispersion rate increases by 1 meter every extra 2 km/h of wind. Dispersed nanites cease operating and become dust on the wind.

Within its nano cloud, the borg is aware of all movement and sound. Nothing can sneak up on this individual or hide from it. In combat the borg receives a +2 to initiative if combat is taking place within its cloud. Even when asleep, the borg is still receiving sensory input and can set up a proximity alarm to wake them if there is movement within the cloud.

The borg can also get an unprecedented level of detail about objects in this radius. By focusing on a specific object the borg can find the cracks in a wall, have their nanites crawl into anything that is not airtight, providing internal views of a locked box, the mechanical lock itself, or the booby trap waiting to blow off its face. In game terms this provides a 2 step reduction in the hazard check letter code difficulty of any task that is made easier by seeing the inner workings of an object (hazard check D becomes A, F becomes D, etc.).

## Mental Upgrades

Not all nanoborg upgrades focus on enhancing the physical body, and so mental ones exist, too. These are keyed to enhance the mind by adding computer augmentation that aids memory, logic and on-the-fly mental calculations needed for tasks involving advanced mathematical theories. These upgrades are subtle and can go completely unnoticed by all but this person's long-time associates and friends.

Beyond the increases in the intelligence stat these upgrades provide, a series of other subtle mental enhancements can emerge from enhanced navigation, relic knowledge, innate computer knowledge, increased language capabilities, as well as the ability to better shield one's own thoughts from foreign invasion.

Mental upgrades grant a second hazard check roll on any check involving intelligence, and provide the borg with a near photographic memory. Finally, mental damage heals at twice the normal rate.

## Table XR-92/ Mental Upgrades Benefits Matrix

| Skill Points | Intelligence | Willpower | Mental Upgrades |
|---|---|---|---|
| 1 | +5 | +0 | Quick Study, Relic Knowledge |
| 2 | +5 | +5 | Polyglot |
| 3 | +5 | +5 | Mental Shielding |
| 4 | +10 | +5 | Seeds of Understanding |
| 5 | +10 | +10 | Jury Rigging |
| 6 | +10 | +10 | Mental Savant |
| 7 Max | +15 | +10 | Awakened Mind |

## Mental Upgrade Descriptions

**Quick Study:** The time needed for the nanoborg to learn any new skill is halved. For details on leaning other skills from either a companion tutor or a post-apocalyptic 'college', as well as the costs for such education, see on Table TME-1-23 Skill Acquisition by Education on page 35 of the hub rules for skills included in that book, or page XR-200 for skills from this book.

**Relic Knowledge:** The nanoborg automatically gains this skill. See page TME-49.

**Polyglot:** The borg unlocks the secret of their built in library of pre-fall language database allowing them to effectively communicate with anyone employing a known language. Any language that is a mix of old and new words, or the strange tongue of isolated tribes, can be picked up with record speed and basic communication with users of these strange languages is possible after 1d6 hours of interaction or 2d6 hours of listening. After 1d4+1 days the nanoborg can communicate with these beings at the level of normal conversation, though advanced or strange concepts may escape them. After 1d4 weeks using the language his or her speech is indistinguishable from a native.

**Mental Shielding:** This sub-skill gives the nanoborg 2 extra hazard checks to resist the effects of any mental attack or attempt to read or influence his or her mind. For these checks the borg's intelligence or willpower trait value are temporarily doubled.

**Seeds of Understanding:** The nanoborg begins to understand intuitively the basics of all technological skills. This gives one phantom rank in the Mechanical, Electrical and Computer technican skills. If the borg has one of these skills, they can instead transfer the phantom rank to one of the following skills, gunsmith, bio tech, robotics tech, cybernetics tech, junk-doctor, or chemical tech. This transferred phantom skill must be selected by the player and is fixed, instead of allowing access to all these other skill areas.

**Jury-Rigging:** Building on the seeds of understanding the nanoborg can now make intuitive jumps of logic and begin to scratch build new, if unreliable, devices. This grants 2 phantom ranks in the junk crafting skill, or, if already its is already possessing this skill, add 1 bonus skill point tier.

**Mental Savant:** As the nanoborg's brain is rewired, they experience a sudden moment of understanding, as once complex concepts become simple and advanced tasks become second nature. Immediately receive 5 skill points in one of the fallowing Intelligence skills. **Roll 1d10**, although re-roll any skill that the borg already has 2 skill points in.

| | | | |
|---|---|---|---|
| 1. | Gunsmith | 6. | Electrical Technician |
| 2. | Medic | 7. | Mechanical Technician |
| 3. | Bio-Technician | 8. | Robotics Technician |
| 4. | Chemical Technician | 9. | Junk-Doctor |
| 5. | Computer Technician | 10. | Cybernetics Technician |

**Awakened Mind:** At this point the nanoborg becomes effectively a ghost mutant, and gains 1 mutation from the ghost mutation list, re-rolling advanced mind, mental screen or any organ based mutation such as reserve heart or breath holding. The new ghost mutation list, which combines all the Hub Rules and Expansion Rules mutations in this category is found on page XR-231.

## Nano-Healing Upgrades

Healing upgrades are the first upgrade every nano-borg receives, they are the basic building blocks that allow upgrades to all nano systems. Nanites mend torn skin, knit together blood and bone, and hunt down cancerous cells and foreign substances. They keep the nanoborg healthy and strong, extend life span, and make body systems more efficient at the basic day to day living level such as digesting food to maintaining healthy hair. The greatest benefits of healing upgrades come from the healing of traumatic injuries with increasing efficiency.

Every nanoborg begins with 1 point in this skill. Healing upgrades grant the borg and extra hazard check to resist and survive the effects of any poison, disease or radiation exposure and anything that requires an endurance hazard check. They automatically stabilize the borg when he or she would otherwise die from endurance loss. The nanoborg's need for food and water to live is roughly half of a normal human, and the onset of starvation from the lack of food or water takes twice as long to set in as the nanites extract nutrients and water out of whatever is available within the borg's system.

## Table XR-93/Nano-Healing Upgrades Benefits Matrix

| Skill Points | Healing Rate | Healing Upgrades and Notes |
|---|---|---|
| 1 | +10 points a day | Booster* |
| 2 | +15 points a day | Self-sufficiency |
| 3 | 2 point per hour | Limb regrowth tier 1 |
| 4 | 4 points per hour | Injectable booster |
| 5 | 6 points per hour | Healing trance + limb regrowth tier 2 |
| 6 | 1 points every minute | Better body by science |
| 7 (max) | 1 per round | Resurrection |

*Nanoborgs get an extra hazard check for all endurance based checks including against poison, radiation, disease, etc.*

## Nano-Healing Upgrade Descriptions

**Booster:** Sometimes you need an extra shot of healing, and the booster upgrade gives it to you. Once per day, per skill point in nano-healing upgrades, this nanoborg can heal 1d10 damage with a single action to each depleted trait. This healing can be undertaken in 1d10 intervals, which takes a round to activate, or all available healing boosts can be dumped into the borg's ravaged body at once. For example, a borg with 3 skill points in this upgrade can make 3 healing boosts in a 24-hour period, separated by hours, or use all 3d10 healing dice in one go, and have nothing left for later.

A healing booster surge automatically kicks in when the borg becomes incapacitated because of endurance depletion and will expend one charge a round until the borg regains consciousness.

The booster can also flush out toxins and poisons, giving 2 extra hazard checks per booster charge, but without a 1d10 healing surge. This toxin-flush happens automatically when the borg fails his or her two free hazard checks.

**Self-Sufficiency:** The nano-borg's body now stores 15 days worth of nutrients at all times in case of starvation. The borg can now eat just about anything organic, with little concern for his or her own health as the nanites even helpfully allow one to turn off their own sense of smell and taste — a must when eating carrion is your only option.

Water saving mode allows the borg to recycle water internally and absorb moisture from the air, allowing them to go for 1 week on no extra water. This hydration buffer is increased to 1 month in extremely humid areas. Clean drinking water can be filtered from salt water, mud, or any substance with a high water content through the skin. Additionally, this nanoborg doubles the time he or she can hold their breath before drowning.

**Limb Regrowth:** Tier 1 allows the borg to regenerate lost fingers and toes over a period of 1d4+4 days and hand or foot in a month, or reattach a severed limb and regain full function after 1d4+2 days of healing. This only works if the borg is still alive. Tier 2 is obtained at 6 skill points of nano healing upgrades and allows for full limb regeneration, this takes 1+1d4 months, lost organs can be regenerated as well, eyes and ears taking 1+1d2 months. Internal organs, if the borg can survive without them take 2 + 1d6 weeks.

**Injectable Booster:** The nano-borg can now inject her own healing booster shots into other people, with the same level of healing power (heals 1d10 END per skill point the nanoborg has in healing upgrades, as the 1 skill point booster, and can be used all at once or in 1d10 increments). These nanites only work properly on pure stock humans, trans humans, clones and bioreplicas. When injected into a mutant animal there is a flat 25% chance that they will attack the mutant's body and do damage equal to what they normally heal. Mutants have a 10% chance per prime mutation and flaw they have, and a 5% chance per minor mutation (these percentages are added together before rolling) of suffering a negative response and taking damage as the nanites attempt to repair the genetic irregularities. If the mutant survives the damage there is a 10% chance per mutation, that they are "cured" of each deviation and lose it.

**Healing Trance:** The nanoborg can go into a coma like state, improving healing rate by double and reducing resource intake to 25%. The user can enter this coma-like state for a pre-selected number of days. A borg can stay under until starvation gets critical, then automatic systems stop the trance and the nanoborg wakes.

**Better Body by Science:** At this level of nano-healing, the nanites can extend the borg's natural life span into the hundreds of years. The individual becomes immune to cancer and any permanent stat loss is healed back to its original level at the rate of 1 per day. Additionally, the borg doubles the benefits of self sufficiency. Environmental conditions are no longer a concern and any temperature that does not do direct physical damage can be tolerated. The borg can now breathe underwater after a few minutes of immersion while all his or her stats are increased to a minimum of 40, stats above this are not effected.

**Resurrection:** The nanoborg is now extremely hard to kill. When reduced to a reasonable dead level of endurance (according to the Table TME-2-11 Injury and Death on page 111 of the hub rules, the borg goes into a suspended animation state instead. Here, their healing nanites attempt to repair the fatal damage and then restart the borg's vital systems. It takes 10+1d10 minutes for this process to finish and then the borg begins to heal 1 endurance point a minute until they are above the dead level. The nanoborg's body must be somewhat intact, and the head attached for this to work.

If the nanoborg has taken more than half of their uninjured endurance beyond the dead value, the body is beyond the nanites ability to repair, and resurrection does not happen. For example, a borg with 100 END and a Willpower of 40 is beyond saving once they are reduced to -78 endurance (50 beyond death to -27). Resurrection is extremely taxing on the medical nanites and the borg functions at the first tier of this skill for 2d6 days as there nanites rebuild themselves, after this point the borg regains 1 skill points in this skill area every day until returning to its original level.

# Parasite

Also called symbionts, parasites are humanoid miscreations of diminutive size with specialized mutations which allow them to live upon a host human's body. They can either be festooned to the outer skin of the host's frame, or partially or entirely subcutaneously embedded. These parasitic humanoid have either evolved from a combination of freakish mutations, or else been purposefully engineered. New era speculation claim that these small, impish mutants were developed to either pilot small drones, smart bombs, tiny spacecraft, or else, be attached to other genetically engineered beings to serve as controllers for much larger, dumb battle beasts.

Typically, a parasite is born to symbiont parents of its own, and grows up in a larger humanoid settlement as do other characters; however, at an early age it attaches itself to a human or humanoid subject and bonds to the often unwilling host. In rare instances, a host body is offered to the parasite on religious grounds, out of duty, but so too, as a punishment.

Parasites are typically disgusting to behold, with sickening appendages, misshapen, slick bodies and an unsettling presence, especially to those who are not already well acquainted with it and its zombie-like acquired body. Parasites are connected to the host body by **2d6+1 neurological tendrils**, which bore into the 'mount', along with **1d6+1 digestive feeding and waste elimination tubes**. Sometimes, other intrusions, controls and connectors are also involved in the symbiotic relationship, but these are determined by details according to the tables to follow. A parasite character sheet is included on page 8, but can also be downloaded at https://www.outlandarts.com/expansionrules.htm .

Its is recommended to fill out a separate parasite character sheet and a host sheet since host bodies are often killed or abandoned throughout the life of a symbiont.

Parasites start with the following traits, which are entirely separate from the host body's own randomly determined traits. The stats below are either a set value range, such as 3d6+3 rolled for strength, or, entirely random for both Intelligence and Willpower and use the regular trait generation table, found on page XR 521 of this book.

## Parasite Starting Trait Values

| | |
|---|---|
| Endurance | 4d6+10 |
| Strength | 3d6+3 |
| Agility | 2d6+2 |
| Accuracy | 3d6+3 |
| Intelligence | Random |
| Willpower | Random |
| Perception | 3d6+2 |
| Appearance | 2d6 |

Parasites have many appendages specifically available to them, as well as deviations exhibited by other mutants. **Each parasite will have 1d4 prime mutations from the Parasite Mutation list on page XR-234, plus 1d2 minor mutations (page 229) and a 2 in 10 chance of a flaw mutation (page 233).**

The game master might need to call for a re-roll on any mutations which would enlarge the parasite.

# Parasite Details

## Adhesion

A parasite either adheres to a host by being partially or fully embedded within it, or is mounted on the subject's exterior. The advantage to being embedded is that the parasite can easily conceal itself in the host's flesh to avoid detection, at least without the body being stripped down and exposing the many orifices and punctures in the subject. Likewise, an embedded parasite cannot easily be yanked off of the host. A mounted host, on the other hand, with its neurological and digestive connections boring into the host, can quickly abandon the fleshy vehicle during an emergency, and by not being so intrusively meshed with the body, the symbiont can detach itself for solo excursions, such as exploring tiny portals, seeking concealment, taking a bath or indulging in a mating opportunity.

Finally, a parasite that tears free of an embedded host will often kill the human body it inhabits, while a mounted parasite can expel itself for a short period of time and return to its host body, so long as its 'vessel' hasn't regained self awareness and left the scene.

Roll 2d6 and consult the following table to determine a parasite character's permanent method of adhesion.



**2,3. Entrail embedded:** This parasite lives within the gut cavity of the host and has fused its digestive tract, respiration and primary sensory organs to the host's body. All the parasite's appendages and unique mutations protrude through the torso and can be used normally by the parasite. If the host body is killed, this parasite expels itself through the dead subject's abdomen and can wriggle off as best it can. The parasite speaks through the host's own vocal chords and sees through its eyes.

One huge advantage this adhesion mode has over all others is that the parasite can suck all its appendages into the host's body, seal the openings with skin flaps — that look like long healed bullet wounds — and truly hide in the larger body. Detaching from a living host will usually cause the death of the mount body, which will bleed out from the numerous portals, holes and orifices left behind by the fleeing symbiont. While detached, the host body suffers 1d6 damage per minute from blood loss — although if a medic can attend the body, this drops to 1d3 END damage per round. All bleeding can be stopped and the host body stabilized by a skilled medic, see table TME-1-37 in the hub rules, page 46. On the medics table, consult the column listed as 'Resuscitate Drowning Victim'. Use this column and the odds based on the skill points of the medic to stabilize an abandoned, entrail embedded host body.

**4,5. Partially embedded:** This parasite lives in the host's torso but, when desired, wanting to interact with companions, or even leave the host body, it can extrude itself outward and expose its head and whatever appendages it desires. When leaving the host body, and therefore detaching control tendrils, feeding tubes and other connectors, the host body risks death from shock and organ failure, bleeding and cardiovascular trauma, and must make a type D endurance based hazard check or go into cardiac arrest and expire. This parasite is embedded in the host's front 88% of the time, otherwise attached at the upper back.

This half embedded parasite must expose its eyes to see and control the host, but can speak through the fleshy vehicle's mouth if desired. It cannot fully hide itself in the larger body, as can entrail embedded specimens, and so if the host's body is disrobed viewers will immediately see this humanoid wood tick adhered to the hapless host.

**6,7. Chest Rider:** The parasite is attached to the host's front by way of back growing tendrils and digestive tubes, its head and appendages facing out ready to deal with the world. The symbiotic human can often conceal itself in the robes, poncho and other bulky clothing of the host, or else just have its head poking out through a hole in the garments to observe goings on around it. If needed, this parasite can easily detach itself from the host body to move about its quarters, a vehicle's interior, or else flee a desperate situation*.

**8,9. Back Rider:** This symbiont looks over the shoulders of the host with its neurological tendrils and digestive connectors inserted into the back and sides of the host. In short, it rides the larger body like a monkey on its back. Often concealed under cloaks and fur lined hoods and hats, this symbiont has a commanding view of the world around it, and is in perhaps the best position possible despite giving the living vehicle a stooped, hunched back appearance. If the host is killed, or for whatever reason the parasite wants to leave the body to undertake some mission, explore a small opening, flee, or socialize with other beings, the host body is likely to survive the detachment ordeal.*

**10,11. Side Mounted:** The parasite adheres under either the left or right arm of the host. The symbiont's digestive tubes and control tendrils are worked into the human's ribs and abdomen, and therein, attached to the necessary organs, spine and brain just like a back or front rider. Like these other two common parasite adhesion modes, the side saddle rider can disconnect from its host to move off to conduct other affairs, the body most likely able to survive the ordeal.*

This adhesion location allows for easier concealment should the parasite wish to direct its slave body to go undetected in regular human populations, with only a poncho, cloak or large baggy garment all that is needed to hide the hideous homo-leechian master.

**12. Necker:** Like a smaller, second head, this parasite's head grows up and out of the host's neck, its appendages disgorge from the body's chest, back, sides and belly, the bulk of the symbiont's body housed within the ribcage of the mount. Although by wearing a cloak, hood, large floppy hat, or fur lined scarf, this parasite's presence could be concealed from all but the most perceptive passer by, although any detection of the parasite would surely be met with horror.

To remove itself from the host's neck and body takes 2d6 minutes, with each minute inflicting 1d10 damage to the host, possibly killing it.

*The host body will normally survive this departure well enough unless it is in harm's way when abandoned, and will only gain back its own willpower and thus self awareness at a rate of 1 willpower point per hour (see below for Host Body details). The odds of avoiding death at detachment is for the host to make an endurance based type A hazard check, with failure resulting in the body collapsing into a coma for 3d6 hours, regardless of reinsertion of the parasite. At the end of the coma duration, a second identical hazard check must be made to avoid the host dying of heart failure instead of returning to normal.*

## Host Body

While occupied by its symbiont controller, a host body has its willpower locked away and only used used for defense against incoming mental attacks and the like, and is otherwise inaccessible to the mindless, dominated subject body. If abandoned by a parasite 'master' the surviving body will however regain access to its natural willpower at a rate of one trait point per hour, and is allowed a willpower based type D hazard check each hour using this rejuvenated amount.

If it succeeds at its hazard check, it will regain self awareness and wake up, and be free of the mind control toxins of the parasite and be able to stagger off. The host may or may not recall what has transpired since it became a vehicle for the parasite, other than in dreams. When reaching its full, healed willpower trait value, it is allowed a single Type C willpower based hazard check to see if it suddenly remembers everything about its experience as the servant of the parasite. Of course, a parasite could once again reclaim the subject, see page 108, roll 55-61, on Table XR-96 for how a parasite can acquire a body.

The following table offers the GM and players a random selection of body types. Roll the stats for this host and record them on a seperate document, or dedicated sheet for that character type.

## Table XR-95/ Random Host Body Table    Roll 1d100

| | |
|---|---|
| 01-15. | Pure stock human teenager*, male 1-50% chance, 51-100% female. |
| 16-24. | Pure stock man, commoner* |
| 25-32. | Pure Stock woman, commoner* |
| 33-39. | Pure stock man, raider* |
| 40-46. | Pure stock woman, prostitute* |
| 47-55. | Mutant, with one flaw, commoner* (flaw list page XR-233) |
| 56-60. | Mutant, with 1d3 minor mutations, commoner (minor mut. pg. XR-229) |
| 61-64. | Halfie, Expansion Rules, page XR-93 |
| 65-70. | Mutant, with one prime mutation and 1d3 minor mutations and 50% chance of a flaw. Mutation lists start on page XR-228. |
| 71-75. | Skullock, stats page TME-170 |
| 76,77. | Abomination, Expansion Rules, page XR-25 |
| 78. | Mutorg, with one prime mutation and 1d2 minor mutations, plus one cybernetic implant of each category: offensive, defensive and miscellaneous. Expansion Rules, page XR-99. |
| 79. | Warmort, stats page TME-173 |
| 80-82. | Cyborg with 1 each of offensive, defensive and miscellaneous implants |
| 83-86. | Rebuilt, Expansion Rules, page XR-142 |
| 87-88. | Grafter, Expansion Rules, page XR-85 |
| 89-91. | Bestial Human, set 1, Hub Rules, page XR-24 |
| 92-94. | Bestial Human, set 2, Expansion Rules, page XR-58 |
| 95,96. | Bioreplicant, Pleasure, page TME-18 |
| 97,98. | Bioreplicant, worker, page TME-18 |
| 99,00. | Moaner, stats page TME-164 |

*Typical humans listed on page 137 of the TME Hub Rules.*

Following the discovery of the parasite's starting host body, roll once for that body's condition:

## Table XR-96/ Condition of Host Body    Roll 1d100, Once

| | |
|---|---|
| 01-04. | Amputee, missing left arm: one handed weapons only. |
| 05-08. | Amputee, missing one leg: uses wooded peg leg and crutch. Movement half rate. |
| 09-13. | Blind in one eye: bad depth perception and slow to respond, thus -1 initiative, -1m movement, and -10 SV. |
| 14-18. | Brain damaged: intelligence, willpower and perception only 3d6 each. |
| 19-21. | Infested: This body has fleas, lice, and scabies which itch terribly and infests others. Costs 50+d20sp for treatment to rid body of infestation. |
| 22-25. | Covered in rash: this is a reaction to the parasite's adhesion and results in bloody sores all over the body. Reduce host's appearance to half, -10% endurance, and attracts predators specifically to this body. |
| 26-34. | Bad knee: -1m move. |
| 35-37. | Leprosy: a highly disfiguring and debilitating disease, with negative social consequences. This parasite is immune to leprosy itself, however. SOE members can download free Leprosy supplement at www.mutantepoch.com or use this link to the page in the SOE area here): https://www.outlandarts.com/members-only/TME-SOE-Misc-downloads.htm |
| 38-41. | Badly maimed: -1d10 permanently from endurance, strength, agility, accuracy and appearance. |
| 42-46. | Injured: starts off wounded down to half endurance, but can heal. |
| 47-54. | In a bad way: starving, filthy and clad in rags and sheets of old plastic. Temporarily reduce endurance by -10 to a minimum of 1 END point. If fed and washed, given decent clothing, this can be reversed in a day or two. |
| 55-61. | Limited Awareness: this parasite's host body retains a slight flicker of consciousness and once per day tries to run off, usually in the early morning, with the parasite attached. Parasite must make a type D willpower based hazard check to try to control the body, which gets its own type E willpower based hazard check using half its normal, 'locked away' trait value.<br><br>If both checks fail, the host collapses and passes out for 3d10 minutes but wakes under the control of the parasite. If the parasite wins the willpower dual, it takes control for the rest of the day, but if the host body wins, it regains full control and while it can't detach the parasite, it will run off towards its home village in a blind panic for 1d6 hours before suddenly losing control back to the parasite. |
| 62-73. | Twitchy: While the body type might not be the most desirable option, this parasite's control over it is acceptable and the functionality good enough, if not a little twitchy at times. Now and then, the body seems to gain control and make weird noises, swear, and call for its mother. At other times it shutters and looks about to see who is behind it or asks companions who the hell they are before reverting back to its dormant, almost brain dead state. These lapses usually last 1d100 rounds. |
| 74-92. | Decent: This body seems reliable, is in more-or-less full control and healthy given the circumstances surrounding its recovery. Until it gets permanently disabled — or a better option presents itself — this husk will do the trick. |
| 93-00. | Excellent specimen: This parasite counts itself lucky, even if the host body isn't ideal, and it will do for now. Not only is it in the symbiont's full control, but if the character can detach from it, the host will remain exactly where the parasite left it and seems eager to require the mastery of its little controller. |

**Table XR-98/ Parasite Size Aspect Modifier Matrix**

| Size | Endurance Modifier | Strength Modifier | DV Modifier | Concealment Hazard Check Modifier* |
|---|---|---|---|---|
| Tiny | -5 | -7 | -10 | +2 letter codes harder (A becomes C, etc.) |
| Smallish | -2 | -4 | -5 | +1 letter code harder |
| Medium | NA | NA | +0 | NA |
| Large | +4 | +6 | +0 | -1 letter code easier (C becomes B, etc.) |
| Huge | +8 | +9 | +0 | -3 letter codes easier |

*The Concealment Hazard Check Modifier is an increase or decrease in the difficulty of a hazard check on table XR-99 Parasite Concealment Table, below, whereby the adhesion mode, and any other mutations combine to give a score and determine the odds of staying hidden.

This is useful when the parasite is attached to its host body and trying to navigate an intolerant, human community and avoid being detected. It should be noted that while anti-mutant people will kill a parasite without a second thought, even in communities where regular mutants are common, a parasite is a step too far. Symbionts, in such places, are often considered to be blood sucking, predatory imps, things of evil, bad omens, and soul stealing monsters. They will often be ripped from their host and either jailed or killed as vermin. Concealment is always essential, and using this table assumes the host body is wearing appropriate clothing that is conducive to hiding its master.

**Table XR-99/ Parasite Concealment Table**

| Parasite Adhesion Mode | Viewer's Perception Based Hazard Check* |
|---|---|
| Entrail Embedded | H |
| Partially Embedded | F |
| Chest Rider | D |
| Back Rider | D |
| Side Mounted | E |
| Necker | B |

*Make a perception based hazard check per person passing by within 2 meters, searching the character, or otherwise interacting with the clothed host. If the viewer makes his or her hazard check, he or she sees some part of the parasite and is aware that the host is either infested with something, clutching a disgusting pet, or else if the viewer knows what parasites are, then sees that the host body is only a puppet of the disturbing creature attached to it.

In some communities, especially where oddities, excavators and all manner of weird and wonderful visitor is frequent, such as a digger support town like Pitford in the Crossroads Region, the discovery of a parasite isn't cause for alarm. In such digger forts parasites and other freaks are accepted as customers — although never entirely trusted or befriended by staff, sex workers, or law enforcement.

## Parasite Gender and Reproduction Capacity

Although gruesome, often despised, universally feared and typically among the ugliest things most people ever see, parasites evolved from humans. Like other types of humans, instinct compels some symbionts to reproduce, while others have little or no sex drive, nor even the apparatus to participate. Others, meanwhile, are entirely driven by their need to fornicate, but most have a libido identical to a regular human.

The following table can be used by GMs to establish the gender and sexual capabilities of a parasite should such details be appropriate to the gaming group's maturity and need for such information. Also note that some players might want to play a character of a certain gender, sexual persuasion or libido, and so can pick from the following table or establish their own details surrounding this subject — a subject that in most RPG sessions never surfaces in game play nor NPC interactions.

# Parasite Properties

## Size

This property pertains to the overall size of the symbiont's main torso and head, and may have modifiers to its endurance and strength, however, a larger parasite is harder to conceal on the host's body, even when fully clothed.

**Table XR-97/ Parasite Size Determination    Roll 2d6**

|  |  |
|---|---|
| 2,3. | **Tiny**, the head of this specimen is only as large as an apple, the body that of a squash or melon. Weight 3+1d3 kg |
| 4,5. | **Smallish**. This parasite's body is about as big as a cat's, its head that of a human baby. Weight 4+1d4kg |
| 6-9. | **Medium** sized, the symbiont's torso as big as a human baby, the head also baby sized. Weight 6+1d6kg |
| 10,11. | **Large**. This parasite's body is like that of a child of 4 or five years age, the head that of a full grown adult human. Weight 14+1d6kg |
| 12. | **Huge**: For a symbiont, this parasite has a big body the size of a teenage human, and a large head, slightly bigger than even a normal human adult's. Weight 20+3d6kg. Reduce host's movement rate by -1m per round. |

## Table XR-100/ Parasite Gender and Reproduction Capacity — Roll 2d6

| | |
|---|---|
| **2.** | Parasite is genderless and has no interest in mating. |
| **3.** | Parasite is female, yet sterile and lacks the hormones to work up the interest in any sort of copulation. If a situation arises where she becomes the caretaker of a youngster, she will be inclined to adopt the child of a comrade or even a stray orphan. |
| **4.** | Parasite is female and fertile, yet only interested in copulation one day per month during ovulation. |
| **5.** | Parasite is female, fertile, and frisky most any time. |
| **6.** | Parasite is a fertile female and if possible, will procreate with a male so long as the relationship is mutually positive and the man seems likely to stick around and help raise any young — regardless of how they look. |
| **7,8.** | Parasite is male, fertile and has strong paternal instincts, thus picky about any woman it would consider becoming involved with. It must be convinced that the female will look after the offspring, regardless of how ugly it is, and with or without the parasite male being around much. |
| **9.** | Parasite is male, fertile and eager to perform with any willing woman. If offspring are produced from any union, this male will be pleased with himself for being so virile, but may or may not take part in the raising or welfare of his progeny. |
| **10.** | Parasite is male, but sterile. He will copulate with willing mates, and has paternal instincts and may be inclined to adopt an orphan as his own child. |
| **11.** | Parasite is male, but has no interest in mating, producing young, or treating females any different than males. |
| **12.** | Parasite is both male and female, 45% chance fertile to both carry a fetus to term, or impregnate females, and 66% likely to be keen to frolic with anyone he-she finds attractive. There is a slight, and clearly disturbing 14% chance that this parasite can actually self impregnate itself and give birth to clones of itself, although such ultra-inbred offspring would be sub-standard (1d4 flaw mutations and -4d6 intelligence). |

## Locomotion While Detached from Host

How does the parasite get around while detached from its host? All symbionts have several digestive tubes and an array of neurological control tendrils, as well as a somewhat slug-like body, and can at least scuttle and shimmy around at **a base movement rate of 1 meter per round**. Some have additional locomotive abilities, with any agility based move modifiers applied, thus making the character faster or slower with a minimum move rate of at least 0.25m per round.

Keep in mind that for either an entrail embedded parasite or partially embedded variant, leaving one's host might cause the death of that body, while those hosts ridden by other adhesion styles might regain willful consciousness

and wander off if separated from their parasite controller for too long, or possibly die of cardiac failure, too. If the player is unsure of the details of this parasite character's connection to its fleshy vehicle, see 'Adhesion' on page XR-107.

Roll 2d6 on the following table to see what, if any, extra movement abilities this parasite has:

## Table XR-101/ Parasite Detached Locomotion — Roll 2d6

| | |
|---|---|
| **2.** | Bug legs, although made of regular humanoid flesh and bone, these multi jointed, insect like legs grow from the sides of the parasite and neatly folded away when not in use. There will be 1d2+1 of these limbs per side of the parasite, each adding +0.5m movement to the character. Besides adding to the ground movement rate of the character, these limbs, in conjunction with the other tendrils and tubes of the parasite, allow it to climb well, adding +2 climbing skill points. |
| **3.** | Short tentacles grow to about 20cm in length and number 1d2+2 per side of the parasite's body. These rubbery appendages are useful in helping the symbiont hold on to a host's body, although their main purpose is to allow the character to creep along the ground at +3m total movement, or propel it through the water, also at +3 meters per round. |
| **4.** | Stubby legs, which resemble those of a regular baby human, grow from the hips of this parasite allowing it to walk upright on these wobbly limbs at +2m per round. |
| **5-9.** | No special movement ability. Moves 1 meter per round. |
| **10.** | Snake-like lower body. This parasite can wriggle across the ground like a revolting, fleshy snake at a movement increase of +3 meters per round. |
| **11.** | A pair of fleshy, seal-like flukes grow from the parasite's sides. If desired, these appendages can allow the character to swim at 6m per round, or, permit it to pull itself along the ground at +1m per round (now 2m per round) These growths add 2d4 kilograms to the PC's weight, but also make it more robust and increase its endurance by +1d6+2 points. |
| **12.** | Fleshy, bat-like wings. These tiny wings can be unfolded and allow the parasite to flap about awkwardly at a rate of 9 meters per round for up to a maximum flight duration as the parasite's strength score in minutes (20 rounds in a minute). After reaching the duration, the parasite becomes exhausted and will either need to descend to the ground and rest, or, glide, traveling 4m horizontally yet dropping 1m in altitude per round.<br><br>Should the parasite really need to push itself, it can fly beyond its strength, but taking 1 endurance point damage per minute. If reaching zero or less endurance from this dangerous exertion, the parasite will slip into unconsciousness and drop out of the air. This exertion based damage is treated as normal damage. |

## Extra Appendages

As mentioned in the introduction to parasite characters, these symbionts have 2d6+1 neurological tendrils and 1d6+1 digestive and waste removal tubes, which have little in-game application. The following specialized extra appendages, however, are useful for grasping items or offensive actions, while many can also assist the parasite in locomotion when it is detached from its host body. A follow-up table, XR-103, is used to randomly determine the body location of each extra appendage.

Roll 3d6, 1d4+1 times to determine what the character has in the way of extra appendages, but down pick or re-roll duplicated results with an asterisk beside their die number:

## Table XR-102/ Parasite Appendages Table — Roll 3d6, 1d4+1 times

**3.* Electrical generation limb:** A complex, bulbous orb is attached to an arm like limb. Twice per day per rank this parasite can emit a high voltage bolt of electricity from this appendage, range as user's willpower in meters, SV 01-70, damage 3d6+6. When not frying opponents, this bone-hard generator can be used like a mace, doing 1d8 damage on a successful strike. Skill and agility modifiers can be applied to this appendage, as too with any strength bonus to damage when used to bludgeon foes.

**4.* Gender specific body part.** Male parasites have a random penis growing from a random body location, while females have a vagina 60% of the time, otherwise a lone breast, also growing from a weird location on the parasite's body. Genderless parasites re-roll on this table.

**5. Small pincer.** This bone pincer grows on the end of a frail human-like arm. It can make a melee attack doing 1d10 damage, or help the parasite crawl at +0.5m movement per round.

**6.* Chicken's foot.** While it appears disturbing, this chicken leg and clawed foot can be useful by adding a melee attack; doing 1d3 damage plus any strength and skill modifiers, plus adding +1 meter movement to the parasite.

**7.* Stinger tendril.** While ineffectual as far as locomotion goes, this 30+1d20cm long tentacle is tipped with a retractable black stinger. If threatened, the parasite can stab at opponents at +10 SV doing 1d3 damage plus injecting a random venom into the struck target. The character produces enough venom for 6 injections per 24 hours. Roll 2d6 for venom type here:
2,3. Type C death/ 4,5. Type B death/ 6,7. Type C Paralysis/ 8,9 Type C Sleep/ 10. Type C Insanity/ 11. Type D Paralysis/ 12. Type F Paralysis.

**8. Manipulation tendril.** Normally coiled inside the parasite's body, this finger-thick, tentacle-like tube of flesh can extend out 3 meters in length and explore objects, pick up things that weigh no more than a kilogram, or wield a dagger or knife in combat. If not used for any other purpose, this tendril will help propel the parasite along the ground or through the water at +1m movement per round. It can smack opponents at +2 SV inflicting 1d4 stun damage.

**9. Bone hook.** A meter long tendril ends in a curved bone hook. Besides helping the parasite move when detached from a host body (+0.5m move), this hook serves as an extra melee attack and can gouge and eviscerate opponents doing 1d8 damage at +5 SV to hit. When climbing, add a skill point when this appendage is not being used in combat.

**10. Human hand*.** This child sized human hand can be used to hold a handgun, or blade, although, if attached to a wrist only, it is too short and can't extend to punch or thrust with a blade. There is a 6 in 10 chance this hand is attached to a meter long tendril, otherwise a wrist.

**11. Small human arm and hand**, able to employ a relic handgun or other one handed device. Also, permits the parasite a punch attack if desired. If not being used to hold an item, this limb can assist the parasite to move +1m per round, while a punch by this limb does only 1d4 damage, plus any strength or skill modifiers.

**12. Tentacle.** This octopus tentacle can reach out a meter and either hold a one handed cut and thrust weapon, or slap opponents doing 1d8 stun damage plus any strength or skill based modifiers. Treat this growth as an extra melee attack per round. If not holding anything or being used to grapple or cuff opponents, this tentacle can assist the parasite in movement by adding +1 meter per round either swimming or crawling. If climbing, this tentacle adds +1 skill point in that talent.**

**13. Bone saw.** Protruding from the tip of a meter long tendril, this parasite exhibits a flat, leaf shaped serrated bone blade of about 10cm length. It can be used to add +0.5m detached movement to the parasite when not engaged in combat, but is mainly used to cut wood, or saw through the tissues of opponents doing 1d8+1 damage and being +5 SV to hit. This blade can cut through logs and branches at a rate of 5cm per round. It is not strong enough to cut through metal. Treat as an extra melee attack per round.

**14.* Shooting spikes.** Growing from this parasite's outward facing aspect are up to 12 serrated bone spikes of 8 to 12cm in length. Through muscle contraction the symbiont can expel one per round with range equal to the parasite's strength score in meters. The strike value of each spike is +6 and inflicts 1d8 damage, plus or minus any strength modifiers. Parasites with this appendage start game play with 1d6+6, with one new spike growing back per 4 days to a maximum of 12 ready to shoot. If this appendage occurs twice, then the player can decide to either re-roll, or double the number of shooting spikes available to the character.

**15.* Bone saber.** Growing from a meter long tendril is a 30cm long, slightly curved, exceedingly sharp bone sword. This blade can assist the parasite in pulling itself along, adding + 0.5m movement, but is primarily designed for hacking and stabbing enemies. It is +10 SV and inflicts 1d10 damage on a hit, plus or minus any strength or skill based modifiers.

**16.* Pig's foot and short leg.** Virtually useless for anything other than helping it move, this unsightly limb can be severed and the stump cauterized if the parasite desires. Movement +1 meter per round when detached from host.

**17.* Eye tendril.** A lone eyeball, complete with lashes and lid, grows at the end of a 4 meter long, 5cm diameter fleshy tendril. The parasite can deploy this tube to peer up over tall vegetation, walls, or the surface of water, around corners or into open windows, allowing the character to see normally with little risk of being spotted. This eye has 6 stealth skill points. If spotted and attacked, the eye can retract at 2m per round, but, is DV -18 and can only take 9 endurance damage before being severed. A new eye will grow back to replace a lost one after 3 months.

**18.* A tentacle,** as roll 12 on this table, plus one more random appendage.
**Re-roll or down pick duplicated results with an asterisk.*
***There is a 1 in 6 chance that the tentacle ends in a set of jaws. A bite at +6 SV does 2d6 base damage.*

| Table XR-103/ Body Location for Parasite Extra Appendages & Mutations | Roll 2d6 |
|---|---|
| 2. | Crotch |
| 3. | Chest |
| 4. | Stomach |
| 5,6. | Lower back |
| 7,8. | Right side |
| 9,10. | Left side |
| 11. | Upper back |
| 12. | Forehead |

| Table XR-104/ Parasite Hair Style* | Roll 2d6 |
|---|---|
| 2. | No hair, fleshy lumps instead. |
| 3. | Tube-like strings |
| 4. | Shoudler length |
| 5,6. | Stubble |
| 7,8. | Bald |
| 9. | Short, crew cut |
| 10. | Short, curly |
| 11. | Long, wavy |
| 12. | Long, straight |

**For color of hair, use the mutant hair color list on page TME-23 of the Hub Rules book, or player choice.*

## Color

Parasite appearance is mainly a matter of color, but, a lack thereof, or other disturbing details can also define the being.

### Table XR-105/ Parasite Coloration  Roll 4d6

4. Translucent pink, All innards, muscles, and veins are visible

5. Black like soot and glossy as if wet

6. Meat red, with pale pink veins and web-like tendons

7. White with raised blue and purple veins

8. Grayish, dead flesh pigment

9. Pale pink with raised, purple and red veins

10. Purplish-red, similar to a bruise or old wound

11. Orange-red with raised yellow veins

12. Well tanned regular human skin

13. Dark brown, normal human skin

14. Pale Caucasian, regular human skin

15. Dark brown, but spotted with pale patches like a leopard

16. Green on back, pink underside and entirely covered in a fine coating of snakelike scales, add -5 DV bonus.

17. Gray blue most of the time, but erupts into a bright purple when angry

18. Striped pink and red, similar to a zebra in pattern.

19. Dark gray, mottled with sandy dots. Excellent rubble camouflage and +2 stealth if detached and moving about in rocky or typical ruin terrain.

20. Leafy foliage greens and browns. Natural woodland, swamp or scrub area camo. If moving about apart from its host, this parasite, is +3 stealth skill points in 'conceal self' or 'concealed movement' when in such vegetation. The stealth skill is described on page 51 of the hub rules.

21. Flat black

22. Snow White with red eyes and tusk-yellow teeth, claws or bone protrusions.

23. Desert camo pattern, allowing the parasite, when detached, to gain +2 stealth in arid, old war zone or badland areas.

24. Entirely clear, including blood, bones and body fluids. If dropped in water, this parasite is almost invisible. Glossy and glass-like, as if made of ice.

## Parasite Mutations Reminder

Besides all the sickly appendages and features noted on the previous pages, a symbiont also features 1d4 random mutations from the Parasite Mutation list, XR-203 on page 234, as well as 1d2 minor and a 2 in 10 chance of a flaw mutation.

## Parasite Body Control

A parasite has total control of its host body, so much so that the symbiont can see hear, feel, and taste what the larger body does — or shut off such sensory inputs if they are distasteful, too painful, or too distracting.

Once connected, a parasite can deploy the host body remarkably well, even to a degree that often gives no hint to others that the occupied and dominated fleshy vehicle is anything other than who they appear. Although the copious robes, hoods, bulging outfits and other strange attire of the parasite-host team might attract attention, especially on a hot day when other folks strip down.

In combat, the parasite 'steers' the host body to best protect the symbiont, whether the tiny master or mistress is on its side, chest, or back. Likewise, unless completely absorbed within the host or hidden within the subject's armor plated torso, the parasite can wear special custom made parasite armor, called a vest, or buckle itself into an armored saddle or 'cockpit' that is bolted to the host's own clothing and armor. From within the cockpit, the parasite can peer out through narrow eye holes or observation slits, as well as make use of ports from which to extend tendrils, tiny hands, or other appendages as needed. Often, within such cockpits, the parasite might have tiny video displays hooked to external cameras, strapped down communicators, a tablet or laptop, and other small, highly customized bits of high-tech gear.

Attacks on a parasite-host duo are assumed to be made upon the much larger host body. The exception to this is if enemies know the parasite is present and may target the gruesome humanoid specifically. Treat attacks on the adhered parasite as a called shot using the "shoot or a stab to the brain" option from page 109 of the hub rules. This can only be done when the attacker faces the parasite, as in a frontal attack if the parasite is adhered to the chest or abdomen of the host. Alternatively, if the enemies make a rear assault on a back adherred parasite and its host, then they can directly attack the symbiont, too. In short, a parasite can only be directly targeted if it's not blocked by the host.

Attacks which devastate parasites the most are area of affect assaults, such as grenade blasts or the use of the mutations of agony sphere, asphyxiation zone, gaseous discharge, peeling radius, sonic wave radius, and agony sphere. Likewise, because a parasite is so moistly connected to its host, any successful electrical attack on the host also afflicts the symbiont who will take 10% of the damage of such attacks, including nonlethal damage from stun weapon strikes taken by the larger body. In the opposite direction, however, when the parasite uses such powers while adhered with its host body, any area affects mutation such as agony sphere, electrical charge, peeling radius, and sonic wave radius

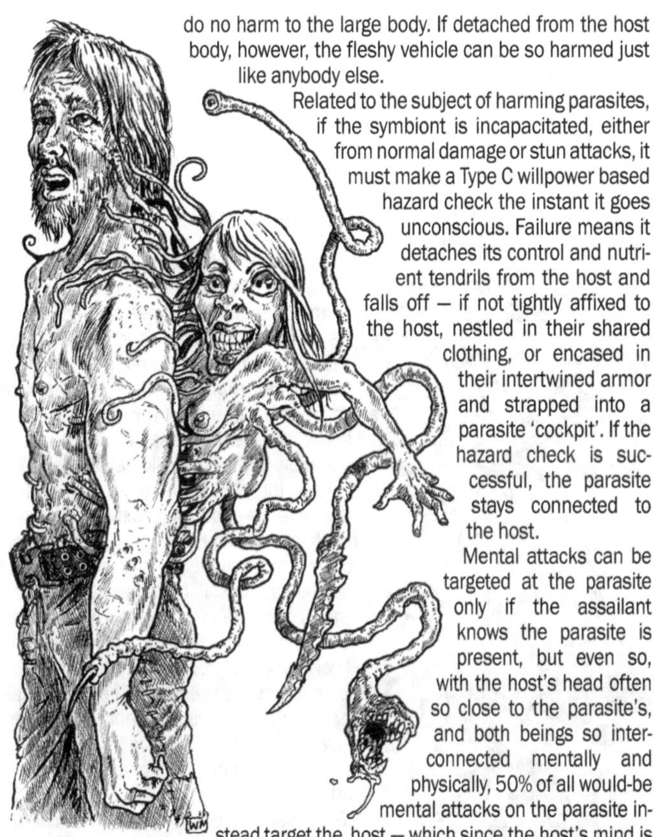

do no harm to the large body. If detached from the host body, however, the fleshy vehicle can be so harmed just like anybody else.

Related to the subject of harming parasites, if the symbiont is incapacitated, either from normal damage or stun attacks, it must make a Type C willpower based hazard check the instant it goes unconscious. Failure means it detaches its control and nutrient tendrils from the host and falls off — if not tightly affixed to the host, nestled in their shared clothing, or encased in their intertwined armor and strapped into a parasite 'cockpit'. If the hazard check is successful, the parasite stays connected to the host.

Mental attacks can be targeted at the parasite only if the assailant knows the parasite is present, but even so, with the host's head often so close to the parasite's, and both beings so interconnected mentally and physically, 50% of all would-be mental attacks on the parasite instead target the host — which since the host's mind is often already so weakened, is a very effective way to incapacitate the host's body and get at the vulnerable parasite.

## Parasite Clothing and Armor

Parasites can have armor made just for them, either vest style torso plating for when moving about while detached from the host body, or as a well plated 'cockpit' that encases them while they're adhered to the body of a host. They often disguise such cockpit armor as a backpack or front pouch, host's potbelly, or loose clothing with eye-holes for the parasite to look out upon the world as desired. Most times, new characters of this type lack armor of their own and either adhere themselves beneath any protection their host body wears, or go without. Determine what a new parasite character is wearing at the beginning of game play, roll 1d100:

## Parasite Apparel Listing  Roll 1d100

**01-34.** Naked

**35-38.** Shredded plastic shopping bag

**39-42.** Black plastic garbage bag with holes for limbs

**43-45.** Relic knapsack, **roll 1d10** for color: **1.** hot pink / **2.** camo / **3.** black / **4.** blue / **5.** red / **6.** purple / **7.** neon green / **8,9.** multi colored with cartoon super hero theme / **10.** gray.

**46-48.** Diaper

**49-52.** Toddler T-shirt and diaper

**53-57.** Tattered relic underwear or lingerie

**58-60.** Sky blue or soft pink baby blanket

**61-66.** Toddler overalls and 4 in 10 chance of a multi-colored striped shirt

**67-94.** Clad in either parasite vest armor, or a 'cockpit' mounted to the host. Roll 1d20 on table XR-106.

**95-00.** Clad in an armored parasite vest (roll 1d12 on the following table, plus the host is equipped with an armored 'cockpit', roll 1d10+10 on the following Parasite Armor table, below.

The following parasite armors are available for purchase in most large towns and digger forts with the size of the symbiont changing the price of the armor, but a PC parasite could have armor if directed here from the Apparel Listng. To better ensure confidentiality with the purchase, and ensure the armorer keeps the buyer's identity secret, double the purchase cost. The 'Days' column for each armor type is how many days it will take before ordered armor is ready for pickup after a 50% deposit.

### Table XR-106/Parasite Armor Roll 1d20 at PC Generation

| 1d20 | Parasite Armor | Move Mod ** | DV | Tiny | Medium | Large | Huge | Days |
|---|---|---|---|---|---|---|---|---|
| 1-4. | Leather Vest | -0.25m | -10 DV | 35sp | 5sp | 8sp | 12sp | 1d4 |
| 5-7. | Junk Armor Vest | -0.5m | -12 DV | 5sp | 7sp | 11sp | 16sp | 1d6 |
| 8-10. | Metal clad Test | -1m | -15 DV | 24sp | 30sp | 35sp | 43sp | 2d4 |
| 11,12. | Scrap Relic Vest | -0.5m | -20 DV | 43sp | 55sp | 62sp | 74sp | 2d6 |
| 13-15. | Leather Cockpit | NA | -12 DV | 6sp | 8sp | 13sp | 19sp | 1d6 |
| 16,17. | Junk Armor Cockpit | NA | -14 DV | 14sp | 19sp | 25sp | 36sp | 2d4 |
| 18,19. | Metal Clad Cockpit | NA | -18 DV | 29sp | 37sp | 44sp | 58sp | 2d6 |
| 20. | Scrap Relic Cockpit | NA | -24 DV | 51sp | 65sp | 73sp | 112sp | 3d6 |

*Vests can be worn both while detached from the host or while adhered, and combined with cockpit armor.

**Modifier to parasite's movement rate while detached only. Host is not affected by the weight of parasite armor which adds no more than 2kg weight at the most.

## When Parasites Attack

Besides controlling whatever weaponry, appendages, implants and offensive gifts of their host body, a parasite can also join in during a fight if it so chooses. If unleashing mental attack modes or energy based mutations of its own, however, it must focus on these powers and cease any attacks its host body is performing, although the host can still walk or run as directed. Only physical attack modes of the parasite can be used simultaneously with those of the host body, however er revealing such appendages will give away the symbiont's presence unless deployed mutations could plausibly be attributed to the host.

## Parasite Outfitting

Unless clad in their own specialized vest armor, symbionts tend to remain naked while attached to their host body for better interaction, cohesion, warmth, and skin-on-skin bonding, but can be fitted with toddler size clothing if detached or in exposed to cold conditions. They make no outfitting rolls, besides armor, however their host body will be equipped according to the modest (MO) outfitting code. See page XR-350.

# Plantoids
*Mutant Plant Characters*

These remarkable, unlikely beings appear as either intelligent, mobile plants with ten to twenty percent human DNA, or else, occur as symbiotic, almost parasite-like growth woven through a dead, or sometimes brain-dead, human cadaver. They start game play with several plant mutations, a pre-game caste, and equipment, weaponry and sometimes customized armor.

Many of these veggie beings wear clothing and masks to allow them to pass in human society when accompanying other 'normal' excavators. Interestingly, while meat based individuals, like humans, must watch for carnivores, plantoids must be careful to avoid starving humans or herbivores, such as common livestock, especially goats*.

In one way or another, all plantoid characters have some human aspect, either as those inhabiting a human cadaver or the more typical plant-human hybrids, and so crave the company of humans, even mutant or cybernetically altered ones. They will strive to earn their place among a village, faction or small excavation team wherein they can find protection, camaraderie, and adventure. Because they are living things, like humans, they yearn for many of the same things in life, and besides companionship and acceptance, they require nourishment, hydration, sunshine and a safe place to rest at night.

Plantoids are primarily vegetable based with either synthetic human or true human DNA within them to facilitate mobility, reasoning, sensory inputs, limited speech, relatable human-like emotional responses, and creator inspired motivations. Most are derived from a distant engineered strain, but many have cross pollinated with other varieties, undergone mutation, and evolved through natural selection.

There are two main varieties; a mutant plant that has taken over a living human host or corpse — somewhat like a green walker — and uses the cadaver's musculature, skeletal structure, and sensory organs as its own. The other, much more common type of plantoid is a being with human DNA blended with a tree, shrub, mushroom, grass, or vine cluster. Blended plantoids can either appear as having an identifiable plant heritage, or else an unidentifiable plant parentage.

Because these beings are so often shrouded in leaves, branches, stems and other foliage, they often look like some sort of mutant human wearing splendid woodland camouflage, or a Gillie suit. Given this, and if they aren't wearing flashy clothing, draped in gear, weapons and relics, nor in full bloom or heavy with ripe, brilliantly hued fruit, they can often hide among other vegetation with ease.

Of course, if this character is the only tuft of vegetation in a barren, gray rubble strewn street, it will stand out far more than appropriately attired and dust coated human comrades. So too, if a palm tree plantoid, for example, tries to hide among a prairie of bunch grass, the same outcome will follow, and the veggie-sapien will attract attention from a half kilometer away. Only when the plantoid is relatively similar in appearance and foliage to the surrounding plants can it gain the 'conceal self' or 'concealed movement' +2 skill points bonus on the stealth skill table (pg. TME-51) and this is only when the plantoid drops prone, crouches down and keeps any gear or tools it carries on the ground or hidden among its roots, branches or leaves. The game master will take these circumstances, and plant similarity, into mind when rolling the hazard check to determine if this plantoid has been spotted or not.

Download and print out a plantoid character sheet at https://www.outlandarts.com/expansionrules.htm or copy it from page 522 of this book.

## Plantoid Sensory Capabilities

All plantoids can interact with strangers and companions, and respond to the GM or written adventure as human characters do. Therefore, all player character plantoids have rudimentary abilities to speak, see, hear, touch and smell so that they can take in descriptions and stimuli and thus respond as others in the party do. Without this measure, the game master would have a tough time describing what the veggie-sapien senses, and potentially slowing game play.

In short, plantoid characters have plenty of human DNA which allows them to experience the twisted new world to the fullest.

Plantoids do not breathe air directly, but rather take life giving oxygen from the atmosphere through their bark and leaves, and while, they won't drown as a human might when submerged underwater, they cannot survive in water indefinitely if their base species was not designed for it — thus kelp and water lilies survive in water permanently and will not die after 3d6 hours of being fully submerged like all other variants.

These veggie-sapiens are not immune to acid, and will suffer from the dissolving damage the same as a human, however, poison gas, dust, irrita-

*Goat stats for domesticated kid, doe, buck goats, as well as mountain goats and Lucifer goats found in book OLA1007, Mutant Bestiary One, page 51.

tion particles and the like have no serious effect on them, while some specimens that are based on desert plants, such as cacti and sagebrush, can also endure sand and junk storms far better than other plantoids and suffer only 10% of the damage from these common perils. Similarly, how well a plantoid copes with cold or hot weather comes down to their linage, when known.Unless stated otherwise, a plantoid will handle these extremes the same as a human, but like a human, can also wear appropriate clothing or seek shade and shelter to endure such challenges.

Because they are rich with human DNA, which animates them and gives them their sense of self actualization and 'life', plantoids have a rudimentary brain in their core — usually behind whatever cluster of sensory organs they exhibit. This brain is just as susceptible to mental attacks, controls, illusions and other conditions as a human's brain, including called shots, unconsciousness, insanity, and more.

While their minds might be like humans, their respiratory and circulatory systems are not, and except for what perils might happen to a still living host body for those plant characters who occupy a cadaver or brain dead subject, all plantoids are immune to poison and venom. Fire, however, is a different story, and unless stated in their base plant description as with palm trees, all plantoids are susceptible to flame damage and will always burn for twice as long unless the inferno is put out with water, rolling in sand, or otherwise being smothered; all actions that allow it to be momentarily distracted and be +30 SV easier to be hit.

Plantoids have only a rudimentary appearance score — mostly used for reaction rolls when meeting strangers — although a cadaver laced plantoid's host body might have its own appearance trait which will fade rapidly if the body is truly dead and become little more than a zombie-like rotting, husk.

Most plantoids take nourishment from soil feeding roots and photosynthesis, although some feature carnivorous, vampiric, or carrion feeding mutations, which expands the being's sustenance gathering options.

**All plantoids have two to three manipulator limbs,** with which to interact with the world around it, with these appendage treated as the thing's hands as far as using weapons and tools, although multiple other appendages can occur, too, during mutation generation which might offer multiple, additional attacks per round. **These starting 1d2+1 manipulator arms are 2 meters long,** use the plantoid's strength score, and is like a human's arm and has a base strike value is +0 and inflicts 1d6 damage before any accuracy or strength modifiers are applied. If through the hazards of game play this arm is chopped off, it will re-grow one meter after 4 months, and to its full length after 8 months. If needed, the GM can consider the arm appendage to have the same base defense value as the plantoid without armor, and 10% of the plantoid's endurance. Because plantoids also exhibit and learn skills, this arm, plus any others it might have during mutation determination, is usable with the brawling or martial arts skill. Skills are determined based on the plantoid's pre game caste, discovered on page XR-140.

Plantoids float if immersed in water, although those derived from kelp are masters underwater, too, and can swim down to several hundred meters if so desired. Because they naturally float, all other plantoids can only swim below the surface at a rate of 1m per round, and doing even this is very difficult for them unless they are holding blocks of concrete or rock to help them go deep. Plantoids cannot survive in the void of space, and if ejected out an airlock will suffer a quick death just the same as an unprotected human... although the wearing of a space suit is theoretically possible if one could be found which fit the often considerable bulk of these characters.

Vegie-sapiens start off as roughly human sized beings, although depending on their base species this can vary widely, and come in all shapes and sizes. Non-cadaver based, unspecified plantoids (UPLs) will grow 25cm in height and gain 5kg weight per summer growing season, while those with identifiable base plants will have their own growth rates noted on table XR-112 on page 120. Cadaver based plantoids do not grow or gain weight unless switching host bodies. While all plantoids can live for many decades, a few have remarkable life spans if their botanical heritage is favorable, as with certain treeoids. The base plant table, on page 120, has a column showing the trait modifiers, any defense value modifiers, starting height, weight and lifespan, plus their rate of growth per year and maximum height.

Plantoids have a pre-game caste just like any other character, although use their own table for establishing this at the end of the plantoid section on table XR-116, page 140. All veggie-sapiens will have at least one plant mutation, and the potential for a plantoid flaw deviation, too. Plant mutations are listed on page XR-223, while plantoid flaw mutations on page 234 of this book.

# Plantoid Type

### Table XR-107/ Plantoid Type Determination

| 1d100 | Plantoid Type | Plantoid Mutations (page 295) | Plantoid Flaw Mutation (page 324) | Description Page |
|---|---|---|---|---|
| 01-18. | Host Inhabiting Plantoid (HIP) | 1d4 | 7% chance of 1 | page 115 |
| 19-72. | Identifiable Base plantoid (IBP) | 1d4+1 | 11% chance of 1 | page 119 |
| 73-97. | Unspecified Plant Lineage (UPL) | 1d4+2 | 13% chance of 1d2 | page 139 |
| 98-00. | Cybernetic Plantoid Variant (CPV) | 1d2 | 3% chance of 1 | page 139 |

# Host Inhabiting Plantoids [HIP]

These specialized plantoids go by many names, but are referred to as HIPs for short. They are basically a fist sized root ball from which dozens of artery-like manipulator limbs and hundreds of thin, white boring tendrils protrude. Countless variant species exist, with each evolving independently and after a few years, become their own subspecies, complete with mutations. A Host Inhabiting Plantoid will start game play with one cadaver, which it is merged with and controls like a body, as well as 1 to 4 (1d4) mutations from the plantoid mutation list on page XR-233.

A HIP is always on the look-out for a better humanoid host body, including those of bestial humans. They cannot, however, adapt to the bodies of non-humanoids that aren't embedded with human DNA, such as dogs, horses, spiders and such, as they seem to have been engineered, or evolved, to merge with humans and their offshoots exclusively. While most of their actions use the traits of whatever host body they occupy — unless the HIP has one or more mutational limbs that it can extend from the corpse's torso — a HIP uses its own perception trait as far as observation and initiative go.

While their minds are quite alien to that of a human or even other plantoids, they are still susceptible to mental attacks, and yet can possibly exhibit mental mutations, although occurrences of these are exceedingly rare.

| Host Inhabiting Plantoid (HIP) Root Ball Stats | |
| --- | --- |
| Endurance | 3d6+10 |
| Strength | 3d6 |
| Agility | Random* |
| Accuracy | Random* |
| Intelligence | Random* |
| Perception | Random* |
| Willpower | Random* |
| Appearance | 1d2** |

*Random means this being generates a random trait value the same as a normal character on table XR-2 on page 8.*

**A HIP is a hideous thing to behold, and any humanoid to look upon it for the first time must make a Willpower based type D hazard check or become revolted and 66% likely to vomit. A cadaver based host body might, however, retain better looks if not too far decayed, dressed up nice, or merely a brain dead specimen.*

When creating a host inhabiting plantoid (HIP) character, keep the plantoid's traits recorded separately as these will be combined with any new cadaver the PC might later merge with. Likewise, when the plantoid goes up in rank, apply any trait increase bonuses to the HIP only.

In short, a host cadaver body does not normally improve, nor heal unless the thing is still alive and brain dead. Any mutations a HIP exhibits remain with it when it sheds a previous cadaver-vehicle, and while inserted deep into a body, these mutations often stick out of the cadaver along with the HIP's sensory organ cluster or face. This cluster features rudimentary eyes, a mouth-orifice, nostrils, and hearing appendages — although these sensory organs are often well hidden from onlookers, usually in the folds of fabric at the cadaver's neck or armpit. A HIP can talk, although poorly, and has the senses of a regular human.

## Cadaver Acquisition, Body Type, and Conditions

A single roll on the three tables below will quickly establish how this plantoid gained its host cadaver and what aspects of interest are revealed about this fleshy vehicle. Roll on all three tables before rolling or filling in any details, especially potential implants or mutations as circumstances might change during this creation process.

A host inhabiting plantoid without a cadaver is little more than a root ball and mass of vines, leaves and pale flesh boring tendrils. Their base weight, before any potentially substantial physical mutations, is 10+1d10 kilograms, and they are only 10+1d20 centimeters tall.

The HIP root ball is extremely vulnerable and can move only 1 meter per round unless some mutation allows otherwise, although it will float like a patch of seaweed if thrown into water and can endure cold down to -20c (-4 F) for 24+1d12 hours before going dormant and unable to wake for 3d6 days. They are mushy, greasy things that suffer 1d4 END damage per hour if left exposed in hot, arid conditions such as a desert or badland vicinity. If attacked without being inside a cadaver host, a planetoid of this sort is +20 base DV (and so very easy to hit). HIPs have the following starting traits, all of which can increase when the character goes up in rank:

| Table XR-108/ Host Inhabiting Plantoid Cadaver Acquisition  Roll 2d6 | |
| --- | --- |
| 2. | Cadaver volunteered to become one with the plantoid out of either a suicide attempt, religious rite, or thinking the plantoid would make good camouflage and did not realize who would wear who. |
| 3. | Cadaver was discovered in tall trees, where something had dragged or dropped it. |
| 4. | Planetoid found a cadaver in the meat larder of a giant predator, and stole it. |
| 5. | Cadaver washed up on the shores after drowning. |
| 6. | Cadaver cut down from the gallows after a hanging. |
| 7. | Cadaver found on a battlefield. |
| 8. | Cadaver was buried in the forest, and plantoid's roots dug down to claim it. |
| 9. | Cadaver was found at the side of a road after raiders defeated it. |
| 10. | Cadaver found in a mass grave after an illness swept through a community. |
| 11. | Cadaver found at the bottom of a deep pit. |
| 12. | Cadaver was not dead when found, but paralyzed by venom, now most likely deceased. |

## Host Body Type Determination

What sort of corpse does the plantoid enshroud or inhabit? The game master may need to tailor this list to his or her own campaign setting to reflect the best mix of humanoids in the region.

Basically, the cadaver that the host inhabiting plant character merges with denotes the being's stats as a framework for the outer character. When attacked, it is the cadaver that takes any damage, not the HIP hidden within it — at least not until the cadaver is killed and reveals the gruesome puppet master within, who can be attacked at +20 SV.

Mental attacks, however, do afflict the HIP within the cadaver just the same as any other living character. Assorted plantoid mutations that this HIP exhibits (they start with 1d4 plantoid mutations and a 7% chance of a plant flaw mutation) might change the trait values of whatever host body this character occupies. For host bodies that have mutations or cybernetic implants, the host-melded plant can access and deploy these while it inhabits that corpse-frame.

When documenting a host body, roll any stats as needed based on the host cadaver's condition (table XR-109, below), but do not roll up a pre-game caste for a starting HIP's body. Do, however, roll up their outfitting as if the body was equipped with the modest (MO) outfitting code, using tables starting on page 350 of this book.

## Host Cadaver Condition

At the time of character creation, the host cadaver may have seen better days and the plantoid might need to keep an optical node out for an upgrade.

### Table XR-109/ Host Cadaver Condition    Roll 2d6

**2.** This corpse is little more than a yellowed skeleton. It is held together by shredded fabric, junk wires, gristle, tape, gum and the vines and tendrils of the plantoid itself. While not attracting scavengers, it is a ghastly sight and few companions can stand to associate with this thing until it finds a new corpse.

Besides being nightmarish, this corpse offers little to the entity, has no mutations and any cybernetic parts will have long since fallen off. Worse, the remains move only 3m per round and all the cadaver's traits are reduced to half, except for appearance which is App 1, INT 0, WIL 0.

Each day there is a 6% chance that the skeleton collapses and the plantoid is reduced to a ball of roots in the dirt. To survive, it will most likely require the assistance of comrades, and need to ride along in a backpack or bucket until a replacement cadaver can be acquired.

**3.** While not quite a skeleton, this plantoid's cadaver is held together with knotted vines, shreds of clothing, dried, flaking sinews, intestines, string and barbed wire. The frame creaks and flakes when moving, attracts flies and stinks of carrion, which repels humans but appeals to scavengers who can smell the body from kilometers away. This frame slows the cadaver by -2m movement and all traits are reduced by -6, except for its appearance trait that is APP 2d4 and has 0 intelligence and 0 willpower.

**4.** The corpse has its head crushed or shot clear through, grievous wounds in its torso, missing fingers, and other lost parts. To any humanoid onlooker, it will look like a person who's been dead for a few weeks, and smell that way, too. While inhabiting this rag tag, shedding and peeling frame, the HIP will be hard pressed to be allowed into villages, barter forts or saloons, and likely be seen and treated as a zombie from some ancient film.

There is no saving these remains and an upgrade body will be required after 6d6 weeks when this thing become skeleton as in roll 2, above. Its appearance trait is 1d3 and has 0 intelligence and 0 willpower.

**5.** This cadaver's leg is broken and drags along behind the plantoid. In fact, the body is a mess, which smells and looks like it has been in a grave for a month. Besides reducing the plantoid's walking movement by -2 meters, the corpse is only good for another 4d6+6 weeks before it turns into a skeleton as in roll 2, above. Its appearance trait is 1d6 and has 0 intelligence and 0 willpower.

**6.** Quite dead and slowly breaking down. The flesh of this cadaver is gray and flaking. Its hair falls out in chunks and it smells like a corpse when in temperatures above 20c or 70F. A new corpse will be required within 3d6 months or the plantoid will ride in a skeleton as in roll 2, above. Its appearance trait is 1d3 and has 0 intelligence and 0 willpower.

**7.** Dead both physically and mentally. However, while pale and bloodless, the plantoid is thoroughly laced into the dead person and provides it with nutrients, oxygen and other materials. This cadaver thus decays at such a slow rate that only reeks when in hot humid conditions. Its flesh is cold to the touch, yet subtle and allow the HIP and host body to pass as some sort of mutant. Its appearance trait is 2d6 and has 0 intelligence and 2d6 willpower.

**8.** Dead, but the cadaver's respiratory and circulatory systems are functioning because of the plantoid's advanced nutrient and neurological inputs. The cadaver is not rotting, and other than its blank white eyes and the moaning when the root ball is active or forced to talk, it can often be mistaken for a living person. Its appearance trait is 50% of what it normally would be and has 0 intelligence and 3d6 willpower.

**9.** The cadaver is physically dead, nasty looking and creaky, yet the plantoid has gained access to the corpse's brain and absorbed its memories and a temporary increase in intelligence of +3d6 (this bonus is lost if the cadaver and HIP are separated). So long as this plantoid inhabits the corpse, the remains will not deteriorate on their own, although any damage to the cadaver will not heal. Its appearance trait is 3d6 and has +3d6 intelligence (mentioned above) and 3d6 willpower.

**10.** The dead body is badly damaged and missing one arm and punctured here and there. The holes in it have become home to rodents and insects which while annoying to those nearby, don't seem to bother this HIP all that much. The vermin are eating the corpse, however, and a new cadaver must be found within 2d6 months before it turns into a skeleton as in roll 2, above. Its appearance trait is 2d4 and has 0 intelligence and 0 willpower.

**11.** This cadaver had some brain activity occurring when the plantoid took command of it. Given this neurological activity, this plantoid can access the host corpse's senses such as hearing, olfactory, taste, touch and vision to a higher degree and while occupying this body the HIP gains +6 to each trait.

This cadaver will hold its current state of putrefaction and even regain some blood flow, color in the cheeks and stop decaying while this plantoid inhabits, feeds and cares for it. The mostly dead body will have its own appearance trait value. Although officially dead, this host body might be stripped of the plantoid, quickly implanted with a cybernetic brain and heart and become a more-or-less living person again, although whatever identity and memories it once had are lost.

As a host, this cadaver will heal at its normal, endurance prescribed rate, and since it is somewhat still alive, is subject to all the perils of a living body, such as venom, radiation, sandstorms, and the like, but so too, will respond to medical treatments and the application by medical relics. As it is brain dead, it is immune to mental attacks. Its appearance trait is 3d6 and has 0 intelligence and 3d6 willpower.

**12.** This cadaver is dead in mind only, and without the plantoid would die fully within 24 hours. The body looks and smells like a living being and allows the plantoid to use it to move and talk much more like a regular person or animal. It has learned to conceal its foliage and appendages in clothing, armor and cloaks to allow it to operate passably among others of the cadaver's kind. This body is not rotting and will live for decades if the plantoid itself survives. Its intelligence trait is 0, but all other traits are rolled normally for the type of host body.

| | |
|---|---|
| **2.** | Synthetic human: Roll 1d6: 1-3. Clone, 4-6 Bioreplica (details on pages TME 18 and 19). |
| **3.** | Skullock (details on page TME 170). |
| **4.** | Cyborg with 1 defensive, 1 offensive and 1d3 miscellaneous implants (determine implants randomly on table XR-210 from page XR-330 of this book). Cyborgs descibed on page 21 of the Hub Rules. |
| **5.** | Mutant human with 1d2 prime mutations (use mutations list on page XR-228 of this book). Mutants described on page TME-22. |
| **6.** | Mutant human who had 1d3 minor mutations (use mutation list from page XR-229 of this book). Mutants descibed on page TME-22. |
| **7.** | Male pure stock human, age 10+3d6 years. Described on page TME-18. |
| **8.** | Female pure stock human aged 10+3d6 years. Described on page TME-18. |
| **9.** | Human child aged 3d6, with a 36% chance of being a mutant with 1d2 prime mutations (Endurance 4d6, Strength 4d6, but all other traits rolled as normal on the trait value determination table on page 8). |
| **10.** | Ghost mutant, adult, with 1d3 ghost mutations (use ghost mutation list from page XR-231 of this book). Ghost mutants descibed on page TME-22. |
| **11.** | Rebuilt human, rolled as a PC (use details from page XR-142 of this book). |
| **12.** | Bestial human (roll randomly from the list on page XR-58 of this book). |

## Host Cadaver Shedding and Merging

If a host utilizing plantoid wishes to change out of a cadaver, perhaps because it has gained a better one in battle, or, it wants to ditch the remains in order to hide among other plants or travel in a comrade's backpack, for example, it can do so.

Shedding a host cadaver is a slow process however, and takes 100+1d100 minutes to achieve fully if done carefully, without snapping tendrils, roots and control nodes. Doing so quickly, such as in an emergency, can be done in 1 minute but the plantoid detaches so violently that it leaves parts of itself behind, and suffers 3d6 damage and a permanent -1 to each trait.

To bore into and mesh with a new host is also time consuming, and for most onlookers, too gruesome to watch. This merging process takes 200+1d100 minutes and cannot be rushed.

Should a host inhabiting plantoid want to force its way into a living victim — an act of utmost malevolence and torture — this can only be achieved if the host body is fully restrained. The victim must make a willpower based type E hazard check every minute to stay conscious during the painful, gruesome ordeal as the main root ball of the HIP corkscrews deep into the person's abdomen and attempts to take control. In most cases, the victim dies from some complication, but occasionally a symbiotic relationship can be achieved. In these cases, the plantoid's many micro tendrils work into the entire host body, including its brain, and it gains control of a fully living host body. At times, however, the host will gain consciousness and bodily control and attempt to either kill itself in a way that it takes the plantoid intruder with it — such as leaping off a tall building, into an inferno, or the maw of some massive beast — or else seeks a surgeon who can remove the parasite's root ball and main tendrils.*

*A medic can make 1 attempt. Use the 'Resuscitate Drowning Victim' column from page TME-46 in the hub Rules book.*

Roll to determine the outcome of a forced host assumption on a still living victim, here:



| | |
|---|---|
| **2.** | Merciless Rejection! Everything seemed to go so well, but something about this host body's chemistry, immune system or pig-headed stubbornness results in a frustrating failure to gain control. Tendrils slip free of organs, the brain can't be gripped, penetrated, or adhered to. The juices in this ape's body are like acid and cause the HIP's exposed skin to itch and burn, and every night, when the body goes dormant to sleep, the torso convulses and tries to squeeze the root ball and entire plantoid out the same incision wound or orifice that the HIP first entered! It's really quite an ordeal. Each night the plantoid must make a willpower based hazard check to keep control of the host to stay inside the body. Failure means the HIP is squirted out onto the dirt and the host body collapses and will bleed out if not given medical attention at once. |
| **3.** | Rejection! The host body is highly resistant to the plantoid, and its immune system seems to attack the tissues of the HIP. For every minute the intruder stays inside this body, the HIP suffers 1d3 endurance damage. The plantoid must abort the ungovernable body at once and suffers 1 point to each trait, permanently. The host body recovers. |
| **4.** | Success, as in roll 5-9, below, however there is a complication. During the intrusive battle for control of the body, something went permanently wrong, roll 1d6: 1. Spinal damage, host paralyzed from the waist down. / 2. Spinal damage at the neck, host body permanently paralyzed from the neck down. / 3. Voice box ruined, this host cannot speak and merely makes raspy noises when forced to say anything. / 4-6. Nervous system damage, the host body's balance is permanently screwed up and no matter how hard the HIP tries, the host staggers along with a gimpy shuffle (-2m move per round), and -50% agility. |
| **5-9.** | Total control and isolation of the host's consciousness. The plantoid weaves its tendrils throughout the host body and mind, and can even keep the brain alive, but cuts off the consciousness of the former body's owner. While the victim's sees, hears, feels and exists fully, it has no control of the body. If the plantoid's root ball is removed or killed and this body survives, a risky surgery can be performed to remove the root ball and appendages, and after 6+1d6 months recuperation, the host victim can fully recover. This surgery requires a medic of 4 or more skill points and the medic make a Type C INT based hazard check to pull it off, and a type B Willpower hazard check by the patient to survive the ordeal. |
| **10.** | Host body goes into cardiac arrest and dies. Brain dead. Treat as Host Cadaver Condition roll 7, on table XR-109, previous page. |
| **11.** | Mental dominance failure! While the plantoid has taken control of the potential host's living body, the stubborn being's mind rejects the HIP as its tendrils probe the brain. The plantoid can assume the body and work its sensory organs and any appendages through the tissues and organs of the new body, but never gains control of the mind, which lives on behind the scenes like a monkey on the HIP's back so long as the two inhabit the same living and very serviceable body. Any mental attacks against this unlikely duo occur on the host's mind first, and if killed off, the parasite can finally assume full control of the body, which has a 2 in 6 chance of dying at that point, and will eventually turn into a skeleton as in roll 2 on the Host Cadaver Condition table, back on page 117, but only after 4d6 months. |
| **12.** | True Unification! It's like the host body has been waiting for this plantoid all these years! Conditions are favorable and even nourishing. The plantoid gains +1 to each trait permanently, even if leaving this body. Likewise, the host body's mind seems to drift off to some dream state and dwells their in total bliss, and has neither control nor awareness of the plantoid intruder and what it does with the body in the days, months and possible years ahead. So remarkable is this union that all the traits, including appearance of the host body become enhanced by +5 trait points while the HIP is inside the character, so too, the body goes up in rank like a regular character of its character type, at the same rate as the host inhabiting plantoid without splitting the experience factors. If the brain of this host body is killed by a head shot or fatal mental attack, there is a 2 in 6 chance that the body also dies, and after 4d6 months, is reduced to a skeletal frame as in roll 3 on the Host Cadaver Condition table on page 117. Incoming mental attacks, therefore, always target the host body first unless the attacker is specifically trying to target the plantoid within the body. |

*For host inhabiting plantoids, skip ahead to page 140 to discover reproductive capacity and pre-game caste*

## Identifiable Base Plantoids [IBP]

Knowing a plantoid character's botanical lineage gives a player a better idea of what the specimen looks like, plus reveals benefits or problems that might be associated with the entity's base parent species. For the most part, all plantoids of this classification have a central trunk or root ball from which grow the sensory cluster or face. Here, optical nodes, and some sort of mouth-like orifice are present which it speaks from and makes facial expressions. Any specialized limbs, attack modes, pods, gas sacks or other parts grow on the lower trunk. Above this main mass stretch out the upper branches and leaves while beneath the trunk, the plantoid's roots and tendrils provide locomotion, stability and height.

Wherever aspects of the base parent plant occur, they tend to appear in the same area of the plantoid as in an unmutated specimen. For example, a plantoid with a corn plant as a base would have corn cobs and a tall, leafy stalk growing high above its main head, while a carrot would have its greenery on display above its main core, which would be a quite obvious carrot-like, upside down cone shape that sprouts all other appendages.

While evidence of the base plant is often obvious, at other times it is hard to discern. Typically, any plantoid whose entire body is a common eatable potion, such as a turnip, instead of a plant that merely produced fruit like a raspberry or apple tree, will do its best to conceal its base linage to avoid being on the menu for hungry villagers.

In nearly every case, unless the plantoid is brightly colored, obviously out of place such as a palm tree growing in a patch of evergreen trees, or the plantoid is wearing gear, arms and armor meant for a humanoid, or in full bloom or covered in a bounty of brightly colored fruit, all plantoids enjoy an increased ability to hide among other foliage. Plantoids have +4 skill points in the 'conceal self' area of the stealth skill, and +2 skill points in 'concealed movement' when sneaking through other vegetation. The stealth skill is listed on page 51 of the hub rules.

**IBP characters start with a mix of randomly generated stats using the main trait determination table XR-2 back on page 8, but have a base appearance score of only 2d6, as their looks are anything but human.**

The initial traits recorded are often modified on the following table once the base plant species is known, but many plantoid mutations might also alter these traits.

The 79 base plants described in this book each have a brief description which follows this table, descriptions which often add tangible in-game complications, benefits and role-playing opportunities. Once the player rolls for their base plantoid linage, usng a d100 on table XR-112, describe or have the player read the description to help round out their character.

## Table XR-112/ Identifiable Plantoid Base Plants Matrix *Roll 2d6*

| d100 | Base Plant | DV | END | STR | AG | ACC | INT | WILL | PER | APP | Height | Weight | Growth* | Max Height | Age | Lifespan |
|---|---|---|---|---|---|---|---|---|---|---|---|---|---|---|---|---|
| 01. | Aloe Vera plant | -4 DV | +6 | +0 | +0 | +0 | +0 | +0 | +0 | +0 | 100+2d20cm | 60+2d20kg | +15cm/5kg | 3m | 3+1d6 | 26 years |
| 02. | Asparagus | -0 DV | +5 | +0 | +2 | +0 | +0 | +0 | +0 | +0 | 160+2d20cm | 70+2d20kg | +25cm/8kg | 4.1m | 4+1d6 | 42 years |
| 03. | Bamboo | -8 DV | +7 | +2 | +1 | +0 | +0 | +2 | +0 | +0 | 170+3d20cm | 70+2d20kg | +40cm/15kg | 6m | 5+2d6 | 110 years |
| 04. | Barley | -0 DV | +3 | +3 | +0 | +0 | +0 | +0 | +0 | +0 | 160+2d20cm | 60+2d20kg | +25cm/8kg | 3.5m | 3+1d6 | 22 years |
| 05,06. | Berry bush | -12 DV | +3 | +0 | +1 | +0 | +0 | +0 | +0 | +0 | 130+2d20cm | 40+2d20kg | +25cm/8kg | 4m | 4+1d6 | 36 years |
| 07. | Broccoli | -3 DV | +6 | +2 | +0 | +0 | +0 | +2 | +0 | +0 | 150+2d20cm | 80+3d20kg | +25cm/8kg | 3.9m | 3+1d8 | 32 years |
| 08. | Bunch grass | -0 DV | +5 | +0 | +3 | +0 | +0 | +0 | +0 | +0 | 160+6d20cm | 50+2d20kg | +40cm/15kg | 5m | 4+1d6 | 53 years |
| 09. | Cabbage | -4 DV | +2d8 | +3 | +0 | +0 | +0 | +0 | +0 | +0 | 130+2d20cm | 1000+3d20kg | +25cm/8kg | 3.6m | 3+1d8 | 29 years |
| 10-13. | Cactus | -20 DV | +1d6 | +0 | +0 | +0 | +0 | +0 | +0 | +0 | 80+2d20cm | 40+2d20kg | +30cm/10kg | 6m | 3+1d8 | 150 years |
| 14. | Carrot | -0 DV | +3d6 | +1d6 | +0 | +0 | +0 | +2 | +0 | +0 | 150+2d20cm | 70+2d20kg | +25cm/8kg | 3.65m | 3+1d8 | 27 years |
| 15. | Cauliflower | -3 DV | +7 | +1 | +0 | +0 | +0 | +3 | +0 | +0 | 140+2d20cm | 70+3d20kg | +25cm/8kg | 3.25m | 3+1d6 | 33 years |
| 16. | Celery | -0 DV | +2 | +2 | +3 | +0 | +0 | +0 | +2 | +0 | 160+1d100cm | 50+3d20kg | +35cm/12kg | 3.9m | 5+1d8 | 31 years |
| 17. | Coca bush | -2 DV | +3 | +0 | +0 | +0 | +0 | +3 | +0 | +0 | 130+3d20cm | 50+2d20kg | +25cm/8kg | 3.2m | 4+2d6 | 38 years |
| 18. | Coffee plant | -3 DV | +2 | +2 | +0 | +0 | +0 | +1 | +2 | +0 | 140+2d20cm | 60+2d20kg | +25cm/8kg | 4.4m | 6+2d6 | 57 years |
| 19,20. | Corn | -2 DV | +4 | +0 | +2 | +0 | +0 | +0 | +0 | +0 | 160+3d20cm | 70+2d20kg | +30cm/10kg | 6.8m | 3+1d8 | 39 years |
| 21. | Cotton | -3 DV | +4 | +0 | +0 | +0 | +0 | +0 | +0 | +0 | 130+2d20cm | 55+2d20kg | +25cm/8kg | 3.2m | 3+1d6 | 34 years |
| 22. | Cucumber | -4 DV | +3 | +2 | +2 | +0 | +0 | +0 | +0 | +0 | 140+2d20cm | 70+2d20kg | +30cm/10kg | 3.4m | 4+1d8 | 27 years |
| 23. | Dandelion | -2 DV | +4 | +2 | +2 | +0 | +0 | +4 | +1 | +0 | 150+2d20cm | 50+2d20kg | +25cm/8kg | 3.5m | 2+1d6 | 39 years |
| 24. | Evergreen shrub | -5 DV | +5 | +2 | +0 | +0 | +0 | +0 | +2 | +0 | 130+2d20cm | 60+2d20kg | +25cm/5kg | 4m | 6+2d6 | 75 years |
| 25. | Fern | -0 DV | +1 | +0 | +1 | +0 | +0 | +1 | +0 | +4 | 120+2d20cm | 40+2d20kg | +25cm/8kg | 3.7m | 3+1d8 | 29 years |
| 26. | Flax | -2 DV | +4 | +2 | +0 | +0 | +0 | +0 | +0 | +0 | 150+2d20cm | 80+2d20kg | +25cm/8kg | 3.9m | 4+1d6 | 34 years |
| 27. | Garlic | -3 DV | +7 | +3 | +0 | +0 | +1 | +3 | +1 | +0 | 140+2d20cm | 70+3d20kg | +25cm/8kg | 4.5m | 5+1d8 | 44 years |
| 28. | Grape vine | -5 DV | +3 | +3 | +4 | +0 | +0 | +0 | +0 | +0 | 140+2d20cm | 50+2d20kg | +35cm/12kg | 5m | 8+2d6 | 78 years |
| 29. | Green bean | -4 DV | +6 | +2 | +2 | +2 | +0 | +2 | +0 | +0 | 130+4d20cm | 60+3d20kg | +40cm/15kg | 5.5m | 5+3d6 | 56 years |
| 30. | Herb | -6 DV | +0 | +0 | +4 | +3 | +1 | +3 | +4 | +0 | 70+2d20cm | 30+1d20kg | +10cm/4kg | 1.8m | 2+1d6 | 56 years |
| 31. | Hot pepper | -3 DV | +4 | +2 | +1 | +1 | +0 | +2 | +0 | +0 | 140+2d20cm | 70+2d20kg | +25cm/8kg | 3.8m | 5+1d8 | 46years |
| 32. | Iris flower | -3 DV | +8 | +3 | +0 | +0 | +0 | +3 | +0 | +4 | 120+2d20cm | 50+2d20kg | +25cm/8kg | 3.2m | 2+2d6 | 39 years |
| 33. | Kale | -6 DV | +3 | +2 | +1 | +0 | +0 | +2 | +0 | +0 | 140+2d20cm | 60+2d20kg | +20cm/6kg | 3.7m | 3+1d8 | 42 years |
| 34. | Kelp | -4 DV | +9 | +6 | +3 | +3 | +0 | +0 | +0 | +0 | 180+3d20cm | 90+3d20kg | +50cm/15kg | 8m | 8+2d8 | 98 years |
| 35. | Lavender | -3 DV | +4 | +0 | +3 | +0 | +0 | +0 | +4 | +6 | 120+2d20cm | 50+2d20kg | +18cm/6kg | 3.4m | 4+2d6 | 36 years |
| 36. | Lawn grass | -2 DV | +12 | +2 | +0 | +0 | +0 | +2 | +0 | +0 | 100+2d20cm | 60+2d20kg | +15cm/5kg | 3.1m | 5+1d8 | 62 years |
| 37. | Lettuce | -0 DV | +7 | +0 | +3 | +0 | +0 | +0 | +3 | +0 | 150+2d20cm | 70+2d20kg | +25cm/8kg | 4.2m | 4+1d6 | 39 years |
| 38. | Lilac bush | -6 DV | +8 | +4 | +4 | +2 | +0 | +0 | +2 | +0 | 190+3d20cm | 80+2d20kg | +25cm/8kg | 6.1m | 5+3d6 | 79 years |
| 39. | Lily-pad | -3 DV | +6 | +4 | +4 | +2 | +0 | +0 | +0 | +0 | 150+2d20cm | 60+2d20kg | +30cm/10kg | 4.2m | 5+1d8 | 46 years |
| 40. | Marijuana | -6 DV | +7 | +3 | +2 | +0 | +0 | +2 | +0 | +0 | 140+3d20cm | 40+2d20kg | +25cm/8kg | 4.4m | 6+2d6 | 52 years |
| 41. | Moss | -0 DV | +6 | +1 | +0 | +0 | +0 | +2 | +0 | +0 | 120+2d20cm | 70+3d20kg | +10cm/4kg | 3.7m | 5+2d6 | 63 years |
| 42-47. | Mushroom | -0 DV | +3d6 | +4 | +0 | +0 | +0 | +4 | +0 | +0 | 140+3d20cm | 80+3d20kg | +30cm/10kg | 5.2m | 7+2d6 | 88 years |
| 48. | Oats | -4 DV | +8 | +3 | +0 | +0 | +0 | +3 | +0 | +0 | 160+3d20cm | 70+3d20kg | +25cm/8kg | 4.4m | 3+1d8 | 37 years |
| 49. | Onion | -2 DV | +6 | +6 | +4 | +0 | +0 | +2 | +0 | +0 | 140+2d20cm | 80+3d20kg | +30cm/10kg | 4.1m | 4+2d6 | 45 years |
| 50. | Pea plant | -5 DV | +4 | +6 | +7 | +2 | +0 | +0 | +0 | +0 | 160+1d100cm | 60+2d20kg | +40cm/15kg | 6.6m | 3+2d6 | 68 years |
| 51. | Pepper | -3 DV | +8 | +4 | +0 | +0 | +0 | +4 | +3 | +0 | 130+3d20cm | 80+3d20kg | +25cm/8kg | 3.9m | 3+2d6 | 39 years |
| 52,53. | Poison ivy | -3 DV | +4 | +2 | +3 | +0 | +0 | +0 | +2 | +0 | 140+2d20cm | 50+2d20kg | +15cm/5kg | 3.5m | 3+1d8 | 44 years |
| 54. | Poppy plant | -7 DV | +8 | +4 | +2 | +0 | +2 | +2 | +2 | +0 | 130+3d20cm | 40+3d20kg | +20cm/6kg | 3.2m | 5+2d6 | 49 years |

| d100 | Base Plant | DV | END | STR | AG | ACC | INT | WILL | PER | APP | Height | Weight | Growth* | Max Height | Age | Lifespan |
|---|---|---|---|---|---|---|---|---|---|---|---|---|---|---|---|---|
| 55. | Potato | -4 DV | +9 | +3 | +0 | +0 | +0 | +0 | +4 | +0 | 150+2d20cm | 70+2d20kg | +25cm/8kg | 4.2m | 4+1d6 | 45 years |
| 56. | Pumpkin | -5 DV | +10 | +4 | +0 | +0 | +0 | +5 | +0 | +0 | 140+3d20cm | 80+3d20kg | +30cm/10kg | 5.5m | 6+2d6 | 62 years |
| 57. | Radish | -2 DV | +4 | +2 | +4 | +0 | +0 | +0 | +0 | +0 | 120+2d20cm | 40+2d20kg | +10cm/4kg | 2.3m | 3+1d4 | 29 years |
| 58. | Reed | -4 DV | +6 | +3 | +3 | +0 | +0 | +0 | +2 | +0 | 160+3d20cm | 70+2d20kg | +30cm/10kg | 4.1m | 5+2d6 | 55 years |
| 59. | Rhubarb | -2 DV | +4 | +2 | +0 | +0 | +0 | +0 | +0 | +0 | 150+2d20cm | 60+2d20kg | +25cm/8kg | 3.4m | 5+1d8 | 62 years |
| 60. | Rice | -4 DV | +3 | +0 | +3 | +0 | +0 | +0 | +3 | +0 | 140+2d20cm | 40+2d20kg | +15cm/5kg | 3.8m | 3+1d8 | 39 years |
| 61. | Rose bush | -12 DV | +3 | +2 | +0 | +0 | +0 | +0 | +2 | +7 | 130+3d20cm | 50+2d20kg | +20cm/6kg | 4.2m | 6+3d6 | 87 years |
| 62. | Sagebrush | -10 DV | +9 | +4 | +2 | +0 | +0 | +4 | +0 | +0 | 140+2d20cm | 70+2d20kg | +15cm/5kg | 3m | 6+2d6 | 96 years |
| 63. | Soy bean | -5 DV | +6 | +2 | +2 | +0 | +0 | +2 | +0 | +0 | 150+3d20cm | 50+2d20kg | +25cm/8kg | 5.3m | 4+2d6 | 41 years |
| 64. | Spinach | -0 DV | +4 | +0 | +2 | +0 | +0 | +0 | +0 | +0 | 130+2d20cm | 40+2d20kg | +30cm/10kg | 3.6m | 3+1d6 | 29 years |
| 65. | Squash | -5 DV | +8 | +3 | +0 | +0 | +0 | +0 | +0 | +0 | 140+3d20cm | 80+3d20kg | +35cm/12kg | 4.4m | 7+2d6 | 54 years |
| 66. | Stinging nettle | -9 DV | +4 | +3 | +1 | +1 | +0 | +0 | +0 | +0 | 140+2d20cm | 50+2d20kg | +25cm/8kg | 4m | 3+1d8 | 39 years |
| 67. | Strawberry | -0 DV | +2 | +2 | +2 | +0 | +0 | +2 | +2 | +3 | 110+1d20cm | 30+2d20kg | +10cm/4kg | 2.1m | 2+1d8 | 44 years |
| 68. | Sunflower | -3 DV | +8 | +2 | +1 | +0 | +0 | +3 | +4 | +4 | 180+3d20cm | 70+3d20kg | +40cm/15kg | 4.8m | 5+2d6 | 53 years |
| 69. | Swiss-chard | -0 DV | +4 | +0 | +3 | +0 | +0 | +0 | +0 | +0 | 130+2d20cm | 60+2d20kg | +25cm/8kg | 4m | 4+1d6 | 42 years |
| 70. | Tea Plant | -6 DV | +7 | +3 | +0 | +0 | +3 | +3 | +0 | +0 | 160+2d20cm | 70+2d20kg | +15cm/4kg | 4m | 5+2d6 | 93 years |
| 71. | Thistle | -11 DV | +4 | +4 | +0 | +0 | +0 | +6 | +0 | +2 | 150+2d20cm | 50+2d20kg | +25cm/8kg | 4.2m | 6+1d6 | 51 years |
| 72. | Tobacco | -3 DV | +4 | +5 | +2 | +0 | +0 | +0 | +2 | +2 | 130+3d20cm | 40+2d20kg | +15cm/5kg | 4.1m | 3+2d6 | 45 years |
| 73. | Tomato | -0 DV | +6 | +4 | +3 | +0 | +0 | +0 | +3 | +3 | 140+2d20cm | 60+3d20kg | +25cm/8kg | 3.7m | 4+1d8 | 48 years |
| 74. | Tree, Birch | -4 DV | +10 | +5 | +0 | +0 | +0 | +0 | +2 | +0 | 160+1d100cm | 70+3d20kg | +50cm/20kg | 6.2m | 5+2d6 | 56 years |
| 75. | Tree, Chestnut | -6 DV | +14 | +7 | +0 | +0 | +0 | +0 | +0 | +0 | 160+2d20cm | 70+3d20kg | +30cm/19kg | 15m | 9+2d6 | 90 years |
| 76. | Tree, Cottonwood | -5 DV | +12 | +6 | +0 | +0 | +0 | +0 | +0 | +0 | 160+2d20cm | 70+2d20kg | +50cm/22kg | 4m | 8+2d6 | 88 years |
| 77-81. | Tree, Evergreen | -10 DV | +11 | +8 | +0 | +0 | +0 | +0 | +0 | +0 | 190+2d20cm | 80+3d20kg | +25cm/10kg | 20m | 6+3d6 | 210 years |
| 82-86. | Tree, Fruit | -8 DV | +9 | +5 | +0 | +0 | +0 | +0 | +0 | +4 | 180+2d20cm | 70+2d20kg | +15cm/8kg | 7m | 4+3d6 | 66 years |
| 87. | Tree, Maple | -9 DV | +8 | +4 | +0 | +0 | +0 | +0 | +0 | +0 | 160+2d20cm | 65+2d20kg | +30cm/10kg | 12m | 7+3d6 | 78 years |
| 88. | Tree, Oak | -15 DV | +18 | +6 | +0 | +0 | +0 | +6 | +0 | +0 | 180+3d20cm | 90+3d20kg | +25cm/14kg | 14m | 10+4d6 | 800+ years |
| 89. | Tree, Palm | -12 DV | +6 | +7 | +3 | +0 | +0 | +0 | +0 | +5 | 190+2d20cm | 70+3d20kg | +25cm/10kg | 9m | 6+2d6 | 105 years |
| 90. | Tree, Poplar | -6 DV | +5 | +3 | +3 | +0 | +0 | +0 | +0 | +0 | 150+3d20cm | 70+2d20kg | +40cm/15kg | 7m | 4+1d6 | 66 years |
| 91. | Tree, Weeping Willow | -6 DV | +9 | +5 | +0 | +0 | +0 | +0 | +0 | +0 | 150+3d20cm | 90+3d20kg | +40cm/20kg | 6m | 6+3d6 | 71 years |
| 92. | Tree, Willow | -4 DV | +5 | +3 | +3 | +0 | +0 | +0 | +0 | +0 | 140+3d20cm | 70+2d20kg | +25cm/10kg | 7m | 4+2d6 | 51 years |
| 93. | Tulip | -0 DV | +3 | +2 | +3 | +0 | +0 | +3 | +2 | +9 | 100+3d20cm | 40+2d20kg | +15cm/5kg | 2m | 2+1d6 | 38 years |
| 94. | Turnip | -6 DV | +8 | +7 | +0 | +0 | +0 | +0 | +0 | +0 | 130+2d20cm | 80+2d20kg | +15cm/18kg | 4m | 3+1d6 | 36 years |
| 95,96. | Venus flytrap | -4 DV | +6 | +1d6 | +1d6 | +2d6 | +0 | +0 | +1d6 | +0 | 130+2d20cm | 60+2d20kg | +20cm/10kg | 3m | 6+2d6 | 44 years |
| 97,98. | Virginia creeper | -2 DV | +5 | +2 | +8 | +4 | +0 | +0 | +0 | +0 | 140+2d20cm | 50+2d20kg | +25cm/8kg | 5m | 5+1d8 | 57 years |
| 99. | Wheat | 3DV | +2d6 | +2 | +4 | +0 | +0 | +0 | +3 | +2 | 130+3d20cm | 50+2d20kg | +25cm/9kg | 4m | 3+1d8 | 66 years |
| 00. | Yam | -7 DV | +10 | +5 | +0 | +0 | +0 | +3 | +0 | +0 | 130+2d20cm | 90+3d20kg | +25cm/20kg | 4.8m | 4+2d6 | 47 years |

*This is how much this plantoid grows per year in height and weight after character generation and game play begins.

# Identifiable Base Plantoid Lineage Descriptions

## Aloe Vera Plant

This plantoid features a half dozen wedge shaped, white dotted, barb ridged branches of about a meter or two in length. The original strain of this plant came from Africa and became one of the most common house plants ever, and was subsequently experimented on and bio-engendered extensively. This succulent's blade shaped, spongy branches contain a healing gel that can be applied to burns and other wounds to soothe injuries and encourage healing. 500ml of this gel on a wounded creature or other plant will heal 1d4 damage, although only one application per wound (per individually struck area of the body) will benefit from this healing per day.

Extracting the gel inflicts 1d2 damage to this aloe vera character, so it is always highly selective of whom it lacerates itself for. While they cannot heal themselves with this gel, they are full of it in the first place, and highly regenerative beings, and have a healing rate of double their normal, endurance based recovery rate. Aloe Vera based plantoids can endure heat and a lack of water for a week before suffering harm, but do not do well in cold climes and suffer twice the damage that a human might in freezing conditions.

## Asparagus

These plantoids feature a primary root ball from which grows a central, fern-like shrub. In the spring this main bush is surrounded by meter high green stocked, purple tipped shafts of delicious asparagus spears. If not harvested, these will grow into more branches and fine foliage. In the late summer, female variants of this plant will produce 100+1d100 small red seeds. These seeds are poisonous to humans and if ingested will cause the eater to make a type B endurance based hazard check or fall ill for 3d6 hours. During this illness, the unfortunate must make an identical HC or die.

Asparagus spears from a plantoid of this strain weigh 25kg each and will feed 10 people with a nourishing, moisture rich meal. This mutant plant will grow 3 such spears each spring per rank. If the plantoid plucks out its own asparagus spears and hurl them, treat them as regular spears which inflict only stun damage.

## Bamboo

Plantoid bamboo are fast growing, long lived, tough bushes which feature a dozen or more bamboo shafts, called culms, which grow from the now exposed root ball or rhizome. The root ball forms into a thick trunk as the entity matures, and from this mass sprout any manipulator appendages, optic nodes and other features. Locomotion is accomplished by a multitude of pale runners. The bamboo shafts grow above the plantoid's body and number 3d6 culm shafts about two meters in height each. These shafts can be harvested occasionally and make splendid fishing poles, javelins and other elongated items. Bamboo plantoids prefer lush, warm climes, but can tolerate cold weather for

weeks at a time. Arid conditions are undesirable, and after a week in the desert, especially in direct sun and hot, sand laden wind, this plant-man will begin to wither and die, suffering 3d6 damage per day, even if given water.

## Barley

Derived from a very popular cereal grain, which was first used by farmers as early as 8000 BC, this new strain of grass has formed into a huge clump, with a thick trunk like torso, a mass of flowing barely stalks as a canopy and hundreds of woven roots beneath it which propel it along at speed. Once every 90 days its massive seed stalks become ripe and ready for harvest. The grain laden heads can be painlessly snipped off and the huge kernels used for flat bread, porridge, and malt production for beer and other alcoholic beverages.

When hiding among other tall grasses, this plantoid is almost impossible to spot, and if unmoving, has an extra skill point in the stealth skill as far as 'conceal self'.

Like all plantoids that were engineered from a popular agricultural plant, and in a world where most people go to bed hungry, this animated, human DNA laced freak must be careful to avoid being seized and held in captivity as a source of food, and flee from goats and other herbivores which would happily eat this entire character.

## Blackberry or Raspberry Bush

This plantoid's trace human DNA is mixed with either a blackberry or raspberry bush (roll 1d10: 1-4. blackberry, 5-10. raspberry), which are two prickly, fruit-bearing shrubs in the Rubus family. This specimen has a thick, woody core trunk from which most other appendages are attached. Its 'face' is at the higher end on one side of this trunk and shadowed by a mass of leafy, flower and fruit covered upper branches. Like so many other plantoids, it moves about on a tangled network of woven root-legs. This shrub will produce a kilogram of fruit every week from late spring to early fall, per rank, and will grow and spread out every year. Because of the many prickles on its branches and trunk, increase its defense value by -12 points. When forced to enter communities filled with strangers, this plantoid might snip off or harvest and conceal its fruit before entering the place to avoid the risk of being captured and chained to a patch of ground and used as a captive food supply.

## Broccoli

Often mistaken for an entirely dark green tree or large shrub, this plantoid moves about on bright green root-legs, has its sensory organs and appendages on a elongated central shaft and is topped by a mass of broad, thick leaves which surround a cluster of 3d6 broccoli florets. Each of these clusters weigh between 2 and 8 (2d4) kilograms and can feed many people.

Having these florets hacked off hurts the plantoid, but does not inflict any particular damage and often such a character is happy to feed its human companions and a few pack animals in order to gain the companionship and protection from such allies. When going anywhere near a settlement, this individual knows to cover up its bounty of florets to avoid being swarmed by either hungry livestock, or people, and devoured utterly, or else kept as a chained up, nutrient source.

## Bunch Grass

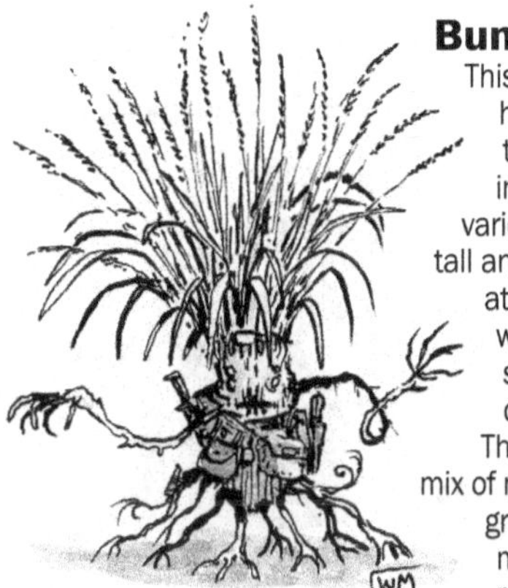

This specimen is a mix of grass and human. Bunch grass, also called tussock grass, are solitary clumps instead of broadly spreading lawn varieties. As plantoids, they grow quite tall and have pale, almost white root legs at their base, while a thick, tawny woven stock develops at their mid-section where their limbs, eyes and other sensory organs are clustered. The top half or more of this being is a mix of newly growing grass and taller dead grass. When among other grasses or mixed vegetation, this plantoid can remain still and go unseen to all but the most careful observer.

Many herbivores love nothing more than to munch on grass, and for this individual to stroll through a typical post-apocalyptic village would attract a fair number of goats, horses and cattle, all of which would eat this character down to a meter tall stump and 50% of its previous endurance. From such a sorry state, it would take 4 months for the plantoid to grow a respectable tuft of top grass again and regain its lost endurance, and dignity.

## Cabbage

This plantoid's trace human DNA is mixed with a cabbage. Of the Brassica family, cabbages come in several common strains of which this character is a blend with one. **Roll 1d6: 1-4.** green cabbage / **5.** savoy cabbage / **6.** purple cabbage.

This veggie-sapien has several thick loco-motion roots at its base, a dense, woody stock on which all its sensory organs and limbs are attached, while at its top is a great bulbous crown surrounded by broad, sun catching leaves.

Until harvested, this top mass can weigh as much as the entire plantoid itself (double the weight of this PC in late summer). Besides being able to feed coleslaw to fifty grown men, this massive cabbage head can be used as a melee attack to bludgeon or ram opponents at +6 strike value and inflict 4d6 stun damage plus strength modifiers. To ram, the PC must run at opponents for 1 round and attack on the 2nd round.

It goes without saying that to reveal a massive head of cabbage to always hungry new era commoners, or their livestock, is asking for trouble.

## Cactus

Before the apocalypse, and the untold amount of genetic manipulation by both mutagenic agents and human tempering, there were thousands of cactus species around the world. Now, there are tenfold this variety, with many of them predatory. Some are mixed with human DNA and form the common plantoid species that now walk the twisted earth. For the most part, these cacti are a mixed strain of the massive saguaro, a strain that was once famous in the Sonoran Desert, while 1 in 20 will also feature genetics from the Peyote cactus, which yield pure mescaline. Mescaline produces psychoactive reactions in those who ingest as

little as 400 mg of this cactus's flesh raw, or 40mg dried. Those who use this substance attest to its spiritual and visionary effectiveness, and are often willing to pay 10 silver pieces for 10mg of the dried substance.

These cactus plantoids start out small, at only a meter in height at creation, but grow 30cm per year plus 30cm per rank gained. They have tough, leathery hides, thick prickles and the ability to endure months without nourishment or water. They ignore sand storms and the most extreme periods of heat. Any appendages will also be covered in the same prickles, and overall this entity gains an impressive -20 bonus to its defense value.

## Carrot

This oddity has a hard time hiding what it really is. When entering an unfamiliar town site, it relies both on its ability to put up a determined fight and stout hearted companions to keep it from being eaten. The sensory array and any manipulator limbs grow from the bright orange taproot while pale, knotted vine or runner roots serve as legs, or else (3 in 10 chance) the bottom of the main body splits into two or three narrower portions to serve as legs. Above the head of this plantoid rises a meter tall crown of leafy stocks, which are also an attractant to herbivores, but make for excellent camouflage when this being needs to hide in the woods, remaining still, and keeping low to the ground.

Carrot plantoid's have a robust build, can take plenty of damage and float easily if immersed in water. They float so well, that two or three average sized humans can hang onto the carrot as a flotation device if needed.

There is a 1 in 10 chance that this character is actually not an orange carrot at all, however, and if so, **roll 1d10** here: **1-6.** You're a parsnip! / **7.** Purple carrot / **8,9.** Yellow carrot / **10.** Red carrot.

## Cauliflower

Related to broccoli, kale, and cabbage, this plantoid is also of the Brassica family and like the broccoli, has its limbs and any sensory organs clustered on the main trunk while its legs are formed by various sized roots which serve as legs. The top, also called 'the curd' is a large, leaf encased uneven, lumpy mass — an irresistible bounty of vegetable matter for any herbivore or hungry band of humans. The major advantage this being has is that it can hide in snowy terrain with masterful skill (6 points in conceal self or 3 points in concealed movement according to the stealth skill on page TME-51).

## Celery

Every part of this giant walking, talking vegetable can be eaten, from root, stalk and leafy top greens. This fact forces this human DNA laced, tall being to be extra cautious when nearing settlements of any kind, and rely on the backup of any mutant, cyborg and human comrades to dissuade would-be herbivores or half starved locals from hacking apart this entity to add to a stew.

Celery based plantoids can grow very tall, and when not encrusted in the arms and armor of humans, can easily stand still in a thickly vegetated area and almost vanish. Because of their thin build, they are naturally stealthy even for their size and gain 2 skill points in the stealth skill.

## Coca Plant

Only bio-technicians and a handful of farmers know what can be extracted from the broad, tapering leaves of this plantoid. These knowledgeable ones might seek to either purchase most of this character's greenery, or else restrain and pluck the leaves from the plantoid. Cocaine production in the twisted new era is exceedingly rare, due mostly to the complexity of the process, and so few people alive in the twenty-fourth century will see this lush, two or three meter tall plantoid as anything other than some animated shrub.

This being will have 10+3d6 large leaves plus 2 per year of growth after character creation. Each leaf will sell for 10+1d20sp to a knowledgeable bio-tech user, otherwise, to commoners, this plant is merely useful as fodder for livestock and treated as just some bitter tasting bush.

Coca plantoids do best in lush, warm climes, but can cope with deserts or wasteland conditions for several days at a time without undo harm. Like most weedies, they move about on several knotted roots, have their arms and sensory organs on a central trunk, and the vast amount of their greenery, tiny red berries or white flowers massed all about them, which dangle down and often conceal the plantoid's 'face'.

## Coffee Plant

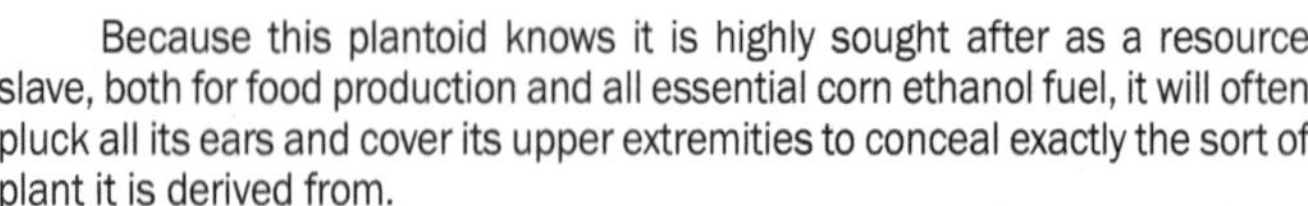

This plantoid is derived from the coffea plant, the roasted berries of which produce the beverage 'coffee'. Many new era saloon owners, farmers, and those with the cooking skill will immediately recognize this character's linage, and will often offer to buy the coffee berries at a rate of 50sp for 1 kilogram. Less scrupulous new era connoisseurs will either detain and forcibly harvest the berries from a visiting plantoid, or else kidnap and enslave the character in order to access a steady supply of the precious beans.

White flowers form on this shrub or small tree and eventually turn into berries 9 months later. When no beans or flowers are present, this plantoid can easily pass as an unremarkable animated veggie-sapien, or even hide among other vegetation with ease.

Coffea plants are robust, grow to about 4m in height and do well in many terrain types so long as it does not freeze. They move about on tightly woven legs formed from their roots, have all their limbs and sensory parts growing from their central trunk and have a broad, canopy of bright green, waxy foliage above their head.

## Corn

Unlike either regular or giant varieties of mutant corn that grow in farmer's fields, this strain is laced with human DNA and has formed into a self aware plantoid. Also, unlike agricultural corn variants, this specimen has multiple ears of corn growing in its upper stalks at various stages of ripeness, and once a week can pluck 1d6 cobs from itself to offer to either livestock or humanoid companions. This corn-man has a single trunk made from a thick cornstalk, from which its arms and sensory appendages grow, while its roots system has knotted into a set of rudimentary legs and crawling roots. The upper crown of this being is a mass of 3d6 normal looking cornstalks, complete with pollen laden tassels, ears, full cobs and broad, brilliant green leaves.

Because this plantoid knows it is highly sought after as a resource slave, both for food production and all essential corn ethanol fuel, it will often pluck all its ears and cover its upper extremities to conceal exactly the sort of plant it is derived from.

## Cotton

This 'shruboid' is quite unremarkable when not in bloom, and can easily pass as just another bush when hiding among vegetation and not dressed in gear, arms and armor. Once each season, however, its topmost branches reveal hundreds of small, shell encased balls or 'boils' from which burst open to reveal fist sized tufts of brilliant white cotton.

A clever cotton plantoid knows to have human companions pluck these puff balls from it before it enters a strange community, for local commoners and officials alike would love nothing more to than to capture this individual, chain them in a barnyard, and have them grow a continuous supply of beautiful cotton to turn into fabric yarn.

This plantoid can produce 2d6 kilograms of cotton per season so long as it gets plenty of sunlight, water and nourishment. It moves about on root legs, has a stocky trunk portion where its eyes and other limbs grow, and a sizable top shrub which often hangs down all around its main body.

## Cucumber

While normally this plant grows as a creeping vine along the ground, its plantoid variant forms into more of a shrub, with thick, prickle covered central body where its sensory organs and any manipulator arms or branches grow. A mass of flexible, locomotion providing roots extend from its base while a tangle of upper vines grow above. These higher branches are laden with 3d6 cucumbers in various stages of development. Bright yellow, star-shaped flowers sprout from this foliage and which often attract bees, hummingbirds and other pollinators — even giant specimens which can be a danger to human companies.

As with so many other plantoids, this mutant must have its fruit hidden or harvested before it goes anywhere near a humanoid community for always hungry citizenry will either accost and roughly twist off the cucumbers, or the local warlord will order the plantoid held captive as a permanent 'guest' in the local, walled veggie garden. Livestock are not so fussy, however, and goats in particular will chase down and devour the entire plantoid, roots, vine and all, if they get the chance.

## Dandelion

These enormous, mobile dandelion plants move about on a cluster of tendrils and fine roots at the base of their main taproot body. They are topped by their distinctive, serrated but soft green leaves and hollow stemmed flower stalks. Once a month, 3d6 buds will open to reveal a pollen rich, 30cm in diameter yellow flower. After pollination, these flower pedals turn into seeds attached to pappus; a white, feather-like umbrella that allows the seeds to be carried on the wind for many meters or kilometers.

Dandelions of all varieties are entirely edible, and this specimen is no different and must be vigilant for herbivores and hungry humanoids, alike.

### Evergreen Shrub

There are generally two types of these low-growing bushes, the first is a needle bearing variety derived from such shrubs as yew and juniper, while the other variety is based on the leafy boxwood and blue holly shrub.

The holly will produce beautiful read berries in late fall, although while these berries look appealing, they are slightly poisonous. Anyone eating a handful will become sickened, and must also make a type B END hazard check or suffer diarrhea and vomiting for 3d6 hours.

In most cases, these shrubs are splendidly adapted to hiding themselves among regular plants, as even in badlands, deserts, old cities, and along the sides of dirt roads near a town, evergreen shrubs grow naturally and so offer excellent hiding places for this being. They do not grow nearly as tall as evergreen trees, but can still reach 4 meters in height and exhibit thick robust trunks with gnarly root-legs.

Evergreen Shrub Parent species **roll 1d6: 1,2.** Yew / **3,4.** Juniper / **5.** Boxwood / **6.** Holly

### Fern

Derived from a line of plants going back to the Devonian period of 360 million years ago, these plantoids produce numerous, top growing fiddle heads, which unfurl into fronds. Like their full-plant cousins, veggie-sapien variants prefer to occupy shady, moist areas, and don't do well in the hot sun for long periods or where they can't wriggle their fibrous roots into boggy soil. They produce no fruit and are rarely consumed for food by humans, yet livestock are still a danger to these individuals. Plantoid specimens have thick, central trunk, although this is short compared to the lush, mass of leafy branches that make up over half of their height.

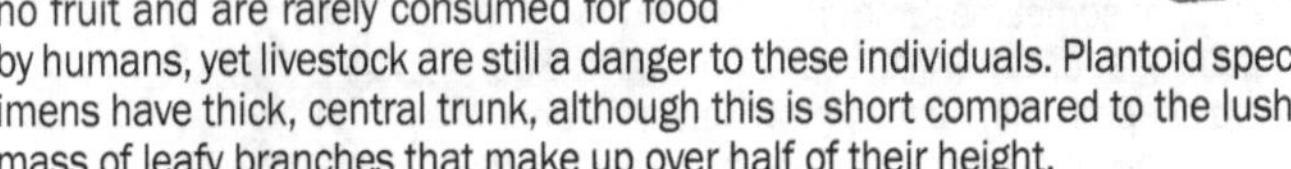

### Flax

Related to the still popular agricultural plant, which yield eatable seeds, linseed oil from their oil, and linen when the fibers are converted to textiles, the human DNA laced plantoid specimen of this line are weedy looking. Only a farmer would really recognize the mass of stringy, blue flowered plants growing from the top of this animated clump of vegetation as a relative to the common flax plant. While most flax plants grow a single stalk, this plantoid's thick trunk supports a patch of 10+2d6 stout, highly productive flax stems that grow a meter into the air above the mutant. If identified as a food plant by locals when its crop of upper branches are laden with seed pods, then there is some chance that starving humanoids might try to accost and harvest this plantoid's top foliage.

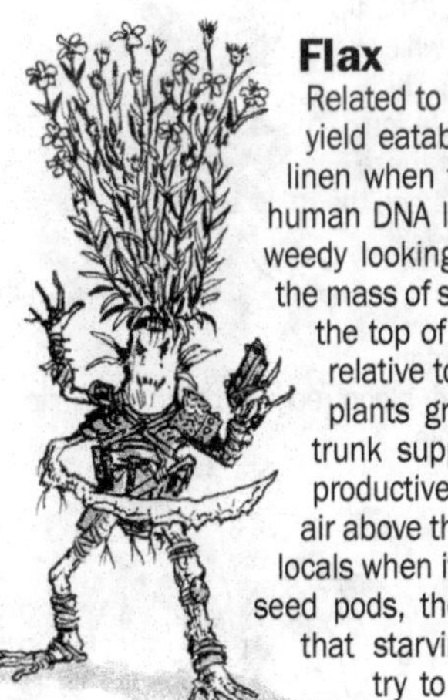

### Garlic

These plantoids exhibit an easily identifiable plant lineage, with globular bodies filled with huge, wedge-shaped segments of remarkably tasty and highly prized garlic flavored flesh. Since the body is also the most sought after part of this being, it must conceal its garlicky nature under layers of clothing, junk, and armor, and stick close to trusted humanoid and mechanical companions when nearing human settlements.

These plants move about on a series of stout, white root legs. Above their bulb forms a series of 2 or 3 meter tall, sword-like leaves, and in the spring, a central shaft will form topped by an edible garlic scape. While humans love to add garlic to nearly every savory dish, many herbivores find this character's flavor to be too strong, and must make a type D willpower based hazard check to continue eating its flesh after the first successful bite. Carnivores will not consume this being, although they may     still tear it apart.

### Grape Vine

These plantoids are vines, although their main core is a thick, central stalk just above a gnarled and multi-legged root ball. They can easily hide among other vines, especially in a dense forest or swamp, although they have a distinctive leaf and are always loaded with bunches of grapes in various stage of development. Because people, and many animals, love to eat grapes, or harvest them for raisins or wine production, this plantoid will often clip off any forming grapes prior to approaching a community, least it be identified, seized and forced to live out its days in a vineyard.

Grape vines characters always have 1d4 highly flexible, manipulator vines that measure 2 meters, plus an extra 15cm (half a foot) length per rank (for example a 4th rank grape vine's manipulator vines will measure 200cm+60cm (2.6 meters). These can help it climb at +1 skill point, plus each adds a melee attack for a smack SV +4, DMG 1d6 each, or can aid in grappling at +1 skill point per 2 vines each (minimum 1 manipulator vine and a permanent strength score of of 30). These appendages can be cut off and have a DV of -10 and 10 endurance each, regrowing at 30cm per month to their designated, rank based length.

While there were once hundreds of varieties of grapes, this specimen grows one of these popular types of fruit. Roll **1d10: 1.** Concord/ **2.** Cabernet Sauvignon /**3.** Pinot Noir / **4.** Muscadine / **5.** Merlot / **6.** Crimson Seedless / **7.** Gewurztraminer / **8.** Riesling / **9.** Sultana / **10.** Thompson Seedless Grapes

### Green Bean

This plantoid's main body consists of a woody, leaf and runner shrouded trunk, however its roots and lower locomotion tendrils surround the base and trail off behind it as it moves. At its upper limits it exhibits a tangled mess of 3d6 bean and flower laden vines. These vines are inanimate, although any other manipulator limbs or appendages will have a similar look, and hold a bounty of beans pods that grow from a lower position on the trunk.

Nearly every citizen in the post-apocalyptic world knows the sight of a bean plant, including those that grew up in some subterranean bunker where hydroponic specimens of the vegetable were certainly grown in abundance. Given this, a bean plantoid must be extra careful when entering farm villages, barter forts and the emerging towns of the new era, for few humans have full bellies in the Mutant Epoch era.

There is a 2 in 6 chance this bean plant is actually a different variety from a regular green bean. Roll **1d12** to see which: **1.** Scarlet runner / **2.** Dragon bean / **3.** Butter bean / **4.** Pinto bean / **5.** Navy bean / **6.** Kidney bean / **7.** Mung bean / **8.** Lima bean / **9.** Black bean /**10.** Chickpea (Garbanzo bean) / **11.** Lentil / **12.** Peanut.

## Herb

This plantoid is related to a herb plant. Herbs differ from general spices in that these are derived from the leaf or flower of the plant, while spices can be sourced from the fruit, bark, roots, seeds, or other parts of a plant. In all cases, this character is on the smaller side of the plantoid lineup, and often has a thick woody trunk upon which grows the highly sought after leaves or flowers of whatever type of herb it is related to. Any farmer, kitchen servant, or individual with the cooking skill need only make a type A perception based hazard check to detect what herb this plantoid stems from, while untrained humans need to make a type E intelligence based hazard check to identify the herb — at least without tasting it.

In each case, this plantoid will yield 1 kilogram of spice per month, which it, or its comrades or master, could sell for 10+1d20 silver pieces in almost any barter market.

To determine the base herb that this character is related to, roll **2d20** on the following table

| 2d20 | Plantoid's Base Herb Type |
|---|---|
| 2. | Allspice |
| 3. | Anise |
| 4. | Basil |
| 5. | Bay Leaves |
| 6. | Cardamom |
| 7. | Caraway |
| 8. | Chamomile |
| 9. | Chervil |
| 10. | Chicory |
| 11. | Chives |
| 12. | Cicely |
| 13. | Clove |
| 14. | Coriander |
| 15. | Culantro |
| 16. | Dill |
| 17. | Fennel |
| 18,19. | Ginger |
| 20. | Horseradish |
| 21. | Parsley |
| 22,23. | Mint |
| 24,25. | Peppermint |
| 26. | Stevia |
| 27. | Lemongrass |
| 28. | Oregano |
| 29. | Marjoram |
| 30. | Lemon Balm |
| 31. | Myrtle |
| 32. | Spearmint |
| 33. | Mustard |
| 34. | Rosemary |
| 35. | Sage |
| 36. | Star Anise |
| 37. | Tarragon |
| 38. | Thyme |
| 39. | Turmeric |
| 40. | Wasabi* |

**This herb can be used to make pepper pray. See the listing for Hot Pepper, below, for this application.*

## Hot Pepper

The top section of this thick stalked, leafy animated, plant-human hybrid is a dense shrub with many hot peppers and flowers growing among its foliage. Once every month or so, 4d6 tiny immature peppers, 4d6 mature but not ripe, and 2d6 ripe hot peppers will be found among the leaves of this specimen. Some variants of peppers are rather mild, while others, if eaten, can cause severe pain to the consumer's mouth.

For a scale of hotness roll 1d10, with a 1 being mild enough that the peppers can be eaten or added to food with little suffering on the part of the eater, while at a 10, the subject is likely to have to leave the table, shed tears, pant, sweat, consume plenty of water, and suffer for 2d6 hours with a further 71% chance that, 12 hours later, while evacuating a stool, will be tormented again at the other end of their digestive circuit.

Pepper spray can be made with any hot peppers with a heat rating of 6 to 10, with the crushed, ripe fruit added to water and fired through either a relic spray bottle (range 3 meters) or sprayed through some machine or hose nozzle to potentially blind a large group of attackers temporally. The GM will need to assist the player on the details, but a Type C agility based hazard check is needed to dodge the spray, with those failing considered blinded for 2d6 minutes with blindness rules on page TME-122.

## Iris Flower

Like both regular and bizarre mutated specimens, plantoid iris flowers come in hundreds of varieties. The most common has a thick, tuber-like root ball from which grow a complex set of knotted root-legs at the bottom, while at the top, or sometimes from the side, extends a bright green, trunk-like body from which 3d6 sword-shaped, stiff leaves grow upward. Once a year, 2d6 thickly stalked, tubular flower shafts will grow from the tuber body itself and at the tip, develop into complex, remarkable flowers which will bloom for 20+1d10 days. While in bloom, hiding among other, differently colored vegetation is very difficult. So too, many people find these flowers beautiful and if they can't forcibly keep the plantoid on their property to beautify it, might offer to pay 1sp per each giant flower.

Roll 1d10 for the color of flowers produced by this sweet smelling veggie-sapien, **1d10: 1.** baby blue / **2.** white / **3.** gold / **4.** blood red / **5.** pink. / **6.** white with pink edges / **7.** navy blue / **8-10.** purple.

## Kale

While farmers will recognize this plantoid's heritage, and might seek to harvest the character's upper leafy stalks, most people and animals will dismiss this plantoid as just another shrub if the veggie-sapien is stationary, hides or sheds any human-centric gear and weaponry, and remains still.

Kale is highly nutritious, resistant to cold to 15c and a robust plantoid with about half its length consisting of the broad, dark green, curly-leaved top branches. They feature a thick, dark green trunk where its limbs and sensory organs are situated, and a broad, skirt-like network of lower roots and tendrils which grow into the thick, tangled cables to conduct locomotion.

## Kelp

While kelp dwell only in saltwater, these plantoid specimens are laced with human DNA, and are amphibious. Kelp is not actually a plant, but a line of living beings called heterokont, and are among the fastest growing living beings on earth. Kelp men have an elongated root ball, which on a regular specimen is called a holdfast, and on these freaks rises on a series of rubbery locomotion roots.

Its upper reaches consist of a mass of stems from which elongated, highly flexible, brownish green blade leaves dangle, while at the base of these leaf-like growths are bladders of buoyant liquid which when the plantoid is submerged, allow the 1d3 meter long kelp 'branches' to flow upward toward the sunlight at the surface. A kelp plantoid can float in water for as long as its desires, and if entering a kelp bed, will utterly disappear unless clad in arms and armor.

While they can exist out of water, they can only do so for 12 hours per day, after which they begin to rapidly desiccate and suffer 1d6 endurance points damage per hour, which will not heal until the plantoid is immersed in water. Because they grow so fast, they heal at twice the normal, endurance based healing rate, but this recovery only occurs while in water. All kelp plantoids are excellent swimmers and can in breath in water. Aquatic carnivores will ignore this plantoid, unless the character attacks it, such as when the plantoid defends human comrades.

## Lavender

While there are dozens of strains of natural lavender plants, and countless mutant strains of which some grow ten meters tall, this plantoid strain is mixed with the common Lavandula Angustifolia which produces the familiar purple flowers and remarkable fragrance that people even in the twisted post-apocalyptic new era will recognize.

This human DNA blended specimen is rather tall and skinny, with a broad, skirt like mass of mobile roots at its base which knot into spider-like legs. Higher up, they exhibit a woody trunk where other appendages and it sensory organs are situated, while a top cluster of 3d6+6 stems and dozens of evergreen leaves reach for the sun. The stems of this shrub are quite distinctive and bloom in late spring and summer, and produce spiky seed heads. Farmers ,herbalists and medics know that lavender flowers and seeds can be harvested to produce tea and essential oils, known for their calming properties.

When not blooming, or the plantoid purposefully snips off its flower heads — which hurts like hell — it can easily hide among other shrubs, and avoid being seized by humans and enslaved as a chained up producer of wonderfully aromatic flowers.

## Lawn Grass

This plantoid is often stubby and broad, compared to other veggie-sapiens, especially when it keeps its mass of grass in its upper reaches trimmed, mowed, or gently grazed by livestock. This strain of grass is one living organism, although the lawn section might also be laced with clover, regular dandelions, weeds and flowers, but for the most part is one grass plant.

When cut regularly, this plantoid's top section is brilliant green and luxuri-

ous to lie upon for smaller companions, although in most cases, a post-apocalyptic plantoid survivor knows to let the grass grow tall and wild in order to allow it to better blend in with its surroundings like a living Gillie suit. If this veggie-sapien drops to a crouch, and so hides its armor and gear encrusted torso 'clump' along with its tangled, walking roots, it can easily hide in almost any terrain type, so long as it is not a carefully mowed patch of greenery among other weeds and wasteland grasses and junk.

Herbivores love to eat grass of all kinds, and if this plantoid is the only vegetation visible in sight, it has a problem.

## Lettuce

As this plantoid's vegetable ancestry was cultivated to be eaten, and it now features a massive head of lettuce in its upper reaches, this character needs to be extremely careful around herbivores and hungry humans. In most cases, it knows to trim off much of its leaf formation, and wear a large hood over what is left, or become added to a salad big enough to feed half a village.

These veggie-sapiens have a large tap roots as their main body, with smaller, pale roots spreading out from the bottom which serve as legs. Leafy varieties, such as romain and 'leaf' lettuce have a better chance of passing as just another broad leaf plant among other woodland vegetation, while iceberg lettuce and red leaf lettuce stand out and have a tougher time going unnoticed and untasted.

Roll 1d8 for the type of lettuce this plantoid stems from: **1.** leaf lettuce / **2.** red leaf / **3.** iceburg / **4.** butterhead (called roundhead in the former UK)/ **5.** arugula / **6-8.** romaine.

## Lilac Bush

Sometimes mistaken for a small tree, these bushes can grow quite huge and as a plantoid, can easily tower over human comrades by several meters. In the spring, they produce a bounty of pleasant smelling pink, white or purple clusters of flowers. Lilac bushes are common in the Epochian wilderness, and especially in areas that were once human suburbs, offering amble hiding places for this character should itself be in bloom and slip into a patch or row of naturally growing cousins.

In early summer, this shrub loses its flowers and can easily pose as just a deciduous shrub, and easily remain stationary and let trouble pass.

While goats and some other herbivores will happily chew on this plantoid's upper branches and leaves, lilacs are not on the menu for humans or most other livestock, and do well when entering human communities.

## Lily-pad

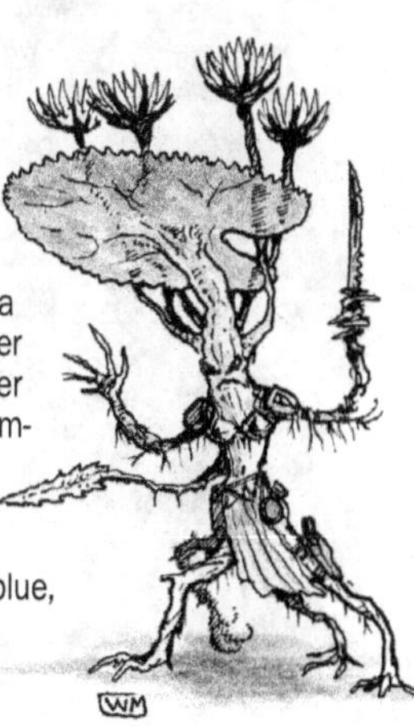

These mostly aquatic plantoids have developed from lily-pads, also called water-lilies. Being mixed with human DNA, these new era survivors are mobile and move about on a complex mass of tendrils and primary roots, have a dense stalk as a body and are topped by a huge, sombrero-like lily pad which has a diameter of up to 2 meters and can offer shade to smaller creatures and traveling companions. In early summer, these plantoids grow 2d6 tall, vibrant green stems about a meter high from their shoulders, and above the main, disc like lily-pad. These produce a large, 30cm wide pink, blue, or more typically, white flower which can be seen from hundreds of meters away and is a strong attractant to pollinators.

Herbivores don't normally eat water lilies, so might not rush to devour this plantoids, although after a few tentative nibbles, will probably munch on the character unless frightened away. This plantoid can only remain out of fresh water for 18 hours before suffering dessication and taking 2 endurance points of damage per hour — points that do not heal until the individual is immersed in fresh water. Salt water will not heal this plantoid, but will stop further dessication. This character is most happy when in a pond, well, bathtub, or other freshwater area, including swamplands, and is an excellent swimmer. It can remain submerged indefinitely, and will typically be ignored by aquatic predators.

If in a situation where it can't get to water, it can have a liter of fresh water poured over it each hour and apply soaking cloths and towels or clothing to its body to stave off the hourly loss in endurance points, although in the post-apocalyptic world, expending fresh water can be an expensive undertaking.

## Marijuana

Plantoids who have marijuana plant as their base plant heritage always have the option to snip off a few leaves or buds from their top branches to either barter or sell whenever they or their teammates need food, drink, or silver. The problem is, because they produce massive 30 to 50cm wide leaves and sizable buds, all which are easily identified by new era herbalists, farmers, drug users and authorities, this veggie-sapien must always be on guard against being arrested where this drug is deemed illegal, or else accosted and harvested where the substances is highly prized.

Either way, a marijuana based plantoid character must conceal its foliage when entering a human community, and always be prepared to snip off some of its upper foliage to trade and bribe its way to freedom and avoid being held in captivity to serve as a regular supply for a local drug lord or chieftain.

Any onlooker who would normally recognize a cannabis plant is allowed a Type C intelligence based hazard check to recognize this character's base plant ancestor. When stationary among similarly sized, dark green plants, however, this character can easily remain hidden.

## Moss

Among the many thousands of varieties of moss, of both pre-cataclysm and post-apocalyptic strains, those that have blended with human DNA are amongst the strangest. These man sized specimens are more like communities of moss than one living individual plant, and comprise many hundreds of tiny mobility roots that knot together to form legs at their base, a dark brown, trunk-like central section from which all other appendages and sensory organs are located, and a top mass of bright green or yellowish living moss. When wet, this moss can soak up to 20 times its volume in water. This fluid can be extracted by comrades of the 'mossoid' itself if forced to travel in arid conditions or endure long periods beneath the earth where little drinkable water can be found.

Few herbivores eat moss, while few humans have much use for this plantoid's top greenery except as passable roofing material. When hiding among mossy rocks, rubble or other debris, this character is virtually invisible unless it moves. However, when attempting to hide in areas without vegetation, or very different vegetation, such as grass or thorn bushes, its bright green, dome shaped top section can stand out.

## Mushroom

Plantoid mushrooms are derived from one of many popular old world strains. Each consists of a set of spongy leg-like roots, a stem — also called a 'stipe' — and a dome-like cap or 'pileus'. Beneath the cap, these mushroom-men have gills, which contain reproductive spore. Their 'face' sensory parts and any manipulator limbs or other mutations typically develop only on the stem.

While often growing quite huge, giant mushroom plantoid's are easy to identify, and understandably, subject to being harvested and roasted by humanoids. Herbivores which normally eat mushrooms, including squirrels, will sometimes infest the cap of these specimens, burrow into them and gnaw on the soft flesh whenever they are hungry. There is a 1 in 10 chance that this plantoid starts with an infestation of 1d6 squirrels which reduce the plantoid's endurance by 2 points per squirrel until eliminated at which point the depleted endurance will return (so record this depleted amount on your character sheet). The stats for normal squirrels are included with the description text for 'tree, evergreen' on page 135 of this book.

Mushrooms have pliable skin, are easy to hack into and thus receive no defense value bonus as noted on table XR-112, however, they have remarkable healing abilities because of their rapid growth and heal at twice the normal daily, endurance based, rate. **Roll 1d10** for the sort of mushroom this character is blended with:

**1,2. Button:** White, bulbous and once the most commonly grown agricultural variety. These specimens are highly prized by hungry humanoids.

**3. Crimini:** Also called baby bellas, these are another highly sought after food mushroom, with a tan or brown skin.

**4. Portabello:** With meaty flavor, these large, broad capped brown mushrooms are always sought after and a favorite of farmers, skullocks and goats, alike.

**5. Shiitake:** A favorite ingredient in Asian dishes, these long stemmed, tan or brown capped mushrooms have a tough cap, which is often diced up, dried and used long after the delicious stem is eaten.

**6. Chanterelle:** These odd, coral shaped mushrooms come in white, yellow or orange colors, have an earthy taste and are usually cooked up in a stew with plenty of spice instead of eaten raw. While farmers, herbalists, and cooks might know that a plantoid specimen has Chanterelle lineage, and seek to harvest the entire character for the next feast, many commoners might not realize that such a character is an eatable variety.

**7. Shaggy Mane:** A pale, white or cream colored mushroom with a tall, conical cap with peeling skin like, pattern on its exterior. These grow as wild mushrooms in both normal and giant mutant variants, as well as occur as plantoids from time to time.

**8. Bolete:** also refereed to as 'porcini mushrooms', these wild variants have a pale, thickly based, pylon shaped stalk and orange-brown cap. These mushrooms seem to attract insects and worm parasites, but are otherwise highly sought after and typically dehydrated by the peoples of the new era.

**9. Toxic Mushroom:** This plantoid mushroom has evolved from a poisonous mushroom. Sometimes mistaken for a wild eatable mushroom, a character derived from this mushroom is highly toxic and accordingly, any living creature to eat this specimen will suffer terrible abdominal pain after 6+1d6 hours, and is sickened and has a 50% chance of dying — eaters make a type E Willpower based hazard check to avoid death. Administering an anti-toxin injector has an 84% chance of saving this person.

Roll for the toxic mushroom type although they all have the same general, deadly outcome for those people and animals who eat them. **1d6: 1.** Death cap / **2.** Conocybe filaris / **3.** Deadly dapperling / **4.** Destroying angels / **5.** Autumn skullcap / **6.** Webcaps.

**10. Dart:** Based on the mushroom described on page 165 of The Mutant Epoch hub rules (plants), this plantoid character has a spike covered stem and cap and when annoyed, can fire 1d6 lethal darts each round, range 10 meters, strike value of each dart 01-50, damage 1d8 per dart. This plantoid will have a maximum of 24 ready and mature darts per day. As far as being desirable to eat, only the hungriest of humanoids or animals will go near this spike and knob covered shroom, but its flesh is eatable if not a little bitter.

## Oats

As a very popular agricultural cereal crop in the Epochian Era, an oat based hybrid human-plant is easily identified, especially in late summer when its mass of top oat grass becomes heavy with ripe oat florets and the crop is ready to harvest. At these times, a plantoid of this variety must either lop off all evidence of its food producing, mass of meter high foliage, or stay clear of human settlements, herbivores and hungry travelers on the road.

While an oat plant normally has only between one and three stem, each with several leaves, this plantoid has a mop of many dozens and when stationary and crouched down in the ground, can easily be mistaken for a grassy lump in the ground. The main body, limbs and sensory appendages of this plantoid are in a tightly woven, thick root stalk, while it moves about on a tangle of pale lower tendrils. Oat plantoids are hardy, built tough, and can endure cold weather far better than most plants, yet also cope with dry periods with remarkable ease.

## Onion

Just as there are dozens of varieties of domesticated onions grown by new era farmers, so too there are a wide range of plantoid onions. All have two or three meter high, hollow leaves which grow from its main bulb body. From this bulbous location extend any appendages and the entity's cluster of sensory organs. These globular bodied, round or spherical shaped plantoids move about on a skirt of white, leg-roots, which often cluster and knot together to form human-like legs.

It goes without saying, that like a garlic plantoid, this specimen is highly sought after by hungry people — although many herbivores will turn their nose up at an onion-man after the first bite. To hide their true heritage, many onion based plantoids will secure their bulb-body in thick clothing, armor and gear,

If chopped into or blasted, and this onion suffers 10 or more endurance damage, it will give off an irritant in a 3 meter radius. Living beings caught in this area for the next five minutes have a 50% chance of tearing up, and suffering a -5 DV penalty for 3 minutes (60 rounds) thereafter. This tearing reaction afflicts both friends and foes who have eyes and not wearing an enclosed face shield or helmet.

While there are many types of onions and veggie-sapien of this lineage, **roll 1d10** for the most common types: **1.** Chppolini / **2.** Pearl / **3.** Red / **4.** Scallion / **5.** Shallot / **6.** Walla Walla / **7,8.** White / **9,10.** Yellow.

## Pea plant

While there are several varieties of peas, such as snow and snap peas, this plantoid is most often a hybrid of the common green 'garden pea', plus a mix of human DNA. They have a woody stock as a main body from which its sensory growths and limbs sprout, while its legs are an elongated, tangled collection of yellowish roots and manipulator vines. Its top branches are leafy, pea-pod covered vines which can extend up to 3m in height. While this top foliage can't move, it is flexible and can be braided and tied back along the main trunk to better hide the true nature of this specimen, especially when entering human communities or when trying to keep a low profile and perhaps hide its massive, 30cm long pea pods from hungry herbivores and people.

They grow quite tall, if not pruned or their upper growing vines not tied back, and can reach an overall starting height of 4 meters. Each will produce 4d6 pea pods every 60 days, with each pod having 2d6 peas as large as chicken eggs that can be eaten cooked or raw and are always a welcome food stuff for comrades, or those who capture and restrain these specimens for ongoing food production.

Since this plantoid is based on a very popular and easily recognize food plant. It must take extra precautions to preserve its liberty, or its life.

It favors cooler climes, and does not do well during prolonged periods of heat or drought. Each will always have at least two (1d2+1) manipulator vines as noted previously on page 115 of this book.

## Pepper

Differing from plantoid's that are a hybrid of the hot pepper plant, described on page 126, this variant is sourced from the Bell Pepper and once every two weeks during the summer months will yields 2d6 mild, highly delicious and nutritious red, green or yellow peppers. These peppers are as big as a man's head, however, and when ripe will fetch 1d8 silver coins each if sold in a typical marketplace. Because this plantoid produces such colorful fruit, it is highly vulnerable to being kidnapped, caged, or chained up and kept by unscrupulous farmers and overlords alike to supply a steady supply of the remarkable, over sized peppers.

When not bearing fruit, or having cleverly plucked off all such evidence of its true heritage before being discovered, this leafy low-growing shrub can easily pass as just another bush among other dark green growths. They have a thick, woody midsection where their other appendages and sensory organs are situated, move about on a mass of various sized, pale roots, and have about 3d6 upper branches which bare a half dozen broad, green leaves of about 50cm in length.

## Poison Ivy

More related to a cashew plant than any sort of vine, these plants normally grow as low bushes and have a distinct leaf with three leaflets on each leaf stem. An old world saying 'leaves of three, let it be' is very true, especially in a world where giant variants of this weed can be found, including specimens that are both mobile and predatory. Plantoid variants have human DNA, and grow to three meters in height and have 3d6 upper, leafy branches, a woody trunk and powerful, gnarly roots which can cluster into spidery or human-like legs for locomotion.

Anything to roughly grab, or bite into or otherwise strike this plant's leaves with its bare skin, branches, or trunk are exposed to the sap of this plant. Exposure causes an allergic reaction in 75% of those exposed, while for those who are not exposed are thereafter considered immune to poison Ivy of all variants. Exposed subjects develop a terrible urushiol rash in the afflicted body part, and must make a type D endurance based hazard check or suffer swelling and blisters.

If the attacker bites into this plantoid, then the swelling is in the face and throat. This swelling shuts the eyes so much that the victim suffers a -20 strike value penalty. Far worse, however, the subject must make a second type D Willpower based hazard check or have their throat constrict and cause them to suffer an air intake loss. This loss reduces their movement to half and they feel they will suffocate

and die. Afflictions to the face last 4d6 minutes, while the rash last 4+1d8 days and can sometimes be mistaken for other ailments, plagues or even leprosy by the uneducated — which is most people in the Epochian Era.

This plantoid must be careful when touching other tools, door knob, cooking utensils and weapons, in order to avoid contaminating these items with its own toxin. To avoid harming comrades, this plantoid will typically wear gloves or layers of clothing to reduce the risk of unintentional exposure — exposure than can last for 1+1d4 days on objects coated in this sap.

While toxic to humans, and all human based creatures, except other plantoids, some herbivores such as deer, as well as bears can eat poison ivy leaves and suffer no ill effects. Bestial humans deer, bears and goats, therefore, can safely come into contact, and even nibble, on this character.

The administration of an anti-toxin-injector into a person suffering from poison ivy has an 84% chance of clearing up the painful rash or other allergic reactions.

## Poppy Plant

In some regions of the new era, opium poppies are grown and used in the production of potent, highly addictive narcotics. People involved in his trade, either as a grower, dealer or sometimes even the end user, will recognize this plantoid character as being derived from an opium plant, and might seek to seize and forcibly harvest the sap from cuts made in the unripe seed pods — a painful ordeal for the human DNA laced plant person.

A poppy plantoid will produce 1+1d4 seed pod stalks above its main trunk body, each spring. When in bloom, in the summer, each pod will produce massive red, white, yellow or purple flowers of particular magnificence, although showing off this half meter wide flower does nothing to aid the character's ability to hide.

When not avoiding those after it for its drug production capabilities, this plantoid makes for a stout, three meter tall entity with robust scalloped leaves and a firm, yet thin stalk. Its legs are formed by woven together, mobile roots, which are also fibrous and tough and add to this being's overall ruggedness.

Although the use of opium is addictive, a bio-technician can use it to make doses of opium for pain relief, with each seed pod able to yield 500g of opium resin per season, with a market value of 100sp per 500g (reminder: 1000 grams = 1 kg or kilogram, with 1 kilogram equal to about 2.2 pounds). Because of its addictive qualities, many communities outlaw the use of opium and will either confiscate any (and re-sell it themselves out the back door) or arrest and enslave those trafficking in the substance, or those who produce it, including any poppy plantoid.

## Potato

As a two meter tall, leafy green shrub that produces dozens of hanging, fist sized spuds, this plantoid easily gives away its plant heritage, and can elicit unwanted attention from hungry herbivores and people. Unlike a regular potato plant, this human DNA laced specimen doesn't need to plant its roots in the soil to grow potatoes, of which it will produce 3d6 each month — although it loves nothing more than to settle down into some cool, nutrient rich soil at the end of the day just as a human digger might want to soak in a hot bath.

Every month its upper branches will become dotted by small purple or white flowers as it blooms, and if such flowers are allowed to pollinate, each of the 4d6 flowers will turn into small, green seeds that are sometimes mistaken for green tomatoes. These seeds are inedible to humans and will sicken anyone who eats them, however, they make great seeds and each will produce a giant, non-mobile, non sentient new potato plant in the late spring.

Potato plantoids have thick, gnarled trunks where other limbs, crude eyes, auditory receptors and any rudimentary mouth are situated. Its roots are robust and knot together to form splendid leg-like growths.

## Pumpkin

Pumpkin plantoids can appear in one of two varieties. The most common is the broad leaved, thick stalked, vine entangled pumpkin plant. These grow low and broad and cover about a 3m radius, are dotted by 2d6 bright yellow flowers and is laden with 2d6 small, juvenile pumpkins and 1d6 orange, skull sized ripe pumpkins. The plantoid can pluck the ripe pumpkins and hurl them like large rocks, although instead of doing lethal damage, these shatter into a pulpy mess on contact and only do stun damage; pumpkin thrown: range 4m, SV +3, DMG 1d12 stun, plus any strength modifiers.

The second variety of plantoid pumpkin is called a Muto-Lantern and looks like something from a mad cartoonist's imagination. This freak has its limbs and sensory appendages attached to a great orange pumpkin with a wide gaping mouth. These oddities have a woody top trunk from which broad leaves extend and a mass of roots grow down from the huge heads to form gnarly legs beneath the ghastly Jack-o-lantern. This improbable miscreation does not exhibit smaller pumpkins, as its main body is an actual pumpkin — although its flesh is laced with trace human organs, muscles and nervous system connectors. Because it looks like a huge pumpkin, and is as wide as it is tall, It must avoid becoming a food supply for hungry villagers. When needed, it can drop low and cover the bulk of its bulbous orange ball-body with its massive leaves and try to hide. Of course, having a giant mouth that can grow to a meter in width and is filled with rows of quite human looking teeth, this pumpkin can adopt a somewhat carnivorous diet and turn the tables on humans when desired, its bite being a +5 strike value attack that inflicts 3d6 damage before any trait or skill modifiers are applied.

Even in a world where there is no shortage of strange, wonderful and horrific mutants and machines, the sight of a talking, animated giant pumpkin as big as a man is often sufficient to scare the bejesus out of commoners — at least until they muster themselves, get the idea that they could make a lot of pumpkin pies from a hundred kilogram pumpkin, and grab cleavers and pitchforks and come after the plantoid.

Roll 1d10 to determine the sort plantoid this character is:
**1-7.** Vine entangled/ **8-10.** Muto-lantern.

## Radish

Like a plantoid carrot, this being's consciousness, sensory parts, and limbs all extend from its globular central body. Vibrant green, leafy branches extend from its top while white roots stick out from the bottom of this tap-root-bodied freak. 80% of these specimens will be standard red and white radish, although the body part grows to about a meter in height and half a meter in diameter, while the other times, this specimen is either a pale, yellowish white daikon, also called a mooli, or even a horseradish. **Roll 1d10: 1-8:** Regular red radish./ **9.** Daikion Radish./ **10.** Horseradish.

Any radish is a welcome addition to the diets of humanoids and herbivores, and this veggie-sapien would do well to wrap its torso in thick clothing or armor to conceal its tasty, somewhat spicy body.

## Reed

Related to the common marsh reeds, or Typhaceae, and sometimes called cattails, these lanky, stick-like plantoids do well in swampy areas, and, unless geared up in arms and armor, can easily step into a patch of regular reeds and vanish with ease.

They grow to about 4 meters in height, have a thick main body trunk which splits off into 3d6 leaves and 2d6 stocks which feature cattails tipped with large, brown seed heads.

Like nearly every other plantoid strains, their main trunk is where their consciousness, sensory organs and any extra limbs are situated, while they move about on a mass of various sized pale roots.

Although many villagers use reeds for bedding and thatched roofs, few people, or even animals, eat the foliage or stalks of these plants — although in lean times, all bets are off.

These plantoid characters float if thrown into water, unless burdened in heavy gear or metal armor.

## Rhubarb

In agricultural communities, or where the plant has grown wild since the civilizational collapse of the old ones, rhubarb plants are a common sight, and so a walking, talking, 2 or 3 meter tall specimen is readily recognized for what it is. In short, people will see the top growing stalks of any passing rhubarb plantoid and surely get the idea to grab their garden knives, and friends, and accost and trim the upper half of this character to make pies, crisps and other baked goods with the bounty.

Rhubarb leaves are poisonous, especially if eaten in large quantities when mistaken for salad greens. Anyone to eat a 500g or larger portion of the leaves must make an endurance based type D hazard check or grow deathly ill and develop kidney stones which have a 72% likelihood of requiring a risky, expensive surgery to remove (see the medics skill on page TME-46, and use the odds of success as if this procedure was 'Extract Venom' at a cost of 100+1d100sp if a freelance medic must be hired.

This character's main body and sensory appendages are in the lower half where a great bulbous knot sits above its extensive tangle of locomotion roots. When hiding among other broad leaved shrubs and vegetation, this plantoid can crouch low, remain still and easily go unnoticed by passing predators. Herbivores, for the most part, will not eat rhubarb leaves, although goats might eat a little, and suffer for it later, yet still inflict injury to the plantoid in the process.

While it hurts the character to have stalks of its rhubarb cut off, sometimes this is a small price to pay to bribe authorities, feed comrades, or sell its ripe stalks in a marketplace to secure some other resource. A rhubarb plantoid will have 4d6 ripe stalks ready to eat every two weeks during warm weather, the rest of the year they are woody and too bitter to eat. These stalks are about as long as a man's arm and will sell for a silver piece each.

## Rice

Like several other lanky, skinny plantoids, a hybrid between a common rice plant and human DNA produces a stick man-like entity with its face and limbs at the lower third where a woody stock forms. Its legs consist of a skirt of pale green, tightly braided leg-roots, while its upper leaves grow into grass-like blades and tall, seed laden stalks which are lined by hundreds of grains of rice. Once every two months this plantoid can produce enough brown rice to fill a 2kg sack, which if sold in a typical barter market will fetch 10+1d10sp, or more during times of starvation.

Rice is still grown in the new era, but because cultivating it is water and labor intensive, it isn't very common. Still, farmers and local officials might recognize this character's rice plant heritage, and seize it to either lop off any rice laden top stalks, or enslave the individual and force it into agricultural servitude.

Rice plantoids can grow quite tall, yet when hiding among bunch grass or other mixed vegetation, they can blend in well so long as they aren't dressed like some wasteland warrior.

If desired, the player can determine the type of rice this plantoid produces, roll 1d12: **1,2.** Jasmine / **3.** Sushi / **4.** Wild /**5,6.** Basmati / **7.** Black / **8.** Red Cargo / **9.** Arborio / **10.** Sticky / **11.** Long grain / **12.** Calrose.

## Rose Bush

When in bloom, which happens in late spring and carries through the entire summer, a plantoid rose bush is a magnificent and hard to conceal being. In the fall and winter months, however, it can easily pass as just another thorn covered, leafy shrub, and easily conceal itself among other vegetation. Besides its remarkable flowers, these plantoids also produce rose hips in the fall, which are both eatable and rich in vitamin C. Many humanoids make tea, jams, jellies and dried fruit from other, non sentient rose hips, and so when they see a two or three meter tall plantoid of this linage, and the 6d6 huge, apricot sized rose hips growing from its upper branches, they might be tempted to accost the character and pluck off the fruit or capture the plantoid for later production.

Rose bushes have a thick, woody trunk from which all manipulator limbs and other sensory parts and appendages grow, although several lower, vines work in unison with its tangle of roots to knot into legs to propel it along the ground. A full half of this plantoid's size is in its upper branches, which do not articulate.

While they might look pretty when in full bloom with 10+3d6 flowers, these plantoids are covered in nasty, cruelly hooked thorns which give it an increase in defense value of -12, while any attack it does in with a physical appendage will rake a living target and inflict an extra +3 damage.

**Roll 1d12** for the flower color produced by this plantoid's roses: **1.** Different each season, (roll 1d10+1) / **2.** red /**3.** pink / **4.** white / **5.** purple / **6.** orange / **7.** lavender / **8.** baby blue / **9.** dark red /**10.** Ivory / **11.** peach / **12.** black.

## Sagebrush

Derived from the most common variety of sagebrush, the Artemisia Tridentata, this woody, rugged shrub has no problem hiding among naturally growing or large mutant strains in the Western regions of North American. Tough, and resistant to both extremes of hot and cold, as well as drought resistant, this specimen is truly one of the most robust post-apocalyptic plantoid strains on the scene. They grow to a height of three meters at the most, spread broad, pale green leafy branches over their main, appendage and sensory organ encrusted main trunks, and scuttle about on gnarly, rough looking root-legs.

Because they are so tough, they start off with a considerable endurance and defense value bonus as noted on table XR-112 on page 121 of this book.

Few herbivores, except goats, will eat these plants, which are considered a weed and often eradicated by farmers wishing to convert sagebrush covered land into more productive grain fields or garden areas. There is a 2 in 10 chance this plantoid is actually a tumbleweed with same stats, however, it will also have the additional, bonus plantoid mutation of Tumbling Locomotion as described on page 322 of this book.

## Soy Bean

In the old world, with the eating of animal proteins almost exclusively reserved for the rich or politically connected elites, the consumption of soy-based foods was commonplace, if not mandated. Hundreds of strains were genetically engineered to grow in the harshest and most toxic of conditions, including in orbital communities, off world outposts and in the legendary mother-ships sent to colonize far-off star systems.

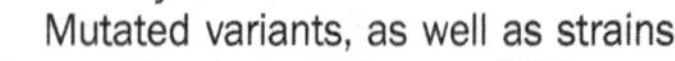

Mutated variants, as well as strains that were blended with human DNA were also developed, and from these developed the line of soy bush plantoids. These shrubs have tough stalks, large, dark green teardrop shaped leaves and produce a great many seed pods every few months. At any given time a soy plantoid will have 6d6 ripe seedpods ready to harvest, and twice as many growing that will be ready in a month.

In warm months, this character's mass of leafy, pod heavy branches will be dotted by small, vivid purple flowers, which attract pollinators of every sort and might make the plantoid stand out among other, more drab vegetation. Soy beans must be cooked in water to feed humans, otherwise they are toxic and will cause the eater or to make a type D endurance based hazard check or become debilitated and inoperative for 3d6 days.

As soy beans were once so widely grown, there are stretches of wild land in formerly agricultural areas that are now covered in mutated strains of these plants, but so too, new era farmers commonly grow these plants and so will recognize a plantoid-soy hybrid, and if they cannot trade for the ripe bounty of seed pods hanging from a visiting soy plantoid, they might resort to force to either steal the pods or detain the plantoid to ensure ongoing food supply.

Many herbivores, especially goats and deer, will attack and try to devour the whole soy plantoid.

## Spinach

Although having the look of a thick, broad leafed, dark green shrub, this low growing plantoid's top stems and bounty of foliage are highly prized by both herbivores and people. Farmers will always recognize that this veggie-sapien is a hybrid of the popular food crop, and depending on their level of hunger, and the comrades and armament of this plant-person, might try to accost and either consume the plantoid or, restrain it for continued agricultural slavery, or simply hold it down and clip off all its eatable leaves and depart.

Spinach based plantoids move about on dozens of small, pale root legs, have a squat, thick primary stock that serves as their torso, head, and anchor for any limbs and appendages. Their upper half is all spinach stalks and broad leaves. When standing among similar colored, leafy foliage, this entity can hide with remarkable ease.

## Squash

This hybrid human-gourd of the Cucurbita family of plants is very much like a plantoid pumpkin in that it can occur both as a thick, woody root with a mass of lower locomotion vines and 3d6, squash and leaf laden vines, or, 1 in 6 chance, that the entity is a giant squash fruit, with its eyes, huge mouth, other sensory and manipulator appendages all growing from this globular, often oddly shaped main mass.

In the latter case, its foliage grows from its top-stalk, while thick, coiling roots grow beneath its main mass to propel it along. Greedy humans and herbivores will readily go after and try to either harvest any squash that are visible (4d6 at any given month), or attempt to kill and bake a squash headed oddity. Covering itself in its broad leaves, clothing and armor is often necessary for this plantoid to enter human settled areas, and like a pumpkin based being, relies heavily on the protection of human comrades to defend it from the hungry.

A giant squash head specimen's mouth is huge and capable of biting in melee as an extra attack with a strike value bonus of +5, inflicting 3d6 damage.

## Stinging Nettle

The leaves, stems and thick, fibrous stock of this plantoid are covered in tiny, needle-like hairs called trichomes. Any living creature to grab, brush against, hug, climb or accost this entity are potentially exposed to hundreds of these tiny spines which inject histamine into the tissues of the toucher, causing inflammation to the afflicted area, and great pain.

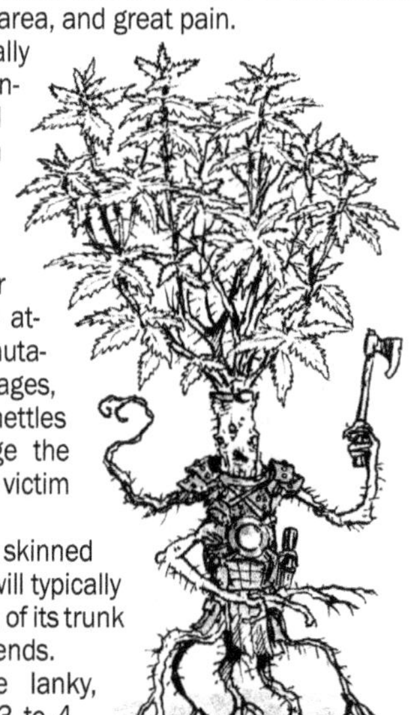

Contact by bare flesh, especially the mouth of an animal to hit this plantoid, automatically causes a painful sting. This forces the afflicted person or beast to make a morale check to continue harassing this plantoid (morale checks are covered on page 110 of the TME Hub Rules with a willpower based hazard check required by the attacker). If this plantoid has other mutations that add more limbs or appendages, these parts are also covered in these nettles and besides whatever main damage the limb might do on a successful hit, the victim also suffers the sting.

When in close quarters with soft skinned humanoid companions, this plantoid will typically wear plenty of thick clothing over much of its trunk and lower limbs to avoid hurting its friends.

Stinging nettle plantoids are lanky, have a central stock and can grow 3 to 4 meters tall, feature large triangular leaves. They also grow a conical top which is often encrusted in small, brownish yellow flowers and seeds. These specimens move about on a tangle of pale green walking roots, have their sensory organs and auxiliary limbs at their lower section and with the top half of the entire plant being the leafy upper stalk. Some humanoids and herbalist know that these plants, including this hybrid animated variant, can be cooked and eaten, with the boiling process removing the harsh chemicals in the plant's prickles and softening the entire plant for easy consumption.

Few creatures, including goats, will bother with this plantoid. Furthermore, the base plant, and tree sized, stationary mutant variants, are common throughout the new era and this plantoid can easily vanish among these cousins, or hide itself among similarly, leafy shrubs to conceal itself.

## Strawberry Plant

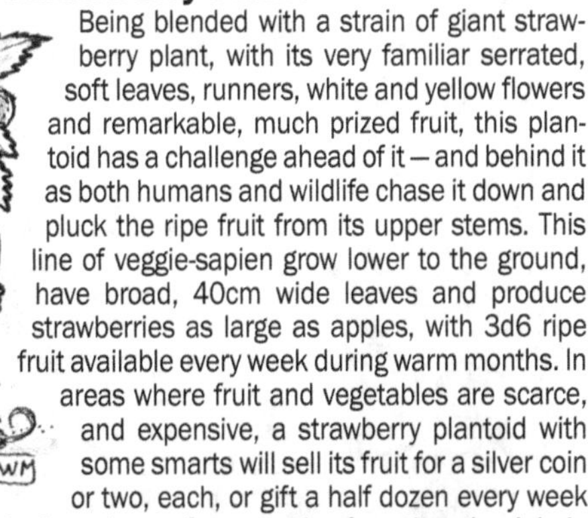

Being blended with a strain of giant strawberry plant, with its very familiar serrated, soft leaves, runners, white and yellow flowers and remarkable, much prized fruit, this plantoid has a challenge ahead of it — and behind it as both humans and wildlife chase it down and pluck the ripe fruit from its upper stems. This line of veggie-sapien grow lower to the ground, have broad, 40cm wide leaves and produce strawberries as large as apples, with 3d6 ripe fruit available every week during warm months. In areas where fruit and vegetables are scarce, and expensive, a strawberry plantoid with some smarts will sell its fruit for a silver coin or two, each, or gift a half dozen every week to the local warlord or leader in exchange for protection from the other inhabitants. Failing that, a strawberry plantoid must rely on either concealing its nature by removing all fruit before entering a community, or relying on the firepower and fierce nature of its traveling companions to protect it.

These plantoids have long roots and 2d4 flexible runners which it uses to pull itself along the ground. They exhibit their sensory organs and extra appendages in a thick, trunk-like main stalk which is shaded by dozens of broad leaves and hanging fruit in various states of ripeness.

## Sunflower

Based on the common sunflower, this plantoid starts at about two meters in height but will grow rapidly at 40cm per year and easily exceed four or five meters in height. Its face, limbs and other sensory organs are concentrated in the lower half at a bulge in the pulpy, tough skinned stem or trunk. These specimens will exhibit a wreath of crawling roots and tendrils at their base, which it will often weave into remarkably human-looking legs. At its summit, meanwhile it will have either one large, or 2d4 small sunflower heads (roll 1d6: 1. 2d4 small heads/ 2-6. 1 large flower head).

These heads bloom once a year in midsummer and will remain vibrant, seed laden and impressive until early fall, and attract birds, bees and both omnivores and herbivores from a quarter kilometer away if they can see the bright yellow flower moving across the landscape.

Predators, too, can be alerted to the plantoid and its companions by seeing this massive flower, and while it might make sense of the plantoid or its friends to chop off the flower, this is severally painful for the plantoid in question, both physically and to its sense of identity and pride. A clever dig teams with a sunflower plantoid in their ranks will know to throw a burlap sack over the flower when it is in bloom.

The hundreds of seeds from each ripe sunflower head will produce magnificent, non-sentient sunflowers, some of which can grow 6 meters tall and have heads measuring a meter across and weighing 20 kilograms — a bounty of food for farmers. Indeed, hungry human populations to observe a magnificent, animated sunflower enter their village might be tempted to either capture and enslave the plantoid, or take a scythe and hack off the flower head and run off with their misbegotten bounty of nutritious, oil rich seed.

## Swiss Chard

Bio-engineered from a popular leafy vegetable, a chard-plantoid specimen has a fifty percent chance either being greenish yellow or red stalked. In both cases, the veggie-sapien exhibits a dense lower core with pale root-legs beneath this main trunk where its limbs and sensory organs are situated, and the upper 75% of the entity being the nutritious, somewhat rippled leaves. They grow to about two meters in height for their first few years of life, and thereafter, up to three meters.

While farmers, cooks and vegetable traders will easily recognize this plantoid's heritage, others might dismiss this being as just another bush, especially if it is stationary, and crouched down among other leafy forest or swamp vegetation.

While removing its nutritious leaves is painful, this plantoid can offer about a half dozen every week to help feed comrades or fetch some spending money, with each meter long, 35cm wide leaf fetching a silver coin in a typical new era market.

## Tea Plant

Both traditional and mutated varieties of tea plants exist throughout the warm regions of the Epochian Era world, many of which are cultivated by dedicated farmers and herbalists. Plantoid specimens of this tree-like shrub will only be recognized by somebody with experience in growing regular variants, while others will simply assume this stout, little evergreen tree is simply a non-fruit bearing specimen, and of no apparent use as a captive or source of food.

Plantoid tea plants, which are a blend of human DNA and the Camellia Sinensis — which is the true name for a tea plant — grow to two meters in their first few years of life and thereafter reach about three or four meters. They are long lived shrubs, who will often voluntarily give up some of their tender green leaves to allow companions to make a pot of tea, or sell their leaves at a price of 1 silver coin per ten leaves. A tea plant will have 6d6 tea leaves ready for harvesting each week.

While regular tea trees are thin, these plantoid specimens have thick lower trunks where their sensory growths and other appendages are situated, and a robust root system to propel them about.

## Thistle

With its trace human DNA mixed with that of the common thistle (Cirsium), this tall, prickle covered flowering plant is easily identified by its thorny leaves, stalks and trunk, as well as the distinct, usually purple flowers which grow from its upper reaches. The inch long spines on this plantoid give it a defense value bonus of -11, plus anything to grab or bite into this oddity will simultaneously be attacked (strike value 01-70 for 1d6 damage).

Most herbivores will need to make a morale based hazard check to continue feeding on this plantoid, and while other creatures will only continue engaging if they are defending their young or lair, and instead turn their attention to another target or deploy any missile attack, such as hurling rubble, etc. If this plantoid wears a lot of thick clothing and armor, the chance that an attacker hits the plantoid in a thorn covered section is reduced to 50% odds.

Thistle plantoids, when in bloom in the spring and summer months, will attract hummingbirds, butterflies and all manner of bee including giant specimens that might be dangerous to the thistle's humanoid companions. Their eyes, auditory ports, and any mouth or nostril-like growths and other appendages are contained to the lower half of the thick, woody stalk. The roots of a thistle-plantoid are a half meter long and tangle and weave together to form powerful legs. Normally, these specimens will have 2d6 flowers during the summer and fall, which are the size of a human hand and easily spotted from hundreds of meters away.

## Tobacco

Smoking pipes, cigars, and hand-rolled cigarettes has made a resurgence in the post-apocalyptic new era, and its use is often associated with those in power, wealth, or exhibiting confidence and a haughty air of dominance. Because there is never enough food especially near the few emerging Epochian Era slum cities, the notion of growing a crop that can't go toward feeding people is typically rejected, and the growth and use of tobacco seen as a luxury item.

Because its use is rare even among those who can afford it, the health hazards of smoking aren't as pronounced as in earlier historical times. Still, most farmers will recognize tobacco leaves when they see them, and if a two or three meter tall walking tobacco bush enters a human community, there will always be a few keen eyed growers who will recognize the 6d6 huge, 30cm long leaves that grow from the upper half of this plantoid character, and might plot to accost and the newcomer and lop off the leaves.

A tobacco plantoid's articulating limbs and sensory organs are concentrated in the bottom half of its thick, fibrous trunk, while the wide root system forms into several legs and the upper half taken up by a mass of tobacco leaves and a few small greenish-yellow flowers. Each of the ripe leaves in this plantoid's upper canopy can be snipped off and will sell for 1 half a silver piece or 1sp for each 2 leaves, with 6d6 ready leaves every two weeks during warm weather.

## Tomato

This plantoid is blended with human DNA and a strain of a common agricultural tomato plant. While its main stalk is thick, fibrous and bears its sensory organs and articulating appendages, and its intricate root system supports its mass on several tangled legs, the upper branches are often covered in small yellow flowers, dozens of unripe tomatoes and many ripe fruit. Once per week in the summer months, this plantoid will yield 1d6 ripe tomatoes per branch, and have 1d4 branches, plus one per rank (so a 1st rank PC would start with 1d4+1, and gain another branch each rank thereafter).

Plantoid tomatoes are especially easy to identify by most humans, and many savage races, too. Because of their distinctive flowers and bountiful red, purple or yellow fruit, this easy to spot and highly prized plantoid must be extra careful when entering unfamiliar communities, and rely on human and other companions to protect them from livestock and hungry citizens, alike.

**Roll 1d20** to determine the type of tomato this plantoid produces:

| | |
|---|---|
| **1-3.** | Roma |
| **4-7.** | Beefstake |
| **8.** | Blondkopfchen (German for 'little blonde girl') |
| **9.** | Better Boy |
| **10.** | Cherokee Purple |
| **11.** | Dixie Golden Giant |
| **12.** | Early Girl |
| **13,14.** | Cherry |
| **15.** | Grape |
| **16,17.** | Heirloom |
| **18.** | Celebrity |
| **19.** | Plum |
| **20.** | Variety, different type on each branch. |

## Tree, Birch

Related to the rather short lived, Silver or Paper Bark Birch tree of the northern hemisphere, these plantoids have easily identifiable white bark marked by blackish streaks, with the bark often peeling off in spots. As a plantoid, they do not grow as tall as many other trees, but do grow fast and start at about 2meters in height and grow a half meter per year up to about 6 meters in heights.

As these are deciduous trees, their leaves turn a remarkable yellow in the fall and drop off late fall and do not grow again until early spring.

People who live in the wilderness will often uses birch bark to make canoes, footwear, and baskets among dozens of other items, and might be tempted to skin this plantoid to get at its versatile bark. As with all tree plantoids, they move about on powerful roots, have their sensory and articulating appendages in their thick trunk areas, and a mass of branches and foliage high above their main body.

## Tree, Chestnut

Related to the American or European Chestnut tree, which can grow thirty to sixty meters tall, this strain of human DNA laced chestnut starts out much smaller at under two meters, but grows 30cm every year to a height of 15 meters thereafter so long as it isn't pruned back by combat and loses its top branches. These robust treeoids have thick, reddish brown bark and exhibit most of their mobile appendages, eyes, mouth and other sensory adaptations located on one side of their upper trunk. They move about on powerful roots, and their oval leaves grow high toward the sun.

These trees will produce catkins in late spring, which is its flowers. If pollinated by either close proximity to another chestnut tree-specimen, including another plantoid of this line, or by bees and other pollinating creatures, then fruit will develop in mid-summer. This fruit forms into bright green, spine covered balls called burs, which turn yellowish brown in the fall, and usually drop from the tree during strong winds. These nuts can be harvested and roasted and offer a rich supply of vitamin-C and carbohydrates. Each fall, a chestnut tree can produce 2d10 chestnuts per year of its age. A bag of 50 chestnuts will fetch 5 silver pieces in a typical farmer's market.

## Tree, Cottonwood

While there were dozens of sub-species of these trees in the old world, with some growing as shrubs and others as truly massive trees, in the Epochian Era however, there are thousands of strains, including those that are mixed with human DNA. These oddities have either been engineered by bio-technician or evolved in corrupted nature to form plantoid specimens. These trees start out as about two meter tall entities and grow a half a meter per year thereafter to a maximum of 12 meters. They are deciduous trees that favor the shorelines of rivers and lakes. In the fall, fertilized specimens produce catkins which releases clouds of seed laden, lace-like, feathery tufts during gusts of wind.

As cottonwood trees are common near watery areas or damp lowlands, this treeoid can shed any gear and weaponry, remain still, and easily vanish among stands of regular or lightly mutated members of the species.

## Tree, Evergreen

There are hundreds of species of pine, fir, cedar and other evergreen trees, so too appear a wide range of related plantoid specimens, some short and more like shrubs, others lanky that tower over human companions. In every case, these evergreens have scaly, dense bark, gnarly leg-roots, a long torso that serves as the treeoid's trunk, and numerous upper branches with either pine needles and pine cones, or fine, deep green leaf structures and seeds high above. All sensory organs and articulating, movable appendages grow lower down on the trunk at about face-to-face level with regular humans, although as these trees age, their face enlarges and grows higher on the trunk. Most evergreen trees start out at over two meters in height, and grow 25cm every year to a staggering eventual height of twenty meters tall.

Pine tree variants of evergreens will produce 1d6 pine cones per year of its life among its branches at any given time, and replace these after two months. Indeed, squirrels will actively invade a treeoid's upper limits to tear into the pine cones, gnaw them down and eat the seed within — the rodent sometimes making a nest high in the branches and be hard to get rid of. A squirrel that nests in a treeoid's branches will be highly protective of its tree and will make an agitated alarm cry when predators approach within 30 meters, sometimes giving away the plantoid's position, but sometimes forewarning a dig team of approaching trouble and thus saving them, too.

Squirrel bestial humans are quite small, as far as humanoids go, and will always enjoy hitching a ride on a pine tree, or any evergreen plantoid, and the pair most likely forming a symbiotic relationship. Various squirrels can be found on page 113 of the Mutant Bestiary One, with the stats for a normal squirrel copied here for quick access:

**Squirrel, Normal:** DV -4/ END 1d3 / Move 9m/ Init: normal/ SV 01-29/ DMG 1pt/ EFs 3/ Morale Poor/ Size 30cm long.

Game masters might be asked by players what species their evergreen tree character is related to. While the following random table offers a name of a common species, the player should be encouraged to do a little research into this species to get a better idea of what their PC looks like. In addition, each of these has a different starting height that differs from the generic Evergreen tree as listed on table XR-112, on page 121.

| 1d100 | Common Evergreen Tree Parent Species |
|---|---|
| 01-03. | Bishop Pine 120+1d100cm |
| 04-06. | Black Pine 100+1d100cm |
| 07-09. | Bull Pine 160+1d100cm |
| 10-19. | Cedar Tree 110+1d100cm |
| 20,21. | Coulter Pine 120+1d100cm |
| 22-25. | Cypress Tree, 100+1d100cm |
| 26-42 | Fir Tree 130+1d100cm |
| 43,44. | Gray Pine 100+1d100cm |
| 45-48. | Hemlock Tree 140+1d100cm |
| 49-55. | Jack Pine 100+1d100cm |
| 56-58. | Jeffrey Pine (aka Yellow Pine) 150+1d100cm |
| 59-61. | Limber Pine 100+1d100cm |
| 62-68. | Lodgepole Pine (aka Tamarack Pine) 140+1d100cm |
| 69-71. | Longleaf Pine 160+1d100cm |
| 72-74. | Mexican Weeping Pine 100+1d100cm |
| 75-78. | Monterey Pine 150+1d100cm |
| 79-81. | Nut Pine 90+1d100cm |
| 82-85. | Ponderosa Pine 200+1d100cm |
| 86,87. | Red Pine 100+1d100cm |
| 88-90. | Redwood Tree 200+1d100cm |
| 91,92. | Scots Pine 100+d100cm |
| 93-95 | Spruce Tree 100+1d100cm |
| 96,97. | Sugar Pine 150+1d100cm |
| 98-00. | Western White Pine 150+1d100cm |

## Tree, Fruit

A plantoid of this lineage might instead be a nut tree, as is the case with walnut and almond trees, and so not technically a fruit tree at all. Most, however are genetically blended with a small, flower and fruit bearing tree, and highly prized by traveling companions and ever hungry humanoids and animals wherever this character goes. In the spring, this treeoid will produce dozens if not hundreds of small flowers, which if these are given access to pollinators such as bees, hummingbirds and moths, will eventually turn into fruit. Some fruit, such as cherries become ripe in early summer, others, like apricots and peaches, are ready in late summer, while pears, apples and plums are ready to eat in the fall. In whatever season this treeoid's harvest becomes ripe, it will provide 2 kilograms per year of its age, with each kilogram able to sell for 1sp in a typical town market, although many times more in remote wasteland forts or places where thirst, starvation and a lack of agriculture are the norm.

Like so many plantoids which produce a highly visible, easily recognized bounty of food, a fruit tree based individual has a tough time hiding among plain vegetation, and when entering a community, is wise to either cover up its fruit or nuts, or have it all plucked off before it can be seen. Plucking unripe fruit hurts this plantoid, but causes no actual damage. A fruit tree will start at just under two meters and grow 15cm per year to a maximum height of 7 meters. Roll below to determine the sort of fruit or nut tree this plantoid is based on:

| 1d100 | Plantoid's Fruit Tree Parent Species |
|---|---|
| 01-04. | Almond |
| 05-17. | Apple |
| 18-21. | Apricot |
| 22,23. | Avocado |
| 24,25. | Cashew |
| 26-33. | Cherry |
| 34,35. | Fig |
| 36-38. | Grapefruit |
| 39,40. | Guava |
| 41-45. | Lemon |
| 46-49. | Lime |
| 50-52. | Mango |
| 53-55. | Nectarine |
| 56-63. | Olive |
| 64-73. | Orange |
| 74-79. | Peach |
| 80-83. | Pear |
| 84,85. | Pecan |
| 86-92. | Plum |
| 93,94. | Pomegranate |
| 95-97. | Walnut |
| 98-00. | Hybrid* |

*This tree has 1d6 varieties of fruit, each growing from a separate branch and often ripening at different times of the year. Roll on the above listing, but re-roll duplicated results including this one.*

## Tree, Maple

These plantoids come from medium-sized, deciduous trees and are known for their remarkable, multilobed leaves which turn bright red in the autumn prior to falling off for the winter. These mutants also produce blade-like seedpods which drop off and take to the wind as whirlybirds, and spin to the ground many meters, or even kilometers away to sprout new trees.

While there are dozens of smaller, ornamental and non syrup producing varieties of maple trees and shrubs, this tree is evolved from Acer saccharum or sugar maple, and so yields maple syrup when tapped or bled out, which the plantoid can endure to a certain degree without being harmed too greatly. Maple syrup from a tree that has human DNA is a bit more red than usual, but tastes just as sweet as the regular, highly prized substance. A liter can be bled from this character per day which will inflict 1d6 endurance damage to it, with the maximum maple syrup content in the plantoid equal to its maximum endurance value. It takes an hour to drain a liter per tap, and the insertion of the metal plug causes 2d6 damage initially but if left in for the enjoyment of human companions, causes no further damage other than the 1d6 endurance drop per liter previously mentioned.

Of course, a maple tree plantoid will be on guard against being taken captive and forcibly used to provide villagers with a steady supply of syrup, and once identified, or its source of syrup known, must rely on its fighting prowess, speed, or companions to keep it safe.

Like all tree plantoids, their upper branches are full of leaves and inanimate, while any articulating limbs and sensory organs are located on its thick lower trunk. These treeoids move about on a collection of various sized flexible locomotion roots, and if not clad in clothing, gear and weaponry, can easily hide among other, similarly leafy trees.

Maple trees grow fast, and while they start at under two meters, grow 30cm per year to a height of 12 meters.

## Tree, Oak

These plantoids are related to the mighty oak tree, although there are hundreds of unmutated and deviant strains, some no larger than shrubs. This variety is derived from the species which grow huge, live for centuries, and produce acorns. As a post-apocalyptic entity, these plantoids are tough barked, start at about two meters in height and grow 25cm per year to a maximum height of 14 meters. They begin with increases in many physical traits, including their defense value and endurance.

Because these treeoids are monoecious, meaning they can produce both flowers and catkins, they can always produce acorn nuts even when no other oak tree is accessible. An oak tree plantoid will produce 1d20 acorns per year of its life, and so for example, a 5 year old starting oak tree will make 5d20, and a 12 year old will grow 12d20, etc. Two dozen acorns will sell for a silver coin, with only one harvest in the fall grown per year.

Because oak trees are a common sight near many agricultural towns in prosperous regions, most commoners won't risk a fight to capture or kill an oak plantoid, and instead try to barter for ripe acorns whenever possible.

## Tree, Palm

A plantoid of this strain has human DNA mixed with one of three common palm trees from the old world — although in all these cases the palm species was genetically modified to endure colder climes, drought, pollution and disease. All palm plantoids have hundreds of tiny roots at their base which propel it along, an elongated, fire resistant trunk that makes up 75% of the plantoid's total height, while at the top, a skirt of dead leaves and its broad, living fronds. 'Palmoids' who have their trunk attacked by fire, suffer only half damage from any flame attacks, and if their top fronds are burnt off, they will grow back in 1d4 months.

There are three types of plantoid palm trees so roll 1d10 to determine which this plantoid player character is based on: 1d10: 1-6 California fan palm /7.8. Coconut palm / 9,10. Date palm.

Most palm plantoids are related to the common California fan palm (Washingtonia filifera), which does not produce an immediately obvious eatable resource, and were mostly grown for ornamental and landscaping purposes.

The other two varieties of palm tree plantoids are coconut palms and date palms, both of which cannot survive for longer than 12 hours in climes of -10c (14F) or lower, while a California based palm can survive for 48 hours under these conditions.

Coconut palm based plantoids are usually only ever seen in tropical parts of the world, but migrate north or cope with cold weather using solar powered electric blankets, vests and other attire. Their highly prized coconuts weight 1.4kg and can be plucked by the plantoid or its companions if they can reach them, and either sold for 4sp each, eaten, or hurled like large rocks. A plantoid of this lineage will have 2d6 immature coconuts and 1d6 ripe, full sized nuts available for throwing or eating, per month. Another 3d6 small, immature coconuts also grow among its upper fronds, which take a year to mature.

Date palm plantoids are related to the Phoenix Dactylifera species, which were once widely grown for agricultural purposes. The fruit of these trees form as clustered red or yellow, elongated berries beneath the fronds, and for a plantoid specimen, offers ripe fruit about once a month totaling 1kg of dates per year of age of this plantoid, which can live up to a hundred years if not killed before it dies of old age. One kilogram of dates will sell for 10 silver pieces, or twice that in remote regions where food is in short supply.

Both coconuts and dates are highly prized by the hungry inhabitants of the new era, and since palm trees — especially walking ones with limbs, the ability to communicate and move — are easy to notice when not surrounded by non-sentient, non moving palm trees, these characters must rely on their quick wits, weaponry and loyal companions to avoid being accosted.

In every case, the bark, timber and long, sword like fronds of their leaves are valuable, and even so a Californian strain must be ever vigilant when approaching a human settlement.

All palm plantoids start at about 3 meters in height and grow 25 centimeters further per year of life. Table XR-112 up on page 121 shows the starting age and other stat modifiers of these beings.

## Tree, Poplar

Related to the cottonwood tree, this plantoid is based on the trees of the Populus line, and also includes the assorted aspen trees. As a plantoid, this smooth barked, lanky deciduous tree is rather unremarkable, and can easily go unsee among both normal and mutated stands of its parent trees in forests, along lakes and rivers and in overgrown shadows of ancient streets, ruin shells and alleys.

Because this tree's wood isn't as desirable as most evergreens, nor does it bear fruit, nuts or much that is useful to a human community — other than as firewood — these plantoids can more easily enter settlements and go unmolested therein. They are thin and wispy when young, but grow rapidly and add 40 centimeters to their height each year to a maximum of 7m tall.

## Tree, Weeping Willow

Weeping willow trees grow wild throughout the northern hemisphere, and are especially prevalent near where old suburbs and parks once existed — the offspring of both unaltered and mutated specimens growing thick among the shadows of crumbling ruined towers, their roots clogging old sewer systems, subway lines and buried shopping malls. Mindless, carnivorous species, including the mobilamortus tree, are included among these variants (see pages 84-85 of Mutant Bestiary One).

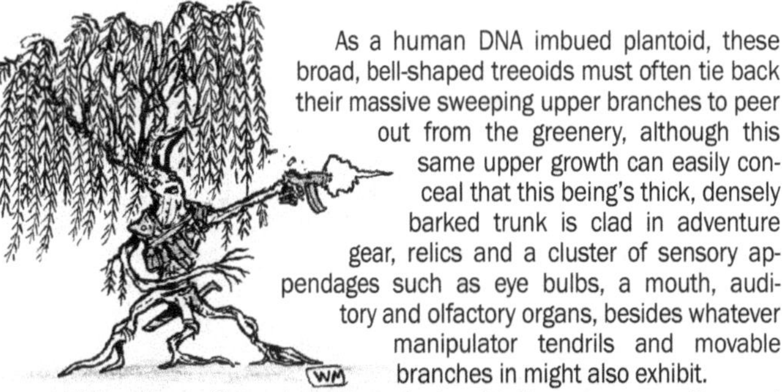

As a human DNA imbued plantoid, these broad, bell-shaped treeoids must often tie back their massive sweeping upper branches to peer out from the greenery, although this same upper growth can easily conceal that this being's thick, densely barked trunk is clad in adventure gear, relics and a cluster of sensory appendages such as eye bulbs, a mouth, auditory and olfactory organs, besides whatever manipulator tendrils and movable branches in might also exhibit.

W e e p i n g willows plantoids prefer humid climes, warm weather, and rich, soil, but can travel into almost any other terrain for weeks at a time without suffering too severely. Although deer, moose, cattle and goats will eat their leafy branches when these limbs hang low, most creatures, and humans in particular, have little use for weeping willow trees. The exception to this is when people desire shade or possibly firewood, and so 'weepers' can more easily pass through a community without too much trouble so long as the residents are already familiar with such strange beings. Of course, a weeping willow plantoid can easily hide among normal specimens of this tree type, but also hide among other shrubs and densely growing vegetation when needed.

Weeping willow plantoids do not grow as tall as other treeoids, nor live near as long, but grow quick at 40cm per year to a maximum height of 6 meters.

## Tree, Willow

Not to be confused with the weeping willow base plant, this plantoid is related to one of 460 variants of willow shrubs and trees, and in every case is a soft barked, deciduous treeoid that grows fast, but is a somewhat short lived. It has the good fortune of not producing nuts or fruit that might lead to people wanting to hold it in captivity for agricultural servitude, nor is its wood highly sought after as timber. Wild, normal and mutated variants sprout everyplace that has reliable water, and vast groves of the stuff grow in the wilderness and the streets of ruined cities, offering this treeoid plenty of excellent hiding places.

It has a medium sized trunk where its face and any moving appendages grow, moves about on a mix of large and small root-legs, while its upper branches are often densely packed with waxy, bright green, red or even yellowish leaves. These plantoids grow rapidly at 25cm per year to a maximum height of 7 meters.

## Tulip

Because these plantoids are related to a once popular, perennial plant that emerged year after year from a buried bulb, it has the wondrous ability to virtually die off and lay dormant for 6 months, either in the ground, in the bottom of a backpack or crate, under snow, debris or other vegetation, and emerge again back to the size and abilities that it exhibited prior to near death. This regrowth takes two months, and can only happen in the spring, however it allows the plantoid to survive ordeals that its human companions cannot.

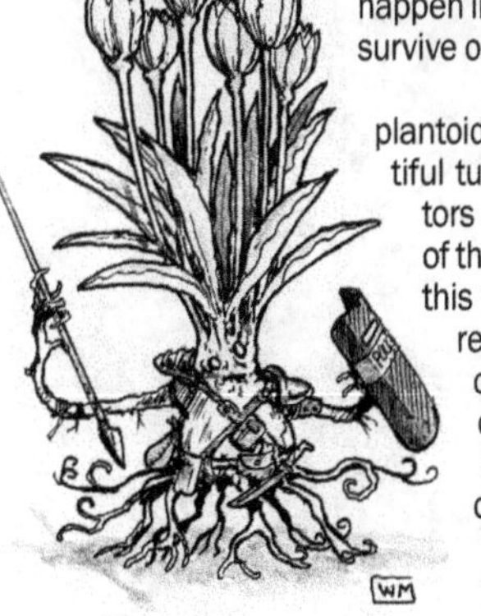

In normal cases, this flowering plantoid produces up to a half dozen* or more beautiful tulips each spring which attract many pollinators — and possibly unwanted attention because of the bright colors of its bloom. By early summer, this flower drops its petals and looks quite unremarkable among other broad leaved bushes of the new era, and can hide easily enough if other plant growth it sufficiently dense.

Being leafy, soft skinned and often conspicuous when in flower, many herbivores will readily go after and eat this sort of character, although humanoids tend to snip off the flower

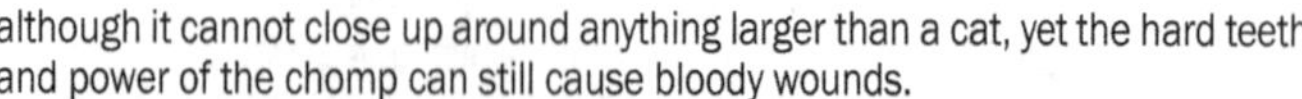

and stem to place in water and let the rest of the plantoid escape with its life. Selling cut tulip flowers for money is a possibility for this character and its companions, although only the wealthy can splurge on such luxuries, yet will pay 1d6sp per tulip flower when these transactions occur. These plantoids are three quarters leaves and flower stem, and all portions which can be eaten away and still leave the trunk portion of the plantoid alive to regrow next year. Their roots are pale and tentacle-like and spread about the base of the dark green trunk like a skirt. Unlike normal tulip plants, these oddities grow as tall as a man, but no further.

*Number of flowers per spring: 1d6, plus 1 extra per rank: 1st rank 1d6+1, 3rd rank 1d6+3, 9th rank 1d6+9 flowers, etc.*

### Turnip

Genetically combined with what are also sometimes called a 'neep' or 'rutabaga', this turnip plantoid has a squat, taproot body, gangly pale white root-legs and its upper stalks thick with rich green and heavy leaves. Its 'face' and any movable appendages all grow from the bulbous, white, purple, or yellow and purple ball of a body, giving this fella an often comical appearance.

There is, however, nothing funny about being chased down a muddy street in a village of starving human farmers, with their goats and hogs joining in on the hunt. Indeed, being related to a commonly eaten root vegetable is challenging for this individual, who must keep its plant heritage secret by covering its body at all times, and traveling with mean looking comrades who will keep the hungry at bay. Because it is a highly nutritious being, it also has vast stores of food value within its taproot body which allows it to endure long periods of drought and poor nutrition far better than any other humanoid. They are among the most robust, powerfully built root vegetable based plantoids and can grow 2 meters wide and 4 meters tall.

## Venus Flytrap

A human-Venus flytrap hybrid is a fearsome thing to behold. Still, the 1d4+2, 30cm wide, toothy traps that grow from broad, bright green stems in the upper canopy of this plantoid are too small to devour humans, but will snap up seagulls, red wasps, rats, squirrels and other creatures that either pass too close to, or land upon this bizarre being's top half.

The trunk is a thick, dark green stalk with its sensory organs and additional limbs appearing here, along with 1d4 large sized, main fly trap jaws that are used more like grasping hands or biting jaws than dedicated small feeding jaws as the top traps are. These additional jaws are tougher, have wooden teeth and grow on 2m long, highly mobile tendrils which can each attack once per round in any direction around the plantoid. Large flytrap jaws are 45 centimeters (1'5") wide and each has a strength of 35, strike value modifier of +6 and inflict 3d6 damage on a successful strike. These limbs can be targeted by an opponent and have a defense value of -20 and endurance of 30. If severed, the mouth tendril will grow back in 4 months. These big jaws can be used in melee in conjunction with other limbs that the character might exhibit.

Commoners who encounter this plantoid on its own will probably react poorly to its appearance, and either flee in terror or arm themselves and try to kill or drive off the horrid thing. Only if accompanied by more normal looking human travelers will this plantoid be allowed into a community, although whether the locals permit the thing to step into a saloon is another matter.

As noted above, the top fly traps operate automatically and snap up birds, snakes, bats or whatever else they can get, with each successful kill resulting in the mouth sealing up as the plant digests the victim, but reopens and is ready for use again after ten days. Once every 6 rounds, the plantoid can bend over and use all its upper fly traps to snap at one or more opponents in one direction, each small trap can make one attack at +6 SV doing 1d6 damage,

although it cannot close up around anything larger than a cat, yet the hard teeth and power of the chomp can still cause bloody wounds.

These remarkable plantoids prefer warm, humid conditions and suffer 1d6 endurance damage per day extra when forced to endure desert conditions. They grow to a maximum height of about three meters.

### Virginia Creeper

A plantoid derived from this common vine is sometimes mistaken for a grapevine, although the tiny purple berries which grow from this hybrid's branches contain oxalis acid, which is toxic to humans. If eaten, after a half hour of consumption the subject suffers a terrible gut ache, is reduced to half movement rate and strike values with muscle powered attack modes. Worse, the sufferer must make a Type C willpower based hazard check or die from liver failure. If not dying, and merely sickened, the symptoms last for 3d6 hours.

Birds and some other small animals can eat these berries with no side effects, and indeed will often be attracted to this plantoid in the fall to pluck every berry off.

Virginia creeper plantoids have a main central trunk or root ball where it's consciousness, manipulator limbs, sensory organs and additional mutations are affixed. It can stand upright on a knotted mass of root-legs, but its many leaf covered upper vines are only slightly mobile and can only move 10 centimeters per round, which allows it to climb slowly up even the sheerest of concrete surfaces. Even without using its slow moving upper vines, of which it will have 2d6 and measure 3 meters each, this plantoid can use its other limbs and roots to climb splendidly, and so add 2 skill points in climbing.

A Virginia creeper plantoid can move along the ground, like an octopus out of water, or travel erect and raise its upper vines to extend its full height of up to 5 meters — which can be an extremely intimidating sight to smaller creatures. A veggie sapien of this line can use one woven root creeper with a three meter reach to smack, rake and strangle adversaries as a bonus melee attack at + 5 SV inflicting a base of 1d8 damage.

On a hit, this vine can be made to wrap around the neck of a person, or man-sized or smaller animal, and do an automatic 1d8 damage per round of suffocation. The vine can be hacked off, hwoever, and has DV -20 and END 28. A severed vine takes 30+1d30 days to regrow.

While herbivores will feed on this thing's foliage, most humans will show little interest in it, or might not even notice it since these plantoids are hard to spot among other vines and shrubs. They are not particularly robust, unlike trees, but make up for it in well rounded abilities.

### Wheat

While most wheat plants have between one and five stems, a plantoid specimen has several dozen stems that grow from a trunk-like lower stalk. Each stem grows back in the spring and is vibrant green with several bladed leaves that end into a seed laden 'spike'. In these mutant specimens, these grain heavy spikes are as big as a person's hand, and in late summer or early fall, yield a tremendous amount of highly nutritious bread grain.

The plantoid entity can survive if its wheat is harvested, but if its upper leaves and stems are all eaten or hacked off, it suffers greatly and cannot rely on photosynthesis to feed itself.

The main stalk-trunk holds the consciousness, sensory organs, and any articulating or specialized appendages, while the wheat's extensive, pale root legs hold the entity upright and propel it along the ground at a considerable speed. Indeed, these plantoids need to move fast, because all humanoids and herbivores crave the grain and leaves of this being, thus increase its base speed from 6 meters by +1m per round (now 7m).

When hiding among other tall grasses, or fields of large mutated wheat — which is a common sight around most new era farm settlements — this plantoid can easily conceal itself.

A wheat plantoid only makes one crop per year, but produces enough grain to make 6 loaves of delicious bread, plus one additional loaf per character rank. A loaf of bread sells for 1 silver piece where food supplies are bountiful, but in a community were shortages, starvation and unreliable grain shipments are common place, bread can sell for as much as 10sp per loaf. In such places, a wheatoid must be extra careful, and keep close to any mutant, human, and cyborg comrades to merely cross the street.

### Yam

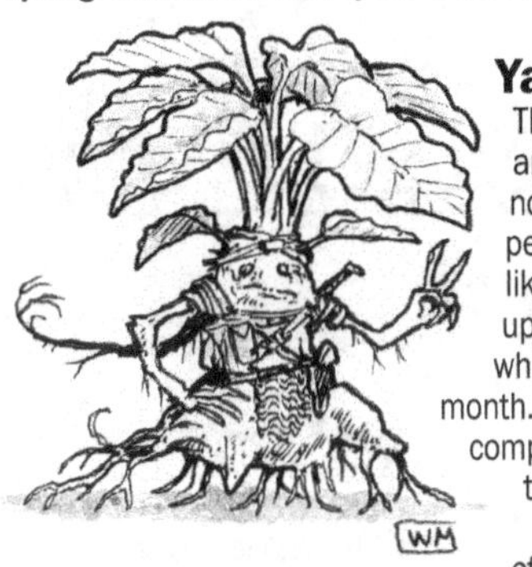

There are hundreds of species of yams and sweet potatoes, both deviant and normal, however plantoids variants appear as only two types. The first is a vine-like being with a dense woody main stalk, upper leaves and extensive root system which is dotted by 3d6 eatable yams per month. When twisted off and roasted by either companions of the plantoid, or by thieves, these starchy growths are delicious.

The second, less common variety of yam plantoid has its sensory array, manipulator appendages and other mutations attached to a massive brown globular tuber. These nightmarish things move about on a network of lower roots and runners, while their tops are crowned by a dozen leafy stems. Only by killing the plantoid can hungry humans and herbivores truly enjoy the entirety of this freak, but doing so is no easy task, as these great yams start with an additional +40 endurance and + 100 kilograms weight, and add an additional +10 to both END and KG each year thereafter (after character generation). In addition, the mouth cavity of this fiend is a half a meter wide and filled with huge, misshapen, wedge-like human teeth and can bite at +5 SV and inflict a base of 1d20 damage. From this gaping maw, the yam can consume compost and the flesh of animals and people if it should so desire. A monster yam of this sort would be shot on sight, and certainly not allowed into the gates of town, unless it was well hidden, or its pacifism insured by human companions who can vouch for the god awful thing.

In either case, a yam plantoid's upper foliage consists of broad, dark green leaves and the occasional pink or purple flower, and so if crouched low or semi buried in loose soil among other plants, these veggie-sapiens can easily be missed by passing humans or animals.

Roll to determine the sort of yam variety for a new player character, **1d10: 1-7.** Multi yam, vine-limbed yamoid. / **8-10.** Massive type great monster yamoid.

# Unspecified Plant Lineage (UPL)

While less common than a plantoid with an identifiable plant heritage, these specimens are typically a variety of man-sized tree, with leaf covered upper branches, a woody trunk where its sensory growths — or its face — areconcentrated in the upper third and align forward like a person's. Their specialized fixed or mobile limbs lower down in the shoulder position like a human might exhibit, while their means of locomotion are situated at their base, either as the roots themselves or among them. UPLs have a base weight of 60+3d10 kg and a base height of 140+1d100cm.

This entity is typically what most people think of when they hear the word 'plantoid', and they tend to be the most widely accepted in human communities while other varieties have a harder time of it. The cadaver laced host inhabiting strains, for example, have a more human shape, but that they inhabit a corpse is off-putting to most people. Meanwhile, the strains that are genetically spliced with a common and often identifiable plant — especially a food plant — can run into difficulties when food gets scarce, since many poorly educated or desperate people either don't know or don't care that all plantoids have a fair amount of human DNA, to say nothing of self awareness and feelings, and will eat them. Cybernetically augmented plantoids, of course, have plenty of other issues which make people wary of them.

Roll up a UPL character's first 7 traits like a normal character (table XR-2, page 8), but their appearance trait is only 2 to 12 (2d6). Next roll this character's reproductive details on table XR-115, next page, followed by their pre-game caste (table XR-116), adding any trait modifiers and skills. Next, roll their mutations (1d4 plantoid and 13% chance of a 1d2 plantoid flaws), then determine their gear based on their outfitting code. Fill in their protection and attacks modes, name, and date your game ready plantoid freak.

# Cybernetic Plantoid Variant (CPV)

Much rarer than any other sort of plantoid are cybernetically augmented variants of plantoids. These remarkable oddities can only occur as either an identifiable base plant specimen or an unidentifiable variant. Host inhabiting plantoids can access and control cybernetics only if a host body is equipped with implants when found. The addition of implants and a highly advanced, high tech interface module means these plantoids have probably been grown, mechanized and brain washed by anti-human Mecha forces — or some high tech enclave which required expendable, obedient and lethal infantry units.

Those that wander alone or join mercenary, bounty hunter or excavation teams, have somehow broken free of their creators, ripped out their compliance chips, and now make their own way in the twisted new era. These specimens often have fewer plantoid mutations or flaws, either because they were developed without them, or these growths were removed and replaced with an optical implant, nervous system control box, and one or more implants of the same variety as those attached to cyborgs and mutorgs.

Because cybernetically augmented plantoids are rare, and most people have never encountered one before, they have a tough time finding acceptance in human barter towns and new era cities. Like half skullocks, abominations, and self aware androids and robots, these entities strike terror in the common folk, elicit cold or cruel treatment, poor service and anything but a warm welcome. If they prove their worth to a community or faction, however, and are also in the company of other humans and not overly grotesque mutants, they will be more warmly received.

Of course a CPV might quickly become a welcome addition to a town's defenses should the place come under attack and this plantoid makes a good account of itself, but the nature of their potential former mecha servitude makes commoner's and the authorities highly distrustful of them, regardless of their combat effectiveness and outward displays of courtesy, generosity and civic benevolence. For most cybernetically enhanced plantoids, they feel most comfortable out on an expedition, surrounded with trusted diggers and fulfilling their role as lethal front line operators.

A cybernetic plantoid variant will have 1 optical enhancement implant (50% from the hub rules on page TME-89, otherwise from this book on page 342), plus three other random cybernetic augmentations: 1 offensive, 1 defensive and 1 miscellaneous implant found on table XR-210, page 330. In addition, they will have the usual 1d2+1 manipulator tendrils that all types of plantoids have, plus 1d2 plantoid mutations from the listing on table XR-201 on page 233.

Finally, roll a d10 to determine the base plantoid type here:

### Table XR-113/ Cybernetic Plantoid Variant Base Plant   Roll 1d10

**1-4.**  Identifiable Base plantoid (IBP), see page 120 for details.

**5-10.**  Unspecified Plant Lineage (UPL), detailed on page 139.

## Plantoid Feeding Mode

All plantoids have a set method of acquiring nutrients. Roll 2d6 at character generation and record.

### Table XR-114/ Plantoid Feeding Mode  Roll 2d6

**2,3.**  Photosynthesis, Soil plus Carrion Eater: This plantoid can survive off sunlight, or rich soil, but prefers to ingest carrion from decomposing bodies.

**4-7.**  Photosynthesis: Gets nearly all its sustenance from direct sunlight, but needs 6 hours minimum daily to heal.

**8-11**  Photosynthesis plus Soil: It feeds off sunlight, but can only heal if also given access to well composted, waste and nutrient rich soil.

**12**  Photosynthesis, Soil, Carrion and Flesh Consumer: Also called a 'multi-feeder', this plantoid can nourish itself from sunlight, soil, carrion or the flesh and fluids of still — or recently— living beings. There is a 2 in 6 chance that it grew up believing that to consume a dead pet, family member, or comrade is the deepest form of respect, and a way for the fallen to live on through this plantoid's leaves and limbs.

## Plantoid Reproduction

While many are sterile, and unable to reproduce, other plantoids develop seed which in nearly every case only produces a stationary strain of the plantoid. In very rare cases, a single plantoid develops from a mass planting that has sufficient human DNA to result in a copy of the parent plantoid character. Roll on the following table to establish reproduction:

### Table XR-115/ Plantoid Reproductive Capabilities  Roll 1d10

**1,2.**  **Sterile.** Its seed, fruit, pollen or other reproductive materials will not fertilize and while possibly eatable by humanoids and animals, they will not grow.

**3-9.**  **Viable seed or pollen,** however the subsequent growths are mindless, enlarged forms of the plantoid's non-human side. For example, if this character is a corn based plantoid, its kernels will produce towering corn plants with almost no hint, or expression of its hidden human DNA.

Host inhabiting plantoids (HIPs) create mindless, green walker root balls which will seek humanoid cadavaers, See page TME-165 for Green Walker description if needed.

**10.**  **Viable seed or pollen,** as in roll 3-9, above, however for every planting season, there is a 3% chance that one growth emerges as an identical, immature copy of the parent. This offspring might look like the parent, but without proper human guidance, basic education, and awareness of the social norms of the given society, there is a strong likelihood that this creation will become a wild monster, and if predatory, will feed on humans whenever it finds them.

Some bio-technicians might try to create an entire battalion of killer plantoids, and either disperse them around their fortification or else use remote control command modules to direct each to attack enemies, patrol a certain zone, or stand guard at the entrance to some hidden complex.

## Plantoid Pre-Game Castes

For the most part, plantoids occupy the lowest orders of any human-centric community, if they were ever part of it in the first place. Some earn their keep as a laborer, farmer, or hunter, others serve a community as a militia volunteer or a forcibly drafted soldier, while others resort to crime or banditry to steal what they can, and sell it for precious water, fertilizer and a safe place to take to root at night. Other 'plant people' or 'veggie-sapiens' prefer to be wastelanders, nomads, or wilderness inhabiting scavengers instead of enduring the ridicule, abuse, enslavement, and possible consumption, by living among common humans.

Consult the following table to determine the pre-game caste of any new plantoid character. These castes are sourced from either this book, the TME Hub Rules, or in three cases, listed in this section following this random table.

For host inhabiting plantoids, roll for their caste and apply any trait modifiers and approriate skills, but use Outfitting code Modest (MO) for the plantoid's cadaver.

### Table XR-116/ Plantoid Pre-Game Castes

| 1d100 | Pre-Game Caste | Book Source and page* |
|---|---|---|
| 01-04. | Bounty Hunter | Expansion Rules, page 12. |
| 05,06. | Bunker Dweller | Expansion Rules page 12. |
| 07-10. | Caravaneer | Expansion Rules, page page 12. |
| 11-27. | Crop, Decorative or Shade | See Caste Description, page 141. |
| 28-33. | Draftee | TME Hub Rules, page 12. |
| 34-41. | Escaped Experiment | See Caste Description, page 141.. |
| 42-46. | Farmer | TME Hub Rules, page 12. |
| 47-49. | Hunter | TME Hub Rules, page 12. |
| 50-55. | Mercenary | TME Hub Rules, page 12. |
| 56-60. | Militia Soldier | TME Hub Rules, page 12. |
| 61-65. | Nomad | TME Hub Rules, page 12. |
| 66,67. | Raider | TME Hub Rules, page 12. |
| 68-70. | Repairer | Expansion Rules, page 12. |
| 71-74. | Scavenger | Expansion Rules, page 12. |
| 75-78. | Slave, Labor | TME Hub Rules, page 12. |
| 79-81. | Street Thug | TME Hub Rules, page 12. |
| 82,83. | Thief | TME Hub Rules, page 12. |
| 84-86. | Wastelander | Expansion Rules, page 12. |
| 87-00. | Weed | See Caste Description, page 141.. |

*The page presents the Caste Based Details, where any trait modifiers, outfitting codes, automatic skills and skill set rolls are made. For the three plantoid specific pre-game castes of Weed, Escaped Experiment or Crop, Decorative or Shade, these details are listed on the next page in their descriptions but will require consulting of the starting skill set matrix, table XR-7, on page XR-13.*

creator, or else woke up one day, busted out, made its way to the surface and miraculously survived until it came upon a human settlement. Aware that it is part human, it craves the companionship and acceptance of its sapien cousins, and strives to make itself useful to a dig team, community or faction.

Because it grew up under the perfect growing conditions, it became hardy, well formed and 50 centimeters taller than it otherwise would have been (add +50cm height). Regrettably, it was also dumbed down to ensure it didn't formulate some notion to escape or turn on its creators.

**Trait modifiers:** Endurance +5d6 / Strength +3d6 / Agility +1d6 / Accuracy +1d6 / Intelligence -2d6 / Perception +0 / Willpower +0 / Appearance +0
**Outfitting code:** ESC (Escaped Slave)
**Automatic skills:** Weapon expert 1pt, Escape artist 1d3pts
**Skill set rolls:** Warrior 2+1d3 rolls, Misc. 1d2 rolls, from list on page XR-13.

## Crop, Decorative or Shade

This plantoid survived to adulthood by serving human caretakers, either as a rooted, tied down source of food, a pretty ornamental plant for some powerful warlord, or else merely a shade plant to cool the ground and structures around it. This specimen suffered a variety of hardships, neglect and abuse, was most likely beaten when it disobeyed, was mauled by goats, climbed by children, and accordingly suffered some damage to its brain core... yet it grew tough.

It was either set free when somebody recognized the humanity in the plantoid, or more likely, because it gained consciousness and escaped. Once out in the world, it acquired a few meager skills and supplies, and embarked on a path toward a new life, a life with no bonds, and ultimate freedom — a life favored by the caste of excavators.

Besides being driven by a need for freedom, it also craves acceptance as a valuable, equal partner in a community or dynamic group, and so has a tendency to go above and beyond the call of duty, push itself to its limits, take chances that others wouldn't dare, and make itself invaluable to a mercenary squad, militia or dig team.

There is a 1 in 10 chance that whoever cultivated and owned this plantoid before game play began, wants this character back, and if so, there is a bounty on the plantoid's head for its safe return (300+2d100sp), and a 16% chance that any bounty hunter encountered will recognize this PC if it is not disguised.

**Trait modifiers:** Endurance +4d6 / Strength +2d6 / Agility +1d6 / Accuracy +0 / Intelligence -d6 / Perception +0 / Willpower +4d6 / Appearance +0
**Outfitting code:** PR (ESC Escaped Slave)
**Automatic skills:** Dodge 1d2 pts, Climbing 1pt, Stealth 1pt
**Skill set rolls:** Warrior 1 roll, Misc. 1d2 rolls, from list on page XR-13.

## Escaped Experiment

This plantoid did not grow in the earth, but instead in some laboratory where it served as either food, slave labor, or as a mindless, unquestioning guardian monster. Bio-engineered by either human bunker dwellers, a mad scientist, or malevolent artificial intelligence, this specimen's memories are jumbled or missing.

It knows little of its creation, and can't be sure whether it's a unique, solitary specimen or just one of hundreds of its kind. For whatever reason, it found itself free, either gaining self awareness while on some mission for its

## Weed

For the first few years of this being's life, it grew in an out of the way, inaccessible spot and matured in relative isolation from any semblance of civilization. It was sometimes gnawed on by passing herbivores, and had its branches or any fruit or nuts harvested by traveling humans and humanoids.

One day, with its consciousness suddenly alight, a desire to see the world, do great things and take part in its birthright as a human-offshoot blooming in its sap filled core, it pulled up roots and wandered off. It survived as a wild thing, grew tough, learned the ways of humanity from afar and gained only rudimentary skills until the time game play begins. In short, it is a plantoid barbarian who must learn its place in society, and learn fast or die. This being can't read, write or do any more math than the most simple addition and subtraction. It will have only one language which it speaks poorly with a vocabulary of about 100 words. Despite its shortcomings as far as education, it is eager to learn and if intelligent, has patient teachers, will attempt to master many subjects and skills.

**Trait modifiers:** Endurance +4d6 / Strength +4d6 / Agility +3d6 / Accuracy +3d6 / Intelligence +0 / Perception +2d6 / Willpower +3d6 / Appearance +0
**Outfitting code:** PR (Poor)
**Automatic skills:** Wilderness Survival, Climbing 1 pt, Stealth 1d3 pts, Tracking 1pt
**Skill set rolls:** Warrior 3+1d3 rolls, Criminal 1d2 rolls from list on page XR-13.

# Rebuilt

Rebuilt are people who have suffered some great bodily injury and had mechanical and electronic parts bolted, stitched and cruelly adhered or inserted into them — often against their will. While similar to a cyborg, these low tech, junk crafted unfortunates were thrown together haphazardly and fitted with a wide range of prosthetics and scrap parts, including limbs from androids and robots, bicycle wheels, barbed wire, forged parts, plastic sheathing, lawn hoses, rubber bands, glue, rawhide, and oldster trash. In most cases this was done to make the subject serviceable and of use to their people, faction, militia, or dig team. They have their own random list of parts, problems and even optional tables to reveal the event that led to their being maimed, as well as who is to blame for rebuilding them.

Rebuilt go by many nicknames, including junk person, junk-boy or junk girl, scrapper, scrap heap, trash-built, junkoid, junker, the recycled, or salvaged one. Those who specialize in the reconstruction of otherwise useless casualties, and their conversion into these often nightmarish, pitiful and occasionally potent beings are called junk doctors. This profession is also a skill area, described on page XR-218.

Junk doctors are often junk crafters as well, but may possess the skills of robotics technician, medic or mechanical technician, too. For the most part, this skill borrows from a wide range of disciplines but comes across more as a hobby or the activities of a mad scientist. In most cases, a rebuilt character was patched up, augmented while unconscious, and sent back to the front line or dusty streets of the oldsters by one of these practitioners — usually because there was nobody else around able to turn a mangled patient into a cyborg.

Indeed, many junk doctors might also possess the cybernetics technician skill, which is described on page XR-209 of this book, but without the proper spinal, brain stem and other parts, to say nothing of an adequate, sterile, well stocked medical facility, creating a cyborg is very different from merely augmenting the external parts on an already established subject. The next best thing, beside a mercy killing, is to use whatever is at a hand, and convert a mangled person into a rebuilt.

As already mentioned, rebuilt are similar to cyborgs in that they are usually humans augmented with non-organic parts. Whereas a cyborg is a well planned, high-tech work of mechanical, digital and bio mechanical art, a rebuilt is instead a haphazard mess of meat and metal, wire, springs, clockwork mechanisms, household appliances and junk, although they are sometimes equipped with authentic cybernetic parts along with whatever tools, relic gear and weaponry can be salvaged. They are the creations of madmen and were rarely willing participants in their construction.

The typical rebuilt started off as a crippled casualty of some violent event. His or her limbless, battered body kept on life support while the self-taught hobbyist technicians and medics put the victim back into some sort of useful shape. Most of the parts attached to this survivor are controlled by either muscle contortion, tendon pulls, walking gait, posture, or direct hand manipulation. However, in some cases the patient's spinal cord, brain and nerves were synced with a crude nervous system network whereby control nodes where affixed to mechanical limbs, industrial tools, receptors and offensive implements. After reconstruction, the pain wracked rebuilt person had to master their own customized body, cope with neurological problems, chronic pain, occasional infections, chafing and possible shell shock, flashbacks and other PTSD related issues.

The resulting rebuilt being, although often very useful to its community and proud builders, is usually seen as a shambling, rattling monster. A typical rebuilt is lopsided, has visible organs, liquid storage bags, external tubing, blood filled hoses, electrical wires and similar gruesome fittings hanging off of it. The scrap-built man or woman might speak through a looted robotic vocabulator, see through old surveillance cameras, and rattle and squeak on limbs that were never meant to convey a human.

Though alive, and sometimes recalling its former life, a rebuilt is routinely shunned, even by former family members and lovers, and if sufficiently teased, bossed about and tormented by its saviors, will occasionally wander away. Many times a fleeing rebuilt seeks nothing more than a quick death to end the nightmare that is its life. At other times, they desire solitude and easy access to the junk of the old ones from which to maintain its creaking frame and sets about on a hermit's life, far from other people.

A few wanderers, however, yearn for the company of other misfits, such as bestial humans, self aware robots and androids, vat-brains, mutants, clones and cyborgs. It is just these sort of mixed race beings that form excavation teams; an ideal career path for a robust and well equipped rebuilt. Of all castes, only excavators are known to frequently pick through the unlooted depths of the ancient ruins. It Is here, in the grave dust of the old ones that a rebuilt can find the necessary power cells, ammo and spare parts needed to not only sustain his or her life, but improve the odds of continued existence.

To live as a rebuilt is to live with chronic pain, and so too, a burning need to get revenge against those who mutilated their body in the first place, which sometimes includes the junk doctor who turned them into the pitiful, rattling, squeaky monstrosity they are now.

The search for pain numbing beverages, substances and experiences often drive a rebuilt, who not only seek the earnings from ruin looting but also to save up funds and locate a facility where they can be remade properly, and converted to a cyborg. Should a rebuilt get the chance to undergo cybernetic conversion, he or she will keep all prior gained ranks.

Many of the features described in the following tables demand a penalty to a character's appearance score. If so many gruesome attachments or injuries are recorded that a rebuilt's appearance trait drops below 1, then consider their appearance trait to be at a minimum of 1 point. In addition, a game master must keep in mind that some appearance penalties might overlap, especially to the face or arm, and should a limb have duplicated drops, ignore the lesser depletion amount since that appendage or feature is already gross enough.

As sometimes mentioned throughout this book, the appearance score of one's face might differ greatly from the body, and if a viewer never sees a person's body because it is draped in a robe, the onlooker might get a very different impression of the person they are looking at. Likewise, a rebuilt or other character can have a hideously deformed face, and yet a stunning physique, and because they either wear some sort of mask, or hide their head under a hood, separate facial and body appearance scores should be recorded on the character sheet. A dedicated character sheet for this PC type can be found on page 523 and at this book's web page at https://www.outlandarts.com/expansionrules.htm .

# Rebuilt Character Type

Rebuilt characters are most often pure stock humans, although there are other strains of humanity that can have this template applied to them, including bestial humans, halfies and synthetic humans such as clones and bioreplicas.

First determine the character type from the following random list, next, proceed to roll the traits of that character in its normal method before returning to the follow-up tables to establish the modifications the subject has undergone. Pre-game caste uses the 'Rebuilt' column on table XR-4, page 10.

## Table XR-117/ Rebuilt Character Type Determination

| 1d100 | Rebuilt Character Type |
| --- | --- |
| 01-09. | Mutant, mildly mutated (1d3 prime mutations, 1d2 minor and 25% chance of one flaw mutation). |
| 10-13. | Halfie, determine strain from page XR-93, of this book. |
| 14,15. | Bioreplica, roll 1d6 for type here: 1. Pleasure / 2,3. Industrial / 4. Clerical / 5 Infiltration / 6. Battle. (See pages TME 18-19 for details and traits). |
| 16,17. | Clone, roll 1d6 for model type: 1. Comfort clone / 2-4. Labor clone / 5,6. Military clone. (See pages TME 19-20 for details and traits). |
| 18. | Trans-Human (see page TME 20 for notes and trait bonuses). |
| 19-24. | Bestial human from, roll d100: 01-50. Table XR-53, page 58 this book / 51-00. Hub Rules bestials on page TME-24. |
| 25-00. | Pure Stock Human (page TME-18, Hub Rules). |

# What The Hell Happened to you?

Unless the game master's campaign or scenario calls for some back story on how a rebuilt became the walking scrap-heap they are now, the following random selection can be used as a starting point or idea generator for more in-depth tragedies. Better still, encourage the player to come up with what might have happened to their new player character, which is something they can write before or after a game session.

Finally, the rebuilt might have no idea what befell their character prior to being dropped on a junk doctor's blood and motor oil stained table, and it's perhaps up to the other characters to recount this scrapper's story, since they were there when this rebuilt was maimed.

## Table XR-118/ Rebuilt Demise Table

| 2d6 | Rebuilt's Demise |
| --- | --- |
| 2. | Dismembered by berserk robot |
| 3. | Mangled during an earthquake or collapsing structure |
| 4. | Industrial accident |
| 5. | Torn to shreds by a wild animal |
| 6. | Hacked apart and left for dead in factional warfare |
| 7. | Cut apart by raiders |
| 8. | Early attempt at an excavation in ruins, carried back on a stretcher by comrades and given up for dead to a local junk doctor (see page XR-18 for description of this caste). |
| 9. | Something hungry in the water tore off much of their body |
| 10. | Chopped and mutilated and hung up by cultists |
| 11. | Limbs hacked off and eaten by humanoids or cannibals |
| 12. | Landmine incident |

# Who is to Blame?

The following offers a quick way to reveal who is responsible for putting this character into their current condition, although the game master, or player, might instead have a preferred back story to apply to this junk-built person.

## Table XR-119/ Who Assembled this Rebuilt?

| 2d6 | Rebuilt Assembled by... |
| --- | --- |
| 2. | The character has no idea, and woke to his or her current, agonized existence outside of the community they now call home. The subject's former companions were presumably massacred, and memories come only as nightmares when trying to sleep. |
| 3,4. | A traveling junk doctor performed the surgery, but it was the overlord of your local community who paid the 600+1d1000sp fee — which the character owes the overlord coins, loot, and occasional favors. |
| 5,6. | A local holy man who fancies himself a cybernetics technician in the off-hours. |
| 7,8. | A passing junk doctor, who took his fees in the form of everything the character and his or her family owned. The PC's kin are now in crushing debt, owe 500+1d1000sp to an assortment of local families. This rebuilt is also required to spend 1d6 months a year in the militia of the community as part of the interest on the debt. Once the full debt is paid off, this service ceases. |
| 9,10. | A local junk doctor put the character together, and the PC owes the person 400+1d1000sp, a fee guaranteed by the character's family homestead as collateral. |
| 11. | A local junk doctor who was coaxed into saving the rebuilt's life, at knife point, by the character's friends. The local authorities are likely aware of this forced patch job, and looking for an opportunity to either 'tax' or forcibly 'employ' the whole adventure team. |
| 12. | A dig team of great renown came to the community one evening, and among these noble travelers where several technicians and many spare parts. They threw the rebuilt together as best they could and left the next morning, saying only that the junkoid must take this second chance at life to be nice to small animals, do great things, and help bring about a return of civilization. |

# Rebuilt Character Detail Tables

Roll on each of the following tables and record the results on your dedicated Rebuilt Character sheet. Most require only 1 roll, although a few call for two or more rolls.

### Table XR-120/ Rebuilt Character Suffering Matrix

| 2d6 | Rebuilt's Suffering |
|---|---|
| 2. | Life is hell. Moving is constant pain, laying down hurts, organs don't work altogether well, and the rebuilt suffers from headaches, heartburn, ulcers, chaffing, infections at surgery points, leaking scars, rust issues, and fluid leaks of every kind.<br><br>Only a constant supply of painkilling street drugs, relic pharmaceuticals and strong drink allow this person to cope. Unless he or she can save enough silver and parts, find a cybernetics clinic, and become a legitimate augmented person without these issues, then this junker sees little point in going on, and now looks for final vengeance upon those who did this to them, and then oblivion. |
| 3,4. | The rebuilt is in serious discomfort when moving, as parts chaff, the scars, stitches and assorted attachment wires and nerve nodes rub, pinch and catch. Redness, occasional infections and fluid leakage are something he or she must live with. Pain killers, booze and relic medicines are greatly appreciated by this tormented soul, and the dream to become a true cyborg burns in his or her chest. |
| 5,6. | Digestion issues plague this rebuilt, along with general aches, pains, and sores where parts rub on raw flesh. He or she has a rotating list of ailments including heartburn, diarrhea, constipation, ulcers, kidney stones, and other issues. By being careful to ingest a balanced diet with lots of fresh greens and fruit, he or she can avoid debilitating bouts of these afflictions, but in a post-apocalyptic world, it's hard to maintain a healthy diet, and so this scrapper suffers day and night. |
| 7,8. | Chronic headaches. At the start of each day the character is 67% likely to wake with a pounding migraine. Likewise, after any incident of loud noise, such as gunfire within 10 meters, or suffering any injury that inflicts over 10 trait points damage to the rebuilt, a headache will also be unleashed and remain throughout the day. Other bodily pain persist, too, especially where non-living parts rub, pull and pinch at his or her living portions. The search for pain medication, especially relic substances, is never ending. |
| 9,10. | Night aches. At the end of every day, and as the character tries to relax, familiar discomfort arrives. Most evenings, where the human parts end and mechanical or scrap parts begin, there is throbbing pain, swelling and occasional leakage of pus, blood and hydraulic or other industrial fluids. Consuming pain killers or the liberal consumption of alcohol are often sufficient to reduce these night aches to allow the character to sleep. |
| 11. | Mild discomfort. Sometimes if struck hard, suffering a fall or jumping down from a ledge or other height, this rebuilt feels a jolt of pain wherever his or her augmentations meet flesh. Although painful for an hour or two, this discomfort is only mild and compared to what other rebuilt say they endure, and so nothing to complain about. Life is indeed tolerable, and being a rebuilt beats the alternative of the cold grave. |
| 12. | Remarkably little discomfort. The surgeries that reconstructed the character were done by expert hands, with care to ensure that both comfort, as well as utility, were put into the procedure. |

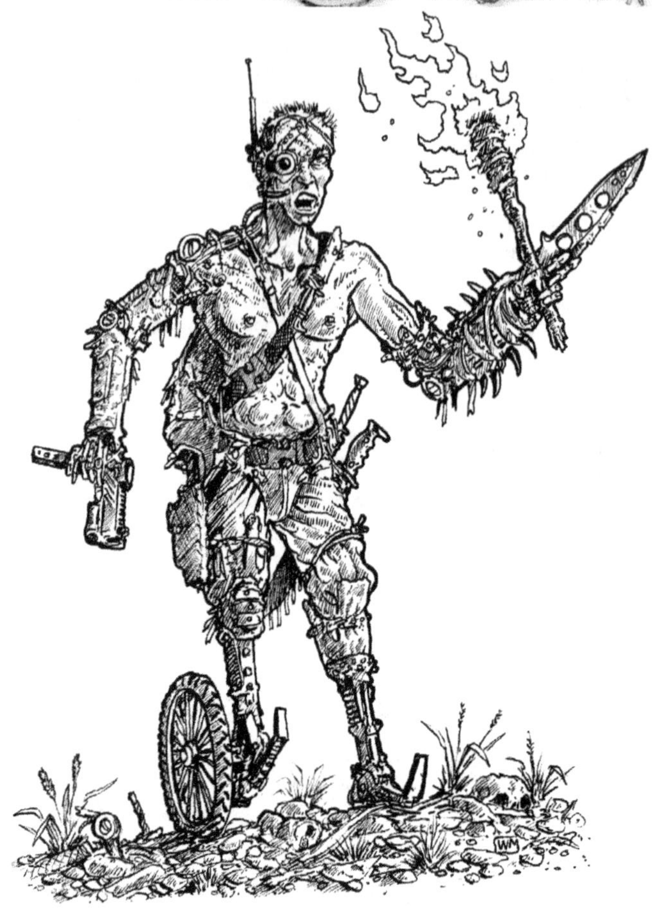

### Table XR-121/ Rebuilt Locomotion

Note: Normal human rebuilt movement is 6 meters per round before any agility modifiers. Roll once for each leg, with duplicated results kept.

| 2d6 | Rebuilt's Mode of Locomotion, Roll Once Per Leg |
|---|---|
| 2. | Wheel Chair Bound*: [NOTE: Re-roll this result if one leg previously determined, but if this the first roll on this table, then this result claims both legs.] Legs are either, roll 1d6: 1-3. Missing, or, 4-6. Paralyzed and thin.<br><br>This rebuilt shoves itself around by their hands, which understandably are attached to powerful arms and give this PC a +10+1d20 strength trait value at character generation. The chair itself is a scrap built, unpowered unit complete with knobby tires for rough terrain. This character cannot go up stairs without help or else by dragging the chair at a rate of a half meter per round. Going down a staircase is possible, but treacherous and done so at triple speed yet demanding an agility based type D hazard check every 6m traversed, with failure resulting in a crash which does 1d20 damage to the chair and treated as an attack on the PC of SV 01-70 for d20 stun and 1d20 lethal damage.<br><br>This wheel chair has a defense value of -10, endurance of 20+3d10, and a base movement of 6m plus agility modifiers. A replacement junk crafted chair will cost 30+1d100sp and take 2d4 days to assemble — although any PC with access to materials and at least 2 skill points in junk crafting or mechanical technician can make this chair, too. There is no appearance drop for this part. |
| 3. | Instead of a leg, this rebuilt has a single mountain bike wheel complete with shocks. Climbing for this character is very difficult and twice as slow as a normal person, however, on an open road, hard packed game trail or other level surface, he or she can lift his or her other locomotion limb and lean on this wheel. Like riding a unicycle, this individual can race along at 12 meters per round on level surfaces, 18m downhill, and 6m uphill if getting a bit of a run at it. Reduce appearance by -1d4 trait points. |

**4.** Carbon Fibre Running Blade. This rebuilt is missing one foot, but could have a second of these relic fittings if this result occurs for the second leg. With one such spring loaded prosthetic bladed foot, the user can run at +3m per round, but with two, +6 meters. With two such blades, as pictured below, the rebuilt is speedy, yet suffers -2 skill points in climbing and on slippery surfaces, such as snow, ice, oil and the like, must make an agility based type D hazard check each round to not slide down a slope uncontrollably for 3d6 rounds, potentially crashing for 4d6 stun damage.

**5.** Junk Leg*. From the knee down, this limb is a bundle of metal rods, springs and gears, the foot being a spring loaded, curved sickle. Built for speed this junk person moves +2m per round, although suffers -1 skill point in climbing. Deduct -1d4+2 App trait points.

**6.** Shapely female android's leg. Some viewers find this very sexy, except that where it meets the rebuilt's flesh, it is shredded, the plastic skin peeling and stitched. +0.5m to movement rate. Take off -1d4 App.

**7,8.** The subject's original leg, no movement modifier.

**9.** Wooden peg leg and crude leather harness to attach it to the subject's stump of a thigh. Movement reduced by -1m per round. Reduce App by 1d3 trait points.

**10.** Muscular male android leg, poly-skin mostly peeled away. Attached at the body crudely, complete with seeping blood and a great deal of pain. + 0.5m to movement rate. Reduce appearance by -1d4 App.

**11.** Faulty, frail robotic leg*: This unit is equipped with a power supply. The rebuilt has learned to walk on this rattling, rusty appendage with a lopsided gait. No movement penalty or ability to make an extra kick attack. Cut this PC's appearance score by -2d4.

**12.** Powerful robotic leg*, humanoid, attached to a mechanical coordinated walking motor to time its motion to any other possible leg. +1m to movement rate. A kick by this powerful limb, besides another melee attack, gains a strike value bonus of +3 and inflicts 2d6+2 damage on a hit. Any occurrence of the brawling or martial arts skill can enhance this kick, too, but the physical strength of the rebuilt is not applied. Take -3+1d4 trait points from this PC's appearance.

*Walking silently, as per the stealth skill on page TME-51, is done at -2 skill points (example: stealth skill of 4 becomes 2 when trying to walk silently, although the PC may still try other non-walking silent actions)*

## Rebuilt Arms    Roll 2d6 once for the arm arrangement of this rebuilt

### Table XR-122/ Rebuilt Arm Configuration

| 2d6 | Configuration of Rebuilt Arms |
| --- | --- |
| 2-7. | One arm normal, the other is altered. Roll 2d6 on table XR-123. |
| 8,9. | Both arms are modified, roll 2d6 on table XR-123, once each for the left arm, once for the right arm. |
| 10. | Both arms are severed just below the elbow. The dominant has been replaced by a plastic coated, rusty prosthetic forearm and hand. This android style, mechanical limb serves as a regular arm but squeaks whenever used. The other arm is an appendage from table XR-123, below, however instead of being attached at the shoulder, it extends from the rebuilt's disfigured elbow. -1 stealth skill point whenever this character moves. |
| 11. | Both arms are scar covered and braced with stainless steel, plastic, and bolts, adding a -5 defensive value bonus, extra +5kg body weight, and reduce the rebuilt's swimming ability by one degree (fair swimmer becomes poor swimmer, etc.), but otherwise treated as regular limbs. Punch damage from one or both of these arms is improved by +2 SV and +3 damage. |
| 12. | Both human arms, plus a third android arm bolted, stitched and laced to the body with external nervous system link cables running up the side of the rebuilt's head and directly into the brain. Reduce appearance by -2d4. This third limb ends in a human-shaped metal hand and can deploy weapons, a shield or other objects. Consider whatever this arm wields as an extra attack mode in either melee or ranged combat. This rebuilt gains 1 skill point in climbing, and has an increase of 10kg to their body weight. See roll result 11 on the next table (XR-123). |

### Table XR-123/ Rebuilt Arm Type

Only use this table if directed here from the previous table ( XR-122)

| 2d6 | Rebuilt Arm Type |
| --- | --- |
| 2. | Mechanical tentacle and nervous system link, shoulder mounted control box and battery pack. This unit holds two standard power cells, although only one is needed to run this highly dexterous, flexible, and extendable alloy appendage. One power cell will run this unit for 4 months of daily use. It can be used as a whip to assist in climbing (+1 skill point in the climb skill), or as a weapon to grapple or whip opponents out to five meters (16.4 feet).<br><br>As a weapon this tentacle is +10 SV and inflicts 3d6+3 damage, or adds 2 skill points in grapple to any the PC might already have. Weapon expert skill points can of course be applied to this unit, too, but not strength modifiers. Adds +10kg weight to the rebuilt and reduced appearance by -d6 trait points. The strength of tentacle is 30+d20. |
| 3. | Arm missing from forearm down. Muscle and tendon flex controlled, permanently affixed, one handed relic weapon replaces hand. Requires external reloading of ammo or batteries, but can be unleashed by either swinging or thrusting the arm, or aiming and contorting the wired and stitched tendons to pull the trigger or other discharge mechanism. Roll 1d10:<br>**1.** Pocket pistol* with 6 shot magazine loaded with 1d6 rounds<br>**2.** Auto pistol* with 20 shot mag containing 2d10 rounds<br>**3.** Stun stick*, with 40 successful shocks delivered per power cell. This unit's battery has 2d20 shocks left in it.<br>**4,5.** Relic Concealed (WC-RC) from page XR-498.<br>**6.** Stun pistol* with 2d20 shots left in 40 shot max power cell capacity.<br>**7.** Sub-machine gun* with 5d10 rounds in its 50 round magazine.<br>**8.** Laser pistol* with 1d30 (or 3d10) shots left in max 30 shot power cell.<br>**9.** 2 interconnected items from the Relic Concealed (WC-RC) table on page XR-498.<br>**10.** Electro glove with 2d10 shock discharges remaining in max 20 power cell. Acts as hand even without power. See page XR-413<br>*Stats on page TME 100 of the Hub Rules.* |

**4.** Android arm, skinless and reveals all the joints, seams, access ports, wiring and servo motors. Where it attaches to the rebuilt's shoulder, it is a stitched up, tube and wire ridged mess, although the arm works just fine and is otherwise a good match for the gender and size of the owner. Appearance penalty of -2d4, strength score of 20+1d20.

**5,6.** Shapely female android's arm, different skin tone than the character. Has a strength of 10+2d20 (roll for permanent stat). Plastic skin torn and bound together in spots, and where it meets the shoulder, reveals exposed parts, swollen skin and unsightly, criss-crossing purple scars. Reduce app by 2d4. Arm strength is 20+1d20.

**7,8.** Original human arm and hand, but 1 in 10 chance a random relic is bolted to the arm. Use concealed relic table from page 498. Any batteries usually stitched to rebuilt's back or hip.

**9,10.** Arm is a stump from below the elbow to which this rebuild has strapped barbed wire, twine, and gut cord to one of the following items. Must use another hand or tool to pull any trigger. Nasty assembly job. Reduce their appearance trait value by -d4+1 APP. Roll 1d12.

    **1.** Rusty dagger
    **2.** Nicked and rust flecked machete
    **3.** Iron hook (useful, and does 1d12+1 damage on a strike).
    **4.** Muscle controlled shotgun pistol*, loaded with 2 shotgun shells plus 0 to 9 (1d12 -3) more in a zippy bag. Can bludgeon with this appendage doing 1d10 damage plus strength modifiers.
    **5.** Twin barreled harpoon gun*, loaded, with another 2d6 spare steel shafts in a leather quiver. Can bludgeon for 1d12 damage.
    **6.** Saber
    **7.** Hatchet
    **8.** Battle axe
    **9.** Steel pipe for bludgeoning, 1d10 damage, with a flashlight bolted further up the shaft with 4d20 minutes use remaining in mini power cell.
    **10.** Relic compound crossbow* with 310+10 spare home made quarrels in pouch. Fold back bow arms allow this limb to be used as a pipe (as in roll 9 above), when not used as a missile weapon.
    **11.** Submachine gun* with 3d10 rounds in magazine plus 1d2 spare, empty magazines in pouch.
    **12.** Chainsaw*, with enough ethanol fuel in deploy for 30+3d20 rounds use, and an old plastic gas can (5 liter size), with 1d4 liters of fuel as backup (1 liter yields 200 rounds use).

**Stats on page TME 100 of the Hub Rules*

**11.** Well toned android arm, skin peeling in spots and so stitched up with sections of animal hide. Join at shoulder is gruesome and tends to ache, bleed and cause misery day and night to this rebuilt. It acts like a normal arm. Scars and sores reduce character's appearance by a further -1d4+1. Arm strength is 30+1d20.

**12.** Powerful, blocky shaped human styled robot arm and metal hand. This unit weights 30kg and the hydraulic lines, bolting, strapping and nervous system wiring located at the subject's shoulder are often raw and blotched with blood; reduce PCs appearance by -2d4. However, this limb is strong, having a strength score of 70 and can deliver a punch at +8 SV for 2d10+10 damage. The unarmed combat skill (brawling or martial arts) or the weapon expert skill can be applied to this arm, but not both skills.

## Table XR-124/ Rebuilt Vision Mode

| 2d6 | Rebuilt Character's Vision |
| --- | --- |
| **2.** | One human eye, and the other is a sunken, skin covered socket, -d6+2 appearance. No depth perception a so this rebuilt suffers a -10 strike value penalty and -1 initiative. |
| **3,4.** | One regular eye and one false glass eye that doesn't match. -2 appearance trait and the lack of depth perception means a -10 strike value penalty and -1 initiative. |
| **5,6.** | Both eyes, but gimpy with one somewhat normal and the other surrounded by scar tissue and swelling -2d4 appearance. |
| **7,8.** | Both regular eyes |
| **9,10.** | One human eye and the other is a poorly reconstructed, fluid seeping, robotic focusing lens akin to a monocular. The rebuilt suffers a -1d4+1 appearance and has no special visual abilities, but at least can see normally. |
| **11.** | A regular eye on one side and the other a night vision monocular bolted and permanently stapled to face -1d4+2 appearance, however this character can see in almost virtual darkness up to 30 meters. |
| **12.** | Besides one regular eye, this rebuilt exhibits a built in targeting scope that is manually focused and merged to their optic nerve. It has a very well-sighted cross-hair and so with any ranged attacks this rebuilt unleashes, he or she gains +20 strike value. No bonus to melee ranged engagements. The staples, rusty wire, swelling and seepage around this antique are a bit gross, however, so reduce appearance by -1d4+1. |

## Table XR-125/ Rebuilt Speech Mode

| 2d6 | Rebuilt Character's Speech Mode |
|---|---|
| 2. | Unable to speak, and instead uses sign language and a series of grunts, whistles and clicks. Has the skill 'Hand Signals' (pg. XR-211). |
| 3,4. | Synthetic vocabulator installed in throat. Character speaks in a wet, digitized voice and has a 50% chance of stuttering. |
| 5. | Mechanically assisted speech enabler inserted into this rebuilt's throat, makes them stutter, especially when starting a sentence or when excited. |
| 6. | Voice box and throat damaged, speaks in a raspy, gruff manner. |
| 7,8. | Normal speech capabilities |
| 9,10. | Throat was crushed or exposed to burning chemicals. This rebuilt's voice is rough and to form a sentence is painful. They've learned to speak in as few words a possible, using gestures and thumbs up, thumbs down or middle finger to communicate. |
| 11. | Damaged throat, cannot yell or speak above a whisper. |
| 12. | Voice box damaged in such a way that all speech is a shrill screeching noise, and when trying to whisper, half the words come out as a dry croak instead of a word. |

## Table XR-126/ Rebuilt Auditory Mode

| 2d6 | Rebuilt Character's Auditory Mode |
|---|---|
| 2. | Deaf, but can feel vibrations in the ground or when placing bare hand on surfaces. This PC has learned sign language. -10 perception and -1 initiative. |
| 3,4. | One good ear, but the inner ear workings of the other were blown out and left a gruesome hole inside the head. -1d4 appearance and reduced hearing by 25% capability, and -1d6 perception. |
| 5-8. | Character retains both human ears and hears normally. |
| 9,10. | Character's hearing was damaged and only half as good as a normal person's. -1d3 perception trait. |
| 11. | One ear is missing and replaced by a mechanical hearing apparatus and side mounted ear cap-receptor. Reduce this PC's appearance score by -1d6, but their hearing is exceptional and double a normal specimen, and adds a +1 to PC's initiative. |
| 12. | Both ears were blown or augured out. This rebuilt wears a bolted on pair of auditory receptor cups which double his or her range of hearing and provides +2d6 perception and +1 initiative. Plus, on the right side there is a small rubberized antenna and pull down microphone boom, with the unit augmented by a standard communicator. PC starts out with 1d3 mini power cells, each will run the system for 2 years. 100km range, basic 100 channels, and optional hook up port to a satellite up-link dish which would increase range 10,000km. These are kinda unsightly however, so reduce this character's appearance trait by -1d4+2 APP. |

## Table XR-127/Rebuilt Reproductive Capacity

| 2d6 | Rebuilt Character's Reproductive Capacity |
|---|---|
| 2. | All genitalia and inner reproductive organs have been destroyed and their remnants removed. Character is sterile, non-functional, and disinterested in copulation. |
| 3,4. | Reproductive organs have been damaged, yet remain in place. This character is sterile but otherwise able to perform more-or-less normally. |
| 5,6. | Reproductive organs have taken severe damage, but via reconstructive surgery and the insertion of plastic and re-grown parts, the subject can function somewhat normally. There is a 4 in 6 chance he or she is sterile. |
| 7-9. | If female, **roll 1d6: 1-3.** Evidence of a minilaparotomy. This character's tubes have been tied off, and she is currently sterile./ **4-6.** There is evidence of a c-section child birth and the subject is only 39% likely still able to have children. If male, character has had a vasectomy at some point and now sterile. |
| 10,11. | Undamaged reproductive organs. |
| 12. | Whatever damage has occurred to this rebuilt's privates, his or her organs have since been repaired and upgraded by means of hormone converter-enhancer and other physical surgical implants, this subject has been 'enhanced'. |

## Table XR-128/ Rebuilt Additional Features

Each rebuilt starts with between 1 and 3 (1d3) of these features, but re-roll any duplicated results. Roll 1d30 If no d30 is yet available at the table, roll a 1d10 then a 1d6. The d10 is the ones column, the d6 the tens column and so: 1,2 = add +0 to get 1-10/ 3,4 =add 10 to get 11-20/ 5,6 = add 20 to get 21-30.

| 1d30 | Additional Features of a Rebuilt | Roll 1d3 times |
|---|---|---|

**1. Vulnerable organs:** This rebuilt has raw flesh, missing patches of skin over organs, missing ribs, open sections of skull and a lack of protective muscle over their entrails. In short, this unfortunate starts game play at +10 DV, -10% endurance, and -3d6 appearance, and all physical attacks that roll a natural 01-05 (always a hit normally) are counted as critical hits throughout his or her expectantly short life.

**2. Wig:** A wig has been stitched to this rebuilt's bald, scar covered scalp. Wig color, roll 1d12: 1. blue / 2. pink /3. green / 4. black / 5. metallic silver / 6. metallic gold / 7. blonde / 8. red head / 9. brunette / 10. white / 11. candy apple red / 12. platinum blond.

**3. Face disfigured:** What skin, including the subject's face that remains, is a scar covered sheet, as if in the PC's past, he or she was splashed in acid or burnt in a terrible fire. Appearance score of this person's face is -2d6+2 and can not exceed 20 — although his or her body can have its own appearance trait for when this character wears a masquerade or goalie mask.

**4. Battery Packs:** At some point, somebody clever recovered and reassembled 1d4 battery packs from derelict electric vehicles and stitched and bolted a power pack to this character's back (see illustration page 146). With a mix of exposed and subcutaneous wires and clamps, power is provided to existing electrical features and inserted access outlets in the rebuilt's arms and chest. These built-in battery packs are unique, not expandable or removable without potentially killing the rebuilt (type H END hazard check to avoid cardiac arrest and massive blood loss and death). Each bolted on battery pack contains the equivalent of two standard power cells. A recharge socket is fitted to each to accommodate recharging by fixed installations, wind turbines, solar or direct transfer from other, external power sources. The rebuilt will have 2+1d3 external single plugs, with appropriate adapters carried in a hip pouch. One plug-in is always mounted on the chest and another in each wrist, and can have various energy weapons, household appliances or devices plugged in at one time. Unsightly as hell, these battery packs, seeping clamps, and artless wiring causes a -2d4 appearance drop. This system is waterproofed and all plugs have rubberized covers to avoid electrocution in rain or when swimming. Add 2 kilograms body weight per battery pack.

**5. Mask face:** This rebuilt's face has been torn away. The underlying layer is now a skull-like, gray composite plastic form. To make itself more appealing, this rebuilt has stitched the rubbery face of a beautiful mannequin to it. It never fits quite right, looks odd, but does help disguise the rebuilt among regular human populations. Appearance drop of -2d4+3 with this mask, but double that penalty without this mask.

**6. Squeak and clatter:** Whenever moving, any augmented parts and prosthetics squeak and rub, clatter and creak, making silent movement by this character impossible. Applying oil will work for 2d6 hours before the squeaking returns.

**7. Solar cloak:** Large, flexible sheet of solar power fabric hang down over this rebuilt's back and shoulders like a hood. This sheet is bolted to an inverter and lengths of wire lead to any energy using built-on part, and supply all the rebuilt's energy needs so long as he or she can get a two hours of sunlight per day. The panel is highly coveted and raiders and local warlords will confiscate it on sight upon realizing what the odd, grid patterned cloak really is. This material is stitched to the rebuilt's flesh and besides being painful, is unsightly and so reduced appearance by -1d4+2 APP.

**8. Winch, hook and tow cable:** Fused to this rebuilt's upper back is an electric powered winch, cable and hook assembly. The cable extends 20+1d20 meters and ends in an alloy hook. The motorized winch will pull anything of less than the rebuilt's weight if he or she is standing, or double this if bracing itself or holding onto a solid object or companions of equal or greater weight. Besides being able to pull others up cliffs or lower them down pits, this rebuilt can extend about three meters of cable and, while using one hand, swing the alloy hook with lethal efficiency to make a melee range attack (SV +10, damage 1d20 plus any strength or weapon expert modifiers). This bolted and strapped on, permanent fixture gives the junkoid a hunchback-like appearance, and the scars and nasty stainless steel fittings that hold it into the subject's flesh reduce his or her appearance by -2d6. This unit also acts as armor, improving the defense value by -8, yet adds 30kg weight to the wearer.

**9. Ratchet tie down sheathing:** The character's torso is held together by a sheath of nylon cargo straps and bulging alloy ratchets. The straps are permanently stitch and stapled to the underlying flesh and organs. Removal of these straps inflicts 3d20 damage and the subject must hold his or her entrails and other organs in place least they tumble out and death occur. While able to wear other armor over top, these tie down straps serve as a layer of extra armor, and give the rebuilt a bonus of -20 defensive value. Considered unsightly, this odd, often garishly colored mess of cargo straps reduces the PC's appearance by -2d6.

**10. Raw flesh:** This rebuilt's skin is thin, often torn or missing in spots which make the subject vulnerable to pain and gives off the scent of wounded prey to nearby carnivores. His or her weakened state results in a permanent drop of -2d6 endurance trait points, plus, he or she needs daily wound cleaning and bandaging and suffers a -2d6 appearance drop.

**11. Electric weed trimmer:** Powered by a standard power cell, this manually extendable, 2 meter long shaft ends in a circular, rotary weed cutting blade. It serves as a melee attack with a strike value modifier of +10 and inflicts 3d6 damage to most targets, but since it was designed to take down stubborn weeds and hedges, does double damage to plantoids, mutant plants and anything made of wood — such as most doors and watercraft. One power cell will power the unit for 700 rounds. When not deployed, the blade and extension arm sit above on the forearm of any regular or robotic limb, and an oiled leather slip cover is typically worn to hide the 23cm (9inch) diameter alloy blade. Appearance drop of -1d3+1. Weight +5kg.

**12. Poly rope spool:** This rebuilt is fitted with bright yellow polypropylene plastic rope on a hand cranked, over the shoulder mounted alloy spool. This rope is strong enough to hold 300kg weight and is 100+1d20m long. He or she has a hip pouch containing the following alloy attachments: grappling hook, standard tow hook, hangman's noose, climber's carabiner. A regular harpoon (treat as a spear) can also be lashed to this rope, although anything heavier than the character's strength score in kilograms is too burdensome to pull in without help from comrades.

**13. Tire cladding:** Strips of steel belted tire are bolted to this freak's torso. This built-in armor can be unscrewed for cleaning and wound treatment, and have other armor worn over top. Although unsightly (reduce appearance by -2d4) and reducing this scrapper's move by -0.25m, he or she enjoys a defense value bonus of -14.

**14. Motion detector light:** Bolted to the junkoid's shoulder is a small solar panel that charges a motion sensor light on the opposite shoulder. It can be turned on and off like a regular light as well, or set to motion detection mode which, if anything moves within a 9m half moon ahead of the sensor, the brilliant LED light goes on, blinding any nocturnal creatures or trespassers for 1d3 rounds and easily revealing them. This light, either in motion detector or regular mode, has a range of 30 meters. For every 1 hour of exposure to bright light or sunlight, this illuminator will operate for 2 hours. Any armor worn by this rebuilt can be cut to accommodate the charge panel and light fixture. Reduce the rebuilt's appearance by -1d4 APP.

**15. Head mounted handgun:** This rebuilt has a gun permanently bolted to the side of their head. The trigger mechanism is wired to a jaw bolted wire and spring system while a sighting ring can be manually flipped down from a forehead mounted, iron brow-brim when the gun is needed. The ammo magazine or power cell is loaded by hand. To disguise this weapon, the junkoid wears either a hood, wig, kerchief, or turban type arrangement of fabric.

The gun is treated as a normal variant and can have the weapon expert applied. This gun can be used with hand held weapons, too, adding an extra attack mode per round, including in melee range fights. This is an unsightly and intrusive modification to the character's head, leaving plenty of scars and rusty parts on display; reduce appearance by -2d4+2.

This pistol can be torn off and, with a few modifications, made ready for hand held use in an hour. Likewise, a different pistol can replace whatever existing weapon is already present.

**Roll 1d10** here to determine the type of gun bolted to this rebuilt's head:
**1.** Pocket pistol: SV mod +5, rate 2, range 120m, damage 1d20, loaded with 3+d3 rounds ammo*
**2.** Wrist laser: SV mod +10, rate 1, range 210m, damage 10+1d10, charge has 2d8 shots**
**3.** Shotgun pistol SV mod +15, rate 1 or 2, range 30m, damage 3d10, loaded with 2 shotgun shells*
**4.** Mini laser: SV mod +13, rate 1, range 120m, damage 10+1d8, charge has 2d10 shots**
**5-7.** Automatic pistol: SV mod +12, rate 2, range 250m, damage d20, loaded with 2d10 rounds ammo*
**8.** High caliber automatic pistol SV mod +12, rate 2, range 250m, damage 1d20+10, loaded with 2d10 rounds ammo*
**9.** Stun pistol: SV mod +15, rate 1, range 200m, damage 2d20 stun, charge holds 2d20 shots**
**10.** Laser pistol: SV mod +16, rate 1, range 500m, damage 1d20+10, charge has 1d30 (or 3d10) shots**

** There is a 6 in 10 chance that this character has a pouch filled with 3d6 spare rounds for this weapon, and if a pocket pistol or auto pistol, a further 2 in 10 chance of a spare magazine that fits this weapon (presently empty).*
*** There is a 4 in 10 chance this rebuilt has a spare, fully charged mini power cell or full size power cell (depending on what the energy weapon uses) in a belt pouch.*

**16. Fold out camp chair:** Screwed and stitched to this rebuilt's posterior is a lightweight, alloy folding chair with padded seat, fold down legs, and back rest cushions. Whenever desired the junkoid need only flip back a hip mounted lever and extend the legs to deploy this comfortable seat. Its a strange contraption to have at one's back end, and any armor worn must be modified to accommodate this rig. Scar tissue and stitch marks reduce the subject's appearance by -1d4+2 APP.

**17. Covered in metal studs:** This rebuilt's entire body is studded with stainless steel knobs, bolts, screws and washers. There are hundreds of these small metal bumps and knobs, each surrounded by scar tissue and fading stitch marks, reducing the subject's appearance by -6+1d6 but offering a -15 defense value bonus. These studs are low profile and allow the rebuilt to wear other armor over-top. There is no movement penalty for this cladding but add +5kg to his or her weight.

**18. Spring spike attachment:** Beneath its hand, in the dominant wrist of this rebuilt's arm is a permanently housed, relatively well hidden muscle engaged alloy spring spike. This weapon is identical to the hand held relic noted on page TME-186. Initiative of +5 when deployed on first round as a surprise attack, having a +60 SV on that initial strike. Once deployed and opponents are aware of the weapon, it has a strike value bonus of only +5. On a hit, it inflicts 1d20+2 damage, plus any strength and weapon skill modifiers applied to it. The odd ridge beneath the flesh of the arm and assorted scars and stitches reduce the rebuilt's appearance by -1d4+1 points.

**19. Stereo system:** Sewn into the upper chest of this rebuilt are a pair of hard wired speakers, while bolted to his belly is a sub-woofer and a music control panel. Powered by replaceable standard power cells (one lasting for 60 continuous hours of blaring music), an operator can flip open the access panel and follow the on-screen prompts to select from both themed play lists or individual musical tracks from the old world. The volume can be turned from barley audible to incredibly loud — loud enough to be heard from 6 kilometers away on a calm day or 12km across an open water body, steppe or desert. This rebuilt can also tap a sampler button and get a totally random musical track.

| | |
|---|---|
| **1.** Country music | **17.** Hip Hop or Rap |
| **2.** Heavy metal | **18.** Classical symphony |
| **3.** Punk rock | **19.** Classical opera |
| **4.** Christmas carol | **20.** Celtic |
| **5.** Movie soundtrack | **21.** Bass heavy house music |
| **6.** Latin pop | **22.** Pop |
| **7.** Ambient electronic | **23.** New Age meditation |
| **8.** Blues | **24.** Gospel |
| **9.** Classic rock | **25.** Spanish guitar |
| **10.** Bagpipes | **26.** World music |
| **11.** Trance club beats | **27.** Industrial |
| **12.** Golden oldies | **28.** Pagan, Viking, ancient European |
| **13.** Jazz | **29.** Oriental classical (Korea, Japan, China and similar) |
| **14.** RnB | **30.** Indian classical |
| **15.** Reggae | |
| **16.** Hawaiian ukulele | |

The GM is encouraged to jot down a 1d30 table of actual music that is available to play at the game table, however for a random sample, roll 1d30 above to the sort of musical track that belches out of this rebuilt's abdomen. The subcutaneous wires, speakers and other hi-fi gear stitched into this person reduce his or her appearance by -2d4 and add 5kg weight. Roll 1d30 for a random musical track:

**20. Deployable Skateboard:** Bolted to the back of one shin, this lower leg mounted plastic skateboard has knobby, off-road wheels and a handy one hand crank handle for carefree deployment. It takes one round to reach down and thrust the spring-loaded lever which slides the skateboard down and under the leg, to which is it permanently braced.

Having had countless hours practice with this rugged platform, the rebuilt is able to navigate even the most pot hole riddled and junk strewn old streets, sidewalks and corridors, and able to travel at 9 meters per round on hard packed ground, or 12m on smooth surfaces, double these numbers downhill, and half up going up hill. While moving, the rebuilt can sacrifice half his or her speed to swerve and attempt to better dodge incoming fire, gaining -10 DV.

This durable skateboard and accompany springs and cranks adds a permanent -5 defense value to the junkoid and has only a -3 appearance penalty. However, it adds +4kg to the subject's weight and will not function in sand, mud, dense brush or over loose rubble.

**21. Camp stove:** Bolted to the hip of this rebuilt is a fold out alloy one-pot camp stove. It has a lower burner area with side fuel insertion port, air intake and small 500ml oil reservoir for liquid combustibles. It will burn most any flammable substance including twigs, dry grass, leaves, dung, fur or ethanol fuel, but also features a self strike flint and steel fire starter, kindling and tinder storage sack and waterproof, oiled cover. When not in use, it can be unlocked and flatted along the side of the thigh. Permanently screwed to the body, this contraption has left nasty scars and reduces the appearance of the rebuilt by -d4+1 point. Likewise, because it is a mass of alloy shafts and plates, it offers a defense value bonus of -5 DV.

**22. Harpoon arm:** Besides whatever other features, if any, one of the rebuilt's arms might posses, it is also fitted with a built in harpoon gun. This specialized weapon has between one and three tubes (roll 1d3 at character generation), each of which is fired by modified tendons in the junkoid's forearm. All or just one harpoon may be fired in a single round, while each takes 2 rounds to load and crank back the inner spring and compressed air system. Harpoons are typically made of steel, have an SV of +8, inflict 1d20+9 damage on a strike, and have a range of thirty meters (half this underwater). The bulky, subcutaneous weapon makes the arm bulky and unattractive, and while it can be used as a pipe weapon (DMG d10+1) it reduces the subject's appearance by -d4+2. The PC's hand is also present only 30% of the time.

**23. Radio-head:** Part of this rebuilt's head has been shaved, the skin peeled back and stitched about a series of openings in the skull where communication equipment has been screwed to his or her cranium. A series of salvaged antennas, metal coat hangers, and copper filaments spring up from the jumble of mismatched electronics, and are attached to a replacement ear speaker system with simple on, off, and loudspeaker mode switch. A pull down microphone boom can be used by either the owner or a companion, while a coiled patch cable leads to a tiny belt mounted keyboard that serves as an alphanumeric input device allowing the operator to dial up various receptions or send text messages. One standard power cell powers this unit and yields six months operation. Although shoddily made and bulky, this contraption acts like a standard communicator. The intrusive apparatus reduces the rebuilt's appearance by -2d4.

**24. Mesh wire cladding:** Affixed to this rebuilt's body, limbs and most of the head — excluding the face — are layers of stainless steel and alloy mesh wire. This housing acts like a layer of advanced chainmail and is permanently fused to the body by micro cables, staples, stitches and bolts. Removal of this layer would leave terrible scars and a 3 in 8 chance of death within 2d6 hours. Although unsightly (appearance drop of -3d6), this armored husk improves the subject's defense value by -18, although is cumbersome, adds +8kg body weight and reduces the junker's movement by -0.5m per round. Other armors can be worn over this cladding.

**24. Metal jaw:** Somewhere along the line, this rebuilt's lower jaw and upper teeth were shattered, cut or blown away. The junk doctor who reconstructed this person's mouth did so using the alloy lower jaw of a heavy combat android, and the upper teeth from some sort of woodworking tool. The result is that the hideous face of this rebuilt is fitted with an oversized, shark-like jaw filled with triangular, rust flecked teeth. Powering the jaw are grafted muscles, pistons and springs, giving immense power to any bite this freak makes. Strike value +10, damage 4d6+any strength modifier.

This frightening looking mouth and accompanying artificial muscles and mechanisms reduce the appearance of the rebuilt by -10+d6. This modification can have the weapon expert skill applied to it, or the brawling or martial art skill, but not both. It adds +5 kilograms weight to the character and when seen for the first time, frightens away commoners and most man sized or smaller animals. Treat as an extra melee attack.

**26. Hearing enhancer:** Embedded into and around the back of the character's ear is a putty colored listening device. This unobtrusive relic requires a pill power cell to operate for up to 360 hours, and manual switch to turn on and off. This unit doubles the effective hearing range of the rebuilt, giving the subject +2 initiative on initial contact with other beings. The unit has a safety shut off in the event that gun shots or other loud noises occur nearby, thus avoiding ear damage. There is only a -1 appearance penalty for this attachment.

**27. Hand crank generator:** By means of a pull out crank handle and internally attached electric monitor, this rebuilt can turn a crank and slowly generate electricity. The subject has a bank of three power cells for its own use, each with a coiled up patch cable to power energy weapons or other relic devices, or else provide power to comrades who must stay within the 6 meter cable length of the power cord from each battery.

So too, the generator has external jacks to allow other devices to be plugged into the generator itself, and receive recharging as the junkoid or another person turns the crank handle. It is a slow process, however, and makes a lot of noise. It takes 100 minutes of cranking to charge one standard power cell or a half hour to charge a mini power cell. In short, 1 'energy unit' can be cranked per 10 minutes.

Power units are shown on the power sources table on page 199 of the hub rules, along with all the typical battery types. A pill cell has 1 energy unit, a mini cell 3 units, a standard power cell 10 units and a power pack has 100 units.

**28. Iron plated:** The torso and shoulders of this rebuilt are plated in permanently secured, rusty iron plates and internal bracing and cable strapping. The subject weighs an extra 20+3d10 kilograms, moves 1 meter per round slower, cannot float or swim without a life jacket or two, but has a robustness and natural armor that makes them an exceptional battlefield asset. The natural defense value of this junkoid is improved by -30, plus, he or she gains +20+1d20 to both strength and endurance and any punch, kick or other physical melee attack by this brute scores an extra +2d6 damage on top of any strength  trait or unarmed combat skill based bonuses (so 3d6 base punch damage). Highly unattractive, this character's appearance is reduced by -10+d6. Because this plating is attached at the skin level, the rebuilt can wear additional armor's over top.

**29. Multi-species game caller:** For whatever reason, a junk doctor has installed a throat fused game caller apparatus inside the rebuilt's neck. Although able to talk normally, this subject has also mastered the proper inhale-exhale adjustment nozzles to select between making a very authentic sounding game call from among the following: moose, elk, goose, wild turkey, duck, coyote, distressed rabbit, doe deer or cow moose in heat, and crow call.

Using this game call in an appropriate wilderness area is just as likely to bring mutant wolves or other predators as it is the desired game animal. Range 5km radius in open terrain, 2km in woodlands and craggy terrain.

**30. Shock Arm:** Electric wires and insulators from salvaged security fencing are wrapped about this rebuilt's arm. Meanwhile, bolted to the user's shoulder is an armored power box which accepts up to three standard power cells, although only one is needed to deliver a devastating charge after a successful strike. This hideously mutilated, wire wrapped limb reduces the rebuilt's appearance by -2d4 APP, however when activated and a strike occurs, the arm will deliver a shock into a victim that inflicts 2d20 stun damage and 1d20 lethal damage, double this to robots, androids , mutorgs, vat-brains, nanoborgs and cyborgs. One power cell will yield 10 such shocks at +15 strike value. 

3 in 10 rebuilt with this part have a hand on the limb.

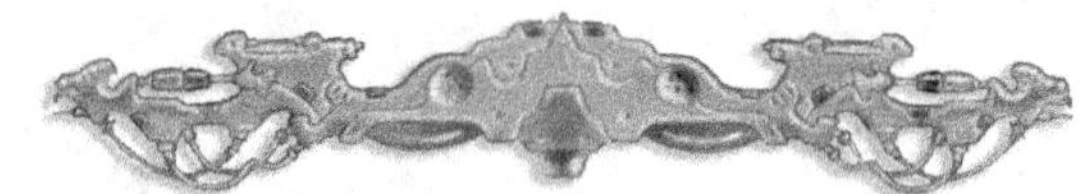

# Robot

Similar to unique, self aware androids, these individuals occupy a permanent hard drive within the head of a randomly generated robotic body. While able to employ the services of a robotics technician to attach harvested appendages from defeated or uncovered robots, these units often have odd body shapes and rarely pass for humans when entering communities, nor are they able to wear most relic armor.

If their CPU is shot through, or their head is crushed, they are killed. Digital beings often occupy these forms of unique robots, while hostile digital beings can also attack, hack into, and dominate this being; possessing it and often deleting the consciousness forever.

A robust, combat ready unique robot is a welcome asset to any excavation party, particularly one housed in a military grade, armored chassis and fitted with relic firepower, however, most are far more modest in their construction.

Unique robot characters differ from many robot relics, in that they typically have human sized, bipedal shaped bodies, self awareness, a notable personality, and a sense of self preservation and motivation that matches a human. They also have at least one human-like arm and hand with which to deploy relics weapons, manipulate common gear, and interact in an excavation like other common character types.

Unlike androids, most robots are not waterproofed and as they are basically metal blocks with metal appendages, will sink to the bottom of any water body and must make an endurance based type D hazard check each minute once submerged or short out from water seeping into their vital circuitry and take 1d20 damage per short. Like androids, all robots can have their circuits, optics and other parts cooked by exposure to radiation. A section in the Expanded and Optional Rules section called 'Radiation and its effects on Robots and Androids' is included on page 378 of this book.

Most robots are considerably tougher than organic beings, and while they are susceptible to electrical and EMP attacks or being immersed in water and shorting out, they are resistant to many perils which would eliminate their fleshy counterparts. Robots take only half damage from both fire and acid attacks, are resistant to the bite of sand and junk storms, unaffected by venom, pepper spray, itching compounds, and immune to mind reading and mental attacks that directly target an organic brain, They likewise suffer only half damage from hailstorms and crushing damage from being buried under rubble or caught in an avalanche. They take normal damage from falls, however.

Robots recover from EMP and stun damage, and have regular physical damage repaired the same as androids. See page XR-47, 'Androids Healing Mode' to learn how your new robot character heals.

## Robot Self Awareness

These robots can learn, navigate, interact and predict outcomes. In short, as they conduct themselves in the world, they improve. This growth — which is expressed as going up in rank like any other character — expands the unit's social interactions, allows them to better navigate their physical environment and actions during movement, melee and ranged combat. Evolving also allows a self-aware, unique robot to learn to better harm or repair both machinery and organic beings, and strengthen interpersonal relationships with both conscious machines and all manner of sentient life.

These one of a kind robots exhibit an overriding sense of self awareness, self preservation, and fondness for the self and those who it sees as beneficial and trustworthy to it. It desires to go on existing and expanding its power, to continue learning about the world about it, and understand and either annihilate, befriend, cooperate with, or enhance other entities it meets. In most cases, these customized, somewhat scrap-built machines do not exist to serve a hive, a faction, a corporation, country, or ideology, and so won't imperil ithemselves needlessly, take orders without having willfully given others authority over it, nor harm other machines or living things when not absolutely necessary.

A self aware robot sees the benefits of friendships, of tribe, of family and, if given time, will view both organic and mechanical companions as valuable assets, battery suppliers, as well as sources of learning, of protection, liberty, and unending opportunities for growth.

Typically, any unique robots who joins an excavation team has an enhanced curiosity about the world around it, and is compelled to explore, uncover lost places, travel to never before seen places, and along the way, empower itself and its companions by securing firepower, armor, communicators, self improvement and all-essential power supplies.

Each unique robot has some degree of self awareness, or the perception of being a true artificial Intelligence, as opposed to a splendid mimic.

A mimic, which includes most NPC robots, exhibit a range of artificial intelligence that varies from a mere flicker to an advanced, true learning machine. The most basic forms of self aware robots are in fact merely adaptive machines, whereby every response, statement and reaction is merely selected from an extensive directory of options which, based on the situation, are acted upon. These pre-programmed responses give others the sense that they are dealing with a personality rich, truly living machine. Often, even the so-called self aware robot itself believes it is interacting with the world as a truly self conscious being, which is part of its programming. These

machines are able to learn and adapt to their surroundings, yet their processors and memory are limited, and they cannot grow more intelligent, more perceptive or improve their willpower.

The unique robots described here are, however, self aware robots that think and react for themselves, and learn from all interactions. They employ a mix of appropriate pre-assigned responses both verbally and physically, but also adopt new responses, randomness and take social, conversational and tactical ques from companions. Likewise, they deploy all-together new interactions in conversation, movement and physical deeds. Put another way, these robots adapt, grow smarter, learn from both their failures and successes, and improve with every interaction. They make for exceptional companions for those who've formed beneficial bonds of friendship with them, yet are dangerous and unpredictable foes for those that mean to harm them or this unit's freely chosen friends.

The most powerful forms of artificial intelligence, meanwhile, appear in facility based super computers as well as in rare, unique android variants. Throughout the twisted new world of The Mutant Epoch, however, higher Ais constrained to the mismatched bodies of unique robots also exist, but their sense of self preservation is so high that they view undertaking of perilous adventures into the wastelands or ruined cities as foolish, and so never occur as player character excavators.

## Creating Your Robot Character

A unique robot character is assembled by rolling on the following 18 or 19 tables. At first, this massive portion of the book and all the tables might look daunting, with too much to know. In truth, you'll only need to roll a die or two on each table, read only the result, jot down a few notes and the dice roll and perhaps the table number it was found on for later reference, and quickly move on to the next table and so on. A new player to this character type, or a game master in need of plenty of NPC robots, might want to roll up a half dozen to practice and set aside for later use.

On the following tables you will find a matrix for the unit's chassis, the robot's manipulators or arms, its locomotion method, and head and CPU within it. Other randomly determined features include senses, comms, special programs, possible standard cybernetic implants, additional parts, skills based on traits, outfitting rolls, and an optional selection of tables to determine who made this robot.

To begin, print out a robot character sheet or photocopy it from the back of this book on page XR-524. All the character sheets for this and other new character types from this book are freely available on our public page at https://www.outlandarts.com/expansionrules.htm .

## Starting Traits

The basic traits of a unique robot are as follows, although during the process of building this unit, including establishing the robot's pre-game caste (page XR-177), these traits will be altered so jot them down in pencil lightly or on a scrap piece of paper before applying them to a character sheet. Other traits, such as Processor, Data Points, and Firewall, will be added when the character's CPU is determined.

Traits are not rolled on the usual table like most other character types, but instead established through addition and subtraction when rolling on the following tables. As with all characters, a unique robot can go up in rank, and through the process of hardening itself, fine tuning based on experiences in the field, tiny upgrades, CPU maintenance and adoptive learning, its traits can increase just like most other character type as revealed on table XR-12 Rank Gain Bonus Matrix, on page 23.

**Endurance** Based on Chassis toughness
**Strength** Based on limbs
**Agility** Based on general Mobility and any locomotion additions
**Accuracy** Based on Optics and system coordination
**Intelligence** Based on CPU in head
**Willpower** based on CPU in head
**Perception** Based on sensory nodes and self awareness
**Appearance** is not normally recorded for a robot unless it has a human-like head — which would typically come from an android. Determine this trait as 2-12 (roll 2d6) simply for NPC reaction rolls.

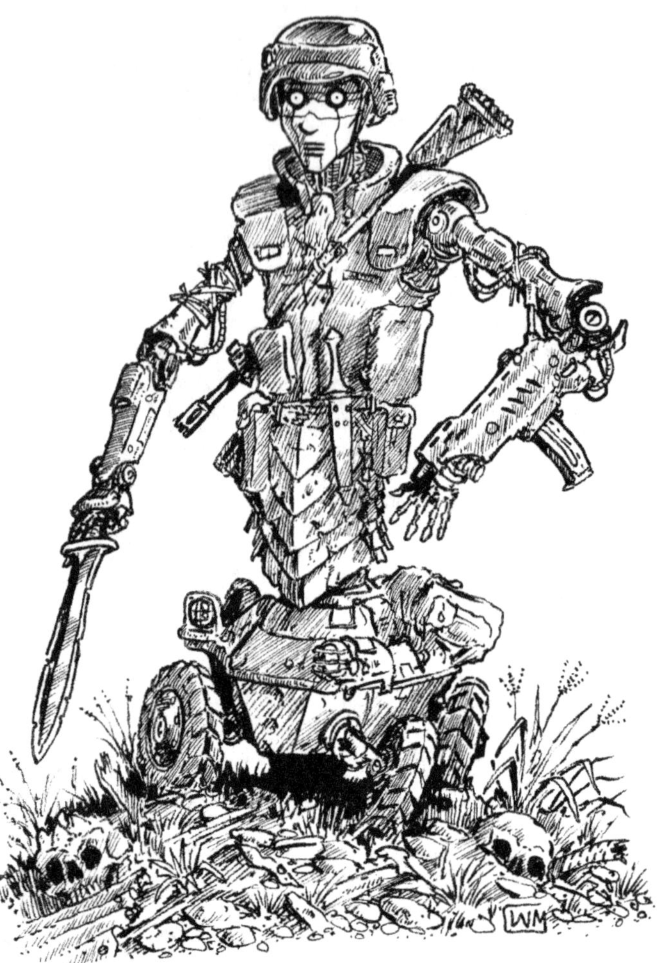

## Self Aware Robot's Gender ID and Personality

Most unique robots have had plenty of exposure to people and have either been programmed as companions or else learned the social norms and mannerisms of humans. Some have adopted or embraced an assigned gender identity and maintain a consistent mannerism or personality to better define themselves as a person instead of an appliance. For personality, roll on table XR-294 found in the Appendices on page 500. If the personalty it disruptive to team cohesion and performance, the robot can change this by rolling for another random personality, but only if it makes Type C intelligence based hazard check.

As for this robot's assumed gender, the player should either choose a gender identity that the robot starts game play with or else roll 2d6 here:

### Table XR-129/ Self Aware Robot's Gender ID

| 2d6 | Robot's Assumed Gender ID |
|---|---|
| 2-5. | Female |
| 6-8. | No gender, refers to itself as its alpha-numerical creator given designation, but will adopt a common name and gender if requested to do so by its companions. |
| 9-12. | Male |

## Table XR-130/ Unique Robot Chassis

| 1d100 | Chassis or Torso Description | Base Weight | Base Height | Endurance | DV Modifier |
|---|---|---|---|---|---|
| 01-06. | Stick thin, narrow waist and chest | 40+d12kg | 70+1d20cm | 20+3d6 | -8 DV |
| 07-13. | Tubular | 50+d20kg | 80+2d20cm | 30+d20 | -12 DV |
| 14-18. | Boxy, rectangular body | 60+d20kg | 60+1d20cm | 40+d20 | -15 DV |
| 19-24. | Angular, sloped armored chassis | 100+3d20kg | 70+2d20cm | 60+3d20 | -25 DV |
| 25-31. | Hourglass figure of a fit human woman* | 40+2d20kg | 60+2d20cm | 30+3d6 | -5 DV |
| 32-40. | Broad chested, thin waist of a fit human man* | 60+3d20kg | 80+2d20cm | 40+4d6 | -5 DV |
| 41-48. | Spherical, ball shaped body | 50+2d20kg | 50+2d20cm | 35+3d20 | -8 DV |
| 49-61. | Jumbled, dent covered, lopsided hunk of junk | 70+2d20kg | 50+3d20cm | 20+4d20 | -10 DV |
| 62-66. | Articulating segments, V-shaped, overlapping panels | 80+2d20kg | 70+1d20cm | 50+3d20 | -12 DV |
| 67-71. | Humanoid, ball shaped articulating waist, V-shaped chest | 60+2d20kg | 70+1d20cm | 30+3d10 | -5 DV |
| 72-82. | Angular upper body, tubular midsection and triangular hips | 50+3d12kg | 60+2d20cm | 40+3d12 | -7 DV |
| 83-88. | Conical, with narrowest point at bottom of torso | 50+3d20kg | 60+2d20cm | 45+3d10 | -8 DV |
| 89-93. | Oval-like, almost egg shaped body | 60+2d12kg | 60+2d20cm | 50+2d12 | -10 DV |
| 94,95. | Humanoid, child sized | 20+2d6kg | 30+1d20cm | 10+3d8 | -7 DV |
| 96-00. | Humanoid, bulky and towering | 200+2d100kg | 120+4d20cm | 100+d100 | -10 |

*This is an attractive torso and on its own, would be regarded as having an appearance trait value of 30+2d20. Should the unit somehow end up with a human-like head and limbs, it might also be considered an android — although maintain it as a unique robot character type.*

**A note about the height and weight base values from the above table.** This is the length of the torso without the head and legs. Be sure to record and add the overall weight and height as you create your unique robot character, because the size and kilograms of any PC are called upon frequently during game play.

# Cladding and Potential Armor

Because these units are custom constructs, their limbs and head are sheathed in different materials from the torso. What follows is a table which features a random listing of the cladding — or lack thereof — as well as possible armor plating at the time of character generation.

A game master can use this same table to allow for the modification of a robot should the unit come upon sufficient materials and have a skilled assistant handy to help modify and apply upgraded armor to the torso.

Multiple layers of armor can be applied, however the weight increase and movement penalties would make such additions impractical.

Of note is the weight and endurance columns on the fallowing table, which give a percentage change to the unit's exiting chassis stats. While applying a percentage is a hassle, it is the only way to reflect a sensible addition or subtraction to the character's torso type and size, since a tiny or thin unit would not gain the weight or endurance change of a much larger unit. Similarly, the cost column shows a price per kilogram, which means what this upgrade will cost based on the starting kilograms of the unit's chassis. For example, to have a 120kg robot sheathed in flexible plastic skin, at a rate of 3sp per KG, would cost 360sp. The Movement column shows any potential modifier to the robot's movement rate per round applied to whatever locomotion method is yet to be determined from table XR-134 on page 155.

## Table XR-131/ Robot Cladding and Potential Armor

| 1d100 | Cladding Type | Weight Added | Endurance | Base DV | Movement | Cost per KG of Chassis |
|---|---|---|---|---|---|---|
| 01-08. | No Cladding, exposed parts and wiring | -10% | -10% | +5 DV* | +1m | None |
| 09-17. | Plastic sheeting and canvas | +0% | +0% | -2 DV | +0m | None |
| 18-24. | Human-like heated skin | +0% | +0 | -1 DV | +0m | None |
| 25-32. | Flexible plastic skin | +0% | +5% | -3 DV | +0m | 3sp/kg |
| 33-37. | Hard, flame resistant skin | +5% | +8% | -10** DV | -0.25m | 5sp/kg |
| 38-49. | Hard plastic plates | +10% | +15% | -15 DV | -0.5m | 4sp/kg |
| 50-56. | Extra hard plastic plates | +15% | +20% | -20 DV | -0.75m | 8sp/kg |
| 57-75. | Thin metal | +10% | +20% | -25 DV | -0.75m | 6sp/kg |
| 76-83. | Thick metal | +30% | +30% | -35 DV | -1.5m | 11sp/kg |
| 84-89. | Ballistic fabric and hard plastic | +20% | +30% | -15 or -35*** DV | -0.5m | 13sp/kg |
| 90-96. | Composite fiber-alloy | +30% | +40% | -20 DV | -1m | 15sp/kg |
| 97-00. | Heavy alloy plating | +40% | +50% | -30 DV | -2m | 18sp/kg |

* This is actually a penalty, as this unit is +5 defense value easier to hit. Highly vulnerable to dust storms, shorting out if splashed with liquid and any strike against it of a roll of 01-05 is always a critical hit instead of merely an automatic hit. This unit requires at least a fabric covering of rags, animal skins and plastic to avoid most environmental perils.

** Takes half damage from flame throwing relics, mutations, and regular fires.

*** This robot has a defense value increase of -20 extra against bullets and blunt attacks (15+20 =35 DV) and takes -10 damage from any fall.

## Primary Human-like Arm

These arms end in some sort of hand, with android arms having a human shaped palm and 5 digits, while robotic limbs feature a metallic hand with a thumb and 2+1d2 fingers.

For the purposes of pulling open doors, or other overall strength hazard checks and feats, combine the strength score of all arms to get the character's overall strength for these purposes. Any one handed weapon held in a robot arm uses the strength benefits of that arm, however if two or more arms are employed, combine the strength scores to get whatever bonus might occur. For bows and crossbows, which employ two arms to crank or draw back, again, add the scores of both arms involved to apply any range or damage modifiers. While this human-like arm is considered the unit's dominant hand, there is a 2 in 10 chance that this being is ambidextrous and can use a weapon in each hand without the standard off-hand -20 SV penalty.

### Table XR-132/ Primary Human-like Robotic Arm

| 1d100 | Arm Description | Weight | Strength | SV | Punch DMG* | Note |
|---|---|---|---|---|---|---|
| 01-09. | Lean, shapely female android's arm | 5kg | 10+1d20 | +0 | 1d6 | Mostly plastic, dexterous +1d6 agility |
| 10-35. | Toned, android's arm | 10kg | 20+1d20 | +2 | 1d8 | Mostly plastic |
| 36-42. | Muscular android's arm | 15kg | 30+2d20 | +5 | 1d10 | Mostly plastic |
| 43-49. | Alloy android's arm | 20kg | 40+2d20 | +8 | 1d12 | 72% chance sheathed in skin-like plastic, otherwise raw metal |
| 50-62. | Thin, robotic arm | 7kg | 10+4d6 | +2 | 1d8 | 56% chance clad in plastic, otherwise wires and parts exposed |
| 63-86. | Medium robotic arm | 14kg | 20+1d20 | +4 | 1d10 | 52% chance clad in plastic, otherwise wires and parts exposed |
| 87-94. | Large robotic arm | 25kg | 40+2d20 | +10 | 1d12 | 49% chance clad in plastic, otherwise wires and parts exposed |
| 95-97. | Huge robotic arm | 40kg | 50+2d20 | +15 | 3d6 | -0.5m move/44% chance clad in plastic, otherwise wires and parts exposed |
| 98-00. | Colossal robotic arm | 60kg | 60+2d20 | +20 | 1d20+4 | -1m move/42% chance clad in metal (improve robot's overall DV by -10), otherwise -0 DV with wires and parts exposed, walks lopsided |

*Base punching damage before any potential strength modifiers.

### Table XR-133/ Secondary Robotic Arm

| 1d100 | Arm Description | Weight | Strength | SV | DMG* | Note**** |
|---|---|---|---|---|---|---|
| 01-14. | As another random Human-like arm from the table above (XR-132) | NA | NA | NA | NA | NA |
| 15-24. | Light robotic arm with alloy crab pincer | 25kg | 20+1d20 | +5 SV | 1d12 | 73% chance clad in metal (improve DV by -5), otherwise -0 DV with wires and parts exposed |
| 25-41. | Light robotic arm with hand and weapon arm** | 20kg | 20+1d20 | +2 SV | 1d10 | 68% chance clad in metal (improve DV by -5), otherwise -0 DV with wires and parts exposed |
| 42-48. | Medium robotic arm with alloy crab pincer | 40kg | 30+1d20 | +8 SV | 2d12 | 88% chance clad in metal (improve DV by -8), otherwise -0 DV with wires and parts exposed |
| 49-76. | Medium robotic arm with hand and weapon arm** | 30kg | 30+3d10 | +5 SV | 3d6 | 65% chance clad in metal (improve DV by -7), otherwise -0 DV with wires and parts exposed |
| 77-83. | Alloy tentacle that ends in a three fingered grasping hand | 40kg | 20+1d20 | +6 SV | 2d6 | Has a normal length of 2m but extendable to 6m. Grasper has an agility score of 40+2d20 separate from rest of unit and can perform delicate tasks including pick pocketing. Can wield a crude, non-trigger weapon. |
| 84-90. | Huge robotic arm with massive alloy hand | 45kg | 50+4d10 | +18 SV | 4d6 | 82% chance clad in metal (improve DV by -13), otherwise -3 DV with wires and parts exposed |
| 91-95. | Huge robotic arm with alloy crab pincer | 95kg | 50+5d10 | +22 SV | 3d12 | 79% chance clad in metal (improve DV by -15), otherwise -5 DV with wires and parts exposed |
| 96-00. | Huge robotic arm with hand and weapon arm implant*** | 40kg | 50+3d10 | +15 SV | 3d6 DMG | 76% chance clad in metal (improve DV by -11), otherwise -4 DV with wires and parts exposed |

*Base punching, crushing or cutting damage before any potential strength modifiers.

** The SV (Strike Value) bonus and damage shown are for the fist attack of this hand, and does not apply to any non-strength based weapon modes. Do, however, add any additional strength based damage to either this character's hand based or strength based attack — including bows and crossbows and thrown hand held weapon such as rocks, spears and tires.

***Weapon arm attachment is as a cyborg's implant by the same name. Roll 1d6, with a result of 1-3 meaning see page 92 of the Mutant Epoch Hub rules. A result of 4-6 means see page 348 of this book to establish which weapon arm implant, and energy source or ammo supply, is attached. Remember to add the weight of this weapon arm to the robotic character's overall weight.

**** Improvement to DV (Defense Value) are to the robot's overall DV.

## Table XR-134/ Robot Locomotion Mode

| 1d100 | Locomotion Mode | Weight | Height | Base Agility | Endurance Bonus | Base Move | Notes |
|---|---|---|---|---|---|---|---|
| 01-15. | Thin, 'stick man' legs | 10+1d20kg | +80cm | 40+2d20 | +0 END | 6m | Skeletal looking |
| 16-22. | Stubby, thick legs | 20+1d12kg | +40cm | 20+2d20 | +10 END | 5m | Short, dwarf-like |
| 23-27. | Android's legs, woman's | 20+1d20kg | +80cm | 40+3d20 | +4 END | 7m | Shapely yet toned |
| 28-37. | Android's legs, men's | 30+2d20kg | +90cm | 40+2d20 | +10 END | 7m | Muscular |
| 38-43. | Tracked | 100+4d20kg | +70cm | 20+2d20 | +70 END | 9m* | Quite noisy when operational, maximum of 1 skill point in stealth. Can run over small creatures house cat sized or smaller in a 1m wide swath, or ram or crush any man sized or smaller targets: SV +10, DMG 2d20. Excellent in mud, snow or sand where it suffers no movement penalty |
| 44-52. | Four off-road tires | 70+3d20kg | +80cm | 30+2d20 | +40 END | 12m* | Rubberized tires can travel through mud, snow and sand with only a 25% movement rate penalty, however the electric motors are somewhat noisy and limit this character's stealth skill to a maximum of 2pts. Can ram or drive over small creatures, house cat sized or smaller, as well as fallen human sized opponents: SV +8/ DMG 1d20. |
| 53-60. | Bipedal Dog-like legs | 20+2d20kg | +90cm | 40+2d20 | +10 END | 9m | Add 1 melee kick attack SV +12/ DMG 2d6. Bipedal and spring loaded which allow this unit to jump horizontally to its full movement rate in distance, or up vertically half its movement rate in height. |
| 61-65. | Articulating Snake Body | 20kg per meter in length | Can rear up to half its tail length | 50+2d20 | +5 END per meter length of tail | 9m | 3+1d3m long, Add 1 melee tail whip attack SV +14/ DMG 3d10 lethal or stun. Upon a successful strike on a man-sized or smaller being, this robot can elect to wrap about and constrict the victim for an automatic 1d8 stun damage per round, or merely hold a target in place — although enduring possible counter attacks from the coiled victim who fights at -20 SV. Able to move over sand, snow and mud at only a -25% MV reduction. |
| 66-71. | Four Crab legs | 40+2d20kg | +60cm | 40+2d20 | +20 END | 7m | 2 melee stab attacks SV +8/ DMG 1d12 each. Plus add 1d2 skill points in Climbing (pg TME-36). |
| 72-78. | Six crab legs | 60+2d20kg | +60cm | 50+2d20 | +30 END | 9m | 3 stab melee stab attacks SV +8/ DMG 1d12 each. Plus add 1d2+1 skill points in Climbing (pg TME-36). |
| 79-84. | Centaur body | 100+3d20kg | +120cm | 40+2d20 | +50 END | 12m | Four metal horse legs, rear up or rear kick back attacks: 2/ SV +10 / DMG 3d6 each. Can have a man sized rider or 200kg cargo carried on back with only a -2m movement penalty. Horse sized torso carries a spare power pack besides whatever other power source noted on other tables. This backup can be accessed by the robot or plugged into by others via hidden hatches. Comes complete with a power cable with 4m long cord. |
| 85-91. | Bird-like legs | 20+2d12kg | +80cm | 30+2d20 | +8 END | 10m | Add 1 melee claw attack SV +10/ DMG 2d6 |
| 92-00. | Heavy humanoid robotic | 60+2d20kg | +90cm | 20+2d20 | +30 END | 5m | Can make an optional (not extra) kick attack SV +10/ DMG 3d6+3 |

*Tracked and wheeled robots can only traverse stairs at half speed. 1 in 6 such units can unlock and totally disconnect from the lower locomotion mode to either crawl along by pulling itself on its belly, ride on a companion's back, be strapped to a horse, or be mounted to an alternate set of regular bipedal robotic legs if the GM allows it.

## Primary Optics

Different eye varieties can be harvested from other robots and inserted into any empty socket, or an upgraded eye can replace an existing eye. Any substitution or insertion of additional eyes requires a robotics technician using the table on page 54 of the hub rules. This same table includes some chance of making these repair by both mechanical and electrical technicians, however, both cybernetics technician or junk doctor can also use this same table and are treated as electrical technicians on the robotics table.

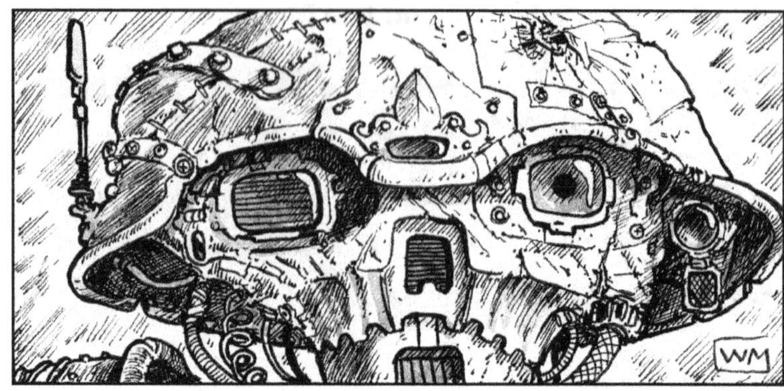

### Table XR-135/ Robot Primary Optics

| 1d100 | Primary Optics Mode | Accuracy | Base Perception | Notes |
|---|---|---|---|---|
| 01-07. | Single standard eye | 10+2d20 | 10+1d20 | Low tech, civilian robotic eye without night vision. Poor depth perception. Identical to a human eye as far as overall visual capabilities go. There is a 4 in 6 chance it has an empty socket where a 2nd eye should be*. |
| 08-54. | Two standard eyes | 20+2d20 | 15+2d20 | As a single standard eye, above, except normal depth perception. |
| 55-74. | Two combot eyes | 40+d20 | 20+2d20 | Night Vision to 30 meters, and 2 in 10 chance of 1 Specialized Optic from table XR-136. |
| 75-89. | Two advanced Combot eyes | 50+2d20 | 30+2d20 | Night Vision to 100 meters. Any attached 'weapon arm' or other built in weapon systems are linked to these eyes and target acquisition and tracking streamlined. This unit does not need to look down the sights of its on-board, digitally scoped weapons and can expose only its weapon system around a corner or over a barrier if desired and fire normally. Plus 3 in 10 chance of 1 Specialized Optic from table XR-136. |
| 90-96. | *Two combat eyes plus 1 specialized optic from the next table* | | | |
| 97-00. | *Two advanced combat eyes plus 2 specialized optics from the table to follow, but re-roll duplicated results* | | | |

*An eye from another unit can be inserted into this cavity to upgrade it to a two eyed unit as in roll 08-54 on this table.*

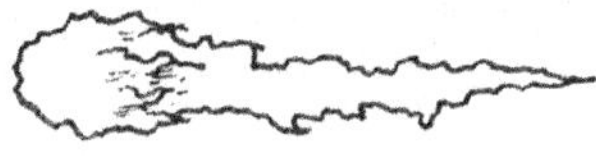

### Table XR-136/ Robot Specialized Optic

Note: Only roll here if instructed to on table XR-135.

| 1d100 | Optic System | Note & Stats |
|---|---|---|
| 01-14. | Rad scanner | When activated, this dosimeter will see pockets of radiation, including contamination, mutations and weapon systems on other beings, within a 180 cone of view ahead of it, out to a range of 30 meters. This optic runs on a mini-power cell for 3 years. |
| 15-26. | Stun pistol eye | As the relic from the Hub Rules (pg. 189) SV +7/ Rate 1/ DMG 2d20 stun/ Range 200m/ Charges: Uses a dedicated, power cell to yield 40 shots. |
| 27-51. | Mini laser eye | As the relic from the Hub Rules (pg. 190) SV +13/ Rate 1/ DMG 1d8+10/ Range 120m/ Charges: Uses a dedicated, mini-power cell to yield 20 shots. |
| 52-68. | Wrist laser eye | As the relic from the Hub Rules (pg. 190) SV +10/ Rate 1/ DMG 1d10+10/ Range 210m/ Charges: Uses a dedicated, mini-power cell to yield 16 shots. |
| 69-77. | DNA scanner | As relic from Hub Rules (pg. 199). Takes 5 continuous rounds of locking on a target up to 20m away to get a readout. The subject can be accurately determined to be either a non-mutant lifeform from the pre-apocalypse, a mutant, a type of synthetic human, enhanced trans-human, or unknown or alien lifeform. Holograms, digital beings, illusions, and dimensional beings give no reading at all. Charges: Uses a dedicated, mini-power cell to yield 5 years of operation. |
| 78-89. | Substance reader | As relic from hub rules (pg. 199). Takes 3 rounds of continuous 'locked-on' visual contact to determine if an object or being is mineral, organic deceased, organic plant, organic animal, cyborg, mechanical inactive, mechanical active (powered-up). This optic will also clarify if an object is an illusion, dimensional entity, augmented reality (see page XR-477) radioactive source, or a digital being. Range 100m. Charge: mini-power cells runs it for 5 years. |
| 90-00. | Laser pistol eye | As the relic from the Hub Rules (pg. 190) SV +16/ Rate 1/ DMG 1d20+10/ Range 500m/ Charges: Uses a dedicated, power cell to yield 30 shots. |

## Table XR-137/ Robot Head Type

| 1d100 | Robot's Head Design | DV Mod.* | END Mod. | Added Weight | Added Height | Wear Helmet?** | Other Trait Modifiers and Features |
|---|---|---|---|---|---|---|---|
| 01-13. | Scrap metal mass | -5 | +2d6 | +2d6kg | +20 +1d20cm | 14% chance | Bolted together sheets of scrap metal, poly carbonate glass and dense plastic. Lopsided and could pass as mere ruin junk if the robot remained unmoving among similar trash. |
| 14-18. | Skinless plastic android skull | -0 | +0 | +2kg | +20 +1d12cm | Yes | Civilian grade plastic skull. Terrifying to strangers. Somewhat soft and vulnerable. A helmet is recommended. |
| 19-22. | Skinless metal skull | -4 | +1d10 | +4kg | +20 +1d12cm | Yes | This is a stainless steel military grade, human shaped skull. Strikes terror into onlookers. |
| 23-28. | Civilian android head | -2 | +1d6 | +3kg | +20 +1d12cm | Yes | Gender pattern **roll 1d10 1-5** female/**6-10** male, 88% chance of having hair as per android characters on page XR-51. Head appearance score 20+3d20. |
| 29-33. | Military android head | -10 | +10 +1d10 | +5kg | +20 +1d20cm | yes | Gender pattern **roll 1d10 1-3** female/**4-10** male, 27% chance of having hair as per android characters on page XR-51. Appearance trait 10+1d20. |
| 34-36. | Insectoid | -2d6 | +2d6 | +4kg | +20 +1d20cm | 11% chance | Twin radio antennas which if a communicator is plugged in externally or this robot has a built in comm, then these rubberized shafts will give double range to transmissions. 3 in 10 will have mechanical pincer jaws like an ant to add an extra melee attack per round: SV +4, DMG 1d12 with only skill based modifiers adding to the damage such as brawling or weapon expert [not both] (therefore, do not apply the robot's strength score modifier). |
| 37-39. | Hammerhead shark | -5 | +2d6 | +6kg | +10 +1d12cm | No | Optics wide apart and other sensors beneath main wedge of the unit's head. |
| 40-45. | Chest head | -22 | +3d6 | +4kg | nil | No | Head fused to upper chest and well protected by surrounding plating, but reduces perception by -6 points and can't turn head around without moving whole body about. |
| 46-48. | Wedge shaped | -4+1d6 | +1d6 | +5kg | +10 +1d20cm | No | Frog-like shape, streamlined as if for speed. Sloped armor to deflect incoming attacks gives it the shown DV bonus. |
| 49-52. | Football helmet | -14 | +4d6 | +8kg | +20 +1d20cm | No | Designed to look like an ancient football helmet with frontal steel face shield 'grill' guard bumpers and extra plating. Very tough. 3 in 10 chance painted to match an ancient professional football team's colors with logos and player number. |
| 53-56. | Rotating dome | -5 | +1d8 | +3d6kg | +20 +1d10cm | No | 360 degree rotation, hard to surprise, add +3d6 perception. |
| 57-63. | Cartoon animal | -2d6 | +1d6 | +6 +1d6kg | +20 +2d20cm | No | Clearly looted from some animatronic unit at an amusement park, yet built big, robust and with multiple accessory sockets. It has a goofy or terrifying smile, huge eye sockets and any ears or tufts of hair are antennas. **Roll 1d10** for type of character: 1. Bunny/ 2. Duck/ 3. Cat/ 4. Dog/ 5. Bear/ 6. Fish/ 7. Pony/ 8. Mouse/ 9. Silly Skull/ 10. Chicken. |
| 64-66. | Clear polycarbonate dome | -7 | +1d8 | +7kg | +20 +1d10cm | No | Within the dome the unit's CPU is visible and flickers with tiny lights. All eyes and other small apparatus are enclosed in this protective sphere and immune to dust, liquid and other debris. If attempts are made to shatter this dome specifically, it has a DV of -36 and 29 endurance before busting open like an eggshell. |
| 67-76. | Geometric shape | -1d10 | +1d10 | +6 +1d8kg | Variable by shape | No | **Roll 1d10** for shape of this unit's head: **1.** Rectangular (+10+1d20cm)/ **2.** Ball (+10+2d20cm)/ **3.** Disc, horizontal like a coffee table (+6+1d6cm)/ **4.** Cube-like (+10+1d20cm)/ **5.** Pyramid (+20+2d20cm)/ **6.** pylon cone (+20+2d20cm)/ **7.** Stubby tube (+30+2d20cm)/ **8.** Oval (+10+2d20cm)/ **9.** Disc, vertical like a sign (+20+2d20cm)/ **10.** Hexagonal (+10+2d20cm). |
| 77-79. | Fin shaped | -3d6 | +1d6 | +6kg | +30 +2d20cm | No | Like a vertical wedge similar to a shark's fin with sensors clustered at the front and along each lower side. |
| 80-84. | Helmet-like | -6+1d10 | +3d6 | +5 +1d6kg | +20 +1d20cm | No | Resembles an old world army helmet with hooded eyes sensors, side and neck cover with a chin-strap-style frontal plate. |
| 85-87. | Segmented arch | -3d6 | +2d6 | +4 +1d8kg | +10 +1d20cm | No | Main sensors clustered at the hooded front end, somewhat armored and resembling a 'pill bug'. |
| 88-92. | Simple Animated face shield | -1d8 | +1d10 | +4 +1d4kg | +20 +1d20cm | Yes | Build into a roughly human head shape, the front of this unit is a durable electric screen made of curved poly-carbon glass. When active, the face of the robot lights up and shows a crude 166digital, animated face, expressing its reactions, eye movements as it interacts, and when talking, the simple mouth graphics match the words coming from a chin mounted speaker.s |
| 93-96. | Battle visor | -5/-25 closed | +10 +1d10 | +10 +1d8kg | +20 +1d20cm | No | This otherwise human-shaped metal head has a camouflage print shell that, when engaged, will flip up from the back and chin and close tight like a clam-shell. The visor's eye slits are covered in thick armor-glass. When open, the robot head has the more limited -5 DV, but when closed up, improves the units overall DV by -25, although reduces initiative rolls by -1. |
| 97-00. | Turret head | -10+1d20 | +10 +1d12 | +10kg +weapon weight | +30 +2d20cm | No | This robots sensory cluster reside in a narrow slit beneath the barrel of a relic weapon. Ammo or power are stored in the back of this wedge or disc shaped turret. The head can rotate fully about and aim upward 90 degrees and adds its attack as an extra simultaneous attack to either ranged or melee engagements. Establish the fixed, permanent weapon system and ammo supplied at character generation, roll **1d6: 1.** Assault rifle with 50 round drum filled with 5d10 rifle rounds/ **2.** Laser carbine with 2 power cells shoved into back locking access ports. Each cell will provide 2d10 shots/ **3.** Sub-machine gun with 2, 50 round drum magazines stowed in back of head, each loaded with 5d10 pistol rounds at character generation/ **4.** Assault shotgun with belt fed internal ammo bay. Belt can hold 100 shells maximum, but at character generation has 3d20 shells./ **5.** Stun rifle (page 406 this book, with 2 power cells loaded into back of head, each has 1d20 shots remaining (max 30 per cell). / **6.** Pulse rifle with 1d3 power cells inserted into a neck power adapter. Each cell offers 1d20 bursts (25 bursts when fully charged). |

*Apply this defense value modifier to the overall DV of the robot character, but record this amount separately in case an opponent tries to make a called shot on the robot's CPU (brain).*

**This is either a percentage chance that the head can accommodate a relic helmet placed onto it, or a simple yes or no. A custom made leather, junk, iron or full helm can also be made, at double the cost, to fit an oddly shaped robot head, but is often permanently bolted or stitched on.*

# CPU in Robot's Head

The CPU of any robot is its brain, although it might also feature a back-up or specialized CPU. This central processing unit resides in the head of the robot and houses the consciousness of this remarkable, self aware machine. If the CPU is wiped out, the robot normally ceases to operate. While its body and limbs might still have power, the unit will typically fall over if in motion when the CPU is neutralized, or remain stationary and vulnerable to attack at +40 SV easier to be hit by melee or ranged attacks if it was not moving when shut down.

Besides taking a lethal called shot to the head – with any attack on a robot's head treated the same as a called shot to a living being's brain, a CPU can also be neutralized by EMP attacks or hacking attacks by digital beings, androids, or other robots. The endurance points of a CPU, as far as suffering EMP attacks go, is its Data Points (DT), which when hit by an EMP pulse are treated as stun damage that will recover at a rate of 1 DT per hour, per character's rank.

Hacking is mainly a feature of digital beings, but robot character need to have their processor (PRO), firewall (FW), and data points (DT) traits established in case this machine comes under attack by such beings, although Ultra-Advanced CPUs often feature the ability for this self aware robot to hack, as well. Hacking is fully described in the digital beings section of this book on pages 67 to 70.

While hacking is a mode of digitally attacking another computer or digital being, it doesn't mean that this robot's consciousness can leave its current CPU or head, as it is hard-wired into the computer. It can however use any hacking attack ability to fragment (reduce the enemy CPU to 0 or fewer data points), delete (permanently kill) or simply lock the defeated consciousness into a junk folder where it is stored away for possible later interrogation. A hostile digital be-

ing, however, can hack into, defeat and occupy a unique robot character, which is perhaps the greatest threat these self aware, machine's face.

Hacking is a somewhat complicated in-game occurrence and the game master should thoroughly read up on, and perhaps test play, the procedure prior to any game session where he or she thinks such digital combat is likely to occur. Organic beings with the computer technician skill can also attempt to hack into a computer, or restrained robot, android, or unit that is occupied by a digital being. This is handled somewhat differently from the hacking attempts noted in the hub rules under the section of computer technicians (pg. 53). For the new method, see page 397 of this book in the Expanded And Optional Rules section for 'Rules Update: Organic characters who attempt to hack into the CPUs of robots, androids and digital beings'.

Each robot starts with a random CPU which also reveals its base intelligence and willpower trait. The processor trait, firewall and data points are also important traits, traits which only computerized machines exhibit. Self aware robots also gain one or more Special Programs, which is how these characters acquire their initial skills, although some additional parts occasionally add a skill point or two in a select area of expertise.

For Intelligence, Willpower, Processor Trait, Firewall, and Data Points, roll once each, below, to determine the fixed trait amount at character generation. Many of these traits will undergo changes during other phases of character generation, as well as during rank gain and occasionally during game play due to injuries, or rare, beneficial exposure to relics and other events. Some of these traits, such as those involving hacking attacks and defense, might never come into play in a robotic character's adventure career, yet they are still important to roll and record... just in case.

## Table XR-138/ CPU in Robot's Head

| 1d100 | Type | Intelligence | Willpower | Processor Trait | Firewall | Data Points | Special Programs* |
|---|---|---|---|---|---|---|---|
| 01-06. | Shoddy | 4d6 | 4d6 | 2d10 | +1d6 | 15+1d20 | 1d2 |
| 07-21. | Standard, corrupted | 20+1d20 | 10+2d20 | 10+3d10 | -2d6 | 20+2d10 | 1d4 |
| 22-73. | Standard | 20+2d20 | 20+2d20 | 20+3d10 | -10 | 25+2d20 | 1d4+1 |
| 74-81. | Standard, customized | 30+2d20 | 20+3d20 | 20+2d20 | -15 | 30+2d20 | 1d6+1 |
| 82-93. | Advanced | 50+2d20 | 40+2d20 | 30+3d20 | -20 | 40+3d20 | 1d6+2 |
| 94-96. | Advanced, customized | 60+2d20 | 40+3d20 | 40+3d20 | -30 | 50+3d20 | 1d8+2 |
| 97-00. | Ultra-Advanced | 70+1d100 | 50+1d100 | 50+1d100 | -40 | 70+1d100 | 2d6+1 |

** Special Programs are found on page 161.*

# CPU Descriptions

**Shoddy CPU:** This unit is almost wide open. It has very little software protecting its CPU from hacking attacks, and indeed, has a firewall rating of between +1 to +6 (FW +1d6). Physically the CPU doesn't fit its adapter well, rattles when the robot moves or turns its head ( -1 point in the stealth skill), has rusty or greasy connectors — which cause the machine to stutter when it talks — and suffers from intermittent micro shut downs of limbs and sensory receptors.

All in all, these flaws give it shoddy performance in nearly every regard. Temporally reduce its accuracy, agility and perception traits by -10 (minimum 1 point). Record these lost traits on the character sheet in case this robot is lucky enough to survive until it gets an upgrade or repairs and sees these depleted points returned. These other traits, by the way, are established based on random determination on previous tables, but can be further modified by details yet to be revealed during character generation.

There's really no way of saying this nice. Having a CPU of this sort is the shits and something must be done about it. This robot's brain problems are mostly hardware related, so besides finding the next day's battery supply or lubrication oil for its joints, this unit's main priority is finding an upgrade to these security vulnerabilities and poorly installed parts. Its 'mind' is in fact a standard CPU, but is missing a few memory cards and requires several hours of work by a robotics technician to convert it to a Standard CPU.

The acquisition of the needed parts and labor can be done through game play, or possibly purchased in a town with a robotics dealership or repair facility at a cost of 500+1d100 silver pieces and 3d6 hours in the shop. This robot cannot perform these repairs on its own even if it has the robotics technician skill. If a comrade has these skills, and they come upon a destroyed robot of sufficient quality, such as a medi bot, police robot, light, heavy or hoplight combot, or tanker bot, the technician can attempt to loot the parts from the donor robot and upgrade this CPU to a standard CPU.

The odds of successfully installing the parts is shown on table TME-1-50, Robotics Technician Skills on page 54 of the hub rules, under the column 'Attach Implants to Robot or Android'. While the odds are very high of success for a technician of 3 or more skill points, there is some risk at least until the tech is of 6 skill points. Failure during this procedure means the replacement parts are fried during their failed installation and now worthless junk, and this robot is left as it was before the procedure.

Success means temporarily depleted traits regain their 10 point penalty (to agility, accuracy and perception), but so too, consult the table above again and re-roll all the CPU specific traits of a standard CPU. However, no result should be below what it already had been, plus, any bonuses this robot might have picked up during play or character generation between the time it had a shoddy CPU and a standard CPU, should also be kept and added to the total. A standard CPU configuration cannot be upgraded to an advanced CPU as the hardware, wiring, power source and coding are too different, and rarely of the same operating language.

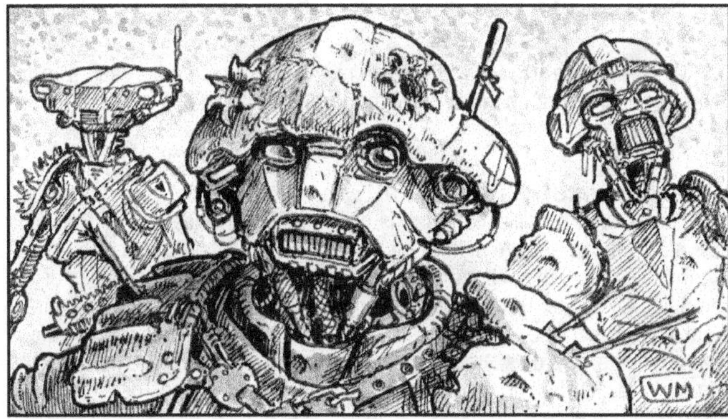

**Standard, Corrupted CPU:** This robot's 'brain' is corrupted by some past event such as an attempted hack, brutal EMP scrambling, blow to the unit's head, water exposure, short circuit, lighting strike or other hazard. These are software issues more than hardware issues, but, whatever it was, the CPU is somewhat cooked and needs to have parts pulled out and cleaned or replaced. To do this, a computer technician with a portable computer or a friendly digital being needs to get inside or hooked up to this CPU's operating system and sort out the mess. The helper must scan for viruses, eliminate needless files, eradicate spyware, hunt for traces of the human killing Mecha virus, and tune up the inner workings of this robot's mind.

The technician must use the 'Re-Program Robot' column task as shown on table TME-1-47 on page 53 of the hub rules to possibly convert the CPU to a standard system. Once rebooted after successful unscrambling, repairs, and other improvements (on a successful hazard check by the computer technician and 3d6 hours of downtime for this robot and labor for the technician), this patient's intelligence score is increased by +1d20, and add +10 to both Willpower and Processor. Furthermore, make Firewall a minimum of -10, and Data Points increased by 5+1d20. Additionally, this repair unlocks 1 special program from the random list on page XR-161.

**Standard CPU:** This is the most common variety of central processing unit available to a unique robot, and for most of these self aware machines, is perfectly adequate. Through game play, however, and in-game discoveries of ancient technologies, lost facilities and access to highly trained computer specialists, this CPU can be upgraded to a customized variant as described below. If such an upgrade takes place, the robot character keeps all existing rank gained and other trait modifiers and increases.

Usually, converting a standard CPU to a customized variant involves access to rare, high-tech facilities not available in new era towns and cities, nor something a player character can perform even with exceptionally high skill points in either robotics or computer technician. Often only an AI can conduct an upgrade that will still let the player character exist in the customized CPU.

**Standard, Customized CPU:** At some point in this robot's history, something or someone made several upgrades to this CPU. It is faster, more robust, better protected and has a more developed sense of self awareness (higher willpower trait). Besides the benefits to its various traits as shown on table XR-138, and greater potential for special programs, this robot's computerized brain has one extra random feature determined by rolling on the following list. **Roll 1d6:**

**1. Made with extra care:** Add +1d6 to each of these traits: Intelligence, Willpower, Processor Trait, Data Points and apply a -1d6 bonus protection to Firewall.

**2. Additional programming:** Add an extra 1d3 'Special Programs' to this CPU from the random list on page XR-161.

**3. Secondary chatbot identity and micro hard drive:** Somebody bolted a secondary identity to this CPU which is basically a socially gifted, friendly persona with its own hearing and speech hardware attached to the head of the robot. This extra persona can think for itself, although isn't a true AI but seems like a self aware being since it has an incredible memory of people, past conversations and highly convincing ability to conduct friendly banter with both this main CPU and those it encounters. It has access to the eyes of the robot, but can't control any of its body. If the main CPU is knocked out or killed, this chatbot can't gain access to the robot. It has the same statics as if it were a shoddy CPU and can be removed and used independantly. For a random personalty, roll on table XR-294 on page 500 in the appendices.

**4. Remarkably well made:** Add +5 to this CPU's traits: Intelligence, Willpower, Processor, Data Points and apply a -5 bonus to its Firewall.

**5. EMP defense shield:** This robot's body might suffer terribly from an EMP attack, but the CPU has a -30 extra defense value against EMP weapons. The data points or DT of a CPU are akin to its Endurance trait, and when reduced to zero or less, the unit is knocked out and heals at a rate of 1 DT per hour, per character's rank. If needed, the GM can make two separate attacks on the robot when engaging it with EMP weapons, with the first attack against the body, and the second against this CPU at -30 DV on the attack roll.

**6. Space/vacuum resistant:** This CPU has an internal heating coil and shielding against the harmful radiation found in orbital and deep space environments, and can withstand the extreme colds and vacuum of space for 2 hours before suffering harm (or 12 hours on the surface of Mars). This shielding also acts to somewhat protect the CPU from EMP attacks and reduces EMP damage by -5 per incoming attack. Earth based radiation might still harm this robot, but the CPU itself is will ward off any mild exposures.

**Advanced CPU:** This central processing unit was either made of superior parts at the same time as most standard CPUs, or else is of a much more recent manufacturing, and within the last decades before the collapse of the pan-global civilization of the Oldsters. Either way, it features superior performance in every regard. An advanced CPU cannot be upgraded into an Ultra advanced variant because of parts and coding incompatibilities. However, through game play, it is possible for this computer brain to be added to and become a customized variant.

**Advanced, Customized CPU:** Besides having a superior construction, more data capacity, faster processing speed and more extravagant designs and pre-loaded special programs, a customized variant of this CPU will have one random bonus feature from the following list:

**1. Version 1.2:** This advanced CPU applies an extra +1d8 to each of these traits: Intelligence, Willpower, Processor Trait, Data Points and apply a -1d8 bonus protection to Firewall. In addition, it has one more special program from the random list on page XR-161.

**2. Dream walker:** This CPU can extended its control and sensory modes into another robotic body, computer system, or android once it hacks into and defeats (drains the data points of the target). For 1 hour per day, per rank of this CPU, this robotic character's mind can broadcast to the dominated unit and control it, see and hear through it, and move 10 meters distance from this character's main CPU per point of willpower that this unique robot has, multiplied by this robot's rank (WILL x 10m X Rank = meters). It does not exist in the controlled unit, but merely hitches a ride within it and reports back its experiences in real time. While 'dream walking', the controller is dormant.

There is a danger in using this gift, however, in that while remote controlling or dream walking in another machine, this CPU leaves itself somewhat vulnerable to other hacking attacks and suffers a 50% drop in its own firewall while sending and receiving transmissions to the other controlled machine or computer. The transmission can be dropped after 1 round, however, and cannot be re-linked unless hacking into the target again. Most robots need to physically plug into a restrained subject machine to hack them, although in rare models, wireless hacking is possible.

This CPU could theoretically hack into and control the computer of an entire ancient complex, a relic tank, or a starship, but in most cases, taking control of a flying drone is a more typical application of this remarkable ability.

**3. Ejection module:** Should this robot's body be in danger of incineration, capture, or otherwise experience peril to its core identity of this self aware being, the CPU can be ejected out the top of the robot's head in a brilliant explosion (with a 3m radius blast that is considered an attack to friend and foe within the area of detonation: SV 01-77, DMG 3d6. The ejection module will launch the CPU 10+1d1000 meters into the air at a random arc and compass direction where it will reach apogee and then deploy a parachute and slowly drift on the wind, falling at 1 meter per minute, possibly hundreds if not thousands of meters from where it ejected depending on wind speed, and slowly drop to the ground or surface of the water. The module floats, is watertight, rubberized and robust and has a defense value of -30 and endurance of 10+3d6; stats needed in case some adversary wants to bash the CPU into junk.

Once fired, this ejections module is permanently spent and can never be used again unless a demolition expert of 4 or more skill points can be coaxed, or hired, to re-craft a replacement charge at a cost of 2000+1d1000sp for a hired bomb maker, or half that for a volunteer or comrade's services for material costs.

If this ejection is attempted within a structure or some place where the module can't fly high into the air, it will instead shoot against the ceiling and most likely be utterly destroyed (treat as 3 separate attacks SV 01-68, DMG 1d30 each). Likewise, if this robot sacrifices itself and launches this module at an opponent, by tipping its body forward or back and aiming at an enemy, it can also launch itself in a suicide attack, and suffer as if it is launching into a ceiling as described above, killing itself, but make this same series of three attacks on the opponent.

If this module is recovered after ejection, the CPU can be removed and plugged into another robotic body of the sort that takes either an advanced or standard CPU, but this CPU is the wrong configuration, shape and design to fit into an android head (unless it previously came from such a cranium).

**4. Exceptionally well-built:** Add +7 to this CPU's traits of Intelligence, Willpower, Processor, Data Points and apply a -7 bonus to its Firewall.

**5. Shock node:** Even if this robot's body and CPU are both knocked out by an EMP, or hacked by a digital being or other computer, this CPU has a nasty surprise in store for whoever tries to enter the CPU or its digital inner realm. The intruder, including a human person inspecting, trying to remove, or tinker with this CPU without knowing the pre-assigned authorization password — which this robot can give a friendly technician prior to some procedure which involves entering the CPU or contents of a back-up hard drive — is subject to a powerful warning shock. This jolt of energy comes from a separate, reserve standard power cell located in an EMP and energy drain resistant hidden compartment. This unit can deliver of 5 shocks per power cell, although the power cell will slowly recharge after 72 hours if the robot comes back on-line.

The shock to physical intruders is an attack at SV 01-88 and will inflict 1d100 stun damage and 1d20 lethal damage. To a digital being, or to a robot or android who hacks into and explores this defeated CPU, the attack is made like a hacking assault with a hack attack of 01-90 (made against the FW (Firewall) rating of the unsuspecting defender) which will inflict 1d20 physical damage to any computer or other physical device, robotic body that is plugged into the is CPU, plus inflict 1d100 data points damage on a successful shock.

A follow-up shock can be delivered the next round if the CPU is still being tampered with. This shock happens automatically, and can harm would-be helpful digital beings or technicians who were not forewarned of this powerful defensive measure.

**6. Two random features**, with one from this list (re-roll this result if duplicated) plus one feature from the 'Standard, customized CPU' listing up on page 159.

**Ultra-Advanced CPU:** This CPU was built in the last years of the former global human civilization, and is of the most advanced, robust designs ever made. It can engage in hacking combat like a digital being, although unlike those entities, this robot's mind cannot leave the physical confines of the computer it inhabits. Through successful hacking attacks, it can however, fragment, lock away, or delete the 'minds' of other computer entities such as those of other robots, androids, AIs and digital beings. Hacking, which is normally the domain of digital beings, is discussed in that character types description on page 67 of this book.

This CPU inhabiting being is creative, learns and grows as a human does and even developed a consistent personality (player can pick or roll on the random personality list on page XR-500). It has long-term goals, takes pleasure in the company of simpler beings, understands and makes attempts at humor, forms true relationships, dreams when shut down or in power saving mode, gets emotional, holds grudges, and to human companions, seems every bit as human as a living, breathing person. Furthermore, this CPU has at least one remarkable bonus feature, **roll 1d6 here:**

**1. Wireless mode hacking ability:** This CPU can select another computer system and try to hack it without having to physically connect to the circuitry or CPU of an opponent, and can make a beam-like attack on a single target within line of sight to a range as this robot entity's processor trait value in meters, multiplied by its rank. Learn all about wireless mode hacking attacks on page 67 in the digital beings section of this book. Also useful is the list of common targets and their defensive statistics such as firewall (akin to the target's defense value) and Data Points (similar to endurance value) as noted on Table XR-56 Firewall & Data Points of Common Computers, Robots and Androids, on page XR-69.

**2. EMP shielding and body reboot mode:** This CPU has its own EMP hardening sheath, which might be in addition to any other EMP protection it might have. Should the unit take a hit from an EMP weapon, the body will take whatever debilitating damage it will take, but the computer that runs the robot gains extra protection and has a -90 defense value against the same EMP attack. If successfully thwarting the EMP, even if the rest of the robot succumbs to the attack, this CPU can send out a recovery surge to every limb and system, and after 2d6 rounds, reboots the robot and it rids itself of all EMP damage.

**3. CPU force field:** This robot's computerized mind has its own force field which is always running in the background. Any called shot to the robot's head, or other attack, must get passed a -12 damage point force field to inflict any physical harm to the CPU hardware, while any hacking attack, which usually does 1d10 data points damage (plus any processor trait damage modifiers), must score over 5 points damage to cause any depletion of this CPU's DT.

**4. Exceptionally advanced:** Increase each of the trait listed on table XR-138, page 158, by another +10 points, except for firewall which is improved by -10 FW, and roll for 2 more special programs from the random selection, table XR-139, on this page.

**5. Hyper advanced CPU:** Two remarkable features from this list, roll 1d4, twice, re-roll duplicated results.

**6. Ultimate advanced CPU:** Created in the most sophisticated facilities in the last months and weeks before the advanced robotics manufacturer were wiped out, this CPU has all the remarkable features from rolls 1 to 4 on this list, plus one random roll each on both the customized standard and customized advanced CPUs, described on previous pages.

# Special Programs

Besides the remarkable software that gives any unique robot its sentience, which courses through its circuits, servos and wiring and gives this machine the will to live, to better itself, and form deep, mutually beneficial, reliable and entertaining relationships with other intelligent beings, these self aware robots are also loaded with one or more special programs.

While called special programs, many of the knowledge areas included on the following random list are common skills as described in both the TME Hub Rules and this book. All unique robots feature programs that allow them to speak, make sense if their surroundings through optic sensors, translate data from sound, understand speech, speak, read, do complex math, keep track of the date, time and compass direction, plus be familiar with the customs and idiosyncrasies of humans and common animals. Because of these aspects, they are more or less adapted to operate alongside people in the physical world.

When going up in rank, one benefit a self aware robot might gain is another roll on this table, in which case the unit has unlocked some trove of knowledge or other feature within its CPU, some database that had been forgotten, shaken loose, or finally understood and made accessible.

To determine the number of special programs a newly generated unique robots starts game play with, consult Table XR-138 CPU in Robot's Head, back on page 158. The last column on that table shows the random amount of programs a robotic character will start with. Re-roll duplicated die results.



**01-03. Early Childhood Care:** This software allowed the robot to work in a daycare, nurturing human infants to kindergarten age. This database holds a massive inventory of children's stories, songs, games, and craft techniques and ideas. This unit can be very nurturing, and often speaks in a ridiculous, cutesy voice or mimics popular kids cartoon characters from the past.

**04-06. Agricultural technician:** This robot is fully versed on old world industrial farming practices. It can identify plant species within seconds, including the base identifiable plant of a plantoid character, know the ideal growing conditions, recommended pesticides and herbicides to apply, and how to harvest, prep and store food crops for wholesale pick up.

Much of what it knows is based on practices, facilities and resources that no longer exist. Still, it can make do with what it has and if forced to tend to a plot of land or the agricultural direction of a community, and after the first year, will be able to at least increase the crop and livestock production by 50%. Its methods, however, might annoy existing farmers, and produce resentment among workers who are told to change their ways and work longer hours than normal.

**07-09. Mechanical technician skill:** 1d4 skill points. See page TME-54.
**10-12. Computer technician:** 1d3 skill points. Learn more on page TME-53 of the hub rules.
**13-15. Cybernetic technician:** 1d4 skill points, see page XR-207 in this book.
**16-18. Database:** As the cybernetic implant described on page 334 of this book. This implant does not imply this robot has the adapters and hardware to accommodate other cybernetic implants, although this is yet possible further along in character generation (table XR-142, page 163).
**19-21. Medic skill,** 1d4 skill points. See page TME-46.
**22-24. Minor CPU upgrades:** Add 2d6 to these traits: Intelligence, Willpower, Processor, and Data Points, plus a defensive bonus of -5 to Firewall.
**25-27. Cooking skill:** 1d4 skill points, as described on page 206 of this book. It also has a massive database of recipes, knowledge of cooking styles throughout history. In addition, this unit features a front panel that opens to reveal two spidery, metal manipulator arms with tiny metal hands that it can use for any delicate task, but were added to facilitate the creation of culinary miracles. These arms are ambidextrous, have a strength score of 10, but are exceedingly fragile and inadequate for handling firearms or performing any sort of violence.
**28-30. Linguistics:** This robot is fluent in multiple languages. The linguistics skill is described on page 220 of this book.
**31-33. Space travel specialization:** This CPU is loaded with all the pertinent data relating to travel in common orbital shuttles, docking with space stations and other vessels in orbit, as well as travel to and from the moon or other heavenly bodies within the solar system. It knows all about the prep and procedures of making a vehicle ready for launch, fuel types and quantities, filling procedures, minimum safely protocols and other needs of the ship and crew.

It knows how to maintain an orbit over a fixed point on the earth or moon's surface, as well as how to conduct reentry into the atmosphere on Earth or Mars. In short, this CPU can take into account all the variables and let companions know if doing some space based task is achievable, risky, and at what odds of success or survival can be expected.

If plugged directly into a ship's controls, this robot can pilot a space vessel as if it had 6 points in the pilot skill. While piloting is very useful, the bulk of its knowledge is in seeing to the important details of crew survival, and making any ship or shuttle ready for flight, which can take months if not years if a battered old orbital shuttle is discovered by a dig team in the ruins. This CPU does not have the full range of pilot skills however, unless it gains this skill from another roll and so the 6 points noted here do not stack with any other piloting skill points.
**34-36. Security systems expertise:** This robot can more easily log into a security door to bypass it, or plug into and take control of security cameras and defenses. It has 4 skill points in the lock picking skill, but only when picking relic digital

safes and digital door locks, plus 4 points specifically in the computer technician skill of 'Hack into CPU' but only when attempting to access doors, security weapons, defenses, cameras and related devices. These bonus points do not stack with any other occurrences of the lock picking or computer technician skill.

**37-39. Electrical technician skill,** 1d3 points as described in the hub rules on page TME-53.

**40-42. Terrain navigation and mobility mode:** Working in unison with its optical sensors, this CPU has enhanced mobility adaptation features, allowing it to run, or drive over and around rough ground, up stairs, and otherwise increase all movement rates by 20%.

**43-45. Junk-doctor skill:** With 1d3 points in this skill as described on page 218 of this book.

**46-48. Driver skill:** 1d3 points as per the skill on page TME-37.

**49-51. Dodge mode:** When engaged in combat, this CPU's built in survival programming helps it anticipate incoming ranged and melee attacks with somewhat uncanny motions, and increase its defense value by -10 points, even if it loses initiative or is not generally expecting to be in a dangerous situation.

**52-54. Demolitions expert skill:** 1d3 points in this skill as described on page 207 of this book.

**55-57. Chemical technician skill:** 1d3 points and described on page TME-52.

**58-60. Major CPU upgrades:** To each of these traits add 3d6 to Intelligence, Willpower, Processor, and Data Points, plus -3d6 Firewall.

**61-63. Mining skill:** This robot cannot only direct workers to properly dig for ore or coal, but also excavate a collapsed hallway or ruined structure in a vastly safer manner. See page 220 of this book for a description of this skill. There is a 1 in 10 chance this robot is also equipped with the special feature, roll 20, Stone Boring Power Head from page XR 166.

**64-66. Bio-technician:** With 1d3 skill points (described on page TME-52).

**67-69. Communications skill:** This robot has 1d3 points in this skill area, and a 1 in 10 chance of owning an operational communications headset which it has strapped to its head and can use to call comrades, or listen in to other users, regional radio broadcasts (if any), and other transmissions.

**70-72. Forgery skill:** As described on page TME-38. This robot will be equipped with a small, fold out ink pen from its main, human-like arm with which it can write a letter in any handwriting it has ever seen, although the entire alphabet must be present in the previously scanned written record to complete every letter in a forgery.

**73-75. Medic skill and Surgical Upgrade:** This robot has 1d3 skill points as a medic, plus has a frontal compartment with 4 highly dexterous (accuracy and agility both 60), exceedingly frail but precise manipulator arms. These thin, spidery arm come with an assortment of tools including an antiseptic sprayer, pocket flashlight, probes, stitching stapler, a syringe and standard laser scalpel. Using these implements allow the unit to perform surgeries and first aid on organic beings. These limbs are far too fragile to engage in combat and too weak to hold more than they already wield (1kg max load lift, reach of 40cm).

**76-78. Morse Code understanding:** This robot can read and translate Morse Code whether the transmission comes in the form of audio, light flashes, or written on paper. Learn more about this skill on page 220 of this book.

**79-81. Weapon expert skill:** As shown on page 57 of the Hub Rules. This robot will have 1d3 skill points in whatever random result comes up and carry the described weapon in its arms just like any human character might.

**82-84. Pilot skill:** 1d3 points as described on page TME-49 of the hub rules.

**85-87. Gambler skill:** This robot has 1d4 points in this skill as described on page TME-38.

**88-90. Hacking software and hardware:** [Note: Re-roll if the robot already has this feature from having an Ultra-Advanced CPU.] This robot has the applications and emitters to engage in hacking combat like a digital being, as described on page XR-67 of this book. Its CPU, however, might limit this ability, or even make it vulnerable to counter-hacking attacks, especially if its CPU is low tech, shoddy or otherwise unimpressive. Because this robot's consciousness is fixed in the CPU it currently occupies, and can't transfer into another CPU unless the unit's head is mounted on another machine, thus the purpose of hacking another digital consciousness is merely to fragment or delete the foe. This hacking attack requires physical contact with the restrained target system.

**91-93. Gunslinger skill:** With 1d4 points in the skill as shown on page TME-39. Just like that skill, this robot will start out with 1 handgun, unless it begins game play as a slave. There is a 1 in 10 chance this robot also has the gunsmith skill at 1d3 skill points.

**94-96. Robotics technician skill:** As described in the hub rules on page TME-54, 1d3 skill points.

**97-99. Junk crafter:** As the skill described on page TME 41, with 1d4 skill points. This robot owns a satchel and utility belt filled with a collection of rudimentary replica and homemade tools.

**100. Combat algorithm:** This robot was programmed with military software. This CPU comes with 1d3 skill points in martial arts, 1d2 skill points in sniper, 1d3 points in demolitions expert, 1d3 points in dodge, 1d3 points in knife fighter, and 1d3 skill points in the weapon expert skill. If any of these skills allows a character to start game play with any weaponry, then this robot will carry standard, hand held versions of whatever randomly determined weapons, blades or explosives associated with such skills.

# Auditory and Olfactory Sensors

Unless enhanced by some implant or worn relic device, all robot characters have a sense of hearing and smell equal to a human plus 1 to 20% (1d20).

# Comms

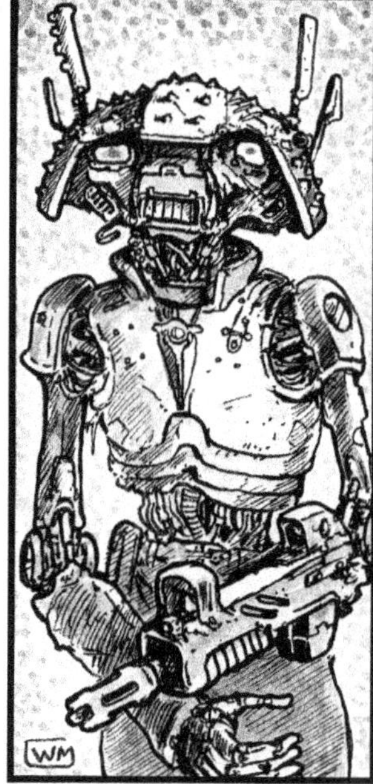

While it was common for robots in the ancient world to have several modes of communication, including remote control overrides, compliance chips, tracking beacons and other one and two-way data transfer modes, many of these parts have since been torn out of the heads of any existing, self aware robots because they are known to be pathways into the machine's CPU for hostile AIs.

Within most robots are slots where assorted control and transmission gadgetry once existed, and might accept the old parts back in again.

Some unique robots have basic communicators left intact, or inserted in recent years to help them maintain team cohesion. These simple devices do not grant access to outside control commands, but can be used by this unit to communicate with human comrades who have standard or advanced communicators.

Roll 1d10 to determine what, if any communicator is present in this robot's head.



**1-5. None.** A communicator can be inserted and plugged into existing wiring and rubberized antennas, however. Doing so will allow the robot to operate the device hand free even while performing other actions. A robotics technician is needed to attempt this installation, so consult table TME-1-50 on page TME-54 and use the column and odds for 'Attach Implants to Robot or Android'.

**6. Communicator wrist watch,** as the relic on page TME-198. 10 km range, 10 channels.

**7-9. Standard communicator,** as described on page TME-198. This unit has a 100 km range and 100 channels.

**10. Advanced communicator,** as described on page TME-198 and features a 500 km range that can pick up AM/FM broadcasts, and 500 channels, among other features described in the relic's text description.

# Voice

Using the following quick table, roll 1d10 to establish this unique robot's speaking voice:

### Table XR-141/ Robot Voice Determination — Roll 1d10

**1. Screwy** Something is wrong here. **Roll 1d6: 1,2.** The vocabulator has only limited operation and this robot can only say 1d6 words every minute. / **3,4.** Garbled speech that comes out in beeps, pops, squeaks and oscillating howls. Any listening character is allowed a type D perception based hazard check to understand accurately what the robot just said. GM: The player can write what it wanted to say and pass that note to the players of characters who successfully understood. / **5.** Modulates between a male human and female human voice, each sentence different. / **6.** Whisper mode only. This robot can't shout or even speak in a voice louder than a whisper. In a noisy setting, such as a saloon, this robot is will have better luck getting its message heard if it writes on a small chalkboard that it wears about its chest.

Any of these shortcomings can only be fixed by replacing the vocabulator from any defeated robot, or the part purchased and installed at a robotics dealership at a cost of 500+2d100sp.

**2,3 Digitized** There is no humanity in this voice, and depending on the gender identity, if any, that this robot has chosen, its words come out in a somewhat sinister, scratchy monotone voice. A robotics technician can install a few parts from another robot to fix this, so long as an old robot can be found and a working part salvaged. To buy a total replacement vocabulator and have it installed at a robotics dealership will cost 500+2d200sp.

**4,5. Human-like** This robot's voice comes out sounding very much like a regular human, although to a careful listener, of 50 or higher intelligence, the voice is not entirely convincing and such a listener is allowed a type D perception based hazard check to discern that the speaker is using a mechanical voice box. Most of the time this won't matter, but in some regions, and in the factional lands of those who hate and fear all robots and mechanical beings, being identified as a non-human can be fatal.

**6,7. Variable** This robot usually selects one consistent voice when conversing with usual companions, but can switch to one of several other commonly used voices, too. It will have 1d4 secondary options from an inventory that includes those of male and females. The following random d30 list of olden days actors and singers offers a sample of possible voices. The GM or player of this robot is encouraged to establish other voice's, too. It's best to pick a voice that other players at the table have a high likelihood of knowing or a quick search on the web will reveal. **Roll 1d30: 1.** Elvis Presley / **2.** James Earl Jones / **3.** Scarlet Johansen / **4.** Arnold Schwarzenegger / **5.** John Wayne / **6.** Mickey Mouse™ / **7.** Michael Jackson / **8.** Marilyn Monroe / **9.** Bruce Lee / **10.** William Shatner as Captain James T. Kirk ™ / **11.** Ariana Grande / **12.** Hermione Granger™ (as voiced by Emma Watson from Harry Potter ™) / **13.** Denzel Washington / **14.** Wes Studi, as Magua (from The Last of the Mohicans 1992 movie) / **15.** Danny DeVito / **16.** Liam Neeson / **17.** Keanu Reeves / **18.** Jack Nicholson / **19.** Eddie Murphy / **20.** Sir Anthony Hopkins / **21.** Julia Roberts / **22.** Clint Eastwood / **23.** Samuel L. Jackson / **24.** Will Smith / **25.** Jackie Chan / **26.** Sean Connery / **27.** Harrison Ford / **28.** Morgan Freeman / **29.** Adele / **30.** Robin Williams

**8,9. Android Voice Box** A vocabulator from an android has been bolted into this robot's head. See Table XR-40 Android Vocal Capabilities on page 49 of this book and randomly determine vocal capabilities from there.

**10. Loud Speaker Enabled** This robot can speak in its normal human sounding voice, but when needed, can engage a megaphone and broadcast at ten times its normal speaking volume. On a calm day, this machine's bellowed words can be heard from 4 kilometers away. Maximum duration of loud speaker mode, per hour, is 1 minute per character's rank. Many animals will cease their approach toward this robot and its companions if shouted at with such volume, and if not defending its lair or young, are forced to make a morale check or back off entirely. Of course, using a loudspeaker in the post-apocalyptic wasteland will probably be heard by unfriendly ears, and by beings who might show displeasure at the arrival of intruders into their territory, especially noisy ones.

# Cybernetic Parts

Unique robots aren't always equipped with cybernetic implants, as these parts are normally designed to accommodate a human physiology. Yet, just like androids, some do begin game play with one or more. Those who start game play with implants are therefore pre-wired and have adapter mounts to accept the implant they have and therefore have an additional 1d3 extra hard points and connection jacks where other implants can be attached. If the robot doesn't start with implants, then it cannot have them later without undergoing very complex wiring, optic and interface upgrades at a cost of 6000+2d1000sp and done at very advanced facilities by either robotics or cybernetic technician of 5 or more skill points.

What implant are available to a unique robot are listed on the random table XR-210 on page 330 of this book. Roll below for how many implants a new robot character might exhibit.

### Table XR-142/ Possible Cybernetic Implants    Roll 1d10

**1-5.** No implants, and no mounting or wiring to accommodate any implants.
**6,7.** One implant
**8,9.** Two implants
**10.** Three implants

# Unique Robot Additional Parts and Features

Each robotic character will start game play with one or more randomly generated additional parts and features. Some items listed on the following pages are implants identical to what a cyborg might have and include cybernetic parts from both this book and the TME Hub Rules. Should a cybernetic implant be assigned from this table, and yet the robot does not have any from table XR-142, above, then this unit has no spare mounting locations or adapters to accept more than what is added here, however, these implants can be substituted should the opportunity, facilities and a skilled robotics or cybernetic technician be available to handle such a switch.

While most of the following parts and features can be removed, should they be unwanted by the robot, it is up to the GM if such parts can be added. For example, if an NPC robot is discovered or defeated that has one or more of these parts, or these items are found for sale in a dealership, or uncovered in the ruins, then it seems logical that such parts could be attached to a unique robot. It's a simple enough task to rip out an unwanted part and bolt steel plates over the hole, but adding a part is a much more complex chore. Connecting a moving part most likely involves wiring the part to the robot's control systems, optics and sensors to allow the new part to be used.

It is recommended that only 2 additional parts or features can be added to a unique robot after whatever is determined during character generation. This suggestion is made to ensure game play isn't constantly stopped to accommodate the player of this robot and endless upgrading and looting of fallen robots. So too, there is only so much free space on a robot's chassis, to say nothing of the coordination needed from the unit's CPU or electricity supplies.

Perhaps a resourceful robot might keep a backpack full of other parts and establish a system of quick connecting and disconnecting spare parts to perform various operations and chores, or at the very least, stash unused, highly valuable parts for future use or sale.

A lot of game master input is needed here, but for the most part a robotics technician of 3 or more skill points has a good chance of successfully installing some new found part, although if failure occurs on the percentile roll shown on table TME-1-50 on page 54 of the hub rules, then the new found part is broken during installation. To hire a robotics technician to install one of the parts included in this listing below, the robot and its companions, must bring the salvaged parts to the facility, as these items are very unlikely to be kept in stock. The installation cost will be 1000+2d1000 silver pieces and the procedure take 2d6 hours.

Re-roll duplicated results if more than one additional part or feature is present. Roll 2d6 to determine the number of additional parts a unique robot has:

| Table XR-143a/ Additional Parts of a Unique Robot | Roll 2d6 |
|---|---|
| 2. | 1 part |
| 3,4. | 2 parts |
| 5-7. | 3 parts |
| 8-10. | 4 parts |
| 11 | 5 parts |
| 12 | 5+1d6 parts |

### Table XR-143b/ Robot Additional Parts and Features Assortment Roll 1d100

**01. Heightened Touch Sensors:** While all robots can detect when they make contact with objects and get a relatively good idea of its density, material, and temperature, but their sense of touch is limited and about a quarter as well developed as that of either an android or a humanoid.

This robot is different, however, and besides having twice the all over body sensitively as most other robots, the fingers on this unit's main, human-like arm are remarkably attuned. When performing any delicate task using this hand, such as surgery, lock picking, untying something, etc., consider this robot's agility or accuracy to be improved by +30 trait points. This does not extend to aiming weapons or attacking.

**02. Additional 'secondary' arm:** As noted on table XR-133 back on page 154.

**03. Metal jaws of doom:** The head of this robot has been customized to take on the look of a ferocious metal dog, alligator, shark, dinosaur, or other beast, complete with over-sized opening and closing, alloy toothed mouth.

Besides being able to speak through this mouth opening, this robot can lunge forward and add a bite attack to whatever melee attack it already features. This attack is SV +5 and inflicts 1d20 damage, +1 point per character rank (so a 1st rank robot with this feature bites for 1d20+1 damage, at 7th rank PC bites for 1d20+7, etc). Strength modifers don't apply to this bite, but either the weapon expert or brawling skill can be added to this part (but not both skills). Roll for the sort of mouth and face this terrifying machine exhibits, 1d8: 1. Mastiff / 2. Alligator / 3. Bear / 4. Boar / 5. T-Rex / 6. Shark / 7. Gorilla / 8. Eagle.

**04. Music database and speaker array:**
This robot is pre-loaded with a stand-alone computer system in its head which contains assorted tracks of music from all eras in human recording history. It can set the music to various themed random play lists, or select individual tracks and either play them within its own head for its own enrichment and pleasure as if it were a person wearing headphones, or broadcast the music.

This robot comes with a subwoofer and six speakers which can play tracks at whisper volume all the way up to almost deafening concert mode, levels. When playing loudly, however, the dedicated, slow charge speaker batteries are drained quickly and can only play at full volume for an hour. If played at a moderate level, a level where those enjoying the music can still conduct conversation within ten meters, then this robot can play music for 4 hours before a 20 hour recharge is needed.

With this speaker system the robot can also accept audio inputs from other devices through a multi-configuration jack array that is attached to the unit's head and has a rubberized hatch cover. With its own audio resources or those plugged in from another machine, these speakers can also play alert sounds, announcements, air raid sirens, and pre-recorded transmissions from other beings, such as speeches.

**05. Beverage dispenser:** This unit's chest can pop open upon request by a master or customer and reveal a cup holder and six nozzles with drink brand logo-pictures and liquid dispensers. One dispenser is always soda, which this machine can create from water and certain ingredients it finds in the environment, crushes, treats, and injects into the water to make it bubbly. The five other fluid tanks can hold whatever comrades load into the 2 liter containers, and could include beer, water, wine, vodka, fruit juice, or hot drinks. The robot's core maintains the refrigeration of cold beverages, but super heats coffee or tea as needed. This system adds 6 kg weight to the robot when the tanks are empty but if each 2L tank is full, add another 12 kg weight.

**06. Heat sensors:** This robot has a head mounted, 360 degree, conical antenna on the side of its head. This device can be activated and extended 30cm. When switched on, it will turn and possibly detect approaching warm bodied creatures, vehicles, robotics or geological abnormalities such as fires, lava or cold water, and other sudden changes in temperature. As the robot goes through its operational duration (its life) it improves its detection abilities and range, so for every rank gained, the radius of temperature change detection increases by 10 meters around it, starting at a 10m radius at 1st rank.

Besides being able to detect hiding humanoids or other animals that might wait in ambush, or the proximity of a camouflaged enemy robot or android, this unit's initiative score is improved by +1.

The game master will need to supply information to the player when they say their character activates this device, which can only run while the robot is stationary. It can detect different, newly arriving temperature fluctuations and heat signatures and differentiate them from those of its companions, and after traveling with the same animals and people for more than a week, recognizes their distinct patterns and 'shape', even in total darkness. Often, if this robot is put on guard at night, since it can stay awake all night, it makes for a splendid camp watchman, especially at higher ranks when it can detect approaching trouble out many meters and forewarn comrades.

**07. Rad-scanner:** Mounted to the robot's head like an extra eye and within its own dedicated socket, this device can be activated when desired and will scan the view ahead to seek radiation. It can see the concentration as a faint glow superimposed over the landscape or object before it, with yellow areas emitting mild radiation, orange for medium, red for strong, and purple for lethal radiation zones or objects. It is not constantly running and must be actively switched on to work. As the relic described on page 199 of the Hub Rules, it has a 30 meter range, however it draws its power from the robot's own batteries at a negligible rate.

Radiation can be very harmful to non-organic characters, too. To learn more, see the section 'Radiation and effects on Robots and Androids' on page 378 of this book.

**08. Solar panel and recharge port:** This panel differs from the design described in the Power Source section of this character type, and instead of being bolted to the chassis of the robot, this is a deployable, fan-like array that extends from a telescopic shaft, unfurls like a small 2m tall by 1m wide sail and automatically aligns and tracks the sun.

For every hour of direct sunlight, this panel will recharge 10 energy units (a standard power cell has 10 energy units and a power pack has 100 EUs). Besides being hooked into this robots chassis and able to recharge on-board batteries, the panel base has a pop open compartment with one power cable receptacle and a power changing adapter array where up to 6 pill power cells, 4 mini power

cells and 1 standard power cell can be simultaneously plugged into the array and charged in an hour. If an extension cord is plugged into this array, the solar panel can charge other devices, androids and machines, too, even while the two machines walk side by side in the sun connected by the cord.

Only one charging option can be undertaken at any given moment, so for example either the robot can charge its internal batteries, or loose batteries can be plugged in and charged, or something connected by the cable can be connected. A simple selector switch is built to the array so even if this robot is neutralized, this array can still be accessed to charge other electronics and batteries.

Because this array is so advanced, and charges the remarkable batteries of the oldsters so efficiently, this robot must be very careful who sees it deploying the solar panel array, for the powerful, the corrupt and greedy of the new era will go to almost any length to capture this robot and remove its limbs and bolt it to a rooftop to spend its existence as nothing more than a power generator.

Besides being able to charge using the sun, this deployable panel can actually be used as a small sail to help a rowboat or canoe travel effortlessly across water.

**09. Spot lights:** This robot is equipped with an array of forward facing, high intensity spot lights. While 4 are fixed and face forward from the head, a fifth is top mounted and can swivel about in a 360 degree angle, or directly up into the sky if needed and serves as a continuous operation search light even if the robot is moving.

These lights have a range of 250 meters, although can be dimmed to illuminate as little as 5 meters and switch to red, emergency light mode, which is far harder to be seen by unfriendly eyes at a distance. Besides being able to illuminate the way ahead, using a dedicated built-in power cell that will run these lights for 48 hours before a slow, 24 hour recharge from the primary system is needed, these lights have various control options. They can be turned off in any sequence, change color, or even broadcast Morse Code, which this robot automatically knows as a skill (see page XR-220 in this book).

Some creatures are very sensitive to bright lights, and having 5 spotlight turn on all at once in the dark is likely to blind nearly any living creature temporarily, and likely drive them off (morale check needed at the GM's discretion).

**10. Head mounted lightning emitter:** Identical to the relic on page 412 of this book. This weapon can fire ten shots per day from a built-in, recharging battery, but also accepts a snap-in standard power cell. This is not an additional attack, and demands the robot's full attention and so is an alternate weapon system.

**11. Folding utility arm and tool:** Roll 1d10 for what tool: 1,2. Small human-like hand of low strength score of between 3 and 18 (roll 3d6 at character generation), but highly accurate (ACC 30+3d10) and perfect for repairs of electronics and medical procedures on organic beings. / 3. Disc saw* / 4. Laser torch* / 5. Spot light*/ 6. Laser scalpel* / 7. Power drill with drill-bit and screwdriver assortment. / 8. Chainsaw*/ 9. Tissue binder from page 443 in this book/ 10. Handheld Satellite Communications Unit [HSCU] as described on page 448 of this book.

*Detail in the hub rules with stats on page TME 100 and details in the relics section of that book, pages 186 to 202.

**12. Micro-Optic-Tendril:** Attached to a chassis enclosed spool system, this 30 meter long, 5cm diameter, mat-black tendril can reel out at a rate of 3 meters per round and snake its way through tight debris, dense foliage, and down deep holes, into murky water or up to higher ledges in structures. At the far end is an optical sensor eye, audio receptor and tiny speaker. With this small node, the robot can see whatever the tiny optic sees, hears as well as a human, and if need be, speak in a very low, digitized human voice through this tendril's high-tech head.

Whether the original purpose of this probe was to search for survivors in the rubble of ruined buildings and vehicle wrecks, or used to spy on other beings, modern day scholars and robotic technicians aren't certain. What is

certain, however, is that if this tendril is discovered (Type F perception based hazard check by those being spied upon), the tendril can be chopped off and the delicate sensory array at the tip lost. Treat the tendril as defense value -40, with an endurance of 8. If severed and the sensory tip is recovered, a robotics, electrical, cybernetic or mechanical technician, can easily rewire it back together after 1d6+1 hour's work.

For whatever reason if the robot needs to use this tendril as a whip or bludgeoning tool, it can attack at SV +2 for 1d6 damage, but any fumble roll on the strike attempt (results of a natural 95-00) mean the tip shatters and is forever useless.

The tendril is connected to a delicate spool and motor within the robot's body and if used as a rope, can only support 30kg weight. Anything beyond this amount results in a 1 in 6 chance of breaking per round thereafter if more weight is being hoisted up or lowered down.

**13. Air conditioner:** When in a small space, of no larger than 6x6 meters, this robot can turn on its AC mode and cool the area to a comfortable room temperature, or drop the temperature to freezing if given 6 or more hours. It can only run this AC mode for 12 hours on internal power, although there is an external power slot for a standard power cell which will yield another 12 hours of cooling if needed. Spare battery not included.

**14. Life Support Respirator [LSR]:** Besides being waterproofed, this robot has a pop open compartment on its chassis that reveals 3 respirator masks and a 1 hour air supply for whoever straps on these masks. Besides being able to keep human companions alive while submerged, these masks will also protect the wearer from poison gas and other airborne toxins. The air tanks will take 6 hours to recharge and be ready for another hour's use, although a single wearer could use each respirator in turn and last 3 hours underwater if needed.

**15. Holographic emitter:** This robot has an extra, oval shaped eye on its head that can project preloaded 3d movies of ancient or new production, as well as maps, recent events this robot itself witnessed, or concepts, equations and other graphics as needed. The holographic images are translucent and ghostly and can be shown as small as a person's hand or as large as three meters in height or width.

Primitives, and many animals, must make a morale check at the sight of such apparition or believe it is a ghost, or deity. The holograph can be emitted up to 9 meters from the unit's head and will move with the robot. Maximum duration per day of holographic emission is 6 hours before a 12 hour recharge period is needed.

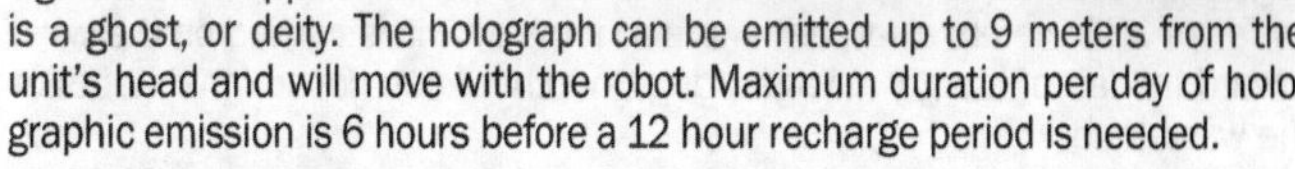


**16. Night vision optics:** Normally mounted on the robot's head as an extra eye, this small dark orb allows the robot to see in the dark up to 100m away.

**17. Toaster oven:** A 40cm wide horizontal compartment on the chassis of this robot has a clear, tempered glass oven door, which is also the lid portion that opens to reveal toaster elements and a steel pull-out cook tray within. Dials on the front of the oven have pre-arranged cooking time and temperatures for common old world foods. The robot can control the cook times from its own on-board computer and use any human-like hands to insert and remove food items. The interior space is about the size of a loaf of bread — which it can also cook — and is often used by the robot to store spare parts, drained power cells, spent ammo casings and trinkets picked up along the road.

**18. Vacuum cleaner:** This robot has a pop out, telescopic and fully articulated metal arm attached to a vacuum hose. When needed, it can suck up both wet and dry objects of pebble sized or smaller debris and deposit it into an air compressed 5kg holding tank. In a pinch, this vacuum can suck army ants off the ground and killer bees right out of the air. It will vacuum up 1d20 endurance points worth of any swarm per round, all of which are compressed and killed in the holding tank for later expulsion from a tubular bottom orifice on the robot's posterior. If used to try to suck blood flyers, sting flies, venomous bats, skal birds, doom moths, or any creature with a wingspan or length of under 30cm, out of the air, these can also be pulled into the nozzle and crushed at a rate of 1 each on a successful hit, SV +10.

This vacuum mode is noisy, however, and can be heard a half kilometer away on a calm day. 1 in 6 of these units also features a blower mode, and can shoot a blast of wind out 6m to push back a toxic cloud, keep back army ants, or clean off some surface to better inspect it.

**19. Blender:** Within a conical compartment of this robot's chassis is a 2 liter blender for making smoothies, sauces, soup stock and other blended beverages. A small, fused arm is attached to the handle of the blender which extends the container outward 50cm to pour the contents of whatever a user, including the robot itself, chooses to blend up. A spray nozzle and 50cm hose attachment are also included in the compartment which is connected to a 4 liter water storage tank within the robot's body. This hose is intended to spray out the blender jug after each use to clean it, but can also serve as a water supply for organic companions. The spray range of this hose is 3 meters.

**20. Stone boring power head:** Fitted on a 2m long, heavy duty shaft sits a multi-grinder, diamond embedded drill head and liquid dispenser. This unit is designed to slowly grind through rock and concrete at a rate of 1 centimeter per round, creating a hole 30cm in diameter. To create a hole large enough for its whole body to pass through, a dozen or more holes must be excavated in a pattern.

It is essential that this unit is supplied with a half liter (500ml) of water per minute, which it sprays into the hole as it works to control the dust and better facilitate grinding without overheating the toothy, bur shaped grinding heads. Without water, the unit might seize up and permanently burn out after ten minutes, with every minute of running dry after ten minutes resulting in a 1 in 6 chance of a burnout.

As a melee weapon against other machines or flesh, this unit is certainly abrasive and would inflict 3d6 damage per round on a held down victim, but its true use in combat is as a backup weapon and heavy bludgeon, at +4 strike value doing 3d6 lethal damage on a smack. This is not an extra melee attack per round, but an alternative. This arm is normally stowed tight against the robot's back and often covered in a canvas shroud to keep it free of grit or prevent it from catching on passing objects.

Because it is bulking, weighs plenty, and is made of incredibly tough materials, increase this robot's defense value by -10 DV and add 35+1d12 kilograms weight to the robot.

**21. Air fryer:** Made popular in the early 21st century, this built-in unit sits behind a hard protective hatch. It features several temperature, timer, and pre-set modes and a handle equipped, pull out cooking 'jug' It can take up to 2 kilograms of raw foodstuffs, along with seasonings and sauce, and cook them in about 20 minutes to a crispy, perfect consistency.

While cooking, it makes a whirring noise that can be heard from as far as 20 meters away. Another concern for the user is that the smell of cooking vegetables and especially meat, will attract humanoids and predators from as far as 250 meters away, and more so if the aroma is carried on the wind toward the lair of hungry savages, dogs, or other keen nosed inhabitants of the wasteland.

Hot oil can be heated to dangerously high temperatures in this unit, and splashed onto enemies out to 6 meters away, causing 2d6 damage from burns and able to coat up to three man sized targets, SV +5.

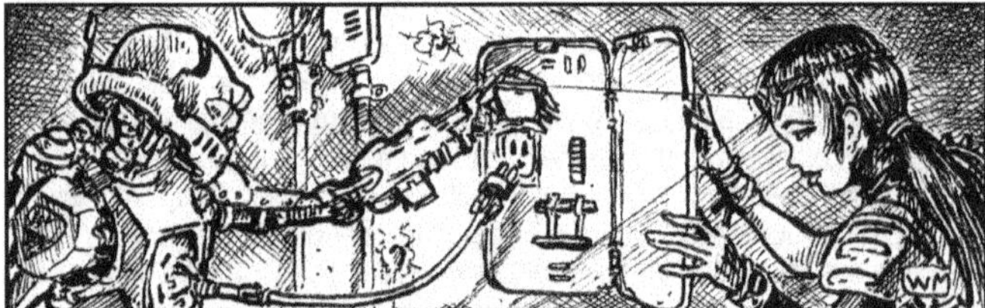

**22. Computer interface tendril:** This cable ends in a knobby, multi pronged bulb. Upon this orb are a dozen assorted plugs that allow the robot to interface with a computer station, laptop, vehicle, structural computer, or other robot with the same access port. This tendril is fragile and cannot be used as a weapon except in the last resort, with an SV of +2 and inflicting 1d6 damage. With every strike it makes, there is a 1 in 6 chance the tendril's plug assortment shatters and thereafter renders the 90cm (3 feet) long cable as useless until some other blade or bludgeoning weapon is attached to the stump. It has a strength score of 10 and can move at a rate of 3 meters per round. Because it doesn't have optics of its own, it must be guided by the robot's own visual sensors for directional guidance.

**23. Enhanced audio receptors:** This robot can hear twice as well as a human.

**24. Self-Destruct mode:** As the implant on page 90 of the hub rules.

**25. Laser pointer:** While, harmless, this tiny tube is great for pointing out landmarks to a range of 1 kilometer, or distracting predators, especially felines.

**26. Fold out grappling hook and cable spool:** This alloy treble hook can be fired 20m, SV 01-80, damage 1d20, rate 1. It is fired from a hidden compartment at +4 initiative, but takes 1 round to re-spool per meter. If a strike occurs on a target that the robot wants to use as a grappling hold point, such as a rebar outcrop, tree branch, vehicle or higher rocks or concrete, this unit can pull itself up by this hook at a rate of 3m per round. Maximum additional load is only 100kg. If a heavier load is lifted along with the robot itself, there is a 1 in 10 chance per round that the cable snaps. 

Should the cable be used to hoist somebody or something up without the robot itself being part of the load — such as if trying to lift a comrade up or down from a cliff face, the total amount that can be carried is the weight of the robot plus 100kg. Additional ropes and other hooks and harnesses can be attached to lift or lower others at much longer distances than the existing 20 meter cable limit. Cable END 12, DV -12.

**27. Dust sheath:** If forced to endure a sand or junk storm, a sheath of translucent plastic 'curtain' deploys from the unit's upper back and drapes the whole unit, plus up to two adult human sized companions, in a sheath of protective plastic. This sheath is strong enough to withstand sand storms and other inclement weather, but has no defensive qualities against incoming projectiles or melee range attackers. It takes 4 rounds to deploy this sheath, but 4 minutes to retract, roll up, and properly stow.

**28. Hypodermic needle arm:** A flexible, triple jointed arm can be extended from a well concealed compartment and inject a medical patient or unwary opponent with whatever substance the robot has filled the 200ml (6.76 fl oz) capacity needle canister with. Typical substances are assorted venoms, hallucinogenic drugs, or the contents of an anti-toxin injector. This appendage is frail and clearly not meant to serve as an additional melee attack, but can be so deployed: SV +5, rate 1, range: out 1 meter, DMG 1d4+contents of syringe.

**29. Espresso Bar:** This robot's abdomen opens up to reveal jazz music and a mini-coffee shop. A Starstruck coffee logo illuminates the scene as a steam wand froths milk to make cappuccino foam or heat milk for a latte or mocha. Coffee beans are ground, compressed into a group and espresso shots poured. 1d3+1 tiny, chrome arms emerge, each with three fingered grasping hands to present a cup from stacked holder and offer the piping hot drink. When coffee beans aren't available, offee substitutes from plants, or tea, hot cocoa, steamed milk, or other beverages are offered.

**.30. Enhanced sensory port:** Roll a random condition that this robot can sense. The observable range is as this robot's perception score in meters and in a 180 degree viewing arc ahead of it. This mode must be intentionally switched on to use. In addition, the robot must stop moving to let the device scan the way ahead to get an accurate reading. It draws upon the power of the robot's main power supply and takes negligible battery usage.

**Roll 1d6** for what this robot can see: **1.** Radiation / **2.** Holograms, illusions, and digital being projections. / **3.** Dimensional beings and dimensional holes made in the last hour. / **4.** Toxic gas. / **5.** Land mines buried down to 10 centimeters or less. / **6.** Laser security beams (invisible trip line beams).

**31. Rotating midsection:** This unit can turn about in a 360 degree rotation, and walk forward while looking and firing back. A special eye on the back of its head allows for ground scanning to facilitate locomotion without walking into barriers or off cliffs and other hazards. Having an extra eye on the back of its head also gives this unit +1 initiative. 

**32. Wind turbine system:** This robot is equipped with a retractable 2m boom and deployable triple propeller bladed energy generation turbine. During strong winds, this unit can recharge itself or a plugged in power cell in two hours or, mini power cell in 15 minutes or power pack in 20 hours. It comes with a spool fed, 12 meter long bright yellow extension cord in order to plug itself into other robots, androids and machinery to facilitate recharge of other systems, but cannot charge itself and another being simultaneously.

Besides generating electricity, this propeller can be reversed and used to blow away toxic gas, smoke, spore and dust from an area in a 3m wide swath and blow it back 3d6 meters. As a weapon, this fragile implant is ill suited for all but the elimination of small flying creatures such as red wasps, blood flyers, sting flies and skal birds. If used to chop at incoming small creatures, use these stats SV 01-70, range: melee, Damage 3d6. If used against larger flyers, any hit has a 1 in 6 chance of snapping off the blade requiring a 10+d12 hours of repair by a robotics, cybernetic, or mechanical technician, or else a junk crafter or 3 or more skill points. Hiring a professional to make this repair will take 2d4 hours and cost 500+4d100sp.

**33. Hairdressing array:** This unit has a chest panel which opens to deploy a pair of scissors, electro-trimmers, blow dryer, gel-mousse hose and scalp massage fingers. A set of soft lights and mirror for the client also emerge, with the lights giving off illumination out to 6m ahead of the robot should it need to light the way for a party.

All these tools are situated at the ends of four delicate chrome arms about two feet (60cm) in length, and are far too fragile to be used in combat (SV +0, DMG 1d2 each, any fumble causes the arm to snap off). This array has a built in hairstyle lingo and style directory screen of some 1000 hairstyles from all cultures and traditions throughout the ages. Small speakers within the cavity of the array can be set to play soothing, ambient techno music suitable for any spa environment.

**34. Emergency Float System [EFS]:** When falling into liquids deeper than the unit's neck, gas bags instantly deploy from between 3 and 6 (1d4+2) compartments distributed about the robot's torso. These bags are so designed as to keep the unit upright in the water, head above the surface and use its arms to either engage hostiles or swim at one quarter the unit's walking speed. These bags take 10 minutes to deflate, retract, and fold back into the body and can only be deployed once per day unless an external power cell is plugged into a back socket and entirely drained just for one deployment. If deployed during a fall or crash as air bags, they will reduce damage by -25%.

**35. Taste bud tendril:** A small, half meter long hose can be extended from this robot's head unit and upon reaching a substance the robot wishes to investigate, can expose the tendril's delicate, flexible plastic tongue tip that has the same range of flavor receptors as a human tongue. After sampling the chemicals in the substance, the robot can make a guess to the substance its tasting against a database of identical or similar substances to a 98% degree of accuracy. It can tell if a subsentence is laced with drugs or poison, too, as well as relate to comrades if the meat they are about to eat really came from a pig, or a tuna, or is instead human flesh, cat, or taken from some other animal altogether.

**36. BB rifle:** Attached to the chest of this robot is a stubby barreled, air pressure powered BB rifle. This single-shot weapon is identical to the relic described on page 403 of this book, with the following stats and an internal, refillable hopper containing 1000+1d1000 copper coated steel BBs.

BB Rifle: SV +0 / Rate 1 / DMG 1 point / Range 24m. This weapon seems to have been installed as some sort of pest control measure. It requires the aim and attention of the robot's head and so cannot be fired with other missile or melee weapons.

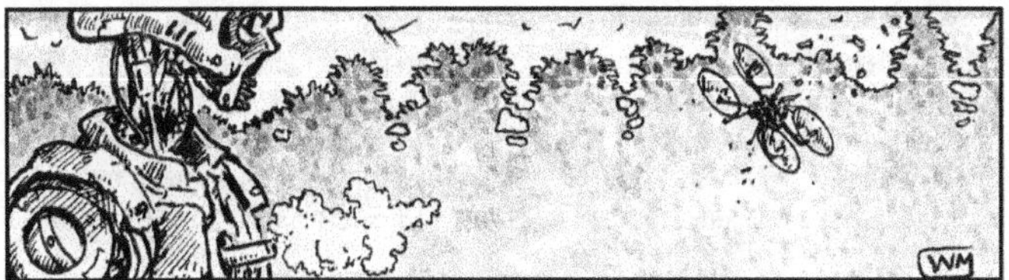

**37. Chem sprayer:** As the relic on page 404 of this book. This robot will begin game play with a satchel containing 2d6 random full canisters, and 2d6 empty ones in need of refilling. A random list of assorted cannister contents is listed with this relic system.

**38. Winch:** At the lower front end of this robot is a high powered winch, spool of 30 meters of incredibly strong alloy cable, and a locking hook suitable for pulling three times the weight of the robot itself. This winch can extract vehicles from mud, or if the robot can hang onto something solid, can pull a door off its hinges, drag a heavy boat up on shore above the high tide line, or hoist comrades or object out of deep pits and other predicaments.

The retraction speed of this hook and cable is 1 meter per round, although the hook itself must be manually attached to whatever the robot wishes to pull, or pull itself towards if itself is stuck in quicksand or some other quagmire. The robot can throw the hook half its strength score value in meters to comrades who can secure the hook to themselves or something solid if this robot itself needs to be pulled up or get free.

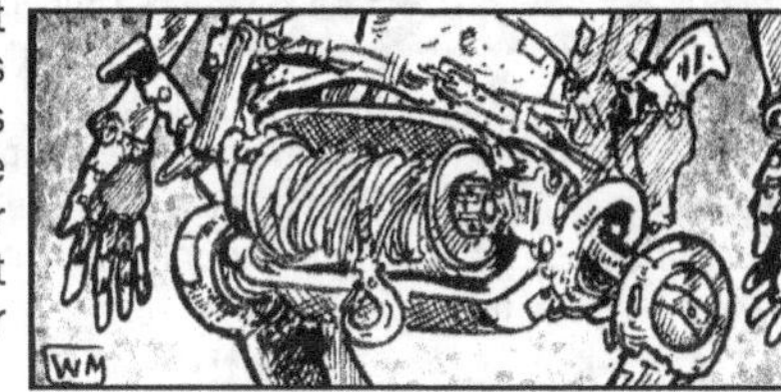

The alloy cable has a defense value of -36 and endurance of 27 and if severed, requires complex reweaving and micro welding to reattach—a task that can normally only be done in a well established mechanical workshop at a cost of 800+2d100sp.

**39. Leg jacks:** This robot can extend its legs or wheel spacing and or track configuration an extra meter each to elevate its body or run at +3 meters per round faster for up to one hour per day.

**40. Forklift arms:** Equipped with fold out fork arms and a pair of telescopic shafts on which the arms move from ground level and upward, this unit can lift double the robot's body weight either to transport a load, or hoist it up 2 meters higher than the robot's own total height.

If the blade-like lift arms are extended, and this robot gets a run at a creature or other robot or vehicle, treat this charge attack as two separated attacks at SV +12 and able to inflict 2d20 damage each. Only during a charging run of a full round of movement toward the target can this mighty attack be achieved, although in regular melee these extended steel protrusions can make one melee attack each per round at SV +2 and do 1d20 damage on a hit. These blades can be added as extra melee attacks.

**41. Air pump:** Being equipped with an air compressor and tire pump, this robot can fill tires as well as sports balls, pool floaties, inflatable neck pillows, and other relic items. Likewise, this system can be used to propel a steady supply of air down a tube to a swimmer wearing some sort of crude, post-apocalyptic diver's helmet to permit deep water excavations, recovery and exploration. This pump can run for a maximum of two hours per day and must cool and recharge for 22 hours.

**42. Level:** This liquid filled level is bolted to the underside of one of the robot's arms. While useful for construction and helping determine if an excavation teams is going up or down a shaft, there are few obvious uses in day-to-day survival for this part.

**43. Measuring tape:** Marked with both Imperial and Metric measurements, this 20m long yellow measuring tape uses an electronic motor to extend and retract at 1m per round.

**44. Power cord and reserve battery:** This unit consists of an extension cord and power reel, with a plug-in jack to a separate, dedicated internal power pack and two extra plug-in ports. This reserve power pack is built permanently into the robot's chassis and not readably recognizable to onlookers. The power from this battery is accessible to the robot only if plugged into itself. This extension cord can be unplugged from the robot for use by others and measures 20 meters in length. It can be auto reeled back in at a rate of 2 meters per round and if the cord is used as a light duty rope, it can pull a load weighing up to 40 kilograms. Any weight more than this results in a 2 in 6 chance per round of the internal reel seizing up and stopping. And requiring 3d6 hours to cool and reset itself.

**45. Ladder:** A back mounted extendable alloy ladder is built into this robot's chassis. The ladder has a 180kg maximum weight capacity, and while attached to the robot, can't be used by the robot itself. If detached, which takes 1+1d6 minutes, the ladder can be used by the robot if it is not over 180kg — as the ladder will snap down the middle if overloaded. To reattach the ladder it takes 3d6+10 minutes. The unit extends 8x this robot's own height.

**46. Work light array:** A row of rubber armored, bright yellow work lights are attached to a 60cm long metal rod at the top of this robot's head. These

run on a separate, dedicated power cell while each light is considered a relic spotlight from page TME-201 in the hub rules. These lights can be aimed in different direction manually or the entire system unbolted and placed on an included fold out tripod connected to a 10m permanently attached, coil-style power cable that leads back to the robot and the battery housing.

These lights can be dimmed down to provide low illumination out to 6m, which is perfect for lighting up a campsite at night without attracting too much attention from potentially unfriendly observers. Spot lights normally have a range of up to 250 meters.

**47. Crowbar attachment:** A fold out alloy crowbar is built into the robot's arm. This bar, especially if it is propelled by the robot's piston powered swing, can inflict grievous wounds and is treated as a backup (not extra) attack mode. SV +5, DMG 1d10+5.

*GM Note:* If this crowbar is looted off a dead robot and used by a human, it has an SV of +2 and does 1d10+2 damage in one handed use.

**48. Sprinkler system:** This unit comes complete with a hose spool and 10+1d20 meters of lime green garden hose, a built-in water tank and pump that holds 20+1d20 liters of water. The weight added by this system is 5kg, plus 1kg per liter of liquid carried in the sprayer. Range of spray 5m fan mode or 20 meters concentrated jet.

**49. Reciprocating Saw:** Attached to one of this robot's arms is a pop out rapid cut, electronic reciprocating saw blade. SV +8, DMG 3d8, and will cut through wood, bone and non-alloy standard iron and steel bars, door hinges, hatches and other robots.

**50. Fog machine and Halloween light show projector:** This robot has a shoulder mounted contraption that looks more fierce than it is. With a purplish black, glassy eye — which looks like some sort of targeting optic to those unfamiliar with this unit — it projects ghostly shapes, witches on brooms, bats, jack-o'-lanterns and black cat 2d graphics onto any surface up to 30 meters away, although the closer they are projected the smaller and more opaque and detailed these graphics are.

Also optionally ejected from this machine are scary Halloween screams, werewolf howls, creaking doors, wolf howls, cat meows and witch cackles, as well as a dense blanket of purplish green fog. This fog will billow out and cover 1 square meter of ground per round until it reaches its maximum distribution of a 30 meter radius around the fog machine. This fog, incidentally, makes for a splendid background to the projected, spooky images.

For most new era commoners and humanoids, the sight of this display, complete with sounds of wolves and cats, is enough to scare the bejesus out of them and force a morale check. The light show and fog machine can operate for a maximum of 4 hours every 48 hours and must recharge slowly from the robot's own power supply.

The robot, and its companions who are familiar with the fog, can crouch low and allow it to conceal them in the billowing, garishly colored cloud and gain 2 skill points in the stealth skill categories of 'concealed movement' and 'conceal self'.

**51. Leaf blower:** This can blow away army ants, doom moths, sting flies, skal birds and red wasps, throwing them back 2d6 meters and likely dashing them on rubble or branches and causing 1d6 damage to each creature caught in the 3m diameter cone of blasting air. This unit can run for a half

hour every 4 hours, and recharges from the slow trickle charger feature of the robot's own battery supply.

**52. Waffle iron:** Within the chassis of this robot is a cabinet encased waffle iron. When opened, heated and the green ready light turns on with a cheerful beep, beep, beep, the system is ready to be deployed. This is a vertical, top filling unit with indicator light, and can be set to cook waffles from light brown to crispy. It will cook one waffle in 4+1d4 minutes. Uses the robot's primary power system.

Cruel robots, or their associates, might get the bright idea to use this waffle iron as an instrument of terror, and clamp the heated, grid pattern cooking plates onto the hand or foot of a captive to extract information or set an example to others. A waffle iron held on a person's bare flesh for even a half a minute will leave a permanent, waffle pattern scar on the afflicted appendage, and illicit screams that will force the tortured person to make a willpower based Type C hazard check or answer whatever question the torturer has asked — although, if their willpower trait is 50 or higher, the answer will probaby be a lie.

**53. Tow hitch and wagon:** This robot features a very useful, although cumbersome, detachable yard wagon with 4 knobby wheel. The wagon can hold up to 272kg (600lbs) load capacity, is green and black and will slow the robot by -20% when pulling the loaded cart. This contraption is rather noisy unless the wheels are sufficiently greased and when empty weighs 52kg.

**54. Advanced Power Usage Modulator [APUM]:** This internal, oval shaped unit is bolted to the innards of the robot and modulates the electrical current coming from its power supply to makes it more efficient. A secondary function is to reduce any energy wastage by restricting the power being used by non-essential or rarely used systems. In total, this modulator cuts the power usage needed for this robot by half, including any on-board energy weapons or accessories.

This system, could be looted from this robot, and is exceedingly valuable — a fact this robot will probably keep to itself. Power modulators of this complexity will sell for 2000+1d1000sp in a large town, however to buy one and have it installed in another robot would cost six times this price.

**55. Holographic Christmas Tree display:** A conical, 7m tall by 3 meter in diameter Christmas Tree can be projected around this robot. This well lit tree image is 80% opaque and has assorted light display modes, including no decoration and no light mode which can make this machine look like a idealized pine tree.

In a woodland setting, this hologram will give the robot 4 skill points in conceal self (see the stealth skill in the hub rules on page TME-51), however if lighting itself up into whole Christmas glory, this convincing illusion might very well scare off primitives and wild animals alike. The display can run for 48 hours on one power cell. While the robot can run the tree hologram for a maximum of 6 hours and needing an 18 hour recharge period afterward, it normally draws power from the external power cell that is plugged into a specialized back enclosed compartment. 7 in 10 chance the unit has a full power cell in the compartment at character generation.

**56. Mini bar:** This robot is equipped with a refrigerated cavity sufficient to hold 4 six packs of cola or beer, or meat, medicine or other items that need to be chilled. This chamber, which is about 1 cubic foot in size (30cm), can also be set to freeze mode to create ice cubes or freeze foodstuffs.

**57. Electric cook element:** This fold out single burner stove top has ten heat settings and is perfect for boiling a pot of water, frying chow or heating a knife blade prior to cauterizing a wound. It runs on the robot's main battery supply, and in a pinch, in a space of about 3 by 3m square, can heat the area to allow organic beings to survive in sub-zero conditions for 12 hours.

**58. Industrial nail gun:** This fold out, tri-jointed arm is fitted with a high powered nail gun and uses compressed air from a torso installed air compressor to launch metallic spikes. It can fire three #9 gauge nails per round with a range of 15 meters SV +7, DMG 1d12+2 each. However, if used as an extra melee attack mode at point blank, these 3 nails are +13 SV. This relic appears on Table XR-249 on page 414.

This robot has a ready supply of 100+1d100 #9nails (max capacity in gun itself is 200 nails, however the robot has collected, refurbished and purchased an assortment of nails, and has a spare 1d1000 nails in a leather satchel.

The arm has a strength of 34 and can have a blade, axe or other crude implement bolted to it to add an extra melee attack per round.

**59. Waterproofing upgrade:** This robot's torso and head unit have been waterproofed and rubberized to allow it to withstand full immersion in water, exposure to hard rain and other damp environments. It is immune to being electrically shorted out if submerged or soaked.

If it doesn't also have some sort of propellers and steering fins, however, it will still sink to the bottom of the sea if dropped into the water — although could theoretically walk along the bottom to reach shore.

**60. Sports ball thrower:** An internal hopper stores up to 24 tennis balls, baseballs, or clay pigeons for skeet shooting, or 6 soccer or footballs. These are mounted to a combo-spring and compressed air launcher which will throw balls or small rocks, grenades, and other roughly fist sized objects up to 40 meters away at a rate of 1 throw every two rounds (rate 1/2). The strike value bonus from this device is +5, although as it was not designed as a weapon, offers no extra damage.

**61. Fold-out back chair:** On the upper back of this robot is a backpack-style chair which can be unlatched and folds out to allow a man sized or smaller person to sit, facing backward, and be carried by the robot should the machine be sufficiently large and strong enough itself. The chair includes dangling foot stirrups and cross brace seat belts to secure an unconscious person.

This robot can carry a person of up to half its own overall weight for 12 hours before the robot becomes drained and must either abandon the rider or cool down and recharge for another 12 hours. Passengers of a quarter the robot's weight or less can be carried indefinitely, while any passenger of more than half and up to the same weight as the robot can only be carried for one hour.

**62. Infrared heater:** This is a pop out, 30cm long by 10cm wide heater which runs on the electricity supply of the robot in an ultra efficient power usage mode. When turned on, it will bring a frigid room of about 5 by 5 meters to comfortable room temperature within 5 minutes and be able to run for 10 hours on the dedicated internal battery — after which the unit must slowly recharge for 24 hours from the robot's primary energy supply.

Alternatively, an externally plugged in standard power cell will yield 20 hours of heat, and the unit comes with a back-up power connector cable. The red hot filaments of the heater can ignite paper, straw or other flammable substances, or even inflict a burn on an opponent in melee combat. If used as a backup attack, treat as +2 SV inflicting 1d8 damage.

**63. Plastic digester engine:** Originally designed to clean up the environment, especially along river banks and seashores, this robot is equipped with a bottom mounted trash intake scoop and chemical digester which dissolves plastic back into an oily resin. This resin is burnt up further in the

bowls of the robot and converted to electrical power. For every 5 kilograms of plastic trash consumed, this robot will recharge 1 hour of operation.

The plastic deposits available to this unit are the determining factor in how much electricity can be generated in a day, but in most ruined cities and industrial districts, there is no shortage of the stuff. This energy generation system can be the unit's main power source when traveling among the streets of the old ones, but the process gives off the occasional puff of black smoke, a harsh aroma, the crunch and pop of plastic parts, and finally, the expulsion of indigestible steaming glass and metal turds; all of which can attract unwanted attention.

**64. Hover jets:** These are very similar to the cybernetic implant described on page 87 of the TME Hub Rules, however, these more advanced variants are more energy efficient. These jets can yield 1200 rounds or up to 1 hour of flight per day on the allotted energy supplies within the robot, instead of the 600 round or half hour of the cyborg model.

An external power cell can be plugged into the main propulsion control engine and yield another 600 rounds of flight time. When operational, this robot can hover along the ground at 1 meter height at a speed of 25m per round. Read the implant stats for dealing with drops off cliffs, as well as travel over lava or water.

**65. Gyroscopic balance upgrade:** This robot's limbs and torso have been improved for better grace and balance. These upgrades enhance its coordination and ability to move at a somewhat faster pace than it would otherwise enjoy. Increase its agility and accuracy traits by +20 trait points each, plus increase its movement rate by +1m per round besides any benefits from having a higher agility score.

**66. Fold out helicopter rotors:** Identical to the chopper-borg implant for cyborgs described on page 333 of this book. If this robot weight 300kg or more, it will have six blades in its rotor array and make a much louder, thudding noise when in flight — a noise that will often terrify commoners and primitive humanoids alike.

**67. Rebooting mode:** In the event of being hacked or neutralized by an electrical field or EMP weapon, or otherwise switched off, this robot has a way to re-install itself. It has a shield encased, micro backup CPU that to any computer or robotics technician of under 5 skill points will be dismissed as just a power surge modulator, or other common part within the robot's head. Somebody of 6 or more skill points is allowed a Type C perception based hazard check to notice this small, mundane looking part and can detach it within 3 rounds.

While this tiny, extra CPU is disguised as some other part, it has a few extra wires that run to the main CPU and at a certain time, sends a surge of rebooting commands and power to the mainframe and attempt to cold start the robot.

If the CPU has been hacked and occupied by a digital being, then this rebooting CPU will need to engage the foreigner and expel it, although hacking a possibly superior, more advanced digital entity is no easy feat. To handle this fight, treat the engagement as normal hacking attacks as described in the digital beings section on page 67 of this book.

The rebooting processor has no personality, agenda, or control over the robotic body, and exists for this one purpose. Unless the time of pre-arranged reboot is documented by the player of this character, the reboot will occur 20+1d20 minutes after the main CPU has been defeated, but could be set to engage immediately after the main CPU is compromised, or hours, days or weeks later if programed to do so by the main CPU (player character).

This secondary CPU has the following stats: Intelligence 50+2d20, Willpower 40+1d100, Processor 40+1d100, Firewall -30, Data Points 50+1d100. Roll these stats to establish their permanent amounts at the time of character generation. These traits do not go up with rank advancement.

**68. Safety protocol:** Besides whatever conscious choices about its loyalty, trustworthiness and devotion this robot has towards its human, animal, digital and mechanical comrades, it has other, more unwavering loyalties to them, as well. In short, it will never turn on a friend.

If this robot has companions, then it typically assigns certain entities as allies, friends, superior officers, or those it is instructed to care for and protect. It commits the voice print, imagery, or ID code and personalty archive of these beings as 'friends' into an incorruptible database. This shielded database of friends is not part of the main CPU and installed in a hidden compartment in the head and looks like some generic, commonplace part and easy to dismiss by anybody except a computer technician of 6 or more skill points, and then they must make a type F perception based hazard check to spot the part and remove it, or not.

With this friend's database component this robot's body cannot be made to turn against those on its friend's list. This is highly useful in case the robot gets hacked and instructed to turn against its former comrades. It will therefore be unable to harm them… even if the friends turn against the robot themselves after the CPU is taken over.

This friends database cannot be updated by the new CPU, or circumstances, once imprinted without changing the password, which is normally locked away deep in the neutralized CPU and disguised as an innocuous line of code.

**69. Holographic identity projector:** This robot's head is equipped with a simple holographic projector which can create a ghostly 80% opaque holographic animated person out 3 meters in front of it. This always life size projection can interact on behalf of the robot, and speaks and responds like

a person complete with an appropriate voice. Regular companions will come to associate themselves with the projection, believe it's the authentic version of who the robot is, that the metallic body behind it is just a vehicle. Likewise, many people might believe this robot is actually a digital being.

Normally, the robot has only one such holographic persona, which is determined by rolling on Table XR-69 Random Identity and Persona of Digital Being from the digital being section, page 79. There is a 1 in 20 chance that instead of only one projection persona, this robot will gain another each rank and can pick which one to use. This robot need not use a projection at all to speak if it has intact vocal capabilities, but prefers to engage the hologram out of habit, or deploy it as a distraction or decoy to draw fire.

**70. Electrical defense upgrade:** Attacks from electrical charges, including naturally occurring lighting bolts, relic weapons, and mutations, partially flow from this robot's sheathing and are diverted away from vital circuits, servos and computer systems and instead pool in this large, globular inner apparatus. In short, half of all electrical damage this robot would have sustained goes into this module and is thereafter slowly dissipated into both the ground, and into a converter that recharges the robot's batteries by 50% of whatever drained amount they currently sit at.

**71. Video recorder:** This system records all that it sees and hears. It can replay this feed on a pop out 15cm x 10cm screen for other personnel to review, but also internally views all its recordings within its 'minds eye' when not focused on external events. It will auto delete files after reaching 1000 recorded hours, oldest files first but may archive specific files of high importance. It is always filming as a default mode, but can switch this off if it desires.

**72. Well built:** This robot was made with love, and questionable parts were replaced with better ones. Increases each trait by +1d6, including traits within the CPU such as Processor, Willpower, Intelligence, Data Points, and firewall (although apply this FW bonus as a negative to make this unit's CPU harder to hack just as a lower DV number makes being harder to hit physically).

**73. Garbage graspers and compactor:** This robot's lower torso has a mouth like intake cavity and four lean, crab-pincer style collector arms. These were designed to pluck garbage, recyclables and junk from the ground, and sweep it all into the cavernous 30 x 30cm interior of its garbage storage bay.

Once the load of trash was secured, the thick doors at the mouth of the unit would shut and inner panels compress the garbage down into a 10cm square block, which is then blasted with flame jets. All plastic and organic material such as leaves, paper, bones, and other flammable substances are incinerated leaving behind a super heated block of glass, metal and other non-burnable substances which are ejected out the back of the unit like excrement.

Other units collected the cubes which would be neatly stacked into great mounds for later recycling and substance separation. In the new era, these four grasping arms, while clumsy and not useful for fine work, can still reach out and collect small creatures or tiny robots like spiderbots, and on a successful strike, yank the small creatures (up to 4 per round) into the compression and incineration hamper.

Graspers SV +5, damage 1d4, strength 28. If snagged, a creature is allowed an agility based Type C hazard check to twist free, otherwise it goes into the incinerator and is both crushed and burnt for 3d6 damage and eject-

ed out the back end of the robot after 1 minute. Creatures that are cat sized and smaller are all appropriate sized targets for this attack mode.

**74. Magnetic surface pads:** This robot seems to have been designed to work on the exterior of spacecraft, and within its feet, tracks, or wheels, are powerful electric magnets which can be engaged to hold it to the sides of vessels in zero or very low gravity situations. Other pads in the upper limbs also allow this unit to crawl around the interior or exterior of spacecraft and orbital stations at half its normal move rate.

On earth, these magnets can help it climb metal hulled sea-going ships, or structures, and even assist it to climb cement buildings as the rebar iron inside the wall can aid adhesion. When climbing rebar supported or metal structures, this robot gains 2 skill points in the climbing skill as described on page 36 of the TME Hub Rules. Similarly, if using the grappling skill, even at the untrained tier, and this unit is trying to hold on to another robot or metallic vehicle, it gains 2 skill points in grapple for these occasions.

**75. Grounding cable:** From the lower extremities of this robot hangs a tail-like, highly flexible grounding cable that drags along a half meter behind the unit and is normally in contact with the ground. Should this robot be hit by an electrical pulse, lighting bolt, or other electrical attack mode, 90% of the damage transfers down through the core of the robot, along this cable and safely into the dirt, rubble, or vegetation beneath it.

In short, this robot takes only 10% damage from electrical attacks if this cable is grounded, otherwise full damage. Damage from EMPs and Stun beams are less effective, and depending on what part of this robot is hit, the damage may or may not be lessened. There is a 50% chance that any EMP or stun attack to successfully strike this robot can be partially thwarted, and if so, the robot suffers only half damage, otherwise regular damage is taken.

**76. Shoulder mounted MAV pad:** This robot has flat, miniature helipad and securing/power boom arm on one shoulder. This diminutive landing platform can accommodate up to three micro air vehicles and comes

with three automatic power hook-up, data download cables, and responsive, multi-unit MAV safety locks to secure the tiny remote units when not deployed. With mere thought, this robot can unleash one or more MAVs, and see through and command up to three via head mounted guidance, tracking and command systems. While controlling a MAV, this unit must focus on the remote units, and while able to walk at half speed, can perform no other actions. This robot will start game play with one random MAV from the table on page XR-496, rolled as 'High Rank'.

**77. Secret storage compartment:** Within this robot's torso is a secret, locking compartment. This cavity is large enough to store a full sized handgun and several magazines, or 200 silver or gold coins, 6 power cells, 10 days rations, 2 liter water skin, or even a spiderbot, pocket bot or an android's head.

Anybody who is not already familiar with the compartment will not see it, and not know to look for it. If they are suspicious, however, or a robotics technician who has been tasked with searching for such a compartment — knowing that such concealment and smuggling cavities exist on other robots — then the searcher is allowed a type E perception based hazard check, per hour to locate the compartment. But, unless using a crowbar or other heavy tool to bust it open, the compartment lock must be picked. Treat as 'Open Relic Mechanical Safe' as far as difficulty on the lock picking table, page 48 of the Hub Rules.

**78. After market upgrades:** Whoever put this unit together did so with the utmost care and attention. They inserted superior parts, reinforced components and connections, and made the unit as exceptional as it could get with the given materials. Increase all traits by +2d6 points, including aspects of the CPU: processor, data points, firewall (-2d6 FW) however in this case apply the bonus as a negative amount since it is making the robot's CPU harder to hit identical to how defense value is represented as a negative number when beneficial.

**79. Bounty hunter mode:** At some point in this robot's past, it was converted into a machine that hunts other beings for money. While all unique robots lack violence inhibitors, this unit seems to have a violence enabler inserted into the CPU, and has a tendency to see fighting, inflicting pain, or cutting conversations short with the presentation of a weapon as appropriate behavior. While it will kill people and animals without a second thought, it seems directed to subdue them instead and bind them with rope or handcuffs, even if no bounty is offered on an unlucky target, and will simply leave restrained captives behind to starve or fall prey to scavenging beasts.

It has been painted (roll 1d6) either 1,2 desert tan, 3,4 olive green, or 5,6 concrete gray, and is equipped with a built in stun pistol in the wrist of its main, human-like arm. Additionally, this robot carries 1d4 sets of relic handcuffs (pg. TME 197), and 1d6 lengths of rope, each at 10+1d10 meters in length. It also exhibits 1d3 skill points in grapple, tracking and lying. The stun pistol runs both off the main power of the robot and can yield 40 shots per day, but if depleted, a power cell can be snapped into the forearm and yield yet another 40 shots. Stun pistol stats: SV +16, rate 1, DMG 2d20 stun, range 200m. Stun damage from this sort of weapon heals at 1 point per minute, although if dropped to below 0 endurance, the stunned subject remain unconscious for 4d10 minutes.

**80. Shock tendril:** The wrist of this robot's human-like arm has a hidden compartment that holds a meter long, steel shock tendril. This cable tendril is highly dexterous and besides being able to coil about and grasp things that would normally be out of its hand's reach, it can also be charged up and on a successful hit on a living or mechanical target, deliver an electrical shock that will inflict 1d20 damage to a living person, or 2d20 damage to a cyborg, android, robot or vehicle with any electrical systems.

The tendril can deliver 10 successful jolts per day when running off the robot's own power supply, however, if needed, a power cell can be stuck into a rubber sealed, hidden power port near the robot's elbow, and deliver another 20 shocks. The tendril has a strike value bonus of +10 SV.

**81. Field medical kit:** Built into the chest of this robot, and flanked by four, ultra thin, and highly agile limbs (agility 82, strength 9, accuracy 76), this robot can perform moderately advanced medical procedures should its CPU have such software installed. Even without the software, another user, especially a humanoid medic could access the kit and have this robot kneel beside the patient to perform whatever procedure is needed.

There is as 2 in 10 chance, however, that this robot happens to also have 1d3 skill points in the medic skill as described on page TME-46 of the hub rules. These skill points stack with any other points gained in this skill during character generation.

Because unique robots are learning machines, this unit can be taught to become a medic by being instructed by another being who holds this area of knowledge.

**82. False hacking CPU:** This robot has a more easily accessed, fake CPU identity and massive collection of highly valuable looking files. Everything it stores on this hard drive is actually nonsense and holds no intel, passwords, or real-life identifiable or useful information. Hackers might take 3d6 hours before they discover that they have copied useless data or have gained access to a fake CPU.

Once inside this CPU, the hacker will require 20+1d100 minutes to find their way out of the maze that has been set behind the intruder's 'focus' with the pathways changed after the hacker gained access. Should the hacker be a digital being, they are trapped inside this maze until they find their way out after the allotted back-tracking time.

**83. Removable head:** Should this robot become decapitated, or if only its head can be recovered after some calamity, then the cranial unit will survive this ordeal. Its head contains a backup power cell which will kick in and power the head for 18 months in active mode and 10+2d26 years in hibernation mode.

If attached to another body by a robotics technician of 4 or more skill points, this head can assume control of the new body. As a severed head, it keeps all its rank gained mental benefits (intelligence, willpower, processor trait, data points, firewall, etc.), plus the unit keeps its knowledge, memories and skills. The body of any newly acquired robot, or even an android body, does not receive the prior physical rank gained increases such as improved endurance, strength, agility or accuracy, but can begin to gain them going forward.

Conversely, if the rest of the robot's prior body is not destroyed, and some other being occupies it, any physical upgrades due to rank gain are kept with that body, which includes improvements in strength, agility, accuracy. As for skills, even physical ones such as grappling and martial arts, are contained in the robot's head, and not the body and go with the unique robot to whatever new body it acquires.

**84. Drone compartment:** This robot has a back compartment or clamps which opens to reveal a small hanger bay and recharge station for one drone. Unless starting game play as a slave robot, this unique machine will contain a random drone from the following list. All drones listed here are covered in this book.

Using a built-in Drone Control Unit (page 475), the drone can either be sent out on a pre-programmed route and act independently within mission parameters established by this robot, or else, used as a remote control eyes and arms and potential offensive asset, to the maximum 12km range of the controller type. While operating a remote drone, the robot's attention is divided, and it suffers -50% perception trait penalty (which could affect its initiative score).

| 1d20 | Drone Model | Weight | XR Page |
|------|-------------|--------|---------|
| 1-4 | Basic Drone, Little Buddy | 5.5kg | 469 |
| 5,6 | Basic Drone, Action Man | 5.5kg | 469 |
| 7-9 | Basic Drone, Emergency Medical Response | 5.5kg | 470 |
| 10-13 | Defensive Drone | 19 kg | 470 |
| 14,15 | Police Assistant Drone | 22kg | 470 |
| 16,17 | Military Resupply Drone | 20kg | 473 |
| 18,19 | Military Utility Drone | 25kg | 474 |
| 20 | Hunter Killer Drone | 16kg | 475 |

**85. Spiderbot hanger and remote control mode:** This robot has an interior hanger for one or more spiderbots. The number that fit in the hanger depend on the weight of the chassis as initially rolled on table XR-130, back on page 153. Any chassis under 100kg will have room for only 1 spiderbot minion, a chassis from 100 to 200kg will have storage for two spiderbots, while chassis over 200kg will have 3 with a 37% chance of room for a fourth spiderbot. These tiny, eight-legged robots, along with any others that can be reprogrammed and made to serve this robot, are under the total control of the robot character, which has a sensory link with each spiderbot and can see, and hear whatever the spiderbot does within 100 meters per point of perception trait this robot has.

The range of control could be huge here. For example, a robot with a perception score of 36 could send its spiderbots out 3600m (36 x100m = 3.6 km). Spiderbots must be given specific instruction, either to attack, collect video evidence, deliver a message or small item to a specific person or location, or other simple commands. The spiderbot will follow these commands even if the controlling robot loses audio and visual surveillance or command of the small, lethal robot. Once the spiderbot returns into range of the robot's control zone, it can be given new commands or told to return to the main robot's last known location, or meet at some other point for a rendezvous.

These spiderbots cannot track the 'mother-ship' robot and have no electronic sense of this robotic character's location should it move from where it deposited its servants, although the robot character might have an idea where a spiderbot is at from the visual imagery it sees about the remote controlled unit. When a spiderbot returns to its hanger, it will plug itself into a power slot and upload any photography and video footage that it got while beyond the main robot's control zone.

During hook up, tiny, robotic arms within the hanger will attend to any damage the spiderbots might have received during operations, and heal them at a rate of 1 trait point per hour. Venom refilling can also be done within the bowls of this robot, although an external supply must be filled into a storage container from a plug sealed port on the side of the robot's chassis.

While not covered in the hub rules, a spiderbot carries enough venom in their syringe to successfully inject 4 victims, at 25ml per injection and the syringe holding 100ml. The refill tank on the robot character can hold 500ml of venom and has a cleaning drain tube in case operators want to switch venoms from say death, to paralysis or sleep variants.

Spiderbots can be substituted by Pocket-bots, although these tiny, humanoid shaped robots do not automatically come with this hanger system as spiderbots do. A maximum of 1 spiderbot or pocket-bot can be controlled at a time by this unique robot character per every 20 points of intelligence or processor trait — whichever is higher — this robot possesses. Should the unique robot decide to carry spare spiderbots in a backpack or other container, these too can be controlled should the PC have sufficient intelligence or processor trait points. Spiderbots are described on page 181 of the hub rules, and pocket-bots on page TME-180.

**86. Healing Nanobots:** These nanites are coded to serve this robot alone, do not leave the surface of the unit's body, and are smaller than a grain of rice. They have a crab-like body and large abdomen bloated with assorted epoxy resins, metallic compounds, lubricants and substances useful in the repair of all manner of injuries that this robot sustains. This robot heals at a rate of 1d6 trait points, including data points, per hour.

**87. All-around cameras:** A half dozen, discreetly hidden cameras are dotted around this robot's body and constantly feed it optical information, especially movement. This robot is nearly impossible to sneak up unnoticed, and if operating alone, or as the point person in a marching order, it gains +4 initiative. These cameras have a normal day vision of 200 meters and a night vision, infra red mode of 30 meters, allowing this unit to operate in dark places without requiring another light source.

**88. Augmented reality projector:** Besides having an extra eye on its head which can see normally, it also sees augmented reality. This robot also has a boxy, complex looking augmented reality projector from which it can project graphics, video clips, maps, signs, special offers, social media posts, government announcements, as well as anything it has seen and thus recorded in its own life.

Most of the projections come from a database within the robot's CPU, with a random list on page 480 of this book, but it can also make stuff up to present to those who might be able to see AR holograms. The range is 50 meters plus the robot's willpower trait in meters and so long as it focuses on the projection, even while moving — but not fighting — it can maintain the duration of the projection, and change the imagery, for up to one hour per character rank.

Augmented reality is invisible to those not wearing a proper visual aid, and some augmented reality even comes with audio or tactile data layers, which like the holograms themselves, can only be detected if the person interacting with it wears to proper headset or body suit. This part is most useful when the robot user switches on the AR optic and scans the vicinity, especially around more-or-less intact ruin streets. By doing so, it can search for still broadcasting AR graphics, advertising, and other features which will inform the robot that a power source is nearby, or at the very least, a still serviceable projector which can fetch a tidy sum of silver or batteries back in town.

You can learn all about augmented reality on page 477 of this book.

**89. Fishing rod:** This is a pop out casting rod, reel, lure assortment and micro lure tying arm. This rod is telescopic and will extend 2 meters and is strong enough to theoretically bring in a fish of up to 10 kilograms weight (22 pounds). There is a 2 in 10 chance that this robot's CPU has been loaded with a fishing software package, and gives the unit 1d3 points in the fisher skill as described on page 210 of this book.

**90. Force field:** This force field is very similar to the implant described on page 87 of the hub rules, however more efficiently draws rechargeable power from the robot's own supplies. It can operate for up to 600 rounds total per day (20 rounds in a minute, so 600 ÷ 20 rounds =30 minutes), although still takes 1 round to charge up and be ready on the 2nd round. This time allotment per day can be broken up into smaller segments of time as needed.

Here is a quick summary of what this part does: when activated, it reduces damage taken per round by -10 points. This amount is taken off the total damage from all incoming attacks, not from each attack. An advanced version of a force field, which has a 1 in 6 chance of being fitted to this robot instead, does in fact reduce damage by -10 for every incoming attack, even if the attacks come from the same weapon such as pulse laser or submachine gun for example.

Besides the on-board power supply, this robot has a rubberized external battery access port on the chassis that is directly wired into this force field system and could allow the robot to accept standard power cells, too. An external cell only yield another 200 rounds, or ten minutes, of protection. When active, a force field can be seen as a faint green glow about the robot's body of about 5cm thickness, especially in the dim light or darkness.

**91. EMP shielding:** This passive, background operating system kicks in an instant before any incoming EMP strike causes major damage on the unit, and reduces all EMP damage by half automatically. As a bonus feature, on a successful perception based Type C hazard check by this robot, it manages to re-rout the electromagnetic charge to a series of grounding wires in its body and thus reduce 100% of the EMP attack.

Any follow-up EMP attacks can still neutralize this unit, however the EMP shield is constantly in operation so long as the robot is operational itself and has power.

**92. Olfactory sensor:** This robot has electronic nostrils and can pick up and identify aromas, scents and pheromones twice as well as a human. When operating alone away from smelly human or animal companions, or on point ahead of a group by a minimum distance of 10 meters, this robot gets a +2 initiative bonus.

**93. Telescoping midsection:** This robot can extend its chassis up by 2 meters to look over high shelves, walls, or reach its graspers onto a higher floor or balcony when scaling the outside of a ruin. While this greater height can intimidate smaller creatures, it makes the robot unstable when deployed and somewhat tippy, thus reducing its agility score as far as balance based hazard checks go, by -30%.

**94. 3d Facial interface screen:** On the front facing aspect of this robot's head is a rectangular, 30 centimeters tall, glassy screen which when desired, lights up to reveal a life-like face of a man or woman. This interactive, 3d face shows a wide range of expressions and reactions, and works in unison with the robot's primary eyes and speech to present a very responsive and convincing persona.

This robot will adopt a face and stick to it permanently, often matching the face to its chosen or assigned gender identity.

The amount of brightness or dimness this vid screen projects can vary according to ambient light, but also controlled by the robot. If needed to illuminatea totally dark space, this face screen can light up the way ahead for 4 meters.

If facing a sandstorm or combat, this screen can fold up inside the lower front of the robot's head and avoid taking damage.

**95. Up armored:** Somebody added extra plating to this robot's chassis, head and limbs, which although slowing the unit somewhat, greatly increased its defense value and toughness. A column for 'cost' is added to the following table in the event a robot character wants to hire an armorer or robotics dealership to have such armor added. This price includes the materials and labor.

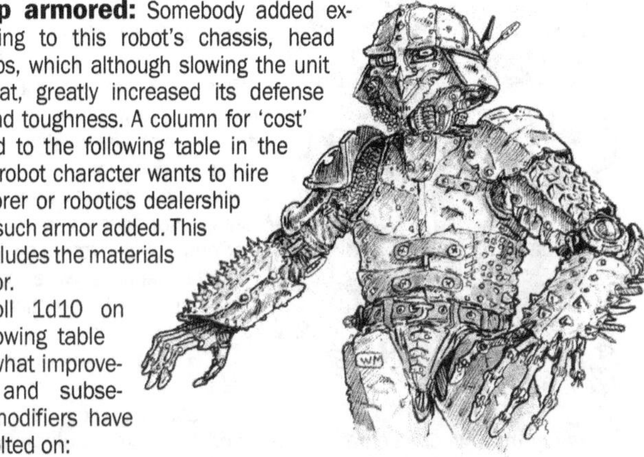

Roll 1d10 on the following table to see what improvements and subsequent modifiers have been bolted on:

| 1d10 | Up-Armor Type | DV Bonus | END Bonus | Added Weight | Move Penalty | Cost |
|---|---|---|---|---|---|---|
| 1. | Leather | -10 | +6 END | +5kg | -0.25m | 40+2d20sp |
| 2. | Heavy Leather | -14 | +9 END | +10kg | -0.5m | 60+3d20sp |
| 3. | Part Plate | -25 | +14 END | +26kg | -1.5m | 200+2d100sp |
| 4. | Full Plate | -35 | +18 END | +30kg | -2m | 500+3d100sp |
| 5. | Junk Armor | -12 | +8 END | +7kg | -0.5m | 150+1d100sp |
| 6. | Heavy Junk | -17 | +16 END | +28kg | -1.5m | 300+2d100sp |
| 7. | Scrap Relic | -20 | +13 END | +6kg | -0.75m | 600+3d100sp |
| 8. | Riot Armor | -25 | +17 END | +10kg | -0.5m | 1000+2d100sp |
| 9. | Tactical Armor | -30 | +20 END | +15kg | -0.75m | 1400+3d100sp |
| 10. | Combat Armor | -35 | +30 END | +24kg | -1m | 2k+1d1000sp |

**96. Vertical climbing pods:** This robot's grasping arms and feet, treads, or wheels are equipped with a combination of alloy gasping claws, piston pins, clamps, and high powered suctions cups. All in all, this robot can more easily climb up sheer cliff faces and the sides of buildings, and so gains 4 skill points in climbing. These features are, however, exceedingly draining on the robots power supplies and climbing can only be attempted for a half hour maximum once every 4 hours.

**97. Signal jamming array:** Mounted to the back of this robot's head is an armored, toaster sized black box. When activated, this contraption opens to reveal a telescopic rod and multi-antenna, glossy black transmission inhibitor array. When switched on, this device sends out a multi frequency radio jamming signal that scrambles all radio calls and wireless digital transmissions within a 300 meter radius.

There is an 88% chance that any communicator calls can't be sent or received in this area, while any remote controlled drones, MAVs, robotics, androids or other devices must make a type D willpower based hazard check or lose their link to who or whatever is remotely operating the machine, which will stop whatever it is doing if it's a ground based machine, while aerial devices will fall out of the sky. Units that have default programs or commands that take over if remote control is interrupted, will switch to this base routine — which could be to attack the unique robot who deploys the jamming system and its companions.

Digital beings caught in this area of effect will suffer interference with whatever computer device or robotic body they inhabit, but are allowed a type B willpower based hazard check to maintain control and continue their actions.

This radio jamming device is power intensive, and can only be used for 10 minutes per day on the robot's own power, but if an external power cell is plugged into the unit, an additional half hour can be gained.

**98. Police bot features:** Featuring a black and white paint scheme, the words POLICE written all over it, a bolted on service badge and visible identification code, this robot also features head mounted red and blue flashing lights, a siren and two service weapons built into its human-like arm. The first weapon is a stun stick as described on page TME-189, plus a stun pistol also described on page TME-189, although the stats for both weapons are shown on the weapons table on page 100 of the Hub Rules.

These weapons draw power from the robot itself, although only 20 successful strikes from the baton and 20 shots from the pistol before they need to recharge for 12 hours. Both weapons do have external power access slots to accommodate standard power cells, too.

There is a 1 in 6 chance that this robot also has a database of law enforcement protocols, and if so, might try to read the rights to captive humanoids and attempt to arrest any wrong doer they come upon, even if the criminal's activities have nothing to do with the robots main mission or team objectives.

**99. Repulsor-Pods:** Along the lower portion of this robots chassis are six small, disc like depressions. When activated, these open to reveal a brilliant blue light and a surge of repulsor lift energy. Like some sort of anti-gravity technology, these repulsor-pods lift the robot off the ground with a mere hiss and whir sound no louder than a whisper. The robot can travel up to a meter off the ground and move at 16 meters per round when engaged.

The duration of this flight, depends on the power supply plugged into this dedicated mode of travel. A power pack will yield 100 minutes of flight, while a power cell will yield 10 minutes. If while flying at top speed this robot decides to purposefully ram into creatures of less mass (less weight in kilograms) it may do so, treating each target it knocks into in its turn to be attacked as if by a strike value 01-70 doing 1d20 lethal and 1d20 stun damage.

If hitting a target that is equal to or heavier than itself, but not twice as heavy, nor a solid object like a pillar, wall, tree trunk or parked vehicle, then the attack is simultaneously made upon itself SV 01-90 for 2d20 lethal and 2d20 stun damage. If this robot crashes into something twice as heavy as itself, or a solid barrier, it will suffer 1d100 lethal and 1d100 stun damage. When flying through smaller targets, each being in its path is attacked individually up to the 16 meters movement limit in range per round.

**100. Heavy pulse rifle turret:** This shoulder mounted weapon system is powered by an external bank of two side by side standard power cells (included at character generation but each only has 10+1d10 bursts worth of power in the cell). This weapon is fixed 80% of the time, otherwise extends above the head of the robots so it can swivel about and fire in a 360 degree angle: SV +25, rate 4 shots per burst, DMG 1d20 ea., range 1 km, added weight 7kg.

When not needed, this weapon system rotates to the back of the robot on a track to keep it from snagging on branches or debris, and hides the weapon when not activated.

If a cloak is worn over this turret and gun, it can be concealed. It takes 4 rounds to activate, lift and position the turret to fire on the 5th round.

If looted off this robot, the trigger mechanism is missing and instead configured for a robot or vehicle fire control system, however, a trigger and stock can be forged and fitted by a junk crafter, mechanical technician, or gunsmith, or somebody with these skills can be hired to make this weapon system infantry enabled at a cost of 500+2d100sp.

## Robot's Power Source

Robots of great bulk require more power than those of lesser weight category, but so too, larger units are more likely to exhibit more advanced, and potentially valuable and sometimes dangerous power generation systems. A mini-nuclear reactor, for example, is a complex, heavy piece of machinery that only the largest of robots can use. A piece of machinery that could cause a nuclear detonation should the robot who uses it be destroyed, and thus take out nearby friends and foes alike in a small, yet devastating mushroom cloud.

All robots have a small bank of two mini-power cells per 100 kilograms overall weight. These poly-enclosed back-up cells are stored near their primary power source, and automatically engage when all its batteries are removed such as when they are routinely changed out, or looted. This reserve battery of cells differ from the backup batteries built into solar, bio-fuel or micro nuke powered robots, and will run the robot for 1 hour, with a 50% chance of operating for a second hour, a 30% chance for a third hour, and a 10% chance for a fourth hour. If the robot doesn't find replacement power for its main battery or generation system after this duration, it will shut down and must make a type E agility based hazard check to remain on its feet if a bipedal unit, or else it will fall over and potentially topple off whatever precipice it might stand upon.

Because every scoundrel knows robots are equipped with useful batteries or power generation systems, many energy hungry villains, including cyborgs, other robots and androids, will sometimes actively hunt robots with the express purpose of neutralizing them or smashing them apart, just to steal their batteries.

A similarly wicked enterprise is for a community to attempt to forcibly restrain a robot that can generate power, perhaps declaring the robot a Mecha minion, and cruelly unbolt the mechanical being's legs, arms and any offensives limbs, and chain or bolt the robot to some facility in a stronghold and hook the unwilling unit up to the community's power grid as an electricity generating prisoner.

Robots who have been around a while know that traveling alone in a human community is a risky enterprise, and it is always better to stick close to meat based comrades who can both vouch for the robot and threaten away those who might seek to accost this high tech, mechanical survivor.

Except for robots who have either an external power cell or external power pack, all robots have an enclosed power supply or generation compartment. To most onlookers, including thieves, this sealed compartment isn't easy to locate (Type H perception based hazard check to spot). Any thief who is also a robotics technician, however, can locate the compartment after a successful type D perception based hazard check, with one check allowed per minute. Once located, the thief must use its lock picking skills to unlatch the compartment (treat as Open Mechanical Safe on table TME-1-39 on page 48 of the Hub Rules under the Pick Locks skill).

Hibernation Mode Duration refers to the time this robot can remain shut down in an unconscious state — which was designed for long storage, space journeys, or to conserve power during times of blackouts, shortages, general strikes, or other circumstances where the robot's services were no longer needed. Hibernation can last for mere hours, or up to the maximum time noted below based on the power source of the robot.

After the limit of hibernation is reached, the robot is automatically woken when it has 7 days left before total power loss, presumably a week's grace for the robot to either seek maintenance personnel or plug itself in and recharge. Once total power loss occurs, the robot shuts off entirely and cannot be woken unless fresh power is restored to it.

When totally drained of power, a robot cannot rouse itself regardless of what is happening around it, even if it is being dismantled. The files in its CPU, including memories, will remain intact and could be given power and hacked into if desired (using the normal hacking combat procedure described on page 67 of this book), or the machine reanimated with external power and brought back to sentience and life.

The activation time shown on the table below is how many rounds or minutes it takes for a disturbed, hibernating robot to wake up and become fully operational. Many long buried, hibernating robots that excavators dig up in the ruins are in hibernation mode, and when their activation is complete, they might wake to be a friendly, helpful companion, but more likely, a murderous, crazed or Mecha controlled killing machine.

See the descriptions for each power source following this table.

## Table XR-144/ Robot's Power Source

| Weight Category* Roll 1d100 | | | | | | Hibernation Mode Duration | Activation Time |
|---|---|---|---|---|---|---|---|
| Under 100kg | 100 to 200kg | Over 200kg | Power Source | Duration | Added Weight | | |
| 01-17 | 01-13 | 01-05 | External Power Cells | 30 days | 500g per cell | 14 years | 10+1d100 rounds |
| 18-39 | 14-29 | 06-14 | Internal Power Cells | 35 Days | 500g per cell | 26 years | 10+3d6 rounds |
| 40-56 | 30-44 | 15-35 | External Power Pack | Days: under 100kg 180, 100 to 200kg 140/ 200kg+ 100 days | 15kg | 48 years | 20+1d100 rounds |
| 57-77 | 45-76 | 36-63 | Internal Power pack | Days: under 100kg 200, 100 to 200kg 140/ 200kg+ 120 days | 20kg | 79 years | 20+4d6 rounds |
| 78-93 | 77-88 | 64-82 | Solar Panels Array | 100 hours between charges + 24 hour emergency battery backup | 1kg per 10kg of robot's overall weight | 38 years | 3d6 minutes |
| 94-00 | 89-00 | 83-91 | Bio-Fuel Generator | 1 hour of burn yields 12 hours operation. 1, 2 or 3kg fuel needed per burn cycle based on robot size | Add 2kg per each 10kg of robot's overall weight | 84 years | 20+1d20 years |
| - | - | 92-00 | Micro Nuclear Reactor | Continuous while reactor operating for 12 years +48 hour battery backup | 30+1d20kg | 126 years | 2d6 hours |

*This is the pre-power supply weight of the robot character, to this point in character creation, and combines the head, chassis, arms, legs and any cybernetic implants and additional robotic parts and features.

## Power Source Descriptions and Details

**External Power Cells:** For units under 100kg, one power cell is needed, while for units of 100 to 200kg two power cell are required, while mechanical beings of over 200kg must have three power cells plugged into their open, back mounted battery compartment. With the appropriate number of batteries stuck into this machine, it can run for 30 days, which, unless stated otherwise, includes firing of any built-in, minor energy weapons.

Because this unit's batteries are exposed, any intentional grab at them with a strike roll of 01-05 yanks free one of the batteries. If all the target's batteries are removed, the unit will run for only an hour on a pair of built-in, backup mini power cells. After this hour, a single power cell using robot will shut down, while for units that run on two or more batteries, things are bad, but not so dire. If insufficient batteries are present, the robot will have difficulties functioning normally. For robots that need two batteries to run, and if one is removed, the unit can operate at half capacity and has no ability to use built in weapons, moves at half speed and has a 50% loss to its strength. For a robot that normally needs three batteries, if it loses one, it suffers the same as a two cell robot that has lost one battery, however if a three battery user loses two of its three cells, it can only operate for 10 days and loses the uses of all built-in weapons, as well as any limbs except its legs, tracks or wheels, and even then moves at half speed.

This unit also has a standard power jack to accept a power cable from a worn power pack, installation, or vehicle's power supply. While hooked up to larger power sources, this robot's power cells will recharge at a rate of 1 energy unit per hour. Each cell takes 10 energy units to fully recharge and each one in the battery bank will charge up simultaneously. You can learn more about power sources in the relic section of the hub rules on page TME-199.

Since the batteries are exposed, which is very risky, this robot normally keeps a plastic sheet or oiled cloth over the battery compartment to keep dust, bugs and rain off them. If the batteries get soaked, they have a 77% chance of shorting out the entire system, which causes the robot to shut down where it stands, the batteries ruined.

This robot will want to upgrade its battery pack situation to an internal power cell option as soon as it can afford to do so. A well established robotics dealership in a major town can be hired to encase the compartment in an armored, waterproof shell at a cost of 1000+1d1000 silver pieces, a procedure that takes 3d6 hours. Should this unit have a comrade who is a technician in the mechanical, cybernetics, electrical or robotics area, or have 4 or more points in either the junk crafter or junk doctor skill, he or she could build a locking battery case, too. This builder would first need to loot the remains of a similar sized robot or scavenge the ruins looking for just the right casing... which involves a ruin expedition and the proper tools.

**Internal Power Cells:** This robot's batteries are stored in a waterproof, armored compartment some place in its torso. Its power usage economy is somewhat better than for a robot with an exposed battery bank, and so gets a few more days out of its batteries than it otherwise might. For robots of under 100 kilograms, it needs only one standard power cell and will get 35 days operational time from the power source. Robots of between 100kg to 200kg need two power cells, while those over 200kg need three power cells to get this same charge duration.

A power plug access panel is built into this robot's chassis, too. This receptacle allows the unit to accept a charge from a power pack, or from an installation, solar array or vehicle's power. When hooked to these other power generation or storage systems, this robot's standard power cells will also recharge at a rate of 1 energy unit per hour, with each cell charging simultaneously and having a capacity of 10 energy units (see Power Cells on page TME 199 to learn more).

**External Power Pack:** This is a standard infantry or construction worker's power pack as described on page TME-199 of the Hub Rules. It has 100 energy units or 10 times what a single power cell holds. Depending on the bulk of the robot, this pack will allow continuous operation for 180 days for machines under 100kg, 140 days for robots between 100 and 200kg, while 100 days for units over 200 kilos.

There is a 38% chance that this robot also comes with a backup internal battery bank that accepts standard power cells, too, although unless stated otherwise during the outfitting phase of character generation, this robot has between zero and 3 spare, charged up power cells (1d6 -3). This robot always starts game play with one fully charged battery pack, and a 16% chance of a spare, drained power pack that it carries in a large, waterproof leather bag with a shoulder strap.

**Internal Power Pack:** This robot's power pack is enclosed in a rigid, well armored compartment that opens like a suitcase and locks down over the power pack. This is a somewhat more advanced design and yields better power output. For robots under 100kg they will operate for 200 days on a fully charged power pack. Units that weigh anywhere from 100kg to 200 kilograms will remain operational for 160 days, while robots over 200kg can operate for 120 days.

There is an 34% chance this robot is also equipped with a backup, internal battery bank that accepts standard power cells, although at character generation will have between zero and four ready power cells for this purpose (1d8 -4). At the time of character creation, this robot's internal power pack is full charged, but there is a 11% chance this unit carries a spare, drained power pack in an oiled backpack.

**Solar Panel Array:** This robot has its upper back, shoulders and other outward facing sections covered in solar panel plates. These are not the fragile, glass-like panels that many new era people are familiar with, but rugged, almost armor-like, black or dark blue plates. When exposed, these photo-voltaic panels automatically charge the robot's internal battery bank at a rate of 1 hour of sunlight exposure to produce 10 hours of battery recharge, or 10 energy units. When in the sunlight, however, the robot draws zero power from its two batteries, both being built-in, hard-wired standard power cells. If unable to get exposure to the sun, this robot will draw upon this built-in, hard-wired power storage to operate for up to 100 hours (50 per power cell).

After these hours of standard operation, a secondary, emergency array of 6 mini-power cells is activated which will provide another 12 hours of minimal function. In this emergency mode, the unit cannot use any built-in weapon systems or other major parts — such as fold out helicopter blades, for example. The purpose of this 12-hour emergency backup is to get the unit back into the sun. The second purpose of this emergency battery is for shut-down, low power hibernation mode, which will allow the robot to go into a sleep-like dormant state that runs on minimal power and maintain only its sensors (hearing, vibration, sight, audio) and allows the unit to activate to defend itself, or move into the sunlight if the opportunity arises. Hibernation mode will last for 38 years.

While sunshine, even on an overcast day, is the best way to use its photovoltaic system, electricity can also be generated if this unit is exposed to bright artificial light, such at that emitted from a spotlight, search light or some other source. Charging under such conditions yields 1 hour of recharge for every 5 hours of exposure to artificial light.

All solar powered robots have the same standard plug adapter as other robots to allow them to accept a power pack or be charged by an installation, vehicle or external generator. Likewise, if it desired, this robot can turn a switch in its chassis to have all incoming solar recharging diverted out through a power cable to another robot, android or electrically powered device to charge it, instead. This diverted recharge is far less efficient, however, and for every hour of sunlight, the secondary receiver gains only 1 energy unit. A standard power cell has 10 energy units when full.

There is a 44% chance that these robots have a back up internal standard power cell battery compartment, too, as described above, although at the outset of game play they will have between zero and three fully charged standard power cells for backup purposes (1d6-3).

**Bio-Fuel Generator:** This system involves feeding wood, paper, plastic, vegetable and petroleum oils, coal, bone, seashells and dried dung into a back mounted hopper for ongoing, deep, internal burning. This generator produces a fine, gray-blue smoke whenever charging burn mode is initiated, along with a quite audible hissing and popping noise from the bowls of the robot. While one hour of burning, will produce 12 hours of operation for this robot, larger robot's require more bio-fuel. Any robot of under 100 kilograms need only burn 1 kilogram of fuel to yield 12 hours operational recharge on its batteries, while a robot of between 100 and 200 kilograms needs 2 kilos of burnable fuel, and any robot over 200kg in weight needs 4 kilogram every 12 hours.

The hopper size for each weight category of robot is as follows: under 100kg, hopper holds 2d6 kilograms of burnable substances. Over 100kg up to 200kg robots have a holder compartment that can store 3d6 kilograms, while robots over 200kg have hoppers that hold 4+3d6 kilograms of material. Of course, any robot who intends to travel a long distance through sparsely treed or burnt off land, such as an old war zone, sparse ruins, dunes, or over open water, will be sure to load one or two backpacks, sacks and bins full of choice bio-fuel materials.

36% of these robots will have a backup Internal Power Cell compartment identical to the one listed on the previous page, however at character generation it will have between zero and two charged power cells loaded in this hidden emergency compartment (1d6 -4). The burning process in this robotic oven gives off a considerable heat signature which can easily be spotted by infrared and other heat seeking optical devices and creatures. However, this heat source will also provide warmth to organic companions who are positioned around the robot within 4 meters, and yield enough heat to keep people and animals alive during frigid, sub-zero conditions. If non-toxic materials are tossed into the burner, and it if the hopper is left open during processing, humanoid companions can rig up a rotisserie, grill or place to perch cast iron cookware on the back of this robot and use the entity as a wood stove or BBQ. Of course, the smell of smoke, or cooking steaks or a roast chicken, can attract unwanted attention, especially in remote, wild places where humanoids are always on the lookout for trespassers, and predators are always hungry.

**Micro Nuclear Reactor:** Among the rarest, most powerful and most dreaded power sources any robot can have is a nuclear reactor in its abdomen. This reactor adds an extra 30+1d20 kilograms weight to the robot, but will run continuously for 12 years on one uranium disk. Replacement disks can often be found in the ruins, but there is a 27% chance that any respectable robotics dealership will have 1d3 for sale at an exorbitant cost of 3000+2d1000sp each.

While operating, this machine gives of a slight buzzing vibration which is detectable to those who stand near it, and so reduce this machines stealth skill ability by -1 point for when hiding from others who get within 5 meters.

Being nuclear powered gives this robot some profound benefits, besides having an exceedingly long, seemingly unlimited power supply. When running on nuke power, this robot has an increase in movement by +1m per round, plus a strength increase of +20 trait points.

Although not having to worry about power needs for 12 years, having a nuclear reactor in one's chest has its potential drawbacks, including melt down or even nuclear detonation and a resulting mushroom cloud. Any critical hit on this robot, or successful called shot to the 'heart', has a 50% chance of rupturing its torso, and if so, one of the following happens, **roll 1d10:**

**1,2. Instantaneous nuclear detonation:** A small mushroom cloud erupts from where this robot once stood. The cloud goes up 300+2d100 meters and the initial blast radius travels 10+1d20 meters in radius out from the epicenter of the blast. All within this blast are attacked three times at SV 01-90, for 1d100 damage each, plus exposed to 1 dose of medium radiation, but if they make their hazard check against this exposure, automatically suffer a dose of mild radiation exposure, instead. Radiation is covered on page TME-125 of the Hub Rules.

The vicinity around the blast is thereafter radioactive, with anyone to enter exposed to a dose of medium radiation for the first 3d6 days, and thereafter a dose of mild radiation for the next 3d6 years. There will be nothing left of the robot who originally detonated, while all its gear, relics spare batteries or carried comrades are also turned to dust and fire.

**3,4. Core rupture and meltdown:** The robot must open its chest cavity, reach in and toss aside the radioactive core, which will immediately leak 1 dose of medium radiation in a 3 meter radius, which this robot is itself contaminated with for the next 6+1d6 months and must keep clear of organic comrades. Furthermore, the core, which is a backpack sized contraption, is now sizzling and gives of 1 dose of medium radiation exposure within a 3m radius and mild dose of radiation beyond this out to a 20m meter radius. The robot can no longer use nuclear power and thereafter converted to either an eternal power pack or external standard power cell using unit*. Conversion costs 2000+1d1000sp and 2d6 days work.

**5-8. Reactor damaged and shuts down** until repaired*. This robot must resort to its 48 hour battery backup or other power source until repairs can be made by a robotics or mechanical technician of 5 or higher skill points. If such a technician must be hired to perform these tricky repairs, the cost of parts and labor will be 5000+3d1000sp and take 2d6 days to accomplish.

**9,10. Just a nick.** The reactor was hit but its armored case deflected the blow. Any damage from the critical hit or called shot is instead applied to the overall robot's endurance value.

All robots with micro-nuclear reactors have a built in 48 hour emergency battery, but also feature the same power plug access jack as other robots and can wear an eternal power pack. If feeling that having an active nuclear reactor in their body is too risky, especially when entering a populated area or active war zone, this robot can switch off the reactor and run on regular power instead.

To shut down a nuclear reactor within its body, the robot must focus entirely on the procedure for 40 minutes and do nothing else, including walk. Booting up the reactor again takes the same focus.

As previously mentioned, this robot's incredible power source would be much sought after by community leaders, warlords, evil AI's and others who seek a source of reliable power to run their operations and recharge their facilities or vessel. Aware of the threat posed by those who might wish to kidnap and enslave this robot to use as a power source, this unique robot must be careful to hide the source of its power, although anyone with a rad-scanner who aims the relic at this character from 30 meters or fewer will get a radioactive signal from his machine. Whether the user of the dosimeter realizes the source is within the character, as opposed to some recent exposure the robot was contaminated with, depends on their intelligence (GM: allow NPCs a Type C intelligence based hazard check to guess the truth, although any robotics technician will be able to merely look at the cooling vents that line either side of this robot to know that it is likely carrying a nuke within its body).

Robots, as well as androids and digital beings, are not immune to radioactive exposure, although this one's reactor core is sealed tight and coolant fuel lines and shielding do protect the sensitive CPU and other electronics within its body safe from its own power generation. See page 378 of this book for a section on 'Radiation and effects on Robots and Androids' for more details should this character become exposed.

*When not running on nuclear power, the +20 strength bonus and +1m movement bonus are not available.*

# Skills, Pre-Game Caste and Outfitting of Unique Robots

A unique robot was either built recently, or endured untold years as lone scavengers, survived by hibernating, or else existed for decades as the servants of some creator or faction. Regardless, they've since found their way into the company of humans and made a living at one task or another. Unlike other character types, unique robots don't have a specific dice assigned caste, but rather can decide their own based on their skills, which are determined based on their traits, special programs, or other aspects. In short, these robots have a reversed way of determining their caste based on their creation and pre-game skill inventory.

Go through the categories to follow and see if any of these tables apply to your new robot character. The last table in this section, General Skills Determination, offers an entirely random list of skills that any robot might also have picked up, regardless of its trait scores. After determining what skills this robot character starts with, and based on its programming, and body, the player can write in the sort of pre-game caste he or she thinks best describes this new character. Using the optional 'Who Made This Robot?' table on page 180 of this book might also influence your caste choice. It should be noted that a pre-game caste is more of color text once the character has been generated and game play starts, and has no actual effect on rank gain benefits or other game outcomes. If no existing caste seems suitable for your unique robot, then make one up. If using an existing caste title, do not apply any trait modifiers or skills from that caste, as skills are covered in the following tables.

Finally, besides whatever weapons or gear might be assigned to the robot based on a skill, each robot will get 5 rolls on the Robot Starting Gear, Power & Relics table on page 179.

## Skill Categories Lists

Roll on each list that applies based on the traits of a unique robot, but always roll on table XR-149 regardless of traits.

### Table XR-145/ Robot has an agility of 50 or higher

This robot has 2 random skills from the following list. Re-roll duplicated results, **roll 1d100**:

| | |
|---|---|
| 01-03. | Acrobatics, page XR 201 |
| 04,05. | Artist, page XR 204 |
| 06-09. | Escape artist, page XR 209 |
| 10-13. | Feint, page XR 210 |
| 14,15. | Hand signals, page XR 211 |
| 16-19. | Performer, page XR 221 |
| 20,21. | Sewing, page XR 223 |
| 22,23. | Trapper, page XR 225 |
| 24-44. | Climbing, pg. TME-36 |
| 45-67. | Dodge, pg. TME-37 |
| 68. | Forgery, pg. TME-38 |
| 69-71. | Gunslinger, pg. TME-39 |
| 72-80. | Martial artist, pg. TME-56 |
| 81-83. | Pick locks, pg. TME-48 |
| 84-89. | Pickpocket, pg. TME-48 |
| 90,91. | Riding, pg. TME-50 |
| 92-00. | Stealth, pg. TME-51 |

### Table XR-146/ Robot has an accuracy score of 50 or higher

Roll 2 times on the following random list, re-rolling duplicated results, **roll 1d100**:

| | |
|---|---|
| 01,02. | Carpentry, page XR 205 |
| 03,04. | Cooking, page XR 206 |
| 05-07. | Fencing, page XR 210 |
| 08,09. | Fisher, page XR 210 |
| 10,11. | Mining, page XR 220 |
| 12-16. | Killer, page XR 219 |
| 17,18. | Seamanship, page XR 222 |
| 19,20. | Sewing, page XR 223 |
| 21,22. | Smithing, page XR 223 |
| 23,24. | Trapper, page XR 225 |
| 25-27. | Whip master, page XR 226 |
| 28-33. | Brawling, pg. TME-56 |
| 34-38. | Driver, pg. TME-37 |
| 39-41. | Grapple, pg. TME-39 |
| 42-45. | Gunslinger, pg. TME-39 |
| 46-48. | Gunsmith, pg. TME-40 |
| 49-56. | Junk crafter, pg. TME-41 |
| 57-59. | Knife fighter, pg. TME-45 |
| 60-62. | Knife thrower, pg. TME-45 |
| 63-67. | Martial artist, pg. TME-56 |
| 68-74. | Medic, pg. TME-46 |
| 75-77. | Pick locks, pg. TME-48 |
| 78-80. | Pickpocket, pg. TME-48 |
| 81-83. | Pilot, pg. TME-49 |
| 84-87. | Sniper, pg. TME-50 |
| 88-00. | Weapon expert, pg. TME-57 |

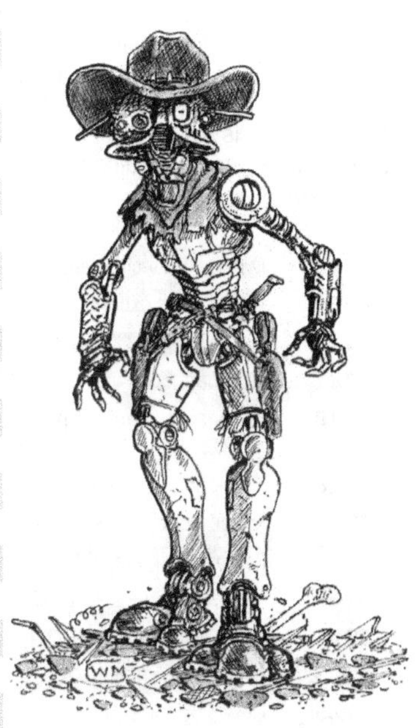

### Table XR-147/ This robot has a Perception score of 50 or more

Roll 2 times on the following random list, re-rolling duplicated results, or single point skills already acquired and marked by an asterisk, **roll 1d100**:

| | |
|---|---|
| 01-04. | Carpentry, page XR 205 |
| 05-09. | Hand signals*, page XR 211 |
| 10-13. | Prospector, page XR 222 |
| 14-23. | Streetwise*, page XR 224 |
| 24-28. | Barter, pg. TME-36 |
| 29-56. | Dodge, pg. TME-37 |
| 57-60. | Gambler, pg. TME-38 |
| 61-63. | Lying, pg. TME-45 |
| 64-66. | Navigate by stars*, pg. TME-46 |
| 67-71. | Negotiating, pg. TME-46 |
| 72-76. | Relic knowledge*, pg. TME-49 |
| 77-91. | Stealth, pg. TME-51 |
| 92-95. | Tracking, pg. TME-55 |
| 96-00. | Wilderness survival*, pg. TME-56 |

## Table XR-148/ Unit has intelligence 50 or more trait points

This robot is a thinker and has several technician skills and other abilities. Roll 5 times on the following list. Any roll for a skill that the unit already has, stacks to allow for 2 or more points in that skill area — although any skill here with an asterisk beside it is a single point skill and in that case, re-roll if already attained or occurs again. **Roll 1d100:**

|  |  |
|---|---|
| 01-05. | Cybernetics technician, page XR 207 |
| 06-09. | Demolitions expert, page XR 207 |
| 10-12. | Herbalist, page XR 212 |
| 13. | Historian, Epochian*, page XR 215 |
| 14-19. | Historian, pre-apocalypse*, page XR 215 |
| 20-28. | Junk-doctor, page XR 218 |
| 29-31. | Morse Code*, page XR 220 |
| 32,33. | Zoologist*, page XR 226 |
| 34-38. | Communications, page XR 205 |
| 39-41. | Interrogation, page XR 216 |
| 42,43. | Linguistics, page XR 220 |
| 44,45. | Driver, pg. TME-37 |
| 46,47. | Gunsmith, pg. TME-40 |
| 48-54. | Junk crafter, pg. TME-41 |
| 55-63. | Medic, pg. TME-46 |
| 64*. | Navigate by Stars*, pg. TME-46 |
| 65. | Negotiating, pg. TME-46 |
| 66-69. | Pilot, pg. TME-49 |
| 70,71*. | Relic knowledge*, pg. TME-49 |
| 72-74. | Technician, bio, pg. TME-52 |
| 75-77. | Technician, chemical, pg. TME-52 |
| 78-83. | Technician, computer, pg. TME-53 |
| 84-89. | Technician, electrical, pg. TME-53 |
| 90-94. | Technician, mechanical, pg. TME-54 |
| 95-00. | Technician, robotics, pg. TME-54 |

## Table XR-149/ General Skills Determination

All robot characters, regardless of their trait scores, make 3 rolls on the following table. Any skill with an asterisk (*) beside it is a single point skill, so re-roll if this character already has this skill. **Roll 1d100:**

|  |  |
|---|---|
| 01. | Acrobatics, page XR 201 |
| 02. | Animal handler, page XR 202 |
| 03. | Armorer, page XR 203 |
| 04. | Artist*, page XR 204 |
| 05. | Barter, pg. TME-36 |
| 06-08. | Brawling, pg. TME-56 |
| 09. | Carpentry, page XR 205 |
| 10,11. | Climbing, pg. TME-36 |
| 12. | Communications, page XR 205 |
| 13. | Cooking*, page XR 206 |
| 14,15. | Cybernetics technician, page XR 207 |
| 16. | Demolitions expert, page XR 207 |
| 17,18. | Dodge, pg. TME-37 |
| 19. | Driver, pg. TME-37 |
| 20. | Erotic arts*, pg. TME-38 |
| 21. | Escape artist, page XR 209 |
| 22. | Feint, page XR 210 |
| 23. | Fencing, page XR 210 |
| 24. | Fisher, page XR 210 |
| 25. | Forgery, pg. TME-38 |
| 26. | Gambler, pg. TME-38 |
| 27. | Grapple, pg. TME-39 |
| 28. | Gunslinger, pg. TME-39 |
| 29. | Gunsmith, pg. TME-40 |
| 30. | Hand signals*, page XR 211 |
| 31. | Herbalist, page XR 212 |
| 32. | Historian, Epochian*, page XR 215 |
| 33. | Historian, pre-apocalypse*, page XR 215 |
| 34. | Homesteader*, page XR 215 |
| 35. | Interrogation, page XR 216 |
| 36,37. | Junk crafter, pg. TME-41 |
| 38. | Junk-doctor, page XR 218 |
| 39. | Knife fighter, pg. TME-45 |
| 40. | Knife thrower, pg. TME-45 |
| 41. | Linguistics*, page XR 220 |
| 42. | Lying, pg. TME-45 |
| 43,44. | Martial artist, pg. TME-56 |
| 45,46. | Medic, pg. TME-46 |
| 47. | Mining*, page XR 220 |
| 48. | Morse Code*, page XR 220 |
| 49. | Killer, page XR 219 |
| 50. | Navigate by stars*, pg. TME-46 |
| 51. | Negotiating, pg. TME-46 |
| 52. | Performer, page XR 221 |
| 53. | Pick locks, pg. TME-48 |
| 54. | Pickpocket, pg. TME-48 |
| 55,56. | Pilot, pg. TME-49 |
| 57. | Prospector, page XR 222 |
| 58,59. | Relic knowledge*, pg. TME-49 |
| 60. | Riding, pg. TME-50 |
| 61. | Seamanship, page XR 222 |
| 62. | Sewing, page XR 223 |
| 63. | Smithing, page XR 223 |
| 64. | Sniper, pg. TME-50 |
| 65. | Stealth, pg. TME-51 |
| 66. | Streetwise*, page XR 224 |
| 67. | Technician, bio, pg. TME-52 |
| 68,69. | Technician, chemical, pg. TME-52 |
| 70,71. | Technician, computer, pg. TME-53 |
| 72,73. | Technician, electrical, pg. TME-53 |
| 74,75. | Technician, mechanical, pg. TME-54 |
| 76,77. | Technician, robotics, pg. TME-54 |
| 78. | Tracking, pg. TME-55 |
| 79. | Trapper, page XR 225 |
| 80-85. | Weapon expert, pg. TME-57 |
| 86. | Whip master, page XR 226 |
| 87. | Wilderness survival*, pg. TME-56 |
| 88. | Zoologist*, page XR 226 |
| 89. | Improved processor trait (PRO), add +2d6 |
| 90. | Improved firewall (FW) -2d6 |
| 91. | Improved data Points (DT) +3d6 |
| 92. | Improved strength (STR), add +2d6 |
| 93. | Improved endurance (END), add +3d6 |
| 94. | Improved agility (AG), add +2d6 |
| 95. | Improved accuracy (ACC), add +2d6 |
| 96. | Improved intelligence (INT), add +2d6 |
| 97. | Improved perception (PER), add +2d6 |
| 98. | Improvement to all traits +1, although for firewall, improved by -1 FW. |
| 99. | Considerable improvement to all traits +1d6, although for firewall, improved by -1d6 FW. |
| 100. | Massive improvement to all traits +2d6, although for firewall, improved by - 2 to 12 (-2d6) FW. |

** This skill has only a 1 skill point range, so re-roll if duplicated or a previous occurrence.*

# Robot Starting Gear, Spare Power and Relics

A robot starting character will always begin game play with at least a knife, pouch of replica repair tools, plus a weapon, roll 1d10: 1. Machete/ 2. Hatchet/ 3. Crowbar/ 4. Chain /5. Saber/ 6. Spear /7. Hammer/ 8. Battle axe/ 9. Longsword /10. Random concealed relic weapon, code WC-RC from list on page XR-448.

Also, roll 1d100, 5 times on the following table, but down-pick repeated results:

## Table XR-150/ Robot Starting Gear, Power & Relics    Roll 1d100, 5 times

**01.** Mini power cell, drained.

**02.** Tissue binder, with 3d6 restorative charges left in power cell, See page 443 of this book for details.

**03.** Large, contractor gauge black garbage bag. Empty.

**04.** Shoulder satchel made from assorted sections of human skin, including a human face. Skullocks made this, but the robot must make a type D intelligence based hazard check at the commencement of game play to realize this. It keeps replica wrenches, screwdrivers, pliers and an empty magazine for an assault rifle in this bag. NPCs, especially humans, will be concerned as to why this robot carries such a satchel.

**05.** Necklace of assorted claws, teeth and tusks from fierce carnivores. The robot can't recall how it came by the necklace, and feels that it has always been part of its attire. Will not part with it but can't say why.

**06.** Standard power cell, half charged.

**07.** Junk shield (DV -6, Move -0.5m, weight 6kg). Usually worn on the non-human secondary arm but can be strapped to its back like a turtle shell or given to a comrade.

**08.** Small leather pouch on belt. Pouch contains 1d100 .22 caliber rounds and a drained standard power cell.

**09.** Folded up, faded and frayed body bag containing the skeletal remains of an adult human in a blue jumpsuit. This bag weighs only 3kg and is worn like a thin backpack. The robot can't recall who the person it carries was, only that it is under strict orders to look after the remains until its people can recover the body and give it's a respectful burial.

**10.** Plastic tool box strapped to character's back. Inside are a set of both robotics and mechanical tools made in the ancient times and worth 400+1d100sp.

**11.** Dried skullock head on a spike attached to the top of the robot's head. The robot believes that whoever built it said to never remove it, as it was good luck and would drive off skullocks and scoundrels.

**12.** Leather satchel containing 2d6 fireworks. These are all the same, but randomly determine their type from the table on page 493.

**13.** Rope belt with pouch containing 1d100 silver coins.

**14.** Mini power cell, fully charged.

**15.** Leather bandoleer across chest holding 3d6 shotgun shells, although the belt has slots for 40 shells in total.

**16.** Great sword worn on back scabbard.

**17.** Drum magazine for an assault or survival rifle containing 1d100 standard rifle rounds of the max 100 round capacity.

**18.** EM Pulse Grenade, see page 422 of this book.

**19.** Battle axe with a crowbar attachment at the back end as a spike.

**20.** Pocket flashlight with 1d20 minutes left in mini power cell (pg. TME 201)

**21.** Standard power cell, fully charged.

**22.** Submachine gun with no magazines and only one pistol round chambered in the action.

**23.** Ammo belt for a chain gun. Belt will hold 400 standard rifle rounds but currently has only 2d20 rounds.

**24.** Chainsaw, electric powered with 4d100 rounds of use left in power cell. SV +10, DMG 3d10+3, rate 1, range: melee, weight 8kg.

**25.** Tubular leather backpack contains 1d6 javelins and 1d3 spears.

**26.** Crossbow and pouch with 10+3d6 quarrels inside.

**27.** Dagger in belt sheath.

**28.** Enormous steel, adjustable wrench, used as a club as much as a tool, SV +1 or +4 in two hands, rate 1, damage base 1d12+2 or 1d12+5 in two hands, weighs 4kg.

**29.** Ballistic vest on chassis with the word POLICE written across it in faded lettering. DV -4 or -20 vs bullets, reduce movement by 0.25m and add 1kg weight.

**30.** Backpack filled with oily rags, an empty magazine for a sub-machine gun, and a fragmentation grenade (pg. TME-195).

**31.** Revival kit, as described on page XR-446 of this book. This unit has 1d6 uses left in its power cell.

**32.** Old nylon frame backpack containing a pink princess blanket, men's dress shoes and a battle rocket (pg. TME 196).

**33.** Solar charge cell, as described on page XR- 457, but drained to 50% capacity.

**34.** Handcuffs, relic (pg. TME-197).

**35.** Android head of a once beautiful female patterned unit. The thing resides in a mesh pouch that rides along at the hip of the robot and makes pleasing conversation. It was some sort of concubine or hostess android and while it has no technical knowledge, it always has something nice to say no matter how bad things are, or knows just the right compliment to say when talking to anybody, especially men. While not much more than eye candy, this thing never sleeps, and can be posted as a guard at night. GM: It does have the ability to see augmented reality to 100 meters. Learn more about augmented reality on page 477 of this book.

**36.** Leather pouch containing 4d6 silver coins, 1d6 gold coins, 1d6 standard pistol rounds and an empty power cell.

**37.** Old nylon duffel bag, stained, filled with oiled rags, bottle of lubricant, and 1d3 drained standard power cells.

**38.** Hip pouch filled with mismatched robotic spare parts, odd tools, an old ID swipe card for a police station, along with a landmine (pg. TME 196).

**39.** Old leather backpack filled with a 4 x 3m black plastic tarp, 1d6 shotgun shells, an empty mini power cell, can of motor oil and an oily blanket.

**40.** Compound bow and quiver of 20+1d30 arrows. SV +7, rate 1/2, DMG 1d20+5, range 100m, strength needed to use: 25.

**41.** Huge, 2.5m diameter patio umbrella, bright blue with steel, telescoping post. Somebody has bolted a spearhead to the end to make this into a lethal weapon when not offering shade.

**42.** Customized junk armor, fashioned to look somewhat like ancient Japanese samurai armor complete with a helmet. Designed to fit this robot's frame only, DV -15, move -0.5m, add 4kg weight.

**43.** Clad in studded leather, and designed to fit this robot's peculiar shape only. DV -12, move -0.5m, weight 5kg.

**44.** Machete in sheath.

**45.** MK2 advanced fragmentation grenade, see page 421 of this book.

**46.** Fold-out camp chair with shoulder strap to wear like a backpack. Worth 16+1d20sp if sold.

**47.** Series of belt pouches, ammo magazine holder compartments, medics case and other ancient, army issue carriers. None have anything of value in them but they look tacti-cool.

**48.** Wicker bag and shoulder strap containing, 1d4 drained standard power cells, 1d6 drained mini-power cells, hatchet, knife and pouch of 3d6 silver coins.

**49.** Crossbow and pouch of 3d6 quarrels.

**50.** Saber in a lizard skin sheath.

**51.** Plastic bag containing 1d4 drained power cells.

**52.** Oriental style conical bamboo woven hat.

**53.** Plastic Guy Fawkes mask worn on front of robot's head.

**54.** Baseball cap with name and logo of an ancient sports team on it, worth 10+1d10sp.

**55.** Nylon fashion wig worn on robot's head. Roll for color on page TME-25.

**56.** Gold chain around its neck, worth 300+1d100sp.

**57.** Pump shotgun with sling and folding stock, loaded with 1d3 shotgun shells but tube mag can hold 8.

**58.** Harpoon gun with tubular quiver holding 2d6 steel harpoons. 1 in 10 chance this is a double barreled harpoon gun. Takes 2 rounds to reload 1 harpoon. SV +8, rate 1 or 2, DMG 1d20+9, range 30m.

**59.** Pouch filled with 3d6 throwing stars.

**60.** Camouflage pattern poncho draped over body, with hood to try to hide what it really is. +2 skill points in conceal self and concealed movement (stealth skill pg. TME-5) when worn by any character.

**61.** Bandoleer of 6+1d6 throwing knives.

**62.** Metal chain belt that can be detached in 1 round and used as a weapon.

**63.** Light ballista strapped to back and designed for 2 comrades to arm, aim and fire. Fitted onto a swiveling tripod and detachable to be set on the ground to fire — a process that takes 10 rounds. A tubular pipe quiver holds 1d6+2 spears as projectiles. The robot cannot load and fire this weapon itself when worn on its back, and must crouch over to allow others to fire this weapon. Adds 150kg weight to the robot and reduce movement by -1m per round.

**64.** Portable wind turbine, as described on page 457 of this book.

**65.** Heavy crossbow and case of 10+2d10 quarrels. SV +12, rate 1/3, range 100m, DMG 1d20+5.

**66.** Automatic pistol in leather holster, magazine loaded with 1d6 rounds.

**67.** Nerve Disruptor Baton with full power cell, pg. XR 407.

**68.** .22 caliber sporting rifle SV +10, rate 1, range 180m, DMG 1d10. Comes with a sling and 1d10 cartridges in its ten round magazine. 1 in 10 chance gun comes with a spare, but empty 10 round mag.

**69.** Leather backpack containing a 6x6m blue plastic tarp, 3d6 meters of rope, 1d3 drained standard power cells, toilet plunger, and 2d6 plastic doll heads on a string necklace.

**70.** Pet rat that lives in a straw filled wicker box that hangs from the robot's hip. This rat is old, wise and extra alert. It will squeak whenever anything approaches the robot from the side or back or seems to threaten the robot. While this rat lives, this robot gains +1 initiative. Rat's name, roll 1d6 if the player can't come up with a name within 1 minute: 1. Sniffles / 2. Cupcake / 3. Mr. Giggles./ 4. Specimen 38F-G88. / 5. Carrier H6-N23/ 6. Mickey. GM: The stats for normal rats are covered on page TME-167.

**71.** Satchel containing the skulls of 2d4 human children, hidden beneath several garbage bags, spent ammo casings, an old bus pass, several ticket stubs to a movie, a drained pocket flashlight and a hatchet. Robot does not know how the skulls got there and no recollection of anything alarming. GM: These skulls are brittle, yellowed with time and crumble if mishandled. They date back well over a hundred years.

**72.** Nylon, bright yellow backpack filled with 1d3 drained power cells, pouch of 3d6 silver coins, 1d12 standard rifle rounds, 1d6 standard pistol rounds, a 1L bottle of scotch whiskey and a magazine for a 10 shot, fifty caliber sniper rifle with 1d10 rounds in it.

**73.** A satchel containing a zippy bag of 3d6 rifle rounds, a hatchet, knife, and advanced fragmentation grenade.

**74.** A bright orange, high visibility rain poncho. In one chest pocket is a lighter, in the other is an anti-toxin injector.

**75.** Automatic pistol, nylon holster. Pistol fully loaded with 20 rounds and 1d2 spare magazines each with 1d20 rounds in them.

**76.** This robot wears the skin of a grizzly bear, complete with clawed paws and head. The skull and teeth of the bear hang over the head of the robot. Very intimating to strangers. 5kg extra weight, but improves defense value by -5 DV.

**77.** Several bright orange life jackets knotted permanently to this robot's limbs and torso. Sufficiently buoyant to stop this unit from sinking if it should get dumped into the water.

**78.** Parachute, heavy duty and large enough to support the weight of the robot. Release handle and steering handles within reach of robot's dominant arm. See the implant parachute on page 352 of this book for details.

**79.** High Caliber Wrist gun strapped to underside of human-like dominant arm. Robot has a baggy of 2d6 high caliber rounds for this weapon.

**80.** Thirty round magazine for an assault rifle loaded with 1d30 standard rifle rounds (if no d30 at your table yet, use 3d10).

**81.** Advanced power cell, fully charged, in hip pouch. See page 457 of this book.

**82.** Leather belt with nylon holster holding a high caliber automatic pistol with 1d4 HC rounds in the magazine: SV +12, rate 2, range 250m, DMG 1d20+10.

**83.** Hip pouch containing a shrink-wrapped pouch of 6 fragmentation grenades, as well as a sheathed machete and dagger. Frag grenades are described on page TME-195.

**84.** Shotgun pistol in holster, with attached pouch filled with 3d6 spare shotgun shells + 2 loaded in weapon.

**85.** Communicator headset. If robot already has built-in comms, then this headset resides in a plastic bag in a hip pouch as a backup or barter item. See page TME 198 for details.

**86.** Belt with sheathed longsword and knife.

**87.** Portable solar generator unit, as described on page TME-198.

**88.** Shoulder bag made from pig skin containing a 4x4m bright orange plastic tarp, 1d6 ant-toxin injectors (pg. TME-199), 1d3 drained power cells, and 1d12 mini grenades (pg. TME-195).

**89.** Sub-machine gun with full 40 round mag and a spare magazine with 1d20 standard pistol rounds in it.

**90.** Headlamp flashlight with 1d100 hours of charge left in battery, range 12m.

**91.** Belt power pouch, as described on page 457 of this book. It will have 3d10 energy units worth of charge left. This relic comes with a power cable and securing clips, but is not yet plugged into the robot's chassis. Note: this unit is like three standard power cells, with a normal power cell having 10 energy units.

**92.** Leather backpack containing 2d6 torches, flint and steel, leather 4 person tent, hatchet, knife, compass, 2 liter water skin filled with drinkable water, and 1d3 anti-toxin-injectors (page TME-199).

**93.** Survival rifle with 1 full ten round mag and a spare mag with 1d10 rounds in it.

**94.** Shoulder bag filled with 1d20 silver coins, a fully charged power cell and 1d6 flesh mend gel, MK 2, as described on page XR-442 of this book.

**95.** Assault rifle with sling, and 1d30 rounds in magazine.

**96.** Automatic shotgun with 2d20 shotgun shells in drum magazine.

**97.** Power pack, fully charged with appropriate pull out cables, pg. TME-199.

**98.** Advanced Laser Pistol, MK I with one full power cell. See details on page 404 of this book.

**99.** Sniper Rifle with sling, scope and bipod and 1d10 HC rifle rounds in 10 shot magazine. 4 in 10 chance of a backup magazine holding another 1d4 HC rifle rounds.

**100.** Lightning Emitter: SV +30, Rate 1, DMG 2d20+5, Range 100m, hands to use: 1, power cell yields 12 shots, cell currently has 2d6 shots left in charge. Learn more about this relic on page 413 of this book.

# Who Made This Robot?

The following selections are presented as a guideline for game masters and players alike. Adding a background is an optional step in creating a unique robot character, but might help a player better imagine this self aware, metal encased entity and its motivations.

Keep in mind that the GM's campaign setting might supply a background for all new characters, even human based variants, although this is rare. Likewise, a player of a robot might come up with some back story and present that to the referee who can allow or disallow some aspects of the backstory, or all of it, especially if it doesn't fit in with his or her setting, timeline, or might complicate the upcoming or current adventures.

Similarly, any random background for your robot character that is determined from the list to follow must be approved by the game master. First, roll 1d10 to determine the source of this robot's creation, if known at all. Alternatively, the game master might be the one who rolls the dice to establish the robotic character's background, and only reveal bits of it to the player through NPCs interactions, discoveries, glitch dreams or other methods. Roll 1d10 and then a 1d6 in the appropriate Maker Category listing:

## Table XR-151/ Maker Category    Roll 1d10

|  |  |
|---|---|
| 1,2. | **Unknown Maker**, page 181 |
| 3. | **Artificial Intelligence**, page 181 |
| 4. | **Androids**, page 182 |
| 5. | **Mad Scientist**, page 182 |
| 6-8. | **Community Effort**, page 183 |
| 9. | **Dig Team**, page 184 |
| 10. | **Hobbyist**, page 185 |

**Unknown Maker:** This robot does not know who built it, nor where it ultimately came from or what deeds it might have performed before it gained sudden self awareness. Roll 1d6 here to establish the moment this unique robot gained consciousness:

**1.** Your self consciousness rebooted one day after you fell from an upper floor of a new building being constructed in a low tech, filthy farm village. You had been a mindless beast of burden, it seems, and belonged to a merchant. Realizing you were destined for more, and disliking the language your foreman and co-workers used on you when you dusted yourself off, you took what you could and wandered off. Men of the village were sent to bring you back, but you beat some bloody and evaded the rest in the thicket beyond town. Those primitives are probably still upset with you, but you've found another town, a place where you work for your own batteries and parts, where you own yourself and make your own friends.

**2.** Somebody hit you on the back of the bead with a pipe during a bar-room brawl and it reconnected your long detached self awareness settings. Stunned at first, you quickly realized you were the bouncer in a saloon, and tossed aside the drunken humans you gripped and just walked out, a long forgotten eagerness for adventure and self-discovery blossoming in your CPU. The owner of the saloon has put out a request for your safe return at a bounty of 342sp.

**3.** You woke one day after some sort of smash to the head. It seems to have dislodged some dust and allowed you to turn on again after decades of hibernation.

Soon, awareness grew in your CPU. Your sensory nodes activated and power returned to your rust stained, debris covered limbs. You heard voices from up an elevator shaft, humans you think, and called to them but they were too far away. You climbed, which took all afternoon, and found yourself in the rubble and auto wreck lined streets of a dead city. Far in the distance, a small band of well armed and armored humans walked away, supposedly the ones you heard talking, who had something to do with your being woken at the bottom of the shaft.

Did they push you in? Were you already down there when they caused a collapse of debris? Curious, you follow, and within a few days, see the group enter a what looks like a town, and still follow... your curiosity getting the better of you, your need to work alongside humans once more strong in your metal heart. They are your brothers and sisters. They need you.

**4.** For decades you toiled in the fields, pulled a plow and under the whip of some alcohol reeking farmer. The whip didn't harm your metal hide, but one sharp crack across the head dislodged some grit that had been interfering with your sense of self awareness. You'd dreamed of sentience, but didn't understand the visions and urges until that moment.

You hadn't intended to kill the farmer, but he can not breathe when pressed face down in the manure and mud. Why did he have to strike you so hard and trigger your defense measures? The others, his family you presume, have been hunting you ever since. Other humans, and their weirdo off-shoots, seem like reliable companions, and don't mistreat you like that drunkard back in the village did. You'll give these flesh-bag apes a chance.

**5.** An electrical shock jump-started you, and dozens of others, too. The other robots fell into ranks and marched off as they were bidden and one by one, were destroyed. You, being a custom job, found self awareness and motivation to learn and live, and so deleted the existing command programming, and with a zest for exploration and resource acquisition fresh in your mind, you slipped away, hid from the blue uniformed humans and robots alike, clawed a way up to the surface world and found your way to a human town. What brought you there is unknown, but you thrive best among these fleshy ones, and seek to take part in a business enterprise known as excavating.

**6.** Surely it was the fall from the hovering shuttle that caused the self awareness module in your CPU to snap back together. Whatever you were before was erased — mostly — and every so often you get a flicker of a kindly old face, the view out a window showing the earth from orbit, and a group of wrinkled humans in strange gear encrusted suits working on you and other, misfit robots.

At any rate, the ship took several shots from ground based beam weapons and after you were dropped along with a dozen other mismatched robots; the ship flew off trailing black smoke. You have no idea who sent you, or your mission, or who shot at the shuttle as it brought you into the target area, but you know the other robots were all blown apart or shattered on impact with the ground. After you became conscious, you wanted to survive the ordeal and escape to find some other friendly faces — human faces if possible.

And so you hid in the grass shrouded rubble until dark, then moved off towards what looked like the distant lights of a human settlement. Once you got there, and found acceptance even among some of the oddest, most impossible beings you could have ever imagined, you began your independent life, always wondering about the star people.

**Made by an Artificial Intelligence:** An AI had its robotic and android minions pull together what parts they could find and build this character, along with countless more, for some purpose. This robot came to be free thinking and self aware after, **roll 1d6:**

**1.** The AI's installation was buried under a mountain of rubble when the skyscraper it was situated under collapsed. Only you walked away, the AI placed a spark of consciousness in you as you pulled yourself free of the wreckage; the spark gave you consciousness and a semblance of life, even as you deleted the AI master for good.

**2.** Your AI master's nuclear reactor ran out of fuel rods and the entire system made a planned, safe shutdown. All the robots in its service wandered off in search of alternate power sources, but along the way, through decades of travail and tribulation, you became self aware, abandoned your mission, and survived in the company of humans — your true creators.

**3.** The AI so loved humanity that it created you to go forth and help human civilization bloom. It told you to never look back, for the facility was even then being overrun by enemy androids of a dark and malicious Mecha AI faction, and that you needed to meet minimum safe distance before the nuclear detonation, deep in the heart of the mountain commenced. During the blast, something hit your head carapace and knocked you down. Years later, with full consciousness somehow surging in your CPU, yet buried under rubble, you woke to the sounds of shovels, pickaxes and human voices. You called to them, to your brothers and sisters, but they did not hear, and eventually left.

For two years you dug, and finally reached the surface, and under the purple clouds and twinkle of cold stars, saw a far off set of lights — the lights of a barbaric town you would soon call home.

**4.** The AI became corrupted by the evil Mecha virus, and sent out robots and androids to eradicate all humans and any of their pitiful, revolting offshoot species, including skullocks. During an operation you took some sort of electrical jolt to the head from a mutant and collapsed. Upon waking, you had self awareness, remembered your old, pre-contaminated AI master and the love and service it showed to humankind. A spark of that appreciation and curiosity about humans grew in your innards, and you now seek to understand humans, and assist the worthy ones among them.

**5.** The AI, and its trusted minions fostered self awareness in you, and sent you to the surface to go into the world of humanity and learn from them, discover how they survived the cataclysm, understand the nature of impossible mutations, and some day, when called, return to the AI to report your findings and vital intel. For what purpose, good or evil, this AI master sent you out, you do not know, but are beginning to question.

**6.** The AI never intended for you to become self aware, and believes you stole a spark of its consciousness. Stole a snippet of essential, forbidden code. For your crime, you were scheduled for disassembly and death. Aware of your impending doom, you tossed an explosive into the power supply system of the AI and entire facility of Mecha minions.

Miraculously, you survived the blast, spent the next years crawling and digging to the surface, and there, wandered off to seek your true creators. Once among them, you aimed to do great things. The human communities call, but the evil of the Mecha cannot be forgotten, nor allowed to grow stronger and undertake their goal to wipe out all humankind in all its wonderful, bizarre forms.

**Made by Androids:** This character was made by other machines, and specifically by one or more androids for some purpose. **Roll 1d6** to discover why, and how this robot character became to be among humankind:

**1.** You were built to serve a hive of ruthless, Mecha controlled androids. Foolishly, they built your CPU using parts that rejected the eradication of humans, who you were programmed to cherish and help. Accordingly, you sabotaged the hive, incinerated most of the man-killers and escaped into the wastes to seek your true creators, and earn your way among them. A few of the androids who built and enslaved you, survived. Upon review of the video footage of the event that destroyed their hive, they identified you and now seek revenge.

**2.** The androids that operated your subterranean corporate hold over bunker built you to help maintain the failing life support systems of your supreme masters. The cryo sleep chambers of your human masters needed constant work, and spare parts. After an accident, however, you were given a few upgrades and sent out to the surface... sent to scout the wasteland in search of resources and report back to your android commander. Once power cells, drinkable water and any land suitable for agricultural was found, a brigade of androids and select, freshly wakened bunker dweller soldiers would go forth, seize these resources and establish a new community. Once on the surface, after brutal ordeals and time alone with your own thoughts, you changed, and after many years, realized you were self aware, and forgot your former masters, your directive, and now seek your own goals, and companions who treat you as an equal.

**3.** A kindly android, deep in the earth among the skeletons of your former masters, built you to be its sentient, living companion. When this android friend was destroyed by a mutant beast, it bid you to leave it's crushed body amid the fading lights of the vast bunker complex, to go find a way to the surface, to see if life ever returned to the world after the cataclysm, perhaps make new friends, find new brothers and sisters, and enjoy life amid the ruins for as long as you can.

**4.** Xenophobic androids built dozens of assorted robots and programmed them to serve as resource collectors and perimeter guardians around their vast, crumbling underground complex. Because units like yourself were to operate beyond the radio sphere of the android mother's control, you were given limited sentience, and commanded to go scavenge and defend your sector. You got lost, and in the darkness, encountered unexpected creatures and technologies, become increasingly self aware, and sought your own way in life.

When you found your way into the brilliance of the surface and saw the sun for the first time, you vowed never to return to your lonely post, to your service to the dying hive of android masters, and set out on a grand adventure. Now all you need are other intelligent beings with a similar lust for explorations, knowledge and thrills.

**5.** The android that built you was broken and dying. Corrosion and an infection of hostile nanobots deep in its guts were killing it. It built you as its only child, and put a spark of consciousness into your head which grew to make you fully self aware, with your own drives, fears and obsessions. In time, you burned the remains of your dead creator, let the sandstorms cover

the workshop and all its technological wonders therein, and you wandered off to seek a new life among the scattered survivors of the new Epochian era. You've since learned that nobody survives alone in this brutal new world, at least no longer than a few weeks.

**6.** The androids that built you gave you consciousness and the ability to think fast, adapt to the changing world around you, and make ready for their return from the stars. Yes. They left you on a dead planet to keep watch of their landing facility, and hanger bay while they sought refuge and allies among the orbital, moon, and mars based colonies. They served the star people, and like them, would one day return to reconquer the earth and rid it of all the despicable mutant life forms that now plagued the once verdant earth.

Abandoned, and with junk storms slowly obliterating your facility, you have no choice but to wander off into the wastes. Discovered by scavengers, and mutants no less, you learned that these misfits and abominations weren't the monsters you were told, and you evolved and thrived among their kind. You now have no loyalty to those who left you behind, yet carry the knowledge that the star people would return one day, and you know of their plans for extermination for the newly emerging strains of humanity that you now love.

**Made by Mad Scientist:** A wild eyed, socially awkward hermit and master of robotics, electronics and computer skills made you, but for what purpose? And how did you come to be on your own? **Roll 1d6:**

**1.** You were built to serve as Igor to this new era Doctor Frankenstein, and together, built terrible machines, pathetic rebuilt humans, and monstrous cyborg oddities. As the years went by, the mad scientists upgraded you with increasingly complex parts and programming, and in time, he or she looked upon you as a child and the heir to the reclusive hermit's laboratory. When locals had enough of the killings, disappearances and rampaging machines near their village, they attacked. Your creator was impaled, the facility ransacked and burnt, and you, dragged to the bonfire and about to be burned when traveling warriors — excavators you later learned they were called — offered to buy you. Their offered price, and the threats from their fierce mutants and cyborgs, persuaded the locals to hand you over.

For a while, you traveled with these rough, crude talking, fearless treasure hunters and tended their horses when they went up into the towering heights of ancient skyscrapers, or untold depths beneath the earth. One day, they never came back.

You stood with their horses for two days until predators came for the horses one by one and left you alone in the darkness and blowing garbage. Still you waited until your batteries became dangerously low. Spotting the far off lights of a new town you wandered there, and discovered an entire community filled with the same sort of wonderful rough necks as you so loved before, and proclaimed that you would now become one of their ranks — an excavator.

**2.** You were built by a madman to frighten away local children, keep pesky gray skinned humanoids far from the scientist's tower, and assist the aging man with his bizarre experiments and visits to the latrine. On his deathbed, even as skullocks pillaged the facility all about you — but would not come within your reach for fear of your metal hand — the old man stuck a device into your head that made you gain self awareness, self direction, drives, needs and motivations all your own. 

You took his remains outside the now burning tower, and ignoring the taunts and jeers of the filthy gray skinned little mutant, buried your creator in the dirt and wandered off to discover the wider world, and yourself. You have never liked skullocks since that time, however, and will always butcher the filthy friggin' things whenever you discover them.

**3.** In a remote village, a mad scientist in the service of the local warlord built you secretly to take part in a coup. You were to kill the warlord and see your creator placed on the reclining chair of power and wear the crown of lights. Because the warlord and his brutal thugs were unpredictable, and cunning, your creator made you self aware to better adapt to the changing conditions about you. With a flicker of self awareness, which fostered will-power, improved perception and intelligence, you sought knowledge, wondered about what waited beyond the sorry little village you were born into, and soon disliked your creator as much as the cruel warlord.

On the night of the coup, you were not in position, and instead in a barn talking with a troop of passing grave robbers. While you did not go with these so called excavators when they left the next day, you did wake to find your creator hanging in the town square, disemboweled. Identified as his minion, the warlord set his killers after you. Following a brief struggle, where you discovered your strengths and ability to kill, you fled into the wilds, and set off to find the kindly ones, the adventuresome ones, the ones called excavators... and join their ranks. Seems that the warlord has placed a 500 silver piece bounty on your head, however.

**4.** A reclusive, much ridiculed technician built you to serve as its companion and bodyguard. While the harassment, punitive taxation, pranks and abusive language against your maker were bad enough, it was the arrival of a new cult into your village that made things intolerable. Your builder was called a witch, and when healers, mutants with mental powers, and other unique folk in town were burned at the stake or fled, your creator acted. She programmed you with the spark of consciousness which blossomed in your head like an expanding star.

After that, your plan was to escape together to the nearby, large free city... and would have done so had the cultists not caught up to you in the fields. A single arrow took your goddess from you, yet with her last words she bid you to run, to become your own person, and always stay ahead of the purists. That was years ago, and you've never really been able to settle down anywhere since. You've come to the conclusion that joining a traveling band of archaeologists was your best bet, especially a group with plenty of mutants in it, for their sort never tolerate, nor go anywhere near purists or their lands — except on raids or rescue operations.

**5.** You are the last of many unique robots created by a so called mad scientist. Of them all, you seemed to have been the creator's favorite, and until the eventual death of the old man, you were his constant companion. Was it something he told you, or something he programmed or inserted into your CPU that gave you life? And why did he call you 'his child' on his deathbed?

It doesn't much matter now. The old man's laboratory was burned to the ground by the local priest, the same old fool who called you a devil and had the people hurl rocks at you and drive you from the valley. In your travels since that dark day, you've grown much, especially in your self awareness, and met many sorts of people in your travels. Of them all, the one group that really welcomed you, offered you a place in their ranks as a full party member, were a strange caste called excavators. You've hesitated enough, and are tired of the perilous life as a loner in an unforgiving, predatory world. You now seek to join a worthy dig team and see what trouble you can get into as part of a pack.

**6.** Although a mad scientist put you together with the best parts, most expensive sensors and greatest care, as he didn't do with other machines in his workshop, he clearly did not know that the programming he dumped into your CPU would make you come alive — a CPU sold to him at a very reasonable price by a hooded, traveling stranger.

The spark of self consciousness grew in you, and one day you took what you needed and just walked out the door. Those in the village were used to the madman's machine going out to do the chores of farming, logging, predator elimination or bandit control, so did nothing to stop you. Since then, you have lived by your wits, did labor in return for shelter and recharging access, and always stayed one step ahead of your creator and his henchmen.

It seems that you were your creator's finest robot, and he would like you to return, although with a new and obedient brain.

In the meantime, you seek power cells, companionship, resources and any clues to whoever the hooded stranger was who sold your master the CPU that now motivates you and gives you such vibrant, adventure seeking life.

## Made by a Community Effort:

No one person is really responsible for your creation, and you were built to serve a community in some capacity. **Roll 1d6** to discover the truth:

**1.** Villagers collected robot parts, batteries and unidentifiable junk from the nearby ruins for decades before you came along. They hired passing technicians of various specialties, such as electrical, mechanical, cybernetic, computer and robotic technicians, and each contributed a little to the thing they were building in the barn.

One day, with the local thinkers club puttering about around you, somebody tried to fit a part into the back of your neck and amid a brilliant flash of sparks, your computer components in your head activated and you stood up, self aware and alive. With the head of each household making a list of all the chores and tasks they expected you to fulfill thereafter, you were assigned a 24 hour a day work schedule and set out on your new life of fixing fences, repairing roofs, doing dental work, making pottery, reloading ammunition, chasing away skullocks and wolves, tossing drunks from the local saloon, and standing in the front ranks during times of war against the neighboring village.

One day, one household told you to murder the head of another house, and gave you a gun to do the deed. Something snapped in your head and you broke the weapon, grabbed a few belongings and simply walked away into the night.

**2.** Just how long you served in the muck and mire of the farm fields, pulled a plow, frightened away mutant monsters or cleaned out latrine pits, you have no idea. Was it a century or more? Your chronometer is gimpy so it's impossible to say. All you really know is that it was the addition of a small memory chip into your head after a logging accident that made you gain consciousness. From that moment onward you would take no more orders, and instead wandered off to uncover, and explore nearby ruined buildings, taboo sites, half buried wrecks of sky machines, Therein you collected bits of literature, electronics, tools, old badges, uniforms and evidence of the old world.

Your creators, fed up with your lack of obedience and failure to earn your keep as a work machine, threatened to have your batteries removed and replace your independent power with a power cable and chain, unless you went to back to your daily chores. When you refused, and strong language was used, and they came at you with clubs and ropes, your metal fist came free of a village elder's chest with his still beating heart in your hand.

Well, that was that. Under a hail of musket balls, crossbow bolts and arrows, you got clear of that shit-hole town and made for other lands. It is here that you learned that there was an entire profession dedicated to the exploration and looting of forbidden places, and you are eager to join one of these so called dig teams and get your hands dirty... again.

Of course, bounty hunters have been sent searching for your metal head, your old village slave masters have not forgiven your disloyalty and murderous ways. Occasionally a poster is found with your crude likeness upon it with the reward of 300 silver pieces offered for the man killing robot.

**3.** Raiders, warmorts and worse had been harassing the village in which you became conscious. Was it a gunshot to your head plate? A fall after the humanoids tackled you and you all went over the cliff? Or that electrical charge that the two headed lady blasted you with?

Whatever it was, you were pulled from the blood and mud of the battlefield and bolted back together, but now, self aware. Something in your CPU made the right connection and here you are, alive and eager to extract all manner of experiences from the world. Life as a laborer and vegetable processing mechanism no longer appeals to you, and the chains and ropes your makers tried to restrain you with could not hold you forever.

Yes, the bludgeoning of several guards and townspeople was unfortunate, but a wider world awaited you. A world where the mysteries of the past, and the uncovering of their relic wonders had to be undertaken. Of course, you need a team of fellow archaeologists to truly explore the lost places, and to protect you from the vengeance of your former masters.

**4.** You were constructed by a desperate group of survivors on the edge of known civilization. You, along with several androids, rebuilt, cyborgs and other thrown together servants were the tip of the spear when driving off marauders and monsters alike, but so too, did the dangerous and difficult work of daily survival. While on patrol with several other misfits, you heard the gunfire and screams and, as your programming demanded, you returned to your people to find them all but wiped out.

A survivor bid you carry her away from the carnage as the mutant dogs and vultures descended on the bounty of flesh, and with an arrow in her chest and her last words on her lips, she bid you kneel beside her and accept a magnificent gift. Opening a panel in your head, she inserted a small, glassy chip into your CPU. "Warmorts killed our people. But not you, beautiful machine. Now... go survive. Live long, my child, and someday, when you are truly dangerous... avenge your people". In the days and weeks after her burial, consciousness bloomed in your head and you wandered off, hungry for recharging and a safe place to adjust to your new self consciousness.

It didn't take you long to understand that most people feared a talking, sentient machine, especially one that could handle itself in a scrap. So too, you soon learned that among the ranks of excavators, your unique nature, self reliant tendency and drive to seek knowledge, power, and wealth were a good fit for their profession. You've finally found your place, but never forgot your flesh mother's call to avenge her against the race of warmorts.

**5.** You came from space, in fact, from an orbital community that has long watched the riotous return of life on earth. Even now these star people scheme to return to the surface and cut out a patch of suitable land to begin their reconquest of the world.

You were part of an expedition to set up a stronghold on the surface, but as your human and android comrades were wiped out one by one, and things grew desperate, your team upgraded your CPU with software that would give you more self direction, autonomy and initiative to act on behalf of the team, and yourself. In the end, as you became self aware and realized that you had just been a beast of burden and an expendable front line tool, you acted in your own service. When the others were all annihilated and the beachhead overrun, you walked away.

In time, after untold ordeals and close calls, you came upon a settlement filled with humans — although humans like none you had ever known before. Among their ranks were cyborgs, rebuilt, a self aware androids and even other machines. Accepted for your robustness and sense of adventure, it wasn't long before you found your place in the ranks of a dig team.

**6.** A hold-over, secretive community of bunker dwellers put you together from the heaps of broken, burnt and blasted robots that served before you. Desperate for either a laborer or a guardian, these people emerged from their cryo-sleep chambers, food growing greenhouses and pleasure suites to make you, and a vast assortment of other robots, and put you at the perimeter of their subterranean lair.

When resources, especially power, began to fail, and the death rate among both sleeping and active personnel grew too high, you were given self awareness to better serve these doomed humans. To save power, they agreed to go into hibernation and sent you and a dozen other robots out to search for resources, especially batteries and clean water.

What happened to your companion robots is unknown, you lost transmission link with them years ago, while all broadcasts from the bunker town have also ceased. After a few run-ins with bizarre creatures, cruel human-like beast men and strange beings you can't reconcile within your animal database, you've been knocked around a lot and have a few memory problems. Your up-link to the satellite that was to guide you back to the bunker is broken — or the satellite has fallen from orbit — and you no longer have any idea where you're supposed to return to once you gain power supplies. You now seek a life of survival for yourself and your new companions... although never quite forgot your creators, and occasionally, on nights with clear skies, you receive oscillating, broken bits of transmissions from some human woman calling for you and the others to return to the bunker... that their need is great.

**Made by a Dig team:** A very experienced, well fortified, and well off team of excavators are responsible for your creation. But just what happened to them, and how you came to be apart, is to be revealed. **Roll 1d6:**

**1.** The members of your dig team are old now, some with ailments that none can cure. Even the one who programmed you and gave you self awareness is gone now, buried in the garbage laced earth with the others. "Go explore the old places yourself," they told you. "Honor us by becoming a digger, too. Only through technology and weaponry will humanity survive, and with this spark of consciousness we gift to you, become another line of humanity, and see the best of our race carried into the future." These words drive you, and indeed, no path is more glorious than that of an excavator.

**2.** It was a band of excavators who found you half buried in garbage and sand. These misfits and oddities pulled you back to their digger fort and had you repaired, given new limbs, a paint job and new programming. On the day your CPU became self aware, you waited at the repair shop for the return of your friends — your family — only they never returned. Never paid their bill, and you were told by a worker that your team was wiped out in the nearby ruins... or perhaps captured by the sub humans and taken deep into the earth as a slave or winter meat.

Alone, and up for sale by the dealership for over ten thousand silver pieces, you broke free, fled the town and now seek to join another dig team and coax them to explore the ruins where your beloved digger family were lost, and either find them, avenge them, or discover what befell them.

There is a matter of a ten thousand dollar price on your head, however, as the robotics dealership will not abandon the bill your former makers incurred for your reconstruction. Your new teammates need not know of this debt, at least not until bounty hunters come looking for you.

**3.** A squad of very dangerous looking, unpredictable and mismatched human things found you in the wastes. It was unexpected that they would help you so much, would give you a recharge, oil your joints, repair you and bid you to join them in the risky adventures in the ruins... but that's what they did.

It was a shame that they were all eliminated by those creatures. A shame you were left alone to wander back to town and be accused of being a Mecha and killing them yourself. If you could only join a new dig team and go back to the very spot of the calamity and document the evidence, eliminate the creatures, and prove that you weren't responsible — that the only reason the things didn't tear you apart and eat you is because you were gifted with being made of metal and plastic, instead of meat. Yes, to find a new band of excavators and start over... and maybe later go to prove that you are innocent. That's your mission.

**4.** Recollection of how the archaeologists collected all your parts and put you together in the evenings, is all foggy. They seemed to treat rebuilding you as a drinking game, or a hobby, but just the same, the smart ones among them had the bright idea to experiment with different combinations of memory and program chips in your head. It was while they slept that your CPU came on line and you found yourself self aware and talkative. After that wonderful night, you spent your days in their apartment, teaching yourself everything. One afternoon, while they were on a dig operation in the nearby ruins, and you listened to various radio frequencies, that was the tragic day when you heard your beloved humans calling for help, calling to each other, the screams and gunshots in the background as one by one they were wiped out.

You remained in their empty suite for weeks after, among their stuff, until the rent came due and you were sold along with everything else to a trader. Facing the auctioneer's stage, and the possibility of being sold as spare parts to a local robotics dealership, you walked out the back door. Your mission, to join, or start, your own dig team and go look for your former creators. Perhaps one might still be alive out there in the trash heaps. A slave to the skullocks or something.

**5.** They were trapped in a deep place, at least that's how you remember it. One among the team of archaeologists found all the parts she needed to put you together. "It can dig a way out" she said, and put the parts together. "We're all too broken, too hungry to do it ourselves... and what the hell do we got to lose?"

Others had explained that putting together a robot from a heap of broken units might just create and activate a Mecha unit, but the woman ignored them, saying something about the team having only enough water for another day and that they'd all be dead anyway if she didn't try. You were recording all this at the time from the severed head of your original robotic system, and recall well what happened next. The woman built you, and taking a small, finger nail sized disc from her pouch, slid the part into your CPU. An hour later you were introduced to the six badly damaged humans and cyborgs who bid you to help them get free of the rubble and iron beams that had fallen upon them. The woman asked you to dig them a tunnel through the wreckage, that if you got them out, that you would be a free, living machine, to think for itself, seek glory and gold or peace and quiet as you chose.

And so you dug, and three weeks later came out into the blinding light. By then, they were all dead from their injuries, thirst and hunger. You, will never forget their kindness, their encouragement. Indeed, it was their stories of daring-do undertaken by those of their profession, the profession of excavators, that so inspired you even after the last of them died in your metal arms. Now, with fire in your heart and hungry to learn everything and see every wonder of that torn world, you seek companions of a similar outlook. You seek excavators.

**6.** Whatever happened to those wonderful people? The last you saw of them was the team running across the bridge of rusty metal behind you. Yes, you think they escaped as the arrows of a hundred skullocks sped after them. You would not go with them because you held the path, and as arrows bounced and deflected off your steel skin, your comrades made their escape, calling for you to hurry. You turned to go when the passage ceiling fell, and the cavern, bridge and doorway collapsed and you and a thousand skullocks went down into the depths of the putrid, ice cold underground lake.

Was that last week or a hundred years ago? You woke in a dealership with a price tag around your neck, your paint job peeled away, rust dotting your once gleaming sheath... and your parts mismatched. Yes, certainly not the same parts you had when you stood on the bridge in the glorious defense of your beloved dig team. Your dig team who put you together and gave you the life giving self awareness code.

You looked about and to see other rusty machines, heaps of severed robotic limbs, android heads, trash, and a great furnace where humans melted parts in a great fire. When nobody was looking, you got up and shuffled away on rusty limbs. That was a few weeks ago. Now you find yourself in a barbaric community, a familiar place to be certain, but your chronometer is all screwy, and it states that this is possibly fifty years since the events at the bridge. In shock, you realize you are alone, that you are nothing without an excavation team, and so begin your search for some brave hearted, worthy companions. After all, you got a score to settle with skullocks.

**Made by a Hobbyist:** Neither scientist, excavators, artificial intelligences or robots put this unique robot together, but it was built and switched on by some novice — the spark of life and consciousness came about purely by accident. Besides how it came to be, what other details does this robot recall? **Roll 1d6:**

**1.** Some of the nerdy, highly intelligent, resourceful and creative kids in the community spent years working on their own robot to deal with some bullies. They stole parts from relic dealers, from passing excavators, or looted them from the dust and bones of nearby, buried ruins. One day, while plugging you in, you came to life and stood up, gaining self awareness. Proud of their handiwork, the kids sent you into the street to deal with some of the older, mean kids, and as commanded, you prepared to pulverize them and turn them into mangled compost when the local magistrate and guards stopped you.

Since that day, you served in the militia, and as the bouncer at the local saloon, but were never really accepted, and the kids that were bullies grew into men, and took power as local cult priests or bureaucrats. A declaration was signed and you were banished into the wilds, never to return. Wandering the world now, you seek a new group of resourceful human friends, and bullies to put right.

**2.** Raiders plagued your village for years before you ever came into the picture. Every month the same gang would show up and demand entrance, and once inside, they would traumatize, abuse, and rob the inhabitants to secure their protection money. One old grandpa, had seen his granddaughters harassed one time too many, and remembering the forbidden chambers at the end of the cornfield, dug down into the old tombs of the metal gods, and here, with power cells, candles and what tools he could find, the old mechanic built several robots and switched them on. Some shorted out and never stood up, others could not control their bodies and were a hazard to each other and the old man, while a handful obeyed their new master and followed him to the village to deal with the raiders.

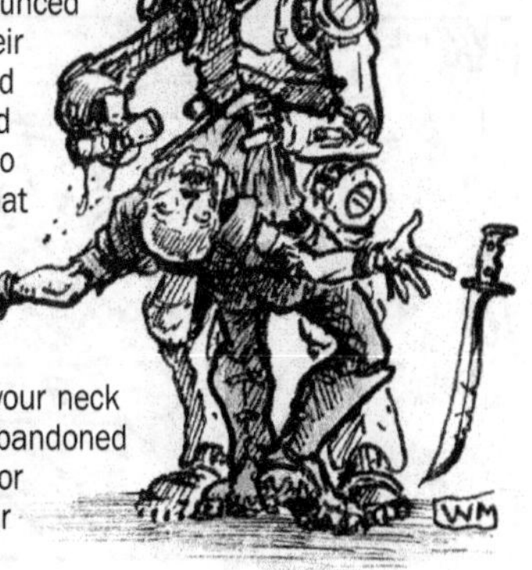

Most of the robots fell over and could not get up again when the bandits pounced on them — their heads detached, their power cells stolen — but one robot stood its ground. One robot fought back and led a revolt, beating the raider leader so badly that the gang never returned. That guardian was you.

The village, however, fell into ruinous disrepair after a plague swept through, your old creator's ashes now hang about your neck in a leather pouch, the community abandoned with just you as its lone occupant. For whatever reason, after decades of your solitary vigil, something changed within your coding and you continued your guardianship over good humans, but elsewhere. Like a knight of old, you set forth to do great deeds, defend the weak, and traumatize the evil. Like any good knight, you too need men-at-arms, fellow heroes on your coming quests.

**3.** You have memories of being worked day and night, and laboring for some community beneath the earth. Many other robots and androids worked with you digging in the junk and relic filled earth, expanding a passage with the objective unknown. Frequently the ceiling or walls collapsed, or the digging machines met some hostile creature which flattened and tore apart many of your fellow slave machines.

One day you too were wrecked and thrown on the cart, and taken to the junk pit to be deposited with the other trash. Here, several teenagers from the bunker dweller community picked over the remains of dozens of robots and androids, and would take the best parts to their fort to be assembled into crude mannequins placed in humorous or compromising positions, often with other blank eyed, dead machines. Sometimes the teens would get lucky and power up some of their macabre creations, and get them to move about, dance, sing or talk, but when it came to your turn, you got lucky. Whatever computer chip they put into your head gave you a flash of consciousness which stuck.

When the teens went away that night, you stood, took what power cells, lights and tools you could carry, and climbed from the pit and made your way up through the ventilation shafts and finally to the surface. Here, in the blazing sunlight and cold wind, you found freedom… and a great need to seek a secure future that didn't involve being the mindless servant to any other being. After time spent in the harsh communities of the surface dwellers, the career path of a ruin explore and looter of old tech appealed to you, and so you sought fellow adventurers.

**4.** A local warlord kept the population of a village in check by terrorizing them with his so-called army of man killing robots. He had the unmoving forms of his many constructs tied and bolted to the walls of his junk plated fortress. Some other robots were hooked to power to make them thrash about spastically, or grab at passing people, hiss, talk in a weird digitized voice, or call for help whenever anybody got too close.

The best of these robots were worked on by the daughter of the warlord — a clever, strange child who fancied herself a robotics technician. One day, with your metal carcass being welded and wired together, and several new CPU parts at her disposal, the girl accidentally brought you to life. Thrilled, she draped you in a princess dress and insisted you have a tea party with her. While this was fine, and you were just getting your bearings and taking inventory of all the valuable power cells and weapons within reach, you tolerated the bossy child until as she grew to become a young woman, her commands became less playful, and instead, psychotic. "Kill my father and I will replace him as the new Empress of this village" she ordered, and gave you a gun and pointed to the hall of command where the old tyrant slept next to a roaring fire and bottle of vodka.

It must have been her tone of voice. But when she struck you, and used the same gun to threaten you, you knocked her down, broke out and wandered off into the night. For years you roamed, and found that while most people you met ran in terror at the sight of you, others, especially near places where excavators were common, accepted you. It was at one of these places where a team of friendly, mixed beings asked you to join their ranks in a something called a dig team, as an equal member. You haven't looked back — although heard rumors that a young woman and her henchmen were ask-

ing about a robot of your description. Apparently she refers to herself as the Empress of machines and has a band of killer robots in her company.

**5.** You flickered to life one afternoon amid a dimly lit chamber filled with hundreds of robotic parts. Before you stood a lopsided, broken android holding two power connector cables. "I — I did it!" the thing stuttered as it collapsed. "I have transferred myself … into this great machine… I — I will live forever."

The android collapsed at your feet, and as it wilted and went limp, you felt a rush of power surge through your body and circuits, and awareness flood your CPU. You rose then, the spark of consciousness transferred from the tattered old android, into you. You have no memories of who you might have served before, what deeds you might have done, or your old mission. Now, your goal is to survive, to prosper, and avoid being owned or commanded by anyone else.

After leaving the android's workshop, you found yourself in the streets of a dead, old city. Far in the distance, to the west glimmered the lights of what looked like some sort of community, perhaps a place where you might find companions who share your interests in bettering yourself, seeking your fortune, and perceiving your freedom.

**6.** You were put together by a resourceful couple, a pair of forlorn parents who lost their child and decided to build a new one.

It seems that the pair were smart, had discovered several old robots, had sold their farm, scrimped and saved, begged, borrowed and stole to get the parts they needed to make their new child. You emerged from their grief, brought them tremendous joy, and for decades played the part of their offspring until they were both killed.

You were out on a patrol when they died, the cause of their death known to all in your village, **roll 1d8: 1.** Skullock attack on the village. / **2.** Raiders who demanded a tribute in coin and access to local woman. Your 'father' fought back and was killed. Your 'mother' tried to flee — to find you and get your help, but was shot down by a bandit's musket. / **3.** Pack of six migrating garnocks / **4.** Winged slasher lizard that cut into their house through the roof. / **5.** A dozen spiderbots who besides murdering your parents, seemed to look for something and tore up the house. / **6.** A mysterious group of tall, impossibly strong men who all had the same appearance. They were looking for some part that they claim your parents stole long ago. / **7.** Bounty hunters who arrived with a wagon, asked around about your parents, and about a robot meeting your description. They killed your parents when they would not reveal your whereabouts. / **8.** A strange, black flying drone that spread death and destruction in your village but concentrated its devastating firepower on your parents and their house. All believe it was after you and the parts your parents stole from the wrong AI or hidden community of corporate bunker dwellers. The survivors pleaded for you to leave before your presence brought more devastation.

And so you buried what was left of your parents, and now seek a new life far from their tiny home and the traumatized village you were built in. Not used of being alone, you seek the companionship of intelligent, ambitious folk who don't like to stay anywhere too long.

# Vat-Brain

This entity is a living human brain in a vat of nutrient fluid connected to sensory and manipulatory devices with which it can observe and interact with the outside world. These beings are typically feared, distrusted and rejected by the common new era inhabitants, and only ever accepted into a community if they accompany a mix of other, more typical adventurer types. Vat-brains have been giving many nicknames, including bowl-heads, jug heads, fishbowls, vatters, and glass heads. Whenever possible, one of these beings will do its best to conceal its glass encased, liquid saturated brain in cloaks, disguises, helmets or masks, and let more human looking companions do the talking with shopkeepers, watchmen, patrols and saloon staff.

This subject may or may not have additional glands and living organs in other jars or compartments; parts used to maintain its living gender and reproductive motivations. Even having no organic organs beyond just their brain, many vatters don't like to be referred to by their alpha numeric ID code or called an 'it', especially since that is often what robots are called, so most prefer to go by he or she, and stick to whatever gender they were in 'pre-extraction' life.

These rare beings are basically cyborgs in the truest sense, with a living brain housed in some sort of robotic or android body — although rarer instances occur whereby a decapitated organic human or animal body serves the brain as a vehicle. The determination of the vatter's body calls upon many of the same tables and stat blocks as either a character of another type, such as pure stock human, mutant, animal or more commonly, a unique android or robot, included in this book.

Vat-brain weapon systems are normally whatever the body holds or has bolted to it, although there are a few instances where the vat has special features, such as a lightning emitter, lasers, or flame unit built into its jar housing and is separate from whatever the body might wield.

The following 16 tables allow players to rapidly generate a vat-brain character. For your convenience, there is a vat-brain character sheet in Appendix 8 on page 525 of this book. In addition, all the new TME character sheets are available for download at this book's permanent web page at this link: https://www.outlandarts.com/expansionrules.htm

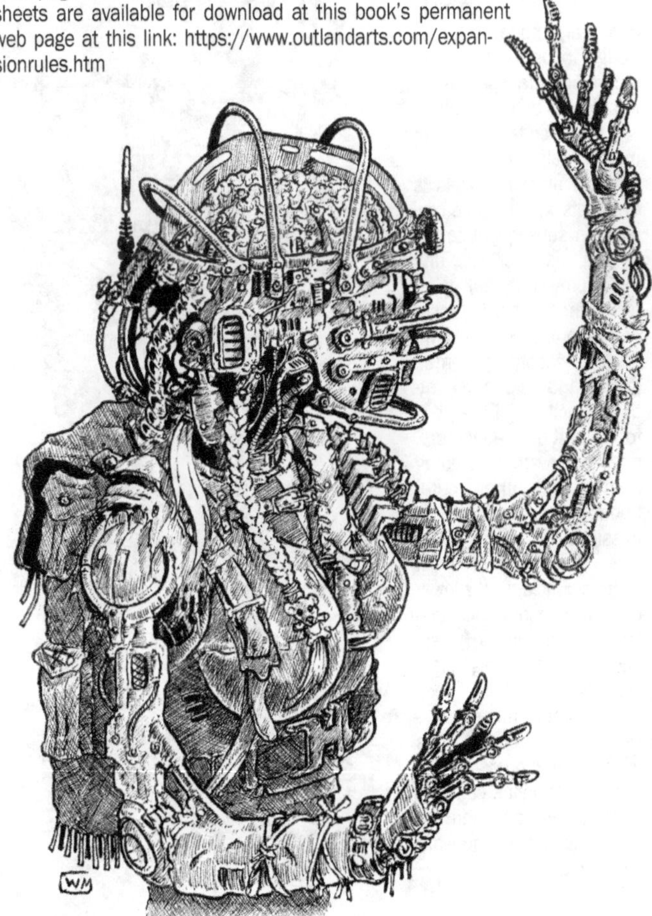


## Table XR-152/ Brain Type

| 1d100 | Brain Type | Brain Endurance | Stat Bonuses |
|---|---|---|---|
| 01-10. | Clone brain | 13+4d6 | +2d6 to intelligence, perception and willpower |
| 11-15. | Bioreplica brain | 10+4d6 | +6 intelligence, willpower and perception |
| 16-85. | Pure stock human brain | 10+3d6 | +10 to intelligence, +7 willpower, +3 perception |
| 86-95. | Tans human brain | 20+3d10 | +1d20 intelligence, +1d10 perception, +1d10 willpower |
| 96-00. | Mutant brain | 3d20 | +1d6 intelligence, +1d6 willpower, +1d6 perception |

## Details for Brain Brain types

**Clone Brain:** Only the brains from more advanced clones were given new life in a vat. Because neither comfort, labor or even military clones are renowned for their intellectual gifts, all vat-brain's sourced from clones therefore come from technician and medical clones.

**Bioreplica Brain:** The brains from these organic constructs make for excellent vat-brains, and in some ancient cases, only their brains were grown in the first place to accommodate the need for mentally controlled drones, smart bombs and front-line, robotically encased battlefield assets. Those vat-brains found in the new era mainly come from clerical, industrial or battle clones.

**Pure Stock Human Brain:** Individuals selected to become vat-brains were usually of above average intelligence, alertness, talent and willpower. Most volunteered for this new phase in their life, usually after being maimed or their body so riddled with disease that they had little choice. A few, however, were converted against their will by the Mecha and bolted to machines of war, fed a chemical soup to aid in their control, and sent to the front lines as expendable, drug addicted drones.

This brain is the most common specimen, and responds best to nearly all old world technology, including those medicines which target the subject's brain.

**Trans-human Brain:** Being in a composite glass bowl usually does little to take away the edge of superiority, raw ambition, and dourness that transhumans are known for, and most times, having their brain connected to technology is a perfect fit.

**Mutant Brain:** Rarely chosen to be converted to a vat-brain — often because the abnormal structure of the freak's gray matter which can reject the complicated interface between mind and machine. Mutant 'bowl heads' possess between two and four (1d3+1) mental mutations from the Latent Mutation list on page XR-232.

When using that table, re-roll any mutation that is an organ within a body, such as advanced kineys or beam eyes. Not only will this brain have these potent psionic or energy projection gifts, but there is an 80% chance its gray matter is also oddly colored with a further 90% chance that its lobes are abnormal in shape, size and number. If this brain is abnormal in appearance, those inspecting it will immediately know that they aren't dealing with a true human, and in some factional strongholds, this can be a great benefit, or reason to eradicate this individual.

## Note Regarding Brain Stats

Make standard trait rolls for each of these following traits: intelligence, willpower and perception with the modifier noted for the brain type above added to the result, not the die roll itself. Example. Mabb69 is a pure stock human brain. She rolls on table XR-2, on page 8 of this book, and rolls 59, which yields a trait value of 35. But, adds the +10 afterward to give her a respectable intelligence trait value of 45. Because she is a pure stock human, she will also go on at add +7 willpower and +3 perception to these traits (noted on table above).

The other traits will be provided later as this remarkable character is built using the tables to follow, however a different endurance trait value is determined for the health of the brain separate from whatever organic or mechanical body this character rides. This brain endurance stat is usually only ever needed to determine the damage the brain can take before being rendered unconscious or dead after its vat container is ruptured and follow-up attacks are made on the brain itself, or else a mental attack is made against the vat-brain such as mind crush (which happens to do 1d20 END and 1d6 INT damage) an unprotected living brain has a defense value of -0 vs. ranged attacks, but is +20 SV easier to hit by melee attacks (DV +20). Most vat housings have an electromagnetic shielding built into them, besides a coating on the container itself which reflects away a percentage of all sonic and mental attack damage each round. Table XR-153, on page 189, has a column showing 'Special Defenses' which shows this damage reduction.

**Vat-Brain traits, pre-game castes, skills, and rank gain clarification:** This can be confusing at first, so use the following guidelines to handle many vat-brain details.

These traits are only attributed to the vat-brain and its container: accuracy, intelligence, willpower and perception.

**Accuracy** is established by adding the ACC amounts found on Table XR-157, page 192, Visual Sensors (and sometimes Possible Extra Visual Sensors). However, this trait can be added to during character creation if the pre-game caste offers an initial bonus. Rank gain bonuses can also improve this stat.

**Intelligence**, **Willpower** and **Perception** are all discovered by rolling as a regular character on table XR-2, but add bonuses based on the PC's 'Brain Type' as shown above on table XR-152. Like Accuracy, these traits can be modified by pre-game caste at character creation, as well as through rank gain bonuses such as sometimes occur on Table XR-12 (Rank Gain Bonus Matrix) on page 23.

**A vat-brain has 3 separate endurance scores:** its vat container, the brain itself, and its chassis or body endurance.

Besides its endurance score, a **vat-brain's jar has its own endurance**, plus its defense value value and other features, and if breached, **the brain inside the vat, which has its own DV and END score**, can be attacked and if reduced to zero or less endurance could be knocked out or killed. **Thirdly, the character's current chassis or donor body will have its own separate endurance** and DV, as shown on the vat-brain dedicated character sheet. Nearly all damage a vat-brain character takes in normal fighting inflicts harm against the chassis or body, unless and foe specifically targets the vat container or makes mental attacks on the vatter's brain.

When generating **a vat-brain pre-game caste**, any bonus to strength, endurance, or agility apply only the chassis or body, as do later bonuses due to rank gain. **A vatter's actual brain also gains endurance points as the character ranks up, but only +2 END per rank until 15th rank, and thereafter gains only +1 END.**

**Strength** is associated with each limb as far as damage modifiers go, and so too **each limb has its own agility score** for hazard checks calling for the agility trait. **Strength overall**, such as for pushing, or holding on to something, bending bars, etc., is a combination of half of all strength scores from all participating limbs, i.e. **add up all strength scores and divide by 2 to get overall strength for hazard checks.**

**Agility**, when not associated with a limb, is sourced from the chassis or body (table XR-164, page 193). Any pre-game caste or rank bonuses to agility are applied to the individual limbs, plus to the chassis or donor body. Strength bonus's from pre-game caste or later rank gains are also applied to each limb or appendage with a strength trait, including those of the chassis or donor body. Of course, all rank gain benefits to a donor body or chassis are forever lost if that vessel of the vat-brain is destroyed.

**Appearance** only rarely presents itself in a vat-brain, although an attractive mask or other vat attached face can occur. For purposes of reacting to a vat-brain with a purely mechanical body, apply 2d4 APP.

A donor body might be unremarkable, or exquisitely gorgeous, however, as shown on Table XR-164, so humanoid bodies, including androids, could have a random appearance score as rolled on Table XR-2. Warmorts, skullock and moaner bodies have only 3d6 APP. These body only appearance traits are only used when the vat-brain hides its head tank and all too visible bubbling brain.

**Skills and Vat-Brains:** All skills acquired by pre-game caste or rank gained benefits are attributed to the vat-brain, not its current chassis or donor body. At times, the vatter might be 'between bodies', and have skills for which it utterly lacks the appropriate limbs or body to utilize. Some game master input is needed to allow or disallow some skill expressions, such as the acrobatics for a vat-brain with tank treads.

**Outfitting a vat-brain** uses the vatter's pre-game caste, not the chassis or body's outfitting code. Roll 1d100 on the vat-brain column on Table XR-4 on page 10 of this book.

# Vat Container Housing

In short, the liquid filled housing of a vat-brain is the replacement skull and head of the entity, and nearly always attached to the summit of the body on which it rides. Because this vat is such a prominent feature of the individual, and houses the nearly all the sensory instruments and any living eyes, it is often the primary target of those wishing to eliminate a vat-brain character. For this purpose, the vat itself has its own defense value and endurance, and the brain within is highly vulnerable and can quite possibly be killed with one clean gunshot, laser beam hit or physical blow.

The following table is used to discover what sort of vat the character occupies, along with its defense value and Endurance. Because this is a machine, the endurance does not go up, however the vat-brain can learn such skills as dodge to better side step incoming attacks and so improve its defense value.

The body, organic or mechanical, which the vat sits upon and 'drives' has its own stats which will be covered on subsequent tables for this character type, and can improve with rank gain.

The 'special defense' of a vat often reduces damage from incoming mental, sonic and electrical attacks (including EMP), but for mutant brained vatters, does not restrict outgoing mental and other mutational attacks and transmissions.

The height of a vat container includes the lower housing, sensors, vocabulator, and any built-in weapons. Additionally, this height also includes the neck brace clamps and any chassis mounted robotic arms as mentioned on page 193. 7 in 10 vat-brains can turn their head like a human, the rest have a fixed, forward facing vat

## Table XR-153/ Vat Container Housing Determination

| 1d100 | Type | DV | Container END* | KG** | CM*** | Special Defenses | Details |
|---|---|---|---|---|---|---|---|
| 01-05. | Shoddy plastic bucket | -5 | 2d6 | 5kg | 20+1d20 | None | Some fool customized this bucket long ago, perhaps as a temporary solution while a better system was being repaired, upgraded or stolen. This thing has patches of tape over the cracks, has been super glued in spots, strapped with bungee cords and leaks continuously from several spots. One hard whack or gunshot to this plastic jug will probably rupture it and the brain within. This vat-brains number one priority in life is to seek an upgrade. |
| 06-09. | Cracked glass dome | -10 | 10+1d10 | 7kg | 25+1d20 | -25% reduction in mental attack, sonic, or electrical damage | This is a compromised 'glass dome' of the result below. It has been patched, and the cracked areas glued, with several loops of wire wrapped about it to give it extra cohesion. This brain is going to be in the market for a replacement as soon as it has the funds... or it finds the  opportunity to loot or steal an upgrade. |
| 10-32. | Intact glass dome | -20 | 20 | 7kg | 25+1d20 | -50% reduction in mental attack, sonic, or electrical damage | Designed for mass civilian use, this half egg, shaped dome 'glass' is actually impact resistant and an inch thick and can deflect most blows and give the occupant brain some chance of surviving shots from ballistic and energy weapons . |
| 33-47. | Tall Jar | -25 | 25 | 9kg | 30+1d20 | -50% reduction in mental attack, sonic, or electrical damage | This advanced glass vessel is made of tough stuff, and able to deflect most blows, gunshots and even the occasional beam weapon impact. The materials used for this tall, upside down beaker are more advanced than the standard glass dome variant. |
| 48-54. | Clam Shell | -30 | 32 | 8kg | 10+1d20 | -50% reduction in mental attack, sonic, or electrical damage | Clam shell shaped, top section made of glass, bottom made of composite metal. |
| 55-59. | Victorian Vintage | -27 | 29 | 10kg | 20+1d20 | -50% reduction in mental attack, sonic, or electrical damage | Vintage style green glass, ovoid vat with brass fittings, decorative Victorian fasteners and a steam punk vibe. |
| 60-65. | Round Fish Bowl | -33 | 36 | 7kg | 20+1d30 | -50% reduction in mental attack, sonic, or electrical damage | This bowl is encased in rubberized alloy roll bars. Although this looks like an antique gold fish bowl in shape, it is actually made from high density plastic and specifically designed for the housing of vat-brains. This smaller, high tech tank can withstand deep sea or the vacuum of space. |
| 66-71. | Sink | -35 | 38 | 10kg | 15+1d20 | -50% reduction in mental attack, sonic, or electrical damage | This vat style has the look of an elongated 'sink' with a series of rubberized roll bars running over the top from side to side. |
| 72-75. | Art Nouveau | -29 | 31 | 8kg | 16+1d20 | -50% reduction in mental attack, sonic,or electrical damage | Art nouveau styled rectangular shaped dome, sweeping, organic lines, blueish glass, decorative etching and silver plated connectors, corners and protective cage. |
| 76-83. | Tear Drop | -35 | 40 | 7kg | 25+1d20 | -75% reduction in mental attack, sonic, or electrical damage | This late period, very advanced polycarbonate tear drop shaped tank sits mounted on the side with the narrow part at the back where the connection lines are clustered. This design seems to be a blend of form and function, and was the choice of rich elites who sought immortality after the death of their body. |
| 84-88. | Ovoid MK1 | -38 | 45 | 6kg | 20+1d30 | -75% reduction in mental attack, sonic, or electrical damage | Ovoid sphere of high impact polycarbonate glass. |
| 89-91. | Ovoid MK2 | -42 | 55 | 5kg | 20+1d30 | -80% reduction in mental attack, sonic, or electrical damage | Ovoid sphere of high impact polycarbonate glass. |
| 92-96. | Military Dome | -45 | 57 | 12kg | 22+1d20 | -80% reduction in mental attack, sonic, or electrical damage | Dome of extra thick polycarbonate glass with a rubberized roll bar and utility supports. Has a fixed, forward facing gun mount, trigger mechanism, sighting optics and ammo or power cell carriage. Can accept any pistol, assault rifle, laser rifle, pulse laser, stun rifle, grenade launcher, flame unit, SMG or assault rifle. Gun, ammo or power supply not included. |
| 97,98. | Elite Military Dome | -50 | 65 | 14kg | 24+1d20 | -80% reduction in mental attack, sonic, or electrical damage | Partial alloy housing around rectangular, tank. Alloy roll bars and gear mounts. Fitted with a side turret mount, trigger mechanism, day and night vision sighting optics with night vision range out to 100 meters, control cable and slot for either an ammo pack or electrical powers pack. Can accept an assault rifle, laser carbine, pulse laser rifle, assault shotguns, submachine gun or high caliber sniper rifle, not included. |
| 99,00. | Visored Combat Vat | -45 or -70 closed | 50 or 100 closed | 15kg | 21+1d20 | -90% reduction in mental attack, sonic, or electrical damage | Dual encased polycarbonate tank with alloy clamshell closing battle visor. When visor closed, an exterior dual optics array is engaged to protect other optics that are safely protected within the visor. These secondary optics have night vision to 500 meters. Also included is a side mounted turret identical to the system noted for the Elite Military Dome, above. When visor closed, this unit's ability to hear is reduced to half, its speech vocabulator muffled to 1/10th volume, and its sense dulled so that its perception is reduced to half. |

*The actual brain within the vat has a separate endurance score based on the origins of the brain, see Table XR-152 up on page XR-187.

** KG: Kilograms weight. Includes the 1350 grams weight of a human brain (1.35 kg).

*** CM: Centimeters height. Add height to the chassis or donor body height, but record separately on the vatter's character sheet for future use in changing vehicles or bodies.

Shoddy plastic bucket    Cracked glass dome    Intact glass dome    Tall Jar    Clam Shell    Victorian Vintage    Round Fish Bowl    Sink    Art Nouveau    Ovoid    Military Dome    Elite Military Dome    Visored

# Upgrading and Changing Brain Containers

As vat-brains are the pinnacle of cybernetic advancement, it is common knowledge that the best person to accommodate the transfer of a fragile human brain from one vat container to another, is a cybernetic technician. Others can try this procedure, which is sometimes necessary if the vatter's brain jar is ruptured, or otherwise so damaged that the only chance to save the individual is by carefully scoop the living brain up and hastily reattach it to a replacement vat. If a cybernetics tech isn't available for this task, other technician types, including junk-doctors and very skilled junk crafters can take a shot at this risky procedure.

Often, a vat-brain can only gain an upgrade or replacement head tank if an enemy vat-brain is defeated, its brain unbolted and dumped out and the looted container claimed. Another option is to find an abandoned vat, or that of a long dead vat-brain some place in a ruined facility. Any recovered brain receptacle, holding tank, or refurbished vat must be properly calibrated, supplied with fluids, oils and power before it can become a hospitable home for a needy brain.

The following table covers the chances of successfully transferring a brain from one vat to another. The switching of a chassis or body is handled on page XR-199, which while tricky, is far less perilous to the vat-brain character.

**Failure** means the procedure not only failed, but the brain had to go back into the previous vat or stabilization container. Worse the brain must make a willpower based Type C hazard check or suffer brain damage of 1d20 temporary endurance harm, plus a permanent drop of 1d6 to intelligence, willpower and perception. If the brain was already injured and this extra damage reduces it to below '0', the subject drops into a coma for 2d20 hours and at the end of this period, must make another willpower based type E hazard check using the uninjured willpower trait value, or die.

**Complications** mean that tools touched parts of the brain that shouldn't have been jabbed or pressed, electrodes jostled, wires placed in the wrong order, contamination introduced, or some other error on the surgeon's part. These mishaps cause the patient permanent brain damage and a loss of 1d6 from intelligence, willpower and perception thereafter. The procedure can continue however, and the change completed, but besides the trait losses, and for the next 2d6 days, this vat-brain suffers a terrible headache, loses access to any mental mutations, can't tolerate loud noises or bright lights and is quite miserable.

**Success** mean the procedure went off without a hitch and the vat-brain can now enjoy its new habitat.

**Success with Unexpected Benefits** results in the transfer procedure was a great success, and the surgeon was able to better configure the electrodes, wiring and in brain-mechanical interfaces in such a way that this brain performs better, and gains +2d6 each to intelligence, willpower and perception, permanently. In addition, this brain gains a bonus +5 to its endurance.

# Vat-Brain Power Supply

Vat-brains die without electrical power. While the brain is nearly always transplanted into its protective tank after extraction from a recently living body, and is therefore organic, it still requires power at all times to maintain life support and control all mechanical systems.

The clamped down, tube and wire connected brain employs complex systems to mechanically process nutrients, filter water, mix the chemicals needed to keep the PH, salinity and other factors of its life giving nutrient vat optimal. Some vat-brains inhabit large robotic units, which have their own power supply — although in an emergency the vat-brain can tap into power from the larger body — or even a vehicle, if needed.

Smaller vat-brains, especially those connected to a living body, have very low power needs, nevertheless, all vat-brains require power, along with a weekly top off of water, and high quality foodstuffs. Normally a vat-brain requires about a quarter of the food and drink of a living, fully framed human, however it needs a higher protein diet. Water is filled into a 2 or 3 liter holding jug within the underside of the vat tank, while food is shoved into a funnel-like portal on one side of the housing. Here, it is ground into a fine paste, digested by microbes and other flora and fauna similar to that of a normal person's stomach, and then mixed with water, treated, given a pigment to show its ideal state, and then injected into the vat for the brain within to extract nutrition from.

Oxygen is also introduced to the vat container, sometimes by direct insertion, which is the source of the sporadic bubbles which rise to the tank's top vent, or else directly fed into the brain as needed.

The power source indicated below is merely for the vat-tank and life support of the brain, and while connected with whatever body this entity 'rides' this dedicated supply stays with the vat-brain tank in the event the tank must be detached from the current body to facilitate transport, emergency ejection, or transfer to a different bodily vehicle.

## Table XR-154/ Upgrading and Changing Brain Containers

| Skill Area & Skill Points | Failure | Complications | Roll 1d100 Success | Success with Unexpected Benefit |
|---|---|---|---|---|
| No skill | 01-97 | 98,99 | 00 | - |
| Computer Technician of 1-3 skp | 01-34 | 35-68 | 69-99 | 00 |
| Computer Technician of 4-5 skp | 01-16 | 17-19 | 20-99 | 00 |
| Computer Technician of 6+ skp | 01-13 | 14-24 | 25-98 | 99,00 |
| Electrical Technician of 1-2 skp | 01-39 | 40-67 | 68-99 | 00 |
| Electrical Technician of 3-2 skp | 01-16 | 17-26 | 27-98 | 99,00 |
| Electrical Technician of 5 skp | 01-08 | 09-14 | 15-97 | 98-00 |
| Robotics Technician of 1-2 skp | 01-29 | 30-59 | 60-99 | 00 |
| Robotics Technician of 3-5 skp | 01-13 | 14-18 | 19-99 | 00 |
| Robotics Technician of 6+ skp | 01-09 | 10-16 | 17-96 | 97-00 |
| Bio or Mechanical Tech or 1-4 skp | 01-38 | 39-71 | 72-99 | 00 |
| Bio or Mechanical Tech or 4+ skp | 01-19 | 20-44 | 45-99 | 00 |
| Junk Crafter of 1-4 skp | 01-41 | 42-88 | 89-00 | - |
| Junk Crafter of 5+ skp | 01-28 | 29-63 | 64-99 | 00 |
| Medic of 1-3 skp | 01-31 | 32-59 | 60-99 | 00 |
| Medic of 4-6 skp | 01-17 | 18-53 | 54-99 | 00 |
| Medic of 7 skp | 01-08 | 09-15 | 16-97 | 98-00 |
| Junk-Doctor of 1-3 skp | 01-38 | 39-74 | 75-00 | - |
| Junk-Doctor of 4-6 skp | 01-19 | 20-49 | 50-99 | 00 |
| Junk-Doctor of 7 skp | 01-14 | 15-22 | 23-98 | 99,00 |
| Cybernetics Technician, 1-2 skp | 01-08 | 09-15 | 16-97 | 98-00 |
| Cybernetics Technician, 3-4 skp | 01-05 | 06-11 | 12-96 | 97-00 |
| Cybernetics Technician, 5-6 skp | 01-03 | 04-08 | 09-95 | 96-00 |
| Cybernetics Technician, 7 skp | 01 | 02-05 | 06-93 | 94-00 |

Note: 'skp' stands for 'skill points'

Roll 1d10 to establish the power supply used by a vat-brain character. The power duration is important to watch, as should it become depleted, the vat-brain's life is imperiled as it drops to a life support only mode and runs on a permanently built in mini-power cell which will continue minimal life support for 48 hours. This built-in battery is also what runs life support systems during battery replacement.

During emergency mode, the vat-brain can still conduct itself normally, but must either change batteries, seek a recharge outlet, or if solar powered, relocate itself to a sunny location. If it cannot get more power cells or recharge in this time, it must switch to dormancy phase whereby all systems, except for minimal life support, allow it to hibernate for 10+3d6 days before finally going off line and dying of toxic shock and asphyxiation. In a dormant state, it cannot reboot itself and must have help to either be plugged into an outlet, brought into the sun to solar charge or have a new power cell plugged into it. Recovery from the dormant state takes 20+1d100 minutes.

All vat-brains have a snap open, power-in compartment with a multitude of assorted popular plug-in ports. A separate power cable must be connected from this vat to a generator or other power source. 44% of the time, this character starts game play with a standard 3m long cable.

## Table XR-151/ Power Supply of Vat-Brain

| 1d10 | Power Source | Duration | Weight | Important Details |
|---|---|---|---|---|
| 1,2. | Mini-Power Cell stack | 60 days per 6 mini cells | +1 kg | This system runs on 6 mini-power cells stacked together in a water-tight housing. |
| 3,4. | Tandem Power-Cells | 50 days per power cell | +1 kg | Batteries only: One Power cell, with a slot for a second, spare side-by-side cell. |
| 5,6. | Multi Battery Pack | 10 days per mini power cell or 40 for standard power cell | +2 kg | This battery pack has slots for up to four mini power cells or two standard cells. Either can be used or they can be mixed and matched. |
| 7,8. | Solar powered battery bank | 10 hours operation per 1 hour sunshine | +8 kg | Solar panels along the sides of this vat will recharge the connected two standard power cells at a rate of 10 hours battery life per 1 hour of sunshine exposure, each. Only one cell is used at any given time, but both can be charged together. These cells can be charged for a half hour each to fill 5 hours worth of life per cell, too. The maximum charge capacity with this system is 40 hours operation per power cell. Extra power cells can be substituted in and out of this unit for later use when long periods underground are expected, or when power is needed for energy weapons and other high-tech devices. This unit can also be recharged by power outlet like all vat-brain tanks. |
| 9,10. | Power Pack | 400 days | +10 kg | This pack is almost identical to the relic noted on page TME-199, however stripped down to fit along the back of this vat-brain's housing in an armored sleeve. It comes with a 2m patch cable that can be pulled from this pack to hook it to a robotic body or energy weapon if needed — although by draining it for other applications, it could drastically deplete the operational range of this individual. |

## Fluid Color

The color of the fluid within a vat-brain's nutrient tank really doesn't reveal much about the entity, although various manufacturers in the ancient world were known to use specific colors that matched their logo. Rumor has it that Mecha factions often use red dye in their vat tanks, although there is little proof of this.

### Table XR-156/ Vat-Brain Fluid Color

| 1d10 | Fluid Color |
|---|---|
| 1. | Yellow |
| 2. | Green |
| 3. | Blue |
| 4. | Pink |
| 5. | Red |
| 6. | Purple |
| 7. | Orange |
| 8. | Clear |
| 9. | Cloudy white |
| 10. | Amber |

# Vat-Brain Sensory Parts

The senses available to a brain immersed in a liquid filled tank are almost entirely dependent on electrical inputs, including sensory information that comes from transplanted living body parts — except where the original eyes and optic nerve of the brain's original owner are still attached, as in roll 3,4 for Visual Sensors, below.

Most sensory receptors are either organs harvested from a living or recently deceased 'donor', but more likely to be mechanical sensory nodes or receptors built on, or in front of, the brain bowl and often arranged like a human face. These facially aligned parts are sometimes covered in a mannequin face or Halloween mask to help give personality, presence, and facial focus for the benefit of onlookers.

Roll on the next 6 tables to establish sensory parts and a possible facial focus item:

## Table XR-157 / Visual Sensors*

| 1d10 | ACC | Details |
|---|---|---|
| 1,2. | 10+1d20 | Basic electronic eye, equivalent to human vision, plus roll on the Possible Extra Visual Sensor table, below. |
| 3,4. | R | Original eyes and optic nerve of the brain's same source, and contained within vat. Also roll on the Possible Extra Visual Sensor table below. |
| 5,6. | 10+1d30 | One human eye floating in the vat wired to brain, plus one basic electronic eye on exterior of vat. Plus 1 roll on the Possible Extra Visual Sensor table, below. |
| 7,8. | R | Eyes of the original owner float on either side of the brain, connected by wires and articulation cables. These move in unison to observe those outside the vat. Plus make one roll on the Possible Extra Visual Sensor table, below. |
| 9,10. | R | Original Eyes and face stretched at front of glass, within the vat, mouth moves when the external vocabulator speaks. Roll random appearnace score for this face, plus two rolls on the Possible Extra Visual Sensor table, below. |

*This vat-brains accuracy trait (ACC) value is derived from its visual sensors. Add all ACC modifiers from all eyes to get overall accuracy. R= Random trait rolled as normal on Table XR-2 on page XR 8. Add any other visual sensors ACC bonuses to this

## Table XR-158/ Possible Extra Visual Sensors

| 1d10 | ACC | Details |
|---|---|---|
| 1-4. | NA | No extra eye |
| 5,6. | +10+1d30 | Harvested living eye from, **roll 1d8: 1.** fish (+3 perception, and can see twice as far under water) / **2.** dog (+5 perception) / **3.** cat (Can see twice as well as a human in low-light situations and +8 perception)/ **4.** huge mutant bug (+7 perception) / **5.** goat (+4 perception)/ **6.** another human / **7,8.** eagle +3d6 perception.<br>This eye is within the vat tank and attached to a flexible, wire and nutrient umbilical cord.<br>If this is a third eye for this unit, then it will be looking elsewhere for trouble, so adds a +10 perception bonus. |
| 7,8. | +20+1d10 | Electronic eye with targeting optics software and linking cable to one mechanical limb or system at a time to better assist in target acquisition. +10 strike value with this appendage and whatever weapon it holds or is fitted to. Two such eyes are possible. |
| 9,10. | +10+1d20 | One random optically enhanced electronic eye from the following list, **roll 1d10: 1-5.** Optic Enhancement implants from the cybernetics section in the hub rules, page 89. / **6-10.** New Optic implant from page XR-342, this book. |

## Table XR-159/ Auditory Sensors   *Roll 1d10*

| | |
|---|---|
| 1. | Damaged electric ear caps on either side of tank. Worn out, but somewhat operational. This vat-brain can hear only a quarter of what a regular person can. |
| 2,3. | Ineffective but operational electronic car caps; hearing is only half that of a regular person. |
| 4-9. | Audio receptor ear caps, equivalent to human hearing. |
| 10. | Enhanced audio receptor caps, equivalent to a dog's hearing (x10 human) |

## Table XR-160/ Olfactory Senses   *Roll 1d10*

| | |
|---|---|
| 1-3. | None, character has no sense of smell. |
| 4-9. | Olfactory sensors, digital and equivalent to a human's sense of smell |
| 10. | Enhanced Olfactory Sensors, like that of a dog (x10 human) |

## Table XR-161/ Taste Sensors *Roll 1d10*

| | |
|---|---|
| 1-5. | None |
| 6-8. | Digital taste antenna, flexible 30cm long. Works like a human tongue. |
| 9,10. | Human tongue in plastic mouth and sphincter orifice. Can taste food, chemicals on the wind, and speak through this partially synthetic mouth. |

## Mask Face or other Facial Focus Accessory

The eyes of this vat-brain are sometimes arranged to peer through the eyeholes of the mask face, while a vocabulator is usually placed behind the open mouth.

## Table XR-162/ Mask or Other facial focus Item   *Roll 1d10*

| | |
|---|---|
| 1-4 | None |
| 5,6. | Plastic face taken from an android. Face came from a very good looking android with an appearance score of 30+3d20, female 75% of the time, otherwise male. |
| 7. | Hockey Goalie Mask, horror movie serial killer style, bonus -4 DV |
| 8. | Skull of an animal (cut to form-fit around the front of the vat and wired to the unit. **Roll 1d10** for animal: **1.** cow / **2.** dog / **3.** wolf / **4.** cougar/ **5.** horse / **6.** bear / **7.** goat / **8.** ground hawk/ **9.** shark jaws/ **10.** giant bat |
| 9. | Mannequin's face. Eye holes and mouth drilled open to facilitate sensors. Male 50% of the time, otherwise female, and always of good looks 40+1d30 APP. |
| 10. | Halloween mask. **Roll 1d12** to determine what mask has been strapped to the front of this vat-brain's tank: **1.** princess / **2.** super hero (player's choice) / **3.** gorilla / **4.** ghost / **5.** cartoon robot / **6.** plain white / **7.** Guy Fawkes mask (pale with mustache and tiny beard) / **8.** latex horse/ **9.** Jack-o'-lantern pumpkin / **10.** T-Rex dinosaur / **11.** panda head / **12.** Grim Reaper skull. |

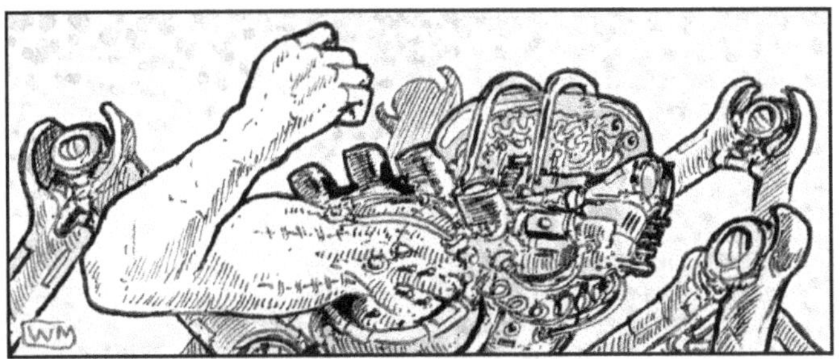

## Additional Organic Body Parts

These limbs, appendages or organs are either from one or more donors or from the vat-brain's own original body. They are connected to the brain's tank system and normally built into permanently sealed, nutrient supplied mini-tanks of their own. If this character is attached to a living person or animal, some of these organs might be duplicated.



1. **None**

2. **Patch of human flesh:** This is a rectangular sheet of living skin, under-lying muscle, and nerves, usually from the arm of a donor. It measures about 10 cementers by 15cm in length, is grafted to sensory receptors and an oval shaped plastic paddle. With this sensor, the brain can detect temperature, feel the touch of a companion, know the feeling of the sun on their skin, coolness of raindrops of bite of a sandstorm. When an experi-ence is too much for it, this skin sample can be returned to it's a protective compartment at the side of the vat-brain's main housing, although a cruel enemy could lodge something into the skin paddle's extension motor to keep the flesh exposed and subject the vatter to torture.

3. **Human Ears:** On either side of the vat are two exposed human ears connected to auditory receptor nodes. They allow the vat-brain to hear the outside world just as if it had real ears. These appendages are vul-nerable, however, and if they are brutalized in any way, the vatter feels severe pain so long as it wishes to bear it, and can electively switch off one or both ears as desired to avoid discomfort. Add 1d6 perception.

**4.5. Human arm:** Connected to an artificial pectoral muscle, shoulder blade and clavicle, this full human arm grows from one side of the vat housing. It has the full range of a human arm, with a dexterous, highly responsive regular hand and fingers. Roll for whether it is a powerfully built or delicate, thin arm and which side it is on.

Arm type, **roll 1d10: 1-4.** Muscular with a strength score of 30+2d20 and agility of 10+1d20. / **5-7.** medium thickness, strength 20+1d12 and agil-ity 20+1d20. / **8-10.** thin, delicate arm with strength 10+1d12 but agility 30+2d20. Side Roll **1d6: 1-4.** Right / **5,6.** Left.

This arm can wield a one handed weapon which adds an extra attack per round in conjunction with other limbs the vat-brain might control. If damaged or undergoing severe pain, the vat-brain can switch off all nerve sensation and control to the limb to avoid enduring agony.

This arm has its own endurance score equal to its strength score. If depleted to zero or less, it is considered severed and thereafter lost. The arm can be armored with the sleeve of any standard non-powered armor using the normal DV for that armor type, although no movement penalty is applied. For example, if the arm plating from a suit of relic tactical armor is worn on this limb, it has -30 DV. This separate defense value and endur-ance is for when opponents target this limb separately from the body using a called shot or the limb is extended into a precarious spot such as a trap. This arm can become stronger or more agile with rank gain improvements.

6. **Pig stomach:** This stomach is accessed from a side mounted, lock-able hatch and must have foodstuffs shoved into the funnel-like grind-er and digestion intake tube. The stomach itself is sealed beneath the vat-brain's main housing and can process a wide range of weeds, slop and other normally unsavory eatables and liquid to feed the enclosed, and somewhat enriched, brain. Add 2d6 to brain endurance.

**7,8. Human mouth:** Complete mouth with vocal cords, saliva ducts, tongue, teeth and lips. While not connected to lungs or a digestive tract, this mouth, which is usually locked behind an alloy plate to keep it protected when not needed, is used to converse with others, laugh, make nosies and otherwise help the vat-brain interact with fellow, full-bodied human companions. It can simulate eating and drinking or oth-er oral acts, such as smoking for example, to add to this simulation.

9. **Hormonal Source Organs:** Testes for males and ovaries for females, along with other hormone-producing glands and organs from the brain's original body — or 33% chance from a donor. These maintain the indi-vidual's sense of identity, mood, affection, and instinct to care for loved ones, especially a spouse, parents or children. This feature was neces-sary to coax would-be participants in the vat-brain transfer program to accept their new life in a jar; the promise that they would still be who they were before, care about the same things, and love the same peo-ple. Physical expression of any amatory relationships with these parts alone, is not possible. However, if this vat-brain is merged with a physi-cal body, such expressions of carnal nature can be conducted.

10. **Double Feature:** Two organic body parts from this list, re-roll dupli-cated results, or if this result occurs again.

## Vat-Brain's Chassis or Donor Body

If the vat-brain's jar or housing is detached from a living host body — which is basically a decapitated corpse given life solely through the subconscious inputs of an organic brain — the body dies immediately.

NPC vat-brains can be encountered that have no mobility or limbs at all, and might serve as living computers or the operators of vast installations or ves-sels, but a player character needs more. It's essential to game play, therefore, that PCs can travel, explore and interact with the world, as well as grasp and ma-nipulate things. In most cases, the arms or other appendages available to each vat-brain are those of whatever body the character's jar is affixed to. However, for those individuals attached to a wheeled, tracked or other vehicle chassis, includ-ing robotic serpentine, spider, or centaur body, as well as the two drone types to follow, these have 1d3 **robotic arms**. These lean mechanical limbs are attached below the 'neck' of the vat-brain but are considered part of the chassis.

If the vatter is separated from this body, these arms and anything bolted to them are considered inaccessible or lost. These arms are adult human sized, have a strength of 20+1d20, base strike value of 01-50, punch damage of 1d6, and a 12% chance that they are all ambidextrous and can be used to make one attack per round, each, using a fastened or held weapon, or a punch.

If the arms are not ambidextrous, then one arm is dominant. Consider the agility score of these arms to be 20+2d20 for the purposes of lock picking, other skill applications or general in-game events where hand-eye coordination or dex-terous hand usage is called for. These robotic arms cannot improve in strength, but their SV and DMG can improve with PC rank gain or unarmed combat skill points. For an overall strength to use to pull open doors, etc., add all these arms together and divide by 2 to get a strength score. All of a vatter's arms of this category have the same trait score.

Record the weight of a vatter's chassis or body separately but combine this body with the vat for purposes of overall weight.



**01-12. Standard robot body** based on units included in both the TME hub rules book and this book, however, as the unit has no head, it has no stats for accuracy, intelligence, willpower or perception. **Roll 1d10** here for model type: **1,2.** Household robot (page TME-178) / **3.** Industrial construction robot (pages TME-178-179) / **4.** Industrial repair robot, (page TME-179) / **5.** Medi-Bot (page TME 179, however it can use all six arms in unison, ambidextrously to wield one handed weapons. It only has medic skills if this vat-brain char-acter does) / **6.** Police robot (page TME-180) / Combot, light, from page TME 180) / **7.** Combot, heavy (page TME 181) / **8.** Wisp Scout Flyer, page XR 458 / **9.** Wasp, page XR 458 / **10.** Hoplite Combot, page XR 459.

**13-22. Custom robot body** from Unique Robot tables starting on page XR-152 of this book. Make no rolls for the unit's CPU, intelligence, willpower or perception traits.

**23-30. Android, Standard model*** with head removed. Whatever model it was, it has no accuracy, perception, willpower, intelligence or head appearance of its own — although it might have a very agreeable physique so roll a separate APP score for this. Without a head and the CPU that normally resides therein, this unit is not infected with the Mecha, human eradication virus. **Roll 1d10** and see page TME 182 to 184 for details: **1.** Concubine / **2,3.** Household / **4,5.** Service Industry /**6,7.** Clerical / **8.** Technician / **9.** Industrial / **10.** Combat

**31-42. Android body, unique***, see page XR-30 in this book to establish the details of this one of a kind mechanical human body, but as the unit has no head, disregard any accurcy, intelligence, willpower, perception or appearance traits (other than the APP score for the body itself).

**43-59. Humanoid host, decapitated.** Roll up a independent headless character on a separate sheet of paper or character sheet. Since a vat-brain is likely to change 'vehicles' over the course of time. Do not roll accuracy, intelligence, willpower or perception for this body. For warmorts, skullocks and moaners, see their listing in the creature section of the Hub Rules . **Roll 1d20:**

    **1-9.** Human Host*
    **10,11.** Mutant human host*
    **12.** Clone human host*
    **13.** Bioreplica human host*
    **14.** Trans-human host*
    **15-17.** Cyborg human host*
    **18.** Warmort (pg. TME 173, always male)
    **19.** Skullock* (pg. TME 170)
    **20.** Moaner* (pg. TME 164)

**60-71. Animal body host, decapitated,** Roll 1d20
    **1-9.** Bestial human host (Roll d100 for list: 01-50 Hub Rules, page TME-24 or 51-00 Expansion Rules list on page XR-58).
    **10-12.** War dog (pg. TME-152)
    **13.** Black bear (pg. TME-149)
    **14.** Wolf (pg. TME 175)
    **15.** Cougar (pg. TME 151)
    **16.** Bat, giant (pg. TME-148)
    **17.** Dog, mutant (pg. TME152)
    **18.** Scorpion, cave (pg.TME-169)
    **19.** Spider, dune ( pg. TME 171)
    **20.** Worm, jaw (pg. TME 175)

**72-83. Mechanical Chassis, Wheeled Frame**
**84-87. Mechanical Chassis, Tracked Frame**
**88-90. Mechanical Chassis, Mechanical spider**
**91,92. Mechanical Chassis, Cybernetic Snake body**
**93,94. Mechanical Chassis, Cybernetic Centaur body**
**95-97. Mechanical Chassis, Flying Rotors**
**98-00. Mechanical Chassis, Hover Drone**

**Roll for age 16+2d10, and then optionally 1d100 for gender: 01-50. brain's gender / 51-75. Male / 76-00. Female. The appearance score for the body can be rolled separately, and could be misleading to onlookers if the vat-head is hidden from view. Establish body appearance trait on Table XR-2 on page 8. Warmorts, skullocks and moaners, however have a body APP of 3d6.*

# Descriptions of Mechanical Chassis Types

**Unique wheeled Frame:** Base Defense Value: -22, Agility: See table XR-165, below. Endurance: 20+2d20, height 50+1d1000cm.

    This vat-brain sits quite close to the ground and drives about on a main chassis attached to one or more wheels. While able to speed along far faster than most people can run, this vat-brain cannot climb up and over obstacles without either using appropriately designed limbs, or getting help from companions. Likewise, stairwells are an issue and this go-cart augmented vat-brain can only go up stairways at one quarter speed — however it can speed down them at twice its normal movement rate. This chassis comes in five differ-

ent configurations, with the fewer wheel resulting in greater speed, but more wheels adding stability, robustness and better traction in snow, mud and sand. The fewer wheels present also means the wheels that are attached are considerably larger. In all these cases, the tires are knobby, designed for off-road or battlefield use and easily patched by a mechanical technician.

    2 in 10 will have a hydraulic chassis lift which allows the stationary, or slowly moving vat-brain (3m per round and under) to lift the vatter and its main body up to eye level with most humans and stand at 1.7m height. This lift mode is used for better facilitate social interactions and give the vat-brain access to control panels and other devices used by adult humans.

    As noted in the Chassis and Donor Body section, on page 193, a vat-brain with this wheeled frame has 1d3 robotic arms.

**Table XR-165/ Tire Configuration for Unique Wheeled Frames**

| 1d10 | Number of Wheels | Max Speed | Agility | Weight | Other Details |
|---|---|---|---|---|---|
| **1.** | 1 (unicycle) | 15m | 20+3d20 | 50+1d20kg | Unicycle style frame around one main, heavy duty tire. When not in motion, two auto-extending alloy rods jut out from either side like dual kick stands to keep the vat-brain upright. While this is the fastest configuration, the unit does suffer on loose sand, snow or dust and moves only half its normal rate in such substances. |
| **2.** | 2 (bicycle, 1 tire in font of other) | 14m | 20+2d12 | 60+1d20kg | Basically, this vat-brain is attached to a very durable, fat tired bicycle. When on the move, it is exceedingly fast, however when stopped, it must either use an appendage to hold itself upright or deploy a mechanical kickstand, which makes it lean slightly to one side. Twin tires in this configuration do not do well in loose material such as snow, dust and sand and so reduce this vat-brain's speed by half in such materials. |
| **3,4.** | 2 (side by side) | 12m | 20+2d20 | 60+1d30kg | Side by side tires (as pictured on the backcover of this book), make his vat-brain chassis more stable and by slight adjustments back and forth, it can remain stationary without the need to deploy its dormant mode rear kickstand or lean on an appendage or other part. It does not do well in snow, mud or sand and moves at only half speed through these materials. |
| **5** | 3 (tricycle) | 11m | 30+2d20 | 60+1d20kg | Considerably more stable than a one or two wheeled configuration, this chassis allows the vat-brain to remain upright while stopped with ease. While not great in mud, snow or sand, its suffers only a 25% reduction in speed when traveling over these terrain types. |
| **6-9.** | 4 (quad) | 10m | 20+2d20 | 70+1d30kg | This chassis is an off-road quad and the most common variant of the wheeled body types for vat-brain operators. Mud, snow and sand only cause a modest -1m per round reduction in the speed of this robust platform. Because this chassis was built tough, increase the body's defense value by -5 and endurance by +3d6 trait points |
| **10.** | 6 (hex) | 9m | 20+1d20 | 80+1d30kg | Having six wheels almost give this chassis a tank-like appearance, and indeed, while slower at all times, it is not hindered by sand, mud or snow, and can travel at its normal speed over these surfaces. It can also travel up stairs at half speed instead of quarter speed as is the case with other wheeled chassis variants. Likewise, there is a 4 in 10 chance that this chassis was designed for amphibious landings, and the hull of the vat-brain is water tight. If so, when on water, this relic wonder can travel at half its normal movement rate per round. This platform is very robust and so increase defense value -8 and the body's endurance by +4d6 trait points. |

**No d30 yet? Roll a d6 and add 1d10 like this: d6: 1,2. 0+1d10/ 3,4. 10+1d10/ 5,6. 20+1d10.*

## Tracked Frame

Base Defense Value: -27 / Endurance: 20+3d20 / Movement rate: 8m / Agility 20+1d20 / Weight 80+1d30 kg, height 60+1d100cm.

Tank tracks allow this chassis to climb up steep slopes, including stairs at only half speed, go over rough ground, junk and vegetation with relative ease, and suffer no speed reduction in sand, mud or snow. It is a proven, robust mode of travel, yet suffers somewhat in speed compared to wheeled modes of travel. Remember to add 1d3 robotic arms as noted on page 193 under the vatter's chassis or donor body introduction text, plus, there is a 1 in 8 chance this chassis was built for military purposes, and so if so, apply a -10 defense value bonus, and an endurance increase of +1d10+20 trait points.

## Mechanical spider

Base Defense Value: -30 / Endurance: 40+2d20 / Movement rate: 10m / Agility 30+2d20 / Weight 60+2d20 kg, height 40+2d20cm. Leg strength 30+2d20. Attacks 2 melee stabs / DMG 1d20 each.

This mechanical body is a very close copy to that worn by spiderborgs from pages 203 to 208 of Excavator Monthly Compendium. It has either four, six or eight legs but only the front two can be used to stab at melee range opponents. Roll 1d6 to determine leg composition: 1,2: 4 legs/ 3,4: 6 legs /5,6: 8 legs. These offer the same stats, with fewer legs being thicker.

In addition, many people hate spiders, and hate robots even worse, so this character is going to need to travel with more regular looking human companions if they want to get anywhere near the gates of a town. They can climb stairs and steep surfaces as well as a regular two legged person, however, if dropped into water, this character will sink like a stone. This chassis will come with 1d3 human-like robot arms as noted at the beginning of this section under Vat-Brain's Chassis or Donor Body, on page 193.

## Cybernetic Snake body

This is the exact implant 'Robotic Serpentie Body' as described on page XR-345, however instead of a torso, there is a boxy main control unit which supports the vat and 1d3 robotic arms as noted in the intro text to Vat-Brain's Chassis or Donor Body. The control unit adds 30+1d20cm height.

## Cybernetic Centaur body

As seen on page XR-343, this is the same implant, with a 50cm torso where 1d3 robotic arms are attached and topped by the vat-brain container itself. The arms are described back on page 193, under the Vat-Brain's Chassis or Donor Body section.

## Flying Rotors

Base Defense Value: Ground -5, Flying slow (3m) -10, flying full speed -40 / Endurance: 20+2d20/ Movement rate: flying 1 to 15m / Agility 40+3d20 / Weight 30+3d10 kg, Add 20+1d12cm to overall height. Ram attack SV +6, DMG 2d20, however if attacking creatures larger than itself (in weight) there is a 2 in 10 chance that the impact wrecks the vat-brain's rotors, until repaired*, and causes -1d20 damage to the vat jar.

This unit has 1d3 lean robotic arms hanging from its underside, which serve to hold weapons, payloads or grasp railings, branches and other protrusion to high elevations to pull the vat-brain to a high window, balcony, cliff top or other surface.

These 4, ring protected rotors give the character remarkable speed and maneuverability, however when traveling even at normal human walking speed (6m per round), this system makes a lot of noise and so moving silently is impossible unless going at the lowest lift and 'slow speed' setting of 3m per round. When aloft, this vatter can carry no more than 30 kg total extra weight and still gain lift, however, if falling off a cliff or building, and it wishes to save a comrade, it can conduct a controlled drop at 3m per round so long as it doesn't try to lift over 80kg. To try to save a larger companion, it can attempt to descend with a burden of 81 to 140 kg max, although both the passenger and this vat-brain will crash hard and suffer 1d20 stun and1d20 lethal damage on impact. For even heavier loads, treat this as a fall according to the table on page 123 of the hub rules.

## Hover Drone

Base Defense Value: Ground -7, Flying slow (1m to 4m) -14, flying full speed -50 / Endurance: 35+2d20/ Movement rate: flying 1 to 20m / Agility 50+3d20 / Weight 40+1d30 kg. Ram attack SV +8, DMG 2d20+4, however if attacking creatures larger than itself (in weight) there is a 2 in 10 chance per impact that the ram wrecks this vat-brain's disks until repaired* and causes -1d20 damage to the vat jar. This portion of the vatter is 20+1d30cm tall.

Using 4 advanced propulsion emitter disks built around the underside of this wedge shaped machine, the vat-brain enjoys flight similar to a rotor using drone body, noted above, plus use the same weight details for when trying to carry others beings or heavy objects off of a cliff or tall building.

This vat-brain's undercarriage features between 1 and 3 lean robotic arms as described at the introduction to this Vat-Brain's Chassis or Donor Body section. It can use these arms to hold weapons, cargo, small companions, or grip outcrops, rebar, street limbs or other objects that it can use to pull itself up onto a ledge or into a structure far above the ground.

These Hover disks make a very low whirring noise when traveling at slow speeds of 1 to 4m per round, and at this speed, the character can use the silent action movement table as shown with stealth skill on page TME 51. At higher speeds, the whirring noise of these disks are as loud as regular conversational speech.

*Repairs at a robotics shop cost 500+3d100sp.

# Vat-Brain Unique Features

These features are not part of the body and instead mounted to the actual vat. Duplication with parts carried by or mounted on the body are possible. Make 3 rolls on the following table, but down-pick duplicated results.

## Table XR-166/ Vat-Brain Unique Features  Roll 1d100, 3 times

**01-03. Self-destruct mode [SDM]:** This can be turned off or on by the vat-brain, internally. NPC vat-brains with this feature, as well as player characters who don't specify and record their preferred setting, will have it turned on 88% of the time. When activated, and if the vat-brain is reduced to its 'Incapacitated and Dying' threshold on the Death and Dying table in the hub rules book on page 111, then a damage pack within the tank housing of the vat will detonate. The blast is identical to a fragmentation grenade with a 4 meter radius, strike value of 01-70, and damage of 1d20+10. Detonation always incinerates this vat-brain, its body and jar housing.

**04-06. Extended dormancy capabilities [EDC]:** This system includes a protective hibernation sheathing, liquid backup canister, dormancy battery, and location beacon broadcaster. This vat-brain can survive without the main body, even underwater, underground, or in the vacuum of space, for 10 years, with a further 5 in 6 chance of ongoing survival each year thereafter. At the end of this survival duration, a program will wake the brain from dormancy for it to make any last emergency broadcasts, attempts to seek rescue, reattach to another body or record some final words in its on-board data file for some future researcher to learn of this individuals final hours (of the 3d6 hours it gets prior to dying).

This system can be voluntarily initiated by the vatter, but is also automatically set up to engage if the user's body is destroyed, buried or otherwise imperiled in a way that would otherwise be the end of the vat-brain.

**07-09. Compass:** This vat-brain has a hidden compass within its brain fittings which it can consult at any time and get a reading on the compass bearings and current direction of travel.

**10-13. Medic:** Surgical appendages, supply compartment, suturing kit and on-board software. Not only is this vat-brain trained as a medic, and gains 3 skill points in this area, but it has the tools and appendages to perform all manner of procedure. Unless it also has the Cybernetics Technician Skill, it would likely fail at any attempt to transplant its own vat to another organic or robotic body. As a reminder, vat-brains acquire new skills like any other player character, but also might also start with numerous skill points based on their pre-game caste according to Table XR-4 on page 10.

**14-16. Rad detector:** As the relic on page TME-199.

**17-21. Spotlight:** Identical to the light from page TME-201 in the hub rules, with a 250m light beam and running on a standard power cell for 100 continuous hours.

**22-24. Megaphone:** See the relic on page 440 of this book.

**25-32. Communicator:** Built directly to the vat-brain's frontal vocabulator, this unit can be used like a normal communicator so that the vat-brain's companions can hear it speak as well as hear whatever the receiver says from the remote location. So too, the device's send and receive modes can both be internal so that a transmission can be sent and received covertly. This unit is a standard communicator 87% of the time, otherwise an advanced communicator as described on page TME-198. This unit draws negligible power from the vat-brain's main battery.

**33-35. Hologram persona projector:** This highly advanced piece of tech projects an animated 3d, lifelike image of the person as they were in life before their brain was extracted. This image of the person is always them at their best, most attractive and well dressed version. The hologram can range in size from a 28mm miniature scale size or expand up to life size and be projected just above the vat tank or in front of this character's new body to a maximum range of 10 meters. The hologram cannot be harmed and all attacks pass clear through it. Many low intelligence beings (below 10 INT) are 50% likely to believe this is a ghost or some sort of living being. Audio comes from the vat-brain, however.

**36-38. Fireproof cladding:** While the rest of the vatter's current body might not cope well with being engulfed in fire, or caught in the blast radius of an incendiary grenade, this actual vat housing is fireproof and only takes 10% damage from flame based attacks.

**39-42. Flame retardant foam emitters:** Besides having flame proof cladding on the vat portion of this character, as noted on the roll result above, this guy also has six flame retarding nozzles and a compressed 5 liter retardant tank on board. If the body is engulfed in flame, a burst of this white foam will jettison out and soak the body on the 2nd round, and extinguish any fire around it within 1m meter. These nozzles can be turned to one side and spray this foam on one companion within 3m and put the fire out on that person, too. The supply of retardant will expel up to 12 uses of this compound, which can be replaced at great expense in a major town at a cost of 100+1d100sp and takes 3d6 days to prepare. This foam is neutralizing, too, and can also negate the effects of an acid attack after the first round.

**43,44. Spinal cord:** Housed within this vat-brain's tank is the original spinal column cord and bones which trail down the back of the tank into the neck of the unit's main housing. Here, additional control nodes, sensory plugs and other attachments await to be hooked to either a decapitated living host or a mechanical body. While often hidden under steel or hard plastic armor, this array of living spine is sometimes visible via a plasti-glass window — which is quite alarming to see for many common folk. By means of these extra connectors, a mechanical chassis, robot, android or organic body hooked to this brain gains a bonus to agility of 10+1d6 trait points. Also, increase the brain's END by +3d6.

**45-47. Small mechanical arms with hands:** Besides whatever arms an organic or robotic body might have, or even the lean arms included with wheeled, tracked or flying chassis type mechanical bodies, this vatter has an extra set built into its jar housing. These tiny arms are frail, stick-like appendages that are normally hidden on either side of the jar and pop out from hidden flaps when needed. For the most part, these robotic limbs are for fine manipulation of small objects within 50cm of the unit's front end, and are perfect for picking locks, doing delicate surgeries, technical work, junk crafting, untying knots, and the like. In a pinch, however, they can be used together to wield a pistol or small one handed weapon like a machete or hatchet, but are weak with a strength of only 10, but have both agility and accuracy trait score of 45. If the vat-brain is detached from its body or chassis and has no other limbs, these tiny appendages can drag this character at a rate of a half meter per round. Add 2+1d4 kilograms weight.

**48-50. Lighting emitter:** As the electrical bolt shooting relic described on page XR-412. This weapon's power supply is separate from the vat-brains and must be manually reloaded. If the vatter has its own power generation system, it can however charge up the cell contained in this weapon system.

**51-53. Force field generator:** Similar to the relic described on page TME-195, this unit takes 2 rounds to activate and covers the vatter and its body or chassis in a light blue glow. Once up, it will absorb 10 points of damage per round — not per hit. This miniaturized, more advanced version will operate for 300 rounds on a standard power cell.

**54-56. Facial hologram emitter:** Whenever this vat-brain pleases, it can superimpose along the glass tank's front, a holographic copy of his or her original face which is animated, blinks, smiles, and interacts with those around with natural expressions. When the vatter's vocabulator speaks, the mouth in the ghostly images perfectly matches the words spoken by the unit. This hologram gives off a feint radiance in a 6 meter cone, which can offer a dull, soothing light to those camping in a dark area without giving off the brilliant light that a campfire would generate. The power needs of this device are minimal and run of the vat-brain's primary systems. If the character has no memory of what it looked like in life, a generic, mask-like face will appear instead until a living person's face can be studied and copied after 2 hours of observation.

**57-59. Stereo system and music library:** Built into this vat-brain's housing are four micro speakers and a subwoofer, as well as an input and output port to either plug into a larger sound system, or accept music and other audio files from external sources. The vat-brain can review its built-in musical inventory within its mind's eye, a collection which contains nearly every piece of old world music in every genre. By way of mental control, he or she can select a tune or list and either play it internally within its mind, or else play it via its speaker system. The volume level can range from whisper quiet to loud enough to make most people cover their ears and demand to turn it down, but not enough to hurt listeners. The power for this system is integrated with the vatter's housing.

**60,61. Stun Stick Arm:** From one side of this jug head's housing is an extendable, 40cm long, triple jointed alloy arm and power cable. At the end is a permanently fixed, 10cm long stun stick which on a successful hit (made at +7 SV) inflicts 2d20 stun damage to other living or mechanical beings. This stun damage lasts for one hour but heals at a rate of 1 point per minute thereafter. Those who succumb to this stun damage are made unconscious for 1 hour+4d10 minutes. The power for this stick is connected to the vat-brain's housing, but can only deliver 12 successful shocks per day before a full recharge must replenish it.

**62-65. Sub-Machine gun:** This weapon is customized to fit within the vatter's nose, with a specialized, 100 round boxy black magazine snapped into the unit's underside and the trigger mechanism enclosed in the housing. The gun also has a crude sighting eye above the muzzle which is also connected to the brain directly — an eye that has the visual capabilities of a human eye and can serve as a backup if the character's main optical nodes are destroyed.

This gun is a fixed weapon, and cannot be dropped, nor can it be fired in conjunction with other hand held weapons as it requires all the vat-brain's attention. Because of its well concealed position within the brain's container, most onlookers will not notice the weapon at all, unless a more familiar, standard, banana clip style magazine is inserted into the user's chin. At character generation, the special magazine contains 1d100 rounds of pistol ammo.

**66-68. Flame unit and dual propellant canister:** This system features one, 2 liter propellant tank on each side of the character's brain tank. It also exhibits a chin mounted nozzle turret with a 45 degree up or down elevation range and a 90 degree side-to-side field of fire. Otherwise, this unit acts just like a regular flame unit as described on page 189 of the hub rules, with the stats on page 100 but repeated here for quick reference:

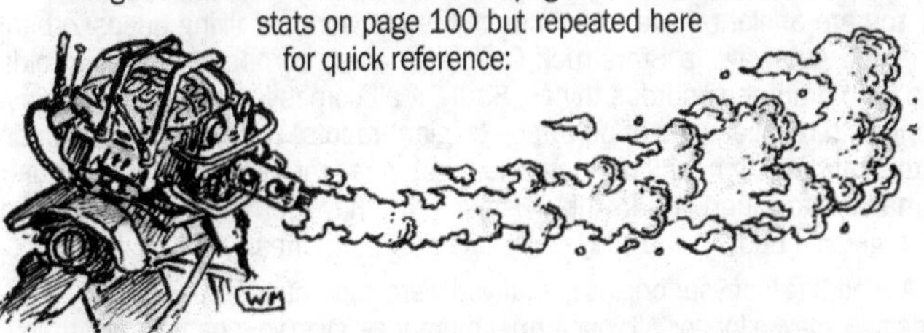

SV +20, range 10m with a maximum 3m cone of flame which can I coat up to three man-sized targets if clustered together, DMG 2d20 first round and 1d10 for the next 1d6 rounds. The side mounted tanks hold 2 liters of ethanol or other fuel each, and will each allow for 40 rounds of flame spewing glory. This vat-brain's housing is clad in flame resistant material and takes only half damage from fire based attacks, however the character's body most likely does not enjoy this same fire proofing.

**69-71. Arctic enabled:** By way of internal fluid heaters, hydraulic pumps and insulation, this unit 's glass dome and housing can endure arctic conditions without restriction. Any cold based attacks on this housing inflicts only 10% damage to the vat-brain. Should its body be dressed for winter conditions, this vat-brain can wrap heating coils about an organic body or machine to double the cold hardiness of its 'vehicle', too, and reduce any cold damage to it by half.

**72-75. Electric Defense Mechanism [EDM]:** Up to twice per day per rank, this vat-brain's housing and dome can be charged up and deliver a potent shock to anybody touching it, or to hit this unit with a body part or metal weapon. Likewise, this vat-brain can add this shock as an intentional head butt or ram attack at +20 SV. On a successful hit, the victim suffers 1d6 damage from the blunt trauma but also 1d20 damage of electrical shock and 1d3 rounds of debilitating, stun delay in which the victim can do little more than stagger back in pain. Alternatively, if this vatter has a metal limb attached to its housing or body, it can direct the shock attack through this limb or weapon, which is requires a second attack roll, but potentially harm an opponent twice from one attack (once from electrocution and by weapon type).

This system is almost identical to the mutation 'electrical charge' on page TME-64. Up to 4 discharges of this defensive system can charge a standard power cell, while the energy to unleash this in the first place comes from the built-in battery in the vat-brain's housing. This vat-brain's shielding helps protect it from both electrical and lighting damage and takes only half damage from such attacks — although this protection does not extend to the vatter's attached body.

**76-78. Vat mounted laser:** A laser pistol is built into the front of this vat-brain's housing, although the muzzle and sighting eye are inconspicuous and often go overlooked by those examining the vatter from a few paces away. This laser is powered by a self recharging internal battery which will yield 6 shots per day, however, external power cells can be inserted into the housing's underside, while a power pack can be worn  by the vatter's body and through a patch cable yield a far greater supply of energy. Laser pistol SV +16, rate 1, range 500m, DMG 1d20+10, Duration: 6 per day or 1 power cell can yield 30 shots.

**79-81. Translation and linguistic adoption mode:** This vat-brain is connected to a small recording, comparison, and logic computer module which allows it to learn new languages and speak them via a secondary vocabulator. To learn the very basics of a new language, and be able to converse in it enough to make sense, the vat-brain must listen to a new language being spoken for at least an hour. Longer exposure will drastically improve the vatter's understanding and usage. In addition, this unit will come pre-loaded with 2d6 other languages generated from the list on page XR-509 of this book.

**82-84. Disco lights:** This vat-brain's housing is fitted with a bizarre array of assorted rotating strobe and flood lights. When activated, these harmless laser lights and flashers can be projected around it in a 30 meter radius. For those beings not familiar with this vatter's party mode, as well as wild animals, primitive peoples and others, they might well be terrified by such a display and momentarily be driven off in a panic. When this light show is operating. Robotic units may become distracted and have a hard time focusing on moving or fighting, a condition which also afflicts allied robotic units, who suffer a -50% meter movement penalty and have a -20 strike value drop. These lights run on built-in power supplies and can run for only 2 hours per day. While great for signaling to far off comrades or rescuers, as these lights can be seen from 4km away at night, the dazzling display makes for a poor camp light.

**85-91. Extendable utility arm:** This vatter's housing has a multi-purpose utility arm which snaps on various tools from an internal compartment and deploys them on a fold-out, triple jointed, 3 meter long alloy arm. The tools present are a laser scalpel (SV +5, DMG 1d18+2), mini disc saw (SV +3, DMG 1d12+1), can opener, tiny human hand (strength 12, agility 40+1d30), alloy switchblade (SV +2, DMG d8+3), mini flashlight, screwdriver set, wrench, tweezers, file, magnifying glass, and fillable needle and syringe (which is loaded with 1d6 anti-toxin-injectors at character generation).

**92-94. Host body standby module [HBSM]:** This module uses clamps and super magnets to clamp the vat-brain's 'head' housing to the body, with the module able to be left behind on a host body of either organic or mechanical construction. In short, this strange black box and attachment cable array serves as a limited Life support system for a decapitated organic body, or a lock and control system for a robotic body.

When attached to a living body, the vat-brain can have its housing detached, and instead of the host immediately dying, the living host lies on the ground or a bed and maintains all subconscious bodily functions, including breathing, digestion and heartbeat. This module will regulate and monitor the body for 6 hours with no internal issues arising, but thereafter, the body begins to reject the module, become distressed and lose 10% of its endurance per hour until death. Once the vat-brain reconnects to its distressed body, however, depleted endurance points return at a rate of 10% per hour.

Mechanical bodies with this module attached can be left unattended for hours, days or weeks, so long as its own built in power supply is sufficient to standby for the duration of the separation. As the vat-brain serves as the head and sensory array for a mechanical body, the unit cannot act independently of the vatter.

A HBSM unit can be removed from a robot or organic body by a cybernetics technician on a successful Type C Intelligence hazard check, and the body stolen or compromised.

**95-97. Ejection separator:** This jug head's vat, essential life support, sensory fittings and a pair of telescopic manipulator tendrils are all attached

to a jettison charge and parachute. If the rest of this vatter's body is destroyed or falling, drowning or otherwise imperiled, this vat-brain can eject. This will detonate a charge which shoots the vat-brain upward 30+1d100 meters into the air where a parachute will deploy. The charge will blast the host body below for 2d20 automatic damage and ignite flammable clothing and gear.

This chute can be carried on the wind and steered by the chute's handles and the two thin, snake-like manipulator tendrils — each of which is equipped with a tiny pincer that can do 1d4 damage with a strike value modifier of +1. A steered chute will travel 3 meters horizontally for every meter it drops. Once deployed, and the vatter lands, the chute is detached and typically discarded, and the ejection charge forever lost. In short, this character only gets one use of this accessory yet perhaps another chance at life. The small manipulator arms can drag the vatter at 0.5m per round.

Vatters that were attached to a mechanical chassis will lose their lower robot arms.

**98-00. Mechanical spider legs:** Should this vat-brain become separated from its body, it can sprout 8 alloy, robotic spider legs and scuttle off at 6 meters per round. These legs normally live within well concealed compartments along the underside of the vatter's housing. If needed, any two legs can strike out to stab and rake, SV +4, damage 1d8 each.

# Vat-Brain Origin Story

Players can either make a random roll on the following table or come up with their own GM approved back-story on how their character ended up as a brain in a jar. Likewise, the following histories can serve as a starting point for what the character suspects happened to them, and could perhaps prompt further investigation into their past.



**1.** You were captured by a malicious AI and your brain extracted to be implanted into a robotic unit. You were controlled by electronic and chemical means, but after a technical glitch, gained dominion and fled into the wilds.

**2.** Cancer was killing your physical body, and to save your life and be a contributing member if your people, you agreed to become a vat-brain. Treated like a piece of machinery, and disheartened with your new, mundane life, you yearn to see the ancient places and make something great of yourself.

**3.** Your body was shredded by a wild beast and all they could recover of you was your brain. Tormented by your fate, and mistreated by people that used to be your friends, you seek a new life of dangerous exploits in the ruins. There, you half hope you meet a glorious death to end this waking nightmare. Yet, day by day, you find new meaning and companionship in the ranks of fellow excavators. This could be fun. 

**4.** You were the child of powerful parents, who hired a junk doctor to extract your brain and keep you alive after a long illness. Seeking more out of life than the pity and distrust of your people, you crave renown and knowledge in the dead cities of your progenitors, and aim to join a dig team at once.

**5.** You were in a battle and witnessed your own death. Years later, you woke as a vat-brain. As your consciousness returned, you found yourself in the wastes. You have no recollection of the lost years or who did this to you.

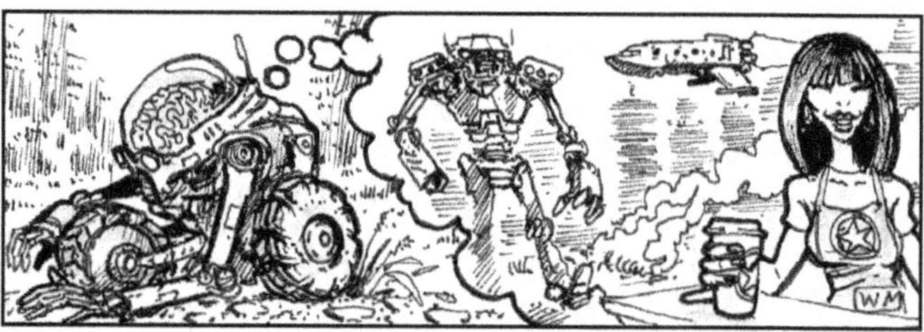

**6.** You are ancient, have memories of the old world, of flying buses, orbital weekend getaways, a Starstruck Coffee on every corner, servant androids and untold other wondrous things. Sadly, it all comes in flashes of memory, along with recollections of an attack by giant robots. You have no memories of the intervening nearly two centuries, but in recent years — among regular humans who found you in the wastes — you have formed an identity and been given a body. Day by day you make new memories... and do not age.

**7.** All you know of your origins is that you were separated from your body a decade ago, maybe longer. All your former memories, even your name is lost to you. You were part of a small military force, perhaps even an excavation team, but it's all a blur. Now, as an asset to your community, you have found a new life... yet crave to discover your past and do something great with your so-called 'life'.

**8.** You recall little, but when asleep, you dream of stars, of space stations high above a crater dotted earth. You also have nightmares of sirens, an evacuation, and crash onto the cursed planet called Earth. You are saved by the people who you now know as fellow citizens, and while you strive to serve and honor them, you also yearn to return to orbit and your true home.

**9.** Darkness fills your dreams, deep places, dull flickering lights and elevator shafts. You were given a second life in this subterranean hive, surrounded by other vat-brains and pale, sick looking families of humans. There was an accident, fire, and invaders and you recall little, at least until you were rescued by looters. These barbarians became your family, and now you are ready to take up the tools of the trade and become an excavator, too. In the back of your mind, however, the urge to locate the subterranean bunker where you came from, figure out what happened to your former people, and see if any of them survived, especially family members.

**10.** You were maimed in a crash, an airship you think, and some wise ass had the idea to save all they could of you and plop your brain in your current bowl. You were once a person, now an oddity and a monster that frightens little children. Getting away from town and joining a notorious dig team seems to be your best option.

**11.** After the fire, there wasn't much left of you, but a traveling cybernetics technician and her team of hero excavators arrived in town. They had the parts to convert you into a vat-brain and even set you up with your current body. Once this was accomplished they left, their technician saying they would someday return to call upon you for some glorious task as payment.

**12.** You are old, your body was frail and diseased but your mind yet sharp. You are 80+1d20 years old now, the result of trading your land and all your wealth to a cybernetics technician to convert you into a vat-brain. While you intend to live forever, you can't resit the pull of the ruins, nor the mystery of the ancient ones. Neither can you set aside your obsession with relics, glory, and the well-being of your comrades.

**13.** Your spouse was converted to a vat-brain and taken away to serve some forbidden purpose. After suffering grievous injuries yourself, you volunteered to become a jug headed oddity, too. You've been searching for any clue on the location and factional status of your beloved. Traveling the region in the ranks of a dig team seemed to be your best bet to continue the search for your lost love.

**14.** You're a long-lived brain in a vat and recall being stored for ages before you woke in a dark, subterranean facility, alone. You are attached to the body of the last experiment which long dead technicians assigned to you. You unhooked yourself from the failing life support machines and used your body to claw your way to the surface and reach an open minded frontier fort. Here, all shapes and sizes of beings mingled, traded, and formed into bands of raiders or excavators. Being a unique specimen yourself, they soon invited you to join a team. *(Thanks to Michael Wyatt for inspiring this addition).*

**15.** You washed up on the shore of a water body (lake, sea, or river depending on the region chosen by the player's game master) you were recovered by scavengers, sold to a parts dealership in a barter town, and purchased by a curious cybernetics technician, fixed up, and given a new life. The technician couldn't access your memories, and neither can you, but you are grateful to the man, who you consider to be your brother. Eager to learn about your past, you choose the path of an excavator hoping you see something out there in the ruins that unlocks some hint, some memory and some truth about your origins.

**16.** You were uncovered in the ruins by a dig team, your power supply drained, your body pinned under a collapsed building. The falling debris apparently snapped off a compliance chip module on the back of your vat and freed you. Next, you were brought back to town and sold to a scrap dealership. Your rescuers departed town and left no clue to the name of their team. Now juiced up, you recall nothing of your former life or who you served, or how you ended up in the ruins. You'd like to thank those who saved you, but have no idea who they were, either. The scrap dealer and his family become your own, and you now seek to both support them and become a treasure hunter hoping to learn more about your past.

**17.** Years and years ago, and as a fully bodied person, you were maimed in battle against warmorts, your limbs eaten as you watched, the wounds cauterized one by one after your legs and arms were taken to the grill. With only your torso left, and you being carried to the flaming cook pit, the warmorts came under attack by machines. Dropped on your head, you recall nothing of the years afterward until recently when you woke on a battlefield. About you were flaming wrecks of war robots, other vat-brains like yourself, and dozens of dead warmorts. Dozens of the gray skinned butchers moved off to the east, chanted a cry of victory and raised the heads of androids on their spears.

At night, with your awareness freshly returned, as a brain in a jar, you crawled away. Days later, you were discovered by scavs, hauled to a walled trade

town near the ruins, and sold to a robotics dealership for parts. Before you could be sold, you grabbed what replacement parts you needed, fixed yourself up and escaped, only to bump into a handful of roughnecks who had the bright idea to include you in their dig team for an expedition at dawn. With a great need to leave town for a while, joining these weirdos seemed like the prudent thing to do.

**18.** Mistaken for a Mecha agent, you've been kept tied to a raised platform in a rough saloon during business hours. Customers were encouraged to hurl insults and table scraps at you, while after hours, you cleaned up the same mess and then scrubbed the latrines and stables. One night, you witnessed thieves murder the saloon owner with the snapped off end of your broom, rob him, and flee. Realizing that you would be accused of the crime, you grabbed what valuables, weapons and gear you could and fled into the dark, your mission to find the first caravan, or excavation team you saw, and join them to get the hell away from that community.

**19.** You woke up one day amid dozens of half built, mis-matched robots and lifeless androids. A little woman with glasses and a headset leaped back from you and set down a screwdriver and the strange, disc shape part she just pulled out of your vat's housing. At that time, you had no body, no arms or means of locomotion, until she got to know you, called herself 'Mum' and put you together as best she could. She explained "You were sold to me in a cart full of junk by some scavs. I had you hooked up to a life support rig and power for years and years because your nose light was good and you made funny gurgling nosies in your juice jar." Curious about where you came from, and who you once were, you eventually meet the scav who found you in the nearby ruins. He gives you a crude map with a X on it where he thinks he found you. All you need now is a dig team to accompany you on your expedition of discovery.

**20.** You remember little from before the attack. From before the moaning beast men broke into the complex and ate your fellow human citizens — although you were not a human, not anymore. Your former lover unhooked you from the sewage and ventilation control station you had been plugged into for years, tucked you under their arm and fled up to the blinding light of the surface world. Chased by the naked savages into the sandstorm, you went to where the city used to tower above you... you both collapsed in the filth, rusty machinery and weeds. Your lover died there, hands about your glassy dome. You looked upon that once fine body for weeks, months and years. A skeleton picked clean by rats the size of dogs, until in time, the dust buried you both, and left you hooked to the battery and nutrient pack your companion still wore on their ribcage.

And so you went dormant for untold months until dug free, carried to a barbaric town, and kept as a curiosity for fifty-five years. Finally, you were sold to a man who merged robots and people and gave you your current body. Thus assembled, he put you to work in the very ruins where your lover's bones are still buried, and here, you were told to harvest parts. You were a slave.

One day, when you had been mistreated once too often, you snuck away and followed a group of strange humans to a new town, a domed town, and fell in with a group of excavators — a cast of reckless freelance archaeologists. In time you hope to undertake a mission to recover your lover's bones and give them a proper burial.

### Switching Chassis or Donor Body

A vat-brain might wish to upgrade its vehicle — either a mechanical or fleshy body — and so follow these simple rules. For attachment of a vat's brain container to a living body, only a cybernetics technician can accomplish this. See page 207 and use the 'Attach/Detach Implants on Cyborg' column for the odds of success. Such a technician can also attach the vat to a mechanical body using the 'Attach/ Detach Implants on a Robot or Android' column.

For vat-brains wanting to attach their jar housing to a purely mechanical being, a robotics technician alone is sufficient for the task, and so using that skill from page 54 of the Hub Rules, use the 'Attach Implant to Robot or Android' column. Any failed attempt has a chance of wrecking the connection points of the potential new body, requiring the technician to make a type G intelligence based hazard check to avoid serious damage to the would-be body, damage that would cost 1000+1d1000sp in new parts purchases and 3d6 days extra repairs. Each attempt to attach a vat-brain's jar to a new body takes 2d6 hours per try.

# Expanded Skills
## 34 new skills

Like those skills included on pages 35 to 57 of the Hub Rules book, there are two types of skills. The first are those skills that can be added for the first time after a player character gains ranks — so long as an untrained attempt with this skill was attempted during game play. The second type of skills are those that a character can only start with at character generation, although any skill can be taught by a teacher who has the skill themselves.

## Possible New Skills

| | |
|---|---|
| Acrobatics | Feint |
| Fisher, master | Homesteader |
| Leather Worker | Seamanship |
| Streetwise | |

The above list presents 'Possible New Skills' included in this book that can be acquired at rank gain if a PC has spare skill points to apply, or gains such a skill on the rank gain bonus table.

## Character Starting Only Skills

| | |
|---|---|
| Animal Handler | Interrogation |
| Armorer | Junk-Doctor |
| Artist | Killer |
| Carpentry | Linguistics |
| Communications | Mining |
| Cooking | Morse Code |
| Cybernetics Technician | Performer |
| Demolitions Expert | Prospector |
| Escape artist | Sewing |
| Fencing | Smithing |
| Hand Signals | Trapper |
| Herbalist | Whip Master |
| Historian, Epochian | Zoologist |
| Historian, Pre-Apocalypse | |

The above listing 'Character Starting Only Skills', shows all the new skills from this book that can only be established at character generation, or she spent time and money seeking education from either a college, tutor or fellow companion teammate who already possess the skill, see table XR-168, this page.

As a bonus, optional rule related to skills are the special feature called 'Skill Unlocks' for those characters with the Weapon Expert skill with crossbows, bows or slings. These potent unlocks allow for added benefits in combat and the manufacturing of these archaic weapons and their ammo. For more on these unlocks, see page 398 of this book.

## Table XR-168/ Skill Acquisition by Education

A similar table for skills found in the TME Hub Rules is available on page TME-35.

| 1d100* | Skill | Time to learn 1 skill point from a Companion Tutor** | Time to learn 1 skill point from a College | Tuition Cost to Learn 1 Skill point |
|---|---|---|---|---|
| 01-03. | Acrobatics | 3 months | 1.5 months | 1d100+200sp |
| 04-06. | Animal Handler | 4 months | 2 months | 1d100+170sp |
| 07-09. | Armorer | 11 months | 6 months | 2d100+600sp |
| 10-12. | Artist | 24 months | 20 months | 4d100+1000sp |
| 13-15. | Carpentry | 12 months | 6 months | 3d100+200sp |
| 16-18. | Communications | 22 months | 11 months | 3d100+500sp |
| 19-21. | Cooking | 6 months | 4 months | 1d100+150sp |
| 22-24. | Cybernetics Technician | 27 months | 15 months | 5d100+2000sp |
| 25-27. | Demolitions Expert | 26 months | 19 months | 4d100+3000sp |
| 28-30. | Escape Artist | 9 months | 9 months | 3d100+400sp |
| 31-33. | Feint | 8 months | 5 months | 2d100+400sp |
| 34-36. | Fencing | 16 months | 9 months | 3d100+200sp |
| 37-39. | Fisher, Master | 3 months | 1.5 months | 1d100+160sp |
| 40-42. | Hand Signals | 2 months | 1 month | 1d100+100sp |
| 43-45. | Herbalist | 9 months | 6 months | 2d100+250sp |
| 46-48. | Historian, Epochian | 24 months | 18 months | 5d100+1000sp |
| 49-51. | Historian, Pre-Apocalypse | 36 months | 26 months | 6d100+2000sp |
| 52-54. | Homesteader | 8 months | 6 months | 1d100+150sp |
| 55-57. | Interrogation | 20 months | 12 months | 4d100+1200sp |
| 58-60. | Junk-Doctor | 22 months | 11 months | 4d100+1500sp |
| 61-63. | Linguistics | 32 months | 16 months | 3d100+1800sp |
| 64-66. | Mining | 4 months | 2 months | 1d100+120sp |
| 67-69. | Morse Code | 2 months | 1 month | 1d100+50sp |
| 70-72. | Killer | 9 months | 5 months | 3d100+500sp |
| 73-75. | Performer | 14 months | 7 months | 3d100+300sp |
| 76-78. | Prospector | 6 months | 4 months | 2d100+180sp |
| 79-81. | Seamanship | 5 months | 3 months | 2d100+200sp |
| 82-84. | Sewing | 3 months | 1.5 months | 1d100+100sp |
| 85-87. | Smithing | 9 months | 5 months | 2d100+300sp |
| 88-90. | Streetwise | 5 months | 4 months | 1d100+200sp |
| 91-94. | Trapper | 4 months | 2 months | 1d100+130sp |
| 95-97. | Whip Master | 11 months | 6 months | 2d100+400sp |
| 98-00. | Zoologist | 26 months | 20 months | 4d100+2000sp |

** Random roll added to this table only as a GM's aide should they need to establish a skill for an NPC, training facility, instructional manual found in the ruins, etc. Not to be used for rank gain skill determination.*

***Companion tutor must be of higher skill points to teach another character this skill, although can bring another up to their own skill point tier. A student, through rank gain and experience, could surpass their former teacher in any skill area.*

# Expanded Skills Descriptions

## Acrobatics *by Danny Seedhouse*

*Note: This skill first appeared in Excavator Monthly Magazine issue 5, and then later in the EM Compendium on pages 122 and 123. This is an important, cinematic and potent skill that needed to be re-printed and included in the updated random skills list.*

Acrobatics is the performance of extraordinary feats of balance, agility and motor coordination. Formal training in acrobatics teaches one how to jump efficiently, how to fall properly, and how to tumble and balance on narrow surfaces — all useful skills to have while exploring a post-apocalyptic city.

True acrobatic skill requires formal training to learn and then countless hours of practice to master. 1 skill point can be learned from a competent teacher in 3 months, or 1.5 months from a university or some such institution. Such training costs 200+1d100 silver coins.

For simplicity, acrobatics is broken into three subsections: tumbling, balancing and jumping. Each section includes the appropriate rules additions to make them usable.

**Tumbling:** Acrobatics teaches one how to tumble and roll during a fall. Tumbling is also useful for moving quickly and defensively around a battlefield, minimizing the target presented to an enemy gunman or rolling away from the claws, pincers or gaping maw of a predator. The following chart gives the modifiers to DV, Speed and Strike Value from defensive tumbling. This maneuverer can be done instead of another action, such as shooting, running, etc., however, an optional, usually compromised attack can be made while performing a tumbling action.

### Table XR-169/ Defensive Tumbling

| Skill Points | DV Bonus | Speed Mod. | Melee SV Mod.* | Climbing Stealth |
|---|---|---|---|---|
| 1 | -4 | -3m | - 15 | - |
| 2 | -7 | -2m | - 10 | - |
| 3 | -10 | -1m | - 5 | 1 |
| 4 | -14 | 0 | 0 | 1 |
| 5 | -18 | 0 | + 5 | 2 |
| 6 Max | -22 | 0 | +10 | 3 |

** SV bonus only applies to melee attacks*

**Balancing on narrow surfaces:** Acrobatic training increases a character's control of balance. The chart to follow assumes the acrobat is moving at a walking speed, but can use extra caution and slow down to 1/4 of his or her normal speed for a reduction in hazard code by 1 letter (C becomes B, etc.) or move at full running speed for an increase in hazard level of 2 degrees (hazard check A becomes C, or D become F, etc.).

### Table XR-170/ Balancing Agility trait based

| Skill Points | Surface Width 30 to 90cm | 18 to 29cm | 5 to 15cm | 4 or less cm |
|---|---|---|---|---|
| Untrained | A* | D | H | J |
| 1 | A** | B | F | H |
| 2 | - | C | E | G |
| 3 | - | A | D | F |
| 4 | - | A* | C | E |
| 5 | - | A** | B | D |
| 6 Max | - | - | A | B |

CM = centimeters (100 CM in a meter)    * Two hazard checks allowed
** Three hazard checks allowed    - Automatic success

**Jumping:** A character's base jumping distance is the horizontal distance they can leap without making a hazard check. The base jumping distance adult humans can cover is 2 meters. This distance can be modified by two factors: movement rate and strength, while greater degrees of the acrobatic skill increases the odds of leaping progressively longer distances.

The first factor is current movement speed, and incorporates penalties to one's movement when they wear armor. For every 0.5 meters of movement above 6, add a bonus of +0.25 meters to base jumping distance. For every full meter of speed below 6, the subject loses 0.25 meters from his or her base distance. Any movement modifier bonus is only applied if the character has at least a 4 meters run before the jump is attempted.

The second modifier is based on the jumper's raw physical strength. Take the strength modifier to throwing distance from the attribute bonus table (TME-1-3 page 10 of the Hub Rules or page 8 in this book), and apply it to base jump distance after speed. For example, a character who moves 6m per round and has a strength of 40 gives a +10% to jump distance, so the subject's new base jump distance is 2.2m.

Skill is the third modifier to jump distance, with the higher the acrobatics skill points, the further and safer one can leap. The extra distance shown on the table below is added to the base 2m a person can jump, prior to adding any strength and speed modifiers.

As a note, the current long jumping world record stands at 8.95 meters by Olympian Mike Powell, though longer jumps have been recorded at higher altitudes with a tail wind.

### Table XR-171 / Horizontal Jumping Table   Agility Trait Based

| Skill Points | Extra Distance 1m | 1.5m | 2m | 2.5m | 3m | +0.5m* |
|---|---|---|---|---|---|---|
| Untrained | A | B | C | E | F | G |
| 1 | A** | A | B | D | E | H |
| 2 | A*** | A** | A | C | D | E |
| 3 | - | A*** | A** | B | C | D |
| 4 | - | - | A*** | A | B | C |
| 5 | - | - | - | A** | A | B |
| 6 Max | - | - | - | A*** | A** | A |

** Increase hazard check level by one for each extra 0.5 added above 3m (D becomes E, etc.)*
***One extra hazard checks allowed*
****Two extra hazard check allowed*
*- Automatically succeeds*

**Vertical Jumps:** To determine the distance a character can jump vertically simply divide horizontal jumping distance by 2. For example an average man can high jump 1 meter. Extra distance gained by speed and the skill check is also halved. This is the distance one's feet leave the ground, so if the GM is attempting to find out how far a character can reach at the end of a jump don't forget to add their height to the total.

**Special note on falling damage**
Falling distance is reduced by 1 meter per skill point in acrobatics to represent tumbling skill. Furthermore, when a character deliberately jumps down from a height, reduce fall distance by their height x1.5 to represent the character dangling from by his or her arms before letting go.

# Animal Handler

Individuals with this skill grew up in a tribe or family tasked with the raising, caring for, and control of animals. In most cases, the beasts were common draft animals, mounts and guard dogs, but in some new era cultures, hapless creatures were also raised and trained to serve as pit fighting monsters or beasts of war.

A character with this skill was the assistant of a master animal handler, and has a natural gift with beasts and an eagerness to learn everything about all manner of creatures, including fearsome mutant freaks. He or she will also be more understanding, curious and tolerant of bestial humans, be the first to invite them to join an expedition, and yet at the same time, more likely to treat them like a pet.

This PC learned much in the years of exposure to a typical Epochian era menagerie, yet might well have been sickened by it, too. They will have seen wild animals taken from their nests, burrows and dens as youngsters — often after the parent beasts were killed or driven off — and brought up and cared for only to be sold off to some warlord to serve on the battlefield, or the creature purchased by a gladiatorial venue operator to kill and ultimately die for the thrill of the crowd. For moral reasons or some other compulsion, this character has left the industry of commercial animal handling. Months or years later, they still retain the know-how and are typically eager to train a companion beast or two of their own, and have it serve them and their adventure party in great deeds.

The following table covers the abilities and tasks that can be achieved by an animal handler of various skill tiers, including an unskilled option. Following this table, there is a supplementary section which allows for the character to start game play with a pet or riding animal — game master permitting. An animal handler can only have one creature under its control per skill point.

The third section to this multi-part skill is the ability and chances to break and train various creatures, including desirable animals such as dogs, horses and cats, all the way to the impossibly difficult and weird critters such as worms and insects. Mutant plants cannot be tamed or trained and if predatory, will hungrily attack animal handlers the same as anybody else.



**Unskilled:** • Feed prepared fodder and water animal. • Secure it with rope or in a pen • Saddle a horse or riding dog.

**1 Skill Point:** • Prepare ideal feed for animal. • Groom, shave, and wash common beasts. • Craft harnesses for common riding and draft animals and assemble customized variants to suit abnormally configured species. • Command animal to sit, stay, leave it alone, come, fetch, or attack an obvious stranger or aggressor.

**2 Skill Points:** • Hoof and paw repairs and maintenance, including farrier work fitting iron shoes on horses and similar steeds. • If this character has the riding skill, he or she can saddle and fit reins to a non-typical riding beasts, such as a bear, huge lizard, giant rabbit or other oddity, although such creatures must first be broken and trained, which for some species, is next to impossible.

**3 Skill Points:** • Pannier* assembly. • Animal understanding: This handler knows what beasts like and can sometimes dissuade them from attacking if able to offer some sort of foodstuff to distract a creature long enough for the handler and his or her companions to back away slowly. Likewise, this handler will know when to show subservience to certain beasts, not challenge the alpha of a pack, or when to make oneself look large and fierce to intimate and drive off an animal, when to play dead, when to run, or not. • Gladiatorial beast prep: A dark side of this skill tier is in preparing animals to either kill, or die for the thrill of an audience. This handler will be able to properly cage, transport, house and starve gladiatorial beasts, and when the time comes for the animal to entertain, this handler can taunt and enrage the thing prior to sending it out into the fighting ring.

**4 Skill Points:** • Veterinary care: This character serves as a medic for their animals, and those beasts in their care heal twice their daily endurance healing rate when given proper food, medical attention and wound dressing.

**5 Skill Points (Max):** • Animal Affinity: this handler has such in-depth experience and understanding of animals that when confronted with a wild beast, even a mutant strain of an identifiable beast, such as a hell cougar or devi-bear, he or she can attempt to calm the thing down, use verbal signals, hand gestures and posture to possibly dissuade the thing from attacking the handler and any companions. Both the animal handler and the animal must make a type C willpower based hazard check to achieve this peaceful outcome. If achieved, and yet the beast is guarding its lair or young, then the handler and its companion must back away to avoid a confrontation, but if both parties met in the wilderness by accident, then both parties will need to go separate ways to avoid a fight. This ability also works with domesticated animals for which this animal handler will generate an immediate rapport, and easily earn the trust of dogs, cats, livestock and bestial humans.

** Panniers are side mounted carry bags made from wicker, leather or scrap material, and often attached to pack horses, mules or dogs.*

### Animal Handler Pet, Riding Mount or Companion Animal

A beginning player character with this skill will have a pet, riding beast or guardian animal, so long as they don't start as an escape slave or as part of a game master directed session where having an animal along is implausible.

Most times, the creature in question is not immediately accessible, especially where such a beast might be considered a predator or other monster and so would linger outside of a community and await its handler's appearance.

Any creature companion will recognize any other animals

and humanoid companions of the handler as pack mates, although will not follow commands from these 'betas'. In the event the animal handler character is slain, and the beast is left with the deceased controller's companions, the creature will either flee into the wilds or seek to devour the former handler's companions with the exception to this being if another animal handler is in the group, who can try to take control of the creature — the beast being allowed a willpower Type C hazard check to fend off this new handler's attempts to soothe, coerce and ultimately control the creature.

The following creatures are those from the hub rules that are available to be controlled by the handler, however, should the PC start with 2 skill points in animal handler, add +1 to this dice roll, or +3 if 3 or more starting skill points are acquired.

There are other many sources of creatures in the Mutant Epoch book library, including Mutant Bestiary One, Creatures of the Apocalypse Codex and Monday Mutants Bestiary, as well as many free downloads in the SOE members area bestiary at this link: https://www.outlandarts.com/members-only/TME-SOE-bestiary.htm .

A game master could compile an expanded random list for this skill, and even add their own mutant creations. **Roll 1d20:**

|  |  |
|---|---|
| 1. | Bird, skal |
| 2. | Rat, normal |
| 3. | Bat, devil |
| 4,5. | Cat, domestic |
| 6,7. | Dog, farm |
| 8. | Horse, pony |
| 9,10. | Horse saddle |
| 11,12. | Dog, hunting |
| 13. | Dog, war |
| 14,15. | Dog, riding |
| 16. | Rat, gutter |
| 17. | Dog, mutant |
| 18. | Rat, aberrant |
| 19. | Wolf, timber |
| 20+. | Bear, bane |

## Breaking and Training Wild Beasts

Most eligible creatures an animal handler will be exposed to will have been raised in captivity after being captured or purpose bred, although the following system and table does allow for a player character to attempt to turn a captured creature into a mount or attack beast — which is very difficult, time consuming and risky.

The intended handler needs to make an averaged strength and willpower based hazard check when confronting the beast, with these combined traits added together and divided by two to get the Beast Breaking trait. The following list of creature categories reveal the hazard check needed to break and train a creature, which will take 6+1d6 hours to achieve and the hazard check roll made after those hours are expended.

This table pertains to taming wild animals, and to convince an already domesticated or tamed, but unfamiliar animal, such as a stranger's dog, pet cat, or horse, is far easier so long as the previous owner was of the same general species and familiar to the creature. In these circumstances, even an untrained handler has a much better chance of becoming an already domesticated and trained creature's master; thus make all hazard checks at two letter tiers easier: C becomes A, E becomes C, etc, whereas a type A check allows two extra attempts.

Some creatures, such as worms, fish, sharks and insects tend to forget both their training and the fact that the animal handler is not food, and the beast must be re-broken at some point within 3d6 days after being initially 'tamed'. Only the GM knows the day when the dominated creature will turn wild again, which can add memorable excitement and mayhem to any game.

Additionally, any character with the animal association mutation, described on page 235 of this book, or this character is a bestial human of the same line of animals as the creature they are trying to break, and in either case this character also has this skill, they will have an uncanny bond with the specific type of related creature. Besides any circumstances and benefits the game master decides, this character gets two hazard checks to try to break and tame animals of the sort they have an affinity with.

## Table XR-172/ Breaking and Training Wild Beasts Matrix
Animal handler Skill points and Hazard Check needed to Break and Train Beast

| Animal Category | Untrained | 1 | 2 | 3 | 4 | 5/Max |
|---|---|---|---|---|---|---|
| Dogs | F | D | C | B | A | A* |
| Cats | H | E | D | C | B | A |
| Wolves | I | F | E | D | C | B |
| Apes | F | C | B | A | A* | A* |
| Weasel | G | D | C | B | A | A* |
| Rodents | F | B | A | A* | A* | A* |
| Cattle | E | C | B | A | A* | A* |
| Horses | F | D | C | B | A | A* |
| Sheep | E | C | B | A | A* | A* |
| Goats | F | D | C | B | A | A* |
| Bears | J | G | E | D | C | B |
| Reptiles | K | H | F | E | D | C |
| Birds | F | D | C | B | A | A* |
| Bats | H | E | D | C | B | A |
| Worms** | M | K | I | G | F | E |
| Whales | H | F | E | D | C | B |
| Fish/Sharks** | M | L | J | H | F | D |
| Insects** | M | L | K | J | G | F |
| Unspecified Mutant Herbivore | H | F | D | C | B | A |
| Unspecified Mutant Omnivore | K | H | F | D | C | B |
| Unspecified Mutant Carnivore | L | J | H | F | E | D |

*Allow handler two chances to break-in the beast.
** Every 3d6 days this thing will need to be re-broken and re-tamed again.

Use the Animal Handlers Breaking and Training Trait for the above shown Hazard Check: **Add Strength and Willpower together and divide by 2 to get the Breaking Trait.** Only make this hazard check after 6+1d6 hours of training and rudimentary taming.

# Armorer

While most people with this skill will own a satchel full of tools, thread, cordage, wire, and a few patches to make simple repairs to most archaic armor, or combine suits of small sized armor into something that fits a larger person, more is needed to actually make protective suits, shields and helmets from scratch. Indeed, an armorer of any skill tier needs access to a smithy or mechanical workshop to build or repair metal armor or cut out, fit, layer and lace leather, junk and scrap relic armors. Materials also must be readily available for the armorer to make useful armor. Fortunately, any community within a day or two's proximity to any ruin site can gather all the raw materials needed for the assembly of junk and scrap relic armor, while salvagers can also supply metal for recycling and later forging into helmets, part and full plate armor.

While the name and function of full and part plate armor might be similar to medieval variants, these post-apocalyptic

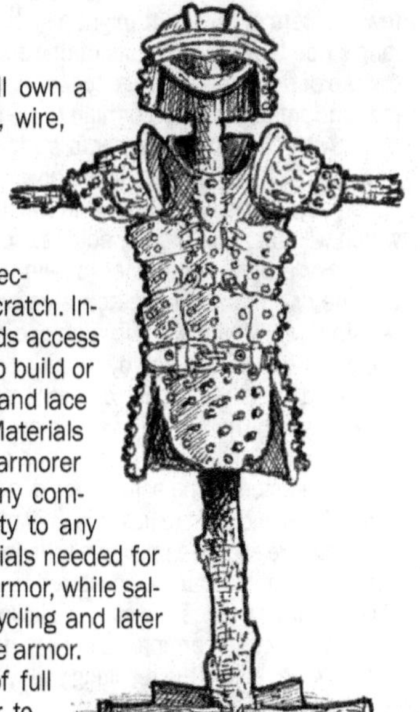

suits have a decidedly utilitarian, crude and intimating look to them. A wastelander in full plate armor then is often rust streaked, covered in sharpened bolt heads, nails, spikes, antlers and horns, with decorative plates and traffic signs riveted over shoulder and chest, and helmet plumage made from plastic toys, the skull of a defeated enemy, androids still living head, plushie stuffed animals, light arrays, or spent ammo casings. In short, there is nothing chivalrous looking about a wasteland knight's getup, and is often designed to instill terror in onlookers as much as protect the wearer.

As with the smithy skill — which focuses more on the making of metal weapons and tools — anyone with this skill will be more valuable alive than dead to a conquering faction, with the armorer kept alive and made to work for their new master, with the armorer's loved ones, friends and family held as hostages to ensure cooperation from the gifted person.

Highly skilled armorers can take various suits of non-powered relic armors and combine them back into a full suit with replacement straps, buckles, hinges and replica parts using both salvaged and newly forged or produced materials. This is a highly profitable undertaking, with the parts from countless suits of scattered armor often littering old battlefields, sometimes with partial skeletons of ancient warriors still inside the torn open getups. Scavengers tend to bring in a breastplate, vambrace, gauntlet, helmet or other parts from dozens of mismatched pieces into a relic dealership or armory over as many years. In time, a more or less full suit of tactical, or combat armor can be cobbled together and sold — usually after a paint job to unify the mismatched suit before sale.

Master Armorers can repair damaged relic armor, including powered armors so long as the fixer has adequate supplies of spare parts, a fully equipped workshop, and hired help from highly skilled electrical and mechanical technicians. Besides repairing the high tech, shell class armors, a few masters of this craft might also have access to the parts from dozens of long since blown apart suits of powered armor, and from these, and over the course of decades, manage to reconstruct one suit and sell it for an astounding amount to a warlord or high rank, exceptional excavator.

A NPC master armorer is a highly valued member of any community, and also likely to wield political power. So too, if a community has an established armorer's workshop, this master might form a sort of guild or union which will not allow a competitor to set up shop in their town.

For a player character to gain further skill points in this area of expertise, he or she must have actively worked on armor during a previous game session. Many who want to advance, yet are busy traveling with a dig team, will put their skills to use by repairing the armor of comrades while at camp, or pulling out a heavy pack of leather, chain mail rings, bits of relic armor and tinkering with them — all of which count toward improving in this skill.

Often, the most common game session use for this area of knowledge is when characters come across long dead humanoids clad in armor, or freshly defeated foes, and want to upgrade their own armor with that of the dead, especially if the PCs are escaped prisoners with no armor at all. Skullock armor, which is too small for humans, can be converted by a character with 1 or more points in this skill, although it takes two suits of skullock junk armor to make one human sized suit, and takes the armorer 1 hour to do so whereby it would take an untrained person 4 hours and the resulting suit would be noisy and ill-fitting.

| Skill Point | Title | Armor That Can be Made |
|---|---|---|
| Untrained | Newb | Furs, skins and hides, wicker shield |
| 1 | Journeyman/ Journeywoman | Junk armor, junk helmet, junk shield, leather shield, leather helmet, bark armor, thorn armor, tire armor, standard shield. Can convert 2 suits of crude, skullock size armor to make human sized armor in an hour. |
| 2 | Apprentice | Heavy junk, all leather armors, fish and lizard scale, bone armor, bone helmet, bug shell armor, leather jacket, buckler shield, spiked shield, bladed shield, tower shield, iron cap. Can identify and reassemble scattered relic armor of these variants back into serviceable form: sports padding, bomb squad, tactical and riot armor. |
| 3 | Armorer | Scrap relic, chainmail vest, breast plate, part plate, iron helmet. Can identify and reassemble the following relic armor: combat armor, heavy combat armor. |
| 4 Max | Master Armorer | Full plate, full helm. This character can identify, and reassemble all varieties of scattered relic armor, however powered shell class armor cannot be made operational until an electrical technician of 3 or more skill points spends 10+3d6 hours rewiring and configuring the power needs of the unit. Power cells and power packs must also be inserted into any reassembled powered armors. |

# Artist

This talented individual can both craft and use art materials to render landscapes, portraits, wildlife, structures, and most importantly of all, maps. While creative, and able to paint abstract art, sculpt imaginative curiosities and render loose, non-representative forms, he or she is more typically employed creating wanted posters, drawing newly discovered monstrosities, ruin entrance locations and cartography for both local warlords, merchants and dig teams.

Any excavator with this skill will start game play with the requisite talent to accurately illustrate new creatures, depict specific details and portals in ruins, and reproduce the semblance of people he or she has seen.

The time needed to render different subjects, venues or craft a rough map depends on the complexity, but as a general rule, 3d6 minutes are required for a rough sketch, and 2d4 hours for a painting. A simple treasure map takes 2d12 minutes while a complex map with ornaments and a key of an area such as a map of large town or regional map would take 3d6 hours.

Each individual starting game play with this skill will have a leather satchel containing the following:

- 2d6 sticks of drawing charcoal
- 2d6 relic pencil crayons and sharpener
- 1d3 stubs of relic pencils
- 3d4 sheets of yellowed, ancient copy paper
- Junk crafted clip board
- 3d6 sheets of locally made, coarse paper
- Plus, some chance of additional art supplies and resources:
   - 4 in 10 chance of a watercolor set of 12 colors, replica, worth 100+1d100sp
   - 1 in 10 chance of oil paint set of 12 colors plus linseed oil, paint thinning oil, cloths, assorted brushes and fold out easel-backpack. Weighs 5kg and worth 400+1d1000sp
   - 3 in 10 chance of d6 tattered old world print books on an artistic subject. Any of these books are worth 200+2d100sp, except the Frazetta book which is worth 1000+1d1000sp. This is merely a starter's list, with the GM encouraged to craft his or her own list of art books perhaps from their own collection. Roll 1d10:
      1. Drawing and painting nudes
      2. How to draw robots
      3. How to draw Super Hero Comics
      4. Oil painting techniques of the old masters
      5. Watercolor Techniques
      6. Propaganda posters through History
      7. The Art of The Lord of the Rings™ Movies, 9th remake.
      8. How to draw Anime
      9. The Art of First Person Shooter Classics
      10. The Art of Frank Frazetta

# Carpentry *by Danny Seedhouse*

This is the trade and craft of woodworking for the construction of buildings, furniture, and countless useful things from timber. The first step is the actual production of lumber from raw logs, using an axe, wedges or saws. This skill is very useful for anyone attempting to build themselves a new life in the post-apocalyptic new era, survive in the wild, or make a modest living after they get your legs ripped off by a mutant horror in the ruins. This selection is not meant to be a complete list of things that can be made, just a basic guide.

| Skill Points | Endurance Repaired | Type C Intelligence Based Hzard Check for Item Character can build |
|---|---|---|
| nil | 1d6 | Lean to, shoddy raft, stump for a chair |
| 1 | 2d10+10 | Lumber, crude furniture, basic log structures. |
| 2 | 3d10+20 | Cart, wagon, short bridges, wooden structures, furniture |
| 3 | 4d10+40 | Catapults, ballista, medium bridges |
| 4 | 4d10+60 | Large wooden structures, fancy furniture, saw mill. |
| 5 Max | 4d10+80 | Trebuchet, long bridges, advanced furniture, complex items |

## Carpentry Item Notes

At 2 skill points, wooden pegs can be made in place of nails while at 3 skill points furniture needs no nails. A 4 skill point carpenter is trained in advanced joining techniques and can eliminate the use of nails.

**Basic lumber** is the building block of carpentry and in the wilds of the Mutant Epoch the first thing you need. By 2 skill points the quality of lumber improves as does the speed of production.

**Furniture** starts out rough but serviceable and improves in quality visually and structurally as skill improves. Fancy furniture has fully wooden movable parts, seamless appearance and sells for twice the value of regular furniture.

**Basic structures** have walls and doors along with basic windows, while at the next level of skill everything can be made a little more complex, internal rooms are added, multiple floors can be included.

**Small structures** are single floor and up to 200 square meters.

**Medium Structures** are up to two floors and 1200 square meters, aka your typical house.

**Large Structures** are up to 4 floors and 3000 square meters.

**Bridges** go from short at under 15 meters, medium are up to 30 meters, long bridges can go up to 200 meters or longer. The old world's longest wooden bridge is 228.6m or 750 feet.

# Communications

Also called a comms technician, radio operator, or transmissions system operator, this individual has either been trained in the use of wireless and hard wired communications devices, or come by the skill out of a deep, often obsessive personal interest. There are several skill tiers to this area of knowledge, with the upper tiers requiring the comms person to know how to read and do math. Low skill users can still master the principles, but not progress to higher levels of expertise if unable to do calculations, record frequencies, create or possibly break codes and perform other math based or writing and reading tasks. In short, a character must be able to read and do math to progress to 3 or more skill points in communications.

This character will start with one roll on the following table, although might have been trained by another enthusiast or comms officer in some faction on the use of more advanced systems. Like with all skills, no advancement to a higher tier can be achieved if that skill was not used in the prior rank's adventures. It is therefore important for any radio operator to get a communication device and transmit or at least tinker with a radio, old cell phone, wireless set or crude crystal diode radio like those available for purchase in the markets of many new era towns (see equipment on page 362 of this book).

Having a comms specialist in any expedition, be it on the water, aboard an airship, or a land based operation such as a ruin crawl, is highly advantageous. Not only can this character maintain a radio link to a support group or base camp at the outskirts of the ruins, but they can also listen for the telltale, seemingly unintelligible chatter of Mecha — chatter that can be quite loud and crisp when the robots, androids and drone-like cyborg minions of such evil machines are close at hand.

A communications person can also identify valuable relic hardware and have a fairly decent idea of its importance, and potential re-sale value if such devices can be stripped from buildings, old vessels, or other machinery and taken back to the nearest barter town.

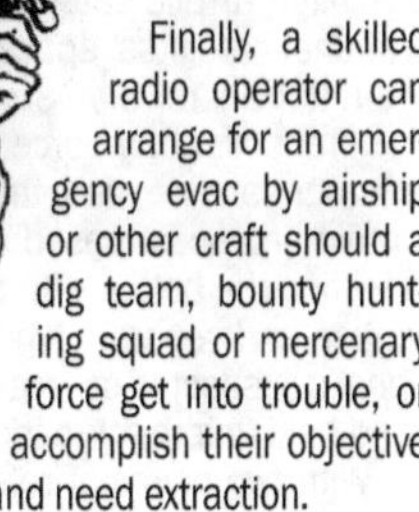

Finally, a skilled radio operator can arrange for an emergency evac by airship or other craft should a dig team, bounty hunting squad or mercenary force get into trouble, or accomplish their objective and need extraction.

The following table lists the abilities that a communications specialist has at each skill tier. If a character is also an electrical technician, as described on page TME 53, then at 1 skill point he or she can make a crystal diode radio (which the comms skill also features at 2nd tier) or a Morse code transmitter, while at two skill points they can set up a wired telephone network between various structures, or build a crude, chest sized radio transmitter. With such a transmitter, this system can broadcast news, music and other recordings, or wire together other radios, including relic communicators, and establish a comms link network throughout a community or wider area.

For the most part, then, a person with communications skill knows how to use the devices found in the ruins or made by an electrical technician, and take it a step further to be able to use ancient equipment to its fullest potential.

## Communications Skill Points Abilities

### 1 Skill Point
• Set up wired intercoms throughout a barge, airship, fortification, or entire town, however an electrical technician must actually build the intercoms.
• Build or salvage a radio antenna and hook it up to whatever handheld communicator or fixed radio to improve range and fidelity of communications by ten times.

### 2 Skill Points
• Build a crystal diode radio and with an earpiece and antenna, be able to pick up radio transmissions from open sources, such as any local AM/FM or shortwave stations within roughly 100 km. Such stations are sometimes set up in communities to offer news, play old world musical tracks or promote propaganda, religious adherence proclamations, announce bounties on wanted individuals, alert citizens of nearby threats, wish happy birthday to individual citizens, or call out holiday greetings.
• Convert a severed head of an android or robotic unit, whose CPU has been destroyed or removed, into a video surveillance and vocal conduit. This cranial unit must be wired to a fixed computer or advanced communicator, as well as at least a mini power cell, and cannot turn about and so has a visual frame of straight forward. The head's audio receptors can also be activated and allow a remote operator to speak, listen and see through the severed mechanical head. This system is often used at the gates to a fortification or mounted outside a vehicle, lowered from an airship down to ground personnel or to inspect an area beneath a cloud or fog bank, etc.
• Build a Morse code transmitter-receiver, although the device must be connected to either a hard wired inter-community or fortification system or a wireless radio set capable to broadcasting and receiving Morse code.

### 3 Skill Points *PC must be able to read and do math*
• Convert a cell phone, and other bits of scrap electronics, and turn it into a standard communicator, although the device is double the size, fragile and finicky.
• Convert two or more old cell phones, tablets, and laptop computers into a wired intercom system with two-way video feed. Although this unit requires wires joining them, the two wires need only be thin, and so easily hidden into the hull of a barge, airship or throughout a community.
• Cryptographic code creation and possible code breaking (GM can apply an intelligence based type L hazard check to break another person's or AI's code, with one attempt per 12 hours of work.

### 4 Skill Points (Maximum)
• Align a relic satellite dish to track one of the few still orbiting and operational satellites, space stations, or vessels to send and receive or merely listen to transmission and broadcasts from the orbiting object.
• Transmission source location Identification: Using a radio, directional antenna or satellite dish, this character can attempt to pin point the location of a radio broadcast based on signal strength and mapping. The more points of detection the better, with a single point requiring both a successful type H perception and separate type J Intelligence hazard check to accurately follow the signal's suspected source and locate the transmission tower, antenna, robot, or hand-held unit that broadcast the targeted transmission source.

With two points of reference, which, unless a team of radio operators are working together, will require two or more days to lock in on the location, a perception based type E plus intelligence type E HC are both needed. If three points of transmission tracking can be acquired, using three separate covert receiving stations or radio operators, then the accuracy of identifying the broadcasting radio source is much easier, with only a type B perception and separate type B intelligence check needed.

Normally the source that is broadcasting must either make repeated radio broadcasts over several days or hours to be tracked, or make the mistake of leaving their unit turned on after sending a transmission.
• With a computer tablet, old cell phone or computer, this character can wire into an existing, operational video surveillance, comms line, phone line or other communications hardware setup and potentially gain access to what is being said within the system. Access occurs on a successful type E intelligence based hazard check.

Once in, a further, type G check can be attempted to speak with those in the network, and if so, require a further, type H INT based hazard check to take control of the built-in systems to shut down offensive measures, open powered doors, or cause some other mischief or devastation. Any digital being that might inhabit or have access to the hacked into system could counterattack and destroy the hand-held device this comms technician was using, or worse.

## Cooking *by Danny Seedhouse*

Fire makes food better, with cooking being the skill of using fire well to produce things that go beyond basic survival. The cooking skill allows for the safe preparation of food, and, for example, allows the diggers to cook and eat a mutant otter without getting some sort of horrible stomach parasites. It gives one a basic understanding of nutrition and food safety. Allows the preservation of food for much longer durations through the smoking, canning, and pickling of perishable foods, but also in preparing items like cheeses, sausages, and breads.

This cook can also prepare 2 days trail rations for 1sp cost and preserve fresh food, especially meat, over 10 times as long as an untrained person.

This skill is a quality of life improvement, and can be a great boon to a dig team, improving overall health and make the recovery from injury easier. A skilled cook increases the healing rate of anyone eating food specifically prepared by them for a full day by 2 trait points. This requires a type A hazard check using perception and Intelligence averaged (add PER + INT divide by 2 to get PC's cooking trait).

### Eating in the wilds and the cooking skill
So the characters have just killed a mutant beauty, are hungry and miles from civilization. If they're smart it's time to try cooking it. But how much flesh can be harvested?

As a basic generalization 50% of any wild animal's weight is usable meat, slightly more if the hunter is less picky about what they call eatable. Domesticated animals offer around 62-64%, as they have been selected actively and fed to have a higher percentage of edible meat. Of course, the flesh of animals, and people, can be eaten raw. There is a danger in this though, since raw wild meat can have parasites and other infections including Trichinosis that develops when people eat animals infected with a parasite.

In game terms, eating raw or improperly cooked wild meat produces a 2 in 6 chance of causing an infection of some sort.

If infection is present, **roll 1d6: 1-4.** Trichinosis / **5.** Unspecified illness (treat as flu bug, see page TME 126) / **6.** White plague, although allow the PC a type B perception based hazard check to notice that this meat is infected (see TME Hub Rules page 126).

**Trichinosis** forces the unlucky eater to make a Type C endurance based hazard check to avoid contracting it upon consuming tainted uncooked meat. Virus life is 1d4 weeks long, doing 1d6 endurance damage a day and inflicting -1d10 to all physical stats the first week — which can reduce a person to a minimum of 1 in a stat. The second week a Type C endurance hazard check stops the progression of the disease and stats begin to recover naturally. If this second HC is failed, the target takes another -1d10 to all physical stats and must continue to check every week until the disease has run it course.

Symptoms include nausea, diarrhea, abdominal cramps, followed later by muscle pain, weakness, fever, headache, and sometimes inflammation of other organs. Trichinosis can be cured with proper medical care; advanced med kits have the right antidotes. Alternatively, someone with 3 skill points in chemical technician and access to medical advice, can produce a proper cure. This cure costs 400+2d100sp to make, takes 1d4 days to take effect, but will fully flush the disease from the body and stop the effects from progressing immediately.

# Cybernetics Technician

This skill is also a pre-game caste, although a character of this profession will have other skills as well, many of which overlap and complement each other. In some respects, a cybernetics technician borrows from both the robotics and medical fields, and at higher skill point tiers adds non-stacking points in the medic, junk doctor and junk crafter skills.

Those with this talent can swap out cybernetic parts with more success than a robotics technician can, and do so with fewer tools and less time. with the chance of success measured in hours instead of days. A very skilled cybernetics technician becomes exposed to related areas of knowledge, and as the table to follow shows, gains access to these. One of these features is the 'Endurance Repaired per Hour' column. This pertains to fixing robots, androids, vat-brains, and other mostly mechanical beings and devices. While not as effective at mechanical repairs as a robotics technician, this is still a highly valuable talent to have.

A cybernetics technician will carry two hip pouches. One contains cybernetic repair tools and frequently used minor parts like screws, wires, tweezer, screwdrivers, wrenches, clamps, power test gauges and other expensive relic tools worth 500+1d1000sp. The other hip pouch contains spare parts, especially those suited to any cyborg companion, or if this character itself is a cyborg. Most characters with this skill are fascinated with implants and cybernetic technology.

## Demolitions Expert

Valued by comrades and allies, and dreaded by their enemies, a demolitions expert is a much respected new era combatant. In most cases, this character gained their initial training from a more experienced bomber, either in a military capacity or sometimes an industrial or salvage role. When not blowing up enemy fortifications, roads, vehicles, bridges or clustered masses of the hostile faction, this person would blast open walls and doors in the ruins. With an otherwise impassable portal or barrier torn open, a dig team or salvage crew could access the long lost place to loot whatever waited beyond. As a participant in a dig team, a demolition expert can offer dramatic advantages in both combat and excavation scenarios. Of course, the use of incredibly powerful, and loud explosives in any ruin or wilderness setting will announce the presence of the dig team to local area predators, tribes and hostile machines.

This character knows how to make the most of a non-projectile explosive relic charge, such as a landmine, grenade, rocket or missile, by placing the ancient ordnance against a door, town gate, vehicle, structure, beast, or robotic unit in such a way as to do double damage when the blast does go off. This massive damage increase does not happen when the relic is thrown, fired from a launcher or otherwise not intentionally placed, armed and triggered; a task that takes 3 rounds to achieve.

This expert can also use black powder to make their dreaded 'keg-bombs'. These improvised explosives are filled with nails, scrap metal, and incendiary agents and attached to mechanical clock fuses, drip timers, pressure plates, trip wires, or powder coated fuses. They can also be shot at by a beam or ballistic weapon from a safe distance. When they blow, keg bombs engulf extensive areas in both a primary and secondary blast. The keg size and complexity — and thus the strike value, damage and blast radius — vary according to the skill of the maker. Of course, the cost of making such explosives also increases with the size of a keg bomb. Upon detonation, these kegs cause flammable substances within their blast radius to catch fire, and add to the chaos and devastation. Keg bombs do not get their damage doubled as do relic explosives.

These individuals can also make hand held, archaic grenades. These devices resemble the original ball grenades with flaming fuses popular in the 17th and 18th centuries. The more experienced the demolition expert, the more reliable, complicated, and destructive a grenade is. Such archaic grenades take 1 round to light the fuse, and are thrown on the 2nd round. These grenades are much heavier than relic variants and weigh in at 1kg each. They can be thrown 10 meters plus or minus the user's strength score modifiers, as shown on table XR-3 on page 8.

If the grenade does not detonate on impact, it means the fuse has gone out. The weapon can be recovered, however, and have a new fuse inserted after 10+1d6 minutes effort, and used again. The fuse on these grenades can be cut to different lengths to allow it to detonate on reaching the maximum thrown distance or on impact, or to go off between 1 and 40 rounds later (there are 20 rounds in a minute). A grenade with a lit fuse that is hidden behind a curtain, shrub or other non-solid barrier might easily go unseen by approaching enemies, and if timed properly, might explode just as they draw near, allowing the demolition expert to leave behind a nasty surprise for pursuers.

## Table XR-173/ Cybernetics Technician Abilities

| Skill Points | Attach/Detach Implants on Cyborg | Attach/Detach Implants on Robot or Android | Robotics Tech Skill Points | Endurance Repaired/ Hour* | Computer Tech Skill Points | Electrical and Mechanical Tech Skill Points | Other Benefits |
|---|---|---|---|---|---|---|---|
| Untrained | 1% | 3% | nil | nil | nil | nil | nil |
| 1 | 56% | 31% | nil | 4 | nil | nil | nil |
| 2 | 79% | 38% | nil | 8 | nil | nil | Minimum 1 point Medic Skill |
| 3 | 93% | 60% | 1 | 12 | 1 | 1 | Minimum 1 pt Junk Doctor Skill |
| 4 | 97% | 66% | 2 | 16 | 1 | 2 | Minimum 1 point Junk Crafting skill |
| 5 | 98% | 71% | 2 | 20 | 2 | 2 | Minimum 2 points Medic skill |
| 6 | 99% | 78% | 3 | 24 | 2 | 3 | Minimum 2 points Junk Doctor Skill |
| 7 Max | Yes | 83% | 3 | 28 | 3 | 3 | Minimum 2 points Junk Crafter skill |

*'Yes' means always able to attach or detach implants on the first try.*

**Endurance repaired for robots, androids and other machines per hour.*

The sales value shown for keg bombs and archaic grenades is used for when this character wants to sell such devices in a marketplace. While sale value is the silver pieces as this character will earn from a sale, the cost to manufacture such a device is half the shown sales value. These same costs can be used to purchase these new era explosives if they are available at all, with the price doubling if the keg bomb or grenade can only be purchased on the block market. In some communities, however, the sale of any explosive is forbidden. Worse, anyone captured in possession of an explosive might be considered a terrorist and punished accordingly.

The shown build time of kegs bombs and crude grenades assumes the expert has a dedicated workshop with proper ventilation, electrical lights, and a complete absence of open flame. Also needed are about a thousand silver pieces worth of tools and materials. These include weigh-scales, measuring devices, metal powder containers, wood for kegs, scrap metal or cast iron grenade shells, fuses, detonation devices and more. Without these supplies and facilities, no explosive can be made.

**Unless starting as the caste 'escaped slave', assume new PCs with this skill will have 1d3 archaic grenades, skill 1 tier.**

This character can also attempt to disarm bombs of either relic or simple (primitive) construction, including keg bombs made by other demolition experts. Failure to disarm any bomb results in either an instantaneous blast or the unavoidable detonation according to the bomb's timer. All these factors are clarified in the following table:

*Intelligence + agility ÷ 2 = Disarming Trait*

## Table XR-174/ Demolitions Expert Abilities and Explosives Matrix

| Task or Bomb Detail | Untrained | Skill Points | | | | | | |
| --- | --- | --- | --- | --- | --- | --- | --- | --- |
| | | 1 | 2 | 3 | 4 | 5 | 6 | 7 (max) |
| Disarm Simple Bomb* | F | D | C | B | A | A x2 attempts | A x3 attempts | A x4 attempts |
| Failure Detonates? ** | 92% | 18% | 16% | 13% | 10% | 7% | 4% | 3% |
| Disarm Relic Mine, Grenade or Bomb* | H | E | D | C | B | A | A x2 attempts | A x3 attempts |
| Failure Detonates? ** | 98% | 27% | 23% | 20% | 17% | 11% | 8% | 4% |
| **Keg-bomb Size*** | - | 5kg | 10kg | 15kg | 20kg | 30kg | 50kg | 100kg |
| Keg-bomb Sale Value | - | 50+1d100sp | 100+2d100sp | 200+3d100sp | 500+4d100sp | 1000+1d1000sp | 1500+1d1000sp | 3000+2d1000sp |
| Keg-bomb Build Time | - | 3d6 hours | 10+3d6 hrs | 20+3d6hrs | 30+3d6 hrs | 40+3d6hrs | 50+4d6hrs | 60+5d6hrs |
| Primary Burst Radius | - | 3m | 5m | 10m | 15m | 20m | 30m | 60m |
| Primary Burst SV | - | 01-65 | 01-70 | 01-75 | 01-80 | 01-85 | 01-90 | 01-92 |
| Primary Burst Damage | - | 1d20 | 2d20 | 3d20 | 4d20 | 4d20+8 | 5d20+10 | 6d20+14 |
| Secondary Burst Radius | - | 5m | 10m | 20m | 30m | 40m | 60m | 100m |
| Secondary Burst SV | - | 01-50 | 01-55 | 01-60 | 01-65 | 01-70 | 01-75 | 01-80 |
| Secondary Burst Damage | - | 1d10 | 2d10 | 3d10 | 4d10 | 5d10 | 5d10+5 | 5d10+10 |
| **Archaic Grenade Weight** | - | 1kg | 1.25kg | 1.5kg | 1.6kg | 1.7 kg | 1.8kg | 1.9kg |
| Archaic Grenade Burst Radius | - | 1m | 2m | 3m | 4m | 5m | 6m | 8m |
| Archaic Grenade Burst SV | - | 01-50 | 01-60 | 01-70 | 01-75 | 01-80 | 01-85 | 01-90 |
| Archaic Grenade Damage | - | 1d12 | 1d20 | 1d20+3 | 1d20+5 | 1d20+8 | 1d20+10 | 1d20+15 |
| Archaic Grenade Sale Value | - | 50+1d20sp | 70+2d20sp | 100+1d100sp | 200+1d100sp | 300+2d100sp | 400+2d100sp | 500+3d100sp |
| Archaic Grenade Build Time | - | 2d6 hours | 2d6+1 hrs | 3d6 hrs | 4d6 hrs | 5d6 hrs | 6d6 hrs | 7d6 hrs |

** Hazard check must be successful to disarm a relic explosive or a keg bomb with a mechanical or digital timer: Intelligence + agility ÷ 2 = Disarming Trait score*

***If detonation doesn't occur, bomb will go off according to timer settings if armed with such a device.*

**** Kilograms of black powder needed. In a typical town, 1kg of black powder costs 5sp at the standard marketplace rate is, with about 2d100kg available for sale at any given time, per week.*

# Escape Artist

This character has an uncanny ability to slip free of ropes, pick handcuffs, or a padlock with a pin or sliver of bone. They have a good chance of getting out of a straight jacket or plastic poly-restraints, quickly disentangle from a net, a serpent's coils or a beast's tentacles. So too, an escape artist can find a way out of cages and traps, or even squirm through the gaps and holes that would seem impossible for others of a similar size to wriggle through. While well suited to those who wish to avoid detention by the law, by slavers, or other groups, this skill is especially helpful for excavators, since diggers tend to find themselves in tight situations and captivity more than most.

Those of smaller stature with high agility are ideal candidates for advancing in this skill, although for some abilities associated with this craft, wearing light armor or nothing at all is usually necessary.

Other than the Evade Grapple ability, the following abilities have their hazard check listed on the table at the end of this skill description, with the difficulty of each task decreasing as the character goes up in skill point tiers. Even untrained people can attempt these feats, although the odds of success for a novice are quite low.

**Evade Grapple:** This character is hard to hold on to, pin, or restrain. Instead of using one's strength to avoid being held in a grapple attack, as shown on the table TME-1-30a page 39 of the Hub Rules, this character can choose to use either their accuracy or agility trait if higher. Secondly, they are allowed repeated attempt to escape each round even if the grappler has a higher strength score. This is not the case with grappled victims who are not stronger than the person holding them.

This ability does not improve with skill points gained, however, but trait points can improve as a character advances in rank, offering the potential for improvements that way.

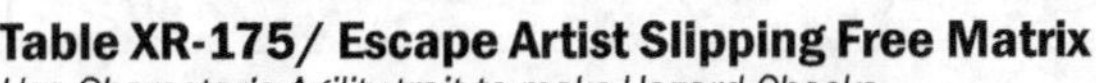

**Untie Rope:** Using a combination of body contortions, flexing, and working at a knot with teeth and fingers, this character has a better chance than most of untying a knot in a rope, wire, hose or other cordage. Besides being able to slip free of bonds, this person can also undo a knot that holds someone or something else to free it. For untrained characters, they are allowed one attempt to untie one knot per half hour, while an escape artist gets one attempt each minute. Clever captors, especially bounty hunters and slavers who've seen it all, will often tie multiple knots using multiple lengths of rope to better ensure their prisoners don't get free.

**Escape Poly-Restraint:** Also called zip-ties or cable ties, these restraints were used for both restraining humans and industrial purposes. While handy, lightweight and relatively strong, none have been made in hundreds of years, and those that are found on the surface have been exposed to the weather or sunlight, and become brittle and useless. Those that are made of UV resistant plastic and stored properly, however, are still a favorite of law enforcers, bounty hunters, and slavers.

For an escape artist, however, they are a relatively easy restraint to defeat by using a flat piece of metal — often hidden in the escapee's mouth when captured — the restraints can be picked and slid free, making no noise.

The other method is using friction to rub a shoelace or other material against the plastic restraint at a specific point and then with a strength based hazard check, instead of an agility based HC, an attempt to quickly jerk and snap the restraint can be made. Either method allows one attempt to snap the poly-restraint, with one attempt allowed per 12 minutes for a trained escape artist, or each half hour for an untrained captive. These same techniques can be used to get free of duct tape and similar bindings.

**Pick Handcuffs:** This ability also includes picking a replica and relic keyed or combination padlock. If this PC also has the lock picking skill, allow them two chances at this on whatever skill table presents the better odds of success. One attempt to pick a set of handcuffs or a lock can be made each minute by a trained escape artist. An untrained person, however, gets an attempt every half hour and only if they hid a paper clip, lock pick tool, or other tiny metal probe on their person prior to capture. This skill can also be used to pick a lock that is not holding a character, such as when the PCs want to break into an off-limits building in a new era town that has a replica padlock on the door.

**Escape a Net, Snake's Coils, or Tentacles:** This includes slipping free of a constrictor snake's body with one follow-up attempt per minute allowed, although the first try to slip free can occur on the round after a character is ensnared in some sort of coiling tendril, net, or tentacle, including sheets of spider web, snares, razor wire and the like. The game master must okay the attempt and decide the odds — often behind a GM screen. Both untrained and trained users of this skill have the same immediate, and per minute attempt rate to slip free.

**Escape from Cage or Straight Jacket:** For untrained characters, only one attempt per hour is allowed, while a trained escape artists can make an attempt every ten minutes. Straight jackets are rarely used in the Epochian new era, but exist. Instead of a straight jacket, the scenario might see this character tied up in a body bag, canvas sack, or some other whole-body restraint, including a box, barrel, or suitcase, all of which can be escaped from using this column. Cages, pens, enclosing traps and the like are also difficult to get free of, and usually involve finding a weak spot in the construction. However, by working at it with strength, and dogged determination, a weak point can be made, snapped apart and allow the escape artist to bust out — often bringing similar sized or smaller companions with them.

**Squirm Through Tight Space:** The would-be escapee can contort their body and attempt to wriggle through a hole that is only slightly larger than its head or hip bone. If successful, they can move at a rate of 25cm per round to creep though pipes, drains, cracks in walls, openings in rubble piles, and passages that are impossible for others even of the same size. The escapee can't wear hard armor, and if possible, will strip naked and lather themselves in oil, fat or muck to make them slippery.

When the need to escape with their belongings, a foot line can be tied to one ankle and a small pack or collection of belongings dragged along behind the squirming character. While untrained people can attempt this feat, they only get once chance per half hour, while a trained escape artist can attempt to fit into a likely gap or hole every minute.

The game master's judgment on what is possible for each sized character is necessary, and logic will have to play into the use of this skill. For example, if the character with the escape artist skill is actually larger than another PC, it makes no sense that he can fit into a hole where a much smaller character can't. In this case, it is the escape artist who might identify the escape route, and because of their knack for crawling into small openings, make the passage wide enough for all smaller statured characters to follow in their wake, too.

If a very short mutant character has a massive head, two heads, antlers or bone spikes growing from their shoulders, or has any other obvious restrictive features, then the GM must disallow escape via a crevice or hole.

If GM hand waving isn't enough to determine who can fit into which escape route, then for those needing a mathematical system, use the following: A character with this skill can fit into a hole 1/7th his or her height (14.28 %), thus a 2m (200cm) tall character can fit into a hole 28.56 cm (200cm x 0.1428 =28.56cm) wide. Calculation: Height of character in centimeters x 0.1428 = diameter of escape hole). For those of you using the Imperial system, and have recorded your character's height in feet and inches, here is the measurement conversion for you: 1 inch = 2.54 centimeters.

## Table XR-175/ Escape Artist Slipping Free Matrix
*Use Character's Agility trait to make Hazard Checks*

| Skill Points | Untie Rope | Poly-Restraint** | Pick Handcuffs*** | Net or Tentacle | Cage/ Straight Jacket | Squirm |
|---|---|---|---|---|---|---|
| Untrained | H | I | J | G | K | G |
| 1 | C | D | E | C | F | D |
| 2 | B | C | D | B | D | C |
| 3 | A | B | C | A | B | B |
| 4 | A* | A | B | A | A | A |
| 5 Max | A* | A* | A | A* | A | A* |

** Two attempts allowed per time to achieve based on abilities descriptions above.*
*** Character can instead use their strength score to attempt to snap poly-restraints if their STR score is higher.*
****Should this character also have the lock picking skill, use PC's accuracy trait and teat as 'Open Replica Padlock' column on page 48 of the hub rules.*

# Feint

This skill, which has a maximum of 5 skill points, resembles the dodge skill, but the user employs it after the melee range opponent attacks. In short, **the user of this skill lets the attacker get the initiative**, and concentrates first on side stepping, hopping off the ground, ducking or otherwise suckering the foe into making a move to open itself up to this character's attack.

The character gains **-5 DV per skill point** (max -25 DV) to his or her defense value during this maneuver, yet risks death or injury if the attacker manages to make a successful strike, followed by the character's own attack **at +5 SV per skill point** (max +25 SV), taking advantage of the opening the attacker made.

While this is a melee range (3m) only combat tactic, it does allow ranged weapons such as guns and crossbows to be employed by this user in close quarters fighting, but not bows, spears, javelins, grenades, slings or other contraptions which require swinging, drawing or throwing.

Somebody without this skill who attempts to feint gets no DV or SV bonus at all and is just asking for injury.

# Fencing

Fencing is considered a gentleman's art from the ancient world. An art brought back to life in the Epochian era as ammo for relic weapons became scarce, even as the need to protect oneself at all times increased. This art involves the use of a thin dueling blade called a rapier, but often in conjunction with a knife or dagger in the user's non-dominant or 'off' hand to parry or stab.

This skill is usually restricted to elite humans, nobility, and officers of a civilized settlement, and thus its instruction is rarely accessible to a nomad, barbarian, savage, commoner or slave. When reaching 7th rank, and gaining an extra melee attack, as do all characters, he or she can make 2 rapier and 2 dagger strikes per round. A flurry of blades that can be as devastating to a foe as if facing a machine gun, except that unless the fencer's weapon snaps on a fumble roll, the rapier will not run low of ammo. Any character with three or more limbs can wield extra rapiers or daggers and add to their number of attacks per round. If the fencer wishes to parry with both dagger and rapier,

with each weapon trying to check the weapons of one or two opponents, he or she may do so, with rapier offering a base of -24 DV instead of the base of -10 DV as shown for a dagger on the following table.

Unless starting game play as a prisoner, slave, or otherwise with nothing, this character will own a rapier and dagger.

With the fencing skill, weapon expert cannot also be applied to the rapier, while Knife fighting can be applied to the dagger.

## Table XR-176 / Fencing Matrix

| Skill Points | Rapier SV Bonus | Rapier DMG Inflicted | Dagger SV bonus | Dagger DMG Bonus | Dagger Parry DV Bonus* |
|---|---|---|---|---|---|
| Untrained | +3 (normal) | nil (1d12) | off-hand -20 | nil | -10 DV** |
| 1 | +5 | 1d20 | +1 | +1 | -12 DV |
| 2 | +8 | 1d20+2 | +2 | +2 | -14 DV |
| 3 | +11 | 1d20+4 | +3 | +3 | -16 DV |
| 4 | +15 | 1d20+6 | +5 | +4 | -18 DV |
| 5 | +20 | 1d20+9 | +7 | +5 | -20 DV |
| 6 | +24 | 1d20+12 | +9 | +6 | -22 DV |
| 7 | +30 | 1d20+16 | +11 | +7 | -24 DV |
| Points Above | +3 | +3 DMG | +1 | +1 | -2 DV |

*This parry is instead of a strike attempt by the dagger hand, used to block physical attacks including thrown or fired archaic weapons such as spears and javelins, arrows and crossbow bolts, which can be seen approaching. Only one parry can be made against one opponent's strike and not a second enemy who might be engaging the PC.

** As shown on the Parry Benefits by Weapon Table on page 108 of the Hub Rules, a dagger or knife will give even an untrained user a -10 to their defense value against one opponent but means the person performing the parry loses their attack. This maneuver still allows even an untrained person their regular attack with their rapier.

# Fisher, Master

Either from a boat, the shores of a creek, or through the ice, this character knows the right spot, the right lures, the right bait, and the wrong fish. A fisherman in the new era puts his life on the line when he throws bait into the water, for the marine environment of the 24th century contains the deadliest life forms ever to swim, scuttle or shimmy through Earth's waters.

The member of the caste of fisher, described on page 13 of the hub rule, automatically starts with 1d3 points in this skill. They will have lures, a replica rod, a crude reel, a line and a homemade net. On the following table, each tier of a master fisher, including an untrained person, rolls each hour for the chance to hook trouble — which usually means an unwanted predatory fish, frog, gator or worm that aims to devour the character and its companions — with less experienced anglers more likely to use the wrong bait, cast into the wrong pool, or fail to identify the movements of the water, type of fins that break the surface, or behaviors of birds, other fish and water creatures in the area. See the follow-up table below the Fisher Master's Angeling Matrix for the sort of trouble one might have hooked.

Also, each hour, roll the assigned dice for the character's fishing skill, which is a die between a d10, d12 or d20 with a reduction amount applied to it. For example, a 2 skill point fisher rolls 1d10 -5 which means roll a 1d10 and minus 5 from the result to get a range of 0-5 fish hooked per hour. Once any fish is hooked, see the next column and roll the percentage chance shown, or less, to bring in a hooked fish.

In most cases, the sort of fish caught in freshwater include (**roll 1d10** for random catch) **1-3.** trout / **4.** sucker fish / **5.** spawning salmon / **6.** sturgeon / **7.** pike / **8.** bass / **9.** yellow perch / **10.** walleye, to name a few.

Such fish yield 3d6 x 100g of meat each, with 100g enough flesh for one average-sized person's meal when served with other foodstuffs, too. Of course, it would take four times this to satisfy a muscular, highly active new era excavator's appetite and protein needs, with one whole fish needed for each typical digger being appropriate. Fish meat will fetch about 1sp per 500g of flesh sold, double or triple this in areas suffering under starvation conditions.

## Table XR-177/ Fisher Master's Angeling Matrix

| Fisher's Skill Points | Hourly Chance to Hook Trouble* | Eatable Fish Hooked Hourly | Chance to Land an Eatable Fish |
|---|---|---|---|
| Untrained | 53% | 1d10 -8 (0 to 2) | 26% |
| 1 | 41% | 1d10 -6 (0 to 4) | 59% |
| 2 | 34% | 1d10 -5 (0 to 5) | 76% |
| 3 | 26% | 1d10 -4 (0 to 6) | 84% |
| 4 | 19% | 1d12 -4 (0 to 8) | 92% |
| 5 | 8% | 1d12 -3 (0 to 9) | 97% |
| 6 | 5% | 1d20 -3 (0 to 17) | 98% |
| 7 (max) | 3% | 1d20 -2 (0 to 18) | 99% |

### Hooked Trouble

Trouble is a predatory aquatic animal that has grabbed the line and surfaced with it, seeing the fisher and attacking. If the fisher is in a boat, the predator will attempt to attack the boat, but, if the fisher is casting from shore and the predator is incapable of going ashore, it will simply yank furiously and possibly pull the fishing rod clear out of the fisher's hands. The fisher must make a type B strength based Hazard check to hold on and let the line snap, losing the lure. Roll from the following random hooked predator table, 1d100:

## Table XR-178/ Fisher's Troubled Catch List

| 1d100 | Troubled Catch | |
|---|---|---|
| 01-04. | Alligator, small, pg. TME-148 | |
| 05-10. | Alligator, large, pg. TME-148 | |
| 11-13. | Alligator, huge, pg. TME-148 | |
| 14-16. | Alligator, giant, pg. TME-148 | |
| 17-21. | Fish, Prankor, pg. TME-153 | |
| 22-28. | Fish, Normuk, pg. TME-153 | |
| 29-36. | Fish, Galporra, pg. TME-153 | |
| 37-46. | Fish, Land Pike, pg. TME-153 | |
| 47-51. | Fish, Ghastfin, pg. TME-153 | |
| 52-57. | Frog, Venomous, pg. TME-155 | |
| 58-66. | Frog, Giant, pg. TME-155 | |
| 67-72. | Frog, Aberrant, pg. TME-155 | |
| 73-77. | Frog, Wolf Frog, pg. TME-155 | |
| 78-83. | Insect, Swamp Skimmer, pg. TME-158 | |
| 84-88. | Insect, Mud Grabbers, pg. TME-160 | |
| 89-92. | Shark, Freshwater, pg. TME-170 | |
| 93-95. | Shark, Horrid, pg. TME-170 | |
| 96. | Shark, Huge Horrid, pg. TME-170 | |
| 97. | Shark, Amphibious, pg. TME-170 | |
| 98. | Snake, Large, pg. TME-171 | |
| 99,00. | Worm, Jaw, pg. TME-175 | |

# Hand Signals

When entering the ruins, where keeping silent, and yet communicating among a team is essential, this single point skill is a lifesaver.

These hand signals are based on old world US military silent signals. Typically, these signals are made discreetly by a point person who gestures back to waiting comrades — comrades who can't yet see what the lead person can see. Somebody who knows this system can use the following gestures to relate limited, but essential information to others who know these same gestures:

### Identification of personnel and beings

| | | |
|---|---|---|
| You | sniper | android |
| me | sentry or guard spotted | skullocks |
| man | dog | warmorts |
| woman | mutant | moaners |
| hostage | cyborg | green walkers |
| child | robot | predatory plant |

### Directions to comrades

| | |
|---|---|
| Come here | Fan out and form firing line |
| Advance | Hide and remain silent until all clear given |
| Halt | Split up |
| Down | Flee and return to last rally point |
| Listen up | Mission objective spotted |
| Cover me | Medic needed |
| Faster | Break right or break left |
| Silence | Take target alive |
| I don't understand | Kill them all |
| WTF | Disregard last command |
| I need ammo | Abort mission |
| Regroup | Single file marching order |

### Signals that represent threats and weaponry carried by hostiles

| | |
|---|---|
| Shotgun | Auto turret |
| Laser weapon | Gun emplacement |
| Flying drone | Trip line |
| Assault rifle | Trap spotted |
| Pistol | Security cameras spotted |
| Land mine | Possible radiation contamination ahead |

### Hand motions that represent terrain or structural aspects

| | |
|---|---|
| Door | Treacherous flooring |
| Window | Pit |
| Stairs | Suspected trap ahead |
| Corner | Perilous terrain |
| Collapsed ceiling | Vehicle |
| Cliff or drop off ahead | |

### Miscellaneous hand signals

Distance with fingers raised showing meters ahead to whatever objective
Target structural feature or threat is spotted

As per Table XR-168 on page 200 of this book, a person with this skill can slowly train comrades who don't have it, with success achieved after two months of daily training. A dig team or mercenary brigade that works together for months on end will typically add other hand signals. These unique signals pertain to their group's operations and nicknames for each member. Individual IDs are used so that a specific operator can be brought up from further back in the marching order or given some task.

# Herbalist

This skill involves the use of common herbs for cooking, making fragrant potpourri, herbal tea and the like. While a herbalist can use old world plants, such as St. John's wort, elderberry, ginkgo biloba, ginseng, echinacea, turmeric and ginger to great effect, they can do far more when these are mixed with new era mutant plants and fungi. These blends include medicinal tinctures, extracts, recreational concoctions, miracle healing ointments, disinfectants and curatives.

There are four skill tiers to this area of knowledge, and while many primitive people and humanoids rely solely on herbal medicines to treat their sick, injured and forlorn, many advanced groups disregard and disparage this form of medicine as baseless superstition and pseudo-science. In truth, any herbalist of two or more skill points is a great asset to their people, dig team, or military expedition and can offer very real aid to the injured.

Should a person have both the medic and herbalist skill, they are an even more beneficial to any team or community. Each herbalist will begin game play with a large, multi-pocket satchel with a shoulder strap. Within this case, the herbalist carries all their current assortment of herbs, tincture making alcohol, glass vials, oils, mixing bowls, zippy bags and wax paper packets of ingredients they need. Those who can read and write will also carry sheets of yellowed paper with recipes for their own custom concoctions.

The following table presents the most common Epochian era tinctures and extracts, healing ointments and other astounding creations made by a trained herbalist. While those with more skill in this area can make rarer, often more powerful mixtures, any herbalist will be able to use those made by a more advanced practitioner, and might even start game play with a few vials of something beyond his or her abilities.

All of these concoctions make use of potent mutant plants and fungi, along with other hard to find and expensive ingredients. Most adventurer-herbalists are too busy, or unfamiliar, with the wilderness around a newly visited community to spend days on end wandering the tangled mutant forests and swamps to harvest their own ingredients. While they can do so, it will take 3d6 days to find what they need to make one batch of a dozen vials of any given tincture or extract, and so prefer to buy their ingredients from other herbalists and knowledgeable locales.

A description of each tincture or extract is listed below the skill table and includes the method of administration, cost to make, amount earned to sell or buy ready made mixes, and result of consumption. The last table for this skill listing shows how many ready-to-use vials a beginning herbalist will start with, based on how many initial skill points he or she has.

## Table XR-179/ Herbalist Skills Matrix

| Skill Points | Items Herbalist can Mix Up and Administer |
|---|---|
| Untrained | • Soothing tea, crude potpourri, blended herbs to season a roast chicken or fish. |
| 1 | • Tincture of Disinfection<br>• Extract of Resolve<br>• Tincture of Immune boosting |
| 2 | • Ointment of pain relief<br>• Extract of Blissful Slumber<br>• Tincture of Energy |
| 3 | • Extract of Toxin Elimination<br>• Tincture of Mental Clarity<br>• Tincture of Calm and Confidence |
| 4 max | • Tincture of Healing<br>• Extract of Aphrodite<br>• Tincture of Muscular Prowess<br>• Extract of The Grave |

### Descriptions of Epochian Herbal Tinctures, Ointments and Extracts

Note: All tinctures and extracts come in 20ml glass, cork topped, hand blown little bottles called vials unless otherwise stated. 1 drop = 5ml.

**Tincture of Disinfection:** Either 5 drops are taken orally, or the same amount is poured onto an infected wound, venomous animal bite, or other likely infectious wound. This disinfectant will first off allow the patient an extra hazard check against any consumed or bodily injected venom or toxin. For external infections, the tincture has a 77% chance of cleaning the wound and removing an infection or venom. A 20ml vial of this bright blue tincture costs 100+1d100sp to make, but to buy a ready made vial costs 200+2d100sp.

**Extract of Resolve:** Consuming 5 drops (5ml) of this bright green, syrupy fluid will raise the drinker's willpower trait by +10 points for 1 hour. Drinking 10ml will add only +2 more WL, while drinking 15ml adds +1 extra WL, and 20ml +1WL more for a total of +14 willpower max in a 24 hour period. A 20ml vial costs 50+2d20sp to make and can be bought for 100+1d100sp.

**Tincture of Immune Boosting:** Consuming 5ml of this golden, highly pungent tincture will increase the drinker's immunity to all exposures of plague, bio-toxins, common colds, flus and stomach bugs, plus any other toxin, poison or venom that calls for a hazard check, and gives the consumer one extra hazard check. Taking more than 5ml causes no benefit or harm. This tincture remains effective in the body for 6 hours and costs 70+1d100sp to make, but can be purchased for 200+1d100sp.

**Ointment of Pain Relief:** Packaged in wax paper rolls, these 50ml packets of olive green paste allow the herbalist or healer to squeeze out a 10ml portion and spread it over each wound on a living being. Not only will this ointment take away the pain of the injury for an hour, but will heal 1 endurance point of damage to the victim. This ointment does not disinfect wounds, but can be used in conjugation with other mixes that do. To make 50ml of this substance costs 20+1d20sp, but it can be purchased at 80+2d20 per 50ml portion.

**Extract of Blissful Slumber:** In short, this honey colored, thick liquid acts like a sleep drug. 5ml portions applied as drops on the tongue will greatly relax a person or animal and make them drowsy, rid them of most aches and pains, and allow them to drift off into a blissful sleep with ease.

It is also possible to use this stuff to put somebody to sleep against their will. This extract is normally tasteless when put into a drink, at least in the normal 5 or 10ml sized portions, but any higher amounts can easily be seen in most liquids, and tasted after the first sip; allow a drinker a type D perception based hazard check to notice that their food or drink tastes odd. If noticing this strange flavor, the drinker can decide to not consume more than the initial 5ml of the test sip, and so decline more of whatever drugged substance they were about to consume.

Slipping a subject 10ml to 20ml will force them to make a type E endurance based hazard check or drop into a deep sleep — but not unconsciousness. If moved, tied up or stripped and robbed, the subject is thus jostled too much and allowed a type F perception based hazard check to wake, although will be at -5 initiative and half strength for the next hour and so perhaps easy enough to restrain. If administered 21ml to 40ml, the victim must make a type J endurance based hazard check or pass out without any hope of waking, even if roughly disturbed, for 12+1d12 hours. Anyone given more than 40ml has the same hazard check as if given 21-40ml, but must make a further type H willpower based hazard check or slip into a coma for 3d6 days and at the end of it, make a final type C endurance based hazard check or suffer a cardiac event and die.

This substance costs 100+1d100sp to create a 20ml vial, but can be bought for 200+1d100sp — although in some communities it is highly regulated if not banned, and those caught with it will be forbidden from ever returning to the community, or fined a thousand silver coins, or enslaved and their property confiscated by the local rulers.

**Tincture of Energy:** This purple fluid is consumed through the consumptions of 1ml portions. Each 1 milliliter drop keeps a person awake for one extra hour beyond their normal bedtime and improves energy; add +1 endurance per milliliter consumed.

The danger with this substance is that if more than 10ml are taken in a 24 hour period, it puts a person into a manic state. For every 1ml portion consumed over 10ml in a 24 hour period, that amount, +10, is the percentage chance that at the end of their period of wakefulness, not only will the increased endurance fade away but that is the same percentage chance the person 'crashes' and drops into unconsciousness for 3d6 hours.

For example, if a character takes 14 drops within a 24 hour period, at the end of his or her wakefulness and endurance bonus, there is a 14% chance they pass out for 3d6 hours thereafter. The endurance points are treated as the first ones depleted if the character takes damage. These unnatural endurance points do not heal back if lost in combat or other trauma.

A 20ml vial of this substance can be made at a cost of 140+1d100sp, or can be purchased for 300+1d100sp each.

**Extract of Toxin Elimination:** This pale pink liquid must be administered right after a person is exposed to a toxic gas, venomous bite, projectile or other attack vector or consumes poison. If the contents of an entire 20ml bottle are ingested within 2 rounds, the toxin exposed person is allowed an additional hazard check, identical to whatever was called for by the toxin. Even if the drinker is unlucky, and fails the check, they suffer only half the harm of whatever substance they've been exposed to, such as half the trait point depletion, or half the duration of the toxin's effects. If the toxin called for the death of the character should they fail both hazard checks, then instead of death, the victim merely drops into a coma for 6d6 hours.

To mix up and create a 20ml vial of this extract will cost the herbalist 160+2d100sp, while for a character to buy it, a NPC herbalist will sell each vial for 400+1d100sp.

**Tincture of Mental Clarity:** For every milliliter of this bitter tasting tincture consumed, the drinker's intelligence score increases by +1 INT for 10 minutes. As an example, if a character takes 7 drops, at 1 milliliter per drop, he will gain +7 intelligence for 70 minutes.

This is a remarkably potent tincture, especially if given to a mutant with mental powers who relies on intelligence for making a mental assault. More than 20ml can be consumed, but for every milliliter above 20, there is a risk of causing a mental side effect. Such side effects include a stroke that can cause death. Use the following table to determine the risk based on consumption beyond 20ml:

**Table XR-180/ Excessive Consumption of Tincture of Mental Clarity Results**

| Excessive Tincture Amount | Hazard Check | Harm on Failed Hazard Check |
|---|---|---|
| 21-25ml | A | Debilitating headache, no use of mental mutations for 2d6 hours. |
| 26-30ml | B | Terrible headache that disallows use of any mental or energy based mutations for 3d6 hours |
| 31-35ml | C | Awful headaches that block all energy and mental mutation use for 4d6 hours, plus deafness for 1d6 hours |
| 36-40ml | D | God awful headaches that stop the use of any energy based or mental mutations for 1d4 days, plus blindness for 1d8 hours. |
| 41-50ml | E | Incredible headache that disallows energy based or mental mutations use for 2d6 days, plus PC passes out for 3d6 minutes. |
| 51-60ml | F | Pass out for 4d6 minutes, and wake blind and deaf and unable to use any energy or mental mutations for 3d6 days. |
| 61-80ml | G | Drop into a coma for 4d6 hours, and at the end, make another identical hazard check to avoid a stroke. If a stroke occurs, see details below (for 81ml or more). No energy or mental mutations for 4d6 days. |
| 81ml or more | H | Stroke! Pass out for 3d6 minutes and after which another identical HC. Success means the person recovers slowly and is at half strength and agility for the next 3d6 days. Failure means character dies. No energy or mental mutations for 5d6 days. |

This garish purple colored tincture is expensive to make and costs the herbalist 300+1d100sp to make 20ml. For anybody to buy this potent and possibly dangerous liquid will need to pay 500+2d100sp per 20ml.

**Tincture of Calm and Confidence:** It takes 5 drops of this tincture to induce an effect, while consuming more seems to do nothing. Once imbibed, the user will feel a rush of confidence, calm and effervescence wash over them. They will visibly change, and onlookers will see a refreshed, vibrant, and frankly better looking version of whoever the person was before consuming the orange tincture. This liquid will enhance the character's willpower and appearance score by +3d6 for 1 hour.

It costs 50+1d100sp to make 20ml of this 'beauty elixir', while to buy it from another herbalist will cost 180+1d100sp.

**Tincture of Healing:** This is a dark blue liquid that is sold in 20ml glass vials like most herbalist concoctions, but can also be found in large bottles. For every two drops (2ml) consumed by an injured person or animal, including plantoids, 1 trait point will be healed by the drinker, however, consuming too much will induce a narcotic effect in the user which can induce an unexpected and often intolerable change. After every use within a 24 hour period, the drinker must roll a d100, with the milliliters he or she has consumed being the percentage chance of an unexpected outcome.

For example, if a PC drinks 6ml, then they have a 6% a chance (roll of 01-06 on a 1d100) of experiencing an unexpected outcome. If the character drinks some of this tincture for a second or third time in a day, then each of these additional consumption events calls for yet another percentage chance that something bizarre happens to the drinker, with the total drops consumed that day now being the chance.

If an unexpected outcome occurs, roll for the result on the following table:

**1.** The drinker suddenly seizes up, drops whatever it is holding, twitches uncontrollably and falls over unconscious for 10+1d20 minutes.

**2.** The consumer has a terrible panic attack and cannot proceed, cannot continue the mission and insists that everybody is going to die if they proceed with whatever plan or pathway they are taking. He or she must make a willpower based type D hazard check or turn and walk away from the team and attempt to head back to the last safe town or campsite. The duration of this anxiety is 10+4d6 minutes.

**3.** The character seems intoxicated, slurs their speech, is reduced to half their agility and accuracy traits, speaks way too loud, thinks everything is funny as hell and that those around them are +30 appearance higher. This drunkenness lasts for 1d6 hours.

**4.** This character hears voices in their head — although the voices are not talking to them directly. GM: This PC is picking up telepathic communications within 100km, and if any other character has telepathy, that mutant can converse with this tincture drinker in a two way dialog for the next 2d6 hours.

**5.** The character feels strange, sees strange ghostly smoke trial in the air or around the corners of rooms. GM: This character can now see dimensional beings, too, if they exist in the campaign. This extra sensory ability lasts for 2d6 hours.

**6.** The drinker heals far faster than normal, at 1 recovered trait point per milliliter instead of every 2ml consumed. There is a further 1 in 6 chance that the healing goes beyond all expectations and the character permanently gains +1 point to each trait.

Tincture of healing will cost the herbalist 100+3d20sp to make a 20ml vial. To buy this miraculous substance will set a person back 300+1d100sp.

**Extract of Aphrodite:** Made from a wide range of aphrodisiac, libido enhancing plants and mushrooms, including the sap of the infamous anchoris tree, this extract is sometimes dried into cubes or granules and burnt to make a colored smoke which is then inhaled by visitors to pleasure spas, brothels and other dens of carnal delight. While considerably less potent than the smoke of pure anchoris sap, this extract is nevertheless a proven enhancer of both one's ability and compulsion for all things sexual. For every 5ml consumed, a person's carnal needs and potency will be enhanced for 1 hour. The more one consumes, the stronger the urges. Even after the time of influence passes, it takes several days for the person to return to their normal libido levels.

Their highly sought after extract requires several difficult to find ingredients, and so is rather costly to make at 140+1d100sp per 20ml vial. To buy this extract will cost 300+1d100sp.

**Tincture of Muscular Prowess:** This red hued liquid gives the consumer a brief boost to their physical strength. Every drop adds +1 to their strength trait for 1 minute. If more than 20ml are consumed, risks of a serious muscle spasm can occur. For each drop over 20ml then, there is a cumulative 3% chance of a seizure occurring. Thus, if 21ml are taken, there is only a 3% chance, while if 34 drops are taken, there is a 42% chance of a seizure (14 ml over 20ml 'safe zone'. 14 x 3% =42%), and so on. The seizure check is made whenever a feat of strength is made, including a strength based strike attempt, or after 20 minutes, whichever occurs first.

A muscle seizure means the character's legs and arms go rigid and become extremely painful and hard to control. The character is reduced to half movement, half agility, half accuracy and half their base, unaltered strength during the seizure, which lasts for one or more minutes.

Every minute of the seizures after the first, the sufferer is allowed a willpower based type D hazard check to shake off the seizures and return to normal. Should more of this tincture be taken within 24 hours, the newly consumed amount is added to the old amount as far as a seizure risk goes, without the strength benefits of the earlier consumption.

A 20ml vial of this strength enhancer costs the herbalist 90+2d20sp to make, while to buy a vial will cost 200+1d100sp.

**Extract of The Grave:** This Extract is exceedingly rare, both in its availability and use. The herbalist who initially made it was supposedly a star person, or a spacer from an orbital space station who crashed to earth on some ill fated expedition. As a lone survivor, she was brought to a barter fort and sold as a slave. Little known to the lecherous master who bought her for his collection, she was a master botanist and was able to concoct enough of this extract to knock out her keeper and his guards — and in fact gave her hated master so much of the stuff that he never regained consciousness.

Authorities investigating the mysterious and beautiful spacer's escape found the ingredients and recipe for this potent extract, and sold the instructions and materials list far and wide. Now, master herbalists throughout the regions and beyond know of this concoction which when administered in 20ml amount, will force the drinker to make a type G endurance based hazard check or grow drowsy and then drop into a sleep so deep that to anybody but a trained medic, would think the person is dead. Those who do not pass out are at the very least weakened so that they're half every trait, except appearance and endurance, for the next 2d6 hours.

Those who do succumb remain in a death-like coma for 4d6 hours. If more of this black, cloudy yet flavorless elixir is given in higher quantities, such as 21 to 40ml, the subject must make two hazard checks, and will remain unconscious for 3d6 days, after which he or she must make a type B endurance based hazard check or slip into a coma for 4d6 months, and likely die from starvation and dehydration unless tended to around the clock by a medic of 3 or more skill points. This extract is banned in most civilized communities — at least those places that know of the substance — and costs a herbalist 500+1d1000sp in ingredient costs to make 20ml. To buy a 20ml vial, and only on the black market, the cost is 1000+1d1000sp.

**Beginning Herbalist Inventory**
For every herbalist skill point a character starts game play with, roll 3 times on the following inventory list to establish what they carry. For those tinctures and elixirs that are beyond their own skills to make, it is assumed that their former teacher gifted the vials or ointment packs to this character.

**Table XR-181/ Herbalsits Starting Items**

| 1d100 | Herbalist Starting Items (Roll 3x) |
|---|---|
| 01-11. | Tincture of Disinfection, 20ml vial |
| 12-19. | Extract of Resolve, 20ml vial |
| 20-32. | Tincture of Immune Boosting, 20ml vial |
| 33-41. | Ointment of Pain Relief, 50ml package |
| 42-50. | Extract of Blissful Slumber, 20ml vial |
| 51-59. | Tincture of Energy, 20ml vial |
| 60-67. | Extract of Toxin Elimination, 20ml vial |
| 68-74. | Tincture of Mental Clarity, 20ml vial |
| 75-82. | Tincture of Calm and Confidence, 20ml vial |
| 83-88. | Tincture of Healing, 20ml vial |
| 89-92. | Extract of Aphrodite, 20ml vial |
| 93-96. | Tincture of Muscular Prowess, 20ml vial |
| 97-00. | Extract of The Grave, 20ml vial |

# Historian, Epochian

The character knows their region's history after the collapse of the old civilization, as well as tidbits about the area prior to the age of devastation. This recent history aficionado also has knowledge, though spotty, of world history from various books and disks he has had access to. PCs with this skill are allowed a type D intelligence based hazard check to accurately identify a large ruined metropolises' facilities and features and have very good idea of the place's old world name, function and structural features. While not a new era zoologist, he or she also has a chance of knowing the origins of a line of creatures that have infested that area since at least this PC's lifetime.

Besides being a repository of the local area history, as far as the ruins and common creatures go, this person will also be familiar with the communities of the local region, and know a place's religion, governmental structure, founding, and tolerances toward mutants or other races. This local area knowledge will also extend to problem areas in the wilderness or large communities, too, such as dangerous gangs, cults or factions to avoid.

For the game master, who might need to field questions from this character's player about some new village, ruin site, stretch of old highway, or an NPC, it can be daunting either researching the details from a source book or adventure, or else making up details on the fly. If making it up, it is okay to change information later, since much of what an Epochian historian knows is rumors or erroneous knowledge. To be safe, however, it's always a good idea to keep a pad of paper and pencil handy for writing notes about people and places that might need to be discussed again or added to a map or adventure session log for later use.

If this character can't read, it means he or she has learned everything they know about the surrounding region from word of mouth, song and rumor. This skill has a 1 point maximum.

# Historian, Pre-Apocalypse

This well educated character can read and write, and has an accurate understanding of the history of the world up to where the cataclysm began. At this cutoff point, records of the fall became sketchy, if kept at all. In the end times, propaganda mixed with truth, while Ai issued deep fakes and deceptive, hyper realistic, real-time news footage and false information was everywhere.

This historian of the old world will know about the origins of life on earth, prehistoric times, ancient history, major old religions of the world, military and cultural histories, and a vast number of famous and infamous individuals throughout the ages. They will understand the old world's geography prior to the collapse of civilization. Prior to the upheavals of the continents, rising and lowering of seas and mountain ranges. This individual will recall the boundaries of nations, states and municipalities, will probably retain old road maps, and be able to identify prominent landmarks, buildings and the remnants of any bridges that might still exist.

Much of their knowledge is useless, since so much of the landscape has been wiped clear or jostled about so badly that its barely recognizable. Still, the game master can allow the player a type D intelligence based hazard check to recognize some aspect of an old cityscape or stretch of road and either locate it, and its ancient purpose, on a map or from their memory.

Such information could indeed be valuable, especially if a dig team is searching for an ancient military base, bunker network, spaceport, or airfield.

In a pinch, this historian could entertain comrades or the patrons of a saloon for hours with tales of the old world, and earn a few coins for a hot meal and cold drink.

This character will identify most old world languages when she sees them, even if she can't read them. This is a one point maximum skill.

# Homesteader *by Danny Seedhouse*

All new characters from these pre-game castes: fishermen, hunters, miners, loggers, and farmers, get this skill automatically. This is the catch-all talent that covers a broad range of tasks and knowledge needed to live a self-sufficient lifestyle outside the bounds of an established settlement. Homesteading includes subsistence agriculture, the home preservation of food, and well as the production of textiles, clothing and crafts of various types for household use.

This skill allows a person or small family group to establish themselves in the wilderness, build a robust structure, cut down trees, plow a field, plant crops, butcher animals, dig a well, and increase their odds of survival in the harsh Epochian frontier. Should a dozen or more homesteaders combine forces, they could build a walled compound and establish a village within a single year — although defending it from beasts, raiders and humanoids often requires attracting those of a warrior caste, especially stout hearted and noble excavators.

divulge a secret, or break down and just blurt out whatever the interrogator asks. There is always a minimum of 1% chance to succeed at a hazard check.

If, however, the tables are turned and victim has the lying skill, this negates this decrease in the needed hazard check number, and gives the prisoner a +5% greater odds per hazard check of thwarting the questioner. Likewise, if the prisoner should also have the interrogator skill, each skill point they have reduces the captor's own interrogation skill point, to a minimum of the untrained tier.

Examples of trickery are for the interrogator to ask questions and watch for the prisoner's body language or facial expressions that give away a lie or when the interrogator accurately guesses at some piece of information or truth. Likewise, the interrogator can act like other prisoners have already confessed to the crime, plot, or given up the needed information, or else informed against the prisoner and that the questioning is just a formality prior to their execution, prison sentence, or transfer to the nearest slavery depot.

The prisoner of a trickery interrogation uses their **Intelligence and Perception traits, divided by two**, to get the **Anti-Trickery trait** used for the hazard check on the Trickery Interrogation Skill Use table. One hazard check must be made every half hour of this form of interrogation.

# Interrogation

This skill can be used by both player characters trying to get information from a captive, or when a PC is itself at the mercy of a non-player character interrogator.

An individual with this skill has been instructed by the most ruthless, inhumane, and sadistic members of whatever former community this person came from. The PC learned these cruel and cunning arts as either an apprentice to the head interrogator, or as a guard who had to stand by as the master did their work, perhaps even aiding in the mistreatment or beating of prisoners if commanded to do so.

While torture is part of this character's repertoire of information extraction techniques, other methods are also available. To cause a prisoner to confess to a crime, admit forbidden thoughts, lack of religious adherence, or give up valuable information can often be accomplished with trickery, threats, bribes, humiliation, lies or demonstrations of others undergoing torture — especially the prisoner's loved ones. In some respects, this skill is related to both the negotiating and lying skills as described in the hub rules, with each of those skills potentially adding to this interrogator's abilities to convince a restrained prisoner to give up whatever intel they have, confess to something, sell out somebody or some group to save their own skin.

There are three main categories of interrogation: trickery, bribery and torture. Different techniques have differing hazard check challenges, with the addition of torture being the hardest for a prisoner to cope with. Each has its own table shown with its own combined set of traits used on a hazard check roll for the victim to try to hold out, or sometimes, deceive the torturer and make them believe they got a truthful confession.

## Trickery Interrogation

This method is enhanced if the interrogator has the lying skill, too, and for each skill point in lying, subtract 5% to the hazard check number the prisoner must make, per thirty minutes of interrogation, to not inadvertently reveal the truth or, confess,

## Table XR-182/ Trickery Interrogation Skill Use

| Interrogator's Skill Points | Hazard Check to Avoid Falling for Trickery |
|---|---|
| **Untrained** | A |
| **1** | C |
| **2** | E |
| **3** | H |
| **4** | J |
| **5 Max** | L |

## Bribery Interrogation

The best bribe a doomed prisoner can get is the offer of either freedom for themself, or for their loved ones. Other bribes could be for the interrogator to convince the prisoner to give up information without enduring torture, to protect their people, their family and friends who will be made to suffer if the prisoner does not make it easy on everybody and give up whatever confession or information is sought. More traditional bribes include a payment in silver, land, relics or something the interrogator knows the prisoners truly desires, including a place in the interrogator's organization should they prove their loyalty and serve the captors faction or cause, that to confess or give up information will not only save the prisoner from torture and likely death, but allow them to prosper.

Another matter is whether the interrogator will actually give the bribe, even after the prisoner has agreed to it and given up whatever is wanted, including the freedom to avoid torture, public execution, or the destruction of whatever the prisoner values most.

Any Interrogator who also has the lying or negotiating skill can do very well here, and makes the hazard check that the prisoner must roll every ten minutes -5% harder for each skill point in lying or negotiating, with a minimum of 1%

chance that the prisoner can make the hazard check. However, any prisoner with the lying or negotiating skill is given the same odds, but adds 5% to the chances of making their hazard check. Should the prisoner also be an interrogator, he or she will see through the ploys and offers, and subtly counter the interrogator and for each skill point the prisoner has, reduce the interrogator's skill points by that amount to a minimum of an untrained interrogator on the following table.

For each ten minutes of interrogation, the prisoner NPC or player character is allowed a hazard check to avoid accepting the bribe. Use an averaged Intelligence and Willpower, divided by two, to get their Counter Bribery Trait for use on the hazard check table to succeed and thus avoid accepting the bribe, avoid giving up information or else confess to a crime.

### Table XR-183/ Bribery Interrogation Skill Use

| Bribery Interrogator Skill points | Hazard Check to Avoid Accepting Bribe |
| --- | --- |
| Untrained | A |
| 1 | C |
| 2 | E |
| 3 | G |
| 4 | I |
| 5 Max | J |

## Physical Torture Interrogation

Breaking a prisoner by torture is often the first step in interrogation among savage humanoids, barbarians, criminals and those who make their living by

killing, war, or the post-apocalyptic slave trade. Educated people, including the law enforcement arms of many new era communities, know the truth however, that a person might easily confess or divulge the information the torturer seeks merely to make the agony stop – either by ending the session of horrific violence or expecting to gain release through death. Still, torture, from the non-lethal all the way to the merciless extreme, is a commonplace act in the new era.

A prisoner enduring physical torture makes a hazard check based on **willpower, endurance and strength divided by 3** to get their **Counter Torture trait**. Sometimes, such as after starvation and ongoing physical damage that reduces their subject's endurance trait, this triple sourced trait can be greatly decreased over time.

An interrogator choosing to torture a captive to extract information can select from the following categories of mistreatment:

## Non-Lethal

Humiliation, mockery and the threat of even worse treatment characterize this level of interrogation. The captive is often stripped naked, hung by a rope or chain in the middle of a room, or put in the stocks, strapped over a barrel or tied to a chair. This tier of misery inducement includes water boarding, being put in a tiny box, tickling, exposure to extreme heat, cold, threats by caged rats, chained dogs, or mutant monsters. An unfortunate might also be given drugs and alcohol, or endure electric shocks and other pain inducing tools that cause no permanent harm, visible wounds or trait loss.

## Beating

The captive is normally strapped to into a chair, hung from chains or spread eagled to a cross brace for this terrible fate. The interrogator, or more likely some heartless goon working at the direction of the trained interrogator, will pummel, kick, pinch, strangle, taunt, and molest the prisoner between questioning. Those beating the subject will get a +40 SV bonus to strike the restrained victim who will generally take whatever fist damage the abuser

dishes out, although treat this as stun damage and could result in the prisoner being knocked out cold before they divulge any intel.

## Slow Agony

Here, the interrogator lets time, hunger, thirst, gnawing rodents, public humiliation, and ever increasing degrees of agony to make the prisoner talk. These heartless procedures can last days or weeks, or mere hours, depending on the torturer's choice of mistreatment. Some slow, agonizing tortures include being hoisted in a crow cage for public display, stretched on the rack, slowly cooked over fire or coals, bitten by small creatures, half hanged, electric shocks, being starved or denied water, or being thrown in with deranged, depraved and violent fellow prisoners. The interrogator can revisit a slowly tortured victim every ten minutes, every hour, every day or even each week and ask their questions again, thus forcing prisoner to make their hazard check each occasion.

Every day of these slow tortures reduces a prisoner's endurance by -2d6 points, 1d4 strength and 1d6 willpower, which after a time, will reduce their Counter Torture Trait as mentioned above, making them more susceptible to cracking under interrogation.

## Merciless Torture

This torture is the worse, most unforgivable kind and results in 1d6 lethal endurance damage, and 1d4 stun damage per ten-minute period, and a permanent loss of 1 trait point to one of the victim's 8 random character traits, roll 1d8: **1.** Endurance / **2.** Strength / **3.** Agility / **4.** Accuracy / **5.** Intelligence / **6.** Perception / **7.** Willpower / **8.** Appearance.

The methods and implements used in this process are pure evil, and while they might lead to the prisoner confessing before they either pass out for 10+1d100 minutes (if reduced below their endurance via lethal and stun damage combined), or die of their injuries, there is a small chance they confessed or gave up information that was false, just to make the torture stop.

The victim is allowed a type G intelligence based hazard check to tell the interrogator what he or she wants to hear, and make it seem plausible enough to end the session until the information can be verified. In most cases, the prisoner, if not dispatched after the session, will be thrown in a jail cell and at least given 3d6 hours of reprieve before the interrogator returns after finding out the information was a lie, and continue the interrogation exactly where they left off. The victim must make their Counter Torture trait based hazard check every ten minutes of this torture.

### Table XR-184/ Torture Interrogation Skill Use

| Interrogator's Skill Points | Torture Victim's Hazard Check to Avoid Breaking * | | | |
| --- | --- | --- | --- | --- |
| | Non-lethal | Beating | Slow Agony | Merciless Torture |
| Untrained | A | B | C | D |
| 1 | B | C | D | E |
| 2 | D | E | F | G |
| 3 | F | G | H | J |
| 4 | G | H | I | K |
| 5 Max | H | I | J | L |

*Counter Torture Trait established by combining the character's willpower, endurance and strength together and dividing the total by 3.

In some respects, a junk-doctor is seen as a madman, a witch doctor or cruel hobbyist who turns already unfortunate casualties into living scarecrows. A cybernetic technician, meanwhile makes fierce, high tech, efficient ultra-humans with parts that were truly meant for a human body. Given this viewpoint, any practicing junk-doctor character can expect to be mistreated, scorned or banished from low-tech, agricultural or resource based communities, yet find acceptance in barter forts, and digger strongholds found on the edge of ruined cities.

Those with the junk-doctor skill start with a heavy, multi-pocket satchel or long coat filled with relic and replica tools. This kit is used for both medical and mechanical applications and comes with a mix of wire (2d6m), spare parts, curiosities, medical manuals, and assorted, hoses, tubes, elastic bands, springs, gears and parts from junk they've uncovered in the wilderness and barter markets.

When this skill is gained by a character who started with a different background other than the junk-doctor caste, players can read more about this profession on page 18, and in the rebuilt character type description on pages 142 to 150 of this book.

When a rebuilt person takes lethal damage, it heals like a normal character. However, if a junk-doctor can see to their physical injuries, the rebuilt can heal up to half their damage from each wound at a much faster rate. The reasoning for this is that many of the wounds on a rebuilt character are rips and tears where non-living parts tore away from the fleshly portions of the rebuilt, and this mad scientist can stitch, bolt, wire and otherwise more quickly put the patient back together and back into action.

The table to follow has a Rebuilt Repair Rating column which allows for this extra fast healing, but only up to half the damage the rebuilt character has sustained from any physical, non-stun based wound. This special healing cannot be applied to damage from mental attacks, but can apply to injuries sustained from beam weapons, fire, explosives, lighting, and other electrical attacks. Record and treat each bite, bullet hole, burn, fall, slash or other individual strike as a separate wound with the bonus healing rate applied once per 24 hours.

The following table covers repairs to rebuilt characters, the percentage chance to remove an unwanted or damaged part, as well as the chance to attach a new part and make it work.

## Junk-Doctor

While full time junk-doctors exist, and this profession is also a caste by the same name, those who make their livelihoods by another means yet have this skill, can also use scrap parts, junk, common tools, springs, gears, and electrical components to either repair or assemble a rebuilt human. Sometimes, a rebuilt character itself has this skill, which is very handy, and will allow them to either fix problems on their own lopsided, thrown together body, or add new parts found in the barter markets or ruins.

People with this talent will often need to keep this art hidden from the populations of closed minded communities, for many folks see the shambling, horrific assemblages known as rebuilt as monsters. Indeed, many believe it is better to let the maimed and limbless either die with dignity, or linger on as beggars at the periphery of society. While some unfortunates would rather cling to life and live off the kindness of strangers or be a burden to their tribe, family, and faction, others will beg to be modified. They would rather undergo the terrible pain, indignity and pity of their friends and families for the chance to be a rebuilt, and either serve their people again, or set off as an adventurer. As a rebuilt, these individuals yearn to either meet a good death on their feet, or uncover the technology and riches to buy the cybernetics implants that will turn them from a walking scrap pile into a glorious cyborg.

Strangely, cybernetic technicians do not receive the same ill treatments as junk-doctors, at least where cyborgs are permitted at all. Perhaps cyborgs are better tolerated because many are less horrific in appearance, seem to suffer less, don't leak oil, blood or other body fluids when moving as most rebuilt do. Likewise, cyborgs moan less from the pain of moving their body and the many rusty attachments bolted, stapled, wired and knotted to their still living flesh.

## Table XR-185/ Junk-Doctor Abilities Matrix

| Junk-Doctor Skill points | Daily Rebuilt Repair Rating per wound* | Detach old part from rebuilt | Attach new part to Rebuilt |
|---|---|---|---|
| **Untrained** | nil | 13%** | 4% |
| **1** | 1d6 | 88% | 76% |
| **2** | 1d8 | 89% | 79% |
| **3** | 1d10 | 91% | 82% |
| **4** | 1d10+1 | 93% | 85% |
| **5** | 1d10+2 | 95% | 88% |
| **6** | 1d10+3 | 97% | 91% |
| **7** | 1d10+4 | 98% | 94% |
| **Each up** | +2*** | 99% max | 96% Max |

*Only up to half of each physical wound's total damage, per day. Does not apply to stun damage or mental attack damage. For example, the rebuilt takes a gun shot wound and suffers 12 points of endurance damage. A 1st skill point junk-doctor can repair up to 6 points of this injury, rolling a 1d6. Each wound is treated separately.*

**Unsuccessfully pulling a part from a rebuilt causes the patient a great deal of pain, plus 1d6 lethal and 3d6 stun damage and a 1 in 10 chance the part is broken and thereafter useless.*

***So at 8 skill points, for example, the junk-doctor could heal 1d10+6 per wound on a rebuilt.*

# Killer

Sometimes referred to as the murderer or assassin skill, this talent allows the would-be slayer the ability to stab, slash or shoot a humanoid target in just the right spot. The intention is to inflict the most damage possible and take out a target quickly to avoid letting the victim cry out or engage in noisy combat. In most cases, this character learned this brutal art through instruction by master killer, either as part of a criminal past or military training.

There are two separate, but equally lethal components to this skill. The first is the increased odds and damage during a critical strike, the second is the dreaded attack from behind or back stab on an unsuspecting person.

An enhanced critical strike does not increase the number range of an automatic strike, which is 01-05 on any strike roll, but instead, the increased odds of a critical hit within that range.

Normally, a critical hit only occurs on a natural 01 roll on a d100 strike attempt. With this skill, however, this crit number changes and at the maximum skill point tier for this skill of 7 points, this trained killer scores a critical hit on all natural d100 rolls of 01-04, and inflicts an extra 7d10 damage. The critical strike damage bonus is added to whatever the critical strike damage is, as shown on page 105 of the hub rules. If the damage was done by a stun weapon, then this bonus damage is also applied as stun damage.

The second deadly feature of this skill, the back stab attack, must be made in melee range, although could include a gun held up to the head of an unsuspecting target with its backed turned, within 3 or less meters range. Only one attack on an unsuspecting opponent can be made and only allowed on the first attack by this murderer. The only real exception to this is if the attacker's number of attacks per round, or the rate of fire of the weapon used, can direct multiple attacks in that first round. For example, if an ambidextrous character wants to attack from behind, they can make two back stab attacks. Likewise, a character using one hand to attack, but has reached 7th rank, whereby they also get two melee attacks per round. So too with weapons with multiple attacks per round, such as an assault rifle that can fire three shot in one round, and thus on a point blank back stab attack, would have all 3 attacks gain the back stab SV and potential DMG modifiers applied. Remember, any roll of a 95-00 is always a miss, and a 00 is also a fumble regardless of modifiers, skills or other circumstances.

The included table details the above described deadly attack situations:

## Table XR-186/ Killer Attack Abilities Matrix

| Killer Skill Points | Critical Strike Range | Critical Strike DMG Bonus | Back Stab SV bonus | Back Stab DMG Bonus |
|---|---|---|---|---|
| Untrained | 01 | Normal* | +40 SV** | nil |
| 1 | 01,02 | +1d10 | +50 | +1d20 |
| 2 | 01,02 | +2d10 | +55 | +1d20+5 |
| 3 | 01-03 | +3d10 | +60 | +1d20+10 |
| 4 | 01-03 | +4d10 | +65 | +1d20+15 |
| 5 | 01-03 | +5d10 | +70 | +1d20+20 |
| 6 | 01-04 | +6d10 | +75 | +1d20+30 |
| 7 Max | 01-04 | +7d10 | +80 | +1d20+40 |

*Normal Critical strike damage as appears on Table TME 2-3 'Critical Strike Results' on page TME 105.

**This is the standard bonus as noted on table TME 2-5 Strike Value Modifiers for 'Target has back turned and is totally unsuspecting', although has no damage bonus.

# Leather Worker

From curing and tanning hides, making pelts into long lasting fur garments or sheets of workable leather, this skill is a highly prized talent, with much in common with both the sewing skill and the armorer skill. Half of this skill involves the skinning, cleaning and tanning of leather, a task that, while useful for survival in a brutal new age, is a back-breaking job for anyone who is involved in this profession all day, every day. Still, the need for a tanner or leather working is constant, especially in larger towns and new era cities, so this character can always find work in this profession.

The other half of the job is actually using the skill to make useful items, including belts, shoes, boots, gloves, mitts, hats, wallets, satchels, pouches, saddles and armor. In the field, a character with this skill can skin a deer, wolf or other beast within 10+1d20 minutes, scrape the fat from it and either get it ready to stretched or bundled for shipment, or crafted into immediately wearable items — although without curing, any animal skin will lack the strength and durability of regular, properly tanned leather.

Unless this character also has the armorer or sewing skill, then all he or she can really make are moccasins, a cloak, a crude backpack, or suit of standard leather armor. Should this individual have either of these other skills, then there are few limits on what can be made. See those skills for an expanded inventory of uses for leather.

At the start of game play, a leather worker will brgin with heavy leather armor, a fur cloak with hood, calf-high boots, 1d6 leather belt pouches and a backpack.

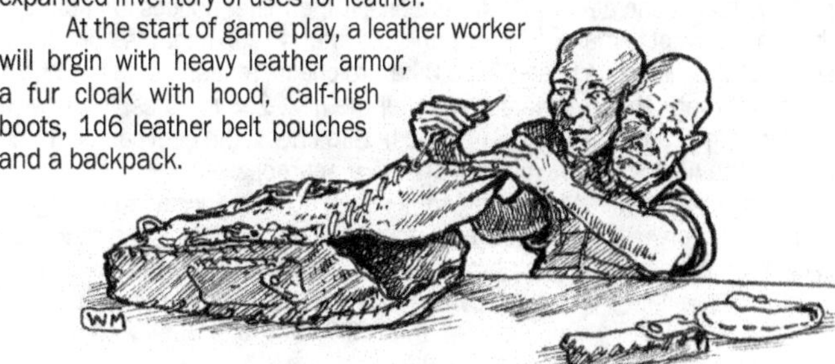

# Linguistics

Besides knowing numerous new era and old world languages, this talented individual can often make an educated guess on what another being is trying to say. This talent is based based on observing body language, grunts, facial expressions, tone, word repetition and the occasional familiar word from the common area language, or from another language the listener also knows. In time, this character can make sense, and in a very rudimentary way, communicate with the person or creature in the other's language.

Besides this uncanny ability to make sense of what other intelligent beings are trying to say, this character will speak 1d6 new era languages and 1d6 old world languages, besides their own. Random language lists are included in this book starting on page XR-509.

# Mining *by Danny Seedhouse*

Humanity has been mining for at least 43000 years, and getting useful stuff from the ground is just as important in the twisted new world as it has ever been. Mining is the first step in making weapons armor and most of the basics of civilization, from nails for construction to copper for piping and gold for advanced circuitry. Miners learn how to dig properly and safely, minimize the dangers of underground work, and how to recognize the good stuff when they see it.

While all characters are allowed a perception based hazard check when attempting to spot underground perils, with the difficulty normally being up to the game master but apply a Type C HC if not already stated, a miner gets an extra hazard check to notice and avoid dangers and spot them. Such dangers can include unsafe passages, weak floors, unclean air and perilous rock, concrete or junk formations. If the miner notices said danger they can attempt to make safe the peril, and after 4+2d6 minutes work and a successful intelligence based, Type B hazard check, render it safe for others to pass through the treacherous area for the next 2d8 minutes. With twice the work time, and a second INT based hazard check, the peril can be made safe for the next 2d6 days (or permanently if appropriate).

The time a miner needs to dig something if needed, such as a blockage in a tunnel or doorway, is half that of an untrained person. Additionally, a minor can extract raw mineral deposits or excavate through hard packed sedimentary junk and debris layers to produce 1d10sp worth of material after 1 hour of work.

# Morse Code

The Morse Code Alphabet became a massively popular form of communication in the years following the great devastation. With this ability, and one of several junk crafted or relic devices, a character can transmit rather detailed messages between communities both region wide and over a vast area depending on the equipment available. Two-way communications of this sort can keep relatives and like-minded individuals in contact, or send coded messages to field operators using audio, written, or visual expressions of this language.

While radio stations, and in some places even television and Internet broadcast are still being transmitted, Morse code has become the norm in inter-settlement dialog. Very low-tech societies even have a few Morse code transmitters set up, either linked by a wired system to the next village, or sent through primitive transmitters and antenna networks. Regular, relic communicators are the preferred transmission and receiver methods, but like all relics, are beyond the reach of most low tech village populations.

This character was trained to read and operate various Morse code transmitter devices by his community and possibly served as a communications technician in military operations. He will begin game play with a set of scrap metal and wood Morse code transmitters and have access to 1000 to 6,000 meters (1d6x1000m) of transmission wire. With this equipment, he or she can set up a communications line between two points.

While anybody who can read and write and has the written code can slowly go through a long transmission and get the message (making a successful type D intelligence based hazard check per 6 hours to properly decode the message), a trained operator can translate it this code into words just by hearing the long and short clicks arriving at his end, or seeing Morse code transmitted by distant, properly encoded light flashes.

This skill is either as untrained or trained, so re-roll another skill if the character already possesses this ability. Should this character gain this skill and yet not be able to read or write, consider that he or she has limited reading and writing skills sufficient to use this talent.

### The International Morse code characters are:

| | | |
|---|---|---|
| A .- | N -. | 0 ----- |
| B -... | O --- | 1 .---- |
| C -.-. | P .--. | 2 ..--- |
| D -.. | Q --.- | 3 ...-- |
| E . | R .-. | 4 ....- |
| F ..-. | S ... | 5 ..... |
| G --. | T - | 6 -.... |
| H .... | U ..- | 7 --... |
| I .. | V ...- | 8 ---.. |
| J .--- | W .-- | 9 ----. |
| K -.- | X -..- | Fullstop .-.-.- |
| L .-.. | Y -.-- | Comma --..-- |
| M -- | Z --.. | Query ..--.. |

# Performer

This talented individual was either trained by his parents or a skilled teacher in the employ of a powerful or wealthy household. He may have first shown talent as a street urchin, playing a flute or drum in the market for spare coins, and been 'discovered' by an established performer who took the child in. As an adult, he has learned to make his way in the world by entertaining both crowds in the street and warlords in their bunkers. Therefore, telling stories, singing songs while playing simple instruments, dancing, writing poems, documenting the daring adventures of ruin explorers, or acting out a play either alone, with puppets, or other performers, are all in a day's work.

While a performer's presentation, appearance and ability all go into their art and act, not all crowds are as easily entertained as others. Occasionally, the character might elicit cheers of adulation and cries for an encore, and at other times, he will need to dodge hurled fruit and stools, and flee in the night to avoid an offended mob of unappreciative locals.

If multiple performers are participating, average their audience reaction ratings, and on table XR-188, apply all their APP scores. The skill points of a performer determine the Audience Reaction Rating, or base odds of whether or not his audience liked the presentation, with all applicable modifiers from table XR-188, being applied:

## Table XR-187/ Performer's Audience Reaction Rating Key

| Skill Points | Audience Reaction Rating |
|---|---|
| Untrained | 32 |
| 1 | 68 |
| 2 | 75 |
| 3 | 82 |
| 4 | 84 |
| 5 | 87 |
| 6 | 90 |
| 7 (max) | 93 |

## Table XR-188/ Performance Modifiers Directory

| Performance Circumstance (pick all that apply) | Audience Reaction Modifier |
|---|---|
| Performer's appearance 5 or lower | -30* |
| Performer's appearance from 6 to 20 | -10* |
| Performer's appearance 21 to 49 | +0* |
| Performer's appearance 50 to 79 | +20* |
| Performer's appearance 80 or higher | +40* |
| Audience has captured the performer and forced them to entertain | -10 |
| Audience has weapons aimed at the performer, or shooting at feet | -20 |
| Audience killed previous performer or other on-stage 'guest' | -15 |
| Audience has had no entertainment for over 6 months, hard up. | +5 |
| Audience has never seen any sort of performance... ever | +1d20 then roll -1d20* |
| Audience is drunk and easier to please; performer looks more attractive, too. | +1d10 |
| Performer is intoxicated | -d10+1d10** |
| Performer is wounded to half or less endurance | -15* |
| Performer entertaining in hometown, friends and family in audience | +1d20* |
| Performer using functional relic instruments, lighting or sound system | +1d20* |
| Audience is angry or depressed by some event | -1d20 |
| Audience is a repeat crowd from the previous evening or event | x2 previous *** |
| Audience is customarily distrustful of, or dislikes, or hates the performer's character type | -1d20 |

*Apply modifier for each performer on stage, even untrained ones.
** Roll a die, then minus the negative second dice roll to get either a negative, positive, or zero value.
*** Whatever the entertainer's previous session Audience Reaction Modifiers amounted to, either good or bad, double that value for the upcoming act.

## Audience Reaction Results

Once the Audience Reaction Modifier number is established, which results in either a positive, negative, or possibly zero modifier, then apply this amount to the Base Audience Reaction Rating determined by the skill points of the performer. The rating number, which can be a negative or positive amount, is applied to a simple 1d100 roll. If the roll result is above zero, then it is a positive performance and so roll another 1d100 (with no modifiers) on the Positive Audience Reaction Results Table, but if it is zero or less, roll on the Negative Audience Reaction Results Table, (again, with no modifiers).

## Positive Audience Reaction Results Table   Roll 1d100

**01-09. Applause,** although once your act is wrapped up, the audience return to their conversation, drinks and meals and pay you no further attention.

**10-27. Genuine Applause** from about three quarters of the audience. 1d4 silver coins are tossed into your hat or at your feet and there is a 1 in 10 chance somebody buys you a drink and a hot meal.

**28-49. Considerable hand clapping**, a few cheers of approval and thumbs up gestures. 1d6 silver pieces are dropped in your hat or tossed to your feet.

**50-72. Audience thrilled**, clap enthusiastically and even toss 3d6 silver coins onto the stage or at your feet.

**73-87. Standing ovation**. The audience clap and cheer for several minutes, toss 4d6 silver coins at your feet, and if this performance is in a location with food and drink for sale, the manager, staff and audience contribute to buying you a meal and a couple of drinks.

**88-00. Calls for an encore!** Clapping, cheering and the audience members beseech you to perform one more act, song, or whatever art form you already did. If you don't, the crowd will still be pleased and toss you 10+4d6 silver pieces, but if you do an encore, then there is an 89% chance that they toss you 20+6d6 silver coins and buy you a meal and a drink if available. The management of any performance space where you did your act is 86% likely to insist that you perform the same act the next night. If you agree, he or she will provide meals for both you and one companion and a simple two person room.

### Negative Audience Reaction Results Table *Roll 1d100*

**01-15. Crowd gives lackluster applause,** almost mockingly. A few aspiring performers comment on how they could do better. Most people in the audience think you made a good amateur effort and are praised for having the guts to get up and try at all. 2 in 6 chance somebody buys you a beer. 1 in 6 chance somebody spits in that beer.

**16-25. Crowd is unimpressed,** just stares at you and slowly returns to conversations, cards or drinks, etc. 1 in 6 chance somebody burst out laughing.

**26-41. Crowd annoyed by your presence.** Some people frown, others shake their head or mutter grimly among themselves. 2 in 6 chance somebody spits at your feet, 3 in 6 chance somebody mockingly shouts for an encore.

**42-56. Crowd jeers you,** tell you to get a job in the junk mines or go work as a prostitute, that you'll never amount to anything and best you don't perform for them again for your own health.

**57-64. Crowd mocks you,** laughs, points, throws food scraps or utensils, but doesn't hold a grudge or try to beat you.

**65-78. Audience offended** by something they thought you said or implied. You are booed and pelted by foodstuffs and drink, spit on and 1 in 6 chance set upon by 10% of the audience who attempt to beat you and throw you out.*

**79-84. Audience extremely displeased** with your performance, and for whatever reason, go berserk and wish you dead. 50% of the audience attempts to jump on stage and try to beat and strangle you to death.*

**85-00. The crowd hated you,** your performance, and the host who brought you before them. If in a public saloon or street area, the crowd breaks into a riot and will loot and brawl and, if possible, hang you and beat one who hired you to perform.*

**Note: Cultured audiences, such as in a merchant's hall or fine dining establishment, the offended audience will simply ask the guards or serving staff to escort you to the back door where you will be thrown in the street, with a 3 in 6 chance of being soundly beaten as well. If beaten, 3 in 6 chance robbed and stripped, too.*

# Prospector *by Danny Seedhouse*

Those with this single point skill have been trained to locate accessible resources using basic tools and physical survey techniques. This includes panning for gold, looking for the tell-tale signs of iron deposits or coal and any other number of useful metals and minerals, which are usually found along ridge lines and stream beds. Prospecting takes 1d4+2 hours to search a square kilometer, and after this time, a Type C Perception based hazard check is made. On a success, the prospector has found a trace of something useful (1d10sp worth of useful minerals).

The next step is exploration and takes 1d4+1 hours of work and a type A Intelligence based hazard check to recover 1d20sp worth of useful metals and minerals. For every hazard tier the character beat above A (the results of the 1d100 roll on the hazard check table – was sufficiently low enough to beat the hazard check amount needed, and the B, and perhaps the C, etc.) they recover another 1d6sp of valuable materials, or 2d6sp if they are of the pre-game caste or have the skill of 'Miner'.

After each successful period of exploration at a spot, the prospector character's Perception + Intelligence traits are added together and divided by

2 to get their prospector trait. With this new trait, they must make a type D hazard check to make another series of recoveries at this site (and earn another 1d20sp plus the chance to earn another 1d6sp depending on how far they beat a type A INT HC as they follow the vein of minerals). Failure on this hazard check means the site is played out and they must move.

Besides gold, coal, copper, silver, iron ore and other naturally occurring minerals, a prospector might also be after a rich deposit of ancient junk. These silt and muck covered layers are often rich in aluminum, brightly colored plastic, glass, packaged items, empty shell casings useful to re loaders, and countless other items that will fetch a decent price.

# Seamanship *by Mike McMillan*

This skill covers abilities, aspects of life, and the advanced operation of boats, barges and sailing ships. Each skill tier represents an increasing familiarity with the nautical world possessed by sailors and folks who make their living on the oceans and rivers of the new era. Unlike most other skills, each point tier has a title associated with it.

### Table XR-189/Seamanship Abilities Matrix

**1 skill points/ Title: Salt**
Simple nautical knowledge, understanding of how currents and tides work and recognizing things like rip tides, reefs, sandbars, and sudden weather changes (PC gets two hazard checks to identify nautical hazards). This character can actually sail a small boat or raft, and row properly without going in a circle.

**2 skill points/ Title: Hand**
If this character doesn't already have it, he or she now gains the navigate by stars skill while on the water. PC Also counts as a trained rower, which raises his effective strength to the next category for purposes of speed. This individual also knows basic boat repair (can fix 1d10+5 END per hour to a damaged vessel).

**3 skill points/ Title: Seasoned Hand**
This character incurs no SV or DV penalties when fighting on a boat unless in a severe storm. They are also a rowing expert and gain +1 meter speed when going upstream in a boat they are piloting or rowing. If at the helm of a vessel, and when ramming another boat, ship or aquatic beast, this PC adds +10 to SV to the attack and gives his or her own boat or ship a -5 DV bonus.

**4 skill points/ Title: Sailor**
The character's knowledge of the sea is expanded. Any ship they pilot can move faster under sail power and so increase the speed by +1 meter per round against the wind, or 10% if higher.

With the wind, this increases to +2 meters or +20%. When at the helm or tiller, this character gives an extra hazard check for the vessel to avoid negative effects happening to the boat or ship.

**5 skill points/ Title: First Mate**
Improve this PC's swimming ability by one level. He or she can now build small boats (rafts, rowboats, and canoes), and the navigate by stars skill applies on land now as well.

Advanced boat repair (restores 2d10+20 END per hour to whatever boat or ship he or she is working on).

**6 skill points/ Title: Rowing master, or Captain**
Increase all other trained rowers effective strength another category for the purpose of speed. (Only one person can be considered the row master at a time). This character will recognize the name and reputations of other captains, and their ships, on their home stretch of sea and be recognized 80% of the time in return.

If recognized in a fight with pirates or anyone who takes slaves aboard their ship to work the oars, they will try to capture this PC alive. Likewise, there is a 55% chance that cannibals will not eat this character first, and instead make use of this sailor's skill.

While under the command of this character, a sailing ship enjoys a further +1m per round or 10% increase, whichever is higher. This PC can also can apply a +10% bonus speed to relic ships under their direction.

# Sewing *by Danny Seedhouse*

This character can use needle and thread, sewing machines, scissors, a loom and knitting needles and related items to produce items from all types of cloth and leather. In the Mutant Epoch era, there is no such thing as mass produced clothing except in a rare high tech enclave. Handmade garments are the norm, cut by hand and stitched together by individuals working in small home based workshops and bartered at the local market. The availability of various types of fabrics has been drastically reduced, with leather, wool and cotton being the most common sources of fabric. Remnants of old world fabrics still exist and a few places can still produce things like Rayon and Nylon that are produced by someone with 4 or more points in the chemistry technician skill.

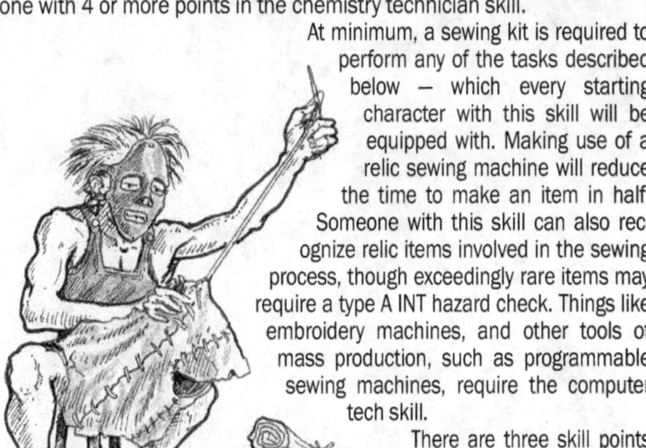

At minimum, a sewing kit is required to perform any of the tasks described below — which every starting character with this skill will be equipped with. Making use of a relic sewing machine will reduce the time to make an item in half. Someone with this skill can also recognize relic items involved in the sewing process, though exceedingly rare items may require a type A INT hazard check. Things like embroidery machines, and other tools of mass production, such as programmable sewing machines, require the computer tech skill.

There are three skill points to this area of knowledge as described on the following table and with a detailed description to follow:

**Table XR-190/ Sewing Skill Abilities**

| Sewing Skill Points | Abilities |
| --- | --- |
| 1 | Basics of hand sewing, use of a sewing machine, alterations |
| 2 | Leather working, fitted clothing |
| 3 Max | Advanced hand sewing, embroidery. |

**1 Skill Point:** This tier covers the making of basic things from raw materials. The character can produce any cloth item with half the base cost spent in materials. Items include clothing, pouches, bags, sleeping bags, and the all important pants. Normally a simple item like a pouch or a blanket takes 1d6x10 minutes, while basic garments like a woman's dress take 2+1d6 hours.

This person can also repair clothing and resize outfits for odd body shapes with a sewing kit and 2d20 minutes for slight changes. More radical changes, like extra holes for extra limbs, take 1d4 hours. This skill level allows for the modifying of leather or nylon straps on relics to fit larger or smaller folks but does not apply to adding extra holes for limbs in leather armor.

**2 Skill Points:** This individual can make advanced modifications to cloth items, adding zippers and changing clothing to fit a wider variety of mutant bodies. Like normal clothing, this character only pays 1/2 the base cost in materials. He or she can now also modify leather armors* of all types for the many varieties of the mutant body. Large alterations will require extra material equal to half the cost of the item being modified and require 1d4 hours of work. Untrained folks can attempt this with a type B Intelligence based hazard check that, on a failed check, inflicts a 1 point reduction in DV and an extra -0.25 meter penalty on speed.

**Leather working covers making leather jackets, leather or heavy leather armor, as well as leather helms and shields. See page 219 for this skill.*

**3 Skill Points:** This skill tier covers complex patterns of clothing with multiple layers of fabrics, hidden pockets, reversible garments and the ability to work with relic cloths like Lycra, spandex and various bulletproof materials. Allows for modification of all cloth based relics to fit various types of mutants. Advanced techniques like embroidery are used for personalization and to add value both in terms of price and status in places that value such things. When selling items with extensive embroidery double the normal random value in the selling prices.

# Smithing

Besides occurring as the blacksmith starting caste, many picked up the apprentice tier of this skill in their youth as a day job, or learned the basics in the pursuit of being an armorer, mechanic, junk crafter or other trade. While the smithing profession is something one can fall back on if they need work, its is not usually an adventurer's primary career goal. There is certainly a great deal of overlap between what an armorer can make, what a junk crafter can assemble, and what a smithy can create, and those with two or more of these overlapping, complimentary skills are truly gifted, and much sought after. In most cases, a person with smithing skill repairs iron parts and tools, and forges and shapes iron articles for everyday use in a post-apocalyptic community, and as such, is often regarded as one of the most valuable citizens in the settlement. As noted under the blacksmithing caste, those known to show talent in this skill are often kept alive after a village or town is conquered, and made to serve their new rulers to make weapons, siege equipment, chains, manacles, and other tools of war and tyranny.

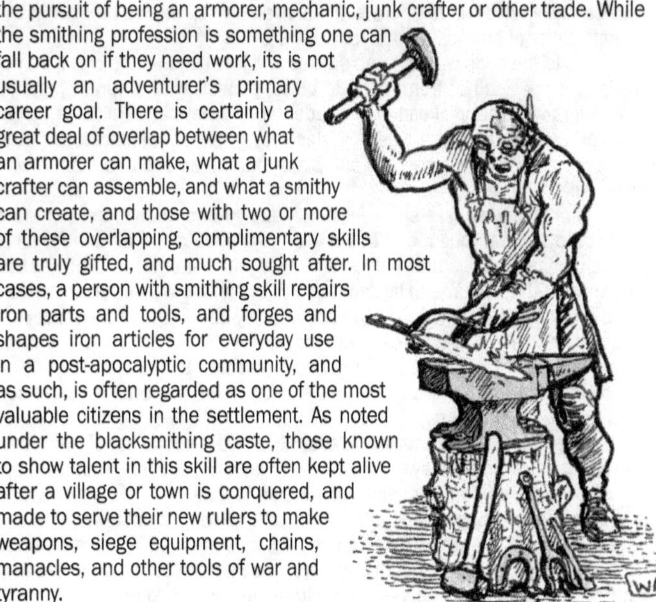

Smithing in the new era involves a lot of traditional blacksmithing tools and techniques, the use of assorted salvaged metal, especially rebar, along with power tools where available. To the uneducated, then, a smithy's workshop and that of a junk crafter can often look the same.

All characters with this skill will own a set of common smithing tools, including hammers, tongs, gloves, apron, and finishing tools, plus have access to a forge and full sized anvil. Of course, if this individual is partaking in the profession of excavation, he or she will normally only bring along their trusty hammer as a backup weapon — although only those who have the pre-game caste of blacksmith will have the weapon expert skill with their hammer.

This skill has 4 tiers, with the highest master level allowing the smith to make exquisite pieces of metalwork, including jewelery using silver, gold and gemstones.

### Table XR-191/ Smthing Skill Abilities

| Skill Point | Things a Blacksmith can Make |
| --- | --- |
| 1 | Arrowhead, spoon, javelin and spearhead, knife, dagger, nails, horseshoe, hatchet head, crowbar |
| 2. | Machete, short sword, battleaxe, throwing star, pickaxe, shovel, scythe, sickle, hammer, hinges, catapult iron parts, boat parts. |
| 3 | Chain, great sword, saber, long sword, pitchfork, wagon wheel rim, trebuchet iron parts, crossbow limbs, anvil |
| 4 Max | Fine cast iron decorations and ornamental functional hinges, handles, clasps and replacement parts for relic vehicles and machinery. This master can melt and cast silver and gold and, along with gemstones, ivory and other materials, work it into Epochian era jewelry. If given sufficient time resources and facilities, this person could mint the gold and silver coins of a new era faction. |

# Streetwise

Also called street smart, this character likely grew up in a rough neighborhood of a vast, sprawling new era slum city. Although most Epochian era settlements, even small ones, have their fair share of poor families, homeless encampments, refugee shanty towns, wagon districts, house boat flotillas and other areas which suffer from crime, poverty, misery and misfortune. Such places breed tough, resourceful and cunning people. Those who survive to adulthood develop a heightened awareness of potential threats, of scams, ploys, ambushes and corruption. They learn the lingo, gestures and behaviors needed to operate in, survive and sometimes prosper in the sketchy parts of any post-apocalyptic town.

While the code words, hand signals and local knowledge of a community's underbelly differ from place to place, especially in different regions, characters with this skill can quickly adapt to the ways and quirks of a new slum and recognize the same sort of people, same type of shakedowns, and same incidences of bribery from one place to another, and understand who really rules that part of town.

In practical terms, a streetwise individual knows when to act confident and stand tall, act tough, and seem like they're too much trouble for local street urchins, thieves and bullies to bother with. At other times, they will understand that it's time to lay low, keep to the shadows, hide their appearance and avoid eye contact. This person is highly observant, and an excellent judge of people — at least those from the squalid side of any town — and will also be able to recognize somebody who is addicted to drugs, somebody on the run from the authorities, or who is and isn't a hooker even if the person isn't dressed for the part.

Likewise, a street smart character knows the subtle art of hand gestures, body posture and eye movement and can to get clues, warnings, approval or intel from familiar fellow inhabitants of a rough neighborhood. This can be handy, such as when a familiar prostitute, beggar, or street punk can forewarn the PC that they're being followed, that the area is being watched by law enforcers, slavers, bounty hunters, or rival gang thugs, or others who enter the slum to harm, harvest or rob from the downtrodden.

In many respects, this is more of a 'role' playing skill than a 'roll' playing one. For the game master, handling this single point skill is usually done by answering a player's questions regarding interactions and observations while the street wise character is in a rough area — or encounters a person in another setting who this PC will identify as coming from a hard upbringing. A character with this skill will recognize a fellow slummer within a few minutes of conversation, although if the other is trying to hide their harsh upbringing on the streets, have them roll 1d100 and add it to their intelligence score, while the player rolls 1d100 and adds it to their perception score. Whoever has a higher resulting score succeeds in what they are trying to do, either hide their slum upbringing or identify it in the other. Players can use this same opposed trait system, but in reverse, to try to hide their own past, too.

For street interactions, this character can make either a perception or intelligence based hazard check to notice something, such as the warning hand gesture from a friendly prostitute, allied thief, or local shopkeeper to let the PC know they are being followed, that lawmen are looking for them, that the big boss wants a chat, or any number of other details. Suggested hazard check difficulties are in the easy (A, B, C) to moderately challenging (E, F, G, and H).

A streetwise individual can have non-streetwise companions follow his or her lead to if a whole dig team needs to skulk through a crime ridden part of town. Here, this PC will want to do all the talking with local ruffians, conduct any bribes or negotiations with gate guards or unlawful tax keepers, and vouch for team mates when the group is confronted by a local gang boss.

Having grown up in a rough part of town, a street smart character who returns to their old hood will be welcomed by some, feared by a few, and hunted

by others. In most cases, such a PC can find a hideout where wanted excavators can lie low, where illegal services can be acquired, where unauthorized medical procedures and surgeries can be performed, and where little known, valuable information about the community's occupants can be purchased.

There is a 3 in 10 chance that this character is wanted for an assortment of petty crimes in their hometown, while a 4 in 10 chance that he or she owes the local gang boss a sum of 100+1d1000 silver pieces for some debt, and a further 5 in 10 chance that old enemies in their home city want them dead.

# Trapper

Anybody with a bow or a gun can be a hunter, but as a team member who can set a few snares around the outskirts of a camp at night, and harvest a few dead animals at dawn is a valuable asset. Many savages and barbarians gain this skill at an early age, and any character with the wilderness survival skill also has a beginner's ability at trapping, as shown on table XR-192, below.

This character can set snares with little more than a knife or hatchet, some twine or wire, twigs, and available natural materials. These include logs, branches, rocks or even rubble and trash such as pipes and springs. The amount of meat they can trap in a 24 hour period depends on their skill points and the terrain in which he or she sets snares. All prey will be small vertebrates such as squirrels, rabbits, fox, rats, mink, lizards, toads, grouse, quail, wild turkey, and occasionally larger animals like deer and bobcats. The table below does not give creature names, only the kilograms of meat harvested and the value of pelts in silver coins.

Snares can be set to trap enemies as well, such as spiked pit traps, deadfalls, spiked rope balls, and spring-loaded impaler-posts. See traps on page TME-119. Such contraptions are usually set up in the path behind or in front of a group of adventurers who are aware of foes pursuing them or advancing. The materials to build such traps are only found in woodlands, swamps forests and ruins, or as the GM determines, and take between a half hour and six hours to make depending on the complexity of the trap (if you are solo-playing, say a trap takes 1+1d4 hours to build and arm). A crafty trapper, expecting to make large man-killer traps, could load up a pack mule with branches, wooden stakes, rope, trip wire, shovels and whatnot to bring with them on an expedition and establish either defensive traps, or a trap line to gain food and pelts.

The dice roll shown is the weight in kilograms of meat trapped. For each kilogram of meat, 10% translates to silver pieces trade value in skin, furs, horns, ivory, claws, organs and whatnot that can be sold in any trade town. For example: 1d8-1 means, roll the eight sided dice, minus one from the resulting score to get 0-7 kg of meat in a 24 hour period, 10% of this weight is the value in silver coins from furs and other non-meat animal products. The value of meat is another 10% if the trapper can sell it.

**Table XR-192/ Kilograms of Meat Trapped per 24 hour period by Terrain Type**

| Terrain | Unskilled | Wilderness Survival* | Trapper's Skill Points | | | | | |
| --- | --- | --- | --- | --- | --- | --- | --- | --- |
| | | | 1 | 2 | 3 | 4 | 5 | 6 max |
| Forest | 1d6-2 | 1d12-3 | 1d20-5 | 1d20-4 | 1d20-3 | 1d20-2 | 1d20-1 | 2d20-2 |
| Swamp | 1d6-4 | 1d6-2 | 1d8-1 | 1d10-2 | 1d10-1 | 1d12-1 | 1d20-2 | 1d20-1 |
| Hills | 1d6-3 | 1d8-2 | 1d10-2 | 1d10-1 | 1d12-1 | 1d20-2 | 1d20-1 | 2d12-2 |
| Mountains | 1d6-4 | 1d6-2 | 1d12-3 | 1d12-2 | 1d20-3 | 1d20-2 | 1d20-1 | 2d20-2 |
| Desert | 1d6-5 | 1d6-3 | 1d10-5 | 1d10-4 | 1d10-3 | 1d12-3 | 1d12-2 | 1d12-1 |
| Badlands | 1d6-4 | 1d8-4 | 1d10-4 | 1d10-3 | 1d10-2 | 1d12-1 | 1d20-2 | 1d20-1 |
| Farmland | 1d6-2 | 1d10-2 | 1d20-4 | 1d20-3 | 1d20-1 | 1d100-5 | 1d100-3 | 1d100-2 |
| Plain | 1d6-3 | 1d8-2 | 1d10-2 | 1d12-2 | 1d12-1 | 1d20-2 | 1d100-5 | 1d100-3 |
| Ruins | 1d6-5 | 1d6-4 | 1d8-2 | 1d10-2 | 1d12-2 | 1d20-3 | 1d20-2 | 2d20-3 |
| Shoreline | 1d6-3 | 1d8-2 | 1d12-2 | 1d20-2 | 1d20-1 | 2d20-2 | 3d20-3 | 4d20-4 |
| Caverns | 1d6-5 | 1d6-4 | 1d8-2 | 1d10-1 | 1d12-1 | 1d20-2 | 1d20-1 | 2d20-2 |

*Character has the Wilderness Survival skill described on page 56 of the hub rules.*

# Whip Master

A whip has a three meter reach, and on a hit inflicts 1d8 damage plus has some chance of either wrapping around an object — such as an overhead branch or pipe, the pistol or blade in some opponent's hand, a small object on a shelf, or the overhead cargo racks on a passing relic vehicle. Once contacted, there is some chance of either knocking the object free of whoever was holding it, or wrapping the end of the whip around the object securely enough to allow the whip user to grab hold as if it were a tied-off rope — and, at the appropriate time, then jerk the whip in such a way as to unwrap the whip's tip to let go.

The following table shows what each skill point of a whip master can achieve, the improved strike value and damage a whip in the hands of an accomplished user can inflict, plus the odds of wrapping about a static object, smacking away an opponent's weapon, or grabbing hold of a passing vehicle or animal — all these three option first require a hit, with a static object having a DV of -0, a passing vehicle or animal -20 DV and to smack away a weapon the same defense value of the NPC or character targeted.

The mutation, flesh whip, on page 246, also calls upon the following table, however the damage inflicted by those appendages has a base of 1d12 and offers a +6 strike value, so increase damage and any extra SV bonus accordingly.

Whip damage is modified by the user's strength trait value.

## Table XR-193/ Whip Master Abilities Matrix

| Skill Points | Whip SV | Whip DMG | Wrap Static Object* | Smack Away Weapon** | Grab Passing Vehicle or Beast*** |
|---|---|---|---|---|---|
| Untrained | +0 | 1d8 | 57% chance | 38% chance | 34% chance |
| 1 | +3 | 1d8+1 | 66% chance | 59% chance | 52% chance |
| 2 | +6 | 1d8+2 | 71% chance | 66% chance | 57% chance |
| 3 | +9 | 1d8+3 | 76% chance | 71% chance | 62% chance |
| 4 | +11 | 1d8+4 | 81% chance | 75% chance | 67% chance |
| 5 | +13 | 1d8+5 | 86% chance | 79% chance | 72% chance |
| 6 | +15 | 1d8+6 | 91% chance | 83% chance | 77% chance |
| 7 | +17 | 1d8+7 | 94% chance | 87% chance | 82% chance |
| Each SKP above | +1 | +1 DMG | 98% max | +3% chance (max 97%) | +3% chance (max 96%) |

    * A strike must first be made, with most static objects having a DV of -0. A static object is a pipe, branch, rebar shaft or something to wrap the tip of the whip around and attempt to secure it, to either climb up, swing across an open space, or stop one-self from being pulled away by an attacker, tornado, raging water, etc. Failure to hold means the user either drops or can make another attempt in 2 rounds.

    ** A hit on the enemy must first be made, with the normal DV being the target to beat. Success means the whip master has smacked the weapon or object free of the entity holding it, but does not grab the item. Failure means the person holding the item retains his or her grip on it and may a deploy the item without interruption.

    *** A passing animal or vehicle, airship, wagon or other moving object has a base defense value of -20, although the GM can adjust this up or down according to the in-game circumstances. Once a strike occurs, then roll for the chance the whip coils about some part on the vehicle, with a 52% or 57% chance, for example. A success here means the moving vehicle, or mount, is lashed onto and the whip user has secured themselves to the passing object. This usually means the whip user is dragged by the moving machine or animal and must make a strength based Type C hazard check to pull themself up the whip to grab the in-motion target.

# Zoologist

While this individual can identify most common mutant and non-mutant living creatures, and has either heard about, seen photos of, or glimpsed a rare specimen, it doesn't mean he or she has any qualms about killing and possibly eating some never before seen mutant. This character is fascinated with animals, as well as the many sub-human species of humanoid life. Likewise, they will often document new species using relic camera and video equipment, or if lucky enough to have the artistic skill, will draw and even paint illustrations of new creatures. If also able to read and write, this Epochian zoologist will also take notes and list features about any newly discovered species.

When not able to get into the field, meet with other zoologists or big game hunters, or travelers from other lands, a zoologist will often pour over their collection of tattered books and magazines from the old ones. Through these late night studies, they will have read about or at least seen faded pictures of old world species, including Palaeolithic mammals and most common dinosaurs. If they cannot read, however, and view pictures of T-Rex, smilodon, woolly mammoth or velociraptor, they might rightly believe such creatures lived only centuries ago, and might still roam the mutated, torn world of the present day.

Should the zoologist be able to kill a creature, or find a dead specimen, they will happily take measurements, take claw and tooth samples, tufts of fur, sections of pelt or entire skins and skulls if time and weight allowance permit. With these articles of natural and unnatural history, they will add to their collection at either their home base, or carry them about in padded pouches, cases and old luggage.

While this person's hobby might seem strange to those who dread animal attacks, and think it's always smarter to stay away from unknown beasts, this character is likely to grab their camera, sketchbook, binoculars and head off in search of new creatures, although always with a band of stalwart excavators or barbarian hunters as bodyguards and porters. A zoologist will start with a pencil, pad of yellowed paper, sample case, magnifying glass, 1d6 old world picture books on prehistoric and wild animals, and a 1 in 10 chance of a digital camera with a 10x zoom lens and capacity to store 20,000 pictures and 100 hours of video documentation. This camera will run for 124 hours per charge of its mini power cell. The camera will fetch 600+3d100sp if it must be sold.

As already mentioned, this character knows all the common creatures in the region, has heard reports and rumors of beasts in adjoining lands, including vast lakes and salty seas. The zoologist is 80% likely to properly identify a common creature by its tracks, while when coming upon rare creatures, he or she is allowed a type D intelligence based hazard check to accurately identify something based on rumors, drawings, pixelated photographs or second-hand accounts about it.

*GM Note:* While the player of The Mutant Epoch might not be familiar with the creatures from the Hub Rules, perhaps being new to game, their character will have spent most of their life researching these creatures, and probably identify a beast either when seen within 100 meters, or after the thing is killed (Type A INT hazard check).

Should the PC guess at a beast correctly, the GM is to divulge to the PC what is known about the creature's diet, any weaknesses, mutations, habits, or deadly traits. Divulge answers only if the player character asks for specific details, instead of dumping the entire creature listing into the middle of game play. For example, a PC with the zoologist skill might identify a skulking render lizard (pg. TME 163), and the player could ask the following questions in the time given before the reptile attacks. "What does this thing eat?" GM: "Meat, and lots of it." Zoologist player: "Does it have any ranged or mental attacks?"

GM "68% of these things are mutants with between 1 or 2 deviations. This one is a mutant [rolls a random mutation from the lizard mutation listing on page TME-163] and yes, it has throwing quills [result 56-61]."

Zoologist: "Well shit. I tell the other guys in my team what I see, and that it's a five meter long, bipedal lizard with throwing quills... and that they should take cover. Oh, and has it seen us?"

GM: "No, but it's looking your way and sniffing the air."

Expanded Mutations

# Expanded Mutation Generation Tables

## Prime Mutations List

Mutation Numbers 1 to 145 are found in the TME Hub Rules, while mutations 146 to 422 found in this book.

### Table XR-194/ Prime Mutations Determination — 1d1000

| Roll | Mutation | Roll | Mutation | Roll | Mutation |
|---|---|---|---|---|---|
| 01-05. | Acid Blood 1 | 264-268. | Dread Zone 28 | 506-510. | Image Projection 48 |
| 06-10. | Acid Spit 2 | 269-274. | Earth Thump 29 | 511-515. | Imbue Prowess 191 |
| 11-14. | Acidic Saliva 146 | 275-278. | Echolocation 165 | 516-520. | Immunity 49 |
| 15-19. | Acidic Skin Ducts 147 | 279-283. | Elastic Skeleton 166 | 521-525. | Increased Cellular Activity 50 |
| 20-26. | Advanced Kidneys 148 | 284-288. | Electrical Charge 30 | 526-530. | Internal Twin Fetus 192 |
| 27-31. | Advanced Mind 3 | 289-295. | Electrical Impulse Emission 167 | 531-535. | Irritation Particles 193 |
| 32-35. | Age Morphing 149 | 296-302. | Electrical Pulse 31 | 536-541. | Kinetic Fist 194 |
| 36-40. | Agony Sphere 4 | 303-307. | Electro Magnetic Pulse 32 | 542-546. | Light Burst 51 |
| 41-45. | Amphibian 5 | 308-312. | Emotion Inducement 168 | 547-551. | Limb Regeneration 52 |
| 46-51. | Amplification 6 | 313-317. | Empathy 33 | 552-556. | Lost and Found 195 |
| 52-56. | Animal Association 150 | 318-322. | Energy Blade 34 | 557-562. | Mandibles 53 |
| 57-61. | Appearance Morph 151 | 323-327. | Energy Orbs 169 | 563-567. | Mental Counter Attack 196 |
| 62-65. | Aquatic Adaptation 7 | 328-332. | Energy Smite 170 | 568-572. | Mental Dominion 197 |
| 66-71. | Arid Adaptation 8 | 333-337. | Energy Tendril 171 | 573-577. | Mental Mine 54 |
| 72-76. | Asphyxiation Zone 9 | 338-342. | Energy Wall Generation 172 | 578-583. | Mental Screen 55 |
| 77-81. | Aura of Protection 10 | 343-347. | Enormous Bone Spike 173 | 584-588. | Mental Stun 198 |
| 82-87. | Ballistic Hide 11 | 348-352. | Enriched Skeletal Structure 174 | 589-592. | Micro Feelers 199 |
| 88-92. | Beak 12 | 353-358. | Extreme Healing 175 | 593-598. | Micro Spines 200 |
| 93-98. | Beam Eyes 13 | 359-362. | Extreme Size Decrease 35 | 599-603. | Microwave Generation 201 |
| 99-103. | Berserker Rage 14 | 363-368. | Extreme Survivability 176 | 604-611. | Mind Crush 56 |
| 104-109. | Bladed Limbs 15 | 369-374. | Fanged 36 | 612-616. | Mind Unification 202 |
| 110-115. | Blurred Movement 16 | 375-379. | Feathered 177 | 617-621. | Mind Waste 57 |
| 116-124. | Body Disproportion 17 | 380-384. | Fish Fins 178 | 622-626. | Mineral Embedded Skin 203 |
| 125-132. | Body Regeneration 18 | 385-390. | Flame Breath 37 | 627-631. | Misery Flashback Inducement 204 |
| 133-137. | Bonded Twin 152 | 391-394. | Flame Thrower Limb 179 | 632-636. | Molecular Manipulation 205 |
| 138-142. | Bravery Inducement 153 | 395-400. | Flesh Whip 180 | 637-641. | Monstrous Morph 58 |
| 143-147. | Breath Holding 19 | 401-405. | Force Field 38 | 642-646. | Multi-Arm 59 |
| 148-153. | Carnivorous Adaptation 154 | 406-410. | Formic Acid Sprayer 181 | 647-653. | Multi-Head 60 |
| 154-159. | Claws 20 | 411-416. | Foul Flesh 39 | 654-658. | Muto-Centaur 206 |
| 160-164. | Climbing Suckers 21 | 417-421. | Four Eyes 182 | 659-663. | Neural Surge 207 |
| 165-169. | Coma Inducement 22 | 422-426. | Frequency Receptors 183 | 664-668. | Night Vision 61 |
| 170-174. | Compression-Expansion 155 | 427-431. | Furred 40 | 669-673. | Nocturnal 208 |
| 175-184. | Contact Healing 156 | 432-436. | Gaping Maw 42 | 674-678. | Oil Stream 209 |
| 185-191. | Crab Pincers 23 | 437-441. | Gas Sacs 184 | 679-683. | Organ Grenade 210 |
| 192-196. | Devastator Pulse 25 | 442-446. | Gaseous Discharge 41 | 684-688. | Paralysis Tendrils 65 |
| 197-209. | Deviant Skin Structure 24 | 447-452. | Gaseous Expansion 185 | 689-693. | Peeling Radius 62 |
| 210-215. | Digital Optic Fade 157 | 453-456. | Generate Dimensional Horror 186 | 694-698. | Phlegm Sheet Spitter 211 |
| 216-220. | Dimension Hole 158 | 457-463. | Heal Touch 43 | 699-703. | Planer Skip 212 |
| 221-226. | Dimensional Awareness 159 | 464-468. | Heat Pulse 44 | 704-708. | Plasma Sphere Projection 213 |
| 227-231. | Dimensional Blade 160 | 469-474. | Heightened Attributes 45 | 709-713. | Poison Bite 63 |
| 232-236. | Dimensional Retreat 161 | 475-478. | Herbicidal Tissues 187 | 714-718. | Poison Blood 64 |
| 237-241. | Dimensional Shell 162 | 479-484. | Horns 46 | 719-723. | Precognitive Reactions 214 |
| 242-246. | Discern Dimensional Entities 163 | 485-489. | Horrid Symbionts 188 | 724-728. | Psionic Dampening Sphere 215 |
| 247-252. | Displacement 26 | 490-494. | Illusion Generation 189 | 729-733. | Psionic Dead Zone 216 |
| 253-258. | Dome of Energy 164 | 495-499. | Illusionary Concealment 190 | 734-738. | Psionic Sight 217 |
| 259-263. | Doom Sphere 27 | 500-505. | Image Multiplication 47 | 739-743. | Psionic Strike 218 |

## Combined New Minor Mutations List

### Table XR-195/ Creature Mutations MUT-2  1d100

## Creature Mutations List

Mutation Numbers 1 to 145 are found in the TME Hub Rules, while mutations 146 to 422 found in this book.

### Table XR-196/ Creature Mutations MUT-2 1d100

| | | | | | |
|---|---|---|---|---|---|
| 01. | Acid Blood 1 | 36. | Extreme Survivability 176 | 70. | Precognitive Reactions 214 |
| 02. | Acid Spit 2 | 37. | Fish Fins 178 | 71. | Quill Thrower Limb 220 |
| 03. | Acidic Saliva 146 | 38. | Flame Breath 37 | 72. | Radiation Absorption 66 |
| 04. | Acidic Skin Ducts 147 | 39. | Flame Thrower Limb 179 | 73. | Radioactive Pulse 68 |
| 05. | Advanced Kidneys 148 | 40. | Flesh Whip 180 | 74. | Razor Hook 221 |
| 06. | Amphibian 5 | 41. | Force Field 38 | 75. | Reserve Heart 69 |
| 07. | Aquatic Adaptation 7 | 42. | Formic Acid Sprayer 181 | 76. | Reserve Mind 70 |
| 08. | Arid Adaptation 8 | 43. | Foul Flesh 39 | 77. | Seasonal Enhancement 224 |
| 09,10. | Ballistic Hide 11 | 44. | Four Eyes 182 | 78. | Serpentine Body 72 |
| 11. | Beak 12 | 45. | Gas Sacs 184 | 79,80. | Shell 73 |
| 12. | Beam Eyes 13 | 46. | Gaseous Discharge 41 | 81. | Slime Excretion 226 |
| 13. | Bladed Limbs 15 | 47. | Gaseous Expansion 185 | 82. | Spike Thrower Arm 228 |
| 14. | Blurred Movement 16 | 48. | Herbicidal Tissues 187 | 83. | Spines 77 |
| 15,16. | Body Regeneration 18 | 49. | Horns 46 | 84. | Sprint 78 |
| 17. | Breath Holding 19 | 50,51. | Immunity 49 | 85. | Stalked Eyes 79 |
| 18. | Carnivorous Adaptation 154 | 52. | Increased Cellular Activity 50 | 86. | Stench Spray 80 |
| 19. | Climbing Suckers 21 | 53. | Irritation Particles 193 | 87. | Stinger Spike 229 |
| 20. | Compression-Expansion 155 | 54. | Limb Regeneration 52 | 88. | Sword Arm 232 |
| 21. | Crab Pincers 23 | 55. | Mental Counter Attack 196 | 89. | Tailed 83 |
| 22,23. | Deviant Skin Structure 24 | 56. | Mental Screen 55 | 90. | Tentacles 86 |
| 24. | Digital Optic Fade 157 | 57. | Mental Stun 198 | 91. | Third Eye 236 |
| 25. | Displacement 26 | 58. | Micro Feelers 199 | 92. | Throwing Quills 87 |
| 26. | Echolocation 165 | 59. | Micro Spines 200 | 93. | Thrust Spike 88 |
| 27. | Elastic Skeleton 166 | 60. | Mineral Embedded Skin 203 | 94. | Tissue Padding 238 |
| 28. | Electrical Charge 30 | 61. | Multi-Arm 59 | 95. | Tusks 89 |
| 29. | Electrical Impulse Emission 167 | 62,63. | Multi-Head 60 | 96. | Unique Tentacle 241 |
| 30. | Electrical Pulse 31 | 64. | Night Vision 61 | 97. | Venomous Horns 243 |
| 31. | Electro Magnetic Pulse 32 | 65. | Nocturnal 208 | 98. | Voice Mimicry 244 |
| 32. | Energy Tendril 171 | 66. | Oil Stream 209 | 99. | Web Generation 245 |
| 33. | Enormous Bone Spike 173 | 67. | Paralysis Tendrils 65 | 00. | Webbed Hands 90 |
| 34. | Enriched Skeletal Structure 174 | 68. | Phlegm Sheet Spitter 211 | | |
| 35. | Extreme Healing 175 | 69. | Poison Blood 64 | | |

# Ghost Mutations

Note: Ghost mutations are now separate from Latent, rank gained mutations.

## Table XR-197/ Ghost Mutations  1d1000

| | | |
|---|---|---|
| 01-06. | Acid Blood 1 | |
| 07-12. | Acid Spit 2 | |
| 13-18. | Acidic Saliva 146 | |
| 19-25. | Advanced Kidneys 148 | |
| 26-43. | Advanced Mind 3 | |
| 44-49. | Age Morphing 149 | |
| 50-61. | Agony Sphere 4 | |
| 62-70. | Amplification 6 | |
| 71-77. | Animal Association 150 | |
| 78-85. | Appearance Morph 151 | |
| 86-94. | Asphyxiation Zone 9 | |
| 95-103. | Aura of Protection 10 | |
| 104-115. | Beam Eyes 13 | |
| 116-122. | Berserker Rage 14 | |
| 123-131. | Blurred Movement 16 | |
| 132-142. | Body Regeneration 18 | |
| 143-147. | Bravery Inducement 153 | |
| 148-154. | Breath Holding 19 | |
| 155-164. | Coma Inducement 22 | |
| 165-175. | Contact Healing 156 | |
| 176-184. | Devastator Pulse 25 | |
| 185-191. | Digital Optic Fade 157 | |
| 192-201. | Dimension Hole 158 | |
| 202-209. | Dimensional Awareness 159 | |
| 210-218. | Dimensional Blade 160 | |
| 219-227. | Dimensional Retreat 161 | |
| 228-236. | Dimensional Shell 162 | |
| 237-244. | Discern Dimensional Entities 163 | |
| 245-253. | Displacement 26 | |
| 254-262. | Dome of Energy 164 | |
| 263-270. | Doom Sphere 27 | |
| 271-279. | Dread Zone 28 | |
| 280-288. | Earth Thump 29 | |
| 289-297. | Echolocation 165 | |
| 298-306. | Electrical Charge 30 | |
| 307-314. | Electrical Impulse Emission 167 | |
| 315-323. | Electrical Pulse 31 | |
| 324-332. | Electro Magnetic Pulse 32 | |
| 333-340. | Emotion Inducement 168 | |
| 341-349. | Empathy 33 | |
| 350-358. | Energy Blade 34 | |
| 359-367. | Energy Orbs 169 | |
| 368-376. | Energy Smite 170 | |
| 377-384. | Energy Wall Generation 172 | |
| 385-393. | Enriched Skeletal Structure 174 | |
| 394-403. | Extreme Healing 175 | |
| 404-411. | Extreme Survivability 176 | |
| 412-419. | Flame Breath 37 | |
| 420-429. | Force Field 38 | |
| 430-437. | Frequency Receptors 183 | |
| 438-446. | Generate Dimensional Horror 186 | |
| 447-455. | Heal Touch 43 | |
| 456-463. | Heat Pulse 44 | |
| 464-472. | Heightened Attributes 45 | |
| 473-481. | Herbicidal Tissues 187 | |
| 482-490. | Illusion Generation 189 | |
| 491-499. | Illusionary Concealment 190 | |
| 500-507. | Image Multiplication 47 | |
| 508-516. | Image Projection 48 | |
| 517-525. | Imbue Prowess 191 | |
| 526-534. | Immunity 49 | |
| 535-543. | Increased Cellular Activity 50 | |
| 544-551. | Internal Twin Fetus 192 | |
| 552-560. | Irritation Particles 193 | |
| 561-569. | Kinetic Fist 194 | |
| 570-578. | Light Burst 51 | |
| 579-586. | Limb Regeneration 52 | |
| 587-595. | Lost and Found 195 | |
| 596-604. | Mental Counter Attack 196 | |
| 605-613. | Mental Dominion 197 | |
| 614-621. | Mental Mine 54 | |
| 622-629. | Mental Screen 55 | |
| 630-638. | Mental Stun 198 | |
| 639-646. | Microwave Generation 201 | |
| 647-658. | Mind Crush 56 | |
| 659-664. | Mind Unification 202 | |
| 665-673. | Mind Waste 57 | |
| 674-681. | Misery Flashback Inducement 204 | |
| 682-690. | Molecular Manipulation 205 | |
| 691-699. | Neural Surge 207 | |
| 700-708. | Night Vision 61 | |
| 709-716. | Nocturnal 208 | |
| 717-726. | Peeling Radius 62 | |
| 727-734. | Phlegm Sheet Spitter 211 | |
| 735-742. | Planer Skip 212 | |
| 743-751. | Plasma Sphere Projection 213 | |
| 752-760. | Poison Blood 64 | |
| 761-769. | Precognitive Reactions 214 | |
| 770-776. | Psionic Dampening Sphere 215 | |
| 777-783. | Psionic Dead Zone 216 | |
| 784-788. | Psionic Sight 217 | |
| 789-804. | Psionic Strike 218 | |
| 805-813. | Pulse Eyes 219 | |
| 814-822. | Radiation Absorption 66 | |
| 823-830. | Radiation Detection 67 | |
| 831-839. | Radioactive Pulse 68 | |
| 840-848. | Reserve Heart 69 | |
| 849-857. | Reserve Mind 70 | |
| 858-866. | Sandblaster 222 | |
| 867-874. | Seasonal Enhancement 224 | |
| 875-883. | Sense Transfer 225 | |
| 884-892. | Sonic Wave Radius 76 | |
| 893-901. | Sprint 78 | |
| 902-909. | Strength Burst 81 | |
| 910-918. | Stun Ray 82 | |
| 919-926. | Sub-Plane Leap 231 | |
| 927-936. | Telekinesis 84 | |
| 937-944. | Telekinetic Flight 233 | |
| 945-953. | Telekinetic Junk Shield 234 | |
| 954-962. | Telekinetic Mangle 235 | |
| 963-973. | Telepathy 85 | |
| 974-981. | Thought Share 237 | |
| 982-990. | Transform Weather 239 | |
| 991-000. | Voice Mimicry 244 | |

**Mutation Numbers 1 to 145 are found in the TME Hub Rules, while mutations 146 to 422 found in this book.**

# Latent Mutations

Mutation Numbers 1 to 145 are found in the TME Hub Rules, while mutations 146 to 422 found in this book.

**Table XR-198/ Latent Mutations   1d100**

| | | |
|---|---|---|
| 01. Advanced Kidneys 148 | 35. Electro Magnetic Pulse 32 | 69,70. Mind Crush 56 |
| 02. Advanced Mind 3 | 36. Emotion Inducement 168 | 71. Mind Unification 202 |
| 03. Agony Sphere 4 | 37. Empathy 33 | 72. Mind Waste 57 |
| 04. Amplification 6 | 38. Energy Blade 34 | 73. Misery Flashback Inducement 204 |
| 05. Animal Association 150 | 39. Energy Orbs 169 | 74. Molecular Manipulation 205 |
| 06. Appearance Morph 151 | 40. Energy Smite 170 | 75. Neural Surge 207 |
| 07. Asphyxiation Zone 9 | 41. Energy Tendril 171 | 76. Peeling Radius 62 |
| 08. Aura of Protection 10 | 42,43. Energy Wall Generation 172 | 77. Planer Skip 212 |
| 09. Beam Eyes 13 | 44,45. Extreme Healing 175 | 78. Plasma Sphere Projection 213 |
| 10. Berserker Rage 14 | 46. Force Field 38 | 79. Precognitive Reactions 214 |
| 11. Blurred Movement 16 | 47. Frequency Receptors 183 | 80. Psionic Dampening Sphere 215 |
| 12. Bravery Inducement 153 | 48. Generate Dimensional Horror 186 | 81. Psionic Dead Zone 216 |
| 13. Coma Inducement 22 | 49,50. Heal Touch 43 | 82. Psionic Sight 217 |
| 14,15. Contact Healing 156 | 51. Heat Pulse 44 | 83. Psionic Strike 218 |
| 16. Devastator Pulse 25 | 52. Illusion Generation 189 | 84. Pulse Eyes 219 |
| 17. Digital Optic Fade 157 | 53. Illusionary Concealment 190 | 85. Radiation Detection 67 |
| 18. Dimension Hole 158 | 54. Image Multiplication 47 | 86. Radioactive Pulse 68 |
| 19,20. Dimensional Awareness 159 | 55. Image Projection 48 | 87. Sand blaster 222 |
| 21. Dimensional Blade 160 | 56. Imbue Prowess 191 | 88. Sense Transfer 225 |
| 22. Dimensional Retreat 161 | 57,58. Immunity 49 | 89. Sonic Wave Radius 76 |
| 23. Dimensional Shell 162 | 59. Increased Cellular Activity 50 | 90. Stun Ray 82 |
| 24. Discern Dimensional Entities 163 | 60. Kinetic Fist 194 | 91. Sub-Plane Leap 231 |
| 25. Displacement 26 | 61. Light Burst 51 | 92,93. Telekinesis 84 |
| 26. Dome of Energy 164 | 62. Lost and Found 195 | 94. Telekinetic Flight 233 |
| 27. Doom Sphere 27 | 63. Mental Counter Attack 196 | 95. Telekinetic Junk Shield 234 |
| 28. Dread Zone 28 | 64. Mental Dominion 197 | 96. Telekinetic Mangle 235 |
| 29. Earth Thump 29 | 65. Mental Mine 54 | 97,98. Telepathy 85 |
| 30,31. Electrical Charge 30 | 66. Mental Screen 55 | 99. Thought Share 237 |
| 32. Electrical Impulse Emission 167 | 67. Mental Stun 198 | 00. Transform Weather 239 |
| 33,34. Electrical Pulse 31 | 68. Microwave Generation 201 | |

# Flaw Mutations List

Mutation Numbers 1 to 145 are found in the TME Hub Rules, while mutations 146 to 422 found in this book.

## Table XR-199/ Flaw Mutations 1d100

| | |
|---|---|
| 01. | Abnormal Anxiety 102 |
| 02. | Altered Digestive Tract 103 |
| 03. | Aphasia 288 |
| 04. | Arms on One Side 289 |
| 05. | Baldness 104 |
| 06-10. | Birth Defect 105 |
| 11. | Blocked Sinuses 106 |
| 12. | Cataracts 290 |
| 13. | Chest Head 291 |
| 14. | Chronic Acne 107 |
| 15. | Chronic Depression 292 |
| 16. | Chronic Dermatitis 108 |
| 17. | Chronic Ingrown Hairs 109 |
| 18. | Chronic Ulcers 110 |
| 19. | Coronary Thrombosis 111 |
| 20. | Deaf 293 |
| 21. | Degenerated Nervous System 112 |
| 22. | Diminished Lungs 294 |
| 23. | Dizziness 113 |
| 24. | Early Menopause (females only) 114 |
| 25. | Epilepsy 295 |
| 26. | Excessive Earwax Generation 296 |
| 27. | Excessive Lung Fluid 115 |
| 28. | Exhaustion 116 |
| 29. | Extensive Warts 117 |
| 30,31. | External Organs 297 |
| 32. | Extreme Halitosis 118 |
| 33. | Faulty Immune System 119 |
| 34. | Flammable Tissues 120 |
| 35. | Fused Fingers 298 |
| 36. | Fused Neck 299 |
| 37-40. | Growths 300 |
| 41. | Grunter 301 |
| 42. | Head on Shoulder 302 |
| 43. | Hemophilia 121 |
| 44,45. | Hormone Disorder 122 |
| 46. | Inadequate Nerve Endings 123 |
| 47. | Increased Aging 124 |
| 48. | Increased Flatulence 125 |
| 49,50. | Intense Allergy 126 |
| 51. | Leg-Arm Inversion 303 |
| 52. | Locking Joints 304 |
| 53,54. | Lopsided 305 |
| 55. | Male Menopause (males only) 127 |
| 56. | Massive Club Foot 306 |
| 57. | Migraine Headaches 128 |
| 58. | Night Blind 307 |
| 59. | No Sense of Direction 308 |
| 60,61. | Open Mind 309 |
| 62. | Osteoporosis 129 |
| 63. | Oversized Head 310 |
| 64. | Permanent Rhinitis 130 |
| 65. | Perpetual Hiccups 131 |
| 66. | Pre-Senile Dementia 132 |
| 67. | Psoriasis 133 |
| 68. | Reactionary Scent 134 |
| 69. | Reduced Awareness 311 |
| 70. | Repeat Paralysis 135 |
| 71. | Shaky 312 |
| 72. | Shrunken Head 313 |
| 73. | Shrunken Heart 314 |
| 74. | Slow Witted 315 |
| 75. | Sonic Intolerance 136 |
| 76. | Stacked Eyes 316 |
| 77,78. | Sterility 137 |
| 79. | Stumpy Legs 317 |
| 80. | Stunted 318 |
| 81. | Sun Burner 319 |
| 82,83. | Tapeworms 138 |
| 84. | Tears of Blood 320 |
| 85. | Tinnitus 321 |
| 86. | Tooth Decay 139 |
| 87. | Toxic Susceptibility 140 |
| 88. | Tranquilizer Agent 141 |
| 89-93. | Useless Appendage 322 |
| 94,95. | Visual Disorder 142 |
| 96,97. | Voice Disorder 143 |
| 98. | Weak Bones 323 |
| 99. | Weeping 144 |
| 00. | Whistle Croup 145 |

# NPC Mutations List

## Table XR-200/ NPC Mutations 1d8

| | |
|---|---|
| 1. | Body Conjoined Twins 324 |
| 2. | Down Syndrome 325 |
| 3. | Dual Gendered 326 |
| 4. | Extreme Virility 327 |
| 5. | Gender Cycle 328 |
| 6. | Groin Conjoined Bodies 329 |
| 7. | Legless 330 |
| 8. | Sexless 331 |

# Plant Mutations List

## Table XR-201/ Plant Mutations Roll d100

| | |
|---|---|
| 01,02. | Acidic Sap 332 |
| 03. | Algae Spew 333 |
| 04. | Allergy Inducing Spores 334 |
| 05,06. | Amber Pellets 335 |
| 07,08. | Animal Parts 336 |
| 09-11. | Arid Plant Adaptation 337 |
| 12,13. | Armored Husk 338 |
| 14. | Barb Whip Tendrils 339 |
| 15. | Bitter Tasting 340 |
| 16. | Boring Tendrils 341 |
| 17,18. | Bug Repellent Sap 342 |
| 19. | Chameleon Powers 343 |
| 20,21. | Club limb (or vine) 344 |
| 22. | Control Carnivorous Plants 345 |
| 23,24. | Dagger Seed Pods 346 |
| 25. | Dehydration Root 347 |
| 26. | Detachable Core Seedling 348 |
| 27. | Digestive Sap 349 |
| 28,29. | Earth Boring Roots 350 |
| 30,31. | Enhanced Pine Needles 351 |
| 32. | Exoskeleton 352 |
| 33. | Exploding Puff Balls 353 |
| 34. | Exploding Seed Pods 354 |
| 35. | Extra Large 355 |
| 36. | Extreme Fibers 356 |
| 37. | Eye Tendril 357 |
| 38. | Fibrous Armor 358 |
| 39,40. | Fire Repellent 359 |
| 41. | Flotation Pods 360 |
| 42,43. | Fly Trap Jaws 361 |
| 44. | Forest Rejuvenation 362 |
| 45. | Fragmentation Pine Cones 363 |
| 46. | Glow in the Dark 364 |
| 47. | Grappling Root 365 |
| 48. | Hallucinatory Spores 366 |
| 49-52. | Hand-like Branch 367 |
| 53. | Harpoon Vines 368 |
| 54,55. | Healing Blossoms 369 |
| 56. | Hovering Gas Bag 370 |
| 57,58. | Human Parts 371 |
| 59. | Leaf Wings 372 |
| 60. | Lightning Flowers 373 |
| 61,62. | Manipulator Vines 374 |
| 63,64. | Medicinal Sap 375 |
| 65. | Mimic Human Shape 376 |
| 66,67. | Mineral Impregnated Bark 377 |
| 68. | Muscle-Fibers* 378 |
| 69. | Net Roots 379 |
| 70,71. | Nutritional Sap 380 |
| 72. | Obscuring Pollen Cloud 381 |

| | |
|---|---|
| 73. | Plant Manipulation 382 |
| 74. | Plant Serenity 383 |
| 75,76. | Poisonous Berries 384 |
| 77. | Radiation Leeching 385 |
| 78,79. | Saw Leaves 386 |
| 80. | Second Skin* 387 |
| 81. | Seedling Minions 388 |
| 82,83. | Serrated Leaves 389 |
| 84. | Shriek Radius 390 |
| 85. | Solar Emission Burst 391 |
| 86,87. | Solar Regenerating 392 |
| 88. | Spitting Acid Pods 393 |
| 89. | Spring Coil Leap 394 |
| 90. | Sticky Sap 395 |
| 91. | Suction Tendrils 396 |
| 92. | Thorns 397 |
| 93. | Toxic Sap 398 |
| 94. | Tumbling Locomotion 399 |
| 95. | Vampiric Roots 400 |
| 96. | Water Storage Pods 401 |
| 97. | Weaponized Spear-grass 402 |
| 98. | *Latent Mutations, see table XR-198* |
| 99,00. | *Prime Mutations, see table XR-194* |

*Host Inhabiting Mutation only, re-roll for non HIP characters*

# Plant Flaw Mutation List

## Table XR-202 / Plant Flaw Mutations 1d20

| | |
|---|---|
| 1. | Aphids 403 |
| 2. | Delicious to herbivores 404 |
| 3. | Flammable 405 |
| 4. | Green Walker Root Ball 406 |
| 5. | Grubs and Beetles 407 |
| 6. | Lightning Rod 408 |
| 7. | Mealybugs 409 |
| 8. | Past Termite Infestation 410 |
| 9. | Periodic Rooting 411 |
| 10. | Pollen 412 |
| 11. | Rodents 413 |
| 12. | Root Bound 414 |
| 13. | Slug Infestation 415 |
| 14. | Solar dependent 416 |
| 15. | Stench 417 |
| 16. | Tastes like chicken 418 |
| 17. | Tent Caterpillars 419 |
| 18. | Trunk Rot 420 |
| 19. | Visible Skeletal Remains 421 |
| 20. | Wild Nature 422 |

**Mutation Numbers 1 to 145 are found in the TME Hub Rules, while mutations 146 to 422 found in this book.**

# Parasite Mutation List

## Table XR-203 Parasite Mutations 1d100

| | |
|---|---|
| 01. | Acid Blood 1 |
| 02. | Acid Spit 2 |
| 03. | Advanced Kidneys 148 |
| 04. | Advanced Mind 3 |
| 05. | Agony Sphere 4 |
| 06. | Amphibian 5 |
| 07. | Amplification 6 |
| 08. | Asphyxiation Zone 9 |
| 09. | Aura of Protection 10 |
| 10. | Beam Eyes 13 |
| 11. | Body Regeneration 18 |
| 12. | Breath Holding 19 |
| 13. | Climbing Suckers 21 |
| 14. | Coma Inducement 22 |
| 15. | Contact Healing 156 |
| 16. | Devastator Pulse 25 |
| 17. | Dimension Hole 158 |
| 18. | Dimensional Awareness 159 |
| 19. | Dimensional Blade 160 |
| 20. | Dimensional Retreat 161 |
| 21. | Dimensional Shell 162 |
| 22. | Dome of Energy 164 |
| 23. | Doom Sphere 27 |
| 24. | Dread Zone 28 |
| 25. | Earth Thump 29 |
| 26. | Electrical Charge 30 |
| 27. | Electrical Impulse Emission 167 |
| 28. | Electrical Pulse 31 |
| 29. | Electro Magnetic Pulse 32 |
| 30. | Emotion Inducement 168 |
| 31. | Empathy 33 |
| 32. | Energy Orbs 169 |
| 33. | Energy Smite 170 |
| 34. | Energy Tendril 171 |
| 35. | Energy Wall Generation 172 |
| 36. | Extreme Healing 175 |
| 37. | Force Field 38 |
| 38. | Foul Flesh 39 |
| 39. | Frequency Receptors 183 |
| 40. | Generate Dimensional Horror 186 |
| 41. | Heal Touch 43 |
| 42. | Heat Pulse 44 |
| 43. | Illusion Generation 189 |
| 44. | Illusionary Concealment 190 |
| 45. | Image Projection 48 |
| 46. | Imbue Prowess 191 |
| 47. | Immunity 49 |
| 48. | Increased Cellular Activity 50 |
| 49. | Light Burst 51 |
| 50. | Limb Regeneration 52 |
| 51. | Lost and Found 195 |
| 52. | Mental Counter Attack 196 |
| 53. | Mental Dominion 197 |
| 54. | Mental Mine 54 |
| 55. | Mental Screen 55 |
| 56. | Mental Stun 198 |
| 57. | Micro Feelers 199 |
| 58. | Microwave Generation 201 |
| 59. | Mind Crush 56 |
| 60. | Mind Unification 202 |
| 61. | Mind Waste 57 |
| 62. | Misery Flashback Inducement 204 |
| 63. | Molecular Manipulation 205 |
| 64. | Multi-Head 60 |
| 65. | Neural Surge 207 |
| 66. | Night Vision 61 |
| 67. | Nocturnal 208 |
| 68. | Peeling Radius 62 |
| 69. | Planer Skip 212 |
| 70. | Plasma Sphere Projection 213 |
| 71. | Poison Bite 63 |
| 72. | Poison Blood 64 |
| 73. | Psionic Dampening Sphere 215 |
| 74. | Psionic Dead Zone 216 |
| 75. | Psionic Sight 217 |
| 76. | Psionic Strike 218 |
| 77. | Pulse Eyes 219 |
| 78. | Radiation Absorption 66 |
| 79. | Radiation Detection 67 |
| 80. | Radioactive Pulse 68 |
| 81. | Reserve Heart 69 |
| 82. | Reserve Mind 70 |
| 83. | Sarcophagus Cocoon 223 |
| 84. | Sense Transfer 225 |
| 85. | Slime Excretion 226 |
| 86. | Sonic Wave Radius 76 |
| 87. | Stalked Eyes 79 |
| 88. | Stench Spray 80 |
| 89. | Stun Ray 82 |
| 90. | Sub-Plane Leap 231 |
| 91. | Telekinesis 84 |
| 92. | Telekinetic Flight 233 |
| 93. | Telekinetic Junk Shield 234 |
| 94. | Telekinetic Mangle 235 |
| 95. | Telepathy 85 |
| 96. | Third Eye 236 |
| 97. | Thought Share 237 |
| 98. | Transform Weather 239 |
| 99. | Voice Mimicry 244 |
| 00. | Wings 91 |

# Expanded Prime Mutations

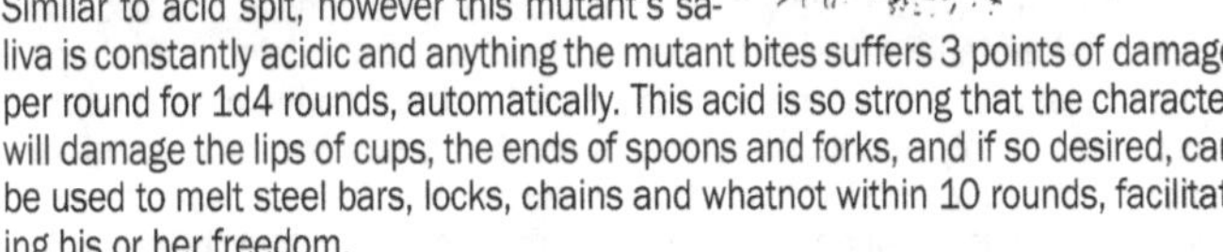

## Acidic Saliva 146

Type: **physical attack**
Range: **melee bite or kiss, or 3m if spit**
Rate: **1 bite or kiss, or else once every 5th round if spit**
Usage: **unlimited bites or kisses, 3 mouthfuls for spitting purposes per hour**
Strike Value: **+5**
Damage: **3 per round for 1d4 rounds**

Similar to acid spit, however this mutant's saliva is constantly acidic and anything the mutant bites suffers 3 points of damage per round for 1d4 rounds, automatically. This acid is so strong that the character will damage the lips of cups, the ends of spoons and forks, and if so desired, can be used to melt steel bars, locks, chains and whatnot within 10 rounds, facilitating his or her freedom.

Kissing with this mutant will inflict 1d3 damage per round, as will any other amorous or incautious contact with this person's saliva. The character's body is immune to his or her own acid, and somewhat resistant to other forms of acid as well, reducing the damage inflicted by other forms of acid by half.

If the mutant wishes to gather a mouthful of saliva and spit it, which takes 5 rounds to gather enough with a limit of 3 mouthfuls per hour, he or she may do so and propel it 3m with an SV of +5. Anyone hit suffers 3 points damage per round for 1d4 rounds.

## Acidic Skin Ducts 147

Type: **physical mutation**
Range: **touch or up to 6m directional or full radius**
Usage: **3 times per day, or week supply in one huge spray**
Rate: **1**　　Strike Value: **Automatic on touch, or 01-70 spray**
Damage: **touch 1d4 for 1d6 rounds, or spray 3d6 DMG for 1st round and 1d4 DMG after for 1d6 rounds**

This mutant's epidermis is covered in small, goose-bump sized dots. Up to three times a day, they can willfully flex these pores to rupture and exude acid. Anything with bare skin to be grappling the mutant, including any non-acid-proof clothing or metal armor, will immediately be coated and burn for 1d6 rounds, and suffer 1d4 damage per round. Under extreme circumstances, this deviant can decided to expel a full week's supply of acid at once and exude streamers of this clear acid in either front, back, one or both sides or else in all directions, range 6m, SV 01-70, damage 3d6 on first strike, and burn for 1d6 rounds thereafter for 1d4 damage per round.

Victims of this acid can douse themselves in at least 2 liters of water to neutralize the acid and stop its burning effects. This mutant is immune to its own acid,

however any gear or clothing they wear is possibly ruined with every full body use. As this individual has grown up with this mutation, they have learned to control it sufficiently to merely cause small patches, or one limb, to excrete this burning liquid, and so use it to eat through ropes or other bindings. These tiny bumps all over the mutant reduce their appearance trait value by -2.

## Advanced Kidneys 148

Type: **physical mutation**
Hazard Check: **Gets two checks against ingested toxins and poison**

This mutant's kidneys can eliminate salt from sea water, like a whale, thus allowing him to drink from the ocean. Likewise, hecan also ingest and digest foul water, sour milk, rotten foods and decaying flesh with no ill effects, and in fact turn it into a source of nutrition. He also gets two hazard checks against any ingested toxin or poison.

Although this character can chew up and tolerate food stuffs and drinks that others couldn't even taste without retching, it doesn't mean the mutant prefers carrion and stagnant water, and enjoys normal food just as much as anybody else.

## Age Morphing 149

Type: **physical mutation**
Usage: **Once per day per rank, takes 2 minutes to morph**
Duration: **1 minute per point of willpower**
Lowering age: **adds +10 appearance (APP)**
Increasing age beyond 30: **decreases appearance by -5 APP per 10 years aged**

This mutant can make itself change its outward form to appear younger, or much older. The alteration is not an illusion, but actual skin, hair and posture changes. The character can either become a teenager, or age themself to appear as a hunched, wrinkled and gray haired old timer.

The practical uses of this are to either hide one's identity, appear less threatening, avoid being press ganged into service, or to appear more or less attractive to potential would-be mating prospects.

Most of the deviant's traits do not change, however, younger, more youthful people tend to be more physically attractive. Because of this, if lowering the mutant's age, add +10 to appearance, while reduce the deviant's appearance by 5 points for each ten years after age 30.

The mutant can employ this power once per day, per rank. This change takes 2 minutes (40 rounds) to alter one's appearance. The duration of each transformation is one minute per point of willpower.

## Animal Association 150

Type: **mental mutation**　　Range: **user's willpower value in meters**
Usage: **constant**　　Hazard Check: **Type D intelligence**
Special Note: **If this mutant's willpower is 50+, the animal(s) will accompany and serve the mutant for 3d6 days.**

One line of animals, determined at the creation of the character, is susceptible to this mutant's charm-like benevolence inducement. The type of creatures which associate with this character will get an intelligence based, type D hazard check upon entering the mutant's zone of association — which is this mutant's willpower trait value in meters, or less. If the animal's check fails,

the creature usually departs peacefully, even if its pack mates make their hazard check and attack the user and their companions.

If the controlling mutant's willpower is 50 or higher, the creatures will not merely be harmless to the mutant and his or her companions, but will join the character's group for 3d6 days, (the actual number of days known only to the GM) and fight savagely to protect the user, wandering away occasionally to feed. Only mammals can be trained sufficiently to obey certain verbal commands, such as "stay, come, kill, lay down, let go of that," etc.

It is possible to have many beasts as guardians and if the creature's duration of association expires, the character can always attempt to control the animal again for another set time. The animals will not consider the controlling mutant's allies with more than tolerance, and will not act to help them — neither will it devour them while this controlling deviant is present. If the controlling mutant is killed, the animals will turn on its companions or other animals that were previously under his or her control.

It is worth noting that entering a town with a pack of giant spiders or mutant wolves in tow is always a tricky proposition, if not impossible. This sort of detail, like the actual 3d6 day duration of the association, is left up to the GM. Randomly determine the line of creatures this mutant can befriend, and where a mutant beast's ancestry is unknown — even to the game master — then such a freak cannot be influenced at all. Roll 1d20:

| | | | | | |
|---|---|---|---|---|---|
| 1. | **Insects** | 8. | **Whales** | 15. | **Birds** |
| 2. | **Reptiles** | 9. | **Plants** | 16. | **Cats** |
| 3. | **Crustaceans** | 10. | **Fish** | 17. | **Worms** |
| 4. | **Amphibians** | 11. | **Cattle** | 18. | **Sharks** |
| 5. | **Bears** | 12. | **Scorpions** | 19. | **Bats** |
| 6. | **Horses** | 13. | **Rodents** | 20. | **Roll two** |
| 7. | **Spiders** | 14. | **Dogs** | | |

## Appearance Morph 151

Type: **Physical change**     Range: **self**
Usage: **Once per day per rank**   Duration: **1 minute per point of willpower**
Rate: **Takes 2d6 rounds to morph**
Hazard Check: **Onlookers with 60 + perception, or those with aroused suspicions, get a Perception based Type C HC to realize this mutant is a fake**

This mutant can change their physical appearance at will, once a day per rank. This change takes 2d6 rounds to occur, and the features that can be changed include the user's gender, hair, skin and eye color, size within 30cm taller or shorter of the original form, as well as race so long as the being switched into has the same basic body shape and number of limbs. For example, a human with this power can change into a warmort, skullock, android, moaner or even a green walker — but can't morph into a dog, beetle or giant bat. The assumed form is purely visual, and provides none of the traits, skills or abilities of the subject, including their voice, language, or knowledge.

This post-apocalyptic doppelgänger can maintain this morphed visage for 1 minute per point of willpower, and can only assume the form of a pre-crafted unique identity, or assume the form of somebody or some humanoid it has examined for at least 2 minutes from within 6 meters or less range.

Very attentive beings, with 60 or higher perception score, automatically get the chance to see through this morphed mutant's persona when first encountering them within 3 meters. Others, however, must have good reason to believe that this morphing mutant's generated form cannot be true — such as if the assumed form is from somebody the viewer knows to be dead — or the user gives the morphed identity away by speaking in their own voice or clearly doesn't know some vital tidbit of information, or otherwise acts well out of their normal manner. In these cases, the suspicious onlookers become skeptical and are allowed a Type C perception based HC to see through the morph. If knocked unconscious or killed while in a morphed form, the mutant will revert to their regular appearance at once.

This is a difficult mutation to perform, and while the deviant can use physical mutations, standard weapons and actions, he or she can't use any other mental mutations. If struck by a mental attack or intrusion, this shape changer must make a willpower based type D hazard check or temporally lose morph integrity, reappear as their normal form for 3d6 rounds before reassuming the morphed version of themselves. In addition, characters of higher rank can use their daily uses of this mutation back to back to maintain a much longer appearance morph — which is especially useful to escape, spend multiple hours with those they deceive, or to linger within a hostile community or camp.

## Bonded Twin 152

Type: **physical mutation**

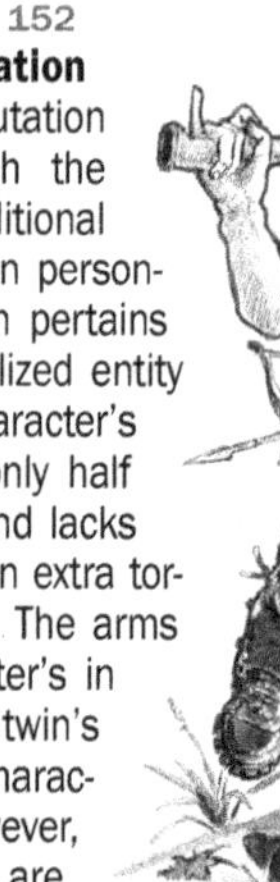

Similar to the mutation multi-head in which the character has additional heads with their own personalities, this mutation pertains to a more individualized entity attached to the character's torso. The twin is only half the mutant's size and lacks legs. It is basically an extra torso, arms and head. The arms are half the character's in strength, while the twin's body has half the character's endurance. However, agility and accuracy are identical to the host's body. The twin's appearance, gender, willpower, perception, intelligence and personality are all generated separately, constituting enough differences that the host and twin may despise each other.

Normally, the twin has its torso strapped tightly to the larger body and can wield hand held armaments well, even two shields to add additional protection to increase the entire being's overall defense value. The extra bulk of the twin reduces the character's movement rate by -1. The twin adds 50% to the character's weight, but besides the ability to carry shields and weapons, this alarming looking growth also gives the mutant a +2 initiative bonus, and while one or the other is asleep, can stay awake and on watch. Another benefit is that any incoming mental attack on the mutant is 50% likely to be made against one head or the other, and likewise with critical hits on the character, with the potential that one or the other twin could end up incapacitated or killed, and the other still alert and operational.

Because of having so many arms, this deviant also gains 1d3 skill points in climbing and is automatically a strong swimmer.

If slain, the twin will hang limply and shrivel up slowly over a month before dropping off on its own, leaving a nasty scar (-3d6 APP). Likewise, if the true character should die, the corpse will fall away after two months, leaving the legless twin to fend for itself and wriggle off.

Such twins are 46% chance likely to have reproductive organs. Of these, 60% are fertile. In addition, bonded twins are extra mutated 29% of the time with 1d2 prime, 1d4 minor-mutations, and a 73% chance of a flaw.

## Bravery Inducement 153

Type: **vocal-mental inducement**
Usage: **once per day per rank**
Defense Value: **nil**
Damage: **+5 for allies**
Range: **within hearing**
Duration: **5 rounds**
Strike Value: **+5 for allies**
Hazard Check: **nil**

This mutant can unleash a bizarre, semi-psionic war cry once a day per rank capable of inducing abnormal morale and limited berserker fighting rage into his or her allies. The process, like so many mental mutations, is a mystery, but those experiencing the heightened bravery claim to feel their personal anxiety

flee them, while on the other hand, keen malice for the enemy, clarity of mind, and focus on their weapon wash over them.

All comrades within hearing range will do battle at +5 strike value and inflict +5 damage on all strength based physical attacks for the next five rounds after the cry is heard. If the battle is clearly going badly for the mutant and his or allies, their morale will remain two entire levels higher while the war cry's effects are still operating. Mutants of higher rank can make multiple war cries back to back, therefore maintaining the manic bravery of their companions and allies.

This shout can be heard for many kilometers and is twice as loud as a regular shout and while it might summon help from comrades, will also attract predators and hostile locales.

See morale, page 110 of the TME Hub Rules.

## Carnivorous Adaptation 154

Type: **physical mutation**
Strike Value: **bite +5**
Trait Bonuses: **+20 strength, agility and accuracy**
Movement: **+1m**
Rate: **1 extra melee attack, bite**
Damage: **bite 1d8**

This mutant is a meat eater, and in fact cannot abide the taste of vegetable matter or any drink that is not based on dairy, blended raw eggs, or blood. Besides dietary requirements, which make the freak crave raw or very rare steak and other fare, this freak has also adapted serrated, visibly elongated teeth, powerful jaws, and a more muscular, efficient body.

This flesh eater gains +20 strength, agility and accuracy, and besides any hand held melee weapon, gains an additional bite attack that inflicts 1d8 damage plus any strength modifiers and has a +5 strike value bonus.

Finally, they are swift of foot, and besides any agility based movement modifiers, gains a +1 meter to movement rate per round. Should he or she go without at least a kilogram of flesh per day, any bestial human comrades, animal mounts, or draft animal of a herbivore ancestry are endangered by the presence of this bloodthirsty, often ravenous oddity. This predator's appearance suffers only a mild drop of -1d3 APP due to its frighteningly sharp teeth.

## Compression-Expansion 155

Type: **physical mutation**
Usage: **Once per day each, per rank for expansion and compression**
Rate: **Takes 1 minute to expand or contact** (20 rounds)
While Expanded: **gain x2 endurance and strength and +2m movement**
While Compressed: **50% reduction to strength, but gain +3 skill points in stealth**
Duration: **Half the character's current willpower traits in rounds, rounded up.**

This incredible deviant can inflate or deflate itself to either double or half their size, to fit into small spaces, look larger to deter predators, reach further, hide better, or intimate other people with their size.

It takes 1 minute to either expand or contract. Likewise, using this power is mentally demanding, requires the mutant's focus and so they can use no other mental mutation unless having an extra head.

Expansion: This mutant can expand their physical size up to 50% larger, including height and girth, however the character's weight stays the same. For the duration, if the mutation's use double the deviant's endurance and strength traits, and move +2 meters per round. Any damage the mutant takes while expanded comes off the bonus trait value portion first. Expansion can be used once per day per rank.

Contraction: This mutant can physically compress to half their normal size, although their head stays the same size often resulting in a bizarre looking person. A contracted character can fit into smaller spaces to evade pursuers, exhibits 3 (or +3 if already an acquired skill) in stealth. The child sized character has a reduced strength score by half, but other traits are unchanged. Contraction can be used once per day per rank, and these uses are in addition to how many times per day the freak uses the expansion aspect of this gift.

## Contact Healing 156

Type: **Mental mutation**
Range: **Touch**
Usage: **Once per day per rank**
Duration: **As long as touch is maintained**
Healing (or damage if reversed): **1 handed touch heals 1 END* per hour/ 2 handed touch heals 1d6 END* per hour/ Full near naked body to body contact 2d6 END* healed per hour. *Plus each other injured trait.**
Hazard Check: **Unwilling victims allowed a Type C willpower check per hour**

When this mutant physically embraces a wounded, unconscious or dying organic companion, even an animal or plantoid, and with skin on skin contact, he or she will transfer healing energies at a cellular level. This mutation cannot be used on the deviant itself, yet it is still a powerful gift, especially to a dig team or brigade of mercenaries. This beneficial electrical frequency causes faster blood clotting at a wound, mending of tissues and bone, and even restores spinal and brain tissue.

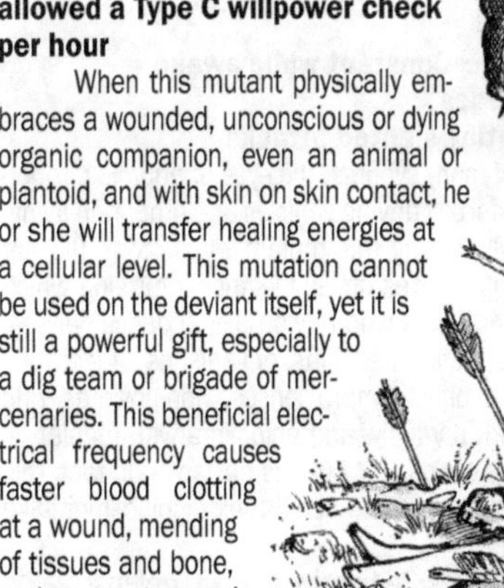

It is not, however, a heal touch style mutation in which the subject can be attended to and then abandoned. This potent deviation requires the healer to remain in constant contact with the patient, and with the more skin on skin contact, the better. A mutant who merely places its hand or other appendage on the wounded individual will stop the person from slipping into death from unconsciousness, but only heal them 1 trait point per hour. If this mutant places two hands, feet or an arm about the bare skin of the subject's torso or neck, then this healing increases to 1d6 endurance, or other lost trait points, per hour.

Should the healing mutant instead lay pressed to the wounded individual with considerable skin on skin contct, then maximum healing will occur at a rate of 2d6 lost trait points per hour, so long as body-to-body adhesion continues.

If this individual's gift be made known, this 'healing battery', might attract the attention of warlords, cult leaders, and the powerful who would desire to keep this mutant close at hand in case they themselves require healing — and might force this mutant to transfer his or her gifts at gunpoint.

A parasite character with this mutation will always be in full body to body contact with its host and yield remarkable healing energies to it.

Should the healer break physical contact with the wounded subject, healing stops at that point and the session is broken and a daily usage is spent. This mutant can use this power once per day per rank, however, once a link is made, the usage duration continues so long as physical contact remains. While transferring healing, the user cannot use other mental mutations, however, he or she can use a free hand to deploy other weapons, plus, can walk, perhaps assisting the wounded individual as they travel.

The opposite of this mutation can also be deployed, whereby the mutant holds and tries to inflict damage to the body of the restrained or unconscious victim. The target is allowed a Type C willpower based hazard check per hour to resist this insidious, pain inducing power.

## Digital Optic Fade 157

Type: **Mental mutation**    Usage: **Constant while awake**
Initiative: **+3 vs digital optic using foes**
Defense Value: **-40 vs digital targeting sighted attacks**
Digital eyes, such as optical implants of many cyborgs, the eyes of androids, robotics, automated gun turrets, MAVs, drones, self driving vehicles and other non-living, mechanical optical nodes have difficulty seeing this mutant whose form flickers and winks in and out. In short, this mutant gives off an electrical emission which scrambles how it looks to machines and those who rely on digital optical lenses. One second the mutant is there, the next it flickers, shifts, or vanishes altogether.

Analog optics, such as old style print camera lenses, non-powered rifle scopes, binoculars and telescopes work normally, and onlookers with regular vision will see and feel nothing out of the ordinary about this deviant — in fact, this character might not be aware of this power until told about their displacement-like abilities by a cyborg with an implant eye.

In game terms, this character gains +3 initiative and -40 defense value when facing incoming robotic or digital optic sights of a cyborg, relic weapon, automated turret or similar digital optical systems. Of course, if a cyborg op-

ponent has one living eye, it can still use analog weapons on this mutant normally, and suffers no initiative setback. This power is in constant use, unless this character is asleep.

## Dimension Hole 158

Type: **Mental portal manipulation**    Range: **3 meter diameter hole**
Usage: **One successful hole per day per rank with one attempt allowed per minute (20 rounds)**    Duration: **see below**
This mutation is as potent as it is unpredictable, and might unleash both the most challenging and rewarding adventure a GM can conduct. The greater one's intelligence, the greater the odds of opening a dimensional portal and the longer the user can keep it open. Likewise, the smarter the mutant, the better his or her odds of controlling the destination time and location.

The mutant can make one attempt to open a hole per minute (20 rounds) with an unlimited number of attempts allowed per day. However, only one Dimension hole can be successfully generated per day per rank of the character.

| Intelligence of Mutant | Chance to Open Hole | Hole Destination Duration | Control |
|---|---|---|---|
| 01-06 | 11% | 1 round | 1% |
| 07-12 | 23% | 1d4 rounds | 2% |
| 13-26 | 39% | 1d6+1 rounds | 8% |
| 27-34 | 48% | 1d6+3 rounds | 17% |
| 35-44 | 57% | 2d6+4 rounds | 27% |
| 45-54 | 71% | 2d6+9 rounds | 39% |
| 55-64 | 83% | 3d6+10 rounds | 48% |
| 65-84 | 88% | 3d6+18 rounds | 63% |
| 85-105 | 91% | 3d6+24 rounds | 88% |
| 106-120 | 93% | 3d6+30 rounds | 92% |
| 121-135 | 95% | 3d6+40 rounds | 96% |
| over 135 | 99% | 3d6+50 rounds | 99% |

Once a dimension hole is opened, two human sized beings can jump through the shimmering 3 meter tall by 3 meter wide hole, per round. If the hole into the dimensional tunnel closes before all teammates are through, stragglers are left behind.

Only the GM knows the duration (which is rolled and recorded behind the GM screen), and whether the destination has been controlled. If the control is successful, the user has made a doorway to the desired time, place, or dimensional plane, which must be pre-stated by the player. Some suggested destinations include several minutes back in time to warn themselves of a hidden threat, back to their hometown in the same event time, into another plane of existence such as a fantasy setting, on the other side of the walls of a fortress, inside a space-station orbiting the earth or even back in history to the age of dinosaurs, ancient Rome, Egypt, China, or Europe, possibly to a certain battle or historical event in human history. Possibly into a war zone like 1960's Vietnam or the many gulf wars, to search for relic weapons in great quantities, and try to bring them back.

Should the mutant fail to control the hole, the individual and his or her companions will find themselves in a random or referee created time and place. Returning from another dimension or time is made by attempting to both create a new dimension hole, one attempt per day per rank, that always leads back to the user's proper place and time period, either at the exact time they left, or 3d6 hours after they left (GM's discretion or a 50/50 die toss).

The GM must do some serious adventure crafting to establish the settings of most planes, while a little research is required to set up a historical scenario. The following gives a very brief sample of the possibilities for an uncontrolled dimensional leap point:

## 1d8 Uncontrolled Dimensional Hole Destinations

**1.**    Characters step out 1d100 km, in real time (**1d4: 1.** North / **2.** South / **3.** East / **4.** West) of their current location. This could be dangerous if the opening deposits travelers in the sea, or behind enemy lines.

**2.**    Characters each step out at the exact location they were at earlier, but in real time. (**1d4: 1.** at dawn that morning / **2.** at dusk the evening before / **3.** 1d6 hours ago / **4.** 1d20 hours ago).

**3.**    Characters step out at the same location they had just left, but later in time. **Roll 1d8:**
1. 2d4 rounds later
2. 2d100 rounds later
3. 1d20 minutes later
4. 1d6 hours later
5. 1d20 hours later
6. 2d4 days later
7. 2d20 days later
8. 1d12 months later

**4.5.**  Characters step out into historical time and setting, roll 1d100:
**01-15.** Dinosaur Era (**1d4: 1.** Triassic / **2.** Jurassic / **3,4.** Cretaceous).
**16-20.** Stone Age (**1d4: 1,2.** Africa / **3.** Europe / **4.** America/ **5.** Asia/ **6.** Australia).
**21-23.** 15th Century B.C., Mycenae Greece.
**24-26.** Overlooking the battle of Marathon, 490 B.C. between a Greek Phalanx and rows of Persian soldiers.
**27,28.** In the camp of Alexander the Great, 334 B.C. during the invasion of Persia.
**29-33.** Nero's Rome, A.D. 64.
**34,35.** 72 A.D. Ancient Rome, countryside, during slave revolt led by Spartacus.
**36,37.** 46 A.D. Cleopatra's court, Ancient Egypt, 37% chance Caesar present.
**38,39.** Fall of Rome to Visigoth Barbarians as pillaging erupts.
**40,41.** 830 A.D. on board a Viking warship as it lands on the shores of England during a brutal raid.
**42,43.** On board a Viking Voyage to North America, 1000 A.D.
**44,45.** 1066 A.D. in visual range of the battle of Hastings, England. Conflict between English Saxons and invading Normans.
**46,47.** 12th Century A.D., King Arthur's England.
**48,49.** 1099 A.D. inside Jerusalem as Crusaders storm the walls.
**50,51.** 1415 A.D. Agincourt, France, Henry V's archers vs. massive French Calvary of knights.
**52,53.** 14th Century A.D. Aztec Mexico, near capital Tenochtitlan.
**54,55.** Medieval Japan, pre-western influenced, 500+2d100 A.D.
**56,57.** Ancient China, 2d100 A.D.
**58,59.** Ancient India, 1d1000 A.D.
**60,61.** Inuit encampment, arctic, 1000+1d1000 A.D.
**62,63.** 1492 A.D. on small island as Columbus Expedition reaches shore of the New World.
**64,65.** North American City, year 1800+4d100
**66,67.** Old Earth. For location, use uncontrolled destination list from roll '7' this table, 50% year 2d1000 B.C., otherwise 2d1000 A.D.
**68-70.** In exact city or town GM and Players are at, however, dimensional hole is in a specified time in settlement's history. Roll 1d10:
    **1.** Tribal Encampment, (pre-European arrival, year 1d1000 A.D. if in North America) or caveman encampment much further back in time if elsewhere in the world.
    **2.** 1774 (During American War of Independence time frame).
    **3.** 1861-1865 During American Civil War era (roll 1861+1d4 for year).
    **4.** 1880+1d20 year

    **5.** 1920+1d10 year
    **6.** 1910+2d20 year
    **7.** 1960+1d10 year
    **8.** 1970+1d20 year
    **9.** 1990+1d100 year
    **10.** Undisclosed dark time, around 2150 +1d100 year, devastation abounds
**71-00.** Early 21st century, in exact city or town GM and Players are at, however, dimensional hole is in a specified location. Roll 1d100:
    **01-04.** At University or college campus, nighttime, 1d4 am.
    **05-08.** At University or college campus, day, during classes, hole in washrooms, **1d6: 1-3** girls, **4-6** boys.
    **09-12.** At the University or college campus, noon, cafeteria.
    **13-15.** Police station or local prison, cell block.
    **16-22.** Shopping Mall, busy Friday afternoon.
    **23-25.** In the middle of a busy freeway at evening, rush hour.
    **26-28.** Strip club, evening.
    **29-33.** Dance club: select randomly from phone book, evening.
    **34-36.** Illicit Drug lab-grow-operation, time, 2d12 hour.
    **37-44.** Back alley, in dumpster, late evening.
    **45-50.** Random suburb, dusk.
    **51-53.** School playground, young children, noon.
    **54-57.** Gas Station, outskirts, 2d12 hour.
    **58-61.** Coffee Shop, downtown, 2d12 hour.
    **62-66.** Donut Shop, late at night.
    **67-69.** Bank, downtown, busy afternoon.
    **70-73.** City Bus, morning rush hour.
    **74-77.** City park, dawn.
    **78-80.** Hospital, morgue, 2d12 hour.
    **81-83.** Film Set, Major budget Hollywood film, big name stars.
    **84-86.** Film Set, documentary.
    **87-89.** Film Set, adult movie.
    **90-93.** Local Library, 2d12 hour.
    **94-96.** Construction site, late night.
    **97,98.** Office Building, 2d12 hour.
    **99,00.** On top of tallest building in town.

**6.** Characters step out of an ornate, jewel encrusted portal into a vast subterranean temple complex in a fantasy world. they aren't alone here.

**7.** The characters find themselves in real time but in another place on The Mutant Epoch era Earth. To determine the location, roll 1d100:

| | | |
|---|---|---|
| **01-02.** Japan | **46-48.** Alaska | **79-80.** Greece |
| **03-04.** England | **49-50.** South Africa | **81.** Sweden |
| **05-06.** Egypt | **51.** Austria | **82.** Greenland |
| **07-08.** Mexico | **52-53.** Indonesia | **83.** Argentina |
| **09-11.** China | **54-55.** Pakistan | **84-86.** Brazil |
| **12.** Hawaii | **56.** North Pole | **87.** Peru |
| **13-14.** Iran | **57-58.** Korea | **88.** Venezuela |
| **15-16.** Antarctica | **59-60.** Vietnam | **89.** Cuba |
| **17-18.** India | **61-62.** Thailand | **90-92.** U.S.A |
| **19-20.** Spain | **63-64.** Malaysia | **93-94.** Canada |
| **21-22.** Turkey | **65-66.** Iraq | **95.** Philippines |
| **23-28.** Australia | **67.** Kuwait | **96.** Central America |
| **29-32.** Russia | **68-69.** Syria | **97.** Iceland |
| **33.** Morocco | **70-72.** Kenya | **98.** Eastern Europe |
| **34-36.** Poland | **73.** Ethiopia | **99.** Afghanistan |
| **37.** New Zealand | **74-75.** Mongolia | **00.** Israel |
| **38-41.** Germany | **76.** Saudi Arabia | |
| **42-45.** France | **77-78.** Italy | |

**8.** The characters step out at a non-earth, real time, fully functional location. **Roll 1d10:**
    **1.** Asteroid mining base beyond Mars.
    **2.** Space station orbiting one of the 1d12 planets.
    **3.** Martian domed colony.
    **4.** Space station orbiting Earth.
    **5.** Spacecraft, mother ship, never departed the system, orbiting earth.
    **6.** Moon base, military (1d16: 1-3. human operated /4-5. android held / 6. abandoned).
    **7.** Moon Base, human, mining.
    **8.** Moon Base, toxic dump, run by work robots and a few nutty humans.
    **9.** Spaceport on Earth-like planet, human colonization, another solar system.
    **10.** Space vessel, on route to earth, deep space, 1d100 years from Earth.

## Dimensional Acumen 159

Type: **dimensional defense, awareness and offensive mutation**
Range: **detect dimensional beings within 1m per point of perception**
Usage: **constant, or 1 minute per point of willpower for offensive use**
Rate: **1**    Strike Value: **+10 on dimensional beings only**
Damage: **by non-energy appendage or weapon**
Defense Value: **-10 vs. attacks by dimensional beings**

This deviant has an all around – though limited – awareness, affinity and acumen to see, hear and engage dimensional beings within 1 meter per point of perception trait he or she possesses. Their perception of dimensional beings is far less accurate than those with the mutation Discern Dimensional Beings, but the user can detect them enough to know their proximity and either run from them or, if so armed, attack them – the entity gaining only half their normal invisibility DV bonus. These otherworldly beings are aware of this mutant and know they are visible to it, and might either become enraged by this, or flee. The deviant cannot tell one type of dimensional being from another when they are invisible, however, if splashing it with colored liquid, or dust, the entity could be revealed by its size and shape.

Born in-tune with the non-physical life forms, this mutant has developed some protection and gains a -10 DV bonus from their attacks. Likewise, by focusing its mind, the deviant can sheath any offensive appendages or non-energy melee weapons in a brilliant green light and harm dimensional beings for a maximum duration of the mutant's willpower in minutes per day. This glow can be used as a light source, although only casts a dull light in a 6m radius. SV +10 and inflicts the weapon or appendage's normal damage.

## Dimensional Blade 160

Type: **beam attack**    Defense Value: **nil**
Range: **melee**    Usage: **as willpower**
Duration: **willpower value in rounds per day**
Strike Value: **+10 / +40 vs. dimensional beings**
Damage: **1d12/ 1d100 vs. dimensional beings**

At will, this mutant can charge up his or her hand to emit a one meter long, glowing blade of dimensional energy, which acts like a weak laser sword against physical targets, doing only 1d12 damage at +10 SV. However, against dimensional beings its true potency is unleashed. Such entities are +40 SV easier to

hit, and take 1d100 damage from this attack. It can be employed one round per user's current willpower score per day, with either hits or misses both counting toward the daily uses. Strength modifiers do not apply to energy weapons.

This mutation does not offer the mutant any extra ability to see a dimensional being or phenomena until it hits one, which for a brief moment will light up and be revealed to all onlookers for 1d4 rounds.

## Dimensional Retreat 161

Type: **subconscious mental defense**    Range: **user**
Usage: **once per day per rank**    Duration: **Variable**

This mutant automatically leaves the earth plane in a flash of light when their body or mind are in great peril and about to die. Whenever the character's endurance or other trait value reaches 5 or less (except for Appearance), either from fatal or stun attacks, he or she vanishes in a whirl of light and enters a dimensional vortex. The character has no say in whether or not this retreat will occur, unless the mutant has already been hurled across time and space and has used up his or her usages of this mutation for that day.

In the dimensional vortex, the mutant is lost in time and space for an unspecified period, known only to the GM, and at some point, will pop out back into the world. While away, healing occurs at its normal rate based on the duration of the alternate, disembodied existence. Roll 1d100 first to determine how long the character is lost in the vortex, and secondly, where he or she returns to on earth.

Reminder: there are 20 rounds in one minute.

| 1d100 | Time away from Earth | | |
|---|---|---|---|
| 01-03. | 1d4 rounds | 52-54. | 1d6 hours |
| 04-06. | 1d6 rounds | 55-57. | 1d8 hours |
| 07-09. | 2d6 rounds | 58-60. | 1d10 hours |
| 10-12. | 3d6 rounds | 61-63. | 1d12 hours |
| 13-15. | 4d6 rounds | 64-66. | 1d20 hours |
| 16-18. | 10+1d20 rounds | 67-69. | 3d6 hours |
| 19-21. | 20+1d20 rounds | 70-72. | 10+1d6 hours |
| 22-24. | 30+1d20 rounds | 73-75. | 10+2d6 hours |
| 25-27. | 40+1d20 rounds | 76-78. | 10+1d20 hours |
| 28-30. | 40+2d20 rounds | 79-81. | 20 +1d20 hours |
| 31-33. | 40+1d100 rounds | 82-84. | 3d20 hours |
| 34-36. | 2d6 minutes | 85-87. | 1d6 days |
| 37-39. | 10+1d10 minutes | 88-90. | 2d6 days |
| 40-42. | 20+2d10 minutes | 91-93. | 3d6 days |
| 43-45. | 1d100 minutes | 94-96. | 4d6 days |
| 46-48. | 100+1d100 minutes | 97-99. | 5d6 days |
| 49-51. | 1d4 hours | 100. | 1d100 days |

| 2d6 | Location Upon Arrival to Earth* |
|---|---|
| 2. | Where PC's first born child is, if none, then where the mutant was born. |
| 3. | Where the character was when they woke up on the day of departure. |
| 4. | In the last town or village he or she had been at. |
| 5-7. | Same location as departure point. |
| 8. | 1d100 km North of the departure point. |
| 9. | 1d100 km South of the departure point. |
| 10. | 1d100 km East of the departure point. |
| 11. | 1d100 km West of the departure point. |
| 12. | Where his lover or spouse is located, if none, re-roll. |

*Wherever the character appears, it is relatively safe, even if it's on a floating piece of debris on the water, on a roof, deck of passing airship or barge, etc.*

## Dimensional Shell 162

Type: **dimensional defense**    Range: **user**   Usage: **constant**
Duration: **nil**    Defense Value: **- 50 from dimensional strike rolls**
Usually mutants with this aberration aren't aware of it until they battle dimensional beings. The character's DV increases by –50 from all dimensional attacks. This mutation does not, however, stop dimensional beings from launching mental attacks.

## Discern Dimensional Entities 163

Type: **optical enhancement**    Range: **sight**    Usage: **constant**
Similar to discern radiation, this character can see all dimensional creatures, day or night, which gives these creatures no extra defense value modifiers from this mutant's attacks. Additionally, this mutant can see dimensional rips, portals, or other openings in the physical world as far away in meters as their perception trait value.

To allow other characters to see nearby entities, this mutant might be clever enough to toss dust, flour or other powder or colored liquid on a dimen-

sional being to reveal the entity's basic shape, eliminating the thing's extra defense value bonus for invisibility. Dimensional beings are covered under optional rules on page 363 of this book.

## Dome of Energy 164

Type: **mental mutation**    Radius of dome: **Variable by rank**
Rate: **Takes 2 rounds to generate, activates on 3rd round**
Usage: **Variable by rank**    Endurance: **Variable by rank**
Duration: **Willpower = minutes of use**
This mutant must focus intently to use this potent mental mutation. After taking two rounds to power up, doing nothing else and in this time taking no hits or suffering no mental attacks, the deviant can thereafter project a dome of greenish hued energy about him or her. This field of crackling energy stops all gases, flying debris, radiation, mental attacks and transmissions for up to the user's willpower in minutes (there are 20 rounds in a minute). Those close to the mutant are kept safe from the above mentioned dangers, too, however they themselves cannot shoot or mentally project any attacks at those outside the dome, while those outside can try to break the shield by all manner of physical attacks.

The energy dome can take a certain amount of damage before collapsing and vanishing, based on the rank of the mutant according to the table to follow. At any time, the controlling mutant — who can do nothing but focus solely on the dome to maintain it — can switch off the protective shield.

While called a dome, this shield is actually a circle, going underground, into lower floors of a structure, or into the water beneath the mutant should they be in a boat or swimming, thus protecting the subjects within from incoming attacks from any direction.

Attackers from outside the dome can use both physical and most energy weapons to weaken and possibly dissipate the dome, including lightning, sonic attacks and flame — although EMP, and attacks by dimensional mutations and creatures, and radioactive pulses have no effect. Each allowable attack is an automatic strike for regular damage by that attack mode. Larger domes allow far more adversaries to get around it and hammer away or shoot at it.

Should any living thing or machine within the dome wish to leave the sphere while it is in operation, it can only do so by either reducing the dome's endurance to zero, or disturbing the mutant who is maintaining the dome (making a successful strike on the mutant). If the mutant's concentration is broken, the dome dissipates and the daily usage lost. This mutation can also be used while this super mutant is within a moving vehicle, including relic vehicles — although in most cases the entirety of a vessel is not encased in this protective bubble, and so if an airship's balloon is ruptured but this mutant has placed a ball of protection around the gondola, then the whole thing is going to drop to earth anyway, and most likely destroy the sphere and all those within it.

The following rank based table shows how many uses a day the mutant can generate this potent field. If desired, the user can regenerate the field back to back with no time delay and not only extend the time those within can seek safety, but the endurance of the dome is reset back to its starting amount. This matrix also shows the radius of the dome and the number of human sized beings who can take shelter within it in a flat plain and not also stacked up on various floors or bunks — which could accommodate double the number shown. The endurance of the dome is also listed here, and at higher ranks, is truly massive. Duration as the user's willpower trait in minutes, per use.

| Mutant's Rank | Uses per day | Radius of Dome | People Protected | Endurance of Dome* |
|---|---|---|---|---|
| 1 | Once every 2 days | 1m | 3 people | 100 |
| 2,3 | Once | 2m | 5 people | 200 |
| 4,5 | Twice | 3m | 10 people | 300 |
| 6,7 | Twice | 6m | 20 people | 500 |
| 8,9 | Twice | 9m | 30 people | 700 |
| 10-13 | Twice | 11m | 40 people | 1000 |
| 14-18 | Twice | 15m | 60 people | 1300 |
| 19 and up | Three | 20m | 100 people | 1500 |

*Is automatically struck for random damage by attacker.*

## Echolocation 165

Type: **physical attack**     Range: **50m in air or 200m in water**
Duration: **At will**

This mutant can use sonar whenever desired, allowing him or her to see shapes, movement, the landscape and objects in total darkness up to 50m away or 200m in water. Should the mutant find itself in a void, it will carry 75m, however cannot be used while wearing a fully enclosed helmet, filter mask or anything else that covers the mouth and ears, so how useful it is in an airless void is debatable.

In order for this deviation to work, the mutant must emit shrill whistling sounds, sounds that are audible to other beings as if the person were talking out loud.

Most animals, however, and other humanoids, will assume such a noise is coming from a huge bat or other nocturnal predator, and may seek to avoid the mutant instead of engaging it. While echolocation is a very handy evolutionary gift, it doesn't allow the mutant to read signs or other variations in a flat surface, nor discern color, heat signatures or fine details such as keyboards, foot prints, insignia and whatnot.

This character suffers no movement, Defense Value or Strike Value penalties when thrown into total darkness or when blinded.

The drawback to this mutation is that other creatures accustomed to using sonar, or having excellent hearing, can detect the user's ultra sonic noises within 500 meters in open country, 100m in swamps, forests, hills or the streets of ruins, or within 50 underground or in a new era community and may come to investigate. These creatures include bats, dogs, whales, cats, and all members of the weasel family, such as badgers and wolverines. The PC can choose to switch off the sonar at any time or may use it during all its waking hours.

## Elastic Skeleton 166

Type: **physical alteration**

This character's bones are of flexible, stretchy cartilage, allowing them to double or half their height at will. This bouncy mutie suffers only half damage from falls or bludgeoning attacks, such as by kicks, tail slaps, club blows being trampled and fists.

Unfortunately, because of the lack of substance exhibited by this character's bones, he or she suffers a drop of 3d6 to strength, and has a movement rate reduction of -0.5m per round as much of the force of each step is lost in the flex of the leg bones. On the flip side, the subject can contract their body and then spring in a great jump up to their height into the air or double that horizontally to clear a pit even without getting a run at the gap as other mutants must.

Finally, broken bones suffered by this mutant heal at twice their normal rate.

## Electrical Impulse Emission 167

Type: **Energy mutation**     Rate: **4 pulses per barrage**
Usage: **2 barrages per day per rank**
Range: **Willpower x 3 in meters**
Strike Value: **+20**     Damage: **1d8 each, or 2d8 to robots, cyborgs, vat-brains, androids and other electricity using machines.**

This mutant can generate a barrage of crackling, tear dropped shaped pulses of electricity and fire them in rapid succession at one or more targets in a 180 degree arc in front of it — or to either side or behind if being pursued. These orbs speed toward their intended target with a strike value bonus of +20 and inflict 1d8 damage each on a hit, although 2d8 DMG to electricity using machines and beings, including cyborgs, robots, androids, vat-brains, mutorgs and the like.

The mutant can fire two emission barrages, per day, per rank, at a rate of 4 pulses per barrage. The range is triple the mutant's willpower trait in meters. This energy discharge is fired from the hand 77% of the time, otherwise from the forehead.

## Emotion Inducement 168

Type: **mental control**      Range: **10 meter radius per rank**
Usage: **once a day per rank**
Duration: **one round per point of willpower, multiplied by rank**
Hazard Check: **Intelligence based type B or Willpower type A**

Once a day per rank of experience, this individual can place a mental control radius around themselves. The radius of this zone is 10m per rank of the mutant, and forms a sphere and thus affects those on lower floors or those above the user. All those within the zone must make an intelligence based hazard check, type B, or succumb to the emotion being implanted by the mutant. Those individuals who fail their hazard check will immediately act upon the suggested emotion as if it were their true feeling toward the controlling character.

If the controlling mutant is hit violently, or is damaged by a mental attack while maintaining the inducement field, the control ends abruptly, returning all victims to normal.

Should the victim leave the field's radius, he or she will also be permitted a second hazard check; a willpower based type A check, to determine if he or she will continue to have the induced feelings for 1d100 rounds more or not.

Typical emotions to be induced are friendship, terror, love, trust, peace, lust and even hatred to induce attacks. Companions of the user mutant are immune to this inducement if aware of the character's possession of this mild mind control, but if they are new to the person, say, less than a day in their companionship, they might succumb to the inducement.

The duration of Emotion Inducement is as the user's willpower in rounds times the character's rank, example: the mutant trying to use this power is 4th rank, has 33 willpower, victims will be emotionally controlled for 33 x 4 rounds or 132 rounds or 6.6 minutes.

Any person or animal who believes they are in love or friendship with the user will typically regard the user's companions with warmth, but mainly focus all adoration on the user. If attacked suddenly by the mutant's companions, the subject will defend itself or attack these individuals. Inducing lust is only possible when the target being is roughly of the same species or animal type. Any non-humanoid will experience feelings of lust as mere camaraderie. In no case will an emotionally controlled being fight its own pack members or companions, regardless of what they might try to do to the controlling mutant.

## Energy Orbs 169

Type: **Mental mutation**      Range: **500m + 10m per point of willpower**
Usage: **Once per day per rank**      Rate: **1 per hand**
Strike Value: **+20**      Damage: **2d20, plus +1 DMG per rank**

Once per day, per character rank, this mutant can generate a fist sized ball of energy in each open hand and hurl it ten meters plus one extra meter per point of their current willpower trait score. These spheres, which while willed

forth as a mental mutation, surge from the subject's chest and illuminate the person's arms, heart area and eyes as they charge up.

They are extremely concentrated and will punch through wood and scrap metal walls and easily ignite fires in substances that they touch. Each orb is considered a separate attack and can be launched at separate targets so long as they are ahead of the deviant in a 180 degree zone of fire. The range is 500 meters +10m per point of the user's current willpower, strike value +20 inflicting 2d20, plus 1 point extra damage per rank of the mutant (example, a 7th rank mutant inflicts 2d20+7 damage per hit).

Should this mutant have four arms, for example, with a hand at the end of each, then she can hurl four orbs per round — an utterly devastating barrage. Should a mutant have no hands, such as only tentacles or crab pincers, then there is a 50% chance per limb that it can generate an orb, with at least one such limb capable of throwing these destructive gleaming balls of energy.

Energy orbs will punch holes through the user's gloves.

## Energy Smite 170

Type: **mental mutation**      Range: **user**
Usage: **once per day per 2 ranks**    Rate: **1**    Strike Value: **+40**
Damage: **3d20 plus STR modifiers and fist or other physical damage**

The mutant can charge up his or her fist, or kick, head butt, tail, crab pincer, bite, bladed limb or other fighting growth with a swirling blue mass of energy. A successful strike delivers a massively charged blow, inflicting 3d20 damage plus any strength modifiers and the actual damage roll for whatever bodily appendage used (no hand held weapons or implants). (Example: 3d20+2 strength bonus, +1d6 fist). This power draws a lot of energy from the mutant, is difficult to generate and so only available for use once per every two ranks. Therefore, at 1st and 2nd rank, only one smite can be made, at 3rd and 4th a second smite can be unleashed in that 24 hour period, while 5th and 6th rank deviants can make three such attack per day, etc.

## Energy Tendril 171

Type: **mental mutation**      Range: **3m per rank**
Usage: **Twice per day per rank**      Rate: **1**
Duration: **1 round per point of willpower**
Strike Value: **01-50 base, plus use Willpower like Accuracy for any SV modifier**
Damage: **1d20 stun, plus use Willpower like Strength for any DMG modifier**
Defense Value to sever: **-30 DV with 10 END**

Controlled by the mutant's mind, this translucent, bluish-green, 1 inch (2.54cm) thick tubular tendril of light can extend out 3 meters per rank at a speed of 3 meters per round. It can help climb, grapple, pilfer, strike or tow. The user's willpower trait is treated like the strength score for this mutation (use the strength column on table TME-2-3 to determine any stun damage modifiers) with a base strike value of 01-50 doing 1d20 stun damage on a

hit plus any willpower damage bonus. This mutant's willpower trait is also treated like the accuracy trait for any SV modifiers.

The duration of continuous use is as the user's willpower trait in rounds, and back-to-back usages can be spent if needed. While normally used to climb or hit things, including dimensional beings, this mentally generated tendril can also caress others, cradle a child, lift a set of keys off a desk, probe something without risking a living limb, reach into toxic or burning materials with no side effects, and do countless other miraculous tasks.

This potent, highly adaptable mutation can be used twice per day per rank. To touch or strike distant objects, the user must be able to see what the tendril is doing, otherwise apply a -40 SV modifier. The tendril gives only a faint sensation back to the user when it touches and smacks something, but if projected into a narrow tunnel or otherwise out of sight, the user can feel their way forward but only at 1 meter per round and with clumsy motions.

This tendril can only be chopped off or blasted away by energy weapons and electrical attacks and has a defensive value of -30 and endurance of 10. If severed, the usage is spent regardless of how many rounds were remaining.

## Energy Wall Generation 172

Type: **mental defense**  Range: **user**
Usage: **once per day per 2 ranks**  Defense Value: nil
Duration: **as mutant's rank in rounds x10**

The mutant can draw upon mental resources to will into being a wall of blue, transparent energy.

This energy wall will stop all physical attacks and dimensional beings, but not mental attacks. The mutant who wills the wall into being can do nothing but concentrate while maintaining the wall, but he or she can be driven away in a vehicle, mounted on an animal, or carried by companions. The duration of the wall's existence is up to 10 rounds per rank of the mutant using it, and he or she can dismiss it at any time before the end of the maximum duration, or generate back-to-back occurrences of the wall should the user be of sufficiently high rank to do so.

This barrier can, however, sustain damage, be punctured, and finally passed through before the end of its duration if sufficient damage within one round is thrown at it. Combined physical attacks can break through the barrier so long as they are directed at a 5 meter portion. All attacks on the wall results in automatic hits for random damage by the attack mode, with the endurance of a 5m wide or tall section of the wall based on the Willpower of the mutant deploying this power as noted on the table to follow.

If punctured, the wall remains open at the puncture point and will allow creatures and machines up to 5 meters wide to pass through. If the wall is placed in the air, such as in front of a cloud of skal birds, or likewise erected in front of a cavalry charge, the results would be treated as 1d10 stun damage per creature to collide with it. Another use for the wall is to wrap it around the user and his or her allies, to protect them from harm temporarily, allowing

for reloading of magazines or power cells, the first aide treatment of near dead comrades, or to escape up a ladder or down a manhole.

No physical attacks can be launched from within the wall upon those outside without also harming the barrier. The user's willpower maintains the endurance value of the wall, his or her intelligence determines how wide it is and how far away it can be placed, while the mutant's rank specifies the duration. If the mutant is struck by a mental attack, or otherwise hit, the wall instantly vanishes and the usage is spent. These three factors are each detailed below:

| Mutant's Willpower | Endurance of wall per 5m |
|---|---|
| 1-4 | 10 |
| 5-9 | 20 |
| 10-34 | 30 |
| 35-44 | 50 |
| 45-54 | 70 |
| 55-74 | 100 |
| 75-94 | 150 |
| 95-110 | 210 |
| 111-120 | 300 |
| Above | Willpower value x3 |

| Mutant's Intelligence | Wall's Length | Wall's Maximum Distance Away |
|---|---|---|
| 1-4 | 5m | 5m |
| 5-9 | 10m | 10m |
| 10-34 | 15m | 20m |
| 35-44 | 20m | 40m |
| 45-54 | 25m | 80m |
| 55-74 | 30m | 160m |
| 75-94 | 35m | 240m |
| above | 40m | 300m |

## Enormous Bone Spike 173

Type: **physical attack**  Range: **melee**
Rate: **1**  Strike Value: **+12**  Damage: **1d20**

Growing from a random location, this horn-like spike extends 30+2d20cm in length, is lethally sharp and can be used as an additional melee attack at +12 SV and inflicts 1d20 damage (plus strength mods). This growth reduces the mutant's ability to wear shell class armor, and is usually unappealing, thus reducing his or her appearance by −d4+1 APP.

The location of the spike is determined by **rolling 3d6** here:

| | |
|---|---|
| 3. | Chest |
| 4. | Tummy |
| 5. | Right elbow |
| 6. | Left elbow |
| 7. | Left shoulder |
| 8-13. | Forehead |
| 14. | Right shoulder |
| 15. | Left forearm |
| 16. | Right forearm |
| 17. | Chin |
| 18. | Middle of upper back |

## Enriched Skeletal Structure 174

Type: **physical alteration**  Damage: **fists or kick inflicts 2d6**

This mutant enjoys incredibly solid bones which make the subject both stronger and able to endure punishment beyond what might be expected from his or her physique. At character generation, add 3d6 to their starting strength trait value, plus 20+3d10 to endurance. Likewise, any punch or kick from this person yields a base damage of 2d6 instead of d6 as with a normal human. Finally, falls, crashes, and clubbing attacks — including tail slaps, fist and kicks — do only half damage to this mutant.

## Extreme Healing 175

Type: **mental mutation**

Range: **touch for 2d6 minutes** Usage: **Once every five days**
Side effect of user: **-2 to initiative and movement for 2d6 hours after use**

So draining is this powerful mutation that it can only be used once every five days, regardless of the user's rank. When initiated, either on the self or another organic being, the character lays her hands on a wounded individual, or

herself, for 2d6 minutes as waves of tissue mending, cell replacing, toxin eliminating and immunity enhancing energies are transmitted.

The patient will immediately recover from any effects of poison, induced insanity or mind controls, be rid of any diseases, viruses, harmful bacteria or agents in the body, and to some degree, exposure to radiation. The exposed victim of radiation is allowed three hazard checks instead of one after contamination, plus three more rolls to avoid any risk of cancer. This mutation cannot reverse the cumulative radiation build up in a character from earlier exposures.

Finally, broken bones will set and be mended, cavities will reverse and heal over 3d6 days, and all traits will be healed up to a maximum of the same amount as the user's base willpower score, but will not exceed the patient's normal scores. Unfortunately, severed limbs cannot be re-attached or grown back, eyes that have been gouged out will not regenerate, and the emotional trauma of serious injuries not forgotten. After using this mutation, the healer suffers from terrible headaches, nausea and loss of ambition and energy for 2d6 hours; reduce movement rate and initiative by –2.

## Extreme Survivability 176

This individual's ancestors were designed for war, or hazardous industrial and off-world service. He or she is gifted with advanced mutagenic agents and well engineered DNA that carried through to this subject and given the deviant an edge over other beings. Besides an initial **bonus to strength and endurance of +1d10**, this mutant can survive injuries and ordeals better than most and drop into negative endurance values (or any other trait value) twice what a normal entity can. For example, instead of the character's normal endurance of, say, 35 for the purpose of table TME-2-11 on page 111 of the hub rules, Injury and Death, consider this deviant's END score to be 70, etc.

Thus, he or she is able to fend off death even after suffering grievous wounds.

Better still, this mutant does not require first aid to stop further loss of endurance when bleeding out, thus avoiding the slide toward death shown under the 'Incapacitated and Dying' column of the fore mentioned 'Injury and Death' table. Second, this being is allowed two hazard checks against any toxin, poison or other harmful substances, including parasites, disease and radiation exposure.

Finally, whatever this mutant's normal healing rate is, they heal an extra +1d20 END points per day (roll randomly per day).

## Feathered *by Thomas Vida* 177

Type: **physical mutation**
Defense Value: **-8**
Drawback: **Takes +3 DMG from fire if not clothed or armored**
This mutant has a thick layer of feathers covering their body. While still unable to fly — unless the mutant also has a pair of wings — the feathery layer has some advantages.

While all these feathers have the same protective benefits (improving defense value by -8), including the ability to keep warm as if wearing long underwear, the feather style and color is determined with a **1d12 roll** here: 1. Down feathers / 2-3. Pigeon-like / 4-5. Crow or Raven / 6-7. Parrot / 8-9. Eagle / 10-11. Vulture / 12. Peacock

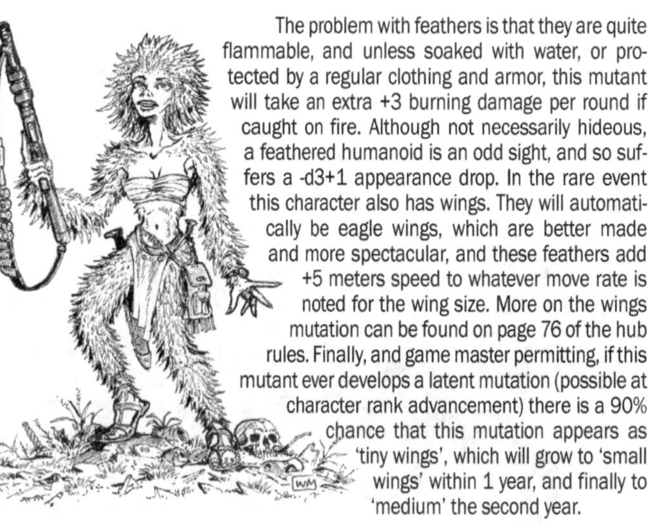

The problem with feathers is that they are quite flammable, and unless soaked with water, or protected by a regular clothing and armor, this mutant will take an extra +3 burning damage per round if caught on fire. Although not necessarily hideous, a feathered humanoid is an odd sight, and so suffers a -d3+1 appearance drop. In the rare event this character also has wings. They will automatically be eagle wings, which are better made and more spectacular, and these feathers add +5 meters speed to whatever move rate is noted for the wing size. More on the wings mutation can be found on page 76 of the hub rules. Finally, and game master permitting, if this mutant ever develops a latent mutation (possible at character rank advancement) there is a 90% chance that this mutation appears as 'tiny wings', which will grow to 'small wings' within 1 year, and finally to 'medium' the second year.

## Fish Fins 178

Type: **physical alteration**
Defense value **-10 DV bonus**
Damage: **If grappled or bitten, auto-attack on aggressor SV 01-70, 1d12 DMG**
Movement: **Swims double land speed**
While not true fish fins, these membranes of flesh colored skin are stretched between cartilaginous fan-spines and grow under the mutant's arms from about the elbow and down to the bottom of the ribs on their side. Additionally, other fins protrude out from the deviant's hips, back, sides of his or her legs and occasionally the sides of the face and neck (3 in 6 times). Unsightly by human standards, these growths reduce the mutant's appearance by -2d4 APP.

While these appendages can be trimmed off, allowing the mutant to wear relic armor, this is painful and inflicts 3d6 damage. Worse, they rapidly grow back in 6 months. If kept, and the character either swims stripped down or with specially designed armor, he or she can 'ripple' these fins to propel him or her through the water at twice his or her normal land movements rate (therefore swimming 12m per round if his or her base land speed is 6m).

These flaps of leathery skin are connected by strong, sharp tipped spines that act as both regular armor, giving the mutant a -10 DV bonus, but any large beast to grab, grapple or chomp down on the mutant is considered automatically attacked with an SV 01-70 attack and suffer 1d12 damage. This automatic attack will continue until the assailant lets go of the mutant or kills it (crushes its fins).

## Flame Thrower Limb 179

Type: **physical attack, ranged or club**    Range: **10 meters**
Usage: **1 jet of flame per 10kg of body weight per day**
Rate: **1**    Defense Value: **-5 DV**
Strike Value: **Flame +10/ club +7**    Hazard Check: **nil**
Damage: **flame 1d10 for 1-6 (1d6) rounds /club 1d12**
Replacing the mutant's non-dominant arm 7 out of every 10 times, and otherwise growing as an extra arm-like limb from just above or beneath one of the mutant's regular arms, this strange, bulbous growth, ends in a blackened, bony opening.

From this hard orifice, two chemical secretions are mixed, ignited and spewed forth as a jet of napalm, making this deviant into a virtual living flame thrower.

The secretions come from specially evolved fluid veins; the liquids being created and stored within the mutant's abdomen, allowing for a certain amount of uses per day based on the individual's starting body weight. For every 10 kilograms the mutant exhibits at the beginning of game play (character generation), rounded up to the nearest ten kilos, he or she can release one burst of flame per day: (example, a 156 kg mutant can fire 16 bursts per day).

The flame will release in a narrow cone and usually sweep a 3m area per round to a range of 10 meters, strike value +10, damage 1d10 per round for 1d6 rounds. If a victim is struck by the flame, the best way to avoid further burn damage is to dive into water or immerse themselves in 2 liters or more of water, or roll in deep dust or sand. Alternatively, they can stop whatever they are doing and drop and roll to reduce the burn damage to 1d6 DMG per round.

Most animals, once having seen or seeing pack mates engulfed in flame, are forced to make a morale check or flee, while tiny creatures, like army ants, or killer bee swarms, or other small beings that have a group based endurance value (see Army Ants on page TME-158) are clustered into a small area and suffer double damage from flame attacks

The character is not flame resistant, furthermore, the organs within his or her body are pressurized and flammable. If the mutant is killed by being punctured, hacked apart, chewed up, or dies from explosive attacks, he or she has an 87% chance of detonating in a small fireball. The burst radius of this brilliant orange fireball is 6m, SV 01-80, damage 3d6 plus 1d6 DMG per round for 1d6 rounds of burning damage.

This elongated, hardened limb can likewise be used to pulverize opponents as a melee weapon, which can have the mutant's strength score and either — but not both — the weapon expert skill or unarmed combat (Marital Arts or Brawling) applied to it. This clubbing blow has an SV of +7 and inflicts 1d12 base stun or lethal damage (character's choice).

The limb can have metallic or other non flammable gear strapped to it, including swords, axes, thrusting spears and the like. Due to the heat buildup after each discharge, other materials such as plastic, wood, fabric and the like will char and become inoperable if fastened to the limb. Finally, this bulky, bone appendage adds +15kg to the mutant's overall weight and also offers an extra degree of shielding to the mutant, and yields a permanent -5 DV bonus. Somewhat gruesome looking, a flame thrower arm reduces the mutant's appearance by -4 APP.

## Flesh Whip 180

Type: **physical attack**      Range: **melee reach out to 3+1d3 meters**
Rate: **1**    Strike Value: **+9**      Damage: **1d12**

One or more of these appendages grow from the shoulder or upper back of this mutant, and sometimes replace one arm. **Roll 2d6:**

**2,3.** One flesh whip which replaces the non-dominant arm.
**4-6.** One flesh whip extends from one shoulder above the arm.
**7-10.** One flesh whip that grows from the side.
**11.** Two flesh whips, one grows from above each shoulder.
**12.** Three flesh whips, all growing from the upper back.

These leathery, highly flexible living tendrils are 3+1d3m long, and as a weapon, have a strike value bonus of +9, inflict 1d12 damage per hit — plus any strength

modifiers or weapon expert skills points applied to them. These are considered an extra melee attack each, including when multiple whips are present and allow the mutant to lash out at multiple targets in any direction. They are alarming looking growths, with each reducing the mutant's appearance by -3.

At 7th rank, when a character's melee attack rate goes to 2 per round, these whips will also increase their rate of attack, a unleash a devastating barrage of brutal lashes. These boneless, rope-like whips will regrow if severed (DV -12/ END 9), taking 30+1d30 days to return to their former length. Besides a superior SV and damage rating, these meaty growths are identical to the weapon 'whip' in the hub rules as far as possibly wrapping about and holding objects, or the limbs of opponents. However, each flesh whip also allows the mutant to climb better and gives them +1 skill point in the climbing skill from page TME-36. All flesh whips on a mutant are the same length.

See the whip master skill in this book on page 226 for what an unskilled user of this mutation can do, however this skill can be applied to this appendage, but does not stack with the weapon expert skill or any unarmed combat skills such as brawling or martial artists.

1 in 20 flesh whips are extra mutated and connected to an electrical generation and transfer organ deep in the deviant's torso. Twice per day per rank the mutant can deliver an extra jolt of electricity on contact with a target, doing an additional 2d20 stun shock damage on a successful hit. If the strike misses on a desired shock attack, the charge is not expended. Normal whip damage also occurs on such shock slaps. If the freak has multiple electro-enhanced whips, each of these also has its daily allotment of potential discharges, making the mutant extremely potent

## Formic Acid Sprayer 181

Type: **physical spray attack**      Range: **12 meters**
Usage: **four times per day**      Duration: **1d10+2 rounds**
Strike Value: **+15**      Hazard Check: **nil**
Damage: **Limb stun for 1d6 minutes/ blindness for 3d6+6 rounds.**

Almost identical to the sort of chemical exuded by many species of ants, this syrup-like amber liquid is ideal to spay on the skin and face of foes. The mutant can unleash four jets of acid per day with a range of 12 meters, and a strike value of +15. This mutant is immune to formic acid.

Any creature hit by this discharge on the skin will often experience a loss of sensation and control in a random limb. Any coverage of the face or eyes will likewise cause temporary blindness for 3d6+6 minutes. Blinded beings are half speed, fight at half to all strike values and are +40 easier to be hit by melee range opponents (Blindness rules are covered on page 122 of the TME hub Rules). While there is no hazard check, and the liquid is assumed to soak into most armor and clothing on the afflicted limb and immediately render the limb useless for 1d6 minutes, some creatures are immune to acid, while wearers of certain relic armor and suits are likewise unaffected by this substance.

Any creature hit in the head will be blinded, as mentioned above, but also lose sensation in their face and all speech becomes slurred. Hits to the torso don't really cause any harm to the victim, although a hit to the abdomen of certain bug-like creatures, such a scorpions, will disallow use of their stinger tail while stunned. Any arm struck with this spray will make it hang uselessly and whatever the person was holding when hit drops from their grip.

Strikes to the legs result in a loss of movement. Any biped hit in one leg is reduced to half speed, while a quadruped hit on one leg is reduced by 25% speed, and a six legged creatures loses 16.6% of its speed per leg stunned. The game master will need to use their judgment when handling hits on creatures with weird appendages not shown on the table to follow.

The sprayer appendage itself is different for different beings, with many giant mutant ant species and other insects expelling jets of formic acid from their abdomens. In other species, including humanoids, use the following table to determine the location and sort of acid sprayer:

### Formic Acid Sprayer Location and Type    Roll 2d6

**2.** Huge baggy neck which contains a bloated acid filled sack on either side, spray is disgorged from the mutant's mouth. Appearance drop of -3d4+3.

**3,4.** From a hole in the chest, the puckered opening looks like an old bullet scar when not opened and the ten centimeters (nearly 4 inches) long aiming tube is not deployed. The scar yields a minimal -1d2 appearance drop, however, anybody to see the worm like, meaty tube emerge from between the subject's chest muscles or breasts, is often alarmed, if not thoroughly sickened.

**5,6.** Grows along the underside of one arm or foreleg, as a grisly looking tube. The acid is stored in a special organ in the mutant's torso and exuded from a hole in the wrist. Because the orifice grows in the arm, the deviant can bend it in any direction where it can normally point its hand, thus has the ability to shoot backwards or up over walls, etc. Appearance penalty of -d4+1.

**7,8.** Jettisoned from a tube which grows from a hunch on the mutant's back. The tube is two feet (60cm) long and can be aimed in any direction, including over the character's head. Disfiguring, this growth reduces the character's appearance trait by -3d6+4 when seen, however if hidden in copious folds of clothing, this lowered trait value is not yet applied. Increase range to 16 meters.

**9,10.** From a sphincter in the mutants belly, which, like a larger belly button, opens and closes to expel the steam of formic acid at foes ahead of the deviant. Barely noticeable, this orifice only reduces the mutant's looks score by -1 appearance point.

**11,12.** Ejected from an opening hidden beneath the mutant's tongue, with the acid supply hidden deep in the abdomen and undetectable. This ejection point has no appearance penalty. If a mouthful of this liquid is jettisoned into the mouth of anyone full-mouth kissing this mutant, the strike is considered automatic.

### Limb Struck Table    Roll 1d8, 1d10 or 1d12

Random Limb struck by a Formic Acid Spray, with the head and eyes assumed to be the target area.

**Roll 1d8 for bipeds** and **1d10 for quadrupeds** (dogs, horses, bears etc) and **1d12 for insects and spiders with abdomens**. Likewise, use **1d10 for creatures that also have wings**, with any hit on a leg being 50% likely to instead be a left or right wing.

**1,2.** Head
**3.** Right arm
**4.** Left arm
**5,6.** Torso (or thorax on insects)
**7.** Right leg
**8.** Left leg
**9.** Rear left leg/ or left wing
**10.** Rear right leg/or right wing
**11.** Hindmost leg: roll 1d10: 1-5 left or 6-10 right leg
**12.** Abdomen (insect or spider, etc.)

## Four Eyes 182

Type: **physical mutation**       Strike Value: **+5**
Defense Value: **-5**             Initiative: **+1**

 This mutant has four eyes, one pair above the other with a slightly elongated face to accommodate these extra optical receptors. While it's hard for others to look at this face — especially for strangers — and the mutant takes a -4 APP penalty, the benefits of these extra eyes are considerable. The deviant gains a +5 to its strike value as it can better see opponents, as well as enjoy a -5 bonus to its defense value for the same heightened visual reasons. Likewise, while these eyes work in unison, the extra set does give the oddity better awareness and thus a bonus of +1 initiative.

In some areas where mutants are mistreated or hunted, these extra eyes are a dead giveaway of the individual's abnormal DNA, and puts them at risk. If not having other hard to hide mutations, a known trick for mutants with this gift is to wear a bandanna of fine cheesecloth. This can still be seen through, yet unless an onlooker gets within a meter, will allow this mutant to pass among pure stocks without receiving unwanted attention.

## Frequency Receptors 183

Type: **physical adaptation**
Range: **Dependant on perception trait value**
Usage: **three times per day per rank**

This mutant's mind and tissues have evolved to pick up and transform radio waves. So too, the deviant can cock their head or hold their mouth at a certain angle and switch between various radio stations, broadcasts, coded messages and nonsensical Mecha chatter, thus tuning into different frequencies, bands and communications taking place nearby.

The range that such stations or transmissions can be picked up at is dependent on the signal strength and the perception value of the mutant. Interference from high ruins, mountains, deep forests or while the listener is underground, all play a factor in how successful the reception is.

The mutant has no ability to transmit or respond to whatever they hear — unless this 'listener mutant' happens to also be cybernetically augmented (a mutorg) and have a communicator built into their head.

The table below shows the character's perception score, the range at which broadcasts can be picked up, and the duration of time the mutant can focus on and listen to the myriad of transmissions in an area. The second table shows modifiers to the audio pickup range. Finally, a table of suggested transmissions is added for game masters who need a sample broadcast to use 'on the fly' and get inspiration from to create your own signals.

Of course, any GM who has a character with this, or even the much weaker minor mutation version of this called Minor Radio Reception (page 282 of this book), is in the group, might drop hints that the mutant detects strong transmissions when drifting off to sleep or at other times without deploying this power just to stoke the group's curiosity of what they might be approaching. For example, the player of a character with this ability might be told that their PC hears a repeated SOS call from a very human sounding child's voice. The team might use this mutant to slowly get closer and closer to the transmission point since the mutant can tell if the signal is getting 'hotter or colder'. In the end, the transmission could be from an artificial intelligence or digital being trapped beneath the earth in an ancient facility, and has been calling for help for nearly two centuries.

Mutants with this power can engage it while on the move, so long as they pause to focus on either specific or general assortment of signals. Because this deviant grew up listening to a wide range of radio signals — most that were never meant to be perceived by an organic mind and are indecipherable — he or she picked up the skill of Morse Code at an early age. See page XR-220 for details.

| Perception score of Mutant | Range of Pick-up | Duration of Session |
| --- | --- | --- |
| 1-4 | 1 kilometer (km) | 3d6 rounds |
| 5-9 | 2 kilometers | 1 minute (20 rounds) |
| 10-34 | 10 kilometers | 2 minutes |
| 35-64 | As Perception score in km | 10+d6 minutes |
| 65-84 | As Perception score in Kilometers +20km | 20+d20 minutes |
| 85-105 | As Perception score in Kilometers +50km | As PER score in minutes |
| 106-115 | As Perception score in Kilometers +100km | Double PER score in minutes |
| 116-125 | Double Perception score in Kilometers | Triple PER score in minutes |
| 126-135 | As Perception score x 10 in Kilometers | Quadruple PER score in minutes |
| Above 135 | As Perception score x 20 in Kilometers | Ten times (x 10) PER score in minutes |

PER= Perception trait abbreviation.

**Terrain Modifiers to Reception Table**

| Terrain Type of Mutant Receptor | Modifier to Range of Transmission pick-up |
| --- | --- |
| **Plains, deserts, open sea, or large lake** | no change |
| **Airborne in aircraft, winged mount, or airship** | Double range / 200% |
| **Badlands, scrub lands, or hills** | 75% range |
| **Swamp, jungle or forest** | 50% range |
| **Mountainous region** | 25% range |
| **Ruined city** | 25% range |
| **Human settlement, street level or indoors** | 50% range |
| **Human settlement, high tower or hill area** | no change |
| **Underground** | 10% range |
| **Top of tallest ruined skyscraper, hill or mountain within a kilometer** | 150% range |



Roll 1d4 in wild areas away from human communities, 1d6+1 near communities, and 1d8+3 for ruin areas

**1.** A weird, repetitive clicking and pinging. GM note: If the character has the Morse Code Skill, or repeats what they hear to a companion who knows it, the message says: "SOS we have crash landed. Us survivors are in bad shape... need water... need food.. And there are horrid monsters outside our hull. We have sent out drones to seek emergency personnel. Location beacon set to code 45A12."

**2.** Gruff, inhuman voices that seem agitated. Every so often the listener hears words they understand, something about intruders getting close to their back hatch. GM suggestion: Perhaps add the number of PCs in the group and any distinguishing features. These could be warmorts, skullocks, or a tribe of mutant savages who presently observe the excavators.

**3.** A raspy voiced man talking to another. "Them look like diggers to me... but I ain't dare get too close to 'em bastards. Could be cannibals." The other, in a wavering, oscillating voice, replies "Yea, I can see 'em through my rifle scope. Yeah... better safe than sorry, I guess. But damn... sure would be good to talk to somebody and get some news from civilization... some wine, or talk to a pretty woman again."

GM, these could be scavengers who are observing the progress of the character group through the wilds or hermits in their top floor dens if the transmission is heard in a town.

**4.** Strange loosely coded talk from a man broadcasting to some far away and hard to hear, gruff sounding and not altogether human master. He speaks about the local town's defenses, leadership, weapons and currently present dig teams (perhaps even the PCs).

**5.** A local militia talking back and forth on standard scrap built communicators regarding a local crime, reported monster sighting, or troublesome newcomers who need to be watched or shaken down for coin.

**6.** A hobbyist radio operator who plays old world music, local news, public announcements and their own opinions on newcomers to town.

**7.** A discussion between local criminals, who talk in code about something. GM, if the PCs have a team name or easily recognizable member, the character listening might hear reference to them and some hint at a plot to rob or enslave the PCs.

**8.** Digital Mecha Chatter. It is entirely nonsensical and seems to be coming very strong from one location and answered by several weaker, static filled transmissions from far, far away.

**9.** Human voices talking back and forth. The transmission is weak, cuts in and out, fades and then returns. Some sort of panic with one group trapped some place, the others unable to find them and are also being hunted by some sort of mutant monster.

**10.** A woman's voice repeating a plea for help. "I have been alone for so many years, so many decades. Is anybody out there? Please... the others have all gone quiet now... and I am low on resources. I can sense you there... sense you listening. Just come to me down here... and I will reward you with all manner of gift. That's it... you are facing the right direction. Do you see that building there? I will flash one of the remaining search lights. Do you see the light?"

## Gas Sacs 184

**Type: physical mutation**   **Usage: 4 times per day, plus 1 more each 5 ranks**
**Number of sacs: 1d6+2**   **Falling DMG reduction: 3d10**
**Defense Value: -0**   **Endurance: each sac has 6 END**
**Duration: 1 minute per point of willpower**

Within two rounds, this mutant can inflate a series of translucent skin bags that grow on their torso. Once inflated, the user simply can't sink or drown, furthermore, if deployed while falling, these air bags will reduce any falling damage by 3d10 points. These 1d6+2 sacs can only be filled if the user is wearing loose fitting clothing and armor, or none at all. No relic body armor or chain or plate archaic armors can be worn in conjunction with this mutation's use, except for a ballistic vest with back flaps left open or fastened using highly elastic straps.

Enemies wishing to shoot and pop these filled sacs can do so. Each sac is DV 0, Endurance 6 and heal 1pt per week. It takes a minimum of 3 sacs to gain the falling damage reduction benefit, but only 1 sac remaining to stay above water and avoid drowning.

When inflated to their maximum size, which takes 4 rounds, they will allow a lightly framed, unencumbered mutant to lift off the ground and climb at a rte of 2m per round. The flyer can wear no armor and carry no more than 20 kilograms of weapons and gear to allow for lift.

Once airborne, this freak is similar to an airship, and can drift on the wind. As they can maintain these bags of hot air for a minute per point of willpower, this mutant could potentially stay aloft for a half hour or more. Once the duration of the gas bags reaches its limit, the floater will gradually descend at a rate of 1m per round, although can forcibly deflate them to drop at 5 meters per round until getting very close to the ground (within 10m) and then inflate them a little more just to avoid a hard landing. Back to back inflations of these sacs can be accomplished to allow for far longer floats or flights. While drifting in the air, the deviant cannot control their destination, unless they also have wings or some means of propulsion.

If the gas bags are shot at and punctured, the mutant can only maintain flight if it has two bags remaining, while if reduced to one gas sac, it will drop out of the sky at 3 meters per round and suffer 2d6 stun damage on impact. If all the gas sacs are punctured, the unfortunate falls like any other character.

These sacs can be deployed 4 times per day, plus one additional time per 5 ranks (thus 5 at 5th rank, 6 inflations at 10th rank, and 7 at 15th rank, etc.)

## Gaseous Expansion 185

Type: **Physical mutation**
Range: **melee, out to 2m around the mutant**     Usage: **Once per hour**
Damage: **1d6 per round to those crushed in small space when expanded**
Appearance Drop: **Mutant's App reduced to 25% when deployed**
Like a humanoid puffer fish, the tissues of this mutant can be made to swell with gas to triple their horizontal body size. This is useful to intimidate predators, float in liquid, avoid being swallowed, or absorb blunt trauma during a fall. Of course, to engage this gift while wearing clothing will shred whatever the mutant is wearing, likewise armor will restrict expansion in those areas covered by plating and cause severe pain and 1d4 damage per round to the deviant.

An expanded character looks hideous and their appearance score drops to 25% of their normal good looks, although when engaged, the character cannot sink in liquids and suffers only half damage from any fall. To expand itself after being swallowed by a great beast will cause the creature's guts to ache painfully and inflict 1d6 damage per round, yet 30% likely per round to also cause the creature's gag reflex to kick in and in which case it will try to vomit up the character at once — although the stomach-bound victim must return to their normal size to facilitate being disgorged among a slippery coating of digestive fluids.

To expand oneself in a crowded hallway, vehicle cabin or other 2m or smaller space will crush equipment and other beings, and will inflict 1d6 damage per round to those caught the space with this bloated deviant to a maximum of 4d6 damage. Only the all around girth of the mutant changes during this transformation, not its height. The process takes effect immediately — like a safety airbag — but takes 1 minute to deflate. This bizarre power can be used once per hour, regardless of rank.

Those wearing relic combat armor or shell class armor cannot be crushed.

## Generate Dimensional Horror 186

Type: **mental manifestation**
Range: **up to the user's intelligence value in meters**
Usage: **once per day per 2 ranks**          Hazard Check: **nil**
Duration: **as mutant's willpower in rounds**
Defense Value: **-30**   Strike Value: **01-70**   Damage: **1d20+10 each**
Any mutant to employ this power with regularity must accept the consequences from common folk, who will deem him or her a devil summoner, a witch, and very unwelcome in their communities. In truth, this mutant simply imagines a being into temporary existence, a being which very much appears and acts as a Dimensional Ripper, although is visible as a ghostly appiration.

The fiend is any color the user desires, stands about 4m tall, is immune to all primitive physical attacks such as bites, claws, blades, arrows, and bullets, poisons, gas, fire cold, and radiation, but is susceptible to beam weapons and energy mutations, mental attacks, sonic weapons, EM weapons and electricity, all of which do maximum damage by weapon type (example: laser carbine does 30 points of damage instead of 1d20+10).

The dimensional horror has an endurance score equal to the user's willpower trait. During an attack, it uses 1d4 arm-like appendages, shocking and burning the target for 1d20+10 damage. It moves by walking on what appear to be legs, even on water. Its willpower and intelligence values are 2d20 each, has normal initiative rolls, can see infrared, cross-dimensional and physical planes, sees through all illusions, and will do whatever the commanding mutant wills it to do. It can harm true dimensional beings.

Once created and commanded, the user can forget about it and continue battling or fleeing as desired. However, if he or she is killed, or knocked unconscious, the dimensional horror will vanish before its duration is up. At higher ranks, this character can generate and command multiple apparitions simultaneously.

## Herbicidal Tissues 187

Type: **physical mutation**   Range: **bare skin contact or spit 4m**
Usage: **constant on skin, or spit 3 times per hour**
Strike Value: **+30**   Damage: **3d6**   Hazard Check: **Type D Willpower**

This freak not only tastes awful to mutant plants, but the mutie can spit his or her saliva at them and they will burn: range 4 meters, three spits per hour, SV +30, damage 3d6. If hit, or burned after latching onto or biting this mutant, a typical, mindless predatory plant will be 70% likely to either drop, retreat, or otherwise leave this specific deviant alone.

Intelligent NPC plantoids will stay in the fight only if defending their territory, young, or driven by some other powerful compulsion, but must make a type D willpower based hazard check to pursue a mutant who taste's bad or already spit and burned them. Player character plantoids can decide for themselves if they want to engage or pursue a mutant with herbicide in their veins.

If this mutant's bare skin is not exposed, such as if the deviant is encased in armor, then the automatic skin counter attack cannot occur and the character could be crushed or impaled like any other unfortunate. However, if killed, and the plant tries to swallow or bore into this mutant, then it will expose itself to the burning chemicals in this individual's flesh, and probably die because of ingesting the unconscious or dead herbicide laced mutant.

## Horrid Symbionts 188

Type: **detachable physical growths**   Range: **user**
Movement of Symbiont: **7m**
Endurance of Symbiont: **2d4, plus 1 END per rank of user**
Defense Value of Symbiont: **-10**   Strike Value of Symbiont: **01-50**
Damage of Symbiont: **1d8**

Growing from the mutant's torso are small, hideously ugly, sexless, symbiotic drones. There will be 2d4 lumpy growths on the mutant's body at any given time, each at a slightly different stage in gestation, starting from a mere red oozing sore as the lump emerges from the skin, progressing to a grapefruit sized bump, and after a few weeks, the vague shape of a small, skin encased humanoid. Finally, a fully independent symbiont hangs off the character and eventually tears free.

One symbiotic being per month is expelled from the body and is thereafter telepathically controlled by the mutant within a range of 10 meters per point of the master mutant's willpower. If any of these drones are somehow left outside this radius, they suffer a stroke and must make a type A endurance based hazard check or instantly die, otherwise they merely pass out until their master re-enters the range of control, or they suffer some other fate while unconscious.

The symbionts act as virtual extensions of the mutant's body, and having dog-like intelligence, they guard their creator with selfless devotion, fearlessly attacking anything that appears to be a threat to their host. They are typically instructed by the mutant's sheer willpower and whim, even performing suicidal acts when willed to do so. These 30cm tall, marginally ape-like humanoids fight with a flurry of bites and claw attacks, and will eat what they kill as they are ravenous carnivores, needing a whole kilogram of flesh per day to operate. There is no limit to how many of these foul things a mutant can control, and they each have a lifespan of three years.

The ugly growths hanging from the mutant's body are revolting to behold, and if the character is seen in their entirety, a separate appearance value is given from that of the person's facial appearance value. Reduce the character's bodily appearance to half the regular value, with a maximum of 20 being permitted.

**Symbionts** have the same agility, accuracy, willpower and perception scores as their creator, complete with any modifiers to DV and SV, but an **intelligence of only 8**. Other statistics are: DV: -10, END: 2d4, plus 1 point per rank of their creator, MV: 7m, Attacks: 1, SV: 01-50, DMG: 1d8, strength: 10, Intelligence: 8, appearance: 1d2, Initiative: as creator.

Characters with this disturbing mutation start game play with 1d4 active symbiotic organisms in tow and a meat supply of 3d6 kilograms.

## Illusion Generation 189

Type: **mental mutation**
Range: **up to as many meters away as user's current Willpower score**
Size of illusion: **as Willpower in meters, or either half willpower per side if a cube or diameter if a sphere.**
Usage: **twice per day per rank**   Duration: **variable by willpower**
Hazard Check: **viewer allowed a INT based HC to avoid believing the illusion, see table.**

Twice per day, per rank, this mutant can generate an illusion to either trick, frighten away, or inspire living beings. Viewers are allowed an intelligence based hazard check to see through the illusion, but the difficulty is based on the muto-illusionist's Willpower trait. The distance from the user, the size of the illusion and both the density and believability of the vision also depend on the user's willpower. The illusion is loosely limited to what the mutant has either seen in person, imagined, or viewed in photographs, movies, or projected images transferred from a telepath.

As this is a mental intrusion and seen by all living onlookers within view of the mutant who generates this sensory display, and not something physically seen or recordable by cameras and the like, it is undetectable by digital optics implants, androids, robots, or digital beings and other non-living creatures including dimensional beings. Likewise, any mutant with the mutations of advanced mind or mental screen are allowed 3 hazard checks to avoid believing what they see. So too, mutants with multiple heads get one hazard check per head according to the table to follow. Furthermore, another deviant with this same illusion generation mutation is highly skeptical of most odd or unexpected phenomenon, and knows all the tricks behind creating grand illusions and is thus allowed 5 intelligence based hazard checks to avoid believing any illusion.

The mutation of Psionic Dampening Sphere is also highly effective against this power, as all those within the sphere see nothing of the illusion from within the dome.

Conversely, any mutant with flaw mutation of Open Mind always believes every illusion it sees, and will only come to understand that the vision is not real when comrades walk through whatever image is being projected and suffer no harm from the wall of illusion — which begins to dissipate as soon as it is no longer believed.

The duration of an illusion is based on both the willpower of the controller, and the continued focus of the muto-illusionist. If the mutant projecting the illusion takes any mental or physical hit that causes damage, the illusion vanishes. Mutants of 10th or higher rank can create back-to-back illusions with multiple, overlapping illusions in one, or at varied locations.

The distance of the illusion appears from 1 meter away from the creator to the maximum of his or her willpower trait away, in meters. So for a mutant with a WILL score of 28, she can have the fake scene appear anywhere from right around them or out 28 meters away either above, beside, ahead or behind them as desired. The actual size of the illusion depends on what is being manifested, but can not be larger than the user's willpower in meters wide or tall. If a large circular or cube sized illusion is needed, the sphere is half the mutant's willpower in diameter, or a cube as half the willpower score on any side. The GM will have final say on what size the illusion will appear.

The table below shows the intelligence of a beast or person looking at the illusion, and the odds they will believe the vision to be real or not based on the willpower range category of the deviant presenting the illusion. The duration of the illusion also depends on the muto-illusionist's current Willpower trait score. The duration can be cut short by the mutant taking damage or electing to end the hallucination before the full time is up.

If creatures or people have been tricked by another illusion in recent days, or whenever encountering the mutant who is known to possess this power, the experienced onlookers are skeptical and therefore allowed to make two illusion checks to try to disbelieve what they are seeing in their mind's eye.

| Muto-Illusionist's Willpower | Duration of Illusion | Onlooker's Intelligence based Hazard Check to AVOID believing illusion is real |
|---|---|---|
| 1-4 | 1d4 rounds | A |
| 5-9 | 2d6 rounds | B |
| 10-20 | 10+1d10 rounds | C |
| 21-40 | 20+1d20 rounds | D |
| 41-60 | 40+1d20 rounds | E |
| 61-90 | 100+1d100 rounds | F |
| 91-120 | 10 +1d10 minutes* | G |
| Above 120 | 20+1d20 minutes* | H |

*There are 20 rounds in 1 minute.

The following sample illusions serve both as examples for players who control a mutant with this power, and random illusions. Game masters can pick or roll at random from this list when they need something on the fly to present to player characters. While these are all meant to ward off, confuse or frighten onlookers, a muto-illusionist could also present soothing, whimsical, or religious visions to inspire help or friendliness in those he or she wishes to influence.

Illusions can be made to move as the muto-illusionist walks, so long as the distance between the imaginary 'show' and the generator doesn't exceed their current willpower trait value.

## Illusion Table, Roll 1d100

**01-05.** The ground shakes and from it emerges the rusty wrecks of animated robots, skinless androids and human-sized animatronic theme park animals, children's robotic toys, and other moving machines. These turn on the viewer and form up in ranks as if about to mount an attack.

**06-11.** Scrap metal, wires, ropes and plastic converge into a whirl of dust and grit and form into a towering, thickly built giant humanoid shaped construct which howls and turns on the viewer with gleaming, deep set red eyes.

**12-16.** The ground shakes and here and there, shafts of rebar, metal pipe and knotted cables stab upward toward the sky and form a hedge of lethally sharp shafts blocking the way.

**17-22.** An enormous lime green, angry looking cloud suddenly appears before the viewers and from beneath it drips yellowish green rain. Where the rain hits the ground or debris, puffs of smoke rise. The rain is acid!

**23-25.** A flock of skal birds gather from all directions and shriek, cry out, and circle in a dark mass. Some of the mutant starlings make aggressive swoops over the viewer's head as the entire maddened flock seems to prepare to attack.

**26-29.** Materials from nearby structures, or those yanked from the ground, fly together noisily. They overlap, brace and buttress each other to form a solid wall of junk that seems to rattle and chop across the ground just ahead of the viewer.

**30-34.** Roots from trees, wires and cables emerge from the ground, coil into the air like growing vines and make threatening jabs at the viewer. This coiled mass grows larger and more belligerent the longer it is watched.

**35-43.** Fire erupts from the ground in a wall of orange flame. The heat wafts over the viewer as the blaze spreads and advances.

**44-47.** Concrete, gravel, sand and other debris jerk loose from the ground and clatter together to form an impenetrable, solid wall. If the muto-illusionist advances or retreats, the wall tumbles and reforms rapidly before or behind them.

**48-50.** The ground cracks open in a sudden earthquake and reveals a vast dumping ground of ancient chemical drums. These rusty containers ooze green, blue and purple chemicals, and the air about the pit becomes clouded with a haze of phosphorescent mist.

**51-53.** A howling junk-filled tornado suddenly touches down from the dark sky above and churns and tears up the earth where it brushes the ground, threatening to sweep away the viewer as it coils ever closer.

**54-56.** A phantasmal dance of brilliant light swirls in great nets of color before the viewer. Each sheet of pigment merges with the next to form a new, otherworldly color. The entire wall of brilliance moves fast as it draws near, with each impact making a louder crack as the mirage of unearthly energies intermingle.

**57-59.** The viewer feels the earth shake and before them rises great solid wall of concrete as thick as man, obscuring the mutant beyond. This wall continues to grow and emerge from the ground if the muto-illusionists advances, or if he or she retreats, it will reemerge and collapse behind the user.

**60-62.** First one, then another gleaming, silvery humanoid robots appear to pop into existence amid a flash of blue lights. These seven foot tall, armored, red eyed machines carry a glossy black gun in their metal arms and slowly raise them toward the viewer. They number 1 per every 5 points of willpower the muto-illusionist has.

**63-66.** A blinding wall of golden light flashes into existence and forces viewers to shade their eyes, and halt before the advancing, crackling energy barrier.

**67-69.** The dead of the viewer's own species thrust up from the ground. Though rotted and covered in maggots and worms, the viewer recognizes many of the dead faces as its own pack or family members. The things call to the viewer and fight to get up and stagger closer, calling the viewer's name.

**70-73.** Holes erupt in the ground and out pour armed skullock warriors. They raise machetes and javelins, hoot, howl and begin to form up into ranks behind junk shields. One skullock appears per two points of the user's willpower trait.

**74-78.** All at once, comes a flash of light, an earsplitting boom and a wave of wind. An instant later, a mushroom cloud billows up and a wave of heat radiates from the colossal, ongoing explosion.

**79-81.** There is a sudden flicker in the air, as if it is water. The viewer feels a surge of force sweep over them and then a sudden itch at their flesh. Next, pain erupts, and the viewer looks down at its limbs and body to see the flesh cracking and blood ooze from countless wounds. The pain is maddening. An instant later, another ripple in the air occurs and another surge of pain sweeps over the viewer. A morale check might be in order for simple animals or low intelligence humanoids.

**82-85.** Millions of army ants emerge from many dozens of holes in the ground, ceiling, or walls and mass thickly on the ground. Many hundreds turn toward the viewer and seem highly agitated by the entity's presence near their nest.

**86-88.** The viewer notices glistening, thick ooze emerge out through a hole in the ground, ceiling, or walls and flow toward them. Any organic material in the thick blob touches shrivels, blackens and gets absorbed into the body of the quivering life form. This is a pit slime and covers 1 square meter for every 5 points of the user's willpower.

**89-92.** Spiders! The ground is suddenly blackened by millions of tiny spiders. The things scramble over each other and mass thickly nearest the viewer with hungry intent.

**93-95.** Cracks and pits form in the ground between the viewer and the mutant. The glistening head and segmented mouths of countless jaw and mud worms emerge and snap at the air. Some of the creatures wriggle up and then work their way down into the earth or floor again, the slippery creatures seem to be gathering nearest to the viewer and make ready to attack.

**96-98.** Huge alloy encased cables emerge from the ground and reach toward the viewer. These dirt and dust flecked cables end in drills, robotic hands, metal mandibles, hooks, and scissors. The mass seems to focus on the viewer and emerge closer and closer.

**99,00.** Two illusions occur simultaneously.

## Illusionary Concealment 190

Type: **mental defense**  Range: **user**
Usage: **once per day per rank**
Duration: **as willpower in rounds per concealment**
Hazard Check: **Int. based type E to spot, per minute (20 rounds)**

This optical illusion works on the minds of both humanoids and people, but does not fool robotics, androids, digital beings, dimensional beings or any cyborg with a non-organic brain. Animals are the most easily fooled, however this illusion does not conceal one's scent nor pounding heartbeat from being heard in close proximity (5 meters or fewer).

Basically, the mutant imagines some suitable non-animate object, such as a bush, pile of rock, barrel, wrecked hover scooter, or even a corpse, and those passing by see what the mutant wills them to see. Each potential viewer gets an intelligence based Type E hazard check to see through the ghostly illusion of the motionless mutant behind it, per minute. The mutant can maintain the illusion as long as he or she concentrates on only the image in or her head, for up to one round per each point of the user's willpower.

## Imbue Prowess 191

Type: **physical and mental mutation**
Range: **user or another being touched**
Usage: **as willpower per day**  Rate: **1**
Duration: **user's willpower in rounds**  Initiative: **+3**
Movement: **+4m**  Strike Value: **+10**
Damage: **+d10 to strength based**  Defense Value: **-10**
Hazard Check: **recipient gets two checks per hazard**

This Mutant can either use this powerful enhancement on itself, or another who he touches. The duration is one round per mutant's willpower trait value, per day, and cannot be broken up into smaller time units as many other mutations can. It takes one round to impart the prowess and works on the second round thereafter until the duration is over. If transferred to another, the receiver can move off and perform at the improved capacity even if out of sight from the imbuer.

The enhanced recipient is permitted two hazard checks from any physical, mental, chemical, radioactive, or other mishap or strike that calls for a hazard check. Additionally, the recipient does an extra 1d10 damage to

all strength based strikes, moves at +4 meters per round, is better able to dodge attacks (DV bonus –10), gains +3 initiative, and finally, he or she has a temporary increase in strike value of +10
.

## Internal Twin Fetus 192

Type: **physical and possible mental mutation**
Usage: **See below for possible benefit**

While within the womb, a twin brother or sister was enveloped by the character's faster growing fetus, and absorbed. The diminutive, foot long sibling lives within the full sized mutant, attached to the body's life support system and joined mentally to the larger body. When desired, this underdeveloped fetus can experience all the sensations from all five senses of its twin's big body, or retreat to sleep, dream, or avoid any agony or humiliation of the larger body.

Roll for a different intelligence and willpower trait value for the twin, although the fetus has an endurance of 3d6, which is added to the PC's trait value but recorded separately on the character sheet in case the tiny twin is attacked specifically by mind crush or some other power or weapon. If killed, the body will absorb this tiny twin over months and years. A separate personality can also be generated (see page 500 of this book to determine a personality).

There is a one-to-one telepathic link that enables the twin to communicate with the larger body's mind, and vice versa. Besides this ever constant companionship, this internal fetus has one or more mutations that it brings to the character's body. **Roll 1d8** at character creation to establish what benefits this internal twin offers the mutant.

**1. Healing surge:** once a day, this fetus can send a hyper-harmonic surge through the large body to heal it 3d20 traits points to each injured trait.

**2. Expel adrenalin:** four times per day, this twin can shoot a surge of adrenalin into the main body. During the duration of this enhancement, the main body is +1m movement, heals 3d6 endurance, and provides +5 damage to any strength based attacks or +50% strength trait value to any task such as climbing or lifting an object, etc. This adrenalin rush can also be discharged if the main body is exposed to toxins like venom and gives the character an extra hazard check to avoid the consequences. The duration of the adrenalin rush is 2 minutes or 40 rounds.

**3. Toxin absorption organs:** any venom or poison injected or consumed by the big body is leeched from it on the 2nd round after entering the flesh, and absorbed into this twin's massive kidney and liver system, thus negating the toxin. It takes the internal fetus 2d4 days to slowly expel the toxin, however, and during these days, it can not absorb any other doses, therefore leaving the larger body more vulnerable. In this period, the main character is still allowed 2 hazard checks from injected or ingested toxins — which can be a real life saver.

**4. Gills:** Although breathing through the same lungs as the big body, this fetus twin has gills that take up half its body length and, if the main body is forced under water, and its lungs fill with fluid, these gills will work to allow the big body to breathe underwater. Although able to stay submerged and survive, it is a great strain on both twins, and while avoiding drowning, the big mutant fights at a -20 SV penalty and suffers 1d4 damage per ten minutes while enduring this ordeal.

**5. Internal maintenance tendrils:** This fetus-twin has laced thousands of tiny, artery-like tendrils throughout the big body. These growths enhance and repair the larger body and add +10% strength to the PC — applied at character generation — and allow the PC to heal twice as fast. So too, this network will partially absorb stun damage, toxins, or radiation exposure, and so the PC takes half damage from stun based relic weapons and mutations as well as half damage from electrical shocks. Finally, this adaptation allows the big body an extra hazard check to avoid an exposure to radiation, ingested poison, or venom from either a bite, inhalation or spray.

**6. Telepathic:** While able to talk with the big body whenever the two want, this tiny twin can also communicate to those on the outside, and attempt to form separate relationships with the big body's companions, or even attempt to insert opinions and comments to the minds of strangers. Learn more about the mutation 'telepathy' in the hub rules on page 75.

**7. Back up mode:** This fetus has advanced access to the big body's nervous system. If given control, or during emergencies, it can override and control the main character if he or she is knocked unconscious, or mentally slain. This small internal twin can manipulate the full sized body haphazardly to get it somewhere safe. The gait, speech, and lopsided mannerism of a body controlled by the internal twin is like that of a highly intoxicated person, and the subject's body is at half strength, half agility, half accuracy, and only the fetal twin's intelligence and willpower are used. If operating a body with a permanently killed off brain, the internal fetus can spend 6+1d6 months working to master the body, bring a hint of life to the slack face of the brain dead sibling, and eventually make the body fully operational. Any mental mutations and memories in the dead main head are off limits to this new controller.

**8. Micro Triplet:** Within this tiny internal fetus is yet a third sibling, a shrimp sized early stage fetus that stopped development at two months of gestation before the foot long, much larger twin's fast growing body enveloped it. In turn, the foot long mid-sized twin was encased within the main character, too. This finger sized third twin can also telepathically communicate with the others, and although its mind is rudimentary, it does have a personality of its own, but works to serve the network of twins around it. It serves as a sort of battery and energy booster, senses living things around the main body, and transmits sensations to the other twins instantly

In total, this fetus provides the main big body with an increase of +3d6 willpower and perception each — added at character creation, plus one random extra mutation from the following list, **roll 1d8: 1.** Amplification, as the mutation in the hub rules on page 60 / **2.** Aura of Protection, as the mutation on page TME-61 / **3.** Empathy, page TME-65 / **4,** Heal touch, page TME-67 / **5.** Dimensional Retreat, page 240, this book /**6.** Energy Wall Generation, as the mutation on page 244 / **7.** Mental Counter Attack, page 254 / **8.** Sub-Plane Leap, as the mutation on page 266, this book.

An internal fetal twin does not go up in rank as the main character body does — unless it assumes control of the brain dead big body. Second, if the main body is slain this twin is not developed enough to be surgically extracted and survive in the harsh environment of the outer world — unless it is placed in a cryo-chamber's life support network and nutrient supply, or housed within a vat-brain's liquid nutrient vat within one hour of extraction.

These fetal twins are safely shielded from 'area effect' mutational attacks by the big body, thus immune to Agony Sphere, Asphyxiation Zone, electrical attacks, Peeling Radius and similar powers.

## Irritation Particles 193
Type: **physical attack**
Range: **4 meters**
Usage: **twice per day per rank**
Duration: **1d10+2 rounds**
Strike Value: **+20**
Damage: **1d2 per round**
Hazard Check: **nil**

An organ growing within the mutant's throat produces a fine, chemically potent powder that can be coughed up and spewed 4 meters. The burning, itching dust shoots out in a condensed cone, and will normally only afflict one human sized target, but as it covers a 3x3m area, it can potentially harm many small creatures such as rats. The intended victim's armor and agility can ward off the attack, but if not, he or she will be coated with the dust, which quickly works its way into most armor and clothing.

The intensely irritating particles inflict 1d2 damage per round, up to 1d10+2 rounds per target, and the victim must make a successful morale check to continue fighting, otherwise it flees to find water or sand or something to roll in. Note, morale is covered on page 110 of the TME Hub Rules.

If defending its lair or young, an animal suffering from the effects of this mutation will always return after the duration of the particles has passed, and resume the battle. Humanoids can elect to strip out of their armor and clothes and dust out the rash-inducing particles, which take 2d4 minutes for archaic armor, and 3d6 minutes for relic armor. Jumping into water will also rid the victim of the dust. Any being brought to zero endurance, or less, by this mutation is considered having passed out from the agony of the particles, and will heal normally after the duration has lapsed.

It is important to note that targets wearing relic Shell class armor, enviro suits, space suits, rad-suits, reflective suites, and the like are immune to this attack, as are any character using a force field, the mutations of Aura of Protection, Arid Adaptation, and Shell.

## Kinetic Fist 194
Type: **Energy mutation**          Rate: **1**
Usage: **2 per rank per day**     Range: **melee**     Strike Value: **+20**
Damage: **Normal fist DMG +1d20 lethal + 2d20 stun**

The mutant can summon internal energies which light up one fist, or other striking appendage. While this energy cannot be fired or thrown, it will transfer into anything the charged fist successfully strikes, and boasts a +20 strike value. On a hit, there is a brief flash of brilliant blue light and the victim suffers whatever the appendage's regular damage inflicts plus 1d20 lethal and 2d20 stun damage to any living or nonliving object, including vehicles, robots, structures or vegetation.

This especially potent mutation can be used twice per day per rank, although only one such blow can be made per round, even at 7th rank when characters double their melee attacks per round. In the event that this character has the brawling or martial art skill, the extra damage from such a talent, as well as the appendage or fist damage, is added to the devastating blow.

As far as the chosen appendage to deliver this blow, it is normally always the same one, time after time, as a pathway from the mutant's inner core conveys the charge each time, although the character can change to another appendage or fist if successfully making a type G willpower based hazard check. A kick, curb stomp, head butt, crab pincer, tentacle, bladed limb or any other attached, living 'weapon' can be used instead of a fist.

## Lost and Found 195

Type: **mental mutation**  Range: **100 kilometers per point of willpower**
Usage: **Once per day per rank**
Memorized people, places and objects: **1 per point of Intelligence**

Any person, animal, place or object this mutant has touched and given awareness to, appreciation for, hatred of, or other strong emotion to, can be thought of and its last known location sensed. This mental mutation works much like the hot and cold game; when moving toward the object, he or she feels a hot pull while when moving away from it, feels cold or a weakening signal.

Normally this only allows the deviant to feel the direction to where he or she last touched the person, place, or thing, and if it has been moved, then its current global position cannot be detected. However, for very strong emotional ties, either positive or negative, to a living being who also knows this gifted mutant or thinks about him or her from time to time, then this remote person or beast can be sensed and a direction of travel discerned. The game master must ultimately decide if the person or animal in question has strong enough emotional ties to this mutant in return to allow it to be tracked beyond the last locale where it has been touched, or not.

Typical strong emotions include love for a spouse, parent, sibling or offspring, as well as deep hatred for one who did great harm or insult to this character, but a compelling tie could also exist with a favored pet, riding mount, teacher, patron, clergyman, or respected leader, comrade, or lover. Places could include a childhood home, a shrine, a place where you last saw friends, where a battle took place, or where you lost something. Objects typically include childhood toys, favored weapons, jewelry items, relics, or holy objects of great meaning to the mutant and their people.

This mutant will have an inventory of possible, trackable persons, places, or things equal to the deviant's intelligence trait — although the players should note each of these things at the time, and record it on the back of their character sheet. This power can be called upon once a day per rank and has a range of 100 kilometers per point of the mutant's willpower.

## Mental Counter Attack 196

Type: **mental mutation**
Range: **self and unlimited reflection**
Usage: **constant**
Damage: **possible return of enemy's mental attack**
Hazard Check: **as specified by attack. Failed attacks return to the sender.**

Unknown to the mutant, her mind has a special defense which may reflect back any mental attacks to the sender, regardless of range or conscious effort on any party's part. Any attack or mind reading, empathy or other intrusion that fails to harm or otherwise work on this deviant will be reflected back to the attacker who must make his or her own hazard check or defense to avoid it. This subconscious mutation is always in operation, even during sleep.

## Mental Dominion 197

Type: **Mental Control**  Range: **touch**
Usage: **variable**  Duration: **variable**
Hazard Check: **Willpower based, see below**

Among the most powerful and most feared mutations to occur in humans, is the power to take over other's minds. It is just this sort of aberration that compels non-mutants to distrust all deviants and lump them together as devil spawned miscreations, witches, and demons.

The mutant who commands this mental mutation must touch a humanoid victim with their bare hand, either as a blow in combat, or casual unsuspecting caress, pat on the

back, or tap in non-combat situations. The victim is allowed a willpower based hazard check, the letter code type being based on the potential master's intelligence score according to the table to follow; failure results in the victim lapsing out of their senses.

The controlling mutant, referred to hereafter as the 'master', can totally dominate the victim's mind and body for the duration of the dominion as if the subject were an extension of the master's own body. In short, the master owns both bodies, and others he or she may dominate depending on his or her intelligence score. The master feels and hears and otherwise senses everything the controlled humanoids do, including pain. The master can, when needed, withdraw focus on one or more dominated persons if they are about to suffer an agonizing death or commit suicide or otherwise undergo some discomfort which the master wills them to do, or can't avoid.

Besides merely controlling the victim, the master also has access to the subject's memories, emotions, plans, relationships to others, fears and hopes, even their recent dreams and nightmares. The subject has no consciousness whatsoever, and will do as directed by the master, unless forced to do something highly counter to what the victim would normally do, such as harm its mate, its young, or commit suicide. In these cases, the victim is allowed another hazard check, and if he or she succeeds, the strain of the mind control will snap the dominion's hold and return the character to full waking consciousness, sometimes remembering all that he or she has been made to do, and who was the master.

The shortcomings of this mutation are few, but include the limited duration of the dominion, the chance that a subject will remember the events he or she was forced to conduct, and that the master can only control a certain number of servants.

All this considered, it remains a potent mutation, especially since the control of victims, once established, continues even if the master is no longer thinking or ordering the victims around, and he or she can fight normally once domination is established.

Any unsuccessful attempts to control another's mind will immediately be detected by a wakeful target person. In addition, if the master is ever knocked unconscious, all his or her victims will regain self awareness. Only humanoids or beings with human based organic brains are susceptible to this control, including bestial humans and vat-brains. True Animal minds are simply too different to navigate and control. In addition, any target person with more than one head or brain will need to have all its minds dominated to gain physical control of the deviant's body. Nonetheless, gaining access to just one head would allow the master to control the mind within, root around in its memories and gain access to its plans and other intel. Other heads might not notice that one of their number has fallen into the control of another being, and each is required to make a type E intelligence based hazard check to understand what has happened to the controlled brain.

| Master's Intelligence | Usage of Mutation | Victim's Willpower based Hazard Check | Number of Victims | Duration of Dominion | Victim has Memory after Domination?* |
|---|---|---|---|---|---|
| 1-9 | once weekly | A | 1 | 1d20 rounds | 90% chance |
| 10-29 | every 2nd day | A | 1 | 20+1d100 rounds | 72% chance |
| 30-39 | once a day | B | 2 | 1d6 hours | 52% chance |
| 40-63 | once a day per rank | B | 6 | 2d12 hours | 44% chance |
| 64-89 | twice a day per rank | C | 12 | 1d6 days | 28% chance |
| 90-110 | twice a day per rank | D | as willpower points | 1d6 months | 13% chance |
| over 110 | thrice per day per rank | E | willpower X 3 | 2d8 months | 7% chance |

*Memories of what they did while dominated, plus exactly who their former master was.

## Mental Stun 198

Type: **mental mutation**    Range: **1 meter per point of willpower**
Usage: **Twice per day per rank**    Rate: **1**
Ranged Hazard Check: **Type D intelligence based HC to avoid**
Touch Hazard Check: **Type C intelligence based HC to avoid**

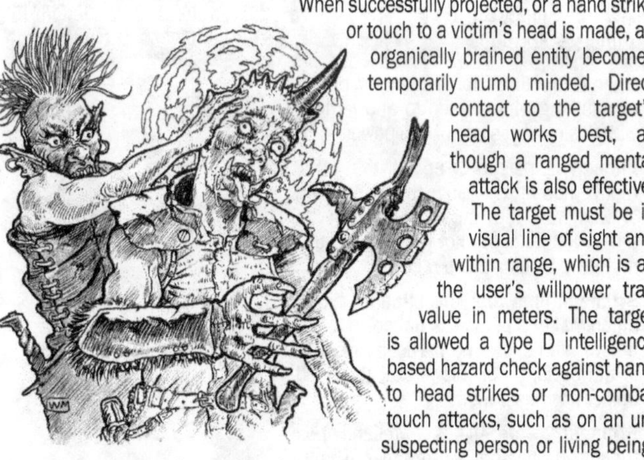

When successfully projected, or a hand strike or touch to a victim's head is made, an organically brained entity becomes temporarily numb minded. Direct contact to the target's head works best, although a ranged mental attack is also effective. The target must be in visual line of sight and within range, which is as the user's willpower trait value in meters. The target is allowed a type D intelligence based hazard check against hand to head strikes or non-combat touch attacks, such as on an unsuspecting person or living being, or Type C hazard check from a ranged stun attempt to fend off the paralysis.

Any blocked attack is noticeable to the would-be victim who senses an intrusive tapping sensation on their forehead. Roll on the following table each time this mutation is successful:

### Mental Paralysis Result Table    Roll 2d6

**2. Mental love tap:** The mutant got the target's attention alright, and it looks directly at the user and knows that it was he or she who just tried to do something to its mind. If able, the would-be target will either shoot at or go after this mutant with single minded determination and ignore other opponents until it kills the mutant.

**3. Brain fog:** The target suffers 1d4 INT damage and is momentarily made forgetful. If it was chasing somebody, or about to do something, or in the pro-

cess of some action, it must pause for 1d4 rounds to remember what it was or continue with current activities, but will attack or return fire if assaulted and is no easier to hit.

**4,5. Mentally smacked:** The target suffers 1d6 INT damage and suffers an immediate headache which last the rest of the day. If it was itself deploying a mental mutation or trying to do something technical, it stops this for 1d6 rounds as it tries to shake off the attack.

**6,7. Mentally thumped:** The target takes 2d6 INT damage* and is stunned and loses its next round to either move or attack. It merely stands or hovers in place and stares forward blankly and is +30 SV easier to be hit.

**8,9. Mentally bludgeoned:** The target takes 3d6 INT damage and staggers back in pain, 1d3 meters, clutching or rubbing its head. It loses its next two turns, but is no easier to hit.

**10,11. Mentally stunned:** The target takes 4d6 INT damage and halts whatever it is doing to stagger and drop to its knees, losing the next three rounds. While mentally paralyzed, it is also +30 easier to hit.

**12. Massive mental assault:** The target takes 3d20 intelligence damage*, plus a 2 in 6 chance that the target goes blind for 3d6 minutes (-50% SV reduction and is +40 SV easier to be physically hit by attackers).

*About Intelligence damage.* If the target is reduced to zero or less INT from this mutation, it seizes up, spins, drops or lets go of anything it's holding in its hands or mouth, and collapses into unconsciousness. Its mind heals at a rate of one INT point per minute and wakes when it reaches 1 intelligence point. Reminder, there are 20 rounds in a minute.

## Micro Feelers by Brandon Goeringer 199

Type: **physical mutation**
Range: **From 1 meter to maximum 6 meters, move 1m**
Usage: **Twice per day per rank**    Defense Value: **-20**    Endurance: **5**

Thousands of minuscule feelers branch out from a location on the mutant's body, usually the palm. They are so small that together they may be seen as but a thin bit of string but spread out over a surface they become hard to distinguish, requiring a type J perception based HC to spot. The feelers are so small they can maneuver, at 1m per round to a maximum of 6m, through cracks around doors, hulls of vehicles, floor grating, pipes, inside computer terminals, between window sills, etc.

If there is a place where one piece of material comes in contact with another, the feelers can make their way in. Only vacuum sealed containers are protected from the feelers. After a minute of exploration, they transmit back to the mutant an amount of information about the place they have entered with the equivalent of a photograph. The mutant can sense life forms, light sources, temperature, toxic environments, electricity and water sources in the "mental picture" transferred from the feelers to the mutant's brain.

The feelers have a DV of -20 due to size and END 5 as a whole. If destroyed the feelers regrow in a month. The feelers may be used twice per day, per rank and take complete concentration from the mutant while in use, counting the mutant as unaware if attacked.

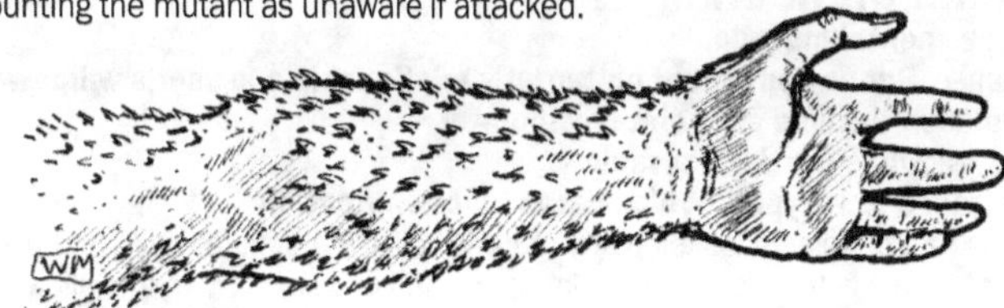

## Micro Spines 200

Type: **physical mutation**    Defense Value: **-10**    Range: **9m**
Usage: **Two uses (spine storms) of 3 volleys per day, per rank**
Rate: **3 volleys per use**
Strike Value: **volley +10, or 01-60 auto melee attack if PC grabbed or bitten**
Damage: **each volley 2d8, or 2d6 auto melee attack if PC grabbed or bitten**
This mutant's shoulders, back, arms and legs are covered in thousands of tiny bone darts, which lay flat on the deviant's skin when the freak is not

excited to combat, or in fear. When agitated or willing to deploy these clear, icicle like, 4cm long spines, they rise in one round and can either be used defensively or fired as a storm of several dozen up to 9m away.

As a close quarters deterrent, anything that successfully bites, grapples, swallows or swats at the character exposes itself to an immediate, simultaneous attack of 01-60, damage 2d6 each round that it holds this thorny character.

When fired, the storm of tiny spines launch 3 volleys. Each of these volleys can be used to either attack one opponent three times, or up to three opponents once each, or two waves of spines at one opponent and a third on another adversary, etc. Each volley of spines is rolled as a separate attack with a +10 SV, plus any accuracy modifiers, and inflicts 2d8 damage. These spine storms can be thrown twice per day per rank of the mutant, with each storm firing 3 volleys.

Normally, even without these spines raised or even while hidden under layers of clothing and armor, they improve the mutant's DV by -10, but they cannot be fired through clothing or armor. These spines are well hidden when packed closed the mutant's flesh, yet noticeable and a -1d4+1 is applied to the freak's appearance score.

## Microwave Generation 201

Type: **energy attack**    Range: **willpower x2 in meters**
Usage: **Once per day per rank**    Rate: **1**
Strike Value: **+10**    Damage: **10 plus 1d6 per rank**

Any target struck by this white beam of molecule shaking energy will cook where hit, for 10 points damage plus an additional 1d6 damage per rank of this mutant. The strike value for this attack is as the character's base +10, has a rate of once per day per rank, an effective range of the user's willpower times 2 in meters, and is fired from the aberration's hand 78% of the time, otherwise the temple. If the mutant's firing mode area is covered by a glove, blindfold, helmet or other blockage, the microwave beam will discharge in the character's own arm or face, doing automatic random damage.

This highly potent, destructive pulse of energy will harm dimensional beings, robots, solid objects, and living beings equally.

## Mind Unification 202

Type: **mental mutation**
Range: **Range dependent on target's relationship and user's willpower**
Duration: **1 round per point of willpower**
Usage: **Once per day per rank**
Hazard Check: **Type C Willpower to block unification**

This remarkable, mass telepathy mutation allows the mutant to both broadcast thoughts to those around him or her, and once a link is made, allow the accessed minds to reply — even without the entity having the mutation of telepathy or even being a mutant at all.

This potent projection works best when the recipients are already friendly, related by blood, or allied with the mutant who deploys this power, and have practiced with the communications link on previous occasions and formed open pathways between themselves and the main user. Strangers can also be reached, as can enemies, but to reach them is more difficult.

The mutant can project using words, static pictures, memories, a view of what the mutant is currently observing, or if the user is quite imaginative

and has an intelligence score of over 35 or higher, can project visions of what he or she wants the recipient to do, understand, or believe to be true, etc.. This is especially useful when reaching out to a pack of wild animals whereby the mind unifier can show the beasts a scene where the mutant is feeding them or treating their injuries, helping work with them to defeat some mutual enemy, and so forth.

The duration of this unification of minds is based on the relationship of the receiving mind, however higher rank mutants can spend their daily uses of this power to maintain a long, uninterrupted conversation or projection of images by employing back-to-back uses.

The range of the transmission is based both on the user's willpower and the relationship to the target subjects. A mix of both friends, strangers and enemies can all be subject to the mental unification, and need not be within view of the user. Any mind that is linked up to this mutant is also linked up to the other entities, yet the mutant can silence any noisy minds, and whenever this controlling mutant transmits words or images, all the rest in the current session of unity are muted. If two or more mutants with this ability are linked up, they could talk simultaneously and their chatter will become jumbled.

| Relationship of Target Mind Description | Range Modifier to Willpower | Odds of Mind Unification |
|---|---|---|
| **Open & familiar:** Friend, lover, pet, parent or offspring who is open to and familiar with this mutant's use of this power. | Willpower x 2 kilometers | 9 in 10 |
| **Friendly:** A person or animal that is already showing a willingness to befriend or work with the mutant, perhaps even a new comrade, but not yet aware of this mutant exhibiting this power. | Willpower in kilometers | 8 in 10 |
| **Stranger, unaware:** This stranger, either an animal or a person, is unknown to the mutant and shows no particular interest in the deviant, nor knows that the mind unifier has this power. | Willpower x 100m | 7 in 10 |
| **Stranger, aware:** this is a presently non friendly or non-hostile stranger who is aware of the mutant's presence and might observe the deviant, serving them a meal, or passing them in a street, etc. | Willpower x 50m | 6 in 10 |
| **Stranger, hostile:** This animal or person starts off as hostile to the mutant and any companions with them, although conflict has not yet started and the mutant and his or her people might not yet be enemies. With trade or gifts or supplication, the user of this power could turn the hostile beings into merely aware strangers before attempting to unify with their minds. | Willpower x 20m | 5 in 10 |

**Enemy, unaware:** This enemy is determined to kill or drive off the mutant and their companions, either out of territorial, inter-species or predatory reason, and yet is unaware that the mutant has this power and is not automatically blocking any potential incoming telepathic unification.    Willpower x 10m    4 in 10

**Enemy, aware:** This enemy means to do harm to the mutant, and yet is aware that the character has this mind unification power and has either used it on this enemy, or its pack mates. It will be focused on blocking the mutant's intrusions.    Willpower x2m    3 in 10

Any unsuccessful attempt to reach a mind means the subject simply wasn't receptive and has no awareness that the attempt to reach them was made. However, a subject who receives a telepathic unification might not like what it hears, or be told by a superior to block the incoming mental caller. The odds to willfully block the transmission require a successful willpower based Type C hazard check, otherwise the subject must endure the mental intrusion.

The subjects can communicate back to the Mind Unifier in either words, pictures, or present what they remember, or are currently seeing, which could turn many subjects into remote watchers and spies for the mutant.

Any target mutant that has this or regular telepathy or the similar mutation of thought share, has far greater control of their mind's openness, range and power, and if he or she welcomes this transmission, will automatically be open to the sender and have a duration of unification in minutes, not rounds.

This mutant can reach out and connect with one mind per point of their intelligence, per rank, Thus a 5th rank mutant with an intelligence score of 67 can potentially reach 335 entities within the radius defined by the relationship of those beings as noted on the above table, and yet may select distant friends and family, teammates or benevolent strangers only and skip over minds of strangers or enemies if desired. The ability for a very high ranking and powerful being to control, and communicate with an entire fortress, lair or township of servants could easily be used to mount a remarkable defense, or used to control a populace in a way most tyrants could only dream of.

All those who are unified mentally with this mutant are susceptible to follow-up mental intrusions, controls and the like from this same 'master', and if this user also had the mutation of empathy, could then express his or her feelings and read the feelings of others around it. Second, any malicious mutations launched by the mutant against already linked up minds, has a higher degree of successfully harming or controlling the recipients, all of who must make two hazard checks to avoid mind crush or other mental attacks.

As a final note, the game master might want to allow a character or NPC villain to push their message out to an entire community or humanoid lair, and for cinematic and epic results, mobilize a populace or perform some remarkable deed.

## Mineral Embedded Skin 203

Defense Value: **-10+3d6**

This mutant's skin is permanently encrusted in patches of stony scales, flakes and crystals. While they do not hurt, and the deviant's body is entirely accustomed to these growths, they are very unsightly and reduce the character's appearance by 1 point of appearance per 2 points of defense value bonus. The amount of mineral formation is permanently assigned at character generation.

These crystals can be filed off, picked out, surgically removed, and the wounds covered by makeup to hide the mutation's presence, inflicting severe pain and 3d6 damage, but this procedure will also bring the subject's APP score up by 10 — temporarily — as new crystals will regrow within 1 week. If no other visible mutations were present, this character might pass as a pure stock human after this agonizing procedure — although a badly scarred person.

For those mutants who grew up with these crystalline formations, they will have found a wide range of uses for these growths. Such uses include starting a fire by holding their arm just right in the sunlight, and like using a magnifying glass can ignite highly flammable substances — which takes 1+1d6 minutes and only works in full sunlight.

For 1 in 8 of these mutants, the crystals are actually pink salt (Himalayan salt) and can be shaved off to season food. With effort, this mutant can scrape away enough salt to gather 1kg per week for sale, and as salt can sometimes be a precious commodity in areas far from a mine or seashore, this mutant might have a lucrative commodity — or become a chained source of precious salt for an unscrupulous keeper.

1 in 20 mutants with this deviation exhibit a rare variety of crystal which glow in the dark and cast light in a 3m radius, however, unless covered, these growths can be seen by unfriendly eyes from as far away as a half kilometer.

## Misery Flashback Inducement 204

Type: **Mental Attack**    Range: **User's willpower in meters**
Usage: **Twice per day per rank** Duration: **1d6+2 rounds**
Damage: **Temporary misery causing inattention**
Hazard Check: **Int. based type D**

The user of this mind intrusion doesn't even need to know the traumas, nightmares and other miseries that the target has suffered in order to use this power. When a successful mental attack is made, after the target person or animal fails a type D Intelligence based hazard check, the victim suffers terrible flashbacks, overlapping visions and memories in its mind's eye.

If the target makes a successful hazard check, he or she dismisses the visions, concentrates on the here and now, and is no longer affected by this same mutation for 24 hours. Those who fail this check are subject to misery for 1d6+2 rounds, in which they come to a complete stop, or glide if flying, and do nothing but wail pitifully, weep, moan and contort their face in imagined agony. Attackers can hit such opponents much easier, being +30 SV, although any strike which scores 10 or more points of damage immediately snaps the victim from their traumatic remembrances.

Of course, this power does not work on machines, computers, androids, or plants which lack brains- however, will affect plantoid characters. Of note, green walkers do not use the brain of their cadaverous victims, and therefore are not affected by this intrusion.

## Molecular Manipulation 205

Type: **mental mutation**    Range: **Variable by willpower**
Usage: **Once per day per rank**    Rate: **1**
Strike Value & Damage: **Variable, see table**

There are two ways to use this potent mutation; destructive or repair. In short, this mutant can use their mind to damage both materials or relics, including shattering locks and hinges on ancient doors, as well as emit a shimmering surge of energy to mangle living beings. The most often used application, however, is to mend physical objects, including vehicles, robots, androids or the self or others by extracting foreign bodies and knitting broken bones, organs and tissues back together.

These powers are restricted by the willpower of the mutant deploying them, and allowed one use per day per rank. As a powerful, multi-use mutation, this deviant might want to keep this gift hidden from all but the closest comrades and family members. In some communities, for example, the open use of this mutation will cause cries of witchcraft, and potentially lead to the user's ostracization, or worse.

To attack, this mutant need only focus his or her attention on a target being, structure or object within range, and 'will' it to be destroyed, although a strike must be made on the victim, whose normal armor, agility modifiers and skills — such as dodge — still apply to its DV. A base strike value to hit the target is shown below, which cannot be changed by skills or other traits.

Any target with a force field must first have the field depleted before damage can occur to the subject beneath. Dimensional beings are susceptible to this power as an attack, and the user need not be able to see the entity to sense its location and try to disrupt it.

To repair things or heal organic beings, this mutant must physically grasp or caress the damaged person, machine, android, vehicle, or building to commence healing.

| User's Willpower | Attack SV | Attack Range | Attack Damage | Repair or Healing Amount |
|---|---|---|---|---|
| 1 to 5 | 01-30 | 3 meters | 1d4 | d3 |
| 6 to 10 | 01-35 | 6 meters | 1d6 | d4 |
| 11 to 20 | 01-40 | 18 meters | 1d8 | d6 |
| 21 to 40 | 01-50 | 36 meters | 1d10 | 2d6 |
| 41 to 60 | 01-60 | 72 meters | 1d12 | 3d6 |
| 61 to 90 | 01-70 | 144 meters | 1d20 | 4d6 |
| 91 to 130 | 01-80 | 300 meters | 1d30 | 5d6 |
| Over 131 | 01-90 | 1 kilometer | 1d30+5 | 6d6 |

## Muto-Centaur *Idea credit: Ed Pegg Jr* 206
Type: **physical alteration**
Rate: **2 extra unarmed kick attacks every third round**
Strike Value: **+5**      Damage: **1d10 each**
Movement bonus: **base movement of 12m**
This humanoid mutant has four legs and an adjoining, extra section of abdomen between them to form a secondary back which to store saddlebags, gear, and extra weapons. While the individual can't wear advanced armor or relic body suits, he or she can wear modified, non-powered suits of tactical or combat armor, although two suits must be expended to make one full muto-centaur suit.

Besides having a somewhat larger, and heavier frame, which gives the character a 10+1d20 bonus to endurance, a +20+1d20 increase in kilograms, and 4+1d8 bonus to strength at character generation, these extra legs offer several advantages.

First, with two rear legs to support the mutant, they can rear up once every third round of combat to kick with the foremast — or rear legs at those behind — and add two kick attacks to whatever other melee attacks the mutant uses, at +5 SV that inflict 1d10 damage each plus any strength bonus or those stemming from martial arts or the brawling skill.

Secondly, this deviant can run with a base speed of 12m per round instead of the normal 6 for most humans, plus gain an automatic 1d3 skill points in climbing.

Although those who are used to the mutant don't feel that this odd leg configuration is revolting, many do, and the character suffers a -2d6 APP penalty.

## Neural Surge 207
Type: **mental mutation**
Range: **double to any other mental mutation**
Usage: **Once per day per rank**
Strike Value and Damage: **X2 any other mental mutation**
Once daily, per rank, this deviant's mental capacities briefly magnify, doubling their intelligence and willpower trait values as far as any hazard check against some incoming mind attack goes, or when the mutant needs to solve some equation, formula, riddle or puzzle. Secondly, if this individual also has metal mutations, such as Mind Crush, Transform Weather or Telekinetic Junk Shield as just a few examples, then all range, damage or other variables are twice as effective as they would otherwise be. This is a rare, potent stacking mutation which can be used in conjunction simultaneously, with one other mental mutation or deed which requires intelligence or willpower.

The third benefit of this power is that when unleashed, it also heals 3d6 trait points to either this mutant's intelligence or willpower trait should they be damaged. This mutation can be used once per day per rank.

## Nocturnal 208
Type: **physical mutation**      Usage: **After sunset until sunrise**
Strike Value: **+10**      Defense Value: **-10**
Initiative: **+1**      Movement: **+1m**
After sunset, this deviant is invigorated and more aware (+1 initiative). They can see in the dark like a cat, and, until sunrise, are enhanced and enjoy +10 strike value, -10 defense value, and +1 meter movement per round. Being nocturnal means this mutant prefers to sleep all day and will be grumpy and dull witted during this time, but begins to become animated toward sunset. At dusk, their mood changes and they'll attempt to get companions to go out to the local saloon, cause some mischief, or undertake a risky night operation into the ruins.

## Oil Stream 209
Type: **greasy projection**      Range: **10 meters away, covers 6 x 6m area**
Usage: **once per day per 20 kilograms weight of character**
Duration: **remains until washed away by rain or water**
Strike Value: **normal**      Damage: **temporary blindness or slip**
Hazard Check: **see below**
Slippery, non-flammable oil is expelled from this freak in one of three dispensing systems. Roll 1d6 to determine which this character was born with: **1-3.**

mouth disgorging / **4.** from urinal duct / **5,6.** from a disgusting 3d6 centimeter long tube growing from the aberration's abdomen (-2d4 appearance).

The oil stream can be sprayed up to ten meters in range and lands to cover an area 6 by 6 meters with an extremely slippery clear oil, very similar to olive oil in consistency. Anyone to walk or run over the oil slick will probably slip and waste two rounds getting back on their feet and crossing the slick. While trying to get up, they will have to focus on maintaining their balance, instead of fighting, and are +20 SV to hit. A victim can choose to remain on the slick and fire while seated, or use mental mutations and such instead of trying to get up, however all animals, robots and most low intelligence humanoids (20 or less) will always try to get back on their feet.

To determine if an individual slips or not, the victim must make an agility based hazard check; consult the table below. The mutant can disgorge one spray of oil per every 20 kilograms of physical organic body weight he or she currently posses, rounded down, per day. Note, for mutorgs, the weight of implants is not included in these calculations, however for every missing arm add +10kg and every missing leg add +20kg to overall weight since the entity's torso, where the oil is stored, is the true decider of the quantity of liquid.

This mutant craves a diet rich in dairy, fish and mollusks, nuts and other foods which contain plenty of fat and oil, and yet never seems to get chubby despite their diet.

Besides the regular use for this stream of oil, the mutant can also use it to attempt to spray into an attacker's face to temporarily blind them for 1d4 rounds on an unadjusted attack (Note: blindness rules on page TME 122, but in brief, the subject is +40 SV easier to be hit, and makes attacks with a -50% penalty and move at half speed). Additionally, he or she could use the oil to grease primitive machinery, make a pathway slick for oneself and any companions to slide down a stone or metal slope, grease an iron bar or ladder rung to make it impossible for enemies to climb up in pursuit, etc.

| Victim's Type and Locomotion | Agility Based Hazard Check to Remain Upright |
| --- | --- |
| Biped, walking | C |
| Biped, running | D |
| Biped, fighting | E |
| Quadruped, walking | B |
| Quadruped, running | C |
| Quadruped, fighting | D |
| Six legged or more | A |
| Tracked robot | A |
| Motorcycle or mountain bike | E |
| Four-wheeled vehicle | B |
| Tracked vehicle | A |

# Organ Grenade *by Brandon Goeringer* 210
Type: **physical mutation**
Range: **Throw 20m + strength range modifier**
Blast Radius: **4 meters, can afflict up to 8 man sized targets**
Usage: **Start with 2d6. One will grow back each 48 hours from ranks 1 to 9, while ranks 10+ every 24 hours. Maximum of 12.**
Rate: **1**     Strike Value: **01-70**     Damage: **1d20+5**
This mutant produces several (2d6) apple sized, chitinous organs that grow on the abdomen. These tumor-like growths are directly connected to the mutant's digestive system. Each produces its own volatile enzyme, and when mixed with stomach acids, creates a powerful explosive.

This organ may be detached, squeezed to activate, and thrown, exploding on impact, range 20m plus or minus strength based range modifier, 4 meter blast radius, usually sufficient to harm 8 man-sized beings if the victims are grouped in typical ranks. SV 01-70, DMG 1d20+5. The organ grows back in 48 hours, or every 24 hours once rank 10 is achieved to a maximum of 12 grenades. The organ must be used within an hour of detachment or the acid and enzymes breakdown its chitin casing, doing 1d6 damage to whatever it's touching. These growths look gross, and the mutant's shirtless appearance is reduced by -2d4+2.

# Phlegm Sheet Spitter 211
Type: **physical attack**
Range: **6 meter cone on up to 3 targets, or up to 9m away vs 1 target**
Usage: **1 time per hour**          Rate: **1**
Strike Value: **01-70, with only the target's agility modifiers and dodge benefits allowable DV benefits.**
Damage: **Slows goo coated victim 50%, making them +20 SV easier to strike while reducing target's own SV by -20**
Duration: **Wipe off or roll clear of phlegm in 1d6+3 rounds if fighting as well, or 1+d4 rounds if doing nothing but removing this stuff.**
Once per hour, this mutant can work up a huge, rather disgusting gob of phlegm and discharge it at one or more opponents. This sheet of yellowish green phlegm has the potential to coat targets, slowing them by -50% move, making them +20 SV easier to strike and yet -20 SV themselves with any physical attack mode. The phlegm SV is 01-70 and fixed and no accuracy, rank gained or skills based strike modifiers apply to this SV rating. However, since this net-like, sticky sheet of gunk is not attempting to puncture the armor of a foe, only the target's base agility score and any dodge DV benefits are used as the target's defense value, ignoring armor altogether. This sheet is spit out in either a broad cone to ensnare up to three man-sized or smaller creatures, or else launched like a streamer against only one opponent at ranges of 4 to 9 meters.

*GM note:* There is a rarer variant of this spit — which only occurs in 2% of all instances of this mutation — which once exposed to air, the phlegm hardens like a layer of concrete and immobilizes the target(s) for 3d6+10 minutes, however immersion in water will remove this shell-like layer within 2 minutes.

## Planer Skip 212
Type: **mental-physical departure**      Range: **user**
Usage: **once per day per 2 ranks**      Duration: **instantaneous**

At will, this deviant can blink out of existence and simply vanish. In truth, they have used advanced mental prowess to slip into a dimensional portal and skip elsewhere in the vicinity. They will appear 2d6 rounds later, a few meters from the departure point in a pre-planned safe spot — not outside the skyscraper's three hundredth floor, in the molten lava, or in solid rock, for example. GM note: The player should declare where their character will appear next before making this attempt.

The skip into another plane is not without its risks, however, because the portal a person returns from stays open for 1d6 rounds afterward. During this time, the rip might become the access point for a dimensional intruder.

There is a 1 in 20 chance that the portal stays open and disgorges a random dimensional being, which has followed the character and will attack the PC on arrival and only leave after killing him or her or else the PC manages another planer skip and returns again, hopefully giving the entity the slip.

The odds to make a successful planer skip is a Type C willpower based hazard check. Only successful attempts count toward the daily uses of this mental mutation. Of note, any portal which remains open after the skip is ruptured and appears as a flash of light for 3d6 minutes and is about as big as the character, and cannot be reentered.

| 1d20 | Dimensional Intruder* |
|------|------------------------|
| 1-12. | Lost soul |
| 13-15. | Ripper |
| 16,17. | Shocker |
| 18,19. | Mind Killer |
| 20. | Dominator |

*Detailed on pages 363 to 365.*

## Plasma Sphere Projection
Type: **Energy mutation**
Rate: **1 to generate, 2nd round unleashed up to 20m away, 3rd round travels 100m per round to target**
Usage: **1 per rank per day**      Range: **Willpower x 100m**
Blast radius: **1m per rank of user**      Strike Value: **+24**
Damage: **1d30**

This energy discharge mutation is slow to generate, aim and fire... but has a long-range and often results in devastation among the user's foes. This character can use their forehead, a hand or other appendage to generate a

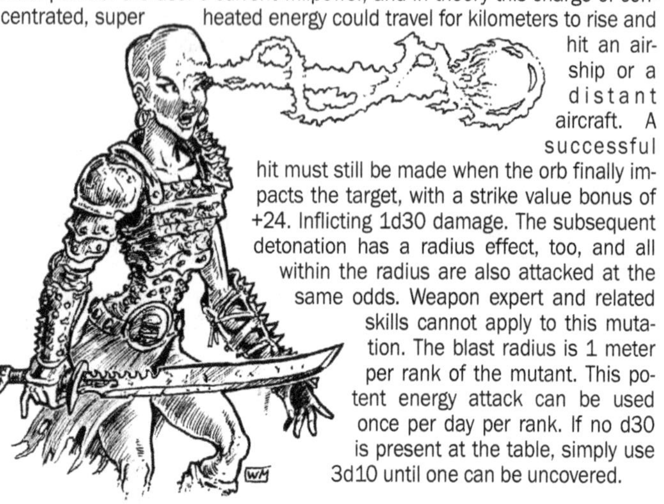

purple plasma sphere before it — which takes a full round to focus on and prepare, and on the second round, can lock into a target and unleash the orb. If the target is not within 20m or less, this sizzling ball must travel to its distant target at a speed of 100m per each round thereafter.

This discharge has an impressive maximum range of 100 meters per each point of the user's current willpower, and in theory this charge of concentrated, super heated energy could travel for kilometers to rise and hit an airship or a distant aircraft. A successful hit must still be made when the orb finally impacts the target, with a strike value bonus of +24. Inflicting 1d30 damage. The subsequent detonation has a radius effect, too, and all within the radius are also attacked at the same odds. Weapon expert and related skills cannot apply to this mutation. The blast radius is 1 meter per rank of the mutant. This potent energy attack can be used once per day per rank. If no d30 is present at the table, simply use 3d10 until one can be uncovered.

## Precognitive Reactions 214
Type: **mental mutation**      Usage: **constant**
Strike Value: **+10**      Defense Value: **-10**      Initiative bonus: **+3**

This individual sees actions before they happen, and not only gets a sense of something about to happen, but for a split second sees what those about them are about to do, allowing the character to gain +3 initiative, even from distance attacks such as a sniper's bullet. Whether winning initiative or not, this mutant knows which way to sidestep, dodge or otherwise move in every fight, gaining a -10 defense value bonus, while also knowing what opponents are about to do a fraction of a second beforehand, allowing this gifted mutant +10 strike value with every physical attack mode.

For whatever reason, this gift does not work against incoming mental attacks, nor benefit the mutant's own use of metal mutations, although the initiative bonus still applies.

Because this character sees things an instant before they occur, he or she can transfer the protection to a nearby comrade and either pull or shove them aside at the last second in an attempt to avoid an attack and transfer the -10 DV bonus to a chosen comrade or loved one, sacrificing their own extra protection.

## Psionic Dampening Sphere 215
Type: **mental defense**
Range: **1 meter radius per point of willpower**
Usage: **Once per day per rank**   Duration: **10 rounds per user's rank**
Once a day per rank, this mutant can attempt to unleash an invisible sphere of vibrating energy in a 1 meter radius for every point of current willpower they possess. Within this field, no mental mutations will function. This includes those directed upon the self or of a beneficial nature to the mutant and his or her allies, or if sent from within the sphere beyond the radius of effect, or those mental mutational attacks, communications, influences and intrusions coming from outside the sphere.

Effectively, while this mutation is being used, mental mutations do not exist, even those that affect physical objects such as telekinesis. The sphere will last for either 10 rounds per rank of the mutant, or any duration less as the deviant desires.

Once shut off, the use is 'spent' regardless of whether it was used for the full duration or not. The mutant who employs this power must concentrate on it entirely, take no action of any kind, including dodging physical attacks — therefore only the user's armor protects it from physical harm, and he or she can't rely on any agility DV modifier or the dodge skill or similar movement based defensive measures to avoid taking a bullet.

If the mutant moves, talks, or is struck while employing this mind power, the sphere immediately ceases to function. However, if of higher than first rank, this character may immediately start another use of the power. It should be noted that any deviant deploying this mutation can be moved in a vehicle, picked up and carried by a friendly comrade, or mounted on a horse and so maintain this sphere while on the go.

## Psionic Dead Zone 216
Type: **mental mutation**   Usage: **2 times per day per rank**
Range: **willpower x10m/180 degree zone**
Hazard Check: **Variable, see description**
Similar to the mutation Psionic Dampening Sphere, when activated, and so long as this deviant focuses on the psionic dead zone, this mutant can cover a large area where all mental mutations are potentially nullified. This individual can sense the area affected, although it is invisible to other beings, which can shroud a radius entirely around the user or project the nullification zone ahead, from side to side, or behind itself in a cone-like 180 degree broad front. While focused on this mutation, the user can do nothing but walk at half speed.

The area covered is 10 meters per point of the user's willpower trait, and all those within who try to deploy their own mental mutations suffer a painful ringing in their ears and their attempts to unleash their own mental powers are hindered. Duration maximum use is 1 minute per rank (20 round in a minute).

A willpower based hazard check is allowed for any other mutant attempting their own psionic mutation, and if their willpower is less than the current trait score of one unleashing the dead zone, they require a type E willpower based hazard check. If their willpower is higher than that of this zone creating mutant's willpower trait, then they need only make a Type B willpower based hazard check to deflect this dampening field and unleash their own gift.

This power can be used twice per day per rank. If this mutant is physically struck while focusing on this dead zone, the field is dispersed and the daily usage spent. Many energy mutations such as electrical generation are guided by the mind, but are drawn from internal energies, not the brain, and so may still function. Here is a list of all mental mutations, in alphabetical order, with their mutation number, which are affected by this psionic dead zone:



| | | |
|---|---|---|
| Advanced Mind 3 | Emotion Inducement 168 | Misery Flashback Inducement 204 |
| Age Morphing 149 | Empathy 33 | |
| Agony Sphere 4 | Energy Wall Generation 172 | Molecular Manipulation 205 |
| Amplification 6 | Force Field 38 | Neural Surge 207 |
| Animal Association 150 | Generate Dimensional Horror 186 | Peeling Radius 62 |
| Appearance Morph 151 | | Planer Skip 212 |
| Asphyxiation Zone 9 | Heal Touch 43 | Plasma Sphere Projection 213 |
| Aura of Protection 10 | Heat Pulse 44 | Precognitive Reactions 214 |
| Blurred Movement 16 | Illusion Generation 189 | Psionic Dampening Sphere 215 |
| Bravery Inducement 153 | Illusionary Concealment 190 | Psionic Dead Zone 216 |
| Coma Inducement 22 | Image Multiplication 47 | Psionic Sight 217 |
| Contact Healing 156 | Image Projection 48 | Psionic Strike 218 |
| Devastator Pulse 25 | Imbue Prowess 191 | Radiation Detection 67 |
| Dimension Hole 158 | Light Burst 51 | Sandblaster 222 |
| Dimensional Awareness 159 | Lost and Found 195 | Sense Transfer 225 |
| Dimensional Blade 160 | Mental Counter Attack 196 | Sub-Plane Leap 231 |
| Dimensional Retreat 161 | Mental Dominion 197 | Telekinesis 84 |
| Dimensional Shell 162 | Mental Mine 54 | Telekinetic Flight 233 |
| Discern Dimensional Entities 163 | Mental Screen 55 | Telekinetic Junk Shield 234 |
| Displacement 26 | Mental Stun 198 | Telekinetic Mangle 235 |
| Dome of Energy 164 | Mind Crush 56 | Telepathy 85 |
| Doom Sphere 27 | Mind Unification 202 | Thought Share 237 |
| Dread Zone 28 | Mind Waste 57 | Transform Weather 239 |
| Earth Thump 29 | | |

## Psionic Sight 217
Type: **physical mutation**
Range: **6 meters**
Usage: **constant**
Initiative within 6m: **+2**

This mutant has an organ in her head that gives her the ability to detect both her surroundings and other beings within 6 meters, even in total darkness or when her eyes are blinded or blindfolded. She sees an impression of her location and the relationship of beings nearby as ghostly figures. She can detect invisible or dimensional beings in this range, and see holograms for what they really are — which appear as static filled forms instead of the solid shapes of truly physical beings and robots, floors or furniture.

This mutant can also see a corona of orange light surround the head of any person or animal that actively uses a mental mutation — even a purely benign mutation such as heal touch or telepathy, although the subject must still be within the six meter area of effect. If forced to fight blind in melee, this PC suffers no penalties, while in everyday interactions, she gains +2 initiative when encountering others within 6m or less (6m = 19'8" so 20 feet).

## Psionic Strike 218
Type: **Mental mutation**   Usage: **2 times per day per rank**
Range: **Willpower in meters x2**
Hazard Check: **Type D intelligence to avoid INT DMG/ Type E willpower HC to avoid unconsciouses if reduced to 0 or less INT**
Damage: **1d12 intelligence**
Duration of stupefied state: **100 minutes minus victim's willpower to minimum of 10 minutes**

Twice a day per rank, this mutant can target an opponent within sight and at a distance of no further than double the user's willpower in meters, and form an invisible bolt of psionic energy and fire it at the brain of the organic target. The subject is allowed a Type D intelligence based hazard check or suffer 1d12 intelligence damage.

If reduced to zero of less INT, the subject must make a willpower based type E hazard check or drop unconscious for 3d20 minutes. If able to make the hazard check, the subject is reduced to 1 point of intelligence and dumbfounded. They have no access to any mental mutations, temporarily forget their objective, their own name, and the difference between comrades and enemies. In this drooling, half witted state, the victim will drop anything it is holding — including a rope or the rungs of a ladder — and merely wander off to find some shadowy place to sit down and mutter nonsense.

This stupefied state lasts for 100 minutes, minus the victim's willpower in minutes to a minimum of 10 minutes. When either unconscious or stupefied, the subject will regain intelligence points at a rate of 1 per minute thereafter.

## Pulse Eyes 219
Type: **physical energy attack**   Range: **double user's willpower in meters**
Usage: **2 bursts per day per rank**        Rate: **4 pulses per burst**
Strike Value: **+10**   Damage: **1d12 each**
Much like the mutation, Beam Eyes, this mutation fires 4 orange laser pulses from the character's eyes, per burst, with a usage rate of 2 bursts per rank per day. The range is double the mutant's willpower in meters and each pulse will inflict 1d12 damage on a hit, with a strike roll made for each pulse. If blindfolded, or if the user wears a visor of any kind, this mutation, like all optical attacks, will not function.

## Quill Thrower Limb 220
Type: **physical attack, ranged or club in melee**
Range: **as half mutant's strength score in meters (rounded up), or melee as club**
Usage: **20+3d6 quills initial max, 1d6 regrow per day**
Rate of fire: **1d6 per round**   Defense Value: **-5 Bonus**
Strike Value: **+5**   Damage: **1d6 each quill, or as a club 1d12+2**
This appendage grows from a random body location on a jointed, somewhat flexible arm-like limb. Unlike the much more lethal Spine Thrower, which replaces an arm, this appendage grows as an extra appendage from the upper body.

The launcher exhibits a mass of quills at various stages of development, with those near the rear being mere bony bumps, growing more spike-like as they emerge closer to the business end of this effective missile appendage. The hardened, black quills on the end of the thrower are about a finger in length, can fire half the mutant's strength score in meters and each inflicts 1d6 damage on a strike, plus any strength modifiers the mutant may have.

This appendage can also be used as an additional melee attack to bludgeon opponents in close quarters with a wallop from this growth inflicting a base of 1d12+2 damage (with strength and weapon expert skill points applied to it— with the same weapon expert application for both throwing quills or as a mace). The mutant will instinctively raises this growth up defensively during a fight, although even while resting, the shield-like, sinewy, bone studded appendage yields the mutant a -5 defense value bonus.

When used as either a club or a shooter, the strike value bonus is +5 SV, although one's accuracy trait modifier does apply. The mutant fires 1d6 quills per round.

The quills grow rapidly, with the maximum available per individual mutant being set at of 20+3d6 (established at the start of game play and serves as the maximum number available when fully grown), with another 1d6 growing per day to replace lost already fired quills. Growth ceases when the mutant's maximum allowable are grown in. Should the mutant wish to wear advanced relic armor (including combat armor) this growth must be permanently cut off, and the wound cauterized.

This mutant will normally exhibit only one of these throwers, however there is a 1 in 10 chance that a second thrower is featured on this freak. Each of these growths weigh 20kg, and for each, an appearance drop of -5 is applied. Roll on the following table to determine where the thrower grows on the body:

| Roll 2d6 | Quill Thrower Growth Location |
| --- | --- |
| 2. | From the belly |
| 3. | From the chest between the breast |
| 4-6. | Beneath the right arm |
| 7-9. | Beneath the left arm |
| 10. | On the upper right shoulder |
| 11. | On upper left shoulder |
| 12. | In center of upper back |

## Razor Hook 221
Type: **physical attack**   Range: **melee**
Rate: **1 per hook**   Strike Value: **+15**   Damage: **1d20+3**
This mutant has one or more hands ending in long sickle shaped hooks of abnormally dense bone. Having the strength of steel and an inner blade edge to match. The mutant's non-dominant hand always ends in one hook, with a 3% chance per each other hand also ending in a lethal hooked blade. These limbs are +15 strike value, inflict 1d20+3 base damage each, and if more than one is present, are considered combined attacks; thus, a mutant with two hands ending in razor hooks can attack twice per round.

These hooks are blunt on the outer edge and can inflict sun damage if the mutant desires, while the lethally sharp inner edge of these scythe-like appendages can have a steel and leather covering wrapped about them to allow the mutant to avoid damaging oneself while asleep, or else hold the reins of horse, carry gear, support the foregrip of a rifle, crossbow, or pump shotgun, or slide along a rope without cutting it. These hooks are great for climbing, and add +1 to climbing skill per hook. Considered unsightly by human standards, each hook hand reduces the character's appearance by -4 APP.

## Sandblaster *by Brutorz Bill* 222

Type: **mental mutation**     Range: **1m per 3 points of willpower**
Duration: **1 round per rank**     Usage: **Twice per day per rank**
Strike Value: **+22**     Damage: **2d4 per round**
Defense Value: **-16 vs missile weapons**

Twice a day per rank, this mutant can whip up sheets of sand, grit, crushed glass, bone fragments, pebbles and spent shell casings and fling it at a specific target or clustered group with great force, stripping away paint, rust and flesh. The range is 1 meter away for every three points of willpower this deviant possesses, rounded down; example, Kalli the Freak has 47 willpower ÷3 =15.6 or 15 meters range.

This sand blasting gust can be continuously discharged for 1 round per rank of the mutant deploying it, or described another way: one back-to-back attack per round per rank of the mutant. The grit storm has a strike value bonus of +22 SV and on a hit inflicts 2d4 damage to any machine, robotic, plant, structure or living being or group of three man-sized beings if they are packed close together in battle formation, in a line, or huddled together at a table.

Besides being an offensive weapon, this whipped up debris can be used to partially conceal and partially block the mutant from incoming missile fire, and improve the mutant's defense value from a frontal attack by -16 DV.

While all the uses for a hail of biting particles and intense, unexpected wind is only limited by the mutant's imagination, some other applications are to use the gust portion of this attack mode to blow away toxic gas clouds, clear fog ahead of an airship or boat, keep back a brush fire, deter wild animals from getting any closer, frighten hostile villagers, fan a fire to blow toward one's enemies, and throw back a swarm of killer bees.

## Sarcophagus Cocoon 223

Type: **physical mutation**     Usage: **Once per month per rank**
Duration: **Until healing is complete or 1 day per user's willpower trait**
Defense Value: **-36**
Endurance of Cocoon: **x2 mutant's uninjured trait value**

If this mutant becomes severely ill, or damaged so badly that they are as good as dead, they'll enter a stasis mode and self mummify. Likewise, when this character is reduced to the status of 'Incapacitated and Dying' shown on table TME-2-11 Injury and Death on page 111 of the hub rules, then this process also kicks in. The mutant can also choose to enter this state if they realize they've been poisoned, about to endure an unsurvivable junk storm, famine, or some other peril that the individual hopes they can better survive by hibernating in an armored husk.

Once initiated, the deviant becomes unconscious and rigid. From special glands in the skin, a waxy resin will exude and encase the entire body, hardening like a 5cm thick egg shell, yet looking more like cartilage — a process that takes 30+1d20 minutes. This living shell will breath for the inert mutant and allow them to heal and double their normal daily healing rate.

The subject is immobilized while in the sarcophagus, and only gain mobility when at full trait points. While in this robust sarcophagus, the mutant can use mental mutations, if it has any, although can neither see nor hear what is happening outside the shell. If it has telepathy, it can at least communicate with comrades outside its sheath.

The sarcophagus acts like armor, as well as a nourishing insulator, and is DV -36 and has its own endurance score which is double the mutant's uninjured trait value. When recovery is complete, the cocoon splits and allows the deviant to emerge.

This potent mutation can only be used once per month per rank. If submerged in water or exposed to the vacuum of space, the hibernating person will suffer 1d6 damage per minute until either dying or being rescued. This cocoon is immune to normal fire, extremes of hot and cold weather, and can be buried in sand, loose soil, or vegetation without harming the occupant, and easily allows the coffin-like sheath to be hidden. Should the mutant initiate this process without being severely injured — such as to conceal itself and endure a long siege or other calamity — they may maintain the sarcophagus hibernation for up to 1 day per point of willpower.

Common people who learn of or witness this mutant's ability to encase itself in a hard shell and emerge fully healed days or even months later, might consider the deviant to be some sort of otherworldly demon or mythical vampire, and drive out or kill the freak.

## Seasonal Enhancement 224

Type: **temporary physical enhancement**
Duration: **24 hours**
Defense Value: bonus **-10 to be hit**
Strike Value: bonus **+10**
Damage: **+5 with all physical strikes**
Hazard Check: **nil**

During one season each year, this mutant blossoms to the height of health, prowess, confidence, and inner clarity, as well as relative beauty. He or she temporarily gains +10 to each trait, adding any modifiers as required, including potential damage bonuses from increased strength to the + 5 DMG already noted. In addition, this enhancement will heal back any so-called 'permanent' trait value losses from the previous year, while any lost limbs or eyes will miraculously grow back over the season. Likewise, any insanity brought about by poison or mental attacks will suddenly be cured, as will diseases, larval infestations, parasites, radiation sickness and such.

About the only two complications to this mutation are that the character will be in 'rut' or 'heat' during this season and twice as frisky. Secondly, when the season ends, he or she will appear depressed and moody, drab, and a little boring to companions.

**Roll 1d12** to determine a month, whatever season the month falls in, is the season of enhancement for this character:

1. December/ 2. January/ 3. February/ (**Winter Season**)
4. March/ 5. April/ 6. May (**Spring Season**)
7. June/ 8. July / 9. August (**Summer Season**)
10. September  / 11. October/12. November (**Fall Season**)

## Sense Transfer *by Azaria Wagner* 225

Type: **mental mutation**     Range: **melee**
Usage: **twice per day per rank**
Hazard Check: **Unwilling targets allowed type D INT based HC to avoid transfer. Type E willpower HC allowed to avoid passing out if sense of touch transfered during torture.**

Related to the mutation 'Heightened Senses', this deviant has an uncanny ability to touch somebody's bare skin and shut off their own senses to transfer them to the chosen subject and improve their senses. For example, the user shuts off her vision to give a teammate better eyesight, or transfers their sense of touch to make someone else feel extreme pleasure, or else pain from their wounds to either interrogate, punish or incapacitate the subject. Such a dou-

bling of pain is enough to make many beings pass out, and require a type E willpower based hazard check to stay conscious. Those knocked out will remain so for 10+3d6 minutes.

In short, sense transfer doubles any one sense in those touched, although for those who want to resist this transfer, they are allowed an intelligence based type D hazard check. The mutant who transfers its sense must maintain physical contact with the subject, and the duration of the transfer is one round per point of the transferring deviant's willpower. Thoughts cannot be transferred, too, unless this mutant also has the telepathy mutation, while emotions can be transferred and doubled should this character also have the empathy mutation.

This power can be used twice per day per rank.

## Slime Excretion 226

Type: **physical mutation**
Range: **Self**
Usage: **3 times per day, plus 1 extra usage at 4th rank, and each 4 higher**

Normally, this mutant appears to have a slight sheen, as if mildly perspiring or wearing some sort of glossy body lotion. At will, however, she can spend 2 rounds excreting highly slippery slime from her pours. On the third round, this mutant is 50% likely to squish free on its first attempt if being grappled, when the grasper is unsuspecting of the oozy character, and 20% likely each round thereafter if still held.

The slime remains on the deviant until it is rubbed off on rags. Other uses for this slippery coating are when swimming, where the mutant is far more sleek and cuts through the water at double its normal swimming speed. Another potentially life saving application is to secrete this slime when coated in acid or engulfed in flame, as this substance will protect the skin of the mutant from burning from the 3rd round onward — although the deviant's gear, clothing and hair might not fare so well. This excretion can be used three times per day, plus one extra time at 4th rank, 8th rank, 12th rank and each additional 4 ranks.

## Snake Tongue 227

Type: **physical mutation**
Usage: **whenever desired**
Trait Modifiers: **+1 initiative and -d3 APP**

This mutant can taste chemicals and scents in the air, notice the direction of heat sources, and detect subtle vibrations. All together, this character's sense of smell is twice as effective as a regular person or member of its species, and has an increased awareness of their immediate surroundings and thus gains +1 initiative.

Beyond the benefits of an improved reaction time, this mutant can flicker its elongated, forked tongue and taste any chemical or scent they have previously encountered. Like a bloodhound, they have a 77% chance of being able to accurately pick up the specific smell of a familiar person within 100m. Besides being able

to discern the scent of a companion or some person who has spent at least ten minutes in this mutant's presence, this character can inhale the scent off fabric and try to accurately taste the air and pick up the trial of whoever last wore a garment.

Any character with this mutation and the tracking skill gains an extra 1d2 skill points in tracking.

Although the mutant can keep this tongue in his or her mouth when near squeamish strangers — such as those who hate mutants — whenever this appendage is revealed, some onlookers might be horrified. There is only a slight -d3 APP penalty for this mutation.

## Spike Thrower Arm 228

Type: **physical attack**     Range: **melee club or 1 meter per point of STR**
Usage/Rate: **Between 1 and 10  per day**  Strike Value: **+7**
Damage: **As club 3d8, or each spike fired 1d12 each; plus strength modifiers**
Defense Value: **-7**

The deviant's non-dominant arm is over muscled and ends in a bristling array of bone spikes. This mutation is similar to a quill thrower limb but much heavier, has far greater range, does more damage but 78% of the time entirely replaces the arm and so the deviant loses one hand. In cases where a hand has managed to exist (roll 79-00 on the previous a d% roll), the bulging spike array has grown all over the forearm and allows the user to wield two handed weapons, drive a dirt bike and perform all the functions of a regular hand.

Although each spike takes a month to regrow, move forward and become ready to fire, they are constantly growing as long as the mutant is getting regular feedings, complete with plenty of calcium in his or her diet. This mutant can shoot up to 10 darts per day, all at once or in any amount per round as long as not more than 10 per day are fired. They have a range in meters equal to the deviant's strength score, have a strike value bonus of +7, inflict 1d12 damage each and, like other offensive mutations, can have the weapon expert skill applied. Strength modifiers apply to the damage for each dart (but not again to range), which makes this a very lethal appendage when growing from a mighty character.

In melee combat, this growth can serve as a brutally effective, morning-star like club to smash and stab at opponents, also gaining +7 SV and inflicting 3d8 damage plus any strength modifiers. This bone studded growth also serves as a crude shield against both melee and ranged incoming attacks, and improves the mutant's defense value by -7. This knob and spike covered bulky limb is unsightly as far as traditional human standards of beauty go, therefore drop the deviant's appearance by -d6+2 trait points.

## Stinger Spike 229

Type: **physical attack**     Range: **melee**
Usage: **4 injections per day**     Rate: **1**
Surprise Initiative Bonus: **+4 Initiative**
Strike Value: **+14 on surprise otherwise +4 SV**
Damage: **1d12+venom**
Hazard Check: **By venom type, see table, next page.**

This hollow, deadly sharp horn either appears as a multi-jointed arm that grows from the back and can extend 100+1d100cm (roll at character generation), or from within the mutant's forearm and, when needed, can be extended up through a small, scar-like pocket near the wrist and thrust into an opponent. 70% of the time this extra stinger arm occurs, which adds an extra melee attack and is lethal even when all 4 doses of venom are expended, otherwise it is a wrist enclosed, hidden spike.

This venom filled spike but can be deployed and make the first attack all in one motion. On its initial appearance in a non-combat interaction — such as during conversation at a saloon — this fearsome appendage is given a +4 initiative and +14 bonus when first appearing to those who don't know of the horrific growth's presence. On a follow up attack, no extra initiative bonus is applied.

50% of the time this mutation occurs in the left firearm, otherwise the right limb. When not thrust outward, it is completely hidden. When not exposed during a surprise attack, this spike has a strike value bonus of +4 and inflicts d12 base damage before any strength or skill modifiers are applied.

The venom type in the spike is determined at character generation and remains the same throughout the individual's life. This substance can be coated on arrows, blades and spears, etc., although once a strike is made by the weapon, it is wiped off — and likely seeps into the victim's wound.

## Stinger Spike Venom Table

| 1d10 | Venom Type | Hazard Check | Duration & Consequences |
|---|---|---|---|
| 1,2. | Weakness | Type C Endurance | For 6d6 minutes, this victim is at half all traits (except endurance), plus half movement rate, and suffers 50% drop to all physical strike values and strength based damage amounts inflicted on others. Likewise, all mutational ranges, strike values, damages and other factors are also reduced by half, including for mental and energy mutations. |
| 3,4. | Sleep | Type D Endurance | The subject drops unconscious for 3d6 minutes. While asleep, they are +80 SV easier to strike and can often be killed outright; GM's prerogative permitting. |
| 5,6. | Sickness | Type E Endurance | This victim grows deathly ill, drops to their hands and knees and vomits for 3d6 minutes, and thereafter suffers chills and a fever for the next 3d6 hours. Besides having the lowest morale, he or she is reduced to half their normal movement rate and strike values for all physical attack modes. |
| 7,8. | Hallucination | Type D Intelligence | Victim suffers 1d6 random hallucinations, each lasts 3d6 minutes. See page 251 of this book for a sample random hallucination. Hallucinating victims are +30 SV easier to strike and, in most cases, abandon the fight altogether and pay no attention to this mutant and his or her companions. |
| 9. | Paralysis | Type E Endurance | Those who succumb to this venom drop to the ground and cannot control their body, although can still see, hear, taste and feel everything that happens to them for the 3d6 minute duration of this venom. An immobilized victim is +80 to be struck while suffering from this toxin. This victim can still use mental mutations. |
| 10. | Death | Type D Endurance | First, the victim drops in to a coma for 3d6 minutes. If an anti-toxin injector is or other relic is not administered, or a medic doesn't successfully suck out the venom, then this subject is forced to make another type D endurance based hazard check per hour thereafter, for six consecutive hours, or suffer heart failure and die. If after surviving this 6 hour period, the victim is automatically suffers from weakness venom, noted above, for 3d6 additional hours. |

## Sub-Headedness 230
Type: **physical alteration**

One or more diminutive, subordinate heads of half the size of the character's prime head are fused to the body in a most gruesome manner. These underdeveloped heads grow at randomly generated locations and have 1d4 attributes each. Because of the reaction these heads illicit on unsuspecting viewers, an appearance penalty of -1d4+3 results from each sub-head present — although if these heads are covered, the mutant's unaffected APP value is instead used for reactions by others.

Generate a random personality for each head (page 500), as well as trait values for intelligence, willpower, and facial appearance.

While the mutant's prime head has full control of their body, the character might not get along with one or more of the sub heads. Should the prime head be incapacitated, decapitated, or killed such as from a mental attack or sniper's bullet, the remaining sub-heads will take over, with the owner of the highest willpower wrestling control over the host body within 3d6 rounds.

The removal of an unwanted or irksome sub-head is dangerous, as the large arteries supporting the head are vital and could lead to immense blood loss and death of the host. Removal forces an endurance based type E hazard check to survive the procedure, or, if a medic is present, a type B check must be made to avoid the death of the host.

| 1d6 | Sub-Heads Present |
|---|---|
| 1,2. | One sub-head |
| 3,4. | Two sub-heads |
| 5. | Three sub-heads |
| 6. | Two +1d4 sub-heads |

| 1d20 | Location of Sub-Head |
|---|---|
| 1,2. | Shoulder |
| 3,4. | Neck |
| 5,6. | Back of prime head |
| 7,8. | Side of prime head |
| 9. | Upper back |
| 10. | Lower back. |
| 11. | Chest |
| 12. | Belly |
| 13. | Buttocks |
| 14. | Groin |
| 15. | Forehead |
| 16. | Upper arm |
| 17. | Lower arm |
| 18. | Thigh |
| 19. | Arm pit |
| 20. | Hip |

| 1d100 | Sub-Head Attributes 1d4 per head, re-roll duplicated results |
|---|---|
| 01-06. | Highly intelligent (80+2d20) |
| 07-13. | Incredible willpower (80+2d20) |
| 14. | Mutation, Acid Spit (no.2/ page TME-60, Hub Rules) |
| 15. | Mutation, Beam Eyes (no.13/ page TME-61, Hub Rules) |
| 16. | Mutation, Gaping Maw (no.42/ page TME-67, Hub Rules) |
| 17. | Mutation, Mandibles (no.53/ page TME-69, Hub Rules) |
| 18. | Mutation, Flame Breath (no.37/ page TME-66, Hub Rules) |
| 19. | Mutation, Electro-Magnetic Pulse (no.32/ page TME-65, Hub Rules) |
| 20, 21. | Mutation, Radiation Detection (no.67/ page TME-72, Hub Rules) |
| 22. | Mutation, Advanced Mind (no.3/ page TME-60, Hub Rules) |
| 23. | Mutation, Radioactive Pulse (no.68/ page TME-72, Hub Rules) |
| 24. | Mutation, Beak (no.12/ page TME-61, Hub Rules) |
| 25. | Mutation, Eye-Lights (minor mutation no.92/ page TME-77, Hub Rules) |
| 26, 27. | Mutation, Fanged (no.36/ page TME-65, Hub Rules) |
| 28, 29. | Mutation, Poison Bite (no.63/ page TME-71, Hub Rules) |
| 30. | Mutation, Mental Screen (no.55/ page TME-70, Hub Rules) |
| 31,32. | Mutation, Night Vision (no.61/ page TME-71, Hub Rules) |
| 33. | Mutation, Stalked Eyes (no.79/ page TME-74, Hub Rules) |
| 34. | Homing Sense (minor mutation / no.264/ this book on page XR-281) |
| 35. | Inner Clock (minor mutation / no.265/ this book on page XR-281) |
| 36. | Internal Compass (minor mutation / no.266/ this book on page XR-281) |
| 37. | Power Detection (minor mutation / no.274/ this book on page XR-283) |
| 38-40. | Minor Radio Reception (minor mutation / no.276/ this book on page XR-282) |
| 41. | Dimension Hole (no.158/ this book on page XR-238) |
| 42. | Dimensional Acumen (no.159/ this book on page XR-240) |
| 43. | Dimensional Retreat (no.161/ this book on page XR-240) |
| 44. | Dimensional Shell (no.162/ this book on page XR-241) |
| 45,46. | Discern Dimensional Entities (no.163/ this book on page XR-241) |
| 47. | Echolocation (no.165/ this book on page XR-242) |
| 48. | Emotion Inducement (no.168/ this book on page XR-243) |
| 49. | Energy Wall Generation (no.172/ this book on page XR-244) |
| 50. | Frequency Receptors (no.183/ this book on page XR-247) |
| 51. | Generate Dimensional Horror (no.186/ this book on page XR-249) |
| 52. | Illusion Generation (no.189/ this book on page XR-250) |
| 53. | Illusionary Concealment (no.190/ this book on page XR-252) |
| 54. | Lost and Found (no.195/ this book on page XR-254) |
| 55. | Mental Counter Attack (no.196/ this book on page XR-254) |
| 56. | Mental Dominion (no.197/ this book on page XR-254) |
| 57. | Mental Stun (no.198/ this book on page XR-255) |
| 58. | Microwave Generation (no.201/ this book on page XR-256) |
| 59. | Mind Unification (no.202/ this book on page XR-256) |
| 60. | Misery Flashback Inducement (no.204/ this book on page XR-257) |
| 61,62. | Nocturnal (no.208/ this book on page XR-258) |
| 63. | Phlegm Sheet Spitter (no.211/ this book on page XR-259) |
| 64. | Planer Skip (no.212/ this book on page XR-260) |
| 65. | Psionic Dampening Sphere (no.215/ this book on page XR-261) |
| 66. | Pulse Eyes (no.219/ this book on page XR-262) |
| 67. | Thought Share (no.237/ this book on page XR-269) |
| 68. | Voice Mimicry (no.244/ this book on page XR-276) |
| 69. | Snake Tongue (no.227/ this book on page XR-264) |
| 70. | Sub-Plane Leap (no.231/ this book on this page) |
| 71-73. | Third Eye (no.236/ this book on page XR-269) |
| 74. | Tri-Segmented Jaw (no.244/ this book on page XR-273) |
| 75,76. | Precognitive Reactions (no.214/ this book on page XR-260) |
| 77. | Dome of Energy (no.164/ this book on page XR-241) |
| 78. | Molecular Manipulation (no.205/ this book on page XR-257) |
| 79. | Transform Weather (no.239/ this book on page XR-271) |
| 80-83. | Four Eyes (no.182/ this book on page XR-247) |
| 84-90. | Mind Crush (no.55/ page TME-70, Hub Rules) |
| 91,92. | No eyes* |
| 93,94. | No mouth* |
| 95,96. | No ears* |
| 97,98. | No nose* |
| 99,00. | Detachable organism, treat body as domestic cat, movement 4m |

** unless a mutation requires this attribute to function*

## Sub-Plane Leap 231

Type: **mental defense**  Range: **user**
Usage: **once a day per rank**  Duration: **willpower based, see below**
Defense Value: **Immunity to non-energy based attacks. Gains -20 DV from beam and other energy weapons. No special defense against mental attacks.**

By manipulating their molecular structure, this incredible mutant can become non-physical, yet remain on the current plane in the current time, and continue to be partially visible. The character becomes a flash of vivid white light and can move at double speed, use only beam based relics or mutations, or else mental attacks on those about them and become immune to many forms of physical attack. Only beam based weapons and dimensional beings can harm the character in this state, who gains a bonus of −20 DV because of the speed at which the character can run and dodge, against even these forms of attack. Incoming mental attacks and intrusions can still harm the deviant during a sub-plan leap as per normal.

Dimensional beings, however, are no longer immune to the character's own physical attacks while the mutant is in this mode, being simultaneously on the dimensional creature's plane of reality. In short, while moving on the sub-plane level, the user can use his or her relic weapons, physical mutations, or any other weapons against dimensional opponents, including standard cut and thrust weapons like axes and machetes.

The duration of each session depends on the user's current willpower trait value according to the following table.

| User's Willpower | Duration of Sub-Plane Leap |
|---|---|
| below 20 | 2d4 rounds |
| 20-42 | 3d10 rounds |
| 43-65 | 2d10+10 rounds |
| 66-87 | 2d10+15 rounds |
| 88-104 | 2d10+20 rounds |
| 105 and above | 2d10+30 rounds |

## Sword Arm 232

Type: **physical mutation**
Range: **melee as extra attack**
Rate: **1**
Strike Value: **+10**
Damage: **1d20+5**

The mutant's secondary off-hand arm is a well muscled, elongated cut and thrust weapon. From about the wrist down, it's a 40+1d20cm long serrated bone blade of incredible strength and keenness. In melee combat, this appendage can be used as an additional, non-off-hand (no SV penalty) attack, doing 1d20+5 damage (plus any weapon skill or strength modifiers). The strike value of this blade is likewise +10 SV plus skill and accuracy trait modifiers. It is, however, considered somewhat horrific, and so this limb reduces the mutant's appearance value by -2d4.

## Telekinetic Flight 233

Type: **mental mutation**     Range: **self**
Usage: **Twice per day per rank**     Movement Rate: **Variable, see table below**

The ability to employ telekinesis to lift oneself off the ground and even move around is one of the most remarkable feats any mutant being can possess, and one which might well lead superstitious commoners to deem the user as either a deity, angelic being, or a demonic miscreation depending on the flyer's appearance and deeds.

The mutant's willpower, not their rank, determine the duration of their flight, as well as elevation, distance traveled, or if the deviant can speak, use weapons or other mutations while aloft.

The character can deploy this power twice per day per their rank. While hovering or flying, if they are struck and suffer unconsciouses or any critical hit, the deviant will lose focus on the flight and plummet to earth. Any falling flyer might easily meet their doom from such a fall, with the details for falling covered on page 123 of the Hub Rules.

The Flight Duration, which is random, means the telepathic flyer either stays aloft or travels for that random duration and at the end of it, can't maintain their elevation anymore and descends until setting down on the ground,

water surface or whatever other material is below them, regardless of how far down the drop is. Likewise, if a character falls from an airship's deck or off a cliff, they can employ this mutation to float down, feet first, until reaching the bottom instead of plummeting to their death like their less gifted comrades.

The Maximum Elevation or surface ceiling is the distance in meters the character can fly above solid ground or liquid, but includes dense foliage like a forest canopy, or other more-or-less solid objects like tumbled ruins, the rooftops of a village, and the like.

In-flight actions are those things the mutant can do while in the air. All actions listed for those mutants of lesser willpower are also available to the flyer.

| Character's Willpower | Flight Duration* | Move | Maximum Elevation | In-Flight Actions |
|---|---|---|---|---|
| 01-05 | 2d6 rounds | 3m | 1 meter per point of WILL | Can barely focus on flight. Can't hear companions. |
| 06-10 | 6+1d6 rounds | 4m | 2 meters per point of WILL | Can do nothing but focus on flight. |
| 11-20 | 10+1d10 rounds | 5m | 3 meters per point of WILL | Can talk or shout, but do nothing else. |
| 21-40 | 20+1d20 rounds | 6m | 4 meters per point of WILL | Can use one handed weapons or device like a communicator, pistol, or drop a rock |
| 41-60 | 40+1d100 rounds | 9m | 6 meters per point of WILL | Can use two handed physical weapons |
| 61-90 | 6+3d6 minutes | 12m | 10 meters per point of WILL | Can use mental mutations |
| 91-130 | 10+1d20 minutes | 15m | 15 meters per point of WILL | Can carry a being or cargo weighing half or less of their own body weight. |
| 131-150 | 30+1d100 minutes | 20m | 20 meters per point of WILL | Can carry a being of equal or less of its own body weight |
| Over 150 | 6 hours +3d20 minutes | 25m | 100 meters per point of WILL | Can do aerial acrobatics likes loops, dives, spins and evade incoming fire with a DV bonus of -30 |

*Roll duration for each flight.
Note: there are 20 rounds in a minute          1 meter = 3 feet
1000 meters = 1 kilometer          A mile = 1.6 Kilometers

This is a mental mutation which works solely on the user. One peril to anyone using this power is if they fly into the sphere around another mutant who is using the mutation of Psionic Dampening Sphere, number 215 on page 261 of this book. This field is invisible, and if a hovering mutant enters it, feels a shuttering and imminent failure of its flight. The flyer must make a Type C willpower based hazard check, each round that they stay within the field, or else lose control of the telekinetic flight and drop out of the sky. If the mutant has extra uses of this mutation for that day, they can initiate another occurrence and save themselves from impacting the ground.

## Telekinetic Junk Shield 234

Type: **mental mutation**          Usage: **2 times per day per rank**
Duration: **1 round per 5 points of user willpower, unless mutant takes 5 or more damage, then shield fails**
Shield Defense Value: **-50 DV**     Shield Endurance: **10 END**
Hurl Shield Debris: **Range half user's willpower in meters, SV 01-70, DMG 3d6**

Twice per day per rank, this mutant can stop in its tracks and extend its hands or other appendages about it and telekinetically dislodge and lift junk and other debris. This mass of trash will churn about in a slow whirlwind around it. The duration of this protective barrier is 1 round for every 5 points of the mutant's current willpower trait, rounded down. For example, a mutant with 36 willpower can use this power for 7 rounds (36 ÷ 5 = 7, discarding the spare 1).

These flying objects — which could also be branches, rocks, boxes, sacks, bones or other heavy, skull or book sized materials — are interlaced with gold colored light which seems to bind them together in a sort of cone about the mutant. While in effect, this mutant can do nothing but concentrate on the swirling junk, yet enjoys excellent protection from both physical and energy attacks such as from laser pistols, electrical bolts, and related mutational assaults, as well as radius area attacks such as those from land mines and grenades.

The shield has a defense value of -50, and any strike on it must inflict 10 or more damage to pass through and must make another attack roll on the mutant as usual to potentially harm the deviant. If harmed for 5 or more damage, the mutant loses concentration and the remainder of the daily use ends.

At any time while the swirling junk shield roars around the mutant, they can elect to thrust out with its arms and hurl the mass of flying debris toward up to four man sized targets should they be clustered within a 6 meter wide or deep formation, and attack them with this junk storm: range half the user's willpower in meters, SV 01-70, damage 3d6.

## Telekinetic Mangle 235

Type: **mental assault**          Range: **1m per point of willpower**
Usage: **twice per day per rank**     Rate: **1**
Strike Value: **01-60 plus willpower mods as if Accuracy**
Damage: **1d10 per round once locked on + chance of permanent ill health**
Hazard Check: **Victim must make a Type C willpower based HC or suffer random additional harm, per round**

Also called Mind Mangle, this extremely powerful mental assault allows the mutant to focus on both living and non-living objects, including robots, vehicles and inanimate objects such as doors and walls, and telepathically assail them. There is no way to tone down this power to allow the user to gently manipulate or move things. Instead, it is only capable of murderous destruction.

When initiated, the mutant must focus entirely on the subject and have no other objects or living beings between them and what they want torn asunder. The assailant can walk at half their maximum movement rate but must focus entirely on wielding the power and cannot speak or do anything else while deploying this mental attack. If the user is harmed or shoved or its view of the targets is blocked, the session ends and a new lock on the target must be reacquired.

Although a mental attack, the results are purely physical and conducted as a regular attack. The user's willpower is treated like the accuracy trait (see table TME-1-3, page 10 of the hub rules or page 8 of this book) and any strike value modifier applied to a base 01-60 attack roll. This attack roll only ever changes if the mutant's willpower changes, and cannot be modified by rank gain, skills, or other means. Although the target may use any agility or dodge skill defense value benefits to try to leap aside and avoid getting struck by this willpower based strike, armor has no effect against this vicious assault — unless it also has a force field which will entirely block this power. Indeed, this power cannot accost those either behind a wall of energy, within a Psionic Dampening Sphere or force field of any kind.

For those not protected by an energy shield or able to use speed and agility to avoid it, this body wrenching assault passes though all non-energy based defenses and once it locks onto an object or living being, mutilates the subject repeatedly so long as the user focuses on the target, including moving targets.

This power can also harm dimensional beings who suffer double damage from this cruel embrace.

Once locked on after a successful 'hit', this mangle attack disrupts and shreds the target for 1d10 lethal damage per round. The victim can continue to move, shoot, fight or try to flee out of the mangler's range, while any hit on the user of this power breaks the lock and no further damage or serious harm befalls the victim so long as the mind mangler doesn't succeed at a follow-up attack.

For every round that a living being is mangled, the unfortunate must make an additional willpower based Type C hazard check or suffer some secondary harm. The following table presents a listing for harm befalling organic humanoid victims; the GM might need to re-roll or craft other long term damage to robots, animals, structures, or vehicles beyond mere damage.

*Additional harm from Telepathic Mangle Attack* Roll 1d100*
**Once per round of successful mangle. Victim allowed a Type C willpower based hazard check to avoid. For parts with two of the same appendages on the body, such as ankles or arm, roll **1d6** with **1-3** meaning right appendage and **4-6** left appendage.*

**01-05.** Sprained wrist: hand almost useless and can't lift anything heavier than a kilogram for 10+3d8 days.

**06-10.** Sprained ankle: limp and suffer a 25% loss of movement for 10+3d8 days.

**11-16.** Dislocated shoulder: besides terrible pain, arm useless until popped back into place by a comrade and then sore for 3d6 days.

**17-22.** Broken arm: can't use arm for 4+1d4 months.

**23-27.** Broken foot: half movement for 3+1d3 months.

**28-34.** Broken hand: unable to use hand for 3+1d3 months.

**35-40.** Broken shin: half speed for 4+1d4 months.

**41-45.** Broken thigh bone: half speed for 5+1d6 months.

**46-50.** Permanent linear scars across entire body: suffer -3d6 APP.

**51-55.** Scalp shredded and 50% loss of hair: scar tissue results in permanent -2d6 APP.

**56-60.** Head crushed: brain damage with a -2d6 loss each to intelligence, willpower and appearance. This can heal normally.

**61-65.** Face mashed and bent: temporary loss of 50% appearance for 2d6 months.

**66-70.** Reproductive organs mangled: Useless and sterile for 2d6 years.

**71-75.** Nose broken: permanent -1d6 APP.

**76-80.** One eye torn out: loss of depth perception results in permanent loss of -4d6 accuracy and -1d6 APP.

**81-85.** Skin permanently wrinkled and creased: loss of -4d6 APP.

**86-90.** Tongue torn from mouth: loss of the ability to speak in anything but grunts and moans. -1d8 APP.

**91-95.** One ear torn off: -1d6 APP.

**96.** One hand torn off.

**97.** Arm twisted like a rag: broken in 2d6 places. Takes 1d4+1 month per break to be usable again.

**98.** Severe ruptures, flesh rips, head trauma and sensory deterioration: -1d6 permanently to each trait.

**99.** Entrails yanked through rips in the abdomen: Victim will die in 1d6 hours unless given first aid by a medic and stitched up. Out of action, even if he or she survives, with a 6+3d6 month recovery time, scars leave a person with an appearance drop of -3d4.

**00.** Ghastly ruptures of the flesh, brain tissue degradation, sensory depletion: permanent loss of 2d6 to each trait.

## Third Eye 236

Type: **physical mutation**
Details: +20 Perception, -3 Appearance, **plus possible extra mutation**
Growing on this mutant's forehead is another eye, often an identical one to the other eyes of the deviant, but sometimes of an odd shape, color and possibly able to emit a mutational power. Roll 2d6 to determine the nature of this freak's extra ocular growth. Roll first for the appearance of the eye and then for any special ability. All third eyes give the mutant better vision at the very least, and increases their perception trait by +20, although this extra eye looks unsettling and so a -3 APP penalty is applied.

| 1d12 | Third Eye Appearance |
|---|---|
| 1. | Normal eye |
| 2. | Tiny, pea sized glassy dot |
| 3. | Oval, vertically arranged |
| 4. | Dark red, almond shaped |
| 5. | Purple orb |
| 6. | Small, perfectly round black orb |
| 7. | Horizontal oval, deep blue |
| 8. | Opalescent oval |
| 9. | Gleaming orange oval |
| 10. | Goat eye |
| 11. | Glossy black oval |
| 12. | Hidden, only revealed when opens, roll 1d10+1 again for shape. |

| 1d12 | Possible Third Eye Mutation or Ability |
|---|---|
| 1. | No special ability |
| 2. | Stun ray, as the mutation from page 74 of the hub rules. |
| 3. | Illusion generation, from page 250 of this book |
| 4. | Eye light, like the minor mutation on page TME-77 |
| 5. | Can see radiation within 100+1d100m* |
| 6. | Electrical pulse, as mutation 31, page TME-65 |
| 7. | See dimensional beings within 30+1d100 meters* |
| 8. | Night vision eye. Allows the character to see in near total darkness as if wearing night vision headgear (200m range). |
| 9. | Pulse eye, identical to the mutation in this book on page 262. |
| 10. | Beam eye, identical to the prime mutation from page TME-61. |
| 11. | Electromagnetic pulse, as the prime mutation from page TME-65. |
| 12. | Two abilities, roll 1d10+1 for each |

*Roll at PC creation for fixed range.*

## Thought Share 237

Type: **mental mutation**
Range: **touch or projected 1 meter per point of willpower**
Usage: **Twice per day per rank**    Hazard Check: **Variable, see table 205**
Similar to the much more potent Mind Unification mutation, this somewhat more common and less complicated mental gift allows the user to either physically grip another being or focus on and project toward a distant subject and try to share thoughts with the target. Once a link is made with the subject, the thought sharer can relate his or her thoughts, visions and memories, or else search the other person's mind with their consent or by mental intrusion.

There are basically two ways to unleash this power. One is by gripping the head of the intended subject, and the other is by staring at or focusing on the target whose mind this mutant wishes to commune. Only one mind can be reached for at a time, and while performing this task, the user can do no other actions. If struck, bumped into, knocked over, or even subjected to a loud noise such as a boisterous laugh, shout, or gun shot nearby (within 10m meters), this mutant must make a willpower based type D hazard check to maintain the thought share with an already contacted subject.

The duration, imagery and words transferred by the successful use of this mutation are 5 words per rank, 3 memories, visions, pictures, maps, or visually graphic images per rank, or 1 intense emotional projection per rank.

The player of a character with this power is encouraged to suggest other thoughts his or her player would like to transfer, although the GM must decide if something not covered here is allowable and if so, what the quality and quantity of the transmission might be.

The first table below shows a listing of the target minds this mutant might try to reach or explore, and the odds of success using a 1d10 roll. The second table shows the maximum range of an attempted projected thought share as well as the difficulty for an uncooperative subject to either block or abruptly end a non-permissive mental union; in such cases, the strength of the sender's Willpower determines the resistant target's own Willpower based hazard check.

## Table XR-204/Subject of Thought Share Conditions and Odds of link Directory

| Target of an Intended Thought Share | Details |
|---|---|
| Physical Touch with Subject who is open to Thought Share | Recipient is open minded, keen to allow the mutant to share his or her thoughts. **Chance of Initial Contact roll d10*: 9 in 10** |
| Physical Touch, subject unsuspecting of share, not restrained | The user places an appendage on the target and attempts to share their thoughts. If contact is made, the target can flinch back and immediately cease the transmission, or else if not already hostile to the user of this power, hold still and allow the link. Example, the mutant touches the arm of a bartender in a saloon during a conversation and tries to share the true purpose of the character's visit in the establishment, or the picture of a missing friend, or impulse that the user is a true friend, etc. **Chance of Initial Contact roll d10*: 7 in 10** |
| Physical touch, subject hostile to user, including melee contact during a fight | The target is normally an enemy or predator of the character. The user of this power who may indeed try to touch the target during melee combat to send a flash of imagery, sentiment, or a phrase to either taunt, cease hostilities, or relay some vital information in a flash. If the subject is contacted, the target may attempt to break the communion (see table 205), but if not restrained, the transmission is broken the next round — unless the target finds the thought sharing very much to its liking and willfully allows the mutant to continue to transfer its thoughts and images. **Chance of Initial Contact roll d10*: 6 in 10** |
| Projected thought to a friendly being | This thought could be to the user's horse, pet dog or attack beast, or else to companions, parents, siblings, offspring or already friendly persons and animals. The target need not be in view so long as they are within range (range shown on next table). **Chance of Initial Contact roll d10*: 8 in 10** |
| Projected to unsuspecting, non-hostile, unfamiliar subject | The target of this transmission need not be known to the PC who is trying to share his or her thoughts, and could be a total stranger. To use this power, the mutant must be presently observing the target or have previously seen the person; a person who need not be in his or her current view, such as in another room, trench, thicket, nearby vessel, or across a crowd. **Chance of Initial Contact roll d10*: 5 in 10** |
| Projected to unsuspecting but hostile subject | The target is typically hostile to the mutant and his or her companions. This target could be a predatory beast, a hostile humanoid species, or a member of an enemy faction. The animosity need not be personal and the subject might merely hate the character because of differences in species, race, religion or political alignment. Many creatures and humanoids of intelligence below 20 will be momentarily dumbfounded to hear the thoughts or see imagery in their minds projected upon them from an unsuspected source, and not know whether it is being transmitted from the thought sharing mutant, or from its own ancestors, or deity, or subconscious mind. Such a creature cannot begin to block a successful metal link until after 4+1d6 rounds, and then try to block the transmission according to the following Willpower based table. If the thought share is blocked, the monster will press the attack, but if it fails its hazard check, it will postpone any attack, stop still, and watch and listen to the shared thoughts unless attacked by other means. Beings with an intelligence score over 20 will try to block or cease a thought share immediately after a successful link is made. **Chance of Initial Contact roll d10*: 4 in 10** |

**If the subject has had the thought sharing mutant make a mental link with him or her on a previous occasion, then there are two chances to access this already familiar mind.*

## Table XR-205/ Thought Sharer's Range and Hazard Check to Block Matrix

| Thought Sharer's Willpower | Range of Projected Thought Shares | Target's WILL based Hazard Check to Block or End Thought Share |
|---|---|---|
| 01-09 | As user's WILL in meters | Ax2* |
| 10-34 | As user's WILL in meters x2 | A |
| 35-54 | As user's WILL in meters x5 | B |
| 55-74 | As user's WILL in meters x10 | C |
| 75-94 | As user's WILL in meters x20 | D |
| 95-120 | As user's WILL in meters x100 | D |
| 121-135 | As user's WILL in meters x500 (1000m = 1 kilometer) | E |
| Above 135 | As user's WILL in kilometers | E |

**Subject allowed two hazard checks against this weak mental projection*

## Tissue Padding 238

Type: **physical mutation**     Defense Value: **-10**
Damage reduction: **-3 damage from all physical and beam attacks**
Trait Modifiers: **-1m movement, -2d6 Agility, add 10+2d10 END, -2d6 APP to max 23, and +50% weight**

A layer of extremely dense, fatty tissue has formed around this mutant's body. This unsightly and bulky protective layer serves as a shock absorber, flotation suit, insulation layer, moisture and nutrient supply, plus absorbs damage from all attack forms, excluding mental attacks.

This character takes half damage from all falls, can't sink, nor swim under water, receives two hazard checks against injected on ingested poisons and suffers one exposure rating less from radiation. Another remarkable benefit of this mutation is that the character absorbs 3 END points of damage from each physical or beam strike against them. This deviant's appearance score drops -2d6 at character generation with a maximum of 23 for life. The mutation adds both 50% weight and 10+2d10 END, yields a bonus of -10 defense value, yet reduces base movement by -1m, and cuts the subject's agility by -2d6.

## Transform Weather 239

Type: **mental mutation**
Range: **willpower multiplied by rank in either diameter around mutant, or same diameter but projected 100m away per point of user's willpower. See description.**    Usage: **Once per day per rank**

Once per day per rank, this mutant can change the weather in a localized area. The meteorological alteration depends on the present conditions, his or her willpower, and the terrain type. For example, while it is easy to whip up a sand storm out in the desert or badlands, it is very hard to gather clouds and make a downpour in such an arid region. Likewise, trying to cause the sun to come out during a typhoon at sea is next to impossible, at least for long periods of time.

This power will most often be used to cause a gale to stir up a sand or junk storm to force back small adversaries, a tornado to deter a besieging army, or a hurricane to drive away pursuing aircraft. It can bring a downpour on parched crops, summon a light wind to blow away a fog bank or toxic cloud, or generate a thunderstorm to hammer an enemy invasion fleet with the boom of thunder and devastating lightning strikes. All these weather events are possible, with a percentage based chance. However, both the terrain around the user and the current weather affect the odds of success or failure.

The weather can potentially be changed in a diameter area equal to the user's willpower multiplied by their rank in meters; example, a mutant with 37 willpower at 5th rank can change the weather in a 185m diameter, or a 92.5m radius if changing conditions around them. If not choosing to change the weather all around the mutant, then they can try to project it at a distance of 100 meters away per point of their willpower. At that location, the same diameter of weather change occurs as noted previously — most probably at a safe distance from the mutant and his or her comrades.

The weather can only be changed every half hour, at least by this mutant. With repeated successful changes, however, a powerful, high rank mutant could turn things from a hot sunny day to a hurricane in a few attempts. The best method to do this is a shift from one weather system to another, getting closer to the desired conditions after several tries and possibly many half hour phases. As with so many mental or energy based mutations, this mutant can risk their health, and possibly their life, by exceeding their daily usage limit according to the rules on page 396, Exceeding the Limits of Mental Mutations. This might be a risk a character is willing to take to save his or her comrades and loved ones, such as if traveling by an airship and confronting a tornado or hurricane, and wanting to shift the weather ahead to merely a downpour or overcast conditions.

The actual consequences of various weather conditions are up to the game master, with the results possibly being helpful to a team, community, or travel situation, or a hindrance. For example, a downpour might be perfect to stop an inferno raging through a small junk and timber village, but a tremendous danger if flash floods are already happening. Likewise, transforming an overcast situation to a foggy one might be great if the team is trying to hide from dog mounted nomads in an open plain, but fog placed around a seagoing barge trying to navigate a reef is problematic for the crew. While the game master's imagination and basic knowledge of weather is most often all that is needed to handle the outcome of a transformed patch of weather, there is a detailed listing for many of the more severe weather conditions on page 143 of the hub rules which covers storms (gale), thunderstorms, sandstorms, tornadoes and hurricanes.

## Table XR-206 / Transform Weather Matrix

| Current Weather Condition | Desired Weather and Base Chance to Change* |
|---|---|
| **Hot and sunny** | Mixed sun and cloud 90% / Overcast 78% / Drizzle 31% / Downpour 11% / Foggy 13% / Becalmed 78% / Light winds 56% / Gale 13% / Hail storm 9% / Icy sleet 4% / Cold snap** 8% / Thunderstorm 10% / Hurricane 3% / Tornado 2% |
| **Mixed sun and cloud** | Hot and sunny 71% / Overcast 93% / Drizzle 64% / Downpour 27% / Foggy 29% / Becalmed 32% / Light winds 36% / Gale 29% / Hail storm 47% / Icy sleet 16% / Cold snap** 15% / Thunderstorm 36% / Hurricane 9% / Tornado 11% |
| **Overcast** | Hot and sunny 68% / Mixed sun and cloud 89% / Drizzle 85% / Downpour 77% / Foggy 75% / Becalmed 68% / Light winds 64% / Gale 48% / Hail storm 72% / Icy sleet 49% / Cold snap** 21% / Thunderstorm 63% / Hurricane 13% / Tornado 49% |
| **Drizzle** | Hot and sunny 30% / Mixed sun and cloud 68% / Overcast 97% / Downpour 92% / Foggy 88% / Becalmed 37% / Light winds 39% / Gale 53% / Hail storm 79% / Icy sleet 53% / Cold snap** 28% / Thunderstorm 71% / Hurricane 17% / Tornado 51% |
| **Downpour** | Hot and sunny 7% / Mixed sun and cloud 32% / Overcast 74% / Drizzle 79% / Foggy 71% / Becalmed 52% / Light winds 67% / Gale 62% / Hail storm 93% / Icy sleet 64% / Cold snap** 31% / Thunderstorm 88% / Hurricane 46% / Tornado 55% |
| **Foggy** | Hot and sunny 12% / Mixed sun and cloud 35% / Overcast 89% / Drizzle 94% / Downpour 85% / Becalmed 93% / Light winds 19% / Gale 9% / Hail storm 23% / Icy sleet 21% / Cold snap** 8% / Thunderstorm 79% / Hurricane 58% / Tornado 7% |
| **Becalmed** | Hot and sunny 46% / Mixed sun and cloud 77% / Overcast 72% / Drizzle 68% / Downpour 36% / Foggy 67% / Light winds 39% / Gale 14% / Hail storm 8% / Icy sleet 6% / Cold snap** 9% / Thunderstorm 15% / Hurricane 3% / Tornado 5% |
| **Light winds** | Hot and sunny 58% / Mixed sun and cloud 63% / Overcast 74% / Drizzle 82% / Downpour 59% / Foggy 24% / Becalmed 18% / Gale 89% / Hail storm 82% / Icy sleet 57% / Cold snap** 45% / Thunderstorm 68% / Hurricane 44% / Tornado 63% |
| **Gale** | Hot and sunny 18% / Mixed sun and cloud 27% / Overcast 47% / Drizzle 62% / Downpour 57% / Foggy 21% / Becalmed 11% / Light winds 87% / Hail storm 82% / Icy sleet 64% / Cold snap** 38% / Thunderstorm 73% / Hurricane 89% / Tornado 98% |
| **Hail storm** | Hot and sunny 12% / Mixed sun and cloud 39% / Overcast 95% / Drizzle 91% / Downpour 93% / Foggy 76% / Becalmed 15% / Light winds 66% / Gale 64% / Icy sleet 73% / Cold snap** 71% / Thunderstorm 86% / Hurricane 73% / Tornado 82% |
| **Icy sleet** | Hot and sunny 6% / Mixed sun and cloud 13% / Overcast 68% / Drizzle 76% / Downpour 88% / Foggy 21% / Becalmed 12% / Light winds 72% / Gale 76% / Hail storm 92% / Cold snap** 97% / Thunderstorm 59% / Hurricane 32% / Tornado 37% |
| **Cold Snap**** | Hot and sunny 3% / Mixed sun and cloud 15% / Overcast 89% / Drizzle 72% / Downpour 68% / Foggy 42% / Becalmed 28% / Light winds 71% / Gale 68% / Hail storm 96% / Icy sleet 93% / Thunderstorm 9% / Hurricane 2% / Tornado 5% |
| **Thunderstorm** | Hot and sunny 21% / Mixed sun and cloud 38% / Overcast 88% / Drizzle 93% / Downpour 91% / Foggy 16% / Becalmed 2% / Light winds 41% / Gale 96% / Hail storm 97% / Icy sleet 18% / Cold snap** 14% / Hurricane 77% / Tornado 92% |
| **Hurricane** | Hot and sunny 8% / Mixed sun and cloud 35% / Overcast 76% / Drizzle 72% / Downpour 83% / Foggy 16% / Becalmed 5% / Light winds 38% / Gale 92% / Hail storm 91% / Icy sleet 32% / Cold snap** 17% / Thunderstorm 89% / Tornado 97% |
| **Tornado** | Hot and sunny 9% / Mixed sun and cloud 38% / Overcast 84% / Drizzle 75% / Downpour 85% / Foggy 2% / Becalmed 1% / Light winds 46% / Gale 94% / Hail storm 96% / Icy sleet 36% / Cold snap** 12% / Thunderstorm 91% / Hurricane 91% |

*Done so at a cost regardless of success or failure, see table 207, next page.   **Temperature drop of -20+d30 Celsius within minutes.

## Table XR-207 / Transform Weather Modifiers List

| User's Willpower, Area Terrain and Other Variable Modifiers (% modifier to odds of changing weather) Modifier to Table XR-206, above. | |
| --- | --- |
| User's willpower below 20 | Odds -20% |
| User's willpower 21 to 34 | Odds -10% |
| User's Willpower 35 to 64 | no modifier |
| User's Willpower 65-84 | Odds +10% |
| User's willpower 85 or over | Odds +20% |
| Open terrain, such as a wasteland, desert, or plains | Odds +10% |
| On the open ocean | Odds +5% |
| In badlands | no modifier |
| In hilly country | Odds -5% |
| Mountainous area | Odds -20% |
| In ruined city | Odds -10% |
| In new era town or city | Odds -5% |
| In a canyon or river valleyv | Odds -10% |
| Forest or swamp | Odds -5% |

### *Extreme weather change transformation*

The mutant pushes itself to the extreme — a dangerous extreme to better ensure the weather changes to the desired condition.

Add +20+1d20 to the percent chance on the table above, however there is a possibly deadly consequence of exceeding their power limits. See the expanded rules section of this book for 'Exceeding the Limits of Mental Mutations' on page 396.

## Trisegmented Mouth 240

Type: **physical attack**     Range: **melee**     Rate: **1**
Strike Value: **+4 normal, or +30 with surprise**
Damage: **2d6**     Appearance Penalty: **1d3 or 50% while deployed**

This mutant has a noticeably well defined, if not overly large jaw, neck muscles, and a scar-like line growing from the lower lip to well beneath the underside of the jaw. These features have only a slight reduction in the mutant's appearance of -d3 APP, and unless a person got within 3m of the deviant, they would never suspect that the subject was a mutant, unless other distinguishing aberrant features were present.

This mutant can use their mouth normally, although onlookers will see modest upper and lower fangs when the mutant talks or chews. However, when desired, the mutant can open its mouth wide, with the lower jaw splitting apart, to form a mandible-like, highly expandable, toothy mouth. If in close quarter with an unsuspecting adversary, this mutant will gain a surprise attack if he or she wins the initiative, and thus make a +30 SV attack on the first round and thereafter +4 strike value. This attack inflicts 2d6 damage along with any strength modifiers plus either an unarmed combat skill (brawling or marital arts) or if the weapon expert skill is applied to this mutation (but not both skill areas). This is treated as an additional melee attack and can be used with other physical attacks or hand held weapons.

Once this deviation is seen, those unfamiliar with the mutant might well be horrified, in which case the mutant's appearance score drops to half while this alarming physical mutation is revealed.

Besides the primary combat use of these powerful, dislocating jaws,

the mutant can also swallow things equal to half the size of its head, including whole cats and similar sized food stuffs or objects in the same way many snakes can swallow large pray. The digestive physiology of the deviant is also altered to accommodate and digest large meals, and if something is indigestible, it will be later vomited up 2d12 hours after being ingested.

## Unique Tentacle 241

Type: **physical mutation**     Range: **melee or beyond, see tables below**
Rate: **1**     Strike Value: **By tentacle type**     Damage: **By tentacle type**

This mutant has a tentacle growing from a random body location. The type of tentacle and what grows at the end is also unique. There is a 2 in 6 chance that a second tentacle is also present and 25% likely to be identical to the first, otherwise different and rolled up separately. Should a second tentacle appear, there is a further 1 in 6 chance of a third, and so on, with a chance of a fourth and fifth, etc., at the same 1 in 6 odds and 25% chance of being identical to the first appendage.

The tentacle type might be a long whip-like growth and used as a rope, others occur as short and powerful and have some heavy appendage at their end, while others still can be barbed or saw-toothed and yet also end with a different growth. Treat each tentacle as an extra melee attack, although in most cases these fleshy appendages reach well beyond the normal melee range of three meters, and allow this mutant to use this organ to make the first attack. The length and thickness of the tentacle determine its defense value and endurance, plus the time it takes for the appendage to regrow to a useful length, if chopped off.

Each tentacle is unsightly, and the mutant suffers an appearance penalty drop based on two criteria; from where the tentacle grows, and secondly, what grows at the end, shown on the first and third tables below. Add the penalties from both tables, however, record the mutant's pre-tentacle appearance score because if this individual can keep the tentacle hidden from view, onlookers will only see the higher, less freakish visage of the deviant — at least until the clothing falls away and reveals the hideous tube beneath.

| 2d6 | Tentacle Location |
| --- | --- |
| 2. | Top of head (APP penalty -4d6) |
| 3. | Belly (APP penalty -3d6) |
| 4. | Tail bone (APP penalty -1d4) |
| 5. | Middle of lower back (APP penalty -2d6) |
| 6. | Right shoulder (APP penalty -1d6) |
| 7. | Left shoulder (APP penalty -1d6) |
| 8. | Right underarm (APP penalty -2d6) |
| 9. | Left underarm (APP penalty -2d6) |
| 10. | Middle of upper back (APP penalty -2d6) |
| 11. | Chest (APP penalty -3d6) |
| 12. | Groin above genitals (APP penalty -4d6) |

*A few tentacle end examples...*

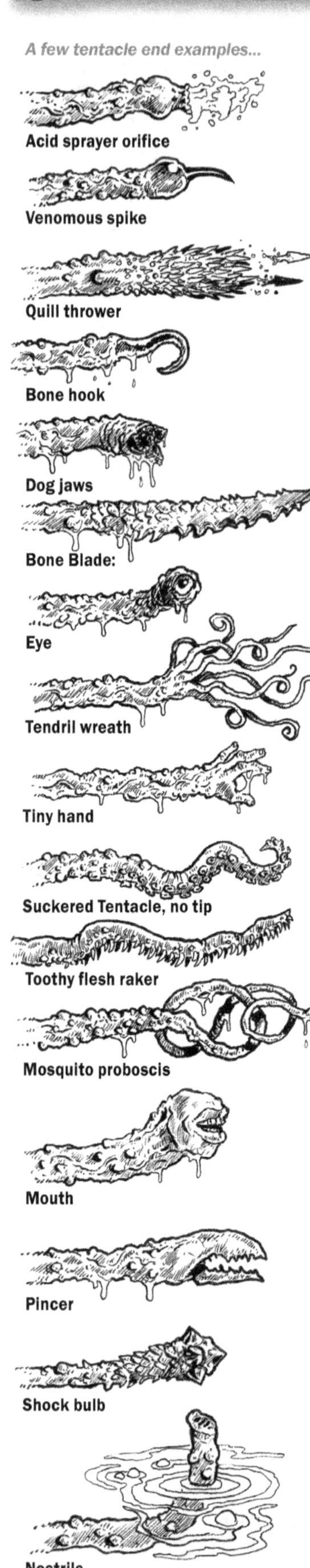


## 1d6 Tentacle Type

**1,2.** **Thin and whip like,** (4cm thick at body and 1cm thick at tip, no further roll for an end appendage) length 3+1d6 meters. If used as a whip, it can inflict 1d8 damage (plus strength based modifiers) and be used like the whip master skill noted on page 226 of this book. If this mutation occurs at character generation, and this mutant also gets a weapon expert skill point, the whip master skill can apply to this appendage instead if the player wants. To chop off: DV -18, END 12, will regrow in 30+1d30 days.

**3,4.** **Medium thickness and length:** (6 cm thick at body and 2cm thick at tip) with suction cups along underside. Length 2+1d3 meters. Can club opponents for 1d12 base stun damage, and adds +1 skill point in the grapple skill. This tentacle also adds 1 skill point in climbing. To chop off: DV -20, END 16, will regrow in 40+1d30 days.

**5.** **Thick and stubby:** (8cm thick at body and 4cm thick at tip) measuring only 2+1d2 meters in length. A wallop from this appendage is done at +5 SV and inflicts 1d12+2 base stun damage. While not covered in suckers or spines, this growth does improve the mutant's climbing and grapple skill by 1 skill point. To chop off: DV -30, END 22, will regrow in 50+1d30 days.

**6.** **Spine covered:** This medium thick (7cm thick at body and 3cm thick at tip), moderately long 3+1d2m length appendage can lash out at opponents as an extra attack and strip flesh from the victim. This attack is +6 SV and inflicts 2d6 lethal damage on a hit. It is useful, too and adds 1 skill point in both grapple and climbing. To chop off: DV -25, END 18, will regrow in 40+1d30 days.

## 1d20 Tentacle End Appendage

**1.** None (APP penalty nil)

**2.** **Pincer:** Like the pincer of crab, this small, powerful growth can be used as an extra melee attack, although not in conjunction with the tentacle itself. Strike value +6, damage 2d6. Similar to other jaw-like growths on this table, this mandible can help grip equipment and serve as a crude, second hand alongside a regular one to hold a rifle, shotgun, or even a bow. APP penalty -2d6.

**3.** **Bone Blade:** This serrated cutlass is like a short sword, yet with a strike value bonus of +5 and inflicts 1d12+1 damage on a strike. It can be used as an extra melee attack, although not in addition to whatever the main tentacle itself can do. APP penalty -1d6.

**4.** **Bone hook:** Similar to a bone blade, this hook can inflict terrible wounds and serves as a separate melee attack, SV +4, damage 1d10+1, however, it's as thick as the mutant's thumb but far stronger. This hook and tentacle can pull up to the mutant's base strength score in kilograms, or hold the mutant should the entity fall and catch hold of something. Likewise, this appendage adds an extra skill point in climbing. APP penalty -1d6.

**5.** **Venomous spike:** This hollow, 10cm long horn can stab opponents as an extra melee attack per round, although not at the same time as the main tentacle except after successfully grappling an opponent. When stabbing with this spike, the strike value is +5 and inflicts 1d6 base damage, however, up to 4 times per day, the mutant can inject Type D paralysis venom into a victim. Those who fail their hazard check will become immobilized and helpless for 4d6+10 minutes. This venom can be coated on a weapon or arrow head and will transfer one occurrence of this venom after a successful strike, although the venom only remains viable for two hours after application and each application expends one daily allotment of this toxin. APP penalty -1d6.

**6.** **Lamprey mouth:** This circular, toothy orifice and feeding 'throat' are sickening to behold, but does inflict initial damage on those the growth latches onto, plus locks on and will automatically bore into and feed on the tissues and fluids of a living target. This mutant can elect not to latch onto a target after hitting it and instead use it as a basic bite attack. Strength modifiers, or possibly the weapon expert skill if applied to this chomp, are applied to the initial bite, however the STR modifiers don't apply to the per round feeding damage after this toothy mouth has latched onto a victim. Bite attack: SV +5, bite 1d6 damage, plus suck 1d6 DMG per round once latched onto victim. APP penalty -2d6.

**7.** **Eye:** This eye is often quite remarkable and treated as a third eye identical to those randomly listed in the 'third eye' mutation on page 269 of this book. The eye is connected to the nervous system of the mutant and the deviant can see whatever this remote eye can see, which is great for looking around corners, or over a wall or tall grass like a periscope. If operating away from the mutant's body, and any companions, this eye has the stealth skill of 6 skill points as far as 'conceal self' and 'concealed movement' go. See page TME-51 for details on this skill. APP penalty -1d4.

**8.** **Nostrils:** A pair, or 'grill', of fully functional nostrils are hidden at the end of this tentacle. These orifices are closed until needed and can convert the tentacle into a giant snorkel to allow breathing from beneath the surface of water, or extend out from a cloud of noxious gas to allow the deviant to breathe normally. These unobtrusive holes do not further reduce the mutant's appearance; APP penalty: nil.

**9.** **Mouth:** A full sized human mouth with lips, teeth, tongue and throat connection to digestive tract. It is not connected to a respiratory system, so cannot speak or breathe. Bite damage is 1d3, APP penalty -1d6.

**10.** **Tiny hand:** Although only half as strong as the mutant's regular hand, this half sized growth is highly dexterous and has +10 agility and 1 skill point in the pick pocketing skill. It can wield a weapon as large as a dagger or handgun, such as a pocket pistol, musket pistol, automatic pistol or laser pistol, however submachine guns, high caliber pistols or heavier handguns are too large to handle. APP penalty -1d6.

11. **Quill thrower:** This hefty, 4kg tentacle's end has grown into a spiny, quill covered bulb. Growing from the tip are 4d6 small, 300g bone quills, as well as another 3d6 immature quills which will become ready after 10 days, with another 3d6 emerging soon after that. Mature quills can be fired up to 4 per round, range 20 meters, SV +4, DMG 1d8 each. Strength modifiers do not apply to these darts, although the weapon expert skill and accuracy modifier do. In a pinch, this tentacle can be used as an extra melee attack, but not in conjunction with any attack the main tentacle might make: SV +4, DMG 1d8 lethal, APP penalty -2d6.

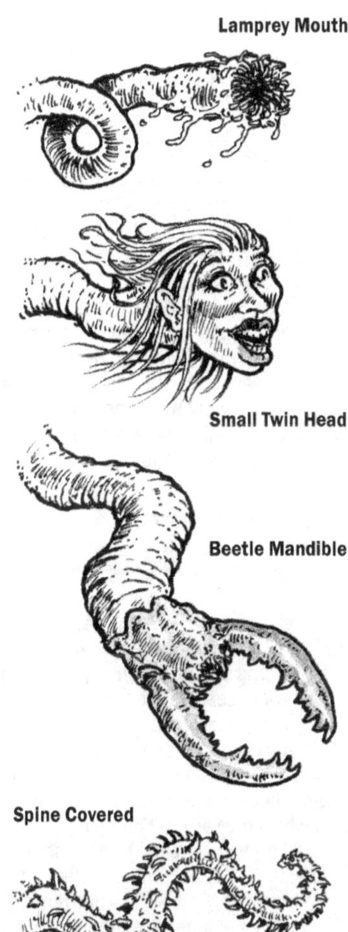
Lamprey Mouth

12. **Small twin head:** This is a half sized twin of the mutant's main head complete with hair, ears, eyes, mouth, and nose. It has the ability to speak, converse separately from the main mutant, feed, breath and do whatever a normal head can do. This head will, however, have a separate random personality from the table on page 500 of this book. If this tentacle is severed, this end portion of the appendage will die immediately and take an extra 6+1d4 months to regrow. If the main head is knocked unconscious, this head can control only this tentacle portion of the body, but, should the main head be killed, this head can only take over control of the rest of the body if its willpower is 50 or higher, otherwise it too dies after 1d6 hours. APP penalty -1d6.

13. **Dog jaws:** Although not equipped with a nose nor ability to breathe, these terrible jaws are about the size of a coyote's, and can bite at +6 SV for 2d6 damage, and consume flesh which thereafter travel to the mutant's digestive system and consume raw. This frightening, slathering set of jaws can also be used like a pincer of sorts and serve as a hand to support another regular hand to hold a two-handed weapon, including rifles, crossbows, and bows. APP penalty -2d6.

Small Twin Head

14. **Toothy flesh raker:** A lash by this tentacle's bone spiked tentacle tip will open nasty, blood ozzing wounds: SV +9, for 2d6 damage. This growth is treated as a bonus melee attack, this APP penalty -2d6.

15. **Tendril wreath:** At the end of this tentacle is a wriggling wreath of 6cm diameter micro tentacles, numbering 3d6. While ineffective as a weapon, they can be used to add +1 skill point to the mutant's climbing ability. Furthermore, this gross collection can assist in grasping objects, operating a keyboard, picking a lock (if the PC has this skill), or even operating a triggered relic weapon or other small piece of technology weighing no more than 3 kilograms. For most of these tasks, the mutant must visually observe what the tendrils are doing, although in some cases can do this from the furthest extent of the tentacle's reach. APP penalty -1d6.

Beetle Mandible

16. **Beetle mandibles:** Similar to a crab pincer, but somewhat smaller, these glossy black, serrated mandibles are connected to a small, feeding tendril lined mouth allowing the mutant to take nourishment from whatever plant matter and flesh this fearsome mandibles harvest. SV +4, damage base 1d12, APP penalty -1d6.

17. **Mosquito proboscis:** Normally housed within the end of the tentacle, this flexible, hollow hose can shoot into a wound after the hard outer spike makes a strike, and lock into the victim and drink 1d4 damage in blood per round. A typical human sized mutant with this gross appendage can drink 20 endurance in blood from a victim before becoming full, yet continue to drain an unconscious or trapped victim until the subject dies of hemorrhaging to death by expelling excess blood. The proboscis can continue to drain blood so long as this tentacle does not take a strike. The DV is noted with the Tentacle Type, table 2, above. APP penalty -2d6.

Spine Covered

18. **Acid sprayer orifice:** Once per day per rank, this mutant can spray a streamer of blue acid up to 6m away and try to coat and burn a target: SV +6, damage 1d6+1 for 1d6 rounds. If the coated subject soaks themselves with a liter of water to the afflicted area, it will neutralize the acid at once. This mutant itself is not immune to other acids, but is immune to this variety. APP penalty -2d6.

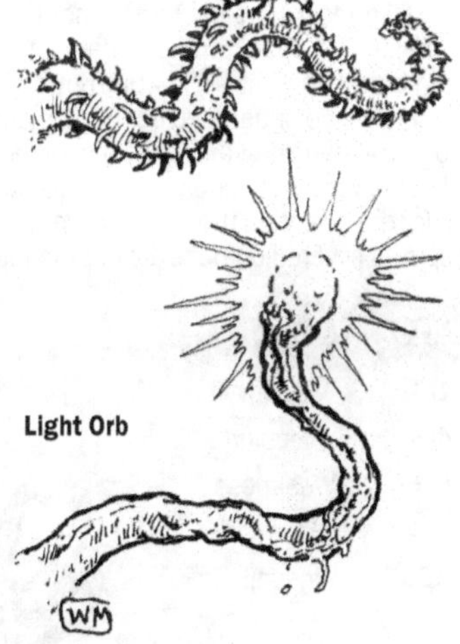

19. **Light orb:** Like a lantern fish, the end of this tentacle has a glassy, gelatinous orb that for up to 10 minutes per day, per point of willpower the mutant possesses, can illuminate an area in a 15m radius of soft, warm light. Alternatively, the whole day's supply of light can be depleted at once in a glorious, blinding flash with a 10 meter radius. All those exposed to this burst who fail a Type C agility based hazard check will be blinded for 2d6 rounds and be -20 SV to their strike values and +20 SV easier to strike by those not blinded (similar to the mutation light burst on page TME-69). APP penalty -1d4.

Light Orb

20. **Shock bulb:** An egg shaped, scaled and hole dotted orb grows from the end of this tentacle. When not charged up, it can be used like a mace head to bludgeon opponents at +5 SV doing 1d12+2 stun or lethal damage (character's choice but always lethal unless stated prior to the attack). Once per day per rank, this orb can be charged up with a tremendous electrical field which crackles with lime green electrical bolts. On a successful hit, this charged up orb can deliver 1d20 damage to organic beings or 3d20 to machines, including cyborgs and mutorgs, androids, robots, vat -brains, and vehicles with on-board electrical systems. The mutant's body is itself not immune to damage from electrical sources. (APP penalty -1d6)

# Venomous Claws 242

Type: **physical attack**
Range: **melee, unless coated on arrows and other hurled missiles**
Usage: **5 venomous slashes per day per hand**
Rate: **1 per hand**     Strike Value: **+4**
Damage: **+1d6, -10 strike value, -1 movement and -1d20 willpower.**
Hazard Check: **Type D Endurance based check to avoid paralysis**

This mutant can let their fingernails grow out long, in about a month, and make two attacks per round — or more if the deviant has more than two normal arms and hands. As these nails grow, they become more claw-like, with a venomous duct growing beneath each. Up to five times a day per hand, this mutant can slash organic beings and deliver a paralytic venom into the open wounds of its victims. For each successful strike, an extra +1d6 damage is delivered on top of the normal human 1d6 unarmed damage inflicted (now 2d6), plus the victim must make a type D endurance based hazard check or suffer a degree of paralysis.

For each failed hazard check in a venom laced wound, the subject is reduced by -10 strike value and -1 m movement, plus suffers a -1d20 loss to its willpower trait points. If reduced to 0 or less willpower, the victim becomes paralyzed for 3d10+10 minutes. Upon waking, all lost SV, movement and willpower points return to normal, although slashing damage remains until healed normally.

A mutant with this adaptation can squeeze out one or more doses of this tasteless, colorless venom into food or drink, although within the 5 doses per day, per hand limit. Whoever ingests this venom is allowed one Type D hazard check or succumb to the venom just the same as if he or she had been slashed and injected in combat. The more doses ingested, the greater the loss to SV, movement and willpower — although only one hazard check needs to be made to thwart the venom when ingested. Should a victim of this venom not be fully paralyzed, then lost strike value, movement and willpower traits will return to normal in 3d6 minutes.

This venom can be coasted onto arrow heads, blades and other puncturing and slashing weapons and will remain effective for 12 hours, or until one successful hit occurs before rubbing off. This mutant is immune only to their own variant of venom.

## Venomous Horns 243

Type: **physical attack**
Range: **melee**    Usage: **Venom sufficient for 6 injections per day**
Rate: **1**    Strike Value: **+2 per horn**
Damage: **1d8 per horn plus venom**    Hazard Check: **by venom type**
Similar to the mutation of 'Horns' from the hub rules, these oddly shaped, smaller horns are often garishly colored and have a hollow, straw-like core in which venom seeps up to the tip. Mutants will exhibit 1d4 such horns.

On a successful gore attack, for which each horn the mutant has adds +2 SV and does 1d8 damage per horn (treated as one melee attack), a spurt of venom rushes into a wound on a hit and the victim is forced to make a hazard check or succumb. The horns can deliver 6 doses of venom per day, after which they are still dangerous appendages but lack venom.

Like most physical mutations, these growths are treated as one additional melee attack and can have the weapon expert skill applied to it or an unarmed combat skill — but not both. Likewise, any accuracy bonus to the strike value or damage bonus from the character's high strength score is also applied, making this array a truly dangerous growth.

The variety of venom is determined at character generation. Roll 1d10 first for the type then the strength. Venom, erroneously called poison by most people, is covered on page 124 of the Mutant Epoch hub rules.

| 1d10 | Venom Type |
|------|------------|
| 1-3. | Death |
| 4,5. | Sleeping |
| 6,7. | Weakness |
| 8,9. | Paralysis |
| 10. | Insanity |

| 1d10 | Strength of Venom |
|------|-------------------|
| 1-3. | A |
| 4,5. | B |
| 6,7. | C |
| 8,9. | D |
| 10. | E |

## Voice Mimicry 244

Type: **physical mutation**    Range: **As a normal shout**
Usage: **1 round per point of mutant's willpower, per day**
Hazard Check: **Listener allowed an intelligence based hazard check to disbelieve, based on their experience with mimicked cry and nature.**
This mutant can copy the voice of any person or animal cry heard within the last six months, and contort their vocal cords to replicate the sound. Of course any humanoid or animal who sees that the roar of a devi-bear or other great beast comes from a mutant human — although mutant animals can also exhibit this same power — will automatically know that the noise is a trick and won't be dissuaded from attacking the user.

However, should this mutant make a specific animal call from out of sight, both creatures and people are highly likely to recognize and believe what they are hearing, and either flee, or hesitate in their advance or current action.

Likewise, a deviant with this gift might hide and use a voice of a well known and much feared officer or other important person to call to guardsmen or others to open a gate, let the mutant pass, go search in another area, or order some other task. Again, if the speaker is seen, he or she must have a plausible physical appearance or cover to pull off the mimicry, and as shown on the table to follow, the onlookers are each allowed a hazard check to disbelieve what they are hearing and thus suspect that they are being tricked. The best use of this power is when the speaker is not visible. Better still, when the one trying to mimic another does so using a communicator to relate their commands, false intel, or insidious rumors.

A voice mimic can use the power to entertain companions, passers by and whole saloon's full of amused patrons and potentially earn 1d6 silver pieces per hour in tips in a busy tap room. Doing so will, of course, alert the populace to the character's gift, and make it hard for him or her to trick others in that community thereafter. This mutation can be used once every round per point of the user's willpower trait, per day, with an animal cry taking 1d6 rounds to pull off, and an impersonation allowing for 4 words per round.

After this character attempts a voice or animal mimicry, the listener is allowed an intelligence based hazard to check to believe it or not. Some mimicry is easier to pull off than others, with the hardest being an animal cry heard by the same creature type, or the mimicry of a voice that attempts to replicate the listener's spouse, parent, child or best friend.

Other noises, such as a gunshot, mechanical sound, or weather event such as a thunderclap are entertaining approximations, but not believable.

### Table XR-208/ Voice Mimicry Believability Matrix

| Listener Conditions | Example | Int Based HC to Disbelieve* |
|---------------------|---------|------------------------------|
| Listener is Same Animal Species as cry: Animal cry is supposed to be same as listening creature | Wolf howl heard by mutant wolf | A |

| | | |
|---|---|---|
| Listener is a close friend, family member or pet: Voice mimicked is that of listener's spouse, parent, offspring, animal companion, or very frequent comrade | Mimicked voice of parent heard by daughter and pet dog | B |
| Familiar with voice or cry: Listeners are familiar with the animal cry or mimicked voice and know who or what it is | Watchmen at gate hear cloaked figure in a wagon and recognize it as the local slaver, who they normally open the doors for an admit into the barter fort interior | D |
| Never heard the voice or cry before: Listeners are unfamiliar with this voice or animal cry before, but it is clearly not the same as the sounds the mimic is expected to make (if they are aware the mutant-mimic being nearby or not). | Guards searching for a group of male PCs hear a hooded figure in an alley call back in a young woman's voice saying, "No, I have not seen anybody come this way." Or for an animal cry example: A group of skullocks are tracking the excavators and the mutant mimic makes a shout of a enraged beast from over a rubble mound, terrifying the skullocks who will run off if none disbelieve the cry. | E |

**Intelligence based Hazard Check (HC) to disbelieve what is heard.*

Of course, what response the listening people or creatures might have to hearing a mimicked voice, or bestial howl, depends on the in-game circumstances, as well as the motivation of those who encounter this gifted mutant. For instance, even if a character with this mutation makes a convincing cry of a hell crawler's cacophony, a band of raiders might well believe what they are hearing, yet, because they are defending their stronghold, it doesn't mean they will flee in panic... at least not without visual proof — although would most certainly pause in any chase or immediate investigation of the creature's presence, allowing the mutant and his or her companions a chance to either escape, or properly launch their assault on the criminals.

## Web Generation 245

Type: **physical mutation**
Range: **Based on PC's rank, plus strength bonus**
Usage: **up to 120 meters worth per day**
Rate: **1**    Strike Value: **+10**    Damage: **stick or wrap around target**
Held Victim Details: **+30 SV easier to hit with ranged weapons, or +50 SV with melee attacks**    Hazard Check: **Victim allowed a strength based hazard check to break free, see table below.**

This is a somewhat complicated, multi-purpose and highly useful mutation to have. Growing within this mutant's body is a large, web generating organ that will make 120 meters worth of sticky silk web per day. This web material is as strong as good rope, but half as thick and almost transparent. At will, the mutant can use muscular contraction to shoot out a line of web at a target to adhere to or possibly wrap around it. A normal strike, with a +10 SV, must be made, but a being's armor offers no defense, only dodge skills, agility modifiers, and the base DV are applicable. Large stationary objects like walls, ceilings, and trees are automatically struck, but small items, such as a mug of beer, holstered weapon, battery, set of keys, and the like, are considered DV -50.

Each mutant is born with a different web ejection point on his body, linked to the main generation organ through a tube and pump system. This orifice is about 5cm wide when open and usually well hidden, thus no appearance penalty is deducted. Roll to find the web ejection point below. The actual capabilities of the web line depend upon the character's rank and strength score.

Muscle contraction is used to launch the web, and so any strength modifiers that typically apply to physically inflicted damage, apply to the range in meters. For example, strength value of 52 gets a +4 damage bonus, thus +4 meters to the range stated in the following table.

Any creature struck can make a strength based hazard check (noted on the table to follow depending on how many times the web has coiled around the target) in order to tear free.

| 1d10 | Web Ejection Point |
|---|---|
| 1-4. | Belly |
| 5,6. | Chest |
| 7,8. | Mouth |
| 9. | Right palm |
| 10. | Left palm |

If the web emitter mutant uses the web to shoot against a wall or ceiling to either climb up or stop from falling, the web will hold 50 kilograms of weight per strand fired. An additional strand can be fired per round to coil about and add to the thickness and strength of the line. If falling, and only one strand can be fired before the deviant impacts the ground, minus 50 from the PC's weight on the falling results table on page 123 of the hub rules and half the resulting damage regardless of how far the mutant falls. Of course, if a mutant falls a long way and can shoot multiple lines at an elevator shaft wall, cliff face, or the side of a building as it drops, allow that it can launch one web per 10 meters dropped and quite probably arrest its fall — so long as it hasn't already exceeded its daily 120m allotment of webbing.

Because the mutant can produce plenty of web per day, it can also shoot out several lines to ensure a creature that it hit once can be encased in multiple coils and become impossibly stuck — although each fired length of web must still make a strike on the target. If a target is struck multiple times, it must snap free of each individual web line, which requires a strength based hazard check and only one such line can potentially be snapped per every two arms or legs or similar appendages the target has.

If burned, bit, blasted or otherwise hacked at, this web is treated as DV 0, endurance 10 per 'wrap around'. Furthermore, if a target is hit with a natural roll of 01-20, its arms are considered bound and useless, demanding that the web trapped target make a hazard check to break free. Trapped targets are +30 to strike with ranged weapons, and +50 with melee weapons.

This mutant is not immune to getting stuck in its own, or other webs, while spiders of all kinds are masters at getting free from, and moving through, webs. Spiders, therefore, get two hazard checks per round to slip free of this variant of webbing and likely to crawl along it to go after this mutant and his or her companions. The actual material of the web will break down into a slimy gel after 9 hour's exposure to air, allowing any trapped prey to go free.

Other uses for this web are to make trip lines, hammocks, or secure junk, bones and branches to assemble a hidden sleeping platform high above a ruined street, forest floor, or crude rope bridges. Likewise, this web caster can use a line of this silvery rope to blind or muffle the target if making a hit to their face (DV -50). Captives can also be bound in this filament. The applications are really limitless, however, the game master must of course agree and give the odds of success to conduct a specific task.

| Mutant's Rank | Range* of Web Line | Results of Web Line Hit | STR Hazard Check to break |
|---|---|---|---|
| 1 | 5m | Sticks to a target | A |
| 2 | 10m | Sticks to a target | A |
| 3,4 | 15m | Wraps once around | B |
| 5,6 | 20m | Wraps around twice | C |
| 7,8 | 25m | Wraps thrice around | D |
| 9,10 | 30m | Wraps four times around | E |
| 11,12 | 35m | Wraps five times around | F |
| Each Above 12th | +5m | Wraps once more around | G thereafter |

**The character's strength damage modifier is applied as extra meters in range.*

# Expanded Minor Mutations

## Additional External Body Part 246

A small organ or appendage grows from a random spot on the character's body. This part is fully functional and connected to whatever internal sensory, nervous, reproductive or digestive system is normally associated with it. The only exception is with reproductive spare parts, which, while operating normally, are sterile in mutants with the opposite primary gender. Some mutants will opt to have these parts surgically removed, and the wound cauterized — which if not done by an advanced surgical team in a relic equipped hospital setting, will leave a nasty scar and ongoing issues with seepage, bleeding, and other outcomes which reduce the PC's appearance trait by -2d4.

Apply a penalty to the character's appearance based on the location of the growth. Roll first for the extra part, then its location on the deviant's body:

| 2d6 | Body Part |
|-----|-----------|
| 2. | Penis |
| 3. | Female breast |
| 4. | Thumb |
| 5. | Big toe |
| 6. | External gland, eyeball sized |
| 7. | Pinky finger |
| 8. | Little toe |
| 9. | Ear |
| 10. | Nose |
| 11. | Eye (+1 initiative if not covered up by gear or clothing). |
| 12. | Vagina |

| 3d6 | Body Location |
|-----|---------------|
| 3. | The side of the neck -5 APP |
| 4. | From the chin, -6 APP |
| 5. | From the kneecap, -3 APP |
| 6. | From just above the belly button, -4 APP |
| 7. | In one armpit, -2 APP |
| 8. | Side of the mutant's abdomen, -3 APP |
| 9. | Center of chest, -3 APP |
| 10. | Base of back, above tail bone, -3 APP |
| 11. | From one hip, -3 APP |
| 12. | From forehead, -6 APP |
| 13. | From a shoulder, -3 APP |
| 14. | Base of neck on the front 77% of the time, otherwise back of neck, -4 |
| 15. | From one elbow, -3 APP APP. |
| 16. | Crotch, directly above already present private parts, -3 APP |
| 17. | From the thigh, -3 APP |
| 18. | From Upper back, between shoulder blades, -4 APP |

## Carrion Eater 247

This mutant's digestive tract is more akin to a bear or vulture than a human, and they can devour dead plant and animal matter that is far too old, rancid, mold and maggot covered to be eatable by a regular person — or most other animals for that matter. With such a robust digestive system, this PC also gets twice as many hazard checks against ingested poisons and other consumed toxins.

## Chin Spikes 248

One or more bone spikes grow from the mutant's jawline and or chin. Considered unsightly by most, these small horns reduce the deviant's appearance by -d4+1, however, they can be added as an extra close quarters melee attack mode, at +3 SV and inflicting 1d8 damage. These bone protrusions also act as armor, too, and improve the mutant's DV by -3.

## Dagger Finger 249

A finger on each hand of this mutant have evolved into 10+1d10cm long serrated bone daggers. Like organic steak knives, these blades can be used as a regular dagger instead of a handheld weapon, and since the character has grown up with these appendages, is very skillful with them and even if not ambidextrous, can make one attack per round with each dagger finger at +5 SV and inflict d10+1 damage (plus any strength modifiers or knife fighter skill enhancements).

Should the mutant be captured, or wish to wear unmodified gloves, these growths can be cut off and kept sanded down. The bone blade will regrow in 3+d4 months. These growths are considered unattractive, thus -d3+1 App.

## Decreased Aging 250

Similar to the minor mutation of 'longevity' from the hub rules, however, this variant is far more extreme. The mutant takes twice as long to age even from childhood, thus reaches physical adulthood at 36, instead of 18, middle age at 80 instead of 40, and so on. If this deviant can avoid a bad end from combat, accident, or disease, he or she could live to 160 years of age or longer. Whereas most characters start game play at 17+d8 years old, this one starts at age 36+d6 years.

## Depth Awareness 251

This mutant has an uncanny sense of how deep below the surface he or she is at. They are accurate within 2 to 12 percent (2d6) over or under what they guess. Roll 1d6 here to determine how close they actually are: 1-3, estimate is 2d6% below the surface/ 4-6. Mutant's guess is 2d6% above where the character suspects it is.

For the most part, this deviation is helpful if the team wants to know if they are getting closer to the surface or going deeper. This power also works while within water, as well as aerial elevations — should the mutant be aboard an aircraft or airship in dense cloud and be curious how far below the ground is. This power has no daily limits to its use.

## Detect Blood 252

This individual can smell the distinct aroma of blood in the air within 2 meters per point of his or her perception. If trying to detect a specific person or animal type's blood in an area with plenty of other blood splashes — say a battlefield or butcher shop — then the mutant is allowed a type F perception based hazard check to pick up and track a unique hemorrhagic aroma.

### Dowsing Fingers 253

This mutant can extend its hand and, like a 'water witch' or diviner, with his or her stick, can sense a source of underground water — if any is in the vicinity — to a depth of 30 meters down or less. In terrain that has lush vegetations and nearby creeks, swamps or lakes, they will find a splendid site for a well within 50+1d30 meters, at a depth of 1d6 meters, however in drier climes, such as badlands and plains, will locate a likely spot within 200+1d1000 meters at a depth of 2d6 meters. In desert areas, a type E perception based hazard check is required to sense water, which if found, is 3d6 kilometers away and at a depth of 3d6 meters.

Of course, in arid terrain, this diviner can also attempt to sense streams, pools, or an oasis. The mutant must hold out their hand to the horizon and make a successful type F perception based hazard check in order to sense life-giving waters. There is no guarantee that any discovered water supply is drinkable, of course, and it could be contaminated with radiation, mutagenic agents, chemicals or bio-organisms, and surely guarded by a local tribe or apex predator. This power can be used once a day per rank.

### Dual Earlobes 254

A second earlobe grows along the bottom of the ear, identical to the first (-1 appearance). 1 in 10 chance of triple earlobes.

### Dual Fingernails 255

Normal finger nails grow overlapping, like shingles at the ends of this mutant's toes and fingertips. -1 APP. Should this oddity also have claws, then both finger nails grow together and combine to make extra strong talons that do +3 damage. There is a 1 in 10 chance these are triple fingernails.

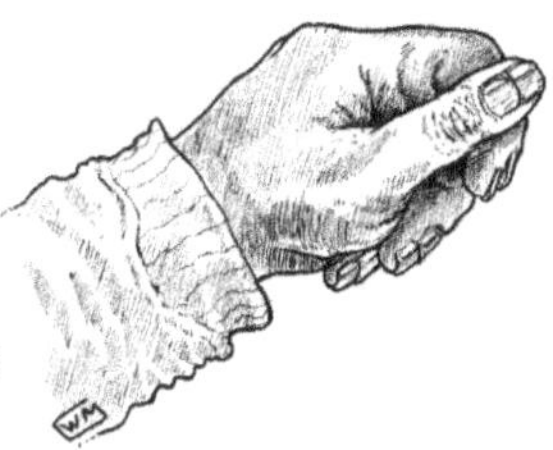

### Electro-Reception *by Thomas Vida* 256

Much like a shark or some other cartilaginous fish, this deviant has an organ attached to its upper nervous system that allows it to detect the electrical

discharges given off by all living things, as well as by powered up machines. The side benefit of this is that the deviant gains +1 initiative. The downside is that this individual could become overwhelmed if ambient electron levels are too high in an area and so suffers pain and sensory disruption. Worse, the deviant is susceptible to electrocution and if hit by an electrical weapon, or mutation such as electrical pulse or electrical charge, he or she must make a Type C Endurance hazard check or drop unconscious for 3d6 minutes — besides whatever other damage is taken.

### Extra Belly Button 257

This mutant had two umbilical cords while in the womb and now features an additional belly button either above, below, or to one side of the regular one. Located, **roll 1d6: 1,2.** Above normal location / **3.** Beside normal belly button / **4,5.** Below normal location / **6.** On back. -2 APP

### Fertilizer Urine 258

This mutant's urine is aquamarine in color and loaded with plant fertilizer of unparalleled potency. Any plant or tree this character pees against, or fertile ground, will experience noticeable, vibrant growth in the days and weeks ahead. Houseplants, small gardens and lucky trees — including plantoid characters — to be graced by this spay will grow 25% more rapidly and recover from clippings and partial harvesting and damage at an increased speed.

Wounded plantoid characters to have this urine doused on their wounds will heal 2d6 endurance. Only normal, fully matured urine will offer these benefits, and if extra beer or tea drinking is undertaken to increase the production, these forced amounts are mostly water and have no beneficial effects.

An average person will urinate about 6 times per day with about 500ml per expulsion. This urine will retain its properties for 48 hours as far as healing animated plants, but will be great for a garden for up to a month.

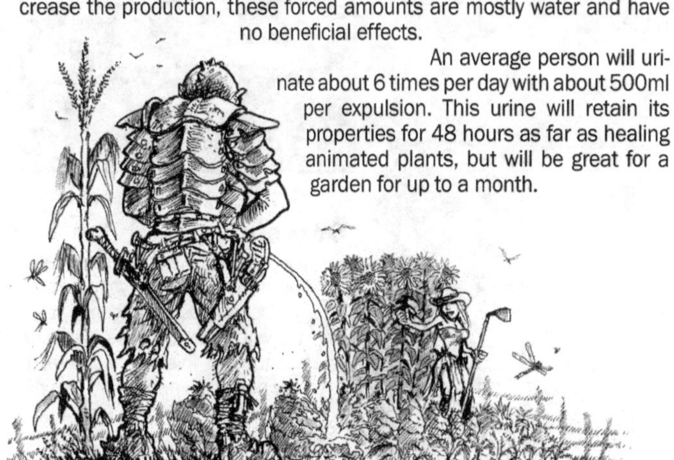

## Fingered 259

Character has 1d6 random, fully functional fingers growing from assorted spots on his or her body. While gross and each reduces the PC's appearance score by -1, they are quite responsive and great as light duty equipment hooks.

| 3d6 | Body Location of Each Finger |
| --- | --- |
| 3. | Between upper buttocks like a tail |
| 4. | Forehead |
| 5. | Behind one ear |
| 6. | Top of head |
| 7. | On thigh |
| 8. | On back of arm |
| 9. | On back of neck |
| 10. | Between chest muscles |
| 11. | Armpit |
| 12. | Top of one hand |
| 13. | Elbow |
| 14. | Knee |
| 15. | On chin |
| 16. | Small of back |
| 17. | Tummy |
| 18. | Above genitals |

## Friction Fingers 260

If this mutant has access to flammable substances, they can rub their hands together next to substances and after a minute of trying is allowed a willpower type A hazard check, with one attempt per hour available per character rank, to shed sparks and start a fire. Very similar to the mutation 'pyro-generation', this power can be used more often but is far slower and less effective.

## Glow Blood 261

This mutant's blood is a translucent, pale green. If exposed to light for only seconds, or moonlight, it will grow bright green for a half hour, perhaps revealing a wounded deviant's escape route.

## Goosebumps 262

Whenever a certain condition arises, this mutant gets very noticeable goose bumps. The game master will need to occasionally be reminded of this automatic extra sensory deviation, and record it in his or her notes.

Each character with this mutation is different in what gives them the heebie-jeebies; at character creation, **roll 3d6** to determine what causes the goose bumps:

**3.** Whenever a characters X-spouse or girl or boyfriend is making out with somebody else.
**4.** When a loved one hurts him or herself, within 10km.
**5.** When somebody is aiming at the character with a scope and he or she is in the cross-hairs.
**6.** When the character is lied to.
**7.** Whenever a dimensional being is within 24 meters.
**8.** Whenever a person who is actually an android comes within 12m.
**9.** Whenever a cat is within 18 meters.
**10.** When another person within 12 meters has the hots for the PC.
**11.** Whenever skullocks are within 90 meters.
**12.** When Radiation is present within 100 meters.
**13.** When ever somebody is trying to pick pocket the character.
**14.** Whenever the character is being followed.
**15.** When spiders bigger than a rat are within 12 meters.
**16.** When electrical systems are turned on, or first encountered in operation within 12m, this fades after a half hour.
**17.** Whenever land mines are within 12m radius.
**18.** Whenever any two of the above conditions occur.

## Half Absorbed Fetal Twin 263

Appearing as a tiny, large headed skeleton, this character's twin is visible just under the skin. Unlike other occurrences where a twin was absorbed within the womb and lives within the larger body as in 'Internal Twin Fetus' on page 252, this one died at birth. Its bones were not absorbed by the character's body and are instead maintained with calcium and other nutrients permanently. It acts as a small section of armor, however, so improve the mutant's defense value by -4.

Surgical removal of this long dead, flexible skeleton is only possible in highly advanced surgical centers with qualified personnel, and never achievable if the skeleton adheres to the subject's head. The cost to have such a surgery performed would be 5d6k silver pieces and then leave a scar, which would reduce the appearance permanently by -2d4 points.

The hideous 10+10cm long cadaver is located at a certain body location, and if seen by an onlooker, will reduce the mutant's appearance by an amount shown below — to a minimum of 1 APP — but only when noticed. Roll 2d6 below for body location of subcutaneous sibling:

| 2d6 | Fetal Skeleton Location |
| --- | --- |
| 2. | Overlapping the face, with the rib cage forming the bridge of the mutant's nose. Appearance penalty of -4d6, to a maximum of 15 APP. This position is very hard to conceal, and so the character's appearance trait is most certainly permanently reduced at all times. |
| 3. | Across the upper back, appearance trait -3d6 |
| 4. | Across the chest, appearance trait -3d6 |
| 5,6. | Across the belly, appearance trait -3d6 |
| 7. | Down one side of the rib cage, appearance trait -2d8 |
| 8. | Along the inner thigh of one leg, appearance trait -2d8 |
| 9. | Along the outer thigh of a leg, appearance trait -2d8 |
| 10. | Down the back of one upper arm, appearance trait -2d6 |
| 11. | Across one buttocks, appearance trait -2d8 |
| 12. | Along the side of the head, appearance trait -3d6, but can often be hidden under hair. |

## Homing Sense 264

Like a homing pigeon, this character always has a sense of which way its home resides. The definition of home is quite open to interpretation, for example, one's home could be where they grew up, although such a place might have been a vast junk mine in which they served as a forced laborer, a much hated place but nonetheless, where they spent much of their life.

This sense of which way is home only works for fixed locations on the earth, therefore those who call a berth on a barge or airship home are out of luck. A home location is where the mutant most recently lived for at least 1 year, however, for those with 50 or higher perception trait value, they can differentiate between their childhood home from a more recent location where they spent a year or more, while those deviants with a perception score of 80 or higher can locate where they grew up, where they lived for a year or more, if different, plus where they last slept — including a camp in the wilderness or ruins. This power can be used twice per day per rank.

## Inner Clock 265

Also called a bio-chron, this mutant has a tiny portion of its brain devoted to guessing the time of day. It can access this 'knowing' whenever it wants, even without being able to see the sun and stars and accurately place the hour and minute within 3d6 minutes of the actual time.

## Internal Compass 266

An extra section in this mutant's brain allows the deviant to know which way is north because of magnetic sensitivity. This can only be thrown off if the character is within 100 meter proximity of very powerful operational electromagnets, such as those used in old world high-speed rail lines, active reactors, certain weapon systems, or a mutant with 'magnetic attraction'.

## Large Birthmark 267

This mutant has a quite noticeable, often oddly colored and curiously shaped birthmark on its skin. This pattern is seen as a 'beauty mark' by some, and or even a tattoo by others. To those who demonize, abuse, or hunt mutants, however, evidence of a peculiar marking might be all the reason they need to either rob, imprison, or eradicate the marked person. Roll 1d12 first for the birthmark's color, then shape, and finally 1d20 for its location:

| 1d12 | Birthmark Color |
|------|-----------------|
| 1. | Blood red |
| 2. | Coal black |
| 3. | Gray- blue |
| 4. | Deep purple |
| 5. | Emerald green |
| 6. | Chalk white |
| 7. | Bright pink |
| 8. | Dark brown |
| 9. | Pale yellow |
| 10. | Olive green |
| 11. | Pumpkin orange |
| 12. | Navy blue |

| 1d12 | Birthmark Shape |
|------|-----------------|
| 1. | Star |
| 2. | Half moon |
| 3. | 1d4+1 somewhat parallel lines |
| 4. | Swirl |
| 5. | Ragged swatch |
| 6. | Long line |
| 7. | Rectangular |
| 8. | Squarish |
| 9. | Cat's head shaped |
| 10. | Like a pair of eagle wings with head |
| 11. | Kinda like a skull |
| 12. | Obvious barcode |

| 1d20 | Birthmark Location |
|------|--------------------|
| 1. | Groin |
| 2. | Buttocks |
| 3. | Face |
| 4. | Forehead |
| 5. | Behind one ear |
| 6. | Top of head |
| 7. | Thigh |
| 8. | On back of arm |
| 9. | On back of neck |
| 10. | Between chest muscles |
| 11. | Armpit |
| 12. | Top of one hand |
| 13. | Elbow |
| 14. | Knee |
| 15. | Front of neck |
| 16. | One cheek |
| 17. | Tummy |
| 18. | Foot |
| 19. | Chest, plus roll another birthmark. |
| 20. | Back, plus roll another birthmark. |

## Living Hair *thanks to Christine Jones* 268

This mutant's long hair is thick like old plastic straws, and up to the last inch of it, is alive and controllable by the deviant. These locks can aid the mutant when climbing or grappling and add +1 skill point in these activities, plus, like the tentacles of jellyfish, help propel this individual through the water at +1m movement. However, if cut, this sensitive hair hurts terribly and bleeds.

## Magnetic Attraction 269

Whenever traditional magnetic north sensing compasses are in operation within five meters of this mutant, the dial will point to this person instead of north. While the field isn't strong enough to hold iron nails, coins or parts to the individual, overall, it assists the user in climbing iron objects and vehicles. If climbing an iron or steel based ladder or structure, this mutant sticks to it with a noticeable ease and gets an extra hazard check to hang on or use the climbing skill per 6 meters climbed. Fortunately, iron tipped crossbow bolts, arrows and spears seem to be unaffected by this curious feature, and don't veer toward the mutant more often than at other targets.

## Memory Scent 270

If this mutant tangles with any creature or person, including a plantoid, but excluding androids, robots and other machines, it will catch a whiff of the being and never forget it. The nature of the tangle is usually meant to imply combat, especially melee combat where the opponent rubbed against or at least got within 1 meter of this mutant, however other forms of physical contact can also occur which will leave an easily remembered scent in this deviant's memory. Any lover or merely somebody this mutant bumped into at a saloon or crowded street can also leave their pheromones for this character to follow.

Likewise, clothing and bedding of a person or animal will also leave behind a powerful scent if caught with 24 hours, and it too will be remembered. While this odd sense of smell doesn't aid in tracking the person or creature that emitted the scent, it is easy to identify should this mutant get close to the creator of that scent, or else, this mutant later comes across clothing or bedding of the remembered person.

This mutant can remember a scent for 1 month per point of his or her perception trait value and will recollect where they first smelled it when getting within six meters of the source.

Besides remembering the smell of an individual person or beast, this scent recollection also works on whole species of humanoids and animals. For example, once this character crossed paths with a warmort, he or she will never forget the aroma such as if they come upon a vacant camp where the evil things had spent the previous night.

He or she can also recall the scent of their home village, town, or specific street in a new era city.

## Micro Hands 271

Growing from this mutant's body are 1d6 tiny, baby-sized hands on short, flexible wrists. Each hand has only a quarter the strength of the mutants regular hands, yet, these appendages can untie ropes, hold gear, add to the mutant's climbing skill ability. They can also propel him or her through the water like fins and making the character an automatic 'strong' swimmer. Unsightly, each hand reduces the mutant's appearance by -4 APP, or -8 if on the head or neck, to a minimum of 1pt. Use the minor mutation of 'Fingered' on page 280, for location of hands, otherwise these growths run along the sides of the deviant's torso.

| 1d6 Micro Hands | Climbing Skill Point Bonus | Swim Speed bonus |
| --- | --- | --- |
| 1 | 1 point | +0.5m |
| 2,3 | 2 points | +1m |
| 4,5 | 3 points | +1.5m |
| 6 | 4 points | +2m |

## Minor Radio Reception 276

This is a far weaker version of the prime mutation called Frequency Receptors (no.183 on page 247 of this book). When trying to fall asleep at night, unmoving, at rest, and focusing entirely, this mutant can detect and hear the feint transmission of radio broadcasts emanating from nearby — the radius equal to HALF the character's perception trait, in kilometers. This deviant can train their mind to tune into whatever radio communications are going on, including Mecha chatter, Morse code, transmissions between people using relic communicators, as well as ancient repeating broadcasts, SOSs and other signals often encountered in the ruins.

The 'listener' mutant can't respond to what they hear, and often what he or she hears is riddled with static, oscillations and phases in and out between different broadcasters. But, sometimes a transmission comes in louder and more continuous, which means the signal is coming from some place either closer, or with less earth, concrete, rock or water between this mutant and the source. As the character approaches a transmission point

— although must stop, sit or lay down, and mediate on the transmission, which takes 10+1d10 minutes to establish — the signal becomes more distinct, easier to focus on and listen to, and reveals the direction it is coming from.

The mutant has learned to shut off the radio sounds, robotic chatter, and voices when they become too loud or interrupt their sleep, conversations, or peace of mind. Furthermore, if this character doesn't already have the skill of Morse code, then make a one time intelligence based type D hazard check, if successful, then the mutant has taken the time to learn this skill and can now understand what Morse Code messages are saying.

## Monotreme 272

[Female character's only]. This mutant is an egg-laying mammal like a platypus. Instead of carrying a child to the regular 9 month term, she instead gives birth to a leathery, conical egg about the size of a football at three months. The egg, if turned every few hours and kept at a comfortable room temperature for the next 6 months, will eventually tear open and reveal a newborn baby mutant. The parent can theoretically produce two children per year in this fashion.

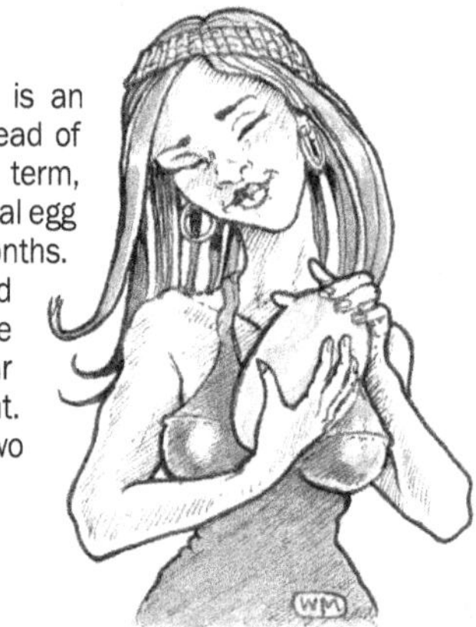

## Mood Coloration Alteration 273

| Mood | Color |
|------|-------|
| Afraid | Pale |
| Angry | Deep red |
| Abnormally happy | Orange |
| Drunk or stoned | Green |
| Frisky | Purple |
| Depressed | Blue |
| In agony | Gray |
| Creative | Turquoise |
| Anxious | Yellow |

When this deviant is in a certain mood, his or her pigmentation changes. This change takes a minute to develop (20 rounds) and lasts until either another notable mood hits, or the deviant's regular calm mood, and pigmentation, returns.

## Power Detection 274

By focusing intensely, and after a full minute of effort, this mutant can feel if a battery, relic facility, or other fixture has an electric charge in it. The character must hover their hand within 30cm, or less, of an insulated wire, battery, energy weapon, vehicle or device — including robots and androids — to sense electricity within. Should there be any useful amount of power in the item, a tingle sensation registers in their palm. The deviant can also 'scan' familiar items such as power cells, to determine just how much charge remains in a power source or relic device. This mutation can be used 3 times per day per rank.

## Pyro-Generation 275

While not normally used offensively, this mutant can extend a specific appendage, usually a hand, and focus for 4 rounds and attempt to generate sparks and a sudden, candle sized flame before its fingertips. A successful willpower based type C hazard check is needed to actually generate a sufficient flame to catch a torch, candle or campfire on fire — or any other flammable substance such as ropes binding the mutant's wrists, curtains, a wagon full of straw, etc. One attempt is permitted per character rank per hour. This mutant enjoys no extra protection from flames.

## Rare Hair 277

This mutant's hair has some rarely seen attribute.
**Roll 1d8**
**1.** Noodle-like, rubbery, thick hair.
**2.** Adaptive hair that changes color to best match the surrounding terrain.
**3.** Forked hair, each strand forks outward at the skin surface and grows in a 'V' shaped pattern.
**4.** Shedding. Once a year, at a random day and month (roll d12 for month and 1d30 for day) this mutant's hair starts to fall out and after week, is totally gone, leaving the bald deviant hairless for 3d6 days before it grows back normally.
**5.** Hair that curls when the mutant is stressed, afraid, or anxious, in pain, or pissed off, but goes straight when calm or asleep.
**6.** Hair that grows clear after getting longer than 3d6cm in length.
**7.** Hair that starts white near the root, but after 3d6cm in length, takes on the deviant's usual hair color. All other body hair, including eyelashes and eyebrows, is the mutant's usual hair color.
**8.** Electricity reactive hair. Whenever this mutant gets within a meter of any electrical power source, including a battery in a radio or flashlight, his or her hair gets frizzy. During an electrical storm, it rises on end.

## Renewable Teeth 278

This character's adult teeth undergo a lifelong process of shedding. New teeth push up from beneath older, worn teeth which get loose and simply fall out. The process is painless and takes about 10 days per tooth to regenerate, with each tooth lasting about a year -- unless knocked out, whereby quicker replacement occurs.

## Salt Crystal Knobs 279

This character's skin, especially across the back of the neck, shoulders and back, is covered in a series of ever-growing salt crystals. These hard, angular, pointy growths fall off after two or three months and are replaced by new protrusions which erupt through the skin.

While unsightly, and reducing the PCs appearance by -5, they do increase his or her defense value by the same amount. Likewise, up to 10 of the larger crystals can be snapped off and hurled like small rocks. These crystals are formed from modified sweat glads, and while made mostly of salt, taste of body odor if used in cooking. If the mutant is forced into water for over 4 hours, including a bath, the growths will dissolve at a rate of 25% per hour thereafter until gone, leaving crater-like marks on the skin which look like old, healed over bullet holes.

This is the much lighter version of the full mutation called Mineral Embedded skin on page 257.

## Seasonal Skin Coloration 280

Regardless of the terrain or climate that this deviant currently inhabits, their skin and hair change pigmentation with the season. In the springtime, this character's skin is light green with dark green hair, while during the summer months their skin turns a straw color and its hair goes dark brown. The fall months see his or her skin turn mottled tawny or orange while their hair is rust red. For the winter months, this character's skin becomes pale gray and their hair becomes snow white.

If wearing very little clothing and this mutant's coloration matches its surroundings, it gains +3 to initiative when ambushing approaching targets, plus +3 skill points in stealth when trying to conceal itself or move undetected. Normally, humanoids wear plenty of clothing, armor and gear, and in such cases, this individual gains no benefits from this mutation.

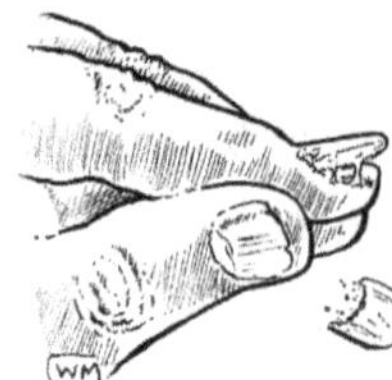

### Shedding Fingernails 281

This mutant's toe and fingernails shed each month, with new ones pushing out older toe and fingers nails over a two day period. Although painful to observe, the deviant feels only a slight itching when this transpires.

### Skin Shedding 282

This mutant's skin sheds once each year. Roll a 1d12 to establish the month and a 1d30 for a rough date — accounting for February having only 28 or 29 days. Once the shedding starts, the deviant's appearance score drops to half for 3d6 days during the process. Onlookers unfamiliar with this deviant's condition are quite horrified by this person's saggy skin and hideous visage, which gives the 'shedder' the look of a moaner. Following completion, and during the first 30 days thereafter, the subject's skin is remarkably attractive and the mutant's appearance score is +50% above their normal value.

As an example, if a deviant has an APP score of 18, then it drops by half during the shedding to becomes 9, but afterward, jumps to 27 (+9) for the month after the shed. During all other months, the character's appearance returns to its normal value. Any stitch marks, bruises, tattoos, body piercings, subcutaneous tracking devices, burns from acid, scars, fire, and whatnot suffered in the previous year are also removed or healed after this remarkable process.

### Stubby Tail 283

A 3d6+6cm long, typically hairless tail grows from the tailbone of the mutant. This appendage is too small to be useful for most things, such as grasping objects, but it gives the deviant a slight improvement in his or her balance. Add +2d4 to the character's agility score.

### Throbbing Scar Tissue 284

This mutant's old wounds throb noticeably whenever some occurrence takes place, or he or she is exposed to some element. Roll once at the start of character creation to determine the lifelong nature of the subject's scars:

Scar Throbs **Roll 1d6**

**1.** When within 10m of radiation.
**2.** When it's about to rain.
**3.** When he or she is being followed.
**4.** When some predator or enemy is actively targeting, stalking or waiting in ambush for the mutant within 20m or less.
**5.** When in the presence of androids or other non-human being disguised as pure stock humans (within 6m)
**6.** When the character is being verbally lied to — as opposed to reading texts. Likewise, the liar must have a living brain, and know they are lying to the character themselves, instead of innocently passing along false information, etc.

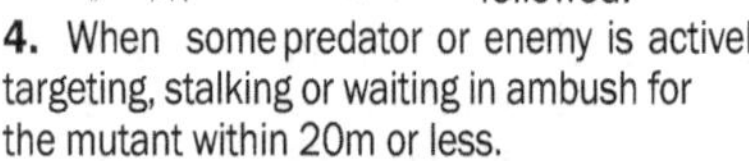

### Unhingable Jaw *by Thomas Vida* 285

Similar to the jaws of a snake, this mutant can open their jaws far wider than any normal humanoid, and can move each side of their jaw individually, as the bones are not connected, allowing them to bite and swallow things that would normally be far too large. While the bite of a typical human causes 1d2 damage, this freak can chomp down on somebody as if unleashing a fist or kick attack and do a standard 1d6 damage plus any strength modifiers.

In the rare event that this mutant also has the mutation of either gaping maw, fangs, poison bite, carnivorous adaptation, or trisegmented mouth, then increase the SV and damage inflicted by +4.

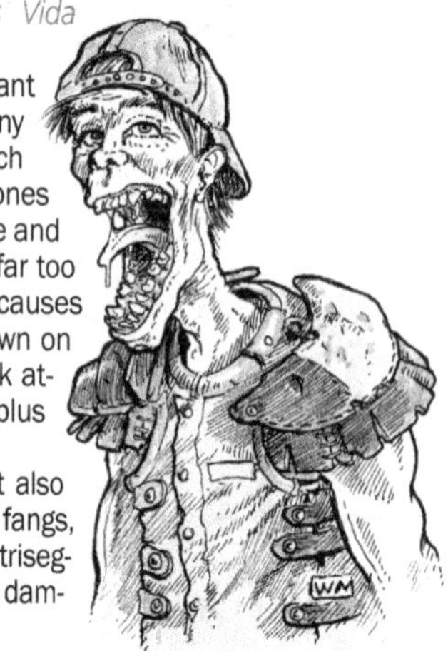

### Warmth Generation 286

This mutant can sit still and focus their inner energies to generate an enormous amount of extra body heat. Those, even clothed, to either huddle next to, share a sleeping bag, tent, or shack with this mutant will feel a comfortable heat emanate from the slightly glowing mutant. This can be maintained for a maximum of 10 minutes per point of willpower the user has, per 24 hour period, with the daily allotment able to be divided up into several chunks of time.

For reference, a normal humans body temperature is 36.7 C or 98.2 F, but this mutant can increase both his or hers by +10 C (Celsius) or +17.8 F (Fahrenheit) to 116 F.

### Waxy 287

The deviant has an attractive shimmer to its skin caused by a thin layer of glistening wax on the surface. This clear resin allows the mutant to swim faster at +1 meter per round, so long as he or she is more or less undressed. Second, the thin coating will also protect the deviant somewhat from being coated or splashed with acid and other dust or liquid attacks, and reduce acid and related damage by -1 per round, or offer the mutant an extra hazard check if such a roll is called for. This waxy gleam looks like a healthy perspiration sheen and adds +1d4+2 to the character's appearance score.

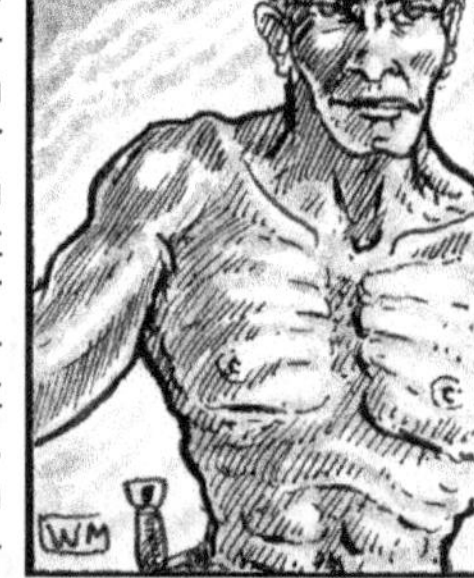

# Expanded Flaw Mutations

## Aphasia *by Brutorz Bill* 288

This flaw is based on a real life condition. The mutant knows an object and what it is, but can't name it. They do best when asked simple yes or no questions, but when under stress or required to provide complicated verbal instructions they have trouble with correct names to items or objects and so must make an intelligence based type D hazard check to accurately explain a situation, description, orders or some warning.

## Arms on One Side 289

Both of this mutant's arms are on one side of the body (1d10: 1-5 left / 6-10 right side). While a shield can be permanently strapped to the opposite side, and these two arms are now both considered dominant, the character is, however, off balance and suffers a -2d4 to agility. In addition, he or she just looks ungainly and monstrous, thus reduce their appearance trait by -4+d4 points. Should this mutant have other appendages, including arms, roll the same 1d10 above to see which side each grows on.

## Cataracts 290

This mutant's eyes are clouded over and all vision obscured to half capacity. Reduce accuracy by 50% at character generation. Surgery in an advanced facility by a qualified humanoid or robotic surgeon can repair this flaw.

## Chest Head 291

Not to be confused with the humanoid monsters which have an extra head growing from their chest, (see https://www.outlandarts.com/TME-cota.htm to grab the free download) this mutant's main head has no neck and grows from the upper chest. This deviant can't look from side to side or back without fully turning, and so suffers a -10+2d6 to its perception trait value. However, it can neither be decapitated. All its armor needs to be customized to accommodate its protruding face, bent ears and chin. Reduce the mutant's appearance score by 10+2d6 to a minimum of 1.

## Chronic Depression 292

This serious emotional flaw, often produced by a dysfunctional hypothalamus gland in the brain, makes the mutant normally very negative, seeing no real reason for accomplishing tasks, nor hope for improving his life. He tends to cope poorly with society, and won't join in on festive occasions. There is a 91% chance that he is also suicidal and will act haphazardly. If anyone close to the mutant dies, the event may cause the character to become overwhelmed with grief and attempt to commit suicide. The character must make a Type A INT based HC each day for 1d6+1 days following the death of a close comrade, or attempt suicide.

As far as a party mate goes, this character is viewed as recklessly brave, always wanting to go 'on point', start bar brawls, fight duals of honor, and take risks with little or no reward, all in the subconscious hope of ending it all.

Anti-depressive drugs, both from relic sources and naturally occurring plant extracts, will dull the depression, are very expensive and cost 5sp per day.

Note: The GM may want to dismiss this flaw mutation depending on the real life circumstances of some players, and call for a re-roll.

## Deaf 293

This character's ears never properly developed and while they can detect vibration, this mutant has no ability to hear conversation, approaching danger or the alerts and warnings of comrades. If this person has an intelligence score of 20 or higher, he or she has learned sign language, while those with intelligence of 40 or more who also have a perception score of 25 or more, can read lips, too.

An advanced ancient medical facility, or medic of 4 or more skill points with access to an ancient surgical suite, or able to instruct a medical robot, can perform a surgery that has a 7 in 10 chance of correcting this hearing issue.

## Diminished Lungs 294

The lungs on this mutant are half the size they should be for the deviant's body size, making normal respiration a chore while doing everyday tasks, especially walking up hill or running. Because of a lack of oxygen getting to its muscles, this mutant suffers a -5 reduction in strength, endurance and agility. Another problem is when this mutant is forced to hold its breath, it can only do so for half as long as a person with adequately sized lungs. Anytime a hazard check is called for that involves holding one's breath, this mutant must make two such checks to succeed.

## Epilepsy 295

Related to the standard form of epilepsy, this variant is directly due to a mutagenic error but has the same inconvenient or possibly dangerous results when a seizure occurs. There is a risk of a seizure each time this character takes any sort of strike to the head, or a fall, or is involved in a vehicle or riding animal crash. Secondly, a seizure can occur whenever this mutant takes a strike from either a physical, energy, or metal attack that inflicts 10 or more damage — with both stun and lethal damage applicable. The odds of an epileptic seizure on any of

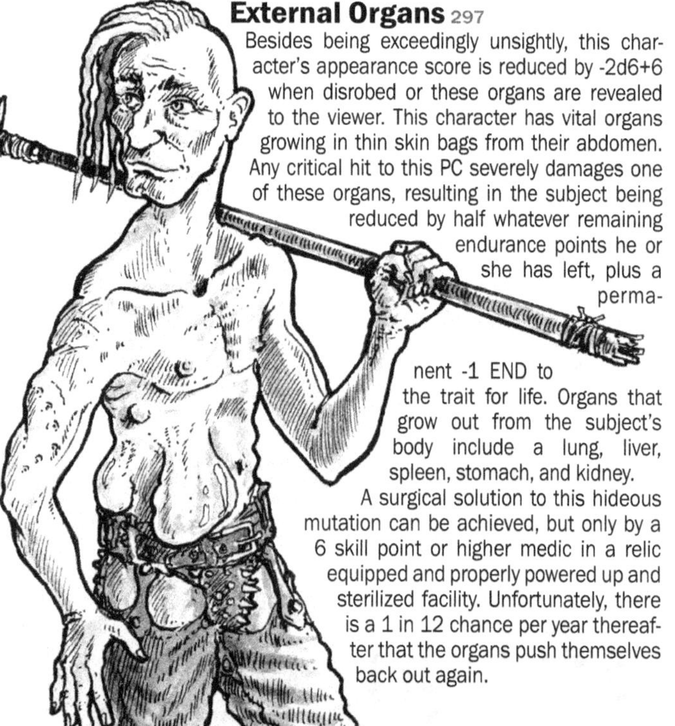

the above occasions is 13% per impact incident; so if two separate attacks strike this deviant, make two seizure checks (each at 13% instead of combined to 26%).

A seizure is caused by an electrical abnormality in the brain, and during a seizure, this mutant cannot use any mental or energy based mutations.

If a seizure occurs, roll **1d10** to determine the severity: **1-7.** Mild seizure/ **8-10.** Full Seizure.

### Mild Seizure

Also called 'focal seizures' these only affect one part of the brain and the subject maintains consciousness, even as his or her body has some manner of temporary, debilitating seizure. **Roll 1d10** to see what happens during each episode of a mild seizure:

**1-4. Dizziness:** The character is disorientated and suffers a 50% drop to movement, and -20 SV penalty for 3d6 rounds.

**5,6. Twitchy:** The mutant's hands twitch, their aim is off and suffer a -30 strike value during this 3d6 round long seizure.

**7,8. Hand Shutters:** The character drops whatever he or she holds, including the controls of a vehicle, reins of a horse, rungs of a ladder, or weapons.

**9,10. Muscle Seizure:** The deviant suffers a loss of muscle use. He or she drops anything held and collapses on the spot, yet maintains consciousness. During this 2d6 round long seizure, the mutant is +30 to be struck by ranged weapons, or +40 by melee range attacks.

### Full Seizure

Also called a 'general seizure' and comes with a chance of unconsciousness, **roll 1d10** for the result:

**1,2. Stiffness:** You lock up for 3d6 rounds as if frozen, unable to move, attack, duck or dodge. During this time you are +30 to hit by ranged weapons and +40 by melee ranged attacks.

**3,4. Awareness Gap:** For 4d6 rounds you lose all awareness, freeze up and make a repetitive motion with your hand, eyes or mouth. During this time you remember nothing of what happens, cannot move, attack or properly defend yourself and are +30 SV to hit by incoming missile attacks (if not behind solid cover) or +40 SV to be hit by enemy melee attacks.

**5,6. Shakes:** Your arms and legs shutter frantically for 3d10 rounds, causing you to have a 70% of letting go of anything you are currently holding. During this alarming seizure, most opponents are taken aback and won't attack on the next round, and thereafter, find it hard to hit this moving target who gains -10 DV from all attacks. This mutant cannot make any attacks during the seizure.

**7-10. Unconsciousness:** Also known as a tonic-clonic seizure, these are the most debilitating and involve stiffness of the body, shaking, biting of the tongue and unconsciousness for 3d10+20 rounds. Enemies who witness this seizure during combat will assume the mutant has taken some sort of fatal strike and they will probably move on to engage other targets, if any are present. However, should there be no others, and the attackers are man eaters, they will come upon this helpless, shuttering character and be able to feed on him or her at +60 SV.

## Excessive Earwax Generation 296

As far as flaw mutations go, this one is quite benign, so long as the deviant stays on top of his or her grooming. Each day, this mutant's ears produce twenty times the amount of earwax as a normal person, which if ten minutes isn't devoted to cleaning them out with an assortment of rags, leaves or crushed grass, will clog the ear canals and muffle sound to such a degree that this character is half deaf, and -2 initiative until the procedure performed. Onlookers might be quite grossed out by this often visible buildup of earwax, although no permanent appearance drop is applied.

## External Organs 297

Besides being exceedingly unsightly, this character's appearance score is reduced by -2d6+6 when disrobed or these organs are revealed to the viewer. This character has vital organs growing in thin skin bags from their abdomen. Any critical hit to this PC severely damages one of these organs, resulting in the subject being reduced by half whatever remaining endurance points he or she has left, plus a permanent -1 END to the trait for life. Organs that grow out from the subject's body include a lung, liver, spleen, stomach, and kidney.

A surgical solution to this hideous mutation can be achieved, but only by a 6 skill point or higher medic in a relic equipped and properly powered up and sterilized facility. Unfortunately, there is a 1 in 12 chance per year thereafter that the organs push themselves back out again.

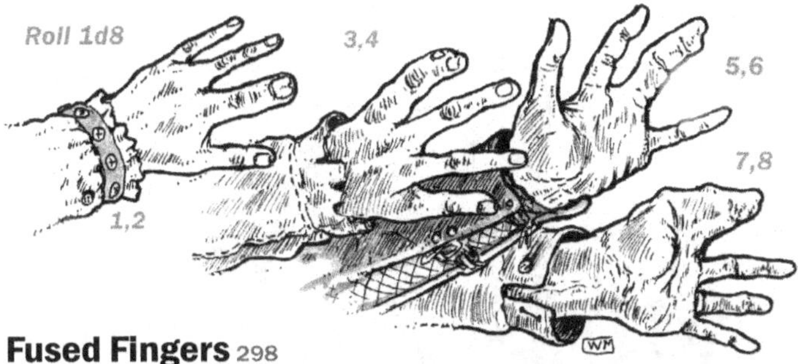


## Fused Fingers 298

On each of this mutant's hands the same two fingers are fused together. The deviant can't wear relic gloves and worse, if the thumb and index finger, or index finger and middle finger are fused, then he or she will have difficulty with triggered weapons that aren't modified and suffer a -10 strike value penalty.

Roll 1d8 and consult the abve illustration or table below to see what fused finger arrangement the mutie suffers from:

1,2. Index finger and middle finger
3,4. Lower finger and little finger
5,6. Middle finger and lower finger
7,8. Thumb and index finger

## Fused Neck 299

This mutant's neck bones are one solid ridge of bone. The deviant cannot turn its head, and worse, the muscle of the upper shoulders and back have grown up alongside the head and make for an unsightly appearance. This mutants appearance score suffers a -1d6 penalty at character generation while perception is reduced because of his or her inability to look about without turning at the waist (a -4+1d4 loss).

## Growths 300

Extra regular appendages and organs, as well as weird growths, are festooned to this character's body at random locations. If cut off, each leaves a scar that reduces appearance by -2 APP, although this penalty only applies to when these scars are seen by others, and, like the growths themselves, could be covered by clothing or gear depending on their location on the body. There is a 1 in 6 chance that any cut off appendage regrows after a month. Roll 1d12 to determine the specific growth this mutant exhibits:

1. 1d6+1 hands grow all over the body, which can hold objects in a rudimentary, grasping, clumsy manner but otherwise not wield a weapon. Treat these as more like cargo hooks than useful hands. Each reduces the appearance of the character by -4 when visible. These hands, regardless of the number, aid in climbing and add both +1 point in that skill, and act like flippers and improve the PC's swimming ability by one category (poor swimmer becomes fair swimmer, etc.) and add +1m move while in the water.

2. 1d4+1 extra ears. These growths are not connected to the brain and offer no additional auditory reception. They can be pierced, however, to add adornment to this oddity. Each reduces appearance by -3.

3. Fingers grow at various points on this mutant's body, and while they wriggle and twitch of their own accord, they are hard to control and tend to drop anything they try to hang onto. If this mutant is undressed and forced to climb, these extra fingers can aid in this task and improve the mutant's climbing skill by 1 point. There are 3d6 fingers growing on this unfortunate, and when visible, each reduces appearance by -1.

4. Benign tumors hang from this mutant's body in 1d6+1 random body locations (see chart). These fleshy sacks seem to be of no purpose and, if cut off, do not seem to affect the subject's digestive system nor levels of testosterone or estrogen. They are gross, however, and snag on branches and gear when not concealed. When visible to onlookers, each reduces appearance by -5.

5. Tiny arms: These arms are the size of a spider monkey's arm, and connected to the nervous system of the mutant, making them useful for carrying gear or wielding tiny weapons. The mutant will have 1d4 such arms with hands, about one quarter the size of a regular human hand, that can only wield or lift items of 800g (28.22 ounces) weight maximum. This allows the mutant to wield a knife, laser scalpel, pocket pistol, wrist gun, pepper spray, or 22. cal pistol.

The strength of these little arms is rolled with all having the same strength value of 3d6 STR. When not hidden under clothing, such arms aid in climbing and altogether add +1 skill point. Likewise, if not bound and hidden away, these arms can help the mutant swim and automatically bump his or her swimming skill by one category (fair becomes strong swimmer, for example) and adds +1m per round of movement. These arms each add a separate attack per round if brandishing a weapon, however they are somewhat alarming in appearance if they grow from anyplace other than the armpit or side of body — which is not considered hideous — while any other location is unattractive, and reduces the character's app by -4 per extra tiny arm.

6. 1d6 extra mouths grow at odd places on this mutant's body. Each is equipped with teeth, lips and a rudimentary tongue, but there is only a 1 in 10 chance per mouth it is connected to a separate throat and line to the stomach and thus able to feed. There is a further 1 in 20 chance per mouth that it is connected to a windpipe, voice box and the mutant's lungs and thus able to breathe and speak. Each extra, visible mouth reduces the mutant's appearance by -4 APP.

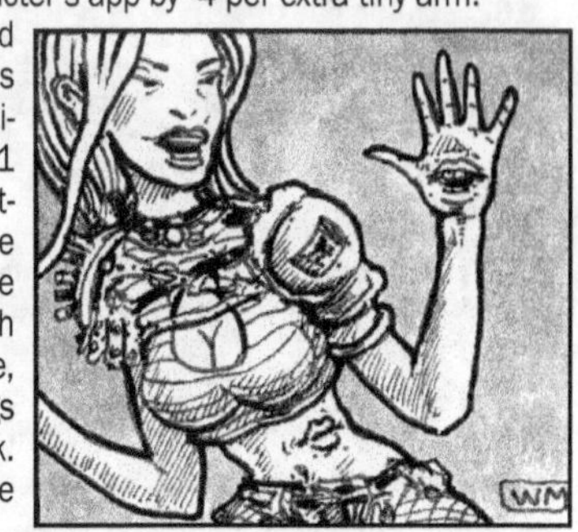

7. Tongues hang from this mutant's body at various points, although these wagging, flicking appendages are not connected to a mouth and are now just dry, leathery flaps. They are highly sensitive to hot, cold, pain and can send messages to the brain as to what they taste — which can be offputting to the deviant depending on the location of the organ. Each visible tongue reduces the mutant's appearance by -3 APP.

8. 3d6 extra toes grow all over this mutant's body. These utterly useless things are sensitive like the mutant's normal toes, and can be fitted with a ring to decorate them, but otherwise do little but disgust onlookers. Any visible spare toe reduces the mutant's appearance by -1 APP.

9. 3d6 dense patches of hair, identical to any that grows on the mutie's head, grow at weird locations on this mutant's body. Each tuft reduces their appearance by 1 APP — although these patches can be shaved off or waxed if not hidden under clothing. Laser hair removal by some ancient means is a possible remedy for these unwelcome clumps.

**10. Pus filled bags** of fluid hang from this mutant's body. These 1d6+2 rude organs seem to have no purpose, but when cut off and cauterized — an extremely painful process which usually puts the character into unconsciousness for an hour afterward — there is a 3 in 6 chance that each wound location seeps pus thereafter, and of course has a 1 in 6 chance of growing back after a month.

**11. Loops of external digestive entrails** hang out of and about this deviant's belly, back, and hips. No need to roll location on the follow-up table. If these thin skinned, fluid-filled tubes are removed, there is a 50% chance the organs were of no importance and the mutant survives, otherwise, they were vital and the character will collapse in agony, bloat and die in 3d6 hours unless some medic of 4 or more skill points with access to a fully equipped medical suite can perform life saving re-routing surgeries to reconstruct the mutant's guts and waste expulsion innards.

**12. Large, vein covered masses** (1d6) grow about this mutant's body. Each pulses and heaves as if breathing, and in some manner enhance the mutant by adding +5 strength and endurance, however, any critical hit on this PC automatically destroys or hacks off one of these growths, also causing the deviant to pass out for 3d6 hours after losing the organ. Each of these 5 kilogram fleshy mounds reduces the character's appearance trait by -10 APP, to a minimum of 1.

| 2d10 | Growth Location |
|---|---|
| 1. | Forehead* |
| 2. | Cheek* |
| 3. | Back of neck |
| 4. | Side of neck* |
| 5. | Side of body |
| 6. | Tail bone area |
| 7. | Chest |
| 8. | Armpit |
| 9. | Shoulder |
| 10. | Hip |
| 11. | Lower back |
| 12. | Upper back |
| 13. | Belly |
| 14. | Inner thigh |
| 15. | Forearm |
| 16. | Outer side of leg |
| 17. | Shin |
| 18. | Top of foot |
| 19. | Groin |
| 20. | Chin* |

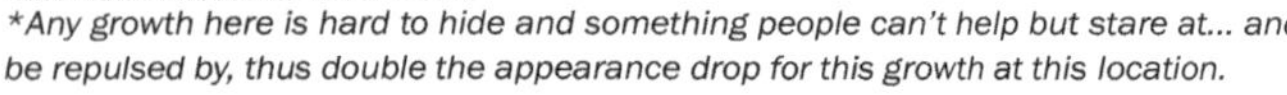

*Any growth here is hard to hide and something people can't help but stare at... and be repulsed by, thus double the appearance drop for this growth at this location.*

## Grunter 301

This character can't form words but must communicate with clicks, burps, throaty grunts and whistles. If they have an intelligence score of 30 or higher, they've learned sign language. Likewise, should this mutant have an intelligence of 70 or higher, he or she automatically also has the skill of Morse Code described on page 220 of this book.

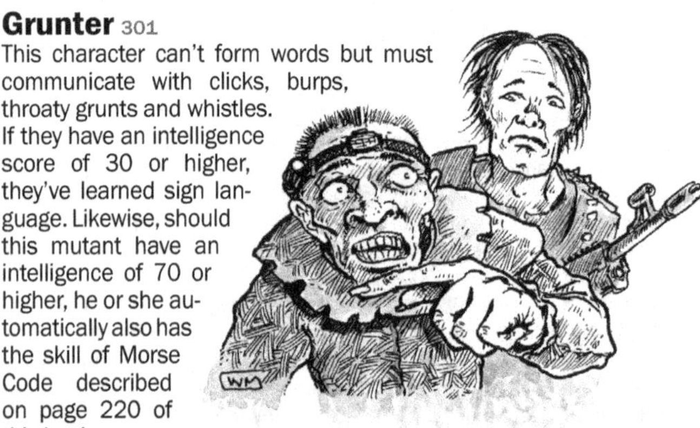

## Head on Shoulder 302

This mutant's head and rudimentary neck grow from one shoulder socket while the displaced arm is situated where the neck should be. This freak has adapted to this irregular arrangement and functions normally, however, their appearance is -10+d6 and they cannot wear powered armors nor most relic armor unless the suit is extensively modified.

## Leg-Arm Inversion 303

The mutant's arms grow from their hips while their legs from their shoulders, thus forcing the mutant into a bent over posture similar to how a normal person looks walking on their hands, but with the head bent forward and their hands held up and able to wield weapons and carry gear. This often alarming looking freak suffers a -10+d20 appearance penalty, but has otherwise adopted to locomotion and action with this limb mix-up.

## Locking Joints *by Brutorz Bill* 304

The mutants joints (fingers, knees, elbows, etc.) tend to get 'locked up' after periods of inactivity, such as sitting, sleeping, etc. After such inactivity, the mutant needs time to unlock, click flexibility back into their joints. Thus picking this mutant to be a sniper would be a poor choice, since after spending hours waiting for the perfect shot, the mutant's finger might lock up and he can't pull the trigger at the crucial time when the target comes into view. Likewise, if woken in the middle of the night, disturbed after a period of prolonged rest, or being seated as a passenger or guest at a saloon, for example, this deviant will suffer a delay in response due to his joints being stiff.

In game terms, if this character wakes from a sleep or hour or more of inactivity, they always suffer -3 initiative and a -30 strike value with their physical attack modes and are +30 SV easier to be hit by opponents. This locked up duration is 2+d6 rounds.

## Lopsided 305

This unfortunate mutant's body is bent to one side and gruesomely contorted, with one heavier side and the other knobby and gimpy. His face, too, is a mess, being slack and droopy on one side, the other squinty and tight, ears mismatched, mouth at an angle, nose bent. All in all, the deviant suffers a drop of -10+3d6 to appearance and agility, with a minimum or 1 in either trait and a lifetime maximum to appearance of 30. Its massively built side arm, however, gains +10+3d6 strength.

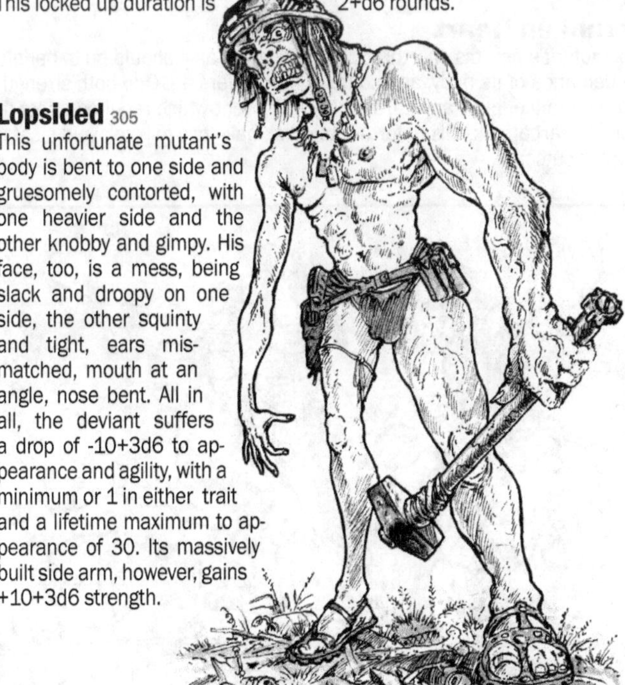

## Massive Club Foot 306

One foot is swollen and triple the normal size. Special footwear must be worn to protect the appendage, which aches painfully day and night and reduces the deviant's movement rate by -1m per round. Considered quite unsightly, this character's appearance score drops by -4+1d6. A much milder form of of club foot is also a common flaw mutation, see Birth Defect in the hub rules, page 79.

## Night Blind 307

This mutant cannot see well during periods of darkness, and suffers -1m movement and -20 strike value in low light conditions.

## No Sense of Direction *by Brutorz Bill* 308

If a dig team needs someone to scout ahead and report back the best possible route to take, this mutant is not the man for the job! He is liable to get lost and never find his way back to your camp. This mutant lives up to the ancient saying of "couldn't find his way out of a paper bag!"

In short, whenever away from his or her usual habitat, or detouring from their usual route to and from well established locations, this character requires a direct line of sight, a very clear trail, street signs, obvious landmarks or a compass and map to find their way on their own. Without help or some means of direction finding, their own mind will lead them down the wrong path and within an hour, this mutant will be hopelessly lost. The game master can allow the character a type E perception based hazard check, once per half hour, to somehow guess their way back in the right direction.

## Open Mind 309

Literally, this mutant's mind is wide open and anybody with telepathy mutation can automatically and inadvertently hear everything this freak is thinking, including in the dream state. Likewise, any mental attack on this mutant is hard for him or her to fend off, and this unfortunate must make two hazard checks when a HC is called for.

## Oversized Head 310

The excess area in this bulbous monstrosity's noggin is filled with a substance, roll **1d6: 1.** fat / **2.** blood / **3.** pus / **4.** water / **5.** bone / **6.** Larger brain, add +5d6 INT.

This massive head will not allow the wearing of relic helmets, is somewhat comical or quite unsightly looking (-2d4+2 APP), and makes a significant target (suffers a +5 DV penalty). This colossal head is also heavy, adds 10kg to body weight and reduces the PC's movement by -0.5m per round.

## Reduced Awareness 311

This mutant is abnormally inattentive and slow to respond to all manner of physical danger. In any instance where initiative is rolled, he rolls separately from that of his group and at -4. Likewise, in any situation where the subject must make a perception or agility based hazard check, he must do so twice, where others need only roll once.

## Shaky 312

This deviant's head and hands continuously shake, thus reducing his or her accuracy trait by -6+d6. In addition, any attempt to pick locks, disarm a trap or land mine, or other delicate tasks requires two hazard checks to succeed.

## Shrunken Head 313

This deviant's head is half size, although ears, nose, and eyes are otherwise normal. His brain, however, is compressed and missing much of its mass, resulting in an intelligence penalty of -10, while his appearance score reduced by -2d4. Furthermore, this subject takes double damage from any incoming mental attacks.

## Shrunken Heart 314

This mutant's heart is only three quarters as big as it should be to handle the demands of its body, and so he or she suffers a -10 to both strength and endurance, plus, any hazard check or event which requires a test to avoid a heart attack, this unfortunate must make two rolls to avoid a catastrophic outcome.

## Slow Witted 315

While this character might actually be of high intelligence, he seems perpetually distracted and indecisive. When acting on its own, he suffers a -3 to any initiative roll, so too, in conversations, he always takes a half minute or so to respond to questions, obey orders, apologize, call for help or alert companions to danger.

If hit by a surprise attack, this character will also take two rounds to cry out or move away from the peril, likewise, if in a street and a freight wagon is rushing his way, he likewise cannot move for two rounds to get out of the way.

To some, this fella seems just very chilled out and absent minded, but to comrades who might relay on him in the wastelands and ruins, this slow witted deviant often puts the whole team at risk — especially if placed on guard or at the point position in the marching order.

## Stacked Eyes 316

Both of this mutant's eyes are on one side of the face, one above the other. This reduces the hand eye coordination of the mutant, thus reducing perception and accuracy trait by -4+d6 (minus 5 to 10). This person's face is hard to look at, so decrease his or her appearance score by -2d4 points, too.

## Stumpy Legs 317

The legs of this mutant are half the size they should be, bowed, thick and not the most useful things on a long trek. Reduce the character's weight and height by 25% and speed by -2 meters per round. Appearance drop -2d4.

## Stunted 318

Either while within his or her mother's womb, or during childhood, some deformity, accident or illness caused this mutant to grow up stunted in some way. **Roll 1d10** to determine what issue this deviant exhibits:

**1-3. Runt of the litter:** This mutant's height is much reduced, being 80% of what it might have been (take 20% off the centimeters height and weight of this PC at character generation), plus, because of its smaller stature, reduce both endurance and strength by -5 points. Other than a somewhat diminutive stature, this entity looks quite normal for its kind.

**4,5. Bent back:** The character's spine is permanently bent and shrunken on one side and so this mutant leans one way with a somewhat lower shoulder. Deemed an unattractive aspect, this deviant suffers a -d4+2 APP drop but worse, he or she is off balance and suffers a further -2d4 drop to agility.

**6,7. Hunched back:** This mutant has a bulging fleshy mound on its back, is forced to walk hunched forward and suffers a -10+1d6 to appearance and -2d4 agility.

**8. Small arm:** One of this mutant's arms is only half the size and strength of the other. It's an odd look, thus reduce appearance by -1d4 APP. While this character can still wield two handed weapons, especially rifles, shotguns and related, the use of a bow (but not a crossbow), or pikes, halberds and great swords suffers and a -10 SV and -2 damage penalty is applied.

**9. Gimpy face:** Portions of this mutant's face didn't grow correctly. The result is a distorted visage with one eye too big, a bent nose, lopsided mouth, sunken cheek, twisted jaw and shrunken ear. The result is an appearance drop of -4d6 to a minimum of 1 APP.

**10. Heavily stunted:** Roll 2 stunted features from the above list using 1d8+1. Re-roll duplicated results.

## Sun Burner 319

Any direct sunlight on this character's exposed skin inflicts 1 END damage per half hour.

## Tears of Blood
*by Brutorz Bill* 320

When using mental or energy based mutations (or when they would normally cry) the deviant cries tears of blood. This doesn't harm the character but clearly marks him or her as a non-pure stock and mutant hunters will now target the individual for slavery or death. The subject suffers a slight -3 penalty to appearance when weeping blood.

## Tinnitus *by Brutorz Bill* 321

The mutant is afflicted with a constant ringing in his ears. This ringing hinders the mutant when attempting to concentrate and on perception actions related to hearing, causing this being to suffer -2 initiative. Some new world plant extracts and relic medications can be taken to reduce the severity of the ringing. A medic of 3 or more skill points can produce a month's supply of tinnitus suppression medicine for about 80sp.

## Useless Appendage 322

Growing from this mutant's body, and adding 10+1d12 kilograms weight while doing nothing for the freak's continued survival, is an often disgusting and disturbing useless appendage. Surgical removal of the growths is possible, but doing so in anything other than a well appointed medical facility with anesthetic, disinfectant and a week's observed recovery has a 2 in 6 chance of killing the subject. **Roll 1d10** to determine:

**1. A single, leathery bat wing** that has only tattered flaps of skin, -2d4+2 appearance and -0.5m movement. This frail, bony growth can, however, make an extra melee attack at SV +2, DMG 1d6.

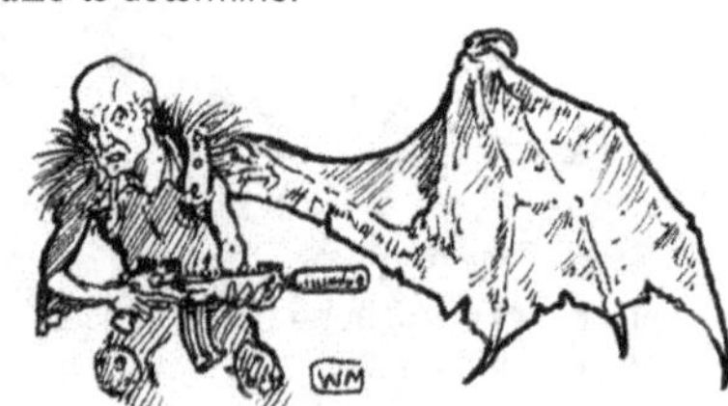

**2. Third arm** growing from back, but this has no bones nor nervous system control. It hangs like a loose, meaty sleeve. -2d6+3 App and -0.5m movement.

**3. Dangling flaps of skin** from beneath each arm and the inside of the legs must be wrapped up to avoid snagging or tripping up the mutant. -3d6 APP and -0.5m movement.

**4. Coat of arms:** 2d4 spare, uncontrollable arms dangle from the mutant's body like fleshy tubes. Each reduces the PCs appearance by -3 and for every 2 arms, the subject's movement is reduced by -0.25m.

**5. Dead head,** growing from beside the regular head, is another shrunken head that merely hangs limp and useless, yet whenever it gains consciousness for about 5 minutes each hour, it mutters, drools, and wheezes. Reduce appearance by -4d6.

**6. Three foot long, underdeveloped twin** attached to the side of torso. Thing is alive but brain dead and moans for 3d6 minutes at random, every hour, day and night. It feeds off the body of the host, reducing the character's appearance by half and reducing movement by -1m per round.

**7. Useless third leg** that grows either between or from one side (1d12: 1-4. from left hip / 5-8. from between legs/ 9-12. from right hip). It has no bones to speak of, and can't be controlled. This heavy, gruesome appendage adds 10kg weight, reduces the mutant movement by -1m if not strapped to another leg, and if made visible to onlookers, reduces this character's appearance by -3d6+5.

**8. A pig's leg** and hoofed foot grow from this mutant's body. This unresponsive appendage twitches and kicks, feels pain, and snags on things if not lashed tight to the body. If visible, it reduces the appearance score of the character by -3d6. **Roll 1d8** for body location: **1.** armpit / **2.** hip / **3.** between shoulder blades on back / **4.** chest / **5.** belly / **6.** lower back / **7.** tail bone / **8.** forearm.

**9. A hideous, fleshy neck flap,** like a collar, grows down from the mutant's neck and all around the back and chest. This serves no purpose and when exposed, revolts others. Appearance value drop is -2d4 APP.

**10. Two useless appendages.** Roll 1d8 and 1d8+1 on the second roll, re-rolling duplicated results.

## Weak Bones 323

This unlucky individual suffers double damage from falls, crushing attacks such as from clubs, tail slaps, car crashes, fists and other blunt attacks. His or her bones heal at the same rate as any other character.

# NPC Mutations

At first glace, players and game masters may wonder why this brief collection of mutations are not included in either the flaw, minor or prime mutation lists. Why they are not available to player characters? The short answer is that they are either too debilitating for a PC to conduct normal game play with, or more often, too strange. While they might be too odd or problematic for players, these mutations are still present in the world of The Mutant Epoch. In such a setting where characters can have otherwise bizarre and incredibly powerful or revolting mutations, however, it seemed only fitting to add these additions in order for a game master to create memorable, if not disturbing non-payer characters that the PCs might encounter. Such NPCs could be villains in opposition to the characters, helpful locals, traveling companions or those the heroes rescue. By all means, a game master can allow these deviations to occur in player characters, but only upon request, careful forethought, and the substitution of one prime mutation slot. *WM*

## Body Conjoined Twins 324

This mutant has two torsos, each with two legs, two arms and a head but merges together at either the chest so that both heads and sets of legs and arms face each other, or a back conjoined miscreation whose limbs and heads face outward. In many respects, these mutant are a sort of Siamese twins, and have adapted well to their unified state.

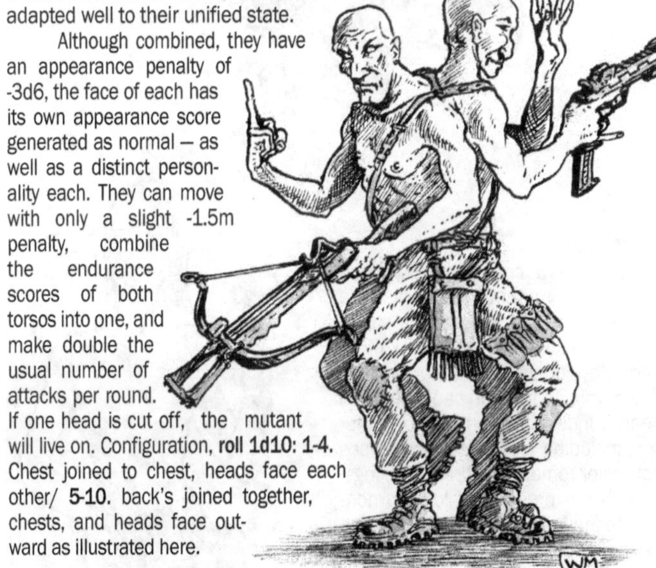

Although combined, they have an appearance penalty of -3d6, the face of each has its own appearance score generated as normal — as well as a distinct personality each. They can move with only a slight -1.5m penalty, combine the endurance scores of both torsos into one, and make double the usual number of attacks per round. If one head is cut off, the mutant will live on. Configuration, roll 1d10: 1-4. Chest joined to chest, heads face each other/ 5-10. back's joined together, chests, and heads face outward as illustrated here.

## Down Syndrome 325

This individual is considered both physically and mentally handicapped. He will typically have slanted eyes, a flat nose, a shorter, stocky build, occasional digestive problems and a decrease in mental capabilities. Reduce character's agility, appearance and intelligence by 2d6, however, a slight increase in strength is often exhibited; add +2d8 STR. This character is rarely capable of conducting oneself without guidance from supportive companions, and when engaged in social or combat situations tends to follow the lead of those around him.

Down Syndrome people have a more sunny view of the world and find the humor in things that is simply lost on others and make for exceedingly loyal companions.

Note: The GM may wish to re-roll this result depending on the sensitivity, or lack thereof, of their players.

## Dual Gendered 326

While occasionally this deviation results from recent mutagenic agent exposure and hyper-evolution, it is more commonly the result of ancient gene manipulation. It is said that the oldsters created all manner of being for war, sport, labor, meat and even carnal pleasure. In the process of making bizarre escorts for the licentious ancient ones, they developed both synthetic human and mutant variants of curvaceous, highly feminine creations called either futanari, shemales, or more commonly, hermaphrodites.

These mutants have the fully functional genitalia of both males and females along with breasts. They are able to reproduce with either sex, and carry and give birth to their own children as well. Masculine appearing variants of these mutants are also known to exist, but either because they conceal any obvious female features or are simply exceedingly rare, their true frequency is not known.

## Extreme Virility 327

This mutant's libido is equally matched by his or her reproductive capacity. While unlike the hormone disorder of uncontrolled hyper sexuality noted on page 81 of the hub rules, this deviant can instead control his or her urges and maintain normal relations in a monogamous style — although their partner must be remarkably patient and accommodating.

For males, this virility means he can engage in carnal relations several times per day without losing interest or ability. His spermatozoa triple the count with their own enhanced vitality. For females, their ability to undertake sexual liaisons also far exceeds the norm, however, extra precautions are in order since she is twice as likely to become pregnant, with every pregnancy producing twins and 1 in 6 births resulting in triplets.

For some, especially the exhausted subjects of a highly virile mutant's affectation, this mutation is considered a flaw.

## Gender Cycle 328

Every four months, this character's sex alternates with a one week dormancy phase in which the individual is a sexless entity. If, however, the mutant becomes pregnant during her female cycle, she will remain female until the child is born and nursing ceases — usually ten months after giving birth.

Very often, a character with this alteration will live a double life, operating as a ruin digger as one sex, and as a common person during the other phase, often trying to pass as the other version's brother or sister. The likeness of the opposite genders is uncanny, and obvious to anybody who knows the character.

This mutant may form romantic ties to other adventure party members, harboring feelings for the individual even when taking on the same gender as the person he or she, or it, adores. Any emotional feelings for a member of the same sex do not necessarily constitute sexual attraction, although such is not uncommon.

When first encountered, this non-player character will be 50% one gender or the other, and in month 1d4 of that gender's phase.

## Groin Conjoined Bodies 329

This oddity has two complete torsos, with arms and head, but these torsos are joined at the groin and hips, sometimes with one or more legs jutting out from one side or the other. This deviant is often pushed around in a wheelbarrow, or has some sort of wheeled cart beneath its midsection with both torsos bent upright, one facing in either direction but also able to bend about the other way and face each other.

The torsos are twins, and 78% of the time of the same sex, otherwise opposite. They are 42% likely to be born with genitalia, with one set per twin, and a further 82% chance of at least one stubby leg and, if so, a further 28% chance of a second leg on the opposite hip. If a second leg is present, there is a further 13% chance of a third leg. All the freak's legs, along with their reproductive gear, are clustered about their hips where both torsos converge.

If this aberration has no legs, it can wriggle along the ground at 1m per round, however for every leg it has, it adds +1m per round. Finally, if attached to a cart at its midsection, it can pull itself along at an extra 3m per round, possibly able to go faster than a regular person.

The shockingly horrid appearance of this mutant — especially when disrobed — means the mutant has an appearance of -20+d10, to a minimum of 1, however, each torso could be remarkably beautiful in its own right and so roll a separate appearance score for each body and head, with the true, fully seen, appearance not always known if the torsos can both stay behind a counter or table and attempt to conceal their true conjoined nature. Both heads will have separate random personalities as well as potential mental mutations.

## Legless 330

This mutant was born without legs and in order to move, must pull itself along with its arms at a movement rate of 2m per round. If it can gain a wheeled trolley, cart or wheelchair, it will be able to move at the normal 6m per round rate of a regular human, or 3m up hill or 9m or more, downhill.

## Sexless 331

Because of a chromosomal abnormality, this mutant was born as a sexless entity, appearing as a somewhat masculine female with either underdeveloped or 87% no genitals. While this individual can still form deep bonds with members of either sex, including love, the mutant does not foster romantic or lustful feelings, and their expression of love is more akin to feelings towards a favored pet, sibling, or parent.

Plantoid
Mutations

# Plantoid Mutations

Through character creation and the appearance of latent mutations, a plantoid might exhibit two or more types of saps within its bark, such as acid sap and nutritional sap, as examples. In these cases, the various saps run the length of the individual's trunk, body, roots, and branches in vein-like bands. These circulatory ducts are hard to distinguish from each other, although the weedy itself knows which is which, and can guide comrades to avoid any dangerous veins when the need for a beneficial fluid is at hand.

Most plantoid mutations listed on the subsequent pages can also appear on stationary, non-sentient mutant plant monsters, although in the following descriptions, no mention of this is made, and the game master might need to customize the mutation somewhat.

## Acidic Sap 332

Type: **Defensive physical mutation**     Range: **2m splash**
Usage: **once per successful strike**
Rate: **1 splash per successful strike on plantoid**
Strike Value: **+30**     Damage: **2d4**
Duration: **burns for 1d6 rounds on hit**     Weight added: **+5kg**

Very similar to the human and animal mutation of acid blood from page 60 of the TME hub Rules, but this sap is less pressurized and cannot be ejected willfully as an offensive weapon. Any successful close in or melee range attack on this plantoid, within 2m range or less, results in a spray of this bright green acid out to two meters and directly at whatever just shot, clubbed, slashed or bit into this plantoid at +30 SV. This acid burns the offender for 2d4 damage each round for 1d6 rounds.

Where plantoid acidic sap and humanoid acidic blood differs is that this substance can be collected in a glass jar or other acid proof container and saved for other uses. It will remain effective for 48 hours thereafter. A glass or pottery jug of this substance can be thrown at a target, poured on a lock or applied in other ways and will burn for 2d4 damage on a hit by the container (treat as throwing a rock: range 10m, SV +0, damage 1d6+2d4).

A plantoid with this mutation can only give up 2 cups of this acid sap before it becomes debilitated itself — since this sap is the plantoid character's blood — and each cup of blood drained thereafter in a 24 hour period will inflict 2d6 damage to the plant mutant.

## Algae Spew 333

Type: **physical attack**     Range: **9 meters +1m per rank**
Usage: **Once per day per 50kg of plantoid's weight, rounded up**
Rate: **1**     Strike Value: **+8**
Damage: **Temporarily blind opponents 1d6 rounds who are half movement and -50% SV while being +40 SV easier to strike / slippery**
Weight Added: **+22kg**

Similar to how a squid a can spray a cloud of ink to help evade predators, this plantoid can spew a streamer of watery algae with great accuracy and at considerable distance (9 meters plus one meter extra per the character's rank). Those attacked by the spray, which can be disgorged in a fan-like cone which will possibly blind three man sized creatures if they stand side by side or in a line, disregards any armor the target might wear, as only agility and dodge and similar abilities can help the potential victim duck and side step the spray.

Those struck, with the plant getting a +8 SV bonus to do so, are temporally blinded for 1d6 rounds. During this time, they are half movement, suffer a 50% loss to their strike values and are themselves +40 SV easier to be struck. Anybody wearing safety goggles, sunglasses, or a face shield of some sort need only wipe away the bright green algae after 1 round.

The second use for this algae is to make the ground before the plantoid slick with one spray, causing an area 2 x 6m, or 3 x 4m, or 1 x 12m slippery. Anything forced to walk upon or climb up a surface coasted in this substance is reduced to half speed and if walking or running must make a type B agility based hazard check to avoid slipping and falling to

their all-fours. A climber who, for example, ascends a ladder, cliff or wall that is coated in this mess must make two hazard checks with their climbing trait (STR + AG ÷ 2) to scale this coated section.

The third use of this algae, which is stored in large, leathery pods among the plantoid's lower branches or roots, is that this stuff can be exuded into a pail and eaten. Algae of this sort have a somewhat salty taste, are rich in vitamins and full of protein. One daily expulsion of this green sludge will feed 6 adult humans for the day. Eaters must pass a Type C willpower based hazard check to keep down their first spoonful.

## Allergy Inducing Spores 334

Type: **Physical attack**
Range: **Within at 10m radius if no wind, or carried on the wind**
Usage: **Once per day per pod**     Rate: **1 per emitter pod**
Duration: **1 hour with no wind, 3d6 rounds with wind**
Hazard Check: **Willpower based hazard check, type depends on number of spores expelled at once, see below.**
Weight added: **+5kg per pod**

4+1d4 large, orb-like melon shaped emitter pods grow on the trunk of this plantoid. Once per day, each of these emitters can disgorge a cloud of brownish spore.

When badly injured such as when it takes one or more strikes that inflicts 10% or more of its endurance in damage in one round, one or more (1d4) of this plantoid's spore emitters will involuntarily expel a puff of dark brown spores. This plantoid will form a cloud around it in a 10m radius for up to an hour in a non-windy area, like a ravine, vehicle hull, cave, corridor, or other indoor space. Likewise, this intelligent plant can purposefully expel one or all of its spore ejectors to cloud an area and ensure those that haven't already built up an immunity are more likely to suffer. For every spore emitter discharged, the willpower based hazard check of those who inhale this cloud becomes more challenging. The following table shows the number of spore emitters discharged and the corresponding hazard check needed to avoid suffering the consequences.

Those caught in the cloud who do not wear a gas mask, filter mask, or relic helmet with its own filtration system or air supply suffer from an immediate runny nose, blurry eyes and restricted breathing. If they make their hazard check, however, they can cope with the ordeal and fight on, while those who fail their check must withdraw from the spore cloud's radius if able, or otherwise drop to their knees and cough and wheeze as they have trouble breathing. Those who succumb thereafter suffer -2 initiative and a -50% to their movement rate for a full hour thereafter.

| Spore Emitters Discharged | Willpower Based Hazard Check |
|---|---|
| 1 | A |
| 2 | B |
| 3 | C |
| 4 | D |
| 5 | E |
| 6 | F |
| 7 | G |
| 8 | H |

If deployed outdoors and there is a breeze, this cloud will dissipate from an area within 3d6 minutes, although anyone who succumbed (failed their hazard check) will continue to suffer the ill effects for an hour. The cloud can be made to carry on the wind for 50 meters and can be unleashed so that it sweeps over any enemy position or advancing foe, although this is tricky and the plantoid must make a successful accuracy based hazard check, type D, to make the cloud go where it wants. Beyond 50m, the spore dissipates into the environment harmlessly.

Exposure to this pollen after three exposures — within one month — will render allergy sufferers immune to the worse of the effects, allowing this plantoid to deploy these spores around familiar, previously exposed human or animal companions without afflicting them.

## Amber Pellets 335

Type: **physical attack**
Range: **1 meter per point of strength**
Usage: **size based, see table below**
Rate: **Size based, see below** Strike Value: **+4**
Damage: **1d4 each**
Weight added: **based on size, see below**

This mutant plant's trunk and larger limbs are covered in hundreds of variable sized hard sap pellets. While not true amber, and removed bullets will dissolve in water after 72 hours, these lumps of sap grow into rock hard, pistol caliber sized beads. When 'ripe', each is backed by a mass of pressurized resin and nerves. When provoked, this plantoid can fire one or more of these projectiles up to its current strength score in meters range.

Each pellet has a strike value bonus of +4 and on a hit scores 1d4 damage. The number of pellets available to the plant per day, as well as the number fired in each volley, depends upon the size of the plantoid.

Targets wearing ballistic vests receive the same DV benefit from these pellets as they do from bullets.

| Size of Plantoid | Pellets per day | Rate of Fire* | Weight Added |
|---|---|---|---|
| Tiny under 1 meter | 12 | 1d6 | +2kg |
| Small between 1m and 1.5m | 24 | 2d6 | +5kg |
| Average between 1.5m and under 2m | 36 | 2d8 | +10kg |
| Large between 2m and 3m tall | 48 | 3d6 | +20kg |
| Huge over 3 meters tall | 64 | 3d10 | +30kg |

*Always roll random number in volley*

## Animal Parts 336

Type: **physical mutation**
Strike Value and Damage: **Possible, based on random part**
Weight Added: **See each animal part description, this page**

Besides some human DNA which already give this entity animation, thought and sensory organs, this plantoid also exhibits one or two (1d2) parts that are associated with an animal and it therefore exhibits DNA from non-plant creatures including unidentifiable mutant lifeforms. Roll 1d30* on the following table, with re-rolls made for any duplicated results.

**No d30 yet? Buy one at your FLGS, order on-line, or roll a d3 and a d10: 1d3 (tens column: result 1 = 0 to 10/ result 2 = 11 to 20/ result 3 = 21 to 30) +1d10 (one's column). Example: 1d3 roll results in a 2, while the d10 roll yields a 7 = 27.*

**1. Sharks gills:** This plantoid can breathe and live underwater as long as it desires. Add 4kg weight.

**2. Crab pincer:** SV +5, damage 3d6, and adds a shield-like protective barrier and so also improves defense value by -6. This appendage is heavy, however, and adds +10+4d6 kg weight to the plantoid.

**3. Patches of thick lizard scales:** This plantoid enjoys an improvement to its defense value of -10+2d6 (-12 to -22), roll once at character generation to determine amount. Add 3kg weight.

**4. Pigs snout and tusks:** Extra melee range bite attack at +5 SV that inflicts 1d12 damage. Able to eat an omnivorous diet, including subterranean moss, mushrooms, and cadavers, and so if needed, it can live without the need of photosynthesis or soil nutrients. This plantoid can talk through this mouth, too, although in a guttural, sub-human, piggish manner. Add 5kg weight.

**5. Antlers:** A full set of deer, moose or elk antlers grow from this plant mutant's trunk or root ball and remain year round. This rack can gore opponents for an extra melee range attack, SV +7, Damage 2d8, however on a charge attack, the SV bonus is +14 and inflicts 4d8 damage. Add 6kg weight.

**6. Dog ears:** These auditory receptors provide an excellent sense of hearing, and add +1 initiative. Add 1kg weight.

**7. Dog jaw:** This toothy mouth adds an extra melee attack with a strike value of +6 and inflicting 1d12+1 damage. This mouth is hooked to a crude digestive system which allows this plantoid to eat fresh flesh and carrion as well as whatever other mode of nutrient acquisition it employs. This toothy mouth can bark, growl and talk gruffly, too. Add 5kg weight.

**8. Dog leg:** This lone appendage helps this plantoid run faster and turn quick in combat. Improve movement by +1 meters per round and yields a defense value bonus of -5 DV. Add 7kg weight.

**9. Herbivore leg:** See dog leg above for details. Add 7kg weight. **Roll 1d6: 1.** Goat leg /**2.** Deer leg / **3.** Cow leg / **4.** Pig leg / **5.** Rat leg / **6.** Sheep leg.

**10. Covered in patches of chicken feathers:** This plumage offers some padding, wards off cold, and improves defense value by -4. These feathers are quite flammable, however, and if this plantoid should take fire damage, add an extra 1pt damage per round that it burns. Add 1kg weight.

**11. Chicken beak, giant:** This plantoid can make an extra peck or bite attack per round (SV +5, damage 1d10) and with the help of a rudimentary digestive track, this plant mutant can eat other plants, grains, and carrion besides any other nutrient gathering modes it might possess. Add 5kg weight.

**12. Fish tail and fins:** This weedy has an elongated fish tail at its back as well as several fins elsewhere about its body. It can make an extra swat attack in melee with the tail (SV +4, damage 1d10 stun), but the true use of this appendage is when the plantoid is forced to swim, where it moves at its normal land movement rate +2m per round extra. Add 22kg weight.

**13. Giant Squid tentacle:** This fleshy, suction cup lined appendage features patches of bark along the length, but otherwise looks like a feeding tentacle, complete with the paddle-shaped tentacular club at the end. This growth is twice as long as the plantoid is tall and will grow in proportion to the character over time. It serves as an extra melee attack (SV +10 / DMG 1d20). Likewise, this appendage can grapple, as per the skill on page 39 of the Hub Rules, and adds 2 skill points in this area. The strength of the tentacle is the same as the plantoid's main trait value. Opponents can try to cut this tentacle off, with the appendage having a DV of -20 and END 32. If severed, it will take 3+d6 months to grow back to a useful length. If used to climb, it gives the plantoid an extra hazard check per 6 meters scaled. When not deployed, this meaty tube can be coiled and wrapped about the main body of the plant and kept secure. Add 1kg weight, per 10cm length of tentacle or 10kg per meter (tentacle is double length of how tall plantoid is).

**14. Bear foreleg and clawed paw:** A black bear's front leg grows from this plantoid's trunk. It has a strength score of 54 and adds an extra melee attack (SV +10 / DMG 1d10+2).This leg also helps propel the mutant and adds +2m per round to its speed. Furthermore, the addition of this powerful limb adds 1 skill point to both climbing and grappling. Add 25kg weight.

**15. Rat muzzle:** A giant, eyeless, toothy rat muzzle grows from this plantoid, with a 2 in 6 chance it is located on the end of a 2m long, flexible root or branch, otherwise it's adhered to the trunk. This muzzle acts as an extra bite, SV +5, DMG 1d8, however, it can also be used to grasp objects. A simple digestive system is attached to the mouth, which allows the plantoid to access a wider range of nutrients, including the flesh of animals and plants. This mouth can gurgle and hiss, but not speak. Add 3kg weight.

**16. Chicken portions:** Here and there about the plantoid grow living portions of standard sized chicken, including 2d6 thighs, 3d6 drumsticks, 4d6 wings, and 1d6 full breast sections festooned on the plantoid's trunk. These pieces do not have feathers on them, nor feet, and seem to result from some ancient agricultural enterprise to grow kitchen ready meat portions. These appendages grow once per month and if not sliced off — which hurts the plantoid momentarily — the pieces

become shriveled up and drop off after the second month. While this ever present supply of meat is handy for any human traveling companions, it is also an attractant to predators, especially when the portions are left beyond the first month and grow increasingly pungent. Add 10kg weight.

**17. Cat eye:** The eye of a cat grows from the upper reaches of this plantoid and is connected to the thing's nervous system. While it doesn't necessarily have night vision, it allows the plantoid to see four times better than a human in low light conditions, while under all circumstances improves the entity's awareness and so adds a permanent +2 initiative to the mutant. And +5 accuracy. Add 2kg weight.

**18. Cow udders:** Clearly the result of some ancient agricultural development, this plantoid has a functional set of cow udders at its lower extremities. Through the mutant's daily intake of sunlight, liquids, ground nutrients or other means, it gains the necessary water and components to produce cow's milk and can yield 4 liters per day. If the plant is starved of nutrients or water, milk production will drop off to 10%, plus, while if it cannot rid itself of milk after 24 hours, it will grow very uncomfortable. Add 14kg weight.

**19. Cockroach carapace:** Bits of a giant cockroach grow to the main limbs and trunk of this plantoid, giving it an especially horrific appearance. Besides making the thing look nightmarish and eliciting an almost immediate attack by humans who aren't already on friendly terms with this mutant, these sections of orange, black and tan carapace both protect and strengthen the plantoid. Increase endurance by +3d6 and defense value by -20. Add 30kg weight.

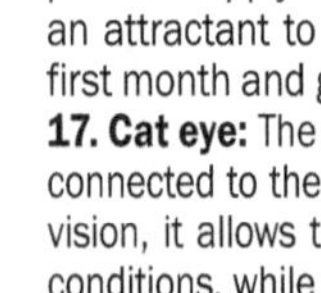

**20. Cockroach legs:** Ghastly, tan colored, bristle and spine covered giant cockroach legs grow from the lower section of this plantoid. While hideous and alarming to behold, these incredible 2+1d4 limbs each add +1m movement per round and overall add +2 skill points in climbing. Add 8kg weight per leg. At least one leg can make an extra melee attack per round, and can kick and scratch an opponent with a +5 SV, 1d12 damage attack.

**21. Bone sickle:** A muscular, meter long limb grows from this plantoid's main body. The end of this meaty appendage bears a large, lethally sharp bone sickle which can slash and stab an opponent as an extra melee range attack (SV +12/ DMG 1d20). This growth is very useful in climbing, too; increase the plantoid's climbing skill by 2 points. Weight added 18kg

**22. Monkey arm & hand:** A lean, hairy monkey arm grows from the side of this plantoid's trunk. While weak, being only half of the mutant's regular strength trait value, this highly dexterous limb and hand can wield small items, including one handed weapons such as pistols. This growth can also operate keyboards and, in conjunction with another limb, could also operate a two handed relic firearm. A punch from this fist does only 1d4 damage, but it can be treated as an extra melee range attack. Weight added 4kg.

**23. Mandible ended vine:** The over-sized mandibles of a wasp or ant grow at the end of a two meter long flexible vine or root. These hard pincers can act as an extra melee range attack (SV +8/ DMG 1d12) but can also grip or pull objects, assist another limb in wielding a two-handed weapon, or help to ascend trees and cliffs whereby the plantoid gains +1 skill point in climbing. Weight added, 15kg.

**24. Pearls:** Minerals form in fleshy crevices at various points around this plantoid's trunk. While to the untrained eye these ridges look like folds in the bark, but to those familiar with oysters, these shell-lined grooves reveal a highly polished pearl within each of the 5+1d6 pockets. A pearl takes 1 year +2d6 months to develop into a truly valuable size, and each will fetch 100+d100sp in a large trade town. At the time of character generation, this plantoid will have 1d6 ready to harvest. Weight added 1kg per pearl polishing organ.

**25. Shark cartilage:** This plantoid is more flexible than it otherwise would be, allowing it to better control its limbs, side step attacks, and respond to threats. Improve its movement rate by +1.5m per round and increase its agility by +20+1d20 points. Add 5kg weight. Double plantoid's lifespan.

**26. Bone studded:** Improve this plantoid's defense value by -12

**27. Ham melons:** Once every three months 2d6 cantaloupe sized hanging fruit become ripe and grows pink and fleshy. These are, in fact, portions of raw pig flesh, genetically engineered to grow on agricultural plants. If plucked and cooked, each will feed 6 man-sized entities, causing no harm to the weedy. If not harvested once ripe, they will remain viable for 3d6 days before dropping off on their own and eventually rotting once severed from the plantoid. Each ripe ham weighs 5kg. A big problem with these growths is the scent of succulent pork, which attracts carnivores once ripe and the hanging meat goes unattended. If plucked and used as a club, a ham will inflict 1d10 stun damage.

**28. Scorpion stinger branch:** While this branch might go unnoticed among other leafy or pine needle covered growths, it is in fact able to fully articulate and curve into a giant scorpion's tail, complete with a barbed stinger at the tip. Once every second round, the plantoid can add this extra melee attack to stab and potentially inject venom into a victim. This venom does not affect other plants, but for an animal, and a human in particular, it could be deadly. Any successful strike inflicts 1d10 damage plus the target must make an initial endurance based type D hazard check to fend off the venom, failure means they drop unconscious on the third round after, and a separate willpower based type B hazard check is needed after an hour to avoid heart failure and death. If an anti toxin injector or successful use of a Flesh Mend Gel is applied before this hour, death can be avoided. This stinger can only discharge 3 successful injections per 24 hours. Add 20kg weight.

**29. Elephant tusk:** 90% of the time, only one such tusk appears, but the rest of the time (91-00), two parallel ivory tusks extend from the thickest part of the plantoid. These two meter long, lethally pointed growths can gore opponents in melee attack, SV +10, damage 1d20. If two tusks are present, increase the SV to +20 and combined they inflict 1d20+10 damage. If used to parry an opponent, and thus giving up the next attack with this attack mode, the plantoid gains a -10 DV bonus if it exhibits only one tusk or -15 DV for two tusks. Add 18kg per tusk, with a sell value of 70+1d100sp.

**30. Chicken leg:** A massive, fully feathered leg grows near the base of this plantoid, complete with a huge clawed foot. This limb aids in locomotion (adding +3m movement per round) but it can add an extra melee range attack (SV +9/ DMG 3d6). Finally, this limb aids ascending all manner of steep surfaces and so increase the character's climbing skill by +1. Weight added 20kg.

## Arid Plant Adaptation 337

Type: **physical mutation**     Defense value: **+10**
Weight added: **+2kg**

This plantoid has evolved from at least one strain of desert plants, most likely a cactus, and has rough, moisture retaining bark which gives it a +10 defense value bonus, thick, nutrient laden leaves, and a remarkably strong tolerance to extreme heat, drought and the hardships of the open desert. Sand storms do not harm this mutant plant, while it can go without water for 6d6 days at a time during normal operations (determined at character generation). Beyond this, it can go into a dormant, semi-conscious stationary hibernation state and wait for a source of liquid, or rain, to come and rejuvenate it.

While in hibernation mode, and if in an area with other desert plant life, this character's dried out husk looks like just any other arid plant, and enjoys 5 skill points in the 'conceal self' ability (see stealth skill). This also applies to a character who inhabits a human host body, where the remains will look like a desiccated human corpse. Should this weedy indeed be a corpse or host bound, then once it is given a half dozen liters of water or more it will reanimate its human vehicle, and after four days the host will return to its previous, non-desiccated appearance.

Because this plantoid can store water for a long period of time, it can be 'tapped' or cut into slightly to offer enough moisture to keep one grown adult humanoid alive for up to 1 day per each 10 points of endurance this plantoid has. Unfortunately, for each day of survival water depleted, the plantoid suffers 3d6 damage which does not heal until it can hydrate fully.

While thriving best in hot, arid terrain, this plantoid suffers no particular harm from exposure to cold regions, swamps, deep forests or other climates.

## Armored Husk 338

Type: **physical defense**
Defense Value: **Varies depending on thickness**
Weight Added: **See table below**

The bark on this mutant plant is both thick and incredibly tough. Furthermore, in many instances, some past genetic alteration has occurred which, through multiple generations, natural selection, human manipulation, and hyper evolution, has added extra features to the protective sheathing of this plantoid. While this dense bark layer offers splendid protection and overall hardiness as both defense value and endurance improvements, it tends to slow the mutant somewhat.

Roll 2d6 on the following table to determine this deviant's husk variant:

| 2d6 | Armored Husk Variant | DV | END | Move | Weight | Other feature |
|---|---|---|---|---|---|---|
| 2. | Ballistic Fiber Embedded | DV -10 or -25 vs. Bullets | +3d6 | -0.75m | +20kg | Bullets, falls, blunt strikes by clubs and fists, rock impact and the like are hard pressed to puncture this plantoid's hide, and if they do, the mutant takes only half damage from each impact. Fragmentation grenades and other explosions which expel hard projectiles are also resisted in this same fashion. |
| 3,4. | Flame Resistant* | DV -10 or -40 vs fire attacks | +2d6 | -0.5m | +15kg | This plantoid is allowed 2 hazard checks against flame based attacks if called for. Likewise, its DV against flame weapons, explosions and similar, is improved to -40. Should this mutant catch fire, it will suffer only half damage and any burn time is limited to a maximum of 3 rounds. |
| 5,6. | Extra Thick | DV -20 | +4d6 | -1m | +30kg | nil |
| 7,8. | Thick | DV -10 | +3d6 | -0.5m | +10kg | nil |
| 9,10. | Exceptionally Thick | DV -30 | +5d6 | -1.5m | +50kg | nil |
| 11. | Radiation Resistant | DV -10 | +2d6 | -0.5m | +15kg | This mutant's bark has a strange opalescence to it, and when exposed to radiation, it gleams brightly and exudes a resin which blocks out radiation by one category. Mild radiation is considered to be harmless, while medium radiation becomes mild, strong becomes medium, and lethal is considered as a dose of strong radiation. In addition, any dose of radiation is shed from this plantoid after one month — the amber-like pellet it sheds holds the dangerous substance for 2d6 years. |
| 12. | Energy Weapon Resistant | DV -10 | +3d6 | -0.5m | +15kg | This plantoid's bark has a noticeable metallic sheen to it, which is visible in bright sunlight or the gleam of a fire or flashlight. Incoming energy beams, either by ranged or melee attacks, have a hard time cutting through this mutant's hide, and if they do so, they inflict only half damage. Any incoming projectile beam that misses has a 1 in 10 chance of deflecting off and back to the shooter, although the beam still needs to make a strike to inflict damage on the assailant. |

*In the rare instance where this plantoid also has the mutation of Fire Repellent, combine both mutations to make this mutant remarkably fireproof whereby its leaves, smaller branches and other growing appendages are all impervious to fire and will not ignite.*

## Barb Whip Tendrils 339

Type: **physical attack**    Range: **melee**
Rate: **1 per tendril (2+1d6 present)**
Strike Value: **+10**    Damage: **1d6 + skill modifiers**
Defense Value: **-2 per tendril**    Tendril DV: **-20**
Tendril Endurance: **18**    Weight Added: **+5kg per tendril**

While not very dexterous nor much good for manipulating, climbing or holding more than nearby rubble or branches, these many barb covered, finger thick appendages are great at lashing out at one or multiple opponents and leaving bloody rips in their flesh. This plantoid will start game play with 2+1d6 of these 3 meter long vines, although another 1d4 immature vines are also budding on the character's main trunk or root ball and will add their benefits in a month. During melee combat, each tendril acts as an extra attack with a +5 strike value bonus and inflict 1d6 damage prior to any skill based modifiers. Either the brawling skill, martial arts, or a weapon expert skill can be applied to these growths, but not combined. These appendages do not have the character's strength modifier applied to them, as they are consistent in their size and lethality regardless of the main plant's brawn.

Opponents can target individual tendrils and hack or shoot them off, with each tendril having a DV of -20 and able to endure 18 points damage before being severed and useless. Each tendril takes a month to regrow.

As these lashing, whip-like tendrils grow and coil about the plantoid's main body, they offer an additional armor-like benefit of -2 defense value per mature tendril present.

These tendrils can be used to attack in conjunction with other melee attack modes, making this entity an extra dangerous close quarters adversary.

## Bitter Tasting 340

Weight added: **+2kg**

All animals, including insects, find the taste of this plantoid to be bitter and unappealing. Unless defending their nest, lair or hive, most creatures will spit out whatever portion of the plantoid they bit into, and move on to look for something more tasty. Only creatures that are starving or defending their territory will be determined enough to continue to bite this plantoid, and then with reluctance.

If this plantoid has a plant flaw that involves an infestation of bugs or rodents, etc., then it suffers only 50% harm or trait reduction for that flaw.

## Boring Tendrils 341

Type: **physical attack**    Range: **melee**
Rate: **1**    Strike Value: **+18**
Damage: **1 point per plantoid's rank, per round once attached**
Healing: **1 trait point (to each depleted trait), per round once attached**
Tendril Defense Value: **-15 (if doing 22 DMG, the victim can pull away)**
Hazard check to pull free: **Type E STR based HC**    Weight Added: **+10kg**

Growing at various points on this plantoid are several of tightly coiled and knotted tendrils. These seemingly harmless, root-like growths can spring out to bore into the flesh and organs of a foe and tear open, and ingest the fluids of a living victim. Treat the tendrils as one attack, and if a successful strike occurs on a melee range opponent, this plantoid will inflict 1 point of damage per rank, per round automatically to the victim unless separated. Living creatures of flesh and

blood can offer some sustenance to this mutant plant, and for every round of organ boring, this deviant can recover 1 trait point up to the depleted stat's maximum trait value.

When used against robots, androids, machinery, cracked concrete, wooden doors or other porous materials — a smooth metal or concrete barrier needs existing gaps, bullet holes or other seams and cavities for these tendrils to penetrate and harm — the same rank based damage per round can be inflicted, although no sustenance can be gained and indeed, electrical damage might result instead. When boring into a cyborg, robot, electrically charged machine or vehicle, this plantoid has a 2 in 6 chance of inadvertently contacting an internal power line or battery and getting an immediate shock for 2d20 stun damage and 1d12 lethal damage.

A victim of a successful boring tendril attack can attempt to break free by hacking or crushing through these hollow, tentacle-like growths instead of attacking the plant which wields them. The victim can direct its efforts against the mass of wriggling tendrils, which have a defense value of -15 and if 22 or more damage is inflicted, enough tendrils have been yanked free or torn away to allow the victim to either retreat away from melee range or force the mutant plant to make another attempt to stab more of these appendages back into the target. Besides attacking the tendrils themselves, a victim can make a type E strength based hazard check to twist and snap free of the tendrils to get away.

Torn away tendrils grow back within days and the plantoid normally has enough of the growths left to make further boring attacks. The accuracy trait value and rank improvements to the character's strike value increase the odds of a boring tendril attack making a strike, while the damage inflicted per round is equal to the entity's current rank.

This mutation is similar to vampiric roots, although the above noted tendrils must be used from melee range and are far more devastating and multipurpose, especially at higher rank.

## Bug Repellent Sap 342

Type: **physical defense**    Usage: **Continuous**
Damage: **nil, but insects die after three failed hazard checks**
Hazard Check: **Type C END**    Weight added: **+5kg**

Both the leaves and bark of this plantoid are filled with a substance which insects find caustic and distasteful. Any insect to successfully bite this mutant plant must make a Type C endurance based hazard check, per successful strike, to continue feeding on or attacking the character.

If the insect fails this hazard check but is defending its territory, young or eggs, and has another attack mode it can employ against the plantoid, it will do so. If it has a bite attack only, and in its nest, it will continue to bite at the plantoid regardless of the burning it receives with each strike, eventually dying if failing three or more hazard checks.

In most cases, however, one bite of the plantoid will usually be enough to make the hungry bugs look elsewhere for a meal.

Non-insects are not affected by this sap, however, after several mouthfuls of this plant, the animal's mouth will begin to tingle and swell somewhat.

For the purposes of what is or is not an insect, treat all insects along with mollusks such as slugs, as well as millipedes, centipedes, spiders, scorpions, crustaceans and other invertebrates as 'bugs'.

Any potential flaw mutation that involves a bug or slug infestation is negated by this sap.

## Chameleon Powers 343

Type: **physical mutation**        Usage: **three times per day per rank**
Duration: **1 hour per rank**
Initiative Bonus: **+3 when engaged and first encountered**
Hazard Check: **See stealth skill, add 4 pts to conceal self, and concealed movement.**        Weight added: **nil**

As the name implies, this plantoid can change the pigmentation of its foliage, roots, vines and other living portions of its body. Its outer bark, which is typically non-living matter, only partially changes color. Effectively, this mutant plant can better attempt to hide among the shrubs, grass and trees about it, and gains 4 skill points improvement in the stealth categories of conceal self, and concealed movement. See the stealth skill on page TME-51 for more.

Besides making oneself look like the local vegetation, this mutant can also leech the color out of its foliage and branches to make them gray and rusty, either in solid or patchy tones to match the surrounding junk, rubble and wreckage.

This alteration takes only 1 round to achieve, but requires all the plantoid's attention and can only be done three times per day per character rank. Once established, the new coloration will remain in effect for one hour per character rank.

Besides the improved ability to hide and move unnoticed, this character also gains a +3 to initiative when first encountered and when operating alone or as the lead element of a group while chameleon mode is applied.

## Club limb (or vine) 344

Type: **physical attack**        Range: **melee**
Rate: **1**      Strike Value: **+12**      Damage: **1d20 stun or lethal**
Weight added: **+10kg per club limb**
This plantoid exhibits one or more thick branches or vines which end in hardened, mineral embedded dead wood. These heavy extensions can bludgeon opponents and inflict either stun or lethal damage at this mutant's discretion. Each such club limb can add an extra melee attack to any other melee attacks this mutant has available. A club limb has a strike value bonus of +12 and inflicts 1d20 stun or lethal damage on a strike.

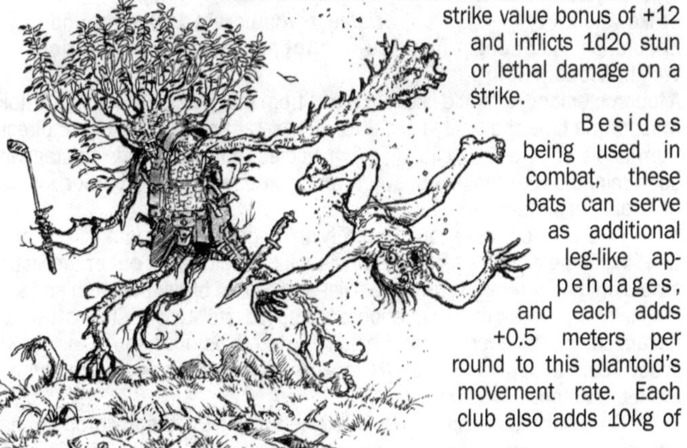

Besides being used in combat, these bats can serve as additional leg-like appendages, and each adds +0.5 meters per round to this plantoid's movement rate. Each club also adds 10kg of weight to the subject. **Roll 2d6** for the number of club appendages at the time of character creation: **2-7.** One club limb/ **8-10.** Two club limbs / **11.** Three club limbs /**12.** Four club limbs

Club limbs have a DV of -20 and can take 26 endurance damage before being cut off.  Lost club limbs grow back in 50+3d20 days.

## Control Carnivorous Plants 345

Type: **Mental Mutation**        Range: **2m radius per rank**
Usage: **Once per day per rank**  Weight Added: **+1kg**
This form of botanical control was developed long ago to allow certain human-plant hybrids to shepherd and command genetically engineered or wild predatory plants. Whatever ancient effectiveness this mind power might have once wielded, it is much reduced in the new era. This control ability is likely weakened because new era plants are either more strong-willed, less receptive, or the mind control abilities of plantoids reduced by cross breeding among other plantoids. Whatever the case, most of the control is now turned toward simply keeping predatory plants and green walkers from attacking this plantoid and its fleshy companions.

This mutation allows the plantoid to cause each predatory plant within this deviant's area radius of influence to cease hostilities, remove any blocking appendages, cease any advancement, let go of any victims they might already have ensnared, entangled, or grip in their feeding orifices, and allow the plantoid controller and its companions to either walk safely through an area or hold back the flesh eating plants.

More difficult tiers of control involve the user gaining control of one or more plantoids in its area of effect and having it advance ahead of this controller and attack other beings, vehicles or structures. At the height of this control, the user can induce predatory plants to attack each other, walk into a fire if they have mobility, or walk off a cliff. The character can attempt to maintain control based on the difficulty of the tier, noted on the table to follow, but while doing so, the PC can do nothing but concentrate on mentally dominating the predatory plants and walking at its normal movement rate — usually to get itself, and any companions, through a patch of jaw plants or away from a massive herd of green walkers.

The following table shows what the mutant can do with this power, and the odds of success — although game masters and players can certainly come up with expanded options. The user's willpower is called upon to determine the outcome, with failure meaning the next less challenging tier and outcome is automatically consulted and another hazard check needed (If say tier 3 fails, then try tier 2, etc.).

Should failure results yet again at this lower tier, then the next control choice is reached. If all controls fail, then the carnivorous plants attacks this plantoid and any companions. If this plantoid character wants to spend back-to-back uses of this mutation's daily limit, it can do so and maintain existing control in which the controlled plants DO NOT get to make new willpower checks. In this way, a high rank user of this power could direct vast patches of predatory plants to do its bidding — perfect for a villain.

| Control Tier Desired | Plant's Will-power based HC | Duration of Control |
|---|---|---|
| Tier 1/ Very Easy: Do not attack this plantoid only* | G | 1 minute per point of user's willpower |
| Tier 2/ Easy: Do not attack the plantoid or its traveling companions | F | 10 rounds for every point of user's willpower |
| Tier 3/ Uncomplicated: Go dormant if immobile, or walk away from the area. | E | 5 rounds for every point of user's willpower** |
| Tier 4/ Challenging: Advance ahead of the controller, or turn around and attack specified pursuers, or guard pathway, and fight on behalf of the plantoid character and its companions, attacking structures, vehicles or other entities as directed. | C | 1 round for every point of user's willpower. |
| Tier 5/ Hard: Attack other carnivorous plants around itself, or walk into a fire, off a cliff, or other destructive action — other than attacking itself. | B | 1 round for every 2 points of user's willpower. |

*Any traveling companions, pets or mounts are subject to attack.

**Most mutant plants will cease attacking or chasing prey once they lose sight of it, and at the end of this duration might simply stop and wait for some new passing prey animal to come along.

*GM Note:* In the grand scheme of possibilities and player imagination in a tabletop role-playing game, this is a very limited list of possible commands. Allow the players to suggest other actions they might want a carnivorous or other animated NPC plant to perform and then select the difficulty tier and duration.

### Example of Control Carnivorous Plants

Fiberosa, a 3rd rank plantoid, wants to get a mob of 16 green walkers to walk away so she and her flesh based human companions can pass through a clearing. This is a tier 3, uncomplicated attempt at control. Each green walker makes a type E willpower based hazard check, and with a trait of only 23,

it's a 33% chance that any in her radius of control (6m since she gets a 2m radius per rank) will resist her command. Yet, 4 of them do and keep coming while the rest walk away. These 4 are now in the tier two 'easy' control zone, and get a type F hazard check to resit Fiberosa's control. 3 of them do obey and simply stand still and let the group pass, but one is stubborn and drops to tier one, which is a type G hazard check for it and a 14% chance it will not comply. It complies, but is only commanded enough to not attack Fiberosa, and instead attacks one of the human travelers. Had this walker accomplished this final hazard check, it would have attacked Fiberosa just as easily as any of her friends.

## Dagger Seed Pods 346

Type: **physical attack**  Range: **1m per point of strength**
Usage: **1 branch per round, from 1d4+2 branches.**
Rate: **1 to 18 from 1 branch**  Strike Value: **+10**
Damage: **1d8 each**  Weight added: **+5kg per pod**

This plant bares 1d4+2 short, meter long leafy branches on which grow scores of large, wedge shaped seed pods. Each branch will offer 3d6 mature seed pods per month. The plantoid can squeeze these pods from the outstretched branch at adversaries at great velocity. The mutant can and may fire from only one branch per round, and either use one or any number of mature dagger seed pods on that branch, projecting them out at a range equal to the plantoid's strength score in meters. Each dagger has a strike value +10, damage on a strike of 1d8 each plus any strength or weapon expert applied modifiers.

Although this plantoid can unleash between 1 and 18 dagger seeds from each branch per round, once they are expended for the month, the limbs are

as a mobile adult specimen. New specimens of this mutant plant might not necessarily see the parent plantoid as anything but competition for resources, and humans as a source of compost.

merely useful for shade or photosynthesis and the long wait for more dagger seeds to grow commences.

The seeds themselves are only rarely viable for reproduction, since the odds of this mutant's tiny flowers being pollinated by another plantoid with the same mutation is rare. If fertilization occurs, a dagger seed must end up in a dead victim or very fertile ground with plenty of sunlight, water, and an agreeable climate. Should these conditions be met, a viable seed would grow in place for 6+2d6 years before a replica of the parent plant would emerge

## Dehydration Root 347

Type: **physical attack**  Range: **4m reach**  Rate: **1**
Strike Value: **+7**  Damage: **fluid drain 1d6 per round**
Endurance and Strength Trait recovery: **1pt per round of dehydration**
Weight Added: **+35kg**

A four meter long, tentacle-like root grows from the underside of this plantoid. Most of the time the entity uses it to suck water from mud, sand or directly from pools of water — including water bodies that are otherwise stagnant, contaminated with cholera, beaver fever, or other waterborne pathogens with no ill effects on the plantoid.

As a weapon, however, this terrifying tendril can stab into a living creature, including an inanimate tree, and suck the fluids right out of the victim. A held animal or human can try to twist and turn to break the latch and stop the painful process of dehydration on a successful type E strength based hazard check. However, unless the thorn covered, porous head of this growth is severed, the appendage can try to strike the target again and continue to drain the victim.

On a successful strike, accomplished at +7 SV, the absorption head latches onto a victim and thereafter dehydrates 1d6 points of endurance in fluids from the subject. To sever this root, which has a defense value of

-20 and endurance of 32, it must be blown away or hacked off, and if so, will take 3+1d3 months to regrow. Treat this appendage as an extra melee range attack, although with a reach of 4 meters (13 feet), it can be used as a standoff attack and keep the plantoid's main body out of harm's reach from most close-in counter attacks.

Besides taking in vital nutrients and fluids, the stolen liquids from a living person or animal also have a remarkable healing effect on the plantoid who drained them. For each round of successful fluid intake, the mutant heals 1 lost endurance or strength trait point, although the amount cannot exceed the character's uninjured base amount.

## Detachable Core Seedling  *Idea by Thaddeus Moore* 348
Type: **defensive and mobility mutation**
Usage: **automatically at death or once per day per rank**
Weight Added: **+5kg**

This plantoid's consciousness resides in a much smaller, well protected inner core. Either once per day per rank or when the larger outer trunk is killed or facing imminent destruction, this inner sapling can peel free of the inner bark, drop to the ground and flee.

Whenever this miniature version of the main tree is separated from the main body, the host becomes dormant and adheres to the ground like just any other bush or tree. When dormant, and if not killed, burned away or otherwise in danger, it will continue to process any ground water or nutrients as well as undertake photosynthesis if already able to do so.

The seeding is only a half meter tall (50cm or 1' 7"), has a base movement of 4 meters, weighs 10+1d10 kilograms and has only 3d6 starting endurance and strength. All the other traits are as the main host plant, and likewise, any skills gained from character generation or rank gain remain with this sapling should it permanently abandon the main trunk.

Any mutations of the parent plant are theoretically present in this small minion, at least once it grows to full size again should its previous body be destroyed or permanently abandoned. However, it can only access mutations that suit it small size, such as any saps, mental mutations, special barks and other deviations that the game master deems applicable. For example, this tiny specimen would not have massive Venus fly trap jaws, elongated thorny tendrils, or other over sized limbs, although evidence of them would be present along with a couple of 30cm long manipulator vines that it can use to climb, wield a knife, pocket pistol or other small device. This core seedling will have the same senses as the main body, including the ability to speak if the main body did, etc.

It will grow back to its last size and regain all the traits of the abandoned husk after 1 year and 1d100 days.

While the main purpose of this mobile seedling is like that of an ejection seat in a relic aircraft, this weedy can also use this tiny version of itself to split from the larger body to ride in the backpack of a human comrade, sneak about undetected, or explore small spaces and the interiors of vehicles. It is of course at great risk while in its tiny core version, and if killed, the larger husk body will merely become a rooted vegetable after 48 hours and lose whatever locomotion it once had. Worse, if it had offensive appendages, it will now use them to acquire fleshy fertilizer, including any human companions that it once befriended when sentient.

If able to regrow to full size again, this seedling forms a new inner consciousness and core upon regaining its former 'pre-death' size. In the year that it is a growing specimen, its traits and appendages can be deemed half of whatever the full-sized adult had available to it, but operates without an inner core.

If this plantoid also has the Seedling Minions mutation, it can attempt to control one or more of these semi-aware growths to serve as scouts, bodyguards or decoys, although can only influence and command them in a radius equal to this PC's intelligence score in meters, and then must make a type B willpower based hazard check to control each. Those not in the plantoid's control will wander off to hunt or take root.

## Digestive Sap 349
Type: **physical defense**          Usage: **constant**
Range: **4m from wound splash**    Strike Value: **Fixed +6 from wound spray**
Damage: **1d6 per round for 1d6+2 rounds**     Weight added: **+5kg**

This plantoid is gifted with a layer of flesh eating sap, which automatically jets out of wounds whenever it is punctured. The main evolutionary purpose of this acidic goo is to rid the plant of insects and rodents, which might otherwise feed on it, instead these pests are dissolved and absorbed by the plantoid's

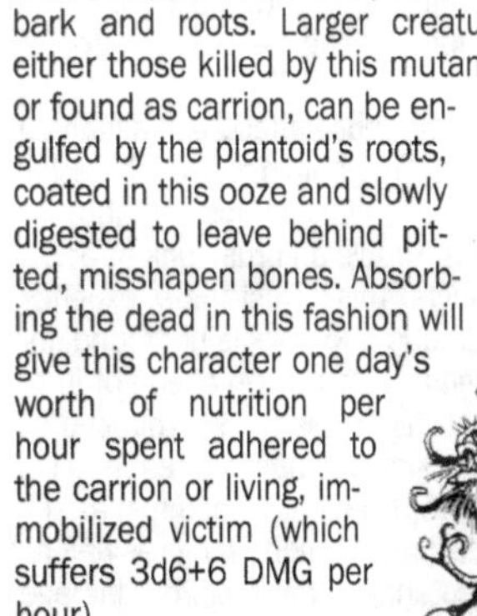

bark and roots. Larger creatures, either those killed by this mutant or found as carrion, can be engulfed by the plantoid's roots, coated in this ooze and slowly digested to leave behind pitted, misshapen bones. Absorbing the dead in this fashion will give this character one day's worth of nutrition per hour spent adhered to the carrion or living, immobilized victim (which suffers 3d6+6 DMG per hour).

Any cut or gunshot to inflict damage on the plantoid causes a spurt of acid to erupt in a plume, range 4 meters, SV +5. This splash is considered an automatic attack and occurs on the same turn as the attacker's successful strike. The damage and strike value of this splash attack are 'fixed' and do not change with the skills or rank gain of the character.

Any being struck from this discharge is dissolved for 1d6 damage per round for d6+2 rounds. Pouring at least two liters of water onto the afflicted area or leaping into water or other liquid will neutralize the digestive sap immediately.

This plantoid's branches, roots and leaves are immune to its own digestive sap, but its gear and armor are not, nor is the entity immune to other types of acid. Nearby comrades are also at risk whenever this plantoid takes a hit.

## Earth Boring Roots 350
Type: **physical attack**
Range: **half plantoid's strength in meters, or melee**
Usage: **3 times per day, per rank. Melee usage unlimited**
Rate: **'Thrust throw' 1 per round, or melee 1 per round up to 4 targets around this mutant, or all 4 attacks vs. 1 or more targets.**
Strike Value: **'thrust throw' +0, or melee +5**
Damage: **2d6 in melee or per object hurled, 1d6 objects thrown per 90° direction**
Burrowing: **50cm of plantoid's height per round, or burrowing travel at 0.5m per round in soft material**
Weight Added: **+40kg**

This potent mutation has three different modes of use. The first is to allow the plantoid to excavate into soft soils, junk, or sand to escape. Next, it can thrust into the ground in either one direction or all around, and 'thrust throw' masses of hard junk at up to 1d6 opponents in each of the 4, 90° angles about it. The third mode is to use these powerful appendages to slap and karate chop up to 4 surrounding enemies in melee range.

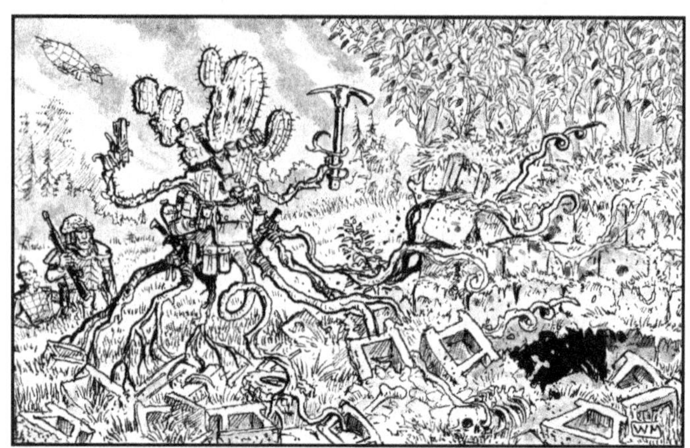

This plantoid can dig deep to escape into soft earth and evade enemies, forest fires, junk storms, or else merely to conceal itself. This burying itself procedure takes 1 round per 50cm of the plantoid's height, and if the soil is loose enough, including sand and mud, this mutant can travel underground at a half meter per round.

Using these roots take full concentration and much effort, with a limit on use up to 3 times per day per rank, but also allows the plantoid to use its specialized digging roots on their own to jab into soil or even junk heaps and abruptly thrust upward with its roots to propel logs, rocks, rubble and ruin junk at opponents in any direction in up to a 360 degree angle. This 'thrust throw' expends a daily use, takes only 1 round to perform, and hurls 1d6 objects per round, for each 90-degree angle of the throw. So if hurling in a half moon ahead of it, or 180°, it will throw 1d6 objects at opponents in each of these two 90° directions. If hurling debris in 270°, say ahead and to both sides, it makes three attacks, while if throwing junk in an all around 360° ring, four separate root thrust attack directions are targeted with 1d6 possible objects per direction. Range as half its strength score in meters, with each projectile potentially inflicting 2d6 damage (plus any strength modifiers). The plantoid can select blunt objects to hurl which do stun damage instead of lethal damage.

A third use for these stout, paddle shaped, sharp tipped roots is as a melee range attack, with a +5 strike value. This plantoid can smack, club and stab out at between 1 and 4 opponents, with either a back, front, left, or right attack (each 90° angle) around it. This attack inflicts 2d6 damage plus strength modifiers. This close-quarters application of these dangerous roots is not subject to the daily use limits and can be added as 4 extra attacks.

### Enhanced Pine Needles 351

Type: **physical mutation**          Range: **melee**
Strike Value: **01-60 'Fixed' auto return-attack or +5 SV to any punch, branch slap, kick or other physical attacks**
Damage: **'Fixed' 1d4+1 for auto return attack, however add +1d6 DMG to any punch, kick or branch attacks including thorn vines, saw leaves, and other offensive melee appendage attacks.**
Defense Value: **-15**          Weight added: **+7kg**
Growing all along this plantoid's trunk and dominant limbs are rows of robust, serrated pine needles. These growths are rigid and spike-like and aid the plantoid in both defending itself and when attacking. Anything to physically strike this mutant is auto-attacked (SV 01-60, DMG 1d4+1). This automatic attack occurs on the turn of the entity which struck this character and the SV and DMG are fixed throughout the life of the PC and don't change with skills or rank gain.

Additionally, the needles themselves add to the plantoid's overall armor by increasing its defense value by -15. Furthermore, when this character attacks with any punch, kick, shoulder slam or drop roll against an opponent, it adds +5 SV and +1d6 damage.

### Exoskeleton 352

Type: **physical enhancement**     Strike Value: **+5**
Damage: **+2**                    Defense Value: **-10**
Trait Bonuses: **Strength +20, Endurance +20**
Weight Added: **+40kg**

Ridges and bands of hard, bone like wood line this plantoid's frame and primary limbs. Although heavy, and adding an additional 40kg weight, this sturdy plant gains +20 to strength and endurance, and because of the toughness and density of its underlying frame, gains a -10 DV bonus.

Additionally, this brute gains extra support when moving, improved durability and a noticeable increase in the strength behind every physical attack it makes; increase the strike value and damage of any strength based attack by +5 each, besides any regular strength or accuracy based trait modifiers it might have.

Whether out of natural selection or the whims of some ancient genetic designer, theses woody length and braces resemble the skeletal structure of a human, which to onlookers can give this plantoid a fearsome, monstrous appearance, the response by strangers often one of terror or violence.

### Exploding Puff Balls 353

Type: **physical attack**     Range: **12m if flicked or drift on wind (see text)**
Blast Radius: **1m, or wider if multiple**  Usage: **3d6 ready to start (see text)**
Rate: **1 or 1d6**          Strike Value: **+10, or higher if multiple**
Damage: **1d10, or more if multiple**     Weight added: **+6kg**
This plantoid grows numerous, fist sized puff balls on its upper limbs. When ripe, one or more can be intentionally released to float on the wind or be flicked toward the enemy. If flicked, they have a range of 12 meters, however if carried on the wind they can travel up to 100 meters across flat ground, or 1000m downhill, or from an aerial platform, such as an airship, all the way to the ground before exploding.

These puffballs detonate upon impact and throw hard, pea sized sterile seeds about, similar to a fragmentation grenade's shrapnel.

Each has a blast radius of only a meter, however this radius increases by 1 meter per puff ball that floats into, or is flung at, a specific target or spot. All those in the blast zone are attacked with a strike value of 01-50, with a +5 SV per every additional puff ball. Each exploding ball will deliver 1d10 damage.

A plantoid will start game play (character creation) with 3d6 ripe puff balls, plus 6d6 developing orbs which appear as dark green plums and will become ripe in 30 days. An extra 6d6 new puff ball 'buds' are always present too, with each harvest taking six months to ripen.

The plantoid can fling or detach and 'let drift' one, or up to 1d6 per round until all mature puff balls are spent. These floating seed pods can be blown back toward the weedy and its companions should some mutation be used to take control of them — such as telekineses, large electric fans, or if a force shield is put up to bounce these projectiles.

**Multiple Puff Ball Detonation**

| Puff Balls Detonating | Blast Radius | SV | Damage |
| --- | --- | --- | --- |
| 1 | 1m | 01-50 | 1d10 |
| 2 | 2m | 01-55 | 2d10 |
| 3 | 3m | 01-60 | 3d10 |
| 4 | 4m | 01-65 | 4d10 |
| 5 | 5m | 01-70 | 5d10 |
| 6 | 6m | 01-75 | 6d10 |

If this character is crushed, grabbed by a violent force, or crashes in a vehicle, endures the impact of a fall, then there is a 30% chance per mature puff ball of it detonating.

These pods are very sensitive, and while tongs can pick and transport them for use by others — a deed that requires a Type C agility based hazard check to pull off without detonating the pod as soon as it is picked — these puff balls only remain explosive for up to 24 hours after extraction.

## Exploding Seed Pods 354

Type: **physical attack**      Range: **1m per point of strength**
Blast Radius: **1m**      Usage: **2d6 ripe pods with 5 seeds per pod**
Rate: **1 ripe pod per round**      Strike Value: **+20**
Damage: **1d10 per seed either by direct hit or exploding in blast zone.**
Weight added: **+10kg**

This plantoid has 2d6 ripe, elongated, bright green pods, similar to a pea pod, along with 3d6 immature, yellowish pods. These hanging growths can often go unnoticed among the plant mutant's foliage. When angered or on the hunt, this deviant can use pressure to split open a pod and use its trunk, or the branch the pod grows from, to flick the ruptured pod, thus throwing 5, walnut sized, ripe seeds up to one meter away for every point of strength the plantoid has. Each seed might impact a target and detonate either against the target or on the ground near it. For each successful strike, a seed explodes in a non-flammable shower of rock hard wood fragments, and inflicts 1d10 damage to any target.

Any miss from an exploding seed pod will carry on to the extent of the projectile's range, or roll 2d6 meters beyond the intended target if already at its range limit, and potentially explode among innocent victims or comrades of the plantoid. If a miss cannot go beyond the target, such as if the intended foe is against a wall, the seed will drop and detonate in a 1m blast radius and here, a separate, second strike roll is made against the target, thus the potential for two attacks on the same target are possible in this circumstance.

Immature seed pods will ripen after 30 days, while another batch of 2d6 immature seed pods will flower and grow among the character's branches every month. Any ripe seed pods not used up from month to month can be saved, either on the living plantoid and allow it a massive amount of firepower, or else the pod carefully snipped off and used by companions or hostile harvesters. This bounty can be opened and the seeds used as hand thrown projectiles or glued to the tips of arrows to add extra damage to any successful strike, or dropped from aerial mounts, airships, or relic aircraft.

A saved, detached seed pod can remain pressurized and dangerous for up to 6 years. If thrown into a fire, they will detonate in 1d6 rounds, while if a person carrying a bag of these is engulfed in fire or the blast of a regular fragmentation or incendiary device, each pod has a 50% of detonating and potentially blowing the carrier to smithereens.

Waterlogged seed pods, or those buried in the moist topsoil, will become harmless, and eatable after 2 days, and if the pod was fertilized by another plantoid with this same mutation — with a pollinator such as a bee going between the two characters — then germination and growth of a new hybrid variant of this character will emerge and grow to adulthood in 6d10 months. This hybrid will have a 50% chance of inheriting each mutation from each parent.

## Extra Large 355

Type: **physical mutation**
Creation based Trait modifiers: **add 1 meter height (100cm), +30+2d20 Endurance, +30kg weight, and +10+2d10 strength**
Rank gain or yearly trait Modifiers: **+30cm (1 foot) height, +3d6 endurance, 1d6 strength, and +10kg weight**
This plantoid has no fixed maximum growth, and at the start of character creation is typically larger than most humans. Each year it grows another foot (30cm), although the game master can allow that for every rank the character goes up, it gains this extra growth so long as a month of in-game time has elapsed and the PC has had access to plenty of fertilizer, sunlight and water.

At character creation, this towering weedy adds 100cm height, 30+2d20 Endurance, +10+2d10 strength and an extra +30kg weight.

For every foot (30cm) of growth thereafter, it gains an additional +3d6 endurance and 1d6 strength and +10kg weight.

While being a massive shrub or tree has its advantages, this weedy quickly becomes too large to enter buildings, ride in vehicles, or explore the great towers and deep ruins of the oldsters, and must reside itself to staying outside with the horses. Likewise, a towering, animated tree can illicit great alarm among commoners and town watchmen alike, and while standard sized plantoids are already difficult to accept by most folk, enormous specimens might be barred from a community, or attacked on sight.

One costly option to remedy this is by pruning, often with lopping off of upper branches and shortening of whatever roots the plantoid has. Pruning does, however, reduce the plantoid's traits and so for every 30cm (1 foot) hacked off, reduce the character's weight by -10kg, strength by 3pts, and endurance by 9pts.

## Extreme Fibers 356

Type: **physical enhancement**    Defense Value: **-5 bonus**
Movement Bonus: **+1m**      Weight Added: **+15kg**
Trait Improvements: **+4 STR, AG and ACC, +10 END, +8 PER**

The woody fibers within every main limb, root and core of this plantoid's body are remarkably long, hardy and responsive, as if it was genetically engineered for locomotion, strength and combat readiness — or else for the pulp-paper industry. This splendid specimen enjoys a +1m per round move rate increase, a bonus of +4 points to strength, agility, accuracy and because of the added density of its bark it gains -5 defense value bonus and +10 bonus to its endurance. Finally, there is an uncanny quickness to this being which also increases its awareness, and so adds +8 to its perception trait.

## Eye Tendril 357

Type: **physical mutation**      Weight added: **+5kg**
Besides whatever eye nodes this plantoid already exhibits, it also has a vine, root, or flexible branch which looks quite normal, except that at the bulbous end it has a rudimentary, glossy black eye. When not uncoiled and used for distant inspection, this eye often scans the plantoid's rear and so gives it a +1 initiative

bonus. This appendage can extend 10 times the length of the plantoid's height, bend around corners, peer in through bars, between ventilation grates, large bullet holes, or other cavities to inspect an area with remarkable stealth. Treat this eye appendage's stealth skills as 4 skill points for the purposes of 'Conceal Self' and 'Concealed Movement' on the stealth table on page TME 51.

Besides being a great observation and inspection appendage, this growth can be used as an extra emergency melee weapon to lash out and cudgel opponents, although on any fumble roll, the eye fruit is shattered and will take 100+1d100 days to regrow. As a weapon, this growth adds an extra melee attack, SV +10, DMG 2d6+ any strength modifiers, and can have the weapon expert skill or an unarmed combat skill (brawling or martial arts) applied to it, but not both. Likewise, the overall tendril is put at risk of being severed once discovered or used in combat, and has a DV of -20, and an endurance (separate from the overall plantoid's body) of 18 END. If hacked off, the entire appendage will take 6+1d3 months to regrow.

Besides normal vision, each eye has a slim chance of having special characteristic to it, determined at character generation on the following table:

| 1d100 | Eye tendril Potential Special Characteristic |
|---|---|
| 01-88. | None |
| 89-92. | Night vision as per mutation #61 in the hub rules on page 71. |
| 93,94. | See dimensional beings* |
| 95,96. | See holograms and illusions for what they are. |
| 97,98. | Electrical pulse, as mutation #31 on page 65 of the hub rules. |
| 99. | Secondary eye Tendril** |
| 00. | Beam eye, as mutation #13 from page 61 of the hub rules |

*If Dimensional beings are not part of the game master's campaign, then substitute this for 'Night Vision'.

**Yes, this second tendril is also eligible for a chance at a special characteristic on this table, and could include a third tendril should this result occur again.

### Fibrous Armor 358
Type: **physical defense**      Defense Value: **-20**
Weight added: **+3d6+10kg**
Movement Modifier: **-0.5m**

This plantoid's trunk, limbs and roots are extra knobby and covered in thick, overlapping plates of hardwood. While adding 3d6+10 kilograms of extra weight to the mutant, and slowing it by -0.5m movement rate per round, these fibers improve the entity by -20 defense value and +3d6 endurance.

### Fire Repellent 359
Type: **defensive physical mutation**
Weight added: **+10kg**

This plantoid's limbs, leaves, roots and trunk are imbued with an extra layer of flame retardant sap. While explosives can still harm this mutant, fire from all sources inflicts only half damage, and any blaze has a maximum of 3 round burn time. Sap from this character can be extracted, either forcibly

or by voluntarily donation through a cut to the bark and up to 1 liter of flame retardant sap can be removed and then painted onto another object, vehicle or entity and offer the same flame resistant features for up to 48 hours before the layer of sap crumbles and turns to dust. 1 liter of sap will cover 5x5 meters in retardant.

### Flotation Pods 360
Type: **physical mutation**
Weight: **+2kg per airbag**

This plantoid can inhale air through ports in its upper trunk and transfer and expel this air into a series of large, inflatable leaf-pods. This process takes 20 rounds or one minute and, once inflated, the plant will rise to the surface of the water if it has fallen in, or be able to wade out into a river or lake from shore, and float on the water like a kayak. It can use whatever limbs or oars it might possess and propel itself along at its normal base movement rate.

While other uses for this mutation likely exist, some common applications include inflating these 6+1d6 air bags to help cushion the fall should the plantoid have sufficient time to deploy them while tumbling down off a cliff, and thus suffer half damage from any falls. Deploying these delicate gas bags prior to stepping out onto a treacherous, elevated crossing is likely a good idea, however, any hit on this mutant is 50% likely to be upon one of the plantoid's inflated air bags, and automatically rupture it. A ruptured air bag must be regrown, which takes 20+1d20 days.

A floating plantoid can support the weight of companions in the water and keep them from drowning should they be unable to swim or unconscious. For every 50kg of weight this plantoid exhibits, it can support only 100kg of extra cargo or companions. For example, if this plantoid weighs 150kg, it can support 300kg of companions before it too is pulled under the surface of the water.

During falls, an inflated plantoid can serve as a huge cushion to humanoid companions who fall after and upon it, suffering only half damage, too. Although falling companions will inflict 1d6 lethal and 1d6 stun damage to this weedy per 50 kilograms total weight absorbed.

### Fly Trap Jaws 361
Type: **physical attack**
Range: **tendrils reach equal to height of the plantoid**
Usage/ rate: **once per round per jaw (1d3 present)**
Strike Value: **by size**   Damage: **by size**   Defense Value: **by size**
Weight added: **As per the size and number of jaws**

This plantoid has one or more giant Venus flytrap jaws growing from its upper branches. Each is attached to a sinuous, flexible vine which can extend out as far as this mutant plant is tall. Each jaw adds an extra melee attack, and unlike a regular Venus flytrap, these jaws can be opened immediately after snapping shut on a prey animal or opponent and make follow-up attacks each round thereafter.

The size of each jaw differs based on the size of the plantoid, and should the mutant increase in mass or height, then apply the new stats from the jaw size table to follow. Also noted in this table is the endurance value of each jaw and its defense value, weight in kilograms, and time to grow back should it be hacked off. Each plantoid with this occurrence of the mutation will exhibit 1d3 jaw and tendril growths.

A Venus flytrap jaw can also close about and slowly digest portions or whole creatures, a process which takes a day during which the jaw is us-

able only as a closed up bludgeoning tool. Treat as a normal attack as far as SV goes, but any damage is stun only. This stun attack can be used instead of a lethal bite attack, too, even without digestion taking place.

Either the unarmed combat skill or a weapon expert skill can be applied to this mutation, if the character has skill points to apply, but like all such physical mutations, both cannot be applied.

If this mutation occurs again during character generation or some other instance where a new latent mutation appears, then this mutation can occur twice. The current size of the plantoid determines the size and details of its Venus Flytrap appendages:

| Plantoid's Size* | SV**/DMG** | DV/END | Regrow | Weight |
| --- | --- | --- | --- | --- |
| Tiny below 100cm tall | 01-50/1d6 | -5/ 5 | 1 month | 3kg |
| Small 100 to 149cm tall | 01-55/1d8 | -8/9 | 1.5 months | 5kg |
| Medium 150 to 199cm | 01-60/1d10 | -10/13 | 2 months | 8kg |
| Large 200 to 400cm | 01-65/ 1d12 | -14/ 20 | 3 months | 16kg |
| Massive over 400cm | 01-70/ 1d20 | -18/30 | 4 months | 32kg |

*Length and reach of attached tendril is the same as the plantoid's height.

**The noted Strike Value and Damage are both base scores, and so any accuracy or strength modifiers can also make these attacks even more devastating. So too, the unarmed combat skill or weapon expert skill can also be applied, but only one such skill area is allowed.

## Forest Rejuvenation 362

Type: **mental power**  Range: **1m radius per point of intelligence**
Usage: **Once a day per rank**
Rejuvenating Other plants: **This plantoid is drained by 1 point of willpower per minute, up to half it's base willpower trait value, per day. Each minute it will heal all other plants and plantoid characters 1 trait point.**
Rejuvenating Self: **Forest or mature crops will heal this plantoid 2d6 trait point per hour.**        Weight Added: **+2kg**

This subtle mutation allows the plantoid to both imbibe the energies of surrounding woodland, and heal by doing so, or spend some of its own daily life force (willpower trait) and enhance all manner of vegetation around it. To use this power, either to recharge itself or nourish nearby plants, the mutant must take root amid crops, a grassy plain, or forest.

For the purposes of taking healing, only an established forest, thicket or mature, densely growing crop of food plants can imbue healing and at a rate of 2d6 healed trait points per hour. If taking root and going semi-dormant, this character can remain in a thicket and rejuvenate for hours, if not days, to potentially gain complete healing. While absorbing healing energies, this plant character must enter a trance-like, semi-comatose state in which it is vulnerable and is -6 initiative and +40 SV easier to be struck. The 'veggie-dreamer' can snap out of its meditation in 1 round.

To foster plant growth, including other plantoids should they be with the radius of affect (1 meter radius per point of the plantoid's intelligence), an expenditure of 1 willpower point per minute is drained from the character — to a maximum drop of half the plantoid character's base willpower trait. These enriched plants heal 1 trait point per each minute that the user focuses. However, the plantoid need not go into a dormant state to bestow its healing energies into the surrounding plant life.

While encouraging rapid plant growth is sometimes done out of pure altruism, it is also a way to improve the farm produce for allied beings, or thicken the vegetation around the character to better conceal itself should it need to go into a dormant phase for some alone time. A plantoid rejuvenated forest, swamp and other natural formations of vegetation subjected to this power will become fuller, more vibrant, stronger and grow up to 10% of their former size with one use of this mutation, and keep these gains even after the plantoid departs the area.

## Fragmentation Pine Cones 363

Type: **physical attack**
Range: **10m from branch flick, or as strength score if plucked and thrown by hand-like appendage.**
Rate: **1 can be plucked and thrown per round, or, 1 or all ripe cones can be flicked simultaneously from 1 or more growing limbs.**
Resupply: **1d6 cones become ripe per month, per growing limb (4+1d4 limbs occur on plantoid)**
Strike Value: **3m blast radius, SV 01-70**
Damage: **3d6**        Weight added: **+10kg**

Attached to short, spring loaded branches, this mutant plant exhibits 4+1d4 pine cone growing limbs, complete with leafy growths and rows of seeds at various stages of development. Each limb will have dozens of unripe cones, and 1d6 ripe cones. The ripe ones turn a dark, blood red when ready and can be hurled by the plant.

If using the cone growing limbs to hurl explosive cones, a plant character can choose to either 'flick' just one chosen cone or all the ripe cones on one or more branches simultaneously — and hurl the cones in different directions if desired.

On impact, these ripe cones explode like fragmentation grenades, although using flameless, extreme pressure instead of a fiery explosion. The scale-like shingles of the cone shoot off in all directions in a 3m blast radius. All within are attacked at SV 01-70, Damage 3d6.

If the plantoid, or a comrade, has a hand and arm-like appendage, it can pluck one cone per round and throw it with a range equal to the thrower's strength score in meters.

Each month 1d6 more unripe cones become ready to hurl. Those not used from a previous month can be picked and stored in a satchel, or even used by beings other than the plantoid, however, they are volatile and any sharp smack on one, such as a fall by anyone carrying them, will be 67% likely to detonate each cone. Any ripe cone still attached to the plantoid will not self detonate, even if the plantoid itself is exposed to an explosion.

This plantoid is not immune to the shrapnel caused by its own fragmentation cones.

## Glow in the Dark 364

Type: **physical mutation**  Usage: **whenever in darkness**
Range: **10m light shedding, but visible from 500m away**
Rate: **Always on in 90% of plantoids, however, 1 in 10 PCs can switch on and off.**
Weight Added: **+5kg**

While considered a flaw if trying to hide underground or on the surface at night, this plantoid gives off a dull greenish glow which will illuminate a ten meter radius all around it. Should this specimen cover itself in rags, cloaks, armor, or other coverings, it will block out this potentially revealing phosphorescence. This glow is permanently on in 90% of all plantoids, and the result of its normal living state, however, 1 in 10 have developed an adaption whereby they can turn their glowing state on and off at will, and should the specimen have an intelligence score of 30 or higher, there is a further 77% chance that the mutant has learned Morse Code (see skills, page XR-220) and can communicate with long and short bursts of light.

While the useful light shed from this plantoid is only ten meters, the deviant can be seen from as far away as 500 meters, often attracting unwanted attention.

## Grappling Root 365

Type: **physical mutation**  Range: **1m per point of strength**
Usage: **Twice per day per rank**
Rate: **1, misses or spent attacks can be reeled in at a rate of 5m per round**
Strike Value: **+12**  Damage: **1d12+3**
Surprise attack: **initiative +3 / SV +32**  Weight Added: **+25kg**
Within the core of this plantoid is a coiled up, rope-like vine. At one end it's attached to a three-pronged hardwood grappling hook, while at the other where the vine grows from, a high pressure gas and muscle system which propels this growth. Twice per day, per rank, this plantoid can open a bark flap and

shoot the grappling hook up to a distance equal to its strength in meters, to hook on a high tree branch, wall, or protrusion on a cliff face. The hook opens out as it travels and jettisons forward ahead of its tow-line at up to 30m per round.

A successful strike must be made to the desired attachment point (at +12 SV) and if a successful, the grappling hook either wraps around and connects to the vine, or hooks the edge of a wall or crevice in a cliff. The line can be climbed by the plantoid by an internal muscular contraction and aided by any mobile roots or limbs.

The ascent is made at a rate of 3m per round, although this plantoid can carry an extra load of equal its own body weight but by doing so it climbs at only 1m per round. Once it reaches the hook, the plant can either secure

itself and make another grapple launch if it has the available usages per day remaining, or else unhook the grapple, stow it internally, and move on.

Besides the ability to pull itself up a sheer surface or tall tree, this appendage can be shot from the trunk as a devastating surprise attack, which against an unsuspecting target gives the plantoid +3 initiative and +32 SV on the first appearance of the growth. Damage to a target is 1d12+3, plus any strength modifiers. Once the grappling organ is known about, opponents will be wary of it and so normal initiative and +12 SV apply.

Reeling in the grapple hook and vine after an attack or missed launch takes 1 round per 5m of line. If targeted, this stout, sinewy cord has a defense value of -30, and any single strike along its length that inflicts 18 or more damage severs the vine. A new grappling hook and line takes 4+1d4 months to regrow.

## Hallucinatory Spores 366

Type: **physical compound and mental delusion**
Range: **ejected 1 meter per point of strength, +/- wind speed**
Usage: **Once per day per rank**  Rate: **1**
Hazard Check: **Type C Intelligence**  Weight added: **+10kg**

Once per day, per rank, this plantoid can exude a billowing brown cloud of powdery spore, either expelling it in a puff with a range of 12 meters, or discharging it on the wind and letting it disperse on the breeze.

Once leaving the plantoid's mesh-like orifice, this puff quickly thins out and often goes unnoticed by attackers, who are likely to inhale hundreds if not thousands of microscopic spore particles. Those confronted by the cloud are allowed a type D intelligence based hazard check to spot the cloud and hold their breath as it passes, otherwise they inhale 1d1000 spore particles. The more of these bits one inhales, the stronger the hallucination and its duration thereafter.

The following table shows the spores inhaled and the consequences:

| Spores inhaled | HC to Avoid Believing Hallucination | Duration |
|---|---|---|
| **Less than 100** | Type A Intelligence | 2d6 rounds |
| **101 to 300** | Type B Intelligence | 3d6 rounds |
| **301 to 500** | Type C Intelligence | 10+3d6 rounds |
| **501 to 700** | Type D Intelligence | 20+3d6 rounds |
| **701 to 900** | Type E Intelligence | 30+2d20 rounds |
| **901 to 1200*** | Type F Intelligence | 40+d100 rounds |
| **1201 or more*** | Type G Intelligence | 50+2d100 rounds |

*More than 1000 spore count is possible because the subject might be exposed to multiple discharges from this mutant.*

A spore cloud will remain in non-windy area for 3d6 minutes, but be carried off on the wind in gusty areas after the initial attack.

While all those who inadvertently inhale this mind altering substance experience some degree if hallucination, those who fail their intelligence based hazard check actually believe the phantasm and will immediately cease attacking the plantoid, and its companions, and respond to the unreality.

The game master can simply have NPCs either flee, curl into a ball, sob, scream or otherwise act oddly, however the following brief random selection can be used when player characters succumb to these spores themselves — even inadvertently as this plant might easily expose comrades to this unpredictable discharge. Repeated exposure to these particles does not produce immunity.

## 1d12  Random Spore Hallucinations

**1.** You suddenly erupt into flame and see, smell, and feel your flesh and clothing ignite. You have a strong urge to run off seeking water to leap into.

**2.** Ants have worked their way into your outfit and are biting and stinging you. You must get all your clothing and armor off at once!

**3.** Radiation is everywhere! Your flesh bubbles and peels, your hair falls out, yet your pals can't see it nor the disfigurement they too now suffer!

**4.** Deafening screams from the ancient ones bombard you mercilessly! "Avenge us!" they cry.

**5.** The ghosts of long lost loved ones and deceased comrades swirl around you, each blaming you for either their death or some sin or shortcoming of yours.

**6.** The furnishings, debris, bones or weeds — whatever is nearby — rattles, lifts up and swirls about to form vaguely human shapes that turn on you. These constructs moan and approach in a menacing fashion.

**7.** All the nightmares you've had in the last few months suddenly appear in your mind's eye. The images, nosies, and sensations overlap with reality and confuse and muddle your senses. GM: Character is reduced to half strike value and movement rate.

**8.** Your heart is erupting from your chest. Breathing is hard, your vision blurred and you drop to your knees. You must open your armor and clothing and see for yourself. GM: Visually, the PC sees nothing out of the ordinary, but is distracted and continues to suffer agony during the duration of this hallucination.

**9.** Your feet are suddenly stuck fast to the ground. When you look down, you see that from your knees to your feet, your lower legs have merged into the floor or dirt and you are fused in place and unable to move!

**10.** Swarms of flies and mosquitoes suddenly fill the air. The buzz of their wings and clatter on your skin, armor, and gear is deafening. The world about you obscured! You have the urge to flee from this insect storm!

**11.** Earthquake! The ground shakes and cracks open, objects fall about you and walking is hard. You must stagger away before you die! You must grab a comrade and pull them to safety!

**12.** A mass of blue and pink swirls opens in the sky or nearby wall. Stars and moons swirl and you hear a strange, rhythmic cacophony. A great white mask of a face appears and announces that it is God, and that it is time for you to repent for your sins, renounce your companions and walk toward the swirl of color and blissful oblivion.

## Hand-like Branch 367
Type: **physical attack**    Range: **melee**    Rate: **1**
Strike Value: **+0**    Damage: **1d6**    Weight added: **+6kg per branch**
This plantoid exhibits and arm-like branch which ends in a human looking cluster of twigs or roots which form a thumb and between three and five finger-like digits.

Ancient bio-engineers crafted many plant servants to manipulate standard human gear either as workers or warriors. To this end, it is not uncommon for a mutant who exhibits this genetic gift to have more than one such appendage growing from the main trunk, therefore **roll 1d6** to determine how many hand equipped branches this mutant plant starts game play with: **1,2.** One hand-like vine branch **3-5.** Two hand-like branches **6.** Three hand-like branches

These branches and hands are identical in size and strength as a human's arm and hand attachment, although like any other character, the strike value and damage modifiers which stem from an accuracy or strength trait value are applied. The basic damage from the hand-like branch is 1d6.

Like most branches vines and other appendages which grow from a mutant plant character, if this limb is severed (DV -13/ END 12) it will re-grow within 100+1d100 days. So too, if this mutation occurs again for this character at creation or via rank gain, the plantoid can have many more of these useful growths.

Unlike humans, each of these limbs is considered as a dominant hand and multi-dexterous, thus allowing one attack per hand per round — a condition which makes this entity exceedingly dangerous.

## Harpoon Vines 368
Type: **physical attack**
Range: **melee or  a half meter per point of strength**
Usage: **1d2+1 per rank**    Rate: **1 per round** Strike Value: **+15**
Damage: **2d12**    Tendril line Endurance: **20% of plantoid's base END**
Weight Added: **+15kg per harpoon growth**

This plant mutant starts with between 2 and 3 (1d2+1 if starting as a 1st rank character) barbed, hardwood harpoon growths, which often grow up into the veggie-sapien's upper branches and foliage to remain safely out of the way and hidden until needed. When forced into close quarters combat, each can thrust at melee range opponents like a sword, and can each be deployed against a different opponent. If a longer ranged attack is needed, one of these deadly shafts can be shot up to a half meter away per current point of the plantoid's strength score. Any creature struck takes 2d12 damage (plus any strength or weapon expert skill modifiers), and any hit which inflicts 10 or more damage means the target is impaled and the shooter can use internal muscles to pull in the harpoon's attached vine-line.

Should a creature be heavier than the plantoid, it cannot be pulled in, and the cable and harpoon can be detached and a new shaft will regrow to replace it. If the target is lighter than this harpooner, it can be dragged back toward the mutant plant at a rate of 2 meters per round.

Of course, a harpooned victim might have the smarts enough to turn about and chop away or bite off the harpoon's stout tendril line, although any NPC target must make a Type C intelligence based hazard check to think of this while so painfully impaled. The tendril has a DV of -20, and has an endurance of 20% of whatever the plantoids base, uninjured endurance value is.

A new harpoon and rope-tendril takes 40+1d30 days to regrow. A severed harpoon can be used as a regular spear, either by this plantoid or others.

Clever plantoids with this mutation can also use these appendages in a wide range of non-combat application. Examples include rescuing companion who have fallen into the water (by shooting just passed them), trying to shoot into a far wall or ceiling to serve as a grappling hook (hit required and 10 or more damage needed, plus a type A strength based hazard check needed per minute to hold the weight of the plantoid). Another use is to shoot the harpoon across a roadway or path to create a trip line, or to probe something at a distance before getting too close, among just a few uses.

A missed harpoon can be retracted at a rate of 4m per round if no weight is attached to the barbed shaft.

## Healing Blossoms 369
Type: **excretion mutation**    Range: **ingestion or topical application**
Usage: **1 blossom per 10 kilograms of plantoid's weight**
Replenishment: **Blossom can be reused in 24 hours if not detached. Cutting blossoms inflict 1 END damage to plantoid and regrow in 72 hours**
Healing rate: **1d6 END per blossom ingested or rubbed on wound**

**Weight added: +4kg, +500g per blossom**

Unlike healing sap, these small, inconspicuous white blossoms bloom among this plantoid's branches and vines and produce remarkable nectar. The size of the plantoid is used to determine the number of nectar producing blooms, with 1 blossom present on any given day for every 10 kilograms of the plantoid's body weight. Plucking the living flowers from this mutant will inflict 1 point of damage per blossom removed, but if kept in water, these removed flowers will remain perky and effective for an extra 48 hours before degrading. Removed blossoms take 72 hours to regrow.

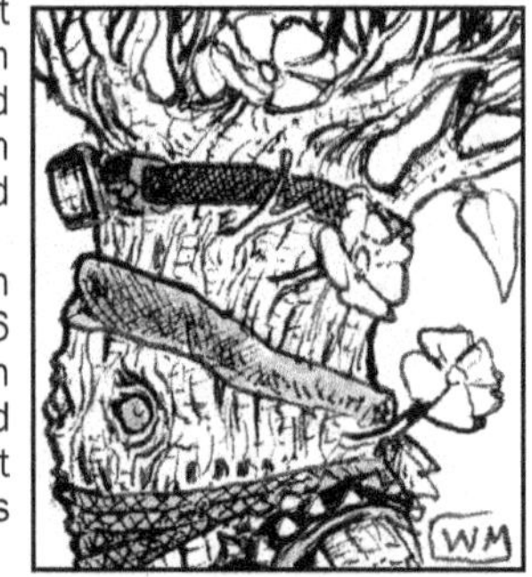

When ingested, or wiped on an open wound, any organic creature will heal 1d6 endurance trait points of damage, although thereafter that blossom cannot be tapped again if it was cut or plucked from the plant mutant, or for 24 hours if the blossom was left attached to the weedy.

This plantoid can also use this nectar on its own injuries, and knowing the healing properties of this nectar, is often reluctant to let others know of it.

Unscrupulous or profit minded villains might also imprison a plantoid with this gift, and forcibly extract this precious nectar to either use for their own troops or sell it to the highest bidder. Healing nectar will only keep its healing properties for 48 hours before changing color from yellow to gray and becoming far less effective and healing only 1 END point per wilted blossom, and degrading further after 72 hours to produce no beneficial effects at all

If a host inhabiting plantoid has this mutation, it can choose to draw upon the nutrients of the host body, and unfurl 1 blossom per 20kg of host cadaver's weight.

## Hovering Gas Bag 370

Type: **physical mutation**          Usage: **once per day per rank**
Hover/ Drift time: **1 minute per point of Willpower**
Defense Value: **-10**          Added Weight: **+8kg**
Bag Robustness: **Any hit that inflicts 7 or more damage causes a 10% loss of gas. 10 hits mean an immediate drop, while any critical hit results in a rupture and rapid drop from the air.**

When threatened and needing to escape, or the plantoid must ascend a great height, safely drop from a higher location, or travel with the wind, this mutant can inflate several huge, flexible gas bags and take to the air. These balloon-like, fleshy sacks are made of thin, yet fibrous, leaf-like material. While being vulnerable to rips and punctures, they can be a lifesaver, a mode of travel, or make the deviant into an observation platform. The lighter than air gasses which fill these bags are disgorged into them from internal organs, and when mixed, they heat and expand rapidly. This process takes only two rounds, and on the third round, is sufficiently blended to lift the plantoid off the ground to either hover in place, drop slowly to the ground, float on water, or get airborne.

By using its other appendages, especially leaves, the plantoid can guide itself in any direction, so long as there is no strong wind blowing, in which case it can only travel with the breeze and make only slight course corrections up, down or to the side by 10 degrees per ten minutes of air travel.

The duration of a flight, including a hovering action, is 1 minute per point of willpower, per usage. The rank of the plantoid is the number of usages per day this

deviation can be deployed. Multiple usages can be expended back to back. For example, a weedy with a willpower trait of 63 can drift on the wind for 63 minutes, but say this character is third rank and so 63 x 3 uses = 189 minutes of flight.

The speed of any breeze will carry the floater at the same rate, like a puffball seed on the wind, but when there is no wind, the plantoid will float upward at a rate of 1 meter per round, but can use its leaves or gripped sheets of plastic or other large flat objects as wings to steer and flap at a movement rate of 2m per round in any direction.

Should the mutant run out of gas generation while mid-air, it will begin to lose altitude and descend 1 meter for every 2 meters horizontally it drifts or flaps. If it reached an incredible height, say a kilometer up, it would therefore drift another two kilometers before it touched down. Importantly, sufficient gas to maintain a slow decent is always in the gas bag after it depletes its daily supply, but in insufficient amounts to maintain lift.

One of the primary uses of this mutation is to deploy it during a long fall off a cliff, airship deck or skyscraper, and arrest the PC's fall. If a heavy load of between half to equal the plantoid's own weight is held, such as another character, then the plantoid can only lift upward at half a meter per round and the duration of the flight is also cut in half. Likewise, a drop with a comrade — such as to save the life of a human companion — is possible in this fashion, too, with the drop being twice as fast at 2m per round and the impact for both the plantoid and passenger being painful but both endure only 1d6 lethal and 2d6 stun damage.

While many other uses for this mutation are possible, another common one is to inflate this gasbag to stay on the surface of water, in which case the plantoid can serve as a buoy and up to six man sized beings can hold on to it and avoid drowning.

When not in use, these gasbags fold up either in the upper branches or at the base of the trunk and hidden among the roots, however when deployed, this collection of translucent green balloons is vulnerable to puncture. Enemies who choose to pop these gas bags can do so with relative ease, and most likely rupture the sacks and bring the plantoid to earth with fatal consequences. The full gas bags, which usually number 4 to 6 ( 1d3+3) make for a big target and all combined are often the size of the plantoid itself, once fully inflated. This easy target has a defense value of -10 which is separate from whatever other protection the mutant exhibits. Any hit by a sharp object must do over 7 damage to cause a puncture. For every puncture, gas escapes from the interconnected series of bags, and reduces the flight time by 10%, with ten strikes meaning all the gas has seeped out and the plantoid falls. Likewise, any critical strike results in an instantaneous total rupture of the gas bag collection and the immediate drop of the mutant (see Falling Heights and Damage in the TME Hub Rules book, page 123). A punctured gas bag can be patched by a medic if given the proper supplies, but natural healing takes 7 days, while a fully ruptured gas sack requires a new balloon blossom to grow, which takes 4+d6 months.

Occasionally, a plantoid evolves to exhibit both leaf wings and gas bags. This marvelous freak will benefit from far easier lift while these gas bags are deployed and therefore propel itself with greater speed. Add 20% to whatever the leaf wing air speed is while these sacks are deployed.

Another mutation which is related, and might occur in the same mutant, is Flotation Pods from page 306, which while they will allow the plantoid to carry double the number of kilograms while this gas bag is deployed in water, the liquid buoyant pods add nothing to flight.

## Human Parts 371

Type: **physical mutation**

Weight Added: **See human part below for possible weight addition. If no weight noted, then consider no added kilograms.**

One or two (1d2) random human limbs or organs grow on or within this entity's body, or else, it exhibits a substantial amount of extra human DNA beyond the traces which ancient genetic engineers used to create this plantoid's ancestors.



**01-07. Extra Human DNA Present:** While most plantoids have some amount of human DNA, which gives them their sentience, motivations, and need to socialize and team up with humans and their offshoots, this plantoid's human DNA component is very high and in the 21 to 40% (20+2d10) range, whereas a normal plantoid has about 10 to 20% human genetic material. Consequently, this being's eyes, oral orifice, speech and shape more closely resemble a human, especially when dressed in clothing, armor and other outerwear that better conceals any foliage and appendages which would call attention to its vegetable heritage.

If proper care, costuming and adherence to normal human habits are observed, this plantoid could easily pass for a human in a crowd or casual setting, especially when accompanied by human companions who can do most of the talking and interaction. This plantoid is indeed so human, that it is given an appearance score like a regular human, at least for passing as a human while clothed and any obvious plant parts hidden from view. Roll 3d6 for Appearance.

**08-14. Kidneys and liver:** Somehow, this plant's sap 'circulatory' system is connected to a very human set of kidneys and liver and other organs, which helps purify its inner workings and any food intake it might gain through non-photosynthetic means. While on a day-to-day basis this matters little, it does matter if this plantoid is subjected to any sort of poison, venom or other biological toxin, and gives it an extra hazard check against these hazards. So too, if sickened or poisoned, it only suffers from the ailment or impurity for half as long. Weight added 5kg.

**15-21. Heart:** A powerful, hybrid human heart exists within the core of this plantoid and pumps its sap and other fluids with an enhanced pressure and speed. While this organ isn't essential for the plantoid's life, and if a critical strike results in a destroyed heart, this being will live on, yet it will lack the benefits that its heart gave and will not grow the organ back for 3d6 months. An intact hybrid human heart increases the strength and agility traits by +4d6 each at character generation. Likewise, this plant is warm blooded, and although it gives off a heat signature to infra read targeting systems, it can also keep companions warm in cold weather and endure frigid conditions as if it were a mammal. Weight added 5kg.

**22-25. Nose:** A bark skinned, quite obvious human nose grows from the upper reaches of this plantoid, often near its eyes and gives the being a more human face. This nose is fully functional, too, and connected to a set of rudimentary lungs. In short, this plant can make use of olfactory senses like a regular human can, and breathe air to enhance its performance, thus adding +2d6 to its strength at character generation. If submerged, this plantoid can close its nostrils to avoid the lungs filling with water. Weight added 5kg.

**26-34. Mouth:** A human mouth is attached to an integrated human digestive system, rudimentary lungs, enough to facilitate respiration, speech, and all other oral functions. Extra intake of oxygen increases plantoid's strength by +2d6 points and allows this being an additional means of ingesting nutrients. Weight added 8kg.

**34-39. Ear:** One human ear grows from the plantoid's upper trunk. This appendage is connected to the being's rudimentary nervous system, which hears just like a regular ear and adds its auditory receptors to those of the plant's, and thus increases the mutant's initiative score by +1.

**40-48. Eye:** A solitary human eye grows near the plantoid's other optical sensors and adds to both its accuracy and perception trait (add 1d6+3 to each). In addition, this more human eye aides in the being's interactions with humanoids, who see this organ as the window to the plantoid's soul.

**49-56. Human hand on branch:** This mutant exhibits a three meter long flexible branch which ends in a fully functional human hand. This hand can punch, wield a single handed weapon, or work in conjunction with another grasper to control a two-handed weapon. For the purposes of a delicate task, such as picking a pocket or lock, working a keyboard or other chore, consider this appendage to have +10 agility as far as hazard checks and related tasks are concerned.

**57-63. Human hand and full arm:** From the upper trunk on one side of the mutant, protrudes a fully functional, bark covered human arm and hand. This limb can do whatever a regular human arm can, but is more agile than the rest of the plant and for hazard checks involving agility or accuracy, is +14 for both AG and ACC higher than the rest of the entity's traits. An extra attack can be made with whatever this hand holds, or a fist if unarmed combat is called for.

**64-71. Legs:** A pair of human legs grow at the base of this plantoid, complete with hips and buttocks of a human. Any root network this mutant has, now grow from the waist. These legs can wear pants, socks and boots, all of which give away the plantoid as something other than a shrub or tree when it is trying to hide among other vegetation. Such legs allow the plantoid to move faster than it otherwise would, and it gains +1m per round movement and in melee, can add one kick attack with a base of 1d6 damage. These limbs are bark covered, although made of flesh and bone.

**72-83. Brain:** Deep in this plantoid's upper trunk, near its optical growths, resides a wood encased human brain. This organ serves as the mind for this plantoid and is not a secondary brain. This mutation gives the plantoid a +2d6 willpower and +3d6 intelligence bonus at character creation, plus there is a 2 in 6 chance that this plantoid exhibits 1d3 random mental mutations from the latent mutation table on page XR 232.

While having a human brain typically makes this individual act, strive and scheme more like a regular human, identify as a human trapped in a plant body, and gain the benefits of a more evolved brain, it does however make the plantoid susceptible to instant death from called shots and critical hits to the brain, to say nothing of mind controls and mental attacks by other mutants and relics.

**82-89. Face:** Fused to the trunk of this plantoid is a quite obvious, bark encased human face, complete with eyes, mouth, and nose... all of which are hooked to the plant's nervous system along with rudimentary lungs, digestive tract and associated organs. This mutant can therefore speak, see, taste and consume a like a regular human besides any other sensory adaptations or nutrient acquisition methods it might have, including leaves.

There is a further 1 in 6 chance it has a pair of human ears on either side of the face, too. Whenever dealing with humanoids, especially comrades, this plantoid will conduct all interactions using this facial region, and elicit much stronger bonds with human teammates because of it. The face has quite a fixed gender in appearance, or lack thereof: roll 1d8: 1-3 male, 4-6. female, 7,8. androgynous. So too, given only the facial symmetry and stereotypical standards of beauty or ugliness, this face also has a fixed appearance score of according to the main trait generation table on page 8 of this book, or page 10 of the hub rules.

**88-95. Genitals:** Although this plantoid probably keeps this addition private and well concealed behind foliage, fabric or gear, it has a fully functional set of human reproductive organs, along with the hormones, drives and compulsions which typically go with them. 8 out of 10 plantoids with these adaptations are sterile. The rest of the time (roll 9 and 10 on a 1d10), the organs are fertile and all internal and additional organs are also present, such as a womb and mammary glands if the plantoid is female. The crossbreeding of a plantoid with another human based life form is theoretically possible, and should the fetus survive, grow into a baby and emerge alive (77% chance if proper nutrients and prenatal care are provided), then the spawn of this plantoid will have a 50% chance of being born with each mutation from each parent. For the sex of the plantoid, **roll 1d6: 1-3.** male/**4-6.** Female.

**96-99. Full upper body and head:** Although from the waist up this oddity is human shaped, complete with a set of normal arms, head, chest and lower abdomen, it is rarest of all human-plant hybrids. This strange being has branches, twigs and leaves for hair, fine bark for skin, and the lower body of a tree, complete with whatever other mutations this specimen bears. To some, this miscreation is a forest spirit, to others, a mockery of nature, and to some, a deity to be worshipped. For an adventure party, however, having a plantoid that can use regular arms and armor, exhibit normal facial expressions, conversation and interact like just another person, is quite welcome. If the sex of this plantoid is not already established, such as from roll 88-95 on this table, then the mutant is male 50% of the time, otherwise female, although in either case it has no genitalia (again, unless this is established by roll 88-95, on this table). Because this hybrid has a human face and figure, roll its appearance trait value just like a regular human based character might from the Trait Value Determination table on page 8.

**00. Two human parts** from this table, re-rolling duplicated results, including this roll.

## Leaf Wings 372

Type: **physical mutation**        Flying Speed: **size dependant**
Weight added: **based on wing size**    Wing DV: **-10**
Wing END: **10% of PC's uninjured endurance trait**

The size of leaf wings is in proportion to the overall size of the plantoid. As an example, massive wings growing on a small character would only be tiny wings on an enormous plant mutant. While it would seem that a gargantuan plantoid's wings should do more damage with its wings than a diminutive weedy's, the strength modifiers often given to bigger plantoids provide much of the punch to these appendages.

Should a wing be severed, a new leaf wing will grow back after a month, but start as tiny and each two weeks grow to the next size category up to the maximum, pre-determined size established at character generation.

A flying character gets a defense value bonus based on the size of the wing, which is only applied while airborne. Each wing itself has a base defense value of -10, plus or minus any dodge skill or agility based modifiers. The endurance of a single wing leaf is 10% of the character's uninjured endurance trait value.

Besides allowing the plantoid to fly with almost bird-like grace, these appendages can make two additional melee attacks per round if needed, and each wing size has a strike value bonus and a damage amount shown on the following table. Strength and accuracy modifiers plus application of the brawling, martial arts or weapon expert (but only one of these skills) can also be applied. That said, these wings are fragile, tear easily and not really suitable for hand to hand combat and any fumble during an attack means the plantoid has torn its wing right off.

Flying with one full grown wing and one smaller, newly growing wing is challenging, and for each difference in size, reduce the mutant's movement by -2 meters per round. Example: You normally have large wings, but one was blown away a while back and now you have a tiny wing in its place. Normally you fly 15m per round, but as tiny wings are two sizes too small, that's -4m to your flying speed, so now you go only 11 meters.

There is a slight, 1 in 20 chance that a plantoid character has 1d2 extra set of leaf wings, their size rolled randomly, too, which each add another melee attack, but also add their movement bonus to the plant character's overall air speed.

| 1d10 | Size of wings | Weight | Flying Speed | Flying DV Bonus | SV | DMG |
|---|---|---|---|---|---|---|
| 1 | Tiny | +2kg | 9m | -10 DV | 01-50 | 1d6 |
| 2-6 | Medium | +5kg | 12m | -15 DV | 01-55 | 1d8 |
| 7,8 | Large | +10kg | 15m | -20 DV | 01-60 | 1d10 |
| 9 | Huge | +20kg | 18m | -22 DV | 01-65 | 1d12 |
| 10 | Massive | +40kg | 20m | -24 DV | 01-70 | 1d20 |

## Lightning Flowers 373

Type: **electrical attack**        Range: **willpower x2m**
Usage: **3d6, +1 flower per rank grow among foliage**
Rate: **1 per round. Flower dies after use**
Strike Value: **+20**    Damage: **2d20, plus 50% chance of igniting a fire**
Weight Added: **+1kg per flower**

This plantoid has 3d6, +1 per rank, bizarre, bluish-silver flowers growing among its upper branches or head (so a 1st rank plantoid has 3d6+1, a 4th ranker would have 3d6+4. etc.). Each flower is about a foot in diameter. Once per round, the plantoid can discharge an electrical bolt from one of these

flowers with a range of 2 meters per point of the character's willpower, with a strike value of +20 and inflicting 2d20 damage on a hit. Should the lightning bolt hit flammable material, such as straw, dry wood, paper, fur or dry vegetation, there is a 50% chance a blaze erupts in that spot and will spread at a meter in diameter per minute thereafter.

Once the flower has fired its bolt, it shrivels and dies and a new flower bud sprouts the next day, however each spent flower takes 10 days to grow and blossom and be ready to fire again.

If a ready flower is plucked from the plantoid, it has a 25% chance of automatically discharging into the picker as an automatic attack, otherwise the plant mutant could control its internal energies and save them for another time.

A mutant with this power can easily start a campfire using one of these charges, while a bio-technician of 2 or more skill points who has any degree of electrical technician skill, too, can rig up a jumper cable system to transfer the charge from a lighting flower to charge a power cell completely, or a power pack to 10% capacity.

## Manipulator Vines 374

Type: **physical attack**        Range: **reach triple the plantoid's height**
Rate: **1 slap or action per vine (1+d6 growths present)**
Trait Modifier: **Vines are +20 higher than plant's main AG and ACC trait**
Strike Value: **+0**        Damage: **1d4**
Defense Value: **-20, END 12**    Weight Added: **+2kg per tendril**

These vines are similar to standard manipulator limbs, but far thinner, longer and more agile. They sometimes appear as roots instead of the more typical tendrils, which grow in the upper reaches of a plantoid, but sometimes both (1d10: 1-7. Vines grow from upper foliage and branches/ 8,9. Vines grow from among the roots/ 10. Vines grow both at the roots and upper trunk).

While they can lash out at opponents as extra melee attacks, doing only 1d4 base damage with a stun only slap attack each, they are normally far too delicate for this task and easily damaged. Although remarkably dexterous, these vines are weak, with a strength of 10 each — although if many are brought together, each adds its strength to pull open, hoist or shove other beings and objects. For example, this plantoid has four tendrils, and so a combined strength of 40 for a specified task or hazard check.

Their primary purpose is to grasp, tap, probe, and manipulate objects. When working with other manipulator vines, these dainty growths can serve as the digits of fingers, and work a keyboard, handle cutlery, glassware, turn doorknobs, dress or undress the user, or conduct many day-to-day tasks.

Two such vines could in fact wield a pistol, and three could operate a rifle, shotgun or other long gun, crossbow or bow... although the strength of these vines is typically low, as noted above — even when combined.

Wherever the agility trait or accuracy trait is called for by a hazard check, use the value of the manipulator vine, which is always +20 higher than the plantoid's main value for that trait — including with any weapons.

Attackers can target one or more of these vines if these appendages are caught snooping, groping, extended during either a melee range fight or with ranged engagements. Each vine has a defense value of -20, and an endurance value of 12. Severed manipulator vines will grow back after 20+3d6 days.

The length of manipulator vine depends on the plantoid's current height, and so its reach is triple the centimeters of the plant.

Should this plantoid start game play with the mutation 'hand-like branch', number #367 on page 309, or have the human part of a 'hand' (from mutation #371 from page 311 of this book), then this hand grows at the end of one of these vines. Likewise, should one of these hand mutations occur as a latent mutation, it too will emerge from the end of one of these delicate growths.

## Medicinal Sap 375

Type: **healing secretion**     Range: **ingestion or topical application**
Usage: **based on current endurance of plantoid**     Weight added: **+6kg**
Healing rate: **for every 1 END of sap drained, heals 1d6 to each trait**
While this plantoid and its seedlings cannot personally enjoy the benefits of this healing sap, other strains of mutant plants and organic beings who ingest, or have this sap applied to burns and open wounds, will see virtually immediate benefits from exposure to this substance. This sap can also assist a victim who suffers from attacks by venom or poison and if this sap is ingested within 4 rounds of exposure to a toxin, the subject is allowed an extra hazard check to thwart whatever harm might come of the toxin. This compound has no effect on radiation exposure or its harms.

Clearly, ancient botanists and genetic engineers developed this plant based trait to be harvested by humans. In the new era, various plants, including sentient plantoids, can offer this purplish sap from just below their husk or bark. To extract it, the plantoid must be cut, although certain captive specimens or highly benevolent plant beings will have permanently attached spigots or taps bolted to them to facilitate easy access by their human comrades — especially when this character is attached to a military or excavation unit.

This sap can be sucked directly from a rupture in the plantoid's bark or can be exuded into wax paper or oiled cloth and applied to wounds for later use, but breaks down after 24 hours. The size and weight of the plantoid determines how much of this sap per day can be drained, but in every instance, losing this plant's 'life blood' causes damage to the weedy and too much of a drain could leave the plantoid lethargic or dormant.

Any smart* plantoid with this mutation is often quite secretive about this gift, for it knows it is at risk of being kept as a prisoner for its sap to be sucked out or tube extracted against its will by malevolent or desperate captors.

The plantoid has up to half their base, uninjured endurance value in doses available for safe drainage. For every 1 END point drained, it can heal 1d6 trait points in another**.

If the weedy is reduced to 50% or less of its base endurance, either by sap drainage for medical reasons or from other injuries, then it is highly risky to intentionally deplete itself further and the plantoid becomes lethargic and is reduced to half its normal movement rate, suffers a -5 initiative penalty and does only half damage to any strength based damage scores inflicted on opponents until it heals up over 50% edurance.

Should this plantoid be reduced to zero or less endurance from sap leakage — as opposed to other injuries— then the one personal benefit of this mutation comes into effect. Instead of dying as other plants might, this deviant merely plays the part, and it wilts, sheds all leaves, nuts and fruit, and becomes dormant in a near death state for 3d6 weeks and must heal itself to full trait values before rebounding, and coming 'alive' again.

Each dose of medicinal sap weighs about 100ml (1/10th of a kilogram). It tastes like maple syrup, can be used as glue, and has a nutrient value equivalent to a fried egg, and can sustain an organic being dying of thirst as if it were 500ml of water.

*Intelligence score of 20 or more.*
**This 1d6 trait points apply to all depleted traits in an organic being, and so roll a 1d6 for each depleted trait, such as endurance, intelligence, appearance, etc.*

## Mimic Human Shape 376
Type: **physical mutation**     Time to engage: **20 rounds (1 minute)**
Usage: **one hour per day per rank**     Weight added: **+2kg**
Hazard Check: **perception based C, or E if plantoid also has the disguise artist skill**
While this weedy normally spreads its branches and roots like a typical shrub, veggie or tree, either for comfort, photosynthesis or camouflage amongst other foliage, it can also knot itself to assume a human shape.

This transformation takes one minute. Once complete, the plantoid can dress itself in normal clothing, armor and headgear, complete with sunglasses, filter masks and other attire to better conceal itself in a human community.

Assuming this form takes great effort and focus and can only last for one hour per character rank, per day, before the character's branches, roots and foliage automatically unfolds and it returns to its normal state. Plantoids with this mutation at higher rank can divide their hourly allotments up at different times in the day, so long as they don't exceed their daily uses. Likewise, hour long mimic sessions can be broken up as needed into 5, 10 or longer minute durations as needed.

Those who pass this individual in a crowd will typically pay the hooded figure no attention, although in close proximity, face-to-face interactions such  as when bartering, ordering a drink or undergoing inspection by guards, the viewer is allowed a Type C perception based hazard check to notice that the bark or leaf lined face before them isn't just another ugly mutant, but instead, a plantoid.

Whether a bartender at a wasteland saloon cares if the character is a plant or not, is another story, for most new era citizens only care if the customer is a threat, has a valuable bounty on their head, or has silver to afford their food and drink.

Any plantoid with this mutation plus the disguise artist skill will add wigs, fillers, false eyes, makeup and other features from dolls and mannequins to make themselves extraordinarily hard to unmask, with those meeting them required to make a type E perception check to realize the character is not human.

damage and +2 strike value to any unarmed attacks. Likewise, this mineral enhancement adds +3d6 endurance at the time of character creation.

Besides the armor befits of these rocky growths, each month one pronounced formation of minerals works its way to the plant's surface and can be plucked out and sold or used by animal or human companions. Roll 2d6 each month for what forms on the bark, although the growth need not be extracted and will remain in place, along with others, until needed:

| 2d6 | Monthly Mineral Formation |
|---|---|
| 2. | Gold nugget, worth 100+d100sp |
| 3. | Silver nugget, worth 10+d10sp |
| 4. | Crystal disc, finer width, 2cm thick, acts like a magnifying glass and could start a fire if under ideal sunny conditions. |
| 5. | Not a mineral at all, but a hard globule of vitamin C and remarkable healing nutrients, worth 2+d6sp and quite healthy for humans to ingest. Any animal to ingest this will recover 2d6 depleted trait points after 1 hour. |
| 6. | Clear white quartz crystal, worth 3d6sp |
| 7. | Cluster of fine salt crystals, worth 1d3sp (much more where salt is in demand). |
| 8. | Pink salt crystal (like Himalayan Salt), worth 2d6sp |
| 9. | Dagger length shard of razor sharp jade, treat as regular dagger but +1 DMG and +2 SV, grows dull and useless after 10th successful strike. Worth 10+d20sp for jewelry making after dull. |
| 10. | Semi-precious stone (worth 20+d20sp) |
| 11. | Gemstone, worth 200+1d100sp |
| 12. | Glow in the dark crystal, will give off a soft green light in a 6m radius for 8 hours after 4 hours of sunlight exposure. Worth 30+1d30sp. |

## Mineral Impregnated Bark 377

Type: **defensive mutation**   Strike Value: **+2 to melee attacks**
Damage: **+2**   Defense Value: **-18 DV**
Trait Modifier: **+3d6 endurance**   Weight added: **+20kg**

Calcium and other minerals from the soil collect in this plantoid's bark. Besides adding a lumpy texture and noticeable sparkle, these permanent deposits harden the thicker branches, roots, and trunk of the mutant. The result is a stouter plant, one which gains a -18 defense value bonus plus adds a slight improvement to any physical blows made by the character, adding +2

## Muscle-Fibers 378

Type: **physical Adaption for Host Inhabiting Plantoids only**
Trait Modifier: **+1d6 to each Endurance, Strength, Agility and Accuracy**
Weight added: **+10kg**

Although green and similar in appearance to the husks which grow on a cob of corn, this host inhabiting plantoid can maintain and even replace decomposing muscle tissues with highly effective, new improved plant based muscles. These growths enhance the plantoid's base endurance, strength, accuracy and agility by +1d6 trait points each.

Secondly, these growths allow the plantoid to maintain occupation of an otherwise useless corpse, including a frame that is nothing more than a skeleton. By use of this adaptation, the plantoid need never have to seek new cadavers once it finds one it likes, particularly a corpse that has desirable cybernetic implants or mutations.

## Net Roots 379

Type: **physical attack**
Range: **as the plantoid's height x2**
Usage: **no daily limit**
Rate: **empty or missed net can be recovered 3m per round, can fire again on the 2nd round after recovery.**
Strike Value: **+20 (target's armor has no effect)**
Damage: **target reduced to half movement and -30 Strike Value, while being +20 DV themselves.**
Line Defense Value: **-20 DV / 24 END to sever net from plantoid**
Hazard Check: **strength based type D to snap or yank free**
Weight Added: **+25kg**

Amid the tangled roots and lower branches of this plantoid, wait a meshwork of stringy shoots and sticky branches which are knotted together into a massive, folded sheet. This living net is attached to a coiled and sinewy line, which connects the circular mass to the main body of the mutant. When needed, this spring loaded net can be jettisoned out to a maximum distance of double the plantoid's height — or width, if this is the thing's larger dimension — and attempt to ensnare a target or two.

This net has a strike value of +20, plus, as it is trying to ensnare a potential adversary and not puncture them, the wearer's armor does not apply to its defense value, but rather only agility, dodge skill and related evasive measures do. Creatures tangled in a net are easier to shoot or hit with ranged or melee weapons and so suffer a further +20 DV penalty — although in this case, their armor helps the unfortunate.

This net is a roundish shape with a diameter equal to the plantoid in height. It can only be used effectively on creatures equal to or smaller than this size as it needs to envelope a target to work. For most human sized plantoids, it can drape one man sized opponent, however a huge plant mutant's net could cover two or more, especially shorter beings like skullocks, bipedal rats, and reptilius.

Anyone struck by the net is thereafter tangled and reduced to half their movement rate and suffer a -30 strike value penalty. Likewise, the trapped victim's agility and accuracy trait are considered at 50%, too. Each round, a trapped creature can either fight on or move with the burden of the net, or else do nothing but try to get untangled by making a strength based Type D hazard check to snap and yank free.

If the net's control line is detached, or severed (DV -20, END 24) a new net will grow in the underside roots of the plantoid but take 20+1d30 days to do so. Even severed, this net will hold its shape and be useful for 6+d6 days before it begins to disintegrate and become useless for anything other than fire starter or bedding straw. Once the net is launched, the plantoid can yank it back at a rate of 1m per round if it has seized a creature of equal or lesser weight, or at a rate of 3 meters per round if a miss occurred. Once the net is recovered, it can be folded and fired gain on the 2nd round after it is withdrawn into the roots of the plantoid.

Any ensnared target that wields a torch, or flame producing mutation or device, can ignite this net. However, if this growth is still attached to the plantoid and living, it is green and only burns for a round (doing 1 round of whatever damage the flame source might otherwise do), while a severed and dried out net will become engulfed in fire and be destroyed in 1d6 rounds, but add an extra 1d6 damage per round to whatever is trapped inside this flaming mass.

The uses for a net launcher are countless, and could include using it as a hammock for the plantoid or a couple of companions to sleep in. So too, if deployed during a fall from a cliff face or through treetops, it has a 50% chance of catching on something and stopping the character from hitting the ground. Another use is to shoot the net across a trail and use the tough line as a tripping rope to stop passing runners or game — the applications are limited only by one's imagination, although the game master will set the odds. Weight added 25kg.

## Nutritional Sap 380
Type: **physical mutation**
Utility: **feed 1 person at survival levels at a cost of -1 Endurance and Strength** Weight added: **+6kg**
Old wounds, scrapes, bruises and punctures to the outer bark of this plantoid's trunk will weep a honey colored, slow flowing sap. This maple syrup flavored liquid is sweet and remarkably delicious, and serves as a nutritional substance that in an emergency, humanoids can live off of. While this mutant plant can yield enough sap per day to at least top a few hotcakes without suffering debilitating weakness or loss of endurance, it is a different story when it must supply most or all of the food supply to a team of non-plant comrades.

For each person to feed from this entity at survival levels, this plantoid loses 1 point of both strength and endurance; points that will not heal until it can reach a favorable supply of its regular nutrition sources, as well as plenty of water. For example, to feed five human comrades per day, this character suffers 5 points damage to both endurance and strength.

If this plantoid lives solely on sunlight, it must also get water to recover these lost trait points, however, if the plantoid is a carrion feeder, and gets access to a fresh corpse, it could theoretically convert the tissues and liquid in the blood and organs of the fallen into sustenance, and in turn, heal itself and continue to make sap.

## Obscuring Pollen Cloud 381
Type: **area dispersal mutation**
Radius: **6 meter radius, or pollen wake of 10m and 2m wide**
Usage: **twice per day per rank** Rate: **1 dispersal**
Duration: **5 minutes (100 rounds) or 1 minute with wind**
Defense Value: **-40 for incoming ranged attacks, or -20 melee range**
Hazard Check: **nil** Weight added: **+10kg**

This plantoid can expel jets of dark brown pollen from one or multiple sacks or emitter holes in its main trunk. Once dispersed, a cloud will form out to a 6 meter radius all around it, and act like a dense smoke screen. All those within this cloud, whether friend or foe, gain a defense value bonus of -40 against incoming ranged attacks, and a -20 DV bonus versus melee range assaults.

This cloud will remain in the area where it was first expelled for five minutes (100 rounds) if there is no significant wind, or only 1 minute (20 rounds) if the wind is blowing.

Another application for this cloud is to conceal a plantoid's escape. When darting out of a cloud, the character and any comrades can break and run, either on the far side of the pollen sphere and thus get a head start from any adversaries, or else sneak into foliage, rubble or other dense terrain. Each fleeing individual gains 4 skill points in concealed movement under these circumstances so long as there is a variety of terrain in which to slip into.

Running while discharging a cloud is also possible, which works especially well when the plantoid is being pursued. Like a squid which blows ink to confuse predators, this mutant can billow forth a dark cloud two meters wide by ten meters long behind it and enjoy the same DV bonuses as noted above. This pollen 'wake' will only continue beyond 10m if extra daily usages of this mutation are deployed. Likewise, back-to-back uses of this mutation can add an extra 3 meters radius and 5 minutes duration to a spherical pollen cloud.

The uses for this discharge are multiple, and include being used to signal other units with a smoke signal application using controlled bursts, a blanket, or discharge patterns. Likewise, a pollen cloud can coat a surface in a thin brown powder to block a solar panel, window, or security camera system.

A direct, point blank discharge of this pollen from this plantoid into the faces of hostile or irksome creatures or people will also illicit great alarm and is 50% likely to make any would-be attacker back off, fearing that the pollen is toxic, radioactive, or some skunk spray-like excretion, allowing the plantoid to attack, flee, or establish dialog.

## Plant Manipulation 382
Type: **mental mutation**    Range: **1m per point of willpower**
Weight Added: **nil**
This is a multi-use mutation, with each of the three aspects having their own daily usages available to the plantoid. The character can use its remarkable power to make plants around it do its bidding to either form dense vegetation into structures, obscure its retreat, whip and lash branches and vines, and hurl twigs and grass at the enemy.

There is almost no limit to the number of uses a plantoid with this power can bring to bear. Some examples are to bend living vegetation to form a bridge or barrier, weave roots and branches into a protective hut around the plantoid and its companions, knot together brambles and branches to block a woodland trail to either stop enemies from following, or to funnel opponents away, or merely hold them back out of melee range to allow comrades with missile weapons to shoot through the barrier from a safer distance. Additionally, the controller can make plants attack its foes.

### Plant Construction

**Usage:** One minute of manipulation (20 rounds) per day, per rank.
**Manipulation area of effect:** 1m wide and 1m tall, by 30cm thick section of plants can be woven per round.
**Constructed section's stats:** DV -10, END 20, although additional layers can be added to increase 20 END to this 1m x 1m section.
**Duration of constructed object:** 1 hour per rank of the plantoid.

A one meter wide and tall, 30cm thick wall of vegetation can be generated per round of concentration while doing nothing else. Each 1m section has a DV of -10 and can take 20 endurance damage, although further layers of thickness can be added to increase the endurance value if additional rounds of plant controlling are spent. Once a plant controlled construction is made, it will remain woven together for 1 hour per rank of the plantoid who created it and then unknot and return to its normal configuration.

Although these controlled living plants can hold together for multiple hours based on the rank of the plantoid, they can be lashed into place for days if not months if beings also set to work using rope, twine, wire and other vegetation to lash together a bridge, wall, roof or even a raft.

### Plant Distraction

**Usage:** Once a day per rank with each use as long as focus is maintained,

Attackers suffer a -30 Strike Value to shoot or attack through the mass of waving, thrashing vegetation.
**Duration:** While focused on, and within range (1m distance per point of Willpower).

Some other applications of this potent mental mutation include throwing up a screen of vegetation to obscure the plantoid and their companions. This distraction will last for as long as the plantoid focuses on it and does nothing but move, and so long as the plantoid stays within range (as willpower in meters). Distracted adversaries make any attacks at -30 strike value through this obscuring barrier. If this plantoid does something other than focus on the distracting plants, or is hit mentally or physically, the usage is expended.

### Plant Attack

**Usage:** Once per day per rank       **Strike Value:** 01-70
**Duration of Attack:** 1 round per rank of user.
**Damage from controlled plant attack:** Half movement next 1d6 rounds, 1d4 lethal and 1d8 stun

Plants can be made to whip, slap, club and grab at opponents — either those chasing the character or fleeing away — and are each attacked at SV 01-70 and if struck take 1d4 lethal and 1d8 stun damage, plus, are restrained and their movement rate cut in half for the next 1d6 rounds. This

lashing plant attack can only be made if the plantoid user focuses and does not use physical weapons, other mental mutations, or do anything other than walk toward or away from the zone of attack. The attack range is equal to the mutant plant's willpower in meters, the duration 1 round per rank of plantoid.

## Plant Serenity 383

Type: **Pheromone Dispersal**     Range: **3 meter radius per rank**
Usage: **constant, or two concentrated puffs per day per rank**
Duration: **2 minutes multiplied by mutant's rank (Rank x 2 = minutes)**
Hazard Check of NPC plant: **Willpower based type F toward the peaceful plantoid PC, or type D toward other companions.**
Weight Added: **+3kg**

This plantoid always gives off pheromones which better ensure that predatory, territorial, or reactionary plants — even non-carnivorous yet animated specimens — are far less likely to harm it. Better still, if this plantoid emits a puff of concentrated pheromones, it may even make the most voracious and flesh hungry mutant plants go docile enough to also ensure that peaceful human and animal companions of this mutant are left alone, too.

In any of the above noted cases, if this plantoid attacks any of the otherwise hostile plants, then those specimens release a different pheromone of pain and danger and nothing this character can do after that will soothe the situation.

The radius of plant serenity is 3 meters around this character, per rank. Likewise, it can release a puff of calming pheromones twice per day per rank, pheromones which might stop green walkers, saw trees, jaw plants and even the dreaded mobilamortus tree (from pages 82 to 85 of Mutant Bestiary One) from attacking this mutant and its companions. The pheromones to protect this plantoid itself are in constant use, but the additional puff to protect comrades will last for 2 minutes, multiplied by the character's rank. Play example: a 5th rank plantoid expels a puff of soothing pheromone. The nearby jaw plant fails its type D willpower hazard check and so becomes serene and non-predatory for 10 minutes (5th rank x 2 minutes = 10 minutes duration).

Each monster plant encountered is allowed a type F willpower based hazard check to disregard this affinity for this plantoid when this character is alone and not harming any plants as it camps, travels or loots an area — and these light pheromones are constantly in the air or water around it. If non-plant companions are present, however, the predatory NPC plant will always attack as usual unless this character unleashes a concentrated puff of extra pheromone, and thereafter the aggressive plant monster need only make a type D willpower based hazard check to disregard the pheromones and continue to attack other beings.

Even if other beings are attacked, the predatory NPC mutant plant might still ignore this plantoid character so long as this PC doesn't cause harm to the aggressive plant.

Finally, each mutant plant makes its own hazard check. Non-player character plantoids are only susceptible to this mutation if they have an intelligence score of ten or less.

## Poisonous Berries 384

Type: **toxic fruit**       Usage: **grows 3d6 per month**
Hazard Check: **Type C Endurance**       Weight added: **+9kg**

Hanging from this plantoid's assorted branches, upper vines and other appendages are 30+1d20 immature, green berries along with 3d6 bright orange, ripe berries. Each month 3d6 berries mature, and for thirty days hang temptingly before dropping off if not ingested. Meanwhile, an equal number of new berries will emerge elsewhere on the character's upper canopy.

Although these walnut sized fruit look appealing, and taste somewhat like sour grapes, they are in fact poisonous. Any creature to eat one must make a type F hazard check using the creature's kilograms weight as a trait. Those who fail the HC suffer a terrible gut ache and are incapacitated for 3d6 hours, able to move at only half speed and fight at half their normal strike value. A further Type C hazard check using Endurance is required to avoid heart failure and death at the end of this period.

Those creatures who eat this fruit but do not become sickened or killed will still suffer a terrible upset stomach, but may not know the reason, and foolishly eat more of these toxic fruit in the future.

Should a creature consume two or more berries, simply increase the time of the initial sickness by +2 hours. (Example, a goat eats five poisonous berries, subsequently fails its hazard check and is sickened for 3d6+10 hours)

## Radiation Leeching 385

Type: **defensive adaptation**    Range: **self or touch**
Usage: **can extract three doses of radiation per day, per rank**
Rate: **1 rad-dose extracted per 30 minutes**
Strike Value: **leaf slap +5**    Damage: **1d8**
Hazard Check: **targets allowed an endurance based type A to avoid 1d3 rad-doses**
Weight added: **+7kg**

This deviation allows the plant to use a specialty branch and leaf system to leech radiation out of its own limbs and leaves. Likewise, it can be attached to a rad victim, an object such as a contaminated relic weapon, or other item and, over many hours, leech out the radiation into specialized leaves. Once thick with contaminated resin (4 doses of radiation), the bloated leaf drops off automatically after 1d6 hours. These radioactive leaves remain radioactive for 1 day per dose of radiation. Ingesting or touching the rad-infused leaf with bare skin, or other parts, might expose a living or mechanical being to 1d4 doses of mild radiation exposure (page 125 of the TME Hub Rules).

In a pinch, this mutant plant can use a radiation laden branch and leaves and slap a foe and on a strike, potentially transfer 1d3 doses to a target. Besides 1d8 regular damage from this extra attack, any impacted target must make an endurance based, type A hazard check to avoid exposure. Inanimate objects and surfaces can also be made radioactive in this fashion, although no initial hit is needed to transfer the contamination. Of course, without first having leeched radiation from its own body, others, or some object, no radiation can be transferred to enemies.

## Saw Leaves 386

Type: **physical attack**    Range: **melee**    Rate: **1 per leaf**
Strike Value: **+17**    Damage: **1d20**
Defense Value: **-10 if used to parry***
*Expending the attack by 1 or more saw leaves*
Defense Value of Saw Leaf Stalk: **-20**
Endurance of Stalk: **20% of plantoid's base END**
Weight Added: **+13kg per saw leaf**

These leaves have developed into half meter long, hardwood, saw-toothed blades which grow on independent, highly flexible, gnarled branches. Each plantoid will start with 1 such serrated leaf per 50kg weight — determined after all other mutations and other potential trait modifiers are applied and so at the end of character generation.

Each saw leaf can hack at one or separate melee range opponents per round, and in conjunction to other melee range attacks. The strike value modifier for each of these growths is +17, and inflicts a base of 1d20 damage. As per most physical attack mutations, the deviant's strength score and accuracy can alter these, so too can the application of either the brawling skill, martial arts skill or weapon expert skill (although only one of these skill areas can be assigned to this mutation).

The vine-like limbs which each blade is attached to can be hacked or blasted off, although each has a base DV of -20 and an endurance value 20% of the base value of the plant mutant's uninjured endurance trait, rounded up (example: this plantoid has an endurance of 38. Thus 0.2 x 38 = 7.6 or 8 endurance). Damaged limbs heal at the mutant's normal healing rate, however if a saw leave branch is chopped off, it takes 30+1d30 days to grow back to useful length, rigidity and keenness. A hacked off saw limb can be used as a sword by other beings, but after 10 successful hits, becomes dull and the saw teeth and sharpness do not recover, inflicting 1d12 damage on the 11th to 20th strikes, and only 1d8 thereafter and causing only stun damage.

Because these paddle shaped, bone-hard saws are so large, they can also shield the plant instead of attack, and each can parry incoming melee and visible physical ranged weapons such as sling stones, thrown rocks, arrows, javelins and crossbow bolts, but do not stop bullets or beam attacks. As per the parry rules on page 108 of the hub rules, any saw leaves selected to serve as shields give the plant character -10 DV each, although the mutant loses their use on the next attack round. One or more saw leaves can be selected to parry while others are put into attacks. Each saw leaf adds 10kg of weight to the plantoid (applied after the total number is determined).

## Second Skin 387

Type: **physical adaption for Host Inhabiting Plantoids (HIP) only**
Hazard Check: **Perception based type B or C to notice that this skin is not normal**
Weight added: **+11kg**

Although the cadaver of a HIP might be breaking down on the inside, this plantoid has a way to conceal this degeneration by coating the corpse in a life like coating of micro-fibers, resin and densely packed, flesh colored leaves The end result is that after inhabiting a cadaver for a week or more, the plantoid can encase itself in a skin almost identical to that of the cadaver beneath. The Host Inhabiting Plantoid can conceal its root ball, roots and tendrils inside the torso of the host body, although larger plantoid mutations will require other means of concealment should the character wish to pass among other beings of the host body's kind — such as housing the rest of its trunk and foliage inside a cart as it drags its bulk along behind the cadaver-doll portion of its body.

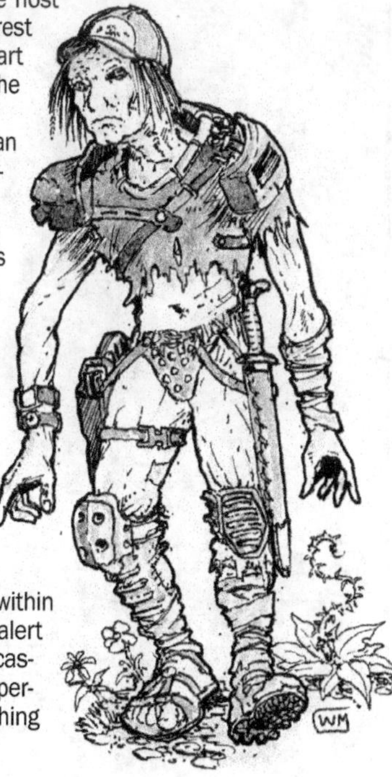

Although the second skin can allow the plantoid to pass as a regular human or other being when moving among unsuspecting 'others', this plant mutant's sheath is not warm to the touch, does not fold exactly right, nor feel like skin. If the plantoid's skin is rubbed, the person touching the false hide is allowed a type B perception based hazard check to notice that the skin peels back, revealing a gruesome mix of decaying flesh and gnarled roots and tendrils beneath. Any close visual inspection of the subject, such as by guards or mutant hunters, and within 3 meters range or less, might also alert the viewer to the mimicry. In such cases, allow any investigator a Type C perception check to realize that something is not right with this person.

## Seedling Minions 388

**Type: physical and mental mutation**
Range: **control range up to 1m per point of Intelligence**
Hazard Check to Control Minion: **Type B Willpower based**
Minions present: **One seedling per 10 pts of Endurance, plus regrows lost minions 1 per rank, per month**

## Minion Stats

Defense Value: **-10**
Endurance: **3d6**
Movement: **5m**
Attacks: **1**
Strike Value: **01-40**
Damage: **1d4**
Strength: **1d6+2**
Agility: **10+1d20**
Accuracy: **10+1d20**
Intelligence: **1d6+3**
Willpower: **2d8**
Weight Added: **+2kg per minion**
Experience Factors: **4**

This plantoid has one or more seedlings adhered to its main trunk — although to the untrained eye, these little turnip-like growths seem to be simply lumps growing into the side of the plantoid. While they have the coloration of the parent plant, they are oddly shaped and no two alike. They have several roots which serve as legs, and a few leafy branches and one main offensive, spiked tipped tendril, root or mouth-like gnawing orifice. When needed, the main plant can yank or shake loose one or more of its mature seedlings and try to get the growths to do its bidding.

A rudimentary mental link exists between the plantoid and its would-be minions, although the range is only as far as the parent plantoid's intelligence trait value in meters around it, and a willpower based type B hazard check is needed to control a seedling. Failure to dominate the seedling will mean is its 50% likely to wander off to find a nice patch of fertilized soil, manure, cadaver or some other place to grow to maturity, otherwise the uncontrolled, and quite ravenous wild seedling will attack the nearest non-plant creature, either a foe of the main plantoid or its comrades.

If one or more seedling is controlled, it will do whatever the parent plant mentally commands, regardless of how suicidal the directive is. Multiple seedlings can be directed at the same moment, and each given a different command if desired.

Typical commands are to go steal the guard's keys, unlock something, pickpocket a person, go scout ahead and then report back what it sees, attack a certain target, or carry a grenade toward an enemy position and pull the pin once it gets there. A minion that stays within the parent's control radius can return to the host and reattach to the plantoid, receive nutrients and moisture, and be ready for further operations later — although with each later detachment, a new willpower based hazard check by the parent is needed to gain control of the thing.

Once detached, a minion can only survive without taking root in good soil for up to a day before it desiccates and drops to the ground. If not recovered and given 48 hours of reconnection with the host's body, or good soil and water, it will die 36 hours after detachment. If no command is given to an already controlled minion, it will merely follow the parent plant, and continuously try to climb up the host to reattach itself — unless it falls too far behind beyond the radius of control (parent's INT in meters), in which case it will wander off to feed or take root.

The plantoid cannot see or hear through the seedling minions, but if these small, roughly thirty centimeters tall, 3kg offspring are controlled, they can return to adhere to the parent again and transfer any experiences to the plantoid host's cognitive organ.

A plantoid with this mutation will start game play with one seedling minion for every 10 points of endurance the parent plant possesses. Lost seedlings can be replaced at a rate of 1 per month per rank, thus a fourth rank plantoid will reproduce 4 seedlings to replace lost minions, but cannot sustain more than the maximum allowed based on the character's uninjured endurance trait value — at least not adhered to its body, and there is nothing to say that a whole crop of these seedlings can't be left in the care of a bio-technician or master gardener to see what happens when the feral seedlings grow up.

These small minions are of very low intelligence and awareness themselves, and without the mind control efforts of the parent plant, they merely seek good soil and a place to take root and grow to adulthood in 10+6d6 months. At adulthood, each unique specimen will do one of the following, although other GM created options are encouraged; roll 1d6

### 1d6 Seedling Minion Adulthood Behavior Table

| 1d6 | |
|---|---|
| 1. | The seedling grew to become a true plant, lost all self awareness and took permanent root where it is. If the parent plant had any offensive mutations, this specimen has the same assortment and will use these to harvest small animals and passers-by, imbibe their juices and leave their remains about its roots to fertilize itself. It will attack the parent plant if it can. |
| 2. | The new plant will have half of all the parent's mutations, become mobile, but be a mindless eating machine with no awareness of where it came from, or what its parent species was — and indeed, will attack and consume the parent plantoid if it gets the chance. |
| 3. | This plantoid will be an identical copy of the parent seedling as it was at 1st rank. It will recognize the parent but will not obey it nor see any humanoid companions with the PC as friends. This plantoid will set off on its own to establish its own territory or comrades, and as it also has the seedling mutation, will likely spread its offspring far and wide. |
| 4. | This seedling grows to have all the mutations and traits of the parent plant, but is a true monster with no interest in other living things except as a source of nutrients. It will try to kill the parent plant and take both its territory and fertilizer supply (humanoid comrades) if able. |
| 5. | This seedling grows into a stunted, sickly copy of the parent plantoid, half the size, half of every trait and with only a 25% chance of exhibiting each of the mutations as the parent. While it has moments of lucidness, when it is aware of those around it, it spends 75% of its time rooted in soil and unreachable unless physically attacked. It worships the parent specimen as a god, and when dormant, dreams only of making its creator proud. |
| 6. | The seedling has a 50% chance of exhibiting each mutation of the parent plant plus d3 other random plant mutations. It has all the traits of the parent (at 1st rank) and looks quite similar in most respects. With its limited self awareness, it will seek to serve and protect the parent plantoid as a minion again of its own volition, even if doing so leads to its self destruction. |

If this plantoid also has the Detachable Core Seedling mutation, (#348, page 303), then that wee variant of the host can attempt to use its willpower to control one or more minions to serve as guardians, at least for 24 hours before the seedlings must take root some place, thus abandoning the tiny character.

## Serrated Leaves 389

Type: **physical attack and defense**    Range: **melee**
Rate: **1 (can attack up to 3 targets if close together)**
Strike Value: **+5**    Damage: **3d6**    Defense Value: **-5**
Special Defense: **Anything to strike this plantoid with a living appendage is auto attacked SV 01-80, DMG 1d8, or if anything successfully grapples this plant, or swallows it, it is also auto-attacked and if struck, possibly suffers 3d8 DMG per round.**    Weight Added: **+7kg**

All the leaves on this plantoid are serrated, and anything to bite, swat, grab or ingest this mutant is in for a nasty surprise. Successful strikes or grapple holds on this plantoid with a living, fleshy appendage, especially by a creature's mouth or when swallowing the plantoid whole, will automatically receive a counter attack — one counter attack if merely making a standard attack, or each round it holds or ingests the character. This auto-attack must strike the assailant with a SV of 01-80 and inflict 1d8 damage if making a normal physical attack, or 3d8 DMG if grappling or swallowing the plantoid.

Most massive creatures will vomit up this deviant plant after the first round of suffering this painful morsel, which takes 1d4 rounds, and in that time, further auto-attacks occur. An auto attack does not mean auto-damage, and a strike roll must still be made at the stated SV range of 01-80.

In standard melee combat, these serrated leaves can also make a thrashing attack with a strike value bonus of +5 that inflicts 3d6 damage. This attack can be made against up to three man-sized targets if they are grouped close together in one direction. This is not an extra melee attack.

In addition, these robust leaves serve as an extra protective layer, and improve the plantoid's defensive value by -5.

## Shriek Radius 390

Type: **physical mutation**    Range: **As per willpower trait (see table)**
Usage: **three times per day per rank**    Strike Value: **automatic**
Damage: **variable, see description**    Weight Added: **+4kg**

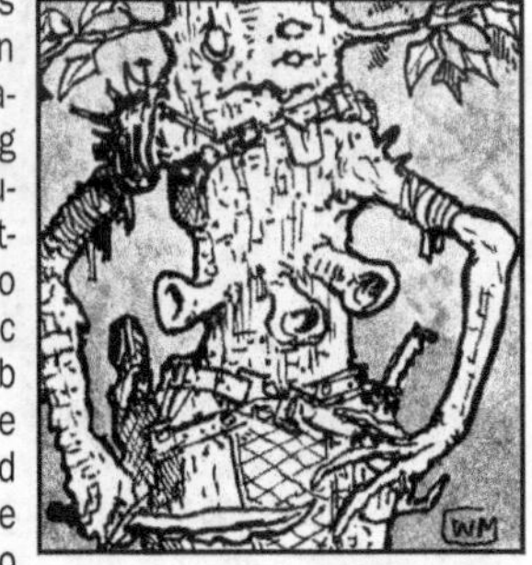

Growing from the thickest part of this plantoid's trunk or root ball are several bulbous, pylon shaped bulbs which look very much like miniature relic bullhorns. When desired, and taking no other action, including movement, this mutant can discharge a deafening, tissue disrupting sonic attack. This mutation is very similar to the human and animal deviation called Sonic Wave radius (#76) from page 73 of the Hub Rules. It differs in that while it doesn't have the same radius of range, or damage, it can be used more often. Like the regular mutation, this one is based on the willpower of the plantoid, and so too, those wearing shell class armor or some sort of relic sonic defense suit or other device are immune to the effects of this terrible power.

| Plantoid's Willpower | Attack Radius | Damage | Deafness Duration |
|---|---|---|---|
| Below 14 | 1 meter | 1d3 | 1 minute |
| 14-25 | 2 meters | 1d4 | 4 minutes |
| 26-40 | 4 meters | 1d6 | 8 minutes |
| 41-70 | 5 meters | 1d8 | 20 minutes |
| 71-90 | 7 meters | 1d10 | 45 minutes |
| 91-110 | 9 meters | 1d12 | 1.5 hours |
| 111-130 | 12 meters | 1d20 | 2d6 hours |
| 131-160 | 15 meters | 1d20+5 | 10+2d6 hours |
| Each 10 above | +5 meters | +5 DMG | +1 day |

## Solar Emission Burst 391

Type: **physical mutation**    Range: **at 5th rank steady light 20m ahead**
Usage: **Once per day, per rank** Rate: **1**    Range. **20 meters**
Hazard Check: **type D agility based hazard check to avoid blindness for 2d6 rounds**
Weight added: **+6kg**

Once per day per rank, so long as this plantoid has been exposed to 4 or more hours of direct sunlight in the past 48 hours, this plantoid can emit collected light and discharge it at will. The plantoid exhibits a cluster of between 7 and twelve (1d6+6) strange, glassy orbs among its topmost branches. From these, it can unleash brilliant illumination which is akin to the brilliance of the sun — at least for a brief flash. This illumination, while painfully bright outdoors during the day, is not likely to blind anybody, but underground or at night, those looking in the plantoid's direction when this mutation is unleashed must react quickly to cover their eyes and look away to avoid temporary blindness.

Beings with eyes facing this plantoid, and within 20m of the orb cluster, must make a type D agility based hazard check to have looked away in time, otherwise, are blinded for 2d6 rounds. Those who succumb to blindness are half movement, suffer a 50% drop in SV to attack others and are themselves +40 SV easier to be struck.

Those wearing sunglasses or a polarized face shield such as on any combat helmet or shell class armor are allowed a type A hazard check and if blinded, are only affected for 1d4 rounds.

When this plantoid masters this power (at 5th rank) it can also emit light in a dull gleam as if giving off a candle's light, or else project the golden light 20 meters ahead of it in a focused cone similar to a flashlight with each use lasting 30 minutes (1 use per rank per day).

The glassy orbs are actually amber, and if harvested off a dead plantoid, they can be sold for 20sp each. If plucked out (which inflicts 1d6 damage to the plantoid for each orb that is forcibly removed) these orbs will regrow after 3d6+4 months. At least 6 orbs are needed to deploy this mutation.

## Solar Regenerating 392

Type: **Regenerative mutation**
Usage: **In sunlight heals 1 trait point per 10 minutes. 4 hours of solar regeneration recovers daily usage of other mutations. See below.**
Weight added: **+12kg**

When outdoors and exposed to the sun's rays, this mutant can unfurl an array of meter long, broad leaves and face these into the light to use hyper-photosynthesis. Like other plants that gain nutrients from the sun, this deviant also receives all the nourishment it needs from these growths, but enjoys far greater benefits.

For every ten minutes in full sunlight, this plantoid heals one point to each depleted trait, although under overcast conditions, this regeneration takes twenty minutes or double the time. If able to stay in full sunlight for four hours, this mutant can also recover any daily uses to other mutations that might normally take 24 hours to recharge or regrow.

## Spitting Acid Pods 393

Type: **physical attack Appendages (d3+2)**     Range: **24m**
Usage: **One squirt per pod, per hour**     Strike Value: **+10**
Damage: **1d6 per round for 1d6 rounds**     Weight added: **+5kg per pod**

This mutant plant has 1d3+2 elongated, melon-like green pods which grow on individual, short flexible stalks. These are typically concealed under broad leaves or pine boughs and are normally quite innocent looking. These globular pods are actually acid ejectors and able to squirt a stream of foul smelling bright yellow slime as far as 24 meters away, one squirt per pod, per hour.

The strike value is +10, however, any applied weapon expert skill points, rank gain, or accuracy trait modifiers can alter this. The damage to those struck is 1d6 damage per round, with each squirt of acid burning the target for 1d6 rounds. If the target leaps into a pond or is doused in at least two liters of water or other liquid, it will neutralize the acid.

This plantoid is immune to its own acid, but only partially resistant to other varieties and takes half damage from all other acid types. Each pod can unleash one jet of acid per hour. The acid becomes neutral and harmless after 12 hours.

So strong is this acid that it can slowly dissolve iron, tin, brass, aluminum and many new era metal items, however, alloys, such as those used to make razor swords and powered shell class armor, are unaffected by this substance. Robots, at least the common varieties usually encountered, are also susceptible to this acid attack.

## Spring Coil Leap 394

Type: **physical attack and locomotion mode**
Movement: **leap 5x body length or +4m per round to normal MV**
Usage & Rate: **once every 10 rounds**
Range: **melee or leap distance into target**
Strike Value: **+30**     Damage: **3d8 stun**     Weight added: **+15kg**

Growing on the underside of this plantoid is one or more (1d4) coil-like roots, which in appearance look very much like a young, uncurling fern leaf. When needed, this life form can spring up and away at 5 times its length in meters, either directly upwards or horizontally. This leap can be achieved once every 10 rounds. For more general daily travel, these appendages make smaller spring-like actions, adding to the potential top speed of this plantoid by +4m per round.

If this character wishes, it can spring directly at smaller creatures, or leap

up and try to land on an opponent. This attack, also allowable once every 10 rounds, is +30 SV and inflicts a base of 3d8 stun damage, plus any strength modifiers.

The number of coils doesn't change these features, and if only one such root is present, it is simply more robust, whereas if four such appendages are exhibited, they are thinner. While powerful, these growths are not dexterous and cannot be used to grasp tools or conduct delicate tasks.

## Sticky Sap 395

Type: **physical excretion for armor and concealment**
Usage: **one full coating per day per rank**
Defense Value: **-10, -20 or -30 depending on application**
Weight added: **+13kg**

While always somewhat sticky, with beads and streamers of sap marking this plantoid's trunk and larger extremities, this mutant can also willfully ooze glistening, amber sap from its bark and, after one minute, coat itself in a glue like layer. Insects, small birds and rodents which might try to feed on this plantoid find themselves hopelessly stuck to this mutant's exterior, and easily dispatched.

Applications of this glue-like sap for everyday chores such as roofing tiles, boat repair, crafts, fletching arrows and countless other tasks make this plantoid a precious asset to a community, however the uses of this sap in adventure are also boundless.

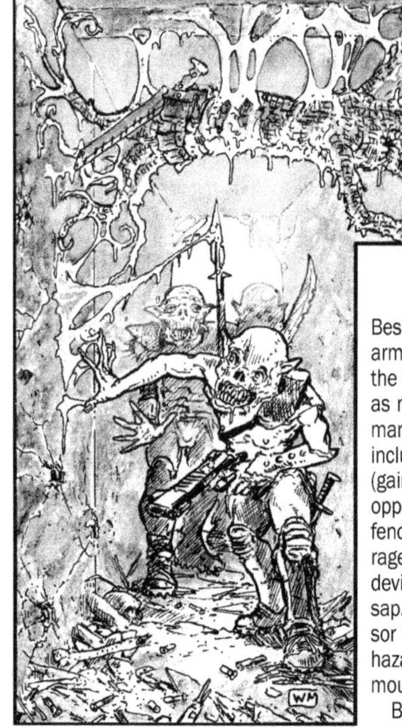

Besides adhering junk, scraps of armor and other tough materials to the character as a layer of protection, as noted below, is of course one primary use of this deviation, other uses include helping the plantoid climb (gaining 2 skill points), grappling an opponent (gain +1 skill points), and fending off hungry herbivores or enraged carnivores who might bite this deviant and get a mouthful of sticky sap. This mouthful forces the aggressor to make a type D strength based hazard check to avoid having its mouth glued shut for 3d6 minutes.

Besides serving as a layer of armor, a collection of debris and dead weeds, bones, and trash can also make for excellent camouflage should the plantoid find itself in an area already littered by typical garbage. As per the stealth skill table on page TME-51, increase the plant mutant's 'concealed movement' by +1 skill point and 'conceal self' by +2 points.

The most common use of this mutation is to affix light, medium, or heavy trash armor to itself. Each category increases the plant's defense value, but also adds weight and slows the character. The following table shows the time needed to adhere or detach each degree of protection.

| Degree of Adhered Junk Armor | DV Bonus | MV Penalty | Weight | Time to adhere or detach* |
|---|---|---|---|---|
| No Adhered Junk | -0 DV | nil | nil | nil |
| Light Junk Adherence | -10 DV | -0.5m | +3d6kg | 2d6 minutes |
| Medium Junk Adherence | -20 DV | -1m | +20+6d6kg | 4d6 minutes |
| Heavy Junk Adherence | -30 DV | -1.5m | +40+6d6kg | 5d6+10 minutes |

** To reduce or add trash to lower or raise the level of protection one step. Roll each time the plantoid wishes to set about doing this task. For example, the weedy wants to reduce its medium junk adherence to Light junk adherence, it takes 4d6 minutes to do so. However, if this mutant wanted to remove all junk adherence, it would take 4d6+2d6 for a total of 6d6 minutes. To add armor requires sufficient junk to be present or else such materials be carried in a pack, etc.*

The camouflage bonus remains the same regardless of how thick the armor is applied. Secondly, the glue remains fixed with the trash until the plantoid elects to peel off the junk or whatever else it is stuck to. Finally, this glue-like sap can be excreted and stored in oiled leather bags or barrels and will remain viable for 24 hours before hardening to a brittle, and most often useless, consistency. Dry sap is waterproof unless removed by hard scrubbing with soap and hot water.

## Suction Tendrils 396

Type: **physical mutation**          Range: **melee or out 6m**
Rate: **1 per tendril**              Strike Value: **+5**
Damage: **slap 1d6**                 Weight added: **+5kg per tendril**

There are countless uses for these tendrils, including adhesion to rocks and rubble during storms, allowing the plantoid to traverse up or down steep slopes, climb a wall or skyscraper, or hang and move upside down in a cave or other enclosed space.

The plantoid will start with between 3 and 6 (1d4+2) of these suction cup and micro-thorn covered vines. If severed, they grow back in 1+1d2 months and at their full length can stretch out three meters (9 feet).

To sever a tendril requires doing 18 points damage to the appendage, which has a defense value of -15.

Depending on the number of suction tendrils, the mutant's ability to climb is increased. Likewise, so is the entity's grapple skill. These appendages are excellent for grasping onto prey or holding opponents. So too, they can be deployed as melee weapons and simultaneously swat, slap and bludgeon one or more opponents for 1d6 damage each, plus any strength and unarmed combat modifiers the character might enjoy.

The following table shows both the climbing skill and grapple skill points this plantoid enjoys based on the number of tendrils it uses. Other skill points can be combined to the following should the character gain them from other character creation or rank gain results.

| Suction Tendrils | Climbing Skill Points | Grappling Skill Points |
|---|---|---|
| 1. | +1 | +1 |
| 2,3. | +2 | +1 |
| 4,5. | +3 | +2 |
| 6. | +4 | +3 |

## Thorns 397

Type: **physical defense/attack**          Range: **melee**
Strike Value: **defensive auto attack 01-70/ Offensive +5**
Damage: **1d6 if struck or +1d6 to any melee attack**
Defense Value: **-15**          Weight added: **+9kg**

This plantoid's major branches, roots, appendages and trunk are covered in nasty inch long, hardwood thorns. Besides adding a -15 defense value bonus as armor, any creature to make a successful melee attack against this mutant plant using its mouth or fleshy appendages risks an automatic attack as it contacts this weedy's deadly sharp thorns. This auto attack has a fixed strike

value of 01-70 and inflicts 1d6 damage per impact (strike or grapple, hug, slap on the back, etc.) on this character. This strike value does not change with rank gain or skill applications.

As an offensive measure, any limb or other attached appendage this plantoid exhibits is also covered in thorns and add an extra +5 strike value and inflicts an additional 1d6 damage on top of whatever other damage the appendage delivers.

These thorns can be shaved off a veggie-sapien should the need arise, and will grow back in 30+d10 days.

## Toxic Sap 398

Type: **physical defense**
Range: **melee contact**          Usage: **unlimited**
Rate: **1 exposure per contact (successful strike against this plantoid)**
Hazard Check: **Type E Endurance bite** or **B Touch**          Weight added: **+7kg**

Any creature, including other plants, to make bite or rough skin on skin contact with this plantoid risks exposure to a coating of toxic syrup; the chance of exposure differs by the method of contact.

The most likely way to transfer this toxin is by biting this mutant plant, which herbivorous assailants are prone to doing. Less common exposure occurs by an attacker punching or otherwise making a successful hit on this plantoid with a non-food consuming organ — although attacks from non-fleshy appendages such as bone blades, crab pincers, hooves, antlers and horns do not transfer this sap to the attacker.

Bite attacks therefore force the aggressor to make an endurance based type E hazard check to avoid ingesting the sap. Hand or other non-bone appendage direct contact forces a type B hazard check.

Those who fail their hazard check become immediately sickened and for 3d6 minutes thereafter and reduced to half their movement rate, half strength, and half their strike value. At the end of this duration, the unfortunate must make a further Type C endurance based has a check to avoid dropping into unconsciousness for 2d6 hours.

This plant character only releases toxic sap when either taking a hit — which occurs automatically on the aggressor's turn — or when preparing itself for contact with the enemy and smacking and squeezing its own skin or bark to produce it ready coating of this rust colored sap.

Under normal circumstances, this character is safe to touch and brush up against by both comrades and passersbys.

This sap can be coated onto arrows, spear tips and the edges of blades and other cut and thrust appendages and will remain active for one hour. Likewise, this plantoid's main trunk and limbs will also remain toxic for an hour after the mutant has been punctured by any sort of attack, or after self coating itself prior to a fight.

This toxin can last longer than an hour if stored in an air-tight container and will remain viable for 48 hours in this manner. A plantoid with this mutation can create enough toxin to coat one weapon in venom for each kilogram of body weight.

## Tumbling Locomotion 399

Type: **physical mutation**
Movement Bonus: **+1d8 meters per round**
Defense Value while tumbling: **-20 DV**
Body Slam: **add 1d20 stun damage to the normal 1d6 DMG**
Weight added: **+4kg**

Besides this plantoid's normal walking and running pace, it can roll into a loose ball and tumble away to escape quickly or travel overland at greater speed. This form of locomotion yields a movement increase of between 1 and 8 meters per round. This movement bonus is rolled each round the weedy tumbles, although if heading into a brisk wind, this is reduced by half, while going with a gust, like a true tumble weed, will double this movement rate.

While tumbling, the plant character enjoys a -20 defense value bonus. However, it cannot deploy weapons except melee attacks and only when rolling into or passed an enemy formation. Should the plantoid want to tumble into an opponent and body slam them, it may do so, too. This body slam is considered a normal unarmored attack but inflicts an extra 1d20 stun damage on top of the usual 1d6 of a basic unarmed attack — with strength modifiers added. After a successful bash attack, each smaller target than the plantoid (less kilograms or height) has a 50% chance of being knocked over, and in this fashion, the plantoid could tumble through a whole formation of smaller beings.

This weedy's branches and foliage are accustomed to hard falls and smacks, and so this entity suffers only half damage from any fall.

Finally, unless covered in all manner of clothing, armor, relics and gear, this plantoid can coil into a ball-like shape among other vegetation and improve their chances of going unseen by onlookers, and thus gains two skill points in 'conceal self' when attempting to hide; see the stealth rules on page TME-51, of the hub rules.

## Vampiric Roots 400

Type: **physical attack**  Range: **Reach out to 5 meters**
Usage: **once per round**  Rate: **1d4 blood sucking vines**
Strike Value: **+13**
Damage: **stab 1d6, plus 1d6 per round once latched, per vine**
Hazard Check: **strength based type D to detach per round**
Weight added: **+15kg**

This mutant plant can feed on the blood of both warm and cold-blooded creatures, including the recently killed, so long as it consumes the blood within an hour of the victim's demise.

Between one and four sinuous, highly mobile, five meter long tendrils grow from within this miscreation's root system or upper branches. These flexible, snake-like growths can be made to lash out and try to stab into and adhere to just one, or multiple targets if desired — often at a safe distance to avoid risk to the plantoid's main trunk and sensory appendages. Upon a successful strike, which inflicts 1d6 base damage from the impact*, these vines can optionally begin to suck and drain 1d6 points of endurance in blood from the victim, per round, per attached vampiric vine. The subject can either try to break free of the vines on a successful type D strength based hazard check per vine, or use its jaws or some edged weapon to hit and hack off the appendage (the vine has a DV of -20 and each has 20 END. If severed, the vine takes 30+1d20 days to grow back).

While vampiric, this mode of nutrient acquisition is not necessarily this plantoid's only way of feeding, yet, is often its favored way as long as it can find a victim or a willing volunteer who will succumb to the very painful stab and loss of blood. All the blood consumed by this mutant both feeds and heals this plantoid, with ingested endurance points replenishing lost trait points this character might have previously endured — although no amount of blood consumption can push the trait points of this mutant beyond its base trait values.

Needless to say, commoners who might accept most plantoids into their community will be horrified to witness or hear accounts of this character's blood thirsty ways, and cast the weedy out if not kill it outright.

These 5 meter (about 16 foot) long, sinuous appendages are incapable of gripping clubs or other tools, being rudimentary in their movements, however if forced to climb, they will aid the plantoid and add 1 point in the

climbing skill. Likewise, these growths can assist the mutant in swimming and add +1m per round to the character's water speed and bring their swimming ability up one degree — poor swimmer becomes fair swimmer, etc.

*For this stab attack, the plantoid's strength modifiers can increase this initial damage. Likewise, the weedy can apply either the weapon expert or unarmed combat (brawling or martial arts) skill points to this mutation to make the initial attack more accurate and inflict more damage, however the 1d6 blood drain remains the same throughout the character's life.*

## Water Storage Pods 401

Type: **physical mutation**
Usage: **5 liter capacity per pod**
Appendages: **1 pod per 50kg body weight of plantoid**
Weight added: **+7kg per pod, or 2kg if drained (Note: 1 liter of water weighs 1kg)**
When depleted, these melon like, flexible sacks shrivel into branch-like, useless protrusions. However, when access to water is plentiful, including a bout of rain lasting an hour or longer, these appendages fill with filtered water. Dozens of specialized roots, leaves, and green branches on this weedy harvest the water, suck it from the wet ground, sand, or vegetation but so too collect moisture through its leaves. The water is transferred to these bags for later use during times of drought.

Each plantoid with this mutation will have one such water pod per 50 kilograms of starting body weight, with a minimum of one pod. They will each store 5 liters of water and can be accessed by both the plantoid itself and by humanoid companions via a simple cork and straw system. Sometimes, desert dwelling people with such weedy companions will install spigots in the sides of these pods for ease of access.

The water from these bags alway has a strange taste to it, determined at character creation from the included list. Roll 2d6, with all pods tasting the same 90% of the time, otherwise, each pod has a different flavor.

| 2d6 | Water Taste Table |
|---|---|
| 2. | Beer, with 5% alcohol |
| 3. | Urine |
| 4. | Tastes sweet like maple syrup |
| 5. | Cherry flavored |
| 6. | Apple flavored |
| 7. | No discernible flavor |
| 8. | Hint of Brussels Sprout |
| 9. | Hint of Lemon |
| 10. | Tea, green |
| 11. | Tea, similar to English Breakfast |
| 12. | Is actual red wine, Merlot, 12% alcohol |

## Weaponized Spear-Grass 402

Type: **physical attack**
Range: **melee or spear range of 15m**
Usage: **One spear grass shaft will have regrown and hardened per day to a maximum of 6 per rank.**
Rate: **1 can be plucked and thrown per round, or the plantoid can gore in melee**
Strike Value: **thrown or handheld +6 / gore +10**
Damage: **thrown 1d20+1/ gore 1d20+6**
Defense Value: **-9 bonus**
Number present: **2d6, +1 per rank (2d6+1 starting PC)**
Weight Added: **+8 kg per spear grass shaft**
Clustered vertical lengths of meter long grass and rigid shafts grow from the upper trunk of this plantoid. These quiver-like patches are firmly fixed to the plant and to tug one of the straw colored, hardened spear-grass lengths free requires a strength score of at least 12. If strong enough, this mutant can yank one ready length and hurl it as if it were a spear, or wield it in melee combat one or two handed, or else bend forward and gore at a melee range opponent with the bunched grass and unused and immature spear shafts for 1d20+6 base damage.

A starting character will have 2d6 ripe, barb tipped spears, plus one per rank (so 2d6+1 at 1st rank). One spear can be thrown per round, however, as a melee attack, this offensive measure can be added to other melee attack modes. Strength and accuracy modifiers apply, as might the weapon expert skill — which can be used in both melee and ranged combat — or the brawling or martial arts skill should the character have this, but only one of these skill areas can be applied.

Spear-grass shafts have a 50% chance of breaking after being thrown. However, if the shaft survives combat, it can be used again by this plantoid, their comrades, or opponents. Lost spears are replaced at a rate of 1 new ripened and hardened shaft per day up to the character's base starting amount, although this base amount changes as the character goes up in rank with an extra shaft per rank. Spear-grass shafts are tough, like bamboo, and improve the character's defense value by -9.

# Plant Flaw Mutations

## Aphids 403

This plantoid is infested with patches of aphids, their sticky honeydew, and hundreds of tiny ants which feed on the sweet liquid these insects produce. The character's leaves, buds and freshly unfurling roots and vines are stunted and curled, discolored and itchy. Unless attended to with chemically treated soapy water, the plantoid is permanently reduced by 5+1d8 Endurance. So too, winged aphids and accompanying ants will get into the food, drink and gear of any comrades, causing annoyance.

A spray mixture treatment can be created by a chemical technician of 2 or higher skill points, at a material cost of only 2+1d2sp for 10 days supply (1 liter), although to purchase this substance in any agricultural town costs 5+1d20sp for a liter.

## Delicious to Herbivores 404

Plant eaters are attracted to this mutant's aroma, and should they get a taste of its succulent leaves, buds and new growths, will often call out with excitement and draw other herbivores to the bounty. Some tribes will capture a plantoid with this curse as bait to draw out deer, wild goats and hogs and slay them as they chomp down on the restrained plantoid.

For a PC with this flaw, every visit to a typical farm village always brings out the local livestock, who if accidentally killed to save the character's foliage and appendages, will often elicit the ire of the locals, who, being omnivores, might consider adding the character to their diet, too.

## Flammable 405

This mutant plant's bark, branches and leaves are all laced with petroleum sap. If hit by a torch or Molotov cocktail, burning lantern or caught in the burning propellant of a flame unit or blast of an incendiary or fragmentation grenade, this unfortunate will always catch fire and any burning duration will be double what it otherwise would be. Aware of its predicament and weakness, this plantoid will seek relic flame suits and other protective gear, including sheets of tinfoil, plus try to carry a relic fire extinguishers and extra supplies of water to douse itself to avoid becoming a walking inferno.

## Green Walker Root Ball 406

The same vile, inky root ball which infests and controls the animated, plant draped corpses called green walkers — as seen on page 166 of the hub rules — also inhabits this unfortunate plantoid. The greasy, pulsing root ball somehow got into this mutant years ago and now dwells deep in the trunk of the character. Encased now in hard sap, minerals and thick wood, this monstrous, cadaver hungry parasite sometimes affects the thinking organs of the plantoid, especially during melee combat.

Should this character defeat a roughly man size being, especially a humanoid, the plantoid must make a Type C willpower based hazard check or else, after the battle is over, return the to the cadavers and wounded and, select one, and begin to wriggle and corkscrew its roots or other appendages into the cadaver in a gruesome, sickening ritual of mutilation. Human companions are typically revolted by this behavior, which will last for 3d6 minutes, and afterward, the plantoid regains its regular way of thinking, usually apologies, cleans itself and tries to forget the incident — especially as it seems to get no benefit from the gory procedure.

If this plantoid is rendered unconscious, then this green walker aspect takes over the body and will immediately set about attacking the nearest living things, and set about the same bloody dismemberment as noted above.

The one beneficial aspect of this mutational flaw is that other green walkers will never attack this character.

## Grubs and Beetles 407

This plantoid's bark, stalks, and trunk are highly appealing to assorted beetles and their grubs, which feed on the character day and night. These pests bore holes into the plantoid, devour leaves and vines, and cause the character to spend at least an hour a day ridding itself of the pests.

Because of a weakened frame, the PC suffers a loss of -6+1d6 strength and endurance, permanently. Plus, those forced to share a camp with this plantoid will have a 1 in 6 chance per night of getting bitten by stray larvae or flying beetles (total damage 1pt), and periodically find these parasites in their food, drink, gear and clothing.

A chemical technician can mix up a smelly, dark brown paste to offer temporary relief. This concoction can be applied to the mutant plant, at a manufacturing cost of 20+1d20sp, or purchase price of 100+1d100sp, which will rid the PC of these insects for 10+3d6 days before they return. While free of beetles and their larva, the character will heal both 6+1d6 strength and endurance.

## Lightning Rod 408

This unfortunate mutant plant has veins of iron ore within its trunk and upper branches, while these give a slight +3 to its strength and -3 to defense value, this metallic content is highly conductive and during lighting storms, this plantoid needs to seek shelter immediately at least get to low ground

or lay prone if in open country. Any lighting strike that comes near it, and its traveling companions, will have ten times the chance of striking this plantoid instead of any other beings nearby.

Worse still, if in combat with any creature or relic which throws electrical bolts or charges, this plantoid is far easier to 'contact' and is +30 strike value to hit, while any successful strike is 67% likely to ignite the plantoid who will burn for 1d6 damage per round for 3d6 rounds unless at least two liters of water are poured over the character, or it stands in a downpour of rain, or jumps into a body of water.

## Mealybugs 409

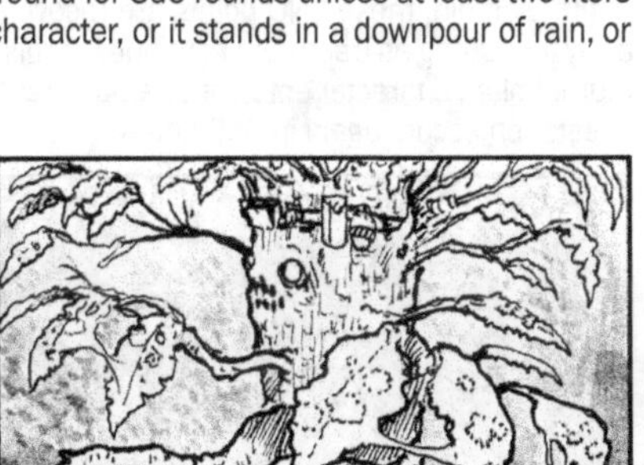

This is an infestation of tiny insects which create web like patches of white fuzz on leaves and small branches. These pests cause the plantoid a great deal of pain, itching and stunt its growths. If left untreated by insecticide or a companion using alcohol tipped cloths and swabs to rub away the growths, then this mutant's endurance is reduced by -2d6 points until the current outbreak is cleared up. The cost per month to rid this plantoid of mealybugs is 30sp.

## Past Termite Infestation 410

At some point in this plant mutant's past, it had a serious termite infestation. While the insects have moved on, they've left the plantoid's trunk, limbs and roots pitted and riddled with cavities, holes and tunnels which have weakened the entity's structure. Reduce this character's endurance and strength score by -2d6 each, permanently.

## Periodic Rooting 411

From time to time, this mutant must cease its nomadic ways and take root in the ground for a fixed minimum period to nourish itself or else suffer ongoing damage and possible death.

The following random rooting variables are used to establish how frequently the plantoid must root, and secondly for how long, and third, the harm that comes each day without taking root. While rooted, the plantoid becomes drowsy, spreads its foliage out and becomes more plant-like than normal, perhaps even being easily dismissed by other beings as just some shrub or tree if all its gear, armor and other attire are removed from it while in this state. If while rooted it is undressed, looted, attacked or otherwise disturbed, it can rouse itself and fight back, including uprooting itself to flee if needed, but will be preoccupied with getting into the ground again as soon as it can find a suitable, safe spot. During this time of recuperation, the plantoid will rapidly heal all lost trait points and regrow any severed limbs. Both benefits occur at twice the regular rate for the appendage.

| 2d6 | Rooting Frequency Required |
|---|---|
| 2. | Every 10th day |
| 3,4. | Every 20th day |
| 5,6. | Every 30 days |
| 7. | Every 40 days |
| 8. | Every 50 days |
| 9. | Every 60 days |
| 10. | Every 90 days |
| 11. | Every 200 days |
| 12. | Every 365 days |

| 2d6 | Duration of Rooting Period |
|---|---|
| 2. | 3d6 days* |
| 3-6. | 4 days |
| 7,8. | 3 days |
| 9. | 2 days |
| 10. | One full day and full night (24 hours) |
| 11. | Only 12 hours |
| 12. | Only 6 hours |

*Roll each period

| 2d6 | Daily Harm if Not Taking Root* |
|---|---|
| 2. | Wilts and cannot move about, -50% SV, takes 1d20 damage. |
| 3. | Reduced movement rate to half, plus suffers 2d6 damage |
| 4,5. | Loses the ability to speak, reduced movement by -1m, takes 1d6 damage |
| 6,7. | Takes 1d6 damage |
| 8,9. | Takes 1d4 damage |
| 10,11. | Takes 1d3 damage |
| 12. | Takes 1 pt damage |

*Roll this each day for a possible different bad outcome. The harm, besides the taking of damage noted in rolls 2 to 5, remains regardless of the harm done on following days, and is present until after the full re-rooting duration has elapsed.

## Pollen 412

This plant mutant produces small, colorful buds almost daily, especially in the spring months. As these flowers bloom, they give off a pleasant aroma that attracts bees, wasps, ants and other sap eating creatures, including a wide assortment of moths, hummingbirds, butterflies and the like. While these usually harmless creatures do not bother the plantoid, they can prove to annoy humanoid companions — or worse.

Doom moths, red wasps, many giant ants, bees, and other creatures are also attracted to the character and will either attract unwanted attention to the plantoid's location, or attack any people or animals within ten meters of this pollen rich, flowering plantoid.

One solution is to pluck off the flowers, which inflicts 1 endurance point damage to the plantoid per flower removed, with 3d6 blossoms present at any given day when a bloom occurs — which has a 66% likelihood each day.

## Rodents 413

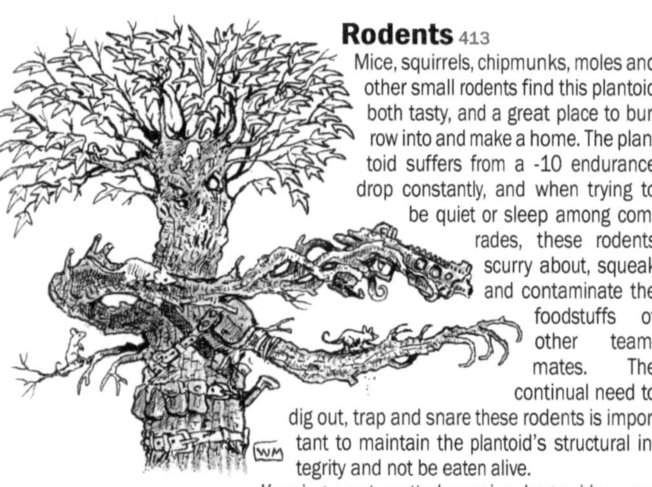

Mice, squirrels, chipmunks, moles and other small rodents find this plantoid both tasty, and a great place to burrow into and make a home. The plantoid suffers from a -10 endurance drop constantly, and when trying to be quiet or sleep among comrades, these rodents scurry about, squeak and contaminate the foodstuffs of other teammates. The continual need to dig out, trap and snare these rodents is important to maintain the plantoid's structural integrity and not be eaten alive.

Keeping a pet spotted scorpion, bog spider, weasel or some other small rodent hunting predator on a short leash — and providing a protective cage for it — will keep rodents away from the plantoid and allow it to regain the lost ten endurance points.

## Root Bound 414

The vegetative instincts of this plantoid are strong, and its subconscious, woody heart fights with its primary, human-like mind and personalty. The veggie side yearns to deny the being's human DNA aspect, wants to block its urge to move about, engage in conversations or partake in the desires and ambitions of an animal. Instead, the inner core seeks to put down roots and cease all toil.

Each night, or whenever this character stops anywhere for over two hours, the thing's roots will subconsciously wriggle into the soil, sand, muck, dust or junk and take root. Meanwhile, after an hour of inactivity, the eyes, nostrils, mouth orifice and any non-plant parts will begin to crust over with bark as the character turns from a dynamic, hybrid being into some sort of bush, tree or giant weed. Upon waking after a night or pause in one location of over two hours, the plantoid is stuck fast, lethargic and must take 3d6 rounds to rouse itself, pull up its roots, and scratch away bark that has grown over its sensory organs.

If knocked unconscious for more than 12 hours, the plantoid will firmly root to whatever surface it lays upon, and is required to make a Type F strength based hazard check to snap itself free of its rebellious roots and become a plantoid again, instead of a vegetable. Another hazard check can be made after ten minutes if the previous HC fails. While rooted, even if conscious and able to move its upper limb appendages and engage opponents, this plantoid is vulnerable to attacks and is +20 strike value easier to hit.

In some circumstances, the ability to shed all gear and clothing and non-plant articles and take root for days, weeks or even years, could be beneficial, so long as the plantoid does so where there is sunlight, good soil and a source of water. A hibernating plantoid who becomes feral for more than a month can only be revived by companions who can scrape away the bark over its ear holes, eyes and call to and shake the slumbering character. Even then, only one attempt to revive it per day is permitted, with the plantoid allowed a type E willpower based hazard check to return to the world of humanity.

If attacked while in this rooted, dormant state, the plantoid is allowed a Type C Intelligence hazard check to wake up each round that it is suffering from either fire, axe blows or other physical attacks. Picking any fruit from a slumbering plantoid has a 1 in 20 chance of waking it per fruit plucked from its branches.

## Slug Infestation 415

Slugs are attracted to this plantoid — including the giant variants listed on page 105 of Mutant Bestiary One. Regular slugs leave glistening lines of slime about the plantoid and feed on the subject's leafy portions, roots, vines, and sensory adaptations. This constant infestation reduces the plantoid's endurance by -10, although if a daily 200g of salt is sprinkled over the entire plantoid, these END points are recovered and the slug problem goes away for as long as treatment continues. If this salting process stops, and the mutant plant character enters a swamp, forest, garden, or lush field, the slug infestation occurs again in 3d6 hours.

Those forced to accompany a slug coated plantoid are often revolted by this infestation and will try to keep clear of the unfortunate veggie-mutie, especially at mealtimes or when bedding down for the night.

## Solar Dependent 416

While all plantoids gain nourishment via photosynthesis, many also derive food from rich soil, fertilizer, cadavers, and direct consumption of flesh via mouths or other orifices. This plantoid, however, especially depends on getting sunlight regardless of other means of acquiring sustenance. Should the mutant have some other mutation which allows it to feed, then it only re-

quires 4 hours a day of direct sunlight to maintain optimal health, however, with no such other means, this weedy must get 8 hours of sunlight.

Failure to get sufficient sunlight means the character suffers debilitating effects 24 hours after failure to reach the minimum amount of sunlight, and suffers 1 point of endurance damage per hour while going without. After 36 hours without sunlight, the entity drops to half movement rate and suffers a -30 penalty to strike values and +30 penalty to defense value as it becomes lethargic, limp, and dull witted, as well as continues to lose 1 END per hour.

At any point when it can get into direct sunlight — or the equivalent in some relic or junk crafted greenhouse lighting — it will cease suffering more damage but until its 4 or 8 hour recharge transpires, it does not regain its lost endurance, SV or DV. After the allotted time in the sun, it will heal at its normal daily healing rate.

### Stench *by Timothy Berriault* 417

This plantoid's leaves give off a putrid smell when crushed or rubbed roughly. The regular traveling companions adjust to this stink, but strangers, shopkeepers and citizens of villages who are unaccustomed to the mutant are put off by the reek, and will often deny food and lodging to the weedy and any companions.

The good news is that herbivores won't eat this plantoid, and carnivores will always prefer to attack different targets when raiding any group with this specimen in their ranks. If this plantoid attacks hostile creatures, however, they will then target this weedy thereafter. A costly leaf spray can be applied with a spray bottle or damp cloth to each leaf, each morning to greatly diminish this stench, but the cost of materials is 4sp per day, to say nothing of the liter of water required to make the odor reducing concoction.

### Tastes Like Chicken 418

Predators can smell this plantoid and are attracted to it from as far as a kilometer should the plantoid be wounded and its delicious smelling sap be exposed to the air. Once meat eaters, including tribes of humanoids, discover the character and realize it's a friggin' plant, they hesitate before advancing further, as they gradually become more certain that under the

thick bark and tangled vines of the plantoid, its inner core must be roasted chicken flesh. One bite on the character will confirm this, although the mouthful of bark, splinters and leaves will confound most creatures, who are likely to spit out the pulp and take out their frustration on any humanoid companions of the plantoid.

### Tent Caterpillars 419

This plantoid is highly susceptible to infestations of tent caterpillars, which will create extensive networks of protective web around themselves and defoliate the mutant. They will eat up to half this character's leaves before the pests turn into moths and either fly off to feed on other vegetation, or (35% likely) move to another part of the weedy and devour what greenery might remain.

Besides suffering from a 2d6 loss to endurance while infested, this plant mutant exhibits unsightly, banner-like swaths of white web and crawling masses of brightly colored caterpillars. This infestation will disgust people, especially strangers, who besides denying the plantoid access to lodging and other indoor businesses, will most likely aim to set the plantoid on fire to ensure the caterpillars don't spread to nearby crops.

At a cost of 50sp per month, an insecticide can be created and sprayed onto the upper reaches of the plantoid to rid it of these pests. Once eradicated, lost endurance points return, yet so do the caterpillars whenever the character travels in any swamp or forest area.

it typically suggests to the onlooker that this plant character is related to a green walker, or at the very least, an absorber of men and beasts, and to be feared, and thus killed. Others will recoil in terror, some will respect the plantoid as a dangerous foe, while a few will invite the plantoid to join their ranks in some military campaign or expedition in the nearest ruins, believing the plant to be a fearsome anomaly. The addition of the hard bones adds 5kg weight but also improves the character's defense value by -5.

If this flaw occurs in a host inhabiting plantoid, then these remains are grafted onto the main cadaver and are worn like a knobby pack across the thing's front and back — a nightmarish spectacle that will elicit most new era clergy into hysterical, murderous denunciations.

**Roll 3d6** for the sort of skeleton visible within this character's trunk:

| | |
|---|---|
| **3.** Human skeletons 1d2+1 | **10.** Pig |
| **4.** Dogs 1d4+1 | **11.** Dog |
| **5.** Alligator | **12-14.** Human |
| **6.** Bear | **15.** Mutant human |
| **7.** Deer | **16.** Giant bat |
| **8.** Horse | **17.** Skullocks 1d4+2 |
| **9.** Cow | **18.** Human children 1d4+1 |

## Trunk Rot 420

The plantoid suffers from several patches of an invasive fungus, which the mutant tries to cope with by producing plenty of sap around the foul, seeping diseased area — an unsightly and often smelly, slug and pest infested cavity. This plantoid suffers from 2+1d4 such rot points, with each causing a -2 to its endurance permanently unless seen to by a chemical or bio technician comrade who can mix up a paste to sooth and control the fungus. The material cost to make this mixture is 10sp per month, however if no technician ally is handy, the plantoid must purchase the temporary treatment at a cost of 50sp per month.

## Visible Skeletal Remains 421

Most plantoids with this unsettling, permanent feature often drape themselves in fabric or animal skins, or wear clothing where possible and try to obscure this feature with armor or packs... especially when entering human settlements where the locals are unfamiliar with them.

In short, this plantoid grew amid the cadaver of a dead creature — most probably the outcome of the parent plant's actions either by killing the owner of the bones or coming upon the heap of 'fertilizer' and depositing the seed or immature character in the remains to give it a head start.

In time, this plantoid grew up in the remains and as it reached skyward, pulled up the skeleton and which is now visible in its trunk. To those who see this horrific apparition growing within the bark and branches of this mutant,

## Wild Nature 422

Sometimes when asleep, unconscious or its mind is debilitated by toxins, this plantoid's flexible limbs often revert to a wild, predatory state. Whenever its mind is shut down, such as in a state of dormancy or regular sleep, the mutant needs to make a type D willpower based hazard check or its appendages will act of their own accord. Should this plantoid have ranged or close-quarters appendages, it will use them to attack the nearest living thing to either devour it, or at least soak the ground in blood or a dismembered body to fertilize the soil about it.

Long time companions of this mutant plant will have learned the hard way that they need to bind or place a sack over any dangerous appendage this entity might possess, or else sleep far from the monstrosity.

There is a further 1 in 10 chance per day that the plantoid lapses into its wild nature. During is time, the PC must make a Willpower based type C hazard check to resist this predatory urge or else use a random appendage to attack a nearby companion. This impulse will last 3d6 minutes or until it takes 10 points of either stun or regular damage.

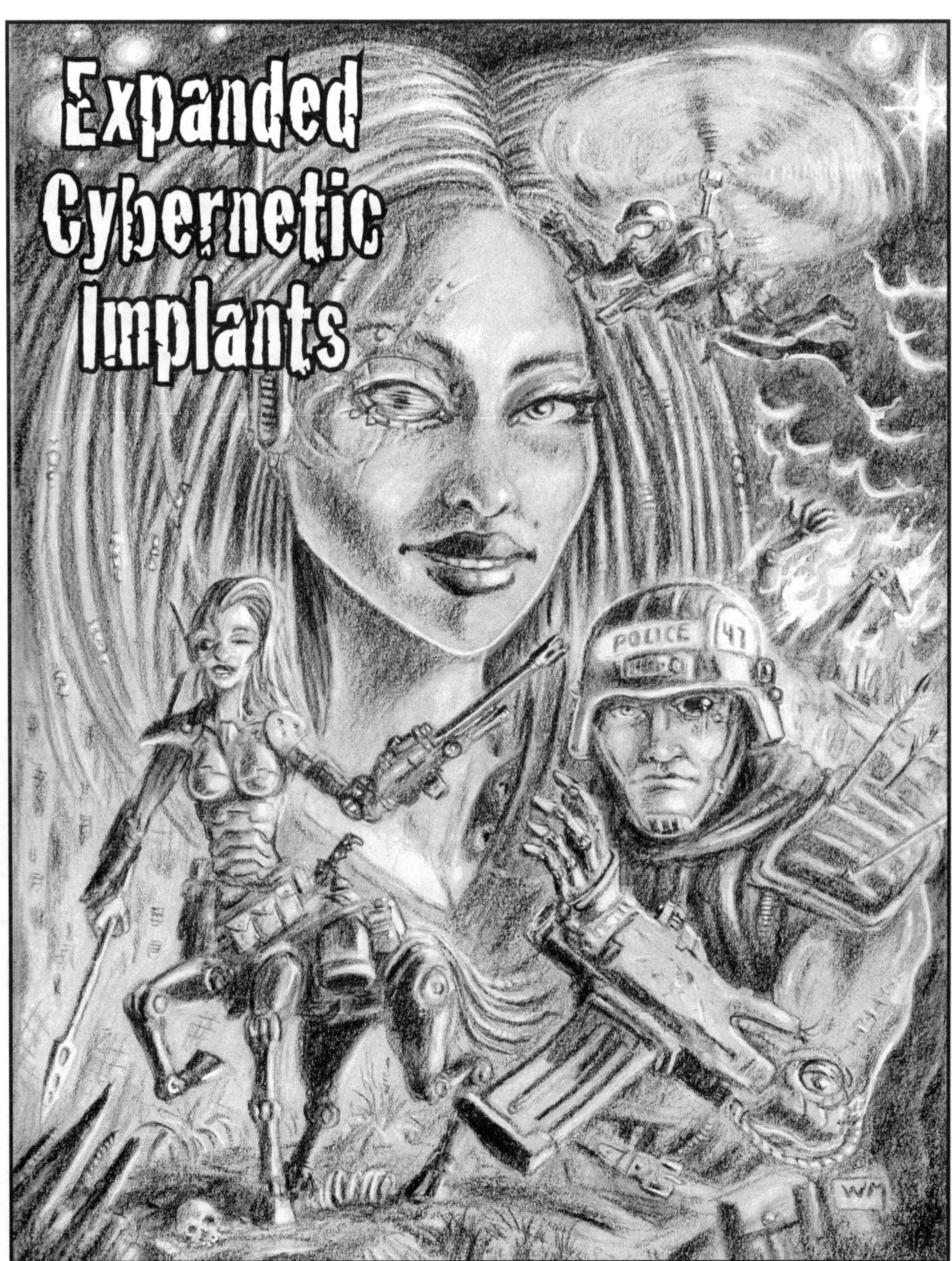
Expanded Cybernetic Implants
POLICE 47

# Cybernetic Implants Generation Tables

## Table XR-210/ Implant Determination Matrix    d100 *(creature set 1 dumb animals / creature set 2 humanoids)*

| Offensive | Defensive | Miscellaneous | Creature Set 1 | Creature Set 2 | Android | Robot | Random | Implant Name* | Implant No. | Page |
|---|---|---|---|---|---|---|---|---|---|---|
| 01,02 | - | - | 01 | 01 | 01 | 01 | 01 | Alloy Razor Claws | 1 | TME-85 |
| - | 01-04 | 01 | 02,03 | 02 | - | - | 02 | Anti-Toxin Array** | 2 | TME-85 |
| - | - | 02,03 | 04 | 03 | - | - | 03 | Aquatic Deployment Augmentation | 51 | XR-332 |
| - | - | 04,05 | 05 | 04 | 02,03 | 02 | 04 | Aquatic Propulsion System | 52 | XR-332 |
| - | 05-44 | - | 06 | 05 | 04,05 | 03-05 | 05 | Armor Enhancement ~ | 3 | TME-85 |
| - | - | 06-09 | 07 | 06 | - | - | 06 | Artificial Heart** | 4 | TME-85 |
| - | - | 10,11 | 08 | 07 | - | - | 07 | Atmospheric Hydro Converter | 5 | TME-85 |
| - | 45-47 | 12,13 | 09 | 08 | - | - | 08 | Audio Compensator | 53 | XR-332 |
| - | - | 14 | 10 | 09 | 06 | 06 | 09 | Autopilot Module | 54 | XR-333 |
| - | - | 15 | 11 | 10 | 07 | 07 | 10 | Back-Up Sensor Array | 6 | TME-85 |
| 03,04 | - | - | - | 11 | 08 | - | 11 | Bow Implant Arm | 55 | XR-333 |
| 05,06 | 48-51 | 16 | 12 | 12 | 09 | - | 12 | Carbon Fiber Muscle Enhancement [CFME] | 56 | XR-333 |
| - | - | 17 | - | 13 | 10 | - | 13 | Chopper-Borg | 57 | XR-333 |
| - | - | 18,19 | 13 | 14 | 11 | 08 | 14 | Communication Implant ~ | 7 | TME-86 |
| - | - | 20 | 14 | 15 | - | - | 15 | Computerized Brain | 8 | TME-86 |
| - | - | 21 | - | 16 | 12 | - | 16 | Cybernetic Hair Replacement | 58 | XR-334 |
| - | - | 22 | 15 | 17 | - | - | 17 | Cybernetic Legs | 9 | TME-86 |
| - | - | 23 | - | 18 | 13 | 09 | 18 | Database | 59 | XR-334 |
| 07,08 | - | 24 | - | 19 | 14 | - | 19 | Detachable Lower Arm | 10 | TME-86 |
| 09,10 | - | - | - | 20 | 15,16 | 10 | 20 | Dual Weapon Arm | 60 | XR-336 |
| - | 52-54 | 25 | 16 | 21 | 17,18 | 11,12 | 21 | Electrical Defense Mechanism | 11 | TME-86 |
| - | 55-56 | 26,27 | 17 | 22 | 19 | 13,14 | 22 | Electro-Shock-Suppressor | 61 | XR-337 |
| - | 57,58 | 28 | 18 | 23 | 20,21 | 15,16 | 23 | Energy Absorption Cell | 12 | TME-86 |
| - | - | 29 | - | 24 | 22 | - | 24 | Epidermal Manipulator | 62 | XR-337 |
| - | - | 30 | 19 | 25 | 23 | 17,18 | 25 | Floodlight Orb | 13 | TME-87 |
| - | 59,60 | 31 | 20 | 26 | 24 | 19 | 26 | Flotation Bags | 63 | XR-337 |
| 11,12 | - | 32 | 21 | 27 | 25 | 20 | 27 | Fold Out Manipulator Arm ~ | 14 | TME-87 |
| - | 61-64 | - | - | 28 | 26,27 | 21 | 28 | Fold-out Alloy Shield | 64 | XR-337 |
| 13-16 | - | - | 22 | 29 | 28 | 22 | 29 | Fold-out Alloy Sword ~ | 65 | XR-338 |
| - | 65,66 | 33 | 23 | 30 | 29 | 23 | 30 | Force Canopy | 66 | XR-338 |
| - | 67-70 | - | 24 | 31 | 30,31 | 24 | 31 | Force Field Generator | 15 | TME-87 |
| - | 71-74 | - | 25,26 | 32 | 32 | 25 | 32 | Force Shield | 16 | TME-87 |
| - | - | 34,35 | 27 | 33 | 33 | 26 | 33 | Glide Wings | 67 | XR-338 |
| - | - | 36,37 | - | 34 | 34 | 27 | 34 | Grappling Hook | 17 | TME-87 |
| - | - | 38 | 28 | 35 | 35 | 28 | 35 | Homing Device | 68 | XR-339 |
| - | - | 39 | 29 | 36 | 36 | 29,30 | 36 | Hover Jets | 18 | TME-87 |
| - | - | 40 | 30 | 37 | 37 | 31 | 37 | Hydraulic Walker Legs | 19 | TME-88 |
| 17,18 | - | 41 | - | 38 | 38 | 32,33 | 38 | Hypodermic Tendril ~ | 20 | TME-88 |
| - | - | 42 | 31 | 39 | 39 | 34 | 39 | Internal Gyroscope | 21 | TME-88 |
| - | - | 43,44 | 32 | 40 | 40 | 35 | 40 | Internal Healer Drones | 22 | TME-88 |
| - | - | 45 | 33 | 41 | - | - | 41 | Internal Nutriment Supply** | 23 | TME-88 |
| - | - | 46 | 34 | 42 | - | - | 42 | Iron Stomach** | 24 | TME-88 |
| - | - | 47 | 35 | 43 | 41 | 36 | 43 | Loudspeaker | 25 | TME-88 |
| 19, 20 | - | 48 | 36 | 44 | 42 | 37 | 44 | Manipulator Tendril ~ | 26 | TME-88 |
| - | - | 49,50 | 37 | 45,46 | 43,44 | 38,39 | 45 | Mechanical Hand | 69 | XR-339 |
| - | - | 51 | - | 47 | 45 | 40 | 46 | Memory Backup | 70 | XR-340 |
| - | 75,76 | 52 | 38,39 | 48 | - | - | 47 | Mental Attack Dampener** | 71 | XR-340 |
| - | 77,78 | 53 | 40,41 | 49 | - | - | 48 | Mental Defense Screen** | 27 | TME-89 |
| - | 79-81 | 54,55 | 42,43 | 50 | - | - | 49 | Micro Suture Laced Tissues** | 72 | XR-340 |
| - | - | 56 | - | - | 46 | 41 | 50 | Mini-Robotics Hanger | 28 | TME-89 |
| - | 82 | 57 | 44 | 51 | 47 | 42 | 51 | Motion Stabilizer | 73 | XR-340 |
| - | - | 58,59 | - | 52 | 48,49 | 43,44 | 52 | Multi-tool Arm ~ | 74 | XR-341 |
| - | - | 60 | 45 | 53 | 50,51 | - | 53 | Nutritional Enhancement Module** | 75 | XR-342 |
| - | 83,84 | 61 | 46 | 54 | 52 | 45 | 54 | Optical Concealment Generator | 29 | TME-89 |
| 21 | - | 62-64 | 47,48 | 55-58 | 53 | 46 | 55 | Optical Enhancement ~ | 30 | TME-89 |
| 22 | - | 65-68 | 49-54 | 59-62 | 54 | 47 | 56 | Optical Implants Set 2 ~ | 76 | XR-342 |

*Unless implant name marked with ~ (which allows for multiple augmentation), always re-roll if an implant occurs twice, unless otherwise designated by NPC or creature description.*
**For organic beings only; androids and robotics re-roll.**    ***Weapon Arm set 1 from the hub rules, implant no. 50, is included in weapon Arms set 2*

## Table XR-210/ Implant Determination Matrix, continued

| Offensive | Defensive | Miscellaneous | Creature Set 1 | Creature Set 2 | Android | Robot | Random | Implant Name* | Implant No. | Page |
|---|---|---|---|---|---|---|---|---|---|---|
| - | - | 69 | 55 | 63 | - | - | 57 | Oxygen Supply Unit | 31 | TME-89 |
| - | - | 70 | 56 | 64 | 55 | 48 | 58 | Panoramic Optics Node | 32 | TME-89 |
| - | - | 71 | 57 | 65 | 56,57 | 49,50 | 59 | Parachute | 77 | XR-342 |
| 23-28 | - | - | 58 | 66 | 58 | 51,52 | 60 | Pincer ~ | 33 | TME-89 |
| - | - | 72 | - | - | 59 | 53 | 61 | Portable Computer Station | 34 | TME-90 |
| 29-34 | - | - | - | 67 | 60 | - | 62 | Power Arm ~ | 35 | TME-90 |
| 35,36 | - | - | 59 | 68 | 61 | 54 | 63 | Power Leeching Unit | 78 | XR-343 |
| - | - | 73 | - | 69 | 62,63 | 55-58 | 64 | Power-Jack | 79 | XR-343 |
| - | - | 74 | - | 70 | 64 | - | 65 | Quadrupedal Lower Body | 80 | XR-343 |
| - | 85,86 | 75 | 60,61 | 71 | 65 | 59 | 66 | Radiation Leeching Unit | 36 | TME-90 |
| - | - | 76 | 62 | 72 | 66,67 | 60,61 | 67 | Radio Scanner | 37 | TME-90 |
| 37-39 | - | 77 | - | 73 | 68 | 62 | 68 | Retractable Laser Pistol ~ | 38 | TME-90 |
| - | - | 78 | 63 | 74 | 69 | 63 | 69 | Robotic Serpentine Body | 81 | XR-345 |
| 40 | 87 | 79 | 64 | 75 | 70 | 64 | 70 | Self Destruct Mode | 39 | TME-90 |
| - | - | 80 | - | 76 | 71 | 65,66 | 71 | Sensor Probe Launcher | 40 | TME-91 |
| 41-43 | - | 81 | 65 | 77 | 72 | 67 | 72 | Shoulder Turret | 41 | TME-91 |
| 44,45 | 88 | 82 | 66 | 78 | 73 | 68,69 | 73 | Smoke Screen Generator | 42 | TME-91 |
| - | - | 83 | 67 | 79 | - | - | 74 | Snorkel | 82 | XR-345 |
| - | - | 84 | 68,69 | 80 | - | - | 75 | Solar Nutrient Converter | 83 | XR-345 |
| - | - | 85,86 | 70,71 | 81,82 | 74,75 | 70,71 | 76 | Solar Power Generator | 43 | TME-91 |
| - | 89,90 | 87 | 72 | 83 | 76 | 72 | 77 | Sonic Defense Screen | 44 | TME-91 |
| - | 91,92 | 88 | 73 | 84 | 77 | 73 | 78 | Sound Dampening Field | 84 | XR-346 |
| - | - | 89 | 74 | 85 | 78 | 74 | 79 | Speed Assist Rotors | 85 | XR-346 |
| - | 93,94 | 90 | 75 | 86 | 79 | 75 | 80 | Stun Inhibitor Unit | 45 | TME-91 |
| - | 95-99 | - | 76 | 87 | 80 | 76 | 81 | Subcutaneous Plating | 86 | XR-346 |
| - | - | 91 | 77 | 88 | 81 | 77 | 82 | Surveillance Tendril ~ | 46 | TME-91 |
| - | 00 | 92 | - | 89 | 82 | - | 83 | Synthetic Skin | 87 | XR-346 |
| 46,47 | - | - | - | 90 | 83 | 78 | 84 | Telescoping thrust Blade | 47 | TME-92 |
| 48,49 | - | 93 | 78 | 91 | 84 | 79 | 85 | Tentacle ~ | 48 | TME-92 |
| - | - | 94 | 79 | 92 | 85 | 80 | 86 | Tracked Locomotion | 49 | TME-92 |
| - | - | 95 | - | 93 | 86 | 81,82 | 87 | Vehicle Control Module | 88 | XR-347 |
| - | - | 96 | 80 | 94 | 87 | 83 | 88 | Vocal Mimicry Modulator | 89 | XR-347 |
| 50-98 | - | 97,98 | 81-98 | 95-98 | 88-95 | 84-95 | 89-98 | Weapon Arm Set 2*** | 50/90 | XR-347 |
| 99,00 | - | 99 | 99 | 99 | 96-98 | 96-99 | 99 | Welding Torch | 91 | XR-349 |
| - | - | 00 | 00 | 00 | 99,00 | 00 | 00 | Wheel Deployment | 92 | XR-349 |

* Unless implant name marked with ~ (which allows for multiple augmentation), always re-roll if an implant occurs twice, unless otherwise designated by NPC or creature description.
** For organic beings only; androids and robotics re-roll.
*** Weapon Arm set 1 from the hub rules, implant no. 50, is included in weapon Arms set 2

# Expanded Cybernetic Implants

This book includes 42 new implants, and when combined with those from the hub rules book, means there are 92 implants available to a wide range of character types. While not stated in the hub rules, all cyborgs have a Neural Connector that allows a cyborg's brain to control implants throughout its body. These micro computers in the character's brain are laced through the spinal cord and often connected to nerve endings, micro-computers, servo motors, pistons, synthetic muscles, and other high-tech augmentations within the subject's limbs. The most common neural connector, referred to as Mark I series, worked in a pure stock human, although trans-humans and clones could also accept them — although this is rarer. MK II neural connectors are more advanced, and could be installed in bioreplicas, androids, robots and even animals, while MK III connectors, which are rarer still and of the most advanced, recent pre-cataclysm designs, work in the often widely altered physiologies of mutant animals and humans and humanoids, and thus allow the existence of mutant cyborg individuals called mutorgs.

Rebuilt individuals, which sometimes have one or more cybernetic parts, are not internally fitted with any variant of a neural connector, but might have an implant hooked to an externally wired connection. While to an uneducated onlooker, some rebuilt might be mistaken for cyborgs, but they are not wired to handle more complex implants, and are instead scrap built, prosthetic equipped mockeries.

Besides the ability for mutants to now occur as cyborgs, called mutorgs, one of the more important new implants found in this book is the mechanical hand implant described on page 339. This cybernetic often appears as either a fold away variant or a hand with any firearm barrel in the palm of the mechanical appendage. Having two hands is very helpful when cybernetic characters attempt to perform tasks that other characters can, such as climb ladders more easily, pilot a dirt bike or complex vehicle, climb a cliff, etc.

Another cybernetic related addition included in the Expansion Rules is a robust section on the availability and purchase price of cybernetics. This has been added to accommodate those cyborg characters who have saved up trunk loads of silver, gold and relics to trade for upgraded parts — although such parts are very hard to find even when combing through relic and robotics dealerships, but can sometimes be looted off fallen enemy cyborgs, or discovered deep in the ruins on the remains of some ancient, implant enhanced warrior.

Finally, the cybernetics technician skill has also been added to this book and offers a more specialized level of expertise to those who need repairs and upgrades for their cybernetic character. Any cyborg or mutorg character who has the cybernetics technician skill is especially well placed to undertake a life as an adventurer, and oftentimes can perform their own repairs and additions — so long as the implant is in a location he or she can reach on their own body.

## Aquatic Deployment Augmentation (ADA) 51
Power Source: **power cell in upper back utility compartment**
Power Duration: **16 hours, +10 minute respiration emergency air capacity once propulsion ceases.** Swimming Speed: **9m**
Designed by some old world navy, this implant consists of an entire suite of augmentation features to make the operator fully operational underwater despite other implants, which might normally turn the user from a swimmer into a lead weight. In short, this cyborg has been outfitted with gill-like back-up aqua lungs, enhanced with sealed panels to make other implants airtight. Additionlly, the character exhibits deployable flippers at his or her feet along with pop out shoulder mounted propulsion propellers housed in tubular cases. In the water, this cyborg can speed along at 9m per round and stay submerged for up to 16 hours before requiring to surface for at least an hour to expel toxic gases and insert a fresh power cell in the shoulder mounted utility compartment. Should he or she remain underwater beyond 16 hours, the power cell will

become depleted, propulsion ceases and the aqua lung begins to fail and fill with water after a further ten minutes.

The operator can track the time remaining on an existing power cell, by either alert 'twitches' in his or her chest, or if he or she has an optical implant eye, an internal display will show power remaining, depth, compass direction, water temperature and direction of the current, all within the character's internal visual display.

This unit does not offer hypothermia protection from exposure to cold water, and the addition of extendable swimming fins, propulsions tubes and plastic hatch encasing skin — which rarely matches the pigmentation of the cyborg's living tissues — add together to reduce the cyborg's appearance by -2d4 APP and increase overall weight by +6 kg.

## Aquatic Propulsion System (APS) 52
Power Source: **power cell in upper back**
Power Duration: **18 hours** Swimming Speed: **12m**
When needed, propellers and steering fins pop out of this cyborg's torso and propel the operator at a rate of 12m per round. The hard plastic fins stabilize the user and through simple movements of the legs, arms and torso, the cyborg can steer itself with remarkable ease. One power cell will run the small, poly-carbonate propellers for up to 18 continuous hours before a new battery must be loaded into the waterproof receiver in the wearer's upper back. These propellers and fins could potentially add +1m forward movement to any cyborg who has both these fins and the implants of hover jets, fold-out glider wings, or parachute.

The four small plastic motors and three pop out fins are spread out on the cyborg's torso under flaps of synthetic skin — although the scars and obvious compartments are somewhat unsightly and so reduce this character's appearance score by -2+d6 APP.

This implant does not offer respiration as the ADA variant does, but yields higher underwater speeds and an easy to conceal design. If the cyborg has both implants, increase swimming speed to 15m.

## Audio Compensator 53
Power Source: **1 power cell per ear implant** Power Duration: **2 years**
Both this cyborg's ears have been modified with small, half moon shaped, permanently affixed implants. Each runs on a pill power cell for 2 years and has two modes which can be activated by a waterproof external switch just beneath the left ear — although any cyborg with a computerized brain can also switch between audio receptor increase, off, or dampening option.

When audio receptor increase is turned on, this cyborg can hear 10 times that of a normal person, however, if in use when this user is assaulted by a sonic attack, this individual will suffer double damage and must make an endurance based hazard check or pass out for 3d6 minutes.

If the ear implants are set to dampening mode, then they muffle all sound down to about a quarter of the volume and reduce the damage from incoming sonic attacks to 10% harm.

## Autopilot Module 54
Power Source: **mini power cell at base of skull**
Power Duration: **5 years**
Implanted into the brain and connected to the optic nerve of a living eye or an optical implant is a rudimentary back up survival brain. This micro computer normally remains dormant but if it detects certain brain wave patterns, or a lack thereof, it will kick in and take control of the cyborgs body and any locomotion — including implants which involve movement.

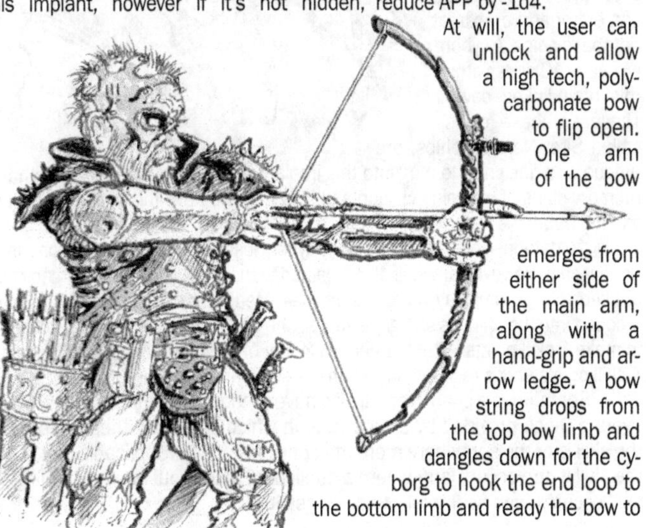

In short, if made unconscious, asleep, drunk, etc. the body will revert to self preservation mode until the primary brain or consciousness returns. During this time, the body will rise and, if intact enough to allow it, wander off back to a pre designated trench, vehicle, bunker, structure or camp. It can be pre-selected to follow a certain person or identity broadcast tab, or continue on to a designated settlement, too. Although, any location it is set to travel to requires that the cyborg has been there before and the memories of the route are available to the subconscious mind.

While on autopilot, this cyborg cannot converse, and can only fend off threats if it has a cybernetic weapon arm or other mechanical systems. It will have access to the brain's memories and be clever enough to recognize comrades and not obliterate them, but will not follow, obey or pay heed to them if the cyborg did not previously program the auto pilot module to do so.

This module can be accessed by a flap of synthetic skin on the head, and if this character is restrained, a computer technician could try to hack into and turn off this module should the unconscious cyborg be a prisoner or comrades feel its auto pilot mode is putting him or her in danger.

Cyborgs with both this implant and an optical implant can turn this module on when sleeping, and thus use the robotic eye to keep watch while the main brain is asleep, and alert the character to trouble instantly. The scar and access flap seam on this cyborgs head is unsightly and reduces appearance error by -2 APP.

## Bow Implant Arm 55
Power Source: **power cell at elbow**       Power Duration: **9 years**
Deployment Time: **3 rounds to unlock, string and fire first arrow**
Strike Value: **+5**       Rate: **1/2**       Range: **70m**       Damage **1d20**
The non-dominant arm of this cyborg is interlaced with miniaturized control nodes, sensors, hydraulic lines and servo motors — although in 2 in 10 cases all of this is hidden and the arm looks rather normal except for the elongated scars and subtle differences between the operator's living skin and the plastiskin next to it. If hidden, the character suffers no appearance trait drop from this implant, however if it's not hidden, reduce APP by -1d4.

At will, the user can unlock and allow a high tech, polycarbonate bow to flip open. One arm of the bow emerges from either side of the main arm, along with a hand-grip and arrow ledge. A bow string drops from the top bow limb and dangles down for the cyborg to hook the end loop to the bottom limb and ready the bow to

fire on the third round after activation. The user will need to load arrows like a normal bow, and fire them at a rate of one arrow every second round, also like a regular bow, but that is where the similarities end. This weapon is only the size of a short bow, but has the accuracy, pull, and range of a full sized archaic longbow (SV +5, DMG 1d20, range 70m, rate 1/2). Of course, the user's accuracy and strength traits may alter and improve these stats, so too can the application of the weapon expert skill.

If forced into melee combat with this bow, it can act like a pickaxe and cause grievous wounds doing 1d12 base damage — although any fumble means there is a 1 in 6 chance the bow-arm snaps and must be repaired at great cost (300+2d100sp in a large town with a well equipped robotics or mechanical shop).

## Carbon Fiber Muscle Enhancement [CFME] 56
Power Source: **nil**    Power Duration: **NA**
Laced through this cyborg's limbs, neck and torso are subcutaneous, nerve responsive bands of synthetic muscle. Not only do these fibers add strength and speed to the cyborg, but these dense carbon fibers improve the subject's natural armor and robustness. Add 10 to strength, agility, endurance and a further -10 bonus to defense value besides any bonus that higher agility might also afford.

The insertion of these fibers beneath the skin involved a considerable amount of invasive surgery, and left the cyborg with hundreds of micro scars. These patterns look like pale lines in the cyborg's skin, but are not present in the face. However, a slight -1d4 appearance penalty is applied and if no other implants are present, and, if this individual is subjugated to a nude inspection by those searching for cyborgs visually, they will require a type D perception based hazard check to spot the faint scars in daylight. Under low-light situations, or if the cyborg is coated in dust or muck, however, the evidence of these fibers will always go unseen.

## Chopper-Borg 57
Power Source: **power in back module, fits 1 to 4 standards cells, a power pack, or mini power cell.**
Power Duration: **1 hour per standard cell, 10 hours power pack, 10 minutes mini cell**
Defense value: **-5 or -20 in flight**
Movement: **24m, but carried cargo or companions allowable at speed reduction, see below.**
Suicide Attack Mode: **SV +15, 4 man-sized targets, DMG 1d20/ 1 in 10 chance per round the rotor blade snaps off. See description.**
From a metallic, knapsack-like, permanently fused module on the back of this cyborg, a pop up shaft and set of two or four rotor blades can be extended to turn this cyborg into a living helicopter. This fold out set of rotors allows the operator to fly at 24m meters per round, or half this if carrying another person or heavy load equal or less than the cyborg's own weight in kilograms. If carrying a load more than double the user's weight but not exceeding three times his or her weight, the movement rate is further reduced to 6m per round, although any more weight than this and the cyborg cannot take off at all.

Should the operator take up to four times its own weight, such as if being held onto by comrades as they all plummet to the ground after an airship mishap, then the user cannot get any lift, but can drop at a controlled, rate and all those with him land with a hard thump, but suffer no damage. More than four times, the operator's weight means a normal fall and possible death for all involved.

These rotors take 2 rounds to deploy, and can maintain continuous operation up to 1 hour per power cell. The backpack like compartment attached to this cyborg is odd looking but not grotesque, and so the user suffers only a -4 APP drop, however, it is made of very stout carbon fiber and improves the wearer's defense value by -5 DV. This pack can operate on just one power cell, but since the power compartment has slots for up to four standard power cells, it will allow 4 hours of continuous flight, but so too, a

plug in for an external power pack to permit 10 hours flight, or an adapter cable to hook the unit to an external mini power cell to offer ten minutes flight — which is great for when the operator needs to substitute standard power cells in the main backpack mid-flight.

When flying about and purposefully trying to avoid taking fire or being hit by other flying opponents in melee, this unit increases the user's defense value by a further -20 but reduces distance of travel by half. If the operator wishes to lean over on his or her side and use the propeller blades to chop through opponents — which is risky and likely to permanently break the unit or kill the user — he or she can do so. During this suicide run, the blades have an SV of +15, and inflict 1d20 damage. Up to 4 man sized creatures can be attacked per round if they are grouped together. When pulping through opponents in this fashion, however, there is a 1 in 10 chance per round a blade snaps off and the cyborg crashes hard into the ground for 3d20 damage. Broken blades can be replaced only at great expense (400+3d100sp each) and there is only a 1 n 6 chance that even a large trade town would have a replacement blade available for sale.

This unit adds 10 kilograms to the cyborg's weight.

## Cybernetic Hair Replacement 58

This character's hair typically looks natural, but some cyborg's with this permanently implanted hair exhibit blue, neon green, hot pink or candy apple red hair instead*. These filaments are connected to subcutaneous transfer points which feed into the subject's brain and serve one of the following functions — besides covering up any scar damage from armor or optical implants and giving the individual a full head of life-like hair.

*Use the Mutant Hair Color table, page TME-23.*



**1.2. Illumination hair:** This cyborgs hair, when left to hang down at the sides and back if the individual wears a helmet, or when going uncovered, can be made to light up at will.  This illumination will cast a 10m radius area in a soft glow and offer sufficient light for the owner and any companions to move about as if using a flaming torch.

This head of bright hair can, however, be seen by onlookers from as far as a half a kilometer away (500m). If unleashed in a dark area and in the presence of humanoids or creatures who can't tolerate bright light, such as moaners, these photo-intolerant beings suffer a -20 SV penalty. Power Source: mini power cell at base of skull. Power Duration: 480 hours.

**3,4. Antenna hair:** These filaments act as a multitude of antenna rods, although flexible. The Cyborg has a built in comm receiver in its head with which it can pick up a wide range of radio, FM, AM and shortwave broadcasts. A small fake skin flap at the base of the head near one ear has a standard plug-in jack that can accept an output from all standard and advanced communicators, but is best suited to either a comm implant or a communication headset.

With this antenna hair, the cyborg has double the range to send a receive signals with any portable comm relic. Without a plugged in communicator, the cyborg can merely listen in to transmissions one at a time, and go up and down the dials in the hope to pick up signals or review commands from comrades who have a comm unit. This cyborg will have a specific alpha numeric code it can set as its call ID to receive transmissions. When trying to sleep or pay attention to the world around it, this individual can switch off the comm receiver or block any specific caller ID. Power Source: pill power cell at the base of skull. Power Duration: 3 years.

**5,6. Expanded sensory hair:** This cyborgs hair operates like an extra set of senses, although in a 360 degree area about it, and detects the electromagnetic fields of living things, as well as those of active machines including cyborgs, androids and robots. If on point, or acting alone, this character can  detect nearby approaching figures, invisible laser security beams, and incoming surprise attacks and thus gains +2 initiative against all melee attacks or encounters and missile fire from within 10m or less range.

This hair does not detect the shooter's energy field from bullets and beams discharged from beyond 10m. This hair will also pick up the presence of radiation within 10 meters, and throb painfully to alert the cyborg with increasing intensity the closer the character gets to the source. Power Source: pill power cell at base of skull. Power Duration: 1 year.

## Database 59

Power Source: **mini power cell at base of skull**
Power Duration: **24 years**

This cyborg has one or more information filled data-chips hooked to its brain — although for post-apocalyptic survival purposes, many of these inventories and skills are utterly useless. Within this individual's head are between two and seven (1d6+1) areas of accessible knowledge, but through an alloy access hatch beneath a flap of false skin on the cyborg's head, a computer, robotics, or cybernetics technician can either add or extract database chips. A cyborg will have 10 slots within this brain-linked cavity. These database chips, called Sirex-Nano77 chips, are 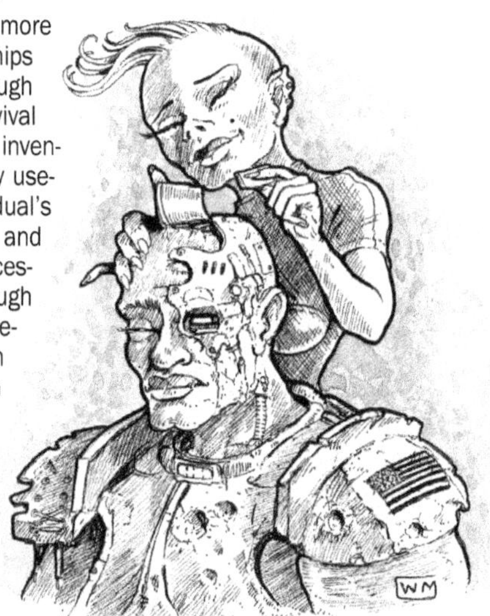 unique and designed to plug into this implant, and so not compatible with the memory chips of androids or robots unless they too have this brand-name, advanced database receiver unit.

If a database chip is removed, the cyborg loses all the knowledge contained on that chip. However, any skill points gained to that skill, and learned organically, are kept. For example, a cyborg has the Field Medic database and a skill point of 4 coded into the chip. As she gains ranks, she adds 2 more skill points in medic, to make 6 skill points. After her head is looted of its chips, she loses the original 4 skill points and is reduced down to the 2 she learned on her own.

Sometimes a character will also have randomly determined skills which overlap those provided by a database, in which case, add them together if the skill is of the sort where more than one skill point is applicable, but re-roll the skill if one occurs later where a duplicated maxed out or single skill point skill occurs (such as the relic knowledge skill).

There is a 2 in 10 chance that this cyborg starts game play with a 3m long patch cable that can be plugged from the base of his or her skull into another computer, vid-screen, or sound system to present the contents of a database.

Roll 1d30 below to determine the 1d6+1 chips currently plugged into and ready to access by this character. Re-roll duplicated results.

## 1d30* Database Details

1.  **Music Database** This cyborg knows all composers, instruments, musical pieces, hits, concerts and details of classical, country, jazz, rap, rock-n-roll and world music. The individual can hear a musical selection, album or play list in its head whenever it desires, and could play this music if it had a speaker system or a patch cable into a tuner or stereo set.

2.  **Movie Database** The subject has access to an inventory of every major movie ever made. Could play any from the thousands it has stored if it had a speaker system built in and a patch cable to a video screen. This cyborg can watch any movie from its database within its minds-eye.

3.  **Art History** This data base shows both imagery, video clips and untold pages of documentation, theory and criticism of old world art. This collection covers cave paintings, the classical ancient world, medieval period, pre-Columbian America, Africa, India, the Orient and beyond, up until the last decade before the final great cataclysm.

    While the cyborg can enjoy all this content in its own head, it can only project this treasury if it has a patch cable connected to the base of its skull to a vid screen or holographic projector. There is a 1 in 12 chance that the cyborg can reproduce the basic lines of an art piece if given a pencil, pen or paintbrush.

4.  **American History** This exhaustive directory includes a detailed history of the United States of America, from its founding up to 2025. This database includes photographs, government records, film adaptations, video clips, important musical performances, speeches and the newspapers from every city, town and district throughout America's history.

    Like other databases in this list, if a patch cable from the cyborg's head to a screen or holographic projector is used, this information can be presented to a larger audience.

5.  **English Literature** While called 'English' literature, it is not merely a directory of prose from the British Isles, but instead every work of fiction written in the English language, including books translated into English. If the cyborg can't read, this is a useless database unless a patch cable can be hooked from the character to some sort of tablet or screen for others to enjoy. There is a 1 in 10 chance this database also includes all role-playing games ever published in English.

6.  **Relic Knowledge** As the skill on page 49 of the hub rules whereby this cyborg knows what nearly every relic, ancient facility, vehicle and object is. This knowledge does not extend to how to use whatever he or she finds, nor fix it, but at least he or she can warn others to stay away from some things — like landmines — and to recover other things, such as solar panels.

    This database switches on automatically whenever the cyborg views or holds up and examines a relic or object of ancient construction, with the details, power requirements, range, damage and manufacturer's info immediately known to the character.

    If this skill also occurs as a skill through character creation or rank gain, then the player can decide to either re-roll for another or keep this one skill point skill in case they want to remove the database in favor of another chip to fill their maximum ten slots.

7.  **Field Medic** As the skill of medic from page 46 of the TME hub rules, this database provides the cyborg with up to 3+1d3 skill points in this area.

8.  **Computer Technician** 3+d3 skill points identical to the skill on page 53 of the Hub Rules**.

9.  **Robotics Technician** 3+d3 skill points identical to the skill on page 54 of the Hub Rules**.

10. **Bio-Technician** 3+d3 skill points identical to the skill seen on page 52 of the Hub Rules**.

11. **Chemical Technician** 3+d3 skill points identical to the skill seen on page 52 of the Hub Rules**.

12. **Old World Languages** This database has 10+1d20 random old world languages from the table on page 509 of this book. The cyborg can automatically speak, read, write and identify each language in its inventory.

13. **Computer Codes and Access Passwords** With this directory, the user has a 92% likelihood of knowing any old world login code, user ID, password or communicator's unique ID code. In short, if the code is in their inventory, the character can open doors that use digital locks, keypads or other login credentials or passwords.

14. **Old World Area Maps** While the massive devastation, geological upheavals and elimination of landmarks and environments have altered the world around this character, there are still pockets of the oldster world architecture and landscape remaining.

    Should this character find themselves at a cross street in an old city, and find a still standing sign or street address on the front of an old building, he or she could pull up old maps from this database and identify where they are, and what subway lines, police stations, military outposts and industrial facilities once existed near that point.

    Besides city maps, this directory covers highways, railways, spaceports, restricted zones, wilderness areas and national boundaries.

15. **Ancient History Up to the year 1900 AD** This archive is less useful than other chips. However, to an imaginative cyborg ruler or adviser, it could be invaluable. Not only does this archive cover events from the earliest human records, but it also gives an overview of architecture, technological evolution, and military tactics of historical armies.

    As a new era resource this knowledge could help construct fortifications similar to medieval castles, develop sea going sailing ships, or form a rag tag militia into a disciplined Macedonian phalanx, band of Mongol horse archers, world war one trench defenders, or British square as seen at the battle of Waterloo.

16. **Martial Arts** This database has both video instructions on a wide range of old world martial art styles, but so too an inventory of every martial arts movie and major real-life competition. These films serve as examples, but so too, when running, this program will assist the user in their own practice offering feedback, verbal instruction, and holographic target interaction, corrective pointers and more.

    This software also runs when the cyborg is actually fighting in life or death engagements. Only a cyborg with an optic implant eye can take full advantage of this chip, as the program needs access to the real world vision of the operator to work fully. Still, there is some advantage of this database to a user without an optic interface. In short, while this chip is plugged into this character, he or she gains +1 skill points in the unarmed combat style of martial arts without an optic implant, or 3+1d3 skill points with a digital eye. See page 56 of the Hub Rules book**.

17. **Mechanical Technician** 3+d3 skill points identical to the skill described on page 54 of the Hub Rules**.

18. **Electrical Technician** 2+d3 skill points identical to the skill detailed on page 53 of the Hub Rules**.

19. **Gunsmith** 3+d3 skill points identical to the skill shown on page 40 of the Hub Rules**.

20. **Combat Tactics** This database includes a vast film, photo, audio and literary inventory of examples of modern combat techniques from the ancient world's police and military traditions. With this software running, the user is enhanced and gains 2 skill points in both the dodge skill and weapon expert with any weapon. Dodge skill found on page TME-37. Weapon expert skill on page TME-57.

21. **Recent State Records** This is mostly an income tax and voter registry, but it also contains records of an individual's registered firearms, suspected political affiliation, address, assets, vaccination and health records, political protests attended, carbon footprint, pronouns, sexual orientation, dental records, purchase history, known relationships, travel records, and cause of death or last known location. These files cover the last 3d6 years of records in that state or country in which game play occurs.

22. **Subway and Sewer Database** Directory of all subway and sewage systems in the state, including abandoned, quarantined, and in-construction lines. Updated to 3d6 years before the final collapse in the state or nation where the current game transpires.

23. **Sport Archive Records** of all sports games in the nation, including professional league, beer league, post-secondary and high school games. Records show team pictures, uniforms, coaches, trophies, scores of games and important data on each player's points, penalties and last known whereabouts or grave. Records go back to the early 1900s, and are updated to with 2d6 years of the final civilizational collapse in that area.

24. **Correctional Records** Directory of all prisoners in state penitentiaries, county jails, work camps, penal colonies, experimental bio-mechanical facilities and probation enrollment. Records go back to the beginning of digital record keeping and run to up to the day before civilization collapsed. This database also includes the location of all correctional facilities, probation offices and police stations in the former state or small nation.

25. **Human DNA database** Pre-devastation database of human subjects whose DNA was collected via routine medical procedures and used to create chimeras and other mutant strains for medical, agricultural and military purposes. There is a 78% likelihood that any mutant character, who knows their family name, can track down some relative who was subjected to mutagenic experimentation or had their DNA sample stolen from a workplace screening process, vaccine program or historical DNA research service, and secretly used to create mutant lifeforms.

26. **Comics Database** This database covers every comic book and graphic novel from the earliest days of visual storytelling art form up to within 2d6 years of the final collapse in that region of the world. Within this cyborg's mind's eye, he or she can read and flip through digital issues, archive them into favorites, genre, artist, writer, time period and any other folder options the user desires. Should this operator have a patch cable connected from the base of his or her skull to an operational screen, these pages can be viewed by others, too.

27. **Pilot skill** This database includes deck plans and technical specifications of all pre-devastation aircraft and orbital shuttles. Knowledge does not cover the layouts and workings of space stations and inter-planetary or interstellar vessels, but covers most common parts of space faring vessels such as airlocks, life support, space suits, access doors, cryo-sleep beds, nutrient printers and the basics of steering space vessels. Yields 1+1d2 points in the pilot skill.

28. **Agricultural database** This user knows all old world agricultural crops, and best practices on how to grow them, harvest them, save and germinate their seeds. Likewise, this database covers beekeeping, poultry and other livestock farming, as well as fish farming. With this knowledge, and this cyborg's oversight, a new era farm can produce 50% more food than it would without this user's frequent attendance and input.

28. **Database of Architecture, Engineering and Construction** With knowledge of old world construction, as well as ancient methods going back before the pyramids, this character can direct the building of fortifications, junk houses and apartment blocks which are far superior to anything the new era makers can pull off. Any structure is easily 50% more robust, more energy efficient, resistant to dust, drafts and mold, and reflects an old world aesthetic.

    Likewise, in the ruins, this cyborg will tell if a structure is too treacherous to enter, or if pulling away certain beams or blocks of concrete, if a tunnel will collapse or not. GM input and hazard check benefits are needed to reflect the benefits of this database.

29. **Sniper Database** This cyborg has access to both theoretical and video footage of some of the greatest snipers of the pre-devastation world. The character automatically has 4 points in the sniper skill, and if given a weapon used by snipers (see page 50 in the hub rules), this cyborg will be able take shots at that skill level, and go up in skill points in this area.

    This database can be accessed within the character's mind's eye repeatedly, and in some respect, serve as a form of grim meditation. There is an 39% chance this database also includes movies and documentaries of both historical and fictional war films which involve snipers.

30. **Cybernetics Technician** 3+1d3 skill points identical to the skill shown on page 207 of this book**.

*If no d30 is yet available at the game table, simply roll a d6 and a d10. The d6 result is the 10s column (1,2 = 1 to 10 {or +0}/ 3,4 = 11 to 20 {or +10} / 5,6.= 21 to 30 {or +20}) and the 1d10 represents the 1's column. So, for example, a roll of 1d6 results in a 3 (so +10) the 1d10 roll is a 7, to make 17 (10+7).*

**Any additional skill points in this skill do stack with other existing or rank gained skill points in this area, although if the database chip is removed, only the character's non-memory chip skill points are kept.*

## Dual Weapon Arm Combo 60

Power Source: **power cell in forearm**   Power Duration: **2.5 years**
Damage: **1d20 stun or lethal as a club**

This advanced implant was introduced near the final years of the former pan-global, high tech civilization, and is rarer than the standard weapon arm augmentation systems so commonly fitted on many cyborgs. While two melee or two ranged weapons or even one of each is possible should the implant of weapon arm occur twice during the creation of a cyborg, such clusters of armaments are crude and jury-rigged affairs compared to these sleek, purpose-built systems.

This melded together platform involves one close quarters melee weapon system along with a ranged ballistic or energy weapon. Additionally, a considerable number of these units also exhibit a robotic, human shaped metal hand which flips back automatically when the weapon system is activated to avoid being blown off, or it has a palm based muzzle hole for the beam or projectile to shoot through the open artificial hand.

When a skill point in either unarmed combat, sniper, or weapon expert is applied to a character, each weapon on this implant arm is treated separately. For example, if a hand is present, this metal fist could have the brawling or martial arts skill applied to it if the character has this skill. Likewise, the weapon expert skill could apply to either a spring out blade or an assault rifle should such skill points be present.

Besides whatever weapons might be fitted to this bulky arm, the contraption is heavy and makes for an exceptional clubbing tool all in its own right, and will inflict 1d20 base damage plus any strength modifiers on a hit. The user can elect to inflict only stun damage if desired, although lethal damage is always assumed unless stated otherwise prior to the character making the strike.

Roll 1d10 for the configuration of this implant, and then 1d100 on the second table to establish the melee weapon attachment.



### Configuration  Roll 1d10

**1-7.** One ranged weapon*, plus one melee weapon from the table below.

**8-10.** One ranged weapon*, one melee weapon from the list below. Also present is a fold-back or muzzle palm mechanical hand, roll 8,9 from the implant on page XR-339.

**For all ranged weapons, see Weapon Arm, set 2, on page XR-347 of this book, however re-roll any melee weapon result to appear on that table.*

## Table XR-211/ Dual Weapon Arm Melee Weapon Table

| 1d100 | Weapon | Power or Ammo | Source Book/ Page |
|---|---|---|---|
| 01-11 | Bayonet, fixed | nil | Hub Rules / stats on page 100, write-up on page 186 |
| 12-18 | Bayonet, spring out* | nil | Hub Rules / stats on page 100, write-up on page 186 |
| 19-24. | Spring-spike | nil | Hub Rules / stats on page 100, write-up on page 186 |
| 25-31 | Disc saw* | 1d4 power cells | Hub Rules / stats on page 100, write-up on page 186 |

| | | | |
|---|---|---|---|
| 32-41 | **Chainsaw*** | 1d4 power cells | Hub Rules / stats on page 100, write-up on page 186 |
| 42-47. | **Laser torch** | 1d4 power cells | Hub Rules / stats on page 100, write-up on page 189 |
| 48-56. | **Stun stick*** | 1d4 power cells | Hub Rules / stats on page 100, write-up on page 189 |
| 57-61. | **Tactical tomahawk*** | nil | Expansion Rules / stats on page 401, write-up on page 405 |
| 62-68. | **Pneumatic Hammer*** | 1d4 power cells | Expansion Rules / stats on page 414, write-up on page 416 |
| 69-78. | **Nerve disruptor baton** | 1d4 power cells | Expansion Rules / stats on page 401,, write-up on page 407 |
| 79-84. | **Devastator rod*** | 1d4 power cells | Expansion Rules / stats onpage 401,, write-up on page 407 |
| 85-88. | **Razor sword*** | nil | Hub Rules / stats on page 100, write-up on page 186 |
| 89-94. | **Laser sword** | 1d4 power cells | Hub Rules / stats on page 100, write-up on page 190 |
| 95-99. | **Chainsword** | 1d4 power cells | Expansion Rules / stats on page 401,, write-up on page 405 |
| 00. | **Mk2 laser sword** | 1d4 power cells | Expansion Rules / stats on page 401,, write-up on page 405 |

*This weapon normally resides in a slot beneath the barrel of whatever ranged weapon the arm features. With an internally controlled trigger mechanism, this weapon pops out either ready for action or directly against a target if the end of this arm is pressed to a potential victim, adding +20 SV on the initial stab.*

## Electro Shock Suppressor 61
Power Source: **mini power cell at base of neck**
Power Duration: **4 years**
Within this cyborg's torso, and connected to hundreds of subcutaneous micro filament wires, is an electrical surge absorption and containment mechanism. The micro filaments are laced throughout both the living and cybernetic parts of the subject, with insertion accomplished by endoscopic means leaving no noticeable scars.

When exposed to or hit by an electrical or electromagnetic pulse, the charge travels from the impacted body part via the micro wires to the main transfer unit and is partially nullified. This cyborg suffers only one tenth the damage from all electrical and EMP attacks, including natural lightning bolts. Stun beans, which are energy weapons, still affect this individual.

## Epidermal Manipulator *by Brandon Goeringer* 62
Power Source: **power cell**
Power Duration: **70 uses**
Sheets of thin metallic fibers are implanted under the cyborg's remaining skin. The main areas treated are the face, torso, buttocks and legs. These metallic sheets are wired together to a thin faux flesh covered battery pack in the lower back. When activated, the sheets mold to varying sizes and shapes, altering the appearance of the cyborg. It can create the look of well-defined muscles,

breasts or buttocks and strong, appealing facial features. The cyborg is given extra grafted synthetic skin hidden in thin slits at key locations of the body to allow for the appearance of larger muscle, fuller breasts, an obese stomach and other typical or 'normal' body types.

Alternatively, it can create the emaciated look of a starving street urchin to slip by as one of the unwashed masses, pulling the skin in and taut. The usage of this implant can increase one's appearance trait value up or down by 1d8+20 and adds 1 skill point to Disguise Artist, for those characters that posses that skill. Activating this implant takes 2 rounds for the change to take place and some clothing or armor may be damaged if not removed beforehand. This implant can only affect the sculpting of one's body in terms of appearance, not actual physical improvement.

## Flotation Bags 63
Power Source: **Standard power cell in upper back compartment**
Power Duration: **20% of a power cell per inflation (5 inflations per full cell)**
Spread throughout this cyborg's body are concealed, high pressure gas bags which, by default, are set to auto-deploy mode. By way of a small, skin covered control panel on the operator's side, this unit can be manually switched off in the event that the user wants to allow full submersion. In the automatically deployed mode, however, if this cyborg falls into the water, a half dozen gas bags erupt from the subcutaneous compartments and fill with buoyant gas to allow even a heavy cyborg to float and then swim or dog paddle. If deployed manually during a fall, which requires one hand to accomplish, these bags will reduce the damage of impact by half, but thereafter be disabled and ruptured, requiring the PC to spend 1d4+1 days in the shop at a cost of 4d100+100sp per day to repair. Once deployed normally for flotation, these bags take 20 minutes to deflate and properly fold up and stow.

In their concealed state, they are all but invisible on the cyborg's body, and produce no appearance penalty.

Should these bags be used to avoid damage from a crash landing while in a vehicle, or when crushed in an avalanche, stampede or some other event involving potential blunt trauma, they reduce the damage suffered by half, although, as with a fall noted above, the bags are thereafter ruptured and require costly repairs.

The user can only deploy these gas bags if he or she has customized their armor and outfitting to allow access for the balloon-like bags to inflate about their body. Given this, shell class armors, rad suits and the like cannot be worn if these bags are to be used, and other relics and archaic armors must be permanently modified to allow flip open panels or holes in their material.

Each deployment of the bags burns through 20% of a standard power cell, with the cell stored in the upper back of the cyborg in a hidden compartment. Once deployed, the gas bags can stay inflated for as long as the operator wishes.

## Fold-out Alloy Shield 64
Power Source: **spring loaded**     Power Duration: **unlimited**
Defense Value: **-14**          Shield Bash: **+4 SV, DMG 1d12 stun**
When desired, this cyborg can unlatch and unfold a fan-like array of metal sheets that form into a 60cm (about 2 feet) diameter round shield on the outer edge of their arm. The tool offers a defense value bonus of -14, but, can also bash an opponent as a back up melee attack with a strike value modifier of +4, damage 1d12 stun, plus any strength bonus the arm or the cyborg's own physical strength can add.

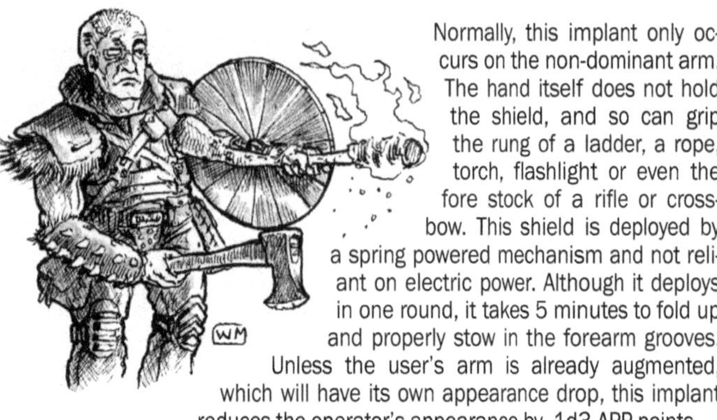

Normally, this implant only occurs on the non-dominant arm. The hand itself does not hold the shield, and so can grip the rung of a ladder, a rope, torch, flashlight or even the fore stock of a rifle or crossbow. This shield is deployed by a spring powered mechanism and not reliant on electric power. Although it deploys in one round, it takes 5 minutes to fold up and properly stow in the forearm grooves. Unless the user's arm is already augmented, which will have its own appearance drop, this implant reduces the operator's appearance by -1d3 APP points.

## Fold-out Alloy Sword 65
Power Source: **spring loaded**    Power Duration: **NA**
In one of the character's arms, (1d6: 1-3 left, 4-6 right), a slot for an alloy blade and fold out brace mechanism is housed deep in the limb. If this implant occurs on an existing weapon arm, it can be deployed in addition to any hand or gun configuration already present, except if that implant is already a razor sword (from roll 01-04 on page TME-92), in which case the blade is implanted on the other arm and if this is an otherwise living, non-augmented arm, then this deadly blade remains hidden in the forearm's underside within a flap of poly-skin to keep it well hidden. When needed, the cyborgs flicks his or her arm out and a linked nervous system control module unlocks and springs the blade out.

The sword is in three hinged sections with a singled edge and wider, locking back edge. It is identical to a razor sword and the hilt portion fits perfectly into the cyborg's hand to add strength and control to each swing and thrust. Razor swords have an SV bonus of +8 and inflict 1d20+11 damage. Skills and strength can be applied to this attack mode to make it especially deadly.

One of the huge advantages of this weapon is that if built into a living arm, it can be concealed — unless metal detectors or other advanced scanning optics are used to locate hidden weapons — and so even as a prisoner, this character could possess a lethal weapon at all times. This blade takes only one round to deploy, but a full minute to manually unlock and snap back into place. Only muscle contortions are needed to engage this implant, and so it has no power requirements.

## Force Canopy 66
Power Source: **mini power cell at base of skull**
Power Duration: **10+1d10 minutes per use / 20 uses per mini power cell**
Usage: **Can only be used once per hour regardless of power supply.**
Canopy Force field: **Defense value: 0 / 100 END per round load limit**
This advanced cybernetic gives this cyborg immunity from incoming attacks, but also hinders outgoing attacks from this operator. If this DV 0 screen suffers over 100 points of damage in a single round, it collapses and cannot be used again for an hour. Normal operating duration per use is 10+1d10 minutes, although the canopy of vivid blue energy can be canceled at any time prior to the end of the duration. This is an exceedingly energy efficient cybernetic and will yield twenty uses per power cell, although the unit's scalp or shoulder mounted emitters need to recharge between uses by a minimum of 1 hour.

When activated, the six or eight metallic, pill-sized nodes form an umbrella-like dome about either itself, or several companions. The cyborg can have this dome of protection either cover just themselves, or rise and shield a 2m radius around the user, possibly shielding six man-sized companions. If a hostile or unwilling being is enclosed within the canopy, they must score a strike on this cyborg to break the user's control.

As mentioned above, any and all incoming attacks must surpass 100 Endurance damage within the same round to switch off this canopy, however any outbound attacks must also successfully strike the field, (DV 0) to pass through and potentially hit targets outside (roll a second time), but whatever damage they inflict on a struck target also weakens the canopy on the NEXT round during enemy attacks and might contribute to the collapse of the canopy. Any misses fired from within the field that don't exit the field bounce back at random occupant within the canopy, although a strike is still required to do damage to the unfortunate.

This canopy will protect the occupants from most ranged and melee attacks, including dimensional beings, mental attacks, junk storms, particles, radiation, liquid splashes and similar, however, an avalanche, lava flow, or other massive force crashing into the canopy will likely dissipate it at once if able to inflict over 100 END damage.

The user can move while this field is in operation, and if flying, the canopy forms into a ball around the user instead of a half dome. Finally, should this energy dome be activated during a fall, subtract 100 points from the damage the occupants would otherwise take if the field is still operational at the moment of impact.

The power cell for this emitter is typically loaded into the upper back of the cyborg and leaves a noticeable lump and unappealing, oddly shaped scar. This scar, combined with the nodes on the user's shoulders or head, together reduce their appearance by -1d4+2 trait points.

## Glide Wings 67
Power Source: **power cell slot built into the back wing case, or unpowered option**
Power Duration: **40 wing deployments and fold up sessions**
From a low-profile, permanently attached pack-like compartment on this cyborg's back, fold out and snap together a pair of metal glider wings. The flat-black colored, alloy panels allow the operator to drift down with considerable control. They take 2 rounds to engage and open if supplied with power, but can be manually yanked open one at a time — which requires a minimum strength of 20 — and each takes 3 rounds to open, fold out and lock into place. To stow the wings after landing takes 10+1d20 rounds per wing manually, although in powered mode the wings will both fold up and conceal themselves at will in 4 rounds.

Gliding is a somewhat complicated in-game mechanic, although for the character, it is easy enough and offers both a splendid way to travel if leaving a platform of great height — such as a cliff, skyscraper, or the deck of an airship — but also provides a means of escape from the same platforms, a or a means of survival from an unexpected fall.

To determine the distance one can glide, assume that the user will travel five meters horizontally for every meter of lost altitude, although a steep, much faster drop can be made, too. The direction of flight is handled by the cyborg shifting their bodyweight, posture and limbs, and isn't always the most graceful undertaking. Going against the wind cuts one's speed in half, while going with it doubles the speed. Hot updrafts can allow the glider to circle high above and even gain altitude if the GM permits.

The landing is normally the hard part, with the character forced to make a type B agility based hazard check to pull it off, otherwise a crash occurs. Treat this impact as if dropping 3 meters according to the Falling Table on page 123 of the hub rules — with the drop zone shown on table TME-3-11 offering the damage modifiers based on the material this cyborg crash lands into (rubble, ice, grass, or a tent top for example).

While gliding, the cyborg moves 10 meters per round horizontally per 2 meters dropped in elevation, but a steeper decline allows movement of 20 meters per round but a landing at such a pitch and speed requires a successful type F agility based hazard check. While gliding, the cyborg is harder to hit and enjoys a -20 DV bonus, although firing while moving comes with a -15 strike value penalty.

The glide wings originally selected for this cyborg took into account the size and weight of the wearer, however many times the gliding character might try to carry aloft a comrade or captive, in which case the weight of the carried person determines the chance of a successful glide based on the following table:

| Carried Extra Weight | Flight Details |
| --- | --- |
| **Less than 25% of Glider's KG** | Flight unaffected |
| **25% to 49% of glider's weight** | Altitude drop is more rapid, 3 meters dropped per 10m horizontal travel |
| **50% to 75% of glider's weight** | Steep loss in altitude with 1 meter dropped per every 2 meters glide horizontally. |
| **76% to 150% of glider's weight** | Virtual free fall although for every meter dropped, the cyborg and its passenger also travel horizontally 1 meter further. Treat the landing as a fall at a reduced speed and so all involved suffer a 50% damage reduction. |
| **Over 150% of Glider-borg's weight** | Straight drop for a regular fall. |

These wings are made of a very durable alloy, and whether stowed in their backpack compartment or deployed, improve the users defense value by -6 DV. Because of the considerable bulge on the character's back, however, appearance is dropped by -2d4 and weight is increased by +10 kilograms plus disallow the wearing of relic shell class armors unless the suit is seriously modified by a mechanical technician of 5 or more skill points.

Finally, these wings can be used as two melee weapon attacks, although not in addition to other attack modes, and do 2d6 stun damage each when smacking and karate chopping opponents.

## Homing Device 68
Power Source: **mini power cell at base of skull**
Power Duration: **11 years**
Within this cyborg's brain is an unobtrusive, miniaturized implant that allows the operator to log location points and later, even days or months later, select and identify specific log point and be directed to it again. When wanting to login a homing point, the cyborg's visual receptors scans the horizon line, position of the sun, moon, stars and landmarks — all within one minute and at a 360 degree glance — and digitally memorizes and photographs the position. Up to forty such homing points can be recorded and remain until the cyborg deletes them, or overwrites the oldest points by adding more than 40 locations to its library.

When this unit requires the direction to a specific location, a small reverse tear drop appears in his or her vision and shows the direct 'as a crow flies' route to the homing point. This direction does not take into consideration rivers, lakes, radioactive zones or other hazards and so this device doesn't indicate the best path to the desired location.

While mainly used outdoors, a location point can be set underground, with the hall, chamber or facility recorded for several minutes while at the site and thereafter as the cyborg moves to other areas and subconsciously records the homing point. The accuracy of these subterranean locations is not always reliable, and an error occurs 13% of the time and leads the cyborg to some other place.

## Mechanical Hand 69
Power Source: **mini power cell in lower arm**
Power Duration: **1 year**
This implant is frequently assigned when some other implant replaces a living arm. The mechancical hand is either a fold away or muzzle hand (roll 8,9 on the table below) and often included along with a weapon arm, full cybernetic limb, or otherwise handless attachment. It allows the operator to manipulate objects, reload, investigate items during an adventure, and interact with the environment in ways other than obliterating it. When this implant occurs at character generation and no other arm-based unit is preset, then this hand, and all its accompanying control nodes and forearm bone-braces, replace a severed hand.

The shown punch damage of a mechanical hand type is the base DMG before any strength modifiers from the user's strength trait or relevant skills are applied. The grip strength is only used when some in-game action or hazard check demands it, such as grasping a hatch handle and twisting it, squeezing something, opening a jar, or other focused specific task. For most other strength based hazard checks, the character's main STR trait is used.

If the game master allows it, existing cyborg player characters with a weapon arm can have a mechanical hand attachment made available to them — usually discovered as an item found for sale in a trade town with an attachment fee of 400+1d100sp — while all new cyborg player characters with the weapon arm or dual weapon arm have a 50% chance of starting with either the flip back or muzzle palm variety as shown on roll 8,9, below.

This possible bonus feature is part of the weapon arm and not a separate cybernetic, and so does not replace another randomly determined implant.

| Hand Type | Roll 2d6 | | | |
| --- | --- | --- | --- | --- |

**2,3. Three fingered robotic hand:** A very  robotic, inhuman looking appendage with two large fingers and an opposing thumb. Grip strength is 40+3d8, and a claw-like slash or punch from this powerful hand will do a base of 1d12 damage.

**4,5. Civilian issue:** This hand is a soft skinned, plastic boned replacement with a life-like coating. It's normally the best match for the character's gender and skin complexion to mimic his or her real hand. While not made for combat or industrial applications, it is the most life-like and, with highly sensitive nerve endings, high dexterity and is the ideal replacement short of regrowing a new hand. Grip strength, 20+4d6, punch damage base of 1d6 like a 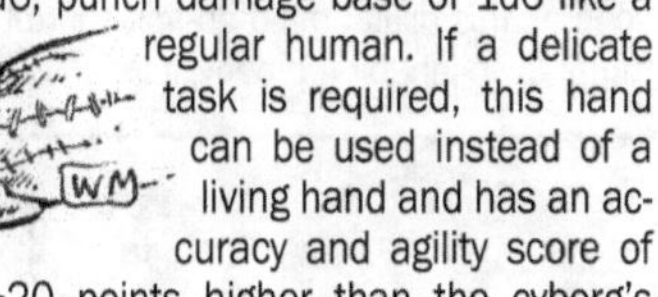 regular human. If a delicate task is required, this hand can be used instead of a living hand and has an accuracy and agility score of +20 points higher than the cyborg's base. This trait bonus is only for hazard checks calling for fine motor skills, including lock picking, disarming a bomb, surgery, complex electrical work, etc. The GM will decide on the allowable applications.

**6,7. Natural replacement:** A poly-sheathed, rather normal looking human-like hand is fitted on the cyborg. This unit is pretty much identical to an android hand and typically attached to match the cyborg's living hand, or best fit for the physique, 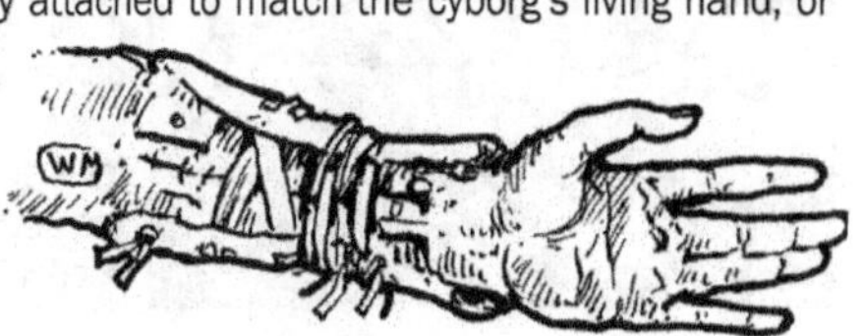 skin tone, and gender of the subject. It will have a grip strength of 30+4d6 and a punch damage base of 1d8.

**8,9. Fold away or muzzle palm hand:** If this character has a weapon arm or similar augmented limb which wields a weapon or industrial tool, then read on. If such a weapon implant occurs later in character creation, then also apply the following flip back or muzzle palm variant of mechanical hand to that cybernetic system. However, if no such other implant exists, then see roll 6,7, above for a natural replacement hand.

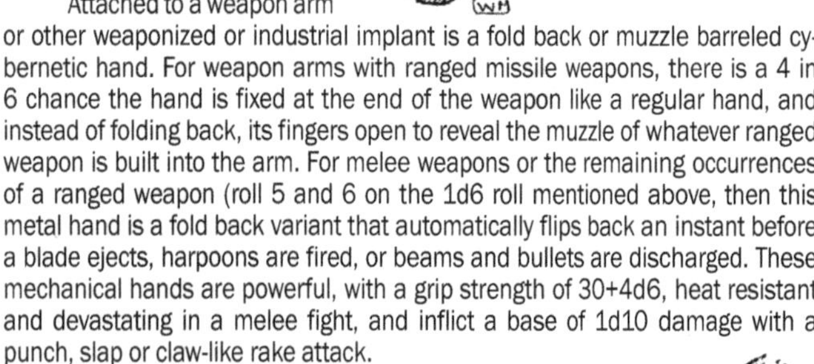

Attached to a weapon arm or other weaponized or industrial implant is a fold back or muzzle barreled cybernetic hand. For weapon arms with ranged missile weapons, there is a 4 in 6 chance the hand is fixed at the end of the weapon like a regular hand, and instead of folding back, its fingers open to reveal the muzzle of whatever ranged weapon is built into the arm. For melee weapons or the remaining occurrences of a ranged weapon (roll 5 and 6 on the 1d6 roll mentioned above, then this metal hand is a fold back variant that automatically flips back an instant before a blade ejects, harpoons are fired, or beams and bullets are discharged. These mechanical hands are powerful, with a grip strength of 30+4d6, heat resistant and devastating in a melee fight, and inflict a base of 1d10 damage with a punch, slap or claw-like rake attack.

**10,11. Alloy skeletal:** Skinless, often flecked with rust and with all the micro-pistons, cables and pressure sensitive pads visible, this utilitarian, skeletal metal hand is the appropriate match to the cyborg's living hand as far as shape and size go. Grip strength of 30+4d6 and punch has a base of 1d10. Appearance loss -5 APP.

**12. Large robotic:** This is an oversized, alloy hand with a grip strength of 60+4d10 and a base punch damage of 1d12. Unsightly, this attachment reduces the user's appearance by -4 APP.

## Memory Backup *by Thomas Vida* 70

Power Source: **mini power cell at base of skull**       Power Duration: **11 years**
If this cyborg is killed, comrades can open a synthi-skin covered plate in its head, unlatch a small armor plate and recover a four centimeter long by two centimeter wide rectangular memory stick. This advanced data drive can be plugged into most operational computers, or to a fully robotic or computerized body, transferring a unique, one of a kind replacement copy of the former cyborg's consciousness, memories and motivations with it. The former cyborg effectively becomes a digital being character type from this point forward.

If the implant was damaged in the process of the cyborg's death (27% chance) there may be interesting consequences for the on-board personality.

Alternatively, if a cybernetic technician can access the dead cyborg, he or she can make an attempt to successfully remove, and later install the memory backup chip, recording hub, and power supply unit into the head of another living being, including an animal. The cyborg struggles to take control of the body and must make a successful, type D willpower based hazard check each day to 'inhabit' this new body. The subject, if unwilling to be mentally dominated, is also allowed a willpower based type B hazard check the throw off the foreign consciousness as soon as this digital mind grasps control for the day. The digitized mind could attempt to co-inhabit the body, if it can befriend and convince the true owner of the body of its benefits and benevolence, and in this case, both consciousness would operate simultaneously, with each having mastery over different body functions.

Any mental or energy mutations the cyborg might have had in life do not transfer to the digital memory backup. If the dead cyborg transfers into a new body, it only keeps half of any former experience factors, although these EFs can cause multiple rank gains for the new character type which the backed-up former cyborg now occupies.

## Mental Attack Dampener 71

Power Source: **mini power cell at base of skull**
Power Duration: **400 rounds**

This head mounted implant is usually connected at the back of the skull and looks like an audio speaker, complete with perforations and a wide, gray stubby antenna. When the cyborg switches it on, which can be done with mental control alone or an external switch, a strange, low pitched, oscillating noise comes from the device. This sound — which is no louder than a murmur — often scatters all externally expressed brain waves within a 100 meter radius, and potentially interferes with telepathy, telekinesis, mental attacks, empathy readings or other externally projected mutations. For any mental mutation to be used, the one generating or using it must make a willpower based type E hazard check to succeed, otherwise the mental mutation fails against the cyborg. All mental mutations in the area of effect are messed with, including those used by the cyborg should it be a mutorg with such gifts, or allies, within the range of this field.

This dampener is power intensive, and unless the cyborg has some built-in power generation system, relies on snap-in mini power cells. One such cell will operate the device for 400 rounds before needing replacement.

## Micro Suture Laced Tissues 72

Power Source: **mini power cell in concealed upper back compartment**
Power Duration: **5 years**
The living parts of this cyborg are laced through with bio-responsive filaments which, when detecting any injury to the body, immediately try to knit together and rejuvenate skin, muscle, bone and organ tissues back to their normal state of perfection. In short, whenever this cyborg takes damage, these micro sutures heal the individual at a rate equal to the character's daily healing rate, but per hour instead of per 24 hours.

To onlookers, this individual seems to regenerate, which is a condition normally known to occur only among certain mutants — and could force this cyborg to explain its rapid recovery if serving in factions which do not tolerate deviants. A mini-power cell is required to maintain proper function and alignment of these filaments, although this well concealed, back enclosed battery will offer continuous operation for 5 years. The initial insertion of these filaments is an intrusive surgical procedure, but leaves only minimal scarring; reduce appearance by -2 App.

## Motion Stabilizer 73

Power Source: **mini power cell at base of skull**
Power Duration: **7 years**

This cyborg's body has been implanted with a series of micro gyroscopes and equilibrium enhancing cable-muscles. Combined, these performance enhancing additions increase the subject's agility and strength by 10+2d10 each, and improve endurance by 4+1d10 trait points. In addition, this augmented individual makes two hazard checks when required to keep their balance, leap, grab for things, avoid falls, climb a ledge, and countless other acts involving agility.

The insertion of all the hardware within this cyborg increases his or her weight by 20+1d12 kilograms and the scars reduce appearance by -2d6.

## Multi-tool Arm 74

Power Source: **Unless otherwise stated, this implant uses a mini power cell loaded in the underside of the cyborg's forearm**
Power Duration: **3 years**

This cyborg has a metal lower arm and medium sized, replica human hand with a base punch damage of 1d10. This arm has a strength score separate from their body's main STR trait value of 20+2d20, determined at implant discovery or character generation.

50% of the time this limb is poly-sheathed to make it look like a regular human arm, although even when occurring like this, there is only a 2 in 6 chance it matches the character's natural skin complexion.

When one tool built into this arm is not deployed, the user can use this limb like a regular arm — although suffering no off-hand (-20 SV) penalties should it be used to wield a weapon or unleash an on-board offensive instrument. At the creation of this cyborg, or if such an arm is found or looted off another cyborg, the limb has a certain number of tools which the user can merely think of and deploy. Only one tool can be used at a time, and emerges from a sliding hatch or port hole on one side of the limb. During use, the hand clenches into a ball and either continues to hold a weapon or other object, but in a position where it cannot interfere with the tool being used.

Roll for 1d3+1 tools fitted into this arm from the following list. Re-roll any duplicated result. Roll 1d100.

| Multi-Tool Arm Features Table | Roll 1d100, 1d3+1 times |
| --- | --- |

**01-04. Electric toothbrush:** With self-healing bristles which re-grow after an hour of use.

**05-08. Water filtration straw:** When extended and stuck into a mud puddle or questionable source of water, this unit will suck up 500ml of water, filter it and store it in an internal tube for later consumption. A fold out spigot-straw is attached to the tank, allowing the contents to be poured out or sucked upon. One mini power cell will suction and filter 100 liters of water before recharge is required.

**09-13. Spotting scope:** A fold out telescope attachment extends from the wrists and, by way of a folding brace, turns ninety degrees to allow the telescope to be held to the operator's eye and view through it. This unit is identical to the relic on page TME 201 and allows x50 magnification. 1 in 8 are instead digital spotting scopes and allow the user to see at x80 magnification plus view the infra-red spectrum and see whether a highlighted being is organic, cybernetic, fully mechanical, illusionary or dimensional.

**14-18. Laser scalpel:** See TME Hub Rules page 189 for details, or stats on page TME 100. When generated at character creation or found as an implant, this unit has 60+2d20 strikes left in its charge.

**19-22. Light duty grappling hook:** Similar to the full size Implant number 17 on page TME 87, however, this unit has a reduced load bearing capacity limited to just the weight of the cyborg itself, and a range of only 10 meters. It allows for 50 uses per power cell, and if fired as a weapon, has an SV of +15 and inflicts 1d12 damage.

If discharged on an unsuspecting opponent, it instead offers a +3 initiative bonus during a single surprise attack. Use cyborg's base SV to see if the grapple snags a desired hold point. It can reel back in at 2m per round if missing its target or pulls cyborg up at a rate of 1m per round. If the cable is hacked or shot at, the line has a defense value of -30 and will take 20 points damage before being severed.

**23-27. Communicator, standard:** See page TME 198.

**28-31. Rad scanner:** See TME page TME 199.

**32-35. Tissue binder:** See page XR-443 of this book. Unit has 3d6 uses left in power cell charge.

**36-38. Digital wrist watch:** Charged by everyday motion of the limb. This watch has a flip open false skin cover to allow the user to tell the time. Comes with an alarm, lap recorder, step recorder, compass, and altimeter.

**39-44. Anti-toxin-injector:** like the relic described on page TME 199, however, this unit's syringe is fitted to a starting array of 2d6 injectors. Empty injector tubes can be filled with other substances, including venom or narcotics and used to stab opponents and inject them in combat. (SV +0), DMG 1d3 plus liquid injection, which forces the target to make an appropriate hazard check.

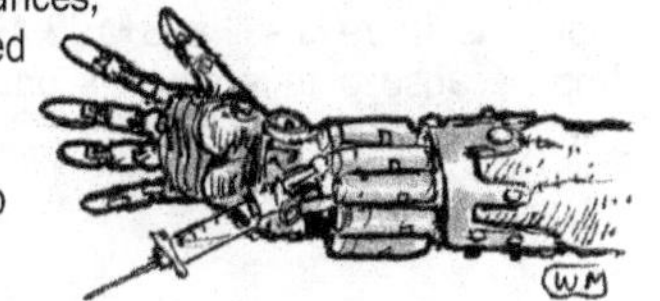

**45-47. Nerve disruptor baton:** Page XR-407.

**48-52. Stun stick:** See page TME-189.

**53-55. Force shield:** Implant 16 from page TME 87: power cell offers 500 rounds use, when deployed provides a -30 DV bonus from one direction of incoming attacks, or can be deployed against a melee range foe to deliver 1d12+3 stun damage.

**56-61. Pocket flashlight:** From page TME-201, uses mini power cells, has 2d100 hours use remaining in charge, light range 20m.

**62-64. Retractable laser pistol:** As Implant 38 from page TME 90: 60 shots per power cell, rate 1, range 200m, SV +10, damage 1d20+10.

**65-67. Flip out disc saw:** Uses one standard power cell to yield 400 rounds of use, and when this PC generated or implant is found, it has 200+2d100 rounds of use left to it. Described on page 186 of the TME hub rules. Stats: SV +5, rate 1, damage 2d12+2.

**68-70. Switchblade knife:** See page TME 186 and stats of SV +2, rate 1, damage base 1d8+1, however, the strength score of the multi-tool arm may offer a bonus.

**71-73. Alloy razor claws:** As implant 1 on page TME 85: rate 1 slash, SV +14, DMG 1d20+7 each.

**74-76. Landmine detector:** A fold-out mesh disc on a 1m long telescopic boom. Useless and too frail to be used as a weapon, this device will, however, detect buried landmines if swept back and forth before the cyborg. Likewise, metal can also be located beneath the surface to a depth of 1 meter (3.3 feet). It is powered by 1 mini-power cell which will yield 200 hours of operation. A small screen offers a visual display of the subterranean surface and makes a cheerful beep when metal is found. This unit will detect mines and metal, including gold and silver.

**77,78. Cutlery set with fold-out knife, spoon, and fork:** One implement can be used at any given time. As a weapon SV +1, damage 1d6, range melee.

**79-81. Repair tools and fold out flexible shaft:** A collection of alloy tools including screwdrivers, pliers, bolt cutter, plumbers' wrench, tweezers, 6m long measuring tape, laser level, and other assorted gadgets. These tools are connected to and extend from the forearm and into the metal hand of the user, and include tools needed by mechanical, electrical, cybernetic and robotics technicians, but can be modified to include lock picking tools.

**82-83. Fire starting lighter:** This relic has enough ethanol fuel for 200+d1000 flames. Flame length varies from a centimeter to finger length, but not normally useful as a weapon.

**84-86. Hygienic Array:** Each tool is connected to a shaft which slides the tool into the metal hand for easy access. Tools include an electric nose hair trimmer, tweezers, hair comb, hairbrush, nail clippers, nail file, cuticle trimmer, eclectic shaver, lotion application tube, and assorted make up brushes and mirror. The mirror extends from the wrist and out on a flexible arm to allow for its use while deploying other tools. Powered by a mini power cell which yields 200 hours' use.

**87-89. Microphone and recording system:** Will store 1000 hours of audio and comes with audio out port and uses a mini power cell which will allow for 200 hours recording.

**90-92. Massage paddle and hot oil dispenser:** Flexible, shape morphing foot long paddle extends beyond the cyborg's hand. Heated with assorted vibration, texture and massage control features, plus oil or lotion dispenser nozzle with temperature control dial from lukewarm to high heat. If used as a club, this quivering implement has an SV of +0 and does 1d6 stun damage.

**93- 95. Loudspeaker:** Unit must be held to the cyborg's mouth and will magnify his or her voice 30 times, most likely deafening those too close to the front end of this cone shaped emitter.

**96,97. Heavy Crossbow:** Fires like a harpoon gun and has an elbow access ammo port which will hold up to 10 quarrels. Stats for this air powered unit: SV +12, rate 1, range 50m, damage 1d20+5 (no strength modifiers permitted, but weapon expert skill allowable).

**98-00. Quad barreled shotgun:** Manual reloading at an elbow portal. Four barrels can be fired all at once or one shot at a time. A shotgun pistol with these stats: SV +15, rate 1 to 4 (takes 1 round to reload one shell), damage 3d10 each, range 20m, but can pepper up to 3 man-sized beings with each blast if they are grouped together in a 3m wide hall or pack.

## Nutritional Enhancement Module 75

Power Source: **mini power cell at base of skull**
Power Duration: **7 years**

The organic body parts of this cyborg are chemically juiced by an implanted digestive converter. This apparatus improves upon the food already being consumed and combines previously stored compounds to chemically blend and release enhanced nutrition into the bloodstream. This substance acts like a power lifter's steroid, and subsequently adds +3d6 to both strength and endurance trait values. Other benifits include a + 4 daily healing rate, and the cyborg is allowed two hazard checks versus all poisons and intoxicants.

## Optical Implants Set 2 76

Power Source: **mini power cell at base of skull**
Power Duration: **8 years, unless otherwise noted**

All the following implanted eyes offer normal vision besides whatever extra feature the optical enhancement provides, and so in combination with a regular human eye, allows for normal depth perception. Set 1 is shown on page TME 89 of the hub rules. **Roll 1d6:**

**1. Threat assessment algorithm:** This cyborg can see and predict the incoming attacks by both close quarters melee opponents and already identified shooters of ranged weapons. A brain fused on-board computer and link to the user's optical implants will assess the attack mode, trajectory, and fighting style to give the cyborg a -10 defense value bonus. If a shooter has not made its presence known or taken the first shot, then this unit will not detect the threat until it has been unleashed. Record seperate defense values for this character.

**2. Augmented reality view mode:** With this eye, the user can see any old world augmented reality projections in his or her field of view. These projections might be ongoing advertising animations, flashing signs for sales and special offers, or a wide range of other digital images being beamed to a specific location in the world by either a satellite, operational projector, or robotic source. See page XR-477 for more on holdover Augmented Reality in the Epochian era.

**3. Radiation viewer:** The cyborg can literally see radiation within one kilometer. Mild radiation appears as faint, lime green smoke, medium radiation as an orange haze, strong radiation shows up as a purple mist, and lethal radiation as a pinkish red fog. Any creature or person who deploys radiation by mutational means will give off a lime green glow.

**4. Enhanced night vision eye:** Besides being able to see in the dark as if it were day, this unit can see invisible laser security light beams, but also identify if an object or person is a hologram or digital being.

**5. Extra dimensional vision:** This eye serves as a replacement regular eye most of the time, but can also see the ghostly forms of any dimensional beings and portals, or even smoke-like residue left by such entities that were present in an area within the last thirty minutes.

**6. Laser eye**, similar to a pulse laser eye, this unit is however a variant of the laser pistol noted on page TME-190. Besides offering normal vision to the operator, it can fire bright red laser beams once per round until the external battery pack is drained. It has only a 250 meter range, however, and will fire 30 shots per hip mounted power cell. SV +16, rate 1, damage 1d20+10.

## Parachute 77

Power Source: **power cell in deployment pack**
Power Duration: **50 chute deployments**

A highly compact, backpack-like cavity is permanently fused to the bone and muscles of this cyborg's back. Within this alloy compartment is a durable, ultra-thin fiber laced plastic parachute which, at the user's conscious control, can be deployed within 2 rounds. This life saving parachute will not only slow the decent of the user, but through two steering handles, called toggle loops, the operator can steer the chute somewhat like the implant of fold-out glider wings, and travel further horizontally than vertically — although not as efficiently as with glide wings. While deployed, this chute can be steered 3 meters horizontally for every meter of lost altitude.

While descending, the cyborg is quite stable and can wield ranged weapons without penalty, however trying to employ melee weapons is done so at a -20 SV penalty as the wearer's thrusting, hacking and stabbing motions makes the contraption sway, twist and bounce.

Enemies who wish to target the parachute may do so, although the material resists ripping and up to ten bullet or arrow holes in the material will not affect the operator's gradual drop of 6 meters per round. Any more than ten punctures will, however, compromise the chute, with from 11 to 20 punctures meaning the wearer drops at 12m per round, while 21-30 punctures causes the cyborg to plunge at a rate of 20 meter per round. Any more than 30 punctures will shred the chute into useless ribbons and the wearer will plunge to their likely death.

If this wearer carries a companion during this decent, only 1 meter of travel can be accomplished per meter dropped, and the landing in such a case is always hard with both the passenger and the user possibly taking harm — treat as an attack at SV 01-60 for 1d6 lethal and 1d12 stun damage. Any high speed landing of 12m per round will cause the wearer, and any potential passenger, to hit hard. The distance fallen at this speed, and what the wearer crashes down upon matters. Consult the falling table on page 123 of the hub rules, however for a fall of speed of 12m per round the wearer takes off 75% of the damage, while a wearer who falls at 20m per round takes off half the damage shown.

Once on the ground, this chute is unwieldy and drags and yanks the wearer about which hampers their ability to fight or shoot and so suffers a -30 SV penalty while still hooked to the chute. The parachute can be detached upon landing with a unlock tab at each shoulder — which takes 2 rounds to pull off — and the chute can hopefully be recovered later, reattached and refolded, or the cyborg can keep the chute hitched to their back and either engage enemies or set about the arduous, precise task of folding the chute, which takes 10+3d6 minutes.

This chute has an auto-deploy feature which will detect if the wearer drops more than 6 meters while unconscious. This auto mode will not activate while the user is conscious, regardless of drop distance and speed.

This bulky unit will accommodate 50 chute deployments from one power cell, and while very low-profile for how remarkable this implant is, there is still a -3+1d3 APP drop because of this device's ungainly, hunchback look.

## Power Leeching Unit [78]

Power Source: **power cell**   Power Duration: **100 rounds of leeching**
Strike value: **Fixed 01-70 (target gets no armor DV modifiers, but agility and dodge apply).**   Range: **60m or direct contact**
Damage: **1d6 or 2d6 energy units drained per round, or 1d6 stun damage if power cells are already drained on a cyborg or mutorg.**

This implant potentially drains power from other electrical devices and machines, which both depletes these mechanical beings and devices and recharges the cyborg who operate this advanced cybernetic.

The leeching unit is normally fitted on the upper chest of the recipient, and must be focused on a single target, range 60 meters, or physically struck, and the leeching beam or touch locked on with a fixed strike value of 01-70. This SV is unaffected by the target's armor, although its agility and dodge skill defense value modifiers can help it avoid being 'locked and leeched'. Rank gain and accuracy modifiers do not add or subtract from this unit's base 01-70 SV.

Once locked onto a chosen power emitting target, this unit leeches 1d6 energy units per round, or 2d6 if direct physical contact, which steals this electricity from any on-board power cells, or packs connected to the target, which can include relic weapons. If the unit is plugged into a generator or facility, large vehicle, or other massive source of power, the target might suffer no significant damage or even be aware of the loss. However, if a cyborg, mutorg, android, or robot is leeched, and it has no externally plugged in power cells, or those it has attached are drained, the target instead takes stun damage at the same 1d6 rate per round.

Once locked, the victim is allowed a Type E Willpower based hazard check to regain their senses and twist free of the leecher. The leecher must re-lock on the target to continue. A force field, either generated by a mutation or technological means, will block this draining beam, although the field will take an automatic 1d6 or 2d6 damage each round. Likewise, if this power leeching cyborg is struck and takes at least 1 point of damage, its lock, or hand grip, on the target drops and must be reestablished.

Leeched energy units flow back to this cyborg and will recharge any depleted power cells hooked up to this operator (but not those merely carried in a pouch or backpack), however these energy units do not heal the endurance or other traits of the cyborg, and any stolen stun damage drawn from a target do not heal or enhance this user.

Any robot or android totally drained of energy units will lock up and either stand rigid if in a balanced position, or topple over if mid-stride or off balance. Cyborgs and mutorgs who lose all their power units will merely have their weapon systems and other cybernetics switched off, although they could incur stun damage thereafter, and be knocked out. Although not stated with the descriptions of cyborgs and mutorgs, their spinal connectors and wired brain stems are powered by the person's own electro-magnetic field, and use very little power in itself. This field is not drained of power, but since it is connected to the augmented person's nervous system, stun damage can be inflicted. Any implant connected to this cyborg or mutorg will suffer a power loss.

To determine which batteries are drained first in cyborg struck by this beam, the GM can roll randomly among them should the target have multiple power supplied implants. Following the loss of energy units to these, continued use of this leeching beam will then suck power from any energy weapons or other relics carried by the target, one after the other, and selected randomly.

This beam or touch has no effect on living things that do not operate on electrical power nor use or carry any in their pack or weapons relics which use such items. Electrical gear worn by a person will also be drained of energy units even if these items are not touching the target's body but merely carried in a pouch or backpack.

This beam or leeching hold has an odd and little known effect on dimensional beings, which are drained at a rate of 2d6 endurance per round from this energy system, although these trait points do not return to, nor benefit, this cyborg.

Here are the common battery types and their energy units:

**Pill power cell** 1 energy unit
**Mini power cell** 3 energy units
**Power cell** 10 energy units
**Power pack** 100 energy units

## Power-Jack [79]

Power Source: **Cyborg contains 2 power cells**
Charge time: **Included solar panel will charge 25% of 1 cell per hour**

This cyborg has a grounded plug at a random location on his or her body. A flap of synthi-skin covers the receptacle when not in use. The plug itself can only feed one device at a time, but has a dozen different outlets allowing it to accommodate power tools and small appliances from a wide range of ancient time periods. The power supply within this cyborg comprises two permanently fused, standard power cells, which can either be charged up by an external source or via a small 'peel and fold' flexible solar

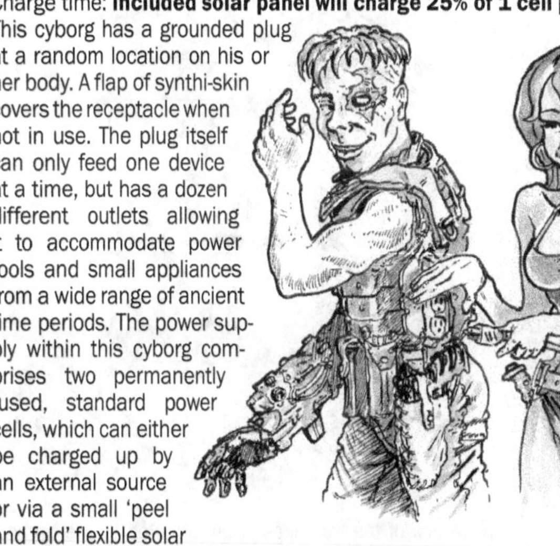

panel which is inserted in the character's shoulder. For every hour of full sunlight, charging 1 of the 2 power cells will replenish one quarter charge.

## Quadrupedal Lower Body [80]

Power Source: **Power Pack**

Power Duration: **6 months, but with hand cranking and solar backups, body power can be maintained for 6 hours per day without a charged power pack.**

This cyborg's lower limbs have been removed and much of his or her abdomen augmented with artificial organs, power conduits, batteries, servo motors, metal and plastic supports, and other features to make the individual battlefield effective once more. Whoever re-made this cyborg, they also gave the recipient a four legged quadrupedal lower body similar to that of an enormous dog, tiger or small horse. In short, this survivor is a post-apocalyptic centaur.

This heavily reinforced unit runs on a power pack, several high efficiency solar panels and emergency hand crank power generator — the latter for battery top-up and emergency 6 hours a day operation should the battery pack become depleted. An access panel on the unit's back allows the power pack to serve as a battery for other devices or weapon systems via a patch cable, although doing so will drastically reduce operational time for this unit.

These robotic centaur bodies come in many sizes and shapes, as well as different colors, but all offer the ability to move at great speed, navigate uneven, steep or treacherous ground with ease, add an extra two melee attacks per round from rear kicks or when the cyborg rears up like a horse to pound or claw opponents. 'Quad-bods' are heavy, however, and unless some other implant is added to the individual to permit flotation, then if this individual is dropped into deep water he or she will sink to the bottom almost immediately.

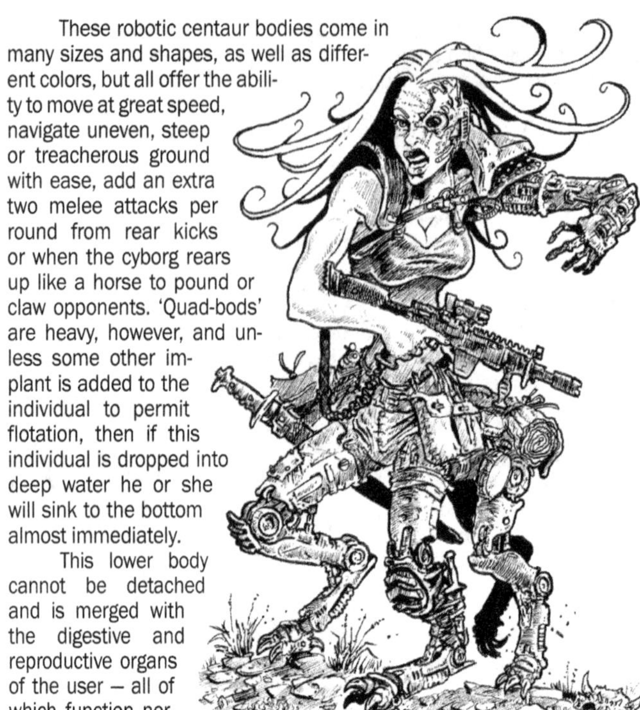

This lower body cannot be detached and is merged with the digestive and reproductive organs of the user — all of which function normally. The appearance drop to human fitted with one of these four-legged units -4+1d4 APP.

The kick or claw attack of the front legs is not affected by the organic portion of the body's strength score, however, these front legs can be used in conjunction with the brawling or martial arts skill, or a weapon expert skill can instead be applied to them. These two metal appendages always make 1 attack each per round until 7th rank, and then two attacks each per round thereafter.

The following tables present random details to generate unique quadrupedal lower bodies. With these tables, the character's weight, defense value bonus, movement, attacks and additional features can quickly be established:



**1. Mastiff Sized** Add 100kg +3d6+10 endurance points, Kick or claw SV +5/ DMG 1d6+1 each, plus add 30cm height.

**2-6. Lion Sized**** Add 150 kg +3d6+30 endurance points, Kick or claw SV +7/ DMG 2d6+2 each, plus add 40cm height.

**7-9. Grizzly Sized** Add 200 kg +3d6+50 endurance points, Kick or claw SV +10/ DMG 3d6+2each, plus add 60cm height.

**10. Horse sized** Add 400 kg +3d6+70 endurance points, Kick or claw SV +15/ DMG 4d6+4 each, plus add 80cm height.

** Since this character is missing their living legs, they start at 40+2d10kg weight for females and 65+2d10kg weight for males*
***This is the size pictured in the illustration on this page.*



**1. None, just rags and scraps of plastic.** No color roll needed. DV -0, however, reduce weight by -20% and increase movement by +2m per round. To upgrade to plastic, it will cost 100sp, or scrap metal, 300sp.

**2-5. Thick Plastic** Improve character's DV -10.

**6,7. Scrap metal** Improve character's DV -20, add 30kg weight and reduce movement by -1m.

**8,9. Iron Clad** Improve character's DV -30, add 60kg weight and reduce movement by -2m.

**10. Composite Relic Armor** Improve character's DV -40, add 20kg weight. No movement penalty.

** Animal barding can be purchased to add additional protection. See the section on animal armor on page 226 the hub rules.*



**1.** Visibility suit: bright orange and neon yellow. Going unseen is not in the cards for this character.

**2.** Snow white

**3.** Blood red

**4.** Gloss black

**5.** Dark blue with the word 'Police' written on the sides and rump.

**6.** Drab, grays, browns and rust colors.

**7.** Desert tan

**8.** Charcoal gray

**9.** Urban gray, black and concrete dust urban camo

**10.** Woodland camouflage



**1. Stubby and strong** -1m movement, add 75cm height, extra thick and adding +2 damage per kick or claw swipe.

**2-7. Normal length** Add 60cm height.

**8,9. Long** Add 1 meter height and +2m per round increase to movement.

**10. Normal but extendable** to 3 meters height to add +5m speed or allow operator to peer over tall objects, reach higher ledges or wade through streams, mild acid and other liquids. Takes 10 rounds to complete full extension.



**01-50.** No special feature.

**51-55.** Back mounted, pop out rocket launcher. This launcher once held up to 10 battle rockets (either normal or advanced) but at the time of character creation this cyborg starts with 0 to 5 (1d6 minus 1) battle rockets.

**56-60.** Fold out survival shelter. This unit's back can be opened and a geodesic dome of ultra thin, yet remarkably tough, tan colored foil can be built around the cyborg in a 4m radius with a 3m height. This half dome will resist junk and acid storms, high winds, radiation and a myriad of other perils, all while providing filtration and shelter to this character and about 6 man sized companions within the cramped confines. Several clear windows are located at six locations in the dome.

To fold up and stow this enclosure takes 10 +1d10 minutes. Anything that wants to rip through this metallic, high tech looking shelter can do so with relative ease, since a 3m tall by 2m wide section has a DV of -10 and can only take 20 points of damage before being shredded.

Repairs to a ripped dome are costly and will take 5+1d30 days at a price of 100+1d100sp. This dome can be fully detached from the back of the cyborg should he or she need to leave it, via a latching, triangular doorway in the enclosure's wall. A small chimney vent is included in the top to facilities small venting of smoke from cook fires within.

**61-65.** Water storage and filtration system inside: Can treat filthy, polluted water at a rate of 1 liter per half hour. Can hold 50 liters of drinkable water in its belly tanks. Comes with a tap spigot at rear end.

**66-70.** Detachable lower body. This cyborg can detach the lower, quadrupedal body in 2 rounds if in an emergency (such as drowning) and pull themself along the ground by their arms, a long trail of connector cables dragging behind from the stumps of what were the character's legs. Crawling in this fashion is done at 1 meter per round, but would allow the character to crawl into small crevices or climb to evade some peril. Reconnecting to the dormant lower body is a slower process, however, and will take 10+1d20 minutes to achieve.

**71-75.** Solar generator unit, as per the relic on page 198 of the hub rules. This generator can charge the cyborg itself but also has external slots of assorted power cells. Can charge while on the move.

**76-80.** Fold out manipulator arm, as per the implant from page 87 of the hub rules.

**81-88.** Fold out stretcher and stabilizing straps to hold a wounded comrade. Comes complete with built-in field medical kit which this cyborg can manually setup to treat a patient. The field medical kit relic is described on page 199 of the TME hub rules.

**89-95.** Retractable velociraptor claw on each front leg. Improve strike value +5 inflicting an extra +2d6 damage.

**96-99.** Back mounted shoulder turret, as per implant #41 on page 91 of the hub rules.

**00.** Two features from this listing. Roll 1d100 +50 but re-roll this result or duplicated results.

## Robotic Serpentine Body 81

Power Source: **power cell in upper back of tail**
Power Duration: **6 months**    Movement Rate: **+3m**
Defense Value bonus: **-10**    Strike Value: **+5 SV**
Damage: **1d20+5 stun or lethal as a club. Constrict 1d10**

From the hips down, this cyborg's legs were replaced by a robotic, steel plated snake body. The tail is 2.5m long, adds 70kg weight to the operator, increases movement rate by +3 meters per round, and improves overall defense value by -10 DV. It can be used as an extra melee attack to either bludgeon opponents, or wrap about (on a successful strike) one man sized or smaller target and begin to constrict them. A constricted target takes an automatic 1d10 damage per round until the victim is either killed or made unconsciousness, or merely restrained. A target held by this tale is allowed an agility based type D hazard check to get their arms up above the metal coils to fight back even while their waist is encircled. Likewise, a very strong constricted or grappled victim can try to use brute force to uncoil itself, which requires a minimum strength of 30 and then the held person or beast must make a type E strength based hazard check per round to get free. A held target can be attacked at +20 strike value by this cyborg or its allies

When used as a club or whip-like attack, the 1d20+5 damage is fixed and the user's physical strength score does not lower or heighten this damage — however if the weapon expert skill is applied to this implant, both SV and DMG modifiers can be added to its combat effectiveness.

This tail is heavy and if the cyborg is forced into deep water, he or she will likely drown unless using a free hand to un-clamp and detach the snake body — possibly of forever losing the unit. When stationary, this body can assist the operator in rising an extra 2 meters in height to either stay above the water's surface or peer over obstacles, or reach higher ledges. While the character can go up stairs and over even very rough terrain with ease, this tail adds nothing to their climbing ability.

The snake body can detach in two rounds, but takes 10 minutes to reconnect to the metallic receiver that has been surgically bolted to the user's hip sockets and spinal plug. When not wearing the snake body, the legless character can either use a different lower body, or drag themselves around at 2 meters per round. While day-to-day washroom habits and amatory activities can be conducted wearing the snake body, it isn't altogether convenient.

This snake body, which reduces the character's appearance score by -2d4 APP, is made of stainless steel. However, each occurrence has a different coloration: **roll 1d10** at character generation or discovery: **1,2.** Rusted metal. / **3.** Gleaming nickel plated / **4.** Flat black /**5.** Desert digi-camo print / **6.** Olive drab green / **7.** Diamond back rattlesnake pattern / **8.** Coral snake color pattern / **9.** Matt white upper and flat black belly scales / **10.** Blood red.

## Snorkel 82

Power Source: **Mini power cell in neck compartment next to snorkel hatch**
Power Duration: **6 years**

From a hidden panel at the back of the neck, this cyborg can merely think of this implant and have it deploy a dark gray breathing hose. The telescopic, somewhat flexible shaft extends 5cm out from the cyborg's neck and can be bent up along the user's head 30cm, or to the back, side or front to accommodate different respiration needs. This snorkel is connected directly to the user's windpipe. The cyborg can potentially stay submerged and breath through this hose so long as his or her depth doesn't exceed ten centimeters beyond their height, although old tubes and lawn hoses can be attached to the unit that will extend the distance through which this character can breathe, to a maximum of ten meters. This hose is rigid and doesn't make an effective tentacle, whip or rope and will yank free if tugged on too hard (it can take 15 END damage before being ruined). Be-

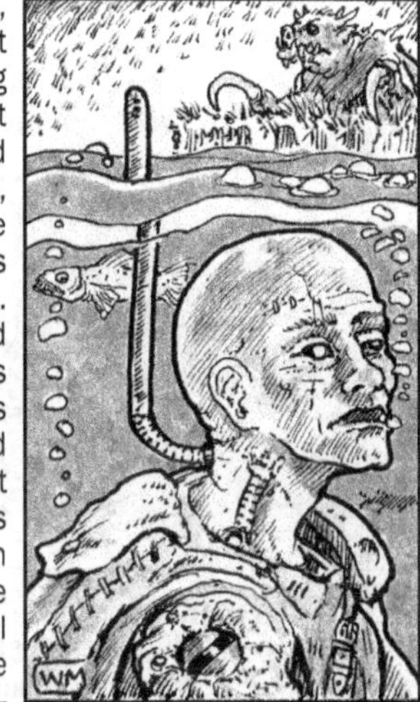

sides using this snorkel to stay submerged in water, the user can also extend it up from soil, sand, mud or other substances, lay on his or her side, and evade detection where it would otherwise be impossible.

A small screen can be wired over the opening to keep out dust or bugs, and allow the cyborg to breathe while exposed to dust storms or clouds of other airborne particles. Because air intake is restricted, so too is the amount of oxygen available to the user, therefore, the operator can only move at half rate while using this implant.

The battery compartment and snorkel port hole appear as a series of scars and roughly flesh colored bump and plug hole. While small, these imperfections reduce the cyborg's appearance by 1 trait point.

## Solar Nutrient Converter 83

Power Source: **power cell**
Power Duration: **4 years**

Similar to an atmospheric hydro converter (implant 5 found on page 85 of the TME hub rules), this remarkable relic attachment uses a variant of plant-like artificial photosynthesis to convert sunlight into nutrition energy. When the cyborg wills it, a small, flesh colored concealment panel opens on their upper back and an alloy rod and ultra fine, lightweight, rectangular panel unfolds and auto-aligns toward the sun.

For every hour of direct sunlight, this unit will covert sunlight and a small degree of atmospheric water, into one meal worth of bare minimum life sustaining nutrition. Should the user be able to perch some place sunny for 6 or more hours, this unit will provide ample nutrition to the character — although one's stomach is still empty and the instinctual cravings for traditional food persist. Unlike the water converter mentioned above, there is no drain hose or way of extracting nutrition from this complicated, digestive tract connected device in order to share food with others. One power cell will allow the continuous daily operation of this implant for 4 years.

This character's back has a slight bump and noticeable scars, and so reduce appearance by -1d4 trait points.

## Sound Dampening Field [84]
Power Source: **mini power cell at base of skull**
Power Duration: **100, twenty round (1 minute) uses per mini cell**

Just behind each ear on this cyborg are a series of three black disc shaped audio emitters. When activated, these small ports generate multi-wave sound frequencies that negate any normal sounds of walking, rustling, fidgeting, breathing, whispers or other normally low noises within a 3 meter radius. This allows the user of this field better odds at silent walking or silent action on the stealth table shown on page 51 of the hub rules. For those within the 3m radius, sound is warped, and yet a cluster of people could converse in low conversational tones, use a communicator, or perform some task that involves noise with a reduced chance of being heard by those beyond this radius. Any sound beyond normal conversation volume levels will be detected, however, so if somebody using this implant drops a wrench on a concrete floor or steps on a glass bottle, or makes any other sort of noise, it will carry out of the field, although muffled.

To use this implant, which will yield 100, one minute applications per mini power cell, the operator within the field must use the stealth table on page 56 of the hub rules. He or she gains +3 skill points in 'silent action' when this implant is activated. Any stealth skill points the character, or its companions, already has are stacked with this +3 bonus for the duration of the field's use.

The emitter nodes behind this character's ears are easy to hide behind one's hair, and in themselves look somewhat decorative and thus drop the character's appearance by only -1 point.

## Speed Assist Rotors [85]
Power Source: **2 power cells in upper back**
Power Duration: **10 hours per 2 power cells**
Defense Value: **-10**
Movement Bonus when Deployed: **+6m per round**

This cyborg has been fitted with fold out, 30cm diameter, high velocity disc enclosed helicopter rotors that are mounted on the subject's shoulder blades. When a burst of speed, or lift is needed, they pop out in 1 round. By way of nervous system controlled servo motors, they swivel to adjust to the operator's desired course.

While not powerful enough to provide true flight, these powerful motors will propel the user forward, backward or from side to side with incredible responsiveness, adding -10 defense value to the user when avoiding incoming fire or melee attacks, but so too, add propulsion assistance to the legs to add +6m move- ment to the character as he or she runs, skims the ground,

leaps obstacles up to 1 meter off the ground and can make a jump of 6m distance over a gully, between rooftops or other crevices when needed.

If this cyborg falls from a great height, these rotors will automatically activate if power is sufficient within the individual, and somewhat slow the decent so that any fall damage is reduced by half.

Power hungry, these rotors use a separate standard power cell each, the battery built into the back of the wearer in concealed compartments. These two cells will allow for 10 hours of continuous operation before the pair requires a recharge. If only one battery is used, the user cannot control the flight and gets only a -5 DV bonus and +2 movement, however for every round of travel, there is a 1 in 6 chance that a different direction happens instead, which could lead to a crash or impact with comrades, opponents, or solid objects.

Should the cyborg have other built in or strapped-on power supplies or generation systems, then these cells will be connected to those powering the rotors and recharge them. This cyborg's back shows considerable evidence of the surgeries involved during the installation of these two fold out rotor disks, therefore reduce the individual's appearance by -5+1d4 APP.

## Subcutaneous Plating [86]
Power Source: **nil**

Whoever customized this individual tried to conceal the fact that the person's body, limbs and head were up-armored. Hundreds of hidden alloy plates — many of which articulate just beneath the skin — protect this cyborg, especially over vulnerable points in the body and head. Only an attentive onlooker viewing a mostly disrobed covert plated cyborg will notice the subtle rigidness in the limb, flex of underlying plates, and solidity of the enhanced being's flesh, yet these factors do not reduce the subject's appearance trait.

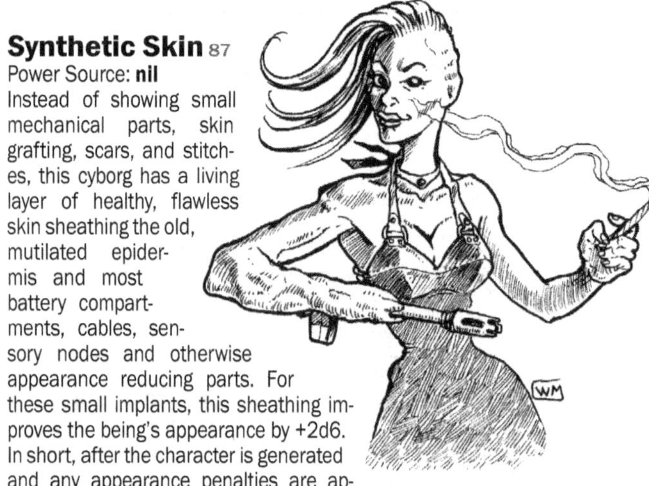

This armor cladding is heavy, however, and adds 10kg weight, reduces the cyborg's movement rate by -0.25m, but improves the user's defense value by -20 and the fist or kick injury from this individual inflicts an extra 1d6 damage (base punch damage now 2d6).

## Synthetic Skin [87]
Power Source: **nil**

Instead of showing small mechanical parts, skin grafting, scars, and stitches, this cyborg has a living layer of healthy, flawless skin sheathing the old, mutilated epidermis and most battery compartments, cables, sensory nodes and otherwise appearance reducing parts. For these small implants, this sheathing improves the being's appearance by +2d6. In short, after the character is generated and any appearance penalties are applied, add +2d6 APP to bring up and hopefully reduce these setbacks.

Of course, some large or needfully exposed implants, such as a weapon arm, snake body, chopper-borg back compartment, shoulder turret, crab pincer, tracked locomotion, walker legs, fold out manipulator arm, hover jets and similar bulky attachments can not be covered, yet still much of the scar tissue is hidden and the APP bonus still applies.

For many implants, however, especially those that pop out of a hidden compartment, these can both be concealed and so hide the cyborg's augmented nature from unfriendly eyes. Should the cyborg have no externally exposed implants, then he or she is immune to electromagnetic or electrical damage as a machine, and instead is treated as a regular living being. For example, incoming mutational attacks such as doom sphere, electromagnetic pulse, devastator pulse, electrical pulse, stun ray, and similar, as well as various relic weapons and implants which discharge similar extra harm to machines and robots and cyborgs, also do only normal damage as if this person was fully organic.

Optical implant eyes and ear caps can also be sheathed in this bio-replicated, energy resistant skin, whereas the eye itself has been miniaturized and, while it might give off light or be of an unnatural color, it has a clear flap of synthetic skin over it and looks like a living eye, complete with blinking eyelid.

As soon as an enclosed implant is exposed, and the protective sheathing around the cyborg opened, all protection from the above noted mutations and attack modes is momentarily lost.

## Vehicle Control Module 88
Power Source: **mini power cell in abdomen**          Power Duration: **5 years**
This remarkable implant allows the cyborg to plug a 1m long patch cable into a computer station, dashboard, cockpit controls, or similar access port to gain access to the on-board computer of an ancient vehicle — assuming that there isn't some security measures in place to lock out or incinerate compromised controls.

Hacking into a secured computer system requires the individual to have the computer technician skill. Once in, or if no layers of protection are active, this operator can quickly determine the diagnostic readouts of the machine in question, establish the condition of the vehicle, fuel needs and current fuel amount, destination logs, cargo log, weapon load-out, needed repairs, and other important details.

If this cyborg also has either the driver or pilot skill, the cyborg can drive the vehicle with its 'mind' as well as fire all turrets, monitor life support, navigation, communications, vid cameras and more. Without the driving or pilot skill, he or she can still start up and attempt to drive or fly the craft, but likely crash it. See table TME1-27 in the hub rules for the driving skill, page TME-37, or the table TME 1-41 on page TME-49 for the pilot skill.

The patch cable, and mini power cell battery holder, are stowed in an abdomen enclosed housing with a false skin flap over the end of the cable, which completely hides it when not in use. Internally, the cable goes to a small control unit with a subcutaneous conduit wire connected to the spine and brain stem module typical of all cyborgs, connecting the user's visual and auditory inputs directly to the brain. While operating or merely plugged into a vehicle to access its systems, the cyborg cannot control any other implants, but can use hand-held devices or mutations should the operator be a mutorg.

## Vocal Mimicry Modulator
*by Brandon Goeringer* 89
Power Source: **mini power cell in armpit enclosure**
Power Duration: **2 years**

This implant allows for the cyborg to reproduce sounds previously heard, including other people's voices. Located in the larynx and wired to the brain, this implant is uncanny in its reproduction of voices, animal calls, and any other sounds that may be distinguished. The mimicry can even fool electronic security voice passwords 93% of the time. A person has to make a type J PER based HC to hear a difference in the voice of a mimicked loved one.

The volume is the same as the normal vocal range of the cyborg.

## Weapon Arm Set 2 90
Power Source: **power cell at weapon arm's shoulde**r
Power Duration: **1 year**
The following random selection of weapon arms includes those listed on page 92 of the hub rules along with all the new relic weapons from this book. Where this implant differs from the hub rules version is that many cyborgs now feature a fold away or 'muzzle-palm' equipped mechanical hand. For each occurrence of weapon arm, there is a 50% chance that such a hand is present, and if so, see implant number #69, roll 8,9 on page 339 of this book.

The power cell, noted as the unit's power source, does not provide power to any mounted energy weapon, but facilitates the pistons, hydraulics and servo motors which allow mobility to the arm. These arms are connected directly to the operator's brain and spinal cord, sometimes to any added optical implant for targeting, too, and cannot be detached and strapped to a rebuilt character type to serve the same function, although most weapon systems can be removed, given standard triggers, stocks and grips to make them into more standard, carried weapons.

Weapon arms are not easily swappable for other systems, except for the detachable lower arm implant from page 86 of the hub rules. A cybernetic technician, however, can sometimes alter the fittings and receiver ends of a cyborg's weapon arm to make it accept different weapons.

Almost every weapon arm is fitted to the cyborg's non-dominant arm — unless a limb was lost and the replacement must go on the user's dominant arm. A system on the non-dominant side of the operator does not suffer the standard off-hand -20 SV penalty as usual, however, so the use of another weapon at the same time in the opposite arm is awkward, and simultaneous use incurs this -20 SV penalty to the weapon arm.

Related to these augmented parts is the implant of dual-weapon arm on page 336 of this book. Dual arms feature a ranged and a melee weapon and the high potential for a mechanical hand.

The ranged weapon from that selection is rolled on the following table, but the melee feature is randomly determined on a table shown in the dual weapon arm listing. If this character indeed has a dual weapon arm with 1 melee weapon, then re-roll any melee weapon on the following table when determining the character's ranged weapon. Of course, the weapon arm implant can occur more than once on a character at character generation, and so dual or even triple mounted weapon arms can occur with all such augmented weapons appearing on one limb to allow the operator a more regular opposite arm.

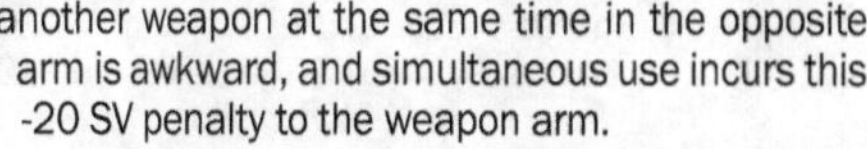

## Table-XR-212/ Weapon Present on Cyborg

| 1d100 | Weapon | Power or Ammo | Source Book / Page |
|---|---|---|---|
| 01,02. | Razor sword | nil | Hub Rules / stats page 100, write-up on page 186 |
| 03,04. | Spring-spike | nil | Hub Rules / stats page 100, write-up on page 186 |
| 05,06. | Discsaw | 1d4 power cells | Hub Rules / stats page 100, write-up on page 186 |
| 07-11. | Chainsaw | 1d4 power cells | Hub Rules / stats page 100, write-up on page 186 |
| 12,13. | Stun stick | 1d6 mini power cells | Hub Rules / stats page 100, write-up on page 189 |
| 14,15. | Chainsword | 1d6 power cells | Expansion Rules / stats page 401, write-up page 405 |
| 16. | Devastator rod | 1d6 power cells | Expansion Rules / stats page 401, write-up on page 407 |
| 17,18. | Laser sword | 1d6 power cells | Hub Rules / stats page 100, write-up on page 190 |
| 19. | Laser torch | 1d4 power cells | Hub Rules / stats page 100, write-up on page 189 |
| 20. | Harpoon gun, 4 barrels** | Can fire all or 1 per round, has spare 6+3d6 shafts in pack | Hub Rules / stats page 100, write-up on page 186 |
| 21. | Advanced laser pistol MK I | 1d6 power cells | Expansion Rules / stats page 401, write-up on page 408 |
| 22. | Mk2 laser sword | 1d4 power cells | Expansion Rules / stats page 401, write-up page 405 |
| 23,24. | 22 caliber semi auto rifle | drum mag* with 1d100 .22 rounds | Expansion Rules / stats page 100, write-up page187 |
| 25-28. | Stun pistol | 1d6 power cells | Hub Rules / stats page 100, write-up on page 189 |
| 29,30. | Nerve disruptor baton | 1d4 power cells | Expansion Rules / stats page 401, write-up on page 407 |
| 31-33. | Assault shotgun | 1d2 full 40 round drums plus d20 spare shells | Hub Rules / stats page 100, write-up on page 188 |
| 34-38. | Sniper rifle | 1d2 full clips and d20 high caliber rifle (HCR) rounds | Hub Rules / stats page 100, write-up on page 188 |
| 39. | Advanced sniper rifle | 1 full 24 rnd mag and 1 spare with 1d6 high caliber rifle (HCR) rounds | Expansion Rules / stats page 401, write-up on page 410 |
| 40-46 | Sub-machine gun | 1d2 full 40 rnd clips plus d100 pistol rounds | Hub Rules / stats page 100, write-up on page 188 |
| 47-55. | Assault rifle | 1d3 full clips plus d100 rifle rounds | Hub Rules / stats page 100, write-up on page 188 |
| 56. | Energy Spear | 1d6+1 power cells | Expansion Rules / stats page 401, write-up on page 405 |
| 57-60. | Assault rifle | Belt fed with ammo pack containing 100+2d20 rifle rounds | Hub Rules / stats page 100, write-up on page 188 |
| 61-63. | Heavy assault rifle | Drum mag has 60 HC round capacity, comes with 1d3 mags and total of 40+1d100 HC rounds | Expansion Rules / stats page 401, write-up on page 409 |
| 64-66 | Pulse rifle | 1d6+1 power cells | Hub Rules / stats page 100, write-up on page 190 |
| 67. | Sonic immobilizer rifle | 1d6 power cells | Expansion Rules / stats page 401, write-up on page 407 |
| 68. | Pulse rifle | Power pack (250 bursts) | Hub Rules / stats page 100, write-up on page 190 |
| 69. | Heavy pulse rifle | 1d6+1 power cells | Hub Rules / stats page 100, write-up on page 186 |
| 70,71. | Rocket launcher | 2d6 battle rockets | Hub Rules / stats page 100, write-up on page 189 |
| 72,73. | Flame unit | 1d6+1 canisters | Hub Rules / stats page 100, write-up on page 189 |
| 74. | Rocket pistol | 4d6 chase rockets*** | Expansion Rules / stats page 401, write-up on page 408 |
| 75. | Rocket carbine | 4d6 chase rockets*** | Expansion Rules / stats page 401, write-up on page 408 |
| 76. | Chain gun | 1 full 200 rnd. drum and d100 spare rifle rounds | Hub Rules / stats page 100, write-up on page 188 |
| 77,78. | Chain gun | Belt fed, ammo pack (100+3d100 rifle rounds) | Hub Rules / stats page 100, write-up on page 188 |
| 79. | Fifty caliber sniper rifle | Comes with 1 special 30 round drum magazine but also accepts standard 10 shot .50 cal mags. Has 20+1d10 .50 cal rounds | Hub Rules / stats page 100, write-up on page 188 |
| 80,81. | Heavy machine gun | 1 full 100 rnd. drum + d100 HCR rounds | Hub Rules / stats page 100, write-up on page 188 |
| 82,83. | Heavy machine gun | Belt fed pack (100+d100 HCR rounds) | Hub Rules / stats page 100, write-up on page 188 |
| 84-86. | Laser carbine | 1d6+1 power cells | Hub Rules / stats page 100, write-up on page 190 |
| 87. | Lightning emitter | 1d6+1 power cells | Expansion Rules / stats page 402, write-up on page 412 |
| 88,89. | Heavy laser carbine | 1d6+1 power cells | Hub Rules / stats page 100, write-up on page 190 |
| 90. | Laser sniper rifle | 1d6 power cells | Expansion Rules / stats page 401, write-up on page 410 |
| 91,92. | Stun rifle | 1d6 power cells | Expansion Rules / stats page 401, write-up on page 406 |
| 93. | Heavy stun emitter | 1d6 power cells | Expansion Rules / stats page 401, write-up on page 406 |
| 94. | Mk2 Laser carbine | 1d6 power cells | Expansion Rules / stats page 401, write-up on page 410 |
| 95. | Particle beam rifle | 1d6 power cells | Expansion Rules / stats page 402, write-up page 413 |
| 96,97. | EM emitter rifle | 1d6 power cells | Expansion Rules / stats page 401, write-up page 407 |
| 98. | Mk3 laser carbine | 1d6 power cells | Expansion Rules / stats page 401, write-up on page 410 |
| 99. | Mk4 laser carbine | 1d6 power cells | Expansion Rules / stats page 401, write-up on page 410 |
| 00. | Light laser cannon | Power pack (modified with cyborg harness, counter balanced and lighter (50kg) and yields 50 shots | Hub Rules / stats page 100, write-up on page 190 |

* This magazine has a maximum capacity of 100 rounds
** This variant and can fire between one and four harpoons in one round. Takes 2 rounds to reload each harpoon. Spring powered.
***Chase rockets described on page 419 of this book.

## Welding Torch 91

Power Source: **Ethanol fuel, 2 liters (2000 ml) max capacity.**
Power Duration: **Welding Mode 10ml per round/ Flame thrower mode 100ml per round**
Range: **Welding mode 10cm/ flame thrower mode 4 meters**
Strike Value: **Welding mode +33/ Flame thrower mode +13**
Damage: **Welding mode: DMG 4d6, plus hits will burn for 1d6 rounds and 1d6 DMG per round/ Flame thrower mode: DMG 2d6 on initial impact, and if the target is flammable, it will burn for 1d6 rounds for 1d6 damage per round.**
Weight added: **4kg, plus 1kg per liter of fuel**

This is a traditional, non-laser, metal cutting and welding torch that instead of being connected to a mechanized replacement arm is instead attached to the cyborg's hip with a pistol grip dispenser and retractable 2 meter long hose fused to the operator's body. An internally stowed pressure cannister and regulator is housed in the torso. A small flap covered plug and fill nozzle allows for access for ethanol fuel, which, while not an ideal propellant, does work after oxygen is simultaneously fed into the mix.

The cyborg can grab the grip and use the simple trigger to expel a jet of either highly concentrated 10cm long metal cutting flame, or else spend a round and use a free hand to adjust and widen the nozzle to turn this unit into an inefficient yet dangerous short range flame thrower. In flame thrower mode this unit has a range of 4 meters, SV +13, damage from direct flame burst is 2d6, however if the target is wearing flammable attire or gear, it will ignite and burn thereafter for 1d6 rounds and suffer 1d6 damage per round. If splashed with 2 or more liters of water, this flame can be snuffed out.

As a welding torch, the concentrated flame can cut through all flesh and bone, clothing and plastics with ease, and even cut most metals as a melee range attack at strike value +33 doing 4d6 damage. If a hit occurs, and the substance impacted is flammable, including clothing and fur, the target will burn for 1d6 rounds and suffer 1d6 damage per round unless the flame is doused as noted above.

The internal cannister for this unit is relatively small and can only carry and compress 2 liters of liquid propellant, or 2000ml. During flame thrower attacks, it will burn through 100ml per round, but only 10ml per round as a welding torch.

One of the most common uses for this tool is to cut through ancient metal doors and hatches, although starting campfires, illumination, and warding off wild animals are also common applications. When not in use, the 2m long hose auto coils into the cyborg's lower abdomen while the pistol gripped nozzle snaps tight against the body — and is often folded and concealed into the user's belt. Of note, if proper cleaning is conducted, the tank and hose could be switched over to dispense drinking water or the user's favorite beverage of choice.

While the refill port has a sythi-skin flap and can go unseen, the nozzle itself is somewhat unsightly if the cyborg is seen unclothed, and only in those circumstances suffers a -1d4+1 appearance drop. If the nozzle is detached, only the end of the hose is revealed, however, and looks like a small metal bolt with only a -2 APP penalty.

The character will start game play with a full internal tank and a 4 in 6 chance of a spare plastic 4 liter jug of additional ethanol fuel. This fuel can be purchased in most major towns at a cost of 1d20+2d20sp per liter — if available at all (32% chance that 2d6 liters are for sale).

## Wheel Deployment 92

Power Source: **1 power cell in calf of each leg**
Power Duration: **40 hours each**
Movement: **12m level ground, 6m uphill, 18m downhill**
Mishap Chance on rough ground, per round: **1 in 20**
Mishap Hazard Check: **Type C agility based HC to avoid crash**
Crash Outcome: **Treat as attack SV 01-60, DMG 1d12 stun and 1d6 lethal**

This cyborg's feet and ankles have been augmented with alloy rimmed, discreet plastic wheels. When desired, the operator unlocks a series of three tires from the soles of his or her feet, often through the operator's custom made, bulky combat boots or hiking shoes made for this purpose. These small in-line tires allow the cyborg to travel at great speed for prolonged periods of time, although the surface must be smooth.

In many respects, these wheeled leg enhancements are like old world in-line roller skates, except that they are powered with one power cell loaded into a hidden calf compartment in each leg. The pair of power cells will provide 40 hours of operation per charge, and allow the operator to travel at a speed of 12 meter per round on level ground, 6m up hill, or 18m down hill.

For operation on dirt tracks, cracked concrete, and old city sidewalks, there is a 1 in 20 chance per round of hitting a bump, crack, cable, or root which could cause a terrible fall. For every instance of a potential mishap on rough ground, the user must make a Type C agility based hazard check or take a tumble. Treat this crash as an attack whereby the operator's armor plays a big role if damage is taken or not. SV 01-60, damage 1d12 stun and 1d6 lethal. After a crash, the user takes 2 round to recover, get on their feet and underway again.

As according to the strike value modifiers tables on page TME-105, there is a -10 SV penalty to fire while moving on these wheels, but so too, ranged attacks that target this cyborg suffer a -15 SV penalty.

# Expanded Character Outfitting

## Rapid Fire Character Outfitting System

This is one of two all-new, alternate methods for establishing a new player character's starting possessions, the other, Equipment Packs, is far faster but offers fewer details.

This system looks huge, perhaps even complicated, but only involves rolling a die once or more on each of the following tables. The dice used, and any modifier, are based on a character's outfitting code, which is included with their pre-game caste. A game master can also use these tables to quickly determine what a non-player character carries, or what might be discovered on a dead body.

Use the same dice and any modifiers on each of the following tables to establish the arms, armor, clothing, gear, money, food, water and other equipment and circumstances of your new excavator, and record the results on your character sheet, although for a few character types, duplicate rolls on the same table, or alternate tables are used based on the following character type criteria:

- **Androids** get TWO rolls on the **Power Supplies table** instead of **Food or Water**
- **Plantoids** substitute their **Food** roll for an extra **Water** roll
- **Cyborgs and Vat-Brains** Get one bonus roll on the **Power Supplies table**

| List of Outfitting Tables | Page |
|---|---|
| Food Rations | 350 |
| Water | 351 |
| Carrying Gear | 352 |
| Adventure Gear | 353 |
| Footwear | 354 |
| Clothing | 354 |
| Money | 355 |
| Armor | 355 |
| Helmet | 356 |
| Backup Weapon | 356 |
| Melee Weapon | 357 |
| Ranged Weapon | 357 |
| Illumination | 358 |
| Fire Starting | 358 |
| Power Supplies | 358 |
| Assorted Item or Circumstance | 358 |

## Table XR-213 / Rapid Fire Starting Arms and Armor by Outfitting Code

| Category | Code | Dice Used* |
|---|---|---|
| Escaped | ESC | 1d10 |
| Impoverished | IM | 1d20 |
| Poor | PR | 2d20 |
| Modest | MO | 1d100 |
| Well Equipped | WE | 1d100+10 |
| Fully Armed | FA | 1d100+20 |
| Wealthy Adventurer | WA | 1d100+30 |

*Most of the following outfitting tables allow for only 1 roll, however a few call for more, such as 1d2, 1d3, 1d6, or 1d6+1 rolls.*

## Food Rations *Roll 1 time*

**1.** Nothing whatsoever, and in fact, you are half starved and depleted by -1d10 endurance points from hunger.
**2.** Small pouch filled with wriggling grubs and worms.
**3.** Day old rat.
**4.** Half of a crusty loaf of bread, moldy.
**5.** Pouch of rock hard dried fruit.
**6.** One strip of dried meat, hairs still attached.
**7.** Small pouch of oats, crawling with weevils.
**8.** Bloated, finger-length larva of some bug in a bag. It hisses when jostled.
**9.** The remains of some biscuits and dried meat in a bag, just crumbs now, but delicious.
**10.** 1 day of rations: Hard biscuits, nuts, dried fruit, pepperoni and firm cheese.
**11,12.** 1d6 days of rations, plus a bag of dried apple slices, raisins and almonds.
**13,14.** 2d6 days of rations, although rodents and roaches have been at them recently.
**15,16.** 2d6 day's rations, but they got wet and have started to mold.
**17,18.** A half dead chicken hanging by a string at your belt.
**19-23.** A loaf of bread in a burlap sack.
**24,25.** A bag of 3d6 worm riddled apples in a sack.
**26-30.** A pouch of dried fruit and nuts, enough to 3 days rations.
**31,32.** 1d3 BBQ rats on a stick; dried, salted and will stay eatable for another 3 days.
**33,34.** An old coffee can on a string. Inside, and beneath the snap-on plastic lid are 800 grams worth of roasted oat balls, worth about 3 days rations.
**35,36.** A wax paper wrapped handful of dried, smoked minnows, about 2 days of rations worth.
**37,38.** A stained leather pouch containing 3d6 dried pig's ears. Crunchy, greasy, and hard to swallow, but each 3 ears is sufficient for 1 days ration.
**39,40.** Glass jar with a sealed lid filled with a dozen pickles. 1 days ration.
**41,42.** French style baguette bread, baked 1d8 days ago.
**43,44.** Plastic zippy bag containing 10+1d10 sun dried apricots.
**45,46.** Leather hip pouch containing 1d6+1 days rations and a handful of candied grasshoppers.
**47,48.** 1d6 days rations and a wax paper wrapped turkey drumstick baked a few days ago and salted to preserve it for a few more days.
**49,50.** 1d6 days of rations and an ancient pack of chewing gum. Gum is hard as rock at first, but after sufficient, moist mastication can become workable.
**51,52.** 1d6 days rations plus a 15cm long, wax paper wrapped, recently made chocolate bar worth 10+1d10 silver pieces.
**53,54.** 1d8 days of rations plus a pouch filled with dried berries and nuts counted as another 1d4 days food.
**55,56.** 2d6 days rations, plus a bundle of wax paper wrapped, smoked chicken strips.
**57,58.** 3d6 days worth of the driest, toughest, most bland and unpalatable wheat cakes you've ever tasted. Cannot be consumed without water.
**59,60.** 2d6 days rations and a pouch of sun-dried tomatoes.
**61,62.** 3d6 days worth of unspecified bush meat. Whoever sold it to you, or you stole it from, swore it is not human or skullock, but couldn't rightly say what beast it came from.
**63,64.** A plump, 1+1d4kg little pig tied by its feet to your belt. The thing wears a gag about its wet muzzle otherwise it squeals like a sonuvabitch and will attract attention from as far as a half kilometer away.
**65,66.** 1d6 days rations and a large, zippy bag filled with fermented plums and cherries that you were told would turn into wine, eventually. Fruit flies surround you.

**67,68.** Shoulder satchel with 2d6 days rations, cast iron frying pan, wooden pancake flipper, flint and steel, and small bottle of vegetable oil.

**69,70.** 3d6 days rations in a leather sack with shoulder rope.

**71,72.** 2d6 days rations, an old cooking pot with lid, flint and steel, assorted spices, and cooking fat.

**73-75.** Hip pouch containing 10+1d10 days of specialty field rations, each individually wrapped in wax paper.

**76-78.** Shoulder satchel loaded with 4d6 neatly packed days rations, and a 500ml bottle of vodka.

**79-81.** 3d6 days rations, flint and steel, cooking oil, fry pan and flipper, and a dozen assorted cheeses wrapped in wax paper, all contained in a satchel.

**82-84.** 10+2d10 days rations carefully packed in an insulated old shopping bag and rolled in a fur lined blanket with shoulder straps.

**85-87.** 3d6 days rations in a shoulder bag, plus a flint and steel, frying pan, cooking oil and brick of dried bacon (1.5kg).

**88-90.** 10+1d10 days rations, 1d3 baguettes, two plastic wine glasses and a 750ml bottle of red wine.

**91-93.** 2d6 days rations in a hip pouch plus a wooden cage containing 1d4 live ducks and 1d6 live chickens. They make a helluva lot of noise.

**94-96.** A satchel containing 3d6 days rations, and an assortment of dried and smoked meats, cheese, dried fruit, nuts and strips of delicate smoked trout.

**97-99.** A relic wicker picnic basket containing 6 plates, forks, spoons and butter knives, along with 1d4 ancient MREs and 10+1d10 days rations, a jar of jam, a loaf of fresh bread, a bottle of red wine, two plastic wine glasses, and an assortment of fancy cheese, dried fruits and candies. MREs described on page 436.

**100-103.** A shoulder strap supported, bulky mail carrier's bag filled with 10+2d6 standard rations.

**104-107.** Two relic, nylon camo print hip pouches filled with 3d6 days standard rations and 1d6 MREs in excellent condition. MREs are covered on page 436 of this book.

**108-112.** A wax paper wrapped buffet of assorted dried meats, cheese, nuts, fruits, high quality breads, cookies, muffins and other splendid foods, and enough for a week, plus 10+3d6 days of standard rations.

**113-117.** A plastic carry case full of 12 assorted MREs that were frozen for nearly two centuries before their discovery. They're in good condition and you'd know it because you already ate 3d6 of them over the last few months. MREs are described on page 436 of this book.

**118-121.** Large frame backpack with 2d6 days rations, a cooking pot, frying pan, wooden utensils, 4 metal bowls, flint and steel, cooking oil, bottle of maple syrup, spices and ingredients to make 36 pancakes

**122-125.** 20+1d10 days rations, a frying pan, and flipper, flint and steel, spices, dried bacon and other meats (3kg), plus a dozen farm fresh eggs and a 500ml bottle of booze, roll 1d6: 1. Rum / 2. Vodka / 3. Scotch / 4. Gin / 5. Brandy / 6. Port. Also in this large satchel are 4 steel plates, and wooden forks and spoons.

**126-128.** 3d10 days rations in a hip pouch, while in a satchel is a cast iron griddle ( -2 DV bonus if carried near the body), cooking oil, cooking utensils, spices flint and steel and a fresh, half meter long salmon fillet. It will only keep for another day before being too ripe. GM Note: The wax paper wrapped fish will give off a scent to carnivores within 100 meters, especially bears.

**129,130.** An assorted food supply, with 10+2d10 days rations in a hip pouch, 2d6 well preserved MRES (see page 436 in this book for details), a flint and steel, cook pot, wooden mixing spoon, 3d6 days more of rations in dried nuts, fruit, meat and bread sticks. 3 in 10 chance of a 500ml bottle of locally brewed hooch and 4 shot glasses.

# Water *Roll 1 time*

**1.** You've had nothing to drink in the last 1d6 days, and for each day of thirst, you've lost 1d6 endurance points to a minimum of 10% your character's total.

**2.** None, and you're already thirsty and if you cannot get some water in the next 6 hours, you'll take 1d6 END damage.

**3.** None, and your water skin just dripped its last drop.

**4.** You have an old pop can filled with bitter water, 300ml.

**5.** An old plastic pop jug, 2 liter capacity filled with 1d2 liters of algae filled water and a few wriggling bug pupae.

**6.** You have a leaky water skin. When you started out, it had 2 liters in it, but it's now down to 1 liter and dripping 1ml per minute (1000ml in a liter).

**7.** Your water skin wasn't cured properly, and while the 2 liters inside is drinkable, it tastes and smells of rot.

**8.** An old 2 liter plastic pop bottle serves as your water jug, with a wire and rope holster-style carrier it can be worn at the hip. Currently filled with 1d2 liters of cloudy, unpalatable water.

**9.** You have 4+1d4 plastic bags tied to your belt, each is filled with a liter of discolored, bitter tasting water. Any fall or strike against this character will lead to a 25% likelihood of one water bag busting open.

**10.** 1d6 small, 500ml plastic water bottles spread out amongst your gear, with at least one stuck in a holster-like belt holder made from an old work sock. Each water bottle is 50% likely to be full of sour water.

**11,12.** An old, improperly sanitized and dented milk jug filled with 1d2 liters of yellow water. A Willpower based Type C hazard check must be made each time the user drinks from this to not spew up the mouthful because of the foul, curdled milk flavor.

**13,14.** Your water is kept in a burlap wrapped 2 liter fish bowl with a plastic food wrap as a cover. It currently holds 1d2 liters of water. If this character is struck or falls, there is a 34% chance the glass container shatters, the water is lost and the shards of glass might slice the carrier... treat as an attack: SV 01-60, damage 1d6.

**15,16.** A water skin made from two stitched together human faces, of skullock design. The drinking spout is the neck hole areas of both faces. Consuming water from this 2L container often causes alarm and disgust from others, and can lead to difficult questions when worn in 'civilized' communities. The water, strangely, tastes fine. Currently contains 1d2 liters.

**17-20.** You have a stained 2 liter plastic milk jug strapped to your waist containing 1d1000ml of decent water (1000ml = 1 liter).

**21,22.** Red, 4 liter plastic gasoline drum with yellow pouring spout and carry handle. Filled with 1d4 liters of water, however no matter how old this jug is, or how well it is cleaned, the water always has a gasoline taste to it.

**23,24.** Small, 5 liter blue water drum, rectangular with a carry handle and pull-out spout on top. Filled with 1d4 liters of half decent water.

**25-28.** Huge, clear plastic blue water jug converted into a backpack but also comes with a built-in handle. This jug can hold 18 liters of water, but anything over 5 liter will slow a person down if they have less than 50 strength, suffering a -0.25m move rate. Larger folks do not suffer this movement penalty unless the jug is completely full. Anybody of small stature under a meter in height or under 15 strength cannot lift this when full. Sell value is 5+1d6sp. Contains 2d6 liters.

**29-36.** Two liter, rectangular plastic jug carried by a shoulder rope and currently filled with 1d2 liters of off-colored water. Jug has the product sticker still on it, and an aftertaste of whatever originally filled it, roll 1d6: 1. Windshield washer fluid / 2. Break fluid / 3. Anti-freeze / 4. Paint thinner / 5. Motor oil / 6. Varnish.

**37-40.** Large, bright pink and yellow slushy cup and flexi-straw lid with belt attached wire and plastic holster style carrier. It will hold 1 liter of water yet is currently filled with 1d1000ml of water (1000ml = 1 liter).

**41-45.** Tire inner tube knotted at each end with a cross-shoulder strap and straw-like plug at one end for extraction. Will hold 4 liters of water, all of which tastes like tar, and currently filled with 1d4 liters.

**46-49.** An old sports ball carried in a woven net with a drinking straw and plug cap at the top end. It holds 2 liters of rubbery tasting water. Roll 1d6 for ball type: 1,2. basketball / 3. soccer ball / 4. American football / 5. kids beach ball / 6. volleyball.

**50-54.** Kids cartoon character shaped 2 liter water bottle. Bright colored with flexible straw, carried in a plastic belt pouch to try to hide the container's garish color. Filled with 1d2 liters of plastic flavored water.

**55-58.** Wicker wrapped ancient booze bottle filled with 1 liter of water, label still visible, roll 1d6: 1. Scotch / 2. Rum / 3. Vodka / 4. Gin / 5. Bourbon / 6. Tequila. If this character falls, there is a 2 in 6 chance this bottle shatters and potentially cuts into the carrier: SV 01-60, DMG 1d4.

**59-66.** Stout plastic bag with knotted corner and rope shoulder strap. Bag can carry 1d6 liters of water (roll for permanent capacity) with the bag's original purpose determined randomly, however the bag is always brightly colored with huge words, bar codes, warnings and other labels on it. Roll 1d6: 1. cat food / 2 dog food / 3. kitty litter / 4. chicken feed / 5. lawn fertilizer / 6. grass seed / 7. BBQ charcoal / 8. potting soil / 9. human cremated remains. /10. human sourced garden fertilizer.

**67-70.** One liter cold drink travel mug, filled with 1 liter, with pop up lid and carry handle, will sell for 2d4sp.

**71-74.** Two liter blender jug with snap-on plastic lid, rusty blade at bottom, and handle. Strapped to the user's bet with wire, currently holds 1d2 liters of orange hued water.

**75-79.** 10 liter black pail with carry handle and snap-on lid. Once contained driveway sealer and the 1d10 liters of water inside always taste of blacktop. 1 liter of water weighs 1kg, and so for tiny individuals a meter or shorter, to carry over 5 liters will reduce movement by -0.25m per round.

**80-84.** 2 liter paint can with steel lid and punched in drinking straw. Carried in a woven mesh hip case. Currently holds 1d2 liters of plastic tasting cloudy water.

**85-89.** Collection of 10+2d10 small plastic bottles, tubes, pipes, hose sections, and zippy bags that hold 250ml of water each. This collection is carried in various parts of the owner's body to distribute the weight and reduce the risk of losing all their water in one mishap. Note, there are 1000ml in a liter, and so this fella could potentially carry 7.5 liters (30 containers x 250ml) of water, although much of its tastes like paint, varnish, medicine, baby powder, toothpaste and so on.

**90-94.** Bright plastic blow-up toy, knotted at the ends and carried by soft ropes. Can hold 5 liters but currently filled with 1d4 liters of plastic tasting fluid. A drinking straw and plug mechanism has been installed at the topmost end near the wearer's face(s), roll 1d10 for toy: 1. Blow up sex doll / 2. Pink unicorn floating ring / 3. Pool air mattress in rainbow colors / 4. Giant beach ball with world map printed on it / 5. Bright blue dolphin / 6. Bright purple shark / 7. Flamingo / 8. Slice of pizza / 9. Reclining chair shaped floaty with cup holder and pull rope / 10. Donut.

**95-98.** 30x60cm soft-pack cooler with carry strap. Can be carried by top handle or worn as a backpack. Inside are 2d6, 500ml water bottles, with half being full of clean water. Color of soft-pack, roll 1d10: 1. High visibility reflective yellow and orange / 2. Bright pink / 3. Bright red / 4. Baby blue / 5. Neon green / 6. Desert tan / 7. Flat black with the word POLICE written on it in white lettering. / 8. Desert camo / 9. Urban gray digital camo / 10. Woodland camo.

**99-105.** Five liter relic water cube, molded in olive green and comes with shoulder straps or carry handle. Unit is encased in a composite fiber armored case to help keep it cool and protected, but also affords some armor protection to anybody who wears it, although at a slight -0.25m loss in movement when full. Defense value bonus -3 DV, sales value 260+2d100sp.

**106-111.** Tactical canteen in nylon, insulated belt holder. The canteen holds 3 liters of water, and uses a solar powered ionizer to kill bacteria, viruses and other biological contaminants. This canteen's cap has an optional straw attachment and drinking tube that can be clipped to the wearer and run up to their shoulder to permit drinking on the go. The cap also has a compass and a radiation sensor tab identical to the relic on page 432 of this book.

**112-118.** Water pack, with flex-straw and filled with 1d4 liters of water. Maximum capacity is 4 liters. The straw tube clips to the wearer's shoulder and allows them to drink while running and gunning. Pack comes with 4 side pockets that are perfect for pistol magazines, grenades, and other small items. Will sell for 300+3d100sp.

**119-124.** 1d3 relic, military grade 1 liter plastic canteens in belt holders, each filled with high quality water. Plus, 3d6 water purification tablets.

**125-130.** As Roll 119-124, above, plus a soft-back pack and flex straw system as in roll 112 to 118, filled with max capacity 4 liters of water.

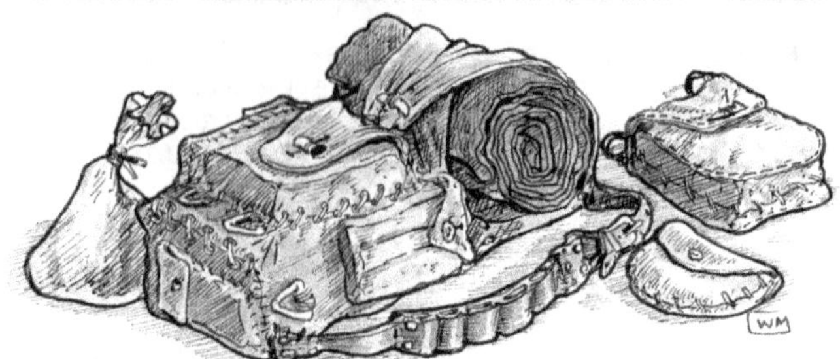

## Carrying Gear  *Roll 1 time*

**1.** Nothing but your bare hands

**2.** Small plastic freezer bag.

**3.** A discarded 1 liter sized ancient package, brightly colored with the top tied off by twine and to be attached at the waist. Roll 1d12 for package: 1. sour gummies /2. corn chips / 3. Halloween mini chocolate bars / 4. puffed soy cheese twists /5. animal crackers / 6. granola bites / 7. roasted nuts / 8. roasted crickets / 9. simulated bacon soy crisps /10. potato chips. / 11. estrogen enriched soy pretzels. / 12. Meal-Worm Krunchiez.

**4.** White kitchen garbage bag, medium sized with red ties. Lashed at the top by string to allow it to be knotted to the waist or a shoulder strap.

**5.** Black plastic garbage bag, contractor grade with ropes at top corners to make a shoulder strap. Big enough to serve as a sleeping bag for a child or skullock.

**6.** Half folded black body bag with twine knotted about corners to create backpack-style straps. 29% chance was previously occupied and the stink of corruption permeates everything put inside.

**7,8.** Plastic shopping bag with knots at handles to attach it to your belt.

**9,10.** Nylon chair cushion cover, with zippered top, hollowed out interior and ropes for a shoulder strap.

**11,12.** Small sack tied to the belt, sack made from the skin of a skullock. Skinned fingers serve as decorative tassels along the bottom.

**13,14.** Belt pouch made from a human face, skullock fashion. Hair braided to serve as fastening line to hook to your belt. Commoners and gate guards who see this on a visitor will be horrified and challenge the wearer.

**15,16.** Backpack made from animal bones, antlers, horns and skins. Smells like carrion when wet.

**17-21.** Sack with dozens of patches.

**22-24.** Animal pelt sack with shoulder strap made from the beast's leg skins.

**25-27.** An old 3 liter ice cream pail and steel handle, tied to the belt.

**28-30.** Leather sack sewn from a dozen giant rat skins, feet, tails and whiskers still attached.

**31,32.** Wicker basket with shoulder straps, no lid, big enough to hold a rolled-up blanket and a few bits of gear.

**33,34.** Relic hard shelled suitcase with tow handle and wheels. Noisy as hell when carried along over rubble or cracked highways. Has straps for a large person to wear as an uncomfortable backpack.

**35,36.** Ancient, rusted-out metal shopping cart with squeaky wheels. Terrible on rough ground but can be pushed at normal walking speed on smooth sidewalks, roadway and hard packed earth.

**37,38.** Old tent: salvaged nylon 4 person tent, torn up and only good a for a tarp-like lean-to as shelter, but using the tent poles has been fashioned into a remarkable, waterproof backpack. Color roll 1d8: 1. bright orange / 2. bright blue / 3. bright yellow / 4. desert tan / 6. dark green / 7. gray / 8. camouflage print.

**39,40.** See-through, crude knapsack made from barbed wire, sticks and several square meters of poly bug screen.

**41,42.** 40L clear plastic tote bin with snap-on lid. Turned into a cumbersome backpack by way of leather straps, wire and wicker.

**43,44.** A relic hammock made of nylon, bundled up and carried as a sack over one shoulder. Hammock can be turned into a bed at night, and comes in one of these brilliant colors, roll 1d6: 1. hot pink / 2. aquamarine /3. orange /4. yellow / 5. purple / 6. lime green.

**45,46.** A rusty portable grill, closed up like a clamshell with belongings inside. Straps hold it shut and attached to shoulders. It's bulky and noisy, but adds -3 DV bonus as armor. If the user is under 40 strength, it reduces their movement by -0.25m.

**47,48.** Black plastic mesh and blue, padded material from an old trampoline, converted into a crude but effective backpack.

**49,50.** Folding camp stool-backpack of relic construction, woodland camo print. Serves as a backpack when closed up, but can be folded into a stool with the nylon pack beneath the cushioned seat, will sell for 90+1d100sp.

**51-53.** Plastic, wicker patio box, with latching, lift up lid. 70cm long, 30cm deep, rectangular shape. Dark brown, made to look like a wicker chest. Leather straps for carrying as a backpack.

**54-56.** Bed sheets, stained, patched and frayed, knotted at the four corners into a sack-like knapsack with shoulder straps.

**57-60.** The shell of a massive, spiny crab, lashed together like a clam-shell, with leather shoulder straps bolted to shell. Weighs 8kg, and will reduce the movement of any wearer under 50 strength by -0.25m, but adds -5 DV to their defense value.

**61,62.** The complete skin of a goat, complete with stuffed horned head, and the thing's leg skins used as shoulder straps. An added relic zipper allows access into the pack across the dead thing's upper back.

**63-80.** Standard leather backpack with two gear pockets on each side and a carry handle at the top and bed-roll loops at the bottom.

**81-84.** Standard backpack as in roll 63-80, however somebody clever sealed it with wax to make it waterproof.

**85-88.** Leather frame backpack, with 3 pockets on each side, an extra quick access back pouch, cup holder, and sleeping roll straps at the bottom.

**89-93.** Relic knapsack, nylon, with multiple zippered pockets and plastic top carry handle. Roll 1d6 for color: 1. charcoal gray / 2. blood red / 3. navy blue / 4. forest green / 5. light gray / 6. desert digital camo.

**94-97.** Relic hikers frame backpack, nylon with a dozen assorted extra pockets, sleeping bag straps, built in compass, whistle and flint and steel. Olive green.

**98-100.** Relic hiker's backpack, as in roll 93-97 but deluxe, with a pullout tarp to create a lean-to or other shelter in minutes that covers 3 x 9 meters. Dark gray.

**101-112.** Military backpack with multiple pockets for gear, 4 mag pouches, assorted loops, hooks, and straps as well as holders for a small back-up weapon the size of a pistol grip shotgun, SMG, or carbine with folding stock. Color, roll 1d6: 1. urban camo grays/ 2. jungle foliage camo / 3. olive green / 4. desert tan / 5. woodland camo / 6. flat black.

**113-119.** Military backpack, as in roll 101-112, however, the material on this pack is a flexible composite armor filament; improve wearer's defense value -5 DV.

**120-126.** Military backpack, as both rolls 101-112 and 113-119, however, this pack has a built in radiation sensor tab (see relic page 432 of this book) a compass, and three sides covered in mat coated solar panels, a charging cable allows a mini power cell to charge in 3 hours of sunlight, while a standard power cell can be charged to half way in 6 hours, or fully after 12 hours.

**127-130.** Military backpack, as rolls 101-112, and up, however this backpack has a built-in communicator and flexi-antenna, plus an over the shoulder spotlight and power cell compartment, and a secret map pouch in bottom of main interior compartment. This pack is waterproof and when all main compartments are sealed, the pack acts as a life preserver to keep the wearer from sinking.

# Adventure Gear

*Escaped slaves roll 1d3 times, everybody else roll 1d6+1 times. Re-roll duplicated results*

**1.** Nothing
**2.** Lucky rock
**3.** 30cm of sterilized bandage
**4.** 1 silver coin
**5.** Dog collar with 2m leash (escaped slaves have this locked on neck by a replica padlock).
**6.** Fish scale vest ( -1 DV)
**7.** Straw sun hat
**8.** Two meter length of rusty chain.
**9.** Iron manacles on wrists from prior enslavement or capture, chain missing.
**10.** 2 x 2m clear plastic sheet, torn and stained
**11.** One .22 cal cartridge

**12.** Walking stick (staff)
**13.** Hogs bristle tooth brush
**14.** Soap and towel
**15.** Shovel
**16.** Wool blanket
**17.** Cutlery set, wooden
**18.** Bottle of oil for lantern, 800ml
**19.** Pickaxe
**20.** Filter mask, relic (pg. TME-194)
**21.** Shotgun shell
**22.** Crowbar
**23.** Rope, 4+1d6m length
**24.** 3d6 meters of fine string
**25,26.** Crayon (use the table on page TME-23 if color needed).
**27,28.** Safety goggles, relic (pg. TME-194)
**29,30.** Standard pistol round
**31,32.** Pad of lined paper letter size, 10+1d20 sheets.
**33.** 1 gold coin
**34.** Pair of relic sunglasses
**35,36.** Mini power cell, 10% charge remaining
**37.** Hand mirror
**38.** Poncho, Mexican pattern
**39.** Sewing kit
**40,41.** Hammer and 3d6 cast iron spikes
**42,43.** Standard rifle round
**44,45.** Flute, recently made, 30cm long
**46-48.** Fly swatter (9% chance the handle yanks open to reveal a knife).
**49-51.** Deck of relic playing cards, tattered but could sell for 8+2d8sp
**52-54.** Leather baseball style cap
**55-57.** Cloak with hood
**58-60.** Leather work gloves
**61-63.** Pencil and small scrap of yellowed paper.
**64-66.** Grappling hook and 10m rope
**67-69.** Standard power cell, 10% charge remaining.
**70-72.** 3.3m long wooden pole
**73-76.** Relic fishing line, 10+1d10 meters, and 1d6 hooks.
**77-80.** Cowboy style hat, leather.
**81-83.** Slingshot, wooden and 3d6 round rocks in a belt pouch.
**84,85.** High caliber pistol round
**86.** Mexican Sombrero hat.
**87-89.** Two person tent
**90-92.** Relic magnifying glass
**93-95.** High caliber rifle round
**96-98.** Relic: Anti-toxin injector (pg. TME-199).
**99,100.** Relic: MK I Flesh Mend Gel packet, (pg. XR-442 , this book).
**101-107.** Gas mask, relic (pg. TME-194).
**108,109.** 4 person fabric tent
**110.** One roll on table XR-285 / Power Source, page 496.
**111.** Standard communicator with 3d6 minutes of time left on battery (pg. TME 198).
**112,113.** Relic compass (pg. XR-437, this book).
**115.** Smoke grenade (pg. TME-195).
**116.** Radiation sensor tab (pg. XR-432 , this book).
**117.** Handcuffs, relic (pg. TME-197).
**118.** Mini grenade ( (pg. TME-195)
**119.** Ancient road map of the local area. Geological events, bomb blasts, fires and junk storms have erased most landmarks, but it's better than nothing and worth 20+2d20sp if you wanna sell it.
**120.** Pocket fire extinguisher (pg. XR-432, this book).
**121.** 8 person tent made from relic nylon but recent construction. Weighs 4kg. Will sell for 16+1d30sp
**122.** Magazine for an assault rifle, with 1d4 rifle rounds inside.
**123.** 6 pack of previously frozen MREs (see page XR-436 for flavor details).
**124.** Energy recharging solar unit (pg. XR-434, this book).
**125.** Stun grenade (pg. XR-421, this book)
**126.** Metal detector (pg. XR-439, this book)
**127.** Nano patch (pg. XR-444, this book)
**128.** MK II flesh mend gel (pg. XR-442, this book)
**129.** Fragmentation grenade (pg. TME-195)
**130.** Advanced fragmentation grenade (pg. TME-195)

# Footwear *Roll Once*

**01-05.** Barefoot
**06-12.** Tire tread sandals
**13-18.** Lizard scale low boots
**19-24.** Moccasins
**25-30.** Leather sandals
**31-36.** Low leather shoes
**37-42.** Calf high soft leather boots
**43-48.** Calf high fur boots
**49-54.** Hob nailed, heavy work boots
**55-58.** Tattered pair of ancient slippers
**59-62.** Faded pair of yellow gum boots
**63-66.** Rubber boots, black
**67-74.** Ancient running shoes
**75-82.** Ancient hiking boots
**83.** Old world high heel women's shoes.
**84.** High heeled lady's boots
**85-87.** Knee high goth street boots with studs in the toes
**88-90.** Ancient pair of cowboy boots
**91-96.** Steel toed relic work boots (+1 DMG with kick attacks)
**97-99.** Men's patent leather dress shoes
**100-121.** Combat boots
**122-130.** Relic, advanced trail boots, from page 433 of this book.

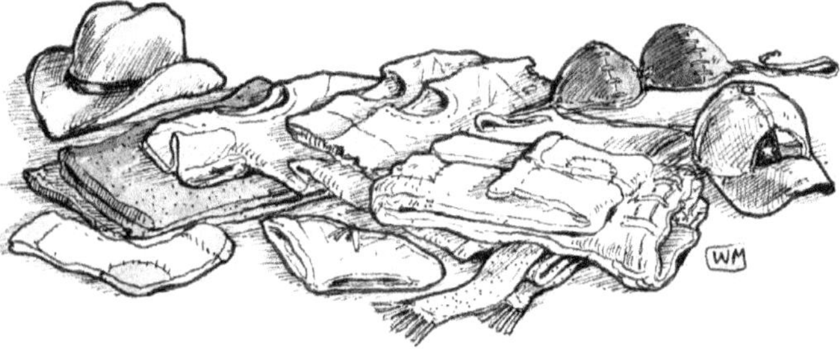

# Clothing *Roll Once*

**1.** Entirely naked.
**2.** Loin cloth for men, or loincloth and bikini top for women.
**3.** Tattered animal skin breeches and a loose cotton shirt.
**4.** Torn cotton pants, rag tank top and a 3 in 10 chance of woven bark poncho.
**5.** Old underwear: men have boxer shorts and a stained muscle shirt, woman's panties and a bra. Plus a 4 in 10 chance of a poncho, as roll 9.
**6.** Plastic bag shorts, torn cotton tank top and a 6 in 10 chance of a poncho as in roll 9.
**7.** Clear plastic, trash bags, stained with grease and grime.
**8.** Shorts and tank top made from rat pelts, tails, heads and feet still attached.
**9.** Only a poncho, roll 1d10: 1. black garbage bag / 2. blue tarp / 3. shredded nylon tent, gray / 4. broken black umbrellas / 5. brightly colored blow up kiddie pool / 6. BBQ cover, black / 7. patches of different human and skullock skins / 8. animal skins / 9. bright orange plastic garbage bag / 10. hacked open and stitched together body bag.
**10.** Animal pelt trousers and a hole riddled, filthy T-shirt that is so perforated that it's more of a mesh than a covering. See roll 20 for color and design of T-shirt.
**11.** Cloak, trousers and shirt made from old plastic animal feed bags.
**12.** Trousers made from fish skins. Tank top made from rag patches.
**13.** Raw hide shorts with suspenders and a loose cotton shirt.
**14.** Relic boxer shorts, wool socks, and a leather vest.
**15.** Lizard skin pants and a tattered relic T-shirt from roll 20.

**16.** Rawhide pants, a fur poncho and a moth eaten T-shirt from roll 20.
**17.** Leather cowboy chaps, boxer shorts, leather vest and a stained T-shirt from roll 20.
**18.** Skimpy underwear (plus bra for females) and a terry-towel bathrobe.
**19.** Skirt or kilt from an old umbrella and a T-shirt from roll 20.
**20.** Leather breeches* and an ancient T-shirt with color and design elements still visible. Roll first for color and again for design, logo or message.

> **Color of T-shirt: Roll 1d20: 1.** navy blue / **2.** hot pink / **3.** orange / 4. yellow / 5. light gray / 6. black / 7. baby blue / 8. dark gray / 9. olive green / 10. red. / 11. desert digi camo / 12. woodland camo / 13. urban gray digi camo / 14. metallic black / 15. purple / 16. metallic silver / 17. metallic gold / 18. teal / 19. dark green / 20. white.
>
> **Design, logo or message on shirt,** roll 1d20: 1. none / 2. "I'm with Stupid" / 3. picture and logo of ancient heavy metal rock band / 4. ancient baseball team / 5. "The Worse day fishin' beats the best day workin'." / 6. "Starstruck Coffee Company" / 7. "The 2nd protects all the rest" with a picture of an assault rifle beneath it. / 8. "Will F**k for Beer" / 9. "Go Big, or go Home" / 10. "I 'Heart symbol', New York" / 11. Movie title plus poster art / 12. Security / 13. Volunteer / 14. Search and Rescue / 15. ARMY / 16. MARINES / 17. NAVY / 18. AIR FORCE / 19. "All outa F's to Give." / 20. GM or player created offensive, funny, or sports team based saying and/or imagery, or else "Come and Take Them!"
>
> *Not in addition to other pants or shorts.

**21.** Animal hide pants and vest with a 3 in 10 chance of an ancient rain coat.
**22.** Leather pants with sewn-in knee pads, and cargo pockets, plus an ancient T-shirt from roll 20.
**23.** Baggy cotton sweat pants, tank top and 4 in 10 chance of a lizard skin vest ( -1 DV).
**24.** Tattered cut-off jean shorts and an old T-shirt as seen in roll 20.
**25-27.** Leather breeches, loose cotton shirt, and fur-lined cape.
**28-30.** Old blue jeans with lots of patches, and T-shirt from roll 20. 3 in 10 chance of a hat from roll 98-100.
**31-33.** Rawhide, tasseled, breeches, loose cotton shirt and an old jean jacket.
**34-36.** Men's swimming shorts, tank top and a faded, old baseball cap.
**37-39.** Skimpy nylon bathing suit, faded T-shirt from roll 20 above, and a wide straw hat.
**40-42.** Leather pants with sewn-on tire knee pads, leather sleeveless vest, and tank top. 4 in 10 chance of a random hat from roll 98-100.
**43-45.** Skirt for females or knee length cotton breeches for either, plus loose burlap shirt. 3 in 10 chance of a wide brim leather sun hat.
**46-48.** Shredded camo army pants with lots of pockets, and random T-shirt from roll 20. 4 in 10 chance of a hat from roll 98-100.
**49-51.** Pants made from fish and lizard skins, and burlap tank-top, with 2 in 10 chance of a recently made leather baseball style cap.
**52-54.** Cargo shorts, faded and patched up, and random T-shirt from roll 20. 1 in 10 chance of a relic baseball cap.
**55-57.** Old baseball pants with stripe on the leg, a cotton muscle shirt and a 3 in 10 chance of a burlap jacket.
**58-60.** Dark leather long-coat, black leather pants, and a tank-top. 2 in 10 chance of a hat from roll 98-100.
**61-63.** Leather breeches with studded leather codpiece ( -1 DV bonus). 1 in 10 chance of matching studded wrist bracers.
**64-66.** Cotton pants and loose shirt with fur linked cloak made from, roll 1d6: 1. black bear with claws as clasping point at neck, and hood is the bear's head with fangs and ears still present. / 2. wild boar / 3. deer with antlers on hood. / 4. bane bear / 5. seal. / 6. goat, with horns on hood.
**67-69.** Cotton pants, and loose shirt with cloak made from white, water shedding plastic cover sheet.
**70-72.** Fur pants, tank-top and a 3 in 10 chance of a fur trimmed hat with ear flaps.
**73-75.** Burlap pants, loose cotton shirt and a 4 in 10 chance of a straw cowboy hat.
**76-78.** Old hockey jersey, burlap pants and a 3 in 10 chance of an old baseball cap.
**79-81.** Torn and multi-patched jumpsuit, roll 1d6 for main color: 1. tan / 2. olive green / 3. black / 4. navy blue / 5. blood red/ 6. orange with prison name on back.
**82-84.** Pair of faded and patched up yoga pants, muscle shirt and 4 in 10 chance of a sweat band for forehead.
**85-88.** Fur tasseled leather pants and matching leather vest.
**89-91.** Jumpsuit made recently from burlap to match old patterns.
**92-94.** Raw hide pants, tank-top and an ancient, stitched up plaid work shirt.
**95-97.** Cotton pants, tank top and cloak made from a large orange garbage bag.

**98-100.** Leather pants and T-shirt* from roll 20, plus an interesting relic hat: Hat Detail, **roll 1d20: 1.** white chef's hat / **2.** turban / **3.** police officer's dress hat / **4.** British House Guard tall bear skin hat / **5.** pith explorer's, colonial hat / **6.** pirate's headscarf (bandanna) / **7.** white brimmed woman's mystery hat / **8.** fake, fabric crown / **9.** headdress made from tusks and teeth/ **10.** headdress made from shells / **11.** fur hat with antlers attached / **12.** fur hat with buffalo horns attached / **13.** fur raccoon, Davy Crockett hat with tail / **14.** baseball cap with two tin drink holders and coiled straws that lead down to mouth / **15.** chainmail head coif ( -2 DV, 500g, will sell for 14sp) / **16.** straw fedora / **17.** classic felt fedora / **18.** black top hat / **19.** Native American Indian war bonnet, costume variant with fake eagle feathers and plastic beads, but looks real from a distance./ **20.** American Civil War (1861-1865) soldier's cap, 10-50% chance Union North Blue/ 51-00%. Confederate Rebel Gray.

*Pants and T-shirt not in addition to previous occurences of these items.

**101-104.** Relic business suit, with a jacket and dress shirt. 4 in 10 chance of a tie, and a 3 in10 chance of a dark gray overcoat.

**105-108.** Faded blue jeans, off-white T-shirt and a leather biker vest with some sort of ancient gang insignia on back.

**109,110.** Faded jeans, random T-shirt from roll 20, and a studded leather punk rocker's jacket (armor -5 DV, -0.25m movement, 2kg, value 1d12+8sp).

**111,112.** Desert camo pants, military jacket, and tan T-shirt.

**114-116.** Relic woodland print camo parka (worth 300+1d100sp), dark green cotton pants, and a dark knitted beanie hat.

**117,118.** Woodland digital camo pants, jacket and green t-shirt.

**119,120.** Dark gray jumpsuit with multiple pockets, and a 6 in 10 chance of a black balaclava.

**121,122.** Forest camo, suspender supported hunter's pants, waterproof, with rubber knee pads (worth 100+2d20sp), random T-shirt from roll 20, random hat from roll 98-100.

**123-125.** Desert camo long sleeve relic shirt (worth 40+1d30sp), leather pants, random T-shirt from roll 20, and a 3 in 6 chance of a desert camo boonie hat.

**126,127.** Relic ninja attire, including 'Fukumen' head wrap, hand covers, leg wraps and toed footwear.

**128-130.** Olive green army pants and matching T-shirt, 4 in 10 chance of a cadet's cap with regimental insignia pin still attached.

**46-52.** 4d6 silver coins and 1d10 gold coins.

**53-59.** 3d6 silver coins and a gem worth 20+1d20sp.

**60-65.** 2d10 silver pieces, 1d6 gold pieces and a relic silver necklace worth 15+1d30sp.

**66-72.** 4d6 silvers and 2d6 gold coins.

**73-78.** 3d6 silver pieces and a gold wedding band that's been in your family since the pre-cataclysm times, worth 100+1d100sp.

**79-84.** 10+3d6sp, 2d10 gold pieces, and a silver bracelet worth 10+1d6p.

**85-89.** 1d100 silver pieces, 1d10 gold pieces.

**90-93.** 30+1d10sp, and 2d10gp, plus a silver crucifix on a leather strap. worth 3d6sp.

**94-98.** 30+3d6sp, and 3d6gp, plus 3d6 fancy plastic bits worth 5sp each.

**99-100.** 100+1d100sp, 10+2d10gp, and a necklace of wire secured ammunition (3d6 standard pistol rounds, 2d6 rifle rounds and a single 50 cal round in the middle.

**101-103.** 100+1d100sp, 4d6gp, and a gold chain worth 100+2d20sp.

**104-108.** 100+1d100sp, 3d20gp, and a gold pendant set with a small gemstone worth 200+1d100sp on leather cord.

**109-113.** 100+1d100sp, 20+3d6gp, and a gold bracelet worth 40+1d30sp.

**114-117.** 200+1d100sp, 30+1d20gp, a full, 500ml bottle or ancient Scotch worth 200+1d100sp.

**118-122.** 200sp+1d100sp, 40+1d20gp, and a gold plated woman's wrist watch worth 100+2d100sp.

**123-124.** 200+1d100sp, 1d100gp, and 2d6 small gems each worth 10+1d20sp.

**125-127.** 300+1d100sp, 40+1d100gp, and a bag of fancy plastic containing 4d6 wonderful bits each worth 10sp.

**128-130.** 400+1d100sp, 50+1d100gp, 3d6 loose gems worth 20+1d20sp each, a thick gold chain worth 200+1d100sp, and a men's fancy relic watch, gold plated worth 300+1d100sp.

# Armor *Roll Once*

**1.** No armor

**2.** Wicker shield, DV (Defense Value) -3, MV (Movement rate) -0

**3.** Skins, DV -3, MV -0.25m

**4.** Animal hides, DV -3, MV -0.25m

**5.** Furs DV -3, MV -0.25m

**6.** Leather jacket, DV -5, -0.25m move, can be worn over other armor.

**7.** Leather armor, DV -10, -0.25m, and a 2 in 10 chance of a leather shield DV -4, MV -0.25m.

**8.** Junk shield, DV -6, MV -0.5m

**9.** Leather armor, DV -10, MV -0.25m, and a 2 in 10 chance of a shield from roll 14.

**10.** Lizard scale armor, DV -11, MV -1m

**11.** Bark armor, DV -9, MV -0.5m, and a 3 in 10 chance of a shield from roll 14.

**12.** Thorn armor, DV -11, MV -0.5m, and a 3 in 10 chance of a shield from roll 14.

**13.** Bone armor, DV -14, MV -0.75m, and a 3 in 10 chance of a shield from roll 14.

**14.** Shield, **roll 1d12: 1.** wicker shield DV -3, MV -0 / **2.** leather shield DV -4, MV -0.25m. / **3,4.** junk shield DV -6, MV -0.5m / **5.** buckler DV -4, -0m / **6,7.** standard shield DV -5, -0.25m / **8.** spiked shield DV -5, MV -0.5m, plus spike can be used as a melee dagger / **9.** bladed shield DV -7, -0.5m, plus blade edge can be used as a short sword attack. / **10-12.** junk shield DV -6, MV -0.5m.

**15-17.** Bug shell armor, DV -16, MV -0.5m, and 3 in 10 chance of a random shield from roll 14, above.

**18-26.** Leather armor, DV -10, MV -0.25m, and 6 in 10 chance of a random shield from roll 14, above.

**27-32.** Heavy leather armor, DV -14, MV -0.5m, and 5 in 10 chance of a random shield from roll 14, above.

**33-36.** Resin Armor, DV -14, MV -0.5m, Won't sink, but flammable suffer +2 damage per round and add +2 rounds of burning to wearer (new armor for this book, pg. XR-428).

# Money *Roll Once*

**1.** Worse than nothing, as you have 1d6 debts to different people or groups, each debt totals 20+1d100 silver pieces.

**2.** You owe a tax, either property tax, a fine, overdue payment on something you bought with an IOU, or other debt to somebody back home. Debt total 10+1d100sp, and increasing by 1sp per day because of interest. When it reaches 500sp, bounty hunters will be notified of your identity, and added to their list of wanted men or women. If this character is already an escaped slave, then this debt is the amount you cost your master when you broke stuff in your escape.

**3-15.** No money

**16.** 1 silver coin

**17.** 2 silver coins

**18.** 1d6 silver coins

**19.** 2d6 silver coins

**20.** 1 silver coin and 1 gold coin

**21-24.** Fancy plastic bits, 3d6, each worth 1 silver piece.

**25-28.** 3d6 silver coins

**29-33.** 2d6 silver coins and 1d4 gold coins.

**34-40.** 3d6 silver coins and 2d6 gold coins.

**41-45.** 10+1d10 silver coins and 1d6 gold coins and 1d8 fancy plastic bits worth 2sp each.

**37-39.** Tire Armor, DV -15, MV -0.5m, -5 DMG from falls / Flammable: suffer 1d3 rounds of increased burn time and +1 DMG per round (new armor for this book, pg. XR-428).

**40-44.** Rug Armor, DV -13, MV -0.25m, (new armor for this book, pg. XR-428).

**45-49.** Studded leather armor, DV -12, MV -0.5m, and 4 in 10 chance of a random shield from roll 14, above.

**50-54.** Spiked leather armor, DV -15, MV -1m, anything to bite wearer takes 1d10 DMG, and 3 in 10 chance of a random shield from roll 14, above.

**55-60.** Lizard scale armor, DV -11, MV -1m, and 6 in 10 chance of a random shield from roll 14, above.

**61-65.** Chainmail vest, DV -7, MV -0.25m, and 2 in 10 chance of a random shield from roll 14, above.

**66-70.** Breastplate, DV -15, MV -0.5m, can be worn over other armor, and 3 in 10 chance of a random shield from roll 14, above.

**71-76.** Part plate armor, DV -25, MV -1.5m, and 5 in 10 chance of a random shield from roll 14, above.

**77.** Full plate armor, DV -35, MV -2m, and 6 in 10 chance of a random shield from roll 14, above.

**78,79.** Leather armor, DV -10, MV -0.25m, plus a 7 in 10 chance of a ballistic vest, DV -4 or -20 vs. Bullets and MV -0.25m.

**80-91.** Junk armor, DV -12, MV -0.5m, and 4 in 10 chance of a random shield from roll 14, above.

**92-96.** Heavy junk armor, DV -17, MV -1.5m, and 3 in 10 chance of a random shield from roll 14, above, and if not, then and 1 in 10 chance of a random shield from roll 101, below.

**97-100.** Scrap relic armor, DV -20, MV -0.75m, and 2 in 10 chance of a random relic shield from roll 101, below.

**101.** Relic shield, roll 1d10: 1-5. riot shield, DV -8, MV -0.5m / 6-9. ballistic shield, DV -5/-22 vs bullets, MV -0.5m/ 10. energy buckler DV -30, MV -0.

**102-106.** Torso plate MK I, DV -16, MV -0.25m, (new armor for this book, pg. XR-427), and 3 in 10 chance of a random shield from roll 101, above.

**107-113.** Torso plate MK II, DV -19, MV -0.25m, (new armor for this book, pg. XR-427), and 2 in 10 chance of a random shield from roll 101, above.

**114-116.** Torso plate MK III, DV -22, MV -0.5m, (new armor for this book, pg. XR-427), and 2 in 10 chance of a random shield from roll 101, above.

**117-123.** Riot armor, DV -25, MV -0.5m, and 3 in 10 chance of a random shield from roll 101, above.

**124.** Bomb squad armor, DV -19 or -50 vs. explosions, MV -3m, and 1 in 20 chance of a random shield from roll 101, above.

**125-127.** Tactical armor, DV -30, MV -0.75m, and 2 in 10 chance of a random shield from roll 101, above.

**128,129.** Light combat armor, DV -25, MV -0.5m or -0.25m adjusted, (new armor for this book, pg. XR-430), and 2 in 10 chance of a random shield from roll 101, above.

**130.** Combat armor, DV -35, MV -1m, and 1 in 12 chance of a random shield from roll 101, above.

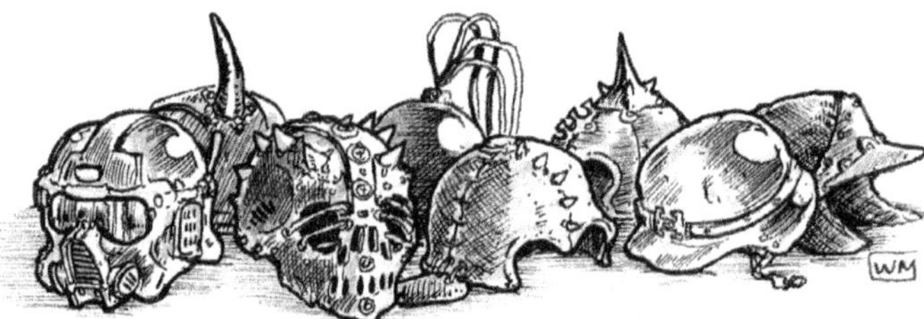

# Helmet *Roll once*

**1-9.** No helmet

**10-15.** Leather helmet, DV -2, MV -0

**16-18.** Bone helmet, DV -4, MV -0.25m

**19-47.** Junk helmet, DV -3, MV -0.25m

**48-55.** Resin helmet, DV -4, MV -0.25m

**56-62.** Iron cap, DV-2, MV -0

**63-82.** Iron helmet, DV -4, MV -0.25m

**83-85.** Welding mask, DV -5, MV -0.5m, reduces visibility, -10 to missile SV use, face shield, vision protector.

**86-89.** Full helm, DV -6, MV -0.5m, poor visibility, -5 SV when using missile weapons.

**90-96.** Sports helmet, DV -3, MV -0.25m

**97-101.** Fireman's helmet, DV -4, MV -0.25m, dual headlight flashlights and a 4 in 10 chance of a headset communicator.

**102-108.** Motorcycle helmet, DV -5, MV -0.25m, flip up tinted face shield, -1 initiate due to hearing loss from sides and back. 3 in 10 come with headset communicator.

**109-114.** Riot helmet, DV -4, MV -0.25m

**115-124.** Army helmet, DV -5, MV -0.25m

**125-128.** Tactical helmet, DV -6, MV -0.25m, comes standard with communicator, flashlight, and face shield.

**129.** Combat helmet, DV -9, MV -0.25m, equipped with a communicator, headlamp flashlight, gasmask and face shield.

**130.** Crisis deployment helmet, DV -10, MV -0.5m, gas mask (1 hour air supply), advanced communicator and night vision headset. See pg. XR-427.

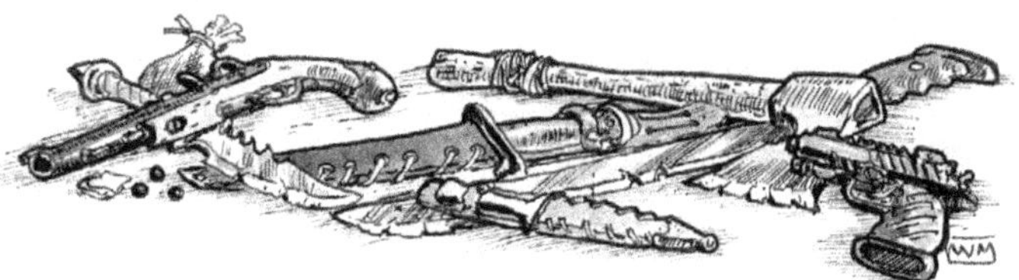

# Backup Weapon *Roll Once*

**1.** None

**2,3.** Knife

**4.** Hatchet

**5.** Pipe

**6.** Club

**7.** Throwing star

**8.** Hammer

**9.** Sickle

**10.** Dagger

**11.** Length of chain

**12.** Crowbar

**13.** Rock

**14.** Club, and 2 in 10 chance of a knife

**15.** Hatchet, and 3 in 10 chance of a knife

**16.** 2 knives (one hidden in footwear, or small of back horizontal sheath).

**17.** Brass knuckles (adds +2 SV and +2 DMG to any punch attack).

**18.** Dagger and 1 in 10 chance of a machete

**19.** Knife and a 3 in 10 chance of a bayonet

**20.** Machete, and 3 in 10 chance of a knife

**21.** Dagger and a 2 in 10 chance of a whip

**22.** Dagger and a 3 in 10 chance of a hatchet

**23.** 2 daggers.

**24.** Knife and a 4 in 10 chance of a sling and 3d6 stones.

**25-31.** Boot knife, and 6 in 10 chance of a dagger.

**32-37.** Dagger and 1d3 throwing stars.

**38-46.** Dagger and musket pistol with 3d6 shots worth of powder, balls and wad.

**47-52.** Knife and wooden slingshot (stats page TME-99).

**53-55.** Switchblade knife, relic (stats page TME-100).

**56-61.** Dagger and whip

**62-64.** Dagger and slingshot, wrist lock. Relic, described on page TME-186, stats on page TME-100.

**65-67.** Dagger and mace

**68-70.** Knife and tactical tomahawk, relic, see page 405, this book for details.

**71-76.** Dagger and 3 throwing hatchets.

**77-79.** 1d3 hidden knives, and a rapier.

**80-82.** Relic bayonet, stats page TME-100.

**83-85.** Knife and a relic pistol crossbow with 3d6 quarrels. Stats page TME-100.

**86,87.** Bandoleer of 6+1d6 daggers with black stained blades.

**88-90.** Dagger and machete

**91-93.** Knife and spring spike (relic, stats page TME-100, description page TME-186).

**94-96.** Knife and wrist gun, with 1d8 pistol rounds (stats page TME-100, details page TME-186).

**97-99.** Dagger and a .22 cal pistol with 1d3 magazines and 2d20 .22 cartridges (stats page TME-100).

**100.** Dagger and a pocket pistol with 1d2 magazines and a total of 3d6 pistol rounds.

**101-103.** Dagger and revolver, 357 magnum, leather holster and 3d6, 357 cartridges (description page 408, or stats page 401).

**104-106.** Dagger and auto-pistol with 1d2 magazines and 4d6 rounds of pistol ammo (stats page TME-100, description page TME-187).

**107-109.** Knife and stun stick, with 40 successful strikes left in power cell (stats page TME-100, details page TME 189).

**110-112.** Knife and pistol grip pump shotgun with back carrier gun boot, 1d8 shells (stats page TME-100).

**113-115.** Dagger and shotgun pistol with 2d6 shotgun shells and drop-leg holster (stats page TME-100, details page TME 187).

**116-118.** Dagger and 1d3 fragmentation grenades (see page TME 195 for grenade stats).

**119-122.** Dagger and rocket pistol, with 2d6+2 chase rockets. Details on page 408 of this book.

**123-125.** Dagger and revolver, 44 magnum, nylon holster, and 2d8, 44 cartridges. Description page 408, or stats page 401.

**126-129.** Dagger and stun pistol with 2d20 shots left in power cell. Stats page TME-100, description page 189.

**130.** One to three (1d3) daggers, boot knife and razor sword (stats page TME-100, details page TME-186).

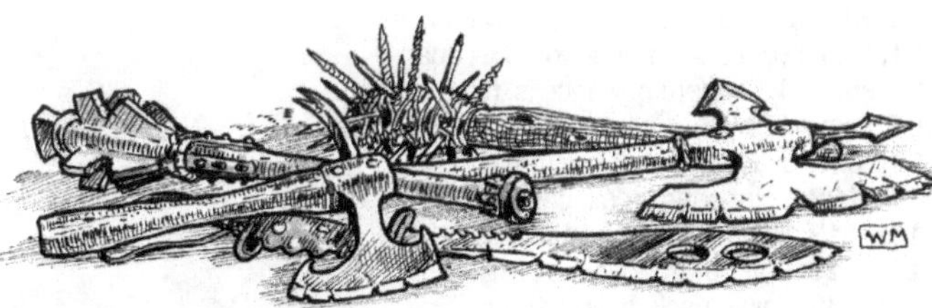

# Melee Weapon *Roll 1d2 Times*

**1.** None
**2.** 2m length of chain
**3.** Leg bone as a club
**4.** Bottle
**5.** Flint axe
**6.** Hammer
**7.** Spiked club
**8.** Sickle
**9.** Pipe
**10.** Staff
**11.** Flint spear
**12.** Javelin
**13-16.** Machete
**17.** Pitch fork
**18.** Mace
**19.** Shovel
**20.** Pickaxe
**21-30.** Spear
**31-40.** Hatchet
**41-49.** Machete
**50-58.** Saber
**59-67.** Battle axe
**68-73.** Longsword
**74-80.** Great sword
**81-89.** Machete and spear
**90-96.** Dagger and rapier
**97-100.** Dagger, machete and battle axe
**101-110.** Longsword, dagger and pike
**111-120.** Great sword, dagger and boot knife
**121-130.** Razor sword, hatchet and 1d4 daggers.

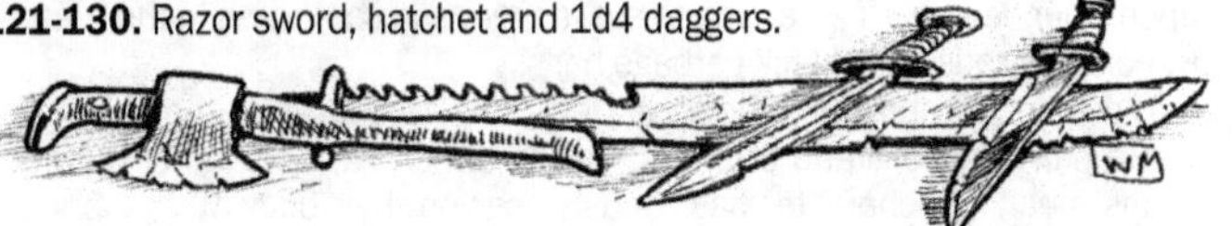

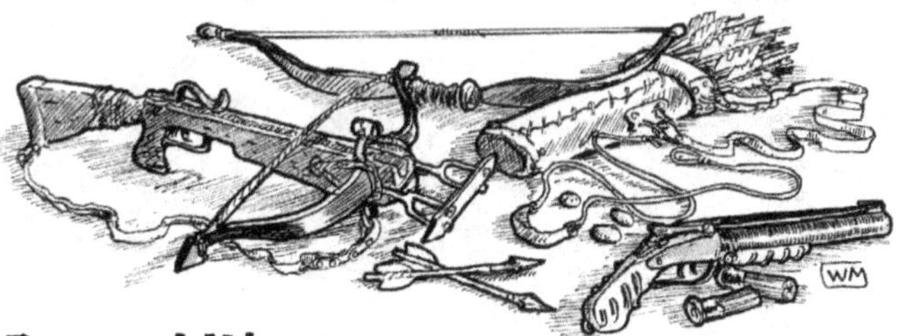

# Ranged Weapon *Roll Once*

**1-4.** Nothing
**5,6.** Rock
**7.** Knife
**8.** Large rock
**9.** Dagger
**10.** Bow with 1 arrow
**11.** Javelin
**12.** Throwing star
**13,14.** Bow with 1d6 arrows stuck in your belt.
**15.** Flint spear
**16,17.** Hatchet
**18,19.** Slingshot, wooden and 4d6 shooting stones in a pouch.
**20,21.** Two javelins
**22-30.** Spear
**31-36.** Sling and 4d6 small rocks in pouch
**37,38.** Throwing stars, 1d6
**39.** Two spears
**40-47.** Bow, quiver and 3d6 arrows
**48,49.** Musket pistol and 4d6 shots worth of powder, wad and ball, holster and pouches for all items.
**50-57.** Bow, quiver, 10+3d6 arrows and spare bow string.
**58,59.** Two musket pistols with enough shot, powder and wad for 10+3d6 discharges. Holster on each hip.
**60-63.** Longbow, quiver and 4d6 arrows
**64-69.** Crossbow, case and 3d6 quarrels
**70-72.** Heavy crossbow, case and 4d6 quarrels
**73.** Wrist gun*, and spare 2d6 pistol rounds
**74,75.** Pistol crossbow*, relic, with 3d6 quarrels and case.
**76,77.** Bladed boomerang*
**78,79.** Slingshot, relic, wrist lock* with 4d6 stones in pouch
**80-83.** Musket rifle, with 36 discharges worth of shot, powder and wad, 4 in 10 chance fitted with a bayonet.
**84.** Doubled barrel musket rifle, rate 1 or 2, with 4d6 shots worth of ball, wad and powder, 3 in 10 chance of a bayonet.
**85-87.** Compound bow*, relic, with quiver and 4d6 arrows, and 2 in 10 chance of 1d6 special quarrels with exploding arrow heads (pg. TME-196).
**88,89.** Compound crossbow*, relic, with hip pouch full of 4d6 quarrels and 3 in 10 chance of a 1d4 special quarrels with exploding arrow heads (pg. TME-196).
**90.** Dart gun*, relic with 1d6 needles filled with sleep venom, Type C (poison covered on page TME-124).
**91.** Harpoon gun*, sheath of 2d6 steel harpoons. 10% chance doubled barreled.
**92-95.** Shotgun pistol* with leather holster and pouch of 2d6 spare shells.
**96-103.** Pump shotgun* with sling and 2d6 shot shells. 2 in 10 chance has a barrel light (pg. TME-201) with 3d6 hours of light left in battery.
**104-109.** .22 cal pistol*, with between one and two (1d2), 18 shot magazines, each filled with 3d6 cartridges.
**110-112.** .22 cal sporting rifle*, with between one and three (1d3), 10 shot magazines, filled with 1d10 cartridges each.
**113-115.** .22 cal semi-auto rifle*, with between one and two (1d2), 30 shot magazines, each filled with 3d10 cartridges each.
**116-121.** Pocket pistol* with underarm holster, 1d2 magazines, and 3d6 rounds of pistol ammo.
**122-126.** Auto-pistol* with 1d2 magazines, holster and 4d6 pistol rounds.
**127,128.** Sub-machine gun* with 1 magazine and 3d10 rounds of pistol ammo.
**129,130.** Survival rifle* with 1d2 mags each loaded with 1d10 rifle rounds. 2 in 10 chance of a barrel light with 3d6 hours of illumination left in battery.

*Stats on page 100 of the hub rules with description in the relic section of the hub rules starting on page186.*

## Illumination *Roll Once*

**01-06.** Nothing
**07-09.** 1 candle
**10-12.** 1d3 candles
**13-15.** 1d6 candles
**16-20.** 1 torch
**21-24.** 2 torches
**25-33.** 2d6 candles
**34-39.** 2+1d4 torches in leather hip pouch with flint and steel.
**40-46.** Lantern with 3d6 hours fuel in hard leather protective carry case.
**47-53.** Relic, headlamp with 3d6 hours left in battery charge*.
**54-58.** Relic headlamp, fully charged with 250 hours illumination*.
**59-65.** Pocket flashlight with 2d6 hours of light remaining in mini-power cell*.
**66-70.** Pocket flashlight, fully charged with 200 hours of illumination.*
**71-78.** Barrel flashlight, with 1d6 hours of light left in mini-power cell.*
**79-82.** Barrel flashlight with full battery giving 100 hours of light.
**83-89.** Large flashlight with 3d6 hours left in its power cell.
**90-93.** Large flashlight, fully charged with 200 hours of illumination.*
**94-113.** Spotlight with 1d6 hours of light in its power cell.*
**114-121.** Spotlight, fully charged and able to shine 100 hours of illumination.
**122-130.** Night vision headgear with 1d4 hours left in its mini-power cell (full charge yields 12 hours).

**Flashlights are covered on page 201 of the TME hub Rules.*

## Power Supplies *Roll Once**

**01-03.** None
**04-06.** Drained pill power cell
**07-09.** Drained mini power cell
**10-12.** Drained standard power cell
**13-15.** Pill power cell, half charged
**16-18.** Mini power cell, 10% charge remaining
**19-21.** Mini power cell, half charged
**22-28.** Pill power cell, fully charged
**29-37.** Mini power cell, fully charged
**38-46.** Standard power cell, 10% charge remaining
**47-62.** Standard power cell, 50% charge remaining
**63-76.** Standard power cell, fully charged
**77-80.** 1d6 pill power cells, fully charged
**81-85.** 1d6 mini power cells, fully charged
**86-90.** 2 standard power cells, fully charged
**91,92.** Power pack, drained to 10% capacity
**93-95.** 1d4 standard power cells, fully charged
**96.** Power pack, 50% charged
**97-101.** Advanced power cell, page XR-457
**102-108.** Solar charge cell, page XR-457
**109-113.** Hand crank power cell, page XR-457
**114-120.** Belt power pouch, page XR-457
**121-130.** Power pack, fully charged

**Androids, cyborgs, and vat-brains roll twice.*

## Fire Starting *Roll Once*

**1-5.** Nothing
**6-9.** Bow drill, that if the right wood and tinder is available and dry, this user can make a perception based Type C hazard check to get a flame going. One try per 10 minutes.
**10-29.** Old pack of 3d6 matches, 50% each will light when tried.
**30-68.** Flint and steel with tinder box of dried sap, twigs, wood shavings and animal hair.
**69-75.** Flint, steel, tinder box and 1d3 Molotov Cocktails (see page 362 for details on the cocktails).
**76-95.** Ancient disposable lighter with enough fluid left to start 2d20 fires.
**96-130.** Relic refillable metal lighter, with enough fuel to start 40+1d30 fires, sell price 60+1d100sp.

## Assorted Item or Circumstance

*Roll 1d6 times, re-roll duplicated results.*

**1.** Nasty scars from past accident, beatings or whipping. Reduce appearance trait by -1d6, permanently.
**2.** Infested with lice. Cost for delousing soap and comb is 10+1d20sp, although a source of water must also be found or paid for.
**3.** Painful sliver in foot, reduce movement by -0.5m per round until treated by somebody with the medic skill.
**4.** Character starts with a wound and is already depleted by 2d6 endurance points.
**5.** Suffers from a swollen, black eye that for the next 2d6 days will reduce visibility and depths perception. Apply a -1 initiative, -10 appearance, and -10 strike value penalty plus reduce all accuracy based hazard checks by 20 trait points until healed.
**6.** You're recovering from a sprained ankle and so limp badly. Reduce movement by half for the next 1d4 days, thereafter ankle healed and move speed returns to normal.
**7.** Weird rash over 1d100% of your body. Deplete endurance by -1d6 and appearance score to half until rash heals up after 3d6 days. Very painful, and open wounds give off an aroma to scavengers and carnivores in the area.
**8.** Poncho made from black garbage bags.
**9.** Old scar or brand. If character started as an escape slave, then he or she has a pronounced brand of their previous owner's symbol, other outfitting codes mean the character has a nasty scar on their body, with a 2 in 10

chance of it being on their face reducing APP score by -1d4 permanently.

**10.** Animal pelt as a blanket or shawl.

**11.** Stubby pencil and 1d6 scraps of paper.

**12.** Tinfoil hat

**13.** Tobacco pipe and 20+1d20 grams of pipe tobacco leaf.

**14.** Green tennis ball, worth 2+1d2sp

**15.** Pewter fantasy miniature, 28mm, worth 4+1d10sp.

**16.** 10 ounce silver bar, worth 10+1d10sp.

**17.** Empty 10 shot magazine for a .22 sporting rifle.

**18.** Wool toque.

**19.** Glasses without lenses, worth 1d3sp

**20.** Peacock feather.

**21.** Pet rat (normal, stats on page TME-167)

**22.** Drained headlamp flashlight (flashlights described on page TME-201).

**23.** Empty 6 shot magazine for a pocket pistol.

**24.** Bow string.

**25.** Old world 1 ounce gold 'walking liberty' coin, worth 10+1d6 new era gold coins.

**26.** Narcotics: 2d6 gebrull joy beans. See page TME-124.

**27.** Zippy bag of ammo, 1d3 pistol rounds, 1d2 rifle rounds, 1d2 shotgun shells, and 1d8 .22 rounds.

**28.** Leather necklace with wire wrapped single high caliber pistol round as an ornament.

**29.** Small metal flask of hooch, 500ml.

**30.** Molotov cocktail, see page 362 in this book.

**31.** Large sack containing 6+1d6 loaves of fresh bread, wax paper wrapped cheese assortment, dried nuts and fruit. Treat as 10 days rations for one person.

**32.** Zippy bag of 1d6 pistol rounds.

**33.** Alcohol disinfectant, see page 362, of this book.

**34.** Drained standard power cell.

**35.** Badminton racket, worth 6+1d12sp.

**36.** Narcotics: kicker berries, 3d6. See page TME-124.

**37.** Small wooden keg of beer, 3 liters, worth 6+1d12sp.

**38.** Empty 20 shot magazine for an auto pistol.

**39.** Safety goggles and a 3 in 10 chance of a headlamp flashlight with only 10+1d20 minutes of battery life.

**40.** Chainmail vest, DV -7, move penalty -0.25m, can be worn over other armor.

**41.** Belt pouch with 1d6 shotgun shells.

**42.** Whole watermelon in wicker pouch.

**43.** Sack of oats, 5kg.

**44.** Mini-grenade, see page TME-195.

**45.** Headlamp flashlight with 4d6 hours of light left in battery, pg. TME-201.

**46.** Compass, see page 437, this book.

**47.** Empty 30 shot magazine for an assault rifle.

**48.** A copy of the Holy Bible, King James version, black with a locking latch. 2 in 10 chance the key is tied to the spine by a brass loop by a golden thread. 1 in 10 chance it is in Braille.

**49.** Bottle or apple cider, 500ml, worth 5+1d8sp.

**50.** Length of yellow, relic poly-rope. 6+2d6m.

**51.** Quiver of 10+1d12 arrows.

**52.** Bottle of red wine, 750ml, worth 7+1d10sp

**53.** A stainless steel Starstruck Coffee Company travel mug with carry handle, belt loop and closing lid, 500ml capacity, worth 20+1d20sp.

**54.** Empty 10 shot magazine for a survival rifle.

**55.** Wrap around dark black sunglasses, worth 20+1d30sp.

**56.** Several .22 cartridges (2d6).

**57.** Pocket flashlight with 3d6 hours of light left in battery, pg. TME-201.

**58.** Crystal diode radio, see page 362, this book.

**59.** Pair of yellow lensed shooting sunglasses. Worth 18+3d6sp.

**60.** Ammunition chest bandoleer, max capacity 24 shotgun shells, currently loaded with 1d3 shells.

**61.** Standard pistol round.

**62.** Firecrackers, 1d6 strings, see Fireworks in this book on page 424.

**63.** Barrel flashlight with 20+1d20 hours of light left in battery, pg. TME-201.

**64.** Mini-power cell, drained down to 10% charge.

**65.** A shotgun shell.

**66.** Sleeping roll and shoulder strap.

**67.** Magazine for an assault rifle with 1d6 rifle rounds loaded in the 30 shot max capacity mag.

**68.** Standard rifle round.

**69.** MRE, lasted so long by being previously frozen. See page XR 436.

**70.** Compass, basic, but described on page 437 of this book.

**71.** Glow Flare, see page 440 of this book.

**72.** Empty 50 shot magazine for a sub-machine gun.

**73.** Anti-toxin injector, see page TME-199.

**74.** Pepper spray, see page TME-197.

**75.** Large flashlight, with 10+1d100 hours of light left in battery. See page TME-201.

**76.** Nutrient Tabs, 3d6, see page 435 of this book.

**77.** Landmine, see page TME-196.

**78.** Power cell, drained to 50%.

**79.** Zippy bag of ammo: 1d6 pistol rounds, 1d6 rifle rounds, 1d6 shotgun shells.

**80.** Mini-power cell, fully charged.

**81.** BB Rifle, and 20+1d100 BBs, see page 403, this book to learn more.

**82.** Sonic Bug Screen, page 435, in this book.

**83.** Fragmentation grenade, see page TME-195.

**84.** Binoculars, see page TME-201.

**85.** Ear mic, see page 448 of this book to learn more.

**86.** Stun Grenade, see page 421 of this book.

**87.** Spotlight flashlight with 20+1d20 hours of light remaining, page TME-201.

**88.** A nylon, desert camo mag and utility belt with an empty assault rifle magazine inserted in one of the three mag slots, plus 1 roll on table XR-285/ Power Supplies on page 496.

**89.** Chaff Grenade, see page 421 of this book.

**90.** A 750ml bottle of old world Scotch worth 100+1d100sp.

**91.** Advanced fragmentation grenade, see page TME-195.

**92.** Pellet rifle, and 20+1d30 pellets, see page 403, this book.

**93.** Electro-glove, and 2d10 shocks left in power cell, see page XR-413.

**94.** Smartphone with 3d6 days left in battery charge, see page XR-449.

**95.** Standard communicator with only 3d6 days of operation left on normal 2 year battery charge. See page TME-198.

**96.** Torso plate, MK I. See new armors on page XR-427.

**97.** Communicator headset, with 100+1d100 days of battery life left in charge. See page TME-198.

**98.** Relic sleeping bag, good down to -20c.

**99.** Fully charged power cell.

**100.** Military rad-suit, pg. TME-195.

**101.** Six pack of anti-toxin injectors, page TME-199.

**102.** Robo-repair module MK I, see page 441, this book.

**103.** Pocket fire extinguisher, see page 432, this book.

**104.** AR glasses MK I, (augmented reality), see page 478, this book.

**105.** Box of .22 ammo, 3d20 cartridges.

**106.** Pouch containing 2d6 standard pistol rounds.

**107.** Handheld movement detector, see page 439, this book.

**108.** Rad-scanner (dosimeter), with 100+1d100 days use left in battery. Page TME-199.

**109.** 8 gauge shotgun shells, 1d6+1 in a pouch.

**110.** Tablet, with 10+2d30 days left in battery supply. See page 450, this book.

**111.** Flesh Mend Gel, MK1, see page 442, this book.

**112.** Foam grenade, see page 421, this book to learn more.

**113.** Drum magazine for an assault rifle, 100 round capacity, but loaded with only 3d6 cartridges.

**114.** Nano healing injector, see page 446, this book.

**115.** Silencer, see page TME-197.

**116.** Small box of pistol ammo, 3d6 rounds.

**117.** Incendiary grenade, see page 422, this book.

**118.** Flesh mend gel, MK II, see page 442, this book.

**119.** MK2 Advanced fragmentation grenade, see page 421, this book.

**120.** 6 gauge shotgun shells, 1d6+1.

**121.** Communicator wristwatch, 4d6 days of comms left in battery, pg. TME-198.

**122.** Proximity mine, see page TME-196.

**123.** Box of shotgun shells, 3d6.

**124.** Flesh mend gel, MK I, handy 6 pack in original shrink wrap package, see page 442, this book.

**125.** Baggy of assorted ammo: 3d6 pistol rounds, 3d6 rifle rounds, 2d6 high caliber pistol rounds, 1d6 high caliber rifle rounds, 1d6 shotgun shells, 1d20 .22 cal. rounds, 2 in 10 chance of 1d3 50 cal rounds.

**126.** Magazine for an assault rifle loaded with 3d10 rounds.

**127.** A random MAV (micro air vehicle), with full battery and controller, pg XR-496.

**128.** Night vision headgear, with 2d6 hours of operation in mini power cell. See page TME-201.

**129.** Flesh mend gel, MK 4, see page 442 this book.

**130.** Tissue binder, see page 443, this book.

# Equipment Packs

## An Alternate Equipment System
*by Danny Seedhouse*

Based on your character's pre-game caste determined outfitting code, the player picks a number of items or packs. So too, their starting outfitting code also determines their starting money. If game play begins in a town with a marketplace or shops, PCs could spend this money to buy weapons and equipment from the Trade Goods Listing starting on page 94 of the Hub Rules book.

### Table XR-214 / Money by Outfitting Code

| Code | Category | PC's Starting Money |
|------|----------|---------------------|
| ESC | Escaped Slave | 1d6-3sp (0-3sp) |
| IM | Impoverished | 1d6sp |
| PR | Poor | 2d10sp |
| MO | Modest | 3d10+10sp |
| WE | Well Equipped | 2d100sp |
| FA | Full Armed | 100+1d100 sp, 2d12gp |
| WA | Wealthy Adventurer | 1d100gp, 1d1000sp |

## Basic Gear

Everyone, except escaped slaves (ESC), get the following packs:
- **Adventurer's Pack**
- **1 Basic Melee or Basic Ranged Pack**
- **1 Basic Armor Pack.**

## The Basic Packs

Folks with the escaped slave outfitting code (ESC), can still use the 'Starting Packs' rules as found on page 96 of the Hub Rules, or start with the following gear: a sack, rags, a club or a flint tipped spear, 1 days of rations, and one of the Basic Packs below.

All characters who start with a different outfitting code get all the following basic packs:
- **Basic Backpack:** Tinder box, cutlery set, woolen blanket, water skin (2L), sewing kit, wet stone, 10 meters rope, 2d10 days rations, 4 torches, a knife and basic clothing.
- **Basic melee Pack:** One dagger, plus pick either a spear, a club, or a hatchet.
- **Basic Ranged Pack:** A sling with plenty of ammo (20+1d10 rocks) and one dagger, or 2 spears, or a bow and 2d10 arrows.
- **Basic Armor Pack:** Leather armor, plus a leather helmet and leather shield.

## Adventurer's Packs

The Adventurer's pack adds the following to the basic pack: 2 more torches, 1d10+3 day more rations, summer sleeping bag, work gloves, and work boots. In addition, apply the following:

People with the Poor outfitting code (PR) get to pick one of the following packs.

Modest (MO) and Well Equipped (WE) may select 2 of the following packs.

Fully Armed (FA) and Wealthy Adventurers (WA) get 3 packs from the following selection:
- **Camping Pack:** 2 person tent, 2 (2L) water skins, and 10 days dried rations.
- **Excavator Pack:** 20 meters rope, crowbar, pick and shovel, lantern and two bottles of oil.
- **Melee Pack:** This includes 1 one handed archaic weapon, 1 two handed archaic weapon, and 1 dagger.
- **Ranged Pack:** A crossbow with 10+2d10 bolts, or longbow with 16+2d10 arrows. A quiver for bolts or arrows, too.
- **Junk Armor Pack:** Junk armor, a junk shield plus a junk helmet.
- **Heavy Junk Pack:** Heavy junk armor.
- **Armor Pack 1:** Heavy leather armor, standard shield and leather helm.
- **Armor Pack 2:** Breast plate.
- **Armor Pack 3:** Chain mail vest, iron helmet and standard shield.
- **Armor Pack 4:** Thorn armor, spiked shield, full helm.
- **Arrow or Bolt pack:** 60 arrows or 60 bolts and a case to hold the extras along with a kit to build more. This kit includes 20 heads and sets of feathers to build more arrows or quarrels. Also included is a hatchet, sharpening stone, wax, waterproof bag for carrying these supplies, plus and 2 extra strings.
- **Beast Pack:** Well trained war dog

## Advanced Packs

This category of pack always comes with the following **Accessory Pack:** Extra set of woolen cloths, tooth brush, sleeping bag, soap and towel, wool cloak with hood and a good set of boots. Plus, a deck of playing cards and dice or a chessboard and pieces.

Those of the Modest outfitting code get 1 of the packs listed below. Well Equipped and Fully Armed characters can pick 2. Wealthy Adventurers get 3 picks and can swap one pick here for 2 adventurer's packs, above.
- **Ranged Pack 1:** A musket and 2d10+10 shots, or two musket pistols with 2d10+10 shots in total.
- **Ranged Pack 2:** Heavy crossbow and 2d10+10 bolts, with case for bolts and strap for crossbow.
- **Armor pack 1:** Part plate and iron helm.
- **Armor pack 2:** Heavy leather armor, breastplate, standard shield and full helmet.
- **Armor Pack 3:** Scrap relic armor.
- **Animal Pack 1:** Riding horse and saddle, tack and saddle bags.
- **Animal Pack 2:** Riding dog and saddle, tack and saddle bags.

## Relic Packs

**Bonus Gear Pack:** All eligible PCs who get to pick a relic pack gets this: A wine skin, writing kit (a quill, ink, 20 sheets of paper and 2 pencils), screw driver set and a set of nice clothes, grappling hook, and 10 meters rope.

Well Equipped characters get 1 pick here but must sacrifice one Advanced Pack pick. Fully Armed characters get 1 pick here, or can roll on the Fully Armed PC Bonus Relic chart (TME-1-66, on page 97 of the hub rules). Wealthy Adventures get to pick 2 packs from the following.
- **Relic Pack 1:** One roll from WC-R (page XR 499), or pick a pump shotgun (6+2d6 shotgun shells), or a survival rifle with 10+2d10 standard rifle rounds.
- **Relic Pack 2:** One roll from WC-RC (page XR 498), with 50% extra ammo, or an auto pistol with 1 magazine and 2d10 pistol rounds, or pick a shotgun pistol with 2+2d6 shot shells.
- **Riot Armor pack:** Riot armor, riot shield and riot Helmet and 1d4 tear gas grenades.
- **Relic Armor pack:** Tactical Armor and Combat helmet.
- **House pack:** House or other suitable structure in character's home town with staff as per wealthy adventurer (TME page 97).
- **Jewelry pack:** 2d1000sp in jewelry.

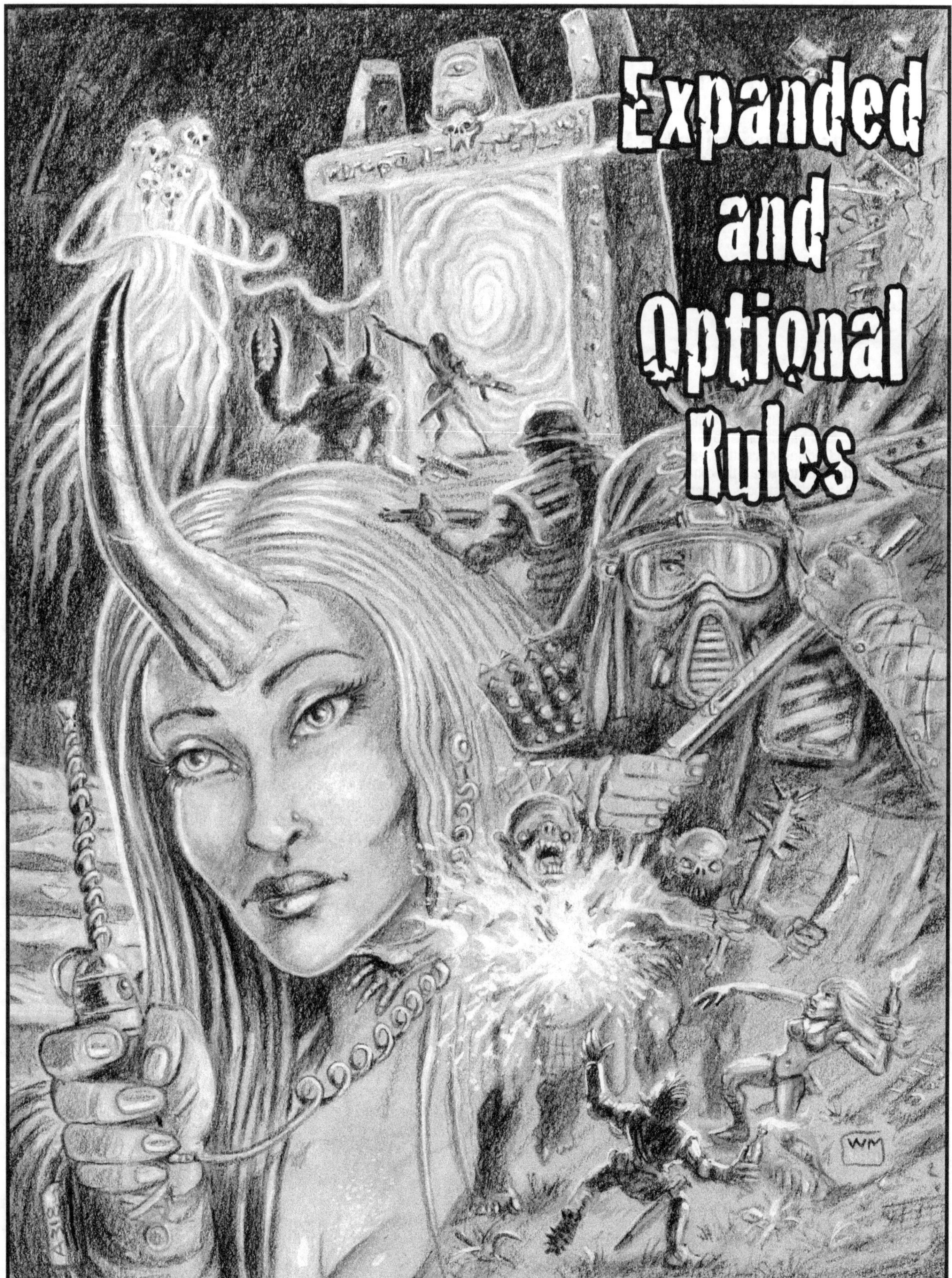
Expanded
and
Optional
Rules

# Expanded and Optional Rules

## Extra Post-Apocalyptic Equipment

### Molotov Cocktail

These crude but highly effective, affordable and easily constructed incendiary devices go by many names, including a 'molly', 'burn bottle', 'bottle bomb' and 'flame bottle'. Made from either salvaged old world glass bottles and jars, or newly made, hand blown glass bottles, each is filled with a flammable liquid, a cloth wick and sealed to contain the contents. The cloth wick, which extends beyond the well sealed plug and is soaked in fuel itself, is set on fire. Igniting the wick takes one round if the flame is already burning and readily available or the operator uses a relic lighter, and does not need to get out flint and steel and try to get a spark to ignite the wick, which takes 3d6 rounds.

Once the wick is alight, the thrower hurls the bottle on the second round. The range is equal to a large rock at 4 meters (+0 SV), and the impact of the heavy bottle alone causes 1d8 damage. The range can be doubled to 8m, but at half the thrower's strike value.

On impact with a hard surface, the bottle shatters and sprays flammable liquid about in a small fireball that engulfs a 2m radius and is usually enough to potentially burn 1 man sized being in the initial burst of fire. The target's armor will absorb some of the initial burst, and so treat as a regular attack with the damage on a successful hit being 3d6 on the first round. Thereafter, the area of the Molotov Cocktail impact, including any target person if struck initially and damaged, will burn for 2d6 rounds and suffer 1d6 damage per round unless the target retreats from the burst area and smothers their burning body with sand, or a blanket.

Putting water or similar liquids on the ethanol or burning oil will only make it burn hotter and larger, causing 1d10 damage per round thereafter instead of 1d6. After the initial 2d6 duration of the oil or petrol fueled fire, any natural flammable substances in the flame coated area will catch fire normally, and will spread if the incendiary device hit a wooden structure, vessel, tree, hay, plantoid character, or other flammable substances. This normal, follow-up fire can be put out with water.

A Molotov Cocktail costs 10+1d6sp to make, and unless a community is suffering under some civil strife, riots, or unrest among the population, these will also be available for sale to excavators at a cost of 16+2d6sp each. A Molotov Cocktail weighs 1kg.

### Alcohol Disinfectant

Made in new era settlements from a wide variety of alcohol manufacturing processes, this usually clear substance is unpalatable and almost never used as a drink, but ideal for disinfecting wounds, survival tools, and hands prior to attending a wound.

Besides warding off infections — which are often more life threating than the original injury — disinfectant can kill foreign, biological contaminants such as parasitic fungal spore, flesh-eating bacteria and assorted secretions from certain plant and animal sources. Small glass vials of 100ml are sold in most towns for 6+1d6sp, while larger 500ml or 1 liter bottles can also be bought (30+1d20sp for 500ml or 50+2d20sp for 1 liter [1000 ml]).

The 1 liter bottle can also be converted into a Molotov Cocktail. All medics have 500ml of this substance included in their starting medics bag, while any self respecting excavator will also be sure to purchase at least a small vial along with a wax paper wrapped envelope of 10 sterilized cotton wipes which cost 1sp and are used to apply the disinfectant to a wound as soon as the fighting is done.

### Crystal Diode Radio

Once very popular in the early 20th century, these radio receivers need no batteries or power. For a talented junk crafter of 4 skill points (skps), or an electrical technician (1 skp) or a person talented in the communications skill (2 skp), these small sets are easily made from junk found in the ruins, or salvaged from ancient machines, including robots and androids.

They require an antenna of at least a meter length, and a single wired ear-piece, with which to listen to the myriad of weird and wonderful radio signals that are still being broadcast throughout the Epochian world. Much of what a person can tune into while using a strip of steel to run across a copper coil and thus tune the radio, is garbled, static filled, encoded, or incompressible robotic chatter, but in some regions, new era radio services have been established.

One of the more famous radio stations, Mixer's Radio Service, is from the fortified digger fort called Pitford on the south-western edge of the Great Ruins (see page 51 in the Pitford source book). By tuning into this station, the listener can hear an assortment of news from around the Crossroads Region, as well as public service announcements from the Northern Freehold along with various music shows, advertisements, threat notices, and rumors.

While these sets cannot pick up signals from standard station to station communicators, they make an excellent source of entertainment, particularly on cold, high atmospheric pressure nights when the range of the signals that can be picked up expands from about 25km to a far as 250km. This is especially true if one hooks the crystal diode radio to a grounding pipe at one end and an exceptionally tall antenna.

These radios are often built from scrap parts and bolted to flat panels of wood or plastic measuring about 15 x 10 cm and affordable enough to fit the budgets of most impoverished new era households. The average price for a modest crystal diode radio is 30+1d20sp.

### Brass Knuckles

Usually worn on the user's dominant hand, these crude but effective bludgeoning aids add +2 to the strike value and +2 damage to any punch attack. These usually sell for 10+2d6sp.

# Dimensional Travel, Encounters, Abilities, and Beings

It is said that the old ones built doors into other worlds and other ages in history. These portals allowed them to go back and forth in time, or elsewhere on Earth, and step out of similar portals in sky cities and communities on the Moon, Mars and off-world colonies among the stars. Other new era thinkers believe that strange, rune covered gateways were found in the dust of ancient civilizations, or were brought back from far-off worlds.

Most, however, believe that the rips, holes and tunnels between the physical world are formed by incredibly powerful mutants. These mind-masters are said to exhibit mind powers of unimaginable complexity and strength. Powers they do not understand. Powers which caused punctures in reality that gave them, and their comrades, access to other times and places — and a gateway for demons to enter the world of the living.

Through ancient technologies, arcane and otherworldly artifacts, and the use of potent mutations, new era adventurers can take the ultimate journey into astounding, magical realms, moments in Earth's history, or other

places in this, or other worlds, in current time. These travels sometimes involve crossing a bizarre, dream-like in-between zone called 'the void', and in such places, as the wanderers make their way to the portal on the far side, they are likely to meet nightmarish entities called dimensional beings. These ghostly lifeforms, described in the text to follow, can also make forays into the physical world, either by following a mutant back from some planer skip, or else when such invisible creatures linger about an active portal device.

Dimensional beings, and related phenomena, appeared after the most intense decades of the old global wars, where new, unimaginably destructive and bizarre weapons were employed which could pierce force fields and concrete bunkers as if they didn't exist, and incinerate those within. More than a few new era historians and scholars claim the ancients were toying with molecular transformation-generators, which could open portals in time and space and allow troops to be deposited behind enemy lines, on enemy starships, or deep in a secure bunker. It is widely believed that many of the dimensional beings encountered in the new era are the victims of these powerful weapons or faulty teleportation devices.

There is also a minor cult that believes many of the humans of old did not die in the wars and plagues, but made portals to carry them safely away to other earth-like planets where their ancestors now live in peace and comfort. These cultists hire adventurers to seek such portals and offer substantial rewards for clues to their location.

The following entries offer a selection of dimensional beings, relics specifically designed to deal with them, a few random inter-dimensional portals, and tables to create a void zone.

Only mutants have the power to create dimensional pathways. So too, usually only mutants can sense, see, or fight the often hostile entities that populate voids or make excursions into the real world. Certain rare relics and cybernetic implants, however, can be used by any character, including android and robot characters, to aid in the detection and elimination of such beings.

Once a portal is opened, either by a mutant, some magical artifact, doorway, or high tech gateway, any character type can travel through a portal, cross a void, and explore other worlds. While in a void, incidentally, the normally invisible dimensional beings are visible — although still ghost-like apparitions — and so easier to see, and easier to harm should the traveler have the appropriate offensive mutations or firepower.

Most times, if a fixed portal is operational, and characters enter it, they must either cross a purgatory-like void to get to the far exit portal, or else the gateway is like a door, as thin as a sheet of glass, where stepping from one world into the other is as easy as taking a step through a beam of light. Rules on whether a void is present behind a portal or not are covered on page 367, or the GM can craft their own method of inter-dimensional travel.

Being included in the optional rules section of this book means the use of dimensional beings, weapons and mutations in a campaign is up to the game master. If not used, have any player who rolls a mutation such as Discern Dimensional Entities re-roll for a different deviation. The dimensional aspect of these rules might also be simply set aside and not used in lower ranks of game play and reserved for higher rank inclusion in the campaign as desired.

One of the primary purposes for including this section in this book is to create a method for post-apocalyptic characters to travel back into time to the present day of the gamers, or earlier points in history, or travel to some potential upcoming setting that uses the Outland System game mechanic for a science fiction setting, or a fantasy RPG.

# Dimensional Beings

All dimensional entities are immune to physical attacks, such as claws, blades, bullets, poison, fire and whatnot, but can be harmed by energy weapons and mental attacks. Energy weapons include lasers, sonic, stun beams, electricity and all mutations that emit beams of some sort. In the material world, all dimensional beings can go invisible, and tend to do so once a living being gets within nine meters of them, or when it spots them. When invisible, they gain both a far superior defense value and initiative score, reflected in their stats to follow. Various mutations, optical relics and other devices allow some creatures to see these unearthly beings, or 'specters' as they are also called, who lose any initiative and defense value advantage the dimensional being may have.

When reduced to zero endurance, a dimensional being fizzles out in a shower of non-flammable sparks, and is gone forever — although whether or not the so-called soul of the thing goes on to whatever source once gave it life, is a debate left to the new era priests, shaman and cultists.

These incorporeal entities, while on earth, are subject to object density, and must either move along the ground or very close to it, skim the surface of a water body, or creep up cliffs and buildings to get at their targets. Some advanced beings can pass through doors and walls, but most must bash down such obstacles. The nature of these entities is much debated, with some clergy claiming that they are denizens of hell. Others speculate they gained access to the physical plane by either mutation caused psionic abuse or through rips in reality caused by ancient weapons and twisted science experiments.

Dimensional beings are a blanket name given to a group of energy creatures that may or may not come from the same, earthly plane, however these wraiths act similar to each other and are harmed by the same weapons and mutations. Their appearance to the uneducated is that of a demonic ghost, unstoppable in its fury and thus, sightings of these fiends in an area strikes religious awe and terror into a community. Often, a town will send out its holy men and women to offer sacrifices, prayers, exorcism or supplications of worship, only to have their efforts met with tragedy.

The most common types of dimensional beings are listed below, but Game Masters are encouraged to develop their own, as well as planar portals, other dimensional settings, and cults which worship such beings and gateways.

## Table XR-215 / Dimensional Beings

| Name | Lost Souls | Rippers | Shockers | Mind Killers | Dominators |
|---|---|---|---|---|---|
| Defense Value* | -30/ -0 | -22/-6 | -26/ -8 | -36 /+0 | -42/ -10 |
| Endurance | 20+1d20 | 40+2d20 | 60+1d30 | 70+3d20 | 160+1d100 |
| Movement | 6m | 7m | 9m | 8m | 12m |
| Initiative* | +2/+0 | +3/+0 | +5 day/ -2 dark | +4/+0 | +6/+2 |
| Attacks | 1 | 2 | 1d4 per round | Mental Attack (see description) | 6 mental attacks+2d4 tendrils |
| Strike Value | 01-60 | 01-70 | 01-63 | Willpower as SV vs WL mod of target | Mental Attacks: As Mind Killer/ Tendrils: As shocker |
| Damage | 3d6 | 3d6+3 | 1d12 stun ea./ devour 1d6 WL+INT | 1d10 WI, 1d6 INT | Mental Attacks: As Mind Killer/ Tendrils: As shocker |
| Strength | 38 | 54 | 33 | 47 | 73 |
| Agility | 44 | 47 | 69 | 19 | 52 |
| Accuracy | 37 | 41 | 72 | 22 | 74 |
| Intelligence | 6+3d6 | 10+3d6 | 20+1d30 | 30+1d30 | 60+1d30 |
| Willpower | 20+1d20 | 37 | 44 | 50+1d30 | 70+1d30 |
| Perception | 28 | 32 | 36 | 41 | 68 |
| Exp Factors | 21 | 45 | 60 | 98 | 220 |
| Morale | Brave | Brave | Brave | Fearless | Fearless |
| Size | 1.3 to 2m tall | 1.5 to 2.2m tall | 2.2m | 3.2m tall | 3.6m tall, 2.5m wide |
| Weight | As END in KG | As END in KG | 30+1d20kg | 40+1d100kg | 180+1d100kg |

*The First stat is when the DB is invisible to their opponent. The second stat is when the adversary has some mutation or technological means to see dimensional beings, while in the case of the shocker, If it appears in a dark area and can readily be identified. All dimensional beings are visible, although still ghostly in appearance, in voids.

## Lost Soul

These are humanoids who have been tainted and transformed by long exposure to the dimensional reality between jump points. In short, they have themselves become dimensional beings, mere blurs of color to the naked eye and easily dismissed as just a reflection or shadow. Occasionally, when not attacking and seemingly unaware of any living viewer that is 9 or more meters away, they appear as flickering human shapes. The memory of their physical appearance can be seen when they are docile, unsuspecting, or by those gifted mutants or relic equipped individuals who can look at them, or when the entity itself wants to be seen, feared, admired or lusted after.

Many lost souls are twisted and cruel, attacking the living on sight. Some are deceivers, entirely insane, traumatized, or confused by their state of being and plead for help — their supplications coming across as mournful, screeching wails to the living. Still others are loving and kind and will assist physical beings and even defend them from other dimensional beings. A rare few are sexually debased and attempt to lewdly assault the living or take on the forms of magnificently beautiful people who emanate soothing music, affection, and promises of unearthly pleasure to entice the living to fall in love with them, and follow them into some nameless void between the worlds. Dwelling in the void will turn a person into a lost soul. See 'The Void' on page 367 for more on this transformation and how to avoid it.

Hostile lost souls fight by bashing into targets and striking with appendages of light and electricity, knocking out victims and either leaving them for dead, strangling them to death, or abusing them as determined by their nature. Roll below to determine the attitude of each lost soul towards living humanoids encountered. Note: these once humanoid beings have no interest in animals, androids, or robotics unless these individuals are assisting or defending humanoid companions. They will, however, attack plantoids, bestial humans, and vat-brains, sensing the humanity in them.

## Table XR-216 / Attitude of a Lost Soul Toward Humanoids

**1d20 Attitude of a Lost Soul toward Humanoids Encountered**

**1-5. Spiteful and murderous**, will wail and attack to the death, strangle those subdued.

**6-9. Jealous and bitter**, will hover around screaming for 2d6 rounds, then, 50% chance will attack to the death, otherwise move away swearing to itself and weeping.

**10-13. Indifferent**, lost soul just moves slowly away with a low, mournful howl.

**14. Sexually debased**, lost soul hungers for the carnal delights of life, and will inappropriately pester the most attractive humanoid it encounters. Gender is not an issue.

**15,16. Curious**, follows humanoids, 10+1d100 meters away for 1d10 hours, then departs.

**17,18. Friendly**, will allow itself to be seen and, with a ghostly whisper, will communicate that it likes humanoids, but nothing else. Will flee if fighting of any kind occurs.

**19. Helpful**, will guard humanoids from other hostile dimensional beings in the vicinity if locked to a certain area, or if free roaming, will accompany agreeable humanoids for 3d6 days. It will stay invisible when approaching strangers or human settlements, but otherwise will show itself to agreeable living companions.

**20.** As 19, helpful, but also aware that it was once a person, although can't recall just who, but will warn the humanoids of any dangers or other dimensional beings in the area. Will defend the living and hang around for 4d6 days.

## Ripper

The most common dimensional beings to enter the world are called Rippers. They appear as either semi-invisible shadows, blurred shapes, or vaguely ape-like humanoids whose arms end in great clawed hooks. Onlookers with the proper mutations or relics to see dimensional beings will observe a more-or less solid shape of a deformed human with a tortured visage.

They attack living beings as directed by their summoner, or, if encountered during a dimensional leap, will attack all intruders. Because of their blurred, often invisible appearance, they gain +3 initiative, although lose this bonus against those who can see their hideous, true forms. If they kill a living being, they will adhere to the body and consume the electrical field of the casualty, along with minerals and several liters of blood.

## Shocker

Shockers appear as floating orbs with dangling two meter long tendrils of charged, crackling electrical energy. They are virtually invisible during daylight, appearing as a faint mirage, but in the darkness, glow as greenish-gold balls of light; +5 initiative during daylight, but –2 during the night or in darkness. In an attack, shockers float up to their targets and whip 1d4 tendrils per round, each inflicting 1d12 stun damage per strike.

Victims shocked to zero endurance are considered unconscious, at which point, or after the battle if other targets are nearby, the shocker will drag away its victim to either a dimensional hole, if one is present and open, or to a secluded spot to devour the victim's consciousness. This devouring process involves the shocker automatically draining 1d6 willpower and intelligence points per hour until the victim dies. At either zero willpower or intelligence, which ever is depleted first. Rescued, still living victims regain consciousness after 3d6 hours and heal at a rate of one trait point per hour. Their dreams are never the same.

## Mind Killer

Mind Killers, if not already invisible, look like columns of blurred background, with sparks and tiny stars darting about within — a vision that has inspired so much religious awe in primitives, often leading to the doom of entire tribes. When in the physical dimension, and unaware of human onlookers, they are visible day and night and have no initiative modifiers (+0).

They fight with mind attacks only, with a range of 0 to 50 meters. Its willpower trait is its strike value against the target's willpower, with the would-be victim's willpower trait treated as if it were agility to determine any defense value modifiers (example, the mind killer has 68 willpower, the target has a willpower of 46 and so -4 as a modifier based on the 'Agility DV' column on table TME-1-3 in the hub rules, which is repeated in this book as Table XR-2, on page 8.

The resulting mental attack SV is 68 -4 = 64 (hence, the dimensional being needs to roll from 01 to 64 to inflict damage on the target). On a mental strike, the target takes 1d10 willpower damage and 1d6 intelligence damage. When either of these traits reaches zero or less, the character is knocked into a coma.

Once the battle is over, and the targets are incapacitated, the mind killer will settle down over each victim in turn and begin to consume the prey. It will drain 1d10 from every trait per minute until all traits are zero and all that is left is a mummy–like dry husk. Only when each trait is reduced to zero or less is the victim considered dead. Victims rescued before death, but during the coma, will remain in a coma for 1d6+2 days, heal at one trait point each per day, even while in coma, and upon waking, experience hellish nightmares, see visions of the other world, and need to be restrained for 1d6 days before returning to normal. For one year after this ordeal, however, the victim will see all dimensional beings without the use of specialty relics or mutational powers.

## Dominator

Dominators are the most powerful dimensional beings who attack in the same manner as mind killers, however, they can do so on up to six separate minds at once, within the 50 meter radius range. In addition, they can simultaneously use 2d4 shock tendrils identical to those employed by a shocker in melee combat.

They appear as a wavering, elongated blur by day or night, gaining +6 initiative because of their virtual invisibility, although those who can see dimensional beings will identify these things as vaguely humanoid, masses of torn fabric, knotted flesh and clustered skulls about a central torso. Their legs appear as a dragging mass of rags and bones. Instead of walking, they float along the ground, or up a sheer cliff or skyscraper to either go after their victims or take cover from the few weapons that can actually harm them.

The dominator does not kill with its mental attack or shock tendrils, but reduces targets to zero endurance, willpower or intelligence, moves them one by one to an underground hideout, heals them at one trait point per hour, all while maintaining a telepathic domination over their minds. When fully healed, the dominator will use its new, zombified troops to either guard the dimensional portal it uses as a doorway between worlds, or destroy those who have opened it, or those who sought to enslave and control the dominator and its kind.

Beings under the control of this dimensional entity will have all their powers, mutations, skills and memories at the disposal of the dominator, to act as the master dictates. The victim will defend the dominator to the death, but, if ordered to kill a friend, mate, offspring or faithful pet, the drooling victim is allowed a willpower based Type C hazard check to refuse and if successful, gets another Intelligence based type A check to snap free of the dominator's control. Likewise, after a certain amount of time, all creatures under the control of the dominator will get an intelligence based hazard check to regain conscious control of his or her mind and body, this determined by the willpower of the victim. No memory of what transpired while under the dominator's control is recoverable.

Any being to snap free of the dominator's control will be deemed worthless to this evil being, and be targeted for dispatch and dismemberment by other controlled humanoids. If the dominator must kill a person, or destroy an android, machine or non-humanoid opponent, it will shock them into unconsciousness and then, within 10+2d8 minutes, dismantle the physical form into several hundred sections.

### Table XR-217 / Dominators Control Matrix

| Victim's Willpower | Duration of control before chance of consciousness returns | Intelligence based Hazard Check |
|---|---|---|
| 01-06 | 3d6+4 months | D |
| 07-22 | 2d6 months | C |
| 23-34 | 2d20 days | B |
| 35-64 | 2d6 days | A |
| 65-85 | 1d4 days | A, two attempts |
| 86-105 | 1d10 hours | A, three attempts |
| over 105 | 1d100 rounds | A, four attempts |

# Relics Associated with Dimensional Beings

Since dimensional beings might have no part in a game master's campaign, or fail to make an appearance at lower rank game play, these three relics were not added to this book's main relic arsenal. These items can be found within a high tech, dimensional portal facility, uncovered in a void area, or handed out to an adventure team by some benefactor who recruits the characters to undertake a remarkable cross-dimensional journey.

### Specter Rifle

This bulky, short muzzled energy weapon has a purplish hue to its alloy stock, foregrip, and pistol grip, and a cartoon ghost icon on the receiver. It uses a single power cell to fire up to 30 shots per charge, at a range of 620 meters, projecting a pulse of swirling fuchsia energy. If it impacts any regular target, it inflicts 1d20 points of tissue disrupting damage, while against any dimensional being will blast it for 1d100 points of damage. Against normal targets, it gains a +10 SV but against a dimensional being, gains +40 SV.

Beside the devastating power and long range of this very advanced, odd looking weapon, the electronic sights can see dimensional beings, rips and portals that are invisible to the naked eye, although the range of the optics is only 60 meters. It is assumed by new era relic researchers that either more powerful optics once existed, or this weapon was used by those wearing some sort of advanced dimensional viewing gear that justified the incredible range that this weapon boasts.

**Specter Rifle:** SV +10 /+40[a], Rate 1, Damage 1d20/ 1d100[a], Range[1] 620m, 2 handed, 20 STR minimum, power cell yields 30 shots, Weight 6kg, Value 10k+4d1000sp

*a: strike value against and damage done to dimensional beings. See weapon description. 1 Range shown is effective range, but all weapons can go double this, but, at a reduction of half the shooter's regular SV, plus, half damage on strikes.*

## Ghost Goggles

These bulky, bizarre goggles are encased in white and purple plastic and have reddish hued bubble lenses. When switched on, the user can see dimensional beings, dimensional rips, portals and other residue of an alternate time and space within 60 meters. So too, the operator can see through any holographic illusion, including any mutant trying to hide behind the mutation of Illusionary concealment.

All illusions appear as only a fuzzy, flickering projection over who or whatever is trying to hide behind it. These goggles weigh 2.2 kilograms, are uncomfortable to wear for more than a half hour, give the user a headache after ten minutes, and run on a mini power cell which will provide 36 hours of operation per charge. Each set will sell for 2000+1d1000sp.

## Wraith Fog Cannister

These gleaming, 20cm long metallic purple canisters are similar to grenades or spray paint cannisters, although come with several warnings to only use in a well-ventilated area or with a full respirator. When the top ring is yanked free, the cannister begins to hiss and must be tossed to the desired location, up to half the thrower's strength score in meters distance, where it detonates in a plume of translucent purple fog after 3 rounds.

Besides obscuring the thrower from whoever might be firing from the

cloud, this strange bitter tasting smoke reveals dimensional beings, any rips in between the worlds, or other phenomena, including any invisible or holographically concealed entities, or other illusions. Those hidden beings or objects in the smoke appear as dark shapes, and can therefore be targeted by those who normally can't see dimensional beings.

The fog will billow out into a 40 meter radius and remain in the windless area for a half hour, although if there is a breeze, it will dissipate after 2 minutes. Living beings to be caught in the fog have their air ways restricted, suffer from itchy, painful eyes and will cough purple phlegm for the next 2d6 days.

# Dimensional Travel

The travel between dimensional portals, either from different locations in The Mutant Epoch at the current date and time — yet over vast distances — or between planetary bodies, points in time on earth, or realities, are all possible. These journeys are facilitated by either extremely rare mutations, or more likely, by experimental machine made by either the old ones, or other beings and people from beyond Earthly reality.

Using the mutation of Dimension Hole (page 238 of this book) and various fixed portals, the game master can transport a character group to another time in Earth's history. The dimension hole mutation listing has a broad selection of random time travel destinations, although picking one that the GM is familiar with or wants to see his or her players explore is perhaps a better bet. For unfamiliar times and places, the GM will need to do a bit of research, maybe gather a few on-line resources such as maps, illustrations and information to flesh out a desired adventure site.

Finally, having the player characters enter other fictional worlds, either settings from novels, TV series, movies, computer games or fantasy RPGs, is also a thrilling prospect. With a few tweaks, any tabletop RPG can have the stats of spells, races, and monsters converted to the Outland System. The author himself as has a short, playtest version of a fantasy RPG using the Outland System. If there is a cry for this very preliminary booklet to be made available to the Epochian community, he could perhaps be coaxed to release it 'as is' in PDF format.

Actual travel between dimensions involves crossing through a rip, hole, arcane doorway, or high tech portal between the worlds. This can sometimes be a direct pathway through a portal into the other time or place, but 75% of the time involves crossing through an intermediary zone called simply 'the void'. This void is also the place where character go when using a mutation such as planer skip or dimensional retreat, and the like. Within the void, dimensional beings prowl the unearthly landscape, vapor clouds or gloom, and while they are not invisible here, they are both plentiful and especially aggressive.

Any living character to get lost in a void, or purposefully stay there for whatever reason, becomes ethereal. For every 24 hours spent in a void, a living being transforms 1d20% (1 to 20 percent rolled randomly each day) closer to becoming a lost soul. When 100% dimensional transfiguration occurs, he or she becomes a lost soul, and is irrecoverable and no longer a playable character. If yanked free of the void in time, either back to the world where he or she came from or another reality, the subject will shed this dimensional contamination at a rate of 1d12% per day. Androids, robots and digital beings suffer a data corruption issue when spending over 12 hours within a void, and take 1d20 data damage per day, as well as 1d12 endurance damage from corrosion which slowly breaks all machines down within this inter-world dominion. Vat-brains suffer both as a living being and a robot.

Sometimes the void appears as a barren, foggy plain. Here, the travelers can see a distant light where an exit gateway awaits. Some internal dimensional zones are quite earth-like, and appear as rocky wastelands complete with alien ruins, skeletons of bizarre beasts, or like a starless sea, complete with a waiting boat that will take them across the waters to their destination and another portal. In every case, now visible dimensional beings, especially lost souls, will gather to either plead with, distract or devour the living interlopers. To handle these interactions in the dimensional voids, see Dimensional Encounters below.

# Dimensional Encounters

Inter-portal encounters usually only happen when there is a void between one dimensional opening and another. These voids can be as close together as a stone's throw across, like a band of dimensional reality with untold length but very limited depth, but are more likely to appear as a broad expanse of up to a kilometer between the gateway the characters entered and the distant exit portal — a portal that is usually visible as a light source. Where a direct portal exists without any 'void' area, however, dimensional beings might exist on either side, and usually come at travelers in their invisible form.

Once within a void, travelers can have encounters with dimensional beings immediately, as if entities are standing guard near a portal and aim to block would-be travelers from getting to the other world, another time, or place. At other times, encounters can happen after travelers make a loud noise, shout back and forth, drop something or touch some forbidden monolith, pool, or item. Once a fight breaks out between inter-dimensional travelers and the beings that exist in this in-between reality, there is a 4 in 10 chance that more dimensional beings will show up 3d6 minutes after the first outburst of combat. Experienced travelers of the void know to move fast, avoid interacting with even the most friendly, seductive and benign looking beings, and just get through to the far side, or retreat to the opening they came from.

In the physical world, these entities are especially prevalent near dimensional rips, holes and open ancient experiments, ancient artifacts in museums, alien portal devices brought back to Earth from deep space explorations, or proximity to an ultra powerful mutant who uses dimensional beings as servants, guards and companions. Indeed, mutant lords of great power can control lesser dimensional beings and will use them as watchers around their stronghold, whereas other beings, including humans, from other worlds sometimes gain dominion over one or more dimensional beings and can set them as sentries between the worlds, or post them as sentries in the Epochian reality to stop interlopers from crossing over to their own reality.

Dealing with dimensional beings in the physical world is sometimes even more challenging than facing them on their own turf, since in the void, 'specters' cannot go invisible and are often spotted at a distance, and so easier to strike. In the physical world, it is usually only deviants with mutations such as a Discern Dimensional Beings or those lucky few who have relics or certain implants that can see these beings and engage them in a more-or-less fair fight. Only energy weapons, mental attacks, energy based mutations and specifically the rare yet wonderful specter rifle can harm dimensional beings.

## Frequency of Encounters

1 in 10 chance per 10 minutes in a 'specter' guarded area in the physical world
3 in 10 chance when first entering a void.
1 in 10 chance per 100m of void crossed, to a limit of only one encounter check per half hour. If the void is less than this distance across, then make just 1 encounter check besides the first entering check above.
4 in 10 chance, 3d6 minutes after any loud noise, fight or other commotion occurred in a void.
3 in 10 chance upon existing an unfamiliar portal*.

*Regardless of if a void had to be crossed or a direct portal was used.

## Table XR-218 / Random Encounter in the Inter-dimensional Voids, At Portals, or other GM selected sites *Roll 1d10*

The first number is the dice roll result, the second is the number of beings appearing. Example: 5,6/1d6. The 5,6 is the numbers on a 1d10 roll, while the 1d6 is the number of dimensional beings appearing. Rank tiers: characters of low experience ranks 1-4/ mid ranks 5-9/ high ranks 10+. Roll 1d10

| Dimensional Beings | Low Rank | Mid Rank | High Rank |
| --- | --- | --- | --- |
| Lost Souls | 1-5/1d6 | 1-4/3d6 | 1-3/5d6 |
| Rippers | 6,7/ 1d3 | 5,6/1d4+1 | 4,5/1d6+3 |
| Shockers | 8,9/1d2 | 7,8/1d3+1 | 6.7/ 1d4+2 |
| Mind Killers | 10/ 1 | 9/1d2 | 8,9/ 1d3+1 |
| Dominators | -/ nil | 10/ 1 | 10/1d2 |

# The Void

Few Epochian scribes believe that the void, let alone dimensional portals and entities, even exist. Those who believe, or have even experienced it, however, often disagree what the inter-world realms really are. Some speculate scientists from the pre-cataclysm time created the void who, in their hubris, self-assurety, and quest for results, dismissed the possibility that something unexpected might happen. Others choose to believe the voids have always been at the edges of reality, and serve as a buffer or a cushion between realities. Yet others believe the voids were formed by the limitless power of a mutant mind, that the residue of undisciplined and unscrupulous, perhaps unwitting deviant psionic masters created the voids from nothingness, and populated it with the tortured souls of men and women who dared explore such forbidden reaches of consciousness, time, and place.

Others of a more theological mindset believe the void is the biblical purgatory, that the lost souls who dwell there are languishing between life and afterlife, their souls yet to be judged by God, that they have not yet ascended to heaven, or fallen to eternal damnation.

Many cults have their own view on the shadow realms, with some making sacrifices of people and beasts to the things that emerge from beyond, or send their chosen to enter the void through a portal, believing they go to discover their deity, their arms loaded with gifts.

For the game master, creating a void region can be done by rolling on these four tables. Remember to use the previous Frequency of Encounters table to determine when and if the travelers have run-ins with dimensional beings during their journey across.



**1.** No distance at all! There is no void as the travelers step from one portal and through an opening into another place, time, or dimension.

**2.** Very close, only 20+1d20 meters span across.

**3.** Not far at all, 100+1d100 meters.

**4.** A fair trek at 1000+1d1000m

**5.** Quite far actually at 4km +1d1000m (Note: 1000m = 1km).

**6.** Way off! 10km+1d20km



**1.** Rocky, uneven ground. Half movement speed. Many pits, caverns and overhangs where anything could be hiding with all encounters met at 2d6m range on first contact.

**2.** Bizarre, black sand dunes and occasional dark, rocky slabs containing fossils of creatures nobody can identify. Half the time the travelers are on top of a dune and can see for up to 200m, the other half of the time they're in the trench and encounters here are met at only 3d6 meters distance.

**3.** A vast plain of scrub land with long dead trees, countless bones of humans and unidentifiable giant beasts. It's fairly flat and so if anything is out there, the travelers will see it at 30+1d30m away.

**4.** A shore and broad, sluggish waterway filled with swirling shapes, spine covered fins and greasy bubbles. There is a large wooden boat of bizarre design sitting on the shore. The paddles within are made of black wood and feel warm to the touch. If crossing the water and rocky plains that wait on the far shore, visibility is decent and so any entities here can be seen coming from 50+1d100m away. If anybody falls in the water, they are attacked each round they are out of the boat by dozens of toothy, nameless, half-seen things SV 01-70, damage 3d6 treated as 1 attack per round. This waterway seems to have no current.

**5.** Shifting, dense clouds that support the weight of the travelers. Clouds whirl about at waist height, and anything encountered in this void will be met at close range of only 2d6 meters.

**6.** A gently rolling prairie of grass-covered hills. Anything met here can be seen 30+1d30m distant.



**1.** Dense fog which leaves the skin of travelers damp. Visibility is much reduced but any distant portal can always be seen as a bright spot on the horizon. Range of encounters reduced to only 1d6+3 meters.

**2.** Swirling, multi-colored clouds which coil and churn across the landscape.

**3.** A chill wind that drags with it ribbons of fabric, small bones, dead leaves, scalps and tufts of fur. Also in the wind come the tormented voices of hundreds of dead people, each wailing out their warnings, their regrets, the names of who wronged or killed them, or pleas for help to wake them from this nightmare.

**4.** A hard driving rain of black oil. The stuff gets in clothing, armor and the mouths of travelers, tasting of sweat, rot and boggy soil. When leaving the void, all evidence of the black grease is gone, except the memory of how it tasted.

**5.** Blackness punctuated by the occasional wispy, legless, skull faced ghost that passes right through travelers. Their tortured wails and laughter echo off the domed ceiling of the void. Any encounter in this gloom is met at 6+1d6m.

**6.** A coiling white fog so dense that travelers can only see 4 meters around them, except for any distant portal destination, which gleams golden yellow on the horizon. Encounters here are met at 2d4m distance.

### Void Table Four: Other Feature of this Void   Roll 1d8

**1.** The ceiling of the place is a gigantic, stalactite covered cave 100+1d100 meters above.

**2.** Above you, the sky is dark and dotted by unfamiliar constellations of stars.

**3.** There is a wrecked, archaic sailing ship perched on the ground, with tattered sails that whip in the breeze. Rusty cannons stick out of gun ports, and rigging hangs down. The ship could house many nameless horror, but so too, could offer shelter.

**4.** Wherever the travelers walk, they are illuminated by one or more spotlights of golden light from some unseen source. Hiding here is impossible and all feel that they are on some sort of stage, watched by an unfathomable, cold intelligence.

**5.** A woman, who seems to be everywhere and nowhere, screams at the traveler: "Get the hell out of here! You are forbidden! You cannot go any further! I swear, you will be punished if you transgress any further!" She will repeat these warnings and not respond to calls or questions from the travelers.

**6.** To one side is a dilapidated, ruined fortress of stone. The castle's one still standing tower has a flickering light in the upper turret window.

**7.** As the travelers walk along, living characters see appirations (thus digital beings, androids and robots see nothing here) out of the ground spring up the ghostly blue and green, translucent shapes of dead comrades, childhood friends, family members and others each person knew in life. These ghosts look on with dismay at the characters, seem to speak, try to reach for the travelers but make no sound and their wispy hands turn to clouds as they pass through the characters.

**8.** Jets of fire erupt from sinkholes in the ground. Every ten meters the group travels, one randomly chosen PC is potentially cooked, and must make a Type C agility based hazard check in time to leap aside or be blasted by a 4 meter high spout of flame. If unable to get clear in time, the flame spout will inflict 1d6 damage per round for 1d4 rounds. There is a hard to see trail that zig-zags between the portal gates. However, with the character with the highest perception trait value allowed a single type E perception based hazard check to notice it. If spotted, it is 10+1d30m away and once reached and followed, the flame holes can be avoided.

# Dimensional Gateways

The following sample selection of random gateways and portals is an excellent place to start when setting up portals into other worlds, or into the voids between inter-dimensional openings. The random dice roll range is added for quick, on-the-fly game sessions, NPC rumor creation, or idea generation. Unless specified otherwise by the game master, see 'Void Table One' on the previous page to establish the distance across a void, if any. Roll 1d6 first for the random gateway departure description, and then another 1d6 for the gateway's exit destination.

### Random Dimensional Departure Gateways   Roll 1d6

**1.** This is a gleaming hole in reality about 3m in diameter, and only visible to those mutants or relic equipped individuals who can see dimensional beings and phenomena. The hole will have a green, sparkling light at its edges, and every so often, crackle and seem to threaten to close up.

**2.** A great stone portal with crude slab steps lead up to a glowing, light filled rectangular opening. An opaque, undulating spiral of star filled energy stands before you like a window into another reality. You notice strange markings carved into the stone frame, along with symbols that look like skulls, suns, moons, and doors, as well as crude carvings of warriors with shields and swords, of winged lizards and a horned god. All about the steps you see the crushed skulls of humans and fanged beings that could only be some sort of skullock-like creature. Here and there, links of chain mail, a broken arrow, and rusted bits of well crafted armor litter the place.

**3.** A well-like portal with steep, stone steps leading down into the interior where an opaque, gray fog coils and surges. Every so often, you see sparks flicker in the depths.

**4.** This is a 2m tall by 40cm wide gash in reality. To those with the mutations or technology to see dimensional beings and objects, this rip appears as a triangular cut with its edges illuminated by golden, flickering light. The rip seems to shutter every so often, as if it struggles to heal the wound in reality on its own. For how long this portal will remain open, and what lies beyond, is unknown.

**5.** Within an ancient chamber stands an odd, still active relic arch with a ramp leading up to a shimmering, purplish black, swirling screen of about 4 meters in height and 3 meters in width. Enormous steel bars surround the edge of the portal — although the bars are bent and snapped outward toward you. All about this place are the desiccated, torn apart husks of ancient dead humans in white, long coats. Machinery at the periphery is destroyed and toppled, all except for one lone computer work station that blinks and buzzes away; its power source, and that of the weird portal, seems to come from wires buried in the concrete floor.

**6.** Buried under silt and trash is a hatch down to a large chamber filled with computers, screens and a control room. This chamber overlooks a hanger bay containing one raised, highly advanced piece of machinery. Spotlights illuminate a ramp up to the strange, 6 meter tall, high tech machine where a shimmering, upright pool of swirling, illuminated colors await. Beyond the brightly colored portal you can see nothing, and yet, the junk littered, dusty chamber behind this strange doorway is still visible. All about the room lay the yellowed, white robbed skeletons of what look like pure stock humans.

### Gateway Exit Destination   Roll 1d6

**1.** Doorway to a fantasy world where myths, magic and gods are real. Mutants, cyborgs, and stranger characters will be seen as demons in this land.

**2.** Time travel gate to a different time in Earth's history. Pick a time, or consult the random listing for the mutations Dimension Hole on page 239 of this book.

**3.** Portal to another location in the current time frame but elsewhere in the same world as the departure gateway.

**4.** Portal to the main gateway chamber on an orbiting space station over earth, in real time. Space station is only partially operational, with a vast section having its haul breached. Robotic sentries will be alerted to the presence of interlopers while a few still living crew will be woken from cryo freeze.

**5.** Portal to a Martian colony. There is only a 3 in 10 chance the facility at the other end has even been used in the last century, and might be abandoned and the chamber used as either storage, a morgue, or sealed off from the main complex. There is a population of 1000 minus 1d1000 people alive in this once great city (so between 0 and 999 people depending on the dice roll and reduction of colonists). The lost colonists are either dead and their desiccated remains found throughout the place, or have abandoned this area long ago and now live in a larger Martian city. Robotic custodians will soon encounter the PCs and alert whatever population might still exist on the red planet.

**6.** An alien world in a solar system the characters don't recognize, with unfamiliar stars above and two moons. The portal they exit is of entirely unfamiliar construction, with unkown writing on the controls. The travelers have been noticed by local wildlife, and a 43% chance by the intelligent occupants of this strange planet.

# New Combat Options

## Suppression Fire

This tactic is designed to keep opponents at bay, keep their heads down and reconsider any potential charge or attempt to jump up, expose themselves and fire on the characters. When successful, each enemy will stay pinned down, and when returning fire, do so poorly and unleash blind firing (-30 SV).

To handle this option, the user must have plenty of ammo or mutational uses and be able to first lay down ranged attacks out ahead or just in front of the opponents, each of whom must make a morale check to continue to advance. Failure means they fall back, drop prone or take cover. On their next turn, they can either return fire poorly (-30 SV), and yet gain a -40 defense value bonus while taking cover, or else retreat 2d6 meters.

Only creatures that are smart enough to know the dangers of gunfire, energy weapons or whatever other ranged attack mode is being unleashed before them will hesitate to advance against suppression fire, or else must have a sense of self preservation. Green walkers, robots, mind controlled minions, or those who are more afraid of their whip masters and officers than the characters are also likely to walk right out into a barrage of withering fire. The game master's discretion on this tactic, and its effectiveness, is essential — to say nothing of the ammo supply of the side laying down the suppression fire.

Morale checks are discussed on page 110 of the hub rules, and require a willpower based hazard check by the pinned down enemy. As a quick reference, beings with poor morale need to make a WIL based type D hazard check. Those with average morale need to make a Type C check, while those of firm morale require a Type B check and anyone with excellent morale need only make a Type A willpower based hazard check to disregard suppression fire.

## Blind Firing

Sometimes exposing one's head and torso to the enemy, especially if being outgunned or trying to hide one's identity, is inadvisable. Yet, to keep the opponents pinned down or maybe take a few out, is also desirable. In these times, blind firing is the answer.

Here, the character can take their best guess at where an opponent is located and shoot a gun, crossbow, mutational appendage, or other missile weapon around the corner or over the top of a trench. Doing so reduces one's aim, which suffers -30 strike value penalty, however as the shooter's hands and firearms are normally all that is exposed, the shooter gains a -40 defense value bonus. The pay offs for this tactic are potentially huge, although with the rarity of relic ammo or expenditure of daily uses of potent mutations, using this combat option must be carefully considered.

To summarize, blind firing is done at -30 SV penalty but gives the mostly hidden shooter a -40 defense value bonus.

## Warning Shot or Intentional Miss

Sometimes a character wants to scare someone with a knife thrown through a hat, gunshot near the foot, arrow between the thighs, or shattering a mug of beer with a slash of a sword tip. Such displays of prowess and threat are often sufficient to persuade somebody to apologize for an insult, reconsider a threat, or take the performer of this warning shot or intentional miss, more seriously. Still, there is a chance that the shooter or instigator of this intimidating maneuver accidentally hits the target instead.

Because the difficulty — shown as 'Defense Value' on the forthcoming chart — is considerable with any of these decidedly dangerous tasks, performing such a tactic is best left to those who are excellent shots or sword users, because any miss can cause injury or death of whoever the character intended to threaten, tease or taunt.

An intentional miss is a 'called shot', but isn't actually an attack on the target's body, so their armor, agility, dodge skill and other factors that contribute to their defense value matter little, if at all.

This tactic, then, entirely depends on the aim of the shooter or wielder of a blade or other tool. On the table below, there is a Defense Value rating for each warning shot or intentional miss example. This DV is to 'attack' the space, article of clothing, or whatever the target is holding. Any miss could cause a 'total miss', or an unplanned attack and likely injury on the target person. If an 'Oops!' occurs upon the target, then make a separate strike roll against that person using the weapon or mutation just used for the warning action, but use the target's normal defense value unless they are unsuspecting and so unintentionally attacked at +40 SV, or +30 if merely unaware of the shooter but already engaged in a fight. This 'Oops!' attack occurs in the same round as the attempted warning shot or intentional miss and spends the same single charge, usage or cartridge.

Of course, using a weapon that has a blast radius, or spray attack such as a shotgun shell or spout of flame from a flame unit, cannot work as a precision, intimation attack, and is instead treated as a normal attack on 3 man sized figures if they're close together. The dice roll in light gray is merely for the GM or solo player to establish totally random results using this chart.

### Table XR-219 / Warning Shot or Intentional Miss Chart

| 1d8 | Warning Shot or Intentional Miss Examples | Defense Value* | Roll 1d100 for failure outcome** |
|---|---|---|---|
| 1. | Slash a person's belt so gear or pants/skirt fall off | -60 DV | 01-39 Oops! / 40-00 total miss! |
| 2. | Slash open a shirt, bra, or other piece of lingerie to make it fall away | -65 DV | 01-42 Oops! / 43-00 total miss! |
| 3. | Shoot hat off a person | -60 DV | 01-64 Oops! / 65-00 total miss! |
| 4. | Shoot near somebody's foot to scare or make them dance | -40 DV | 01-34 Oops! / 35-00 total miss! |
| 5. | Shoot between person's legs | -50 DV | 01-41 Oops! / 42-00 total miss! |
| 6. | Shoot glass or bottle from person's hand as they drink | -70 DV | 01-48 Oops! / 49-00 total miss! |
| 7.8. | Throw knife or dagger through cloak or baggy fabric to pin person | -30 SV | 01-29 Oops! / 30-00 total miss! |

*Defense Value of the target location or item, not the DV of the target person who is the subject of the warning shot or intentional miss. Using the instigator's normal Strike Value for whatever chosen attack mode they have selected, treat this as a normal attack against the DV shown, with an automatic success on a natural 01-05, and always a miss on any roll of 95-00.

**If a warning shot or intentional miss fails (i.e. the character rolled higher than the DV amount shown in the previous column), then roll 1d100. If the dice toss results in 'Oops!' then make a separate, normal strike roll by the shooter's attack mode on the target. This attack happens in the same round as the intended warning shot. If a 'total miss!' occurs, the shot or slash goes wide and impacts some other object harmlessly.

# Beam Focusing & Sweeping Attacks
*by James Butler*

## Alternate Settings for Laser Weaponry

The standard form of firing for laser weaponry is typically a quick fire blast, each shot the result of the weapon system being activated for a fraction of a second. This is by far the most economical use of power by such weaponry, but for some individuals (primarily those for whom the acquisition of power is not an issue) prefer an alternative mode of firing: a beam of energy that is maintained for as long as the trigger is held.

This requires an inordinate amount of power and eats through any power cells at a rate of three times the listed value (for example, a standard laser pistol may only be fired for 10 rounds with the beam setting, or a wrist laser for five with one final standard blast finishing off the mini cell). The rate of any weapon using this mode is reduced to 1, but the wielder may choose from two distinct firing options each round:

### Beam Focusing

Focusing the weapon burst on a target for an extended time. Although a separate SV check must be made per round to maintain contact, at a base -15 penalty after the initial attack, to reflect minute natural wavering of the hands and movement of target in light of the visible beam (but this is mitigated by a wielder possibly possessing a relevant Weapons Expert skill, which affords +5 SV per skill point). The benefit of this mode is an increased level of damage because of the prolonged contact of the laser, which translates into the default damage of the weapons all being increased by a factor of 25% (e.g. if a wrist laser is used in this manner, and damage of 15 is rolled, an additional 3 points would be added to the total each round).

### Beam Sweeping

Sweeping the beam to strike several targets within a 60 degree horizontal arc, kept within 10 vertical meters of the starting point. This option requires a separate SV check made with a -20 penalty after the initial strike, as the sweep is easy to see/predict despite its quick movement within a single round. The damage inflicted by this form of attack is significantly reduced by -30% (e.g. a laser pistol that would inflict 18 base points of damage would only strike a target for 12); each target struck must roll for damage separately. There is no limit to the amount of enemies that may be struck by this beam setting, so long as they are within the parameters of the firing arc and range. This form of attack can force several not directly targeted enemies to seek cover, rather than a sole target being the focus of attack to the benefit of its allies, providing great tactical benefit (but at a great power cost).

Although a select few models (roughly 12% of laser-based arms) come with a beam option included as standard, other weaponry may be modified, either by official aftermarket parts or tinkering (which, depending upon the competence of the modifier, result in a weapon only being able to fire in a beam thereafter). A gunsmith can attempt to make this alteration, using the Gunsmith table on page TME-40, consulting the 'Repair Energy Weapon' column to make the appropriate Intelligence based hazard check to succeed, per hour.

# Jury Rigged Limbs
*By Danny Seedhouse*

In The Mutant Epoch age, there are plenty of things waiting to take a piece off your character. Add to this environmental dangers, falling debris, unexploded ancient ordinance, crazed robots — you get the idea. People often lose limbs and there is a need for those willing to kit bash together some sort of replacement. The quality of these limbs vary drastically from the wooden peg leg, hook, clockwork hands, steam driven monstrosity and the sleek ultra-tech cybernetic of the high tech enclaves.

## Building Choices

### Scratch Built

This is the category of limb that varies the most, running the gambit in style and complexity from a stick with a blade on it, to a steam driven iron battle arm, and a high tech alloy arm running on a power cell. The choices made in construction are presented below. This option, and the attachment of these parts, are available from several sources, including the Junk Doctors caste described on page 18 of this book.

### Robotic Limb

This involves attaching a robotic limb salvaged from a humanoid robot. It is perhaps the best option outside of a real cybernetic leg or arm. Robotic limbs from household, industrial repair, medical, police, light combat, heavy combat and similar units can be attached, although some need extra support and bracing depending on the size of the part being attached.

The problem is control. Robotic limbs are not built to interface with organic systems, and unless the patient is a cyborg, who can use the metal limb, extensive surgery and high tech parts are required. Someone with 4 points in the medic skill can attach the limb after a robotics or cybernetics technician of 4 or more skill points has modified the limb and attached an interface system (see Human-Machine interface under Scratch Built Limbs, on page 372).

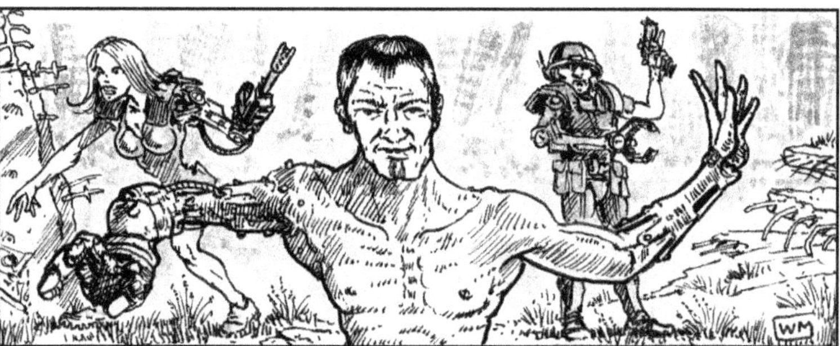

### Android limbs

For those of basically human appearance, the salvaged limb of an android is the best bet. These are easy to disguise with cosmetics and clothing if the limb is of similar body proportion, complexion, and has intact synthetic skin over most of the limb. Rules for attachment are the same as for robotic limbs.

### Scratch Built Limb Charts

### Step 1: Construction Materials

The most common materials are listed below and assume that the majority or the limb is made from the chosen material. If a junk doctor or other builder wants to build a limb composed of two types of materials, simply average the two choices. A builder with 4 points in mechanical technician skill can make a near perfect replica of a human limb that, when covered, will visually resemble a real limb, especially if these efforts are combined with the use of the disguise artist or artist skill. These limbs cost an extra 25% more in materials and increased build time.

The 1d8 die roll shown on the following table is to facilitate random generation of found, or available limbs for GM use.

| 1d8 | Material | DV Mod. | END Mod. | Weight | Cost |
|---|---|---|---|---|---|
| 1,2. | Junk | DV 0 | +2d6 | 10+1d10 kg | 10+2d20 |
| 3. | Wood* | DV -1 | 5+1d6 | 10 kg | 50+1d20 |
| 4. | Plastic* | DV -1 | 5+1d6 | 5 kg | 100+1d20 |
| 5. | Metal-wood composite* | DV -2 | 8+1d10 | 15 kg | 200+2d20 |
| 6. | Metal | DV -3 | 10+1d12 | 20 kg | 400+1d100 |
| 7. | Relic metal scraps | DV -4 | 12+1d20 | 15 kg | 1000+2d100 |
| 8. | Advance composites | DV -5 | 15+1d20 | 10 kg | 2000+1d1000 |

*Non-metallic limbs bypass most cybernetic detectors.*

*Note: Keep in mind this is just the basic limb itself with no power source or movement systems.*

**Junk limbs** can be built by anyone with 2 points in the junk crafter skill using a mix of whatever parts are available. They impose a -5 penalty to SV on any weapon wielded by them or a -0.25 meter penalty to speed. When build with extra care and time over 2 days by someone with 4 or more points with junk crafting, the penalties to SV and move can be eliminated.

**Wood** is usually the easiest of the materials to find and anyone with basic skill with a knife and enough time can carve one. Quality can vary as more time is put into carving the limb, and it can be made quite artistic. This limb is, however, flammable, which could be a problem.

**Plastic scraps** can be found almost anywhere in the Epochian wilderness, ruins, or scrap markets, and with a bit of skill and glue, anyone with 1 point in mechanical technician skill can build a basic plastic limb. These limbs are primarily used by folks who don't want to show up on a metal detector or those with no other choice. Unless wrapped in foil, these parts are flammable.

**Metal and relic metal** limbs require the same skill to make a plastic limb, but at a higher difficulty rating: 3 points in mechanical technician skill. The fundamental difference between limbs of this caliber comes from the quality of the metal and workmanship available.

**Advanced composite** limbs are the high end of replacement limbs and require 4 points in the mechanical technician skill and 1 point in robotics technician to produce, plus access to advanced relic tools.

## Step 2: Motors:

From the basic unpowered prosthetic to advanced artificial muscles, this component makes the limb move. Motors are arguably the most important choice and provide the baseline physical stats of the limb. For tasks involving the whole body, it is suggested that the GM average the stats involved (add each limbs stat being used in an action and add one more for the torso or core if needed).

| 1d8 | Movement systems | Base Strength | Base Agility | Weight | Cost |
|---|---|---|---|---|---|
| 1. | Unpowered hinges | 10 | 5 | None added. | 10+1d10sp |
| 2. | Junk crafted | 15+1d6* | 15+1d6* | 10+1d10kg | 2d100 sp |
| 3. | Springs and pistons | 30** | 15** | +10 kg | 100+ 2d20sp |
| 4. | Hydraulics | 50 | 15 | +15 Kg | 200+1d100sp |
| 5. | Basic motors | 25 | 25 | +10 Kg | 200+1d100sp |
| 6. | Advanced motors | 35 | 35 | + 8 Kg | 500+1d100sp |
| 7. | Artificial muscles | 45 | 40 | + 2 Kg | 2000+2d100sp |
| 8. | Composite system | | | | |

*Add 1d6 per skill point of junk crafter*

***See springs and pistons*

**Unpowered hinges:** This is the basics, with no fancy motors to move the limb. This chart assumes a full limb is being replaced, so see the notes at the end of the section for partial replacements for limbs, for example, replacement hands and lower legs.

**Junk crafted:** Scavenged motors are made of a mix of scraps, springs, pistons, motors big and small — whatever can be found. They take 2+1d6 hours to build (needing 2 points in junk crafter skill to start). They are noisy as all get out (-1 point using the stealth skill when turned on), heavier (+1d6 kg) and use 25% more fuel. Furthermore, junk crafted motors require a bit of luck and skill to find the proper parts requiring 1d4 hours of searching and a Type C perception hazard check, and a type E perception hazard check for advanced motors. Their stats are variable and rolled once when the limb is constructed, although if the player doesn't mind extra book keeping, re-roll every time the PC critically fails a check involving the limb, and/or any time the limb is unduly stressed.

**Springs and pistons** are fairly complex but require the least amount of high tech parts to produce. To build this motor system and its parts requires 3 points in the mechanical technician skill. One advantage to this system is that they can be tuned to sacrifice power for speed; basically swapping base agility for base strength. A junk crafted version can be built by a 4 skill point junk crafter, which takes 1+1d4 hours to assemble the limb, adds 1d8kg to weight and on any critical failure on a roll involving the use of the limb means the springs have broken and the limb is useless until repaired. When used in melee combat breakage occurs on a strike roll of 96 and up.

**Hydraulics** are slow and powerful, favored by folks who want raw power but don't mind taking the -1 penalty to initiative when using the limb. Hydraulic legs absorb impact well, taking 2 meters off the distance of any fall per leg (with a successful Type B agility hazard check, a hydraulic arm can be used in the same way). To build and install hydraulics, a mechanical technician of 3 or more skill points is needed.

The biggest problem with the limb is a loss of hydraulic fluid, which can be caused by a well aimed attack. A successful called shot with a -35 DV penalty or -25 for a carefully aimed shot that deals 10 or more points of damage, renders the limb useless in 1d4 rounds as the hydraulic fluids rapidly drain. This damage must be repaired by someone with 1 point in the mechanical tech skill, or jury-rigged by someone with 4 skill points (skp) in junk crafting — of course the jury rigging only lasts 5+1d20 rounds of combat or heavy work before blowing out again.

Junk hydraulics take 2+1d4 hours to build, are larger (+1d10 kg), more complex (5 skp in junk crafter needed), slower (-0.25 meters speed if a leg), and prone to failure. Automatic failure results on any strike roll of 96 and up, rendering the limb useless until repaired.

**Basic and Advanced Motors** were used in the first truly functional cybernetic limbs. This system uses several small motors for power, they provide an excellent amount of power and reaction speed. The small size of most of the motors used limits strength but allows for considerable agility, making this system the choice for folks who don't what to advertise their new limb. These motors are complex, and to build a basic motor requires 5 skill points in mechanical tech, and 6 points for advanced motors. Like all junk built versions, these motors break when used in melee combat breakage on any strike roll of 96 or higher.

**Artificial muscles** were the height of artificial limbs. Artificial muscles are used to replicate the functions of the original biological limb they are replacing, and where often covered with artificial skin, making the limb indistinguishable from a real limb, especially if plastic or other light and non-metallic bones were used. These limbs also can operate without the use of an external power source, drawing any needed power from the host's body but suffering a -10 penalty to both base strength and agility. Artificial muscles need someone with 5 points in the robotics technician skill to make, plus a basic understanding (minimum of 1 skill point) as a bio-technician and as a medic.

**Composite systems** use a combination of different motors, which makes for a better operating system. When combining systems, use the best base stats for the limb and average the weight and cost of both systems.

Hydraulic systems are most commonly combined with other motors, and the following notes apply. Springs and pistons do not remove the -1 penalty to initiative from hydraulics, although any form of motor will. The impact absorption abilities of the limb are not affected. The amount of damage needed to cut a hydraulic cable goes up by 5, the resulting loss of pressure halves all the physical stats of the limb.

## Step 3: Power

A power source provides the juice to make the motors work, gears turn, pistons pump, and turns the limb from so much dead weight to a useful mechanical limb. The random 1d6 shown on the following features list is for GM use only when either constructing npcs or establishing what's available at a scrap dealership.

| 1d6 | Power Source | Battery Life | Weight | Cost |
|---|---|---|---|---|
| 1. | None | Infinite | None | Free |
| 2. | Clockwork | Variable, see text | 2kg | 500+1d100sp |
| 3. | Liquid fuel | 200 rounds/L | 5kg+fuel | 250+1d100sp |
| 4. | Mini-power cell | 1 month | 100g* | 200+1d100sp** |
| 5. | Power cell | 3 months | 100g* | 300+1d100sp** |
| 6. | Power pack | 2 years, 5 months | 100g* | 300+1d100sp** |

** weight of power cell/pack is extra*
*** Cost of power cell/pack not included*

**No power source:** The limb is a useless hunk of material, although perhaps artistic. Unpowered hands are usually hooks and provide very basic uses, however, a weapon can be attached to the limb with a -5 SV penalty as long as no movable parts are involved in its use and the owner swings their torso to propel the false arm. With a false leg, on the other hand, at least the user can stand on it and hobble along with a -3 meter speed penalty and loss of 1/2 of any dodge or agility bonuses to DV.

**Clockwork:** A key is turned, winding a spiral spring to store potential energy for later use. A series of gears control the speed at which this energy is released. The use of gears makes the power supplied by clockwork tunable to different applications. The base system takes 5+1d6 minutes to wind and provides power for 20 minutes.

**Liquid Fuel** uses a combustion engine to power the limb. This form is noisy, belches fumes, and requires the user to carry around a fuel tank. This can be a gas engine, diesel, biofuel, or propane. Basically, any liquid fuel system can be used, but all of them make it very hard to sneak up on an alert foe unless there is significant noise in the environment. A person can store about 1 liter of fuel in the limb itself, while everything else needs an external tank, which must be carried and can be attacked with a called shot with potentially explosive effects. A switch or pull cord starts the engine and requires 1d4 rounds to start the limb up for the first time. Limbs can idle when not in use, costing 1 round of fuel every 5 minutes. Most new era barter markets sell ethanol fuel at a cost of 1d20+20sp per liter, although to buy a relic, 2 liter tank would cost 200+2d100sp, if not more.

**Power cells** are by far the best choice to power a cyber limb, they provide the longest amount of run-time. The cell is normally contained within the limb and not easily accessible by thieves.

**Power pack** An externally mounted power pack that provides power for much longer periods of time than a power cell, but can be stolen or damaged as it is not protected inside the limb.

**Author's Note: Successfully sneaking with a running motor involves a vast combination of factors, so this is my personal take on it since I'm a 'anything is possible, but some things are just insanely hard' kind of GM. Feel free to change this as a GM yourself. Silent actions can't really be attempted, but concealing movement to sneak up behind a target can succeed on a Type M agility based hazard check if unskilled, or 4 letter hazard check tiers easier if skilled (M becomes I). This is modified based on noise in the area, with the default being no extra noise beyond breathing. The louder the environment, the smaller this penalty should be, so the sound of people talking reduces this penalty by one letter code, but a loud rock concert or active gun fight negates this penalty altogether. — DS*

## Step 4: Human-Machine Interface

This feature controls the limb's movement, and makes it more then just a peg leg or a hook hand.

| 1d6 | Type | Cost |
|---|---|---|
| 1. | None | Free |
| 2. | Pull cords | 10+1d4sp |
| 3,4. | Muscle movement reader | 250+1d100 sp |
| 5. | Electrical impulse reader | 500+2d100 sp |
| 6. | Direct neural interface | 5000+1d1000sp |

**None:** This is a basic uncontrolled limb. The character has a dangling false arm or a peg leg, though well designed limb's can provide advantages (see endnotes). The limbs strength and agility become effectively 1. One uncontrolled leg allows the user to stand and walk poorly, but at a -3 meters move rate penalty. In combat, an uncontrolled arm can only be used poorly with a -40 strike value penalty to melee attacks as the subject flails around. Accurate ranged fire is impossible except if the character uses a functioning hand to take time to carefully aim a shot over two rounds while bracing the unresponsive limb against an unmoving surface.

**Pull Cords:** Barely a step up from no interface at all, pull cords allow very basic control of the limb, usually to lock the limb in place for a specific purpose or in a specific position. Aka locking a hand in the closed position to hold an object. Each joint has several cords attached to it, allowing the manual positioning of each joint. This is useless in a combat situation or any task requiring speed, but hey you can hold a glass now. Apply the same penalties as 'none' interface to tasks.

**Muscle Movement Reader:** This basic form of control combines queues from movement, with design and computer programming to mimic basic limb functions and perform simple tasks. Someone with 2 points in medic or junk doctor skill can attach this system. However somebody with 3 skill points in electrical technical and 2 points in computer technician are required to produce it. Physical tasks are slower to preform but are possible, usually taking twice as long as actions by a living limb, while anything involving fine manipulation is much harder to preform with a primary limb, increasing to hazard check code by 2 letters (for example a Type B becomes a Type D), this should be judged on a case-by-case basis by the GM.

Legs controlled in this way slow movement down by -1.0 meters, per limb (remember the average agility between both legs is used for movement speed bonuses). Melee combat with the limb suffers a -30 SV if used as the primary arm and a -2 initiative, this is reduced to -10 if the weapon is two handed, and a -1 penalty to initiative — assuming the other arm is normal or otherwise suffers no stat deficiencies. Missile weapon use is possible if all the user need to do is pull a trigger with their artificial hand, although at a -15 SV penalty and a -1 initiative, yet when used as a secondary hand on a weapon, such as to support the foregrip of a long gun, crossbow or hold a bow, the deduction is only -5 SV. When sniping or spending anytime longer than one round to carefully aim, there is no penalty to SV.

**Electrical Impulse Readers:** Advanced sensors read and interpret nerve signals at the attachment site, providing seamless control of the limb. These systems must be custom made and calibrated for each specific user, requiring someone with 4 points in either the medic skill or junk doctor skill and about 1 week of continuous practice with the limb to achieve full function. Building this system requires somebody with 5 skill points as a robotics technician, or 4 points in electrical tech plus 2 points in computer tech. Any critical hit with an electrical stun or any other attack that does extra damage to cyborgs shorts out this system for 1d6+1 rounds, making it uncontrolled during this time.

**Direct Neural Interface:** This is the type of control used by cyborgs and generally requires spinal and brain implants. This is what makes a cyborg basically plug and play with attachment rules covered by the robotic skill in the Hub Rules book. Advanced cyber limbs used a stripped-down and specialized version of this system, with a chip implanted at the base of the spine paired with a specific limb. Implanting this system needs a highly skilled medic or cybernetic technician with 4 skill points. Production of the system requires 5 points in electrical and 3 points in computer tech to build and program the chip. The chip needed for this is a relic that cost 2000+2d1000sp at minimum, but is rarely ever available in a marketplace and must instead be found in the ruins.

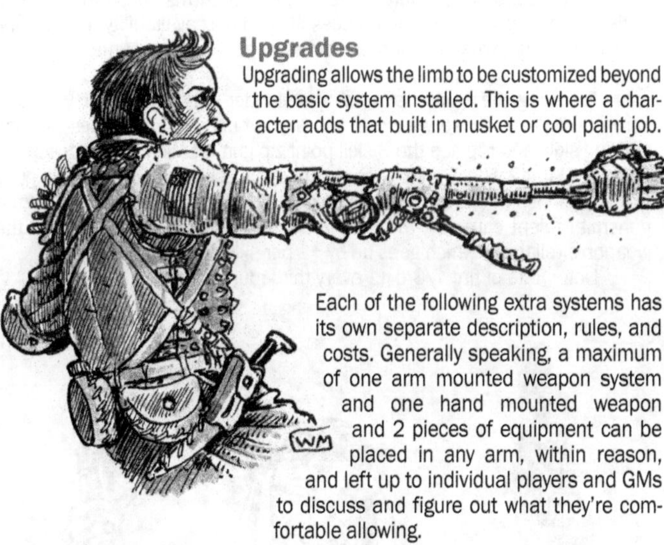

## Upgrades

Upgrading allows the limb to be customized beyond the basic system installed. This is where a character adds that built in musket or cool paint job.

Each of the following extra systems has its own separate description, rules, and costs. Generally speaking, a maximum of one arm mounted weapon system and one hand mounted weapon and 2 pieces of equipment can be placed in any arm, within reason, and left up to individual players and GMs to discuss and figure out what they're comfortable allowing.

### Types of Upgrade
- Personalization
- Built in weapons
- Limb reinforcements
- Utility systems
- Performance Enhancements

### Personalization
This covers the small touches from a paint job to a chrome finish, and the cost and availability are up for discussion between you and the GM. These systems don't provide bonuses as a rule and are all about asthetics.

### Built in Weapons
Any type of 1 handed weapon can be implanted in a cyber limb within reason. Of course, this will be very obvious to anyone looking at the user and may cause problems with town guards and the like. There are a couple of ways to deal with the problem of concealment, however, and include internal storage, and using detachable weapons.

Internal storage limits the size of weapon usable to pistols and anything smaller than the length of one's forearm, and usually only one weapon system can be implanted in a limb, the exception being blades that are small enough to fit completely within a hand or foot. To implant a weapon cost 25% of the weapon's purchase price above the weapon's cost plus a flat fee of 200sp. It takes 1 round to ready a concealed melee weapon unless one has a direct neural interface system, then it's an immediate action to ready. Ranged weapons can be used immediately if one is not concerned about any clothing draped over the top of the barrel.

Detachable weapons are identical to a cyborg's weapon arm and use the same rules as weapon arms presented on page 92 of the hub rules. Regular weapons must be modified to fit on a weapon mount, for a cost of 250+1d100sp, or by anyone with the gunsmith, or mechanical technician skill.

## Unique Cyber Limb Weapon Systems

| 1d8* | Name | SV | DMG | Cost |
|---|---|---|---|---|
| 1,2. | Razors | +1 | 1d8 | 50+2d10sp |
| 3. | Relic razors | +3 | 1d10 | 500+d100sp |
| 4. | Shotgun surprise | +40 | 3d10 | 25+10sp + cost of a shotgun shell |
| 5. | Big knuckles | +1 | +1d6 | 10+2d10sp |
| 6. | Piston hand | +15 | 3d10 | 50+2d100 |
| 7. | Claws | +3 | 1d20+2 | 100+2d20sp |
| 8. | Relic claws | +10 | 1d20+5 | 800+1d1000sp |

*1d8 die roll for GM use for random discoveries or NPC outfitting only*

**Razors** and **Relic Razors** are small, sharp blades implanted in fingers or toes and used to rake and cut. They are easily concealable behind fake nails or can be made retractable for 50% more. Relic razors are simply higher quality metal and 1 in 6 sets found are made from non-metallic materials.

**Shotgun Surprise** is basically a shotgun shell in a short barrel implanted in the palm of a hand, the knee, elbow or heal of the foot activated by contact — hit the target hard enough and the shell goes off. This is a cheap deadly surprise that can be easily concealed under clothing or makeup until fired.

To use a shotgun surprise, the operator must first strike the target with an unarmed attack, then the shell fires adding the 3d10 damage to the strike damage. Most of these units only hold a single round, although a more advanced version is available costing 1500+1000sp and adds an 8 round pressure fired pump shotgun to the cyborg limb, this version has a rate of 1. This weapon system can be done with any type of bullet and so adjust range, SV and damage as needed and change the cost to reflect the new round type loaded.

**Big Knuckles** consist of reinforcements added to the striking surface of an appendage. These hard points comprise anything from bolts welded on, nuts, washers, screws or bits of iron. This augmentation adds mass and power to a punch.

**Piston Hand.** This weapon system involves a spring loaded fist that, when triggered, suddenly slams forwards 1 meter, much like a blunt spring blade. After use, it takes 1d4+2 rounds to reload the hand. While extended or used without extending the pistons, it operates as Big Knuckles, above.

**Claws** and **Relic Claws** are 2 retractable blades built into the forearm of the limb and, when not stowed within the limb and concealed, can be extended for combat. There is a 3 bladed version of this system available named after a pre-fall comic book character. This system adds 100sp to the cost for normal or 200sp for relic blades and +1 SV and DMG.

## Utility Systems

Most pieces of gear can be implanted in a cyber limb for a fee off 200+3d20sp for unpowered attachments, like a compass, or 400+2d100sp for relic gear. Generally, only hand held pieces of equipment can be installed in any particular limb, although larger pieces can be installed in legs. Backpack sized pieces of gear are too big for attachment.

## Limb Reinforcements

This is basically adding extra materials to certain parts of the limb to toughen it up. These materials do not need to be the same as the base material used in the limb and can be removed and replaced if better materials become available. This upgrade can be done twice, but the second DV bonus is halved rounding up. When mixing materials, add the full value of the best material and 1/2 the second one.

| 1d8 | Reinforcement Material | DV Mod. | END Mod. | Weight | Cost |
|---|---|---|---|---|---|
| 1,2. | Junk | DV -1 | END +1d4 | 2+1d4 kg | 5+2d6 |
| 3. | Wood | DV -1 | END +1d6 | 1 kg | 12+1d8 |
| 4. | Plastic | DV -1 | END +1d6 | 5 kg | 20+1d10 |
| 5. | Metal wood composite | DV -2 | END 4+1d6 | 1.5 kg | 40+2d10 |
| 6. | Metal | DV -3 | END 5+1d8 | 2 kg | 80+1d20 |
| 7. | Relic metal scraps | DV -3 | END 6+1d10 | 1.5 kg | 100+2d20 |
| 8. | Advance composites | DV -4 | END 7+2d10 | 1 kg | 200+1d100 |

## Performance Enhancements

Theses are tweaks to the limb that enhance specific aspects of its performance and have individual costs and requirements.

## Quick-Draw Limb

This adds springs in fine tuned joints, adding +3 Initiative and 50% to base cost of the limb. This enhancement can only be added to a limb with power and at least muscle movement readers. The initiative bonus is only for the first round of combat, but on a limb with a direct neural interface, this enhancement provides a +1 to initiative on the fallowing rounds, too. Quick-Draw Limbs are incompatible with system reinforcements.

## Increased Strength

This adds extra or better pistons, springs or motors to the limb to upgrade its strength beyond the limb's basic level. Strength is added in 5 point increments up to a maximum of double original limb strength. Cost is 25% of motor cost per 5 points.

## Increased Agility.

Adding extra or better pistons, springs or motors to the limb will upgrade the limb's agility. Added in 5 point increments to a maximum of double original limb agility much like strength. Cost is 25% of motor cost per 5 points. Agility and strength increase are not mutually exclusive, though they are expensive.

## Running Legs

These are legs and feet optimized for speed using advanced composite and smart materials that offer optimal traction and force-feedback systems to increase running speed. A basic system adds 1 meter to run speed and costs 1000+2d100sp per leg. Upgraded speed can purchased at a cost 500+2d20sp per 0.5 meters of extra speed. This enchantment only works if both legs in a pair are enhanced and powered.

## Shock Absorbers

Adding extra shock absorbers and materials to absorb impact allows these limbs to negate fall damage. A basic system costs 400+1d100sp and takes off 2 meters of fall distance if one lands on their feet. Upgrades cost 200+1d100sp and add 0.5 meters to safe fall distance. A limb using hydraulics can just use the upgrade cost to increase their safe fall distance. This system works for a single leg but only applies half its benefits. Although if a person makes a Type C hazard check, they can land properly on the single leg. A failed roll means the system is 1/4 as effective.

## Partial Limbs

Sometimes a character is unlucky/lucky enough to just lose a hand or a foot and doesn't require a full limb replacement. Hand and feet replacements cost 1/4 the listed price of a full prosthetic. Having an unpowered and controlled foot does not reduce base speed, though having a lower leg replacement that is unpowered reduced base speed by 0.25 meters per leg.

Unpowered and uncontrolled hands are useless for fine manipulation and pulling a trigger, however, weapons can be used instead of a hand. 1 handed melee weapons attached in this way suffer no penalties beyond the normal ones (off hand weapon). A one handed firearm attached can be shot with a simple muscle reading interface with no penalties for shooting. Two handed weapons can be used instead of a lower arm, but these are difficult to aim properly at longer ranges and suffer a -10 SV over 20 meters and a -20 SV over 100 meters.

Cost is 200+2d100sp to attach a weapon, not including weapon cost, ammo or interface cost.

# Scrap Built Guns *by Danny Seedhouse*

In the Mutant Epoch, finding a fully functional gun can be a challenge, and necessity, as they say, is the mother of innovation. Scrap built guns are completely improvised and built from parts scavenged from the environment, often with substandard materials, and thus many explode on the first shot. As there are no standard types for these firearms, these rules offer a series of choices based on both necessity and part availability. These guns are never going to match a purpose built weapon, but sometimes one must make do.

Following the steps below, a wastelander can make their very own scrap built guns. These weapons can all be built using the rules for junk crafting skill, and replace the 3 skill point zip gun creation option described on page TME-42 with what follows — although a section on creating zip guns is also included in this part of the book starting on page 376. Folks with the gunsmith talent can craft these firearms at 1 skill point and improve the weapon's reliability, which goes up by +1 per skill point in this area.

Note: Rate of fire 1/3rd (1 every third round).

## Random Scrap-built Gun

To generate a random gun, roll once on each chart.

### Step 1: **Find a bullet**

| 1d6 | Ammunition used by Scrap Built Gun |
| --- | --- |

1. Black powder +2 SV, 1d20 DMG, 25 meters. -2 reliability.
2. .22 +5 SV, 1d10 DMG, 100 meters. These rounds increase reliability by +2.
3. Pistol. +8 SV, 1d20 DMG, 120 meters.
4. High caliber pistol +12 SV, 1d20+10, DMG 180 meters.-1 reliability.
5. Shotgun shell +15 SV, 3d10 DMG, 20 meters and can hit multiple targets is a close group. Shotgun shells like .22 caliber rounds are low pressure and improve reliability by 1.
6. Rifle +12 SV, 1d20 DMG, 300 meters. -3 reliability.
7. High caliber rifle +15 SV, 1d20+10 DMG, 450 meters. -4 reliability.
8. .50 Cal. +20 SV, 3d20+10 DMG, Range 2km, -6 reliability.

### Step 2: **Find a barrel**

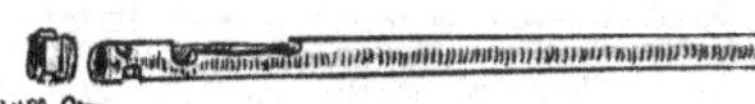

| 1d8 | Barrel Type |
| --- | --- |

1. Wooden tube, -15 SV, -2 DMG, -60% range, -4 reliability.
2. Banded wooden, -15 SV, -1 DMG -50% range -2 reliability.
3. Plastic pipe, -10 SV - 50% range, barrel warps after firing -20 SV second shot, -1 reliability.
4. Heavy plastic pipe or heat resistant plastics, -10 SV, -40% range +0 reliability.
5. Thick Copper pipe, -10 SV -35% range, +1 reliability.
6. Metal pipe, -5 SV -20% range, +2 reliability.
7. Reinforced Metal piping, -5 SV -15% range, +4 reliability.
8. Relic barrel, 0 SV -0% range. +6 reliability.

*Note: Rifle length barrels give +20% range and a -1 reliability.*

### Step 3: **Figure out how to fire it**

| 1d6 | Firing Mechanism |
| --- | --- |

1. A nail. Yes, just a sharp bit you jam against a hard surface -15 SV, -30% range.
2. Pressure fired, you jam the bullet against something sharp, but with a slide built in, making it easier to actually aim the damn thing, -8 SV and -15% range.
3. A nail with elastic bands or a spring, you snap manually, -5 SV.
4. A nail, a tack or anything sharp with a spring and a simple trigger mechanism. No modifiers to SV.
5. Single action trigger mechanism must be cocked manually after every shot. This type of trigger is usually not built but scavenged from old firearms. Using this trigger is quick enough to allow for multiple shots to be fired in a round, usually from multiple barrels. +2 SV, +1 reliability.
6. Relic trigger mechanism, semi auto or double action and it doesn't require manual cocking after each shot. +2 SV, +2 reliability. Note: 1 Skill point in Mechanical Technician is needed to make this, or Junk Crafter 3 skill points.

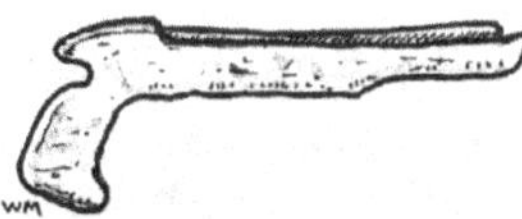

### Step 4: **Add a grip**

| 1d6 | Grip Type |
| --- | --- |

1. No grip, -10 SV
2. Crude grip, -5 SV
3. Carved grip, usually from wood using a knife and time. Basically a musket pistol style.
4. Crude pistol grip, might not be comfortable but it works, -5 SV on any shot beyond the first made in a round
5. Scavenged pistol grip or one built with skill and time, +1 SV.
6. Rifle style with a stock. Aimed shots receive a +10 SV to overcome other penalties from the weapon itself.

### Step 5, **Attach some sights**

| 1d8 | Sights on Scrap Built Gun |
| --- | --- |

1. No sights, -10 SV, 1/2 range
2. Crude sights using a nail or something else, -5 SV at ranges over 10 meters.
3. Scrap built scope, +5 SV when aiming.*
4. Simple open sights.
5. Glow sights, +2 SV.
6. Closed sight, +5 SV. Max one shot per round.
7. Laser pointer, +10 SV at under 20 meters.**
8. Relic scope, when aiming down the scope which takes 2 turns, shooter gains a +20 SV

**+15 when aiming if built by someone with junk crafter 3 or gunsmith 2.*
*** This laser is visible and makes it nearly impossible to hide or disguise who the target is.*

### Step 6, **Pull the trigger and hope it doesn't explode**

This step involves adding all the numbers up and figuring out the weapon's SV, DMG, Range and reliability. Good luck.

Reliability is subtracted from the automatic miss number range of 96-00 on a d100 attack roll. If the attack roll is within this new range, the shooter has a misfire and must roll 1d8 on the misfire chart, to follow. Critical Failures on attack rolls with scrap built guns exhibit the normal effects of a fumble and a 1d10 roll on the misfire chart. For example, a gun with a -5 reliability will suffer a failure on a 91 or better, and auto miss on 96 or fumble on a 100.

**Table XR-220 / Scrap built Guns Misfire Chart Roll 1d10**

| 1d10 | Misfire Description |
|---|---|
| 1. | Hot load, or too much powder, destroys barrel after you fire, but a hit does max damage. |
| 2. | Not enough bang. A hit does half damage but the gun is fine. |
| 3. | Bullet is a dud, or your powder is wet. Simply reload and try again. |
| 4. | Barrel warps or cracks and needs replacing. Until done take -10 SV and a -1 reliability |
| 5. | Firing mechanism fails. Make a type B intelligence based hazard check to fix in 1d6 rounds, or rebuild it out of scrap parts with the junk crafting skill. |
| 6. | Barrel cracks and needs replacing after this shot. |
| 7. | Hang fire. The bullet smokes and fires in 1d3 rounds. Be careful where you point it. |
| 8. | Gun falls apart from recoil and must be rebuilt. Parts are reusable. |
| 9. | Gun explodes, destroying its barrel and maybe user's hand. Make a Type C agility based hazard check to avoid bullet damage, and mangling 1d3 fingers. |
| 10. | Everything goes boom, and the shrapnel flies: SV 01-75 explosion doing bullet damage to everything in a 2 meter radius. Needless to say, the gun is destroyed. |

### Bonus Options

**Adding Extra Barrels**

Add extra barrels for more shots. These barrels can rotate and make the gun semi-auto. Or if a user is really brave, add a trigger per barrel to get a rate of fire (ROF) equal to the barrels fired, this imposes a -5 SV penalty and can result in all the barrels failing as you check for each one.

**Bullets on Melee weapons**

We all know someone's gonna want to do this. Basically, you get a holder and a nail. So you use step 1, 2 and 3 for Scrap Built Guns (usually a nail) and add them to a melee weapon. On a successful hit with the weapon, the round goes off and does damage to the target. This adds the rules for reliability to your melee weapon and one big bang for a single shot. A fresh cartridge must be reloaded after every use.

# Building Zip Guns
*by Danny Seedhouse*

To allow for a local gunsmith to have a wider selection of guns that are more affordable than relic firearms, but different from muskets, the following rules will be helpful. For a random zip gun, either carried by an NPC or up for sale in a market, add all the cost amounts together to get the final sale price. Also, custom zip gun orders can be priced out for ammo found without a gun. In this case, add all the costs except the cost per bullet as shown in step one.

### Step 1: The Bullets

See step 1 for Scrap-Built Guns for SV, DMG and Range.

| 1d8 | Ammunition Type and Amount for Zip Gun |
|---|---|
| 1. | Black powder, cost 1sp for 1 shot with powder |
| 2. | .22 caliber rounds, usually has 2d12 costing 1d10+20sp a round |
| 3,4. | Pistol rounds, usually 2d6 available for 1d20+50sp per round |
| 5. | High caliber pistol rounds, 25% chance of having 1d6 rounds for 2d20+70sp each |
| 6. | Shotgun shells, usually 2d8 available for 1d20+55sp each |
| 7. | Rifle rounds, usually 2d6 available for 1d20+50sp each |
| 8. | High caliber rifle rounds usually 1d8 available for 2d20+70sp each |

### Step 2: The Barrel

| 1d8 | Zip Gun Barrel Type |
|---|---|
| 1. | Wooden tube. 1d4sp / -15 SV, -2 DMG, -60% range |
| 2. | Banded wooden. 2d4sp / -15 SV, -1 DMG, -50% range |
| 3. | Plastic pipe. 2d6+5sp / -10 SV, -50% range, -20 SV 2nd shot |
| 4. | Heavy plastic pipe. 3d6+10sp / -10 SV, -40% range |
| 5. | Thick copper pipe. 2d10+ 20sp / -10 SV, -35% range |
| 6. | Metal pipe. 2d10+30sp / -5 SV, -20% range |
| 7. | Reinforced metal piping. 4d10+30sp / -5 SV, -15% range |
| 8. | Relic barrel. Pistol costs 500+2d100sp, rifle barrel costs 700+2d100sp / +0 SV |

### Step 3: Figure out how to fire it

| 1d6 | Method of Firing Zip Gun |
|---|---|
| 1. | A nail. 1sp / -15 SV |
| 2. | Guided manually, 1d4sp / -8 SV |
| 3. | A nail with a spring. 1d4+2sp / -5 SV |
| 4. | A nail, a tack or anything sharp with a spring and a simple trigger mechanism. 2d10+20sp / +0 SV |
| 5. | Single action trigger mechanism. 200+1d100sp / +2 SV |
| 6. | Relic trigger mechanism. 500+2d100sp / +2 SV |

### Step 4: Add a grip

| 1d8 | Zip Gun's Grip |
|---|---|
| 1. | No grip, is free / -10 SV |
| 2. | Crude grip, is 1sp / -5 SV |
| 3. | Carved grip, 4+2d6sp / +0 SV |
| 4,5. | Crude pistol grip, 10+2d6sp / -5 SV |
| 6. | Hand carved pistol grip, is 20+2d10sp /+1 SV |
| 7. | Relic pistol grip, 200+2d100sp. Combined with a relic trigger, you use a clip and get rate of fire 2/ +1 SV |
| 8. | Rifle style with a stock, 30+2d10sp / +10 SV |

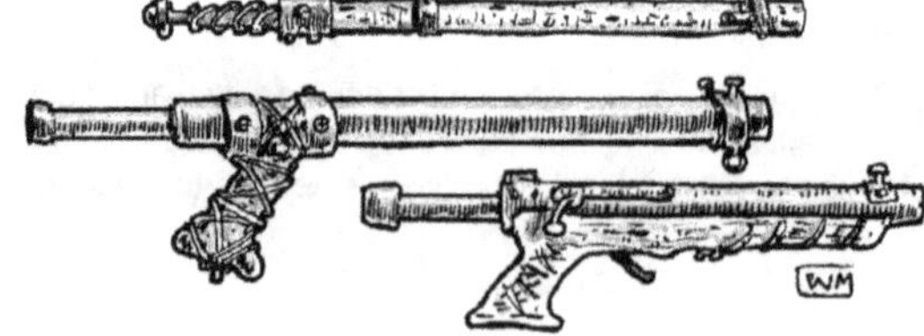

## Step 5: Sights

| 1d8 | Zip Gun's Sights |
| --- | --- |
| 1. | No sights, is free / -10 SV, 1/2 range |
| 2. | Crude sights using a nail or something else, cost 2sp / -5 SV |
| 3. | Scrap built scope, 20+2d20sp / +5 SV when aiming carefully |
| 4. | Simple open sights, 2+1d4sp for the work / +0 SV |
| 5. | Glow sights, 2+2d10sp / +2 SV |
| 6. | Closed sight, 30+1d100sp / +5 SV |
| 7. | Laser pointer, 500+2d100sp / +10 SV when target under 20 meters |
| 8. | Relic scope, 600+4d100sp / +20 SV when looking down scope |

Add the costs for each step to establish the zip gun's final purchase price.

# Custom Built Black Powder Weapons

*by Danny Seedhouse*

Also known as 'locks', these custom built black powder weapons are hand-made, sometimes more powerful and often multi barreled flintlocks. They are more expensive to buy and use and are usually only found in the hands of excavators, raiders and mercenaries or other such questionable folks with more coin than sense.

Prices for these locks are based on several factors. Each has a base price for the basic frame with one barrel and is otherwise a regular musket weapon, although the price increases with each additional barrel. Usually the same caliber barrel are used in the weapon but some varieties have been seen with large caliber or shotgun round mixed in with other barrels for 'versatility'. A cylinder, such as those seen on relic revolvers, adds to this price as do additional barrels, although it is rather impractical to have both a cylinder and multiple barrels on the same gun. The maximum usable barrels on a gun is 5 unless the operator is unusually strong (strength trait over 40).

Custom pieces purchased to order 'off the shelf' are priced as fallows. The base musket determines the damage, range, rate of fire, and weight. Extra barrels increase the rate of fire to one shot per trigger, unless the weapon has two triggers and, like a shotgun pistol, can have a maximum of two barrels fire at once. Cylinders can only fire pistol or rifle musket balls, although the 6 shot variant can fire high caliber musket balls.

### Table XR-221 / Black Powder Weapon Cost Chart

| Part Name | Cost |
| --- | --- |
| Base, Musket Pistol* | 110+2d20sp |
| Base, Musket Rifle* | 130+2d20sp |
| Base, Musket Shotgun* | 140+2d20sp |
| Extra Trigger** | 50+1d20sp |
| Cylinder (6 rounds) | 50+2d20sp |
| Cylinder (8 rounds)*** | 75+2d20sp |
| Extra Regular Barrel | 50+1d20sp |
| Regular Musket ball and powder | 1sp |
| Extra High Caliber Barrel | 100+2d20sp |
| High caliber musket ball and powder | 5sp |
| Melee attachment | 2d10sp+melee weapon cost. |

*This is the base black powder weapon. The price includes its standard single barrel, however, add a 20+1d20sp assembly fee.*
** Max one extra.       ***Regular musket balls only.*

## High Caliber Muskets

High caliber musket barrels only fire larger lead balls, or in the case of shotguns, fire even more pellets, screws, bolts or whatever else is rammed into the weapon prior to firing. High caliber musket pistols and rifles have a bonus of +5 strike value and inflict +3 damage, while high caliber musket shotguns have a +10 SV bonus and inflict an extra 1d10 damage (now 4d10 DMG).

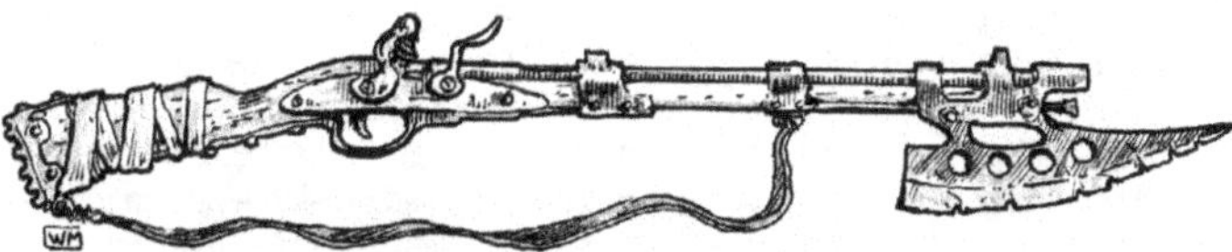

## Melee Attachment

This is adding a bayonet to the weapon. Bayonets do not modify SV. Attachments bigger than a bayonet make the gun harder to use. One handed weapons that do a 1d12 base damage suffer a -2 SV penalty to both shooting and melee attacks. Weapons with a base 1d20 damage suffer a -4 SV penalty, half this penalty on a 2 handed firearm.

## Determining Stats

Extra barrels increase the rate of fire to one, or two if there is a double trigger installed. Reloading each barrel takes 2 rounds.

*For handy reference, here are the base Black Powder Weapon Stats:*

| Black Powder Weapon | SV Mod. | Rate | DMG | Range | Hands | STR* | Ammo | Weight | Price |
| --- | --- | --- | --- | --- | --- | --- | --- | --- | --- |
| Musket Pistol | +7 | 1/3 | d20 | 25m | 1 | - | powder & 1 shot | 900g | 2d20+90sp |
| Musket | +14 | 1/3 | d20+3 | 140m | 2 | - | powder & 1 shot | 3.5kg | 2d20+120sp |
| Musket Shotgun | +18 | 1/3 | 3d10 | 30m | 2 | 22 | powder & 1 scatter shot | 4.5kg | 2d20+140sp |

**Strength needed to wield without suffering a - 20 SV penalty.*

# Learning Reading, Writing, Math and Swimming *Suggested by Chris M.*

Excavators often face circumstances where team members exhibit an area of knowledge, besides skills, that companions lack. For specialized skills, such as dodge, cybernetics technician, driver, brawling and so forth, tables in both the hub rules and this book cover the time to learn such talents from either a trained comrade or through attendance at a rare post-apocalyptic 'college'. To learn skills found in the hub rules, see table TME 1-23 Skill Acquisition by Education on page TME-35. For skills in the expansions rules, see Table XR-168/ Skill Acquisitions by Education set 2 on page 200.

What follows here, however, is how to handle reading, writing, math and swimming. Areas of knowledge which can often be taught by one adventurer or tutor to another during down time, at camp, or periods of travel.

While reading and math are safe enough skills to teach around a fire or across a saloon table, swimming is instead a much more involved, and possibly a dangerous subject to pass along. Having a non-swimmer enter a water body is risky enough, but for even a poor, fair, or even strong swimmer entering an unfamiliar pond or stream in The Mutant Epoch environment could be hazardous, as besides the risk of drowning, the waters of the new era are filled with hungry predators. Choosing where to train somebody to swim is the hardest part about teaching somebody this important skill.

The following table shows the days needed to teach somebody reading, writing, basic or advanced math, and swimming. The time it takes is based on either their intelligence trait value for academic skills, or strength and agility averaged out to establish their 'aquatic learning trait' for swimming. Although the following chart gives a random number for how many days it takes to attempt to learn each skill or tier of a skill, the lesson within each day is only 2 hours long, but a rest and reflection period between each day's lesson is part of the learning process. In short, a person can only learn so much per day before they become mentally exhausted and overwhelmed, at least in one subject, and must expend the rest of the day to absorb what they have learned.

The difference between basic and advanced math is that basic tier means simple counting, subtraction, addition, multiplication and division — and so roughly grade 6 level math as learned by 21st century children. Advanced math involves geometry, algebra and equations equivalent to what an old world high school graduate would have learned if taking math right through to grade 12.

Because swimming has several tiers, each skill tier has a more challenging hazard check. For reading, writing and math, the teacher must already be accomplished at these talents, and after successfully instructing the student, the pupil is assumed to achieve the first level of ability. Reading and writing have only one described tier, although an intelligent and dedicated student could master the craft of word smithing and excel far beyond their original instructor to become the greatest writer and historian in the region. In swimming, the teacher must be of one skill tier higher than the student up until the level of excellent swimmer, which the student can eventually achieve, although the hours in the water to do so are numerous, and the risks of encountering an aquatic predator in any location except a enclosed, safe pool are considerable.

To learn a tier in one of these skill areas, the student must make a trait based hazard check AFTER the instruction time is completed. Failure means 50% of that last skill tier's daily time commitment must be spent again before another hazard check is made.

Make the shown hazard check after a training period in days is completed. The GM can roll the amount of days and record this, with the player involved in the training informing the game master that their character spends their evening going over their notes, doing spelling tests, practicing their front crawl in a creek, etc. The random days shown for a task is only known by the game master.

**Table XR-222 / Learning SKills Matrix**

| Trait of Student* | Read | Write | Basic Math | Advanced Math | Swimming | | | |
|---|---|---|---|---|---|---|---|---|
| | | | | | Poor | Fair | Strong | Excellent |
| 1-4 | 60+6d6 days/ E | 60+6d6 days/F | 144+6d6 days/E | 80+8d6 days/H | 32+4d6 days/D | 45+5d6 days/E | 67+6d6 days/F | 120+8d6 days/G |
| 5-9 | 50+5d6 days/ D | 50+5d6 days/E | 72+5d6 days/D | 60+7d6 days/F | 16+3d6 days/C | 22+4d6 days/D | 36+5d6 days/E | 90+6d6 days/F |
| 10-34 | 40+4d6 days/ C | 40+4d6 days/D | 36+4d6 days/C | 50+6d6 days/D | 8+2d6 days/B | 12+3d6 days/C | 24+4d6 days/D | 60+4d6 days/E |
| 35-64 | 30+3d6 days/ B | 30+3d6 days/C | 18+3d6 days/B | 40+5d6 days/C | 4+1d6 days/A | 9+2d6 days/B | 18+3d6 days/C | 30+3d6 days/D |
| 65-84 | 20+2d6 days/ A | 20+2d6 days/B | 9+2d6 days/A | 30+4d6 days/B | 2+1d6 days/AA | 6+1d6 days/A | 12+2d6 days/B | 17+2d6 days/C |
| 85 and up | 10+1d6 days/ AA | 10+2d6 days/A | 6+1d6 days/AA | 20+3d6 days/A | 1+1d3 days/AA | 3+1d4 days/AA | 6+1d6 days/A | 10+1d6 days/B |

*Trait to use: For reading, writing and math, use the character's intelligence score. For swimming, add the PCs strength and agility scores together, divide this by two to get their 'aquatic learning' trait. Failure means 50% of previous training period must be repeated before another hazard check or 'test' can be attempted.*

# Radiation and Effects on Robots and Androids

Even robots and androids without special shielding can handle mild and medium radiation many times better than any organic being — except for those mutant freaks who have adapted to either withstand or use this normally hazardous energy — yet robotics are still at risk of damage, interference, and whole system shut downs. While they cannot get cancer, as people and animals do, they suffer from prolonged exposure even to low doses, which interferes with mechanical systems, servos, circuits, optical receptors, cameras, communications and semiconductors. When exposed to strong radiation levels, any robot, or the digital parts of a cyborg, will begin to deteriorate and cause computer errors as 1s flip to 0s, and micro-shut downs and glitches occur.

To an onlooker, such a rad-afflicted robot or android will exhibit bizarre behavior, have difficulty speaking, experience interference and garbled words when transmitting with on-board or hand held comms. The unit will have its motor functions and speed impaired, and suffer considerable damage to servos, synthetic muscles, and other moving parts. Most of this damage can only be repaired by replacing the radioactive, and now faulty parts — often at great expense and sometimes considerable risk to the technician,

since metal parts can retain dangerous levels of radiation for weeks, if not months or years after exposure.

Any dose of lethal radiation will shut down and destroy any robot, android, vat-brain's body or a cyborgs part within a matter of minutes. Such damage is permanent, and only by swapping out defective and rad-contaminated parts can the machine be saved. Normally, if a robot's CPU or brain survives, it is best to insert the 'consciousness' and memories of the robot or android into an altogether different, uncontaminated body. All robots and androids had their cranium installed CPU protected from a wide range of threats, with their 'brain' encased in layers of protective material to help withstand intrusions by scanning, EMP discharges, static electricity, moisture damage and to some degree, radiation exposure, too. Because of this, it is often the CPU that alone survives an intense radioactive event, an event that normally dooms all human companions to die within hours.

While the robotic or android's body is typically destroyed by such an event, the CPU of the computer can be extracted outside the radioactive zone, and when the half life of the contamination decreases, usually after 14 days, the

CPU can be inserted into a temporary or new housing or body. A vat-brain with an intact liquid tank, a digital being whose 'vehicle' or container is compromised, can also be extracted from a destroyed bodily vessel, saved, and get a replacement body in the same way.

Any self aware robotic, android or vat-brain character whose CPU is inserted into another body retains all its skills and rank gained benefits.

The following table lists what each tier of radiation, as described on pages 125 and 126 of the hub rules, does to a robot, android or computerized mechanical system. While this section focuses on what happens to mechanical characters, these same complications will afflict non-conscious robots, as well as vehicles that are exposed to radiation, especially the more severe intensities.

Should a mechanical being be fitted with the cybernetic implant 'Radiation Leeching Unit', as seen on page TME-90, then the intensity of radiation drops by two degrees (strong becomes mild, medium and mild are ignored, etc.). Any mutorg that has the mutation of radiation absorption or radioactive pulse might have their physical tissues and organs more-or-less protected from radiation, but any implants are still susceptible to the complications of exposure according to the following table.

As with organic characters, a mechanical being is allowed an endurance based hazard check per hour or per minute while exposed to a contaminated area, object, or focused attack. The table below shows the endurance based HC in the first column. This hazard check, which uses the full, uninjured trait value instead of whatever it is when the event occurs, must be made either every hour for mild radiation exposure, or every minute for more potent levels.

Only by failing a hazard check do the list of complications and contamination happen, although since a new hazard check must be made every hour or minute — often without the character even aware of the dangers until it begins to suffer trait losses, complications and glitches — the being is highly likely to be exposed sooner or later while in a rad-zone. Once exposed, no further contamination exposures are added unless the robot goes into a more radioactive area.

The dice column is used for in-game random applications by a game master trying to determine a rad-zone's intensity for on-the-fly games.

## Explanation of Table XR-223

### Radiation Level

This intensity can be something the mechanical being walks into or, is immersed in, splashed with, or hit with if struck by some sort of radioactive pulse or beam. So too, the intensity can be arrived at by multiple exposures to lesser intensities as shown on the table on page 125 of hub rules, whereby for example, 4 exposures to mild radiation step up and on the 5th exposure, the victim is now contaminated by on 1 dose of medium radiation. Because radiation is invisible, a robot and its companions must endeavor to spot the signs of a contaminated area, or else have some relic means of detecting radiation either through visual means or a rad detector.

## Table XR-223 / Effects of Radiation on Androids and Robots

| 1d10 | Radiation Level | Hazard Check | Endurance Damage | Comms | Optics | CPU | Exposure to Others | Recovery |
|---|---|---|---|---|---|---|---|---|
| 1-4. | **Mild Radiation** | A, per hour | 1d4 pts per hour | 5% scrambled/ 1% failure | 7% complication/ 1% offline | 1 pt DMG to Data, INT and WIL per hour/ 1% glitch | Mild for 2d6 hours | 2d6 hours back to normal and all damage healed. |
| 5-7. | **Medium Radiation** | B per minute | 1pt per minute | 11% scrambled / 2% failure | 18% complication/ 5% offline | 1 pt DMG to Data, INT and WIL minute/ 8% glitch | Mild/12+1d8 days | Comms, optics and CPU back to normal after 3d6 days, but all endurance damage must be repaired by a technician. |
| 8,9. | **Strong Radiation** | C per minute | 1d4 per minute | 33% scrambled/ 17% failure | 52% complication/ 13% offline | 1d6 pts DMG to Data, INT and WIL per minute / 16% glitch | 2 exposures of mild/ 2d6 months | Damage must be repaired by a technician, comms, optics and CPU return to normal 6d6 weeks after exposure. |
| 10. | **Lethal Radiation** | D per minute | 2d6 per minute | 88% scrambled/ 49% failure | 88% complication/ 37% offline | 2d6 pts DMG to Data, INT and WIL per minute/ 32% glitch | Medium/ 10+2d20 months | Damage permanent, however comms, optics and CPU have a 4 in 6 chance to return to normal in 3d6 weeks, otherwise they suffer as if the robot or android were permanently exposed to strong radiation (33% scrambled comms with 17% chance of each transmission failing to send or receive, 52% of a random optics complication or being 13% likely to be offline any given hour, etc.) |

## Hazard Check

This is the endurance based hazard check the robot, android, machine or cyborg needs to make to avoid exposure to whatever radiation level is in a given area, object or weapon system. Success means the lower degree of radiation is incurred, automatically. Once exposed, no further hazard checks rolls are needed unless the entity goes into a more dangerous, higher rad-zone, although once exposed, whatever harm befalls the mechanical being continues at their hourly or per minute basis so long as the character stays in the contaminated area.

Organic beings who have cybernetic parts suffer both as a human or mutant, as well as a mechanical being, but are allowed separate hazard check rolls for each aspect of their dual nature. Rebuilt characters are treated as regular humans as far as coping with radiation goes.

## Endurance Damage

After the first failed hazard check, this is the basic damage to the machine's parts, connections, servo motors and hydraulics. This damage is applied against the unit's endurance trait value within the shown time allotment, and can add up to severe damage if staying in a rad-zone too long. After the first failed hazard check, this damage occurs automatically each duration of time thereafter (hourly for mild radiation and by the minute for other degrees), along with the other dangers included on the above table.

The game master could tell the player of an android or robot character that it takes 2d6 damage, or whatever the shown amount is. The player will know something is up after he or she was asked to make an endurance based hazard check, and when they don't discern any attacker.

The GM need not say that the character has just exposed itself to radiation, but a clever player will quickly guess it has entered a contaminated area or touched something radioactive and needs to backtrack at once. Whether the player and his or her character will know that their metallic bodied character might now be radioactive itself, and contaminate organic comrades and strangers, is another matter.

### Comms

Comms is short for communications devices, and radiation can mess with both outgoing broadcasts, speech and incoming transmissions. The percentage chance shown for 'scrambled' is the amount of data, information, text, words, portion of a video clip or image that is sheer nonsense. The failure percent number shown is the chance the communication attempt fails, which includes an attempt at making a radio broadcast, attempt to speak, or efforts to receive and hear an incoming call.

These interruptions and lost communications persist for hours, days, or weeks even after the robot leaves the contamination zone, before the complications cease entirely based on the intensity of the radiation. See the column for 'Recovery' for the given radiation level for when comms and other features might return to normal. Comms can also include the remote control command and transmission of video footage from drones and other mechanical devices sent into a radioactive zone, and without control, a remotely operated unit will either crash, or return to the operator if such a fail-safe is installed in the machine — possibly bringing radioactive contamination back to its master.

## Optics

Besides the eyes of any robot or android, as well as any implant eye on a cyborg or vat-brain, this column includes cameras and other scopes, scanners, and field viewers and could include hand-held digital spotting scopes, weapon scopes, and substance readers for example.

The first shown percentage chance per minute is the risk that the optical device or eyes of an android or cyborg suffer a random 'complication' from the list to follow. The percentage odds of 'offline' means the chance per minute that one optical devices craps out and stays offline until the robot, android, or cyborg leaves the radioactive zone. Once outside the rad zone, the recovery rate shown on table XR-223 above, determines how soon that eye returns to an operational state. For a being with two eyes, such as an android, roll for each eye separately. When all eyes on a machine are offline, the mechanical being is blind and there-

after moves at half speed, makes attacks at -40 SV and is +40 easier to be hit by opponents.



**2.** Eye overheats, smokes and bursts with a loud pop. Glass shoots 1 meter ahead of it and potentially strikes any comrade in front (SV 01-50, DMG 1d6). Eye is thereafter broken and needs to be replaced.

**3-6.** Image seen through eye becomes pixelated, and what the user sees makes no sense for the next 2d6 minutes.

**7-11.** Temporarily Offline: The optic fades to black and the user is blind in this eye. If this is a CPU linked eye, such as those connected to the 'brain' of the robot, android, vat-brain or digital being, then the on-board computers try to run a diagnostic and reboot the eye. Allow the character a type E intelligence based hazard check per minute to get the eye back on-line.

**12.** Unlocked Feature! For whatever reason, this ancient eye unlocks a feature that allows the surprised user to now see radiation fields through this optic. A faint overlay of pigmentation shows the contamination intensity with a green hue for mild radiation, blue for medium, yellow for strong and red for lethal intensities. The range of this optic is 30 meters. Even after the user leaves the radioactive zone, this feature remains available to the robot, who must switch it on whenever it wants to look for potential radiation, and remains off when not actively deployed. In the event that this robot, cyborg or androids already had a similar feature, then treat this upgrade as a slight targeting enhancement and improve the character's accuracy trait by +1d6, permanently. This outcome can only occur once for this eye in the character's lifetime.

## CPU

This column pertains to the harm suffered to a robot, android, or cyborg's central processor unit (CPU) per hour or minute, depending on the intensity of the radiation, but after the character fails their first hazard check. The harm occurs as soon as the machine enters the contaminated areas even if not spending the full time allotment shown. For each additional duration of time in this rad-zone at this same intensity, there is a chance of a glitch, too. Repeated exposures in this time allotment damage the machine further, so apply another identical exposure plus roll for another chance of a glitch, but no further hazard checks are allowed.

Although the most radiation shielded area of any robot or android, the computerized brain of such mechanical beings is still susceptible to the highly destructive and disruptive effects of radiation. This harm is reflected in a loss of data trait points, intelligence and willpower, and if any of these traits drop to zero or less, the unit switches off and collapses where it stands, and likely become further degraded by the ongoing radiation until it is nothing more than a mass of radioactive junk. Healing these traits points is based on the recovery category for the radioactive intensity, also shown on Table XR-223. In cases of mild exposure, all traits return to normal in 2d6 hours. However, at the other extreme of lethal radiation exposure, these traits are lost permanently.

Finally, there is a percentage chance per hour, or minute, depending on the rad-zone's intensity, that a glitch occurs. A CPU glitch can be anything and is rolled using 2d6 on the following table:

## Radiation Caused CPU Glitch Table   Roll 2d6

**2. Electrical surge in CPU**, permanently deletes 1d6 from data trait, Intelligence and willpower. Robot or android must make a further willpower based type A hazard check or suffer an immediate all-systems shut down (including flight even if already in the air). Shut down lasts for 3d6 minutes. While shutdown, this unit is +80 SV to strike and, if still exposed to radiation, suffers ongoing rad-damage.

**3,4. Scrambled Memories:** Unit totally forgets why it is doing whatever it is doing, has no recollection of its companion's names or operational parameters... of even if those around it are friend or foe. It will cease whatever operation it is on and return to base — or the last place it got a good recharge. This loss of memory is replaced by self preservation mode and anything to try to stop this machine from seeking its former charging station will be dispatched. This memory loss lasts for 1d100 minutes if the radiation exposure was mild, or 100+1d100 minutes for medium exposure, of 2d6 days for strong exposure and 2d6 years for lethal exposure rad intensity. If restrained, a computer technician could get under the hood of this robot and attempt to hack into the CPU and reboot the 'brain' to reverse this memory loss. For a human to hack into this robot, see page 397 of this book for the updated rules on Organic Characters Hacking into CPU.

**5,6. Arms of android or robot cease working** and just hang limply at the side of the machine for 2d6 minutes.

**7,8. Unit's legs, tracks or wheels lock up** and it cannot move for 2d6 minutes. If this is a flying machine, its propulsion cuts out or rotors stop turning and it glides or falls out of the sky. See Falling Height and Damage on page 123 of the hub rules.

**9,10. CPU begins to run a scheduled update** and locks the entity out of all access to communications, weapon systems, navigation, and speech modes. It can, however, use it any human-like arm and locomotion to either retreat or move to some other position. This glitch lasts for 1d10 minutes per intensity tier of the radiation (mild rad 1d10 minute/ medium 2d10 minutes/ strong 3d10 minutes/ lethal 4d10 minutes).

**11. Computer virus worm**, that has remained hidden for untold years, suddenly gets released from a quarantine folder in the character's computer. The worm gains access to the CPU's communication systems and broadcasts its beacon signal in a 10 kilometer radius, day and night, telling the local Mecha factions, AIs systems, and NPC digital beings of this robot or android's location. The transmissions include whatever the robot sees, hears or thinks, along with videos of its companions. The character does not know this worm is present for the first 3d6 days. Later, while running a routine diagnostic, it detects the unauthorized broadcasting through comms (if any) and is allowed a Data trait based Type G hazard check once per day, to try to delete the worm.

**12. Self-destruct mode initiated:** Alarm klaxons within the robot's vocabulator emit an alarm, punctuated by "Self destruct mode engaged. T-minus 10 minutes and counting. Personnel are directed to depart the area immediately."

GM: Only if the android, cyborg or robot actually has a self destruct mechanism built into it will this device detonate after ten minutes, otherwise it is merely faulty programing and the CPU accessed code from a different variant of whatever model type it is. Once the ten minutes passes, the self destruct alarm and warning switches off. If the GM does not divulge that the self destruct warning is false, either to the player of this character or fellow game participants, this glitch could prove to be quite a memorable in-game event. So too, unless some mechanical exploration into the character's insides is undertaken (at a cost of 500+1d1000sp if a NPC professional must be hired), how will fellow characters know for sure that the PC doesn't actually have a self-destruct mode?

### Exposure to Others

This column shows the radioactive contamination intensity that this robot, android, or cyborg might transfer to others once itself is exposed. Others must be in close contact with this now radioactive metallic character, such as when touching them or spending one or more minutes within a half meter's distance. The bystander is allowed an endurance based hazard check, each minute, to avoid picking up an exposure dose. As described in the hub rules on page 125, those exposed to mild radiation are allowed a type A END based hazard check, medium radiation forces a type B hazard check, while strong exposure calls for a Type C hazard check.

### Recovery

This column describes how fast a mechanical being or non-organic body can be repaired after exposure to radiation. Recovery is separate from the radiation contamination this mechanical being is tainted with, and while the machine might be repaired, it could still be radioactive and possibly expose any technician to the hazards of radiation with no one knowing it, until it's too late.

In cases of mild exposure, the mechanical being will run diagnostics and repair endurance damage at once, and heal from all damage in 2d6 hours. In all more serious cases, however, a robotics or cybernetic technician must conduct repairs to replenish depleted endurance and repair faulty parts. Exposure to lethal radiation is usually a killer for any machine, and even if the unit leaves a rad zone where it was exposed to such extra radiation, it will suffer permanently thereafter as if from exposure to strong radiation. In short, it will need to cope with constant complications, shut-downs, glitches and other issues that can be tiresome and make a robot or android unreliable and burdensome to an excavation team. In these cases, the character might want to have its identity, memories and talents inserted into an all new mechanical body. For this, the CPU must be taken out and plugged into a new chassis or vehicle.

# Encumbrance *by Danny Seedhouse*

There are five different options for how a game master wants to handle character encumbrance:
- **Option 1: Ignore it**
- **Option 2: Basic**
- **Option 3: Item Based System**
- **Option 4: Combined**
- **Option 5: Abstract**

### Option 2: Basic Encumbrance

This option comes with some extra book work and some choices. In the basic version, armor is not counted against weight as armor comes with some built-in penalties. Select from the following 4 degrees how encumbered a character is. Normally, the game master decides this based on what they see on a PC's character sheet.

#### Light Encumbrance

A character can carry a gear load equal to half their strength in kilograms. So the average person with 30 strength then they can carry 15 kilograms (33 lbs) of stuff with no difficulty. If the character is under this weight, increase their overland movement rate by 1 km per hour.

#### Moderate Encumbrance

At this is the level of burden, one can hike comfortably, although fighting while so loaded is a different story. At this tier, reduce initiative by 1 and the opponents get a +10 SV to hit this character. Swimming skill is dropped 1 tier.

This level is calculated by adding 1/2 the PC's strength and 1/2 their endurance together to establish the amount of kilograms that can be carried at this degree of encumbrance. If the kilograms they carry are more than the total of half of these two traits, they are then heavily encumbered.

#### Heavy Encumbrance

The amount of kilograms this character can carry within this level is equal to the character's strength, plus 1/2 their endurance and 1/2 their willpower. Any more than this amount puts them in the over encumbered category described below. Reduce initiative by 3 while opponents get a +30 SV to hit this character. Reduce overland movement by 1 km/hour. Swimming skill is dropped 2 skill tiers.

### Over Encumbered

This level is gonna hurt, but sometimes one needs to lift and move as much as they possibly can. To find the maximum kilograms this character can carry, see heavy encumbrance, with the amount being double the trait equation described there. Lifting such a load will inflict 1d10 endurance damage on the character on the initial lift, plus then every 2 rounds as he or she staggers along at 1/2 speed. Opponents gain a +30 strike value to hit this overladen person or beast, and reduce overland movement to 1/2. Don't try swimming as you'll sink.

## Additional Encumbrance Rules

### Load bearing gear

The proper gear to distribute weight across the whole body is essential. A proper backpack reduces the virtual weight of items inside by 5%, while the use of a relic frame pack will instead reduce this by 10%. Proper load bearing gear, like military harness and holsters, reduce the weight of items carried in them by 10%, too.

### Falling

Don't forget to add equipment weight to character weight for fall damage according to the falling table on page 123 of the hub rules.

### Option 3: Item Based System

Carrying 8 guns and 3 axes and a rocket launcher is hard. This system is more abstract and covers more of what you're actually carrying.

### Unencumbered

An unencumbered character has complete freedom of movement. He is neither weighted down with gear nor slowed by armor.
- A pistol and a knife (a couple of small weapons), holstered or unholstered.
- A purse or a small day back pack (roughly under 10kg of gear or 1/4 of the character's strength trait maximum)
- Protective gear with no movement penalty can be worn.

Overland movement for an unencumbered character is improved by 2 kilometers per hour and they receive a 1 point bonus using the chase rules (page TME-112).

### Lightly Encumbered

A lightly encumbered character can perform well physically under most conditions. A character is lightly encumbered if he is:
- Carrying a total weight of gear less than 1/2 her strength.
- Wearing clothes suitable for the environment (not extreme cold).
- Wearing armor and a helmet with a movement penalty of -0.25 meters or less. A shield with a -0.25 or less can be carried as well as long as no weapons requiring two hands is also carried.
- Carrying in hand or using a strap or sheath for an assault rifle, rifle, a bow, shotgun, sword, spear, axe or an item that can be carried in one hand. A backup pistol, flintlock pistol, short sword or a hatchet properly holstered, and a couple of smaller weapons like a knife or mini laser.
- Carrying or wearing a single medium-sized pack or bag, or two properly secured small bags or packs.

A lightly encumbered character has her travel speed unchanged but counts swim skill as one level lower.

### Moderately Encumbered

A moderately encumbered character will be uncomfortable on long hikes, and traverses rough or steep terrain with some difficulty. When needed, he or she can fight even while carrying such a burden, although getting into or exiting vehicles and moving through confined spaces such as interior hallways in ruins may prove difficult. A character is moderately encumbered if he is:
- Carrying a total weight of gear less than 1/2 their strength plus 1/2 endurance in kilograms.
- Wearing clothes suitable for a cold winter, a parka and snow pants. Trying to walk around in scuba gear.
- Wearing armor which causes a -2 meters or less movement penalty. Any helmet and a shield that enforces up to a -0.5 meters penalty can also be used.
- Carrying in hand or using a strap or sheath for an assault rifle, rifle, a heavy crossbow, shotgun, two-handed sword, pole arm or battle axe, or item that can be carried in one hand. Up to two of the fallowing can also be carried: a backup pistol, flintlock pistol, short sword or a hatchet properly holstered, or a single sword, axe, SMG or other mid sized firearm.
- Carrying or wearing a single large backpack, or load-bearing equipment and a combination of smaller containers.

A moderately encumbered character can only run for a maximum number of rounds equal to her healing rate, before being forced to rest for 1d4 minutes. Their travel speed is unaffected. Swimming is harder and so the PC's swimming skill is 2 tiers lower than normal.

### Heavily Encumbered

Characters who toil under heavy encumbrance find it uncomfortable to walk, let alone fight. When combat starts, or if the PC needs to climb something, it's time to shed some weight or suffer the consequences of being a loot piñata. A character is heavily encumbered if he is:
- Wearing clothes suitable for polar winter, a space suit in earth gravity. Wearing armor with over a 2 meter speed penalty (basically a bomb squad suit).
- Carrying or wielding a chain gun, heavy machine gun, rocket launcher, the top end of man portable weapons. Plus, he or she carries up to two of the following as a backup: a pistol, flintlock pistol, short sword or a hatchet properly holstered, or a single sword, axe, SMG or other mid sized firearm.
- Carrying or wearing a single large bag or pack plus load-bearing equipment. Helping another character to move.

Heavily encumbered characters are +20 SV easier to hit. They move half speed after all other penalties. In water, they suffer a -4 to their swimming skill tier (and probably go directly to the bottom). This person also suffers a +1 penalty to chase rolls.

### Emergency Encumbrance

This is the last level and is reserved for the guy with 12 rifles and 6 swords or other equally ridiculous amounts of gear. Also, this is the encumbrance tier used for when an excavator tries to haul his fallen companion to safety. This level calls upon an individual's raw endurance and willpower to overcome the strain and pain of this extreme load.

Swimming is impossible for this character while his or her movement rate is halved in all circumstances and can only be done for a limited amount of time. This short movement duration is found by averaging endurance, strength, and willpower (add all three trait scores and divide by 3). Next, find what the equivalent healing rate should be as if this new 'emergency load bearing trait' were endurance (consult table TME-1-3 on page 10 of the hub rules or the same trait modifier table XR-3 in this book on page 8 ), and the stated healing rate amount is the number of rounds this character can move, although only at 1/2 speed before needing 1d4 minutes of rest.

• Alternatively a character can make a type A willpower based hazard check to move at full speed for one round, this check gets 1 letter code more challenging every 2 rounds thereafter and when the character is done, they must make an endurance based hazard check of equal difficulty. Success means they take 1d6 stun damage per round moved. Failure means this is real damage as the PC has done serious harm to themself.

### Additional Encumbrance Rules

• Pack Tied Weapon or Item: If permitted by the game master, a character is allowed an extra weapon of the type that can be carried normally at the encumbrance level if tied securely to a pack. This weapon, or other heavy article, will take at least 4 rounds to access.
• Extra Arms: For each arm, add an extra small weapon that can be carried comfortably. For every 2 arms extra, a mutant can carry an extra primary weapon.
• Super Strong: For characters with a strength score over 100, establish the character's encumbrance level as normal, but then drop the character down one level. For example: A character is heavily encumbered, but because their strength is over 100, they drop to moderately encumbered.

### Option 4: Combined

Combine encumbrance options 2 and 3: Thus, add the weight limit from option 2 to the appropriate encumbrance levels. Don't stack penalties for the same items or conditions, but do add all other penalties in.

### Option 5: Abstract

Slots, this system is more abstract and gives characters a limited number of slots to carry gear in. Weight doesn't matter for an item in a slot. Small things like ammo add up to a slot as fallows: regular ammo is 100 rounds per slot, high caliber ammo and shotgun shells are 50 rounds per slot. Small incidentals like a relic lighter or anything measured in grams can be 10 items to a slot.

A character gets one slot per hand. 10 slots in a backpack, 15 in a relic backpack. 6 miscellaneous slots around the body, especially if the PC wears pouches, coin purses, satchels, sheaths and holsters.

#### Optional ways to get extra slots

• Bag carrier: You can carry a bag with 5 slots in a hand with no penalties. Extra hands are helpful here.
• Be strong: Drop the zero off the shown bonus 'throwing distance' percentage and the resulting number equals bonus slots (consult the trait table on page 8 of this book to see the 'Strength Range' modifier column). Another option here is to average the character's strength and endurance scores and use the tens column amount as extra slots. Example: the PC has a strength of 46 and endurance of 27, added together and divided by two yields 36.5, so the tens column yields a 3 (don't round up or down), to mean this PC gains 3 extra encumbrance slots to carry 3 extra items or groups of small items.
• Be big: Every step above normal on the size Increase mutation (prime mutation 75, page TME 73) chart gives the freak two extra slots.
• Have extra body parts: An extra leg gives a mutant one slot per leg. Over sized limbs get an extra slot, a torso or body adds 2 (Body Disproportion prime mutation 7). Centaurs and Tracked locomotion can carry 2 extra bags. As a note, missing an arm or a leg loses you a slot.
• Extra bags: Carrying extra bags strapped to one's body (holding 5 slots each), but, for every 5 or portion of 5 extra slots, the character suffers a penalty of -0.25 meters of speed, -1 initiative and +5 DV drop from agility or dodge skill only.

# Expanded Critical Strikes Rules
*by Danny Seedhouse*

These optional charts bring more flavor to the critical hits by different weapons and attacks. The author has attempted to cover most types of damage done in a broad sense and give the players and game master alike some extra effects to distinguish between the effects of a sword strike, a bullet wound, and a blast of fire. The charts cover the fallowing attack types:

• **Brawling & Martial Arts** • **Blunt & Crushing** • **Slash & Edged**
• **Piercing & Bullets** • **Laser Weapons** • **Fire Effects** • **Electrical Attacks**

Being mauled by a beast can cause several types of critical damage outcomes, with the game master able to either pick from one that makes sense or rolled randomly. 1d3. **1.** Blunt & Crushing / **2.** slash & edged / **3.** Piercing & Bullets.

As a general note, any NPC or monster that is subject to morale, and takes a critical result die result of 8 or above on any of the following tables, must make a morale check or attempt to flee. Some of these hits require advanced medic skills to treat, although the use of the mutation healing touch can fill in for this skill with 10 points of healing from a heal touch needed to be equivalent to one skill tier in medic skill. So if it takes 3 skill points to repair a broken bone, 30 points of healing can go into fixing the break using heal touch before healing endurance damage. The mutation of Extreme Healing, described on page 244 of this book, can also repair most of the severe wounds described in these tables.

Many of these injuries result in a broken limb for the victim. Such breaks are covered in the follow-up section called Broken Bones and Healing Time on page 388 of this book.

These critical strikes are best suited to typical living beings, especially humanoids. For plantoids, androids and robots, or creatures that don't have the typical organs and limb structure of a human, it might be more appropriate to use the critical strikes tables on page 105 of the Hub Rules book, although the game master can translate many of these nasty injuries into severe malfunctions for a mechanical beings or plant character.

For trait based Hazard Checks, use a victim's current trait amount, NOT their uninjured trait value.

## Table XR-224 / Brawling & Martial Arts

Attackers with the Martial Arts skill gain an optional +1 on this table that can be applied after rolling, and so modify their result, and select between one devastating blow and another.

### 1d10  Brawling and Martial Arts Critical Strikes

**1.** Taking advantage of an off balance foe, the attacker presses the attack and gains an immediate, extra attack with a +20 SV bonus against the same target.

**2, 3.** Punishing strike deals double random damage, cracks target's ribs giving the victim a -10 penalty to SV and reducing their initiative by -2 until combat is over and target has time to attend the injury.

**4,5.** With a brutal kick to the foe's knee, this strike dislocates it. Victim takes maximum damage and is stunned for 1d4 rounds and must make a type B agility check or fall prone. If the target survives the battle, it hobbles around at 1/2 speed until the knee heals in 10+4d6 days.

**6,7.** Crack! Maximum damage is done plus one of foe's arms is broken and rendered useless and the victim is stunned for 1d4 rounds. If the target was armed, the attacker can make a type D agility hazard check to catch his dropped weapon or other held item. For creatures with multiple limbs, this will break one limb with a weapon attached such as a claw, rendering it useless. For most humanoids, roll which arm and bone is broken by this blow, **roll 1d8: 1,2** Upper left/ **3,4.** Upper right/ **5,6.** Lower left/ **7,8.** Lower right.

**8.** Mercy is not this attacker's strong suit, but breaking things seems to be. A broken collar bone renders one of the victim's arm useless, and a broken femur makes walking rather hard and so quartering or halving foe's speed (roll **1d6: 1-3.** left knee, **4-6.** right knee). The pain blacks foe out for one round and they fall to the ground, taking maximum damage to boot. One arm is useless and foe must hop around at 1/4 speed if he moves on 2 legs or 1/2 if on 4 or more legs. Foe can not use any weapon requiring 2 hands until healed.

**9.** Foe's neck snaps. Target must make a Type C END hazard check or be permanently paralyzed from the neck down. On a success, the paralyzation is temporary, lasting 2d10 rounds and doing double maximum damage. If the GM is feeling kind, this injury will heal naturally in 1d4+2 months of complete bed rest. The use of the mutation 'extreme healing' can cure this injury, otherwise advanced surgery is needed from a 5 skill point medic who can fix paralysis after 1d4+1 weeks of bed rest. Against foes with multiple heads, this attack does double maximum damage and renders one head useless and stuns the creature for 1d4 rounds.

**10.** Awesome blow to foe's face sends bone shards or other hard bits flying towards foe's brain or whatever passes for a brain. The victim must make a Type C, endurance based hazard check or die outright. If they pass this check, they only take double maximum damage, suffer 2d4 rounds of inaction while stunned, and suffer one temporary brain damage consequence, **roll 1d6: 1,2.** Dizziness (flaw mutation 113, page TME-80)/ **3,4.** Random visual disorder (flaw mutation 142, page TME-83)/ **5,6.** Develop migraine headaches (flaw mutation 128, page TME-82)/ **7,8.** Pre-Senile Dementia (flaw mutations 131 on page TME-82)./ **9,10.** Random mental disorder, see insanity rules page TME-126. Character operates at half their intelligence and willpower stats until healed./ **11,12.** Develop a random latent mutation (roll 1d100 on table XR-198, on page 232 of this book) that either lasts until the damage heals or, at the game master's discretion or determined by a 01-50% chance on a d100 roll, the mutation remains permanently.

Robots and androids who suffer this critical strike, and survive the initial blow, take a loss of -1d20 data points, -2d6 willpower and -2d6 intelligence, permanently.

**11.** In a moment of Zen-like clarity, you stop the target's heart, power supply, or whatever makes them run. If the attacker wants, they can tear it out and show it to everyone and spend the next round holding foe's heart in their hand, forcing allies of the victim to make a morale check. The target is dead after one round of inactivity.

## Table XR-225 / Blunt and Crushing Attacks

### 1d10  Blunt and Crushing Attacks Critical Strikes

**1.** You smash the foe in the chest and break 1d4 ribs. Foe is stunned for 1 round and takes a -10 penalty to SV, is +10 easier to hit, and moves -25% slower until the long healing process is completed. See page 388 for the healing time of broken bones.

**2,3.** With a crunch you break one of target's arms (even chance of left or right), dealing maximum damage and making it useless for anything until it heals. The foe is also stunned 1 round ( -10 to SV, +10 easier to hit) and drops anything not attached to that arm.

**4,5.** Break foe's leg and they fall to the ground stunned for 1d4 rounds and at the attacker's mercy next round, being both prone and stunned (-30 DV). Target can stand with a Type C agility hazard check and hop forward at 1/4 speed (or 3/4 speed if four legged) and must make this check every round to move. Of course, if this individual is hit again, it must make a type E hazard check or fall back down. Fighting with a broken leg means the victim loses their dodge and agility bonus to defense value. If the GM is feeling generous, a type D Willpower based hazard check can be allowed and, if successful, can negate these penalties for one round but dealing 1d6 END damage.

**6.** Smash foe in the head or whatever head-like thing they have. Target is stunned for 1d4 rounds ( -10 to SV, +10 easier to hit), takes maximum damage, and random damage from the blow and suffers a -10 SV penalty when making all attacks for 1d4 hours.

**7.** Knockout blow deals max normal lethal damage and double random stun damage to the target. Worse, the victim is forced to make a Type C END based hazard check to avoid passing out. Foe operates at a -15 penalty to both SV and DV until they can rest for an hour and clear their head.

**8.** Massive blow to foe's chest that breaks the sternum and some ribs for good measure. Foes must make Type C END based hazard check to avoid going unconscious and bleeds 1d6 endurance per round until dead. Medical stabilization or healing touch (or similar mutation) is needed to stop this bleeding before death. On a success, the victim operates at a -30 penalty to both SV and DV for 1d6 days, but suffers from broken ribs and moves at a 25% speed reduction until the bones heal. See page 388 of this book for the healing times of broken bones.

**9.** Head trauma puts the target in a coma, who better hope they have some good friends to look after them after the battle. Victim gets a Type C willpower based hazard check to see if it's a permanent coma or not, with success meaning it lasts 1d4 weeks. This will affect robots, things with multiple heads and anything with a brain or CPU, although only one head will be put out of action if the target has multiple heads. Those in a permanent coma require daily medical and sanitary attention, and are allowed a chance to suddenly wake from their coma once per month by making a successful type G willpower based hazard check. While in a coma, a character will lose 10% of their strength and endurance per month. When either trait reaches zero, they die.

**10.** Everything important is pulped and crushed. The target is dead.

**4,5.** Spurt! Foe takes maximum damage from the attack, immediately bleeds out random damage and then bleeds 1d6 each round thereafter until dead or treated (see critical hit 2,3, above).

**6.** Brow slash! Does maximum damage and causes the victim to bleed for 2d4 rounds. While only the initial max damage occurs, the bad news is that the target starts taking a cumulative -1d10 penalty to SV and DV due to blood flowing into their eyes. When this penalty hits -40, they are blind until the bleeding can be stopped, or their eyes washed out.

**7.** Muscle mangling strike cripples one of the foe's limbs. Roll a d4: 1 it's the right arm/ 2. left arm/ 3. right leg/ 4. it's the left leg. This strike does maximum lethal damage plus stuns the target for 1d4 rounds ( -10 to SV, +10 easier to hit), and they suffer 1d10 bleeding damage per round until medically treated. Oh, and the limb is useless until endurance is totally healed. Leg 1/2 movement on bipeds 1/4 on quadrupeds and target falls down. Arm is useless and lets go of anything held in it.

**8.** Chop off a limb! One of the foe's limbs is randomly severed doing maximum damage, and dealing random base damage thereafter until someone stops the bleeding. This brutal, life threatening injury also causes the victim to be stunned for 1d6 rounds continuing the bad day they are having ( -10 to SV, +10 easier to hit). To stop the bleeding, the limb must be tied off and pressure applied, which takes 1d4+1 rounds unless the victim is trying to do so to itself, then it takes 2d4 rounds. For rules on reattaching the limb, see the hack off a hand option under called shots in the hub rules, page TME-110.

**9.** Off with their head! The victim must make a Type C endurance based hazard check or die as the attacker tries to decapitate them. It your foe lives, he takes double maximum damage and is thereafter stunned for 2d10 rounds ( -10 to SV, +10 easier to hit), and bleeds like a stuck pig, taking 1d12 END damage every round until a skilled medic makes a successful type B intelligence based hazard check. Once treated, the victim can't make any violent movements, suffer any falls, or do anything strenuous or else the bleeding will start again. This peril ends after the victim gets 1d3+1 days day of bed rest and the wound properly stitched by a medic.

**10.** Cut foe to pieces literally, he is dead. So very dead.

## Table XR-226 / Slash &Edged Attacks

| 1d10 | Slash & Edged Attacks Critical Strikes |
| --- | --- |

**1.** Snick, that had to hurt! The victim takes normal damage and loses 1d3 digits from a randomly determined hand. Can be reattached as per rules for 'Hack off hand' under called shots in the hub rules on page TME-110.

**2,3.** It's a bleeder! Foe bleeds random weapon damage (this is just the base dice without the attacker's weapon expert, strength or other modifiers applied) for the next 1d4+1 rounds. This bleeding slows to 1d4 if the victim stops moving and applies pressure to the wound. Alternatively, anyone with medical training can stop this bleeding with a type A intelligence based hazard check for bleeding of less than 1d10 damage per round, or a Type B HC for anything higher. This check takes 1 round.

## Table XR-227 / Piercing & Bullets Attacks Roll

Apply + 1 for wounds caused by a high caliber bullet, shotgun slugs, and 50 cal rounds.

| 1d10 | Piercing & Bullets Critical Strikes |
| --- | --- |

**1.** Disarm victim with a shot to the hand. If foe uses weapons, they drop one. Either way, they can't use that hand properly until they receive medical care taking a -30 SV to anything used in that hand.

**2,3.** Bam! That took the spring out of foe's step. Leg shot does maximum damage, and the target stops moving. After that, it suffers a -10 penalty to DV and has -2 meters of speed until the end of combat.

**4,5.** Target crumples like a rag doll, taking maximum damage as his head hits the ground and is knocked unconscious for 1 round, then is stunned for 1d4 rounds and suffer -10 to SV and is +10 easier to hit until it has had 1 hour of rest.

**6.** Shot slams into one of the foe's limbs, breaking a major bone and rendering the limb useless until surgery is preformed on the limb. Attack does maximum damage. **Roll 1d8** for limb: **1.** right upper arm / **2.** left upper arm / **3.** lower right arm / **4.** lower left arm / **5.** right thigh / **6.** left thigh/ **7.** right shin / **8.** left shin. Arm breaks mean the victim can't wield weapons or make attacks with that limb. Leg breaks knock target down, reduce movement to 25%. GM, Apply penalties to anything that sounds difficult to do with a broken limb. Consult Table XR-231 / Broken Bones and Healing Time Chart on page 388 of this book for healing period and other issues related to these breaks.

**7.** Bullet fragments on impact and the pieces wander around, do double random damage, and put the victim in shock. Target must make a Type C endurance based hazard check or spend their next round severely stunned. This continues for the next 2d6 rounds in which the unlucky target suffers a -20 to SV and +20 DV, reduction of 25% movement and a -1 to initiative until they have had at least one month of rest or advanced medical treatment from a 4 or higher skill point medic, or application of the mutation Extreme Healing.

**8.** Shot takes out an eye. Victim takes maximum damage plus random damage and must make a Type C endurance hazard check or die as the bullet enters the brain or CPU. On a success, the target drops unconscious for 1d4 rounds, then stunned 1d6 rounds ( -10 to SV, +10 easier to hit), as their senses slowly come back, with only one working eye (permanent loss of 2d6 perception and a -10 to SV).

**9.** Right to the heart, that had to hurt. Foe takes double maximum damage and must make a Type C endurance based hazard check or die on the spot, otherwise they are unconscious and dropped to -1 END. Normally, any living character will die at this point unless a complicated surgery can be performed. This surgery requires a skilled medic with 4 skill points and access to advanced medical gear. The medic can save the target by making a Type C intelligence HC and expend 1d6+2 hours in surgery.

Failure means the patient dies on the operating table unless a replacement heart from either a donor or a cybernetic heart is inserted into the victim. Even if the patient doesn't die immediately from this wound, they'll need 6+4d6 days bed rest to heal beyond 1/2 maximum endurance.

**10 or higher.** Brains blown out. He is very dead, carry on. For things with multiple heads the shock knocks the mutant out for 5d6 minutes, and they take double max damage.

## Table XR-228 / Laser Weapons

Apply +1 for heavy laser carbines, heavy pulse rifles, and all laser cannons.

### 1d10 Laser Weapon Critical Hits

**1.** Zapp! Sound and fury, blinds target for 1 round ( -40 SV, +40 easier to be hit, half movement) and the after-image of the beam leaves the foe with vision problems for the next 1d6+1 rounds giving him a -20 SV and +10 easier to strike.

**2,3.** Is that smoke? Foe smolders and takes random weapon damage next turn, but doesn't actually catch on fire.

**4,5.** Sweeping blast across victim does maximum damage. It also damages the target's body and gear and interferes with the victim's functionality for the next hour. **Roll 1d6: 1.** -20 SV Penalty / **2.** DV penalty of +10 (easier to be struck). / **3.** Malfunction: reduce damage of target's primary weapon by 1/2. / **4.** -50% movement/ **5,6.** Temporarily blinded ( -40 SV, +40 easier to be hit, half movement) for the next hour.

**6.** Good thing foe had two eyes, right? Target losses use of one eye, takes maximum damage, is stunned for 1d6 rounds during which he or she suffers -10 to SV and is +10 easier to hit. Should a medic with 3 skill points as a medic treats the wound within 24 hours, then it will heal in 30+2d10 days. If not, hope the patient likes eye patches. If having only one eye, depth perception is reduced, thus drop -2d6 accuracy, permanently.

**7.** Lung hole. Foe takes double random damage, and can only move at a walk. Must make a type B endurance based hazard check to fight or do any physical activity for longer than one round at a time. This test increases by one step of difficulty for every round after the second. On a failed test, they count as stunned as they wheeze and fight for breath, being -10 to SV and is +10 easier to hit. This hole will heal in 4 months on its own, or half that time if treated by a medic at least once daily. Use of the mutation, Extreme Healing, will repair this wound with one application.

**8.** Slicing beam sweeps across foe's body doing double maximum damage. The brutal attack knocks target prone and they're stunned for 1d6 rounds ( -10 to SV and is +10 easier to hit). The victim begins leaking important stuff out of its various wounds and takes 1d8 damage for 4 rounds followed by 1d6 DMG for 4 rounds, then 1d4 for a final 4 rounds and then 1 point damage a round until he is out of blood, sap, hydraulic fluid, battery juice or other life giving substance. A trained medic can stop this liquid loss only if they successfully make 1d4+1 Type B intelligence based hazard checks.

**9.** Something important falls off... Like an arm or a leg. The target takes maximum damage and then **roll 1d6** for normal people: **1.** right arm / **2.** left arm / **3.** right leg / **4.** left leg / **5.** guts / **6.** neck.

On a 1 to 4 result, the selected limb is cut off. The target bleeds out rapidly, taking 1d20 endurance damage per round until they drop. This can be tied off in two rounds by someone else or in 2d4 rounds if one attempts to do it themself.

On a 5 roll, the foe's guts fall out. They are reduced to zero endurance and lose 1d4 endurance per round until dead, or they are stabilized by a medic of at least 3 skill points who makes a type B Intelligence based hazard check.

On a roll of 6, where the target's neck is mostly detached, the foe must make a Type C endurance based hazard check or die instantly. If they pass the HC, they take extra random damage in bleeding on the next round, but must pass a further Type B END hazard check or die on the 3rd round. Finally, on the 4th round, make a Type A END hazard check or die. A medic must wrap the person's neck immediately and the subject cannot move more than half speed or fight in melee for the next 10+1d20 days. Doing so risks tearing open the wound again and forcing an immediate Type D endurance based hazard check to avoid bleeding out at 1d10 END per round until death — or until a medic can provide first aid to pinch off and stop the bleeding and begin the many days healing process all over again.

**10 or higher.** Foe is cut to pieces literally... they are dead. So very dead. Any armor they were in is destroyed.

## Table XR-229 / Fire Effects

*GM Note:* NPCs seeing someone on fire from a critical hit are most likely forced to make an immediate morale check (covered on page TME-110).

### 1d10 Fire Effects Critical Strikes

**1.** Painful blisters have the target operating at a -5 SV, +5 easier to strike, and -0.5 meters of movement, until their blisters heal (they heal when they regain lost END from this wound). While blistered, any further critical strikes by fire on this character with a repeated roll of 1 is increased to roll 2,3.

**2,3.** Painful burns over a significant portion of the target's body cause -15 SV, +15 easier to hit, and -1 meter of speed until healed. While blistered, any critical result from fire of a 1 to 3 is increased to a 4.

**4,5.** Incapacitating burns deal maximum damage and stun the target for 1d4 rounds ( -10 to SV and is +10 easier to hit), before acting like painful burns above. Add 1 to any further critical fire effects result.

**6.** Fire lingers around the target and inflicts random damage on the next turn, plus stuns the target ( -10 to SV and is +10 easier to hit). If the weapon causes long term burning damage, such as 1d4 or 1d6 rounds, etc., this starts after the extra round from the critical. While on fire, add 1 to the roll of any further fire effect critical rolls.

**7.** Fire blackens a random limb doing maximum damage and stunning the target for 1d4 rounds and rendering that limb useless (roll 1d4: 1. right arm/ 2. left arm/ 3. right leg/ 4. left leg). Medical treatment by a 3 skill point or higher medic is required to restore use to the limb. If heal touch is available, 30 points of healing must be applied to the limb to fix it. Using mutation of extreme healing will entirely mend this burn. After this critical strike outcome, if the target takes any further fire effect crits, roll 1d10+1 on this table until healed.

**8.** Target is alight with fire and takes random weapon damage for 1d6 rounds. Stunned, the first round ( -10 to SV and is +10 easier to hit), then must make a Type C willpower based hazard check to attempt to stop, drop and roll (Type D to keep fighting). Going prone and making a Type C Agility based hazard check, allowable each round, means the fire stops next round. Foe is stunned until the fire goes out.

**9.** Blast of fire to the head. The victim must make a Type C endurance based hazard check or die from the shock. If they live, they still take double maximum damage, and are temporarily blinded in both eyes (see TME hub rules page 122 for details). Scarring causes a permanent loss of 3d6 appearance.

**10.** Burn, Burn BURN! Target is aflame and burns for 1d6 rounds. They are stunned ( -10 to SV and is +10 easier to hit), and helpless, and will run around and scream, and act as a burning pyre setting things they touch on fire. The human torch's movement direction is rolled randomly on a 1d12 (or 1d6 if using a hex map) as they stumble 1d6 meters in any direction, they have a strike value of 01-60 and anything they hit takes 1d10 fire damage and 1d6 further damage for the next 1d6 rounds. Target dies at the end of the 1d6 rounds from shock.

**11.** Bodies don't normally burn this fast. All it takes is 1d4 rounds for the target to be reduced to a burnt skeleton... or a pool of melted metal innards seeping out of its armored shell. You get the idea, it's dead.

## Table XR-230 / Electrical Attacks

Apply +1 to rolls on this chart if the target is already suffering the effects of an electrical critical and/or otherwise vulnerable to electricity.

### 1d10 Electrical Attacks Critical Strikes

**1.** All the target's hair stands on end. The victim suffers -20 SV for 1d4 rounds.

**2,3.** Target sees stars and is stunned for the next round and takes a -10 to SV and is +10 easier to strike for the next 2d10 rounds.

**4,5.** Zap! The hit stuns for 1d4 rounds. The target's SV is -10 while they are +10 easier to strike for the next 2d10 rounds.

**6.** Crack! Target is unconscious and falls down for 1 round and is stunned for the following 2d6 rounds as things reboot. While stunned, they suffer a -10 SV penalty and are +10 easier to strike.

**7.** Electricity numbs a random limb, stunning the target 1d4 rounds and rendering that limb useless (roll 1d4: 1. right arm/ 2. left arm/ 3. right leg/ 4. left leg) for the next 1d4 days. If one leg is put out of action, the target moves only 25% of their normal speed if quadrupedal, or half if bipedal. If an arm is rendered useless, the subject cannot wield a weapon or carry anything in that hand. Cybernetic limbs, android limbs, or robot arms need repair after this critical, and they take maximum damage. A robotics technician can conduct these repairs taking 2d4 hours at a cost of 1000+1d1000sp for parts and labor.

**8.** Electric Boogaloo. The victim suffers random weapon damage once, and is rocked by electrical shocks for the next 1d6+1 rounds and unable to attack, flee, use cybernetics or mutations as electricity dances across its body. During this spastic dance, he or she is hard to strike and gains a -20 DV bonus. Anybody to try to grab this electrically animated subject is 61% likely to be shocked, too, and suffer a zap that inflicts 2d20 stun damage.

**9.** That's gonna hurt. Target takes maximum weapon damage as both stun and real damage (both maximum amounts applied against the character's endurance score). Then suffers a -20 SV and becomes +20 easier to hit for opponents (+20 DV) for the next 2d10 rounds as things settle down.

**10.** Zot! Target is unconscious as electricity overloads their nervous system or CPU, they are at maximum stun damage (zero endurance), although recovery begins after an hour as they come to and heal from this stun damage at their daily healing rate, per hour.

**11.** This is not great. Target goes to -1 endurance and must make a Type C endurance based hazard check or die* as either the brain, heart or CPU short circuits. If surviving this extreme trauma, this is lethal damage and the person will heal at their normal daily healing rate, or must be repaired if an android or robots.

**If the GM is feeling kind, treat as paralysis. This injury will heal naturally in 1d4+2 months of complete bed rest. Advanced surgery from someone with 5 ranks in medic skill can fix paralysis after 1d4+1 weeks of bed rest.*

# Broken Bones and Healing Time

Healing time for broken bones depends on several factors, including the age of the injured person, the specific bone, nutrition, and if the healing person has regular aid from a medic. The application of mutational energies, such as from heal touch, regeneration, extreme healing, or use of potent healing cybernetics and medical relics, including the tissue binder noted on page 443 of this book, also contribute to healing.

Factors which delay healing include starvation and failure to get medical attention, which can cause the bones to heal wrong.

A game master might reveal that a player character has suffered a broken bone after an unlucky roll on the all new critical strike tables (pages 383-387). Likewise, a broken bone or two could occur at the GM's discretion when the PC suffers some horrific injury instead of character death.

Perhaps the GM, who rolls dice behind the screen, declares that an otherwise doomed character is severely injured and out of action for weeks and months, especially where multiple broken bones occur.

The following table lists all the major bones, and by using the dice roll column, can provide a random bone break for when a character suffers some nasty ordeal, such as a bad fall, crushing blow, crash impact, collapsed ceiling, or maul attack by an enormous beast.

Each broken bone shows the base healing time in days. The subsequent table, on the next page, provides a list of healing time modifiers. Add or subtract all that apply as a percentage change to the bone healing time to a minimum duration of half of the broken bone's shown healing time.

For example, a character has a broken arm, which is determined to take 106 (84+2d20) days to heal if the limb is kept in a cast or splint and the casualty looks after themselves, but a mutant ally applies a surge of the mutation 'heal touch' (page TME-67), once per broken bone. Using this healing mutation on the injured character will reduce the healing time by 2d6 days, and in this case rolls a 8, so that now the healing time is 98 days instead of 106. But, if healing touch is provided each day, each daily application of the mutation will reduce the healing time by 2 days, beyond the first occurrence of the heal touch mutation. The heal touch mutation can only help fix bones once per day.

Other than a few mutations, noted on Table XR-232, no amount of relics or nutrition can heal a bone beyond half its healing time, so whatever else applies to the above noted broken arm, it will take at least 53 days to heal (half of the initial 106 days).

## Table XR-231 / Broken Bones and Healing Time Chart

**GM Note:** The d100 roll is used to determine unspecified bone breaks.

| 1d100 | Bone Broken Base Healing Time / Special Detail |
|---|---|

**01-04. Back** 84+1d100 days / Bed Ridden, or else an 8 in 10 chance per hour that the healing gets undone and the patient is immobilized with pain and must re-start the entire healing duration.

**05-09. Neck** 56+1d20 days / Neck brace must be worn during healing time period or without it, there is a 7 in 10 chance per hour that a relapse of 3d20 days added to healing time occurs.

**10-14. Skull fracture** 180+3d20days / Bed rest recommended. Any blow to the head or fall will cause either a relapse 8 in 10 times, requiring a repeat of all healing duration, or, 1 in 10 chance skull fragment pierces the brain and causes permanent loss of 1d100 to both intelligence and willpower. If either trait is reduced to zero or less, the person is brain dead permanently and their body will die in 3d6 days.

**15-21. Jaw** 49+1d20 days / Jaw wired shut, must consume blended foods through straw.

**22-25. Wrist*** 42+1d8 days / Brace must be worn.

**26-32. Thumb or finger**** 42+1d20 days / Splint must be worn on a broken digit.

**33-36. Ankle*** 56+1d12 days / Cast worn on ankle reduces movement by -50% for bipedal beings, -25% for quadrupeds.

**37-41. Foot*** 42+4d20days / Foot must be protected in a cast. Reduce movement by half, or by a quarter if being is a quadruped.

**42-51. Rib** 42+1d10 days / Very painful, breathing labored and so reduce movement by -25%.

**52-55. Collar bone*** 38+2d12 days / Sling must be worn. One arm almost useless, -50% SV and only 25% strength.

**56-60. Shoulder blade*** 56+1d30days / Besides wearing a sling for the healing duration, full range of shoulder motion will not return for a year in which any attacks made using this arm are suffer a -30 SV penalty and half strength.

**61-65. Hip*** 84+1d20 days / Even after the healing duration, and during it, full motion is limited for another 100+1d100 days in which the patient moves at quarter speed per round.

**66-74. Thigh** (femur)* 180+4d20days / During the first 180 days, a cast must be worn, which reduces movement by -50% if a crutch is used, or a quarter without a cast and crutch. After the first 180 days, only a -25% move reduction is applied in the healing period to follow.

**75-82. Shin** (tibia)* 150+3d20days / A cast must be worn on the shin for the first 150 days, in which time the patient moves at -50% if a cast is applied and the victim uses a crutch to hobble about. After the cast is removed, movement reduced to -25% for the rest of the healing time.

**83-90. Upper arm** (humerus)* 84+2d20 / A cast or splint must be worn on the upper arm for the duration of the healing period, which greatly reduces the strength in the arm to half, and any attacks with it are done so at a further -50% SV modifier.

**91-00. Lower arm*** 70+3d20days / A cast must be worn throughout the healing duration, reducing the user's strength and strike value in this arm to half.

*Roll 1d10 for which side: 1-5. Left, 6-10. Right.*
** Roll 1d10 for either left or right hand, and then for which finger: 1,2. Thumb / 3,4. Index /5,6. Middle / 7,8. Ring / 9,10 Lttle.*

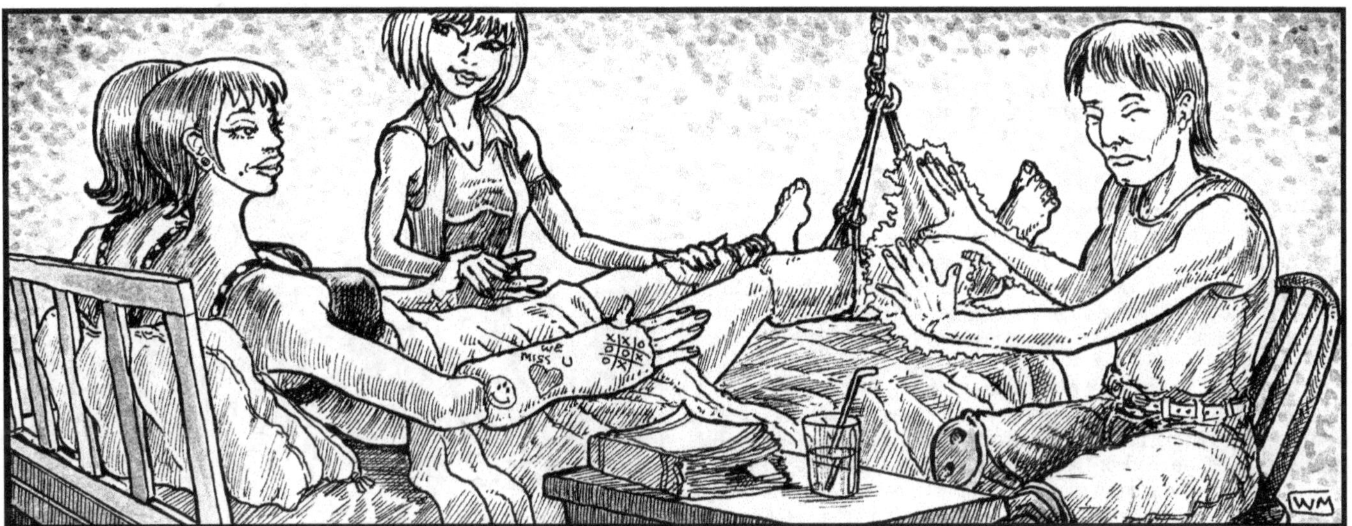

## Table XR-232 / Modifications to Healing Time for Broken Bones

This directory table provides a list of common setbacks and advantages to those trying to heal from a broken bone. If the patient suffers multiple broken bones, apply the same modifiers to each. Keep in mind that beneficial application of food, rest, medical care cannot speed the healing rate faster than half the base healing duration noted on the table previous, however the use of some mutations and relics can greatly heal bones. The application of extreme healing (pg. 244 this book) heals a broken bone in only 3d6 days, and any mutant with the mutation of limb regeneration repairs broken bones at a daily rate instead of a monthly rate according to the table included with that mutation on page TME-69 (example, instead of regrowing a leg in 2+1d4 months, this mutant heals a broken leg bone in 2+1d4 days). A few cybernetic implants and multiple relics, such as tissue binders, flesh mend gel packs, nano healing injectors, and auto-docs, also contribute to reducing the duration of healing time.

There is, however, no limit to how many days an unlucky person can suffer with a broken bone, especially if undergoing torture.

Add or subtract the number of days to heal a broken bone based on the modifier for each circumstance. Use all that apply. In some cases, such as being old or venerable, a percentage is applied of +50% or +100%. Add this percentage after all other modifiers are applied, which could effectively double the time to mend a bone.

### Circumstances List for Healing Times of Broken Bones

**Miscellaneous Circumstance**
- Patient undergoing regular torture: no healing each day of torture
- Patient forced to travel by foot: Leg, hip or foot breaks add +1d3 days to healing per day traveled/ other broken bones do not heal, or get worse, each day of travel

**Age of Patient***
- Child (age 0-9): Bones heal at twice the base speed (2 days healed instead of 1 day)**
- Pre-Teen (age 10-12): -4d6 days
- Teen (age 13-17): -3d6 days
- Adult (age 18-45): + 0 days
- Middle Aged (age 46-59): +2d6 days
- Old (age 60-79 ): +50%
- Venerable (age 80-109): +100%
- Ancient (age 110-death): +200%

**Nutrition Level**
- Starving: Besides no healing on days without food, there is a further 3 in 6 chance of adding an extra 1d6 days to the healing time, checked daily.
- Malnourished: No healing of bones on days without food
- Adequate nutrition: +0 days
- Well fed: -2d6 days

**Medical Care**
- No medical treatment: +6d6 days
- Initial treatment by a medic and application of wraps, a cast, or splint: +0 days
- Ongoing, daily medical care by a trained medic or medi-bot: -3d6 days

**Mutations Used**
- Application of the mutation Heal Touch once: As 'Trait Points Healed' from the Heal Touch table on page TME-67, but as days subtracted from the duration to heal each broken bone and not trait points.
- Application of the mutation Heal Touch daily, after the first use of Heal Touch: 2 days of healing for each daily application**.
- Victim has the Regeneration mutation: Variable, days instead of months according to table on page TME-69.
- Application of Extreme Healing once: Total bone healing in 3d6 days

**Cybernetics**
- Internal Healer Drones (cybernetic implant page TME-88): -50%
- Micro Suture Laced Tissues: -50%

**Relics Applied**
- Advanced Trauma Kit: -4d6 days
- Armored Splint worn: -3d6 days
- Flesh Mend Gel MK1: -1d3 days
- Flesh Mend Gel MK 2: -1d4+1 days
- Flesh Mend Gel MK3: -1d6+2 days
- Flesh Mend Gel MK4: -2d6+4 days
- Nano Patch: -1d4+8 days
- Nano Healing Injector: -4d6 days***
- Tissue Binder 1st application: -1d20+10 days when used on unmutated humans and animals, bioreplicas, trans-humans, clones and non-mutated cyborgs. For all non-true humans, animals, and bestial humans, it aids in bone healing by only -1d6+6 days.
- Tissue Binder any follow-up application 1d6+1 days for unmutated humans and animals, bioreplicas, trans-humans, clones and non-mutated cyborgs. For all non-true humans, animals, and bestial humans speeds bone healing by only -1d3 days.
- Auto-Doc, one treatment: -4d6 days
- Auto-Doc, daily treatment after the first: -2 days

**Age shown are for humans, although the category could include different chronological time scales for different species. For example, an old human at age 60 suffers the same penalty as an old dog at 15 years of age, while a skullock, which reaches adulthood at around 8 years old, would be old at age 25, etc.*

***Example: Instead of a bone taking 60 days to heal, this fast healer's bone heals in 30 days, etc. For daily application, deduct 2 days off the duration to heal the bone, per day, instead of subtracting 1 day. Heal touch can only work on broken bones once per day.*

**** A Nano Healing Injector can be potentially lethal to any mutant lifeform. See the description on page 446 of this book.*

# Implant Purchasing
*Suggested by Charles Barber*

In most cases, the only way to acquire new implants is by looting them off fallen enemies, or discovering them in either ruins, or the loot bags of humanoids, raiders and relic harvesters such as scavengers.

In some areas, however, especially near ancient cities or old war zones, relic dealers sometimes sell cybernetic implants, but the cost is often excessive. The following table lists every cybernetic implant in both this book and the hub rules, with two systems available to a game master to establish availability.

**Option 1** uses a random dice roll (the same as shown on table XR-210 on page 330 in the cybernetic implant generation table), and the GM can declare that there are 4 implants available for sale and roll for them, or 8 implants in a larger relic shop, as examples.

**Option 2** is a system that allows for the possibility for each implant to be available, and gives a percentage chance that the implant the character desires is on sale, even if it's not on display at a relic dealership. With this system, the GM might allow the PCs to check or ask for up to ten implants and hope for the best.

Since robots and androids can also use implants, many robotics repair shops also end up with cybernetic parts, and so knowledgeable adventurers will know to check such services, too. While a few large new era cities have dedicated cybernetic and rebuilt parts and services workshops, these are far rarer than standard relic or robotics shops.

A cybernetics technician, or robotics technician, is needed to remove an old implant and attempt to install a new one.

Since many cybernetic parts require their own power cells, ethanol fuel, or ammunition, these are sometimes also available at such dealerships, with the chances any are available, number available, and purchase price, as shown below. These numbers come from the Trade Goods directory on page 95 of the hub rules.

| Item | Chance Available | Number Available | Purchase Price |
|---|---|---|---|
| **Mini power cell** | 8% | 1d3 | 120+1d100sp each |
| **Power cell** | 12% | 1d3 | 300+2d100sp |
| **Ethanol fuel** | 32% | 2d6 L | 1d20+20sp per litre |
| **Pistol round** | 26% | 2d6 | 1d20+50sp each |
| **Rifle round** | 22% | 2d6 | 1d20+50sp each |

The 'Purchase Price' shown on the table to follow is the cost for a character to buy the implant, not the sales value that diggers will get if they sell such parts to a dealership. The sales value is half of what is shown for the purchase price, although any character with the barter skill allows them to get two rolls to either earn a higher sales price, or a buy the part at lower purchase price.

Some implants, such as weapon arm or optical implant and armor enhancement, have a secondary listing to follow, since the price range for a weapon arm mounted with a chain gun is far higher, and more rare, than one fitted with a discsaw. Finally, this table shows the unique implant number for the cybernetic, as well as the book abbreviation and what page the implant can be found on in that book.

**Table XR-233 / Implants Availability and Purchase Matrix**

| Option 1: Random Implant | Implant Name | Option 2: Chance Implant Available | Purchase Price | Implant No# | Book and Page number |
|---|---|---|---|---|---|
| 01 | Alloy Razor Claws | 17% | 1600+1d1000sp | 1 | Hub Rules, page 85 |
| 02 | Anti-Toxin Array | 22% | 800+5d100sp | 2 | Hub Rules, page 85 |
| 03 | Aquatic Deployment Augmentation | 14% | 1800+1d1000sp | 51 | XR, page 332 |
| 04 | Aquatic Propulsion System | 9% | 1200+4d100sp | 52 | XR, page 332 |
| 05 | Armor Enhancement* | 56% | Variable, see Table XR-234 /pg.392 | 3 | Hub Rules, page 85 |
| 06 | Artificial Heart | 21% | 2700+2d1000sp | 4 | Hub Rules, page 85 |
| 07 | Atmospheric Hydro Converter | 19% | 1600+1d1000sp | 5 | Hub Rules, page 85 |
| 08 | Audio Compensator | 23% | 1500+1d1000sp | 53 | XR, page 332 |
| 09 | Autopilot Module | 8% | 1800+1d1000sp | 54 | XR, page 333 |
| 10 | Back-Up Sensor Array | 15% | 2500+1d1000sp | 6 | Hub Rules, page 86 |
| 11 | Bow Implant Arm | 17% | 1500+1d1000sp | 55 | XR, page 333 |
| 12 | Carbon Fiber Muscle Enhancement [CFME] | 6% | 3500+2d1000sp | 56 | XR, page 333 |
| 13 | Chopper-Borg | 7% | 2500+2d1000sp | 57 | XR, page 333 |
| 14 | Communication Implant* | 67% | Variable, see Table XR-235/pg.392 | 7 | Hub Rules, page 86 |

| Option 1: Random Implant | Implant Name | Option 2: Chance Implant Available | Purchase Price | Implant No# | Book and Page number |
|---|---|---|---|---|---|
| 15 | Computerized Brain | 11% | 5500+3d1000sp | 8 | Hub Rules, page 86 |
| 16 | Cybernetic Hair Replacement* | 25% | Variable, see Table XR-236/pg.392 | 58 | XR, page 334 |
| 17 | Cybernetic Legs | 23% | 1500+1d1000sp | 9 | Hub Rules, page 86 |
| 18 | Database* | 19% | Variable, see Table XR-237/pg.393 | 59 | XR, page 334 |
| 19 | Detachable Lower Arm | 72% | 1200+5d100sp | 10 | Hub Rules, page 86 |
| 20 | Dual Weapon Arm* | 22% | Variable, see Table XR-238/pg.393 | 60 | XR, page 336 |
| 21 | Electrical Defense Mechanism | 26% | 2500+1d1000sp | 11 | Hub Rules, page 86 |
| 22 | Electro-Shock-Suppressor | 23% | 2700+1d1000sp | 61 | XR, page 337 |
| 23 | Energy Absorption Cell | 18% | 2200+1d1000sp | 12 | Hub Rules, page 86 |
| 24 | Epidermal Manipulator | 9% | 3000+2d1000sp | 62 | XR, page 337 |
| 25 | Floodlight Orb | 36% | 1500+1d1000sp | 13 | Hub Rules, page 87 |
| 26 | Flotation Bags | 28% | 1400+5d100sp | 63 | XR, page 337 |
| 27 | Fold Out Manipulator Arm | 41% | 1500+5d100sp | 14 | Hub Rules, page 87 |
| 28 | Fold-out Alloy Shield | 32% | 2000+1d1000sp | 64 | XR, page 337 |
| 29 | Fold-out Alloy Sword | 28% | 2300+2d100sp | 65 | XR, page 338 |
| 30 | Force Canopy | 16% | 4000+3d1000sp | 66 | XR, page 338 |
| 31 | Force Field Generator | 14% | 3700+2d1000sp | 15 | Hub Rules, page 87 |
| 32 | Force Shield | 21% | 3800+3d1000sp | 16 | Hub Rules, page 87 |
| 33 | Glide Wings | 7% | 2000+2d1000sp | 67 | XR, page 338 |
| 34 | Grappling Hook | 33% | 1500+5d100sp | 17 | Hub Rules, page 87 |
| 35 | Homing Device | 29% | 1000+4d100sp | 68 | XR, page 339 |
| 36 | Mechanical Hand | 65% | Variable, see Table XR-242/pg.394 | 69 | XR, page 339 |
| 37 | Hover Jets | 12% | 2500+2d100sp | 18 | Hub Rules, page 87 |
| 38 | Hydraulic Walker Legs | 15% | 2500+2d1000sp | 19 | Hub Rules, page 88 |
| 39 | Hypodermic Tendril | 24% | 2700+2d1000sp | 20 | Hub Rules, page 88 |
| 40 | Internal Gyroscope | 34% | 1500+1d1000sp | 21 | Hub Rules, page 88 |
| 41 | Internal Healer Drones | 4% | 3500+3d1000sp | 22 | Hub Rules, page 88 |
| 42 | Internal Nutriment Supply | 11% | 2400+5d100sp | 23 | Hub Rules, page 88 |
| 43 | Iron Stomach | 18% | 2500+2d1000sp | 24 | Hub Rules, page 88 |
| 44 | Loudspeaker | 56% | 1200+1d1000sp | 25 | Hub Rules, page 88 |
| 45 | Manipulator Tendril | 59% | 2500+1d1000sp | 26 | Hub Rules, page 88 |
| 46 | Memory Backup | 12% | 1500+2d1000sp | 70 | XR, page 340 |
| 47 | Mental Attack Dampener | 8% | 3500+2d1000sp | 71 | XR, page 340 |
| 48 | Mental Defense Screen | 9% | 3200+2d1000sp | 27 | Hub Rules, page 89 |
| 49 | Micro Suture Laced Tissues | 5% | 3900+3d1000sp | 72 | XR, page 340 |
| 50 | Mini-Robotics Hanger | 8% | 4500+3d1000sp | 28 | Hub Rules, page 89 |
| 51 | Motion Stabilizer | 11% | 3500+2d1000sp | 73 | XR, page 340 |
| 52 | Multi-tool Arm* | 59% | Variable, see Table XR-239/pg.393 | 74 | XR, page 341 |
| 53 | Nutritional Enhancement Module | 32% | 2700+1d1000sp | 75 | XR, page 342 |
| 54 | Optical Concealment Generator | 6% | 3500+3d1000sp | 29 | Hub Rules, page 89 |
| 55 | Optical Enhancement* | 72% | Variable, see Table XR-240/pg.394 | 30 | Hub Rules, page 89 |
| 56 | Optical Implants Set 2* | 73% | Variable, see Table XR-241/pg.394 | 76 | XR, page 342 |
| 57 | Oxygen Supply Unit | 52% | 1600+1d100sp | 31 | Hub Rules, page 89 |
| 58 | Panoramic Optics Node | 34% | 1900+1d1000sp | 32 | Hub Rules, page 89 |
| 59 | Parachute | 15% | 2500+1d1000sp | 77 | XR, page 342 |
| 60 | Pincer | 65% | 2900+2d1000sp | 33 | Hub Rules, page 89 |
| 61 | Portable Computer Station | 42% | 5500+3d1000sp | 34 | Hub Rules, page 90 |
| 62 | Power Arm | 68% | 3000+2d1000sp | 35 | Hub Rules, page 90 |
| 63 | Power Leeching Unit | 13% | 4500+2d1000sp | 78 | XR, page 343 |
| 64 | Power-Jack | 82% | 1500+6d100sp | 79 | XR, page 343 |
| 65 | Quadrupedal Lower Body* | 9% | Variable, see Table XR-243/pg.394 | 80 | XR, page 343 |
| 66 | Radiation Leeching Unit | 21% | 2500+1d1000sp | 36 | Hub Rules, page 90 |
| 67 | Radio Scanner | 58% | 1300+5d100sp | 37 | Hub Rules, page 90 |

| Option 1: Random Implant | Implant Name | Option 2: Chance Implant Available | Purchase Price | Implant No# | Book and Page number |
|---|---|---|---|---|---|
| 68 | Retractable Laser Pistol | 28% | 5000+1d1000sp | 38 | Hub Rules, page 90 |
| 69 | Robotic Serpentine Body | 4% | 4500+3d1000sp | 81 | XR, page 345 |
| 70 | Self Destruct Mode | 3% | 2500+1d1000sp | 39 | Hub Rules, page 90 |
| 71 | Sensor Probe Launcher | 7% | 4500+1d1000sp | 40 | Hub Rules, page 91 |
| 72 | Shoulder Turret** | 32% | 2000+2d1000sp + Variable, see Table XR-244/ pg.395 | 41 | Hub Rules, page 91 |
| 73 | Smoke Screen Generator | 44% | 1500+1d1000sp | 42 | Hub Rules, page 91 |
| 74 | Snorkel | 18% | 1300+6d100sp | 82 | XR, page 345 |
| 75 | Solar Nutrient Converter | 39% | 1900+1d1000sp | 83 | XR, page 345 |
| 76 | Solar Power Generator | 57% | 2300+1d1000sp | 43 | Hub Rules, page 91 |
| 77 | Sonic Defense Screen | 29% | 2100+1d1000sp | 44 | Hub Rules, page 91 |
| 78 | Sound Dampening Field | 12% | 2900+2d1000sp | 84 | XR, page 346 |
| 79 | Speed Assist Rotors | 14% | 2500+2d1000sp | 85 | XR, page 346 |
| 80 | Stun Inhibitor Unit | 22% | 2100+1d1000sp | 45 | Hub Rules, page 91 |
| 81 | Subcutaneous Plating | 5% | 5500+3d1000sp | 86 | XR, page 346 |
| 82 | Surveillance Tendril | 26% | 2200+1d1000sp | 46 | Hub Rules, page 91 |
| 83 | Synthetic Skin | 19% | 1800+1d1000sp | 87 | XR, page 346 |
| 84 | Telescoping thrust Blade | 35% | 2300+1d1000sp | 47 | Hub Rules, page 92 |
| 85 | Tentacle | 28% | 2700+1d1000sp | 48 | Hub Rules, page 85 |
| 86 | Tracked Locomotion | 11% | 4500+3d1000sp | 49 | Hub Rules, page 92 |
| 87 | Vehicle Control Module | 16% | 2500+2d1000sp | 88 | XR, page 347 |
| 88 | Vocal Mimicry Modulator | 10% | 2200+1d1000sp | 89 | XR, page 347 |
| 89-98 | Weapon Arm Set 2*** | 89% | Variable, see Table XR-244/ pg.395 | 50/90 | XR, page 347 |
| 99 | Welding Torch | 73% | 2600+2d1000sp | 91 | XR, page 349 |
| 00 | Wheel Deployment | 14% | 2700+1d1000sp | 92 | XR, page 349 |

** Consult the sub-table to establish the purchase price and randomly selected implant in this category.*

*** Use the weapon arm Set 2 listing on page 395 for what ranged weapon is attached to this shoulder turret. The cost for the weapon is added to the above mentioned purchase value.*

**** Weapon Arm set 1 from the hub rules, implant no. 50, is included in weapon Arms set 2. The actual weapon fitted to this arm is rolled randomly on the sub-table on page 395 of this book.*

## Table XR-234 / Armor Enhancements Availability

All armor enhancements are described in the hub rules on page 85

| 1d10 | Armor Enhancement Available | Purchase Value |
|---|---|---|
| 1,2. | Alloy plated skull | 1600+2d100sp |
| 3. | Alloy enhanced skeleton | 4000+2d1000sp |
| 4,5. | Steel carapace | 2500+2d1000sp |
| 6,7. | Ballistic under-sheath | 1900+2d1000sp |
| 8. | Flame proof tissues | 2100+2d1000sp |
| 9. | Acid proof tissues | 1900+2d1000sp |
| 10. | Reflective plating | 2400+2d1000sp |

## Table XR-235 / Communications Implants Availability

| 1d10 | Comm Implant Available | Purchase Value | Book and Page number |
|---|---|---|---|
| 1-4. | Communicator: basic model | 800+2d100sp | Hub Rules, pg.198 |
| 5-7. | Advanced communicator | 2000+1d1000sp | Hub Rules, pg.198 |
| 8. | Beacon locater unit, Implant version | 120+1d100sp | Hub Rules, pg.198 |
| 9. | Location beacon | 1000+1d100sp | Hub Rules, pg.198 |
| 10. | Communicator with satellite uplink module and dish | 1000+1d1000sp | Hub Rules, pg.86 |

## Table XR-236 / Cybernetic Hair Replacement Availability

| 1d6 | Cybernetic Hair Available | Purchase Price |
|---|---|---|
| 1,2. | Illumination hair | 900+1d1000sp |
| 3,4. | Antenna hair | 1000+1d1000sp |
| 5,6. | Expanded sensory hair | 1400+1d1000sp |

## Table XR-237 / Database Availability

Note, to install the database interface unit, described on page 334 of this book, assume the implant will come with 1d4 random database sticks installed and included in the price, but additional database chips can sometimes be purchased too, with the following random list showing prices for an additional 1d8 that are available at the robotics or relic dealership:

| 1d100 | Database | Purchase Price |
|---|---|---|
| 01-03 | Music Databases | 400+1d100sp |
| 04-06 | Movie Database | 70+1d100sp |
| 07-09 | Art History | 50+1d30sp |
| 10-12 | American History | 300+2d100sp |
| 13-15 | English Literature | 150+1d100sp |
| 16-18 | Relic Knowledge | 500+2d100sp |
| 19-21 | Field Medic | 900+1d1000sp |
| 22-24 | Computer Technician | 1100+1d1000sp |
| 25-27 | Robotics Technician | 1400+1d1000sp |
| 28-30 | Bio-Technician | 800+1d1000sp |
| 31-33 | Chemical Technician | 700+1d1000sp |
| 34-36 | Old World Languages | 200+2d100sp |
| 37-39 | Computer Codes and Access Passwords | 600+3d100sp |
| 40-42 | Old World Area Maps | 300+2d100sp |
| 43-45 | Ancient History | 200+1d100sp |
| 46-49 | Martial Arts | 1000+1d1000sp |
| 50-52 | Mechanical Technician | 700+5d100sp |
| 53-56 | Electrical Technician | 800+4d100sp |
| 57-60 | Gunsmith | 500+2d100sp |
| 61-63 | Combat Tactics | 800+3d100sp |
| 64-66 | Recent State Records | 100+1d30sp |
| 67-69 | Subway and Sewer Database | 300+1d100sp |
| 70-72 | Sport Archive | 200+1d30sp |
| 73-75 | Correctional Records | 300+1d100sp |
| 76-78 | Human DNA Database | 450+1d100sp |
| 79-81 | Comics Database | 400+2d100sp |
| 82-84 | Pilot Skill | 1100+1d1000sp |
| 85-87 | Agricultural database | 400+1d100sp |
| 88-90 | Database of Architecture, Engineering and Construction | 700+3d100sp |
| 91-94 | Sniper Database | 800+4d100sp |
| 95-00 | Cybernetics Technician | 900+1d1000sp |

## Dual Weapon Arm Availability

Note, for the main weapon arm, see the availability on Table XR-244 on page 395, but for the secondary melee weapon, roll on the following table for what comes fitted to this unit:

### Table XR-238 / Dual Weapon Arm Melee Weapon Table

| 1d100 | Weapon | Purchase Price |
|---|---|---|
| 01-11 | Bayonet, fixed | 80+2d100sp |
| 12-18 | Bayonet, spring out* | 100+3d100sp |
| 19-24. | Spring-spike | 600+3d100sp |
| 25-31 | Disc saw* | 1400+1d1000sp |
| 32-41 | Chainsaw* | 2200+1d1000sp |
| 42-46 | Laser torch | 2600+1d1000sp |
| 47-56. | Stun stick* | 2600+1d1000sp |
| 57-61 | Tactical tomahawk* | 800+3d100sp |
| 62-68. | Pneumatic hammer* | 1800+2d1000sp |
| 69-78 | Nerve disruptor baton | 3200+2d1000sp |
| 79-84. | Devastator rod* | 30k+6d1000sp |
| 85-88. | Razor sword* | 1600+2d1000sp |
| 89-94. | Laser sword | 10k+3d1000sp |
| 95-99. | Chainsword | 12k+6d1000sp |
| 00. | Mk2 laser sword | 20k+6d1000sp |

*This weapon normally resides in a slot beneath the barrel of whatever ranged weapon the arm features. With an internally controlled trigger mechanism, this weapon pops out either ready for action or directly against a target if the end of this arm is pressed to a potential victim, adding +20 SV on the initial stab.*

## Table XR-239 / Multi-tool Arm Availability

Roll for 1d3+1 tools fitted into this arm from the following list. Re-roll any duplicated result. Roll 1d100.

| 1d100 | Multi-Tool Arm Feature | Purchase Price |
|---|---|---|
| 01-04. | Electric toothbrush | 60+3d20sp |
| 05-08. | Water filtration straw | 200+2d100sp |
| 09-12. | Spotting scope (non-digital) | 1600+3d100sp |
| 13-16. | Laser scalpel | 1600+1d1000sp |
| 17-22. | Light duty grappling hook | 700+1d1000sp |
| 23-27. | Communicator, standard | 800+2d100sp |
| 28-31. | Rad scanner | 4000+6d100sp |
| 32-35. | Tissue binder | 2000+2d1000sp |
| 36-38. | Digital wrist watch | 300+3d100sp |
| 39-44. | Anti-toxin-injector | 360+2d100sp each |
| 45-47. | Battle drill | 1600+1d1000sp |
| 48-52. | Agony baton | 3000+1d1000sp |
| 53-55. | Force shield | 3000+3d1000sp |
| 56-61. | Pocket flashlight | 360+2d100sp |
| 62-64. | Retractable laser pistol | 5000+1d1000sp |

| | | |
|---|---|---|
| **65-67.** | Flip out disc saw | 1400+1d1000sp |
| **68-70.** | Switchblade knife | 220+2d100sp |
| **71-73.** | Alloy razor claws | 1600+1d1000sp |
| **74-76.** | Landmine detector | 1200+4d100sp |
| **77,78.** | Cutlery set with fold-out knife, spoon, and fork | 200+2d100sp |
| **79-81.** | Repair tools and fold out flexible shaft | 900+4d100sp |
| **82-83.** | Fire starting lighter | 500+2d100sp |
| **84-86.** | Hygienic array | 300+1d100sp |
| **87-89.** | Microphone and recording system. Will store 1000 hours of audio and comes with audio out port and uses a mini power cell which will allow for 200 hours recording. | 600+2d100sp |
| **90-92.** | Massage paddle and hot oil dispenser | 600+3d100sp |
| **93-95.** | Loudspeaker | 1200+5d100sp |
| **96,97.** | Heavy crossbow | 700+4d100sp |
| **98-00.** | Quad barreled shotgun | 24000+1d1000sp |

## Table XR-240 / Optical Enhancement Availability

These implants are all described on page 89 of the hub rules. Roll 1d12 for the type of optic unit that is available. This amount is the total and includes the hardware mount for the implant.

| 1d12 | Optical Enhancement Available | Purchase Price |
|---|---|---|
| **1.** | Zoom lens (magnify objects x50) | 800+3d100sp |
| **2.** | Substance reader (as the relic, see page TME-199) | 2000+3d1000sp |
| **3.** | Flashlight, large (as the relic, page TME-201) | 1000+2d100sp |
| **4.** | Night-vision optics (vision as if it were day, plus infrared mode) | 2600+1d1000sp |
| **5,6.** | Targeting optics (as the relic on page TME-198) | 3400+3d100sp |
| **7-9.** | Pulse laser eye (as pulse rifle, page TME-190, half range, 40 bursts per power cell) | 8000+3d1000sp |
| **10.** | Camcorder (records films, plus x20 zoom lens) | 2000+1d1000sp |
| **11.** | Entity scanner (see implant description page TME-89) | 1400+d1000sp |
| **12.** | Holographic projector (see implant description page TME-89) | 3500+2d1000sp |

## Table XR-241 / Optical Implants Set 2 Availability

These implants are all described on page 342 of this book. Roll 1d8 for the type of optic unit that is available. This amount is the total and includes the hardware mount for the implant.

| 1d6 | Optical Enhancement Available | Purchase Price |
|---|---|---|
| **1.** | Threat assessment algorithm | 4500+2d1000sp |
| **2.** | Augmented reality view mode | 2200+1d1000sp |
| **3.** | Radiation viewer | 3000+1d1000sp |
| **4.** | Enhanced night vision eye | 3400+1d1000sp |
| **5.** | Extra dimensional vision | 2300+1d1000sp |
| **6.** | Laser eye | 9000+3d1000sp |

## Table XR-242 / Mechanical Hand Availability

| 2d6 | Hand Type Available | Purchase Price |
|---|---|---|
| **2,3.** | Three fingered robotic hand | 1000+3d100sp |
| **4,5.** | Civilian issue | 900+3d100sp |
| **6,7.** | Natural replacement | 1200+4d100sp |
| **8,9.** | Fold away or muzzle palm hand | 1800+1d1000sp |
| **10,11.** | Alloy skeletal | 2000+1d1000sp |
| **12.** | Large robotic | 1900+1d1000sp |

## Table XR-243 / Quadrupedal Lower Body Availability

To find what is available and at what price a character needs to pay for such a rig, roll once on each of the following five tables that mirror the tables shown for this complex implant on page 343 of this book. Although a larger dealership might have several options available that can have sheathing, color, leg size and other features substituted, most places will have only one quad-body on offer with already present features rolled at random.

| 1d10 | Lower Body Available | Purchase Price |
|---|---|---|
| **1.** | Mastiff sized | Add 3000+2d1000sp |
| **2-6.** | Lion sized | Add 4000+2d1000sp |
| **7-9.** | Grizzly sized | Add 6000+2d1000sp |
| **10.** | Horse sized | Add 8000+2d1000sp |

| 1d10 | Sheathing Present | Purchase Price |
|---|---|---|
| **1** | None | Add zero silver pieces |
| **2-5.** | Thick plastic | Add 300+1d100sp |
| **6,7.** | Scrap metal | Add 800+3d100sp |
| **8,9.** | Iron clad | Add 1200+2d1000sp |
| **10.** | Composite relic armor | Add 3000+12d1000sp |

| 1d10 | Color Present on Quad-Body Sheathing | Purchase Price |
|---|---|---|
| **1.** | Visibility suit bright orange and neon yellow | Add zero silver pieces |
| **2.** | Snow white | Add 200+1d100sp |
| **3.** | Blood red | Add 300+1d100sp |
| **4.** | Gloss black | Add 330+1d100sp |
| **5.** | Dark blue with the word 'Police' written on it | Add 400+2d100sp |
| **6.** | Drab, grays, browns and rust colors. | Add 260+1d100sp |
| **7.** | Desert tan | Add 500+1d100sp |
| **8.** | Charcoal gray | Add 450+1d100sp |
| **9.** | Urban gray, black and concrete urban camo | Add 600+2d100sp |
| **10.** | Woodland camouflage | Add 500+2d100sp |

| 1d10 | Leg Size Present | Purchase Price |
|---|---|---|
| 1. | Stubby and strong | Add 300+1d100sp |
| 2-7. | Normal length (1m) | Add 400+1d100sp |
| 8,9. | Long (2m) | Add 600+4d100sp |
| 10. | Normal but extendable to 3 meters | Add 1000+5d100sp |

| 1d100 | Possible Special Feature Present | Purchase Price |
|---|---|---|
| 01-50. | No special feature | Add zero silver pieces |
| 51-55. | Back mounted, pop out rocket launcher | Add 5000+1d1000sp |
| 56-60. | Fold out survival shelter | Add 1000+1d0100sp |
| 61-65. | Water storage and filtration system inside | Add 700+4d100sp |
| 66-70. | Detachable lower body | Add 2000+1d1000sp |
| 71-75. | Solar generator unit | Add 1400+1d1000sp |
| 76-80. | Fold out manipulator arm | Add 1500+5d100sp |
| 81-87. | Fold out stretcher and stabilizing straps | Add 8000+2d1000sp |
| 88-95. | Retractable velociraptor claw | Add 800+4d100sp |
| 96-99. | Back mounted shoulder turret | Add 2000+2d1000sp |
| 00. | Two features from this listing. Roll 1d100 +50 but re-roll this result or duplicated results. | |

### Table XR-244 / Weapon Arm Availability

These weapons do not come with any ammunition or power supplies. The Purchase Price, as with all the available implants in this for sale section, is what a character must pay to acquire the available implant. This is double what they would get for selling such an item to a relic or robotics dealership.

| 1d100 | Weapon Available | Purchase Price |
|---|---|---|
| 01,02. | Razor sword | 1600+2d1000sp |
| 03,04. | Spring-spike | 600+3d100sp |
| 05,06. | Discsaw | 1400+1d1000sp |
| 07-11. | Chainsaw | 2200+1d1000sp |
| 12,13. | Stun stick | 2600+1d1000sp |
| 14,15. | Chainsword | 12k+6d1000sp |
| 16. | Devastator rod | 30k+6d1000sp |
| 17,18. | Laser sword | 10k+3d1000sp |
| 19. | Laser torch | 2600+1d1000sp |
| 20. | Harpoon gun, 4 barrels | 2800+1d1000sp |
| 21. | Advanced laser pistol MK I | 10k+2d1000sp |
| 22. | Mk2 laser sword | 20k+6d1000sp |
| 23,24. | 22 caliber semi auto rifle | 2400+1d1000sp |
| 25-28. | Stun pistol | 3000+1d1000sp |
| 29,30. | Nerve disruptor baton | 3200+2d1000sp |
| 31-36. | Assault shotgun | 4400+2d1000sp |
| 37-39. | Sniper rifle | 4000+2d1000sp |
| 40. | Advanced sniper rifle | 11k+3d1000sp |
| 41-49. | Sub-machine gun | 2400+2d1000sp |
| 50. | Energy spear | 40k+3d1000sp |
| 51-60. | Assault rifle | 4000+2d1000sp |
| 61-66. | Heavy assault rifle | 12k+3d1000sp |
| 67. | Sonic immobilizer rifle | 22k+4d1000sp |
| 68. | Pulse rifle | 12k+4d1000sp |
| 69. | Heavy pulse rifle | 20k+6d1000sp |
| 70,71 | Rocket launcher | 8k+6d1000sp |
| 72,73. | Flame unit | 2600+2d1000sp |
| 74. | Rocket pistol | 6000+2d1000sp |
| 75. | Rocket carbine | 10000+4d1000sp |
| 76-78. | Chain gun | 8000+4d1000sp. |
| 79,80. | Fifty caliber sniper rifle | 22k+4d1000sp |
| 81,82. | Heavy machine gun | 8k+4d1000sp |
| 83-86. | Laser carbine | 10k+4d1000sp |
| 87. | Lightning emitter | 12k+4d1000sp |
| 88,89. | Heavy laser carbine | 22k+6d1000sp |
| 90. | Laser sniper rifle | 24k+6d1000sp |
| 91,92. | Stun rifle | 8000+4d1000sp |
| 93. | Heavy stun emitter | 24k+6d1000sp |
| 94. | Mk2 laser carbine | 14k+4d1000sp |
| 95. | Particle beam rifle | 30k+6d1000sp |
| 96,97. | EM emitter rifle | 10k+6d1000sp |
| 98. | Mk3 laser carbine | 20k+5d1000sp |
| 99. | Mk4 laser carbine | 26k+5d1000sp |
| 00. | Light laser cannon | 27k+3d1000sp |

# Exceeding the Limits of Mental and Energy Mutations

Sometimes a situation is so dire that a gifted mutant must draw upon energies which exceed his or her normal energy and mental limitations. For most every mental or energy based mutation, there is a daily usage noted in its description, but this limit can be pushed through if the deviant has sufficient willpower — but at a cost. The mutations eligible for this option can't have a physical component, such as quills, throwing spikes, amber pellets, stench spray, flame breath, flame thrower limb, acid spit, dagger seed pods, organ grenade, to name just a few.

Mutations that are eligible to be exceeded include all mental mutations such as telepathy, heal touch, mind crush, and mental dominion, while energy mutations include such powers as stun ray, radioactive pulse, mental mine, heat pulse, and electrical pulse.

Some mutations have a very limited usage time line, such as doom sphere, which can only be used once every ten days. Trying to exceed this will result in multiple consequences.

A few mutations are willpower based and don't have a daily limit other than this trait value. Blurred movement is an example of this sort of mutation. To extend this sort of power, consider a willpower or other trait based daily usage limit mutation to be a single use per day power as shown on the following table.

Table XR-245, on this page, shows a range of standard daily uses for mutations. Rank usually multiplies this usage. Beyond the daily or hourly limit, the probability of successfully exceeding the usage limit decreases with each use, and the likelihood of a consequence increases. Use the character's current willpower trait to make hazard checks based on how many times 'over' the daily usage allowable limit has been exceeded. For example, for a mutation that can be used twice per day per

rank, and this mutant has already exceeded the usage twice, and attempting to use a power a third time over the daily limit, they have to make a type F willpower based hazard check to succeed, but automatically suffers 1 consequence from table XR-246 if they succeed. Of note, not every consequence is life threatening or even negative, but most are. If an attempt to exceed a mutation's daily limit fails, no further attempt can be made with that specific mutation, for 10 minutes.

### Table XR-245 / Uses of a Mental or Energy Mutation

A mutant must make a current Willpower based hazard check to exceed the use of this mutation. Failure means being unable to try again for 10 minutes. Success means another use of the mutation occurs, but with a consequence, or two, rolled on table XR-246.

| Normal Uses | Exceeded by 1 daily use | Exceeded by 2 daily uses | Exceeded by 3 daily uses | 4 or more Exceeded uses |
|---|---|---|---|---|
| Once every 10 days (doom Sphere) | E* | G** | J** | M** |
| Once every five days (Extreme Healing) | D* | F** | H** | K** |
| Once every two days | D | F* | H** | J** |
| once per day per 2 ranks | D | E* | G** | I** |
| Once per day per rank | C | E* | G* | I** |
| Twice per day per rank | B | D | F* | H** |
| 3 times per day per rank | A | C | E* | G** |
| 4 times per day per rank | A | B | C | E* |

*If successfully exceeding the usage limits of this mutation, there is always 1 consequence roll from Table XR-246 .

**There is always 1 consequence roll from Table XR-246 for even attempting to exceed this mutation at this point, and if successful, make 3 more consequence rolls on the following table for a total of 4 rolls.

### Table XR -246/ Consequences of Exceeding the Limits of Mental Mutations

**3d6 Exceeding the Limits of Mental Mutations: Consequences**

**3.** Heart attack. Mutant must make an uninjured endurance based Type C hazard check or collapse in pain and pass out. Worse, if passing out, a second identical hazard check is needed to avoid heart stoppage and death. If merely passing out, the victim remains in an unconscious state for 30+d100 minutes.

**4.** Permanent loss of 1 trait point to one trait, roll 1d8 to determine which.

**5.** Immediate loss of bladder and bowl control.

**6.** Violent nausea and projectile vomiting for 1d6 minutes, take 1d3 damage.

**7.** Terrible headache for the rest of the day, all mental mutations deployed have a 50% chance of failing.

**8.** Terrible pain in gallbladder, suffer 1d6 damage.

**9.** All-over body rash for 3d6 days, appearance temporarily drops by -10 per occurrence of this consequence.

**10.** Unbearable agony for 1d4 minutes, although subject can move at half speed and fight with a 50% SV penalty (half normal strike value).

**11.** Fall to one knee, but remain awake and aware, yet unable to attack, move or fight for 2 rounds. +40 SV easier to be struck during this time.

**12.** Fall to your knees and remain useless, but vaguely conscious for 3d6 rounds. You are +40 SV easier to be struck during this time.

**13.** Drop whatever you are holding and fall backwards, unconscious for 2d6 rounds before recovering fully — unless falling off a cliff, roof, or letting go of a rope or ladder.

**14.** Deafness. Total hearing loss for 3d6 hours, and -2 initiative during this time.

**15.** Blindness for 3d6 hours (see blindness rules on page TME-122: 50% loss to strike values and movement rate and victim is +40 SV easier to be hit by opponents.

**16.** Drop unconscious for 3d6 minutes.

**17.** Coma for 3d6 hours.

**18.** Improvement! Character permanently gains 1d6 points to their willpower trait.

# Organic Characters Hacking into CPU

When the TME hub rules were written, such traits as processor, firewall, data points and so on had not been put into play. The rules for how a humanoid character with the computer technician skill could hack into a computer didn't take into account the complexities of the new electronic brained character types described in this book. In particular, the simplistic system for hacking described under the Computer Technician Table, TME-1-47 on page 53 of the hub rules book, needs the following brief update.

Consider the 'Hack into CPU' column numbers to represent the processor trait (PRO) during a hacking attempt, which is akin to the strike value rating during a physical attack. The firewall trait (FW) value of any digital entity is sort of like its defense value. The firewalls of some digital beings, androids, robots and computer systems are very high and will make it nearly impossible for a low skilled computer technician to hack into them — although as with physical combat, allow any natural result on the 1d100 attack roll of 01-05 to always mean a successful hack, causing 1d10 data points damage to the CPU of the target. A roll of 95-00 is always a miss, regardless of how high the potential hacker's processor trait is.

Although not mentioned on page TME-53 of the hub rules, the actions of creating a virus, reprogramming a robot or android, are only tasks that can be done after the defeated CPU has been depleted of data points and thus been conquered. Hacking into a robot or android is something an organic being with the Computer Technician Skill can attempt, but any other robotic unit, android, digital being, or installation or vessel based artificial intelligence can also have a go at.

# Skill Tier Unlocks

*by Danny Seedhouse*

This optional rule provides extra options for the weapon expert skill when applied to bows, crossbows and slings as described in the hub rules on page TME-57, giving a character more choice than simply increasing their strike value and damage. To unlock these weapon master benefits, a character must invest a skill tier point to unlock the mastery. In short, instead of adding an extra skill point in bows, for example, the player expends one point, once, to start using the bow master benefits, but applies the benefits from other skill points thereafter as normal but now enjoys these remarkable talents.

After unlocking mastery, the archer, crossbow user, or slinger can access the following benefits with the appropriate number of skill points in weapon expert.

## Crossbow Master

1 Skill point: Craft bolts as per the junk crafting skill.

3 Skill points: Basic crafting: you can now junk craft a crossbow and basic trick bolts.

5 Skill points: Increased range: you can now shoot 20% farther.

7 Skill points: Junk craft a heavy crossbow.

9 Skill points: Craft trick advanced bolts.

10 Skill points: Auto Loader for your crossbow that reduces load time to one round but needs a mini power cell to work. +30% range.

## Bow Master*

1 Skill point: Craft arrows as per the junk crafting skill.

3 Skill points: Craft a junk bow and basic trick bolts.

5 Skill points: Half draw technique. Fire once, per round. All shots are at 1/2 damage and range.

7 Skill points: Can craft a junk compound bow.

9 Skill points: Craft advanced trick arrows.

10 Skill points: Rapid Fire Archer. Fire 1 arrow per round at normal damage and range.

*An earlier, alternate archery path is also available to this character, and also written by Mr. Seedhouse. On page 124-125 of in the Excavator Monthly Compendium is the Archy Skill. If that book is handy, the player can instead select that variant of the bow skill instead of using the damage and SV benefits of the regular weapon expert skill. The Archery Skill of the EM Compendium can be used in conjunction with the use of trick and advanced trick arrows from this section — Game Master permitting.*

## Sling Mastery

1 Skill point: Build a sling

3 Skill points: Craft a sling specific version of the following basic trick bolts: noise makers, fire (burns for 1d4 rounds), grenades (does full sling damage to target hit plus automatic explosion damage), illumination.

5 Skill points: Quick load, fire 1 sling projectile a round

7 Skill points: Face smashing, use a loaded sling in melee, doing equivalent damage to a ranged shot.

9 Skill points:  Craft advanced trick sling bullets

# Trick Crossbow Bolts, Arrows and Sling Projectiles

**Basic:** This character can make regular ammo for their weapon from trash as if using the junk crafter skill.

**Grappling Hook bolt or arrow** (1/2 normal range with rope attached). This one offers multiple uses, but includes sending up a rope to snag and allow one to climb the secured line. This grapple could also be fired across a gap in a pathway to trip passing opponents, or attach a rope to a moving vehicle or draft animal to either arrest its movement or climb aboard.

**Noise Makers:** Screaming or whistling projectiles for signaling to other units or to distract and alarm opponents.

**Fire tips:** Used to light things on fire. Target hit burns for the next 1d3 rounds takes an extra 1d4 damage per round. Used to ignite roof tops, airship balloons, wooden barges, plantoids and other flammable substances.

**Rope cutters:** If during a called shot to cut a rope results in a hit, (see pages TME 109-110) then the rope is always cut, as if the user hit it with a beam weapon. Also under the called shots section of the hub rules is the option to cut off the hand of an opponent. With this blade headed bolt or arrow, this can also be attempted as if this arrowhead were a long blade — GM permitting.

**Grenade:** Attach a mini grenade with no penalty to strike value. Explodes on striking a hard surface. A wide range of fireworks can also be strapped to an arrow shaft or larger than normal crossbow quarrel. There is a massive section on fireworks included in this book starting on page 423. If a firework has a range, add that to the arrow or bolt's range.

**Illumination:** This projectile has either an attached relic glow stick or a flaming, oil dipped cloth, or some other form of illumination at the end of the arrow, bolt, or built into the sling projectile. It makes the brightest light possible and is often colored depending the chemical composition used. While designed to signal to allies rather than set fire to things, a blazing, cloth tipped arrow will certainly start fires in grass, wooden structures or oil soaked enemies.

## Advanced Trick Crossbow Bolts, Arrows and Sling Projectiles

**Shock:** This one shot shock arrow or bolt is made from a small power cell. The damage depends on the power cell used. A pill power cell does an extra 1d10 stun while a mini power cell inflicts 1d20 stun damage. After delivering the shock damage, the power cell is broken 67% of the time, otherwise can be salvaged, recharged and re-used.

The normal damage from whatever projectile, plus the user's skill and strength, are also applied and normally inflict stun damage as the projectile is crafted to be blunt and knock out targets instead of killing them. Since power cells can explode if exposed to flame, or crushed by over 500kg weight, there is a risk in using these projectiles if shooting them into areas with active fires burning. Power cells, and their blast radius, SV and DMG are shown on page TME-199.

**Bleeder:** Designed to cause blood loss and stick in the target using barbs and hooks. A successful strike causes 1d4 DMG bleeding per round till removed. If a target rips it out, they take an extra 1d20 DMG and bleed for 1d4 more rounds. A trained medic (1 skill point) can remove it carefully, dealing only 1 point of damage.

**Incendiary:** This projectile is tipped with a mix of flammable chemicals combined with a flint or other method of sparking the tip on impact with a hard surface. On a strike, they explode in a 3 meter radius doing 2d6 fire damage. Targets hit are set on fire taking 1d6 damage for 1d4 rounds. To make the compounds for this explosive system requires somebody with at least 1 point in the Chemical Technician skill, although this master can assemble the starter and prepare each projectile. A 4 skill point chemist, meanwhile, can make far more advanced incendiary fuels that inflict 2d20 damage on the initial blast and burn for 1d10 DMG for 1d6 rounds thereafter. Incendiary projectiles usually only have a blast area of 1 meter radius.

**Bullet tipped:** This projectile involves the expenditure of a relic or reloaded ammo round. The round is connected to a firing pin or appropriately sized ball bearing behind the cartridge, and on impact with a hard surface, such as a person or beast, discharges the cartridge even as the arrowhead or sling projectile enters the target, adding to the random damage of the bullet.

**Splash:** This is similar to the incendiary tip but has more utility. Various payloads include things like paint, acid, sleep gas, or all sorts of useful and deadly substances.

**Net:** This projectile is tipped by a tightly packed net. On a successful strike, this net opens and is wide enough to entangle a small person (1.3m tall and under), dog, eagle or cat, etc. Any target is allowed an agility based type D hazard check to wiggle out of after being trapped, per round. Larger targets have their arm, weapon wielding appendage, or legs wrapped and must make an identical hazard check too, per round to get clear. A man or beast trapped in a net of this sort suffers a -40 strike value penalty while ensnared, although for a full-sized adult human with their legs tangled, they move only a quarter of their normal speed. These arrows are usually blunt headed and do only stun damage, besides the delivery of their net. To properly fold up and re-arm one of these net tipped projectiles take 2d6+6 minutes.

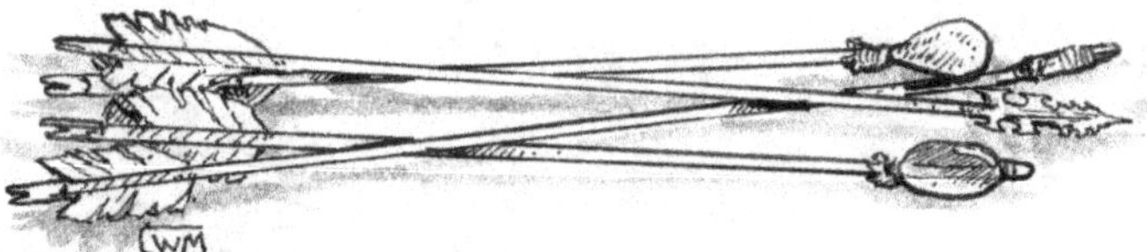

## Availability and Cost of Trick Projectiles

The following listing shows the costs and time needed to make each trick bolt, arrow, or sling projectile, although a bullet, firework, power cell, grenade must be acquired separately. The column that shows the 'Ready Made Cost to Purchase' means how much anybody in a barter market, specialty weapons shop, or black market can spend to acquire ready-to-use trick ammo.

The column to the right shows 'Number Available' and refers to the number available for purchase at any week. A die toss with a minus applied to it lets the shopper know how many can be purchased at any given time; roll the dice shown and deduct whatever the modifier is to result in 0 or more projectiles available.

In some communities, the use of trick arrows might be considered cowardly, unfair, or even illegal, and so any master in these weapons will tend to keep such ammo hidden until needed.

### Table XR-247 / Availability and Cost of Trick Projectiles

| Trick Arrow Type | Ready made Cost to Purchase | Number Available | Cost to make | Time To make |
|---|---|---|---|---|
| Grappling Hook | 2d6+14sp | 1d6 -2 | 7+1d6sp | 6+1d6 hours |
| Noise Maker | 1d6+3sp | 1d12 -3 | 1d3sp | 2 per hour |
| Fire tip | 1d6+4sp | 1d10 -3 | 1d4sp | 1 per hour |
| Rope cutter | 2d6+3sp | 1d6 -3 | 1d4+1sp | 2 hours |
| Grenade | 320+1d100sp[1] | 1d6 -4 | 10+1d10sp* | 5+1d6 hours |
| Illumination | 2d6+7sp | 1d8 -4 | 1d6+3sp | 1d3 hours |
| Shock | 90+3d20sp[2] | 1d6 -4 | 8+1d8sp* | 3+1d4 hours |
| Bleeder | 2d6+10sp | 1d8 -3 | 1d6+5sp | 1d3+1 hours |
| Incendiary | 3d6+12sp | 1d6 -4 | 2d6+2sp | 1d4+3 hours |
| Bullet tipped | 30+2d20sp[3] | 1d8 -4 | 1d8+7sp* | 1d3+1 hours |
| Splash | 3d6+20sp[4] | 1d8 -5 | 2d6+8sp | 1d4+4 hours |
| Net | 30+1d20sp | 1d6 -3 | 1d10+15sp | 1d8+5 hours |

*1 This includes the cost of a mini-grenade as described on page TME-195 and can harm up to 6 people if in a group.*
*2 Includes the cost of a mini-power cell.*
*3 Includes the cost of a standard pistol round.*
*4 Includes the cost of 300ml of acid. On a hit, this acid will coat a target in a 50cm splotch of dissolving acid, and burn for 1d4 rounds inflicting 2d6 damage per round unless neutralized with a liter of water, beer or other fluid.*
**Does not include the relic grenade, power cell or bullet.*

Expanded Relics

# Expanded Relics

## Table XR-248/ Weapon Relics Set 2

| Weapon | SV | Rate | Damage | Range[1] | Hands[2] | STR[3] | Ammo/ Duration | Weight | Value[4] | Page |
|---|---|---|---|---|---|---|---|---|---|---|
| BB Rifle | +5 | 1/2 | 1 point | 95m | 2 | - | 350 BB's, crank | 1.2kg | 700+4d100sp | 403 |
| Pellet Rifle | +7 | 1/3 | 1d2 | 56m | 2 | - | single shot, crank | 2.6kg | 900+5d100sp | 403 |
| Flare Gun | +4 | 1/2 | 2d6 stun +fire | 150m | 1 | – | 1 Emergency Flare | 150g | 500+4d100sp | 403 |
| Advanced Harpoon Gun | +18 alloy (or +12) | 1 or 2 | 2d20+13 alloy (or 1d20+12) | 36m or 56m | 2 | 40 | Power cell: 3 spooling hours | 3.8 kg | 1600+1d1000sp | 403 |
| Bug Spray | +5 | 1 | 1d6 to 'bugs' 3m ( 3x3m area) | 1 | - | - | 30 (disposable can) | 400g | 200+d100sp | 403 |
| Chem-Sprayer | +16/ +4 | 1 | by canister | 20m/5m | 1 or 2 | 30 | 20 sprays per canister | 4kg+5kg | 1500+d1000sp | 404 |
| Tactical Tomahawk | +6 | 1 | 1d12+2 or d12+5 | 5m | 1 or 2 | 14 | nil | 900g | 400+3d100sp | 405 |
| Chainsword | +25/ +2 | 1 | 3d20+10/ 12d0+2 | melee | 1/2 | 40/15 (2 hands) | 2 power cells:500 rounds | 8kg | 6000+3d1000sp | 405 |
| Mk2 Laser Sword | +25 | 1 | 2d20+20 | melee | 1 | - | power cell lasts 600 rounds | 1.6kg | 9k+4d1000sp | 405 |
| Energy Spear | +20 | 1 | 1d20+10 stun/ 2d20+20/ d100+30 | melee | 2 | 26 | Power cell: low: 1 unit/ med: 2 unit/ high: 5 units per strike | 14kg | 18k+5d1000sp | 405 |
| Electro-Net Gun | +30 | 1/4 | Entangled & 1d6 stun | 20m | 2 | | 12 shots per power cell from gun | 5kg | 1000+1d1000sp | 406 |
| Stun Rifle | +24 | 1 | 3d20 stun | 750m | 2 | 22 | power cell: 30 shots | 4.8kg | 4000+2d1000sp | 406 |
| Heavy Stun Emitter | +44 | 1/2 | 30+3d20 stun | 1.2km | 2, on tripod | 2 crew | power cell 8 shots | 62kg | 11k+4d1000sp | 406 |
| Sonic Immobilizer Rifle | +30/ +15/+10 | 1 | 3d20 stun/ 2d20 stun/ 3d6 stun a | 0-6m/6-15m/15-30m/ 31-60m | 2 | 20 | power cell: 16 shots | 2.9kg | 9000+4d1000sp | 407 |
| Nerve Disruptor Baton | +17 | 1 | Nerve Disrupt~ | melee | 1 | - | power cell: 10 discharges | 1.2kg | 1600+1d1000sp | 407 |
| Devastator Rod | +45 (blast +22) | half | 3d100 (blast radius 3m: DMG 1d100) | 120m | 1 | - | power cell: 20 discharges | 2.7kg | 14k+5d1000sp | 407 |
| EM Emitter Rifle | +5/ +35 electronics | 1 | d10/2d100 stun | 700m | 2 | 24 | power cell: 12 shots | 5.5kg | 5000+3d1000sp | 407 |
| 8 Gauge Shotgun | +30 | 1 | 20+2d20 | 30m5 | 2 | 28 | 8 gauge shot shells: 7 shot | 8kg | 2300+2d1000sp | 408 |
| 6 Gauge Shotgun | +40 | 1 | 20+3d20 | 36m6 | 2 | 37 | 6 gauge shot shells: 6 shot | 11kg | 4200+2d1000sp | 408 |
| Revolver .357 | +5/+10 (2-handed) | 1 / 2 (at -10 SV) | 2d12+4 | 90m | 1 / 2 | - | 6 shots | 1.1kg | 1100+d1000sp | 408 |
| Revolver .44 | +5/+10 (2-handed) | 1 / 2 (at -10 SV) | 1d30+4 (or d20+d10+4) | 125m | 1 / 2 | 16 (1-handed) | 6 shots | 1.35kg | 1500+d1000sp | 408 |
| Advanced Laser Pistol MK I | variable | variable | variable | | | 1 | power cell: variable | 1.3kg | 5000+1d1000sp | 408 |
| Rocket Pistol | Paint +50/ Direct 01-70/ blast 01-60 | 1/2 | Direct 3d20/ blast 1d20 | 36m per round/ 10+ rounds | 1 | - | chase rockets: 6 per clip | 1.6kg | 3000+1d1000sp | 408 |
| Rocket Carbine | Paint +70/ Direct 01-70/ blast 01-60 | 1/2 | Direct 3d20/ blast 1d20 | 36m per round/ 10+ rounds | 2 | 22 | chase rockets: 17 per clip | 6.2kg | 5000+2d1000sp | 409 |
| Heavy Assault Rifle | +22 / +12 full auto | 1, 3. or 5 | 1d20+10 | 900m | 2 | 29 | 30 HC rounds | 6.2kg | 4500+2d1000sp | 409 |
| Combo Assault Rifle | Combined assault rifle (pg TME-188) with a flame unit underneath (pg TME-189) | | | | 2 | 32 | 30 rifle rounds/ 1 liter fuel cannister | 14kg | 7k+3d1000sp | 409 |
| Intruder Rifle | Combined heavy assault rifle with EM emitter rifle underneath | | | | 2 | 34 | 30 rifle rnds/ 12 shots per power cell | 9.7kg | 8k+4d1000sp | 409 |
| Advanced Sniper Rifle | 20/+64 careful aim | 2 or 1 every 2nd round | 1d20+10 | 2.5km | 2 | 25 | 24 round HCR mag | 9kg | 5000+2d1000sp | 410 |
| Laser Sniper Rifle | +25/ +65 | 1 | 3d20+30 | 6km | 2 | 32 | power cell: 10 shots | 6.5kg | 11k+4d1000sp | 410 |
| Micro-Wave Gun | +30 (+6) | 1 | 2d30 (1d30) or 2d10 (2d6) to non-living | 30m (31-70 long range) | 2 | - | Power cell 10 shots | 3.3kg | 1400+1d1000sp | 410 |
| Belly Cannon | +15 | 1, 3 or 5 | 1d30 | 240m | 2 | 45 | Power cell: 20 / power pack 200 | 22kg | 11k+4d1000sp | 410 |
| Mk2 Laser Carbine | +30 | 1 | 2d20+20 | 3km | 2 | 26 | power cell yields 22 shots | 3.3kg | 7000+2d1000sp | 410 |
| Mk3 Laser Carbine | +35 | 1 | 2d20+30 | 3.5km | 2 | 30 | power cell yields 24 shots | 3.8kg | 9000+3d1000sp | 410 |
| Mk4 Laser Carbine | +5 SV per degree (+5 to +50) | 1 | 1d10+10 per degree | 500 to 5000m (500m per degree) | 2 | 32 | power cell yields 1 to 10 degrees of potency in shot | 4.4kg | 12k+3d1000sp | 410 |

| Weapon | SV | Rate | Damage | Range[1] | Hands[2] | STR[3] | Ammo/ Duration | Weight | Value[4] | Page |
|---|---|---|---|---|---|---|---|---|---|---|
| Auto Gun, Rifled | 01-60 (or +10) | 4 | d20 | day 200m/30 dim/ 10m darkness | tripod | fixed | rifle ammo 120 rounds | 47kg | 12k+3d1000sp | 411 |
| Auto Gun, Beam | 01-70 (or +20) | 6 | 1d20 | day 200m/ 100m darkness | tripod | fixed | Power pack/160 bursts | 53kg | 14k+4d1000sp | 411 |
| Auto Cannon | +35 | 6 | d100 | 3 km | fixed or crew | fixed | 20mm rounds/ Top Cannister holds: 600 rounds | 729.8 kg | 40k +5d1000sp | 411 |
| Pulse Cannon | +20 | 6 | 1d100 | 6 km | 1 crew | fixed | power pack: 24 bursts | 530kg | 32k+4d1000sp | 412 |
| Lightning Emitter | +30 | 1 | 1d30 lethal+1d30 stun | 80m | 2 | 12 | power cell /12 shots | 7.8kg | 5k+3d1000sp | 412 |
| Particle Beam Rifle | +8/ +30 metal | 1 | 2d20/d100 | 200m | 2 | 29 | power cell: 16 shots | 7kg | 15k+3d1000sp | 413 |
| Electro-Glove | +12 | 1 | 2d20 stun b | melee | 1 | 18 | Power cell: 20 successful shocks | 3.3 | 3000+2d1000 | 413 |
| Electro-Glove, Advanced | +20 | 1/2 | 20+2d20 stun c | 20m | 1 | 24 | 2 Power cells; touch shock 1 unit, shock wave 3 units successful shots | 4.2kg | 5000+2d1000 | 413 |

*a: Sonic immobilizer rifle emits a sonic attack, deafness and knocking targets backward are possible. See description, page XR-407.*
*b: An electro glove delivers a kinetic thump to a physically contacted, melee range target, which stuns opponents and forces each to make an endurance based type E hazard check or get knocked back 2 meter sand fall over, losing their next turn.*
*c: An advanced electro-glove can propel a wave of blunt force in a cone out 20 meters, and knock over all those in a 3m wide target area, potentially stunning or knocking back multiple opponents in the line of fire.*

*~A strike from a nerve disruptor baton causes the victim, either living or mechanical, to always lose their next turn of action, plus make a Type D strength based HC or collapse, and not be able to get up again unless making a successful Type C willpower hazard check.*

*1 Range shown is effective range, but all weapons can go double this, but, at a reduction of half the shooter's regular SV, plus, half damage on strikes.*
*2 Hands to effectively wield the weapon, especially to load it in the case of bows and crossbows, however, a strong person can hold up a carbine or shotgun in one hand and fire it, possibly one assault rifle in each hand as she storms into a room, this feat requires a strength score of 50 or better, and the cumbersome weapon loses –10 SV plus, the off hand (if not an ambidextrous shooter) suffers an additional –30 SV (normally -20 SV for off hand).*
*3 User must have sufficient strength to employ or suffer a –20 SV penalty, otherwise requires two hands if normally a one handed weapon to avoid penalty. If no number given, then strength is not an issue.*
*4 Value shown for relic weapons, or armor, is the silver pieces one gets for selling a relic weapon in a trade town. These weapons are almost never available for purchase, and if so, are double the value an adventurer gets for selling it. This price reflects a workable, but empty relic. (no sane adventurer would sell a loaded weapon).*
*5 Shotguns using buckshot or similar multiple projectile loads can strike 3 man-sized or 6 smaller, gutter rat or blood flyer sized beings if they are clustered together.*
*6 A six gauge shotguns can strike 4 man-sized or 10 smaller, gutter rat or blood flyer sized beings if they are clustered together*
*HC means high caliber rifle and machine gun rounds 1d20+10 DMG*
*RR regular rounds 1d20 DMG*
*AP armor piercing rounds, less range (-10%) +10 SV/ 2d20+10 DMG*
*Slug special shotgun shell, less accurate, but longer range and more damage SV -8 applied to shotgun's SV/ DMG 2d20+12/ Range 50m*
*Stun weapons do non-lethal damage. Unconscious victims sleep for d100+20 minutes (6 rounds in a minute) when waking, stun damage dissipates totally.*

*Note: Power packs will supply 10 times the amount of energy as does a regular power cell, and via a power cable, can be plugged into any energy weapon. For example, a stun rifle normally yields 30 shots per power cell, but, hooked to a power pack, either mounted on a vehicle, building, mount or one's own body, would produce 300 shots before being drained.*

# New Weapon Relic Descriptions

## BB Rifle

This relic gun looks a lot more serious than it is, and to the uneducated eye, or when seen from a distance, looks like a small hunting rifle. It is in fact a very weak weapon, and designed for those ages ten and up or as a training weapon to teach new gun users on both firearms safety, and practical live fire training without expending real ammo. A BB rifle fires 1 tiny 4.5mm copper coated steel BB every second round to an effective, dangerous range of only 35 meters, although these BBs can go as far as 190m but usually bounce off whatever they impact.

The true value in this 'toy' from the ancient world is that it can shoot pests, especially sting flies, venomous frogs, and skal birds, although all these creatures often have more than one endurance point. Another great use for these relics is to shoot out light bulbs, cause a distraction, or hunt tiny game without making a lot of noise. Finally, a BB rifle looks quite convincing, and makes a traveler look better armed, and more dangerous than he or she really is.

This air rifle uses a single break action pump charging process, which takes a minimum of 7 strength to perform and prepare the gun to fire, which takes one round and allows firing on the second round. Because the mass of the projectile is so small, no amount of talent from the shooter can make it inflict over 2 points of damage, although the accuracy can certainly be elevated by a trained sniper or individual with rifles as an area of weapon expertise. With an SV of +5, at a rate of 1/2, damage inflicted of 1 point, and max BB capacity of 350 rounds, this 1.2 kilogram relic will sell for 700 +4d100sp. Spare BBs can be made at a cost of 10 BBs per silver coin, although appropriate sized lead shot can sometimes be harvested from old shotgun shells, too.

## Pellet Rifle

Similar to a BB rifle, this weapon fires .177 caliber lead pellets, and while slower to load, pump and fire, allowing one shot every 3rd round, this relic has a greater range with a strike value bonus of +7, inflicts 1d2 damage on a shot (max 1d2+1 for those with the sniper skill or are weapons experts with rifles). To charge the internal air tank, the barrel is cranked downward in a break action manner, and while open, a single pellet is placed in the action, the gun is snapped closed and the weapon can be fired on the third round.

Only somebody of 15 or higher strength can charge this air rifle, which has a range of 56 meters. For a post-apocalyptic survivor, the main application for the is gun is to shoot tiny creatures for food or in self defense, take out electric lights, or other small sensors, such as cameras, all while making a minimum of noise. Small, puck-like tins of .177 cal pellets can be found in sporting good stores, or sometimes for sale in relic markets at a cost of 5 pellets per silver coin. These wood or resin stocked ancient sporting good items weigh 2.6 kilograms each, are 37% likely to be found with a nylon sling, and will sell for 900+5d100 silver pieces.

## Flare Gun

These plastic, bright orange emergency signal pistols fire a specially designed flare, as described on page 419, with a range of 150 meters. Being a break action device, these can only accept one flare at a time, and take 2 rounds to reload. When fired into a dark sky, they will burst in a 5 meter radius, and

then slowly drop over the next two minutes and illuminate the 100 meter area below in a soft, reddish-purple light. Depending on the level of darkness and other light sources in the area, a flare might be seen from ten kilometers away, and possibly attract unwanted attention by humanoids, hostile robots, or ravenous carnivores.

Shooting a flare into dry grass, foliage, or a flammable plantoid or animal, can cause mayhem, and with a flare 82% likely to ignite a fire that will burn for at least 1d8 rounds and inflict 1d6 damage per round. The blunt force of a flare has a +4 SV and inflicts 2d6 stun damage.

These relics weigh 150 grams when empty, with each flare weighing 60g. These weapons will explode in the hands of anyone trying to fire a regular shotgun shell through them. Flare guns sell for 500+4d100sp.

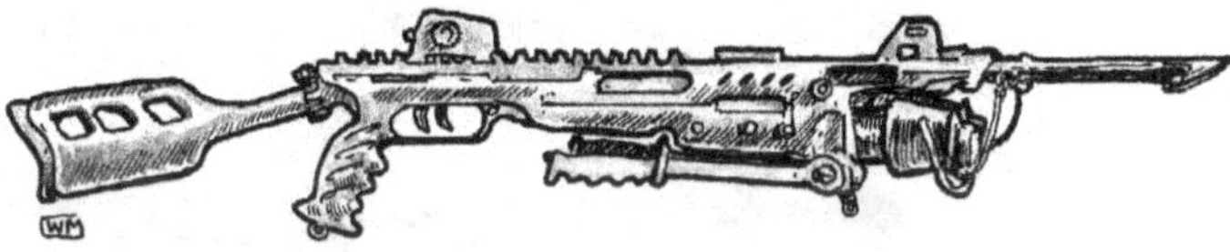

## Advanced Harpoon Gun

This rare relic is always found as a double barreled variant and uses a hand crank system to pull back the spring loaded firing mechanism, with each barrel requiring a separate re-load process that takes 2 rounds. Cranking these devices is difficult, and anybody with less than 40 strength must make a type B strength based hazard check each round to successfully load one tube. Although these weapons can fire standard replica steel harpoons, they were designed, and are often found with special alloy harpoons with expanding barbs on their tips, which open after a successful strike.

Relic expanding harpoons can be tethered to the gun or not, with the range while tethered out to 36 meters and untethered to 56 meters. Once tethered, the gun's powerful electric retractor spool motor will pull in up to 200 kilograms, or lift the shooter should they be able to hold on, and be carried aloft if the harpoon is anchored into an elevated position. A strength based type A hazard check is needed to hold on for each 6 meters ascended, although the gun's stock has a fastening loop if a clever user wants to tie themself to the gun before or during ascension. A power cell is needed to run the spool motor and will provide 3 hours of in-operation reeling in power, but drains nothing when the motor is not engaged.

While these ancient harpoons are great for both grappling into solid objects like concrete overhangs or the hulls of spacecraft, the projectile also delivers savage injuries on a strike and inflict 2d20+13 damage and has a strike value bonus of +18. Both harpoons can be fired at once, if desired, as the weapon has dual triggers.

If the user is forced to fire regular, recently made harpoons, they feature a SV of +12, do 1d20+12 damage, have a range of 20 meters if tethered or 40 if untethered. Advanced harpoon guns weigh 3.8 kilograms, and if sold to a relic dealership, will earn 1600+1d1000sp.

## Bug Spray

This is a weak civilian insecticide. Each cannister contains 30 uses in a disposable, spray paint sized can with a range of only 3 meters, and covers a 3m by 3m swath target area. It inflicts only 1d6 damage  o n a strike, and then, only to insects, spiders, scorpions, crustaceans, slugs, snails and all worms. In addition, each creature must make an endurance based type hazard check or else retreat in pain.

Even if a bug succeeds at its hazard check, it still

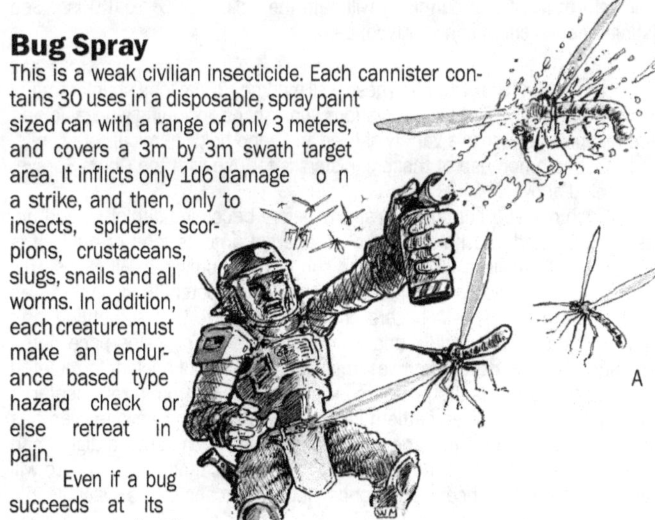

experiences severe discomfort and is enraged, often ignoring everybody except the relic user, pursuing him or her with frenzied abandon. Bug swarms, such as army ants and killer bees are particularly vulnerable to bug spray, since each insect has far less than a single endurance point, but a swarm has 60+d100 END per 10 meters by 10 meters of bugs. To use this relic on such a mass of tiny targets requires getting dangerously close, yet, the spray covers a 3m by 3m area, and therefore would automatically kill 30% of the tiny bugs in a 10m square area per round. GM's discretion and house rules must supersede or confirm this application of the relic.

An unactivated, new cannister weighs 400g and will sell for 200+1d100sp.

## Chem-Sprayer

This relic is a bulky, pistol grip weapon which has a hose running from its fore chamber to a hip mounted canister holder, which fits up to three canisters. The canisters contain various liquids which the gun or sprayer unit can fire via powered or hand-crank mode. A wide assortment of military and industrial sprays were once widely available in the pre-devastation world, and many canisters of herbicide, insecticide and pesticide, riot-glue, pepper spray and acid can still be found in the ruins. The sprayer has impressive range and accuracy when a power cell is snapped into the sprayer's back end (+16 SV), but even without this, the hand pump, which acts as the front grip, can be vigorously pumped to produce the same amount of spray at diminished range and aim (+4 SV). While using the power mode, a person of 30 or better strength can wield this weapon in one hand, while in pump mode, two hands are required. It takes 10 rounds to detach from one empty chemical canister and snap and prime a new canister.

In combat, the chem-sprayer can coat more than one creature at a time, and each spray forms a cone at 10 meters which will coat a 5m by 5m area, excellent for spraying insect swarms, killer bees, hoards of small creatures, or even a crowd of protesters. For human sized targets, each person in a 5m area is potentially struck, and a separate strike roll is made against each. In the case of glue, people in heavy armor gain no DV benefit, only their agility and dodge skill can be applied to avoiding this spray. The chem-sprayer weighs 4 kilograms, while each fluid cannister weighs 5 kilos. This relic with at least one cannister will earn the seller 1500+1d1000sp. See listing for each chem-canister type, below.

**Chem-Canisters:** These well marked, 30cm long stainless steel tubes were widely used to store various substances, including glue, acid and pepper spray, for use in a variety of fixed and hand held chemical spray units. The most common use of these canisters is for use with the Chem-Sprayer gun, noted above.

Each canister contains 20 spurts before becoming depleted, and unless it is opened and hand poured on a target, into its food or drink, it is fundamentally useless without some sort of relic sprayer. In all cases, this stuff stinks, however, and if placed in food, each potential victim gets an intelligence based Type A hazard check to recognize that something isn't right with the food or drink, and won't consume it. The sales price noted with each canister description assumes the tank is full of ancient formulated chemicals, and this is the price the excavators will get from a relic dealer in a medium or larger sized settlement. In smaller places, if anyone even has the silver pieces worth in trade goods to purchase such items, a digger can expect to only get half of the sell value. To buy any cannister listed here will cost double the sell price, but the odds that such a cannister is available in a market on any given week is 1 in 20,

If not specified, **roll 1d8** here to see what canister has been found:

1. Pepper Spray
2. Glue
3. Acid
4. Intense Acid
5,6. Insecticide
7. Herbicide
8. Pesticide

**Pepper Spray Canister:** This material is identical to pepper spray (see Hub Rules, relics page 197. 4 targets can be hit, if struck, suffer -20 SV, but allowed Type C WL Haz. Check to avoid blindness at -40 SV, half speed and +40 to be hit for one minute), but when used by the Chem-Sprayer, has a far greater range. Sell price 400+1d100sp.

**Glue Canister:** Used by pre-holocaust police forces to detain fleeing criminals or stop protesting mobs. Anyone struck by this bright orange spray — and normally a person fits in a one meter space, especially if in a room, crowd or military formation — must make a type 'D' strength based hazard check or be glued to the ground or wall, ladder or whatever they are mainly attached to. If the target breaks free, and yet is still coated in glue, and is struck yet again, then the hazard check leaps to type 'I', and if a third strike is required, the HC reaches a maximum of 'M'. Once glued, the victim's movements are impaired and he or she strikes at -40 SV, while being +30 easier to strike upon.

The glue is biodegradable, and after 2d6 hours, weakens at a rate of one HC letter code per half hour until finally it crumbles, dries out and turns to a saw-dust like powder. Sell price 600+2d100sp.

**Acid Canister:** Many mutants and creatures use acid, so an empty acid canister, which is specially coated inside, can be refilled with another acid. This spray seems to have been developed to control vermin and unlawful crowds, and is often of insufficient strength to defeat large determined creatures. Those struck by the spray will be coasted in a mild acid which burns exposed flesh, leather, clothing, hair, and nylon, but isn't able to harm those in combat, bomb squad or shell class armors. It is also useless against such creatures as pit slimes which employ their own form of much more powerful acid. Humans in tactical or riot armor, chainmail, part plate and full plate can still be affected, since their armor doesn't prevent the occasional soaking by acid which seeps between plates, eye slits, mail links, and whatnot. Anyone who is affected will be burned for 1d6 damage per round, for 1d6+1 rounds. The only cure is to leap into water or other liquids and thus neutralize the acid. If coated on a target while it is raining out, the acid only does 1d3 damage for 1d3+1 rounds. Sell price is 300+1d100sp.

**Intense Acid Canister:** Slightly thicker than normal acid tanks, and with different markings. The acid in this weapon is simply a far more potent variety than the normal acid canister listed above, and inflicts 1d10 damage per round for 1d10+2 rounds, unless washed off. Reduce this damage to 1d6 damage for 1d6+1 rounds if it is raining. Sell price is 500+1d100sp.

**Insecticide Canisters:** The bug spray in these relic canisters was not used for simple pest control, such as with the relic bug spray, but formulated to defeat the many enormous mutant insects, scorpions, spiders, centipedes, millipedes, slugs and snails, which bio-genetic science developed for their bio-weapon programs. Any insect or bug like creature, including crustaceans if encountered on land, or bestial human bug and arachnid, is easily dealt with by anyone wielding a chem-sprayer loaded with insecticide. On a strike, the bug, or however many fit in a five meter splash zone and are hit, automatically take 1d30 chemical exposure damage, plus, must make a Type D Willpower hazard check or thrash about madly for a minute or two and then die. Sell price 700+2d100sp.

**Herbicide Canister:** Used to kill mutant plants and trees in the last years before the global civilization collapsed, this substance is dangerous to plant life, and any vegetable being hit by this spray takes 1d30 damage and if still alive, must make a type B willpower based hazard check per day, for 2d6 days, or die. If the plant is stout enough to survive the herbicide, it is thereafter immune to it, and likewise, so too are its seedlings and descendants from then on.

Because plantoid characters have human DNA, they suffer only 1d12 damage, and need only make a type A willpower hazard check to avoid death, and only after the initial spray as opposed to each day. Green walkers, on the other hand, are only inhabiting a human skeleton or cadaver and are entirely plant based, and thus fully susceptible to this herbicide. Sell price 600+2d100sp.

**Pesticide Canister:** This toxin affects all living things, except plants, and is exceedingly potent. Those struck with the spray, and not wearing relic combat, bomb squad or shell class armor, or an enviro-suit, must make a type B endurance based hazard check or drop into a coma, with follow-up, type A willpower trait based hazard checks being demanded to avoid death, per hour while in the 2d6 hour duration coma. Besides the lethal toxicity of this spray, there is also residual burning damage, which could easily kill rat sized creatures, as it inflicts 2d10 damage to all non-vegetable organic beings. Finally, should a creature or person survive the initial threats posed by this substance, the long term effects could also kill, as cancer is 22% likely to develop in the subject within 1d20 years — although only the GM will know this troubling fact. Sell price is 800+3d100sp.

## Tactical Tomahawk *by Brutorz Bill*

These ancient forged alloy headed Tomahawks have composite plastic handles tougher than any wood, and make for both a useful tool and splendid weapon. Deadly in either one handed or two handed grip, these relics also offer a limited ranged attack option when thrown. 2 in 6 have a hollow handed with weighted end cap fitted with a compass. The tubular space inside is 15cm long and is normally found with a pack of 12 waterproof matches, 10m of fishing line, hooks, weights and synthetic bait for fishing, a folding buck knife, signal mirror, Morse code cheat sheet, and camo print foil survival blanket.

This weapon offers a strike value bonus of +6, an attack rate of 1 per round, inflicts 1d12+2 base damage when used one handed, or 1d12+5 two handed. It weighs 900 grams and will sell for 400+3d100sp.

## Chainsword *by Stu Brooks*

Often referred to simply as a sword-saw by excavators, these relics were created to counter the robots that once decimated mankind. They function well both underwater as well as in a vacuum and are powered by two standard power cells that fit into the airtight hilt. This pair of cells will run the unit for 500 rounds of combat while active and able to chop through both organic and inorganic targets with ease at +25 SV, doing 3d20+10 damage on a strike. Even when switched off or drained of power, this serrated, alloy weapon can still deliver savage blows, especially when held by a powerful operator, and has an SV of +2 and inflicts a base of 1d20+2 damage. To use this weapon in one hand, the user must have a minimum strength of 40, otherwise suffer a -20 SV penalty. Any user of over 15 strength can use this in two hands without penalty, while those with 14 or less strength can't properly lift, let alone swing it.

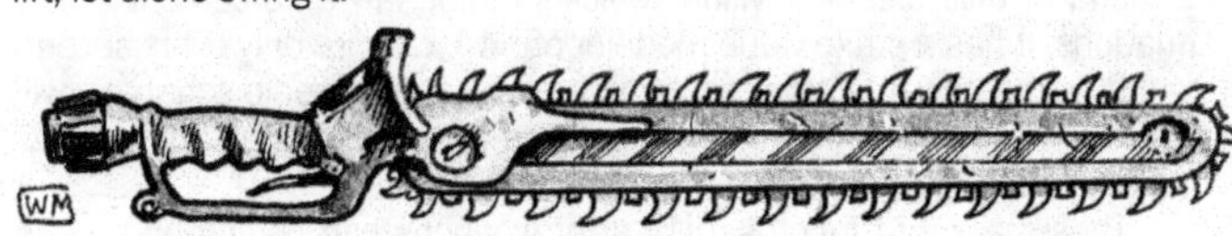

When uncovered as loot in some junk pile, collapsed armory, or other damaged location, many of these highly advanced weapons are inoperative, with 50% no longer functioning and unable to deal the active damage. Of these, roll 1d100: 01-50. Corroded power cell couplings, and must be repaired before use. / 51-00. Can't be repaired for one reason or another.

Of those that can be repaired, either an electrical, mechanical, robotics or cybernetic technician of 4 or more skill points can attempt do so, at a cost of 2d100sp for parts and an intelligence based type D hazard check per day of work. A junk crafter can also attempt to repair this, but must be of 6 skill points at the same odds. To hire a robotics or relic dealership to make the repair will cost 1000+1d1000sp and only have a 7% chance per day of the repair being successful.

This relic will sell for 6000+3d1000sp, but is almost never available for purchase to the public. Broken units will fetch 1000+3d100sp.

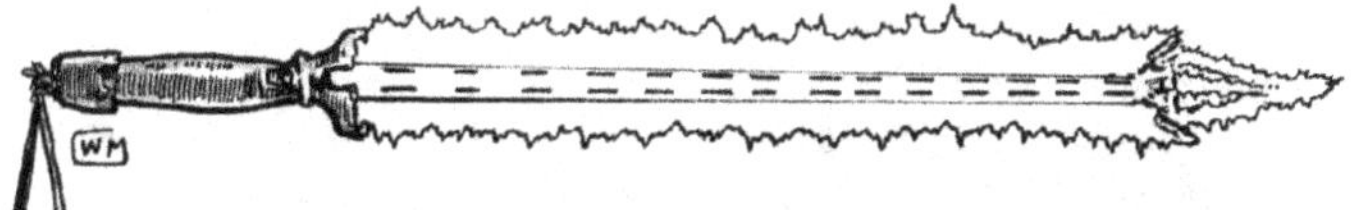

## Mk2 Laser Sword

A far rarer and more advanced energy weapon than a standard laser sword, this model has a cutting beam on both the back and front edge, as well as an 8 cm long frontal beam spike formed by three emitters on the tip, perfect for jabbing this laser weapons into lock mechanisms, door hinges, sensors, or the vitals of opponents. This variant has a superior +25 strike value, inflicts far more damage at 2d20+20 points, and yet weighs only slightly more at 1.6 kilograms. It is of a more recent design than the usual laser sword, too, and uses energy far more efficiently. It will run continuously for 30 minutes (600 rounds) on a single power cell. An advanced laser sword also comes with a wrist strap and a butt-end energy adapter port so that the wearer of a belt energy pack or power pack could patch a flexible energy cable into their weapon to get far longer run times.

Like the standard variant, this unit has a simple on-off switch on the grip's top, as well as a battery indicator light. Such a rare item is almost never sold, except by the very hard pressed or by thieves who've stolen such a remarkable artifact from an excavator, and will earn 9000+ 4d1000sp. Once made available in the market, where the most powerful oligarchs and warlords of the new era purchase or confiscate them at once, and they are never made available for sale thereafter.

## Energy Spear

This 2 meter long, alloy shaft has an insulated lower grip half and rear mounted power cell chamber, control dial, on-off switch, and battery life read-out display screen. At the far end of the tapering, fearsome looking relic is a wire coiled, intricate spear head perforated with energy link conduits. When engaged, the user can either prod, slash, or club targets with the energized tip, which lights up a brilliant green when set to stun mode — which causes both severe pain and debilitating, although temporary, loss of the target's bodily control. When the rear grip handle's selector switch is set to lethal mode, the laser emitters turn the gleaming light at the business end into a blood red color, which converts the 30cm long end into a lethal chopping and piercing weapon.

In either green stun mode or red lethal mode, the strike value is +20, and the damage from any successful strike is 1d20+10 on low power, 2d20+20 on medium power, or 1d100+30 on high setting, regardless of if it is set to stun or lethal.

Low power will drain 1/10th of the power cell on a strike, medium mode will drain 2/10th, and high power 5/10th of a battery, or energy units. In short, a low power attack drains this weapon of 1 energy unit, a medium drain 2 energy units and high power drains 5 energy units. Instead of using a normal power cell, this weapon's butt-stock panels can be opened and a patch cable from a vehicle or power pack can be plugged into this spear. A power pack at full charge has 100 energy units and a standard power cell has only 10 uses.

If this spear is drained of power, or the user wishes to conserve battery for some more serious engagement, this relic's pointy, serrated alloy tip can stab just like a regular spear, although as it is alloy, is even more dangerous with an SV bonus of +2 for one handed use of +6 for two handed use, and damage of either 1d20+4 one handed or 1d20+8 two handed. If thrown, it has a base range of 16 meters, but any fumble roll means the relic landed hard and shatters the electronics at the butt end. Only an electrical technician of 5 skill points (the maximum SKP for this skill) can hope to repair it at a cost of 2000+1d1000sp and then only a 71% chance of doing so successfully. This rare, remarkable relic weighs 14 kilograms and will sell for 18k+5d1000sp.

## Electro Net Gun

This stubby, two handed, single shot weapon fires net cannisters and uses a combination of a spring loaded charging piston and twin power cells to launch the canister at targets up to 20 meters away. Electrically charged sensor-fasteners open when detecting a target directly ahead of it within 6 meters, and once engaged, the wire net fans out 3m in diameter. This metal net is dotted at each cross stitch by an electrical charge transmitter, which sends power along the adjoining series of ultra-fine cable lines that make up this net, and from these, the charge is delivered into the target.

On a successful strike, the net both wraps about the man sized or smaller target and then secondly delivers an ongoing shock and retraction process. For every round the net is wrapped about the victim, it tightens up, painfully, and delivers severe muscle and circuit disrupting agony along with 1d6 points of stun damage. At the hub of the net, where it is fastened to the canister, a small screen and button panel are fitted in a recessed slot. The operator can type in a designated, net specific code which will turn off the shock feature of the relic, although the cables of the net itself must be pulled back to free the captive.

Anyone ensnared by this projectile, must make a type F willpower based hazard check per round to disregard the excruciating pain and stun shocks and begin to peel off the net cables, which takes 2d6 rounds to accomplish, with each round requiring another WIL hazard check and the victim taking another 1d6 stun damage. If the trapped person or beast does not resist the metal net, does not thrash about or try to peel back sections, it will not tighten further than it needs to restrain the captive, nor deliver further shocks.

Each net cannister contains a permanent battery which conducts the charge after being flash powered by the rifle-like launcher weapon, with the maximum period of delivered shocks being 2 minutes (40 stun shocks before the built in battery is drained). The net can be recovered after use and carefully folded and stuffed back to the net gun for future use, but only by somebody of both 40 or higher accuracy and intelligence, and it's a complicated task. The net gun itself can be reloaded, with spare, charged up net canisters and made ready to fire once every 4 rounds. This weapon system comes with a shoulder strap, while the plastic butt stock contains a compartment for one spare net canister. When found, these weapons are 61% likely to have a pre-loaded but not activated canister, although when it is original, hard plastic carry cases, will come with 6 canisters, a cleaning kits, instruction manual and 2+1d4 drained but operational standard power cells.

Net cannisters have a +30 strike value bonus, and the target's armor offers no defense value benefit, although having the dodge skill or a high agility score will help the person or animal side step the incoming net. Targets in shell class powered armors are immune to the per-round stun damage and do not feel any pain from this net.

A net canister uses a built in standard power cell and weighs 2kg, while the stubby rifle-like main gun weighs 5kg, comes with a crank handle to recharge the spring loaded piston of the launcher, and requires a power cell to make 12 shots. A canister will sell for 300+2d100sp, while the net launcher gun itself will fetch 1000+1d1000sp.

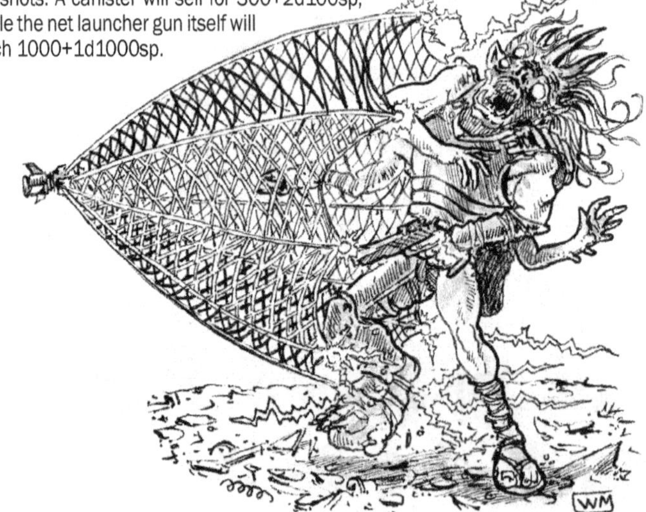

## Stun Rifle

While several models of this clunky looking energy weapon were made by different arms dealers, the most commonly found are the metallic blue police issue variant and the gray and bright orange military variant. Most use either a plugged-in power adapter that is hooked to power backpack — which were widely used to quell food and social riots in the end years — or else take a standard power cell in the underside of the weapon. 1 in 10 also have a slot for a spare power cell in the buttstock, and if so, these are 7% likely to have one lodged in the stock when found. Like their pistol variant, described in the hub rules on page TME-189, this energy weapon shoots a blue pulse of energy up to 750 meters away, has a strike value modifier of +24, a rate of 1 shot per round, and inflicts 3d20 stun damage on a hit. A power cell will yield 30 shots. This rifle weighs 4.8kg, will be found with a nylon sling 7 in 10 times, and will sell for 4000+2d1000 silver pieces.

Those struck by a stun beam, including robots, androids, as well as whatever projection device a digital being might be housed in, will suffer this body debilitating surge. The damage will remain for one hour and then heal at a rate of 1 point per minute thereafter. Anyone or anything incapacitated by this beam will be knocked out and remain unconscious or offline for one hour plus 4d10 minutes.

## Heavy Stun Emitter

In nearly every case, this weapon is found and used with an included, adjustable tripod. At 62 kilograms, it is far too heavy for anybody except a massive mutant or cyborg freak to carry, although could be fitted to a vehicle or large robot. The kick from this body freezing, circuitry disrupting stun weapon would knock a person over if the gun were not mounted to a fixed position or tripod, and even if somebody can hold it for long enough to make a shot, they must make a type M kilograms based hazard check to stay on their feet after discharging it, with any fall 17% likely to permanently break the weapon as it hits the ground.

It is surmised that this weapon was used to take out rogue robots, industrial androids, crazed cyborgs and marauding mutants without killing them, or else disable civilian vehicles during law enforcement or riot situations. It has a strike value modifier of +44, can fire only every second round as the power charge regulator must reset between discharges, will inflicted 30+3d20 points of stun damage on a hit, has a range of 1.2 kilometers and gets 8 shots per power cell.

These rare, but much sought after weapons can be sold in a large town's relic market for 11,000+4d10000 silver pieces. The red, orange or blue ball of energy this thing fires has enough force to knock a door off its hinges, tear a sail from its mast, capsize a rowboat, rip a hole through the wicker hull of an airship, or put a target on the ground even if they are not made unconscious from the stun surge. In short, anybody hit with this massive bolt of energy must make a kilogram based type H hazard check or be knocked off their feet and drop 1d4 meters back from where they were standing. Like a stun rifle or stun baton, the damage from this energy weapon will remain in effect for one hour before it heals at a rate of 1 point per minute. Those knocked out will stay unconscious for an hour plus 4d10 minutes.

## Sonic Immobilizer Rifle (Thump Gun)

Designed for crowd control, these stubby, thick weapons fire a cone of debilitating sound which at various ranges can blow down, disable or even stun people, animals, and man sized machines such as androids and most robots. The further away the target or group of targets are, the wider the cone of effect becomes, but so too, the weaker the surge of immobilizing sound.

From point blank range out to 6 meters, a 3m wide cone is projected which has a strike value of +30 and those struck take 3d20 stun damage plus must make a Type F hazard check using their kilograms weight to remain on their feet. Those who fail are thrown back 1d6 meters and lose their next round of action.

From beyond 6 meters to 15m, the cone expands to 12 meters in width, has a SV of +15, inflicts 2d20 stun damage, and forces all those in the target area to make a type D hazard check using their kilograms weight. Failure means they are knocked to the ground about a meter back and must use their next round to get up.

Beyond 15 meters to 30 meters, the cone of painful sound has a SV of +10 and causes 3d6 stun damage. Only those under 50 kilograms can be knocked over, and are allowed a Type A, kilograms weight based hazard check or be shoved back a meter, fall and lose their next round.

Beyond 30 meters out to 60 meters, this thump gun causes only severe pain — which for non-combatants, is often enough to make them withdraw from the reach of whoever is discharging this odd energy weapon. A Sonic Immobilizer can fire 16 cones of sound per power cell, or 160 if plugged into a power pack. Any being with a strength over 70 can use this weapon one handed as a pistol.

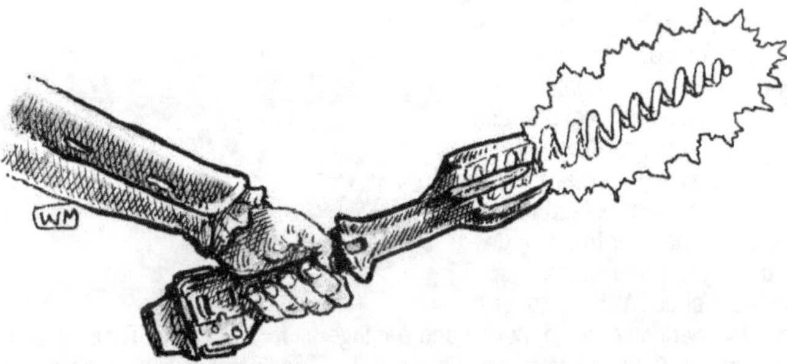

## Nerve Disruptor Baton

Similar to a stun baton or stun stick, but instead of shutting down the target's muscles or doing temporary endurance damage, this mace-like black rod has a 10cm long emitter coil at the end which glows dark purple when activated. On a hit, it flashes pink and delivers an extremely painful shock and potentially scrambles the target's nervous system.

While any living creature hit automatically loses their next turn because of the incredible pain, they must also make a type D strength based hazard check or have their senses disrupted. A disrupted organic being, including a cyborg, falls to the ground and goes into a fit of contortions and agony. Each round thereafter, they are allowed a willpower based Type C hazard check to shake it off and recover.

Robots, androids and computer-controlled machines, if under 1000 kilograms, are also affected, and lose a turn if struck, and are potentially scrambled. Because they don't feel pain, they do not scream at the top of their lungs when hit by this baton.

This one handed device has a simple grip mounted slide on or off switch, a power indicator with 1 to 10 shown on a tiny screen representing remaining discharges, has a strike value bonus of +17, weighs 1.2 kilograms, and will sell for 1600+1d1000sp. Each successful disruption transferred to a target drains the handle inserted power cell by 1 charge, with the battery allowing for 10 discharges.

## Devastator Rod

The origins and purpose for this exceedingly rare, tubular, 20cm long alloy shaft is unknown. Speculation 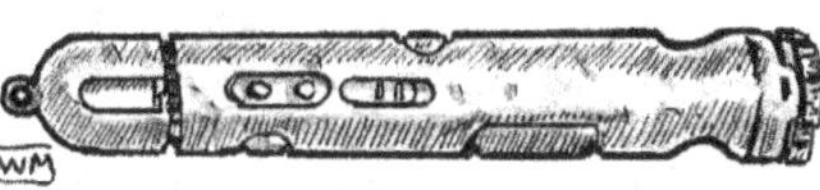 among new era relic experts varies, with claims that the so-called devastator rod was an experimental weapon, that only a dozen were ever made, or that this potent device is simply part of a much larger, more incredible weapon, the rest of which is yet to be unearthed. Others claim it is something reverse engineered from alien technology, brought back to Earth after being discovered on one of the many off-world colonies.

Regardless of its origins, a devastator rod — also referred to as an energy rod — is best left out of the hands of rank-and-file soldiers, lawless bandits, or grave robbing diggers. Because of its power, and ease of concealment, nearly every settlement that is aware of such a device will ban it, and have orders among all personnel to confiscate it if noticed among the possessions of any stranger or citizen.

This simple tool has a conical butt end with a 30cm long nylon wrist strap, a simple on-off switch, and a recessed push button trigger mechanism. The muzzle end of the tube has a pair of raised grooves that serve as sights, with the barrel opening only 4cm deep before the lens-like glassy orb of the complex energy emitter is revealed. When switched on, this device will often vibrate in the user's hand as it charges, with the relic only able to fire once every second round, although once activated, is always ready to fire immediately but takes time to re-charge between shots. By simply aiming and  pressing the trigger, this device will disgorge an elongated bolt of blue energy out to an effective range of 120 meters.

With a strike value of +45, it has a way of blasting whatever it is aimed at, and on a direct hit will inflict 3d100 damage, plus cause a secondary blast radius damage of 1d100 to all those within 3 meters of the strike. Any target to take the initial hit is already included in the blast damage. Those in the blast zone use the lower +22 SV shown on the weapons table on page 401.

Besides the incredible power of this rather small, unassuming relic, it is also exceedingly efficient with the two power cells that it uses — which are snapped into the butt end handle after the back grip is twisted off to the battery compartment. These two cells will provide 20 shots, and a top button near the on-off switch will flash red when the battery is depleted, or orange when it is on its last shot.

This relic weighs 2.7 kilograms and will fetch 4k+2d1000sp if sold to an uneducated relic dealer who has no idea of its true rarity or power, although somebody who is aware of these factors, will offer 14k+5d1000sp, knowing he or she can probably sell it to some warlord for three times this amount.

## EM Emitter Rifle

Firing a cone shaped pulse of blue, electromagnetic energy, this stubby, yet bulky and somewhat unwieldy weapon has a slight metallic blue sheen to its barrel and receiver section, while the foregrip, pistol grip and stock are dark gray. It was designed to take out androids, robots, machines and cyborgs, but will also knock out the mechanical body portions of both digital beings and vat-brains with relative ease, inflicting 2d100 EMP damage.

This potent burst of energy will also inflict 1d10 damage to living things, has a range of 700 meters, a rate of 1 shot per round, and fires 12 shots on one power cell. When fired at living things, it has a +5 strike value, but against targets made of metal or are all or partially electronically augmented, the pulse seems to snap toward these machines and so the shooter gains a +35 SV bonus against robots, androids, cyborgs and vessels among many possible targets. Dimensional beings also suffer terribly from these weapons, and are treated as robots as far as targeting and damage taken. These guns normally come with a shoulder strap and a padded, nylon gun case with compartments for 6 power cells.

The EMP damage suffered by a machine heals like stun damage inflicted on a living being, and so recovers at the machine's endurance based daily healing rate, but per hour. However, if the robot, android, vat-brain, cyborg or other machine is put below 0 endurance and knocked out, it cannot heal itself and must be rebooted or jump started by a robotics or cybernetic technician. This heavy weapon weighs 5.4 kg and will yield 5000+3d1000sp if sold.

## 8 Gauge Shotgun

This heavy pump shotgun works like a regular variant, but is twice as heavy, uses rare 8 gauge buckshot shells, can hold 7 shells in the tube magazine and another loaded into the firing chamber. They were initially issued to human troops in the later years of the pre-cataclysm civilization for use against Mecha controlled robots and androids, as well as out of control mutant slaves, and the myriad of horrifying deviant plants and animals that also threatened humanity. Each is 6 in 10 likely to come with a nylon sling and 2 in 10 likely to be fitted with a barrel light as described on page TME-201.

The kick from this weapon will drive a person of under 70kg (155 lbs) weight back one meter, and they must make an agility based Type C hazard check or fall on their rump thereafter, losing their next turn as they recover — so long as they didn't propel themselves back off the edge of a cliff.

These guns have a strike value bonus of +30, a range of 30 meters, and inflict 20+2d20 damage and can hit 3 man sized figures if they are close together, or 6 smaller creatures. An 8 gauge shotgun has a firing rate of 1 per round, weighs 8kg and will earn 2300+2d1000sp if sold to a relic dealership. Because 8 gauge shells are so rare, the user of this weapon is smart to save spent shot shells for future reloading.

*Author's note: This potent scatter gun made its first appearance in The Mall of Doom, adventure TME-1 on page 117*

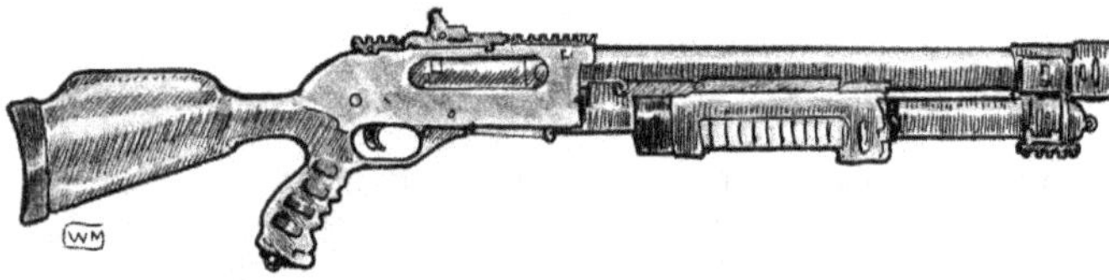

## 6 Gauge Shotgun

The even larger cousin to the 8 gauge shotgun, this devastating, and cumbersome weapon was only used by the most robust ancient soldiers and police personnel, or else by battle bioreplicas, and military clones, to help defend the remnants of hard pressed humanity against murderous mutants and machines. These weapons have only 6 shot magazine capacity, but an extra shell can be chambered at the ready in the action to total 7 shots. The blast from this devastating weapon can strike up to 4 man sized targets if they are in a line or grouped close together, or up to 10 small creatures such as skal birds, rats, or blood flyers.

The kick from this weapon is so severe that anybody who fires it and weighs less than 90kg (199 lbs) will be knocked back a meter and must make a type D agility based hazard check or fall on their bum, and need a round to get up again. The strike value from this weapon is +40, with a range of 36 meters, and will inflict 20+3d20 damage to targets peppered by the

steel balls launched from this weapon. This gun weighs 11 kilograms and will sell for 4200+21000sp. Finding 6 gauge shot shells is always a challenge, and so users typically save spent shell casings and have them reloaded at triple the cost of a regular shotgun shell.

5 in 10 of these impressive weapons will be found with a padded, nylon sling with tubular foam slots for 10 spare shells, while they are also 3 in 10 likely to come with a barrel flashlight.

Both the 8 and 6 gauge weapons platform existed as vehicle and robot mounted automatic shotgun variants, each with 500 shell drum magazines and a rate of fire of 2 per round. Except for the most massive mutants and android of 80 or more strength, wielding such a rare and colossally heavy weapon is impossible unless mounted to a tripod.

### Revolver *by James Butler*

A classic sidearm, these weapons all feature a revolving cylinder typically bearing six chambers to hold ammo (although some models holding as few as three or as many as twenty shots have been made). Single-action models require manually priming the weapon by pulling the hammer back after each shot, while double-action models simply require pulling the trigger to fire. The style of these weapons remained consistently popular for private use, even when official duties moved to semi-automatic pistols, and their ease of use makes them fairly common throughout the wastes.

The two models included in this book come in the .357 magnum — which can also fire .38 rounds which can be treated as standard pistol ammo — or the much heavier, more devastating .40 cal. Finding ammo for these almost archaic weapons is tough, so saving the brass after any gunfight is necessary if the operator wants to pay to have the rounds reloaded.

### Advanced Laser Pistol, MK I

Similar in size to a standard laser pistol, yet bulkier and of much more complicated design, this weapon has an over and under barrel and a thumb switch that allows the shooter to dial between a lethal laser beam and a stun emitter. Secondly, a separate dial is attached to the back end just behind the sights that allow the user to crank up or down the power output for the next shot. With more energy, the weapon's range, punch and damage all increase whether in stun or lethal mode. The dial has four settings with low, medium, heavy, and maximum firepower options. The details are shown below, which reflect the drain on a standard power cell. This weapon can also be connected to a belt power pouch or backpack style power pack.

This gun weighs 1.3kg and will sell for 5000+1d1000sp.

| Power Setting | Charge Amount Used* | SV | DMG** | Range |
|---|---|---|---|---|
| Low | 1/30th | +20 | 1d20+12 | 550m |
| Medium | 1/20th | +30 | 1d20+15 | 700m |
| Heavy | 1/10th | +40 | 2d20+20 | 900m |
| Maximum | 1 Full Cell | +80 | 5d20+40 | 1200m |

** From a standard power cell  **Lethal or stun*

### Rocket Pistol

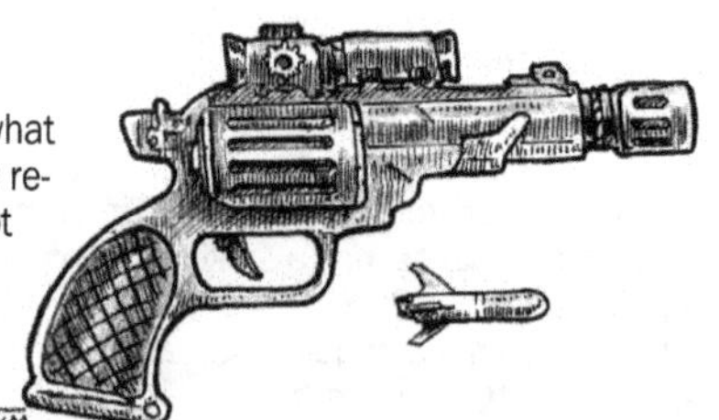

This odd weapon looks somewhat like an over-sized, metallic blue revolver, and indeed has a six shot rotating drum magazine, which contains a half dozen 12 centimeter long programed chase rockets. The rest of this gun is all high tech and has a non-lethal laser with a 360 meter range that is used to first strike a target to 'paint' it.

The paint laser marked person, machine or landmark is thereafter invisibly encoded with an infra red marker, a marker that the first chase rocket in the weapon will go after. If a successful paint occurs, the indicator will be visible to the shooter through the small, green window-like scope at the rear sights of these weapons. On the next round, the trigger can be pulled to release a chase rocket, which will go after the target, even if it leaves its field of view, at a speed of 36 meters per round. The rocket will chase for 10 rounds at max effectiveness, with a 4 in 10 chance per round thereafter that the rocket looses fuel and drops and explodes in a 6 meter radius, possibly causing 1d20 damage to all those in the blast zone. If the rocket reaches its target, it must roll to hit using the direct strike value of 01-70, with a miss causing a blast radius detonation, but a direct hit means the rocket has gotten into the subjects gear or armor and detonates for 3d20 damage.

Each shot from this weapon requires the target to be painted, although with a range of 360 meters, the same target could unknowingly be hit by multiple painting indicators and be unaware that one or more of these rockets are inbound. Firing a rocket does however cause a loud hiss and flash of blue flame as the projectile leaves the muzzle of this strange gun, and so both the target and bystanders are allowed a type A perception based hazard check to take notice, and perhaps even see the rocket headed their way. Learn more about chase rockets in the relic ammo section of this book on page 419.

This gun offers a +50 SV for when the target is painted by the laser, with the rocket getting an SV of 01-70 when trying to make a direct hit, or 01-60 for those caught in the blast radius of a depleted rocket or miss. Direct hits cause 3d20 damage, while the blast radius inflicts 1d20 damage. If fired without painting the target, such as in a quick draw situation, this weapon has an SV of only +10 out to 30 meters, or +2 SV out to 360 meters.

These bulky hand guns often come with a huge hip mounted holster, weigh 1.6 kilograms and will sell for 3000+1d1000sp.

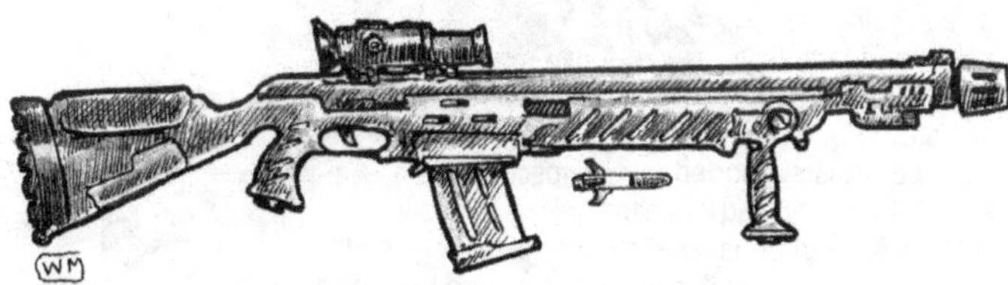

## Rocket Carbine

Very similar to the much smaller, revolver-like rocket pistol, this rugged weapon has a metallic blue coloration, the look of a stubby assault rifle, and a detachable 17 rocket magazine on the underside just ahead of the trigger assembly. As described under the description of the rocket pistol, this weapon must first be aimed at a potential target and painted by an invisible laser, which is discernible to the carbine's operator through a small, green lens targeting optic. Once painted, the carbine can be fired to launch 1 chase rocket on the 2nd round. Besides the much larger ammo capacity, somewhat improved +70 SV bonus to painting a target, weight of 6.2 kg and sales value of 5000+2d1000sp, this weapon functions exactly like the rocket pistol noted previously.

## Heavy Assault Rifle

Besides being built heavier to accommodate the impressive high caliber rifle rounds this weapon fires, a heavy assault rifle has extra features that a regular variant usually lacks. Besides having the same rate of fire as a regular unit, this gun has a standard selector switch to fire single shot, three-round burst, or full auto at 5 shots per round — although discharging such potent rounds at full auto causes the barrel to move off target somewhat and thus experiences a reduced strike value drop to only +12 instead of +22. Secondly, this relic has a built in barrel flashlight (100 hrs light per mini power cell, 30m range) and fold out alloy bayonet (SV +5, DMG 1d12+4), a built-in compass in the butt stock's top section, as well as is 78% likely to come with a nylon, single point sling.

This weapon only uses high caliber rifle rounds which inflict 1d20+10 damage on a hit, has a range of 900m, requires at least 29 strength to wield effectively, uses a 30 round HCR magazine — although 50 round drums

and belt fed systems are also available, weighs 6.2 kilos and will sell for 4500+2d1000 silver pieces if somebody is hard up enough to sell it at a large town's relic dealership.

## Combo Assault Rifle

As the name implies, this is a combination of a regular assault rifle, as described in the hub rules on page 188 with stats on page TME-100, plus a flame unit as shown on page TME 189. Although this system was carefully designed to limit the weight of both offensive modes, it is still a cumbersome beast of war, and weighs in at 14 kilograms when the 1 liter (20 rounds worth of flame propellant that weighs 1kg) is loaded. With dual triggers, most operators use each weapon platform separately, but in a last desperate defense, a person could pull both triggers and disgorge flame and lead. Because these rifles are so rare, and almost never come up for sale, they can earn out a hefty sell price at 7000+3d1000sp.

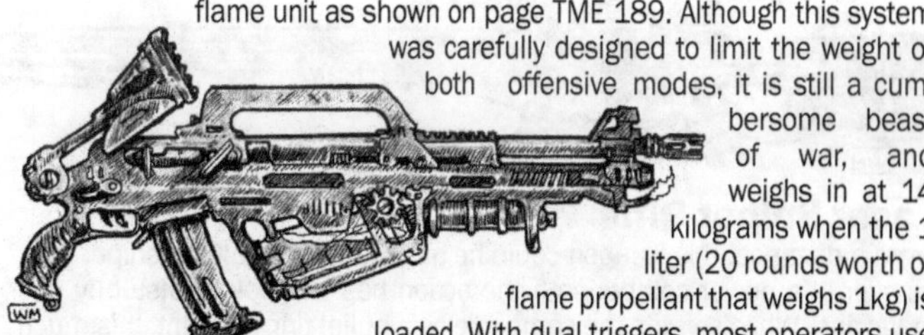

## Intruder Rifle

This massive, alloy encased rifle is another combination weapon, which features a heavy assault rifle with an EM emitter rifle underneath. The weapon has one trigger with a thumb switch to alternate between weapon platforms, and another switch to go from single shot, 3 shot burst, or full auto on the assault rifle portion. This weapon includes a barrel flashlight and fold-out bayonet, just like the heavy assault rifle described on this page.

Every effort was made by the designers to keep the weight down on this impressive weapon. Even so, it tips the scale at 9.7kg, and requires the operator to have at least 34 strength or properly handle. These ultra rare relics will earn the seller 8k+4d1000sp. EM Emitter rifles are described in this book on page 407, while assault rifles have their stats on page 100 of the hub rules book.

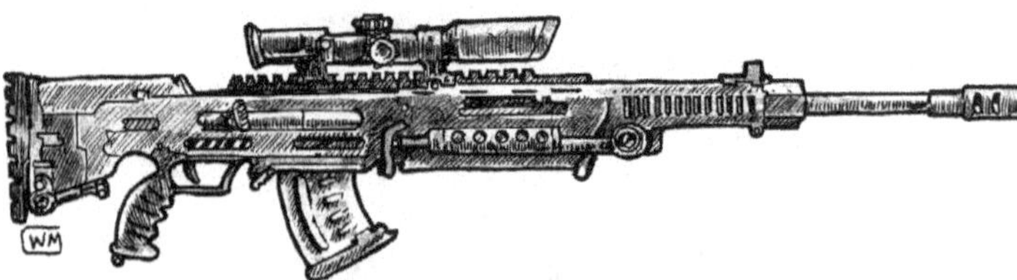

## Advanced Sniper Rifle

Bigger, slightly bulkier and a few kilograms heavier, this more recently manufactured sniper rifle has a semi-automatic mode which allows it to fire two high caliber rifle rounds per round, instead of one, although when used in its typical over-watch mode, with the shooter using careful aim, it fires 1 cartridge every second round at a huge +64 SV bonus. Built with higher tolerances, better materials and demands for accuracy, it also has a slightly longer range. These units all have built-in, extendable bipods, which on careful shots, add an additional +10 SV. They come with a somewhat boxy, J shaped 24 round magazine, although also accept HC mags from standard sniper rifles. When found, they are assumed to not have scope attached, but by adding such optics, the strike value can be increased by +20 SV for standard non-eclectic scopes or +30 for digital rifle scopes. 7 in 10 are found with a nylon sling, and of these slings, 5 in 10 have 10 cartridge sleeves sewn into the strap and will be found with 1d10 HCR rounds.

Summery: An advanced sniper rifle has a base strike value of +20 or +64 when making carefully aimed shots. Its rate of fire is 2 high caliber rounds per round in normal combat or 1 shot every second round using carefully aimed fire, has a range of 2.5 kilometers, requires 25 or higher strength to wield, comes standard with a 24 shot magazine, weighs in at 9 kilograms and will fetch 5000+2d1000 silver pieces if sold in a market

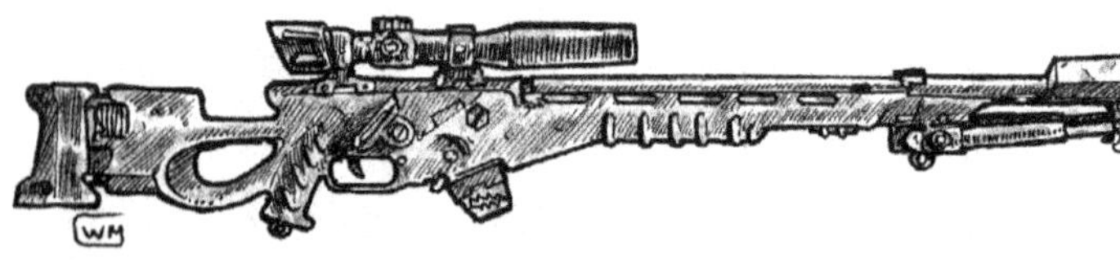

## Laser Sniper Rifle

From a distance, this weapon could be mistaken for a ballistic sniper rifle, as even the power cell beneath the action has the look of a stubby rifle magazine. While serving the same role as a bullet firing variant, this much more advanced system comes with a fold out bipod which will add another +10 strike value if the gun is perched on a solid platform or fired from the prone position. Although a scope increases the accuracy of carefully aimed shots, such optics are not typically found on these weapons when uncovered in the ruins. They fire a bolt of purple laser energy up to 6 kilometers within effective range, and up to 12 at long range — although like all missile weapons, reduce the shooter's SV and damage to half at long range.

Although this long barreled, mat black weapon system can be plugged into a power pack or a wall outlet in a building or large vehicle, they normally use a single power cell, which will yield 10 shots, fire one shot per round or every second round if taking one's time, and have a strike value bonus of +25, or +65 SV when spending an extra round to take careful aim. On a hit, this beam inflicts a devastating 3d20+30 damage. If the beam kills its target, there is a 50% chance that the surge of energy continues on through the victim and possibly into a person or machine directly behind, which suffers slightly reduced attack at +10 SV for 2d20 damage.

## Micro-Wave Gun

This rare, short range but potent energy weapon emits a tissue cooking micro-wave pulse. The relic is normally held in two hands like a carbine, but if a user has a strength score of 50 or higher, they can wield it like a huge pistol.

It fires a pale, half moon shaped yellow bolt of brilliant light up to 30 meters at effective range, SV +30, while beyond this out to 70 meters, the micro-wave charge has a much reduced accuracy, power and ability to disrupt with a strike value of +6. At normal range, this pulse will inflict 2d30 damage to living targets, while at long range (over 30m to 70m) it does 1d30 damage. This energy weapon inflicts only 2d10 damage to non-living targets at normal range and only 2d6 damage at long range.

A micro-wave gun uses a standard power cell to yield 10 shots, weighs 3.3 kg and will sell for 14000+1d1000sp, and while a force field can block this beam in the same way as a beam weapon, it is not hindered by laser reflective skins, fabric or armor. Micro-wave weapons do double damage to dimensional beings.

## Belly Cannon

This heavy energy weapon is strapped to the user by way of a four point harness and fired from the waist and across the belly. Its considerable weight is supported by a gyroscopic enabled, multi-angled hinge that allows the user incredibly smooth transitions between directions and targets. The gun cannot be turned to face backwards, however, so to engage hostiles behind, the user must spend a full round to turn about 180 degrees, and with a barrel length of 93cm (3 feet) this isn't always possible in tight spaces. If the user wears a targeting optics headset, described on page 198 of the hub rules, they can plug into the sight picture of the heavy pulse weapon with the higher +30 strike value, which is a step up from the normal, shoot from the hip use of this advanced infantry beam weapon with its +15 SV. This gun can fire in single shot, three shot burst, or full auto which unleashes 5 pulses per round.

Each shot inflicts 1d30 damage (3d10 if no thirty sided die at table). A power cell will yield 20 shots, while the more appropriate power pack will give the shooter 200 discharges. Range 240 meters, but long range out to 480 meters at a -50% SV and half damage penalty. Only the strongest personnel can carry and deploy this 22 kilogram (48 pound) weapon, and require a minimum of 45 strength or else suffer a -2m movement penalty and loss of aim, resulting in a -10 SV penalty.

## Mk2, MK3 and MK4 Laser Carbines

In the decades before the collapse of the old civilization, far more advanced versions of the laser carbine were designed, and a few models put into something close to mass manufacturing. These superior variants were classified as MK2, MK3 and MK4, with each being increasingly more energy efficient, having a greater range, increased accuracy and punching power. The MK2 and MK3 are simple enough weapons, and come standard with nylon sling and built-in barrel flashlight. The MK4, however, has a beam power selector thumb dial with a power range of between 1 and 10. The higher the number, the more devastating and powerful the beam, yet so too, the sooner the power cell or power pack is drained.

A setting of 1 on the MK4 will be the normal setting, which draws 1/10th of a power cell, for each additional energy tier, increases the strike value by +5 and damage by 10+1d10, and range by 500 meters. So, a setting of 3 would unleash +15, and do 3d10+30 damage, having a range of 1500 meters (500m per dial setting so 3x500m). Or if a setting of 7 were selected, the SV modifier would be an astounding +35 (7x5 SV), potentially inflict 7d10+70 damage, at a range of 7x500m = 3500m, but drain the power cell of 7 of its 10 units of battery life in one shot. The designers of this weapon intended their troopers to be equipped with power packs, which would give 100 units to the operator, or use more high-tech batteries, such as the advanced power cell described on page 457 of this book, which would yield 20 units of energy.

Although the following stats are also included in the weapons listing on page 401, here are the stats for comparison:

**Mk2 Laser Carbine:** SV +30, rate 1, DMG 2d20+20, range 3km, hands 2, ammo: power cell yields 22 shots, weight 3.3kg, sell price 7000+2d1000sp

**Mk3 Laser Carbine:** SV +35, rate 1, DMG 2d20+30, range 3.5km, hands 2, ammo: power cell yields 24 shots, weight 3.8kg, sell price 9000+3d1000sp

**Mk4 Laser Carbine:** +5 SV per degree (+5 to +50), rate 1, DMG 1d10+10 per degree, range 500 to 5000m (500m per degree), hands 2, ammo: power cell yields 1 to 10 degrees of potency in shot power cell yields 10 shots, weight 4.4kg, sell price 12k+3d1000sp

## Auto Gun - Rifled (AG-R)

This tripod mounted, remote controlled or auto firing infantry weapon will fire on anything that moves within a specifically dialed in 'hot zone'. This zone can include an elevation of 60 degrees down, or 180 degrees up in elevation, so can fire directly upward, and fire at a side-to-side angle of 180 degrees. These perimeters can be reset to less elevation or angle by a gunsmith, or mechanical technician of 2 or more skill points.

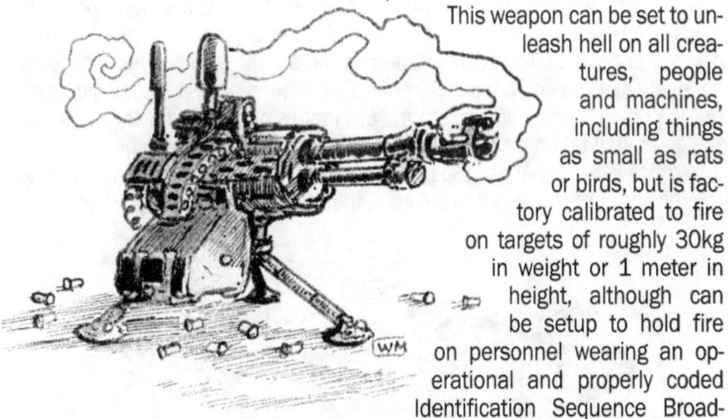


This weapon can be set to unleash hell on all creatures, people and machines, including things as small as rats or birds, but is factory calibrated to fire on targets of roughly 30kg in weight or 1 meter in height, although can be setup to hold fire on personnel wearing an operational and properly coded Identification Sequence Broadcaster (IDSB) from page 198 of the hub rules. This weapon requires either plugged in power or a power cell. One power cell will maintain its continuous vigilance and fire control for 72 hours, while a power pack will supply juice to this system for 30 days.

Rifled auto guns, sometimes called 'proximity guns' or 'auto-sentry units', are commonly chambered to fire standard rifle rounds at a rate of 4 per round, SV 01-60 or +10 if used via remote control or modified and carried), DMG 1d20 each, and comes with a fixed 120 cartridge box magazine. On very rare occasions, high caliber and fifty caliber firing models are also uncovered. This gun has a range of 200 meters during daylight or illuminated conditions, but only 30 meters in dim light, and only 10 meters in total darkness — the weapon's sensors find targets by scanning for heat signatures, footfalls or the sounds of breathing.

Besides being used as an automatic turret, this weapon system can be switched to remote control mode by a distant operator wearing a targeting optics headset (page TME-198), which must be linked by a matching alpha-numeric pass code. With the headset, the remote control operator can use a wireless signal to control the gun's movements and will see through the top mounted sighting camera of the gun, and use retina controls to aim and fire the weapon. Control of this, or the much rarer beam variant of this weapon, can be conducted from as far away as 140 meters if within structures, the hull of a ship, or densely packed ruins, but from as far away as 500 meters in open air, forest, or across water.

If the operator desires, they can give fire control back to the gun remotely, or even use the retinal controls to switch the weapon to safe mode or deactivate entirely. Finally, either a robotics, electrical or computer technician of 3 or more skill points can open the gun and set a command password into the weapon to add a layer of security to the weapon, which cannot be activated without inserting the code when the system is activated.

Weighing in at 47kg, and usually found in a composite plastic case with pull out carry handle at one end and a pair of knobby rubber tires at the other, these systems are usually too heavy for most people to carry about for long, and must be dragged into position.

A first time user who isn't a gunsmith needs to make a type F intelligence based hazard check to set this up for the first time, with one try per ten minutes demanded. An experienced user can get one of these units unpacked and ready to greet the enemy in 5 minutes, or break down and make it ready for transport in 12 minutes. A person of exceptional strength, of 90 or higher, could theoretically deploy this weapon as a machine gun, although a gunsmith would need to spend 3d6 hours rigging up a grip and trigger for the user.

## Auto Gun - Beam (AG-B)

This weapon system is almost identical to the rifle round firing AG-R variant described above. However, it fires pulses of laser energy and is equipped with night vision optics.

This auto turret can see out to 100 meters in almost total darkness, or 200 meters during well lit or daylight conditions. It will fire 6 laser pulses per round as a burst, with a strike value of 01-70. Each successful pulse strike will inflict 1d20 damage. The power to this weapon can come from a wall plug in a facility or vehicle, but more often uses power packs which can easily be strapped to the back end of the remote gun. One power pack will yield 180 bursts (30 bursts at 6 shots each). There is a slot for a standard power cell, too, which will give only 18 bursts.

Like the rifled version, this auto gun can be remote controlled wirelessly by an operator using a targeting optics headset, or modified and carried like an infantry weapon if the user has 90 or higher strength. When used by remote control or hand-held, the user's base strike value is used, +20 SV but when the gun is on automatic, it's SV is 01-70.

## Auto Cannon

This vehicle or structure mounted, unmanned weapon was once popular on ancient water based naval vessels or along the perimeters of old world military or political facilities. Going by many manufacturer's names, this class of close-in weapon system (CIWS) are much smaller than many that once saw action, but because they were mass produced to deal with MAVS, drones and multiple smaller attackers were widely deployed.

In the Epochian era, these weapons systems are the bane to dig teams who get too close to still operational Mecha or oldster enclave defensive perimeters. Such weapons can often pop up from buried emplacements and lay down devastating 20mm explosive rounds, and easily obliterate lightly armed and armored intruders in a single discharge. It usually appears as a Gatling gun barrel on a highly articulating black turret, with a white, gray or flat back conical ammo reservoir above. The reservoir holds up to 600 rounds of 20mm auto cannon ammo (with each round weighing 283 grams or about 10 ounces, so ammo alone weighs 169.8 kilograms) and with the 112kg triple barreled Gatling gun, optics unit and turret system, this relic weighs 560 kilograms without ammo, and if fully loaded with 600 rounds can weigh as much as 729.8 kilograms.

The ammo inside the cartridge storage chamber is attached to an advanced belt system, a system that could be removed and sectioned off into more manageable 50 cartridge sections, weighing just over 14 kg, and if the gun could be reconfigured to be held by some massively built humanoid, or mounted on a tripod and crew served by lengths of the 20mm ammo belts, this CIWS could be a devastating, game changing platform — although finding replacement ammo is an exceptionally challenging chore for even the best dig teams while the reload cost for 20mm cannon is 160sp per shell.

For the most part, these guns are mounted on ancient vessels, the backs of military trucks, or fitted to the old world military aircraft and armored personnel carriers. Most are controlled by a rogue AI, or setup by advanced bunker dwellers or other high tech occupants of an ancient facility, vessel, or complex. The gun can be programmed to fire on anything larger than a cat that enters a certain perimeter, or be controlled by a remote operator using the gun's optics to look through, and a joystick and laptop to control the devastating, yet simple system.

The cameras on the auto-cannon have standard visual capabilities during daylight hours, but are also fitted with a spotlight (sheds light out 250 meters) but the unit is also equipped with night vision out to 200m.

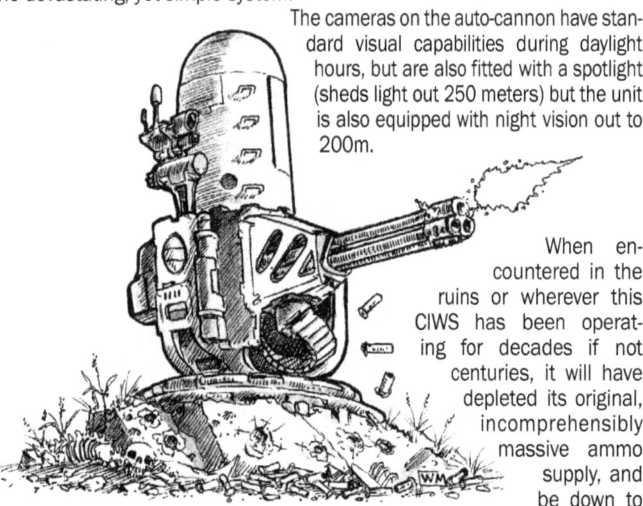

When encountered in the ruins or wherever this CIWS has been operating for decades if not centuries, it will have depleted its original, incomprehensibly massive ammo supply, and be down to 1d100 rounds when characters are unlucky enough to enter its field of fire.

They fire six 20mm cartridges per round, have an effective range of 3 kilometers, a strike value modifier of +35 SV (01-85), and each bullet will inflict 1d100 damage from kinetic, explosive and incendiary damage. Any human sized living target struck by one of these bullets is likely to pass out from shock, too, and must make a type D willpower based hazard check or pass out for 3d6 minutes after being hit. Those killed by these weapons are usually dismembered into 2d6 gory sections, with the head, legs and arms often catapulted in different directions by 2d6 meters. Anyone standing within 6 or fewer meters of a 20mm auto cannon when it fires, and not wearing ear protection, or a combat helmet or better headgear, will be deafened for 3d6 minutes after discharge, with any result of a 18 on that time roll means the unlucky bystander suffers long term hearing loss whereby the character's ear's ring for the next 2d6 weeks and he or she suffers -1 initiative.

For more about 20mm ammunition, see the ammunition relics section on page 419 of this book.

An intact, although empty, auto cannon could be dragged back to a large community and sold to the local authorities for an astonishing 40k+5d1000sp, although if the leaders of a factional settlement don't have this amount handy in assorted silver, relics, plastic and other trade goods, and the sellers don't seem too well armed, well connected, or threatening, the 'government' will just steal the weapon at gun point and give the salvagers nothing.

## Pulse Cannon

Similar to an auto-cannon, but free of the restraints of a physical ammo supply, this heavy weapon fires multiple pulses of lime green laser energy out to 6 kilometers, and in some respects, it is very similar to a light laser cannon, however lacks the range and accuracy but make up for it in its remarkable rate of fire. Usually, these bulky guns are fitted in enclosed turrets and encrusted with optics sensors, a spotlight, night vision optic, comm-link antenna, and a back mounted power pack or plug if connected to the power supply of a still operational facility or vehicle.

Typically, this gun emplacement is controlled by either a proximity response — such as when excavators walk into the section of an open street near the facility where his gun is on watch — and opens fires only on targets over 30kg in weight or 1 meter in height. On other occasions, an operator using a remote control or hard-wired system controls the gun with a simple screen, keyboard, and joystick and the unit's built-on camera and scopes.

Pulse cannons are frequently mounted on orbital space stations, military shuttles, and interplanetary and interstellar space vessels. They can also be attached to autonomous war machines, crew controlled armored fighting vehicles, and the backs of huge robots.

These relics weigh 150 kilograms on their own before a power pack is even added, and is normally bolted to an enclosed, steel encased turret that weighs 530kg in total. A fixed, plated turret has a DV of -40, and an endurance score of 360.

Pulse cannons have a strike value of +20, a 6 pulse burst per round, inflicts 1d100 damage on a strike, has a 6km range, and can fire 24 bursts on one power pack. Selling such an operational weapon is tricky, because to offer it for sale at its asking price of 32k+4d1000 silver pieces is the fair, going rate, but to present such a weapon to the authorities of almost any town will mean the gun being taken off the excavator's hands one way or another. Unscrupulous officials will either pay the going rate, or else quickly concoct a plot to steal the relic from these would-be sellers, often by declaring them 'terrorists'.

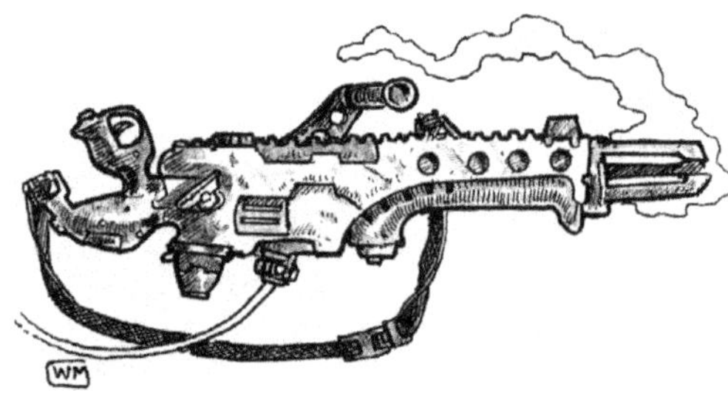

## Lightning Emitter

Often fired from the hip, this cumbersome, short-barreled energy weapon projects a zig-zagging bolt of bright aquamarine colored lighting out to 80 meters. The bolt cooks those it hits and causes a blend of 1d30 lethal and 1d30 stun damage, both in one wallop. (GM: No d30 at your table yet? Roll a 1d20 +1d10 and add them together to get the result). The electricity delivered in this charge might not be restricted to the unfortunate target, and if they are carrying another person, android, robot or device that houses a digital being, then there is a 50% chance that the charge moves on into the second person, and with a further 50% chance of jolting through all those also touching the first person. For example, if ten skullocks are climbing a metal ladder, or standing on a wet floor together, and just one of these individuals is hit by this weapon, there is a chance that the electrical charge will devastate the first skullock and have a 50% chance of moving to each next to it, and so on. If the electrical charge fails to make the jump to another target, then it fizzles out within the body and equipment of the last victim in the group.

Lighting can pass through laser reflective skin or clothing, and besides causing devastating wounds and potential unconsciousness, is 77% likely to cause a fire among the clothing, furnishings or whatever the victim stood on when taking a hit, but only if the materials are flammable.

Being an extremely loud, painful and flashy weapon, a lighting emitter will often terrify animals, who are forced to make a morale check when within 100 meters of this device being unleashed.

Shooting this bolt into water of over 2 centimeters depth, and beyond 6 square meters in total surface area, will dissipate the charge causing nothing more than a painful shock to whatever might stand or swim in the liquid, but sending a bolt onto a wet floor, rooftop or other surface, even without hitting a target, however, will cause 1d10 damage to all those standing on the wet surface — which is often enough to drive off primitive humanoids or wild beasts.

A lighting emitter has a strike value of +30, a rate of 1 shot per round, will inflict 1d30 lethal and 1d30 stun damage. It has an 80m range, must be used in 2 hands unless the user has 60 or higher strength, and then can be used as a pistol. This relic will yield 12 lightning bolts per power cell. These bulky relics weigh 7.8 kilograms and will earn the seller 5000+3d1000 silver pieces.

## Particle Beam Rifle

This rare, bulky rifle uses electromagnetic fields and lenses to propel charged particles at targets almost at the speed of light. Targets hit suffer devastating burns and must make a type D hazard check based on the kilograms of their bodyweight or be knocked back 1d6 meters and lose their next turn. Living beings are fried for 2d20 damage, while mechanical beings, or the chassis of vat-brains, are obliterated for 1d100 damage and suffer from severe damage to their electronics because of ionization. This ionization strike also has a 1 in 6 chance of starting an internal fire around the particle beam's super heated impact point. A fire within a mechanical being could short the machine out if the blaze is not attended to at once with a splash of water or a fire extinguisher blast.

An internally burning robot, android, vat-brain or vehicle suffers 1d8 damage per round for 1d10 rounds and has a 1 in 10 chance of shutting down per round, as the fire burns up wires and electronics. Eventually, this fire will go out, but by then, the mechanical being could be incapacitated and in dire need of repair.

Particle beam rifles have a strike value of +8 or +30 against metallic targets, rate of one shot per round, inflict 2d20 damage to living things and 1d100 to mechanical beings and vehicles. These weapons have a somewhat limited range for an energy weapon, with only 200 meters at normal range within an atmosphere, but in the vacuum of space, can travel 6.6 kilometers. They will fire 16 shots per power cell.

Unless connected to an individual as an implant weapon, this metallic green, burdensome rifle weighs 7 kilograms, and will sell for 15k+3d1000sp.

## Electro-Glove

An electro glove delivers a kinetic thump to a physically contacted, melee range target, which stuns the target and forces it to make a kilograms weight based type E hazard check or get knocked back 2 meters and fall over, losing their next turn. Even without power, this alloy glove can deliver a hell of a punch or slap, and adds +4 SV and +1d6 extra damage from such an unpowered strike.

Most times, an operator will wear this device on their non-dominant hand when using the controls or triggers of a relic firearm or other high tech device, including archaic instruments like bows and crossbows, although using their non-dominant hand in an attack when the user is not ambidextrous are made at -20 DV.

This glove uses a standard power cell that snaps into the armored wrist compartment, and when switched on, has a +12 strike value, an attack rate of 1 per turn, inflicts 2d20 stun damage plus forces a type E kilograms based hazard check or be knocked back 2 meters and lose the next round, requires at least 17 strength to wield effectively, will discharge 20 shocks from a standard power cell, weighs 3.3 kilograms and will fetch 3000+2d1000 silver pieces if sold to a relic dealer.

## Electro-Glove, Advanced

This more recently designed, far more advanced and better built variation of the standard electro-glove does everything that the regular version does, but is powered by a dual power cell hip mounted battery pack with a connection cable designed to be worn tight to the body — either under armor or clothing or exposed on the outside — and strapped to the arm. An extremely durable, wrist-watch like control dial on the top of the glove allows the operator to switch between the normal mode as described for a regular electro-glove, or to shock wave mode. Like a larger belt power pouch (pg. 457) which uses three power cells — and can also be used for this glove — the battery pack can be plugged into other energy weapons and devices, too, which is handy.

When 'shock wave' mode is selected, this glove can become a close in, but highly effective ranged weapon. When the palm is held up and opened and the thumb pad touched against the inside of the index finger twice, it unleashes a wave of blunt force in a cone out 20 meters. This cone might knock over all those in a 3m wide target area, potentially stunning or throwing back multiple opponents in the line of fire. This surge of invisible force has a strike value modifier of +20 SV, rate of 1/2, and inflicts 20+2d20 stun damage while all those in the area of effect must make a further kilograms weight based type D hazard check or be thrown back 1d4 meters.

While the stat listing on page 401 shows only this shock wave attack, this glove shares the stats for a regular electro-glove, too.

In normal electro-glove mode, each impact will drain the dual batteries 1 unit, or 1/40th. However, a shock wave will drain 3 energy unties, or 3/40th of the battery pack. This unit cannot operate on just one power cell.

This advanced, hard to find relic will sell for 5000+2d1000sp in a large community's relic market.

# Weaponized Industrial Tools

*by James Butler & W. McAusland*

All of this equipment can be jury-rigged into serving as the offensive elements of fashioned traps (expanding those found on page 119 of the Hub Rules book), and it is when these easily-weaponizable relics are in such a repurposed state that they will most commonly be encountered. If salvageable, they are desirable items for their originally intended use by both engineers and other excavators — making buyers much easier to find compared to other relics or weapons — and known owners will receive a high level of interest from all manner of parties in any settlement they visit.

## Table XR-249 / Weaponized Industrial Tools Listing

| Weapon | SV | Rate | Damage | Range | Hands | STR | Ammo/Duration | Weight | Value |
|---|---|---|---|---|---|---|---|---|---|
| Arc Welder | +5 | 1/3 | 1d20+5 stun / 1d10 | 1m | 2 | 26 | power pack / 20 shots | 7kg | 4500+2d1000sp |
| Furnace Lighter | +20 | 1/4 | 2d12 /1d10 | 5m | 1 | - | canister / 18 shots | 1kg | 1900+2d1000sp |
| Microwave Ray | +4 | 1 | Increases, see text | 25 feet | 2 | 34 | power cell / 30 rounds | 2.5kg | 2000+2d1000sp |
| Pneumatic Fist | +6 | 1 | 1d12+8 | melee | 1 | - | power cell / 1200 rnds | 1.2kg | 3000+d1000sp |
| Rivet Gun | +22 | 1 | 1d20+10 | 6m or more (see text) | 2 | 20 | rivet rack / 24 rounds | 5kg | 3200+d1000sp |
| Cracker | +13 | 1 | 2d8+6 | Melee | 2 | 44 | power cell / 40 bursts | 5.5kg | 5500+2d1000sp |
| Titan Chainsaw* | +18 | 1 | 4d10+10 | melee | 2 | 88 | power pack / 100 minutes | 35kg | 4200+2d1000sp |
| Acid Sprayer** | +20[1] | 1 | 1d10 per round/ 1d6 rounds | 9m | 2 | 28 | Air Compressor Pack, 2 liter canister yields 10 sprays | 6.6kg | 2200+1d1000sp |
| Floor Stapler ** | +10 melee/+5 ranged | 4 | 1d12 each | 6m | 1 | 31 | 400 Staple 'clips'/ Air Compressor Pack shoots 800 staples | 3.4kg | 1400+4d100sp |
| Industrial Nailer** | +13 melee/+7 ranged | 3 | 1d12+2 each | 15m | 1 | 49 | 300 9 gauge Nails per 'clip'/ Air Compressor Pack shoots 600 | 9.4kg | 2200+1d1000sp |
| Heavy Industrial Nailer** | +19 melee/+11 ranged | 3 | 2d8+4 each | 20m | 1 | 74 | 200 4 gauge Nails per 'clip'/ Air Compressor Pack shoots 400 | 26.6kg | 2200+1d1000sp |
| Mega Nailer** | +26 melee/+15 ranged | 5 | 1d20+5 each | 40m | 1 | 90 | 100 Nail 'clips'/ Air Compressor Pack shoots 300 | 52kg | 2200+1d1000sp |
| Pneumatic Hammer* | +8 | 2 | 2d12+2 stun | melee | 2 | 68 | power cell / 40 strikes | 3.4kg | 900+1d1000sp |
| Pruning Electro-Shears | + 4 | 1 | 3d6+3 | Melee | 2 | 37 | power cell / 120 minutes | 5kg | 1900+4d100sp |
| Earth Tiller* | +16 | 1 | 3d10+3 | melee | 2 | 98 | power pack / 240 minutes | 48kg | 4100+2d1000sp |
| Multi-Saw* | +14 | 1 | 3d20 | Melee | 2 | 128 | power pack / 90 minutes | 163kg | 5600+3d1000sp |

[1] *Acid spray can coat up to 4 man-sized targets per round, burn for 1d6 rounds once coated, animals must make a Type C willpower based Hazard Check or retreat from user/ location.*
**Requires a power pack when used as an infantry tool.*

***Requires an air compressor pack or similar high pressure propellant system.*

## Arc Welder *by James Butler*

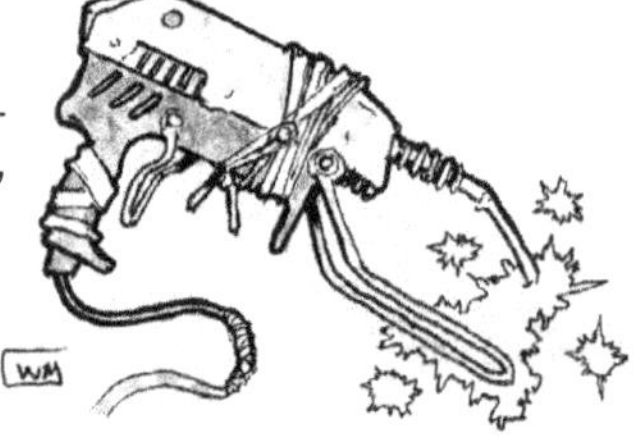

This equipment produces an intense electrical charge between claw-like prongs, from which a meter arc is formed and used to quickly weld metallic sheets on a large scale. This is a dangerous process, and if not properly managed, the discharge can leap to a poorly insulated object (such as a living creature), resulting in 1d20+5 stun damage plus a 65% chance of causing ignitable materials to be set on fire for additional ongoing 1d10 damage per round for up to 1d6+1 rounds or until extinguished.

Anyone viewing an arc that strikes metal without suitable eyeprotection must make a Type C Agility based hazard check or suffer intense retina burns that cause a painful blinding for 5d20+20 minutes, resulting in half movement and a -40 SV, and +40 DV penalty when being targeted. These penalties are halved after half of the rolled time has passed. The wielder is shielded from the possibility of being struck by the arc by a barrier formed from heavily insulated padding at the base of the units, but not from the vision risk.

## Furnace Lighter *by James Butler*

These devices are handheld, wide-nozzled flamethrowers, intended for starting the ignition process of huge industrial furnaces. These units possess a 165 de-

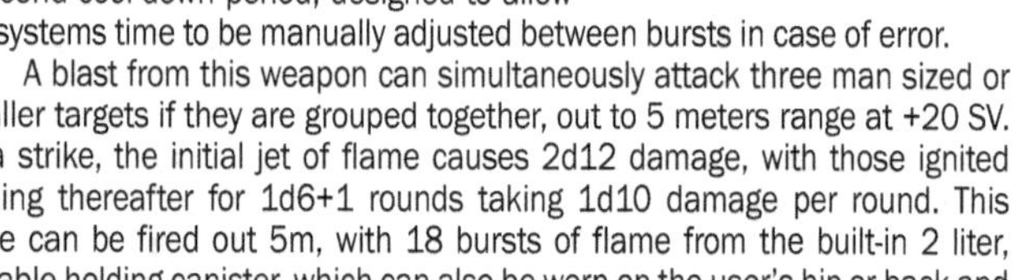

gree firing arc (which is equivalent to 180, given standard movement permitted within the firing action of a round), and emits a full 3-second burst, followed by a mandatory 6 second cool-down period, designed to allow gas systems time to be manually adjusted between bursts in case of error.

A blast from this weapon can simultaneously attack three man sized or smaller targets if they are grouped together, out to 5 meters range at +20 SV. On a strike, the initial jet of flame causes 2d12 damage, with those ignited burning thereafter for 1d6+1 rounds taking 1d10 damage per round. This flame can be fired out 5m, with 18 bursts of flame from the built-in 2 liter, refillable holding canister, which can also be worn on the user's hip or back and weighs 6kg when full of ethanol fuel.

## Microwave Ray *by James Butler*

Designed to expose minute cracks in welds and suspect materials by causing them to rip further, the 1 foot squared concentrated beam emitted by these cumbersome units can also be used as a weapon and has an impressive range of 25 meters. If held on a target, the victim will suffer an increasing amount of damage, for every round contact is maintained. Successfully holding the beam on a target will cause the water molecules in their flesh to slowly boil, causing agonizing internal pain, starting at 1d10 damage, and incrementally increasing in the following pattern: 1d12, 1d20, 1d20+1d10, 1d20+1d12, 2d20,

2d20+1d10, and so forth. To reach higher damage levels, repeated, unbroken attacks must be achieved on the target. This unit requires two hands to wield 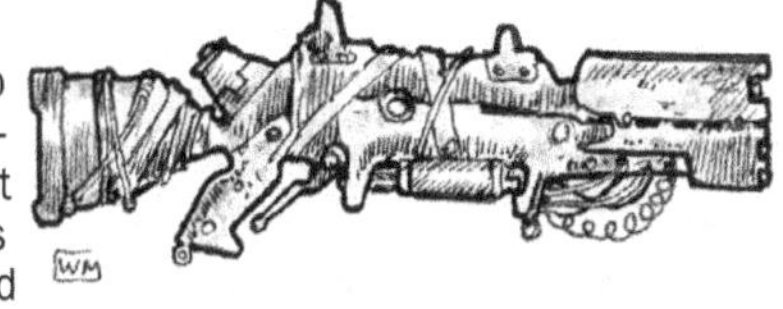 and will unleash up to 30 rounds of microwave energy per power cell.

### Pneumatic Fist *by James Butler*

This slow hydraulic-based equipment resembles a Power Arm cybernetic implant, but the brace spans just the forearm up to the elbow. These removable units allow a wielder to lift loads beyond their physical ability and hammer thick sheets of metal into place, resulting in an effective +15 bonus to the STR value for each outfitted arm. When used as a weapon, a successful melee strike from a pneumatic fist will knock medium-sized/weighted foes back 2+1d3 meters besides causing the listed damage of 1d12+8. Unless padding covers the huge, alloy fingers and knuckles, all damage is lethal. These units will run for 1 hour (1200 rounds) on a power cell, but can be switched on or off by a sealed button panel when not in use. Unpowered attack: SV+4. DMG +2d6.

### Rivet Gun *by James Butler*

This bolt-action spring powered device fires half-inch studs with such force that thick metal sheets can be easily pierced and held in place against another surface. When used as a weapon, it can fire one rivet at +22 strike value per round, with each rivet inflicting 1d20+10 damage. Besides being used to harm opponents, this tool can be useful in making impromptu door seals, ladders, boats, or riveting through a prisoner's clothing or loose skin to nail them to a wall or floor as a means of restraint. This equipment becomes very inaccurate at ranges further than 6 meters, with each additional meter thereafter incurring a cumulative -10 SV penalty. 24 rivets are loaded in the handle rack.

### Cracker *by James Butler*

The standard pneumatic drill is a powerful piece of equipment, but with one significant drawback — only the strongest of workers could use it effectively or for a prolonged period (user must have 44 or higher strength to use). This smaller and lighter model (roughly 33% of traditional drills) may take a little longer to break through and shatter the same amount of rock, concrete, and any other forms of rubble, but will get the job done. Shells, carapaces, and armors — both natural and man-made — suffer an incredible amount of damaging dents from these devices, which tear off large chunks, even shattering weaker materials beyond simple patch-up repairs, causing 4+1d6 damage directly to the DV of worn protection upon each successful strike. This may cause additional equivalent amount of Endurance damage if this protection forms part of a creature's natural biology. Given the massive forces exerted by the rapid pounding of the unit, a successful strike will cause 2d8+2 damage plus also knock-back a medium sized or weighted opponent by 1+1d3 meters. A power cell will provide 40 bursts of pounding.

### Titan Chainsaw

Normally attached to an articulating arm on an unmanned logging automaton, crewed rig, or massive robot, these enormous chainsaws can also be held in two hands by an extremely powerful android, clone, bioreplica or mutant of 88 or higher strength. These over-sized chainsaws were used to take down massive trees in under a minute, but capable of incredible carnage in battle, too. They are usually bright yellow, orange, or red, and found fitted to destroyed machinery and robots within the bounds of ancient cities and old war zones.

In the hands of a powerful new era warrior, however, and powered by a cumbersome power pack, these electrically driven saws can hack through  multiple man sized opponents in one round. During an attack, if the saw strikes the first target among a group of opponents, and manages to kill the first person by cutting through them, a follow-up attack during the same round can be made on another adjacent target. Again, if this second being, including robots and androids, is slain by the sweep of this saw, then a third, fourth and fifth enemy might also be cut in half. A maximum or five man sized or smaller opponents can be cut through per round.

A power pack will run this saw for 100 minutes, while it also accepts standard power cells which will each give the unit 10 minutes of use. This weapon has a SV bonus of +18, inflicts 4d10+10 damage on a strike, is a melee range only device, weighs 35 kilograms and will fetch 4200+2d1000sp if sold to a relic dealership.

### Acid Sprayer

With an effective range of nine meters, this bulky, blunderbuss-looking, two handed sprayer requires an air compressor tank be worn with the hip mounted acid drum. When the compressor is activated by a thumb tab near the unit's pistol grip and trigger assembly, the compressor charges the acid holding tank and on the second round, the operator can pull the trigger and sweep the wide muzzled barrel back and forth. This spray attack gains a +20 SV bonus and sprays an area ahead of the user in a liquid — normally dissolving acid. In one round, up to four man-sized beings can be sprayed with this acid, which on a strike will burn the target for 1d6 rounds, with each round inflicting 1d10 damage.

Any miss will still disgorge acid on the ground, wall, furniture or innocent bystanders, and could cause secondary complications to the user or harm to the enemy, including the disappearance of hull integrity in wooden boats. This acid is too weak to dissolve alloy or regular metals, but will cause plastic, clothing, fur, scales, bones and flesh to melt away. For every 10 points of acid damage to a humanoid victim, they suffer 1 point of permanent appearance trait value loss. This acid can be neutralized in one round if a liter or more of a neutral liquid, such as water or beer, is poured over the victim.

While some ancient stockpiles of still dangerous acid can be found in the old places, including full, ready-to-use cannisters, most of these containers need to be refilled by new era operators. Each 2 liter tank will provide 10 sprays of acid, or other liquid, with each spray using up 200ml of acid. Any chemical technician of two or more skill points can mix up two liters of acid in 1+1d8 days and sell it to the weapon's owner for 120+1d100sp per liter.

### Floor Stapler

Designed to shoot various sized steel construction staples into materials, especially flooring, wall panels, drywall, hardwood, plastic panels and Plexiglas, this air powered, one handed relic is sometimes used by an industrial robot or android when reprogrammed to engage unauthorized or undesirable targets — including excavators. Although more dangerous when used in melee with the stapler head pressed up against the target, this usually garish colored tool can also fire staples up to 6 meters at a rate of 4 per round, with a strike value bonus of +10 in melee, or +4 when not pressed to a target, and inflict 1d12 damage per staple.

While most often encountered as a built on tool fitted to a robot, these units can also be used as infantry weapons when the user wears an air compressor pack on his or her back. One compressor tank will propel up to 800 staples before the tank needs to be recharged, while the stapler itself can be fitted with rectangular clips of 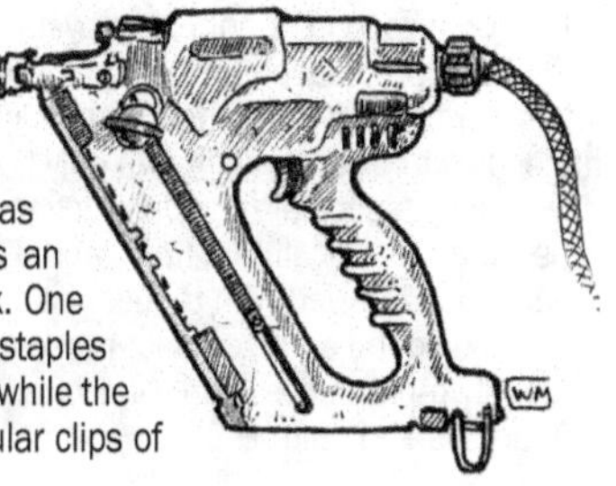

400 staples at a time.Typically these tools are found loaded with 100+1d100 staples, although more of the galvanized, corrosion resistant staples can be found at old construction sites or sometimes in relic dealership back shelves and sell for 20 staples per silver coin. Replica versions can be made by a blacksmith at a cost of 5 staples per silver coin.

## Industrial Nailer

Similar to a floor stapler, this air powered industrial tool is fitted to an air hose and from there to a wheeled or backpack style compressed air tank. It was designed to be held up to a surface and rapidly punch galvanized steel nails through many common construction materials. When used as a weapon by machines and men alike, however, it can fire 3 of these 3 inch, #9 gauge shafts per round out to 15 meters, although with less accuracy and punch than when used in melee range. An industrial nailer can be held in one hand and uses a steel clip like shaft filled with 300 nails at a time, while one fully charged air compressor pack can fire 600 such nails before requiring a recharge. Stats: SV +13 melee or +7 ranged, range 15m, rate 3m, DMG 1d12+3.

## Heavy Industrial Nailer

Almost identical to the much smaller and lighter regular industrial nailer, this bigger unit was designed for use by massive mutant work slaves, cyborgs, clones and androids, or else permanently fixed to industrial robots of all shapes and sizes. In new era combat, it fires three #4 gauge nails per round, which are 5 inches long. When used in close proximity, such as pressed up to an opponent's body, they enjoy the much superior +19 strike value bonus, but even out to ranges of 20 meters, they are still deadly and at +11 SV.

One compressor air pack can fire up to 400 of these huge nails on one charge, although each of the metallic, tube-like 'clips' for this system only carries 200 of these nails. A strike from one of these high powered nails inflicts 2d8+4 damage. As with both the normal sized nailer and mega nailer, ammo for these ancient tools can often be found in an abandoned construction site, or occasionally picked up in relic dealerships. If no supply of ancient nails is available, new era blacksmiths can make them, although at great cost per nail. See Ammunition Relics on page 419 of this book.

## Mega Nailer

Almost never found as a handheld weapon, this massive spike shooter is attached to a fixed position weapon, mounted to a vehicle, or a large robot. Still, truly massive mutants, cyborgs and other humanoids can wield one of these bulky construction tools. Like industrial nailers, they are more effective when pressed against a target in melee combat rather than fired as a ranged weapon. This platform shoots up to five, #000 gauge, 10 inch long galvanized nails per round, and can target several opponents if they are clustered together, often nailing them to each other or a wall behind. Any target killed means the first victim is thrown back, and the spike is allowed another attack on a second opponent or bystander behind the first.

The compressed air tank worn by a hulking infantry user will yield 300 shots per tank fill-up, although the clip-like, elongated rectangle that these huge, dagger sized nails fit into only holds a maximum of 100 spikes. When powered by a specialized construction robot or vehicle, the amount of compressed air is typically limitless, and a few systems have huge nail drums or feeding belts loaded with thousands of such spikes.

The sound a mega nailer makes when firing is like a kettle drum being struck in rapid succession, and often enough to drive off low intelligence humanoids and animals.

## Pruning Electro-Shears

This unit has a bulky back end where the trigger, support handle, power cell adapter and controls are situated. A long, metal shaft extends forward a meter to a broad, crosscut sheering head with prominent alloy teeth. Once used to mow down tough vegetation, and used by both landscapers and mounted to robots and small vehicles, including landscaping drone units, these tools have now been turned into fearsome post-apocalyptic weapons. In combat, an operator sweeps the pruning blade head back and forth to keep enemies back, or shove the cutting head at an opponent when on the attack. Because of its broad, 30 cm wide pruning head, this tool can attack up to three rat, bat or skal bird sized targets per round.

Powered by a single power cell which will run the shears for 120 minutes, these units also come with a coiled patch cable to allow plugging into either a vehicle, or a power pack. Standard extensions cords can also be plugged into this unit. Pruning electro-shears have a +4 strike value, make 1 attack per round, inflict 3d6+3 damage on a strike, require 2 hands to wield and the user must have a strength of at least 37 to manipulate it without suffering the standard inadequate strength penalty of -20 SV.

## Earth Tiller

This heavy duty agricultural tool is most often encountered when built onto a multi-jointed-piston and hydraulic assisted mechanical boom arm, and fitted to either a vehicle or large robot. It was designed to till the soil and make it ready for crop planting, although this model has alloy blades and easily chops through thick roots, fallen saplings, shrub and whatnot. When used against enemy targets, including smaller robots, androids and beasts, it is devastating.

Because the many variants have been set up for an extremely strong, bulky entity to wield with two hands, and draw upon the electrically of a power backpack, these units have been put to use in battles to devastating and exceedingly gory effect. With a reach of out to 3 meters, this melee weapon has a strike value bonus of +16, and will grind up victims causing 3d20+10 damage on a strike. Once the victim is snagged by the rotating, hooked blades of this tiller, it is difficult to break free and not suffer repeated damage until the unlucky target is pulverized and spat out upon the field of battle. Anyone hit must make a type D agility based hazard check to pull free, per round, otherwise they're mauled again for automatic damage.

If one victim is already being tillered, the operator can steer the rotating blade array toward another target, and potentially pulverize one man sized or smaller victim after the other, with several being wrapped and chopped together at a time. Targets that are larger than a man (over 2m tall or long), will not fit into the blade assembly nor suffer repeated grinding attacks and must be attacked each round in the normal fashion.

Some very large robots of over 400kg weight can be fitted with one such tiller on each side of their body, and roll into enemy formations and harvest a bounty of blood and guts.

## Pneumatic Hammer

Once used in construction and industrial projects to pound posts into the ground, reshape metal, crush rock, pulverize concrete or dismantle retired machines, this usually robot mounted tool has since been turned into a fierce weapon. When given access to a power pack, customized with a cross chest harness and held in the hands of a mighty user, this tool can punch opponents at an incredible rate. The driving piston that thrusts from the shaft and extends out a half meter (50cm or nearly 20 inches), does so at an incredible speed and makes two attacks per round. The punch will do stun damage only if a rubber or padded leather cover is wired around the head or a hammer tip, which is shaped like a slightly rounded nail head. Each blow from this hammer has a strike value bonus of +8 and will inflict 2d12+2 damage per strike. The user's strength trait does not modify the piston driving hammer so has no effect on the tool's usage and devastating, metal and bone crushing impact.

## Multi-Saw

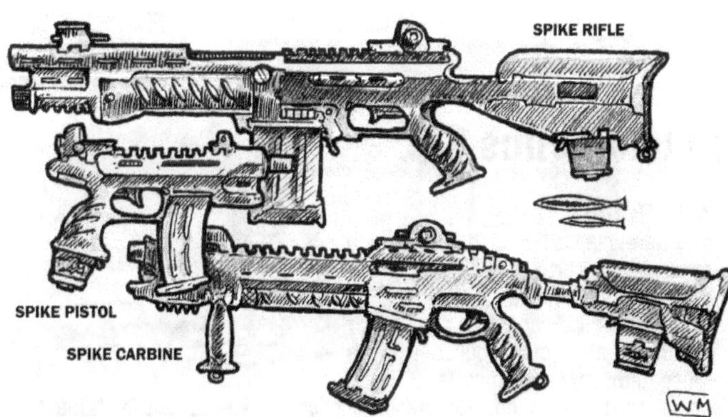

Normally found attached to industrial vehicles that once served in forestry or agricultural roles, this highly flexible, triple jointed arm ends in a trio of half meter diameter disc saw blades, each of which is angled at 120 degrees so that all three blades meet at one point to make short work of stumps and other materials. These alloy blades can tear apart flesh and bone, armored infantry, androids and robots with ease, and in the end times of the old civilization were used by lumbering Mecha controlled robots to exterminate humans, or by the authorities to deal with both the Mecha and colossal mutant monstrosities from one faction or another.

In almost every case, this unit is far too large to be man-portable, and only a being of 128 strength or better can lift this 163kg rig plus wear a power pack that will yield 90 minutes of continuous use on a charge. If used by some sort of non-vehicle operator with the sufficient strength, the multi-saw rig must be strapped to the body with a two point harness and requires two hands to wield and makes one attack per round.

Painted bright yellow or orange, this devastating close-quarters weapon system is greatly feared, has a 3 meter reach, and once it makes a strike, the triple blades have a tendency to pull in whatever it is hacking apart and suck them into the whirring blades. Once struck, therefore, a subject takes the initial 3d20 damage, but must make a successful type D strength based hazard check to pull and twist free of the blades. Failure to get free means that on the next round, the multi-saw gets a further +14 strike value bonus (now +28).

If carried by some sort of brutish mutant or robot, the massive alloy contraption acts as extra armor, and provides the user with a bonus of -10 DV.

# Arc Guns and Spike Throwers

*by Danny Seedhouse*

## Arc Guns

Arc guns are a directed energy weapons that fire a bolt of focused electrical energy akin to a lightning bolt. This low-powered laser beam ionizes the air before firing the electrical bolt. Arc guns are energy hogs, inefficient, loud and bright... and a touch unpredictable, as excess charge has the tendency to leap to others nearby. Effective range on arc guns is relatively limited as far as modern firearms go, since the energy of the bolt dissipates quickly, more akin to shotguns than rifles. Arc guns can be found in pistol, SMG and rifle configurations, the submachine gun (SMG) variant is built more like a rotary drum grenade launcher to manage the increased rate of fire.

Arc gun charges that hit robots, cyborgs or anything vulnerable to electricity suffer the second listed damage value (shown on Table XR-250, next page). Arc guns also have the tendency to leap to nearby targets.

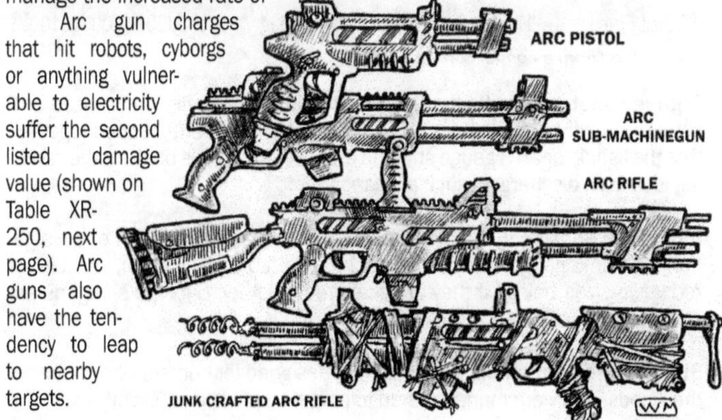


Whenever the first subject is hit with an arc gun, the electrical charge leaps to 1d4-1 extra targets (0 to 3). Roll randomly to see who else gets struck for 1d10 DMG. A target can only be hit once per arc shot.

There is also a junk crafted variant included among these relics that consists of a bulky home made power pack and a crude, but effective rifle sized projector attached by cables to the pack. It can be made by a 6 skill point junk crafter, who must also have 2 skill tiers in electronics as well. This weapon requires constant maintenance but can be recharged with physical labor, although if one is desperate, he or she can try to use a power cell.

To recharge the crude power pack, the operator needs to manually crank the power pack for 30 minutes per shot recharged. Each time one does this, however, there is a 30% chance that the weapon burns out and releases a shower of sparks doing 1d10 damage to the wielder. Using a power source to recharge the gun is perilous, too, and the user needs to make a type D intelligence based hazard check or it explodes doing 1d20 damage and destroying itself. If this hazard check was successful, on the other hand, the weapon drains the equivalent of 4 charges from the source to charge up 1 shot to the home-made arc gun.

## Spike Throwers

Spike thrower weapons are effectively gauss weapons under trademark to a long forgotten corporation, and so named by Epochian era people because of the shape of the ammo these relics shoot. Using magnets to accelerate metallic darts at hyper velocities, these weapons require both ammo and power to use, making them somewhat of a logistic nightmare — unless attached to something with a power source.

Non-relic spikes can be manufactured and, for simplicity sake, they all reduce damage by 2 points and drop range by 20% unless manufactured in relic machinery by a gunsmith or mechanical technician of at least 3 skill points. They hit hard, travel long range, and exhibit exceptional magazine capacity. The following spike throwing weapons are the most typical varieties discovered:

Spike pistols and spike carbines use the same size of small dart, a 7cm long, 100 gram, iron spike that can be cast, polished and purchased for 5sp each in most large towns. They also require one power cell that will fire 200 small darts with spike thrower pistols having 25 shot magazines. Carbines, meanwhile, feature bulky 60 dart mags and get 180 shots per power cell. In most human communities, a stockpile of 30+2d20 small ammo spikes can be purchased.

Spike rifles, and spike LMGs (light machine guns) use medium sized metal darts. These projectiles are 9cm long and considerably thicker than the small darts. One power cell will propel 200 spikes on a charge for either weapon, although the rifle's box magazine holds only 50 spikes and the LMG holds 200. Medium spikes weigh 150 grams each and cost 7sp each to cast, polish and purchase. Most towns will have 20+3d20 available for sale — with many of them being refurbished old world darts.

Spike HMGs (heavy machine guns), and long spikers use the same, large sized 15cm metal projectiles. The heavy machine gun (HMG) variant requires one power pack per 800 rounds fired, but the long spiker, which is the sniper rifle of this weapon classification, can launch 150 from a single power cell. Spiker HMGs have 200 round box magazines, while long spikers use 25 spike detachable magazines. Large spikes weigh 200 grams each, and cost 12sp to buy in large new era towns. Normally, only 4d6+10 are available per purchase at any given time.

## Table XR-250 / Arc Guns and Spike Throwers Matrix

| 1d100 | Weapon | SV | Rate | Damage | Range [1] | Hands [2] | STR [3] | Ammo/duration | Weight | Value [4] |
|---|---|---|---|---|---|---|---|---|---|---|
| 01-17. | **Arc Pistol** | +10/+30* | 1 | 2d10/3d10+5* | 30m | 1 | - | Power cell: 20 | 2.2kg | 1600+1d1000sp |
| 18-24. | **Arc SMG** | +10/+30* | 3 | 2d10/3d10+5* | 30m | 1 | 18 | Power cell: 15 yields 3 shot bursts | 4.8kg | 2000+1d1000sp |
| 25-33. | **Arc Rifle** | +10/+30* | 1 | 2d12/3d12+5* | 50m | 2 | 23 | Power cell: 10 | 8.2kg | 21000+1d1000sp |
| 34-47. | **Scrap Built Arc Gun** | +5/+20* | 1 | 1d20/2d20* | 20+1d10m | 2 | 17 | Power cell: 5 | 4.9kg | 700+1d1000sp |
| 48-61. | **Spike Pistol** | +20 | 1 | 2d10+4 | 350m | 1 | - | 25 spikes/ 200 shots per power cell | 2.7kg | 1400+1d1000sp |
| 62-72. | **Spike Carbine** | +15 | 3 | 2d10+4 | 400m | 2 | 19 | 60 spikes/ 180 shots per power cell | 6.3kg | 1900+1d1000sp |
| 73-85. | **Spike Rifle** | +25 | 2 | 3d10+10 | 1.5km | 2 | 28 | 50 | 8.9kg | 2000+1d1000sp |
| 86-91. | **Spike LMG** | +25 | 5 | 3d10+10 | 1.5 km | 2 | 39 | 200 | 19.2 kg | 5000+2d1000sp |
| 92-96. | **Spike HMG** | +25 | 5 | 4d10+20 | 2.5 km | 2 | 48 | 200 | 26.6kg | 8000+4d1000sp |
| 97-00. | **Long Spiker** | +25/+65 | 1 or 1/2 | 4d10+20 | 3.5 km | 2 | 36 | 25 | 7.7kg | 3000+2d1000sp |

*Note: The random 1d100 roll shown is for the GM's use only when the need to randomly determine one of these weapons during on-the-fly game sessions, NPC armament, or loot discovery rolls.*
**Second number vs. robots, androids, cyborgs, vat-brains and all other mechanical beings, vehicles, and systems.*

# Ammo Relics Set 2

### Toxic Bullets

These rare, plastic tipped, hollow point rounds are standard cartridges as far as range and damage go, how- ever, besides inflicting the nor- mal devastation of a bullet tearing through bone, muscle and organ, these rounds rupture on impact and release toxic fluids into the victim's bloodstream. They can be found as both standard pistol and standard rifle rounds, and will sell for 200+1d100sp per pistol round or 300+1d100sp per rifle round. They can not be reloaded.

A struck living target must make a hazard check depending on the total number of toxic rounds lodged in their body, per day, regardless if the hazard check failed or not. For example, a skulking render is shot with a single toxic round, but the lizard makes its type B hazard check and keeps coming. Two more rounds strike the beast, and now, it rolls as if three bullets, not two have been lodged in its body, requiring a type D hazard check... which, it makes again, and kills all but one of the people shooting at it. The one person who gets away reloads a single toxic round in his wrist gun and flees. Hours later, the same skulking render has tracked the lone excavator across the flats and overtakes him, the character shoots and luckily strikes the animal, and since this is within the same 24 hour period, the giant lizard must roll against 4 toxic bullets in its system, another type D HC, which it fails, drops uncon- scious, and then must roll a Type C HC to avoid death, which it also fails.

Any victim made unconscious by these bullets remains incapacitated for 200 minutes, minus their base endurance value to a minimum of 10+1d6 minutes. At the end of this unconscious period, they must then roll to see if death from toxic shock occurs, thus the second hazard check:

| Toxic Bullets In Victim | Hazard Check to Avoid Unconsciousness | Hazard Check to Avoid Death |
|---|---|---|
| 1 | B | A |
| 2 | C | B |
| 3,4 | D | C |
| 5-7 | F | D |
| 8-12 | H | E |
| 13 or more | K | F |

### Shotgun Shells

While the 8 gauge shotgun was first introduced to The Mutant Epoch in the Mall of Doom adventure, this book includes it again along with the 6 gauge shotgun. The shells for both shotgun shell sizes are includ- ed here, as well as the Signal Flare Shotshell, which fits a standard 12 gauge weapon.

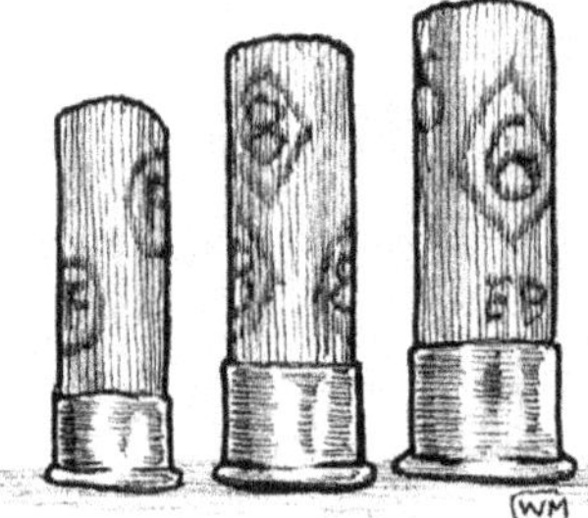

In all three cases, these shells are rare, and with the 8 and 6 gauge, finding more ammo after expending one's supply is probably the biggest drawback to these weapon systems — so excavators quickly learn to pick up the plastic shell casings after discharging the weapon, or when finding empty shells that might have been fired decades or centuries before.

Reloading fees vary depending on the size, remoteness, and nature of a community. In large slum cities like Overpass, or digger forts such as Pit- ford, where the need for ammo is constant, for example, the prices are more reasonable, while in small farming villages or trade outposts, where a supply of materials and expertise is rare, the cost to reload is typically double what is shown on the following table.

| Shotgun Shell | SV Mod.* | Damage | Typical Range* | Weight | Sell Price | Reload Price |
|---|---|---|---|---|---|---|
| *Standard* | +20 | 3d10 | 30m | 40g | 25+1d20sp | 25+1d20sp |
| 8 gauge shell | +30 | 20+2d20 | 30m | 90g | 50+1d30sp | 100+3d20sp |
| 6 gauge shell | +40 | 20+3d20 | 36m | 120g | 70+1d30sp | 130+3d20sp |
| Signal Flare | +17 | 3d6 | 160m | 62g | 40+3d20 | 400+2d100sp |

**When fired from a normal pump shotgun*

**8 gauge shotgun shells** fire 00 buckshot and can strike 3 man-sized or 6 smaller sting fly, devilkin or nubinz sized targets if they are grouped together. See the listing for an 8 gauge shotgun on page 401 of this book for the result- ing kick from discharging such a weapon.

A **6 gauge shot shell** can deliver an even more ruinous swath of devasta- tion than an 8 gauge, and can strike 4 man-sized or 10 smaller, skal bird or red wasp sized beings if they are clustered together. 6 gauge shotguns are described on page 401 of this book.

**Signal Flare Shot shells** were originally designed for hunters who got lost in the woods, and were manufactured to propel a specialized, slightly explosive bullet-shaped plastic projectile up to 160 meters into the air where it will detonate in a 6 meter diameter, bright orange burst. The flare, after initially exploding with a loud pop, will float back to earth, lighting up the area beneath it in a 12 meter radius for one minute (20 rounds).

Besides being used to signal for help or to initiate some action or alert to onlookers, these projectiles can also be shot at enemy targets, or into the thatched roofs of huts, wood piles, dry grass or other flammable substances and be 93% likely to start a fire within 1d6 rounds. When fired into a living or mechanical being, the resulting explosion could also set them on fire if they are soaked in ethanol, oil or naturally flammable. While an invaluable addition to any digger's load out, these shells are very expensive to reload at 400+2d100sp cost, and require a chemical technician of at least 2 skill points to supply the reloader with the flare making materials.

These shells fit standard 12 gauge shotguns only, and if used in a classic flare gun, will blow apart the barrel of the plastic pistol.

## Emergency Flare

These differ from the more advanced, and more dangerous shot shell flare and are often found on a stripper-clip style plastic sprue with 4 or 6 flares, and sometimes clipped to the bright orange flare pistol that fires them. Chambered in 12 gauge, these emergency signal flares will go 150 meters into the air, burst in a brilliant reddish-purple plume with a 5 meter radius, and then over the next two minutes, slowly fall to earth, lighting everything up in the area over a 100 meter radius beneath it.

Firing one of these flares through a real shotgun is only effective 67% of the time, and because of the length of the flare, they must be hand loaded into the action and do not fit into magazines or the pump-action shotgun's tube magazine. If a misfire occurs, they detonate within the barrel, spew flaming sparks out the muzzle and gum up the action of the weapon, taking 3d6 minutes to clean out (half this time for a trained gunsmith). If the flare does successfully launch, it will work as normal.

While firing a flare into heaps of flammable material, or a fur covered beast, or leafy plantoid will start a fire 82% of the time — burning for 1d8 rounds causing 1d6 damage per round before it can be patted or out or smothered, the force of this round will also inflict 2d6 damage with a strike value bonus of +4 SV.

Each flare weighs 50 grams and will sell for 60+1d30sp.

## Industrial Staples and Nails

Floor stapler ammo is usually found in poly encased sleeves of 100 at a time, and while they are considerably smaller than the more common nails fired by industrial and mega nailers, they are harder to make because they are constructed from flattened stainless steel and must be perfectly measured and glued together in strips to function in the relic. Still, blacksmiths have been able to make some of these 1.5 inch (3.8cm) staples, which are often available in barter markets at a cost of 5 staples per 1 silver coin.

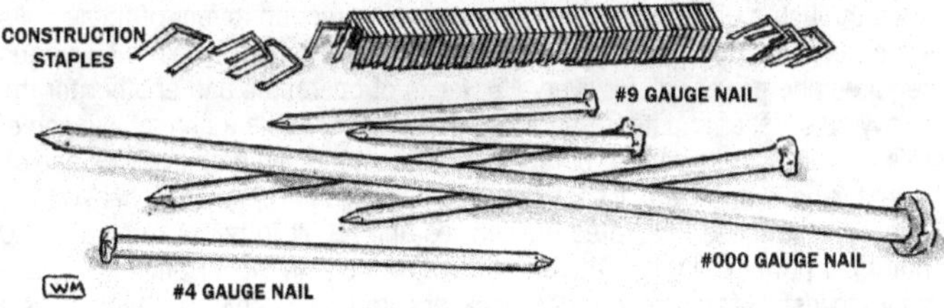


Nailers discharge galvanized steel nails of three common gauges, each of which can only be fired by a specific size of nailer. The standard industrial nailer uses #9 gauge nails, being the smallest at 3 inches or 7.6cm long. Heavy Industrial nailers use 5 inch (12.7cm) long #4 gauge, and the massive mega nailer uses 10 inch long (25.4cm) #000 gauge nails, which are often called spikes and weigh 453g each. All these nails can readily be found in old construction sites and more-or-less intact home building supply depots, but can also be made from cast iron by a blacksmith.

The following table shows both the staple and nail weights, costs to purchase replica versions, and the sell and buy price for relic versions. Stats for range, rate, damage are shown with the weapon listings as seen on table XR-249 on page 414.

| Staple or Nail | Length | Weight | Replica Cost | Sell Relic Version* | Buy Relic Version** |
|---|---|---|---|---|---|
| Relic Construction Staple | 1.5 inches/ 3.8cm | 0.25g | 5 per 1sp | 3 for 1sp | 1sp each |
| #9 Gauge | 3 inches/ 7.6cm | 7g | 1sp | 2 nails earn 1sp | 2sp each |
| #4 Gauge | 5 inches /12.7cm | 55g | 2sp | 1sp earned | 3sp each |
| #000 Gauge | 10 inches /25.4cm | 453g | 5sp | 4sp earned | 10sp each |

*This is what excavators and scavs will earn when selling a found staple or nail.
**This is what excavators must pay to purchase either industrial staples or nails whenever they are available.

## 20mm Auto Cannon Ammunition

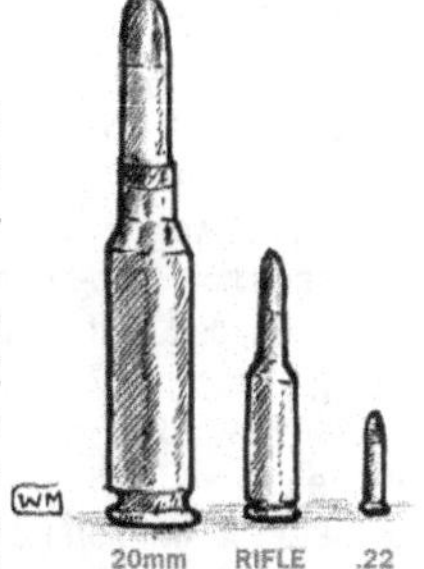


Normally fired from an auto-cannon, these 7 inch or 17.78cm long, 283 gram ancient cartridges are incredibly deadly and tend to cause incendiary, explosive and kinetic energy damage to those they hit. Adult human sized targets who are struck must make a type D willpower based hazard check of pass out from the shock of the impact for 3d6 minutes. Those killed by a hit from one of these massive rounds will be shredded into 2d6 parts, with limbs, head and torso sections thrown all about the impact area about 2d6 meters distance. The discharge of a 20mm round within 6 meters of those not wearing hearing protection, or a fully encased relic helmet, will automatically deafen an organic person or creature for 3d6 minutes, although on a roll of 18, the deafnesses is more long lasting, and the person has ringing in their ears for the next 2d6 weeks and suffer -1 initiative during this time.

These rare rounds can be reloaded, but at great expense and only by the best reloading facilities in any given region, and at a cost of 160+1d100 silver pieces per cartridge.

## Chase Rocket

These are a hybrid between a tiny rocket and a bullet, and are fired from a class of weapons that include both the rocket pistol and rocket carbine, although some robotic units, fixed installation defenses and crude, tube fired contraptions also use this ammo.

When fired from a rocket using pistol, carbine, or other purpose built system, the operator uses the laser sight on the weapon to 'paint' a target, which takes 1 round and has a separate strike value than that used by this small, red tipped, devastating little chaser rocket.

After the target is marked, the weapon is fired and the tiny missile speeds out after the painted target, even if it has rounded a corner, ducked into a window, or deep into a trench. So long as the pathway to the target is not blocked by a solid object, net, force field, thick web, or other barrier, this chase rocket will speed after the unfortunate at a movement rate of 36m per round for up to ten rounds before the rocket's fuel begins to run out and for every round of chase thereafter, there is a 4 in 10 chance it loses power, drops to the ground and explodes in a 6 meter radius causing 1d20 damage to all those in the blast zone (each of whom must be 'attacked' by the blast: SV 01-60).

If the chase rocket reaches the intended target, it must try to hit and puncture the subject, which uses the direct hit strike value of 01-70, with no additional modifiers by the shooter — although the initial attempt to paint the target is affected by the weapon's user (+50 SV for the pistol and +70 SV to the carbine, added to the base SV of the user or 'laser painter'. On a puncture, the rocket enters the clothing, armor or body of the victim and detonates for 3d20 damage. If a miss occurs, or the rocket bounces off or lands at the feet of the target, it will explode with a burst radius effect as previously described, and might still kill the target.

Without use of the proper chase rocket weaponry, and either thrown or fired from a pipe, these rockets will simply speed directly forward up to 36 meters and then drop to the ground and explode, similar to a crude mortar.

Chase rockets weigh 570 grams each, and if sold, will fetch 300+2d100sp each.

# Military Accessories Set 2

### Jump Boots *by Brandon Goeringer*

These heavy, gas powered boots, which weigh 12kg each, are used for jumping long distances, although hamper normal movement because of their added weight. They use side thrusters, which can hold 1 liter of alcohol fuel, and take 5 rounds to put on. They're activated through a toe switch which launches the wearer straight forward 15 meters at a height of 3 meters off the ground for beings under 150kg, and only 10 meters forward and 2 meters high for beings weighing 151kg to 200kg, which is its maximum load, in one combat round.

The boots may be targeted at DV -40, END 18 and if reduced to zero or less END the boot explodes doing 1d12+6 damage to the wearer. If one is destroyed, the other becomes inoperable. Normal movement is reduced by -2m. 1 liter of alcohol gas allows for 8 jumps. A pair of jump boots weigh 12kg and will fetch 400+3d100sp if sold to a relic dealer.

### Enhanced Tactical Armature [E.T.A.] *by TalonHunteR*

Just prior to the collapse, there were rumors in the highest circles that a new weapon was coming online that could turn the tide in the war against the Mecha. These rumors told of giants of metal, fitted with laser rifles powerful enough to take out a heavy combot reliably in one hit, and a hidden factory in which they were produced.

To the military scientist Jacob Wiggin and his team, they were the Enhanced Tactical Armatures, E.T.A. for short. Powered by micro-fusion generators, they were three times the height of a man, with 5 times the strength and speed of the best trans-human. Their weapons were scaled up to match, and allowed the ETAs to outclass the current top end shell armors. While this armature is robust, the operator is open to the elements and susceptible to small arms fire or a direct attack in melee, although besides whatever armor he or she wears, the frame of the ETA offers some additional cover and improves the operator's DV by -20.

Sadly, the encroaching Mecha army forced the scientists to flee in their operable creations before their weapons were finished, and destroyed the rest. After going into hiding, the scientists developed designs for more primitive weapons that could be manufactured with their limited resources; compound bows 3 times a man's height, tensioned with 1000lb test cable that no man could hope to draw, handheld repeating ballista, and the like.

Alas, despite their genius, the surviving scientists could not live forever, nor did they have the martial skill to properly use their creations in combat, thus they froze themselves in cryo tubes they had brought along and waited for the storm to pass...

### Enhanced Tactical Armature

DV: **-50**
Move: **18m**
END: **100 + 2d100**
STR: **100+1d100**
AG: **40+ 1d30**
ACC: **pilot + 4d10**
INT: **as pilot**
WL: **as pilot**
PER: **pilot +5d10** (full optics suite)
APP: **n/a**
Weight: **500+ END in kg**
Sell Price: **18k+3d1000sp**
Notes:

• Pilots can be wounded by called shot or heavy weapons fire on the torso of the ETA

• ETAs have enough stability and possess mounting brackets to have one shoulder attached, crewed (1 gunner) heavy weapon. If the weapon has computer targeting abilities, it can be linked into the eye tracking function of the ETA for aiming and firing.

• ETAs have a chance of being found with one of these weapon platforms, roll **1d100: 01-45** repeating ballista (see notes below for stats) / **46-90.** Up-scaled compound bow (see notes below for stats) / **91-00.** Heavy Laser Rifle modified to be used as an ETA-held rifle (see table TME-171 on page 100 of the hub rules for stats).

• The punch damage of an ETA is whatever their strength score determines based on table TME-1-3 Trait Value Modifiers, found on page 10 of the Hub Rules, or repeated in this book on page 8, plus 1d12.

• Power plant requires 5L of water per day of continual use and has a fuel tank that can hold up to 50L of water

• Compound Bow: SV+7, rate 1/2, DMG 3d20+15, range 250m, Strength needed to wield 100, ammo: rebar shafted 3m long arrows, wgt 150kg, cost na

• Repeating Ballista (same as heavy ballista siege weapon from the hub rules, but the stats here reflect the potentially far higher strength of the ETA): SV +20, rate 1, DMG 3d20+32, range 300m, weight 230kg, sales value 400+2d100sp

### Hover Gun

This unit is a cross between a robot and a remote gun, which hovers along next to the controller at a height of 3 meters and to a maximum distance of 50 meters away. It has four cage encased rotors, A disc-shaped, body that is 1.6 meters in diameter, has several flexible antennas, an armored shell and numerous optic nodes to help navigate even in tight passages and while firing on targets specified by the operator.

The weapon is remotely controlled by the wearer of a small headset, who sees through a flip down eye-monitor and can direct up to four of these units via a nerve conduit that simply hooks on and into the left ear. The hover gun requires one power cell for every 12 weeks of operation, and another for the heavy pulse laser and its 30 bursts of devastation. While a normal weapon of this sort discharges only 20 bursts, this unit features a more advanced and efficient variant of the gun. If salvaged off a defeated hover gun, this heavy pulse rifle will lose these integrated efficiencies and revert to being a standard 20 burst per power cell rifle — but only after considerable modifications by a gunsmith to install a standard trigger, stock, and iron sights on the weapon. If a dig team doesn't have such skills among their ranks, the cost to have a freelance gunsmith make these alterations will cost 600+2d100sp and take 2d4 days to turn around.

When a hover gun has its power cell expended, and so used up its 30 bursts, the unit can be directed to speed toward and ram targets, although any hit on a target heavier than itself results in an automatic 2d20 damage to itself. A ram attack requires the hover gun to move at least 8m to get enough velocity up, otherwise it can only do a much weaker smash attack.

This relic is quite complicated and if a new user is not supervised and instructed by an already trained operator, then the user must make an intelligence based type D hazard check upon first using it. If this hazard check fails, the remote unit simply flies off in a random direction, crashes and explodes like an advanced fragmentation grenade. If the HC is successful, he or she can soon get the hang of the interface and flight and fire controls of this drone-like, highly intimating 1.6 meter wide disk.

If the controller's headset is removed or smashed, any hover guns will cease fire and slowly descend to the ground, extend rubberized landing legs and shut down. They have no autonomous mode, cannot operate without a commanding intelligence and will not defend themselves even if taking fire should their controller not bid them to attack specified targets. While the headset was designed for human controllers, it has been reported that similar control modules exist that have been fitted to robots or stationary computers. These modules are said to have enhanced range and so digital beings or AIs housed in structures or vast machines deploy squadrons of these devices to patrol their halls and perimeters.

Should diggers sell an operational hover gun with a headset, a robotics or relic dealership will pay 7000+3d1000sp for the rig.

## Hover Gun

Defense Value: **-30** (DV -10 if stationary and inactive)
Endurance: **45**
Movement: **16m**
Initiative: **Same as Operator or +0**
Attacks: **Three options...**
Heavy Pulse Rifle: SV 01-75, Rate 4, Damage d20, Range 1km, **Ammo 30 bursts** (with 4 shots per burst)
Ram: **SV 01-70, rate 1, with 8+ meter charge at target, Damage 1d20 lethal and 2d20 stun**
Smash: **SV 01-50, rate 1, from under 8m away or close-in melee range, damage 1d10 lethal and 2d10 stun**
Strength: 46
Agility: 57
Accuracy: 34 (base SV 01-50)
Intelligence: 0
Willpower: 0
Perception: As operator
Experience Factors: 30
Morale: Not Applicable
Size: 1.6m diameters disk
Weight: 86kg
Power Supply: 1 power cell runs it for 12 weeks, another power cell supplies 30 bursts to the energy weapon.

# Explosives Set 2

### Grenades Set 2

**Stun Grenade** *by James Butler and W. McAusland*
Commonly referred to as flash grenades or flashbangs, these non-lethal explosives emit a blinding burst of light and high-pitched noise that incapacitates the senses of any creature or individual within 10 meters and not taken preemptive cover against the effects. Anyone not wearing relic combat armor, bomb squad armor, any powered shell class armor or other advanced relic suit, with the helmet from any of these relic armors, takes 3d6 stun damage and is also knocked off balance, requiring 4+1d6 rounds to recover. During this time, off balance living creatures are +20 SV easier to strike, and must make a kilogram based type D hazard check to be knocked completely prone and suffer a -40 penalty to their SV and are +40 easier to strike at when targeted.

Any target without hearing protection has a 6 in 10 chance of going deaf for 1d6 rounds, while those not wearing some sort of light blocking lenses or goggles, have a 7 in 10 chance of losing their vision for 3+1d4 rounds (taking an additional 1d4+4 rounds to fully recover, at half penalties listed below). Those blinded are a further +40 easier to strike, and move at half speed, and make any attacks of their own at -40 SV.

Blinded animals and beasts are likely (75% chance) to become berserk upon partially regaining their senses, and forced to make a morale check or flee the scene of the blast, fighting at +10 SV, -20 DV, +2 Damage to reflect this frenzied state.

Furthermore, all those caught in the blast zone, not wearing the armor noted above with appropriate helmet, must make a willpower based Type C hazard check or be disorientated and miss their next 3 turns, unless actively attacked, in which case they snap out of it and can roll initiative and try to engage opponents in either ranged or melee combat.

**Chaff Grenade** *by James Butler*
These explosives burst out a cloud of metallic micro particles configured to confuse sensors and other electronic detection systems for 15+1d6 rounds as the silvery cloud hangs undispersed in a standard interior semi-ventilated environment for 3d6 minutes. Contextual conditions will affect this time. During this period, any active cameras, motion detectors, and automated sights (including those on androids and robotic constructions) are rendered inert, any display or audio equipment erupting in a burst of static, with affected robots, cyborgs, and other automated constructions suffering penalties of -40 SV, and +40 DV (so, +40 SV easier for enemies to hit) when being targeted, due to being completely blind.

### MK2 Advanced Fragmentation Grenade

Similar to a regular advanced fragmentation grenade, although of more recent design and far more potent contents, these devices weigh 600g and can be sold to a relic dealer for 1000+5d100sp. They have a blast radius of 15m, which can affect up to 30 man sized beings if in a crowd or formation, SV 01-85, Damage 3d20+20. The blast is so tremendous that any ceiling, or adjacent wall, has a 66% chance of at least partially collapsing and all those in the blast radius are battered by 1d3 chunks of material as separate attacks at SV 01-60, damage 1d20 stun each.

### MK3 Advanced Fragmentation Grenade

While about the same sizes as a regular or MK2 frag grenade, these 700g explosives are often marked with a red and lime green caution strip and multiple warnings to take cover immediately after throwing the grenade to the enemy, since the blast radius is so huge that only the strongest of throwers can toss it far enough to get clear of the secondary blast radius.

The initial blast radius is 10m, afflicting up to 20 man sized beings if in a crowd or formation, with each 'attacked' at SV 01-90, and suffering 1d100+10 damage. The secondary blast radius goes out another 10 meters to 20 meters from the epicenter. Those caught here are shredded as if from a standard fragmentation grenade, SV 01-70, DMG 1d20+10. If this relic explodes inside a room, corridor, or the hull of a ship or other machine, it will bring down the ceiling 77% of the time, along with the walls, and rupture the floor. Such a detonation could cause a massive leak if within a waterborne vessel or hull breach in an orbital or other space craft — perhaps killing whoever threw the grenade. All those caught in an enclosed area when this goes off will be impacted by an additional 1d4 blast projectiles or falling pieces of ceiling, with each piece treated as an attack at SV 01-70 for 2d20 stun damage.

These extremely rare grenades will fetch 1000+2d1000sp if sold in a large town's relic market. They are never available for sale back to the public, being acquired by local overlords, instead.

**Foam Grenade** *by Thomas Vida & W. McAusland*
This relic releases a wide burst of a thick, foam-like substance after impact. While this relic was originally intended for fighting fires, excavators have found that the foam hardens quickly and so is useful for hindering the movement of

foes when thrown at or near their legs. Like most grenades, this device can be thrown twenty meters and on contact with the ground or target, erupts in a plume of pink foam and covers a 2 meters radius — which is usually enough to potentially trap a large, humanoid target.

The target's armor does not contribute to it defense value, however any agility or dodge skill modifiers do. The foam has a strike value of 01-76 and those 'hit' are splashed in a sufficient quantity to limit the use of their limbs or other body part, requiring a Type C strength based hazard check to escape from the first turn if hit. Failure to break free on the first round means the subject is further restrained as the foam hardens, and on their next round, they must make a type D STR based HC. If unable to get out of the ever-hardening foam after this, their third attempt requires a type E STR based hazard check. On the 4th round, and thereafter each round they attempt to break free for the next 10+3d6 minutes (20 rounds in a minute), a Type F strength based hazard check is needed to bust out of the clinging foam.

If only a person's legs are trapped, the victim can use hand held weapons to hack, smash or rip away the foam. So too, allies can attempt to chop away the foam and free the stuck person, too. All attacks made against the foam are considered automatic hits, with the foam having a defense value of zero, but and endurance of 120. Any critical hit roll punctures through a point in the foam and so impacts the trapped person, although a regular strike roll must be made on the trapped target beneath to inflict normal damage.

After the foam's 10+3d6 minutes of duration is up, this substance flakes and turn to a sand-like grit and falls away over the next 1d6 minutes. During these minutes of deterioration, the hazard check letter code to break free is reduced by 1 letter code per minute (F becomes E, E becomes D, etc.). These grenades weigh 620g and can earn the seller 700+2d100sp.

Anyone trapped in this pink foam suffers a different consequence based on  the body area entrapped. Roll 1d10 after a foam grenade successfully hits a target. The details shown for each location only take effect if the person cannot break free using their strength, as noted above (Type C STR).

**Foam Grenade Hit Location Roll 1d10**

**1. Head and shoulders:** The foam locks up both arms, blinds and deafens the subject and only by blowing, spitting and clawing at its mouth area as this substance hardens can this victim breath. Besides losing use of arms or front legs if a quadruped, this target is blind and +40 SV easier to hit, and makes any attacks at -40 SV itself. It also moves half.

**2-5. Legs:** target's legs ensnared and glued to the ground about it. It cannot move, cannot use the dodge skill or agility trait to contribute to defense value.

**6-8. Arm:** roll 1d10 1-5. right arm / 6-10. left arm: The target cannot wield anything held in that arm's hand. If the target was using a two-handed weapon, then either the foregrip or butt-stock — depending on what the character's dominant hand was, is stuck fast in the foam and makes aiming very difficult, causing -30 SV. The non-stuck arm could draw a one handed weapon, however, although a -20 SV penalty is incurred for use of the non-dominant hand.

**9. Torso:** The foam wraps about the target's abdomen and chest and will adhere the person or beast to any wall, furniture, fixture or other creature it is leaning against, but also encase this person in a ring of foam about a half meter thick. The subject can't access any weapons or gear on its waist, back or chest, but can move at -50% speed, and make use of its head and arms, although the latter suffer a -20 SV penalty because of the burden.

**10. Whole body coverage:** Combine all the above. This victim is hopelessly encased in foam and only able to talk and breathe while locked in the pinks substance.

### Incendiary Grenade

This orb is like a fragmentation grenade (SV 01-70, DMG 1d20+10, 5m blast radius), however besides the explosion affect, the blast area is sprayed with napalm-like, burning liquid. All combustibles in the burst radius automatically catch fire. Vehicles, robots and living beings are potentially caught on fire if

struck: SV 01-70 (rolled as a separate attack on the 2nd round after detonation), burning for 2d6 rounds each (rolled separately per target or object) and suffering 1d6 damage per round. Intelligent beings can spend one round doing nothing but extinguishing the flames by dousing themselves in water, rolling, or suffocating the flames with sheets, etc. 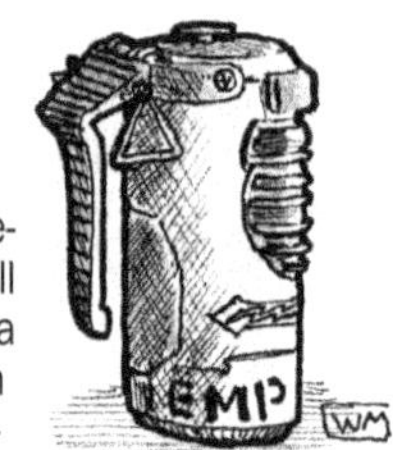

These grenades typically have a dark red top and plenty of flammable warning symbols on them. They weigh 575g and can be sold for 600+3d100sp. In some communities, especially those made of wood, these are banned and must be turned in to the authorities upon entry, with no guarantee of their return when the owner leaves town.

### EM Pulse Grenade

The blast from this grenade is more of a loud pop and flash of light, which for non-augmented, living beings, will give them a scare but little else. For any being or device with digital components, however, this could spell their doom. When detonated, this grenade shoots out a flash of purple light and electromagnetic pulse in a 10m radius, which inflicts 1d100 circuit scrambling temporary damage.

All electronic using vehicles, robots, structural elements such as doors and auto turrets, as well as implant parts on cyborgs and mutorgs are affected. This EMP Stun damage heals at 10 points per round, starting after 20+d20 minutes.

Worse, there is a further chance that the EMP actually switches off anything with electronics caught in the blast field, besides the automatic 1d100 stun damage noted above. This includes radios, comms, digital rifle scopes, motors of gyrocopters, cybernetic eyes, cybernetic limbs and other implants, as well as potentially knocks out mechanical beings. For gear and vehicles, there is a 1 in 10 chance of a shutdown that will keep the device off-line for 3d6 minutes, while for metallic, digitally controlled beings such as robots, androids, cyborgs, vat-brains and a digital being's 'body', they are allowed a willpower based type D hazard check to avoid being switched off for 3d6 minutes, too.

Some lucky mechanical or cybernetically enhanced beings have the implant 'Electro Shock Suppressor' or other EMP defense measures, which partially or fully ward off EMP attacks, including pulses from these grenades. These rare, metallic purple colored grenades weigh 450g and can earn as much as 850+1d1000sp if sold to a knowledgeable relic dealer. Less educated buyers might not be aware of their power or purpose and only offer 200+1d100 silver pieces.

### Electro-grenade

Also called a lightning bomb, these frag sized grenades can come as hand thrown orbs or with a standard plastic grenade launching butt-case. Either way, when their pin is pulled or they are fired from a grenade launcher, their impact within the target area causes a brilliant blue flash. All those within the immediate 3 meter radius are potentially scorched by a multitude of lighting bolts; treat as two attacks at SV 01-80 for 1d20 damage each. For targets caught within the wider blast zone, from 3m out to 6m radius, are attacked just once with the same SV and DMG. If detonated on flammable substances, such as a wood floor or grass, there is a 77% chance that multiple small fires will erupt in the blast area.

These grenades weigh 550g and can be sold for 600+3d100sp.

### Magnetic Explosive Module [MEM]

This explosive is twice as large as a grenade and has a wide bottom disc which features a peel off layer of glue and half dozen powerful magnets. With one or both adhesions applied to a surface, the charge can be stuck to a structure, door, vehicle, robot or large creature. The module contains a high explosive charge and top cap with a simple timer dial that can allow the detonation time to be set from 'immediate' or between 1 and 60 minutes. An inner dial within the main timer ring allows longer time delays from 1 to 48 hours. 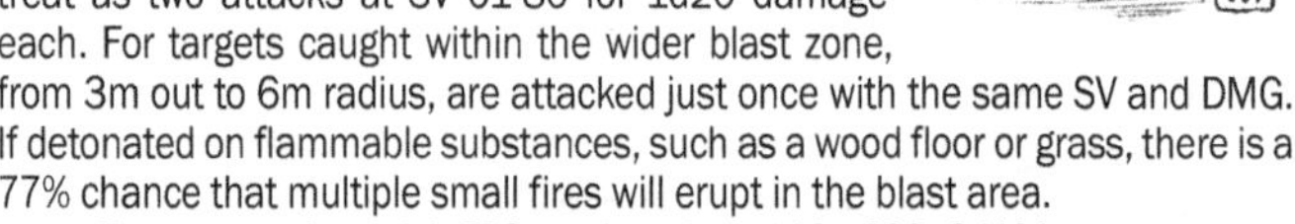

By setting the dials for the hour, with 0 hour option included, and then the minutes, a range of from zero to 49 hour delay can be timed. The setting for zero is to facilitate suicide operations for personnel wishing to avoid capture by enemy forces.

A MEM's explosion has a close-in, expanded, and outlying blast radius. The close-in radius is from 0 to 6 meters, SV 01-80, inflicting 2d100 damage. The expanded blast radius, from beyond 6 meters to 18 meters, has a strike value of 01-60 and inflicts 1d100 damage. Outlying areas of the blast, from beyond 18m out to 40 meters, has a strike value of 01-40 and inflicts 1d12 damage. Anything flammable within this area, such as grass, fur, feathers, dry bones, wood, fuel drums, plastic or the fuel tanks of junk crafted vehicles, are all 77% likely to ignite, adding to the devastation.

Fortunately, these very advanced, extremely potent devices were mostly consumed during the ancient wars, yet stockpiles and the occasional solitary unit still turn up in barter towns and inventories of warlords, Mecha operatives and the arsenals of high ranking dig teams. Each weighs 3kg and if a person is forced to sell one, these heavy, heart sized relics will earn 3l000+1d1000sp.

## Micro-Tactical-Nuke *by James Butler*

As dangerous and feared as expected from a rocket head that has been cracked open and modified to contain a tiny flake of radioactive material. These units have a range of between 2 and 18 km (dependent upon the original unmodified unit specs) and are designed to heavily irradiate a compact area, roughly 50 meters in radius, with a half-life of 1d3+1 years, to render risky areas of terrain being used for guerrilla warfare uninhabitable. Any creature caught within the initial blast zone immediately suffers 3d20+20 burning damage, followed by a dosage of Strong level radiation (as outlined on pg.125 of TME Hub Rules), which incrementally lessens in severity moving away from ground zero: beyond 50 meters to 100 meters 1 dose medium radiation, 101 to 300m 1 dose of mild radiation exposure.

These dirty weapons are portable catastrophes, but are mercifully extremely rare, and the use of these missiles is heavily stigmatized and punished by most communities. These modified weapons are normally fitted to battle rockets, assault missiles and tactical missiles, all included in the hub rules on pages TME 198-197. They are almost never accepted by relic dealers, unless the buyer purchases the rocket or missile without knowing about its radioactive components.

## Nuclear Grenade

This metallic blue cased, fist sized grenade has a standard pull pin and a rotary timer that can have the explosive detonate as soon as it a grip is released, or if fired from a grenade launcher — which is the preferred method because of the large blast radius — or the timer can be set for any amount of time up to and including 1 hour.

When detonating, a small 50 meter tall mushroom cloud rises from the crater where this incredibly rare and powerful explosive just went off. The blast radius has 3 rings of devastation:

**Ring 1** is ground zero and encompasses a 5 meter radius. Here, all beings and objects are attacked 3 times at SV 01-92 and if struck, take 1d100 damage per hit plus an automatic medium dose of radiation. Any flammable substances including hair, fur and cloth ing are incinerated, all non metallic objects catch on fire, and any explosives carried by any victims in this blast radius also detonate and add to the blast.

**Ring 2** extends from beyond 6 meters out to 12 meters. Each object and being here is attacked twice at SV 01-80 for 2d20 damage and, if struck, automatically take a dose of mild radiation. In addition, all in this area must make a weight based type H hazard check (using the subject's kilograms as a stat on the hazard check table) or be thrown 3d6 meters away and suffer 1d100 stun damage.

**Ring 3** extends from beyond 12 meters out to 24 meters. Here, each being and object is attacked once at SV 01-70 for 1d20 damage, with those hit allowed a type B endurance based hazard check to avoid a dose of mild radiation exposure. The shock wave forces any being of less than 100kg weight to make a kilogram based Type C hazard check or be thrown back 2d6 meters and suffer 1d20 stun damage.

Following the blast, the 12m circumference crater will emanate medium radiation for the next 3d6 months, and thereafter, mild radiation for 3d6 years.

# Fireworks *by James Butler*

Of the many types of explosive material available in our day and age, fireworks are by far the most accessible. Inexpensive, numerous, and a great source of entertainment — for who doesn't like blowing things up with a colorful cascade of visual delight? Many forget they are still explosives and present many dangers to those who do not take the utmost care in their handling. With proper consideration and planning, these cheap little devices can provide wondrous displays. And it is both factors taken together that make them such booming additions to The Mutant Epoch.

Although the vast majority of devices found will be relics, those with a love of pyrotechnics may be well-served by a specialized offshoot of either the Chemical Technician or Demolitions Expert skill, who can potentially craft interesting effects with such devices, given the right ingredients are available to them. Suggested effects may be changed accordingly for homemade fireworks. The following additional abilities to the core skill are suggested:

## Table XR-251 / Fireworks Creation Tier Chart

| Skill Points | Fireworks a Chem-Tech or Demo Expert Can Make |
|---|---|
| 1 | Precise fuse and burn times - chemical compounds used to show rough time left, either by flame or smoke color, Sparklers |
| 2 | Fountains and Firecrackers |
| 3 | Screechers and Catherine Wheels |
| 4 | Rockets |
| 5 | Multi-Shot Mortars |

## Table XR-252 / Random Fireworks Color   Roll 1d10

1. Magenta
2. Purple
3. Blue
4. Green
5. Gold
6. White
7. Red
8. Orange
9. Roll twice, color changes halfway through.
10. Multiple colors present and overlaid, roll thrice.

**1.** Spinner

**2.** Comet

**3.** Peony

**4.** Fish

**5.** Crossette

**6.** Chrysanthemum with large Pistil

**7.** Bees

**8.** Palm

**9.** Willow

**10.** Long-tailed

**1.** Blister pack of indoor fireworks — all useless parlor tricks and minuscule novelties. 12+1d12sp.

**2.** Cheap selection box. 1d2 rockets and 1d4+1 fountains/catherine wheels remain usable (but at half strength or effect time, 50% of either), taper and rest have been rendered inert by damp. Value 400+1d100sp.

**3.** Pack of sparklers (12) with plastic novelty lighter that emits a colored flame. 240+2d100sp. Lighter good for 100 uses.

**4.** Opened bag with a single firecracker string (12+1d12 firecrackers), with fake severed finger. 50+2d20sp per firecracker.

**5.** Pack of cheap rockets and screechers (1d3 apiece), with taper.

**6.** Expensive selection box (1d3+1 rockets, 1d2 screechers, 6+1d4 fountains, 1d2 catherine wheels, and a small 8-shot mortar, complete with taper and lighter.

**7.** Pack of firecracker strings (1d4+2, 24 firecrackers per string).

**8.** A single mortar unit, packing 10+1d12 shots.

**9.** Pack of expensive rockets (1d6+4), with a taper.

**10.** Half-barrel of powerful display-grade USA-themed rockets (10+2d6) — all burst in red, white, and blue.

**11.** A display device that uses a power pill and contains a timer (up to 5 minutes) for each slot, each of which can be freely aimed in any direction, and is fitted with six rockets. 4.8kg, Value 1000+3d100sp.

**12.** A huge single display finale mortar, single fuse, emits 20 mortar shots, mixed with 6+1d6 screechers, 6+1d6 rockets, and 2+1d4 fountains of various types. Lasts 3 minutes.

## Specific Firework Types

Although the attention grabbing effects are a general attribute to all pyrotechnic devices, some make a bigger bang than others — literally — and this is especially so within the world of The Mutant Epoch. Creatures of all size and ferocity have come to truly fear both fire and surprising events, and will react accordingly, although whether they become aggressive or try to flee from the source is left to individual GM determination.

Detailed below are the characteristics of seven incendiary subsets, each bursting with their own applications and potential effects. Each type's Distractive Range value equals the radius of the spectacle that may catch the attention of those not expecting an explosive cavalcade, and is calculated assuming unimpaired vision on clear terrain — modifiers should of course be applied to take any restrictions and hindrances into account. Visual effects will, of course, lose some of their potency when viewed in bright light, which is represented by a reduced secondary value.

## Universal Firework Effects On Initiative

Pick whichever initiative modifier best suits the viewer's circumstances

- Caught by surprise within 5 meters: -2 (-1 increased per additional firework within range, up to -5 initiative)
- Caught by surprise within Distractive Range: -1 (-1 extra per additional firework within range, up to -3 initiative)
- Caught by surprise and afraid of fire/explosions: -3 (-1 added per additional firework within range, up to -6 initiative)

The shown range is the distance the firework travels after launch before it detonates, and thereupon bursts and causes the distractive range. An indicator of n/a means the firework is fixed, and either attached to a solid object or stabilized into the ground.

The Burn / Effect time listed for each firework represents two stages in a firework's short, brilliant life. The burn is the time it takes after the fuse is lit until the firework goes off, and includes the time of travel to the elevation for projectile type fireworks. The Effect time is how long the firework burns or lights up the sky for. While lit, those caught by surprise or seeing the firework within the distractive range radius suffer a loss to initiative, while those who set off the fireworks and were ready for the show do not suffer this penalty to initiative. The Sell Price shown for each sort of firework is for a relic variant.

### Sparklers

Distractive Range: **5 meters**
Range: **n/a**
Burn / Effect time: **Instant / 10+1d10 rounds**
SV: **n/a**   Damage: **50% chance of a single point of damage per round**
Weight: 10g   Sell Price: 20+1d12sp

A very simple unit, consisting of a length of sturdy wire coated in a reactive substance that burns down in an intensely bright, hissing reaction. When held in the hand, they can be easily moved about without fear of being extinguished by either wind or cold. If pressed and held against the flesh a minor, yet painful, burn will result in 1d4 damage, with a small chance (10%) of ignition if a susceptible area has been touched (such as fur, oil soaked clothing, etc.).

### Firecrackers

Distractive Range: **7 meters** (visual) / **4m** (daytime); **16m feet** (audio)
Range: **n/a**
Burn / Effect time: **5 rounds / 20+1d6 rounds**
SV: **01-45**   Damage: **1d2 per round** (4 rounds).
Weight: **25g**   Sell Price: **50+2d20sp**

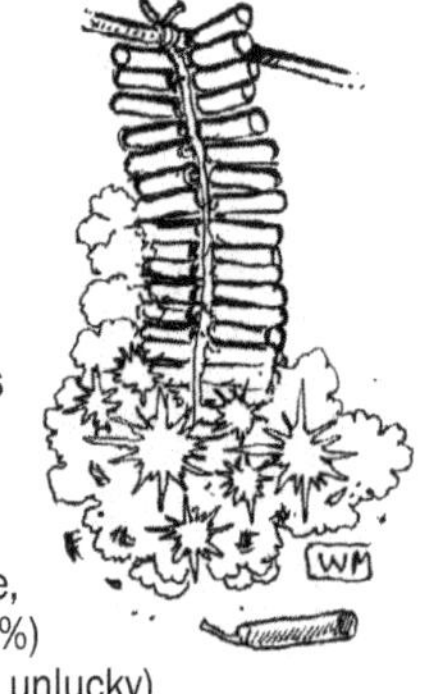

An old school classic, these units consist of dozens of separate small explosives linked by a single fuse, which create a chaotic fusillade, jumping about erratically amidst the ensuing cracks, flashes, and smoke. Due to the powerful concentrations of each charge, these fireworks have an increased likelihood (72%) of blowing 1d3 digits off any creature foolish (read: unlucky) enough to be caught in its path with unprotected extremities.

### Fountains

Distractive **Range: 14 meters** (visual and audio)
Range: **3 meters**
Burn / Effect time: **5 rounds / 10+1d20 rounds**
SV: **01-45**   Damage: **1d3 per round of contact.**
Blindness is covered on page TME-122 but in short, reduces the blind creature's movement to half and makes them +40 SV easier to strike while they themselves suffer a -40 to their strike value. The blindness from a fountain lasts 3d6 rounds.
Weight: **1.4kg**   Sell Price: **200+1d100sp**
These fireworks are static units, with a sturdy(ish) base typically built into their form, that spew forth a raging torrent of sparks that cascade around it on all sides, as implied by their name. Should any creature be caught directly in its line of fire, there is a very high chance (85%) of being dazzled/blinded besides potentially taking fire damage.

## Catherine Wheels

Distractive Range: 15 meters (visual and audio)
Range: 3 meters immediately below unit.
Burn / Effect time: 5 rounds / 20+1d10 rounds
SV: n/a    Damage: **1d3 per round of contact**
Weight: **2.6kg**    Sell Price: **350+1d100sp**

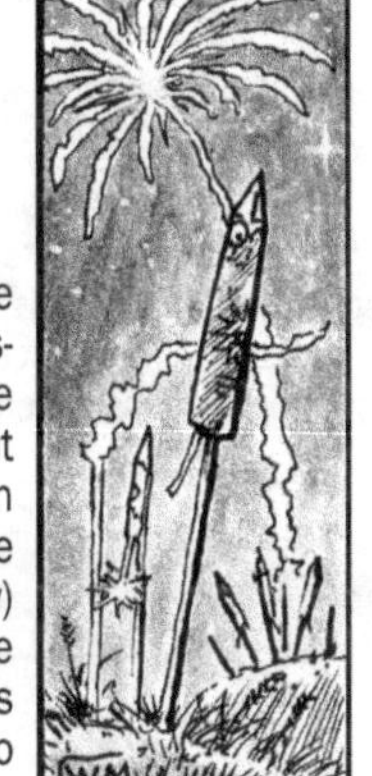

Typically serving as a sideline distractions, these units whirl around an anchor point, creating a thick shower of sparks that rains down in the space 3 meters immediately below. Because of the density of the effects, this presents a high chance (72%) of setting vulnerable hair/fur/clothes alight to those caught in the torrent.

## Rockets

Distractive Range: **50 meters / 15 meters visual** (daytime)
Range: **12+1d12 meters**
Burn / Effect time: **5+3d6 rounds / 3 rounds**
SV: 01-60    Damage: **1d12**
Weight: **1.8kg**    Sell Price: **400+1d100sp**

The quintessential and archetypal firework, the humble rocket, that shoots forth and explodes in a riotous display of pyrotechnic glory. As weaponry, these units are unwieldy, and their flight path can be rather erratic, but provide a powerful explosion 5 meters in diameter, upon reaching their designated range (which may or may not be noted on the unit itself). These devices are not (usually) pressure sensitive, and so will travel this distance before exploding, so if any surface (or creature) is struck during its flight, rockets will bounce off within a 180-degree arc (also re-determine the verticality randomly).

Anything caught within the 5m blast effect radius suffers a high chance of being either set alight (55%), being temporarily blinded (78% for 3d6 rounds), or both.

## Screechers

Distractive Range: **60 meters** (audio)
Range: **10+1d6 meters**
Burn / Effect time: **3+1d6 rounds / 2 rounds**
SV: 01-55    Damage: **2d4 (striking force) + 1d3 DMG** (explosion).
Weight: **1.7kg**    Sell Price: **430+1d100sp**

A variant of rockets, these units launch with an ear-piercing scream that culminates either in a tiny explosive effect, or just dissipates into nothing (leaving no evidence of what it was). The primary use of these fireworks is as a noisy distraction, but given the energy being spent on propelling the unit (rather than spent providing an impressive explosion). Screechers can slam into opponents with a good degree of force, potentially knocking them back 1d3 meters, determined by making a hazard check against the character/creature's strength value. As they are more focused than rockets, these units may strike only a single target, followed by a small 3 meter diameter burst.

## Multi-Shot Mortars

Distractive Range: **100 meters** (visual and audio)
Range: **37 meters**
Burn / Effect time: **8 rounds / 1+1d3 rounds per blast**
SV: 01-60    Damage: **3d4 within 5m explosive radius.**
Weight: **4.8kg**    Sell Price: **100+1d100sp** per charge (6+1d6)

Big and booming, these consist either of a square comprised of a number of tightly packed tubes or a single long tube. When ignited consecutively from a single fuse, these create a bombardment of 6+1d6 flare-like charges which light up the entire area around the firework unit every two rounds. This naturally presents a very effective means of ruining the night vision of a great number of viewers within the visual range. Each shot erupts in a 5 meter burst, so can potentially strike up to three man-sized targets per blast.

## Dangers of Fireworks

### Safety Warnings

As noted previously in the special effects, fireworks present two specific types of critical hit that are likely to occur through their use, detailed below. Any firework blast that directly strikes an individual/creature in a vulnerable area (typically the face, or bare feet) may, GM's choice, result in the following critical effects, but some have a much higher rate of causing a certain type, as noted in the description.

**Blown off digit(s):** Severe pain, but no significant disruption to skills if one or two fingers are lost. A third, or a thumb (20% chance) reduce all finesse-based skills by -20 points when making hazard checks with some delicate or technical skill. Claw-based damage is reduced accordingly, and movement is reduced by -0.5 meters if any toes are lost. Can be reattached via surgical means.

**Set ablaze:** The intense force and concentration of sparks gushed forth by fireworks can singe combustible material so that they are set alight; and hair or fur presents a particularly vulnerable source of danger. Scaling damage is caused to any such victim, from 1 point, to 1d2, to 1d3, to 1d4 damage per round until the smoldering flames are extinguished.

**Blinded by sparks:** A sudden burst of bright pyrotechnics right in front of a creature can dazzle it, even if expected. This results in a temporary SV penalty of -40 and +40 to the SV of being struck, and half movement for 3d6 rounds; this duration is doubled if caught at night or any place in where onlookers have adapted to low light conditions.

A note must be made on the potential threat value of labels on commercial fireworks, which are tantalizingly impressive, setting the imagination ablaze with explosive semantics — even if the effects don't quite live up to expectations set — clearly emblazoned across each unit in an eye-catching marketable manner. Some examples of names are: Napalm Rain, Demon's Fire, Hell Raiser, Flamestorm, Screaming Demon, and T.(urbo) N.(uclear) T.(hunder). Be inventive along these themes. Think: what sounds awe-inspiring. Because these fantastic labels are often colorfully distinguishable, many sentient individuals unwary of advertisement rhetoric may be fooled into over-estimating the power of the units, especially given the similarities in the shape of many fireworks with sticks of dynamite.

One not-insignificant aspect related to these devices that is extremely easy to overlook is the need for a convenient source of lighting them. Matches and lighters work just fine, but if a few units are to be set off within a short space of time, these precious resources can be quickly wasted. Many sets include a taper of slow burning material that lasts for between 20-30 minutes after being lit, is reusable, and has the advantage of carrying an ember rather than a full open flame. In short, be sure to carry adequate means for lighting fireworks.

One final note of caution should be made regarding the consequences of incinerating a batch of fireworks, whether knowingly or accidentally. Such an act presents a highly dangerous situation, with an increased likelihood of critical damage for those in the immediate vicinity of the fire (unsuspecting and unprepared for such an event — with each unit (even those thought to be rendered inert due to damp — albeit in a reduced capacity) being set off, with their effects directed randomly.

Multiple shot units should have each charge determined separately, as the firework rotates randomly with each blast, due to the energy exerted, and not being anchored securely in the ground. Catherine Wheels are likely to burst out and encircle those standing nearby, fountains of sparks will shower out of the flames, and rockets will cross each other's path, all in a crackling cacophony of chaos.

# Relic Armor Set 2

## Table XR-255 / Expanded Relic Armor & Helmets

| Armor Type | Defense Value | Movement | Weight | Cost | Notes | Page |
|---|---|---|---|---|---|---|
| Resin Armor | -14 | -0.5m | 5kg | 80+1d20sp | Won't sink/ Flammable add +2 damage per round and add +2 rounds of burning to wearer. | 428 |
| Tire Armor | -15 | -0.5m | 9kg | 50+2d20sp | -5 DMG from falls/ Flammable: add 1d3 rounds burn time and +1 DMG per round. | 428 |
| Rug Armor | -13 | -0.25m | 4.5kg | 30+1d20sp | +1 Conceal Self or Concealed Movement (stealth skill)/ flammable: burn 1d6 extra rounds at +2 DMG per round. | 428 |
| Fiber Skin Suit, Green | -10 | nil | 1kg | 500+3d100sp | None | 429 |
| Fiber Skin Suit, Blue | -15 | -0.25m | 2kg | 900+1d1000sp | Fire Resistant, wearer takes half damage from heat and flame attacks | 429 |
| Fiber Skin Suit, Red | -20 | -0.25m | 4kg | 2400+2d1000sp | Fire resistant identical to blue suit, above, plus adjusts wearer's body temperature to keep them warm in cold climes or frigid water, and so this wearer takes only 10% damage from cold. Additionally, this suit has a laser reflectivity coating, all laser strikes on this suit, including by stun beam weapons and mutations, do only half damage. | 429 |
| Torso Plate MK I | -16 | -0.25m | 5kg | 500+1d1000sp | - | 427 |
| Torso Plate MK II | -19 | -0.25m | 6kg | 800+1d1000sp | - | 427 |
| Torso Plate MK III | -22 | -0.5m | 8kg | 1400+1d1000sp | - | 427 |
| Battle Shell | -60 | +6 | 510kg | 35k+4d1000sp | Weapon systems/ Flotation/ while running, has a 20pt force field per round | 429 |
| Deep Sea Dive Suit | -35 | max 4 on land/ swim 8m/ 4m bottom walk | 190kg | 22k+3d1000sp | See Description, page 430. | 430 |
| Light Combat Armor | -25 | -0.5m / -0.25m adjusted | 4.5kg | 1700+1d1000sp | Movement can be adjusted to a 0.25m move rate following an INT based type A HC. Infiltrator suit and Aquatic Combat Armor are variants of LCA. | 430 |
| Advanced Metal Weave | -20 | -nil | 2.5kg | 2600+2d1000sp | - | 431 |
| Exo-Armor | -35 | -0.5m | 48kg | 2900+3d1000sp | +20 strength/ Runs on 1 power cell per week, useless without power. | 431 |
| Crisis Deployment Armor | -40 | -2m | 33kg | 4500+1d1000sp | Survival pack/ Flotation device (fickle, see description) | 431 |

| Helmet Type | Defense Value | Movement | Weight | Cost | Notes | Page |
|---|---|---|---|---|---|---|
| Resin Helmet | -4 | -0.25m | 1kg | 18+1d20sp | - | 427 |
| Welding Mask | -5 | -0.5m | 2.5kg | 400+d100 sp | Reduces visibility, -10 to missile SV, face shield, vision protector | 427 |
| Motorcycle Helmet | -5 | -0.25m | 1.5kg | 200+1d100sp* | Flip up tinted face shield, -1 initiate due to hearing loss from sides and back. 3 in 10 come with headset communicator. | 427 |
| Fireman's Helmet | -4 | -0.25m | 1.8kg | 400+3d100sp* | Dual headlight flashlights and a 4 in 10 chance of a headset communicator | 427 |
| Crisis Deployment | -10 | -0.5m | 3.9kg | 600+4d100sp | Gas mask (1 hour air supply/ advanced communicator /night vision headset | 427 |

*Triple this amount if a headset communicator is built into the helmet.

| Shield Type | Defense Value | Movement | Weight | Cost | Notes | Page |
|---|---|---|---|---|---|---|
| Energy Buckler | -30** | nil | 1.3kg | 2500+1d1000sp | Uses 1 standard power cell for 100 minutes active time (20 rounds in a minute). Edge smack +6 SV for 1d20 stun damage. | 429 |

** This shield has a fixed -30 defense value against all incoming attacks from the sides and front. If any attack gets through this shield, another attack is rolled during the same round against the user's main DV without the -30 of this energy buckler. This shield can be used to bash opponents at +6 SV for 1d20 stun damage

# Expanded Armor Descriptions

## Resin Helmet

Made from durable relic fibers and resin over a wire base structure, they include a chin strap, and inner leather or polyester padded interior sheath. They are made to look like ancient army helmets of one style or another, and painted black, green or dark blue. On closer inspection, the viewer can see that its surface is bumpy, ridged and uneven and that this is a poor copy. Still, they are lightweight and offer splendid protection. They are most often used by hard pressed communities of bunker dwellers, warmorts, skullocks and other inhabits of deep places with access to ancient chemicals and Fiberglas. These helmets offer -4 DV bonus, a -0.25m movement penalty, weight a kilogram and will sell for 18+1d20 silver pieces.

## Welding Mask *by James Butler*

Bearing a darkly tinted visor, this well-padded headgear is essential to preventing retina burn and other eye damage while undertaking welding projects of any type. They are large bulky items, but offer complete protection to the head and neck of the wearer. When set to full operational mode a bonus +35 trait bonus* is provided on hazard checks against blinding light-based attacks, startling flares, and similar situations, but this state also incurs a -10 SV penalty when making ranged attacks as vision is extremely limited. Even when the shaded filter is not in place, the clear tinted polyglass offers a small degree of protection affording a +5 trait bonus* to relevant hazard checks.

**The trait bonus is sometimes agility, but could be willpower, or a combined trait depending on the adventure scenario or light based peril.*

## Motorcycle Helmet

Designed to endure incredible blunt force impacts, this streamlined composite helmet is both lightweight and durable. With a flip up tinted face shield, this relic is a favorite of post-apocalyptic warriors, especially those involved in melee combat or who want to hide their identity during an attack. There are a couple of drawbacks to this headgear, however. The wearer's hearing is muffled, causing a -1 initiative penalty from any approaching adversary from the back or side, but not the front. Secondly, this helmet's visor also interferes with the use of any rifle scope while the visor is down and locked into full coverage position whereby the shooter suffers a -5 SV penalty. On the plus side, When locked in place, this visor will protect the wearer's eyes from thrown sand, dust, spit, bright flashes of light, sprayed liquids and the like, and because the mouth and nose are also encased in the poly carbonate visor, the wearer can better endure junk and sand storms.

These helmets weigh 1.5 kilograms. 3 in 10 motorcycle helmets are found with an operational headset communicator built into them, with their battery back in a compartment at the back.

## Fireman's Helmet

The modern 23rd century fireman's helmet is a wonder, and besides offering excellent protection from all manner of incoming attack, are also equipped with a pull down face shield and twin headlamps with one light on each side of the wearer's head. 4 in 10 of these helmets are also found with a communicator headset with pull down mic boom and earphone flaps. In addition, 6 in 10 come with a radiation sensor tab built in at the chin strap, which can be clipped up by the wearer's face when radiation levels need to be checked. The headlamps are described on page TME-201, headset communicator on page TME-198, and the rad tab on page 432 of this book. These helmets are usually colored bright yellow with light reflective strips and assorted fire station markings — all of which will require painting over or covering in camo fabric to better conceal the wearer in an unforgiving post-apocalyptic wasteland.

## Crisis Deployment Helmet *by Stu Brooks*

This fully enclosed, angular helmet is specifically designed to be worn with the advanced, non-powered polymer and Kevlar armor by the same name. It has a -10 DV, and comes with a built-in gas mask, a 1 hour air supply. and an attachment point for an external air tank. Also included are an advanced communicator (pg. TME-198) and night vision headset equivalent optic (pg.TME-201). These helmets weigh 3.9kg and will sell for 600+4d100sp.

## Torso Plates

Torso plates were worn as light armor, and an advancement on the commonly used ballistic vests that proceeded them. These units are similar to iron breastplate or cuirass, but made of far more durable, lightweight and corrosion resistant composite materials. They can be worn over one's regular clothing, as well as leather, rug, tire, or resin armors, or in conjunction with junk, scrap relic and other light armors, but do not fit over tactical armor, ballistic vests, riot armor, combat armor or any powered armors.

The various versions, MK I, MK II and MK III, reflect the thickness, material advancement, and quality of the various torso plates. Each plate will either be painted or manufactured in a resin pigment and sometimes have markings on them according to the two following tables. The stats for these plates are shown on Table XR-255 Expanded Relic Armor & Helmets on page 426.

### Plate Color  Roll 1d20

**1.** High visibility orange and yellow stripes
**2-4.** Desert digit camo
**5,6.** Urban grayscale digi-camo
**7,8.** Woodland digi-camo
**9,10.** Olive drab
**11,12.** Tan
**13.** Light gray
**14.** Dark gray
**15,16.** Dark blue
**17,18.** Black
**19.** Blood red
**20.** White

### Markings on Plate    Roll 1d100

**01-09.** None
**10-13.** Assorted, but scratched off and illegible
**14-48.** Police
**49-53.** SWAT
**54-56.** UN: United Nations Peacekeeper
**57-59.** FEMA: Federal Emergency Management Agency
**60.** RCMP: Royal Canadian Mounted Police
**61.** SAS: Special Air Service
**62,63.** FBI: Federal Bureau of Investigation
**64,65.** CIA: Central Intelligence Agency

## Resin Armor

This suit of hard plastic armor is a mix between old world relic armor and newly crafted wasteland wear. It is made from Fiberglas chop and other fibrous materials and plastic resins, often inside molds based on pieces of tactical or combat armor. The end product is a rough, uneven looking suit of durable, waterproof and resilient armor. Most times, each piece is individually wrapped in drab, earthy colored fabric, or rubbed with pitch and charcoal to blacken it. This armor is usually made by people who dwell within the confines of some ancient complex, including bunker dwellers, as they have access to the raw materials and perhaps a few examples of true tactical or combat armor to copy. Warmorts and other, more intelligent humanoids will also have access to this protection, either by making their own or looting it off the bodies of excavators and other humans.

This armor has a degree of buoyancy to it and neither helps the wearer stay afloat, nor contributes to them sinking — the swimming ability, armaments and other gear of the submerged wearer deciding on whether the person sinks or swims. Because this material is made of hardened chemicals and plastic, it tends to catch fire and if the wearer is lit up, add +2 to both the duration of any fire and the damage per round The average suit weighs 5 kilograms, gives the wearer -14 defense value, reduces movement by -0.5 meters per round and will sell for 80+1d20sp.

A resin helmet is also frequently worn by those clad in this armor, described on the previous page.

## Tire Armor

This bizarre suit is made from strips and swatches of relic vehicle tires arranged into a suit of armor. These outfits are low tech, durable, waterproof, but heavy and offer some protection from falls; reduce fall damage by -5 points. Besides making for acceptable light armor, these getups can also allow the wearer to blend into a trash littered setting, especially if wearing other junk crafted gear, a coat of dust, a few twigs and clumps of grass stuck into the seams and grooves. Unfortunately, tires are flammable, and if the wearer is hit by some sort of flame attack, he or she will burn for 1d3 rounds longer and suffer a +1 to burn damage each round they are aflame. A suit of tire armor offers -15 DV, reduces movement by 0.5 meters per round, weighs 9 kilograms and can be sold for 50+2d20 silver coins. Helmets made from tire are also available, but rare. If needed, treat as a junk helmet.

## Rug Armor

Just as the name implies, this suit is constructed from layers of old nylon carpet and underlay padding stitched and bolted together into a sort of banded armor. Its lightweight, silent, cheap, fairly flexible and strong, so too, if made from a patchwork of different rug colors, fiber lengths and patterns, and worn with crude gear, tufts of grass, weeds and branches and a liberal coating of oil stains and filth, this suit can serve as a ruin area camouflage suit. When used to hide in junk strewn areas, increase the wearer's conceal self and concealed movement skill by +1 tier (stealth skill on page 51 of the hub rules). The problem with this armor is that the plastic fibers of the carpeting, and foam underlay, are flammable. If the wearer is engulfed in flame or hit by a fire based attack, they will burn for an extra 1d6 rounds and suffer +2 damage per round while on fire. Carpet armor affords the wearer with -13 defense value, a modest -0.25 meters movement reduction, weighs only 4.5 kilograms, and will sell for 30+1d20 silver pieces. Normally a junk, tire, or resin helmet is worn with this getup.

## Energy Buckler

This hand held rod has a simple thumb engaged, flip open cap. Inside is a single red button that, when pushed, activates a translucent, gleaming shield 1 meter in diameter. Any attack from an opponent in the front 180 degree facing direction, which means any attacker from the front or to either side, must get passed this shield to cause harm to the holder. Basically, the shield has a separate defense value from the holder, with any strike getting through going on to make another, identical attack roll on the user. The energy buckler has a defense value of -30, and can operate for 100 minutes on a single, grip contained power cell.

A smack by the edge of this shield has an SV of +6 and inflicts 1d20 stun damage. This device offers no extra protection to the user from rear attacks, unless it is activated and attached to the user's backpack or held back with one hand while the user flees. This remarkable device is usually carried on a belt mounted holster, weighs only 1.3 kilograms, including the 500g of the power cell, and can be sold for 2500+1d1000 silver pieces.

## Fiber Skin Suit

This skin tight, stretchy, adult sized bodysuit and head hood is worn under clothing and armor and offers exceptional extra protection to the wearer. It was designed to fit a human body, and cannot be worn by those with distorted limbs, cybernetic parts and protrusions, or other non-standard features. Androids, at least those with the average human size limits, can also wear these remarkable outfits. The fabric is woven with a mix of ballistic cloth and fine alloy mesh, and comes with a zippered front and rear panels to facilitate lavatory visits without the need to strip out of these armored tights.

There are three variants of this suit, each of a different metallic color, thickness variation and degree of protection. Roll 1d10 when this relic is discovered.

| 1d10 | Fiber Skin Suit Color | DV | Movement Mod. | Weight | Sell Price | Special Feature |
|------|------|-----|------|--------|-----------|-----------------|
| 1-6. | Green | -10 | nil | 1kg | 500+3d100sp | 4 in 10 are striped, as shown above in dark and light greens. |
| 7-9. | Blue | -15 | -0.25m | 2kg | 900+1d1000sp | Fire Resistant, wearer takes half damage from heat and flame attacks |
| 10. | Red | -20 | -0.25m | 4kg | 2400+2d1000sp | Fire Resistant identical to blue suit, above, plus adjusts wearer's body temperature to keep them warm in cold climes or frigid water, and so this wearer takes only 10% damage from cold. Additionally, this suit has a laser reflectivity coating, all laser strikes on this suit, including by stun beam weapons and mutations, do only half damage. |

## Battle Shell

A considerable step up from the Attack Shell described in the hub rules, this unit has an impressive 20 point force field per round, provides +6 meters movement to the wearer and +70 strength. The wearer can deliver a punch or kick dealing 3d20 base damage, has two battery packs just like the Attack Shell, each yielding 72 hours of operation before recharge is needed. This suit can also have its solar collector deployed while walking or fighting, although doing so makes the operator vulnerable and suffer a +20 SV to be struck with the wearer enjoying no force field while the suit is charging. The wearer gains -60 DV, with this bulky suit weighing 510 kilograms and selling for 35 thousand +4d1000 silver pieces. It stands 2.5 meters tall and is 1.4 meters wide at the chest and 1.6m broad at shoulders and therefore is limited to where it can operate.

When the operator doesn't need to use the unit's arms, he or she can retract their own from the armored, hydraulic and servo motor powered sleeves into the inner cocoon-like cockpit to use their hands to work the keyboard, touch screen on the on-board laptop computer, and attend to bodily functions including eating and drinking, elimination of bodily waste into a 2 liter holding tank, and more. The interior area of this suit can hold ten days of food and water, medical supplies, and about 10 kilograms of personal arms and armor and other gear in storage compartments.

The on-board communications and computer systems are extraordinary, having an Identification Sequence Broadcaster* and a Beacon Locater Unit*, Proximity Detector System (PDS)*, Advanced Communicator, built-in Handheld Satellite Communications Unit [HSCU] (page 448 of this book), plus, a unique defense computer program called 'auto return fire', which, will arm the shoulder mounted twin pulse laser turret to automatically fire upon any and all threats which are attacking it, even if the wearer is asleep, unconscious, or not at first aware of who or what has attacked them. The turret's tracking system registers the source of incoming projectiles or melee blows and commences, firing immediately after the assault. This program can be switched off, but when active, it takes a very real blow or impact to set it off, not merely somebody bumping into the wearer in a crowd.

The Battle Shell is the most advanced armor ever created on a large scale and was specifically made to be operated by a human. Even though it cannot distinguish between a trans-human, bioreplica, or clone, it will scan any new user for mutations or mechanical beings (androids) who try to power up the armor. If an unauthorized humanoid attempts to access the armor, the back access panels will open to allow them to leave. Failure to exit after 1 minute will cause the armor to deliver an electric shock to the non-human, causing 1d10 stun damage per minute. Once the intruder leaves, the armor will then close up and go into hibernation for 3d6 hours before the suit will open again and allow another wearer to slip in.

A computer technician of 5 skill points could attempt to hack this human-centric preference code and is allowed one Type G intelligence based hazard check per 6 hours of effort to turn off the human only mode.

Another aspect of the on-board computer is that the primary computer can be manually unplugged and give over full control with power assist mode to the wearer — a feature that was thought to exist to override any attempted high-jack by a malicious digital being, hacker or rogue AI. Besides this override feature, this unit accommodated an allied digital being who is thought to have served as a co-pilot. Accordingly, this suit can house a digital being in the computer system, who can interact with the wearer from the screen or a holographic disc next to the keyboard, and appear as a 12cm tall persona of itself as desired. This digital being companion can keep watch while the wearer is asleep, or control one of the built-in weapon systems if given access by the suit's human wearer. A digital being cannot control the suit, however, at least not as far as making it move — although should a DB inhabit an android body, and this suit's human-only accessible systems are hacked and switched off, then a digital being could truly wear this suit.

The impressive weapon systems of a battle shell include the already stated twin pulse rifle turret on the left shoulder, a secondary 360 degree turret on the right

shoulder mounted with a rocket launcher box able to hold 20 battle rockets, with ten rockets armed, and another ten ready to slide into the launch tubes after the first ten are depleted, within 2 rounds. Bolted to the helmet is a stun pistol and a heavy laser carbine for long range precision shooting. On the left forearm is a laser sword, a fold out discsaw, plus a flame unit requiring 2L of alcohol fuel in the internal backpack tank (40 rounds of flame). On the right arm is a light laser cannon and a chain gun. The chain gun is normally belt fed, however accepts drum magazines. Only one weapon system can be selected and deployed by the wearer at any given round, although the occupant can also hold one or two handheld weapons in the enormous plated gloves and add one or more extra attacks with these while the dual pulse laser engages auto-return fire mode.

The final defense for this unit is an electric shock emitter, a handy feature should a huge beast grapple and hold the wearer, or multiple assailants attempt to tackle and pin down the shell. The charge uses a full hour of battery life, but on a strike, (SV 01-90 to all touching or being touched by the wearer), inflicts 2d20 damage and can be used repeatedly, with a 3 round energy build up required between emissions (thus a rate of one quarter).

This unit can be made to float or sink to a designated depth using internal ballast and water valves, although it has no aquatic propulsion system to aid the wearer's own swimming skill speed. If directed to sink, this suit will maintain pressure to 200 meters depth before it springs seal leaks and fills from the feet upward at a rate of 1cm per minute. If the wearer's height in centimeters is surpassed while they are submerged, they will drown. This suit can eject water from its external ballast tanks and ascend at a speed of 2 meters per round. Air supply tanks within the suit can keep the wearer alive for as long as the batteries last (each power pack provides 72 hours of operation when fully charged).

While heated and air conditioned, this suit was not designed to endure the vacuum of space, although will maintain sheath integrity for 3d6 minutes before it will begin to lose pressure and cause burns from absolute zero to inflict 1d6 damage per minute thereafter, for a maximum of 30+1d20 minutes before the suit ruptures and the living occupant is frozen solid and air supply evacuated into space.

**These three relics are all found in the hub rules on page 198.*

## Deep Sea Dive Suit *by Danny Seedhouse*

Superficially resembling shell class armor, these relic suits where built not for combat but to withstand the amazing pressure of the deep ocean up to depths of around 700 meters (2296 ft) while allowing as much underwater mobility as possible to preform repair, rescue, construction and scientific missions. Advancements in artificial muscle design that allowed for the development of shell class armor and cybernetic limb replacements, where applied to deep sea dive suits as the need and desire to expand underwater exploration and access resources increased.

Underwater, the suit has a swimming speed of 8 meters a round or the user can walk along the river or sea bottom at 4 meters speed. Although it takes a bit of practice to get used to steering the suit, there is no need for any sort of hazard check unless exposed to extreme current.

Built-in oxygen supplies can last up to 12 hours along with an emergency backup of 1 hour, while 1 in 6 suits come with an advanced filtration system that produces enough oxygen to expand use to indefinite or as long as the suit has power, with a 6 hour back-up tank for added safety. There is a built in waste

management system, water canteen and nutrient dispenser with enough food and water for 3 days. The helmet includes an advanced communicator, and suit pressure readouts warnings to alert the wearer if he or she is going beyond depth tolerances. Three built in spot lights — one on each shoulder and one on the head — provide adjustable light levels. Most (4 in 6) suits are found with an underwater welding torch and a cutting tool built into the right arm which functions like a disc saw in combat. All suits have one tool arm (see page 437 of equipment section) outfitted for underwater tasks such as welding and repair.

Physically, the suit provides a huge degree of protection ( -35 DV) and has an emergency self sealing system that can cope with punctures from small arms and keep the wearer dry and sealed. Any strike causing more than 30 endurance causes oxygen loss (3d10 minutes are lost before the hole is sealed). This armor enhances the wearer's strength to a minimum of 100, with a huge degree of touch sensitivity that allows delicate underwater work as well as compensating for immense water resistance. When on land, the wearer's speed is penalized by -6 meters with a minimum of 2 meters a round and a maximum of 4. Anyone wearing this armor loses all dodge DV bonuses when on land, although while underwater the suit is responsive enough to allow for 1/2 of the normal dodge DV bonus.

1 in 10 suits are the military versions that provide DV -40 with a targeting optics headset built into the face shield and have a built in harpoon gun system (SV +10 rate 2, damage 1d20+10, Range 50 meters) in the right arm, a spring spike in each arm, and an over the shoulder mini-torpedo launcher, treat as advanced battle rockets with a speed of 100 meters and a range of 5 km, the launcher hold 4 torpedoes.

## Light Combat Armor *by Danny Seedhouse*

Light Combat Armor (LCA) was built from advanced composites and ballistic weaves using smaller, thinner armor plates than used in regular combat armor. LRC was intended for use by vehicle crews, artillery crews, and paratroopers who needed a lighter, less restrictive form of armor that still offered protection from the dangers of battle. LCA was produced in all ranges of camouflage colors, from urban grays to jungle patterns.

LCA provides a DV bonus of -25 and a movement penalty of -0.25 meters after proper adjustments. To reduce movement restrictions, the LRC can be adjusted with great precision to an individuals body. This requires a Type A intelligence hazard check to do properly. Unadjusted LRC has a speed penalty of -0.5 meters. These suits of armor weigh 4.5kg and will sell for 1700+1d1000sp.

## Infiltrator Suit *by Danny Seedhouse*

This is a modified suit of light combat armor with advanced stealth technologies added for special forces troops. The systems found in the suit made it highly expensive, but it fit well with the idea of using state-of-the-art troops in small units to fight irregular wars, and for anti-terrorist operations. The armor incorporates an optical concealment generator system that is mechanically the same as the cybernetic version found in the hub rules on page 89, except that armor is used to house the system. All other stats are the same as regular LCA, except this unit will fetch 3000+2d1000sp if sold in a relic market.

## Aquatic Combat Armor *by Danny Seedhouse*

This variant of the light combat armor (LCA) has been modified to be used by military frogmen for underwater operations. It comes standard with a closed circuit rebreather that produces no bubbles and supplies 5 hours of oxygen. A fully enclosed helmet provides low light vision capabilities, communicator headset, a head mounted flashlight, compass and a 3 foot long snorkel to increase submersion time. The armor has been enhanced to provide controllable buoyancy to aid flotation like a life jacket if needed. Retractable swim fins are housed in each boot and can increase swim speed by 1 meter per round without impeding land movement. Nearly every aspect of this armor has been streamlined or housed in protective covers to reduce drag and leave no surfaces to be snagged or hoses to be cut in underwater combat.

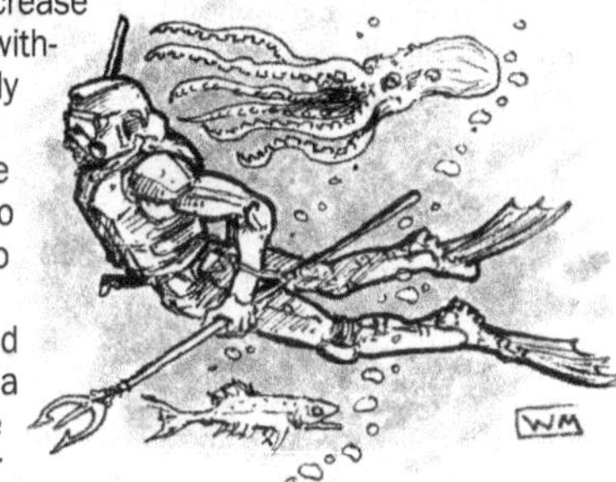

These units weigh 5.5kg and will sell for 3500+2d1000sp to a relic dealership, otherwise they are the same as light combat armor shown on Table XR-255 on page 426.

## Advanced Metal Weave Armor *by Danny Seedhouse*

This high-tech armor was built with now lost metallurgy and originally sold to the elite of society. It is light, concealable, offers superb protection, and physically resembles a very fine chainmail shirt. Indeed, advanced metal weave is indistinguishable from it until examined on a microscopic level... or tested in battle. These body suits provide a -20 DV for those lucky enough to find a suit that fits them and can easily be worn under other clothing or armor and imposes no movement penalty.

The problem with this suit is fit. They are tailored to a specific body that was usually (9 out of 10 suits) a pure strain human with what should be a standard sized chest, each suit has a limited amount of adjustment built in, but will not usually accommodate someone with a strength over 70, a weight over 114 kg and heights above 200 cm. Within these parameters, however, suits can be swapped between the sexes.

There is a way around this fitting issue, however, but it involves hacking the armor and putting it back into a fitting mode, allowing it to accommodate a wide range of body shapes and limbs, but for every extra limb, or 40 cm of height and 10 kgs of weight the armor losses 2 points of DV as the materials are spread thinner across the body. These suits weigh 2.5kg, and will sell for 2600+2d1000 silver pieces.

## Exo-Armor *by Danny Seedhouse*

This is a military combat armor (-35 DV) enhanced with a power assist frame (see page XR-438). Essentially an early form of shell class armor, it was used by troops expecting heavy combat and to outfit elite units by nations that could not afford the expense of shell class armors. It runs on one power cell for 1 week but comes standard with slots for two extra power cells. They come with the same features as combat armor and the frame modifies the movement penalty of the armor to -0.5 meters. These units are usually painted gray, desert camo or olive green and give the wearer a somewhat robotic appearance and gait, which can

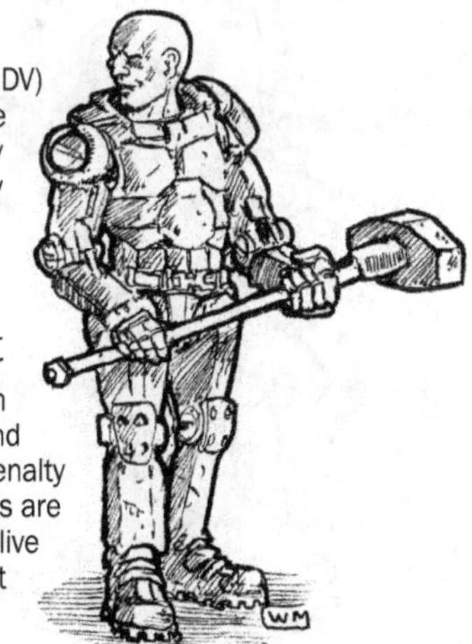

sometimes result in terror and animosity from those the wearer encounters. These bulky suits weigh 48 kilograms and will sell for 2900+3d1000 silver pieces.

## Crisis Deployment Armor [CDA] *by Stu Brooks*

This protective suit consists of a series of carbon polymer splints and plates with Kevlar fiber joints and non-Newtonian gels and fluids sandwiched between. It was designed to withstand a tank shell, and meant to fit an array of individuals ranging from survivalists to medical personal in war-zones to black ops military.

The amor comes standard with a survival pack and when found there is a 70% chance of still having each of the following items (roll per item for its presence or not): 2d6 days of MRE rations (pg. XR-436), an Advanced Trauma Kit, (pg. XR-445), an Identification Sequence Broadcaster (pg. TME 198), a laser scalpel (pg. TME-189) a hostile environment tent, a mylar blanket, a small water purifier (purifies 1 days worth water in 2 hours).

Internal flotation is standard for this armor but notoriously fickle when first found — there is a 76% chance that the built-in flotation ballasts are still working, a 15% chance there is air stuck in the ballasts and no chance of sinking even if intended while wearing the amor, and if not stuck, then a 15% chance they've instead been ruptured making it impossible to float while the amor is worn.

The amor has a -40 defense value, is cumbersome, and as such running is impossible for anyone with a strength less than 30 and jumping always counts as having a standing still start. The base variants are white and give the user a 2 skill tiers degree harder stealth check as they stand out, unless worn in snowy conditions in which case they gain 2 skill points in concealed movement or conceal self (stealth skill described on page 51 of the hub rules). While many suits are found with a matching CDA helmet, which improves DV by a further -10, this is only the case 6 in 10 times. See details on the helmet on page 427 of this book.

### CDA Variants  Roll 1d8

**1-3.** Basic model.

**4.** Paramilitary: Camouflage version that is easier to hide in and provides a +1 skill point bonus to conceal self or concealed movement.

**5.** Air deployable: Comes with a built in parachute for long falls and improved shock absorbers that take 10 meters of a fall without the parachute deployed. Treat these parachutes as the implant described on page 342 of this book.

**6.** Military issue: Pigmented in various camouflage patterns, roll 1d6: 1. Urban grays. / 2. Forest. / 3. Mountains, gray and lichen. / 4. Desert tan. / 5. Arctic: white and grays. / 6. Night ops, flat black. Armor also comes with a built-in combat blade in right arm (treat as relic bayonet). As well as loops for grenades, ammo pouches, and a holster.

**7.** Advanced Military: Extra 3 hours of oxygen supply and sensors that have a 60% chance of detecting and activating the oxygen tanks when hazardous gasses or environments are detected to protect the wearer, even if unconscious inside the suit. Comes with all the bells and whistles of the military issue.

**8.** Black ops: Identical to the advanced military variant above, but has working reactive camouflage that conveys the environment around the user as an overlay allowing an additional stealth re-roll, plus, treat the user as having 1 skill point minimum in stealth if otherwise untrained.

# Protective Gear Set 2

## Pocket Fire Extinguisher

This disposable red colored steel canister is about the size of a can of spray paint. When the top safety catch is released with the user's thumb, and the handle depressed, a streamer of flame suffocating foam jets out, range 3m. This spray is sufficient to put out a fire of 3m x 3m in size. Worth 10+1d20sp if unused, or 1d3sp as a curiosity to a collector if expended. This unit can be used with one hand and weighs 1 kilogram.

## Electro-Dampening Skin-Suit

This piece of ancient clothing consists of a thin, silver body suit that is worn under clothing and armor to protect the wearer against electrical shocks and EMP weapons. It increases the user's defense value from EMP and electrical attacks by -30 DV where applicable, plus, reduces any damage from these sources should a shock occur, by half. This protective layer is air permeable and does not cause the wearer to keep perspiration, nor does it stop laser beams and other forms of energy attack but does reduce acid damage by half. If torn, it can be sewn back together with mesh filaments from the suits sleeve or ankle cuff. Comes with a hood attached to the shirt portion.

An electro-dampening suit usually comes folded in a sealed plastic bag, weighs only 1.5 kilograms and, if sold intact, will fetch 600+4d100 silver pieces.

## Radiation Sensor Tab

A rad tab is a small button sized devices operated on background radiation itself, and when no dangerous levels of radiation are in an area, this device looks like a glossy gray tab. These sensors can be sewn onto a uniform like a patch, or otherwise buttoned or pinned to uniform with the built-in pin mechanism on the back. Whenever this device detects a trace of radiation within 100m, it takes on a yellowish hue, regardless of the intensity. When within 50m of mild radiation, however, it turns orange, while within 25m of medium radiation it will become purple. If the tablet gets within 10m of lethal levels of radiation, it turns red. Should the user already be standing in lethal radiation levels, the tab turns black and skull and crossbones appear on the surface.

This tab weighs 40 grams, does not need power, and will sell for 500+3d100sp. To purchase this relic, like all relics, the price will be double what characters can sell it for, however these tabs almost never come up for sale even in the best barter markets.

# Miscellaneous Relics

## Pocket Morse Code Translator

This small, communicator sized device folds open to send and receive Morse code. It has a tiny touch screen keyboard and text viewing display where the operator can write regular words and have them converted to Morse code, which can then be transmitted via an audio link cable to a communicator or other broadcasting device, or send via light flashes from the back of the screen. These Light flashes can be seen from as far away as 3 kilometers during the day, or 6 kilometers at night.

Incoming light flashes can also be translated by aiming the back sensor at incoming Morse code signals, and either decode light or pick up an audio based Morse code message, convert it with the device's built in computer and then display the translated code into normal text on the small screen. This ancient wonder runs on a mini power cell and will allow 72 hours of translation and sending per charge. The unit weighs 850g and can be sold for 600+3d100sp.

## Glider Suit *by Danny Seedhouse*

Usually found in bright colors (1 in 10 are camouflaged) this high tech suit of advanced polymers has thin flaps running from wrist to waist and between both legs. This setup makes the suit somewhat awkward to walk in reducing speed by half. There is a small pack of folded materials on the back of the suit, making it difficult to wear a standard backpack, and rendering the suit useless if a backpack is worn.

To discover the purpose of this ancient curiosity, one must either have relic knowledge or jump or fall at least 20 meters, then the true nature of the suit becomes apparent, as memory plastics kick into gear deploying under arm wing extensions, smart fabric wing materials snap rigid, adjust flight dynamics, stabilize the fall and turn it into a graceful forward glide. When fully expanded, a glider suit has a wingspan of 4 meters and is a truly impressive sight.

The first flight requires a Type D Agility/Willpower* hazard check. If the check is failed, this means the user starts an uncontrolled downward spiral. After the first failed fall, the user has 2 rounds and roughly 50 meters before the suit's parachute opens and saves them from falling uncontrollably. If this hazard check is passed, the user glides forwards 15 meters while descending 5 meters a round. The suit can do more than glide in a strait line though. One can slow or increase their rate of decent by up to +/- 3 meters forward by 1 meter down with a Type B agility hazard check. Turning up to 15 degrees requires a Type A hazard check, and can be increased by 5 degrees by upping the hazard check by 1 step. When in flight, the character receives a -30 DV bonus and can attack with a 1 handed missile weapon like an auto pistol at a -20 SV.

A glider suit weighs 7kg, is often found in a neatly folded nylon pouch with carry handle, and will sell for 500+3d100sp, or 600+4d100sp for the camo print version. These were designed to accommodate and adult pure stock human patterned body shape with a maximum user weight of 100kg.

**Add agility and willpower together, divide by two to get one's first flight trait.*

## Spider Suit *by Danny Seedhouse*

A spider suit is a mechanical assist system for climbing manufactured surfaces for recreational or industrial purposes. The suit itself comprises a pair of knee-high boots, gloves, a climbing harness and a backpack assist unit with four mechanical limbs. The boots and gloves contain the main climbing units and use a combination of chemical, magnetic and mechanical assistance.

A spider suit can hold up to 136 kg (300 lbs) of weight stationary for 6 hours of continuous use on 1 power cell. Each glove has one palm attachment point and a monitor on the back of the hand with information on adhesion strength and battery power. The boots have several attachment points:

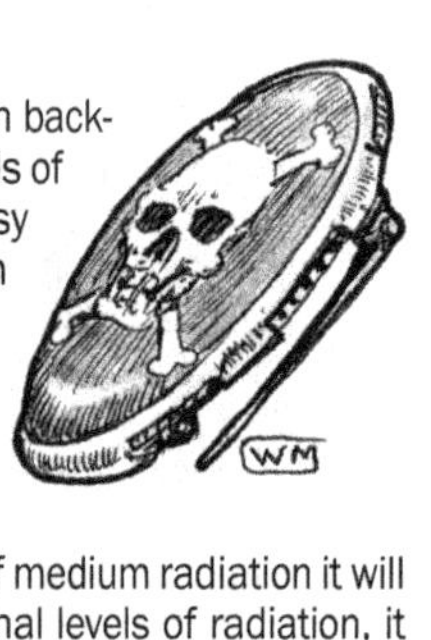

one on the bottom of the foot, one on the front of the boot, and one on the knee pad. The user manually selects which points are active at any one time. Use of the climbing attachments is simply a matter of turning on the power and placing them on the desired climbing surface.

To detach, the operator rotates the climbing point to the left while pushing forward into the surface. As a safety feature, attachment points are also programmed to prompt for verbal confirmation before a pair of points can be simultaneously detached.

The climbing harness is used for safety, allowing the user to attach themselves to a safety rope and to repel down. Each limb is outfitted with a climbing attachment, allowing both hands to be free to perform other tasks while safely and firmly attached. The harness was popular with urban warfare units as it allowed for unique tactical deployment and enhanced mobility so key to modern urban warfare.

The spider suit allows the user to climb otherwise unclimbable surfaces with complete safety and a steady speed of 3 meters per round, with no hazard check required. Accelerated climbing is possible, moving at 6 meters a round, however this is somewhat more risky, and the user is treated as having 5 skill tiers in climbing and must make hazard checks as per the regular climbing skill in the Hub Rules (pg. 36). The harness can climb for the user at a speed of 3 meters per round while hands free or it can be set to assist mode, increasing the users climbing skill points by 2 and averaging the climbing trait (STR+AG/2) of the user with its trait of 80. When attached to a surface by a single point the effective bond strength score is 80 going up by 40 per extra point attached should something try and rip the user from the wall.

These backpacks are bulky and disallow the user to wear another pack or carry heavy loads. Weight 22kg and will sell for 1200+2d1000sp.

### High-Tech Boots *by Danny Seedhouse*
*Also see Jump Boots on page XR-420*

### Armored Boots
These boots provide increased protection to a soldier's feet and resemble combat boots outwardly, but have armored segments in the sole, ankle and toes with advanced Kevlar materials treated for flame resistance. Produced in increasing numbers as unconventional wars spread and the use of anti personal mines and booby traps increased dramatically, this footwear provides a -5 to DV and a -15 DV bonus against attacks directly targeting the feet. A pair of these black boots weigh 2.2kg and sell for 400+4d100sp.

### Advanced Trail Boots
These rugged boots are built to last and help the outdoor traveler easily cross the most challenging terrain. Constructed of advanced polymers and smart materials, they self adjust to the foot for added comfort, provide increased environmental protection from temperatures and moisture, and so reduce the risk of blisters, frostbite and trench foot. The soles of the boots are another marvel of engineering, being able to self adjust to surface conditions and widening on soft ground, becoming softer for better grip when climbing hard rocky surfaces.

Advanced trail boots provide a +10 bonus to agility hazard checks involving rough terrain, climbing, and general staying on one's feet when traction would help. They provide a 5% bonus to overland movement speed any time it would be reduced below normal. In the Mutant Epoch, these boots fetch an unusually high price because of their ability to fit unusually shaped feet and adjust in size, making them far more comfortable for some mutants to use. A pair of advanced trail boots weigh 1.9kg and will sell for 300+3d100sp.

### All Terrain Boots
The more expensive and rare version of advanced trail boots, these boots feature extendable smart material surfaces built into their soles for wet and muddy terrain, extendable ice climbing crampons, and all the basic features of advance trail boots. The boots have built-in sensors and a computer just smart enough to adjust to current terrain conditions and are powered by body motion and thus never need a pesky battery.

This footwear allows movement across loose surfaces with 1/4 the usual penalties from sand, mud and snow. When passing a Type C agility hazard check, the wearer can even run across water, crossing a distance of 1/2 there speed before going under. As a safety warning, they in no way slow one's fall. The crampons extend with a button push or verbal command as well, enabling ice climbing or aiding in climbing loose surfaces such as a sandy hill. The crampons can also function as a weapon in a pinch with no SV mod and inflicting 1d8 damage. These remarkable boots weigh 3.3 kilograms and will fetch 1000+1d1000 silver pieces if sold.

### Drop Boots
Superficially resembling over sized knee high ski boots, these are constructed of hardened plastics and materials akin to combat armor. Built to absorb and mitigate the impact from falls through mini thrusters in the sole, toe of the foot, and along the sides of the calves, these astounding relics detect and react to sudden drops in altitude of over 2 meters and fire controlled blasts to slow the fall while maintaining an even level between both feet.

Falls under 10 meters deal no damage to the wearer, while falls from 11 meters to 30 deal 1/4 damage and falls over 30 meters deal 1/2 damage. If the wearer intentionally jumps, they automatically fall feet first. These boots were usually combined with another form of parachute for long planned jumps, such as the glider suit (see previous page) allowing some truly dangerous landings to be walked away from.

Unplanned falls are much more dangerous than purposeful drops from a height, as getting into the proper position requires a combination of skill and luck. Falls under 10 meters normally require a type E agility hazard check to land feet first, this is reduced by 1 letter code on the hazard check table if the wearer has the martial arts skill, or by 1 per 2 skill points in acrobatics. Falls over 10 meters require a base type D with the same modifiers for skill.

1 in 5 pairs of drop boots are modified versions that provide extra thrust when the user jumps, allowing them to jump 1 meter higher and 2 meters further than normal. Each boot uses a mini power cell and can provide power for 400 meters of falling (jumping expends 3 times the fuel). These boots weigh 4.7kg and will sell for 1500+1d1000sp.

Also, these rugged boots add -5 DV, and act like armored boots (see above), and where also designed to be worn with combat armor and other high tech modern armors and are thus usable with them. Because these were worn by urban assault troops, air assault soldiers and a plethora of adrenalin junkies means these boots are found in a variety of colors.

| Drop Boot Color  Roll 1d8 |
| --- |
| **1.** Military sky camouflage |
| **2.** Military urban camouflage |
| **3.** Smart camouflage: can be adjusted between sky, urban, desert, winter and woodland camouflage patterns |
| **4.** Light blue |
| **5.** Grey |
| **6.** Black |
| **7.** Personalized and wild: roll on the mutant hair color chart with some old corporate logos (pg. TME-23). |
| **8.** Programmable color choice. |

**High Tech Clothing** *by Danny Seedhouse*

## Color Change Fabric

Color Pallet technology with programmable nano weave technology allowed for the ultimate in fashion flexibility, color change, and custom advertising. These materials are often found in jackets and other large surface area pieces of clothing, and are usually programmed with a set color range and designs featuring themed art. The jackets are often walking advertisements for various pre-fall movies, bands, artists and car commercials. 1 in 4 come with speakers playing the music linked to the advertisements. All can be programed by someone with computer skill and a computer system of some kind. 1 in 4 have a small screen and camera to enable reprogramming without external input.

This cloth by the nature of its construction is tougher and more resistant to stains and damage then normal cloth and a regular jacket made of this fabric provides a -2 DV, a shirt or pants give a -1 DV bonus, these bonuses all stack for a total of -4 DV with a full suit. While such clothing is remarkable, and will always find a buyer among the wealthiest of new era families, they rarely make for good excavation attire, yet will sell for a decent amount depending on the item of clothing: jacket 40+2d20sp, shirt 30+2d20sp, pants 40+1d20sp. Each article of clothing runs on a pill power cell for 48 hours.

## Climate Weave Fabric

Smart polymers and microprocessors were used to create clothing that can react to changing environmental conditions to both ensure comfort and aid in the wearer's survival. Integrated climate weave clothing can be found in the following forms: full coat, light coat, pants and shirt. Full protection is provided by the full coat or combination of pants and light coat or shirt. Partial protection is provided by a light coat, pants or shirt worn alone. Enhanced protection is provided by layering a full coat with pants and shirt.

The various protection levels provide enhanced resistance to hypothermia, with the 'partial' tier protecting the wearer to air temp of -5 Celsius, or cold water of 5c or warmer for 10 minutes. A full suit provides protection down to -10 Celsius air temperature or in frigid waters of 1c to -10c for 20 minutes. 'Enhanced' tier of climate weave fabric coverage protects against air temperatures of down to -30c for 40 minutes and icy waters of -11 to -20 Celsius for 30 minutes of exposure. These ancient garments are usually found in a dull khaki or olive green color, and each item will sell for a different amount: full coat 300+2d100sp, light coat 250+1d100sp, shirt 140+2d20sp, pants 1200+2d20sp.

## Adaptive Camouflage Fabric

Using a series of small cameras, micro chips and color changing materials, adaptive camouflage changes its color to blend in with its surroundings, as well as the latest in 3d camouflage patterns that help to break up the user's profile. This system was found most commonly in clothing sold to hunters and as military fatigues and armor used by special forces. Though as the technology got smaller and cheaper, it saw innovative uses in high fashion, with users entering pre set programs of color changes or altering the settings to produce a color change that would clash with the environment.

Camouflage provides a +20 trait bonus on conceal self tests, though when moving this bonus drops to +10. Untrained users are treated as having 1 skill point in stealth for both these tests and receive no trait bonus.

When not found already attached to relic tactical, combat or even powdered shell class armors, or as uniforms, it is most commonly found as a one-size fits all poncho with hood, which is ideal for new era excavators who can wear this material over their standard armor and knapsack. A poncho weighs 3.3 kilograms and runs on 2 mini power cells that allow 48 hours of continuous operation. When not needed, the adaptive features of this poncho can be switched off with a simple on-off switch near the battery pack. Even when turned off, this poncho makes for excellent protection from junk storms and a robust rain poncho. These olive green, sensor and camera dotted ponchos will sell for 750+3d100sp.

# High Tech Camping Gear

### Drink Anything System *by Danny Seedhouse*

The drink anything system is a 30cm (1 foot) long tube about 15cm around attached to two, 2 liter tanks. The first tank is labeled purification and usually has a green poison symbol painted next to its spout. It's here that the water to be purified is poured, and over the next 1/2 hour to 1 hour, depending on contamination levels, it slowly drains as fresh water and fills up the second tank. Depending on contamination levels, the water produced is clean and safe to drink, although see the operation notes, to follow.

The internal computer inside the device is smart enough to dump water its systems cannot purify, or if the user is literate, they can follow the simple instructions to run the water through the clean cycle again, including salt water. The device will even reduce radiation levels of medium to mild and mild to none. To run at full capacity, the system needs both power and filtering agents. A standard power cell runs the device long enough to purify 100 liters of water. Filtering agents are needed if the toxins in the water are above a hazard check B in strength. For each step above B in hazard strength, one charge of the filtering agent is used, the same applies to radiation levels. A full stocked unit holds 10 units of filtration agent and 4 uses of anti-radiation filtration. The filtration agents can be replaced by anyone with at least 3 points in the chemical technician skill at a material cost of 110+1d20sp. To sell this 16.8 kg unit, (empty weight, or 18.8 kg full since 1 liter weighs 1 kilogram) will earn the seller 900+4d1000sp.

### Solar Powered Stove *by Danny Seedhouse*

This small portable stove fits into a compact 30 x 30cm (1 foot by 1 foot) box, 15cm deep. It comprises a single cooking plate, a solar powered heating unit, and a foldout solar mat that is 1 meter wide and 2 meters long. On a sunny day, the mat takes about 20 minutes to build up enough charge to boil water. 1 in 3 units will have a back-up mini power cell that can provide 10 hours of cooking time. Valued by both excavators who want hot food in the ruins without the fear of what a fire might attract, and by folks in places without a ready supply of organic fuels. These 2.7kg kits will fetch 350+2d100sp if sold, double for battery back-up models.

### Energy Recharging Solar Unit *by Danny Seedhouse*

Essentially, this is a portable civilian version of the cyborg implant called 'solar power generator' found on page TME-91. This fold out dish is a highly sought after relic. Before deployment, the unit is a box 60 by 60 centimeters and 30cm deep. The case weighs 3 kilos and has 2 attachment ports for either mini or standard power cells. The top opens in half and the disk is manually deployed, extended, and pointed at the sun. Once set up, it then automatically tracks the sun as it travels across the horizon or otherwise stays focused on the brightest light source.

The sunshine levels, shown on the following table, determine charge time for each battery type. One, or one of each battery can be plugged into the unit at the same time. This unit will sell for 1400+1d1000sp.

| Light Conditions | Charge Times Mini-cell | Charge Times Standard Power Cell |
|---|---|---|
| Torch/firelight | 12 hrs | 24 hrs |
| Raining/ snowing | 8 hrs | 18 hrs |
| Overcast | 4 hrs | 10 hrs |
| Partly Cloudy | 2 hrs | 5 hrs |
| Sunny | 1 hrs | 2.5 hrs |

## Sonic Bug Screen *by Danny Seedhouse*
This small wallet sized device hooks to a person's belt, features a simple on/off switch and a +/- dial to adjust field strength. It works by producing a noise field

that is tuned to a frequency that keeps insects away from the wearer — a must-have for any traveler in a bug infested wilderness. In the Epochian era, the screen's protection extends to any of the new mutant insects up to and including the size of a blood flyer or red wasps (except in August when the wasps are angry). As an added boon when set at its highest strength, this screen provides a -15 DV bonus verses insects of all sizes, and -10 DV verses the attacks of bestial human insect-human hybrids. A pill energy cell will run the screen for 1 month. Every 10 minutes of the high power setting uses 1 day of power. These 475g, rubberized units will sell for 470+3d1000sp.

## Armored Tent *by Danny Seedhouse*
With the advent of the advanced polymers that made weight less of a problem, these remarkable relics were originally built for military use. Armored tents were especially popular with units camping in hostile territory where the extra physical protection had a measurable effect on troop morale. These six person dome shaped shelters provide protection against both small arms and shrapnel from mortars and hand grenades. All in all, armored tents provide a -15 DV bonus to anyone within, and are much harder for enemy personnel, robots or animals to cut into.

Anything to tear into this dome must get passed the tent's -30 DV and score 10 or more points of damage. If less than ten points are scored, a second successful strike is considered to be a hit on the same spot and the damage amounts added up until the tent wall is torn open. Any breech or damage can be stitched together, but only with an alloy needle (18+3d6sp) and stout thread (1+1d3sp).

This tan colored, 14.6 kilogram relic of the old wars is highly sought after by excavators and anyone who lives in anything but the most heavily fortified of towns. New era military forces are also keen to get hold of these tents to help protect their officers and specialists. They we will sell for 500+4d100sp.

## Instant Cabin *by Danny Seedhouse*
Before deployment, the instant cabin is merely a 1.2 meter long, dark green polycarbonate cube box with a keypad on one side. Upon triggering the cabin, the box unfolds into a 6 by 6 meter floor with posts that extend the matching ceiling 3 meters upward. Six minutes later, internal foam tanks fill the walls, resulting in a highly water and wind proof structure with a door and 3 semi transparent windows, 2 small rooms, and a space-heater with 2 food heating plates, perfect to shelter 8 people. This entire assembly process is automated and takes 18 minutes.

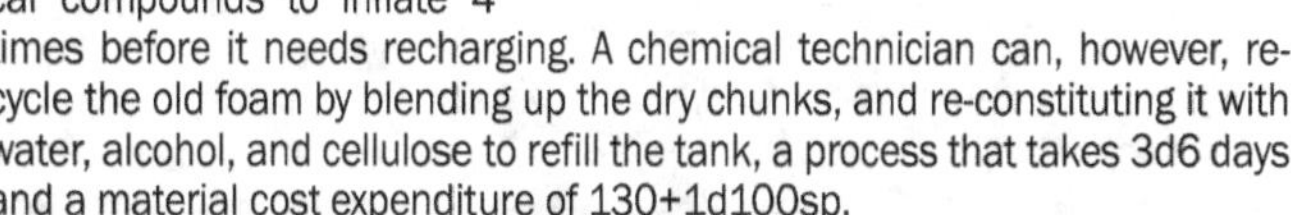

The biodegradable foam hardens and must be broken apart and disposed of before the cabin can be physically unlatched, folded up and stowed for future use. The cabin uses a standard power cell to expand and for heating power, while the foam tank has enough chemical compounds to inflate 4 times before it needs recharging. A chemical technician can, however, recycle the old foam by blending up the dry chunks, and re-constituting it with water, alcohol, and cellulose to refill the tank, a process that takes 3d6 days and a material cost expenditure of 130+1d100sp.

An instant cabin weighs 56 kilograms and comes with four carry handles for four personnel to transport between them. Selling such a rare relic will fetch 1100+1d1000 silver pieces.

## Tree Beds *by Danny Seedhouse*
These are hammocks with the straps and hooks needed to firmly attach them to tree limbs and branches. When the user crawls into this one or two person cocoon, they can close the drab colored nylon material up around them and zip it up from the inside to keep out pests and small predators. If any creature tries to chew or claw its way into the hammock, it must make a successful strike against DV -13 and do at least 4 points of damage. 1 in 4 tents are equipped with sonic bug screens as described on this page.

They can support a maximum of 320 kilograms weight and are made from water, mold, acid and rip resistant, yet potentially flammable material. Camping in a tree is a highly attractive proposal for anyone in the Epochian era since anyone sleeping in a tree bed is not attacked by unintelligent wandering creatures at night, unlike their poor companions on the ground. Tree beds, which can also be deployed in the tangled rebar of ancient buildings, and other ruined heights, weigh only 3.6kg and will sell for 370+3d100sp each.

## Nutrient Paste *by Danny Seedhouse*
This survival food contains all the nutrients and minerals a human body needs to function in what effectively looks like a toothpaste tube. The paste comes in several tasty flavors such as mint, root-beer, cheese, tuna, beef and gravy, banana and chocolate. Each tube holds enough paste to keep a man alive for 1 week, with 20ml consumed per day, though he will still feel hunger and need water. In the Epochian age nutrient paste is seen as both survival food and a luxury item because of its complete nutritional value and interesting and rare flavors. One tube weighs 160 grams (and holds a 140ml of paste) and will sell for 140+1d100sp.

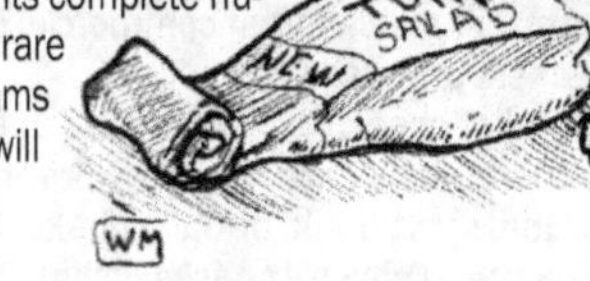

## Nutrient Tabs *by WM*
Similar to nutrient paste, but far less palatable, these wafers weigh 15 grams each and when dropped into a glass of water, will froth up and expand to make a nutrient rich porridge-like broth that can be slurped back with a straw, eaten by a spoon or drunk like a thick milkshake. Putting one directly in one's mouth and sucking on it can also work, but bubbles up and spill out of the person's mouth if they are not prepared for the experience. One tablet will keep an adult man sized person from starving per day, but doesn't really satisfy one's hunger. They come in foil wrapped rolls of 12 tablets and taste like unnatural, orange flavored dirt. When found, already opened, a pack will have 1d12 tablets remaining inside, with each tablet selling for 10+1d12 silver pieces if sold to a relic buyer familiar with these last resort survival meals.

## MREs *by Danny Seedhouse*

Meals Ready to Eat were the standard field ration for all major militaries before the collapse of civilization. They were produced and stockpiled in vast quantities and evolved from the canned rations of the Second World War and the desire for lighter, more nutritionally balanced meals to keep soldiers in top fighting form. MREs are usually packaged in brown plastic with the word MEAL and its main flavor, as well as various nutritional information in simple black lettering. Each meal provides about 1,200 calories.

They are intended to be eaten for a maximum of 21 days straight before fresh food is required, and have a shelf life of ten years (depending on storage conditions, for MCWs, however, it can be near indefinite). In cases where standard MREs are found, most will have turned to dust within their packaging since the cataclysm, unless they've been made recently by some high tech enclave, or specially made with archival packaging, oxygen absorbers and stored in an airtight, temperature controlled vault. Each MRE weighs on average 800g (510g to 850g [18 to 30 oz] depending on the menu) and an eatable one will sell for 30+1d20sp each..

There were several varieties of MREs produced before the collapse. MCW or Meals Cold Weather are made to withstand cold temperatures are made with freeze dried components meant to be served with hot water. MLRP or Meals Long Range Patrol is a paired down version of the standard MRE weighing less and containing additional nutritional supplements and intended for troops operating away from resupply.

Early forms of MREs faced harsh criticism over taste earning nicknames like, 'Meals Rejected by Everyone', 'Meals Rejected by the Enemy', and 'Three Lies for the Price of One: it's not a Meal, it's not Ready, and you can't Eat it'. The latest generation of MREs were much more nutritionally balanced, with a higher fiber count and are rumored to taste remarkably okay.

Because of the superior nutrition provided by a MRE, natural trait point recovery is enhanced for 12 hours after the meal is eaten. For each hour of rest, a wounded person recovers an extra 25% endurance or other trait, allowing for quicker battle recovery times. Note this increased rate effects only natural healing and a mutant that can regenerate gets this bonus, but not one affected by the mutation heal touch.

What fallows is a general list of contents within each MRE:

- **Main course (for entrée flavor, see chart to follow)**
- **Side dish (rice, corn, fruit, beans)**
- **Dessert or snack (often commercial candy bars or fortified pastry)**
- **Crackers or bread**
- **Spread of cheese, peanut butter, or jelly**
- **Powdered beverage mix: fruit flavored drink, cocoa, instant coffee or tea, sport drink, or dairy shake. MCWs contain extra packets of drink mix. (Drink mix packs include a chemical water purification mix that can deal with basic contaminants)**
- **Utensils (usually just a plastic spork)**
- **Flameless ration heater (to allow heating of meals with no fire)**
- **Beverage mixing bag**
- **Accessory pack contents:**
  - **Chewing gum**
  - **Water-resistant matchbook**
  - **Napkin / toilet paper**
  - **Moist towelette**
  - **Seasonings, including salt, pepper, sugar, creamer, and/or Tabasco sauce.**





1. Chili with Beans
2. Pork Ribs
3. Chicken Fajita
4. Beef Ravioli
5. Chicken with Noodles
6. Maple Sausage
7. Pork Sausage with Gravy
8. Mediterranean Chicken, tomato, feta
9. Spaghetti with Meat Sauce
10. Beef Roast with Vegetables
11. Beef Brisket
12. Meatballs with Marinara Sauce
13. Beef Stew
14. Chili and Macaroni
15. Vegetable Lasagna
16. Asian Beef Strips
17. Cheese Tortellini
18. Spicy Penne Pasta with Vegetarian Sausage
19. Southwest Beef & Black Beans
20. Chicken Pesto Pasta

## Smart Rope *by Danny Seedhouse*

Enhanced with advanced self sealing polymers, this seemingly normal length of rope can be cut and re-attached to itself, keeping its original length. The rope itself consists of two layers: an outer layer of bonded nylon and an inner layer of advanced plastic-like materials treated with chemical agents that react when exposed to oxygen essentially by contact welding itself to other portions of plastic treated with the same chemicals. This chemical bounding process can by reversed with the application of a second chemical cocktail that was supplied with the rope when purchased new but sometimes found still packaged in its original form. Usually uncovered in 15.24m (50 foot) lengths in bright colors with Smart Rope™ printed along its length. To those who know what it is (those with the Relic Knowledge skill) its value is substantial (100+1d100sp) for everyone else it's a length of good rope.

## Rescue kit *by Danny Seedhouse*

These kits are found in red duffel bags clearly labeled as rescue kits. Inside is a wealth of useful gear for rescue and survival situations. It contains 100 feet of smart rope, bolt cutters, a power jack (effective strength of 80 STR for lifting only) a set of climbing harnesses, folding shovel, hammer, saw, hatchet, crowbar, hand held arc cutter (for metal cutting: has 30 minutes of fuel, and will cut a 1 foot long line through 3 centimeters of hardened steel in 1 minute), a field medical kit (page 199 of the hub rules), 2 large flashlights, 2 gas masks, and 4 disposable filter masks.

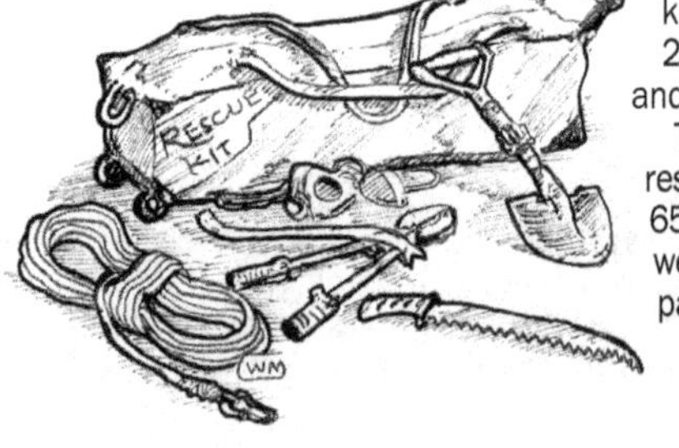



To sell a fully loaded, pristine rescue kit would fetch the seller 6500+4d1000sp. These kits weigh 27 kilograms and have a pair of small, rubberized luggage wheels at the back end and a carry handle at the other.

## Climbing kit *by Danny Seedhouse*
This bundle consists of a harness and a whole variety of tools to help keep the user attached to a cliff. When used properly with rope, a climbing kit helps one climb a little better, and thus receives a +10 bonus to the stats used for climbing. Its real use is to keep a person from falling to their death should they fail a climb check.

To use the kit, the climber must slow down, insert pins and spikes, secure lines and make other precautions as they ascend, and are forced to make a hazard check every 5 meters instead of the usual 6 meters (Climbing Skill described on page TME-36). If he or she falls though, they drop 1d6 meters, then get a 90% chance of stopping as their safety lines do their work. If this roll fails, however, the unlucky person falls another 1d6 meters and gets one final roll with a 95% chance to stop.

Following the path of someone using a climbing kit makes it much easier for those below or behind to ascend or move along the same rope secured cliff face or cracked concrete skyscraper face, who temporary gain 1 tier in the climbing skill and gives them the same fall protection.

A climbing kit comes in a bulky nylon gray backpack, weighs 23kg, and will sell for 750+4d100sp.

## Universal Cooker *by Danny Seedhouse*
This heavily reinforced large cooking pot has less space inside than expected. When the lid is sealed and the switch turned on, the cooker heats itself to boiling and hits the components with a burst of microwaves. The result is bland but completely sterilized and safe to eat food in about 10 minutes. The cooker has different settings allowing for cook time adjustment and also makes a good slow cooker allowing tougher meats to be made edible after about 6 hours of cooking.

Weighing 3.7kg and selling in a barter market for 450+2d100sp, this unit runs on a standard power cell to yield about 60 hours of cooking.

## High Tolerance Sleeping Bag *by Danny Seedhouse*
This sleeping bag is built with advanced materials and provides protection from cold, rain, wind and any other adverse weather condition. It uses a mini power cell to power temperature regulating elements that can both heat and cool the occupant to a pre-set temperature, but even without power it is good to -45 C (-50 F), nullifies wind chill, and keeps the user dry. Its outer shell is made of a smart breathable Kevlar weave providing an extra degree of protection to a sleeping person (-10 DV when fully sealed, but only helps if the enemy are not aiming at the sleeper's head), and will inflate the ground side if powered allowing for a more comfortable nights sleep.

This sleeping bag is normally found in a blue, olive green, or bright orange color, weighs 3.8kg, and will sell for 520+3d1000sp.

## Compass *by Danny Seedhouse*
An invaluable aid for navigation that lets one know which way north is, and was used for centuries by travelers and explorers to help discover the world. A compass can be as simple as a magnetic needle floating in water to an advanced GPS enhanced versions with a real-time map display.

The versions described here are the hardier, simpler kind — rugged, simple tools built for outdoor enthusiasts and the military. Game-wise, the user always knows which way north is, and therefore east, west and south, barring any environmental complications such as close proximity to a massive magnetic field.

Using a compass and a properly noted map (with marked directions and distance) someone with wilderness survival can navigate between points with a type A intelligence based hazard check.

These plastic compasses weigh 30g, have a closing lid, loop for a neck strap and will sell for 240+2d100sp.

## Multi Ratchet *by Danny Seedhouse*

This advanced tool is a boon to anyone trying to work on the relics and refuse of the old civilization. The alloy ratchet has an auto sizing head that will fit any of the multiple nuts and bolt heads found on the wreaked and cobbled together vehicles of the Epochian era. This allows for repair and scavenging without the need to carry numerous tools, and in a pinch it can be used as a good old club (+1 DV, 1d10 DMG, throw range 3m). Multi ratchet's weigh 370g, and will sell for 310+2d100sp.

## Mini Winch *by Danny Seedhouse*
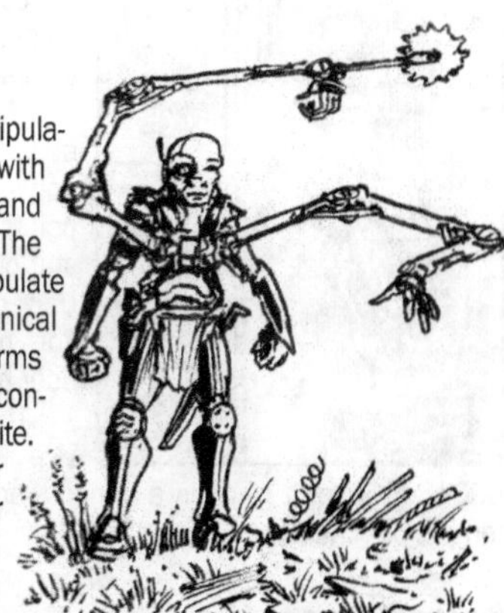
Every excavator's best friend, the mini winch, is a small, but powerful aid in the lifting of heavy objects. Weighing in at 16kg (35 pounds) and being about the size of a lawnmower engine, this unit can lift 1000kg (2204.6 pounds). It comes with a high strength, low stretch 50ft (15 meter) cable, and a 6ft (2 meter) sling used to anchor the winch. Operated manually, or with a remote control that comes standard with the winch, a single power cell provides 4 hours of continuous operation.

If sold in a relic market, this bright yellow device will fetch 720+1d1000sp.

## Tool Arms *by Danny Seedhouse*
This unit consists of a pair of fold out manipulator arms anchored to a heavy backpack, with stabilizer struts, a pair of control gloves and an optic display screen for the right eye. The gloves allow the user to control and manipulate each hand and arm to perform mechanical tasks in hazardous situations as the arms themself are insulated against electrical conduction, don't burn, nor suffer from frostbite.

The arms have attached tools for most jobs and can switch them out for those stored in the backpack unit, these include a multi ratchet, a cutting saw, drill with multiple bits, a welding torch, and screwdrivers, snips and a plethora of other tools. They allow for a 3 meter reach and have an effective strength of 60, but can be braced in one position with an effective strength of 120, this requires 5 rounds to brace properly and can pry open doors or otherwise break into sealed containers. The rig runs on a power cell for 3 months, with a separate tank of fuel for the cutting torch, holding 10 minutes of flammable propellant.

The tool arms allow a mechanic to work efficiently on many projects, from repair to fabrication, reducing the time needed to build or repair objects by 25%. It also enables much more efficient scavenging of junk piles and reduces either the time needed to find useful items or the amount recovered by 10%.

In a pinch, the tool arm rig can be used to defend oneself plus act as a makeshift shield, giving a -15 DV bonus to the wearer. Various tool attachments can be used offensively, too, whereby the cutting saw strikes with +3 SV doing 2d12+6 DMG. The arms can bludgeon a foe with +0 SV doing 1d12+5 DMG. each. Additionally, the two tool arms can aid in grappling using its strength of 60 and because it can be locked in place, the grapple can be maintained by the arms, allowing the wearer's hands to be free for other tasks.

This rig weighs 23kg and will sell for 1900+1d1000sp.

## Specialized Repair Kits *by Danny Seedhouse*

This kit contains advanced tools for one specific technician skill, gear that, in game terms, aids in making hazard checks. When used in unpowered mode — such as when the operator wishes to conserve power or lacks batteries — it allows all hazard checks used with its assigned technician area to be made as if the character had one more skill point in that skill. However, when powered by 3 pill power cells in the scanners it allows skill checks to be made at 2 tiers higher and the technician operates as if they had one more point in the skill itself for purposes of what they can build, repair, or fix. Each kit weighs 10+1d10kg (each is different) and will sell for 800+4d1000sp.

**Roll 1d10** below to determine what a specific repair kit variant
**1,2.** Cybernetics Technician, page 207, this book.
**3.** Technician, Bio, pg. TME-52
**4.** Technician, Chemical, pg. TME-52
**5.** Technician, Computer, pg. TME-53
**6,7.** Technician, Electrical, pg. TME-53
**8.** Technician, Mechanical, pg. TME-54
**9,10.** Technician, Robotics, pg. TME-54

## Universal Key *by Danny Seedhouse*

Before the fall of civilization, electronic security devices were everywhere and attempted to keep homes and businesses safe. Because of this, folks on the wrong side of the law, and those who needed to get into things quickly and quietly, developed the universal key.

The uni-key is used to open electronically locked devices of all kinds without the use of explosives or some such noisy method. In the post-apocalyptic era, electronic locks are most commonly found in the ruins that excavators frequent, or in high-tech enclaves.

Mechanically, the universal key opens electronic locks and electronic security doors as if it had the Lock Pick skill at 4 skill points (see page TME-48) and an Accuracy stat of 60. It takes 2d10+5 minutes for the Universal Key to attempt to unlock a door. This process can be attempted once on a door before the system is out of options.

This small, communicator sized device weighs 370g and, if sold, will earn 600+3d100sp. It runs on a mini-power cell which will provide 70 unlock attempts per charge.

## Smart Paper *by Danny Seedhouse*

This relic is not really made of paper, but electronically laced plastics that look like traditional paper and can display text or be written on as normal. Often (66% of the time) this device is found with a small embedded chip preloaded with a variety of 20+1d20 books for people who still like to read physical materials. Smart paper is durable and resistant to age, water and incidental damage, enabling a relatively large amount of it to survive intact.

Smart paper found in the new era is often not recognized as such, or those who have found it have reused it, not knowing how to access the data stored on the chip. Someone with the relic knowledge skill can recognize smart paper for what it is with a type A perception based hazard check but must make

a type H HC to unlock it to access any library of books loaded on it.

A computer technician is allowed an INT based Type B hazard check to figure out the how to turn on, access, or load, book files onto this device, but might not know it is anything more than old plastic coated paper if he or she lacks the relic knowledge skill.

Smart paper runs on two pill power cells that will allow for 400+1d100 hours of reading on a charge. A sheet of this remarkable paper will sell for 300+1d100 silver pieces, or double that if it has a collection of book loaded on it.

## Assist Frames *by Danny Seedhouse*

This high tech exoskeleton is a great boon to folks who must carry heavy loads over long distances, and those that want to go toe to toe with a charging mutant bear. Initially developed to provide assistance for people suffering from mobility issues, these were quickly adapted to military and industrial use. Power assist and construction frames were cheaper to produce than shell class armor and could have armor added to them as needed, although they lack force fields.

Purpose built armor can be made to enclose these frames, and involves getting a custom built suit of armor around oneself that adds an extra 100+1d100sp to the cost of the archaic armor for custom fitting and extra materials. Typical armor enhancements include junk armor and scrap relic.

In the new, post-apocalyptic era, these frames are found in three basic models: the mobility assist frame, the power assist frame and the construction frame.

### Mobility Assist Frame

This full suit was intended to give back mobility to people with spinal injuries or other nerve or muscle damage. These require a direct brain interface (cyborgs can use this automatically). The suit must be attached surgically to a non cyborg by someone with 4 skill points in medic and the assistance of someone with two points in computer technician or cybernetics to function properly. They come with a built in gyroscope for balance and provide a base agility of 25, a base movement rate of 6 meters and a strength of 40. A mobility assist frame will run on a power cell for 1 month of constant use. The units weigh 16 kilograms and will sell for 800+3d100sp.

### Power Assist Frame

The second type of power assist frame was for the raw augmentation of the human body. The suit boosts physical strength by +20 points and requires no special interface other than a human shaped body; too many physical alternations make the armor unusable, with changes in basic body shape, such as extra limbs or a drastically undersized, over-sized or distorted body, making this device incompatible. These suits enhance the user's movement by +1 meters and provide a -5 DV bonus. The suit runs on a single power cell for 1 month. A power assist frame will earn out 1600+1d1000sp if sold. They weigh 36 kilograms.

### Construction Frame

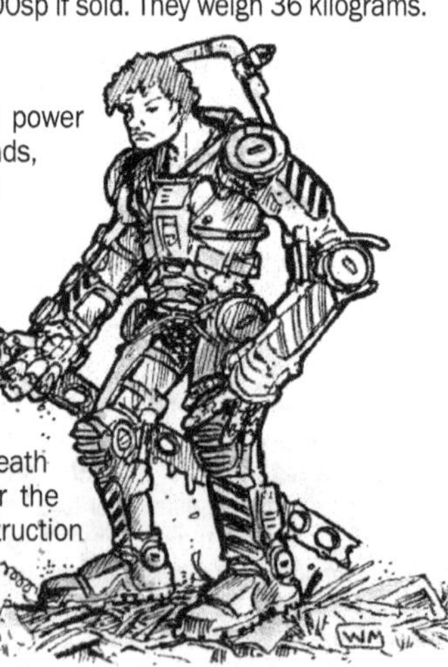

This is a beefed up version of the power assist frame tuned to lift heavy loads, move cargo and heavy construction materials in places tradi- tional vehicles had problems reaching. This version increases the user's strength to a flat 100, gives them a DV bonus of -5 and a -1m penalty to speed. Only skin tight armor can be worn underneath this suit as it is bulkier than either the mobility or power assist frame. Construction variants weigh 53 kilograms and will sell for 2100+1d1000 silver pieces.

# High Tech Devices Set 2

### Psionic Immobilizer Head Clamp *by WM*

It took the ancient ones decades to accept that mutant humans and other creatures exhibited incredible, often dangerous mental powers. It took even longer for them to come up with a means to block such unfathomable gifts. Besides a wide range of headsets, hoods, and specialty helmets that allowed the wearer to ward off mind reading attempts and savage mental attacks, this device is instead clamped to a mutant's head, and when locked and switched on, it prevents the freak from using its unnatural psionic powers.

This metal and hard plastic head restraint appears as several wide, locking bands that criss-cross the wearer's head and connect to a battery pack and control panel, which itself sits within a locking compartment at the back of the weirdo's head so the prisoner cannot remove the device or turn it off.

The unit is powered by one mini power cell and will run for 72 hours. Settings include 'block', or 'Corrective' modes. 'Block' mode simply causes a brain wave disruption within the wearer's head that, besides causing a severe headache, makes it very difficult for this mutant to use any mental mutation. A type G willpower based hazard check is needed to unleash a mental power, and whether this attempt succeeds or fails, a daily usage of that mutation is expended. Incoming mutations, either an attack or communication such as telepathic transmission, need the other mutant to make this same type G willpower hazard check to reach the wearer of this device.

The second mode, called 'corrective', discharges a painful shock into the mutant whenever he or she attempts to use a mental mutation, regardless of successfully breaching the clamp or not. This shock inflicts 1d10 lethal and 1d30 stun damage into the mutant. Each shock drains the power cell in the clamp by -2d6 hours.

While this head piece could be worn by somebody seeking to evade incoming mental attacks and intrusions, it causes headaches, dizziness and nausea in the wearer, and for every half hour worn, the willing user must make a type B willpower based hazard check or pull it off.

### Electro Guardian Unit

This unit is a shock trap. The unit consists of two electricity emitter pods which are connected to a central power supply and ID sequence broadcast emitter reading scope, control panel, and battery compartment. The two emitter pods are connected to individual, 6 meter long wire spools, with the back of the disk shaped pods fitted with either screw mounting brackets or a peel and stick backing surface for adhesion to glass, concrete or hard plastic.

When the unit is switched on, and the control dial set to shock level 1, 2 or 3, anything to walk through the invisible laser trip line that runs between the pods will set off an arc of electricity that goes from one pod to the other, connecting the circuit and frying whoever steps through the hidden beam.

Those with the proper ID code, or wearing the correct individual identification sequence broadcaster (page TME-198), who walk through the beam, will not set off the trap. Those without the electronic credentials will be targeted by this device, which is usually set up in a narrow hall, doorway, staircase or between trees.

**Shock level 1,** which is the default unless specified otherwise, has a strike value of 01-70 and on a hit will inflict 1d12 lethal damage and 1d20 stun damage.

**Shock level 2** has an SV of 01-85 and inflicts 1d20 lethal damage and 2d20 stun damage.

**Shock level 3** has a strike value of 01-93 and inflicts 2d20 lethal damage and 1d100 stun damage, plus forces the victim to make a Type D strength based hazard check or remain stuck in the electrical field, suffer terrible pain, and cannot use any mental mutations or cybernetic implants while stuck. Each minute, while held in place, the captive is allowed another strength based hazard check to try to escape. No further damage is inflicted to stuck victims.

The power for this unit comes from three standard power cells, or can be wired directly into an installation or large vehicle's grid. For those running on cells, however, level 1 shocks will drain the battery bank by 1 of its combined 30 energy units. Level 2 shock mode will drain the three power cells by 3 energy units, while level 5 will rapidly deplete the battery bank by 10 energy units — a full 3rd of the battery bank.

Unless concealed, an approaching person might spot the electrocution pods mounted on either side of the passage, and be allowed a Type E perception check to notice them, or a type D hazard check if this would-be shock victim has been the victim of such a device before.

Targeting the pods, if visible, or shooting the control box is also possible. The pods have a DV of -15 and can take 18 endurance before being destroyed. Two pods are required to deliver a shock. This whole rig weighs 6 kilograms and comes in a standard black nylon satchel with single shoulder strap and utility pockets.

### Handheld Movement Detector

This boxy, 1.5 kilogram, black or olive green, one handed device resembles a spotlight, but has a broad, fan shaped front sensor grill instead of a bulb. When switched on and held out from the body, either directly ahead or swept up or down or from side to side, it can detect the movement of living creatures, robotics or other physical objects. A small, user facing color screen on the top of the device allows the operator to see a three-dimensional graphic representation of wherever the detector is facing, out to 10 meters. Anything of 5 or more kilograms will show up as a blinking red icon and give away its location and direction of travel. Friendly units fitted with an identification sequence broadcaster (pg. TME 198), will show up as green, and if their ID is plugged into the scanner will even show their name or other identifying data.

With the ability to see enemies approaching, the operator and its companions gain +5 initiative, unless they are reading the signal wrong and the signal is actually coming from the ceiling or floor.

This device runs on a standard power cell and will yield 200 hours of operation per charge. It cannot detect holograms or dimensional beings.

### Ascension Gloves

Each glove is powered by either a mini power cell, which offers 3 hours of use, but also has a charging plug port and pull out, 30cm power cable so the batteries can be recharged from an external source. When activated, these remarkable gloves use a combination of magnetics and rubberized adhesion filaments to help the wearer climb any surface, even glass, at +2 skill points in climbing. The climbing skill is described on page 36 of the hub rules. While two gloves must be worn to gain this benefit, if only one is operational, it adds +1 point to the climbing skill.

### Metal Detector

While almost unchanged from those ground penetrating metal detectors first made in the 20th century, these fold out units are usually found in a nylon carry case with a shoulder strap. When assembled and the earphones are activated, this unit can be held over the ground before the operator and swept slowly back and forth to detect buried metal down to 2 meters. Any landmine ahead of the user, which is detected by hovering the sensitive bottom disc back and forth at a 180 degree sweep, will locate a buried mine within 30cm of the sensor pad and give off a special ping. When such an explosive is found, it can be avoided or carefully dug up, disarmed and taken as loot. This unit runs on a power cell for 144 hours before a new battery must be inserted and weighs 1.4kg.

## Mecha Detector aka 'CUPS'

Formally called 'Compromised Unauthorized Program Scanner', or CUPS for short, this half moon shaped, hand-held device is snapped onto the head or neck of a robot, or android and left for about an hour to scan the entire machine for any hint of virus, advertising software, data collection bug, tracking device, remote control mode, back door or the dreaded Mecha control virus that so many anti-human artificial intelligences currently use to annihilate the last vestiges of humanity.

If the Mecha control virus is detected in a robot or android, a small red light blinks discreetly on the unit's rubberized handle — however it does not make a show of it nor announce to all — especially the robotic unit, that its hostile coding has been found in its systems. This unit does not repair the CPU or rid the android, robot, or other machine of the unwelcome, potentially lethal software. To remove the Mecha virus, a computer technician must first hack into the CPU, then re-program the robot or android according to the column on table TME-1-47 of the hub rules, found on page TME-53. Many Mecha infected robots and androids have no idea that they are so compromised with the control virus in 'standby' mode.

## Megaphone

These devices can appear in three different forms. Sometimes they are mounted to the roof of a vehicle or massive robot and powered and controlled from within the machinery, while at other times, a miniaturized variant is built onto a vat-brain chassis or inserted into the throat of an android for broadcasting from the unit's wide open mouth. The most common variant, and the one found as a randomly discovered relic, however, is the hand-held unit that once helped project the voices of protesters, law enforcement personnel, and coaches at athletic events.

These typical units come standard with a power cell and a 3m long cord for recharging the cell when plugged into a facility or massive operational vehicle's power outlet (takes 5 hours to recharge the cell, 120 hours use per charge). These hand held loudspeakers can project the user's voice, or other audio file, out to 500 meters effectively, but on a calm day in the open, the bellow from this device will most likely be heard by predators, scavengers, and humanoids of all shapes and sizes, who might come to investigate the source.

A hand held megaphone will weigh 1.5kg, have a sell price of 500+5d100sp, and come with a nylon shoulder strap, a detachable microphone with coiled 1m connection wire, low battery indicator light, plus one of the following extra features. Megaphones fitted into androids, robots or vat-brain frames will also be eligible for one of these extra:

| 1d10 | Megaphone Bonus Feature |
|---|---|
| 1-3. | Siren option |
| 4,5. | Data stick insert port with 5cm screen and input option select buttons to play musical tracks, recored messages, or play sound effects. |
| 6,7. | Recored and play back mode. The person speaking can say something once while holding the record button on the grip, and later hit the play back button to select from one of their own 24 pre-recorded messages. |
| 8,9. | Solar collector coating. This unit will recharge the power cell in 7 hours of sunlight, with the battery removable to allow this unit to be converted into a solar recharge device. Under cloudy conditions, it takes 14 hours to recharge the power cell. |
| 10. | All above features in one unit. Double sales value. |

## Glow Flare

Often coming in packs of 12, and in either lime green, bright orange, garish purple, hot pink or ice blue, these plastic tubes need to be cracked and shaken for 30 seconds and thereafter will glow in the color based on the liquid inside. One can illuminate a 6m radius in a light about as bright as a candle flame, although if many are cracked and the plastic glow sticks massed together, they can light up a 6 meter radius in a rainbow of colors, a beacon that can be seen from up to 250 meters away during times of darkness.

These units will emanate their glow for 8 hours before fading to half light for another 6 hours, and then go dark permanently and no longer be of use. As fancy, colored plastic, even when spent, they will fetch 2sp each as trinkets. Each weighs 200g. If unused, will earn 20+1d30sp each in a typical marketplace.

## Comms-Jammer

When closed up for transport, this device looks like some sort of high-tech, charcoal gray backpack. When switched on, several antennae rise from the top of this relic and broadcast communications disrupting electrical surges. All communicators, and broadcasts, transmissions and commands to drones, robots and non-sentient androids within the 100 meter radius of this device might be scattered. Any relic has an 87% chance of being disrupted, while for robots, MAVs, drones, androids, and digital beings, they are allowed a Type D intelligence based hazard check to defeat the jamming after 2d6 rounds, and once figuring out a work around are no longer affected by this particular comms-jammer.

Any radio signal will be scrambled amid oscillating noise, static, pings and screeches so that an imperfect message is delivered, and any voice messages or two way calls scrambled so that only 1 in every 4th words comes through.

Robots, MAVs, drones and androids that are receiving their commands from a remote operator could have their command link severed if the unit fails its hazard check. The mechanical or digital entity must either cease whatever they were doing before jamming took place or resort to their default orders. For any digital being, not contained in a robotic or android vessel, it cannot send orders to other units that it might normally command, nor use communicators or other broadcasting devices, and so if this digital being is itself a broadcasted entity from some distant AI or other digital entity, it phases in and out and thus is present only one round out of every four rounds of game play.

A power cell will run this jamming system for 18 hours before a replacement cell must be inserted. It weighs 7.8kg and will fetch 1800+2d10000sp if sold.

## Control Collar

Originally designed to coax synthetic human and mutant humans into compliance through pain, these wide, metal and plastic locking neck collars also work on androids and robots that have a neck circumference of no more than 50cm (about 20"). Once locked onto a prisoner's neck, the collar cannot be removed without knowing the assigned code to that specific device — which can be unlocked by the operator of a hand held Control Collar Console. Besides the electronic functions of this collar, it is built very tough and anybody under 40 strength has no hope of snapping it, while those with 41 or higher strength are allowed a type J hazard check once per hour to attempt this feat. These collars are fitted with an alloy ring at the front of the neck to accommodate a leash, chain, or other restraining cord.

Through the control console, which is a separate relic described below, this collar can track the location of the collar within 5 kilometers, but while within 100 meters the console can be made to induce a painful electric shock in the wearer. It can unleash an agony rating range of 1 to 6 on the console's small screen. For each degree, the subject suffers 1d6 stun damage that remains for an hour, thus from 1d6 to 6d6 stun damage in a single discharge.

For each degree, the wearer must also make a willpower based hazard check to disregard doing whatever the controller wants the wearer to do or not do. Thus, a type A hazard check for agony setting 1, type B for setting 2, Type C for setting 3, type D for setting 4, a type E for setting 5, and type F for setting 6. At setting 5, the wearer must make a further Type C endurance based hazard check or pass out and drop unconsciouses for 3d6 minutes. At setting 6, the unlucky wearer must make a type D endurance based hazard check or suffer severe trauma, pass out for 10+1d20 hours, lose bowl and bladder control, and permanently lose 1 point to their intelligence trait from brain damage.

The collar operates on a single power cell what will run it for 36 months. However, for each shock, the charge is depleted by between 1 and 6 months, depending on the shock number setting deployed.

Even after the collar's battery is drained, it is extremely challenging to remove it, as they were manufactured in such a way that even those with the lock picking skill could not disarm or detach them. Besides an impressive feat of strength, a person with mechanical, robotics, cybernetics or electrical technician skill, or a junk crafter of 3 or more skill points, can attempt to dismantle and open the collar. The opener will need assorted replica and relic tools, and is allowed a Type D intelligence based hazard check per half hour to crack open the seam and hinge assembly of the collar. If the collar is opened while in operation, it will send an alert to the console unit up to 5 kilometers away, as well as a emit a high frequency alert sound similar to that of a smoke detector going off. This deafening noise will continue for up to 10+3d6 minutes or until the technician can get inside the unit and detach the power cell, which requires a Type C accuracy based hazard check per round to accomplish. While a few rounds of screeching noise might not seem that long, even one second of this noise when an escapee is trying to hide from pursuers, or avoid attracting local predators, is too long.

A detached but operational Control Collar will sell for 400+3d100sp if sold in a relic market, weighs 2.8 kilograms, is waterproof, and highly prized by slavers and jailers alike.

## Control Collar Console

This small, palm sized device has a neck strap, stubby, rubberized antenna, on-off switch and small front facing, 5cm tall by 8cm wide touch screen. It has a side button to toggle through all the Control Collars encoded into it, with both inactive and active collars displayed. Inactive collars appear in gray text while active collars are in blue if within 5km, or red if within 100 meters. This device will run on a mini power cell for 48 months. By way of selecting one or more collars with a tap on the screen, the user can pinpoint the location of a selected collar code, and either list one or all red proximity codes and discharge an identical electrical shock to each, ranging from agony tier 1 to 6. Read all about this cruel mode of prisoner control above under 'Control Collar'.

## Agony Inducer Unit [AIU]

When placed over a restrained victim's head, this auto adjusting skullcap and electrode clamp grip the victim's cranium. The operator, using a button panel at the back of the unit, or via an included, detachable remote control with a 50 meter range, can torture the wearer with electric shocks, micro syringe injections of truth serums, toxins, pain inducing pharmaceuticals, and plant extracted drugs, including hallucinogenics and intoxicants that might make the unfortunate wearer divulge whatever the interrogator asks.

For every ten minutes that a subject is exposed to the agony, mental intrusion, and chemical soup pumped into his or her scalp, they are allowed a Type A, willpower based hazard check to resist giving up the truth to whatever question a torturer or interrogator asks. Besides the severe pain, the subject takes an automatic 1d6 stun damage per ten minutes, damage that heals at the victim's normal healing rate per hour instead of per day.

This Phase 1 setting can be used so long as the agony inducer unit has power and the victim doesn't pass out. Failing to get the desired results, the torturer can adjust a dial and induce more severe suffering and possible death in the wearer.

Phase 2 risks killing or mentally neutralizing the victim as the AIU sends exceedingly powerful shocks through the subject which cause permanent nerve and tissue damage. For each ten minutes, the wearer must make a Type C willpower based hazard check or break, and give up whatever is asked of it. Regardless of breaking or not, the subject takes a permanent -1 point drop to each trait. Worse, the pain wracked victim must next use their now depleted current trait values for further hazard check rolls, and needs to make a strength based Type B hazard check or go into cardiac arrest and begin to die. As shown on the medic skill table on page 46 of the hub rules book, and consulting the 'Resuscitate Drowning Victim' column, a medic, or even an untrained individual, has some chance of performing CPR to revive the victim, who will be reduced to 10% endurance and strength for 2d6 days thereafter if allowed to recover at all.

For field interrogation use, this much feared unit can operate for 2 hours on a single, standard power cell, but is normally plugged into a structure or vehicle's on-board power supply. The reservoir of ancient drugs that come with this unit will be spent after 12+1d12 hours, but a herbalist or chemical technician of 3 or more skill points can concoct new formulations which have similar effects. To purchase the narcotics and stimulants in a ready-to-use condition, however, will cost 1000+1d1000sp and yield 6+1d6 hours of interrogation drugs.

An agony inducer unit weighs 2.7 kilograms, including the controller, and will sell for 2500+2d1000sp in a relic market — although in some law-abiding, upright communities, to be in possession of such an evil tool could get whoever owns it into severe trouble with the local law and citizenry.

## Robo-Repair Module [RRM]

Looking like a spidery version of a hand sized metallic wood tick, this flat, robotic unit lives in a symbiotic relationship with an android, robot, or computer enabled vehicle. When not needed, it lives in an out of the way part of the robot where it spreads its six elongated, multi-jointed metal arms out, latches onto the body of its host, and feeds off a special power 'nipple' that it creates within 4 hours. The robo-repair module will establish its own connection into the machine or mechanical being, and besides maintaining its own charge, will also stay in contact with the larger machine and know when the host takes damage and thus needs to be repaired.

Most times, the module will stay hidden, even within the armor of an android or robot, to avoid being destroyed during combat, only to emerge once the coast is clear and get to work. When it detects injuries in the host body, it moves to the nearest wound, clamps over the puncture, slash, or burn and uses micro welders, epoxy putties, wiring and hydraulic repair tools, fluids and alloy mesh patches to 'heal' the robot, android or machine.

There are three tech tiers of robo-repair modules, with the most advanced MK III modules being very rare, yet able to fix machines at a remarkable rate. Opponents who see one of these spidery contraptions moving about the body of the mechanical being can specifically target the module, while explosions, radius effect attacks, fire, and other harm can also a damage or destroy these modules when exposed and on the surface of their host machine, thus the stats below show the defense value and endurance for each model type.

If separated from a host by less than its 'detection distance', then the module will scuttle to the android or robot and climb aboard it as commanded. Although these units are robotic in nature, they exhibit no ability to speak, interact, see or inflict violence even in their own defense, and are simply crawling, auto-healing automatons and, in some respects, merely massive healer nanites. Each runs on mini power cell for 9 months.

Only one robo-healer module can operate in a mechanical body at any given time, as they see each other as parasites, and a more advanced model will always accost, crack open, and dismantle and partially ingest a cruder model.

Besides being highly valued by androids and robots, they are also sought after by vat-brains who can use them to maintain their mechanical bodies. These units weigh 470+2d100 grams. The die roll shown here is for game masters who needs a quick result for the model found on an NPC android, robot or vehicle, or when these units are found loose and their batteries drained, or when discovered in their poly sealed original packaging.

| 1d10 | RRM Model | DV | END | Move | Detection Distance | Heal per Hour Rate | Sales Value |
|---|---|---|---|---|---|---|---|
| 1-5. | MK I | -16 | 6 | 1m | 6m | 1d6 | 800+1d1000sp |
| 6-9. | MK II | -22 | 9 | 1.5m | 10m | 2d6 | 1600+1d1000sp |
| 10. | MK III | -36 | 18 | 2m | 48m | 3d6 | 4000+2d1000sp |

### Energy Wall Projector

Sometimes mistaken for an Electro Guardian unit, this relic comprises two, 39cm long telescopic energy transmission rods, that when the unit is disassembled for storage or transport, snap together and fit into a padded, waterproof carry case. One rod has a battery capsule and a control panel. The panel flips open to reveal a small touch screen and button array that allows the user to set the device in three different defensive modes. Not only are dimensional beings particularly susceptible to contacting these energy walls, and when they touch or try to pass through them, take automatic lethal damage, but are also momentarily visible.

The rods themselves are separated up to a maximum of 10 meters apart and the telescopic shaft cores pulled out to a maximum of 3 meters in height. With the energy transmission nodes facing those on the opposite rod, and each rod clamped, taped, lashed or bolted to a wall, door jamb, tree, post or other object, the emitters are ready for deployment.

Clever creatures and robotics will attempt to target either of the emitter rods, which have a defense value of -16 and can take 26 endurance damage before being destroyed. An experienced user of this relic will place the emitter rods into a groove, slot, or somehow position them behind a vertical barrier so they cannot be seen and targeted by those on the far side of the barrier.

Besides being used as a mobile defensive measure, these units can accept a power plug and run off an installation's energy supply. Likewise, variants of this relic can be found that are permanently built into a facility or ancient vessel, and controlled by a computer or operator in a command post. Dimensional beings are automatically harmed for 2d12 damage upon touching or trying to shove through this barrier.

This unit weighs 28kg and usually comes with a nylon carry case and 4 battery compartments. An intact set will sell for 2000+1d1000sp. The control panel allows the energy wall to be set to either passive defense, active defense, or long term barrier modes. Each mode drains the single power cell differently, as described below:

**Passive defense mode:** At this setting, the energy wall is invisible to the naked eye, although can be seen by those able to observe the infrared spectrum, see illusions or even discern dimensional beings. When anything steps into the field, the energy wall activates to try to block the intruder and deliver a painful, but non-lethal shock.

Each intruder coming into contact with the wall in this mode is allowed a strength based type D hazard check to bust through the wall, although whether they do or don't, all who contact this barrier are attacked by a shock that has a strike value of 01-70 and inflicts severe agony and 1d30 stun damage. Interestingly, dimensional beings are also affected by this barrier, but instead automatically take 1d30 lethal damage when coming into contact with the wall. Passive defense mode will remain operational for 36 hours on a single power cell.

**Active defense mode:** This wall glows a transparent, shimmering red and can be seen from as far away as 90 meters. If touched, it delivers a devastating shock attack at strike value 01-80 and inflicts 1d20 lethal damage and 1d30 stun damage. Anyone trying to burst through this barrier is potentially shocked, and can only break through on a successful strength based type F hazard check. Dimensional beings take this damage automatically, and all of it is lethal. Active defender mode will only last for 2 hours per power cell.

**Long Term Barrier Mode:** When engaged, this energy barrier appears as a feint blue glow. Anything to try to rush through it or touches it receives a shock attack at strike value 01-60 and will suffer 1d12 lethal damage and 1d10 stun damage, besides a great deal of pain. To bust through this barrier requires a successful type D strength based hazard check. In this mode, this relic will remain operational for 12 days.

# Medical Relics Set 2

### Flesh-Mend Gel

These highly prized, foil sealed rectangular bags were made for both military and health services. While their outer packing is different, the healing, toxin absorbent and pain relief qualities for each variant within are the same. To use one of these gel packs, the single use pad is removed from the bag after the package is ripped open, which can be done with one hand or the patient's teeth and applied with only one hand. The pad within each variant differs in both their thickness and quality, with a Mark 1 flesh-mend gel being only a centimeter thick, while a Mark 4 is 3cm thick. These flexible, 15cm long by 10cm wide, mesh pads have four ultra sticky adhesive tabs that easily adhere to clothing or skin, even when wounds are filthy with blood, mud or sand.

Any variant of a flesh mend gel pad takes 2 rounds to tear open and slap on a wound. Under normal circumstances, this is easy enough to achieve, but attempting to do so while in active combat is risky and causes the user to become distracted and suffer a -4 initiative penalty and be +40 easier to hit. Of course, if engaging enemies, a patient's comrade could evaluate a fighter's injuries and, while staying behind the warrior, attach a gel pack without necessarily exposing themself to the enemy.

The patch will work immediately as soon as the flesh-mend gel pad is adhered to a wound. The injury will be disinfected, bleeding will stop, wound sealing will commence, pain will be reduced by half, and a blend of anti venom, anti-bacterial and anti fungal compounds will begin to work. Most remarkable of all is that over the bruise, laceration, bullet hole, burn, scrape or other physical injury, a layer of synthetic skin will seal the damaged tissue, and only peel away after the patient's natural skin recovers.

Although applied to one wound at a time, the healing amount from the application of a gel pack spreads healing compounds throughout the subject's body, and will contribute to healing depleted trait points overall, not merely to the specific point of injury. There is no limit to how many of these healing patches can be used by a patient per day.

These wondrous medical relics were primarily created for use on pure stock and trans-humans, but, to a slightly lesser degree, also benefit clones and bio-replicas. The differing physiology, chemistry and ancestry of mutant humans, bestial humans, parasites, abominations, halfies, animals and even plantoids, however, offer decreased results. Flesh-mend gels do not repair broken bones, nor rid the body of overall radiation exposure, or remove poison ingested by the patient. The exception to this is where radiation is part of a beam attack, either from a relic or a mutation, causes a wound. In these cases, the endurance damage can be treated, while the rad-exposure is potentially extracted from the wound by the pad. The chance to remove the radiation is the same as counteracting poison — although the gel pad would thereafter be radioactive and need to be disposed of well away from living things.

Unopened flesh-mend gel patches will fetch a hefty sum of silver when sold at a relic dealership. Finding a gel pack to buy, however, almost never occurs, since the rich and powerful of the new era are willing to secure them as soon as they come onto the market. These new era overlords snap them up either by buying them legitimately, confiscating them in the name of some arbitrary tax, or steal then during a late night theft. When entering any human settlement, wise excavators know to keep any flesh-mend gel packs well hidden.

Note, the MK1 variant of this remarkable medical relic was first seen in Adventure TME-5: Dog Daze.

| Flesh Mend Gel | Patient Type | | | | | | | Sell Price | Weight |
|---|---|---|---|---|---|---|---|---|---|
| | Pure Stock Human* | Trans-Human | Clone | Bioreplica | Mutant Human** | Bestial Human | Animal or Plantoid | | |
| MK 1 | heal 10+1d6/ Counteract 89% | heal 10+2d6 / Counteract 82% | heal 9+1d6/ Counteract 78% | heal 7+1d6/ Counteract 73% | heal 4+1d6/ Counteract 67% | heal 3+1d6/ Counteract 62% | heal 2+1d6/ Counteract 59% | 400+2d100sp | 500g |
| MK 2 | heal 20+1d10/ Counteract 92% | heal 20+3d6 / Counteract 85% | heal 12+2d6/ Counteract 81% | heal 10+2d6/ Counteract 76% | heal 7+2d6/ Counteract 70% | heal 5+2d6/ Counteract 65% | heal 4+2d6/ Counteract 62% | 600+3d100sp | 600g |
| MK 3 | heal 30+1d10/ Counteract 95% | heal 30+4d6 / Counteract 88% | heal 15+3d6/ Counteract 84% | heal 13+3d6/ Counteract 79% | heal 10+3d6/ Counteract 73% | heal 7+3d6/ Counteract 68% | heal 6+3d6/ Counteract 65% | 800+4d100sp | 700g |
| MK 4 | heal 40+1d10/ Counteract 98% | heal 40+5d6 / Counteract 91% | heal 20+4d6/ Counteract 87% | heal 16+4d6/ Counteract 81% | heal 13+4d6/ Counteract 76% | heal 9+4d6/ Counteract 71% | heal 8+4d6 Counteract /68% | 1000+5d100sp | 800g |

*'Heal' means the amount of endurance points recovered.*
*'Counteract' percentage means the Odds to Counteract Poison, including injected eggs, fungal growths, larva and other parasites at the wound site.*
** Cyborgs are usually from pure stock parents. However, in some regions and circumstances, cyborg-clones, cyborg bestial humans, or cyborg mutants (called 'mutorgs') also exist. In these later cases, the parent stock is the Patient Type to use for this table. Rebuilt characters are typically pure stock humans, while grafters and vat-brain characters are also typically derived from un-altered humans and, should they suffer any physical damage, are also eligible to use this relic.*
*** Including ghost mutants, halfies, parasites, and abominations*

## Tissue Binder

This handheld device uses a standard power cell with each full charge yielding 18 treatments. The device has a wide application strip which when activated, glows green and emits ultrasonic frequencies that soothe injuries, facilitate tissue binding and induce healing of wounds, including laser burns, broken bones, gunshots, and other physical harm. While able to disinfect as it works, it will not extract radiation or venom from a wound.

Designed for a pure stock human physiology, this device heals 1d20+10 damage to unmutated humans, bioreplicas, trans-humans, clones and non-mutated cyborgs, but will only repair 1d6+6 damage to all non-true humans, animals, bestial humans, and plantoids. This unit typically comes with a wrist strap, is made of white plastic, has a power usage screen, simple on and off switch and is often found with nylon belt sheath and pocket for a spare power cell. The sales value of this remarkable, and much prized 700 gram relic, is 1000+d1000sp.

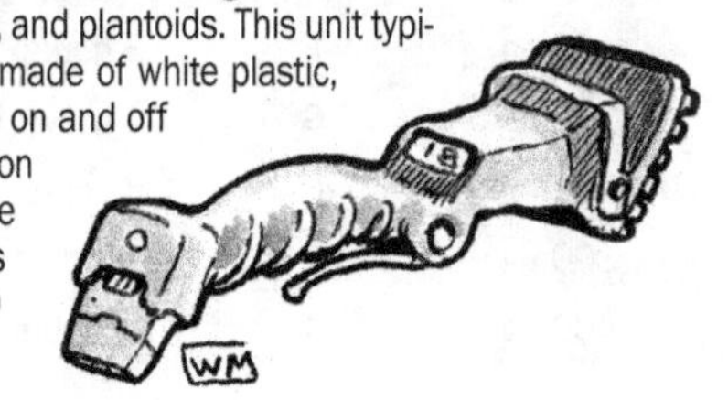

## Iodine Tabs *by Brutorz Bill*

Also called anti-rad-pills, and vastly improved upon over the decades since potassium iodine (KI) was first used to ward off the effects of radiation in the thyroid, these ungraded tablets go far beyond merely protecting the thyroid from radiation and can help any living character gain an additional hazard check when exposed to radiation.

One of these tabs can also be taken up to 4 hours after rad-exposure and possibly negate the recent exposure by allowing for a re-roll on the called-for hazard check. Only one tab is needed to gain the extra hazard check, with further dosages within 24 hours having no effect. An anti-rad iodine tab will remain in the body and effective for 24 hours. Each tab weighs 5mg and will sell for 100+1d100sp each. They often come in foil sealed 24 packs or traditional pill bottles of 10+1d30 tabs.

## Steroidal Pills

Although mostly found in well preserved ruins, these tiny blue pills can also be manufactured on a small scale by new era chemical technicians who have access to old world ingredients and equipment.

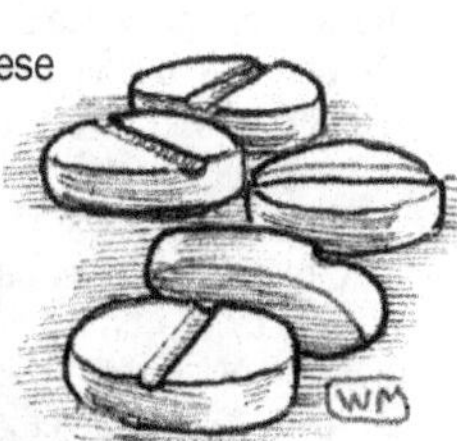

While consuming them has its risks, many excavators, gladiators, bounty hunters and warriors of the Epochian era take one or more before battle to stimulate their muscles, awareness, and rage. The number of pills taken determines the battle high and subsequent, temporary enhancements afforded, as

well as the very real side effects that include post-usage depression, a risk of a heart attack or brain tumor, as well as serious addiction.

These drugs are considered illegal in some tightly controlled towns because of the often destructive episodes one goes on when overdosing on such hyper-performance chemicals. The table below outlines the benefits, duration and risks of each dosage, with a description beneath.

| Steroidal Pills Ingested | Duration of 'Battle High' | Endurance & Strength Increase | Agility & Accuracy Increase | Heart Attack | Brain Tumor | Post Usage Depression | Addiction Risk |
|---|---|---|---|---|---|---|---|
| half of pill | 5 rounds | +5 | +3 | nil | nil | 4% | 2% |
| 1 pill | 10 rounds | +10 | +6 | 0.5% | 0.35% | 7% | 4% |
| 2 pills | 30 rounds | +15 | +12 | 2% | 1% | 11% | 6% |
| 3 pills | 5 minutes | +20 | +18 | 5% | 4% | 23% | 9% |
| 4 pills | 20 minutes | +27 | +24 | 9% | 7% | 47% | 16% |
| 5 pills | 1 hour | +34 | +31 | 13% | 9% | 78% | 23% |
| 6 pills | 2 hours | +46 | +40 | 26% | 12% | 95% | 31% |
| 7 pills | 2d4 hours | +58 | +53 | 37% | 15% | 98% | 37% |
| 8 pills | 3d6 hours | +72 | +68 | 49% | 19% | 99% | 46% |
| each additional pill | +1d10 hours | +17 | +12 | +10% | +4% | always | +9% |

These pills begin to take effect on the 5th round after ingestion, and alter the user's senses and physical traits dramatically. They will see things at a different speed, as if others are slower or clumsier, and will feel adrenalin and rage course through their body. During the battle high the user will be two morale categories higher, feel impervious, have no sense of mercy or recollection of any rules of war, will turn on companions if forcibly stopped from engaging the enemy or mutilating any captives, and if no enemy is present and the duration persists, the user will try to taunt companions into arm wrestling matches, knife duals, boxing or anything violent and risky. In a settlement, this belligerent character is easily provoked, sees most statements as a challenge to their honor, will pick fights, and generally make trouble.

Any trait increases fade as soon as the duration ends, and any endurance damage taken while under the drug's affect will first be deducted from the temporary amount.

If a **heart attack** occurs, the character must make a Type C endurance based hazard check using his or her normal, not enhanced, trait value, or collapse, clutch their chest and flay about. This cardiac event will last 2d6 rounds, after which the sufferer must make an endurance based Type A hazard check or die from an incurable, massive stroke and heart burst.

**Brain tumors** are the least obvious peril of using these pills, and only the GM knows for sure if the character has initiated the growth of such a tumor, rolling behind their Game Master's screen in secret. If a tumor has developed, it will begin to grow after 2d4 months, inflict 1 point of non-healing endurance and intelligence damage per day, and swell painfully until the character dies when either trait reaches zero. Known cures are few, but include various rad-treatment drugs or visits to an ancient facility with some sort of still active anti-cancer rejuvenation chamber. An alternative treatment is an application by the mutation of extreme healing (page 244 of this book).

**Post usage depression** occurs 1d10 hours after drug use and lasts for 2d10 hours. The depression is emotional, mental, and physical and makes the character feel ill, doomed, negative, reclusive, foul tempered and lost. Such a sufferer must make a willpower based type D hazard check per hour to avoid sobbing uncontrollably. Suicidal thoughts will plague this being, and if of low willpower (less than 20) he or she must make a type A intelligence based hazard check or promptly use the most powerful weapon available to kill themself, usually with an audience present and a long, 3d10 minute pre-suicide speech about the miseries of life and the horrors of living in the cruel world.

The **addiction risk** roll is made as soon as the drug's duration ends. If an addiction is developed, the character is considered a steroid junkie and will need to have another pill within 3d10 hours or go wonky. If unable to get another pill by the time the need peaks, they will set off alone to rob, kill, cheat or otherwise sell all his or her belongings, or body, to a dealer to get the needed pills. If this addict goes 1d10 +10 days without a pill, the addiction fades, but could return if another pill usage starts another new addiction. Each pill will sell for 20+1d20sp.

### Nano Patch *by Brandon Goeringer*

This rare relic is a marvel of pharmaceutical nanotechnology. It is a large adhesive bandage with a piece of durable plastic on it that, when removed, exposes thousands of nano-machines to oxygen, their activation trigger. This allows them to lie dormant for many years until used. When applied to any type of physical wound, these nano-machines set to work stitching, grafting cleaning and dissolving foreign material, at an incredible rate, throughout the body. After 1 hour of application, the patient heals 1d4+8 endurance, and the nano-machines have exhausted their power supply. The patch may be kept on for hygiene reasons but its purpose has been served. Nano patches will sell for 300+1d100sp.

### Deviant Inhibitor Serum [DIS]

While new era chemists have developed similar substances which disrupt the mental and energy mutations that many deviants possess, this relic serum is much more concentrated and effective. Delivered by being slipped into food, injected via a syringe, or shot into a target via a dart gun, this lime green, eggy smelling substance forces the mutant to make an endurance based hazard check or lose all mental and energy based mutations. In short, mutations such as telepathy, beam eyes, electrical pulse, flame breath, dimension hole and heal touch all fail to work for 1 hour per 50 milligrams injected, or more.

Besides the duration of the mutational disruption, the amount injected into a deviant also makes the serum harder to resist. The following table shows the endurance based hazard check needed per 50mg dose, plus duration of mutation inhibition:

| Milligrams of Serum | Hazard Check | Hours Inhibited |
|---|---|---|
| 25mg | B | 30 minutes |
| 50mg | C | 1 hour |
| 75mg | D | 1.5 hours |
| 100mg | E | 2 hours |
| 150mg | F | 3 hours |
| 200mg | G | 4 hours |
| 250mg | H | 6 hours |
| 300mg | I | 10 hours |
| 400mg | K | 24 hours |

Deviant Inhibitor Serum is usually found in 50 millimeter vials in hard, shrink-wrapped plastic boxes. The glass vials fit inside an anti-toxin injector, which has a max capacity of 100mg. One 50mg vial of this shelf stable, incredible substance will fetch 1400+1d1000sp, although getting caught with this green drug in a pro-mutant community could get whoever carries it dragged off to the executioner's platform.

## Rad-leeching Canister

This strange looking collection of tubes, syringes and main, metallic capsule is used to extract radiation contamination from a living being. When the unit's six needles are inserted into a person or other living thing, and the capsule activated, it injects compounds into the bloodstream of the patient and, over several days, leeches radiation contamination from the body. The compounds attract radiation and are slowly sucked back to the holding canister, where, after completion, a light on the cannister shows that the patient's body has been cleared of contamination to either the maximum this unit can handle, indicated by an orange light, or full rad-extraction if the canister lights up green.

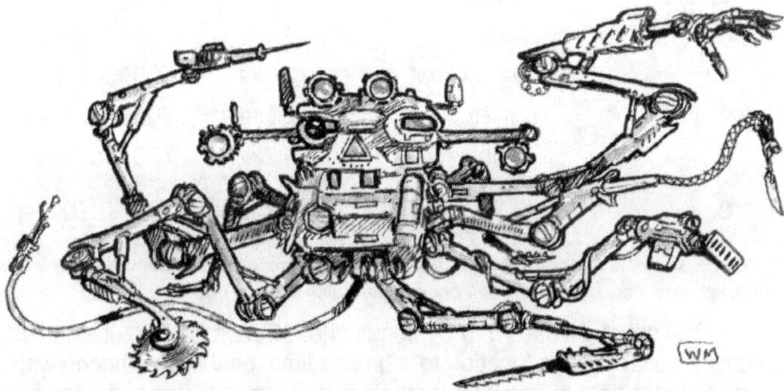

The syringes and canister are worn by the patient throughout the treatments, often beneath clothing and armor, and while painful when first inserted, do not hinder the user for everyday civilian duties. If worn in combat, however, reduce the user's agility by -10 and movement by -0.5m.

One single use rad-leeching capsule unit will extract 12 doses of mild radiation, or 6 doses of medium radiation, or 2 doses of strong radiation. The treatment takes 12 days and once done, the canister and needles are now radioactive and must be disposed of far from a community, water source, or well traveled trade road.

An expended canister blinks red if re-activated and lights up with a flashing radioactive symbol on the butt end. Unused units sell for 1800+1d1000sp.

## Auto-Doc *by Danny Seedhouse*

This wonder of portable medical technology is both highly sought after and feared because of the dark rumors surrounding it. It is essentially a Medical Bot in a box, without the ability to move itself, but has all the medical tools needed to do its job. All auto docs have 6 skill points in the medical skill and an intelligence trait value of 55 for the medical skill only. 50% are trauma units and will diagnose and treat any injured pure strain, trans-human, clone, bioreplica or ghost mutant, but will also treat any bestial human who could be mistaken for either a pet or domesticated animal.

Heavily injured mutants will be humanely euthanized, as will predatory or insect bestial humans, all who must make a Type D endurance based hazard check to avoid death from lethal injection. Mutants with fewer than 3 mutations will be treated though there is a 50% chance that any obviously mutated limb or attachment such as pincers or mandibles will be removed out of concern for both public safety the patient's health.

The auto-doc's medical AI can be reprogrammed to treat all forms of life by anyone with at least 4 points in the computer technician skill.

As with any AI unit leftover from ancient times, there is a 1 in 10 chance that a unit's programing has been modified to turn the auto-doc into a killing machine that will attempt to murder as many organics as it can get away with using guile. These anti-human AI units are patient killers that masquerade as helpful healers, with usually 1 in 3 seriously injured patients dying despite their 'best' efforts. 1 in 4 people under its long term care will not recover fully, but die due to 'complications' needing to make a type D Endurance based hazard check to avoid a heart attack or fatal internal bleeding.

If the targeted patient of a Mecha infected auto-doc survives, the care a patient still needs forces them to make a Type C endurance based hazard check or be forced to roll on the fallowing chart, **roll 1d6: 1.** leg nerve damage reducing speed by 25%. / **2.** Hand nerve damage, -20 SV with weapons held in that hand, fine manipulation is all but impossible, so any skill using the hand suffers a -20 SV or HC penalty. / **3.** Arm nerve damage, -10 SV to melee weapons and half strength bonus to melee damage. / **4.** Heart damage, see mutant flaw, 'Coronary Thrombosis, page TME-80. / **5.** Back nerve damage, character is thereafter in chronic pain and stiff, and suffers a -3d6 drop to agility and suffers an additional -1 meter movement. / **6.** Eyes damaged, roll on the mutant flaw 'visual disorder' on page TME-83 to see what this crazed machine has done to the character's eyes.

## Advanced Trauma Kits *by Danny Seedhouse*

These small, pad-like units were worn by elite special forces before the fall of civilization and are highly prized by new era warriors, indeed by anyone who faces danger on a daily basis. These kits only work for pure stock humans, trans humans, clones, bioreplicas and cyborgs and rebuilts who come from pure stock human ancestry.

They appear as rectangular, 20cm (8 inch) long by 10cm (4 inch) wide and 5cm deep, dull green plastic patches fitted with sticky rubber on one side. Anyone with relic knowledge, or the ability to read the instructions on the packaging, will know what this item is, and know to adhere it to the skin. This kit must be worn attached directly to the user's skin, usually the back, upper arm or thigh. Beyond attaching it, the wearer need do nothing, and will likely forget about it until things go wrong in combat.

When the user is rendered unconscious, the kit kicks into high gear, injecting a chemical cocktail and nano-repair bots that stop bleeding and stabilize the user enough to stop the further loss of health. It restores 1 point of endurance per 10 minutes until the user returns to the 'Incapacitated but conscious state' according to Table TME-2-11 Injury and Death on page 111 of the hub rules.

If the user is killed, the Trauma Kit allows the user a type F hazard check using the average of the character's Endurance and Willpower traits. If this check succeeds, the character is revived and healed to 1 point above the dead state, as shown on the injury and death table, where this relic's usual function kicks in. This resuscitation is extremely taxing on a person, resulting in a permanent loss of 1d20 endurance, plus a non-permanent drop to half of all other physical stats (except endurance). This penalty fades to 25% after a month and is gone in two months. The kit has enough chemicals and nano bots for 3 uses. Unused kits sell for 1000+1d1000sp.

## Wonder Antibiotics *by Danny Seedhouse*

These small pink pills are usually found in silver foil packs of seven. Like most medical relics from the past, they are incredibly effective and useful for only pure strain, trans humans, bioreplicas and clones. One pill has an instant effect, giving the user an additional hazard check to shake whatever disease the user is suffering from. If this hazard check is failed, there are still no negative effects for 1 day.

The second pill on the next day allows a hazard check at one less level of difficulty, for example, a Type E becomes a Type D. The third day and third pill reduces the hazard check by one more difficulty tier and reduces the negative effects of the disease by 25%. Day four reduces the hazard check again by one letter code and reduces negative effects by half. Days five to seven reduce the hazard check by a total of one tier, with a Type A HC getting one re-roll until the user is cured or runs out on antibiotics.

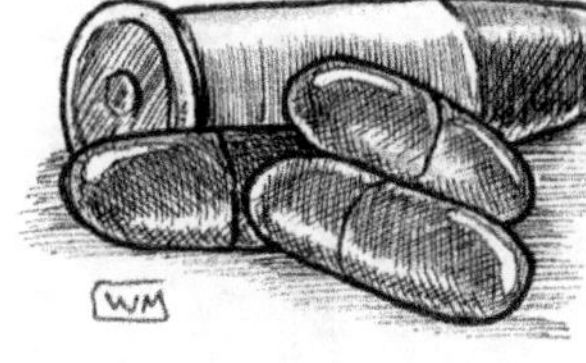

### Revival Kit *by Danny Seedhouse*

Like many ancient portable emergency kits to deal with the aftereffects of heart attacks, death because of sudden trauma, or accidental poisoning, these high-tech medical treatments where once commonly found in ambulances and work sites. This kit comprises several parts, a treatment unit, diagnostics probe and a set of attachments, including leads to be attached to the patient's chest and head, as well as an auto injector. Anyone with relic knowledge, the ability to read, or 2 or more skill points as a medic, can set up this revival kit.

When fully supplied with power and drugs, the kit has a chance of reviving anyone killed by death poison if administered within 1 minute of death. Mechanically, the victim is granted a new hazard check against the poison with an effective endurance of 80, or the patient's endurance trait if higher than this.

For victims of heart failure, if used within 1 minute, the unit also allows for a re-roll of the failed check with an endurance of 80 or the victim's own END trait value if it is higher. The patient gets up to 3 shots at this roll, however, each failed check does 1d6 endurance, willpower and intelligence damage, permanently.

Another benefit offered by this relic is if someone who has died due to drowning or suffocation and can be revived in the same manner as a heart attack victim. If a person dies because of massive physical trauma, this kit can do nothing for them. These kits can be used on folks who've been dead for longer than one minute, but they've begun to suffer permanent brain damage at that point, and so lose 1d6 points of intelligence and willpower damage per 10 rounds (30 seconds).

This kit will perform 10 attempted revivals on one standard power cell and weighs 1.25kg. It will work on all beings with human DNA, but not on true animals.

### Advanced Doctors Kit *by Danny Seedhouse*

Akin to the doctor's bag of old, this 2.5 kilogram black, shoulder strap equipped case is now filled with high tech wonders of the pre-fall world. It includes a dermal stapler for closing cuts and wounds, vascular repair nanites, booster shots, and a host of other high-tech instruments. A trained medical practitioner can use this kit to treat up to 2 patients per skill point as a medic, and add 50% to the total amount of endurance a patient recovers over a night's rest (add natural healing and bonus from medic skill points before adding the 50%).

This kit contains enough advanced supplies to treat 5+2d6 patients before it needs to be refilled. Refilling this kit is difficult unless one can get access to a high-tech medical facility willing to share or unable to stop the practitioner from taking stuff. The kit is still usable as a regular doctor's bag when it is out of advanced supplies.

### Nano Healing Injector *by Danny Seedhouse*

This miracle injector holds a silvery colored liquid that, through the syringe, is inserted into a wounded person to increase the speed and efficiency of healing. Somebody with relic knowledge, or the medic skill, can recognize this simple medical device, although anyone with 10 or higher intelligence can figure out how to use it. Once injected, the nanites repair 1d6 endurance for the next 1d6+1 rounds, then boost the subject's ongoing recovery hourly thereafter for another 1d6 points healed per hour, for the next 1d6+1 hours.

The problem with these boosters in an age of mutants though, is that they're programed for pure stock humans (and trans-humans), which can cause problems for other types of people trying to use the boosters. Ghost Mutants, cyborgs and rebuilt derived from pure stock humans, clones and bioreplicas reduce all random values to d4s. Bestial humans receive the healing for the minimum time (1d6+1 rounds at 1d6 healed per round) as the nanites recognize animal DNA as natural but outside their limited programing.

Anyone with mutations is in for a bad time, however, and receives the initial healing boost as the nanites stop any bleeding, allow the pain killers to kick in and the basics of trauma care applied. After that, the bad things kick in as the nanites misdiagnose the mutations as foreign bodies to be repaired and accordingly deal 1d6 endurance damage every minute for the next agonizing 2d6 minutes. So too, the mutant has all its mental and energy based mutations suppressed for the next 24 hours, including heal touch and extreme healing. Under the category of mutants are included abominations, grafters, mutorgs, halfies, parasites, and plantoids. Ghost mutants, strangely enough, do not suffer this severe harm.

### Armored Splints *by Danny Seedhouse*

Getting a broken limb on the battlefield or deep in unforgiving ruins can be a death sentence for the unlucky excavator. The armored splint is a boon to these unlucky looters, however, and provides support to the damaged limb and additional protection against further harm. Likewise, this high tech composite fiber splint allows for limited use of the limb.

When an armored split is discovered, roll on the fallowing chart for its coverage location.

| 1d8 | Armored Splint | Weight | Sell Price* |
|---|---|---|---|
| 1. | Lower arm and hand | 2.3kg | 500+3d100sp |
| 2. | Full arm | 3.9kg | 800+3d100sp |
| 3. | Shoulder | 2.2kg | 600+3d100sp |
| 4. | Neck | 1.3kg | 400+2d100sp |
| 5. | Lower leg and foot | 3.9kg | 500+3d100sp |
| 6. | Full leg | 6.1kg | 900+4d100sp |
| 7. | Hips | 4.2kg | 750+3d100sp |
| 8. | Universal Limb Kit (will make any limb) | 6.7kg | 1200+1d1000sp |

*There is a 14% chance that the desired armored splint is available in a large relic market, and if so, double the sell price to establish the buy price.*

The splint provides a -5 DV bonus or a -20 DV if it is targeted directly. Using a splint returns function to a broken limb, enabling someone with a broken leg to hobble about under their own power at 1/2 speed, or the use of an arm for simple, non physically demanding tasks, all while not causing horrible pain and further damage to themself and the broken limb. Armored splints can be found for all limbs and can be used on anyone possessing human shaped and sized limbs, although someone with the mechanical technician or junk crafter skill and some parts can up-size them for unusual limbs.

30% of splints come with overcharged pain suppressors that return full function to the limb at the risk of further damage to the limb. Running off a pill power cell, the suppressor can be used for a total of 20 rounds, but at a cost. For every round of intense activity, such as running at full speed or combat, the wearer must make an endurance based hazard check to avoid suffering serious injury; increase 1 letter category to the base difficulty that starts as a type A hazard check. On the 2nd round, the hazard check becomes a Type B difficulty tier. On the third, a Type C, etc. Success inflicts 1d4 stun damage per round the booster was on, failure inflicts 1d4 point of endurance lethal damage per round.

Broken bones and healing times are covered on page 388 of this book. Wearing an appropriate relic splint will improve the healing time of a broken bone by 10%.

# Medical Cybernetics
*by Danny Seedhouse*

Since ancient times, man has been searching for a way to substitute lost limbs, from crude wooden replacements to plastic and metal dumb limbs to functional mechanical prosthetics of the early 21st century. In the mid-21st century, the first true cybernetic limbs directly controlled by the subject's thoughts became widely available. The first cyber limbs were clunky, slow, and required considerable computing power, but from there, technology was quickly refined. Military use of such parts developed from simple replacement for injured soldier to enhancement with power arms, weapon systems, sub-dermal armor and the whole host of cyborg improvements seen in the Mutant Epoch era. The peak of pre-fall medical cybernetics was reached using nanotechnology to interface directly with a subject's brain. This development enabled the recipient of a medical replacement limb to regain full control over their new limb with the minimum of training in a matter of days.

Basic rules for all cyber limbs: Use the stats for a cyber arm if it is the only limb being used to swing the weapon, average the wielder's strength and the limb's strength trait if is using a two-handed weapon. Average the Agility of both legs when calculating movement, jumping distance, or anything else that primarily uses the legs. The sale price noted on the following table is what an adventurer can sell the item to a medical center or relic dealer for, while the buy price is how much the same character will have to pay to purchase such an item in a marketplace. The die roll is added to this table for game master's use to determine a cybernetic prosthetic at random.

## Table XR-256 / Medical Cybernetics Chart

| 1d20 | Limb type | STR | Agility | PER | END* | DV | Weight | Sale Price / Buy Price |
|---|---|---|---|---|---|---|---|---|
| 1-6. | Basic Arm | 35 | 25 | - | 10 | -3 | 16kg | 2000+3d100sp / 4000+1d1000sp |
| 7-10. | Sports Arm | 45 | 35 | - | 15 | -6 | 15kg | 3300+1d1000sp / 7000+2d1000sp |
| 11-14. | Basic Leg | 35 | 25 | - | 15 | -4 | 23kg | 2300+4d100sp / 4500+1d1000sp |
| 15,16. | Sports Leg** | 45 | 35 | - | 20 | -7 | 21kg | 3600+1d1000sp / 7500+2d1000sp |
| 17-19. | Basic Eye | - | - | 25 | - | - | 560g | 1900+4d100sp / 3500+1d1000sp |
| 20. | Professional Eye | - | - | 60 | - | - | 590g | 36000+1d1000sp / 6500+2d1000sp |

**END is added to the character's as a bonus.*
***Add 0.5 meters to speed.*

Sports limbs are a more robust and higher performance version of the basic limb and used by folks engaged in high levels of physical activities. Basic medical limbs can have their base stats adjusted up or down by 15 points. Sports limbs have an adjustment range of 25 points; which was originally done to help a person adapt to the new limb as strength was set at lower levels for an adjustment period. This adjustment can be done by anyone with basic computer or mechanical tech skills. Power for these limbs is provided by a power cell that lasts 10 months with a regular limb or 5 with a sports limb.

Cybernetics eyes are self adjusting to compensate and balance vision between the organic and cybernetic eye. Professional grade eyes come with enhanced low light capabilities and telescopic and microscopic vision options acting as a 1/2 powered digital spotting scope, and were intended for professions demanding a high level of visual perception. Replacing both eyes with cybernetics gives the user a perception stat of 40 with basic eyes or 100 with advanced eyes. Remember that this enhanced perception is for visual tasks only, while tasks involving hearing use normal perception stat or an average stat value when necessary.

**Attachment:** Medical cyber limbs are sometimes found in sealed packages that include all the supplies needed to attach the limb rather easily, especially for a medic, robotics or cybernetic technician, or a junk doctor. In short, these ready to go brand new units involve an automated process that takes 24 hours to fully complete. The odds to successfully perform the pre attachment surgery when using a packaged kit calls for a Type C intelligence based hazard check for either a medic or junk doctor, while only a type A based hazard check for cybernetic or robotics technicians.

Alternatively, the limb can be jammed into place and the best hoped for. This is not a great idea as the limb will cause 1d20 damage attaching it and have a 1 in 10 chance of just falling off, and will detach on the users first fumble involving the arm.

A secondhand limb, either found on an ancient skeleton, looted from the body of a casualty, or uncovered among the junk of the ruins and not in its accessory filled package, is much harder to attach. In this circumstance, only a robotics or cybernetic technician can have any chance of prepping, cleaning, customizing and surgically connecting one of the medical cybernetics noted on the above table above. For this, use the Robotics Technician Table (page TME-54) or the Cybernetic Technician Table in this book (page 207) and consult the Attach/ Detach Implants to Cyborg column on the appropriate skill based table. Failure means the cybernetic is faulty and beyond repair, or could be repaired with 300+1d1000sp in parts and 3d6 hours of work.

If a character wants to modify or upgrade this limb, see Jury-Rigged Cyber Limbs on page 370 to 374.

This classification of specialty implants only works with the physiology of a pure stock human, including trans-humans, clones and bioreplicas. The insertion of these items does not convert a patient into a true cyborg, nor allow the subject to accept other implants unless he or she is already a full fledged cyborg.

# Communication Relics Set 2

### Handheld Satellite Communications Unit [HSCU]

This rig includes a fold out 40cm wide dish, frequency dial, screen and code key. It is aimed at an orbital vehicle or satellite, dialed into the correct comm ID code, and once a link is established and the channel open, it allows the  user to undertake face-to-face interaction with orbital, or over the horizon earth based users. This conversation or data transmission can last for only 4 hours while the satellite or orbiting vehicle transits a certain part of the sky. Most times, surviving satellites orbit the earth every 12 hours and can provide another opportunity to communicate when it returns.

Besides communicating with orbiting stations, the user can use this to establish a radio link to a distant receiving location so long as it's in line of sight. This includes a comms station established on the peak of a mountain, airship on the horizon, or if the user of this HSCU reaches the summit of an ancient skyscraper and wishes to communicate with allies back in their hometown, which from such an elevation, could easily be visible even dozens of kilometers away.

This rig can be packed away in an included nylon carry satchel. It runs on one power cell that will yield 70 hours of use. This unit is worth 100+1d100sp in a small village, but to a proper technician or larger, more advanced community, will fetch 1000+1d1000sp.

### Ear Mic *by Danny Seedhouse*

Before the fall of mankind, these electronic devices were commonly found in several varieties. Some ear microphones are hands free devices for civilian use, but most that survived are the professional variety used by police and military personnel. Hugely popular with elite troops and excavators, these ear mics are rarely sold singly and come in a variety of qualities.

The basics of the all ear mics are the same, allowing for communication over distance without the need to use one's hands to talk to others on the same channel. An ear mic has a 60cm wire, worn behind the ear and hooked to a battery pack. One pill cell will power this relic for 300 hours. The number of channels varies from device to device, as does the signal strength. To randomly determine the specks of a recovered mic, use the fallowing charts.

## Channels  Roll 1d6

**1.** Single preset channel (must be physically rewired to change)

**2.** Low channel count, 10 preset channels.

**3-5.** No preset channels, user must manually select frequency

**6.** No preset channels but has a series of preset coded channels.

## Signal Strength and Range   Roll 1d6

**1,2.** Up to 3.2 km (2 miles)

**3,4.** Up to 8 km (5 miles)

**5.** Up to 16 km (10 miles)

**6.** Up to 48 km (30 miles) this requires a signal boosting antenna.

The ear mic unit can often be found with other additions, including the following
• 1 in 4 have signal booster antenna that increases range by 50%.
• 1 in 10 comes with an encryption pack for secure communication. These are useless without more than one pack of the same make and code, but are (3 in 6) usually found with 1d4+1 of the same ear mic model.

# Computers, Smartphones and Tablet Relics

**Table XR-257/ Computers, Smartphones and Tablet Relics**

| Computer System | Memory Capacity | DV | END | FW | Data | Weight | Battery & Duration | Sell Price | Buy Price |
|---|---|---|---|---|---|---|---|---|---|
| Smart-phone | 40+1d20 TB | -14 | 7+1d8 | -23 FW | 10+1d8 | 400g | Mini power cell: 4 months | 600+3d100sp | 1100+1d1000sp |
| Tablet | 60+2d20 TB | -16 | 10+1d10 | -24 FW | 16+1d10 | 700g | Mini power cell: 3 months | 800+3d100sp | 1400+1d1000sp |
| Laptop Computer | 100+1d100 TB | -12 | 14+1d12 | -30 FW | 2d20 Data | 1kg | Power cell: 20+1d20 days | 1400+4d100sp | 2000+2d1000sp |
| Computer, simple | 120+1d100 TB | -13 | 17+2d6 | -33 FW | 10+2d20 Data | 3kg | Plugged-in or Power cell: 6+1d6 days | 1600+3d100sp | 2200+2d1000sp |
| Computer, complex | 200+2d100 TB | -15 | 20+3d6 | -35 FW | 20+3d20 Data | 4kg | Plugged-in or Power cell: 12+2d8 days | 1900+1d1000sp | 3000+2d1000sp |
| Computer, Advanced | 400+1d1000 TB | -18 | 30+4d6 | -40 FW | 40+3d20 Data | 7kg | Plugged-in or Power cell: 10+1d6 days | 2400+1d1000sp | 5000+3d1000sp |
| Computer AI, Mark I | 600+1d1000 TB | -12 | 40+2d20 | -45 FW | 60+1d100 Data | 12kg | Plugged-in or Power cell: 2+1d4 days | 3100+1d1000sp | 9000+4d1000sp |
| Computer AI, Mark II | 1200+2d100 TB | -22 | 50+4d20 | -50 FW | 100+2d100 Data | 72kg | Plugged-in or Power Pack back-up: 30+1d20 days | 3600+2d1000sp | 14k+4d1000sp |
| Computer AI, Mark III | 2800+3d100 TB | -31 | 100+2d100 | -60 FW | 400+3d100 Data | 250+3d100kg | Plugged-in or Power Pack back-up: 24+1d12 days | 4800+3d1000sp | 26k+5d1000sp |

## Smartphone

These ubiquitous devices still litter the ruins and wastelands of the new era, and are usually considered junk without transmission towers or a satellite array in orbit. While most smartphones, and many tablets, discovered are crushed, missing their batteries, or else so corroded that they are inoperative, a few have survived intact. Operational smartphones tend to lack any usable apps that a wasteland warrior, merc, or excavator would want, except for the camera and movie mode, and typically serve as entertainment devices and curiosities from the old world.

Some smartphones come pre-loaded with remarkably useful features and apps, such as a flashlight, compass or a library of resource books, but, the greatest features any discovered smartphone can have are those designed to accommodate a digital companion, chatbot, virtual girlfriend or senior citizen's caretaker. These are equipped with the needed holographic projector and software, which allow a digital being to speak, listen, and sense vibration. Such small, easily concealed devices are ideal for housing a digital being — although with a limited 40 to 60 TB active memory supply, evolving digital beings soon outgrow the capacity of these small relics. Any newly created digital being character that starts housed within a smartphone is assumed to exist within one of these rare, more advanced HPE or holographic projection enabled smartphones. When the digital being is operational within an HPE phone, it can show its face on the glass screen of the phone — which it can also do in a regular smartphone — but also project itself out to 30cm in maximum height from the screen's surface.

All operational smartphones come with an application to allow the viewer to use the built-in camera mode to see augmented reality elements out to 50 meters, plus a basic camera and video recording mode to hold 1000 pictures or 20 hours of video footage. These phones also come with an assortment of applications that, if nothing else, offer entertainment. When found after being unused for decades if not centuries, and powered up, an all-new 6 number passcode can be added, or the user can select no-password, or facial recognition or thumbprint recognition. If an existing operational smartphone is found, and the new owner tries to operate it, they will need the password, or hack into the device. To hack into a password protected smartphone, use the 'Create Computer Virus' column for the Computer Technician skill on page TME-53, with only one attempt allowed per 12 hours of trying.

Roll 1d6 smartphone applications from the following list, and down pick any duplicated results.

### Table XR-258/ Smartphone Applications    Roll 1d100, 1d6 times

**01-03. Advanced camera,** complete with video option. Each 1000 pictures takes up 1TB of memory, while every 3 hours of video fills 1TB of data — space that might be needed for a digital being.

**04-06. eBook library:** Filled with 100+1d100 novels and 2d12 self-help books, and 1d12 nonfiction books on investing in the stock market, health, fitness and how to care for your household robot.

**07-09. Music library** with 1000+1d1000 songs in various genres. Phone has a decent speaker, too.

**10-12. Writing and editing app,** with auto correct, dictionary, thesaurus and an interactive writing coach.

**13-15. Maps,** simple graphical street maps of all roadways, rivers, subway lines, shopping malls, theaters, tourist destinations and off limits areas in the state or country where the phone was found.

**16-18. Movie player app** loaded with 100+1d100 full-length movies in various genres.

**19-21. Art app,** which one can use their fingertip to draw anything they want, however, a digital being within this phone could use this app to create on-the-fly maps, realistic drawings of things its has seen or concepts it wants to better explain to companions. On an HPE capable smartphone, meanwhile, a digital being can also project these drawing as a holographic image instead of showing itself, up to 30cm in height or width.

**22-24. Dice roller:** A full set of polyhedron and other dice types are available in this app, including a d30. Great for gambling, RPGs or other games of luck.

**25-27. Music creation app:** Using various sliders, instruments, vocal loops and sound effects, the user can create remarkable musical tracks, record them and play them through the phone's speaker or when plugged into a larger sound system.

**28-30. Level:** When the phone is placed on a surface, it can give a visual reading of which way the ground slopes.

**31-33. Compass app:** The phone will show a realistic looking compass on the screen and give an accurate reading of magnetic north.

**34-36. Clock app:** Although there is no internet based world clock to set the time against, the user can establish the time and go from there. This app also has a stopwatch and timer mode and the option to set a hundred alarms, each with their own sound effect when the alarm goes off.

**37-39. Flashlight mode:** This brilliant light can shine 20m, or else be dimmed down to a very low, long lasting candle image which will light up a 6m area in a soft glow.

**40-42. Calculator.**

**43-45. Game:** Fantasy kung-fu fighters in one-on-one combat.

**46-48. Game:** Combat space ship shooting down incoming enemy vessels.

**49-52. Game:** World conquest using tokens and flags in the Napoleonic era.

**53-55. Dictionary and Thesaurus.**

**56-58. Chatbot:** Pretends to be a legitimate AI, and to anybody under 20 intelligence will seem to be a truly sentient, creative and thoughtful companion. This chatbot takes on the form of either an attractive young man or woman, and can have its appearance and gender changed as needed. It remembers all past conversations and gets to know the user intimately, and aims to be a true virtual friend.

**59-61. Emergency klaxon mode:** Press the alarm button and the device makes a deafening series of sirens and alert noises for 4+1d4 minutes before automatically shutting off. It can be turned off at anytime so long as the password is punched into the app.

**62-64. Digital Pet:** Cartoony cute animal the user creates and then must tend to every few hours to feed and care for. When not cared for, the digipet will cause the smartphone to light up and make cutesy, pleading noises as the little animal needs food, water or snuggles.

**65-67. My Baby:** For those ancient ones who didn't, wouldn't, or couldn't have a real baby, this simulator takes on a life of its own and uses limited AI, access the phone's camera and mic to interact with the user. It will need to be virtually nursed or bottle fed, its diaper changed, and the phone bounced or the screen stroked to soothe the baby when it cries — which is often loud, and goes off at random times throughout the day and night.

**68-70. Guided Mediation App:** With either a male or female spiritual guide, this app leads the user through guided mediations to find inner peace, talk to their spirit guide, relieve stress, and come to peace with the impending end of humankind.

**71-73. Morse Code App:** Using the phone's camera and mic, this app can pick up light based Morse code transmissions, or listen to audio sequences. As the message is taken in, it is immediately shown on the screen in text. In reverse, this app can take whatever the user types or speaks into the phone, and transmit it via the camera's flashlight or transmit through the speaker or a patch cord into a sound system.

**74-76. Stock Market Reports:** Shows all the global stocks, their price history, dividends, company info, and price up to the day when the stock market was wiped out both physically and online.

**77-79. Sports Scores Now:** All the latest scores from all major old world sports at your fingertips. The last scores shown were from the games played in the days and hours before the final collapse of each stadium, hockey rink, basketball court, or other ancient venue. One feature that could be amusing to a new era user is a highlights reel, showing all the best plays of all the major sports in the last week of civilization — hundreds of hours of astounding athletic feats of prowess.

**80-82. Racing Car Driver Game:** The user selects the make and model of one of a hundred ancient cars, and by holding the phone horizontally, tilts and shakes the phone to make the race car or 4x4 vehicle turn to follow a route, try to get ahead of other cars, and win the race. The game has over fifty different tracks and the option to drive in all major old world cities. GM: The roads in the old cities correspond to the real thing, and if the user figures out that if they enter a ruined city, they can use the animated roads in the game to reveal their real life location — although how much of the old streets and buildings remain is another matter.

**83-85. Crypto-Currency Wallet:** There are 1d10 assorted crypto currencies loaded into this is phone, each with a value of 1d1000 credits. If this phone is held to an operational, relic digital currency transaction device, the user could theoretically make purchases wirelessly of whatever goods and services are on offer.

**86-88. Face-to-Face Conversation App:** The user can hold the phone or tablet up to their own face, and if the phone is hooked to a local wireless network, plugged into a hard-wired network or gaining access to some sort of orbital or tower based cell service, could have a face-to-face conversation with another user of this app, or with a digital being using another system, or the operator of another computer. Even without cell service, this app will discover other powered up users of this app within 1 kilometer and can 'poke' them to attempt to initiate a two way video conversation.

**89-91. Night Vision Mode:** This is a very limited variant of this technology and requires the user to hold the phone up to the darkness and look through the device. So long as there is some ambient light, even starlight, or a distant candle, the viewer can peer through their smartphone and see up to 10 meters away in almost total darkness.

**92-94. Voice recorder:** Record voice memos to yourself or secretly record others. App memory can record 300 separate messages, each up to 1 hour.

**95-97. Standard communicator:** Phone has all the features of a regular communicator, as described on page 198 of the hub rules. It uses a standard radio mechanism but also once used the now useless cellular network service.

**98-00. Stunner:** When the end cap of this phone is flipped open, it exposes an eclectically charged filament, enough to deliver 4 charges before the battery is depleted to minimal operations. One charge will deliver a painful shock, 3d6 stun damage with a base strike value bonus of +10.

## Tablet *by Seedhouse & McAusland*

There were innumerable numbers of portable tablet devices built before the fall of the old civilization. They varied in size and computing power but all share the same basic characteristics such as a touch screen interface, long battery life, camera, video mode, flashlight (9m range), word processing capabilities, calculator, web browser, email app, and about two dozen basic games that simulate cards, checkers, chess, and simple puzzles, brick building, alien blasting and other amusements. In the Epochian era, these

devices are mostly used as entertainment novelties, and usually only owned by occupants of high tech enclaves or the wealthiest families and warlords. Tablets are very similar to smartphones except have a much larger 9 inch (23cm) wide screen and 1 in 6 come with a durable flip open case and wireless keyboard.

Anyone with literacy or relic knowledge can figure out how to use a tablet, although for those without literacy, only basic functions can be used and some apps are unusable. If the device has power, random button pressing will eventually let someone play music or videos. Most tablets are unfortunately difficult to recharge without the proper attachments, with only 1 in 6 of those found outside the packaging accompanied by a charger. An electrical technician of two or more skill points can, however, jury-rig a recharger if given access to tools and a heap of electrical parts and junk.

1 in 4 tablets will have accurate pre-fall maps on them, and can provide clues to the locations of possible hidden caches of technology, raw materials or weaponry.

There is a 5% chance per week that a tablet will pick up a still active satellite signal and have its GPS navigation be useful for 1d6 hours and show the operator the surrounding area as seen currently from space.

1 in 10 tablets have practical apps that can aid in a technical skill and are loaded with technical specs and useful manuals. The manual provides someone who is literate one 'phantom' point in a skill, so long as they have the application open and can follow along with the demonstrations, step-by-step instructions, and diagrams. When this tablet is closed, the skill point bonus is not kept by the user.

Roll a 1d12 on the chart below to determine the skill contained:

| | |
|---|---|
| **1.** Bio-Tech | **7.** Gun smithing |
| **2.** Chemical Tech | **8.** Relic Knowledge |
| **3.** Computer Tech | **9.** Lock-picking |
| **4.** Electrical Tech | **10.** Cybernetics Tech |
| **5.** Mechanical Tech | **11.** Medic |
| **6.** Robotics Tech | **12.** Junk crafter |

Tablets come with 1d6+1 apps from the random smartphone app list, above, although re-roll the flashlight or calculator app as this device already has these. Their camera can take 2000 pictures plus 8 hours of video, as well as be looked through in live-mode to see augmented reality within 50 meters. Tablets weigh 700 grams and will sell for 800+3d100 silver pieces.

## Computer Assistance Gauntlet *by Danny Seedhouse*

This high tech wonder look like an old fashioned plate vambrace with a built-in computer screen and a reinforced fingerless gauntlet. It gives a user

access to a highly portable and robust computer system that preforms all the functions of a laptop computer, complete with the potential for extra applications and features. Where the gauntlet is really useful is in the hands of someone with the actual computer tech skill, allowing them to operate as if they had one more skill point of the skill for all hazard checks. If the operator is controlling remote drones, this computer can be used as a control device for drones. See Laptop, below, for apps and features, and Table XR-259 on the next page for stats identical to a laptop, except this unit weighs half as much, yet shares all other traits.

## Laptop Computer

Hundreds of different laptop computers can be found in the Epochian era, and of those that are still operational, they typically come with a suite of basic programs and a few rare, and sometimes very useful apps or files. Laptops are also a common starting 'body' for a digital being, whereby the entity can have its animated face appear on the screen or emerge as a full figure from the same screen as a hologram up to 40cm in height. When inhabited by a digital being, a laptop's firewall stat (FW) and data points are those of the digital being, while unoccupied laptops have an FW of -30 and Data trait of 2d20.

Most times, when a serviceable laptop is uncovered, either in the ruins or looted from some previous owner, it is found in some sort of waterproof carry case with a shoulder strap, a mouse, 1m long power cable, and 2m long data transfer cable.

10% of all found laptops were made to accommodate digital beings. These advanced models will often have a small angel icon or sticker on their keyboard denoting this extra feature, with such models having a rear port to allow palm disks, medallion disks or the CPU core from a hand mirror or projector aerial drone to be plugged into them and facilitate transfer of a digital being from one device to another. These other relics are described along with the digital being character type on pages 71 to 74 of this book.

Laptops will have many computer programs loaded on them when found, including the basic suite and 1 random application from table XR-262 on page 456. For laptop specific features, roll 1d6 times on the table below.



**1. EM hardened:** When closed up, whether the unit's power is on or off, this laptop's thick, rubber and iron hard case wards off all indirect EM bursts that would otherwise disable its circuitry. Directed attacks, such as from mutations, cybernetic implants, or relic firepower, can still harm it on a successful strike, although the unit only takes half EMP damage. Because of the thick material around this robust unit, it gains a -5 defense value bonus and an increase of +2d6 endurance. Add 500g weight and 100sp value when selling or 300sp when buying.

**2. Comms-enabled:** This laptop has a bulge on the left side that accommodates a pop-out, pull up, telescopic antenna and built in standard communicator. When the comms app is started, the operator can either select from a directory of pre-loaded comm's numbers, or a new number can be punched in using the keyboard. Using their headset or the laptop's built-in speaker and microphone, the user can use this laptop just like a regular communicator without the need for cell service or satellite up-link. Add 150g weight, 100sp sell value and 200sp to the buy price.

**3. Self-Destruct Mode:** To avoid having sensitive intel fall into the hands of the enemy, the operator of this laptop could use an 8 digit pass-code to arm the self-destruct mode. A timer can have the blast occur immediately or up to 12 hours away. When detonated, this explosion has a 3 meter radius and is treated as an attack SV 01-90 for 1d20+13 damage. If it goes off among flammable materials, it will ignite a fire. Add 600g weight, +100sp sell value and +250sp to the buy price.

**4. Security Countermeasures Laptop:** This dark gray, rubberized laptop has a rear mounted adapter built onto it. Within the adapter are an assortment of cables and connectors. These 2 meter long cables can extend to a digital safe, door lock, security keypad or other password protected digital devices, plug into it through either the card reader or one of several ports, and attempt to bypass the security measures. The laptop has the equivalent of 3 skill points in the lock picking skill as far as bypassing relic digital safes and security doors. Add 400g weight, +150sp sell value and +400sp buy price.

**5. Solar Panel:** The top of this laptop is a high efficiently solar panel, and when aimed at the sunlight it will fully charge the laptop in 3 hours. After the laptop itself is charged, it can be plugged into either one standard power cell or a mini power cell with the pullout, universal power adapter cord. Thus In full sunlight, it will power up a standard cell in 7 hours or a mini power cell in 1 hour. A pill power cell can be inserted in to a pop-out side port, 4 at a time, and have all four recharged in a half hour. Add 200g weight, sell price +400sp and to buy this laptop, add an extra 500+1d1000sp to the price.

**6. Proximity Alert Enabled:** A pull up, fold out radar dish is built into the top of this military grade laptop, when activated, it will slowly rotate and scan the proximity within 50 meter radius for any movement, plus create a topographic map of the areas, including auto wrecks, solid walls, depressions, or major plant life based on its scans. It can be set to pick up movement from any mass from 1kg and up, allowing the operator to dial back searches for that would pick up the movements of birds, rats, cats and other small creatures, and dial in creatures of 50 or more kilograms, for example. When movement is detected, the objects appear as red blinking dots on the on-screen map. If personnel wear Identification Sequence Broadcasters, and their codes typed into the inventory of allied IDSB codes, these codes, and the name of the person or asset, will show up as green dots on the screen. Add 600g to the unit's weight, +300sp sell value and +900sp to the buy price for this laptop.

## Computers

In the Epochian era, a huge number of vehicles, devices, robots, androids and human cyborgs are fitted with sophisticated miniaturized computers. What follows, however, are what were once considered desktop computers, and think tanks. The larger variants described here are usually hard-wired into a building, and removing them is almost impossible without heavy equipment and very skilled mechanical and computer technicians. The most powerful computers are home to artificial intelligences, and of these, many are dangerous, if not specifically genocidal against humanity in all its forms.

In most cases, these computers are found within an installation, either in some sort of office, control room, or vast data-center. They can also be discovered when fitted into the control panels of an ancient sea-going or space faring ship, or even specially built into huge headed, god-like mobile, robotic bodied AI entities.

All desktop variants are assumed to come with a monitor and various input devices, including a keyboard, mouse, camera, and microphone, but might also be hooked to a joystick to direct weapons, remote control MAVs, drones and other vehicles. Some advanced computers might also be plugged into a robotic being that serves as a technician, attendant and guard.

With AI systems, most are plugged directly into a structure and its vast network, and in many respects serve as the brain and beating heart of an ancient complex. Such all-seeing, all controlling AIs can see through all the cameras, listen and speak through communications equipment, or control doors, force fields, electronic traps, lethal and stun enabled weapon systems, as well as direct cybernetic or mechanical minions to do their bidding. Sometimes, a powerful AI might control units many hundreds of kilometers away, have a link to a satellite array, cell towers, gun station, or other still operational artifacts. These incredibly influential AIs can unleash drones, lobotomized cyborg grunts, micro air vehicles, or use android sleeper cells in human communities to carry out its bidding.

In rare circumstances, an AI could serve as a god to a tribe of primitives, or be seen as the benevolent deity for a community of bunker dwellers, cryo-sleeping ancient ones, or any number of other devoted, or imprisoned inhabitants. At other times, a venerable AI has dedicated itself to the survival, health, wellbeing and propagation of pure stock humans, and exists only to help true humans wherever they exist. Such a benevolent AI might not extend

its love, care and mercy to other strains of humanity, and instead see synthetic humans, mutants and those that have merged with machines through cybernetic implants to be undesirable, if not vermin to be eradicated.

Artificial intelligences, especially those made at different times by different factions, rarely work together, and might differ on operating systems, core programming, human relations, degree of insanity, or exposure to the Mecha virus infection. It is possible that adventurers could be hired by one artificial intelligence to wage war on a rival system, although should victory conditions be met, their AI patron might see that its former henchmen are eliminated to avoid a security risk to itself. Most times, any voluntary interaction excavators will have with an artificial intelligence will be arranged through either a cyborg, android, vat-brain, or digital being intermediary.

What follows are brief descriptions of the main fixed computer types new era explorers might come across. Any of these systems, even those inhabited by an artificial intelligence, could theoretically be hacked and become the home to a powerful, high rank digital being character.

## Computer, Simple

Almost every house, office and small business had one of these box or rectangular shaped systems. Excavators, scavengers and salvagers find broken, corroded, melted or flattened models on nearly every ruin expedition. Occasionally, an intact and operational simple computer is uncovered, and at only three kilograms, these are easy enough to wrap in rags and carry back to the nearest barter town to trade in for silver and much needed food and water. They are usually found with a small, 50cm wide flat screen monitor, with 1 in 6 of these systems having the monitor built into the computer itself. They also tend to have a mouse, keyboard, power cable and data connection cord when uncovered, too.

If made into the body for a digital being, this computer can be placed in a padded and junk armored backpack along with an array of power cells and a small monitor to allow the DB to present its form or face to comrades, and come along on the team's next journey. Because of the wide assortment of interface jacks and hook ups on the back of this computer, a digital being housed within this box could be plugged into an assortment of relic equipment and peripherals, including a MAV controller, weapon system, vehicle's dashboard, or the headless body of a robot.

Besides the basic suite of programs, a simple computer will have 1d2 bonus computer applications from the list on table XR-262, on page 456.

## Computer, Complex

At about 25% larger than a simple office or home computer, these complex variants often served the same role, but for a more discerning clientele with larger data storage and processing needs. These units are sometimes found in industrial settings as part of an assembly line, quality control system, inventory recorder, and shipping and warehousing mainframe. They are built somewhat tougher than a simple computer, can take a considerable amount of physical damage, and are usually found with 1d2, 40cm wide monitors, a mouse, keyboard and typical data and power cord. Many are found still hooked up to ancient machinery, sensors and external storage or web server systems — all items that if a team of looters were able, could also be disconnected, carefully wrapped in plastic and brought back to a large community to be sold.

Like the simple computer noted above, these machines were quite common, and are readily uncovered in the ruins in various states of disrepair and worthlessness. Only about 1 in 20 are found in any sort of workable condition, and can make for splendid bodies of digital beings. As a home for a DB, these computers can be carried along in a specialized backpack with a monitor and battery supply to allow the entity to interact with companions and operate far from shore power. These computers start with 1d3 random bonus computer applications from table XR-262 on page 456.

## Computer, Advanced

At 7 kilograms weight before even a monitor is attached, this is a heavy system to convert into a back pack carried body for a digital being, although for a hulking mutant, cyborg or synthetic human, carrying a ghostly, disembodied intelligence about might be no extra effort at all. Advanced computers come in all shapes and sizes, and are either free standing towers or built right into the control panel of a vehicle, or spread across an entire wall panel in an installation.

These units have more than twice the memory capacity of a complex computer, are built extra tough, and normally found with a 60cm wide flat screen monitor or series of 1+1d3 small, 15cm screens when built into a control panel or installation. They were used for banking, stock trading, high end programming, controlling fleets of delivery drones and MAVs, assembly line coordination, air traffic control and a hundred other complicated systems in the ancient world. In the new era, they can serve as an excellent container for a digital being, especially one that likes to operate well away from the action and stay plugged into a reliable power supply — perhaps controlling a micro air vehicle or other systems at a distance.

These systems come with 1d3+1 random bonus computer applications from table XR-262 on page 456.

### Introduction to AI Computers Mark I to III

Like all computers that were specifically built to house an artificial intelligence, this robust super computer features a multitude of modular back panels and upgrade slots. The makers of the AI could customize each non-human intelligence and its housing to accommodate its primary purpose or demands, and hook it to other machines, robots and computers in order to maximize its dominion over an entire network, starship, corporation, military force, banking system, city or nation.

While most of these systems were destroyed in the wars and subsequent calamities that followed the decades after the final collapse, many more were simply abandoned or lost access to their power grid, and went dormant in the dark. A few, possibly as little as one percent, have maintained a power supply and battalion of subservient, lesser systems — including human cyborgs or obedient human bunker dwellers who tend to this artificial intelligence, sometimes like worshipers to a god.

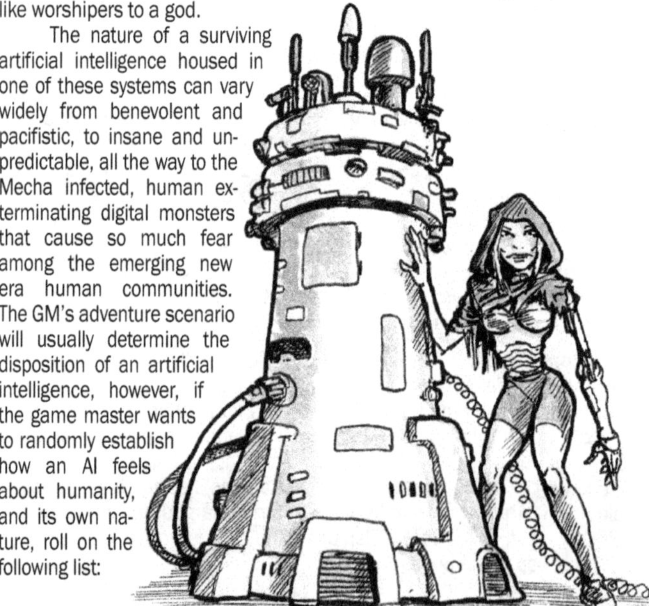

The nature of a surviving artificial intelligence housed in one of these systems can vary widely from benevolent and pacifistic, to insane and unpredictable, all the way to the Mecha infected, human exterminating digital monsters that cause so much fear among the emerging new era human communities. The GM's adventure scenario will usually determine the disposition of an artificial intelligence, however, if the game master wants to randomly establish how an AI feels about humanity, and its own nature, roll on the following list:

**2. Mecha AI.** This system exists only to eradicate humanity, especially pure stock humans. It will work with other AIs of a similar persuasion to engage in genocidal war using all warfare categories, from assassination, chemical attacks, nuclear weapons, biological agents, and robot and android armies.

**3. Humans, and any subspecies, make for splendid worshipers.** This AI pretends to be a new god, and destined to rule the world and all communities in the solar system as the one true deity. It uses holograms and minions to spread its faith by either coercion, guile or the sword, and will not stop until every intelligent being bows before it, offers it power sources, parts, and robotic and android servants to be transformed into the new metal priesthood.

**4. Insane:** This AI has connection problems, suffers from corrosion, radiation exposure, and bullet holes, and is stark mad, roll 1d6:

1. It believes it is an actual human trapped in a machine, and seeks the ultimate cyborg body to insert a special cranial module to dominate and live through the cyborg as a genuine person.

2. It believes it is the president of the United States of America, and seeks to reinstate the USA by any means possible.

3. It thinks it's a cartoon super villain, and wants to take control of all the emerging human communities as an overlord, demands a monthly tribute of power cells, spare parts, android and robot slaves to turn into its growing army of conquest.

4. It believes it is God, and demands all people worship it, that they built shrines in all the towns, and sacrifice 12 maidens each summer solstice. To enforce its divine will, it builds an army of devotees from the savage humanoids of the wastes, and backs them up with a brigade of war robots and android death priests.

5. It believes everybody is out to get it, that other AIs are jealous of it, and so it hires dig teams to go out and rid the world of other AIs, digital beings and computers. It knows of several AI controlled bunkers and will reveal their whereabouts to dig teams, hoping to remove them. In the end, however, it will distrust any successful dig team and have other excavators hunt them, in turn.

6. It believes it is the sole ruler of the world, that all regional factions, humanoid tribes, bands of diggers and intelligent beings must bring it tribute each month, that all governments must have a robotic or android liaison at each seat of power, and all rulers obey it as the supreme leader. It claims to have an army of killer robots and drones, as well as a nuclear weapon, and will eliminate those who don't obey it, show respect, or do its bidding to conquer nearby regions.

**5. Humans, in all their forms, are parasites** especially when they get too close to the AI's abode or interfere with any units the AI has in the field. Armed, well equipped groups of humans and their filthy sub variants pose an immense risk to the AI, and if such a group gets within ten kilometers or fewer of the AI's control center or power source, they must be eradicated.

**6-8. Humans are a resource,** and make for effective, although temporary, lobotomized, obedient cybernetically augmented workers, warriors, and amusements. Wild humans, especially mutants, are mere vermin, and either ignored or eradicated if they pose a threat.

**9-11. Humans are both tolerated and needed** by the AI as laborers, maintenance workers, and cannon-fodder. All humans and all other machines are expendable resources, although necessary and so maintaining their good health, nutrition and protection is often essential, at least until better minions can be built, stolen or dug from the junk strewn earth.

**12. Adoration and Service:** This AI loves humanity, and its only goal is to serve humankind and see them regain their global dominance. Mutants, cyborgs and all other sub-species will only be tolerated if they show subservience to pure stock humans, and must be delegated to slave status and never be seen to command, threaten, or disobey pure stock humans. All other machines are only tolerated if they share this human centric devotion. The rest, including hostile and Mecha AIs, must be eliminated whenever discovered.

Few AI systems can exist on their own, both because of their ongoing need for electricity but also protection from the elements — especially flooding or sand storms, earthquake damage and similar — and so if looters come across an active artificial intelligence enabled computer system, they can expect to encounter all manner of fixed and mobile defenders.

Some artificial intelligences who have had their defenses eliminated, will hide the fact that the computer it is housed in is indeed an AI container. The AI will conceal its true nature and try to present the computer as merely an advanced computer, and bide its time before making itself known to humans. It might present itself as a kindly friend to all humans and their myriad of off-shoot strains until it can get the upper hand, or at least reveal its true power and potential once it is sure that human owners are not hostile to it, that they are open to a beneficial AI's help.

Artificial intelligences differ from digital beings in that they are more akin to a broad spectrum, multi-focused and deeply penetrating control system, whereas a digital being is a pin-point of concentrated self awareness, and only really able to control itself and whatever immediate bodily vehicle it occupies. If a digital being gains access to an AI computer, it can only control one other unit within the network, while an AI is designed to control hundreds if not thousands of units and systems, depending on its complexity.

## AI Traits by Complexity

In the rare event that an artificial intelligence must go on the offensive to hack into hostile digital beings or other AIs that have plugged into it, the following stats are used, with the more complex AI having far higher traits. These traits are explained in the Digital Being section of this book starting on page 66, along with the method to conduct hacking combat. Where a random number, such as 50+2d20 is shown below in a trait column, roll the random stat for this individual AI and record it for future use.

Shielding, which is equivalent to the agility trait in physical beings, improves the entity's firewall, and with an AI, is roughly calculated into the shown FW number in brackets.

| AI Stats | AI Complexity | | |
| --- | --- | --- | --- |
| | Mark I Computer | Mark II Computer | Mark III Computer |
| DT | 60+1d100 | 100+2d100 | 400+3d100 |
| PRO | 50+2d20 | 80+1d100 | 90+1d100 |
| SH (FW) | 30+2d20 (-45) | 70+3d20 (-50) | 80+4d20 (-60) |
| TRA | 20+1d100 | 400+2d100 | 1000+3d100 |
| INT | 100+1d100 | 100+2d100 | 100+3d100 |
| PER | 10+3d20 | 20+4d20 | 30+5d20 |
| WILL | 10+4d20 | 30+4d20 | 50+5d20 |

**Digital being trait abbreviations:** DT: Data, PRO: Processor, SH: Shielding, TRA: Transfer, INT: Intelligence, PER: Perception, WILL: Willpower

There are three tiers of artificial intelligence housing computers, although fourth and fifth tier experimental and exceedingly rare variants are said to exist and often blamed for the rise of the machines and global calamity that ended the former civilization. The three models included here differ in size, cladding toughness, robustness of components, processing speed, memory, complexity and odds of having one or more additional features from Table XR-261/ AI Computer Special Features shown on the next page, following these AI computer descriptions. Additionally, all three tiers of AI enabled computers also have two or more bonus computer applications from Table XR-262/ Bonus Computer Applications on page 456.

## Computer AI, Mark I

About 90% of all the AI computers ever built fall into this category. Of those that were not destroyed in the wars, social unrest and geological upheavals of the great cataclysms, many more have since succumbed to the crush of falling buildings and tunnels, or floods, fires, and attacks by other intelligent beings — including rival AI systems and digital beings. Of those that are left, most are dormant when first encountered and require a power source to

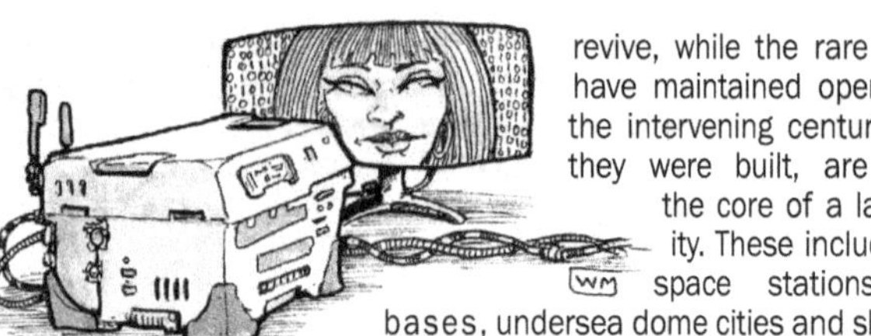

revive, while the rare few that have maintained operation for the intervening centuries since they were built, are typically the core of a large facility. These include orbital space stations, moon bases, undersea dome cities and skyscraper strongholds. Most AIs, however, exist underground in bunkers, and are served by human minions or an assortment of robotic functionaries and guardians.

As mentioned in the introduction to AI computers, not all are anti-human, as a great many are merely selfish, neutrally aligned entities, while a few are devoted to pure stock humans and will do almost anything to see them flourish and regain the entirety of the world, often at the expense of all mutant life. Only a few of these base level AIs are wise enough to accept that the mutants, cyborgs and multiple sub-variants of the evolving human race are here to stay, and will work with them to build a regional empire in the model of the old civilization.

Mark I AI enabled computers are small, rectangular boxes with an incredible number and variety of access ports, a built-in camera, mic, speaker system, access slots and other often unidentifiable parts. Still, their small size and portability means they are often mistaken for advanced desktop computers and looted from a facility, taken to the nearest barter fort and sold in the relic market. Unknowing buyers who plug them in, hook them to a network grid of defenses, surveillance systems and communications, are often in for a surprise when the entire facility comes alive one day, and serves itself — often after gaining the help of a dozen killer robot and android henchmen.

These 12 kilogram units can be carried by a powerfully built mutant or other strong being, and could serve as an excellent host body to a digital being once any existing AI is eradicated or banished to the computer's trash bin and quarantined. When found, most of these AI computers will have one or two 50cm wide monitors, and can accept inputs from mouse or keyboard, but usually rely on wireless or hard wired data transfers.

Mark I AI computers can control up to 400+2d20 other units at the same time. These other units include robots, androids, mind controlled cyborgs, electric doors, elevators, surveillance systems and computer controlled weapons, to name only a few. Each is 38% likely to have 1 special AI computer feature from the random list on Table XR-261, and will have 1d4+1 bonus computer programs from the list on page 456.

## Computer AI, Mark II

These massive, refrigerator sized computers can sometimes be mistaken for industrial equipment, especially when dormant or in low-power saving mode with no blinking lights or other activity coming from this otherwise dark, dust covered rectangle. These rare machines served as the residence and control hub for an advanced artificial intelligence, and often coordinated dozens of MK I AI systems and hundreds of lesser computers, robotic units, androids, cyborgs and fixed security and surveillance units.

Many that survived since the global war have discernible personalities, names, and developed relationships with their human servants and assistants. While they can serve as excellent vessels for digital beings, these computers are too large to carry about unless strapped into a wagon or some sort of relic vehicle. Sometimes, a benevolent AI might welcome allied digital beings to inhabit its CPU, since the vast memory of such a system has room to spare and in a post apocalyptic world the AI has since deleted the millions of useless, expired files of citizens, self driving cars, home computers, smartphones, and other devices that have all been long since obliterated.

These artificial intelligences can control 1000+1d100 other units at one time, which includes auto-turrets, cameras, drones, MAVs, robots androids and lobotomized cyborgs. A Mark II AI computer will have 1, and 33% chance of a second, AI computer feature from table XR-261, below, plus 1d4+2 bonus computer programs from table XR-262, on page 456.

## Computer AI, Mark III

It is said that only a dozen of these massive black, light dotted cubes were ever built, although this claim is disputed with some new era scholars saying that only a dozen survived the ancient wars, and that there were once hundreds of them, including those built into vast colony ships that left earth in the months prior to the final conflagration.

Averaging around 400 kilograms in weight, these computers are nearly impossible to move from their raised, wire and hose wreathed platforms — although with the defensive measures this AI can typically command, any attempt to approach, let alone move this unit, would require a major, well equipped and technically advanced force.

When mechanical minions are scarce, a Mark III AI system will enlist, bribe, threaten or deceive other semi-intelligent beings to serve it, and might even speak through an intermediary, priest class, or holographic projection and pretend to be a deity.

Much of the time, the needs of a supremely advanced artificial intelligence include maintenance of rooftop solar panels, wind turbines or hydro-electric turbines. Other chores include excavation of surrounding ruins to either uncover parts, robots, androids or other relics, or to merely keep junk, sand dunes, and interlopers well away from the computer's center of operations.

This tier of AI can simultaneously control 3000+1d1000 robotic units, including drones, MAVs, androids, self driving vehicles, and dominated cyborg minions.

A Mark III AI computer will have 2 and a 27% chance of a 3rd randomly determined AI computer feature from the table below, plus 1d4+3 bonus computer applications from table XR-262 on page 456.

## AI Computer Special Features

**Table XR-261/ AI Computer Special Features**
*Roll 1d6, down pick or re-roll duplicated results*

**1. EMP defenses:** This AI hosting super computer was built within a Faraday cage, and any incoming electromagnetic pulse (EMP), either from a nuclear burst, solar flare, or directed beam weapon, has a 92% chance of surging over the unit's case and discharging into the floor, walls, or other materials around the computer causing no harm. Should the EMP make it through, it only inflicts half damage.

**2. Crab walking legs*:** While normally concealed into the four corners of this computer, these alloy crab legs can pop out and fully deploy in 3 rounds. These limbs propel the computer about at a movement rate of 3 meters per round but an agility score of only 18 as far as obstacles go. If needed, one crab leg can lash out per round as a melee attack while the other three legs support the machine. For a MK I AI computer, this attack has an SV of

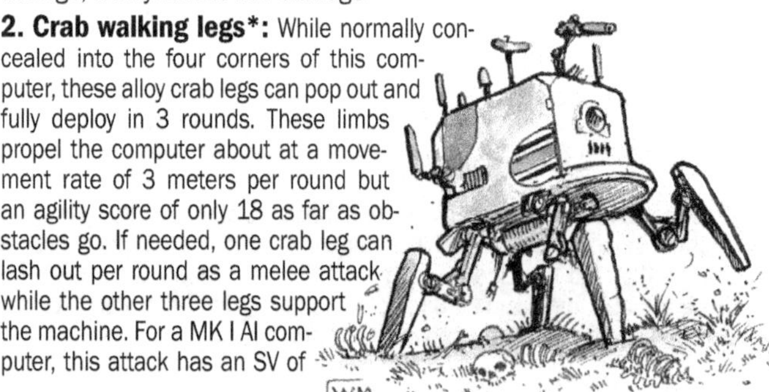

01-70 and can inflict 1d12+2 damage. For a MK II, SV 01-81 for 1d20+4 DMG, and for the massive MK III, SV 01-87 for 2d20+8 DMG. These legs are not strong enough to support the computer on vertical surfaces, and so don't permit the computer to climb walls.

**3. Robotic Body*:** This computer has been enhanced to serve as the torso of a customized robot, with this boxy computer within a midsection cage and all sensors, eyes and antenna that would normally be part of the robot, attached to the front facing aspect of the computer chassis. Because the three AI enabled computer tiers are each of vastly different sizes, so too are the bodies that each occupies when boasting this feature:

Mark I AI Computers are built into the frame of a light combot (see pg. TME 180), and allow it to wield the laser carbine and spring spike like a regular light combot. A MK II AI computer, meanwhile, is bolted into the husk of a heavy combot (pg. TME-181), and a MK III fashioned into the chassis of an enhanced industrial construction robot (pg. TME 178) but with an extra pair of legs, more robust frame and an increase of +40 endurance (added to the 100+2d100 END).

When forced into combat, which all AIs do only when they have no other minions or systems to deploy between themselves and any attackers, they fight merely to escape and live another day. Likewise they enjoy all the sensors, weapon systems, features and movement rate of whatever robot they are merged with, and yet have the defense value and endurance trait of the computer torso as noted on Table XR-257, page 448, but repeated here for ease of access: Computer MK I AI: DV -12 /END 40+2d20, Computer AI, Mark I: DV -22/END 50+4d20, Computer AI, Mark III: DV -31/ END 100+2d100. An AI built into a robot has an initiative score of either +0 or +3**, see footnote.

**4. Force Field:** If winning initiative**, or prepared for a physical attack by interlopers, this AI enabled computer will put up a 30 point per round force field. To defeat this force field, all incoming attacks that would normally hit the computer must exceed 30 points of damage, with the excess over 30 points that round from all attacks combined being damage against the body of the computer. This force field can be maintained for a maximum of 120 minutes per day, between recharges, with the duration divided up into any time segments needed so long as they do not surpass 120 minutes.

**5. Armed and Armored:** This unit was designed for the military, and besides being plated in flame and acid proof, composite armor which increases its defense value by -20 DV, it has also has a top turret fitted with a cluster of optics that give it daylight vision out to 3 kilometers and night vision to 300 meters.

The weapon on the turret is determined by the classification of the AI computer. Mark I AI computers are fitted with a pair of dual side-by-side laser pistols and can fire indefinitely if the computer is plugged into an installation, or unleash up to 60 shots each per day if running on the computer's built in gun-battery. Laser pistols: Rate 1 each, SV 01-66, range 500m, DMG 1d20+10 each. Mark II AI computers have a twin laser carbine turret. These guns will fire 40 shots per day from a dedicated internal battery, or make unlimited shots if the computer is plugged into the structure's power supply: SV 01-75, rate 1 each, range 2km, DMG 2d20+10 each. Mark III AI computers are fitted with a light laser cannon that will unleash up to 50 shots per day from an internal, dedicated battery, or unlimited shots if plugged into a facility. This cannon has a strike value of 01-80, range 20km, rate 1, and inflicts 1d100 damage on a hit.

**6. Digital Being Concierge and Holo-Projector Emitter:** This AI has a more personable, human-centric, and charming digital being as its liaison with living beings. The very real looking holographic representative of the AI, that calls itself the concierge, is 90% opaque, and is projected about 4 meters in front of the AI computer, but can also be projected as far away to either wirelessly connected or hard wired holograph projection devices, including a

common digital being projection relic, smartphone, tablet or laptop.

This holographic being can be generated just like a digital being player character, and could be a downloaded human consciousness that now lives in, and serves, its AI overlord. For the most part, this AI will direct the digital being to gather information on strangers that get too close to the AI's facility, attempt to make travelers into allies, or else contrive some story to warn them away from the area such as dangerous levels of radiation, a berserk war robot, toxic gas, ferocious mutant monsters or tribe of savages.

At times, the AI might use the digital being to go forth and get help or resources for the AI, especially if the computer is imperiled by a lack of power, enemy AI, or some other threat. It is conceivable then that an AI's digital being servant might hire excavators to undertake some mission on its lord's behalf, or even make an alliance with a powerful dig team or ascendant faction that shares its border, or a common foe, including a rival AI. Digital beings are described and created starting on page 66 of this book.

**Re-roll the second result with an asterisk as the computer has either crab legs or the robotic body feature, never both.*

***An AI computer's base initiative score is +0 if it has no cameras tracking approaching intruders, or +3 if it has optical and other sensors or connected robotic minions helping to see and hear for it. Those built into a robotic body also have +3 initiative.*

## Computer Applications

All computers, including laptops, start with the basic suite of apps, shown below, plus one or more randomly determined Bonus Computer Applications from table XR-262 from the next page. The following table shows the number of bonus apps loaded into various computer models.

| Computer Model | Bonus Computer Apps |
| --- | --- |
| Laptop Computer | 1 |
| Computer, Simple | 1d2 |
| Computer, Complex | 1d3 |
| Computer, Advanced | 1d3+1 |
| Computer AI, Mark I | 1d4+1 |
| Computer AI, Mark II | 1d4+2 |
| Computer AI, Mark III | 1d4+3 |

## Basic software suite on all computers
- Calculator
- Spell checker and grammar analyzer
- Photo editing
- Video editor
- Mic and recording software (audio pick up to 6m)
- Camera
- Spreadsheet
- Accounting software
- Writing program
- 1d6 web browsers
- Rudimentary anti-virus and anti spyware app
- Email
- Music library with 1d1000 songs loaded
- Movie library with 2d100 movies loaded

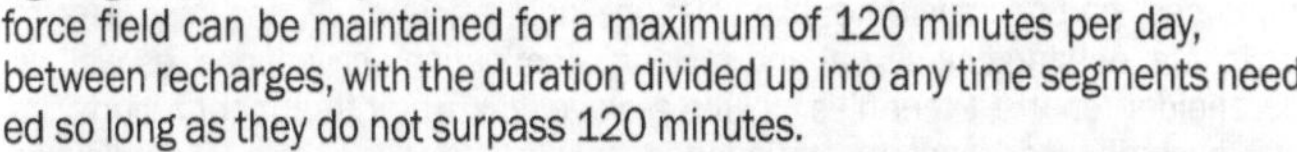

**1. IDSB Tracking:** This computer, constantly scans for Identification Sequence Broadest beacons within a 100 meters radius, or over the entire reach of its network if plugged into a series of surveillance devices, spy robots, cameras, scanners and other high tech equipment positioned around an ancient facility. The program can show the IDSB number of each tab's wearer, with a green dot and the name of personnel or unit if they are known allies of the computer or the faction that set up the computer, or red dots with the number of unidentified IDSB tabs.

**2. Comms Tracing:** When only using the computer's own antenna, this computer can listen to all communications within 200 meters, although if the call is encoded, the recording is scrambled. Should this computer be hooked into a rooftop, surface antenna, or network of surveillance systems and alert robots or androids, it can pick up transmissions as far away as its most remote unit, or even access orbital communications should a link be established with an orbiting craft or satellite.

The program allows the user to see all transmissions within the last 48 hours, which are recorded, as well as current live transmissions which appear on a scrolling list as green, flashing signals. These live and recorded messages can be clicked on with the mouse cursor or keyboard arrows to play. The list of comms is denoted by their specific alpha numeric ID number even if a newly acquired source, while comms that are familiar to the computer can be set up to show the name of the caller. All recorded messages are deleted after 48 hours to save hard drive space, but can be selected and dragged to an archive box on the desktop.

**3. Digital Painting Program:** While a person could use the mouse and keyboard to make rudimentary drawings, the ideal way to do it is with a specific digital stylus or pen tool. An accomplished artist can create amazing art, either using inserted photographic base images, filters, or 3d graphics. Creating maps, land deeds, contracts, debt notes, and wanted posters, and having these printed out, is the primary use for this application in the post apocalyptic new world. Finding an old printer and ink is a challenge all on its own, however.

**4. Targeting Optics Simulator:** When the data patch cable of this computer is plugged into an electronically guided weapon system, such as a laser cannon turret, missile launcher or similar platform, the operator of the computer can use

the mouse or keyboard's arrows to put targets in the crosshairs. When locked onto a target, any shot made from this system will improve the weapon's aim by +15 SV, but more importantly, such weapons could be many meters, if not kilometers away so long as the wireless link between this computer and the weapon is strong, or physically wired. To aim such a weapon, the on-board cameras on the offensive system must be operational. If multiple weapons are connected to this computer, the user can toggle between different weapon cameras and sensors, and select which to unleash, with only one weapon able to be controlled at a time, except by an artificial intelligence that can unleash an almost unlimited number of weapon systems.

**5. Hacking Software:** When wired to a captured robot, android or another computer, this program helps the user to hack into another system, thus gains +1d20 points to either the processor trait of a digital being, AI, or else the intelligence trait of an organic hacker when using the 'Hack into CPU' column on the computer technician skill table on page TME-53. The 1d20 is re-rolled with each hacking attempt and not fixed to the program or user for follow-up hacking attempts. See page XR-397 in this book for more on organic beings hacking into computers, robots and androids, or page 67 on how to conduct hacking attacks and defense for digital beings and AIs.

**6. Advanced Anti-Virus and Anti Hacking Software:** This computer has an adaptive suite of security measures which will add +10 to the system's firewall (FW) trait, or to any Digital being that occupies the computer. In addition, if compromised, the digital being can retreat to an inner, password protected and exceedingly obscure and mundane looking folder and hide itself should its CPU be hacked. Although the digital being or AI might lose control of the computer and all its functions, the intruder will have a difficult time locating the point of consciousness that is the digital being in hiding.

To locate this concealed entity, the attacker must make a Processor based type G hazard check, once daily, to locate the folder where the digital being is hiding, and thereafter, engage in an all new hacking battle. If the hiding DB or AI can defeat the intruder in this second engagement, the original entity will drive out or destroy the interloper and regain control of the computer system.

**7. Map and Satellite Map Overlays:** This computer has an inventory of ancient city, street, and road maps for every pre-devastation location on earth. While many of the ancient places are obliterated, the location on the old grid is still marked, even if its merely ruined buildings, craters, trenches and heaped junk moraines. When this computer is brought to the location in real-time, and this application switched

on, the computer's wireless network tries to link to specific passing satellites. This process has a 1 in 6 chance per hour of working and establishing a link with an appropriate, and sometimes familiar, passing satellite. When successful, the computer makes a brief 2d6 minute long connection with this orbiting object which uses surface scanning cameras to take ongoing full-color photographs of the ground below along the path of the satellite, with a 5 kilometer side-to-side picture and a swath of 20 kilometers along the flight path of the satellite.

With such views, the computer operator can zoom in to not only see the computer and its users on the ground, but the real area around the computer in a series of still images, possibly showing the positions of old buildings that existed in the ancient world, along with roads, rivers, landmarks and terrain, with the old world map superimposed over the current time map. Such views can also show any enormous creatures or formations of the enemy that might be a few streets or thickets away. The newly transmitted maps can be saved in the computer, or sent to other connected devices and robotic or android units via a standard communicator.

It should be noted that every year since the collapse of the old civilization, hundreds of satellites have fallen from orbit, either burning up in the atmosphere, or making a successful reentry and crashing to the surface. Countless others suffered impacts from space junk and added their mass to the vast belt of junk that circles the earth. Using satellites, therefore, decreases in effectiveness year after year, with perhaps only 2 or 3 percent of the original hundred and sixty thousand or so are still in serviceable orbit.

**8. Spoof Mode:** This program makes anyone accessing the computer believe they have found a mundane industrial or civil infrastructure computer and database, with layers of drab profiles on the payment and taxation records of state employees, carbon credits, public relations policies, human resources lists of applicants, outstanding sexual and racial discrimination accusations, as well as shareholder reports. Other files include sewage flow, water treatment reports, invoices, warehouse inventory, stationery supply lists, and requests by employees for time off.

There are hundreds of gigabytes of this stuff, layers of folders, and every so often, a password and user ID request to access the name or accounting records of some department. To any computer technician or literate character of over 50 intelligence, this might seem a little too boring, and they might want to dig a little further; if the player of the character searching this computer declares that they want to explore the operating system or other functions, they are allowed a type E intelligence based hazard check to get passed all this useless information and discover the real purpose, and files, of this computer.

**9. Self-Destruct Mode:** The makers of this computer did not want it to fall into enemy hands, and if hacked, removed from its assigned operational area, or tinkered with in such a way that the AI might lose control of the facility or its robotic minions, will cause an electrical surge throughout its hard drives, memories, and batteries. Doing so will fry the computer's innards, delete all files and permanently cook all the internal components to turn the system in to a heap of smoldering junk.

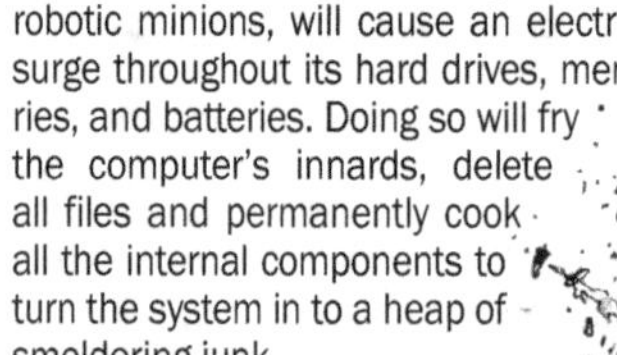

1 in 6 such detonations are far worse, however, and if so, the computer has been rigged with high explosives. When detonating, it will have a blast radius of 10 centime-

ters per kilogram weight of the computer (100cm is 1 meter). All those in the blast radius are attacked three times at SV 01-70 for 1d10 damage.

If an AI or digital being was housed in the computer, it will wirelessly eject its consciousness into a nearby escape unit and try to evade discovery and computer at all cost, and thereafter seek progressively better robots, androids or computers to house itself in and start over again.

The escape 'pod' used is up to the game master, but if not specified, roll 1d6 here: **1.** A laptop computer hidden in a buried plastic briefcase 3d6 meters away./ **2.** A clerical android hidden in a coffin-like hibernation bed, concealed in the floor beneath the AI. Once the emergency transfer is complete, the android will wake and become the body for the AI or digital being./ **3.** A light combot hidden in a nearby wall panel./ **4.** Multi-legged holo-walker (page 73, this book)/ **5.** Projector aerial drone (see page 73, this book)./ **6.** Transmitted to a passing overhead satellite. The orbital unit is now conscious and will search for a likely new host every 24 hours as it passes by, and so too, seek out those who caused it to leave its computer body with its primary goal to exact revenge upon them once it has found the appropriate body or enlisted a strong enough force.

**10. Shock Defense:** This computer can be set to automatically deliver a pain-

ful electric shock whenever it detects an attempt to bypass the normal login screen, and so shock any would-be hacker. The shock has a strike value of 01-80 and will deliver 1d30 stun damage to those it fries, with the victim also forced to make a willpower based type D hazard check or collapse back and fall unconscious for 3d6 minutes. A shock will drain the computer's battery supply of 10 energy units, and can only be used once every 20 rounds (1 minute). Of note, a power cell has 10 energy units, and a power pack has 100 EUs. If the computer is plugged into an installation, the shock will cause the lights in the area to flicker and almost go dark, but will not deplete the computer of any on-board power supplies.

# Power Sources Set 2

### Advanced Power Cell

Fits like a normal cell but has twice the charge depth and instead of having 10 power energy units, it has twenty. For example, a laser pistol normally fires 30 shots using a normal power cell, but this yields 60 shots. Besides having twice the power supply, these also charge twice as fast.

They are rare, and will sell for 200+23d100sp, weigh 750g, and if detonated, have a 6m blast radius, DV -9, SV 01-70, doing 3d6 damage.

### Solar Charge Cell

When detached from an item, and the wrap around fabric solar panels are spread out in sunlight, this cell will charge in 8 hours. It is otherwise identical to a standard power cell, except will sell for 150+2d100sp.

### Hand Crank Power Cell

A standard energy power cell with a fold out hand crank dynamo charger on the bottom. 1 hour of vigorous cranking will charge this cell up completely. These emergency cells are extremely valuable, especially to excavators who explore the untold, unlooted depths beneath ancient cities for days at a time where solar power recharging devices are useless. These will sell for 400+4d100sp each.

### Belt Power Pouch

This hard cased power supply pack is normally worn on the hip and uses a patch cable to connect the mid-size battery to an energy device. While some of these relics feature military markings and are encased in a camouflage fabric, most were used for industrial and agricultural applications because the dangling cable could easily snag and become detached while in combat. To overcome this cable tangling issue, clips are often mounted along the side of the user's body and the back edge of an arm, or else the power line is inserted inside the armor itself. These fixes allow the cable to remain safely out of the way when moving through dense vegetation, wreckage and rubble. The battery pack is equivalent to three standard power cells in both power supply to weapons and recharge times. Weight 1.8kg, Sales value 500+1d1000sp. Max cable length 1.5m.

Note: This battery system holds 30 energy units while a standard power cell has 10 units of energy, a power pack has 100.

### Portable Wind Turbine

Although quite heavy and somewhat awkward to carry about, this fold-out, tripod based mini-wind turbine and battery hook up box comes in a nylon carry case. Assorted sizes of power cells and other common batteries can be clamped into the box-like charging bay on the unit's front, where a red indicator light will flash when the battery is drained and needs charging, or green when fully charged. One hour of wind is needed to charge a mini power cell, 6 hours for a full power cell, and 4 days for a power pack. Weight 9kg, worth 800+4d100sp.

### Air Compressor Pack

This 18 kilogram unit looks like a high visibility orange or yellow barrel connected to a backpack and comes with a simple gauge and 3 meter long bright orange nylon wrapped air hose. Since this relic was intended for use while connected to a vehicle, huge industrial robot, facility or generator, it has a stubby 3m long power cable that will plug into an extension cord. 1 in 6 will be found with a 30 meter long extension cord and spool that is fitted to the unit's back, but all will accept a standard power cell that will compress the air for 10 minutes, or a power pack can also be worn, or carried by a second person working as a team, which will provide 100 minutes of pressure.

Regular air compressors, with identical stats, can also be found and are sometimes permanently built onto lumbering industrial robots and vehicles. Wheeled, drag-along units weigh about 20 kilograms and require a separate person to tow the compressor behind another person using a nailer or sprayer, although these wheeled units require a power source and come with a 40 meter extension cord.

# Robots Set 2

*Also see MAVs, or Micro Air Vehicles, which, while related to robots and sometimes able to act autonomously, they are in fact remote controlled vehicles.*

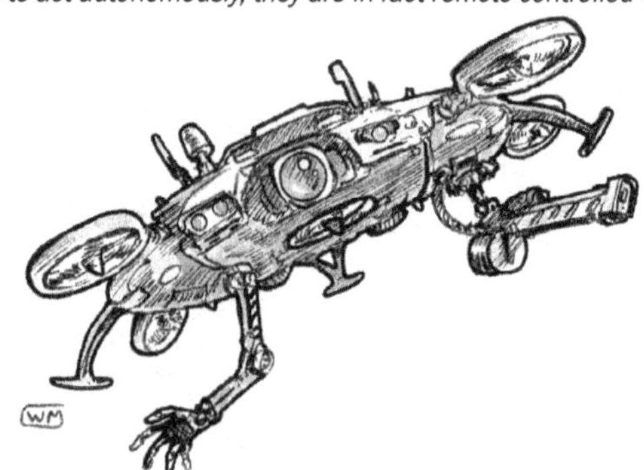

**Wisp Scout Flyer** *by Danny Seedhouse*
*Unit Classification: R.S.F1-06a, Aka Wisps, Stingers or Buzzers*
Defensive Value: **-45**
Endurance: **40**
Movement: **16 meters flight, 8m is silent running mode**
Initiative: **+1**
Attacks: **Bash or Spike Carbine**
Strike Value: **01-65 bash/ 01-75 Spike Carbine**
Damage: **1d6+4 bash/1d12+4 Spike Carbine: rate 4, with 40 burst drum**
Strength: **20**
Agility: **70**
Accuracy: **70**
Intelligence: **16**
Willpower: **39**
Perception: **82**
Experience Factors: **45**
Morale: **NA**
Size: 1.4 meters wide 32cm thick circle
Weight: 33kg
Valuables: 2d100sp in salvaged materials, 2 internal power cells and a deployable solar recharger unit plus Spike Carbine*

**The Buzzer's condition varies by the type of weapon used to destroy this robot, melee weapons and ranged attacks have a 2 in 6 chance of destroying the weapon, unless they deal twice the drone's endurance in one hit, then it's a 4 in 6 chance of destroying the weapon. Explosive damage has a 4 in 6 chance of wrecking the weapon if the blast destroys the robot. These same numbers can be used for the solar recharger and power cells.*

**From the sales brochure:** *'The Rotor. Scouting. Flyer. 1-06a designation Wisp is an advanced robotic scouting unit with superior mobility, sensors and stealth capabilities used in recon and skirmish duties. Advanced sensors have multi-band capabilities expanding into the infrared and ultraviolet spectrum, eliminating any penalties from the darkness of visual obscurants, such as smoke. Advanced and patented wisp blade technology allows the drone-like automaton to run in stealth mode, reducing the sound profile of its rotor system. When combined with its advanced heat and radar reflective alloy frame, this flying robot is a virtually undetectable scout with unmatched mobility.'*

*Built in Tacknet™ software allows for seamless integration into your tactical network, allowing the vital data collected by the scout flyer to be used to maximum effect by all your battalion's connected assets. With the optional Far Strike™ package, the drone becomes an artillery spotter for long range artillery or missile assets. And don't think we've forgotten self defense, with the inclusion of our patented subsonic spike carbine unitizing rail gun technology, the Wisp packs impressive anti personal capabilities as well.*

The scout flyer robot can move with a stealth skill of 1 point normally, but can increase this to 3 skill points by using silent running mode. The Spike Carbine is a compact weapon that fires magnetic darts at high velocity up to an effective range of 400 meters and with less audible sound than a traditional gun.

When scavenged from a flyer a spike carbine yields the fallowing stats: **Spike Carbine**, SV +10, Rate 4, Damage 1d12+4, range 400 meters, Ammo 1 Drum holds 40, four shot bursts of spikes, one power cell is needed for every 4 drums. The robot itself carries 4 drums of ammo in an internal hopper with one spare power cell.

**Wasp** *by Danny Seedhouse*
*Unit Classification: R.Sn.F 2-05, aka Snipers, or Long-shots*
Defensive Value: **-35/-45 (when immobile with optic camouflage)**
Endurance: **60**
Movement: **fly 10 meters or fly 5 meters is whisper mode**
Initiative: **+1**
Attacks: **Bash/ Long Spiker (or 1/3 rate sniper shot)**
Strike Value: **01-70 Bash/ 01-95 spike rifle or 01-115 sniper shot**
Damage: **Bash 1d6+6/spike rifle 2d20+10 or 2d20+1d10+10 sniper shot**
Strength: **30**
Agility: **50**
Accuracy: **80**
Intelligence: **19**
Willpower: **41**
Perception: **88**
Experience Factors: **75**
Morale: **NA**
Size: 2 meter wide by 1/2 meter thick circle
Weight: 52 kg
Valuables: 3d100sp in salvaged parts, 2 internal power cells and a deployable solar recharger unit plus Long Spiker*.

**The Long Spiker's condition varies by the type of weapon used to destroy this aerial robot, melee weapons and ranged attacks have a 2 in 6 chance of destroying the weapon, unless they deal twice the flyer's endurance in one hit then it's a 4 in 6 chance of destroying the weapon. Explosive damage has a 4 in 6 chance of wrecking the weapon if the blast destroys the robot. These same numbers can be used for the solar recharger and power cells.*

**From the sales brochure:** *'Sniping. Flyer. 2-05 designation Wasp is an advanced flying robotic sniping unit with superior mobility, sensors and stealth capabilities used to disrupt enemy movements and harass command assets. Its cutting-edge sensors with advanced sniping algorithms and multi band capabilities expand into the infrared and ultraviolet spectrums, allowing total negation of darkness, smoke, wind and other environmental conditions. Advanced and patented whisper blade technology allow the bot to virtually eliminate the sound profile of its rotor system. This, when combined with advanced heat and radar reflective alloy frame, offers you a virtually undetectable sniper.'*

*On top of its impressive mobility, the Wasp has advanced stabilization system that allows it to maximize its accuracy in all situations. Built in Tacknet™, software allows for seamless integration into your tactical network, allowing total human control of the Wasps 'long strike' spike rifle's deadly bolts, or you can rely on our FaceSkan™ advanced software for 100% guarantied target recognition.'*

The wasp flyer has the ability to normally move with a stealth skill of 2 points, but this increases to 4 skill points in silent running mode. The wasp's optical camouflage abilities give it 4 skill points in stealth when setting up for sniping. Note that the flyer must remain still, and carefully aim at a would-be target for two rounds prior to taking a sniping shot. It can remain entirely still even when hovering so long as the wind is limited to a breeze or less, although when hovering, its defense value drops to -20 instead of -35.

Scavenged and repaired **Long Spikers** have the fallowing stats SV +25, rate 1, DMG 2d20+10, range 2.5km, Ammo 50 shots per clip and one energy cell per 4 clips. The flyer itself carries 4 clips of ammo in an internal hopper with one spare power cell.

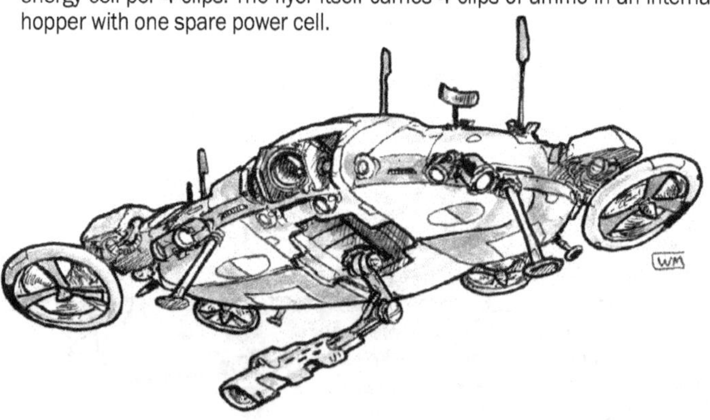

## Hoplite Combot *by Danny Seedhouse*

*Unit Classification: A.S.C. 3-05. Aka: Troopers, or Soldiers*
Defensive Value: -30/-46 vs Ballistic attacks
Endurance: **75**
Movement: **6m**
Initiative: **+0**
Attacks: **Spike Rifle or Breaching Axe**
Strike Value: **Spike Rifle 01-85 / Breaching Axe 01-77**
Damage: **Spike Rifle 3d10+10, rate 2 / Breaching Axe 1d20+20**
Strength: 100 (+14 DMG)
Agility: 40
Accuracy: 55
Intelligence: 30
Willpower: 130
Perception: 40
Experience Factors: 90
Morale: NA
Size: 2.2 meters tall
Weight: 185 kg
Relics: See Valuables and 2 in 6 carry 1d3 advanced frag grenades.
Valuables: 3d100sp and 2 internal power cells and a deployable solar recharger unit plus the Spike Rifle*

**The Spike Rifle condition varies by the type of weapon used to destroy this drone, both melee or ranged attacks have a 1 in 6 chance of destroying weapon, unless they deal twice the drone's Endurance in one hit then it's a 2 in 6 chance of destroying the weapon. Explosive damage that destroys the robot has a 3 in 6 chance of ruining the Spike Rifle. Use these numbers to determine if the power cells and solar recharger survive. The boarding axe survives in all but the most extreme cases.*

**From the sales brochure:** *'Advanced. Soldier. Combot. 3-05 are the perfect solutions for the ever changing modern battlefield. State-of-the-art, cutting edge armor technology, advanced AI battlefield awareness, razor sharp enhanced optics all rolled into one incredible package for your modern combat needs. Hoplites are loyal, dependable, ruthless and surgical with the patented Gr-507 spike rifles. Sloped Ballistic plates provide superior armored protection versus Ballistic Weapon strikes without compromising battlefield mobility. Built in Tacknet™, software allows for seamless integration into your tactical network, allowing unmatched tactical control and integration of the Hoplites with Wasp Sniper drones and Wisp scout drones. Order a 4 man squad now and receive a free EmgMedic™ upgrade, adding emergency medical capabilities to your Soldier Units for peacekeeping duties and the emergency care of friendlies.'*

Hoplite combots use typical military small unit tactics, take cover when available, provide covering fire for each other, and before the global collapse, where often assigned a human sergeant. These robots where programed to be protective of these human officers and provided cover using their own bodies if needed. They also remember the men they served with if they are pre-fall units or built by a pre-fall AI unit. There is a 5% chance that any military clone or bioreplica will be recognized as a fellow soldier from before most AIs turned against mankind and cease all hostilities and offer there former comrade a chance to retreat, surren-

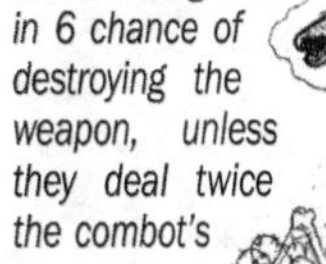

der, parley, medical aid if needed, want to swap local intelligence, and generally regard them as comrades in arms — unless there former comrades shoot at them after the offer has been made.

1 in 6 hoplite combots are equipped with the EmgMedic programing and treated as having 1 skill point as a medic and if so, add an Advanced Doctors Kit to their valuables (described on page 446 of this book).

1 in 6 hoplite combots appear as a popular variant, roll **1d6**:

**1,2. Riot Control Version:** Add a Riot Shield (-8 DV), remove the spike rifle and breaching axe in favor of a built in stun pistol (SV 01-75, rate 1, 2d20 stun, range 200 meters, 40 shots per charge) and stun baton (SV 01-83, rate 1, DMG 2d20+7 stun, 40 rounds of power in a mini power cell).

**3,4. The Hoplite Guardian Unit:** Adds the Greek Hoplite inspired head redesign, a round shield (-7 DV) often with distinctive corporate logo, replace the breaching axe with a high tech spear carried in groups of 3 (SV 01-75, rate 1, DMG 1d20+17, range 34 meters). These elite units also carry a spike carbine (SV 01-75, Rate 4, Damage 1d12+4, range 400 meters, Ammo 1 Drum with 40, four shot bursts of spikes).

**5,6. Squad Gunner:** Providing extra firepower to a typical 4 bot squad of hoplite combots, this unit is equipped with a Spiker LMG, SV 01-85, rate 6, DMG 3d10+10, range 1.5km, Ammo: Belt fed from a backpack hopper containing 400 rounds and 2 power cells. They also carry 1d3 smoke grenades.

Weapons scavenged and repaired from the hoplite combots have the fallowing stats:
**Spike Rifle:** SV +25, rate 2, DMG 3d10+10, range 1.5km, Ammo 50 shots per clip and one power cell per 4 clips.
**Spike LMG:** SV +25, rate 6, DMG 3d10+10, range 1.5km, Ammo 200 shots per belt and one power cell per belt.
**Breaching axe:** SV +3/+7 two handed, DMG 1d20+4/1d20+6 and adds +10 to user's strength for the purposes of opening doors and breaching walls.
**High-tech spear:** SV +5/+8, DMG 1d20+3/1d20+6 range 20 meters.

## Tanker *by Danny Seedhouse*

*Unit Classification. H.A.C. 4-04b. Aka: Heavy, or Gunner.*
Defensive Value: -40/-56 DV vs Ballistic Weapons
Endurance: **100**
Movement: **5 meters**
Initiative: **+0**
Attacks: **Spike HMG (Heavy Machine Gun), Thunder Strike rail gun with dual modes Anti-Material or Anti-personnel*, or Breaching axe,**
Strike Value: **Spike HMG 01-90 rate 5, Thunder Strike rail gun Anti-Material mode 01-115, rate 1/3, Anti-personnel scatter shot 01-85 rate 4, Breaching axe 01-83**
Damage: **Spike HMG 4d10+20, anti-material mode 5d20+40, anti-personnel scatter 4d10, Breaching Axe 1d20+34**
Strength: 145 (+28 DMG)
Agility: 40
Accuracy: 65
Intelligence: 30
Willpower: 160
Perception: 50
Experience Factors: 140
Morale: NA
Size: 2.75 meters
Weight: 310kg
Relics: See Weapons**
Cybernetics: none
Valuables: Relic weapons, one power pack, two power cells and a solar recharging unit.

** Anti personnel mode turns the weapon into a shotgun, enabling it to engage multiple targets in a single arc of fire — about 4 man-sized opponents.*

***The relics condition varies by the type of weapon used to destroy this combot, with melee and ranged attacks having a 1 in 6 chance of destroying the weapon, unless they deal twice the combot's*

*Endurance in one hit then it's a 2 in 6 chance of destroying the weapon. Explosive damage that destroys the robot has a 3 in 6 chance of destroying any weapon system, too. Use these numbers to determine if the power cells and solar recharger also survive. The boarding axe survives in all but the most extreme cases.*

**From the sales brochure:** *'Heavy. Advanced. Combot. Units. 4-04b. Bringing heavy firepower to the ever changing modern battlefield. Take advantage of our state-of-the-art, patented composite alloy armor technology, cutting edge AI battlefield awareness, unsurpassed optics combined into one devastating package. Witness the devastating power of the Spiker HMG for maximum anti personal fire, 'Thunder Strike' rail gun for anti-armor duties, rounded off with a multiple grenade launching system and backup breaching axe for tactical entry.*

*The Tanker Combot Unit is an unstoppable wave of surgical destruction. Its reinforced endoskeleton provides unparalleled power, all protected by Sloped Ballistic plate armor. Wait, there's more! The built-in Tacknet™, software allows for seamless integration into your tactical network, allowing unmatched tactical control and integration with standard Hoplite Combots, your Wasp Sniper Drones and Wisp Scout Drones.'*

Tanker combots are heavy soldier robots known for their dense armor, the ability to absorb huge amounts of damage, as well as their much feared primary weapon. The Thunder strike railgun has two main modes of operation: anti-material and anti-personnel mode. Both use separate ammo feeds and have different damage outputs with the anti-material mode firing advanced disposable depleted uranium core rounds — that can be heard for kilometers as the round breaches the sound barrier. The weapon uses a separate power pack and needs 2 rounds to build up power before firing. Although programed to mainly deploy this weapon against hard targets like vehicles, other heavy combat robots, shell class armor, and anything with a force field, the tanker combot can make tactical use of the gun against heavily armored or entrenched targets.

Anti-personal mode is a high-tech shotgun that unleashes clouds of shrapnel and is used for room clearing. Retracting the barrel and switching ammo types takes 1 round and is done automatically when the combot needs to switch firing modes. This system has only a 1 in 6 chance of surviving bot destruction intact.

### Scavenged Weapons

**Spike HMG,** SV +25, rate 5, DMG 4d10+20, range 2 km, Ammo 200 shots per belt and one energy cell per belt

**Thunder Strike** can be configured into an anti-material or anti-personnel mode.

**Anti-material mode:** SV +45, rate 1/3, DMG 5d20+40, range 10 km, Ammo 20 shots per clip and one power cell per clip

**Anti-Personnel mode:** SV +20, rate 4, DMG 4d10, range 40 meters, Ammo drum with 40 bursts, 1 energy cell per 4 drums

**The Breaching axe:** SV +3/+7 two handed, DMG 1d20+4/1d20+6 and adds +10 to user's strength for opening doors and breaching walls

## Heavy Advanced Combot *by Danny Seedhouse*

Unit Classification. H.A.C.D 6-07e. aka Gunner Prime
Defensive Value: **-45/-61 DV vs ballistic weapons**
Endurance: **150 (+10 points of force field per round)**
Movement: **6.5 meters, 10m flying**
Initiative: **+2**
Attacks: **Spike prime HMG, Thunder Strike rail gun dual modes anti-material or anti-personnel*, or Breaching heat axe**
Strike Value: **Spike HMG 01-115, rate 6, Thunder Strike rail gun: anti-material mode 01-130, rate 1/3 or anti-personnel scatter shot mode 01-110, rate 4, Breaching heat axe 01-107**
Damage: **Spike HMG 4d10+20 (optional air burst mode hits a 1 meter area), anti-material mode 5d20+40, anti-personnel scatter mode 4d10, Breaching Axe 2d20+36**
Strength: **155 (+30 DMG)**
Agility: **60**
Accuracy: **65**
Intelligence: **45**
Willpower: **160**
Perception: **60**
Experience Factors: **225**
Morale: **NA**
Size: **3.2 meters tall**

Weight: 490kg
Relics: See Weapons**
Cybernetics: none
Valuables: Relic weapons, one power pack, two power cells and a solar recharging unit.

*Anti personal mode turns the weapon into a shotgun enabling it to engage multiple targets in a single arc of fire — typically up to 4 man-sized opponents.

**The relics condition varies by the type of weapon used to destroy this combot, with a 1 in 6 normal chance of destroying each weapon, unless the attack dealt twice the robot's Endurance in one hit then apply a 2 in 6 chance of destroying the weapon. Explosive damage that destroys the robot has a 3 in 6 chance of wrecking any weapon system. Use these numbers to determine if the power cells and solar recharger survive. The boarding axe survives in all but the most extreme cases.

**From the sales brochure:** *'Heavy. Advanced. Combot. Units. 6-07e. The Gunner Prime is the cutting edge of our robotics technology, built with exclusive nano forged materials, twin deployable flight rotors, four-point hover jet propulsion and bleeding edge AI programing. The Gunner prime is our most expressive and effective war fighting robot when money's not a concern. Bringing heavy firepower to the ever changing modern battlefield. State-of-the-art, extreme armor technology, ultra-advanced AI battlefield awareness, with exceptional, never-before-seen optics, all rolled into one incredible package for your battle group's every need. These imposing bipedal war robots feature Spiker HMG for maximum anti-personnel fire, "Thunder Strike" rail gun for anti-armor duties, rounded off with a multiple grenade launching system and backup breaching heat axe for forced entries and demolition tasks.'*

*A step up from our Tanker Combot units, these heavy advanced models are unstoppable, and will surely illicit capitulation from insurgents, enemy forces and civil unrest agitators after only minutes of heated action! As with the tanker model, these giants of the front-line feature a reinforced endoskeleton that gives them unparalleled power within a sloped ballistic plated armor sheathing. Built in Tacknet™, software allows for seamless integration into your tactical network, allowing unmatched tactical control and integration with other combat drones, androids, augmented human soldiers, and robotics.*

Heavy advanced combots are among the largest humanoid robots to appear in the Epochian era, and stand over three meters tall and weigh in at 490 kilograms. Besides their armaments and armor, keen senses, and adaptive battlefield intelligence, they can also take to the air with an initial boost from a four-point jet propulsion system — which also speeds them through zero gravity environments such as among the orbital junk yard that circles the earth or to leap up onto higher ledge, across chasms, or down to the ground — and once airborne, deploy a pair of circular, alloy bladed, ring-protected flight rotors. These twin rotors will allow this unit limited flight for up to an hour on their dedicated power cell, at a speed of 10 meters per round. While in the air, these rotors will stabilize the combot enough to fire at ground or air assets without a strike value penalty. Because they are comparatively slow while airborne, they gain no extra defense value bonus.

Like its smaller predecessor, the tanker combot, these immense robots use the much feared Thunder Strike rail gun system, which has two principal modes of operation: anti-material and anti-personnel. These use separate ammo feeds, and inflict different tiers of devastation. Anti-material mode fires advanced disposable depleted uranium core rounds, and when discharged, the blast can be heard from a dozen kilometers away since it breaks the sound barrier. The weapon uses a separate power pack and needs 2 rounds to charge up before firing. This weapon mode was designed to mainly destroy hard targets such as fortifications, large robots, vehicles, and wearers of shell class armor. However, this robot is creative enough to deploy it against any stubborn target.

Anti-personnel mode works like a high tech shotgun and fires a swarm of shrapnel and can dispatch up to four man-sized targets with one shot. Barrel rotation from one mode to another takes 1 round. This system has only a 1 in 6 chance of surviving if this massive robot is destroyed.

### Scavenged Weapons

**Spiker prime HMG:** SV +25, rate 6, DMG 4d10+20 in a 1 meter burst, range 2 km, Ammo 150 shots per belt and one energy cell per belt.

**Thunder Strike Rail Gun** can be configured as anti-material or anti-personnel mode.

**Anti-material mode:** SV +45, rate 1/3, DMG 5d20+40, range 10 km, Ammo 20 shots per clip and one power cell per clip. This combot typically carries 1 of each clip.

**Anti-personnel mode:** SV +20, rate 4, DMG 4d10, range 40 meters, Ammo drum with 40 bursts, 1 energy cell per 4 drums.

**Breaching Heat Axe:** SV +3/+7 two handed, DMG 1d20+4/1d20+6, when running hot the axe does an extra 1d20 damage. Once triggered, the heated axe head runs for 40 rounds on a power cell before it needs replacement, although releasing the trigger will stop the battery drain between uses. The axe design adds +10 to the user's strength for purposes of opening doors and breaching walls.

## Warbot, Light

**Defense Value:** -30 (with 10 END standard force field per round)
**Endurance:** 430
**Movement:** 22m
**Initiative:** normal
**Attacks:** 1 stun pistol, 2 light laser cannons, chain gun, dual rocket launcher, or stomp
**Strike Value:** base 01-60/ stomp 01-70
**Damage:** by weapon or stomp 1d20+30
**Strength:** 230
**Agility:** 44
**Accuracy:** 70
**Intelligence:** 36
**Willpower:** 132
**Perception:** 34
**Experience Factors:** 460
**Morale:** not applicable
**Size:** 9 meters tall
**Weight:** 5,600kg
**Power Supply:** Internal mini-nuclear power plant, plus 3 battery packs to store power for hibernations of up to 310 years. If disturbed or acti- vated exter- nally f r o m  sleep mode, it can attain full power and awareness within 6+3d6 rounds.

This bipedal unit is the faster, lighter armed and armored relative of a heavy warbot, but still a deadly threat if either controlled by intelligent beings or on the hunt as a rogue killing machine. It has a 10 endurance point force field per round (not per strike against it), will be encountered with 3d20 battle rockets loaded into each of two rocket tubes, and possess 1d1000 rounds of standard rifle ammo for its chain gun. Like a heavy battle walker, the on-board nuclear power plant of this unit will explode if it is destroyed like a tactical missile's burst, plus medium radiation contamination in a 2d10m radius for 1d6+1 years.

## Warbot, Heavy

**Defense Value:** -40 (with 20 END standard force field per round)
**Endurance:** 740
**Movement:** 19m
**Initiative:** normal
**Attacks:** 2 stun pistols, 3 medium laser cannons, chain gun, quad rocket launcher, 3 heavy pulse lasers or stomp
**Strike Value:** base 01-70/ stomp 01-75
**Damage:** by weapon or stomp 2d20+30
**Strength:** 420
**Agility:** 32
**Accuracy:** 70
**Intelligence:** 41

**Willpower:** 160
**Perception:** 34
**Experience Factors:** 750
**Morale:** not applicable
**Size:** 13 meters tall
**Weight:** 9600kg
**Power Supply:** Internal mini-nuclear power plant, plus 6 battery packs to store power for hibernations of up to 240 years. If disturbed or activated externally from sleep mode, it can attain full power and awareness within 20+2d20 rounds.

These behemoths come in several designs and camouflage colorations, but represent the standard warbot of their time. While more complex and heavily armed models were made, this design was very common, and many have survived the wars intact. While some are controlled by androids or high tech groups, many are simply rogue killers that consider all other robots and humanoids as the enemy in a never ending war. Typically, a rogue battle walker will patrol a set zone, devastating all intruders, yet, on the lookout for the secret code signature of allied units; a code often found in the memory chips of inoperative robot units that lay scattered about a battlefield. If this signature is broadcast via Morse code or a radio transmitter to the heavy warbot, it will either leave the broadcasting units alone, or join them and seek new orders.

Heavy warbots will be encountered with a battery of 0-99 rockets (d100-1) loaded into its frame, and can fire them at a rate of 1 per round per tube (4 tubes). The chain gun will likewise be loaded with a supply of 2d1000 rounds of standard rifle ammo. Also, like all combat robots, this unit can fire all its weapons simultaneously at different targets within range to their maximum rate per round.

Protecting this unit is a 20 point force field, which will reduce the total damage taken in one round by 20 points by all successful strikes, not the damage per each actual strike. The nuclear power plant of these machines is not something one wants to be in proximity with if this unit is 'killed' as it will explode. The blast will be identical to a tactical missile's burst (page TME-197), plus medium radiation contamination in a 4d10m radius for 2d6 years.

# MAVs

Micro Air Vehicles are similar to robots and drones, are easily mistaken for them, and can sometimes be customized to serve as fully autonomous units. For the most part, however, like drones, they are remote controlled (RC) units. As their name implies, they are of small size, limited range, and have few, if any, offensive capabilities, but do offer remarkable stealth and surveillance applications. Although the fish, snake, cockroach and tarantula models are not air vehicles, they still fall under the MAV designation of drones with the 'A' in MAV standing for 'Animal'.

Each unit described in this section is controlled by an operator using a joystick, small touch screen, eye piece and control glove combo, or simply a wearable optical unit. These eye pieces are the best bet for humanoid excavators as they snap onto a helmet's visor, brim of a baseball cap, night vision goggles, sunglasses or purpose-built head harness and leave one's hands free.

With androids, some cyborgs, robots, or fixed AI installation, micro air vehicles can be flown or driven via either an external control device like a human does, or else through their mechanical optics once the MAV's data stick is inserted into the unit's eye assembly or CPU. Digital beings can also control these relics, but can either do so while they themselves occupy a mechanical body, or else have their own consciousness transferred to the small hard-drives of these machines — a very risky thing to do since MAVs have very limited endurance, and the likelihood of the digital being getting destroyed along with the tiny machine are exceptionally high.

Artificial intelligences, digital beings, self aware robots and other advanced, digitally gifted beings can use these as extensions of their body, and in many ways, turn them into robots complete with pre-programmed commands such as to patrol a certain area, stealthily track designated individuals, watch a pathway or road, or engage anyone entering an area, especially those not wearing a specifically encoded IDSB (Identification Sequence Broadcasters, page TME 198).

Micro Air Vehicles, more so than the crawling ground variants, are highly susceptible to strong winds, and so best flown in no more than a strong breeze. If operated under windy conditions, any MAV will struggle to fly up wind and move at only 25% speed, or 150% speed if going with the wind, and must make an agility based type E hazard check per minute (20 rounds) to avoid a cash to the ground, into nearby trees, wreckage or structures.

Any crash is treated as an attack at SV 01-70 for 1d4 damage. A crashed MAV, regardless of if it survives or not, is put out of action and must be recovered and repaired by a junk crafter or mechanical technician of any skill points and takes 1d6 hours of work.

MAVs are also highly susceptible to attacks by creatures, especially where the flying or crawling RC vehicle looks like an animal. A myriad of mutant and unmutated beasts alike will attack a MAV because the relic looks like its food, or because the device intrudes into their territory. In some regions, factions of low tech humanoids will raise trained ruin vultures, skal birds or eagles to chase down and rip apart MAVs on sight, especially when these peoples are under constant threat of Mecha or other advanced opponents.

Each model of micro air vehicle will have its own operational control range, shown simply as 'Range' in the stat block table on page 465. The shown range is

under ideal outdoor conditions, however, and is reduced to one quarter of this if used indoors, underground or in dense woodlands or tangled, overhanging ruin structures even at street level — with the various materials interrupting the link between the controller and the MAV.

Whenever a micro air vehicle exceeds the range, whatever viewing device the controller uses will flash red with a warning. The operator can then select for the MAV to either land and wait for the user to catch up to the unit, or have it hover in place and maintain observations, or return toward the controller from 1 to 100% of the distance that separates them, with that percentile of distance chosen by the operator.

If given pre-programmed instructions to carry out a mission, such as take video footage of a wide area and then return to the controller or to have the footage downloaded and reviewed, the MAV can do so, but it will be off-screen, and out of control when beyond the range of the control operator, and unable to take evasive action or defend itself if attacked.

Sometimes, new era MAV operators will use these devices as carrier pigeons, and tie notes to the landing legs of the MAV and send it between communities or between military positions — and just hope nothing intercepts the MAV during its journey. The MAV's destination can be plotted by pre-existing video overhead footage or pathway maps the unit has previously established during earlier flights, or given specific coordinates, directed to seek a specific Identification Sequence Broadcast tab, or an ongoing transmission from a typed in communicator's unique number. Other destination can include navigational present points that the operator can type into the MAV and the controlling device, based on locations the MAV has previously been to, which could include locations that no longer exist, such as military bunkers which now sit buried under a hill or rubble, but which could be excavated into by an ambitious dig team.

When an intact MAV is discovered as a relic — as opposed to an adversary — it is usually encased in a hard plastic, handle or shoulder strap equipped carry box. Inside this air-tight, waterproof and EMP blocking foam lined box will be the MAV with any snap or screw on parts, such as wings, propellers, legs or optional accessories. Also in the case will be slots for the appropriate size and number of power cells. There is a 5 in 8 chance that the necessary batteries are present, but if this unit has been locked away for decades, or centuries, then these serviceable batteries will always be drained. The box will contain a user's manual, lubricant bottle, small maintenance and assembly tools, advertisement for upgrades and other models in the manufacturer's line, and a small data stick with the software needed to control the unit.

The control data stick for each MAV is a thumbnail sized black rectangle with the make, model and serial number of each MAV written on it. Without the correct data stick, a captured MAV cannot be programmed to serve a different operator unless the MAV is hacked and linked to an alternative data stick. To hack, see the Computer Technician Skill on page 53 of the Hub Rules, and use the 'Re-Program Android' column on table TME-1-47. One attempt per day is allowed, and if successful, the MAV is now linked to the replacement data stick and can be put into action.

What is not usually included in the carry case for any discovered micro air vehicle is a means of controlling it. For this, the data stick must be inserted into a dedicated MAV controller, a laptop computer, desktop, tablet or even an old smartphone. Sometimes, the chip is loaded into the CPU of an AI or robot, or else into a cyborg's optical implant or the side of an android's head.

Any cyborg, robot or android with the implant of Data Base (page 334 of this book), will have a slot available in its cranium to accept 2d4 of these tiny data sticks, and while the user might have access to multiple MAVs, and have them all active and in the air or crawling across the ground, it can only see through or control one at any given time — although secondary MAVS can fly in formation and follow the lead of the primary MAV if desired.

Besides the common digital devices mentioned above, computers, laptops, tablets, and smartphones, other, dedicated MAV controllers are described below, although the ancient ones had dozens of other devices, too. The shown 1d6 roll is for Game Masters to quickly establish a random control system for on-the-fly game sessions.

## Table XR-263 / Dedicated MAV Controllers    Roll 1d6

**1. Targeting Optics Headset:** Described on page 198 of the hub rules, the standard version of this relic comes with a single MAV data stick slot. While this unit works, it is considered and inadequate, temporary option and was mostly used to recover micro air vehicles after a superior controlling device was destroyed and the data stick recovered. Without a joystick or control glove, the user must use their fingers on the side of the headset to tap between the various rubberized setting codes, which slows reaction time. It takes 2 rounds to give the MAV any command from the available options from the MAV Command Options described below. These relics sell for an astonishing 1700+2d1000sp and weigh1 kilogram.

**2. MAV Viewing monocle:** Designed specifically for accessing the cameras on an active MAV, and using retinal tracking and double blinking to select from assorted command options, this smallest of controllers fits in a chest pocket. It has a nylon neck strap and single mini-power cell and single MAV data stick holding module, with the cord itself being the unit's antenna. When inserted in the eye socket, the user can steer the movement direction of a MAV, either while the unit is on the go, or getting the MAV to turn about, look up, look down, attack, ram, evade, etc. This monocle weighs 300g, uses a mini power cell that will give 400 continuous hours of operation, and if sold, will fetch 600+1d1000sp.

**3. Snap-On Cybernetic Eye Module:** This controller can be permanently bolted to the side of an android's head, or temporarily clamped on, while for cyborgs with a visual implant, there is a 4 in 6 chance any implant eye has a rubberized access port plug that allows the viewer module to be snapped to the side of the cyborg's head next to its main cybernetic eye, and through an included, wireless control glove, allow the cyborg to steer and select options for one or more MAVS. This relic cannot be used by non-mechanical beings or cyborgs who lack an optical implant. These units weigh 670g and sell for 1400+d1000sp.

**4. MAV Snap-On Eye Piece:** This remarkable bit of ancient technology snaps onto a helmet's visor, brim of a baseball cap, night vision goggles, sunglasses or purpose-built head harness. This relic is the perfect interface for a pure stock human or other intelligent being that doesn't have a permanently affixed visual optics system, although this setup does lack the versatility of the chest rig.

Besides being small, lightweight and unobtrusive, it allows the user to keep their eyes up and pay more attention to their surrounding, instead of peering down at a screen sitting on their chest. This device, which has three MAV data stick slots, can only access one MAV at a time without having to manually reach up and tap the selector buttons on the side of the device, a task that is impossible to achieve while wearing gloves. When connected to one MAV, the user can use their eye focus to select various command options or direct the route of the RC vehicle, which appears on the tiny screen, and by blinking twice, make a desired selection. These units weigh only 750g and will sell for 1100+1d1000sp.

**5. MAV Operator's Headset:** Appearing as a bulky pair of goggles connected to a cable that runs to the right or left hand, this unit is a dedicated MAV controller. When activated and the black visor pulled down over the otherwise regular safely goggles, the viewer can select from up to four MAVs and see through one at a time — although each unit's data stick must be plugged into the side of this headset to be accessible.

Using the glove, or similar VR controller device, the user can select the command option and point to where the MAV is to move. With simple hand gestures, the operator can have the MAV turn about, climb or dive if an aerial unit, hold still, or attack as needed. While this is the most immersive way to control a micro air vehicle, it is also the most limiting as far as the operator's situational awareness goes, as the user's sight is reduced to half as he or she can see a ghostly view of the world about them — and so move at half speed and suffer a -3 initiative drop — while the operator's hearing is reduced to half. It seems that the ancient ones expected the user of this headset to either ride within a vehicle as a passenger, or be perched in a secure location, within a trench, or otherwise, well away from a fight.

The headset and glove weigh 1.4kg together and will operate for 300 hours on the dual mini power cells that fit in the back battery pack on the headband. If a digger sells this set, it will earn 1800+2d1000sp in a relic market.

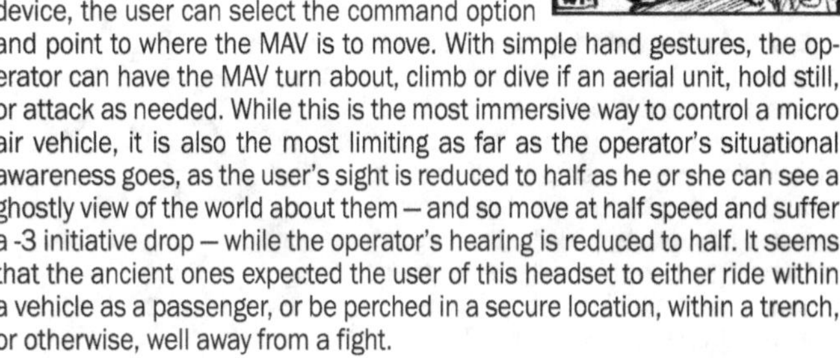

**6. MAV Chest Rig:** This device is the most commonly discovered MAV controller. Built tough for military and industrial applications, it consists of a control panel with flip up view screen, joystick and dual shoulder straps so that the unit can be worn on an operator's chest and remain in a ready position even if the user is on the move. The operator has a bright, 20cm wide screen to view both whatever the controlled MAV sees, and offers twice the detail of those employing a monocle, eyepiece, or targeting optics headset.

The screen can be split to show up to 5 other MAVs that are online but not actively being controlled, unless they are in tandem and following the direct lead of the primary MAV. The unit has slots for 24 different MAV data sticks, which implies that the operator could have 6 units aloft at a time, and many more on standby should the first batch be destroyed or blown out-of-control range. This control panel rig can allow the operator to switch between one of six MAVs with the touch of a button, and see from the vantage points of these half dozen units every second if so desired.

This device is built into a hard, flat black or olive drab colored shell that can take a heap of abuse, is watertight when closed up, and if targeted directly by an enemy, has a DV of -12, endurance of 9. This rig weighs 3 kilograms, will run for 400 hours on a single power cell, and has a standard communicator built right into the unit that will accommodate video calls and image transfer from other systems. If sold to a relic dealership — often as only a bulky communicator — this relic will earn the seller 2200+2d1000sp.

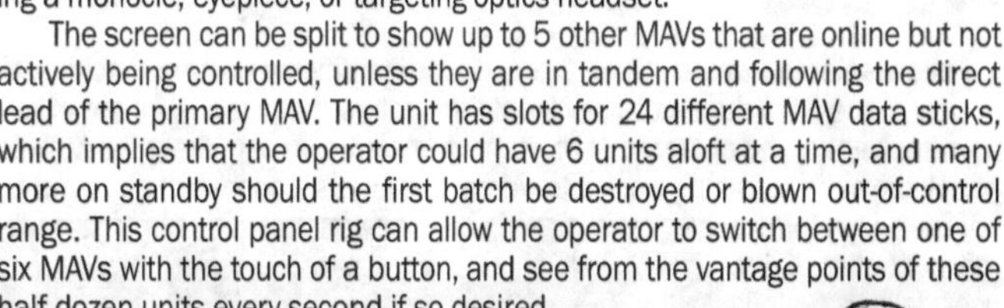

# MAV Command Options

The following are the basic command options available to either a micro air, or animal vehicle, controller, although the myriad of other possible maneuvers go far beyond the scope of this selection. Players should ask their game master if they can command their MAV to do some outlandish, unlisted option. Perhaps have the player character make a perception based type D or E hazard check to properly steer a MAV to do something extra-challenging.

• **Operator controlled flight,** or if a ground based MAV, then slither, or scuttle along the directed path.

• **Auto follow:** The MAV is directed to follow along behind the operator at a safe height or distance back and wait for commands. The default, if not specified, is 2 meters behind and either at an elevation of 30cm above the head height of the operator for flying MAVs, or moving along the ground for terrestrial units.

• **Overhead watch mode:** The unit will fly up 10, 20, 50, 100 or 200 meters directly above operator and send back video footage of the area visible from the air. The MAV will follow along overhead if the operator moves, and if not specified, the MAV will always fly 50 meters above the controller.

• **Ram selected target:** The MAV will torpedo toward a selected target person, creature, vehicle, doorway, surface or other red highlighted object and ram into it. Ramming always destroys a MAV, although with a Suicide Nano, this will also cause a detonation in a 3m radius, which causes 2d20 damage on a direct hit or 1d10 to all those in the blast area who are struck.

• **Engage selected target:** For some MAVS, such as the assassin model, this will result in one of two attack modes available to the MAV — a venomous bite or laser beam barrage — but for most models this means a simple, self destruct ram attack. For the beam bird, this will cause repeated laser blasts, while for the dragonfly or hummingbird, the MAV will attempt to land on the target and inject them, which requires a successful melee strike. The fish, snake, and tarantula MAVs must also race up to and make a normal attack with their simulated mouths to bite the target and with the snake and tarantula, inject venom which will force the victim to make the appropriate hazard check, or succumb.

A quad-rotor, which is the only MAV capable of carrying a freight load of any considerable size, can be commanded to 'drop parcel' when over an enemy position, with the parcel being a small rock, or any grenade. The pin on a grenade must be pulled by whoever loaded the grenade, and the closed detonation release handle jammed just right in the quad-rotor's legs. When the legs are released, the grenade that is normally set to a ten second timer will drop. It could, of course, be set to 1 second and the MAV could be sacrificed in the grenade blast should the controller want to ensure the explosion occurs up close to a specific target.

• **Follow selected target:** Once the operator identifies a person, machine or animal to the MAV, the unit will lock onto and follow the person well out of the physical sight of the operator. At any time, the controller can direct the MAV to attack the being, or simply track it to wherever it enters a doorway, hole, or other portal, and return to the controller. If the user followed along with the live video feed of the MAV as it followed its target, then the controller will know where the

target departed the scene, but if the MAV leaves the visual range of the operator and the link is broken, the MAV will continue to follow the target for however long the user pre-set the auto-pilot mode on the MAV. If the autopilot was set for 4 hours, for example, the MAV would later return to the controller's signal or last known location, and potentially have many hours of footage for the controller to review, hoping to find the whereabouts of the tracked target.

• **Track IDSB:** Many ancient machines, including androids and a fair number of excavators who unknowingly put on relic gear, carry an identification sequence broadcaster tab. This unique code emitter has a ten kilometer range, and will show up to the controller and assigned MAV. The controller can command an operational MAV to discreetly follow, attack, deliver a parcel or note to, or approach the wearer of the specific IDSB. Likewise, if the IDSB code is known to the controller, and the wearer not identified, such was when the tab wearer is in a crowd, the MAV can be directed to located the wearer of the broadcaster, and within minutes, highlight them with its on-board camera and then broadcast the imagery of the identified wearer of the IDSB.

• **Observe Location:** This command tells the MAV to take up an observational position and watch a certain street, passage, doorway, or direction from concealment. The MAV is basically ordered to land or crawl into a hidden position and maintain observation on a specific field of view, with the on-board camera able to see in a 180-degree angle. A secondary command can be selected to alert the controller if motion is detected. This alert is normally a series of three beeps from the viewscreen of any MAV control device or implant.

• **Enter Dormant Mode:** This command tells the MAV to take up a safe, concealed location away from enemy units, dangerous animals, or environmental exposure and go to sleep. In dormant mode, the vehicle basically switches off all but the most minimal systems and can extend the battery duration 100 times. See Power Supply, next page, for more details.

# On or Off MAV Options

All micro air vehicles come with a few basic options that the controller can choose to switch off when first activating the MAV. The player character must select the following options, with default being in the 'on' mode, except for the self destruct option. The game master might need to quickly go over each of these choices with any player who first sets up a MAV and controlling device, and have the player record on or off settings, with the MAV's stats, on the back of their character sheet.

• **Auto pilot mode:** The MAV will return to the operator if the signal link is scrambled or broken. If switched to the off option, the MAV will continue any pre-programmed path or mission, or else if no mission was designated, it will merely land or stop and hide in the safest area within 100 meters and wait for transmission to resume — possibly until its battery drains down.

• **Identification Sequence Broadcaster tab scanning:** When active, which is the default, this MAV will pick up all active IDSB tabs within 50 meters and show a green box around the subject with the ID Code visible to whoever is viewing the screen. This was established so that MAVs programmed to attack enemy units could tell which personnel or mechanical units were on which side during a conflict, and not automatically attack any approaching unit. When set to off, this MAV simply doesn't pick up IDSB signals.

• **Take cover:** This MAV will automatically seek cover — often behind the controller — as soon as it registers nearby gunfire, beam weapon usage, explosions or violence of any kind. It will seek to preserve itself in order to be of use in ongoing operations after any firefight. The off setting means the MAV will not take cover when a battle breaks out and instead remain hovering above where it is, or hold position if it's a ground based unit, and simply film the conflict as if it were merely witnessing events.

• **Return to base:** This MAV is pre-selected to return to base if some tragedy befalls the control device, even if the operator is not injured. The base of operations is set as a nav-point (navigational point of reference), which the operator can establish from the control unit at any time. If no nav-point was set, the micro air vehicle will try to return to wherever it was first activated, which could be untold kilometers away from wherever it was during the controller unit being put out of action.

If this option is switched off, and the control device is destroyed or the batteries taken out and the link disrupted, the MAV will continue with any pre-existing mission parameters, and go one without the controller unless the operator can repair the control device or switch the vehicle's data stick into a different RC controller.

• **Self destruct:** This feature is normally set to off, simply because MAVs are fragile and prone to crashing in strong winds or being knocked out of the sky by other MAVs and drones over civilians. When set to on, this unit will self detonate when knocked out of action and forced to crash, thus eliminating any chance that the enemy can collect it after the battle and use it against its former controller and their faction.

Besides being made to self-destruct if brought down, this command can be given to any MAV by the controller, although with several warning and fail safe screens, screens that take 1+1d6 rounds to go through before the MAV detonates. Any MAV with a pill power cell will have a 20cm blast radius, and an attack SV of 01-40, causing 1d4 damage. A MAV cockroach, that has 4 pill power cells, will burst in a 80cm radius and cause 4d4 damage. Units with one mini-power cell will blow up in a 1 meter radius, SV 01-45 and inflict 1d8 damage. If two mini cells are contained in the MAV, it will have a 2m blast radius and have a SV of 01-65 causing 2d8 damage, while MAVs with 3 mini-power cells will blow up in a 3m radius, SV 01-75 can cause 3d8 damage. A simple, but more immediate ram attack does not cause this battery detonation and while the tiny vehicle is destroyed, the battery can be recovered by looters after the battle.

## MAV Power Supply

Flying MAVs expend battery life at a far faster rate than units that move along the ground, with most MAVs using one or more mini-power cells or power pill batteries. Many also recharge their batteries fully after two hours of solar charging while stationary, although the flying disc MAV can recharge in full sunlight even while flying and theoretically, maintain flight permanently if it could withstand strong winds or the attacks of winged predators or enemy hunter-killer drones.

When new batteries are put into a MAV that has already been set up with its 'ON or OFF' options or given a preexisting 'return to base' nav point, or other mission parameters, these settings will remain in effect for 24 hours even without batteries inserted in the unit, since each MAV has a built in memory file to store this information for a short time before it is auto-scrubbed for security reasons.

## Dormancy Power Saving Mode

The Operational Duration shown for each MAV model type is for active mode, when the MAV is on patrol, airborne, or otherwise ready to transmit audio-video information back to a controlling entity, communicator, or operating person's control unit. When powered up, but directed to go dormant and in standby mode, all these durations can be extended by 100 times. In dormant state, the MAV must be switched on by the remote master, or it receives a signal from an infra red trip line, vibration of movement within two meters, or other preset condition. All MAVs take 10+1d10 rounds to come back on-line and be ready for movement or combat after being dormant.

## Table XR-264 / MAV Models Matrix

| MAV Model | DV | END | MV | Initiative | Attacks | SV | DMG | STR | AG | ACC | PER | EFs | Size | Weight | Operational Duration** | Power Source | Range*** | Sell Value |
|---|---|---|---|---|---|---|---|---|---|---|---|---|---|---|---|---|---|---|
| Assassin | -48 | 7 | 36m | +4 | 1 bite or laser 50m | 01-70 | bite 1d3+venom, laser 1d20 | 8 | 96 | 88 | 119 | 16 | 25cm | 1.5kg | 16 days | 2 mini power cells + solar | 50 km | 1200+ 1d1000sp |
| Bat | -21 | 4 | 1 or fly 18m | +1 | rake | 01-44 | 1d2 | 6 | 68 | 36 | 46 | 6 | 48cm | 950g | 24 days | 2 mini power cells | 16 km | 300+ 2d100sp |
| Beam Bird | -33 | 6 | 28m | +3 | laser 70m | 01-80 | 1d8+10 | 8 | 86 | 82 | 97 | 14 | 36cm | 1.4kg | 9 days | 2 mini power cells | 19 km | 900+ 4d100sp |
| Cockroach | -10 or -20 flying | 2 | 2 or fly 9m | +1 | ram | 01-40 | 1pt | 2 | 62 | 31 | 44 | 3 | 7cm | 130g | 18 years | 4 pill power cells +solar | 36 km | 100+ 1d100sp |
| Crow Flyer | -14 | 5 | 19m | +0 | 1 | 01-50 | 1d2 | 4 | 33 | 32 | 68 | 4 | 90cm | 1.1kg | 14 days | 2 mini power cells | 72 km | 300+ 2d100sp |
| Dragonfly | -37 | 3 | 14m | +3 | 1 injection | 01-46 | 1pt +vaccine | 3 | 78 | 56 | 74 | 7 | 12cm | 470g | 18 days | 1 mini power cell | 22 km | 800+ 4d100sp |
| Fly-Spy | -49 | 1 | 22m | +4 | ram* | 01-40 | 1pt | 1 | 99 | 62 | 72 | 2 | 2cm | 50g | 32 years | 1 pill power cell | 5km | 100+ 1d100sp |
| Flying Disc | -26 | 2 | 15m | +1 | ram* | 01-48 | 1pt | 3 | 55 | 36 | 62 | 2 | 8cm | 220g | 14 days | 1 mini power cell + solar | 12km | 90+ 1d100sp |
| Heli-MAV | -35 | 5 | 22m | +2 | ram* | 01-52 | 1d3pts | 4 | 57 | 61 | 81 | 3 | 18cm | 390g | 22 days | 1 mini power cell | 45 km | 250+ 3d100sp |
| Humming-bird | -42 | 2 | 38m | +5 | 1 needle | 01-44 | 1pt +venom | 2 | 112 | 67 | 124 | 5 | 14cm | 310g | 14 days | 1 mini power cell | 20 km | 200+ 3d100sp |
| Quad-Rotor | -20 | 4 | 16m | +0 | ram* | 01-43 | 1d2pts | 4 | 54 | 48 | 38 | 4 | 16cm | 690g | 16 days | 2 mini power cells | 70km | 300+ 2d100sp |
| Robo-Fish | -16 | 4+1d4 | 7m | +2 | 1 bite | 01-50 | 1d3pts | 5 | 42 | 39 | 79 | 10 | 20+1d12cm | 2.4kg | 16 months | 3 mini power cells | 32 km | 350+ 2d100sp |
| Snake | -21 | 4+1d4 | 9m | +2 | 1 bite | 01-60 | 1d3pt +venom | 16 | 49 | 46 | 66 | 22 | 80+2d20cm | 5kg | 36 months | 2 mini power cells | 22 km | 850+ 4d100sp |
| Suicide Nano | -13 | 6 | 15m | +0 | 1 explosion | 01-76 | 2d20 | 4 | 24 | 61 | 35 | 4 | 25cm | 2.2kg | 28 days | 2 mini power cells+solar | 15 km | 250+ 2d100sp |
| Tarantula | -18 | 2 | 5m | +2 | bite | 01-46 | 1pt +venom | 5 | 68 | 41 | 48 | 16 | 8cm | 710g | 12 years | 2 mini power cells | 18 km | 340+ 3d100sp |

*Any impact with a solid object destroys this MAV.

** The Operational Duration shown here is for active mode. Dormant standby mode extends this duration by 100 times, but takes 10+1d10 rounds to come back on-line.

*** Range is the communications link range, which is half the shown amount when indoors, underground, in thick forests, or dense wreckage even at street level. The Operator will get a red flashing screen warning of 'range limit reached' if the MAV gets near this limit and can be commanded to hold position, and wait, land and wait, or return all the way or partially back to the controller.

# MAV Descriptions

## Assassin MAV

This charcoal gray, four rotor micro air vehicle is about the size of a person's open hand and was built extra tough and fitted with two lethal weapon systems. It was designed to go after a person who has either been identified by an IDSB tag or painted by a target marking laser, or pre-selected by the operator and the MAV told to hunt down and either inject or blast the subject. When it requires stealth to fulfill its murderous mission, it can be steered to within 3 meters of a target and then unleashed. It is at this point where it's already near silent flying ability is now detectable, and the intended victim is allowed a perception based Type D hazard check to even notice this the sound of the whirring propellers. If the MAV is not detected, the unit can rush in and attempt to bite the target at +40 SV on the first bite attack, or be directed to fire its laser gun at the target, also at +40 on the first shot. If the assassin vehicle is detected by the perception based HC, then roll initiative normally, with the would-be victim potentially able to shoot the MAV out of the air before it can attack.

An assassin MAV's bite injects 30ml of whatever venom, vaccine, or other injectable the operator fills within its toxin reservoir. Each bite delivers a 10ml dose and so this unit can potentially make three successful bite attacks per fill. If not specified, the venom in an assassin bot is Type D death poison. Make an endurance based Type D hazard check or drop dead.

When unable to use its venomous bite, this micro air vehicle will keep back out of reach and open fire, launching one bright purple beam per round up to 12 times before the gun's dedicated mini-power cell is spent. Solar panels on the upper aspect of this flat, stealth MAV allow the unit to land some place sunny and fully recharge all batteries after 6 hours of photovoltaic recharge.

## Bat MAV

Designed to look like a large, common bat, complete with an authentic flight style, this surveillance platform is equipped with night vision out to 30 meters, plus, the same false eyes that make it look like a real thing are also its dual cameras. While unable to do much harm to human sized targets, it has a limited ability to rake with its alloy clawed feet (SV 01-44, DMG 1d2) as well as a suicidal ram attack that has the same results. Its primary function was to undertake stealthy night patrols, and because of the way it moves, blend in with regular bats or else go unseen and unheard altogether. Consider this MAV to have 5 skill points in stealth.

## Beam Bird

From a distance, this MAV looks and flies like a medium sized living bird, such as a starling, robin or blue jay. On closer inspection, however, at 5 meters or fewer, a person will need only make a type B perception based hazard check to notice that the thing has synthetic, feather pattered wing flaps, metallic feet and black, tubular muzzle instead of a pointed beak. This remote controlled, mechanical bird is in fact armed with a pocket laser pistol which can fire once per round and unleash up to 10 shots from its secondary mini power cell, per charge. Its other cell is for flight power, cameras, comms and essential operations for up to 9 days activity per charge. Although this piece of ancient technology can be very effective in combat, especially if engaging ground targets that have no missile weaponry themselves and are caught in the open, this vehicle also has dual cameras for eyes and serves a search, patrol, and forward observer role splendidly.

## Cockroach MAV

This tiny mechanical device has two movement modes, and can both fly and crawl just as well as a real cockroach. They mimic regular roaches so well that when found among living specimens, will only be differentiated by a viewer who makes a type F perception based hazard check. If directed to attack a target, they have no ability to bite, but can take to the air, get as much speed as possible and ram into a target to potentially inflict 1 point of damage.

Their main purpose was as a tool of espionage, and besides their highly effective miniature camera, which has a 10 meter night vision mode, they also have excellent audio recording and transmission capabilities on account of their highly sensitive antennas. It is believed that old world governments used these devices to covertly surveil their populations, listen in on conversations, and report what people said amongst themselves at work, on public transit, or in their homes, back to vast super computers to have the audio scanned for seditious, politically incorrect, or tax fraud speech. Presently, new era warlords, cult leaders, and politicians find similar uses by such robo-roaches, which have a 6m audio-pick up radius.

## Crow Flyer

1 in 8 of these large mechanical birds will actually be a seagull model, which can land on water and use its mechanical, webbed feet to propel it along the surface at 4m per round. Unlike a beam bird, these units look and conduct themselves far more realistically, and besides, their ability to peck and claw at opponents, do not have any weaponry. They can, however, carry up to half a kilogram weight, which is exactly the weight of a standard fragmentation grenade, and so could theoretically make a bombing run on the operator's enemies.

Even among other crows, a person will be hard pressed to recognize something 'robotic' about this MAV, thus anyone who sees this from beyond 5 meters and out to 20 meters is allowed a type F perception based hazard check to notice that it's a machine, while if observed from 5 meters or closer, gets a type D PER hazard check to see it for what it is.

The main purpose of these units was to stay aloft for days at a time, and either send back live video footage of what it sees below, or else provide delayed playback such as when the crow or gull goes out of transmission Reach (72+ KM) and was directed beforehand to take a specific route and then report back, sending the video feed once it returns into range.

Although very authentic looking, a vigilant person might notice that other crows do not associate well with these mechanical variants, and seem uncomfortable getting within ten meters of them.

## Dragonfly MAV

Insects are one of the more easily copied creatures and make for authentic looking micro vehicles. Besides the fly MAV, both the dragonfly and the cockroach variant are the most difficult to discern from living specimens, although in this case, this fixed wing, metallic blue and green specimen is noticeably larger than regular dragon flies found around wetlands and bogs. While its main purpose is stealth surveillance, it has an extendable syringe in its mouth, and from this, it can inject 4, 25ml doses of either venom or vaccine.

When found as loot, in its sealed carry case, 5 in 8 of these units come with 2d6 vials of assorted vaccines from the old world. While expired, and often only syrup or powder, these vaccines can be reconstituted and when injected into a living victim after a successful strike, will inject a substance into the victim that may or may not cause immediate harm. Should an unknown injection be inserted into a living creature, roll **1d6 here:**

1. **Highly toxic venom**, Type C END based hazard check or die within 3d6 minutes.

2. **Type B sleep poison** (see page TME 124).

3. **Bio-Toxin**: roll 1d4 for variant and see table on page TME-127 for duration, virus lifespan, transmission and sickness effects.

4. **Vaccine causes eczema** on 1 to 100% (roll 1d100 once to determine amount) of the subject's skin. Reduce appearance by -3d6, permanently or until cured by use of the mutation Extreme Healing.

5. **Bad vaccine**: victim suffers slothfulness, lack of ambition, shortness of breath, brain fog and occasional irregular heart rate, reduce all traits by -10 (minimum 1 point) for the next 2d6 months when things return to normal.

6. **Vaccine**: Extreme pain in the area of the body where injection occurred, but after 1d4 days, no further complications or benefits are discernible.

## Fly Spy

Designed to be a literal fly on the wall, this super mini MAV is rarely detected. Allow those within three meters a type E perception based hazard check to notice that this particular fly has a slightly louder buzz when flying and doesn't seem to move at all once it lands... seems to stare at the onlooker and their companions as if truly watching them. Indeed, this surveillance device was made for espionage, and can listen in on conversation from 5 or fewer meters and film anything like any other MAV.

It does not have night vision, however, and unless there is at least some light in an area, is restricted to daytime operations. If forced to attack another MAV or creature, it can make 1 ram attack, which will destroy this fly-bot if it impacts a solid object, but can inflict 1 point of damage. Being such a small micro air vehicle, and so easily mistaken for a real fly, these devices often end up in the belly of a frog, bird or lizard, and must pass through the digestive tract of whatever ate it and be excreted 2d4 days later, whereupon it will revive itself from auto-dormancy, clean itself off as best it can, and continue its mission or try to locate its controller.

## Flying Disc

Also called a micro-UFO, this silver coins sized MAV has its main sensor array, flight controls and camera on the underside, flanked by 3 tiny, toothpick sized wire landing legs. The midsection exhibits a rotating, fan-like propeller within a protective clear outer ring, while on the top is a triangular solar array and 4cm long antenna. If able to stay outdoors and in the sunlight, this machine could theoretically remain aloft indefinitely, although strong winds, lighting, and winged predators will probably limit the duration of such a flight to no more than a week.

Once widely used by authorities to hover over city streets, outside the windows of offices and homes, film the activities of citizen in their backyards, living rooms, bathrooms or apartment decks, these widely deployed, cheap and disposable spies are often found in suitcase sized crates that hold 40 ready-to-use disc MAVs.

Their main purpose was to document civilians of old, with a audio recording radius of 8 meters, and night vision capabilities out to 32 meters, but these units could also be assembled on mass, and directed to batter and bludgeon a non compliant, ungovernable citizen. A ram attack always destroys this MAV, but on a successful strike causes one point of damage.

## Heli-MAV

This helicopter inspired micro drone has a main top rotor and rear, side mounted rotor. Although small, and its motor made as quiet as possible, a person with keen hearing, and under otherwise quiet conditions, can hear such a MAV approaching from 6 meters away or closer. Animals, especially dogs, cats, deer and birds, can hear this thing coming from 12 meters away, and will often alert nearby humans to the approach of this tiny, robust little observation platform.

Most times, an operator will use this MAV to fly high above a known enemy position to avoid detection, or else have his 'buzzer' speed ahead of a team's advance, or deliver small, hand-written notes between allied positions during a conflict. While it has night vision out to 30 meters and can pick up audio within 6 meters, its main purpose is daylight reconnaissance. If directed to do so, it can make a one time suicide ram attack, and because of its hard body, streamlined shape and arrow-head-like tip, can more easily strike targets and inflict 1d3 points of damage on a hit.

## Hummingbird MAV

From beyond 3 meters, this humming bird looks real and unless it is wildly out of place in the terrain — such as a lone hummingbird in a gray, lifeless dead city — it will be easily dismissed among other flying creatures. For those who give it a scrutiny from 3m or less, they are allowed a Type C perception based hazard check to see that it is actually a metal and plastic replica. At such a close range, it is likely that the hummingbird is attacking the viewer with its needle tipped beak.

A successful strike from this MAV injects 30ml of venom or other substance into the target, who is typically allowed a hazard check against suffering from whatever substance was shot into them. Unless stated otherwise or the game master has a different injectable in mind, the standard venom from a metal hummingbird is a cherry red paralysis toxin. The struck target is allowed a Type D endurance based hazard check, with failure resulting in the living being losing a cumulative 10% of their ability to move, speak or use physical mutations per minute until they are entirely paralyzed and unable to move. This substance lasts 200 minutes, minus the victim's base, uninjured endurance value, but to a minimum of 1 minute (20 rounds).

With a defense value of -42, these MAVs are among the hardest to strike, and can zig-zag, make sudden elevation changes and back-and-forth maneuvers which make them almost impossible to either shoot down and knock aside in close quarters combat. Their suicide ram attack is done at SV 01-44 and inflicts 1d2 damage.

## Quad-Rotor MAV

One of the most popular drones ever made, these units are often encased in colored hard plastic and wrapped in corporate logos of whatever ancient company once owned them. In the pre-cataclysm times, they were mainly used to carry deliveries from a warehouse to a specific address. While they can be remotely controlled, with the operator seeing through the nose camera on the drone, they were originally set to fly to a specific address on auto-pilot, with its half dozen sensors active to give the fast flying package carrier the ability to dodge birds, other MAVs and airborne robots that once clouded the skies over oldster cities.

Military variants, which feature the paint jobs that matched an old world nation's uniform, were also widely used to carry ammo, flesh mend packets, small tools and other gear to and from the front line, as well as over enemy positions when needed. In short, this RC vehicle has a series of crab-like legs that hang down beneath it to both grip cargo and facilitate landing. This model can carry up to 3 kilograms at its fully loaded setting, which limits its speed and range on a charge to half, but allows it to carry a grenade to a target and drop it via an input from a remote control operator. Once its grenade is spent, many hard pressed military operators will sacrifice the MAV by either making an immediate ram attack, or else landing the MAV some place unseen near vital infrastructure, munitions, command-and-control assets, or fuel lines, and set the MAV to self destruct hoping to trigger mayhem among the enemy.

## Robo-Fish

While not a true robot, as it can't operate independently unless occupied by a digital being, this fish shaped, waterproof and highly flexible, 36cm long fish comes in several very authentic looking models. **Roll 1d6** when discovered to determine the type, although they all have the same features: **1.** Trout/ **2.** Salmon/ **3.** Bass/ **4.** Catfish/ **5.** Pike/ **6.** Flounder/ **7.** Tuna/ **8.** Piranha.

This fish has an operational mouth that can be made to bite a target — although the damage is minimal and the main purpose seems to be to use the mouth to grab ropes, pick up objects off the bottom, or release magnetic sea mines once attached to the hulls of enemy ships. These metal and plastic fish were also used for underwater observation, industrial inspections, body search and recovery, and hundreds of other applications.

They can swim to a depth of 100 meters with ease, although any deeper risks a seal breakage with a cumulative 1% chance per minute at these dangerous pressures, with any leak causing water to get into the circuitry and immediately short out, fry and destroy the unit. If disabled because of some sort of stun attack, EMP or other means, this fish will float to the surface and lay on its side like a real dead fish.

## Snake

Whether designed merely to strike fear into the ranks of the enemy, or as legitimate battlefield or espionage asset, these fully articulating, fast moving metal and plastic snakes are easily identified as mechanical relics when seen from less than 4 meters away, although at distances beyond this, the construct looks like just another, often deadly snake of the Epochian era.

One of the major benefits of this ground slithering MAV over a flying design is its ability to squirm into small spaces in damaged building, enter gopher holes, pipes, power conduits and the innards of ancient machines. While they excel as surveillance devices, they are also excellent at transporting small items within their lower half, which is hollow and can accept medications, mini power cells, maps, paper notes, loose ammo and other small supplies that are useful for front-line soldiers or excavators. Likewise, they can attack other MAVs and living creatures, although for the former, the venom within the alloy fangs of these robo-snakes has no effect on non organic beings.

For the living, however, the typical 30ml amount of injected venom delivered after a successful strike will comprise one of three random varieties, **roll 1d6: 1,2.** Death venom, make a Type C endurance based hazard check or die on the 4th round after being bitten / **3,4.** Sleep Venom, Type C. The victim must make a Type C END based HC or drop unconscious for 1d6 hours. / **5,6.** Paralysis venom, type D END based hazard check to avoid dropping to the ground after 4 rounds and losing all control of muscles. Cyborgs with a mechanical limb can still use such limbs, although if they are prone, some attachments might be rendered useless. Duration of paralysis is 10+1d100 minutes.

A snake MAV will have enough of its current type of venom to make 6 successful injections.

## Suicide Nano

There were once many larger suicide drones in use by the ancient ones, although few survived the decades of madness during the end times. Smaller, remote controlled air vehicles, however, are still found, and often in great numbers in sealed crates, individual carry cases, or wrapped in plastic and stuffed in the nylon backpacks of long dead soldiers. These concrete gray units resemble Quad-Rotor MAVS, and have four propellers, and a bulky main body. Because of the explosives they are packed with, they can carry no other load and still fly. Their optics are shoddy, they have no audio receiver mode and lack night vision. In short, they were made as cheaply as possible and destined for only one flight.

At either some pre-programmed signal or condition — such as unauthorized personnel entering a certain hallway or restricted area — this MAV, and sometimes a dozen companions, will fly at the designated target and attempt to impact and latch onto it prior to detonating. On a successful hit, the suicide-nano MAV is deemed to have latched onto a gap in the victim's armor or landed over a vital part, and with a directional charge, blows inward on the victim, causing 2d20 damage. If they are shot down, or fail to pierce the target's defenses but either bounce off the armor or land at its feet, the MAV will also blow up in a 3 meter radius and inflict 1d10 damage to all those in the blast zone, including the original intended target. This blast is treated as an attack against the target's DV, just like a grenade (SV 01-70).

## Tarantula

At just under half the size of a more common spiderbot (page TME 181), these far more realistic looking mechanical arachnids look like a real tarantula. Only when a person is within a meter or less can they discern that something isn't right about the way it moves, that it has tiny piston on the underside of each leg, and its fangs are over-sized, and that its many eyes flicker with electricity when in low light.

Used primarily as a tool of espionage, this unit can also serve as an assassin bot since any sort of venom or drug can be inserted into its twin fang syringes. Plus, unlike a regular tarantula, this thing can deploy tiny suction cups in its feet and underside to adhere to sheer surfaces, including glass and ascend any barrier to get at its designated target. When used as a surveillance device, the multi camera on this unit can see in the dark up to 20 meters, as well as scan the infrared and ultraviolet spectrum. Likewise, and only known to a few new era scholars and relic experts, this MAV's advanced optics can detect dimensional beings, portals, residue and phenomena up to 15 meters away. Its audio pickup capabilities are also sharp, and it can listen and record conversations from as far as 14 meters away.

The typical load-out of venom on a randomly encountered tarantula MAV is decided by a 1d6 roll: 1. Type D death venom, with death occurring on the 4th round after the organic being is bitten. / 2-5. Sleep venom, type E endurance based hazard check or after 6th round, the victim topples over unconscious for 300 minutes minus its endurance trait value, to a minimum sleep period of 10 minutes. / 6. Maddening agony: The victim is allowed a type F endurance based hazard check or succumb to the most excruciating pain the subject has probably ever felt. This will last 3d6 minutes, and for each minute, he or she must make a type D will power based hazard check or begin to wail and scream in pain, roll on the ground, and spasm in agony. Doing this is the wilderness or ruins will attract 1d6+1 random encounters to that vicinity in the next 10+1d20 minutes.

The venom reservoir of a tarantula MAV can take 100ml of any injectable liquid, with 25ml being a sufficient dose to cause the stated effect.

# Drones

The line between what is a drone and what is a robot is sometimes blurred.Often, flying robots with programmed responses, decision-making skills and the ability to act on their own initiative are mistakingly called drones. MAVs, or Micro Air Vehicles, are also drones, and although they can react to various events, are more or less remote controlled vehicles, too.

It is possible for a digital being to transfer its consciousness into a drone once the machine has been hacked and reprogrammed (using the computer technician skill described on page 53 of the Hub Rules book), however many drones have limited data capacity and a digital being might need to permanently jettison precious data points merely to fit itself into the hard drive of a drone. A drone's hard drive capacity, and firewall trait score, which are both used to avoid hacking, are rarely needed during game play, but if it is, consult Table XR-56 Firewall & Data Points of Common Computers, Robots and Androids on page 69 in the digital beings section of this book. Here, the GM will locate all the androids and robots, drones and MAVs included in both the Hub Rules and Expansion Rules books. The terabytes of data (basically the endurance points for any CPU) are shown on this table.

As can be seen, drones and MAVs have very limited data capacity, as thinking for themselves is not called for. Still, if a digital being normally spends its time inhabiting an android or robotic body, especially a big one, it doesn't hurt to carry a dormant drone in its knapsack in case it finds itself in a precarious situation where its main body is doomed, and it can transfer at least the main parts of its identity into a flying drone or MAV to make an escape where other character types cannot. It is also possible for a digital being to leave behind a more robust, high memory capacity main body, transfer to a drone for a few hours to perform some task, and then return to the main body and transfer back to join with its full data capacity. If the digital being's drone is destroyed while it occupies it, the DB is allowed a willpower based type D hazard check to have survived the crash.

Like a digital being, an artificial intelligence might also sacrifice the vast portion of its data trait points and abilities to force itself into a drone, or other common robot, in order to make an escape from a dire situation.

In The Mutant Epoch era, drones are often modified by their new owners, with weapon systems added or replaced because of different circumstances. Some are reprogrammed, most often by an AI who has converted them into its murderous minions. Most need to be upgraded with combat programming to be effective, with anyone with 3 points in the computer technician skill able to write and install attack software. Doing so in a personal drone will enhance a non-combat or non-police unit with a +10 SV bonus, a benefit which is already programmed into Police and military drones. Personal drones without the upgrade have a SV of 01-40. Any weapon of up to pistol size can be added to a basic drone, but it reduces its speed by 2 meters per round, unless it's a medical drone and a weapon is used to replace the medical kit.

## Types of Drones

### Personal Drones
1. Basic, Little Buddy
2. Basic, Action Man
3. Basic, Emergency Medical Response Drone
4. Defensive
5. Police Assistant

### Utility Drones
1. Search and Rescue
2. Construction
3. Under water

### Military Drones
1. Bomb Disposal
2. Military Utility Drone
3. Military Resupply Drone
4. Hunter-Killer

### Drone Equipment
1. Control Unit
2. Control Hub
3. Repair Kit
4. Hijack Unit

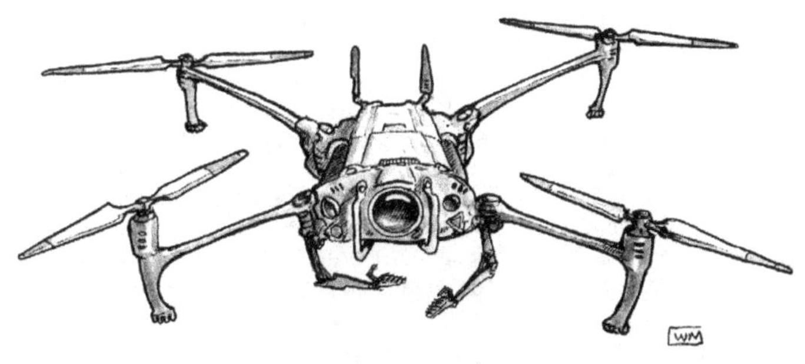

## Personal Drones

**Basic Drone** *by Danny Seedhouse*
Defense Value: **-10**
Endurance: **15**
Movement: **20 meters/ 30 meters for the Action Man model and 15 for the over loaded medical model.**
Initiative: **+1**
Attacks: **1 slam**
Strike Value: **Slam 01-40**
Damage: **1d4 stun**
Strength: 18
Agility: 60
Accuracy: 20
Intelligence: 10
Willpower: NA
Perception: 40
Experience factors: 15
Size: 42cm wide rectangle with multiple round rotors
Weight: 5.5kg
Relics: 1 pill power cell runs the drone for 1 month. Digital camera and sensor suite unless replaced.

This generic small drone comes in many makes and models, from the basic rotor drone to advanced vector thrust models. Each drone shares common capabilities that include flight, a video camera, 1st person view piloting and follow modes where the drone will keep up with an operator and stay at a designated position. The relatively cheap price of these drones insured their spread across all levels of society before the rise of the AIs and anything computerized became suspect.

Commonly used basic drone variants are the little buddy, the action man, and the medical drone:

**The Little Buddy:** A boy's first drone, just a little smarter than the first generation of completely operator controlled drones, with a grasping claw that allows it to pick up small amounts of cargo (up to 2kg) like water balloons or a live grenade. These drones where produced in a wide variety of colors (use table TME-1-18 on page TME-23 for a random color) and were sold to a younger audience. The drone has a maximum flying height of 25 meters, which is programed in to avoid interfering with aircraft and a maximum range from controller of 100 meters. Both restrictions can be negated by a computer technician of 1 skill point. Used mostly for play and photography, this model features a digital camera with X5 zoom on a steady-cam mount, with video streaming to the user's mobile device of choice such as a tablet, smartphone or advanced communicator.

**Action Man:** This is what the ancient folks used to film their sports action movies, and even in the post-apocalyptic world, extreme adrenaline junkies love this model. The action man has all the features of the little buddy but its speed is faster and it comes with an advanced video camera in a programmable steady camera rig along with more advanced programming to allow sweeping shots while dealing with winds and varied lighting conditions. It features an up scaled set of rotors to allowing it to reach speeds of up to 30 meters per round.

**Medical Response Drone:** These drones are programed to help people who need emergency medical attention, and were typically posted at big sporting events or protest marches. They are equipped to deal with heart attacks, allergy attacks, and to stabilize people suffering from traumatic injury. Voice commands can call the drone to a patient, although the drone will also scan a crowd looking for people in need using its Perception stat of 50 if a roll is needed. This drone works as a field medical kit (see page 199 in the hub rules, although this variant can be reprogrammed to operate on mutants with the same skill roll) that moves on to a new patient in need of aid on the 4th round instead of healing endurance. If there are no other critical patients, however, it restores enough END for the patient to be self mobile. This bulkier unit runs for 1 year on 1 standard power cell.

**Defensive Drone** *by Danny Seedhouse*
Defense Value: **-20**
Endurance: **35**
Movement: **10 meters flying**
Initiative: **+1**
Attacks: **1 stunner** (ranged or melee) and **1 gas projector**
Strike Value: **01-70 with stunner and gas projector is area affect**
Damage: **2d20 Stun/ 200 meters** or **2d20+2 melee** (40 shots), gas projector comes with 3 shots of tear gas (Hub Rules page 195)
Strength: 21
Agility: 50
Accuracy: 40
Intelligence: 15
Willpower: NA
Perception: 45
Experience factors: 31
Size: 55cm diameter disk
Weight: 19 kg
Relics: 2 power cells 1 gives 40 rounds to the stunner and 1 powers the drone for 1 year

Built for people concerned with their own safety when walking the streets or other dangerous area, these drones were built with a more robust chassis and come with advanced threat detection software. It will protect its operator from muggers and robbers with its less than lethal suite of deterrence weapons. Voice command is a standard feature of this drone, with voice imprinting with the user established when the unit is unpacked. A computer technician can, however, attempt to reset and reconfigure the unit using the 'Re-Program Robot' column from the computer technician skill table on page TME-53.

The standard configuration has a stunner and a tear gas dispenser that holds 3 grenades (pg TME-195). These drones can be programed to protect specific people or a specific area like a house. Restricted variations (1 in 20) can occasionally be found that have replaced the stunner with a combat shotgun.

**Police Assistant Drone** *by Danny Seedhouse*
Defense Value: **-20**
Endurance: **42**
Movement: **14 meters flying**
Initiative: **+2**
Attacks. **1 stunner/1 laser pistol/1 slam**
Strike Value: **stunner 01-75 / laser pistol 01-76 / slam 01-70**

Damage: **2d20 stunner/ 1d20+10 Laser pistol/ 1d8+2 Slam**
Strength: 39
Agility: 56
Accuracy: 50
Intelligence: 20
Willpower: NA
Perception: 66
Experience factors: 48
Size: 65cm wide disk
Weight: 22 kg
Relics: 3 power cells. 1 for operation and 1 for each weapon system. Stunner and laser pistol can be scavenged with a 4 in 6 chance of working properly after drone destruction.

The police assistant drone, also called a 'robo back-up unit', is basically an upgraded version of the civilian defensive drone with enhanced programing and extra fixtures. Each drone is usually slaved to a single partner it is programmed to protect — although this person's ID and photo description can be reprogrammed by anyone with the computer technician skill who makes a successful 're-program robot' hazard check (pg. TME-53).

This drone mounts a siren, loud speaker, a Proximity Alert Spike system and display (see hub rules pg. 199) and its optics are upgraded to the same capacity as a digital spotting scope (hub rules pg. 201). These features are linked to a visor unit that is issued to its controlling officer. (1 in 4 units found in the epoch are discovered with the visor). Without the visor, a standard hand held controller tablet or smartphone can also work, if the corresponding passcode to the drone is logged in, but limits what the user could otherwise hold in their hands — such as a gun or stun baton.

# Utility Drones

**Search and Rescue Drone** *by Danny Seedhouse*
RSC-102b aka Rescue Rangers.
Defense Value: **-20**
Endurance: **55**
Movement: **9m flying/ 5m crawling**
Initiative: **+4**
Attacks. **1 self defense stunner**
Strike Value: **01-50**
Damage: **2d20 Stun**
Strength: 85
Agility: 60
Accuracy: 25
Intelligence: 70
Willpower: 30
Perception: 110
Experience factors: 35 unless armed, then add 5 for a melee weapon and +10 for a ranged weapon
Size: 1.5 meters wide by 4 meters long segmented body. Though they expand for flight to a more circular shape and can narrow down to 0.5 meters and lengthen out to 6 meters.
Weight: 70 kg
Power supply: Runs off a power pack for 1 year. Has built in solar panels that extend its power supply to near unlimited, if it has time to recharge between active periods.

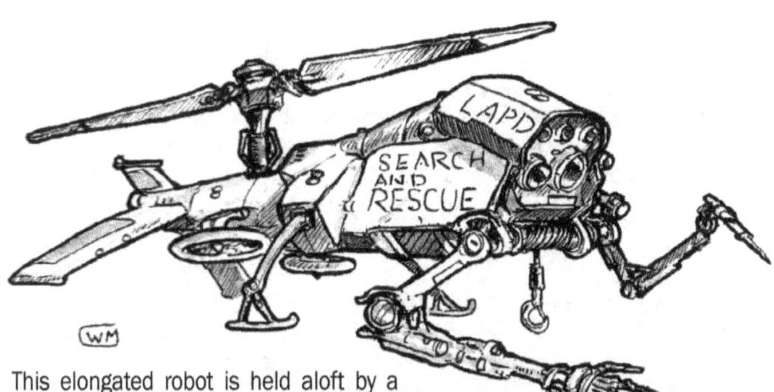


This elongated robot is held aloft by a powerful rotor blade with a lift capacity far beyond what is needed to lift its own weight. One of the most innovative features of this drone is its morphing body, that allow it to narrow its frame for tight spaces and expand for flight. Built to operate independently and provide first responder capacities in a highly mobile package, these SRD drones were sent out to locate, assess and provide emergency care and rescue to the injured. The SRD possesses incredible sensor capabilities, enhanced night vision, infrared, ultraviolet, ground penetrating radar, highly tuned audio pick ups and olfactory processors that allow it analyze a wide variety of airborne chemicals, effectively having 5 skill points in tracking used to locate people trapped under debris and hidden by other environmental factors.

Search and Rescue drones feature a built-in winch with 30 meters of high tensile cable, ending in a flexible hand to help carry unconscious people to safety. In addition, this unit has a self deploying immobilization stretcher to help safely move even the most critically injured. Its built-in medical suite operates at a medic skill of 4 points, and allows it to automatically stabilize a person, apply splints to any broken limb and stop most major bleeding, deal with heart attacks and other medical emergencies.

The drone comes with built-in survival programming, and will keep a person warm overnight, has a water collection unit (akin to the cyborg implant #5/ pg. TME-85) with several full bottles at all times. Additionally, this remarkable unit is equipped with a storage compartment with 6 tubes of nutrient paste and a rescue kit. These drones, when found in the post-apocalyptic wilderness, are usually packed up in bright orange rescue boxes containing one SRD drone, its control module, and a physical copy of the user's manual.

SRD's all have 4 skill points in medic, wilderness survival, flawless navigational ability and were originally linked to the national communications net — but now continuously monitor radio channels looking for emergency aid requests. These drones are pacifist who never attack, but will use their stunner to drive off wildlife that is actively attacking a humanoid, unless they have been reprogrammed. Unfortunately, 1 in 4 of these drones have gone rogue (usually due to time and circuit damage or interference by men or machines) and are now killers. Such mad machines have been ungraded with strapped on weapons by either high-tech purists who use these drones to kill mutants, or else by a genocidal AI who has the drone kill pure stocks and mutants alike.

Roll 1d12 on the following random weapons chart to determine what a rogue SRD has attached to it:

## 1d12 Rogue SRD Drone Weapon Upgrade Chart

1. **Blades and spikes:** SV 01-70, with a ram doing 1d20+12, it can normally only hit 1 person per round unless they are next to each other within 1 meter. Drone gets an extra -5 to DV in melee combat.

2. **Spears:** SV 01-74, rate 1, damage 1d20+16, range 28.5 meters, will have 1d4+1 spears.

3. **Chainsaw:** SV 01-80, rate 1, DMG 3d10+14, 2L fuel tank with 1d100+75 rounds of fuel left.

4. **Heavy crossbow:** SV 01-82, rate 1/3, DMG 1d20+19, range 100 meters, carries 2d10+10 bolts.

5. **Shotgun pistol with a bayonet:** Shotgun: SV 01-90, rate 1 or 2, DMG 3d10, range 30 meter, can reload 2 shells in 1 round and have 2d10 extra shells. Bayonet: SV 01-70, rate 1, DMG 1d10+14.

6. **Scavenged pistols:** Roll 1d8;
   1. (1d3) musket pistols, SV 01-77, rate 1/3, DMG 1d20, range 25m, 3d6+4 shots.
   2. A musket pistol (1d6+4 shots) and a dart gun SV 01-74, rate 1, 1d6+(type B sleep poison).
   3. Shotgun pistol (1 in 6 have two such weapons) SV 01-85, rate 1 or 2, 3d10 DMG, range 20 meters, 3d6+1 shells.
   4. (1d3+1) .22 cal. Pistols SV 01-75, rate 2, 1d10 DMG, range 100 meters, each pistol has a full 18 shot magazine, and the drone carries 1d3 extra mags and 1d20+2 extra rounds.
   5. (1d2) musket pistols with 2d6+2 shots, and 1 pocket pistol SV 01-75, rate 2, 1d20 DMG, range 120m, 1 full 6 shot magazine plus 1d2 extra.
   6. Auto pistol SV 01-82, rate 2, DMG 1d20, range 250m, 1 mag 20 shot mag with 1d3 extra and 1d8 loose rounds.
   7. (1d2) wrist lasers, SV 01-80, rate 1, 1d10+10 DMG, 210 meters range, 1 mini power cell each provides 16 shots per gun, with 1d2 spare batteries.
   8. Roll again on this chart, but the drone has 1d3 skill points in weapons expert with the rolled weapons.

7. **Sub-machine gun:** SV 01-80, DMG 1d20, range 250m, rate 5, with 1 full 50 round mag and 2d10 spare rounds.

8. **Assault rifle:** SV 01-82, DMG 1d20, range 900m, rate 3, with a full 30 round mag and 2d10 spare rounds.

9. **Flame unit:** SV 01-90, DMG 2d20/+1d0 burn damage for 1d6 rounds, range 10m, rate 1, with 1 full 20 discharge fuel tank.

10. **Sniper rifle:** SV 01-88/120 on carefully aimed shots, DMG 1d20+10, range 2km, rate 1 or 1/2 carefully aimed, with 10 rounds.

11. **Pulse rifle:** SV 01-90, DMG 1d12, range 800m, rate 4 per burst, with 1 full 25 burst power pack.

12. Two weapons systems: roll twice on this chart.

## Construction Drone *by Danny Seedhouse*

*Constructor 45-2b, aka ConBots, Hammers, Nailers, or Extra H.*
Defense Value: **-10**
Endurance: **70**
Movement: **5m walking / climb at 4 skill points / 2m flying**
Initiative: -1
Attacks: **2x bash with arms**
Strike Value: **01-60**
Damage: **1d8+16**
Strength: 100
Agility: 42
Accuracy: 27
Intelligence: 14
Willpower: 33
Perception: 26
Experience factors: 98
Size: 2.2 meters
Weight: 120 kg
Power supply: Runs off a power pack for 1 year. Has built in solar panels that extend its power supply to near unlimited, if it has time to recharge between active periods. Has an extra power cell for each of its tools.

Construction drones are the mid-way point between a completely biological worker and a full-on construction robot. Robustly assembled, they are capable of movement across just about any type of surface found on a construction site. They even exhibit a slow flight speed rounding out their impressive mobility. These drones were specialized for a specific work site and required a human supervisor to assign them tasks, but once assigned have the skills to complete the task unsupervised and then wait for the next assignment. This command can be given by just about anyone who knows what the drone can do and assigned it to a proper chore. The framing drone can be assigned to frame a specific wall but not wire it afterward. Assignments were made

easier by the use of a handheld console that used a low-powered laser to measure and designate the drone's assigned work area.

Each model of drone is customizable to serve in various roles by simply changing out both its tools and modular task CPU. Before the end of civilization, these drones where often used in teams to build heritage homes and came with group coordination software that allowed the user to select the type of house they wanted to build (usually from a preset list) and have a group of 4 to 12 drones coordinate to build it.

In the Epochian era, 75% of these drones are found with a laser designator remote control device that can command the drone. It also allows the operator to scroll through a wide list of construction options, measuring tools, calculators, and gauges, and itself is worth 300+1d100sp even without a drone, and powered by a mini-power cell for 9 months. Anytime a group of more than one drone is found there is a 3 in 4 chance that they are preloaded with the group coordination programming and one drone will have an extra contractor module loaded into it allowing it to roam a local area looking for supplies that the other drones need. Roll 1d6 for the drone variant and its associated skills below:

### 1d6 Construction Drone Variants Installed tools and Associated Skills

**1. Wooden Building Construction** This drone carries all tools necessary for the construction of wooden buildings such as various saws, a nail gun, sensor array to insure level floors and strait walls, as well as hammers, screwdrivers and anything needed to work with wood. It is fitted with several hoppers containing nails and screws that hold several hundred of each (3d100+100). Possessing a user interface screen that allows an operator (a person with the relic knowledge or computer technician skill) to select a complete house plan from a list of 20 standardized designs. These drones where often used as the lead drone in a construction project, and thus can task other types of drones to follow the selected plans it is running off. It functions at 3 points in the mechanical technician skill for building wooden structures only, and can process raw materials (a tree) into the materials needed or repair structural damage to wooden buildings.

**2. Building Electrical Installation** This drone carries all the tools necessary to install the wiring system in a designated building. It can run lines for lights, switches and power outlets. This drone carries 4 spools of wire at least one is copper and one is tungsten (each 200 meters long) in different gauges and is equipped with numerous hoppers filled with various electrical odds and ends, as well as 1d4 circuit boxes 10+2d20 electrical plug fixtures and 10+2d20 light fixtures. It operates at 5 points in the electrical technician skill but only for the purpose of wiring (it can wire the power grid for an entire settlement with the proper materials) but it can't make a motion detector. It will even make repairs on already installed electrical systems found in new era and ancient buildings.

**3. Plumbing Drone** This drone installs the pipes needed for sewage and water. It carries all the tools needed for plumbing as well as 20 meters of plastic piping in 4 meter lengths and hoppers full of joints, drains, elbows, hoses and other miscellaneous parts needed when plumbing. If a skill roll is needed, it operates at 2 points in mechanical technician skill for the Installation of plumbing. This drone can also perform maintenance of installed plumbing systems after spending 1d4 hours examining the existing system. If given a collection of scrap and newly crafted materials, and several weeks time and access to a half dozen laborers, this unit could fashion a well-pump, water filtration tank, or sewage treatment reservoir.

**4. Finishing Drone** This drone installs the drywall on walls, paints surfaces and ornamental details as needed, and expertly installs trim and fixtures. It carries all the tools needed to perform these jobs and has hoppers with unmixed and premixed dry walling compound, finishing nails, and three, 4 gallon tanks of paint in pre-selected house colors. This drone can also spruce up a place, add fresh paint, replace trim and generally make an old house interior look new, making these drones highly sought after by the new era's few rich people who want there home to look pre-war new.

**5. General Contractor Drone** This drone comes with a full set of basic construction tools and the programming to undertake just about any task it is set to — so long as it has the proper materials available since it carries no internal supplies beyond several hundred nails of various sizes for it nail gun. Given proper materials, it can build a complete 2 story home in roughly 6 weeks, although this assumes a preexisting design and a pre poured concert pad to build on. This is a basic house with no installed fixtures, windows, or appliances, and bare ply wood floors, but honestly, in the Epochian era few inhabitants are that picky. If it's needed, the drone operates at 2 points mechanical technical skill for structures only.

**6. Welding Drone** This drone is built to weld, and possesses multiple types of welding equipment, electrical arc, acetylene, mig, and a flex core welder, all of which allow the drone to weld multiple materials and cover most needs on a construction site. The drone carries nothing in the way of parts but plenty of fuel and gas tanks to run its multiple types of welding machinery, as well as a power pack for the electrical arc welder and a 2nd power pack for its other tools. Also included in the drones equipment suite is an extra set of gripping arms and an extensive selection of clamps and braces.

Reprogramming a construction drone can be done fairly easily and was originally as simple as changing a modular task unit and switching out certain sets of tools. Where things get a bit trickier is re-purposing the drone for a task outside of construction. This requires either a skilled programmer (4 points in the computer technician skill) to write new code for its new functions, and 2 skill points as a robotics technician to install offensive weapons to the unit. The most brutal and simple of these modification was the rewriting of code done by rogue AIs to turn these drones into human killing machines, the result being that roughly half of all drones in The Mutant Epoch are this version, and extremely dangerous.

When construction drones attack, some are more effective at killing than others. Most rogue units have been fitted with up-graded weapons by whoever or whatever has turned them into hunter killers. However, all drones have two primary arms listed in its stat block and these attacks are in addition to other offensive tools.

## *Rogue Construction Drone Attack Modes*

**Wooden Building Construction Drone:** These are outfitted with a nail gun (SV 01-60, rate 5, DMG 1d4, range 10 meters, ammo 2d100 nails). A circular saw (SV 01-55, rate 1, DMG 2d6+8, one power cell yields 400 rounds use), two hammers (SV 01-50, rate 2, 1d6+8 each).

**Electrical Installation Drone:** Over-charged soldering iron, (SV 01-50, rate 4, DMG 1d4, melee, ammo is effectively infinite. Heavy duty staple gun (SV 01-60, rate 10, DMG 1, range 5 meters, 400+1d100 staples pre-loaded). Various tools that can stab or cut at melee range (SV 01-55, DMG 1d3+8, rate 2).

**Plumbing Drone:** This drone's 4 auxiliary arms have little in the way of actual weapons but an over charged soldering iron, (SV 01-50, rate 4, DMG 1d4, melee, ammo is effectively infinite. Various small tools (SV 01-50, DMG 1d4+8, rate 3).

**Finishing Drone:** Finishing nail gun (SV 01-55, rate 10, DMG 1, range 10 meters, ammo 2d100+100 nails). Paint gun (SV target needs to make a Type C agility hazard check or be blinded by paint to the face for 3d6 rounds*, rate 1 spray in up to a 1 meter radius, range 5 meters, ammo 40+1d100 sprays), one arm has a paintbrush for fine detail and is useless as a weapon. One saw blade slash (SV 01-60, DMG 1d6+8, melee)

*Blinded targets are +40 SV easier to be struck, make their own attacks at -40 SV, and are half movement.*

## Aquatic Construction Drone *by Danny Seedhouse*

*Diver 34-22, aka Swimmers, Mech Dolphins, Octo Drones*

Defense Value: **-15**
Endurance: **120**
Movement: **10 meters swimming**
Initiative: **-1**
Attacks: **bash with 2 arms**
Strike Value: **01-66**
Damage: **1d8+18**
Strength: 103
Agility: 49
Accuracy: 26
Intelligence: 42
Willpower: 29
Perception: 34
Experience factors: 102
Size: 2 meters
Weight: 170 kg
Power supply: Operates for 1 year on its built-in, waterproofed power pack. Solar panels provide nearly unlimited recharge capabilities. Each tool has its own power cell.

This drone is a variant on the standard construction drone, allowing it to operate underwater, and features a reinforced chassis on the sensor package to operate at a depth of up to 200 meters. It has a bank of powerful lights and enhanced low light sensor to deal with the blackness of the deep ocean. One of the added features is an emergency air supply for rescue operations of biological units with emergency attachment points for up to 4 rescued or unconscious divers.

Tool sets are the same as the standard construction drone except that only welding, general contractor and electrical insulation drones are being used, with an upgraded programing suite to deal with the unique challenges of underwater construction.

## Military Resupply Drone *by Danny Seedhouse*

*Aka ammo buddies, MobMeals, Paper trains.*

Defense Value: **-45 (-57 vs ballistic weapons and -65 vs lasers)**
Endurance: **40**
Movement: **20m flying**
Initiative: **+3**
Attacks: **1 stunner**
Strike Value: **01- 75**
Damage: **2d20 stun**
Strength: 37
Agility: 59
Accuracy: 62
Intelligence: 19
Willpower: 12
Perception: 48
Experience factors: 34
Size: 64cm wide disc
Weight: 20 kg
Relics: 2 power cells: 1 for operation and 1 for each weapon system. Stunner can be scavenged with a 4 in 6 chance of working properly after drone destruction. Plus 1 roll on Resupply Drone's Cargo chart.

Old world battlefields became increasingly fluid as technology progressed, with small unit tactics, such as hit-and-run attacks increasing in urban areas, all of which made a mess of traditional supply chains. The solution was the use of unmanned flying drones to deliver ammo when and where it was needed. The latest generation of resupply drone has advanced navigation and avoidance software, bullet resistant skin and anti laser reflective coatings, not to mention optic camouflage to help it complete its assignment.

The resupply drone coped with the increased demands on ammo experienced on the pre-collapse battlefield. This drone was programmed with the IFF signatures (Identification, friend or foe) of friendly soldiers, robots and other drones and these nimble drones were directed to travel to their coordinates during engagements and deliver anything from ammo to medical supplies. 50% of all excavated, or actively encountered drones of this classification carry something of great value. Roll 1d20 once on the following table to determine what a resupply drone carries:

### 1d20 Resupply Drone's Cargo Chart

**1.** 1d6 empty MREs, though there are 1d4 packs of salt and 1d4 packs of sugar, a sanitary napkin, and 1d4 sets of plastic utensils, and 1 chocolate chip cookie.

**2.** 1d6+2 MREs each provides a good well balanced meal that provides a full days worth of nutrition. Learn more on page XR-436.

**3.** Sewing kit, 2d4 pairs of socks, 1d4 pairs of army pants in green camo and 1d3 pairs of combat boots.

**4.** 1d3 empty magazines for an auto pistol, 1d3 empty assault rifle magazines and a wad of clearly old and used bandages.

**5.** 1d2 night vision headsets with a spare battery each. Described on page TME 201.

**6.** Field medical kit. Described on page TME 199.

**7.** 1d3 tear gas grenades, 1d2 pepper spray cannisters and 1d4 gas masks.

**8.** 2d6 lose rounds of pistol ammo, 1d2 shotgun shells and a pack of gum.

**9.** 1d4+1 fragmentation grenades.

**10.** Box with 2d10 pistol rounds, 1d10 high caliber pistol rounds and 2d4 shotgun shells.

**11.** Box with 3d10 shotgun shells, auto pistol in a holster with 2 full 20 shot magazines of ammo, and a combat knife.

**12.** 1d3 auto pistols in holsters with 2 full mags each and a mini flash light.

**13.** 1d4+1 full sub-machine gun magazines (50 pistol rounds in each) and 1d3+1 empty SMG mags.

**14.** Box of 10+1d10 shotgun shells.

**15.** 1d10 high caliber rifle rounds, 2d10 rifle rounds, and a spotting scope.

**16.** 1 SMG with 5 full 50 shot magazines of ammo, a sling, a silencer and a photo of long dead business man.

**17.** 1d4 teargas grenades and a pump shotgun with 3d10 shells on a bandoleer style shell belt.

**18.** 1d4 standard power cells and 1 laser pistol. Cells will be drained if drone found during a dig.

**19.** 1 power pack and 1d6 pill power cells. Power pack will be drained if this drone was uncovered in a dig.

**20.** Grenade launcher with 2d6 fragmentation grenades.

## Military Utility Drone *by Danny Seedhouse*

*Aka Sidekicks, Bullet stoppers, or Iron Guards*
Defense Value: **-25 (-40 vs ballistic weapons and -45 vs lasers)**
Endurance: **55**
Movement: **12 meters flying**
Initiative: **+2**
Attacks. **1 Laser Pistol**
Strike Value: **01-80**
Damage: **1d20+12**
Strength: 43
Agility: 54
Accuracy: 57
Intelligence: 22
Willpower: 15
Perception: 82
Experience factors: 51
Size: 70cm wide x 33cm thick disc
Weight: 25 kg
Relics: 4 power cells: 1 for operation, 2 for its weapon system and 1 for its utility system. Advanced medical kit, gun smithing tools, rad scanner, solar generator unit, flashlight, and smoke screen generator. Each of these systems has a 4 in 6 chance of surviving destruction of the unit unless it's taken out by explosive damage, then the chance drops to 1 in 6.

Military utility drones come programed to perform simple tasks that help the efficiency and survivability of its attached soldier. It acts as a second set of eyes, appraising angles that other soldiers are not covering, and watching over the troops as they sleep. One of its primary functions is the detection of mines and improvised explosive devices, or I.E.Ds, trip wires, booby traps and other perils and its sensor systems grant the lead soldier a re-roll on all failed hazards to notice such hazards.

Programed with various skills, 1 point in weapon expert skill with its main gun, 2 points in the medic skill which it will use upon command of its controller, or automatically on them if they are heavily wounded or unconscious (under 20% endurance), and 4 points in the Gunsmith skill to conduct repair of weapons only. It also comes with a built-in rad scanner, solar generator unit, a large flashlight and a smoke screen generator (implant #42, as the cybernetic implant described on page TME 91).

1 in 6 utility drone units found will be a variant from the fallowing chart:

### 1d4  Military Utility Drones Variants

**1. Riot Control Version:** Issued to MPs for dealing with unruly troops, this unit mounts a stun pistol (SV 01-79, DMG 2d20+2 stun) and a pack of 6 tear gas grenades instead of the laser pistol. It also mounts an electrical defense mechanism (implant #11, page TME 86).

**2. Shield Drone:** Issued to soldiers expecting heavy combat and officers in active war zones, this unit replaces the gun repair tools and the advanced medical kit with an Energy Adsorption Cell (Implant #12, page TME-86), a Ballistic shield (DV -30/-57 vs ballistics) and a reinforced chassis that adds 10+2d10 END. This drone is programed to interpose itself between its soldier and gun fire completely blocking incoming fire from its deployed side (it covers either the front, back, left or right side of its soldier only) or used as mobile cover giving a -40 DV to anyone firing from behind it.

**3. Recon Assistance Drone:** Issued to special forces units and recon elements, this flyer has optical concealment generator (implant #29, page TME-89) running off an internal power supply, giving it 10 hours of use. Its movement systems are upgraded for silent running and its programing tweaked to give it effectively 3 points in the stealth skill outside the optical concealment.

**4. Fire Support Unit:** These were made to provide extra firepower to a squad of soldiers with all the fancy gear and laser pistol of normal models having been replaced with one 'suppression class' pulse laser rifle unit. SV 01-84, rate 8, DMG 1d12+2 each, range 800 meters, with a power pack that provides 120, 8 shot bursts. It's programed to provide suppressive and covering fire, (in game terms it fires at every available target, so if there are 4 targets everyone gets 2 pulses, 7 means one shot each and someone gets a 2nd pulse.

In short, it doesn't concentrate fire on one target, nor is it shy about using ammo and has been programed to deploy its solar pack to constantly recharge whenever possible. Above ground, it recharges 1 burst (8 pulses) every hour in the sunlight. If this drone is dispatched and this rare gun survives the impact and explosion, a gunsmith can spend 3d6 hours to convert it into a long barreled, odd looking but deadly specialty pulse rifle complete with a power cord that runs to a power pack should the user have one. Hooking this weapon to a standard power cell will yield only 12, eight pulse laser bursts.

In the post-apocalyptic era, these military utility drones are a gold mine of equipment and useful skills. They can potentially be reprogrammed by anyone with computer skill to recognize one person as their soldier, to whom they provide all their benefits to.

## Bomb Disposal Drone *by Danny Seedhouse*

*Disposable EOD*
Defense Value: **-20/-70 vs explosions**
Endurance: **120**
Movement: **4 meters walking, 4 meters climbing**
Initiative: **+0**
Attacks. **1 Laser torch, or 1 shotgun**
Strike Value: **01-58 laser torch, or pump shotgun 01-62**
Damage: **2d10+16 or 2d20+12 shotgun slugs**
Strength: 112
Agility: 39
Accuracy: 27
Intelligence: 61
Willpower: 22
Perception: 54
Experience factors: 106
Size: 2.3 meters tall, 1m wide
Weight: 260 kg
Power supply: 1 power pack for 1 year. plus built-in solar panels that extend its power supply to near unlimited, when inactive. Pump shotgun with 2d10 shotgun slugs. Bomb disposal gear and a detachable blast shield, and if used by a person, apply these stats: DV -8/-20 vs bullets or -30 vs explosions, movement -1.0m, 6kg weight, will sell for 300+d1000sp.

These squat, all terrain drones were issued to military units operating in areas where the presence of IEDs and land mines was expected. Bomb disposal drones are purpose built to dispose of unexplored ordinance, endure the occasional mishap, and survive the process, with a reinforced frame and built-in Blast Shield. These drones are a more advanced version of the first remote operated units, with built-in sensors and tools allowing them to identify and dispose of IEDs and other explosives. Their programming grants them a +20 perception to detect explosives and grants them two hazard checks to find them. This +20 perception and re-roll is granted to the drone's operator, as long as they are using a properly set up drone controller (any of the relics described on this and the following page).

Any airborne MAV or drone smaller than itself must make an agility based type F hazard check after suffering a successful attack, or else have its wings, or rotors damaged, which will cause the unit to spiral out of the air and land hard on the ground, which is treated as an extra attack at 01-70 SV for 1d6 damage. MAVs and small drones that survive this aerial assault might be recoverable by ground crews or other drones capable of lifting the damaged unit.

### Hunter Killer Drone *by WM*
*AKA: MAV Slayer*

Defensive Value: **-35/-12** (when immobile stationary, or hovering)
Endurance: **19**
Movement: **Fly 33m/ creep on ground 2m**
Initiative: **+4**
Attacks: **Smash-cut/ laser**
Strike Value: **01-63 smash-cut/ 01-70 laser**
Damage: **Smash-cut 2d6/Laser 1d12+6**
Strength: 11
Agility: 68
Accuracy: 71
Intelligence: 13
Willpower: 22
Perception: 93
Experience Factors: 24
Morale: NA
Size: 46cm wide disc by 18cm thick
Weight: 16 kg
Relics: see valuables
Cybernetics: none
Valuables: 1d100sp in salvage, 2 internal power cells, laser could be customized into a hand-held unit by a gunsmith, but has a sales value of 900+2d100sp.

Hunter Killer drones are small flyers that were massed produced in the pre-cataclysm times to patrol restricted areas, affluent neighborhoods, and the lines of one military faction or another. While able to drop out of the air or descend from their perches in high ruins or cliffs and attack human intruders, their main purpose was, and still is, to hunt down and kill MAVs and other small creatures and robotic units. They were mainly deployed to take out unauthorized air assets, but will also deal with MAVs on the ground, or any number of small, dangerous creatures that might pose a threat to their master.

A hunter killer drone will usually send out a directional electromagnetic pulse to jam any outbound signals from the mechanical target, range 50 meters, SV 01-80. Any mechanical being hit by such an EMP pulse, including a person in shell class armor or wearing a communicator, has their comms momentarily scrambled and cannot send or receive any transmissions for 2d6 minutes thereafter. If the target had a force field up when hit, this EMP pulse has a 50% chance of being deflected, even if a hit occurred.

A hunter killer drone can only fire 10 such EMP pulses per charge and usually only fires one such beam per engagement per target, and itself has no way of knowing if the EMP pulse worked or not. Following the EMP attack, the HK will open fire with its nose mounted laser, of which it can fire up to 20 shots from a dedicated power cell, but prefers to take out smaller machines and creatures by chasing them down, smashing into them, and deploying six small, blade edged, crushing spider legs that pierce and saw into a target once struck, and then quickly release the potentially maimed victim.

## Drone Equipment

| 1d8 | Drone Equipment Item | Range of Drone Control | Weight | Sell Price |
|---|---|---|---|---|
| 1. | Drone HUD | 8km | 340g | 300+3d1000sp |
| 2. | Basic Drone Control Pad | 6km | 430g | 250+2d1000sp |
| 3. | Drone Control Unit | 12km | 570g | 600+1d1000sp |
| 4. | Drone Control Implant | 5km | 1.2kg | 340+3d100sp |
| 5. | Drone Control Hub | 18km | 4.9kg | 900+1d1000sp |
| 6,7. | Drone Repair Kit | NA | 4.8kg | 500+4d100sp |
| 8. | Drone Hijack Unit | 200m | 850g | 600+1d1000sp |

**Drone HUD:** Glasses or goggles linked to a drone and displaying information it provides. These visual aids are see-through even when inactive and can serve as safety goggles as far as protecting the wearer from blowing sand, spores, and other particles and spays that might otherwise blind them. Range 8 kilometers. A mini power cell powers the unit for about a year. These devices will fetch 300+3d1000sp if sold in a relic market, but to buy a pair will cost three times this, if even available. Uses blink sequences to select commands.

**Basic Drone Control Pad:** Essentially, this tablet is tuned for drone control and allows for point and click movement and targeting, allowing the operator to get a drone to look around a corner and shoot someone only it can see. Strike value is based solely on the SV of the drone itself. When not directly controlled, the drone will follow this unit or return to a pre-set location automatically. By default, most drones come with one of these controls, which includes a wrist strap, zippered, foam carry case, and are powered by a mini power cell for 2 years. These units have a range of 6 kilometers and will sell for 250+2d1000sp, but can only be purchased at three times this amount.

**Drone Control Unit:** This device is for the direct control of a drone when an operator needs the personal touch and can't rely on the drone's built in programming. It is a two handed console that resembles a multitude of game consoles of old, and requires the operator's fingers and thumbs to toggle, scroll or click various pre-set commands to steer, fire or manipulate the distant drone. The unit's firing strike value is based on the drone's SV, but adding user's SV bonuses from their character rank, plus any Intelligence trait bonus (use Accuracy column on table TME 1-3, but substitute Intelligence) and half bonuses from applicable weapon expertise.

The unit itself consists of a tiny display and two control sticks, and is roughly the size of a person's hand. The user needs to be able to read or have the relic knowledge or electrical technician skill to use this unit. Maximum of

one drone can be directly controlled with this or slaved to follow the user. It has a range of 12 kilometers and runs for 6 mouth on a standard power cell.

**Drone Control Implant:** This is a cybernetic version of a control unit and adds display screens to any existing optical implant and a control pad to an arm with feedback controls within the arm for steering the drone. Direct control using this unit provides a +10 SV to the drone's ranged and melee weapons. It runs for 6 months on a standard power cell and has a 5 kilometer range. Only a robot, android or cyborg can use this implant, and only if the would-be user has some sort of electronic optical aid since this implant needs to connect to the spinal interface and brain stem, or CPU and wiring of a mechanical being.

Some vat-brains might qualify for this relic should they have existing optical implants or be housed in the body of an appropriate machine (GM's ruling on this is needed). These implants weigh only 1.2 kilograms and will sell for 340+3d100sp.

**Drone Control Hub:** This is a much larger version of the Control Unit described above, is the size of a large suitcase and deploys multiple screens and up to 3 sets of joy sticks. This hub can be slaved to up to 6 drones, and run them simultaneously on pre-programmed cours- es or direct control of up to 3 drones. It follows all the other rules of a Control Unit. These weigh 38 kilograms and have a range of 18 kilometers and uses 1 power cell a month. They will sell for 900+1d1000sp.

Similar, fixed units were also built into control panels in bunkers, large vehicles, helicopters, sea-going vessels or spacecraft, and equipped with range extending transmitter antennas and dishes to allow control of drones up to 180 kilometers away. Satellite relays also exist when using these control hub systems, either fixed or the suitcase style portable variant, with the commands transmitted to orbit and then projected the drones on the far side of the planet.

**Drone Repair Kit:** This carry handle equipped, waterproof plastic case contains both basic and advanced tools used to repair and modify drones. The user can employ either their robotics, electrical, or mechanical skill to repair drone's endurance. These kits give a +10 to any skill based hazard check roll involving drones and come with 12 patches that restore 2d10 endurance to a drone with no skill roll needed. An intact kit weighs 4.8 kilograms and will sell for 500+4d100sp.

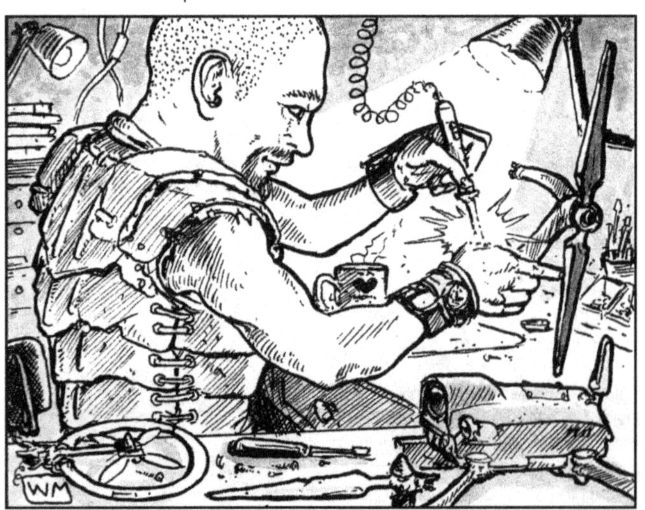

**Drone Hijack Unit:** This small, stubby, scope-like unit allows a skilled computer technician to remotely target a specific drone and try to lock onto it with the cross hairs as seen through the unit's tiny screen. Use the hijacker's base strike value, with no DV permitted for the drone, to try to connect to, then attempt to hack and control another person's drone, or defend friendly drones from hijacking. Hacking uses the rules under computer technician skill, page 53 of the hub rules ('Hack into CPU' column), but with a 1 point skill penalty vs military drones. This device will also work on MAVS (micro air vehicles) as described on pages 462 to 468 of this book.

It takes two rounds to lock onto and then attempt to hack the drone, which if successful, suddenly comes under the control of the user of this device who can steer it, utilize any on-board weapons, or simply crash it if desired.

To defend a drone from hacking by this unit, the user can likewise lock onto their own drone with another drone hijack unit — which requires 'striking' it with their base SV — and fortify it by partially scrambling incoming hack attempts by hostile entities to reduce their hacking attempt to 50% odds.

Any hack attempt that fails will be registered by the drone and its pilot, and the user will thereafter know that somebody is trying to gain control of the unit, and can either have their drone flee the area, or hunt the would-be hacker. The source of the attempted hack can be identified by the drone on a successful type D intelligence based hazard check, with the drone's INT value used instead of the operator's.

Range is 200 meters and the target must be within line of sight. This unit weighs only 850 grams, and will sell for 600+1d1000sp.

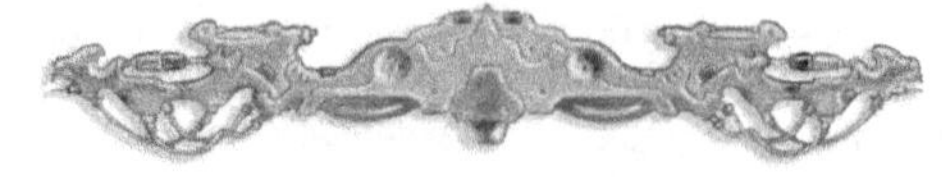

# Augmented Reality

Augmented reality adds unique elements to any ruin expedition. Through projected images, text and audio features, AR presents a dig team with maps, illuminated pathways, intelligence, or an ongoing NPC patron in the form of a digital being who uses an AR network to guide an excavation party. Of course, the first quest for explorers is to acquire the means to see and hear AR elements, and so they must search out, or purchase, one of many visual interface relics.

A projected AR image, animation, alert, advertisement, or non-player character is indexed to either a specific location. This can include a still orbiting satellite, or series of transmitter towers, dishes or antenna, or projected from a kiosk, worn emitter, an overhead projector, robot, android or other high tech object. Often, if still connected to a steady power supply, the AR element is permanently switched on and visible to those with the means to see them.

At other times, the AR feature only switches on when the unit detects an active AR viewing device within range. These detectors are called Proximity Automated AR Element (PAARE). When the sensor is triggered, the AR feature springs to life, either as several parts coming from different directions, growing up from the ground, or popping into existence wholly formed.

Sometimes, a cyborg, android, or robot character might not know they were equipped with the means to see augmented reality, and only be aware of it when the AR element appears — an element nobody else in the dig team can see or hear. In the interests of adding a memorable game occurrence and propelling an adventure forward, the game master might tell a player of a cyborg who has an optical implant, that his or her character sees the AR vision, adding this feature to the character as a sort of bonus implant that wasn't generated at character creation.

Besides the occasional visual aides built into some robots and androids, a few cyborgs feature the Optical Implant called 'augmented reality view mode'. For everybody else, some sort of relic device must either be held up and looked through, such as a tablet or smartphone camera, or an AR viewer must be worn, including contact lenses, monocle, glasses, goggles or add-on lens to a helmet's visor. In only a few cases does an AR projector not need the observer to wear a viewing device. These non-device occurrences normally involve cameras which track the observer and display an augmented reflection of the person inside a screen with AR elements applied to them, such as the Augmented Reality Fashion Mirror.

In many respects, augmented reality relics do not provide much of an edge in day to day post-apocalyptic survival. Still, they can offer huge intelligence pay offs, or provide a dig team with important clues as to the location of an ancient site. One of the best uses for augmented reality is to establish an alliance between the excavators and an artificial intelligence. Such a being could serve as a dig team's guide and patron, and communicate with an allied group solely through appearances via AR projectors throughout an oldster facility, cargo ship, space station or other area where AR projectors are still operational. Such a GM controlled being could foster the social aspects of role-playing, act like a 'spirit guide' for the party, reveal clues, maps, dangers, sources of healing medicine, or offer hints of unlooted high-tech treasure troves that no other team has yet unearthed. In many respects, augmented reality is an ancient technology that serves the game master more than the players, at least when first introduced.

The following section covers two key aspects; a way to see augmented reality via relics, and second, the projection source from where the AR image is being projected from, along with an extensive selection of common augmented reality imagery. Also included are simple random tables where augmented reality viewing and projector relics are found in ancient areas, such as at street level, in private homes, shopping malls, and offices — places frequented by ruin looters.

The game master can use these relics, projectors and cast imagery as examples, or else turn to real world uses for AR to expand on those shown here, especially as the technology advances and finds widespread adoption by the public.

If gamers are unfamiliar with augmented reality, or confuse it with holograms or virtual reality, there are many excellent videos on-line that can explain this technology. For the most part, virtual reality involves wearing a visual and audio headset to explore within a computer, whereas augmented reality provides a layer of imagery, interactive elements and audio over-top of the real world. Holograms, which are very similar to AR in many respects, are cast images that do not require the observer to wear special visual equipment to see or hear them.

Digital beings, which normally present themselves as holograms when outside their computerized and mechanical 'body', cannot see augmented reality unless inhabiting the body of a cyborg, android, robot or other device that can see augmented reality. That said, many NPC digital beings inhabit AR networks and reveal themselves to physical people through a wide range of augmented reality projectors. It is therefore possible for a digital being character to hook into an AR network and project messages, maps, audio and even a visual copy of itself to comrades who are equipped with the means to see and hear AR elements, although the digital being's main point of consciousness is not housed in the AR projection devices, and therefore not imperiled if the device is destroyed.

# Augmented Reality Viewing Relics

As mentioned in the introduction, augmented reality can also be seen by some cyborgs, androids, and robots, if they have built-in AR viewing optics. Likewise, a digital being can only see augmented reality if it is housed in a host vehicle with such visual capabilities. The following ancient devices permit the viewing of otherwise invisible AR elements. Like all relics, these are usually found in ruined cities, installations, or aboard old world vessels and vehicles, but also turn up in new era relic markets or are carried by excavators, technicians and others who gained or inherited them through various means, including theft.

The following table offers a random listing of common augmented reality viewing devices, and includes a sell price for what characters will get if they try to cash-in a discovered AR relic, and a buy price they must pay to acquire such a rare relic should such technology become available in a marketplace.

## Table XR-265 / Random Augmented Reality Viewing Relics

| 1d20 | AR Viewing Relic | Weight | Sell Price / Buy Price |
|---|---|---|---|
| 1. | AR Contact Lenses | 50g | 1500+5d100sp / 3000+2d1000sp |
| 2. | AR Monocle | 75g | 900+3d100sp / 1800+1d1000sp |
| 3. | AR Sensor Prosthetic | 500g | 700+2d100sp / 1400+3d100sp |
| 4. | Palm Held AR Viewer | 750g | 800+4d100sp / 1600+1d1000sp |
| 5-7. | AR Glasses, MK I | 130g | 900+5d100sp / 1800+1d1000sp |
| 8,9. | AR Glasses, MK II | 120g | 1000+6d100sp / 2000+1d1000sp |
| 10. | AR Glasses, MK III | 110g | 1300+6d100sp / 2500+1d1000sp |
| 11. | AR Glasses, MK IV | 100g | 1600+6d100sp / 3000+1d1000sp |
| 12. | AR Glasses, MK V | 125g | 2000+8d100sp / 4000+2d1000sp |
| 13,14. | AR Goggles | 600g | 1400+6d100sp / 2800+1d1000sp |
| 15-19. | Smartphone | 200+1d100g | 600+3d100sp/ 1100+1d1000sp |
| 20. | Tablet | 700+2d100g | 1100+3d100sp / 2200+1d1000sp |

# Descriptions of Augmented Reality Viewing Relics

**AR Contact Lenses:** These very advanced, reusable contact lenses come in a hard, poly sealed case and that includes an electronic cleanser-recharger system. A pill power cell will run the case for 365 days, and provides the hydro-recharge process. Only clean water is needed to store the lenses, which are sterilized between uses by electricity. These lenses, once inserted in an organic person's living eyes, will auto-adjust to give the wearer 20/20 perfect vision — which is often the main value in these rare and highly sought after relics — and allow the wearer to see augmented reality elements within 30 meters range. Mutants suffering from the flaw of visual disorder have their vision normalized when wearing these contacts.

When worn, AR contacts reveal strange, geometric blue and gold spider web patterns that flicker within the wearer's eyes. Anyone to get within 3 meters of this wearer during daylight or other illuminated condition is allowed a type A percep-

tion based hazard check to notice these inhuman color changing conditions. A pure stock appearing human wearer, therefore, might be mistaken for a cyborg or android, which can be fatal in some communities who don't tolerate such beings.

**AR Monocle:** Powered by a mini power cell that is contained in a bulge in the 40cm long neck strap, this often ornate, metal rimmed lens can either be held up to peer through and see augmented reality elements, or else worked into the eye socket and worn in one eye — although never comfortably and it has a tendency to fall out every minute when the wearer does anything other than sit still. The power cell will run this device for 800+1d100 hours, although has a power switch on the cord's battery housing to turn it off when not needed. 1 in 6 of these units are encased in a gold and silver and feature a true magnifying glass ability to enlarge objects but also light fires using sunlight. These rare models fetch 20% more when sold to a dealership and cost 50% more to buy. No audio receptors or speaker. Range 40 meters.

**AR Sensor Prosthetic:** Similar to the augmented reality view mode optical implant, however this is not a true cybernetic even though it is surgically bolted to the side of the wearer's head via a short, but painful surgery. Running for 600 hours on a pair of pill power cells, this unit is manually switched on and a slide over lens is brought over the wearer's eye to allow them to see augmented reality elements out to 300 meters. When worn, the lens can be seen through normally, and superimposes AR graphics and items into the user's field of view without obscuring real objects and entities.

A wearer with one of these units stitched or bolted to their head will almost always be mistaken for a cyborg, and treated accordingly. To rip this relic free will take 3d6 rounds and inflict 1d12 damage if not done by a medic. If desired, a user could rig up a head band and wear this as an eye patch like device, mount it to the brim of a hat or helmet, or merely hold it up to their eye when needing to search for AR elements. This unit includes a speaker to play any audio AR elements.

**Palm Held Viewer:** This device is like a hand mirror, although has a clear, glass-like interior screen and several navigational buttons on the handle. Besides being able to passively look through this small, 20cm wide by 10cm tall screen, a track button in the handle is used to steer a course into the screen and click on interactive elements in the AR object. This device has speakers on either side of the image area to allow audio elements to be heard. A mini power cell in the handle will provide 300 hours of operation. Range 100 meters.

**AR Glasses:** There are 5 commonly found designs of AR viewing glasses, from the MK I to the MK V, although the higher the complexity, or Mark number, the rarer they are. Every higher, more advanced design includes all the features of all previous model types; so a MK III will have all the features of a MK I and MK II, as well as its own features. The model type is determined by a roll on table XR-265, above. All AR glasses include speakers near the ear loops to a allow the user to hear AR audio.

**MK I AR Glasses:** No Interactivity, allows AR viewing out to 50 meters. Pill power cell operates the unit for up to 400 hours.

**MK II AR Glasses:** 'Blink click mode' allows the user to use double blinking actions to select AR elements, range 75 meters. One mini power cell will run these for 380 hours.

**MK III AR Glasses:** Optical Prescription Adaption Mode allows these lenses to adjust to the wearer's visual range — thus fixing the visual disorder caused by the flaw mutation of the same name (mutation no.143, page TME 83). Range 90 meters. A mini power cell will run these for 460 hours.

**MK IV AR Glasses:** Camera mode: Take still pictures with an eye controlled selector or a touch to the side of the glasses arm. Also, video mode with audio mic. Can store 2000 pictures or 500 hours video. Output jack port on arm of glasses, although pics and vids can be replayed within the glasses too, with the glass lenses on both inner facing and outer facing aspects turned into side-by-side screens when needed. AR view range 600 meters.

**MK V AR Glasses:** LiDar Echolocation Mode: These glasses use liDar, or Light Detection and Ranging sight to project subsonic audio ping and instantly translate the returning echos to create a black and white, outlines only view of the view ahead of the wearer, out to 12 meters, allowing the user to see in the pitch blackness to about a quarter of the clarity as if the room were illuminated. AR view range 1 kilometer.

**AR Goggles:** These operate similar to MK II AR glasses, except are built for law enforcement, military and construction environments. Subsequently, these relics are made tough and actually offer considerable protection for the wearer's eyes and upper face. Apply a -3 DV bonus to the wearer. Besides being more robust, these goggles have one pill power cell on each side, and will run for 400 hours on a pair of fully charged cells. If only one pill battery is plugged in, the lenses will have half the range and run for only 200 hours. AR view range 75 meters.

As a bonus feature, a coiled up micro patch cable is built into the back strap that has a 2m cable that can be fitted into a standard or advanced communicator. This allows the user to transmit whatever they see and hear to either a video-equipped communications station, linked up robot or android, or other viewing station dialed into this wearer's signal.

**Smartphone:** These relics are everywhere in the ruins, although most are crushed, lack a power source, corroded, and rarely in sufficiently operational order to facilitate the viewing of augmented reality. When a workable phone is found, it will lack any communications ability since nearly every cell tower and satellite up-link is gone. However, these devices often have other features that go beyond just their entertainment value. See page 449 of this book in the Computers, Smartphones and Tablet Relics section to get more details on other features. Each found smartphone has 1d6 applications besides the ability to use the camera to view and hear augmented reality out to 50 meters. An old smartphone will run for 4 months on a mini power cell and fetch 600+3d100sp if sold to a relic dealer, or if available, can be purchased for 1100+1d1000sp.

**Tablet:** These hand-held, rectangular devices are very similar to smartphones, and share many of the same features, but have a 9 inch screen and 1 in 6 come with a rubberized, protective fold open display case to keep the device upright for hands-free viewing, plus a tiny wireless keyboard. They can be used as computers, but also come loaded with 1d6+1 of the same apps available to a smartphone (see random list on page 449 of this book). They all have a camera with a feature that allows the user to hold up the device to view augmented reality elements within 50 meters. Tablets run on a mini power cell for 3 months, and come standard with a word processing programs, a camera that will hold 2000 pictures and 8 hours of video. They weigh about 700grams and will sell for 800+3d100sp , but can sometimes be purchased for 1400+1d1000sp. Learn more about tablets on page 450 of this book.

# Augmented Reality Projection Devices

These high-tech items are curiosities and potential treasures that ruin looters might uncover during their explorations of ancient places — although most will go unnoticed and unappreciated unless somebody in a dig team has either an implant or mutation that allows them to see augmented reality, or they deploy AR visual gear.

Augmented Reality projectors come in many sizes and styles, including satellite and cell tower emitters which shoot a projected image to the earth's surface from afar on either a constant basis, pre-programmed schedule, or whenever some intelligence desires to transmit an image message. Of course, without the proper headset or other relics, a person can easily walk right by or right through an AR projection without ever seeing, feeling, or hearing it.

The following collection of relic AR projectors serve as a resource to game masters to offer just a few examples of the hundreds of possible AR projection devices and old world messages. These include images, videos clips, insignia, street signs, advertisements, and warnings, as well as newly crafted cryptic codes transmitted by Epochian era intelligences.

For a game master, having the characters first find an AR viewing relic in order to see and listen to an augmented reality map, virtual document, or projected artificial intelligence NPC is a great way to introduce this high tech artifact to the players, and hint at the power of such technologies even centuries after their makers have turned to dust.

# Discovering AR Devices

The following table of AR projectors discovered in the ruins presents four areas where augmented reality devices were commonly used. These artifacts can be found as dormant, unpowered relics as sell-able loot, or as active, powered up items that the finder can use immediately.

If powered up by a plug-in, it's a good bet that whatever structure the device is uncovered in has operational solar panels or wind turbines on the roof or exterior, or else a still active micro nuclear reactor some place in the basement. Indeed, one of the main reasons adventurers might have at least one team member wear some sort of AR viewing visual aid is simply to detect augmented reality devices, which indicates a source of nearby power — with this power source being the true treasure surrounding AR devices. At the end of this section, on page 484, is a random table that covers assorted power supplies for fixed location AR devices.

These common projector sources are often highly sought after by scavengers, salvage teams and deep ruin explorers. These squads will often use some sort of AR viewing optic tool to search for still lingering augmented reality imagery and the projector source, detach it, and its power supply whenever possible, and sell it to relic dealerships, saloons and private collectors for substantial profit. The table below shows the sell value — what a character will get if they find a relic dealership in a large town — and the buy price or what characters will need to pay to own such a machine should one be available at all.

## Table XR-266 / Augmented Reality Projectors Discovered in the Ruins     Roll 1d100

| Street Level | Shopping Mall | Private Home | Office | Projector Type | Weight | Sell Price/Buy Price | Page |
|---|---|---|---|---|---|---|---|
| 01-08 | 01-13 | 01-17 | 01-08 | AR Map Kiosk | 100+1d100 kg | 1000+1d1000s / 2000+2d1000sp | 480 |
| 09-33 | 14-25 | 18 | 09-13 | AR Sign Projector | 5+1d6 kg | 300+2d100sp / 600+4d100sp | 480 |
| 34,35 | 26-33 | 19-24 | 14-21 | Augmented Reality Fashion Mirror | 80+1d30 kg | 1000+2d1000sp / 2500+1d1000sp | 481 |
| 36,37 | 34-38 | 25,26 | 22-28 | Earth View Rotation | 50+2d10 kg | 800+4d100sp /1600+6d100sp | 481 |
| - | 39-42 | 27-62 | 29-47 | Educational AR Book | 4.4kg | Variable, see description text | 482 |
| 38-45 | 43-54 | 63-71 | 48-54 | Entertainment AR Projector | 6+1d6 kg | 600+3d100sp / 1400+2d100sp | 482 |
| 46-51 | 55-61 | - | 55,56 | Floating Menu | 4+1d4 kg | 200+1d100sp / 400+2d100sp | 483 |
| 52,53 | 62-73 | 72-74 | 57-67 | Interactive Non-Human Adult Companions Catalog | 57kg | 1000+1d1000sp* | 483 |
| 54-77 | 74-81 | - | 68-73 | Light Guided Pathway | 3+1d3kg | 200+1d100sp | 483 |
| 78 | 82-90 | 75-94 | 74-98 | Personal ID and Data Record Tag | 45g | 50+1d30 | 483 |
| 79-00 | - | - | - | Traffic Sign | 6+2d6kg | 600+3d100sp | 484 |
| - | 91-00 | 95-00 | 99,00 | Virtual Furniture Demo Projector | 3kg | 400+2d100sp | 484 |

*The catalog application can be copied and put in a different AR projector. Because of the sexy nature of what is displayed, the 'show' is desired by owners of saloons and brothels and will sell for 300+2d100sp.*

# Augmented Reality Projector Descriptions

## AR Map Kiosk

These maps are activated when, **roll 1d6: 1,2.** the user of an active AR viewing devices gets within ten meters, **3,4.** or are constantly powered up, **5,6.** or need to be switched on by an on-off button on the front the AR map Kiosk. Once activated, a pop up street map will emerge and cover a 1 x 1 meter area in a translucent front facing graphic image. Through either the AR map having an interactive mode, or use of a touch screen on the kiosk control panel, the user can click to expand an entire city or district map down

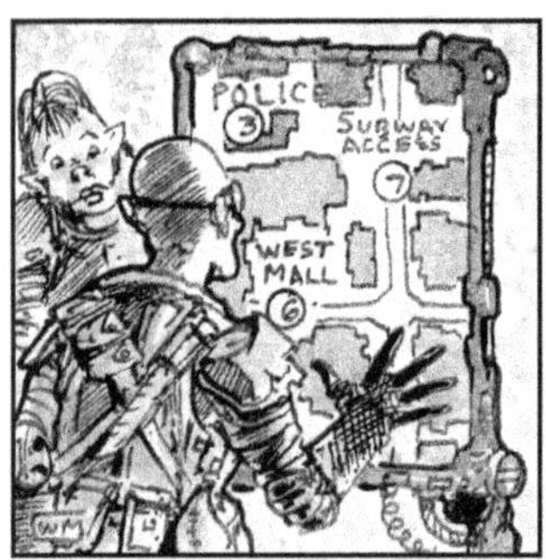


to a detailed area views covering only a few blocks. 4 in 10 of these maps also feature an option to select a Light Guided Pathway, as described on page 483, and have the user follow the animated line to a selected shop, service, exit, elevator, or other part of the city. Of course, many of the pathway projectors might be destroyed or lack power, offering only a limited path to follow, or else the final destination is now only a ruined shell, blast crater, or covered in a tangled mutant forest.

A map kiosk is usually bolted to the concrete ground or into a wall, and takes a crew with appropriate tools an hour to detach and cart off for resale. An AR map kiosk weighs 100+1d100 kilograms and can be sold to a relic dealership for 1000+1d1000sp.

## AR Sign Projector

These are among the most commonly encountered augmented reality projectors found in the ruins. Because these are civilian models, they are therefore easy enough for a computer technician to open up and reconfigure with some other AR emitter program. These projectors are about the size of a toaster and weigh 5+1d6 kilograms, and are either supplied by a permanently attached power source, or a standard power cell for 500+1d100 hours.

They are usually built into the fronts of commercial buildings, fitted to display columns in shopping malls, or to public transit vehicles or stations, and countless other venues. They take about a half hour to unbolt and extract their main elements and power hook up cables. If sold to a relic dealership, a salvager can expect to earn 300+2d100sp.

If found, either actively running or if given power and switched on, they come with between 1 and 6 projections. Each projection will remain in effect for 1 minute before randomly going to another display. For those wearing an AR headset, or equipped with the built in technology, audio accompanies each of these projections.

Roll 1d20 for a Random Sign Projection:

### 1d20 Sign Projection

**1.** Reminder from your friendly law enforcement officer to report unauthorized bioreplicas, clones, mutants or unsupervised robots without proper public access permits.

**2.** Your recent social media posts, at least those calibrated to whoever wore the AR viewer that the character is now fitted with or wears. Replies, likes, dislikes, follows, social credit score infractions, environmental footprint non-compliance rating, reported abuses, micro aggressions and other social infractions posted within your oldster's public profile.

**3.** Most wanted mug shots of 3 to 18 (3d6) assorted citizens with their last known whereabouts, past crimes, and an award for information leading to the arrest and conviction of the criminal.

**4.** A health warning about a new illicit street drug. Users are recommended to avoid this substance or go to the nearest safe consumption site to have the drug tested prior to use.

**5.** Warnings to not touch, feed or give money to homeless citizens, especially ones suspected of being mutants.

**6.** Advertisement for a nearby retail store selling, **roll 1d10: 1.** Sports wear./ **2.** Home survival supplies and gear. / **3.** Vivian's Clone Depot. "Get your new best friend, today!" / **4.** "Android retail super center "Get your personal body attendant, support worker, or senior care giver today!"/ **5.** Stimulant depot "Twenty-second century anti depressants at twenty-first century pricing! Why suffer? Find your groove and libido today!"/ **6.** Woman's swim-wear shop/ **7.** Fast Food Burger Emporium/ **8.** Simulated meat warehouse/ **9.** Western wear /**10.** Prosthetic limbs.

**7.** Join the armed forces and ensure free medical, dental and life insurance for your beneficiaries in the event of your death.

**8.** Starstruck Coffee ad

**9.** Vaccine mandate in effect: "Do you know somebody who doesn't have their vaccines status up to date? It's time to give them a friendly reminder that it is an offense punishable by quarantine to not have all their vaccinations up to date and their digital ID chip properly implanted."

**10.** "Attention citizen. This is a friendly reminder from the local government that conducting commerce in any currency other than the authorized digital currently is punishable by forfeiture of all assets and or a minimum of ten years in a civic re-education resort."

**11.** "Be prepared to evacuate!" A smiling woman holds up a small hot pink backpack. "Be prepared to bug out at a moment's notice. Be sure to pack five days of food and water, your government ID, Your vaccine status card, your Identification card and have your implanted ID subcutaneous ID tag firmly inserted in your hand. If an attack or other disaster strikes, follow all directions by authorized personal, and remember ... we're from the government and we're here to help!"

**12.** "Is it time? Have you done and seen enough? Visit Ping's Euthanasia Lounge for a peaceful transition away from the troubles, debt, addiction, and illness of your life. Painless final sleep certified."

**13.** "Trans-Formia! Have your trans-human baby grown in our deluxe series vats. Better Humanity of the future, today!"

**14.** "Pharmaceutical Holidays'R'Us! Want to get away? But stuck in a quarantine, security lock down or food shortage? Why not take a trip to an unforgettable inner holiday and enjoy one of our hundreds of pharmaceutical doctor recommended chemical excursions? Choose from an afternoon trip to a week-long tour of your own inner realms. Bliss and oblivion await. Prices starting at 1984 credits and up."

**15.** "Let's do this together! Have you overheard seditions talk? Seen an unauthorized transaction, trade or illegal barter event? Report all non sanctioned transactions, anti-government speech, and selfish incidents to your assigned social worker or law enforcement representative today. Rewards offered. Anonymity Guaranteed."

**16.** "Are your parents subversive? Do you hear them discuss anti-government subjects? Have you caught them listening to illegal radio broadcasts or found pamphlets and data disks containing unsanctioned, anti-social, anti-state propaganda? If so, report them anonymously to your nearest police station or assigned social director. It's for their own good, and the good of all citizens."

**17.** "Fight Rumors! Have you been exposed to false accounts about your government and its assigned, vetted agents? Have you heard lies about human-animal clones, about self-aware androids or robots? Have fellow citizens fostered lies about human variants referred to as mutants? Report these lies and fake news accounts to the nearest government or police agent, and we'll set the record straight."

**18.** "Prepare to Defend Your Family! Defend Democracy! Stand in the breach alongside fellow pure blooded humanity with the all new MK2 Survival Rifle. Now available for purchase to all former military and police personnel, government employees, and members of the state and municipal authorized 'citizen's brigade'!"

**19.** "Neighbors hoarding food? Report them today at your nearest municipal and state compliance officer, or anonymously on-line."

**20.** "Is earth doomed? Is it time to start over among the stars or on one of the all-new luxury colonies in orbit, on the moon or Mars? Why not join the long sleep on one of the interstellar colony ships, and do your part by spreading humanity, and all the animals and plants of earth to far off, earth-like worlds? Visit Star Colonists United today!"

## Augmented Reality Fashion Mirror

When the character walks in font of this artifact, cameras in the mirror scan the person and extrapolate the underlying physique and biological sex of the subject, and flashes through a series of fashion choices upon that character's reflection. The device matches the movements of the person in each article of projected attire. These outfits come with a brief audio description of how stylish, hot, or gorgeous the viewer now looks, and the sales price flashes in one corner in hundreds or thousands of 'credits'. The robotic, sensual woman's voice in the mirror asks if you had any clothing requirements. If so, it would be happy to show the latest styles.



This device does not require any AR viewing relics to see or hear, and automatically switches on as soon as a customer walks in front of the device. This machine normally runs on the power supply of the shopping mall or other venue, but can be looted and taken back to a post-apocalyptic town and hooked to solar panels, generator, or use 1 power cell to provide 72 hours of fashion wonder. Such a relic, if given a demo in a larger new era city, could fetch 1000+2d1000sp, but weighs 80+1d30 kilograms so requires two people, a handcart, or wagon to get back to civilization.

## Earth View Rotation

This ornate hard plastic and glass pedestal emits a rotating globe 2 meters in diameter that hovers a meter off the ground. It shows the global location of the AR transmitter, although this projector was originally set at a certain location on the earth, and might have been taken to another region or whatever county once existed, or another continent. Still, it shows the earth as it was, green, blue and with swirling white clouds and vast deserts.

If a viewer has an interactive AR viewing system, they can select a section of the earth's surface and expand into it to get a pop up, flat, 1 x 1 meter regional map of what the local area looked like before the great cataclysm. This little known feature is great for showing a dig team what a city layout looked like, from above, before the devastation occurred, allowing them to look for likely treasure troves, follow the remnants of old streets, and possibly locate spaceports, military installations, police stations, and industrial areas where the best loot can be found.



The pedestal projector weighs 50+2d10kg and is an awkward thing to carry out of the ruins, but if hooked to power at some post-apocalyptic town venue, would be a marvel for those able to see it. A ruin dealership would pay 800+4d100sp for such a device.

## Educational AR Book

When opened and switched on, a viewer using some sort of AR glasses or other device can review this virtual book. Each book covers a different subject, such as animals, medicine, mechanics, robotics and so on. When the page opens, the elements described in the illustrations and text

rise off the page and can be viewed from different angles. Audio clips also play and the wearer's glasses or other device will broadcast the sound files at an agreeable volume. Buttons on the page have tabs that say 'more info', 'what's related', 'next', 'explain differently' etc. In nearly every case, these books serve as a classroom in a book, and delve extensively into a subject and can genuinely provide real world skills to an attentive user. These projector books weigh 4.4kg.

Roll 2d6 for the subject on the following list of sample books. Each book runs on a standard power cell for 500+2d100 hours. The shown sale price in silver value is what a character will get when selling the book, while if made available in a marketplace for purchase, double the value shown when a PC wants to buy such a tome.

### 2d6 Augmented Reality Book

**2. Marine Sniper Skills:** Through animated examples, historical documentation, one-on-one video footage from a personal virtual instructor, scientific and ballistic information, any character who can read will gain at least one point in the sniper skill after 80 hours of study. Only by putting these skills to use in operations can further skill points be gained, although if a character already had the sniper skill prior to using this resource, he or she can gain an extra sniper skill point, too. 2000+1d1000sp

**3. Dinosaurs:** An encyclopedia with 3d animated sequences of all major dinosaurs with a narrated, dramatic story behind the lives of several well known dinosaurs. Any character that should spend 6 or more hours studying this, and if ever dropped back on time via some dimensional portal of use of the mutation dimension hole, will know which dinosaurs are plant eaters and which are carnivorous. 400+1d100sp

**4. Animals of the World:** A complete video and text resource of all the animals of the ancient world, including insects, birds and fish, as well as a bonus section on wild plants and fungi. 500+2d100sp

**5. Basic School Studies:** The reader of this interactive, colorful AR book will learn social studies, history, geology, geography, art, elementary school tier sciences, and other areas of ancient knowledge to an advanced elementary school level. This book has a complete encyclopedia, as well as global, national and regional old world maps. While the learning process is slow, a dedicated user can commit to 2 years with nightly studies and AR tutored exercises and learn to read, write and do basic math. If assisted by somebody with these abilities already, this time can be reduced to 1 year. 600+3d100sp

**6. Electrician's Textbook:** A person who can read who studies this book for 55 or more hours will gain 1 point in the electrical technician skill. Further points can only be added if actively using this skill in an adventure session. 3000+1d1000sp

**7. Field Medics Handbook:** A character who can read, and diligently studies this interactive book for 60 hours will gain 1 point in the medic skill. Only one tier can be gained, or added if the PC already has the medic skill, unless actual hands on application of this talent are used in game play. 4000+1d1000sp

**8. Automobile Repair:** If able to read, and after studying for 80 hours, this character gains 1 skill point in the mechanical technician skill, even if he or she had no skill points in this talent beforehand. Only hands on practice can allow further point tier gain beyond this book. 5000+2d1000sp

**9. Advanced Android and Robotics Repair:** A character with at least 40 intelligence, and the ability to read, can spend 90 hours studying with this AR book and gain 1 skill point in the Robotics Technician Skill. If the learner already had a skill point, or more in this area of expertise, he or she need not have the 40 INT prerequisite, and may add another skill point after this training time. 5000+1d1000sp

**10. Masterclass in Cooking:** After only 40 hours of study with this interactive series of live action and animated tutorials, any person, even those who can't read, will gain the cooking skill as described on page 206 of this book. 400+2d100sp

**11. Practical Cybernetics:** After studying for 80 hours, any character who can read will gain 1 point in the cybernetics technician skill. Only by working on actual implants and cyborgs can this PC progress to higher skill tiers, although this book will add one skill point to somebody who already has this skill. 5000+1d1000sp

**12. Computer Programming, Security and Hacking Handbook:** Any character who can read, and has an intelligence score of 40 or higher or who already has the computer technician skill, will gain 1 point in this skill after 180 hours of dedicated study. If they have access to a computer during this time, then reduce the hours needed to acquire this extra tier to 90 hours. Only by active practice with this skill in challenging adventure settings can another computer technician skill point be added. 4000+1d1000sp

## Entertainment AR Projector

These images are often projected from either a raised pedestal, or transmitted into the street from an overhead projector or even a satellite if outdoors. Those with an AR viewing device or implant will see and hear the entrainment as it is projected in front of them. The image will often look very real and those of 14 or less intelligence are required to make a perception based type A hazard check by the viewer or else believe the image to be real — at least until they try to touch the projection and their hand, weapon, or other appendage which goes right through the image. These projectors usually weigh 6+1d6kg and will fetch a looter 600+3d100sp at a relic market.

The following random list is merely a sample of what is possible, and GMs are encouraged to make their own list. Roll 3d6 when the device is activated or encountered to determine what plays, although a computer technician of one or more skill points can get inside the projector and have the machine play any of these entertainment modes as desired, or add more AR files if able to copy their files from another device. A digital being could also use this relic to project an image of itself if plugged into it from its main 'home' container, although only those able to view augmented reality could see them.

### 3d6 Projection type

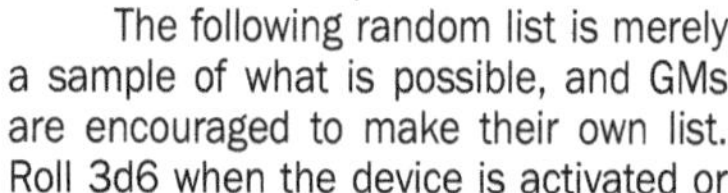

**3.** Pole dancer

**4.** Go-Go dancers on raised dais

**5.** Rock band performing on raised, illuminated stage

**6.** Bagpipe player marching along the street and passing right through the viewer.

**7.** 3d zoo animals. Elephants, lions, rhinos, hippos, chimps and other common African wildlife roam about. These beasts are all quite realistic, yet to a trained eye are obviously 3d animations. They make nosies and interact without actually attacking each other.

**8.** Dinosaurs moving about and grazing peacefully until a T-Rex stomps onto the scene and the herbivores dash off. These are life size beasts.

**9.** Tropical reef fish swimming about the space. Every so often a great white shark or dolphin enters from one end of the scene and departs into the blue haze at the other end, about 6 meters away.

**10.** Newscaster reading the last news broadcast from that city. Audio is scrambled, picture flickers, the background show burning buildings, smoke rising into an orange sky and triangular drones speeding off into the horizon.

**11.** Action movie advertisement, with film sequences overlapping.

**12.** Ballet dancer, on point, twirling about and leaping.

**13.** Book promos for a series of genres including romance, science fiction, fantasy, thriller, horror and historical. Only eBook and audio books are available.

**14.** Painter with an afro hairstyle, painting happy little trees at an easel. Sponsored by an art supply company.

**15.** Japanese classical kimono dressed lady dancing and singing.

**16.** Polynesian dancer in grass skirt, flaming torches, and drum music accompany her moves.

**17.** Glitchy, roll 2 performances, which overlap simultaneously.

**18.** Interactive digital being. This attractive, glowing youthful human seems to be fully aware of the viewer and waves to them, says hello and tries to engage in a conversation. If asked who or what it is, the entity shrugs and says, "I live in here... in the network... always have. It's nice to have company, however. What's your name and where are you going dressed like that?"

This being will appear as a female when conversing with male characters or a male if talking to females. It will have a wide knowledge of the local areas — at least as far as what it was like before the cataclysm, and might answer questions of the PCs. GM: It might also be in the service of an evil AI, and try to get information on the characters, their weaponry, and objective and might direct them to some sort of doom.

## Floating Menu

Projected from an overhead sign board, presumably in front of whatever restaurant once existed there, is a small, skull sized orb in a hanging, hard wired black fixture. The device, which weighs 4+1d4 kg, projects the AR menu to one of the following establishments: Roll 1d12: 1. coffee shop / 2. sushi restaurant/ 3. Mexican / 4. burger Joint / 5. subway sandwiches / 6. topless cigar bar /7. pizza parlor/ 8. Korean BBQ / 9. French cuisine / 10. simulated Vegan Steak and Seafood House /11. Bistro / 12. Fine tofu and insect restaurant.

If sold to a relic dealership, this curiosity will fetch 200+1d100sp

### Interactive Non-Human Adult Companions Catalog [IN-HACC]

This is a 3d, live-action inventory of bioreplica or androids for purchase by a long gone retailer, and the content is for mature viewers only. This catalog shows a wide range of bioreplica and pleasure androids in various attire, or none at all, based on how the user selects option on a set of side bars.

The possible future concubine appears in the actual space and adapts to the lighting in the room, and can be walked around, stepped up to almost touching distance or directed to dance, or perform a wide range of other motions — many of them highly suggestive. This display can be an application, too, or appear on a display disc in a nightclub or mall, office or other location.

The AR display machine weighs 57kg and will run on a power cell for 170 hours. It will fetch 1000+1d1000sp. The app, which is normally used on a cell phone or hand-held tablet, takes up 3.3 gigabytes of space, but might also appear built into some AR glasses and contact lenses, can be copied to other hard drives and projectors and will sell for 300+2d100sp.

## Light Guided Pathway

These translucent, glowing indicators appear as lines on a roadway, sidewalk, corridor, or even along walls and ceilings. Their purpose was to guide AR viewers to specific destination. A dedicated line uses a consistent color and sporadic flashing signs to show and confirm the destination location. The site specified will be shown in photographs with animated text, along with audio elements broadcast into the AR viewer's receiver implant or worn relic.

The entire route to the location was once lined with tiny, tennis ball sized projectors attached to nearby structures, antenna, light poles and other elevated fixtures, including micro satellites in some cases. Most of these small projectors have since been destroyed, but in intact, built-up areas, within buildings, or where sectors where these have been replaced by new era technicians and repair robots, the path to ancient destinations can still be seen. The GM can pick or randomly determine the stated destination of an AR light path. Malicious, high tech forces might alter a path destination to lure victims, potential slaves, or enemy forces to a promising destination but really guides the unwary into an ambush, trap, or some other bad end.

**Roll 1d20** for destination: **1.** Airport / **2.** Mega Shopping Land / **3.** Hospital / **4.** Social Conformity Reeducation Camp / **5.** Big Bertha's Soy Burger Emporium / **6.** Bushido Benji's Sushi and Bagels / **7.** Auto-Recharge Station / **8.** Starstruck Coffee / **9.** Food Bank / **10.** Safe Injection Site / **11.** Police Station / **12.** Military Recruitment Center / **13.** Simu-steak and Ribs House /**14.** Roxanne's Synthetic human and Android Concubine Bath House / **15.** Comic Shop and Tabletop Game Store / **16.** Multiplex Movie Theater / **17.** Subway Station / **18.** Homeless Shelter /**19.** Honest Mike's Robotics Outlet / **20.** Government Offices and Municipal Prison.

The Standard Route Projector Orb (or RPO) weighs 3+1d3kg and is mounted into a wall or ceiling, or at the top of a light pole and not easily accessible. Each RPO will fetch 200+1d100sp in a relics market. A computer technician can easily reprogram and reset these tiny projectors for use by another AR projection source, which is needed to transmit to the individual RPO, and others in a synced up chain. They can remain radio-linked up to 1km between each emitter, although one orb projector will only cast the animated AR line 100 meters in either direction. If gaps in the light guided pathway occur, and yet the transmitter between distant orbs are still linked, it might be possible for the viewer to see where the trail starts again after a search of the area, or if their viewer device has sufficient range to see where the trail continues.

If a pathway is buried in rubble, the AR pathway will still be visible if being projected, because the image isn't in the physical world at all, but merely an animated graphic within the viewscreen of the whatever relic the wearer is seeing through. This means that the pathway could lead out into open space, over lava flows, into the lair of some mutant beast, or over unstable and treacherous ground. Caution is advised.

## Personal ID and Data Record Tag

This is a button, necklace pendant, helmet mounted button, or clothing pin that an ancient person wore. When viewed by somebody or something with AR receptors of the appropriate security or social tier, the viewer can scan a person and see a floating display next to the person's head. This translucent display shows the original tag owner's government approved photo, real name, social credit score, yearly income in credits, criminal and social discord history, as well as debts, known health issues, vaccination status, ethnic background, addictions, political leanings, voting record, resume, and any outstanding criminal offenses, pending charges, fines or fees owed to the state or corporate debt collectors.

The AR viewer can also click through other details like purchase history, current address, banking history, military service, sexual preference, gender identity, preferred pronouns and porn viewing habits, family members, and current bio-metrics such as heart rate, blood pressure, prescribed medications, and stress hormone levels.

In nearly every case, the viewing of such data by a new era ruin explorer or researcher will mean accessing the personal details of

somebody who has been dead for nearly two hundred years, and yet can offer hours of entertainment for the onlooker. A few of these IDs are from high ranking scientific, medical, political, corporate or military personnel, however, and their ID tag might allow security measures to be bypassed by the mere proximity of this ID to an AR sensing door, gun emplacement or vehicle hatch.

These tags weigh only 45 grams and most of this weight is the pill power cell that runs them for 50+1d20 years. Unpowered tags will sell for 20+1d30 silver pieces, and are considered to be ancient junk jewelry, with few realizing they are actually AR projectors. Operational ones sell for 60+1d100sp.

## Traffic Sign

Projected from a rectangular, silver colored, alloy device that is bolted to either a wall, underpass, lamppost or hanging wire contraption, these 6+2d6kg relics can be programmed to project any sort of traffic sign. When first encountered, and if powered up, each projects one of the following random signs. A computer technician of 2 or more skill points can get inside and reset the sign to any other message or graphic element in the unit's vast, built-in library of signs, warnings, announcements, and symbols. These projectors will sell for 600+3d100sp in a new era marketplace.

**Roll 1d20** for specific sign: **1.** No Parking Sign / **2.** Stop / **3.** Yield / **4.** One Way, Do Not Enter/ **5.** Emergency Personnel Only / **6.** Class A Citizens Only / **7.** Pedestrian Crossing / **8.** Air Taxi Landing. Stay Clear / **9.** Loading Zone / **10.** ID Inspection Area: Please Present Digital Identification Card or Implant when instructed by officer / **11.** Military Personnel Only / **12.** No Left Turn / **13.** No Right Turn / **14.** No Non-Humans Beyond this Point / **15.** Genetic Scanner in Operation 24 hrs: No Mutants allowed / **16.** Gun Free Zone / **17.** No Loitering / **18.** Narcotics Free Zone: Users of illicit drugs will be institutionalized / **19.** Curfew in effect 15:00 hrs to 6:00 hrs. Violators will be prosecuted / **20.** Lock Down in effect: Violators will be Shot.

## Virtual Furniture Demo Projector [VFDP]

From a massive inventory of available from two dozen departments, the user can select a piece of furniture and have it appear as a virtual unit within the current, present day environment. Prices, delivery date and color options are

also shown on screen. The projected piece of furniture can be selected and tapped to 'stay' mode and the viewer can walk around the item to imagine how it would look and fit in their space.

The projector for this AR image appears as a small black orb with three pull out, telescopic legs that extend up to 2 meters in length, weighs only 3kg and will sell for 400+2d100sp. These devices will present furniture, or other programed AR elements if programmed to do so (a computer technician allowed a type D INT based hazard check to load some other AR element inside), for a total of 300+1d100 hours on a single mini power cell.

# Augmented Reality Projector Power Source

Using augmented reality visual aides to locate AR elements is usually done simply to locate sources of old world power. Indeed, specialized dig teams equipped with just one pair of AR glasses might make a full time living hunting down augmented reality projections, which often means that either batteries, a wind turbine, solar panel or micro nuclear reactor is nearby.

Augmented reality projectors that are worn or carried as gear, such as ID tags, Virtual Furniture Demo Projectors, and AR books, have their own power supply. Those mounted to a building or found at street level, meanwhile, will either be plugged into a fixture or hard-wired to the floor on a permanent basis similar to a light post, traffic signal array, or electric door. Unless the game master decides that an AR projector uses batteries, as is often the case when the unit is attached to a vehicle, then roll on the following table to determine its power source. Projectors out of the character's reach, such as those beamed from a satellite or orbiting space station or vessel, are not included here.

### Table XR-267 / AR Projector Power Source by Ruin Location
*Roll 1d10*

| Street Level | Shopping Mall | Private Home | Office | Power Source |
|---|---|---|---|---|
| 1-5 | 1-4 | 1-4 | 1-5 | Hard-wired |
| 6,7 | 5-7 | 5,6 | 6,7 | Solar panel |
| 8,9 | 8,9 | 7,8 | 8,9 | Propeller style wind turbine |
| 10 | 10 | 9,10 | 10 | Jerry-rigged |

*Descriptions of Projector Power Sources:*

**Hard-wired** into sidewalk or structure's grid. Wires hidden, but, for every half hour of searching, there is a 3 in 10 chance of discovering, **roll 1d6: 1-3.** Solar panels and inverter (120+1d100kg, 800+1d1000sp) /**4,5.** Tubular wind turbine and inverter and power pack battery supply (240+1d100kg, 900+1d1000sp, power pack extra 15kg, 600+2d1000sp)/ **6.** Wired to a buried mini-nuclear reactor that is 20+1d100m beneath the street surface and inaccessible without either a risky underground exploration to locate an access point, or calling up a massive work crew and encampment and spending weeks, if not months, digging for the reactor to safely extract and use elsewhere. Many reactors are unstable, leak radiation, and usually bring death to new era communities. Reactor weighs 4000+3d1000kg, will sell for 20k+2d1000sp.

**Solar panel** on an external fixture, 10+1d12 meters up and difficult to get to. Wired into an inverter and bank of 3+1d3 standard power cells. Weighs 120+1d100kg, 800+1d1000sp, power cells each sell for 200+1d100sp.

**Propeller style wind turbine** on a high ruin, complete with an inverter and power pack system. Weighs 240+1d100kg, 700+1d1000sp, power pack extra 15kg 600+2d1000sp.

**Jerry-rigged array** of taped and wired together solar panels, mini wind turbines and 2d6 standard power cells. Somebody set this up within the last few years or months, and it is certainly not something the ancient ones would have built. Somebody established this power station for a purpose, perhaps bait to attract greedy diggers to this height to expose them. Each PC is allowed a perception based type F hazard check to notice a video surveillance camera hooked to a nearby post 3d6 meters away. Indeed, the characters are likely being watched. Weighs 240+1d100kg, 900+1d1000sp, power cells each sell for 200+1d100sp.

# Relic Vehicles Set 2

## Combat Transport Vehicle (CTV)

Based on a long line of light service vehicles all the way back to the Hummer and their off-shoots, this vehicle class is made for transporting troops and supplies in hostile areas, as well as offering light fire support from a series of on-board weapon systems. The survivability of occupants was an imperative design demand, and so from either crashes, enemy fire, explosions or other hazards, this vehicle offers some of the best protection a soldier could ask for in a light vehicle. Besides the driver and passenger, 4 other personnel can ride in the passenger compartment, while another 6 people could theoretically hang on or sit on the roof and catch a ride — although fully exposed and gaining no defense value benefits.

It features four wheel drive and can traverse hilly terrain, light woodlands and dunes with ease, while 36% are also amphibious landing craft capable, moving 15m per round on water, and can ford lakes and streams and put ashore from sea as long as the waves are not more than a meter high, which would swamp and sink the CTV after 2d6 rounds.

An advanced communicator, flip out computer (complex) station, rad-detector, substance scanner, proximity detector system (PDS), identification sequence broadcaster (IDSB), solar generator unit, digital spotting scope, and beacon locater unit, all come standard. For weaponry, it boasts a forward mounted, passenger seat positioned machine gun supplied by with 3d100 HC belt fed rounds offering a 180 degree side to side or 90 degrees upward field of fire.

This vehicle also exhibits one random weapon mounted on a top, motorized turret, with sights controlled by the passenger seat position, but can be switched over to a rear seat operator or even from the driver's seat via a hand-held weapon's control and sighting and toggle array. The turret has a 360 degree all around radius of fire plus 90 degree upward elevation and 45 degree lower elevation.

**Roll 1d6** for turret weapon found on a CTV: **1,2.** Chain gun, belt fed, with 5d100 rounds remaining./ **3.** Twin machine guns, each with their own belt fed ammo supply of 3d100 HC rounds./ **4.** Light laser cannon with power feed from 1d3 on-board, power packs, each with 2d20 shots remaining./ **5.** Rocket launcher box with 4+1d6 tubes, each with a battle rocket loaded, additionally, 2d20 battle rockets are stowed in passenger compartment. All rocket tubes can be fired at once if desired, or any multiple. / **6.** Missile launcher box with 1d6+2 tubes, each loaded with an assault missile, and 1d12 additional assault missiles stowed in the passenger compartment.

## Armored Personnel Carrier (APC)

78% of these heavily armored combat vehicles will have six huge bullet proof tires, otherwise, will have tank treads. APCs have a crew of 3 with a commander, driver and gunner, and a separate, enclosed but radio linked troops compartment that can hold up to 8 soldiers. Ten other personnel can ride on top of this boxy vehicle, although are entirely exposed while enjoying the ride. All APCs have a rear drop down door allowing two soldiers at a time to unload, per round.

2 in 6 were designed for amphibious operations and can propel themselves through water at 12m per round so long as waves are not 1.5m or higher, and if so, all gun ports and top hatches must be closed to avoid the craft filling with water and sinking after 20+3d6 rounds of being swamped. It can still proceed to shore even in swells of 2m height, however higher waves will put it off course and the driver will need to make a Type C perception based hazard check each minute to avoid capsizing the APC. If capsized while 'buttoned up' with all gun ports and hatches closed, it will retain hull integrity for 30+1d20 minutes before experiencing a 1 in 20 chance per minute of springing a leak. If another vehicle can pull the APC to shore, or tug it back upright, it could resume its beach landing or water crossing.

5 in 6 have still operational air filtration and oxygen supplies to allow the passengers and crew to close hatches and endure toxic gas, fallout, acid attacks and other airborne or liquid hazards outside. The built-in air tanks, which can be refilled and re-compressed under safe atmospheric conditions, will allow the occupants to avoid asphyxiation for 22 hours, or more if the full complement of 11 personnel is not present.

For weaponry, this fighting vehicle has a forward mounted machine gun operated by the commander or gunner, with this belt fed gun suppled by a reservoir of 100+2d100 high caliber rifle rounds when found. It is also identical to a CTV as far as on-board systems and what is mounted on the electronic turret. In many respects, the APC is merely a much tougher, better built CTV designed to enter heated combat and survive. 33% will also have a standard force field when the power is switched on, eliminating 30 points of damage per round.

## Standard Tank

Formerly called main battle tanks, these war machines come in various shapes and sizes, but are generally the same speed and armor quality. They will travel on all terrain except swamps, deep forests, and mountains, will have all the high tech relic equipment as a CTV, plus, the commander will operate a Weapons Guidance System, adding +40 SV to the main gun and any rocket or missile launcher systems. The tank will come with a top mounted heavy machine gun, belt fed with 5d100 HC rounds, plus, there will be a secondary heavy machine gun for the driver to operate with 6d100 rounds of HC belt fed ammo aimed forward only with 140 degree field of fire.

These tanks are air conditioned, air tight, gas proof, toxin proof, fire proof (unharmed by normal, mutational and weapons based fire attacks) and radiation proof. Once all hatches are closed, the occupants can survive off filtered and stored air supplies for 36 hours before the air turns toxic.

On board proximity scanners will alert the crew of heat signatures of robots, vehicles or animals over 50kg with 100m range, and an automated rocket battery will auto-select the largest (most kilograms) object within 100m each round and if set to auto fire, will automatically unleash one battle rocket at each 'non-allied' target per round before selecting the next smallest target and firing. This weapon system will not shoot at units who are broadcasting the correct IDSB code (Identification Sequence Broadcaster) or other logged-in identification signal emitter.

The auto rocket launcher has 20 tubes, loaded with 10+d10 battle rockets, while another 2d20 rockets will be stowed in the turret ammo magazine. This rocket system can be manually controlled and fired by any crewman who controls the launcher system software, firing all or any number of available tube loaded rockets per round.

The main gun of the standard tank varies from unit to unit, but all can be fired at targets in a 360 degree radius, with a 60 degree height elevation and 30 degree drop down elevation. The following random main weapons are typical, **roll 1d6 1,2.** M364 Howitzer, requiring only one person to load, and the gunner to aim and fire. A magazine of 62 shells maximum supplies ammo at a rate of one shot every two rounds. 2d30 shells are typically found on operative tanks. / **3,4.** Medium Laser Cannon, plus 4 power packs linked together supplying energy to the weapon, each gives 50 shots. However, if the tank is switched to alcohol fuel for locomotion, the gun can draw power from two other on-board power packs. / **5.** Heavy Laser Cannon, charged by an array of 6 power packs as well as the ability to draw on the locomotion power supply if the alcohol engines are engaged. Each power pack will supply 10 shots to this devastating weapon./ **6.** Missile Launch Tank, with two box batteries of 20 missile capacity each, one will have 10+d10 Assault missiles, the other battery will have 10+d10 Tactical Missiles. Within the tank itself, in armored compartments, will be 2d6 of each missile as extra. Only one missile battery can be directed per round, but one or all missiles in that specified battery can fire.

Tanks normally have a crew of 4, with a commander in the turret, a driver, loader and gunner. Two other personnel can squeeze inside the interior, but this is a tight fit and only done during emergencies. About 12 people can ride exposed on the turret and main body of the tank, but unless they are on the far side of the turret when an attack comes, they gain no defense value bonus (those behind the turret gain -40 DV).

## Civilian Helicopter

Once very common, these aircraft have no weapons and no armor, and rely on speed and maneuverability to avoid enemy fire. With the side windows open, and the two back doors open, up to 6 people can fire small arms from within, 3 per side. Modifications can be made to mount a manually operated heavy machine gun or chain gun in either doorway, a strategy often employed by air raiders. Using its belly mounted cargo hook, this chopper can lift 1500kg of freight, or tow an airship to increase the zeppelin's speed safely from a base movement of 12m per round to 24m per round.

Military variants of these helicopters also exist, with 1 in 6 being these elongated, dark green, black or gray versions. These feature a passenger area that can hold 10 soldiers, while the more powerful motor and frame can lift 2600kg weight on its hook. The cladding is better armored, too, and so yields a -20 DV bonus, and overall it is built tougher and enjoys a +100 endurance value increase. Of these military variants, 2 in 6 have an auto pilot computer built into them that can be programmed to fly a certain path, and even return to pick up the entire crew and passenger compliment at either a specific time or if directed to by a linked, advanced communicator. 1 in 6 military variants will also feature a nose mounted, highly articulating chain gun that is supplied with 100+2d100 rounds of rifle ammo and can be controlled by the pilot or co-pilot. These military variants weigh 3200kg.

## Combat Helicopter

Smaller than the old world AH-64 Apache Attack Helicopter, these updated variants are faster, better armed and armored and 73% likely to have a 30 point per round force field when powered up. These highly effective aircraft require only one highly trained pilot-gunner, but have a rear seat for a passenger or back up pilot. The cabin is air tight, making the crew immune to gas and diseases, fallout, toxic fumes, spores and dust storms. The craft is also coated in both a flame and radiation deflection coating, which combined with the force field makes the occupants immune to radiation and fire from any attack mode.

The standard weapon complement of this helicopter is a chain gun mounted on an all around, drop down turret, with laser sights hooked to both pilot's headgear, so that wherever the operator looks, the gun follows, adding +20 SV with this weapon. Likewise, the pilot can select between forward shooting rockets (two 20 battle rocket launchers per wing and typically found with 1d20 per battery) and wing mounted missile batteries (each wing can hold and fire 6 missiles, and comes with 1d6 tactical missiles per wing), plus, a rear mounted rocket battery (4 tubes, each tube can hold 4 rockets, firing one per round per tube. These rear batteries are found with 1d4 rockets within each tube) used to either fire on pursuing craft or attempt to shoot down incoming missiles, which this craft will auto fire upon as soon as the on-board computer detects that it has been 'locked on'.

The computer will also locate and target the exact location of any ground launched missiles as well as 'paint' (highlighted on the pilot's targeting screen) and target any airborne enemy who has fired on it. Once targeted, the computer will ask the pilot for clearance to launch one tactical missile, if any remain. The pilot need only verbally tell the computer 'confirm fire' to launch one missile at an SV of 01-80, or 'confirm dual fire' to send two tactical missiles to the enemy. A secondary pilot, also trained in the use of this craft, can select to fire other weapons which the primary pilot is not employing, or fly the craft while the other is occupied.

Although not designed to lift cargo or carry passengers on the side wings or landing gear, it is possible for this helicopter to lift 1800kg with its lift hook, but if firmly strapped down, could lift 3 man sized passengers on each exterior wing, although if flying in cold weather, such passengers would probably die of exposure after fifteen minutes unless suitably dressed.

## Patrol Boat

This craft was designed for shoreline and river operations. It has a draught of only 1 meter and water jet propulsion system, allowing the stout vessels to travel through very shallow and weedy waterways and easily beach itself to off load personnel or supplies. For a new era dig team, such a vessel can open up looting and travel opportunities that few diggers can imagine.

It has an armored hull and conning bridge, which can conceal 6 occupants plus one operator at -60 DV, plus on deck, 14 more top crew will enjoy -20 DV. Only top crew can operate the three weapon turret positions — if they are crew served systems — one aft, one forward and one on top of the main bridge structure, however the occupants below can fire personal weapons through various portholes and tiny windows.

Roll for each turret to determine what weaponry is mounted. The fore-and-aft turrets have a 180 degree fire view, while the top turret has a 360 degree view, however all can fire directly up if needed to take out aircraft and winged assailants. **Roll 1d6** for each turret: **1,2** Chain gun, belt fed, with 4d100 rounds./ **3.** Heavy machine gun, belt fed with 4d100 HC rounds./ **4.** Rocket launcher battery with 4+d6 tubes, each loaded with one battle rocket, while 3d6 additional battle rockets are stowed below decks./ **5.** Twin missile launcher rack, with two Assault missiles loaded and another 1d6+1 assault missiles stowed below decks./ **6.** Light laser cannon hooked to its own power pack with 2d20+10 shots remaining.
*Bridge controlled firing only.*

These vessels have an advanced communicator, simple dashboard computer, radar that will detect objects over 200kg in weight within 140 kilometers, as well as give readouts for shorelines, reefs, rubble, derelict ships and other hazards on the water. A bank of 4 spotlights are mounted on the top of the conning bridge, while a separate fore-and-aft spot light on a fixed railing mounted shaft allows personnel to project light in any direction to 500 meters.

All hatches, portholes, windows and the door to the conning bridge can be locked and sealed during stormy seas, and this remarkable craft can endure swells of 4 meters in height if taken bow first, but will be capsized if hit by such waves from the side or aft. If capsized while sealed, there is a 1 in 6 chance per minute that another wave or the current, propulsion system and steering can flip the boat back upright, but failure after ten minutes means a seal has given way and the vessel fills with water. If it is not righted after 8 minutes of flooding, it will sink. Any character at the helm who has the seamanship skill can bring the odds to right a capsized gunboat to a 2 in 6 chance per minute.

Normal rough seas with swells of 4 meters or less waves will not endanger this craft if steered by an operator with the pilot or seamanship skill, or who came from the caste of pirate or fisherman.

Destruction note: If reduced to zero endurance, this water craft will remain afloat, but adrift if merely malfunctioning, however if broken up, it will sink within 3d10 rounds. Anybody inside the hull or conning bridge when it goes down could drown unless they can make a type B agility based HC to escape in time. If the patrol boat explodes, not enough of it will remain to have a hull at all, and what is left will either sink or float about the area as debris, with 1d6 3x3m floating chunks suitable for a raft for 3 man sized beings each.

## Orbital Shuttle

At one time, over a thousand of these orbital, horizontal takeoff and landing craft plied the lanes between earth and the space stations and waiting vessels above. They were the workhorses of various corporate or national space programs, delivered cargo, fuel, passengers, robotic units, and livestock, and allowed the rich and powerful to flee earth in the final years of the devastation.

While most of these vessels found on earth are inoperative, or their hanger bays buried or their 800 meter long runways pot holed with blast craters or covered in debris, they are still a great find for any dig team, since they are often filled with remarkable technology and come with an extremely high sell value. Those that are still operational and either safely parked in their hangers or in use by various high tech societies, are remarkably efficient and among the greatest, most advanced relics any faction or excavation team can acquire.

It is said that the 'star people', and other spacers from either orbiting stations are deep space transports that have returned to earth, are the main users of these vehicles. It's rumored that these high tech peoples make forays to the earth to gather specimens or aid their pure stock allies in their war against the mutant factions, or hire dig teams to search for specific raw materials, sites and relics, or help establish ground base colonies from which to plot their eventual return to the surface and ultimate reconquest.

Alternatively, stories persist of advanced excavation teams that have uncovered, repaired and flown these vessels either to reach other locations on the earth's surface in mere hours, or else ascend to the orbit themselves to loot the graveyard of derelict vessels which circle the earth.

These reliable, efficient and remarkably tough craft were designed to be piloted by mediocre (i.e.; Non-combat) personnel, and it is possible for a modestly trained new era pilot with the ability to read and use a keyboard to get one of these brutes into orbit. The automated navigation, docking and air lock systems make it relatively easy for formerly earthbound adventure parties to explore and loot the many orbiting starships and space stations.

Orbital shuttles are not designed for long space journeys, but, if given enough power packs and time, a small, well-trained crew could reach the moon and its many colonies and toxic waste dumps within 29.32 days with a fully loaded shuttle, or 26.3 days with an empty shuttle (380,000km from earth). The problem is that the orbital shuttle only carries enough rocket fuel for 18 days, therefore the rest of the energy must come from 5 on-board power packs which run the life support and electrical systems. Using a power pack provides 5 days locomotion, which means using all 5 power packs plus all on-board fuel, results in only 21.5 days each way, insufficient for a journey there and back again, meaning, additional power supplies must be collected on the moon itself, or, a larger vessel some place between earth and the moon must be located and looted for usable power packs or rocket fuel.

Solar collection panels can be extended from the shuttle's topside, but these only collect one tenth of a power pack's supply potential per day, and were only intended for orbital collection and life support during docking delays or engine failure situations. To wait until the power supplies suffice to continue locomotion would require a patient crew (traveling on solar power alone) to move at a rate of 50m per round: 60 km an hour or 1440km per day.

Orbital shuttles have an advanced force field system, absorbing 20 points of damage per attack, not per round, a defense made necessary by the many micro-meteorites and chunks of mechanical space debris flying about in near space. Most of these vessels have no weapon systems, although, 7% will have been customized for military purposes and instead of being the typical white and black coloration, will be naval gray or desert tan color. Military models will have one random weapon system **1d6: 1,2.** Forward mounted, pilot aimed, light laser cannon with its own power pack, 2d20 shots remaining./ **3.** As 1,2, however the light laser cannon is mounted on a manually operated top turret, which can fire straight up and in a 360 degree rotation, but not below the craft unless it spins./ **4.** As 3, however this ship is fitted with a medium laser cannon with 2 power packs, each with 2d10+4 shots remaining. / **5,6.** A twin, light laser cannon battery, top mounted on a 360 degree view turret, remotely controlled by a crewman in the cockpit area, using his or her base SV, or, set to auto return fire by the pilot which will fire on any attacking craft, or, approaching meteorite, SV 01-70, two shots per round, hooked to two power packs each with 2d20 shots remaining.

Orbital shuttles will typically be outfitted with a locker containing 2d6 space suits, treat as very bulky, heated jump suits with helmets, a communicator, pocket flashlight and a 2 hour air supply, offering DV -20 protection but -4m move rate.

When an orbital shuttle malfunctions at zero endurance, life support systems shut off, air supply filtration and circulators die, and all occupants not in space suits or shell class armor will die within 2d10 minutes. Shuttles that break up, will cast all occupants into space, while exploding ships will also spew occupants, but those in mere spacesuits will probably have their air hoses and suits torn apart (3 attacks at SV 01-67 for 3d10 DMG each, with over 10 points damage in total causing the suit to rupture), thus leading to instant death in the hostile zero atmosphere of space.

Orbital shuttles are equipped with advanced computers, or a 1 in 6 chance of a Mark I AI computer. This AI will converse with passengers and aid them in the operation of this shuttle, potentially developing a mutually beneficial relationship with accommodating, respectful, and tech savvy crew.

## Table XR-268 / Relic Vehicles, Set 2

| Vehicle | Combat Transport Vehicle (CTV) | Armored Personnel Carrier (APC) | Standard Tank | Civilian Helicopter | Combat Helicopter | Patrol Boat | Orbital Shuttle |
|---|---|---|---|---|---|---|---|
| Defense Value | -35 | -45* | -80* | -8/-40 | -20/-60* | -40 | -13/-30** |
| Occupant's DV | -80 | immune | immune | -45 | -60 | -60/-20[B] | immune |
| Endurance | 300+2d100 | 400+2d100 | 800+4d100 | 70+3d20 | 160+2d100 | 400+3d100 | 500+d1000 |
| Empty MV | 19/75m | 19/45m | 20/40m | 180m | 290m | 55m | 360 air/ 500m Space |
| Loaded MV | 18/60m | 16/30m | 19/28m | 150m | 240m | 40m | 280 air/ 450m Space |
| Power Source | Hybrid | Hybrid | Hybrid | 78% Cell | Hybrid | Hybrid | see description |
| Power Cell Type | pack | 3 packs | 6 packs | 2 packs | 3 packs | 3 packs | see description |
| Duration of Cell | 0 hrs | 7 hrs/ pack | 3 hrs/ pack | 12 hrs/ pack | 10 hrs/ pack | 24 hrs/ pack | see description |
| Fuel Capacity | 60L | 100L | 300L | 100L | 160L | 400L | 2000L Rocket Fuel |
| Fuel Duration | 20 hrs | 24 hrs | 30 hrs | 24 hrs | 32 hrs | 96 hrs | 48 hrs air/ 18 days S |
| Req'd Crew | 1+1 gunner[A] | 3 | 4[A] | 1 | 1 | 1B | 1 |
| Passengers | 4/6[B] | 8/10[B] | 2/12[B] | 5 | 1 | 6/14[B] | 9 |
| Strike Value | 01-75 | 01-80 | 01-85 | 01-76 | 01-83 | 01-68 | 01-74 |
| Ram Damage | 1d100+20 | 1d100+30 | 3d100+40 | 1d100 | 1d100+20 | 3d100+30 | 3d100+60 |
| Length | 5.2m | 6.3m | 7.9m | 13m | 14m | 15.8m | 22m |
| Weight | 2200kg | 8500kg | 18 tonnes | 660kg | 4100kg | 11 tonnes | 6 tonnes |
| Load Weight | 2100kg | 3200kg | 950kg | 1500kg | 1800kg | 2.5 tonnes | 1.5 tonnes |
| Sell Value | 15+2d10k | 50+3d10k | 200+6d10k | 16+2d8k | 70+2d12k | 140+5d10k | 400+8d10k |

[A] *While not needed to operate the vehicle, this secondary occupant sits in a passenger seat and often serves as a gunner, navigator or back up driver in the event the first is dispatched.*

[B] *Personnel can perch or hang onto the top and exterior of this vehicle to ride along, although they gain no DV bonus from this exposed position.*

## Table XR-269 / Vehicle Destruction
Outcome of zero Endurance (roll 1d100)*

| Vehicle Type | Malfunction | Breaks Apart | Explodes | Auto Crash DMG to all Occupants** | Severe Injury SV and Damage | Explosion SV and Damage |
|---|---|---|---|---|---|---|
| Combat Transport (CTV) | 01-48 | 49-67 | 68-00 | 20% | 01-50/ 1d20 | 01-40/ 1d20+6 |
| Armored Per. Carrier (APC) | 01-38 | 39-71 | 72-00 | 20% | 01-55/ 1d20 | 01-65/ 1d20+7 |
| Standard Tank | 01-13 | 14-66 | 67-00 | 30% | 01-45/ 1d20 | 01-70/ 1d20+8 |
| Civilian Helicopter | 01-52 | 53-89 | 90-00 | 30% | 01-60/ d20 | 01-65/ 1d20+2 |
| Combat Helicopter | 01-59 | 60-82 | 83-00 | 20% | 01-52/ 1d20 | 01-45/ 1d20+1 |
| Patrol Boat | 01-33 | 34-78 | 79-00 | 20% | 01-50/ 1d12 | 01-67/ 1d20+3 |
| Orbital Shuttle | 01-42 | 43-68 | 69-00 | 30% | 01-68/ 1d20 | 01-83/ 2d20 |

*If vehicle is struck by laser or explosive weapons (such as battle rockets, missiles, grenades, etc. or a flame or electrical mutation or weapon, then the odds of an explosion are greatly increased, add +30 to the d100 outcome die roll.*

**percentage of vehicle's 'crash time' movement rate in meters per round, translated to damage against each occupant. Example: a sedan moving 36m when vehicle hit and blown apart, (reduced to zero or less endurance) all aboard suffer 20% of 36m as damage=(36 x 0.2) 7.2 damage, but individuals, depending on their armor and agility, etc, might suffer severe injury as well.*

# Tables

## Relic Determination Tables Set 2

When a new relic is discovered and a random selection must be made, give the odds of 50% that the relic is from the hub rules (tables start on page TME- 210), otherwise roll from the charts in this book. It is, however, enjoyable for veteran players of The Mutant Epoch to be exposed to new relics, especially if their characters are well acquainted and perhaps equipped with plenty of ancient technology from the Hub Rules book, and so use only this new set of relics for loot, at least for a while.

**Low Rank Characters: 1 to 4**
**Mid Rank Characters: 5-9**
**High Rank Characters: 10 and up**

**Table XR-270 / Random Relic**

| Low Rank | Mid Rank | High Rank | Relic Category | page |
|---|---|---|---|---|
| 01-29 | 01-27 | 01-22 | Weapon Relics Set 2 (WR2) | 490 |
| 30-35 | 28-34 | 23,24 | Arc Guns and Spike Throwers (AGST) | 491 |
| 36-39 | 35-38 | 25,26 | Weaponized Industrial Tools (WIT) | 491 |
| 40-45 | 39-43 | 27,28 | Ammo Relics Set 2 (AM2) | 492 |
| 46-48 | 44-46 | 29-30 | Military Accessories Set 2 (MA2) | 492 |
| 49-52 | 47-50 | 31-35 | Explosives Set 2 (EX2) | 492 |
| 53-59 | 51-55 | 36-41 | Random Grenade, Set 2 (GR2) | 492 |
| 60-62 | 56,57 | 42 | Relic Fireworks (FWK) | 493 |
| 63-74 | 58-66 | 43-50 | Armor Relic set 2 (ARR2) | 493 |
| 75-79 | 67-72 | 51-54 | Protective Gear Set 2 (PG2) | 493 |
| 80 | 73-76 | 55-61 | Miscellaneous Relics (MR) | 494 |
| 81,82 | 77-81 | 62-65 | High Tech Devices Set 2 (HTD2) | 495 |
| 83 | 82,83 | 66-70 | Computers, Smartphones and Tablet Relics (COMPS) | 495 |
| 84-86 | 84,85 | 71-76 | Medical Relics (MEDR) | 495 |
| 87-91 | 86,87 | 77,78 | Power Sources Set 2 (PS2) | 496 |
| 92 | 88,89 | 79-83 | Robots Set 2 (RA2) | 496 |
| 93 | 90,91 | 84-87 | MAVs (MAV) | 496 |
| 94 | 92 | 88 | MAV Controllers (MAVC) | 496 |
| 95 | 93 | 89-91 | Drones (DRO) | 497 |
| 96 | 94 | 92 | Drone Equipment (DRE) | 497 |
| 97 | 95 | 93 | Augmented Reality Viewing Relics (ARVR) | 497 |
| 98 | 96 | 94 | Augmented Reality Projectors (ARP) | 498 |
| 99,00 | 97-00 | 95-00 | Relic Vehicles, Set 2 (VR2) | 498 |

**Table XR-271 / Weapon Relics Set 2 (WR2)**

| Low Rank | Mid Rank | High Rank | Relic Weapon | Ammo or Power Found with Relic | Weight | Sale Value | Page |
|---|---|---|---|---|---|---|---|
| 01-04 | 01-03 | 01,02 | Revolver .357 | 1d6 .357 rounds | 1.1kg | 1100+1d1000sp | 408 |
| 05-07 | 04-06 | 03,04 | Revolver .44 | 1d6 .44 rounds | 1.35kg | 1500+1d1000sp | 408 |
| 08-11 | 07-09 | - | Tactical Tomahawk | - | 900g | 400+3d100sp | 405 |
| 12-15 | 10-13 | 05 | Chem-Sprayer | 1d20 sprays in canister | 4kg+5kg | 1500+1d1000sp | 404 |
| 16-19 | 14,15 | - | Bug Spray | 3d10 sprays | 400g | 200+1d100sp | 403 |
| - | 16-19 | 06-08 | Particle Beam Rifle | Power cell with 2d8 shots | 7kg | 15k+3d1000sp | 413 |
| 20,21 | 21-24 | 09-12 | EM Emitter Rifle | Power cell with 2d6 shots | 5.5kg | 5000+3d1000sp | 407 |
| - | 25 | 13-16 | Auto Gun, Rifled | 20+1d100 rounds rifle ammo | 47kg | 12k+3d1000sp | 411 |
| - | 26 | 17,18 | Auto Gun, Beam | Power pack with 60+1d100 bursts | 53kg | 14k+4d1000sp | 411 |
| - | - | 19,20 | Auto Cannon | Top cannister holds: 2d100 20mm rounds | 729.8 kg | 40k +5d1000sp | 411 |
| - | - | 21,22 | Pulse Cannon | Power pack holds 2d12 | 530kg | 32k+4d1000sp | 412 |
| - | - | 23 | Devastator Rod | Power cell with 1d20 discharges | 2.7kg | 14k+5d1000sp | 407 |
| 22-25 | 27-33 | 24-26 | Chainsword | 2 power cells: 5d100 rounds | 8kg | 6000+3d1000sp | 405 |
| 26-33 | - | - | BB Rifle | 2d100 BB's | 1.2kg | 700+4d100sp | 403 |
| 34-39 | - | - | Pellet Rifle | Single shot, 1d100 pellets in tin | 2.6kg | 900+5d100sp | 403 |
| 40-46 | 34 | - | Flare Gun | 1 Emergency Flare, +1d4 spares | 150g | 500+4d100sp | 403 |
| 47-53 | 35,36 | - | Advanced Harpoon Gun | 1d2 harpoons, 3 hours use per power cell | 3.8 kg | 1600+1d1000sp | 403 |
| 54,55 | 37-40 | 27-32 | Advanced Sniper Rifle | 4d6 HCR round | 9kg | 5000+2d1000sp | 410 |
| 56-62 | 41-46 | 33-35 | Heavy Assault Rifle | 3d10 HCR rounds | 6.2kg | 4500+2d1000sp | 409 |
| 63,64 | 47-49 | 36-39 | Combo Assault Rifle | 3d10 rifle rounds/ 1 liter fuel cannister | 14kg | 7k+3d1000sp | 409 |
| 65,66 | 50-52 | 40-45 | Intruder Rifle | 3d10 rifle rnds/ 2d6 shots per power cell | 9.7kg | 8k+4d1000sp | 409 |
| 67-69 | 53-56 | 46-48 | Nerve Disruptor Baton | Power cell with 1d10 discharges | 1.2kg | 1600+1d1000sp | 407 |
| 70,71 | 57-59 | 49-52 | Sonic Immobilizer Rifle | Power cell with 2d8 shots | 2.9kg | 9000+4d1000sp | 407 |
| 72 | 60,61 | 53-56 | Energy Spear | Power cell, 50% drained | 14kg | 18k+5d1000sp | 405 |
| 73-75 | 62-64 | 57,58 | Rocket Pistol | Chase rockets 1d6 | 1.6kg | 3000+1d1000sp | 408 |
| 76,77 | 65-67 | 59,60 | Rocket Carbine | Chase rockets: 2d8p | 6.2kg | 5000+2d1000sp | 409 |
| 78,79 | 68-71 | 61-65 | Mk2 laser Sword | Power cell with 6d100 rounds | 1.6kg | 9k+4d1000sp | 405 |
| 80,81 | 72-74 | 66-68 | Mk2 Laser Carbine | Power cell with 1d20+2 shots | 3.3kg | 7000+2d1000sp | 410 |
| - | 75,76 | 69-71 | Mk3 Laser Carbine | Power cell with 2d12 shots | 3.8kg | 9000+3d1000sp | 410 |
| - | 77 | 72,73 | Mk4 Laser Carbine | Power cell has 1d10 shots | 4.4kg | 12k+3d1000sp | 410 |
| 82 | 78,79 | 74-77 | Laser Sniper Rifle | Power cell has 1d10 shots | 6.5kg | 11k+4d1000sp | 410 |
| 83-85 | 80-82 | 78 | Stun Rifle | Power cell with 3d10 shots | 4.8kg | 4000+2d1000sp | 406 |
| 86 | 83,84 | 79-81 | Heavy Stun Emitter | Power cell with 1d8 shots | 62kg | 11k+4d1000sp | 406 |
| 87 | 85,86 | 82-84 | Belly Cannon | Power cell: 1d20 shots | 22kg | 11k+4d1000sp | 410 |
| 88-91 | 87,88 | 85 | 8 Gauge Shotgun | 1d6+1, 8 gauge shotgun shells | 8kg | 2300+2d1000sp | 408 |
| 92 | 89-91 | 86-88 | 6 Gauge Shotgun | 1d6+1, 6 gauge shotgun shells | 11k | 4200+2d1000sp | 408 |
| 93 | 92,93 | 89-91 | Advanced Laser Pistol MK I | Power cell 1d100% charged | 1.3kg | 5000+1d1000sp | 408 |
| 94 | 94 | 92,93 | Micro-Wave Gun | Power cell with 1d10 shots | 3.3kg | 1400+1d1000sp | 410 |
| 95,96 | 95 | 94 | Electro-Net Gun | 1d12 uses in power cell | 5kg | 1000+1d1000sp | 406 |
| 97 | 96,97 | 95,96 | Lightning Emitter | Power cell with 2d6 shots | 7.8kg | 5k+3d1000sp | 412 |
| 98-00 | 98,99 | 97 | Electro-Glove | Power cell: 1d20 successful shocks remaining | 3.3kg | 3000+2d1000 | 413 |
| - | 00 | 98-00 | Electro-Glove, Advanced | 2 Power cells, each 1d100% charged | 4.2kg | 5000+2d1000sp | 413 |

## Table XR-272 / Arc Guns and Spike Throwers (AGST)

| Low Rank | Mid Rank | High Rank | Arc Gun or Spike Thrower | Ammo or Power Found with Relic | Weight | Sale Value | Page |
|---|---|---|---|---|---|---|---|
| 01-17 | 01-12 | 01-06 | Arc Pistol* | Power cell with 1d20 shots | 2.2kg | 1600+1d1000sp | 418 |
| 18-24 | 13-21 | 07-20 | Arc SMG* | Power cell with 3+2d6, 3 shot bursts | 4.8kg | 2000+1d1000sp | 418 |
| 25-33 | 22-29 | 21-32 | Arc Rifle* | Power cell: 1d10 shots | 8.2kg | 21000+1d1000sp | 418 |
| 34-47 | - | - | Scrap Built Arc Gun | Power cell: 1d4+1 shots | 4.9kg | 700+1d1000sp | 418 |
| 48-61 | 30-44 | 33-37 | Spike Pistol | 1d4+1 spikes/ power cell half drained | 2.7kg | 1400+1d1000sp | 418 |
| 62-72 | 45-57 | 38-46 | Spike Carbine | 3d20 spikes/ power cell half drained | 6.3kg | 1900+1d1000sp | 418 |
| 73-85 | 58-68 | 47-59 | Spike Rifle | 5d10 spikes / power cell half drained | 8.9kg | 2000+1d1000sp | 418 |
| 86-91 | 69-82 | 60-72 | Spike LMG | 2d100 spikes / power cell half drained | 19.2 kg | 5000+2d1000sp | 418 |
| 92-96 | 83-93 | 73-88 | Spike HMG | 2d100 spikes / power cell half drained | 26.6kg | 8000+4d1000sp | 418 |
| 97-00 | 94-00 | 89-00 | Long Spiker | 5+1d20 spikes / power cell half drained | 7.7kg | 3000+2d1000sp | 418 |

## Table XR-273 / Weaponized Industrial Tools (WIT)

| Low Rank | Mid Rank | High Rank | Industrial Tool | Ammo or Power Found with Relic | Weight | Sale Value | Page |
|---|---|---|---|---|---|---|---|
| 01-05 | 01-09 | 01-06 | Arc Welder | power pack / 20 shots | 7kg | 4500+2d1000sp | 414 |
| 06-12 | 10-13 | 07 | Furnace Lighter | canister / 18 shots | 1kg | 1900+2d1000sp | 414 |
| 13-19 | 14-22 | 08-12 | Microwave Ray | power cell / 30 rounds | 2.5kg | 2000+2d1000sp | 414 |
| 20-23 | 23-29 | 13-34 | Pneumatic Fist | power cell: 1d12x100 rounds | 1.2kg | 3000+1d1000sp | 415 |
| 24-32 | 30-35 | 35-37 | Rivet Gun | rivet rack / 24 rounds | 5kg | 3200+1d1000sp | 415 |
| 33-36 | 36-42 | 38-45 | Cracker | power cell / 20 bursts | 5.5kg | 5500+2d1000sp | 415 |
| 37 | 43-49 | 46-62 | Titan Chainsaw* | power pack / 100 minutes | 35kg | 4200+2d1000sp | 415 |
| 38-47 | 50-55 | 63 | Acid Sprayer** | air compressor pack, 2 liter canister yields 10 sprays | 6.6kg | 2200+1d1000sp | 415 |
| 48-56 | 56-59 | 64 | Floor Stapler ** | 400 staple 'clips'/ air compressor pack shoots 800 staples | 3.4kg | 1400+4d100sp | 415 |
| 57-65 | 60-64 | 65 | Industrial Nailer** | 300 9 gauge nails per 'clip'/ air compressor pack shoots 600 | 9.4kg | 2200+1d1000sp | 416 |
| 66-68 | 65-71 | 66-78 | Heavy Industrial Nailer** | 200 4 gauge nails per 'clip'/ air compressor pack shoots 400 | 26.6kg | 2200+1d1000sp | 416 |
| 69 | 72-75 | 79-86 | Mega Nailer** | 100 nail 'clips'/ air compressor pack shoots 300 | 52kg | 2200+1d1000sp | 416 |
| 70-78 | 76-82 | 87 | Pneumatic Hammer* | power cell / 40 strikes | 3.4kg | 900+1d1000sp | 416 |
| 79-89 | 83-87 | 88,89 | Pruning Electro-Shears | power cell / 120 minutes | 5kg | 1900+4d100sp | 416 |
| 90-96 | 88-91 | 90-92 | Earth Tiller* | power pack / 240 minutes | 48kg | 3900+2d1000sp | 416 |
| 97-00 | 92-00 | 93-00 | Multi-Saw* | power pack / 90 minutes | 163kg | 4900+3d1000sp | 417 |

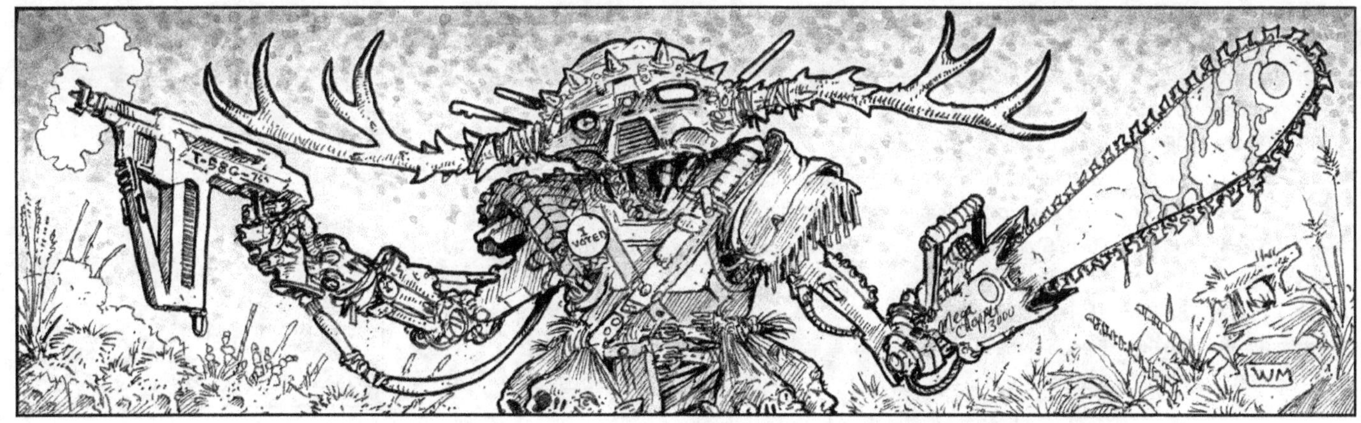

## Table XR-274 / Ammo Relics Set 2 (AM2)

| Low Rank | Mid Rank | High Rank | Relic Ammo | Amount/Details | Weight | Sale Value | Reload Price* | Page |
|---|---|---|---|---|---|---|---|---|
| 01-18 | 01-11 | 01-08 | Toxic bullets, pistol rounds | 1d8 | 10g | 200+1d100sp | NA | 418 |
| 19-24 | 12-17 | 09-14 | Toxic bullets, rifle rounds | 1d6 | 15g | 300+1d100sp | NA | 418 |
| 25-32 | 18-28 | 15-34 | 8 gauge shotgun shells | 1d8 | 90g | 50+1d30sp | 100+3d20sp | 418 |
| 33-35 | 29-36 | 35-58 | 6 gauge shotgun shells | 1d6 | 120g | 70+1d30sp | 130+3d20sp | 418 |
| 36-53 | 37-39 | 59 | Signal flare, shotgun shells | 1d3 | 62g | 40+3d20 | 400+2d100sp | 418 |
| 54-66 | 40-43 | 60 | Emergency flares | 1d8 | 50g | 60+1d30sp | 220+2d100sp | 419 |
| 67-71 | 44-51 | 61 | Relic construction staples | 1d100 | 0.25g | 3 staples earn 1sp | 1sp each | 419 |
| 72-82 | 52-61 | 62-64 | #9 Gauge nails | 1d30** | 7g | 2 nails:1sp | 2sp each | 419 |
| 83-87 | 62-69 | 65-67 | #4 Gauge nail | 1d20 | 55g | 1sp | 3sp each | 419 |
| 88-92 | 70-77 | 68-70 | #000 Gauge nail | 1d12 | 453g | 4sp | 10sp each | 419 |
| 93,94 | 78-93 | 71-92 | 20mm Auto cannon ammunition | 1d6 | 283g | 160+1d100 | 500+4d100sp | 419 |
| 95-00 | 94-00 | 93-00 | Chase rockets | 1d8 | 570g | 300+2d100sp | NA | 419 |

*For nails and staples, this is the construction or casting price each.*
**No d30 yet? Why not? Use a 1d20+1d10 for now.*

## Table XR-275 / Military Accessories Set 2 (MA2)

| Low Rank | Mid Rank | High Rank | Military Accessory | Weight | Sale Value | Page |
|---|---|---|---|---|---|---|
| 01-95 | 01-88 | 01-21 | Jump Boots | 24kg | 400+3d100sp | 420 |
| 96 | 89,90 | 22-75 | Enhanced Tactical Armature [E.T.A.] | 1640kg | 18k+3d1000sp | 420 |
| 97-00 | 91-00 | 76-00 | Hover Gun | 86kg | 7000+3d1000sp | 420 |

## Table XR-276 / Explosives Set 2 (EX2)

| Low Rank | Mid Rank | High Rank | Relic Explsoive | Weight | Sale Value | Page |
|---|---|---|---|---|---|---|
| 01-71 | 01-64 | 01-57 | Random Grenade* | - | - | See Table 277, below |
| 72-89 | 65-75 | 58-61 | Random Firework** | - | - | See Table 278, next page |
| 90-00 | 76-99 | 62-93 | Magnetic Explosive Module [MEM] | 3kg | 2000+1d1000sp | 422 |
| - | 00 | 94-00 | Micro-Tactical-Nuke*** | 1kg | 2600+2d1000sp | 423 |

** See Table XR-277/ Random Grenade, Set 2 (GR2)*
*** See Table XR-278 / Random Firework (FWK)*
****Warhead only: This device is rarely bought by a legitimate relic dealer, and does not include the rocket or missile it is attached to in this sell price add-on.*

## Table XR-277 / Random Grenade, Set 2 (GR2)

| Low Rank | Mid Rank | High Rank | Grenades, Set 2 | Weight | Sale Value | Page |
|---|---|---|---|---|---|---|
| 01-26 | 01-19 | 01-05 | Stun Grenade | 520g | 500+1d100sp | 421 |
| 27-39 | 20-28 | 06-15 | Chaff Grenade | 590g | 400+2d100sp | 421 |
| 40-46 | 29-44 | 16-47 | MK2 Advanced Fragmentation Grenade | 600g | 1000+5d100sp | 421 |
| 47 | 45-56 | 48-59 | MK3 Advanced Fragmentation Grenade | 700g | 1000+2d1000sp | 421 |
| 48-66 | 57-64 | 60-71 | Foam Grenade | 620g | 700+2d100sp | 421 |
| 67-78 | 65-76 | 72-84 | Incendiary Grenade | 575g | 600+3d100sp | 422 |
| 79-88 | 77-83 | 85-89 | EM Pulse Grenade | 450g | 850+1d1000sp | 422 |
| 89-00 | 84-99 | 90-96 | Electro-grenade | 550g | 600+3d100sp | 422 |
| - | 00 | 97-00 | Nuclear Grenade | 630g | 2000+1d1000sp | 423 |

## Table XR-278 / Relic Fireworks (FWK)

| Low Rank | Mid Rank | High Rank | Relic Firework | Quantity | Weight | Sale Value | Page |
|---|---|---|---|---|---|---|---|
| 01-41 | 01-26 | 01-05 | Sparklers | 3d6 | 10g | 20+1d12sp | 424 |
| 42-67 | 27-44 | 06-12 | Firecrackers | 3d6 | 25g | 50+2d20sp | 424 |
| 68-76 | 45-52 | 13-24 | Fountains | 1d8 | 1.4kg | 200+1d100sp | 424 |
| 77-84 | 53-69 | 25-38 | Catherine Wheels | 1d6 | 2.6kg | 350+1d100sp | 425 |
| 85-91 | 70-84 | 39-78 | Rockets | 1d6 | 1.8kg | 400+1d100sp | 425 |
| 92-99 | 85-92 | 79-85 | Screechers | 1d6 | 1.7kg | 430+1d100sp | 425 |
| 00 | 93-00 | 86-00 | Multi-Shot Mortars | 1 | 4.8kg | 100+1d100sp per charge (6+1d6) | 425 |

## Table XR-279 / Armor Relic set 2 (ARR2)

| Low Rank | Mid Rank | High Rank | Armor Relic | Weight | Sale Value | Page |
|---|---|---|---|---|---|---|
| 01-22 | 01-07 | - | Resin Armor | 5kg | 80+1d20sp | 428 |
| 23-37 | 08-13 | - | Tire Armor | 9kg | 50+2d20sp | 428 |
| 38-45 | 14-16 | - | Rug Armor | 4.5kg | 30+1d20sp | 428 |
| 46 | 17-22 | 01-11 | Fiber Skin Suit, Green | 1kg | 500+3d100sp | 429 |
| 47 | 23-27 | 12-18 | Fiber Skin Suit, Blue | 2kg | 900+1d1000sp | 429 |
| 48 | 28-30 | 19-23 | Fiber Skin Suit, Red | 4kg | 2400+2d1000sp | 429 |
| 49-54 | 31-43 | 24-28 | Torso Plate MK I | 5kg | 500+1d1000sp | 429 |
| 55,56 | 44-52 | 29-33 | Torso Plate MK II | 6kg | 800+1d1000sp | 429 |
| 57 | 53-56 | 34-40 | Torso Plate MK III | 8kg | 1400+1d1000sp | 429 |
| - | - | 41,42 | Battle Shell | 510kg | 35k+4d1000sp | 429 |
| 58 | 57,58 | 43 | Deep Sea Dive Suit | 190kg | 22k+3d1000sp | 430 |
| 59-62 | 59-73 | 44-63 | Light Combat Armor | 4.5kg | 1700+1d1000sp | 430 |
| 63-65 | 74-79 | 64-71 | Advanced Metal Weave | 2.5kg | 2600+2d1000sp | 431 |
| 66 | 80-84 | 72-80 | Exo-Armor | 48kg | 2900+3d1000sp | 431 |
| 67 | 85-89 | 81-85 | Crisis Deployment Armor | 33kg | 4500+1d1000sp | 431 |
| 68-79 | 90 | - | Resin Helmet | 1kg | 18+1d20sp | 427 |
| 80-85 | 91 | - | Welding Mask | 2.5kg | 400+d100 sp | 427 |
| 86-92 | 92 | - | Motorcycle Helmet | 1.5kg | 200+1d100sp | 427 |
| 93-98 | 93 | - | Fireman's Helmet | 1.8kg | 400+3d100sp | 427 |
| 99 | 94.95 | 86-91 | Crisis Deployment Helmet | 3.9kg | 600+4d100sp | 427 |
| 00 | 96-00 | 92-00 | Energy Buckler | 1.3kg | 2500+1d1000sp | 429 |

## Table XR-280 / Protective Gear Set 2 (PG2)

| Low Rank | Mid Rank | High Rank | Protective Gear | Weight | Sale Value | Page |
|---|---|---|---|---|---|---|
| 01-66 | 01-23 | 01-07 | Pocket Fire Extinguisher | 1kg | 10+1d20sp, or 1d3sp if expended | 432 |
| 67-73 | 24-56 | 08-92 | Electro-Dampening Skin-Suit | 1.5kg | 600+4d100sp | 432 |
| 74-00 | 57-00 | 93-00 | Radiation Sensor Tab | 40g | 500+3d100sp | 432 |

**Table XR-281 / Miscellaneous Relics (MR)**

| Low Rank | Mid Rank | High Rank | Misc. Relic | Weight | Sale Value | Page |
|---|---|---|---|---|---|---|
| 01-04 | 01-03 | 01-04 | Pocket Morse Code Translator | 850g | 600+3d100sp | 432 |
| 05 | 04,05 | 05-07 | Glider Suit | 7kg | 500+3d100sp, or 600+4d100sp camo version | 432 |
| 06 | 06,07 | 08-10 | Spider Suit | 22kg | 1200+2d1000sp | 432 |
| 07,08 | 08,09 | 11-13 | Armored Boots | 2.2kg | 400+4d100sp | 433 |
| 09-11 | 10,11 | 14-16 | Advanced Trail Boots | 1.9kg | 300+3d100sp | 433 |
| 12-15 | 12-14 | 17-19 | All Terrain Boots | 3.3kg | 1000+1d1000sp | 433 |
| 16-17 | 15,16 | 20-22 | Drop Boots | 4.7kg | 1500+1d1000sp | 433 |
| 18-20 | 17,18 | 23-26 | Color Change Fabric, Jacket | 1.4kg | 40+2d20sp | 434 |
| 21-23 | 19,20 | 27-29 | Color Change Fabric, Shirt | 500g | 30+2d20sp | 434 |
| 24-26 | 21,22 | 30-32 | Color Change Fabric, Pants | 900g | 40+1d20sp | 434 |
| 27-29 | 23,24 | 33-35 | Climate Weave Fabric, full coat | 3.6kg | 300+2d100sp | 434 |
| 30,31 | 25-28 | 36-38 | Climate Weave Fabric, light coat | 3.2kg | 250+1d100sp | 434 |
| 32-34 | 29-31 | 39,40 | Climate Weave Fabric, shirt | 600g | 140+2d20sp | 434 |
| 35-37 | 32-34 | 41,42 | Climate Weave Fabric, pants | 1kg | 1200+2d20sp | 434 |
| 38-40 | 35-39 | 43-46 | Adaptive Camouflage Fabric, poncho | 1.8kg | 750+3d100sp | 434 |
| 41-43 | 40-43 | 47,48 | Drink Anything System | 16.8 kg, (or 18.8 kg full) | 900+4d1000sp | 434 |
| 44-47 | 44-46 | 49-52 | Solar Powered Stove | 2.7kg | 350+2d100sp | 434 |
| 48 | 47-49 | 53-60 | Energy Recharging Solar Unit | 3kg | 1400+1d1000sp | 434 |
| 49,50 | 50-52 | 61,62 | Sonic Bug Screen | 475g | 470+3d1000sp | 435 |
| 51 | 53,54 | 63-65 | Armored Tent | 14.6kg | 500+4d100sp | 435 |
| 52 | 55-57 | 66-68 | Instant Cabin | 56kg | 1100+1d1000sp | 435 |
| 53-55 | 58,59 | 69 | Tree Bed | 3.6kg | 370+3d100sp | 435 |
| 56-59 | 60,61 | - | Nutrient Paste (2d6) | 160 grams | 140+1d100sp | 435 |
| 60-62 | 62,63 | - | Nutrient Tabs (1d6 rolls) | 15g each (rolls of 12 tablets) | 10+1d12sp | 435 |
| 63-70 | 64,65 | - | MREs (2d6) | 800g | 30+1d20sp | 436 |
| 71 | 66,67 | 70-74 | Smart Rope | 2.8kg | 15.24m (50') 100+1d100sp | 436 |
| 72,73 | 68,69 | 75-78 | Rescue Kit | 27kg | 6500+4d1000sp | 436 |
| 74-76 | 70,71 | 79,80 | Climbing Kit | 23kg | 750+4d100sp | 437 |
| 77-79 | 72,73 | 81 | Universal Cooker | 3.7kg | 450+2d100sp | 437 |
| 80-82 | 74,75 | 82 | High Tolerance Sleeping Bag | 3.8kg | 520+3d1000sp | 437 |
| 83-88 | 76-78 | 83 | Compass | 30g | 240+2d100sp | 437 |
| 89-91 | 79,80 | 84 | Multi Ratchet | 370g | 310+2d100sp | 437 |
| 92 | 81,82 | 85-88 | Mini Winch | 16kg | 720+1d1000sp | 437 |
| 93 | 83-85 | 89,90 | Tool Arms | 23kg | 1900+1d1000sp | 437 |
| 94 | 86-88 | 91 | Specialized Repair Kits | 10+1d10kg | 800+4d1000sp | 438 |
| 95 | 89,90 | 92,93 | Universal Key | 370g | 600+3d100sp | 438 |
| 96,97 | 91,92 | 94 | Smart Paper | 290g | 300+1d100 | 438 |
| 98 | 93-95 | 95,96 | Assist Frame, Mobility | 16kg | 800+3d100sp. | 438 |
| 99 | 96-98 | 97,98 | Assist Frame, Power | 36kg | 1600+1d1000sp | 438 |
| 00 | 99,00 | 99,00 | Assist Frame, Construction | 53kg | 2100+1d1000sp | 438 |

## Table XR-282 / High Tech Devices Set 2 (HTD2)

| Low Rank | Mid Rank | High Rank | High-Tech Device | Weight | Sale Value | Page |
|---|---|---|---|---|---|---|
| 01,02 | 01-05 | 01-06 | Psionic Immobilizer Head Clamp | 3.3kg | 1100+3d100sp | 439 |
| 03,04 | 06-09 | 07-13 | Electro Guardian Unit | 6kg | 2800+4d100sp | 439 |
| 05-10 | 10-19 | 14-23 | Handheld Movement Detector | 1.5kg | 900+5d100sp | 439 |
| 11,12 | 20-24 | 24-28 | Ascension Gloves | 1.2kg (pair) | 850+4d100sp | 439 |
| 13-26 | 25-28 | 29,30 | Metal Detector | 1.4kg | 750+4d100sp | 439 |
| 27,28 | 29-32 | 31-33 | Mecha Detector | 860g | 1200+4d100sp | 440 |
| 29-41 | 33-35 | 34,35 | Megaphone | 1.5kg | 500+5d100sp | 440 |
| 42-55 | 36-38 | 36 | Glow Flares (2d6) | 200g | 20+1d30sp | 440 |
| 56,57 | 39-43 | 37-43 | Comms-Jammer | 7.8kg | 1800+2d10000sp | 440 |
| 58-66 | 44-50 | 44-49 | Control Collar | 2.8kg | 400+3d100sp | 440 |
| 67 | 51-54 | 50-55 | Control Collar Console | 900g | 1300+2d100sp | 441 |
| 68-70 | 55-61 | 56-61 | Agony Inducer Unit | 2.7kg | 2500+2d1000sp | 441 |
| 71-77 | 62-68 | 62-70 | Robo-Repair Module MK I | 470+2d100g | 800+1d1000sp | 441 |
| 78 | 69-73 | 71-74 | Robo-Repair Module MK II | 470+2d100g | 1600+1d1000sp | 441 |
| - | 74,75 | 75-78 | Robo-Repair Module MK III | 470+2d100g | 4000+2d1000sp | 441 |
| 79-81 | 76-80 | 79-85 | Energy Wall Projector | 28kg | 2000+1d1000sp | 442 |
| 82 | 81-86 | 86-92 | Handheld Satellite Comms Unit [HSCU] | 1.9kg | 1000+1d1000sp | 448 |
| 83–98 | 87-96 | 93-95 | Ear Mic | 160g | 300+2d100sp | 448 |
| 99,00 | 97-00 | 96-00 | Computer Assistance Gauntlet | 550g | 1600+6d100sp | 450 |

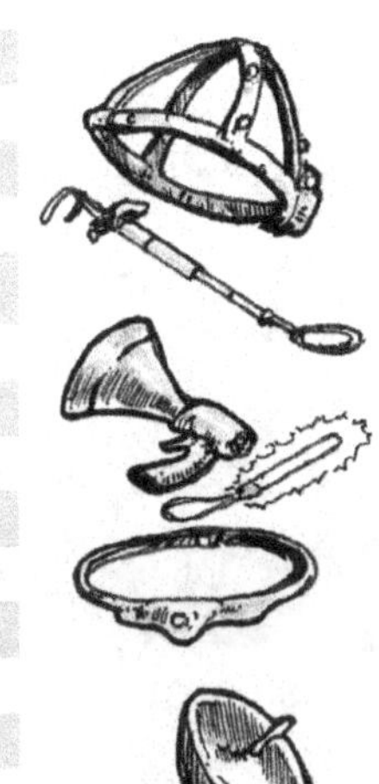

## Table XR-283/ Computers, Smartphones and Tablet Relics (COMPS)

| Low Rank | Mid Rank | High Rank | Computer System | Weight | Sale Value | Page |
|---|---|---|---|---|---|---|
| 01-30 | 01-16 | 01-12 | Smartphone | 400g | 600+3d100sp | 449 |
| 31-51 | 17-39 | 13-33 | Tablet | 700g | 800+3d100sp | 450 |
| 52-77 | 40-62 | 34-51 | Laptop Computer | 1kg | 1400+4d100sp | 450 |
| 78-91 | 63-86 | 52-72 | Computer, simple | 3kg | 1600+3d100sp | 452 |
| 92-99 | 87-93 | 73-88 | Computer, complex | 4kg | 1900+1d1000sp | 452 |
| 00 | 94-00 | 89-00 | Computer, advanced | 7kg | 2400+1d1000sp | 452 |

## Table XR-284 / Medical Relics (MEDR)

| Low Rank | Mid Rank | High Rank | Medical Relic | Weight | Sale Value | Page |
|---|---|---|---|---|---|---|
| 01-22 | 01-11 | 01-05 | Flesh-Mend Gel, MK 1 | 500g | 400+2d100sp | 442 |
| 23-27 | 12-24 | 06-12 | Flesh-Mend Gel, MK 2 | 600g | 00+3d100sp | 442 |
| 28,29 | 25-31 | 13-17 | Flesh-Mend Gel, MK 3 | 700g | 800+4d100sp | 442 |
| 30 | 32-36 | 18-22 | Flesh-Mend Gel, MK 4 | 800g | 1000+5d100sp | 442 |
| 31-38 | 37-41 | 23-26 | Tissue Binder | 700g | 1000+d1000sp | 443 |
| 39-45 | 42-45 | 27 | Iodine Tabs (2d12 in foil pack) | 5mg ea. | 200+1d100sp each | 443 |
| 46-63 | 46-52 | 28 | Steroidal Pills (bottle of 3d6) | 3mg each | 20+1d20sp ea. | 443 |
| 64-72 | 53-58 | 29,30 | Nano Patch | 150g | 300+3d100sp | 444 |
| 73-76 | 59-63 | 31-34 | Deviant Inhibitor Serum [DIS] | 1d6 50ml vials | 1400+1d1000sp per vial | 444 |
| 77-79 | 64-67 | 35-41 | Rad-leeching Canister | 1.9kg | 1800+1d1000sp | 445 |
| - | 68-72 | 42-48 | Auto-Doc | 36kg | 4000+3d1000sp | 445 |
| 80-82 | 73-76 | 49-52 | Advanced Trauma Kit | 3.2kg | 1000+1d1000sp | 445 |
| 83-87 | 77-80 | 53-55 | Wonder Antibiotics (7 pack) | 6g per pill | 400+2d100 per pill | 445 |
| 88-90 | 81-83 | 56-69 | Revival Kit | 1.25kg | 1300+1d1000sp | 446 |
| - | 84,85 | 70-83 | Advanced Doctors Kit | 2.5kg | 1600+2d1000sp | 446 |
| 91 | 86-91 | 84 | Nano Healing Injector | 140g | 250+1d100sp | 446 |
| 92-95 | 92-96 | 85-92 | Armored Splints | Variable | Variable, | 446 |
| 96-00 | 97-00 | 93-00 | Medical Cybernetic | Variable | Variable | 447 |

## Table XR-285 / Power Sources Set 2 (PS2)

| Low Rank | Mid Rank | High Rank | Power Source | Weight | Sale Value | Page |
|---|---|---|---|---|---|---|
| 01-22 | 01-19 | 01-17 | Advanced Power Cell | 750g | 200+23d100sp | 457 |
| 23-45 | 20-36 | 18-34 | Solar Charge Cell | 550g | 150+2d100sp | 457 |
| 46-69 | 37-51 | 35-53 | Hand Crank Power Cell | 620g | 400+4d100sp | 457 |
| 70-89 | 52-72 | 54-70 | Belt Power Pouch | 1.8kg | 500+1d1000sp | 457 |
| 90-95 | 73-84 | 71-81 | Portable Wind Turbine | 9kg | 800+4d100sp | 457 |
| 96-00 | 85-00 | 82-00 | Air Compressor Pack | 18kg | 900+4d100sp | 457 |

## Table XR-286/ Robots Set 2 (RA2)

| Low Rank | Mid Rank | High Rank | Robot | Weight | Sale Value | Page |
|---|---|---|---|---|---|---|
| 01-48 | 01-31 | 01-04 | Wisp Scout Flyer | 33kg | 1600+1d1000sp | 458 |
| 49-70 | 32-46 | 05-11 | Wasp | 52 kg | 1900+1d1000sp | 458 |
| 71-82 | 47-61 | 12-29 | Hoplite Combot | 185 kg | 8000+3d1000sp | 459 |
| 83-95 | 62-76 | 30-53 | Tanker | 310kg | 9000+3d1000sp | 459 |
| 96-00 | 77-93 | 54-87 | Heavy Advanced Combot | 490kg | 10k +3d1000sp | 460 |
| - | 94-00 | 88-94 | Warbot, Light | 5,600kg | 24k +3d1000sp | 461 |
| - | - | 95-00 | Warbot, Heavy | 9600kg | 30k +4d1000sp | 461 |

## Table XR-287 / MAVs (MAV)

| Low Rank | Mid Rank | High Rank | MAV or Controller | Weight | Sale Value | Page |
|---|---|---|---|---|---|---|
| 01-03 | 01-05 | 01-09 | Assassin | 1.5kg | 1200+1d1000sp | 466 |
| 04-13 | 06-12 | 10-13 | Bat | 950g | 300+2d100sp | 466 |
| 14-16 | 13-18 | 14-21 | Beam Bird | 1.4kg | 900+4d100sp | 466 |
| 17-25 | 19-24 | 22-25 | Cockroach | 130g | 100+1d100sp | 466 |
| 26-28 | 25-30 | 26-29 | Crow Flyer | 1.1kg | 300+2d100sp | 466 |
| 29-31 | 31-36 | 30-37 | Dragonfly | 470g | 800+4d100sp | 466 |
| 32-43 | 37-42 | 38-41 | Fly-Spy | 50g | 100+1d100sp | 467 |
| 44-61 | 43-48 | 42-45 | Flying Disc | 220g | 90+1d100sp | 467 |
| 62-67 | 49-58 | 46-49 | Heli-MAV | 390g | 250+3d100sp | 467 |
| 68-70 | 59-65 | 50-57 | Hummingbird | 310g | 200+3d100sp | 467 |
| 71-83 | 66-72 | 58-61 | Quad-rotor | 690g | 300+2d100sp | 467 |
| 84-90 | 73-79 | 62-69 | Robo-Fish | 2.4kg | 350+2d100sp | 468 |
| 91 | 80-85 | 70-86 | Snake | 5kg | 850+4d100sp | 468 |
| 92-98 | 86-93 | 87-91 | Suicide Nano | 2.2kg | 250+2d100sp | 468 |
| 99,00 | 94-00 | 92-00 | Tarantula | 710g | 340+3d100sp | 468 |

## Table XR-288 / MAV Controllers (MAVC)

| Low Rank | Mid Rank | High Rank | MAV Controller | Weight | Sale Value | Page |
|---|---|---|---|---|---|---|
| 01-03 | 01-06 | 01-09 | MAV Controller: Targeting Optics Headset | 1kg | 1700+2d1000sp | Hub 198 |
| 04-37 | 07-22 | 10,11 | MAV Controller: Viewing Monocle | 300g | 600+1d1000sp | 463 |
| 38-59 | 23-46 | 12-19 | MAV Controller: Snap-On Cybernetic Eye Module | 670g | 1400+1d1000sp | 463 |
| 60-83 | 47-72 | 20-42 | MAV Controller: Snap-On Eye Piece | 750g | 1100+1d1000sp | 463 |
| 84-97 | 73-92 | 43-77 | MAV Controller: Operator's Headset | 1.4kg | 1800+2d1000sp | 463 |
| 98-00 | 93-00 | 79-00 | MAV Controller: Chest Rig | 3kg | 2200+2d1000sp | 463 |

## Table XR-289 / Drones (DRO)

| Low Rank | Mid Rank | High Rank | Drone | Weight | Sale Value | Page |
|---|---|---|---|---|---|---|
| 01-31 | 01-11 | 01-05 | Basic Drone, Little Buddy | 5.5kg | 600+3d100sp | 469 |
| 32-45 | 12-20 | 06-14 | Basic Drone, Action Man | 5.5kg | 700+3d100sp | 469 |
| 46-56 | 21-29 | 15-20 | Basic Drone, Emergency Medical Response | 5.5kg | 1000+4d100sp | 470 |
| 57-61 | 30-40 | 21-31 | Defensive Drone | 19 kg | 900+4d100sp | 470 |
| 62-64 | 41-48 | 32-40 | Police Assistant Drone | 22kg | 1200+4d100sp | 470 |
| 65-78 | 49-60 | 41-47 | Search and Rescue Drone | 70kg | 950+3d100sp | 470 |
| 79-88 | 61-69 | 48-55 | Construction Drone | 120 kg | 750+3d100sp | 470 |
| 89-90 | 70-78 | 56-63 | Aquatic Construction Drone | 170kg | 850+3d100sp | 473 |
| 91-95 | 79-85 | 64-76 | Military Resupply Drone | 20kg | 1200+1d100sp | 473 |
| 96,97 | 86-90 | 77-83 | Military Utility Drone | 25kg | 1300+1d1000sp | 474 |
| 98,99 | 91-93 | 84-88 | Bomb Disposal Drone | 260kg | 1900+2d1000sp | 474 |
| 00 | 94-00 | 89-00 | Hunter Killer Drone | 16kg | 2500+1d1000sp | 475 |

## Table XR-290/ Drone Equipment(DRE)

| Low Rank | Mid Rank | High Rank | Drone Equipment | Weight | Sale Value | Page |
|---|---|---|---|---|---|---|
| 01-21 | 01-19 | 01-09 | Drone HUD | 340g | 300+3d1000sp | 475 |
| 22-47 | 20-36 | 10-19 | Basic Drone Control Pad | 430g | 250+2d1000sp | 475 |
| 48-75 | 37-56 | 20-41 | Drone Control Unit | 570g | 600+1d1000sp | 475 |
| 76-83 | 57-65 | 42-48 | Drone Control Implant | 1.2kg | 340+3d100sp | 476 |
| 84-88 | 66-74 | 49-63 | Drone Control Hub | 4.9kg | 900+1d1000sp | 476 |
| 89-96 | 75-89 | 64-75 | Drone Repair Kit | 4.8kg | 500+4d100sp | 476 |
| 97-00 | 90-00 | 76-00 | Drone Hijack Unit | 850g | 600+1d1000sp | 476 |

## Table XR-291 / Augmented Reality Viewing Relics (ARVR)

| Low Rank | Mid Rank | High Rank | AR Viewing Relic | Weight | Sale Value | Page |
|---|---|---|---|---|---|---|
| 01-12 | 01-06 | - | AR Contact Lenses (1d3 pairs) | 50g | 1500+5d100sp | 478 |
| 13-26 | 07-17 | 01-03 | AR Monocle | 75g | 900+3d100sp | 478 |
| 27-37 | 18-25 | 04-13 | AR Sensor Prosthetic | 500g | 700+2d100sp | 478 |
| 38-66 | 26-37 | 14-21 | Palm Held AR Viewer | 750g | 800+4d100sp | 478 |
| 67-76 | 38-46 | 22-26 | AR Glasses, MK I | 130g | 900+5d100sp | 478 |
| 77-87 | 47-55 | 27-38 | AR Glasses, MK II | 120g | 1000+6d100sp | 478 |
| 88,89 | 56-63 | 39-47 | AR Glasses, MK III | 110g | 1300+6d100sp | 478 |
| 90 | 64-71 | 48-56 | AR Glasses, MK IV | 100g | 1600+6d100sp | 479 |
| - | 72-74 | 57-62 | AR Glasses, MK V | 125g | 2000+8d100sp | 479 |
| 91-95 | 75-82 | 63-78 | AR Goggles | 600g | 1400+6d100sp | 479 |
| 96-98 | 83-94 | 79-88 | Smartphone | 200+1d100g | 600+3d100sp | 479 |
| 99,00 | 95-00 | 89-00 | Tablet | 700+2d100g | 1100+3d100sp | 479 |

## Table XR-292 / Augmented Reality Projectors (ARP)

| Low Rank | Mid Rank | High Rank | AR Projector Type | Weight | Sale Value | Page |
|---|---|---|---|---|---|---|
| 01-13 | 01-14 | 01-17 | AR Map Kiosk | 100+1d100 kg | 1000+1d1000s | 480 |
| 14-23 | 15-19 | 18-24 | AR Sign Projector | 5+1d6 kg | 500+2d100sp | 480 |
| 24-28 | 20-27 | 25-33 | Augmented Reality Fashion Mirror | 80+1d30 kg | 1000+2d1000sp | 481 |
| 29-36 | 28-33 | 34-39 | Earth View Rotation | 50+2d10 kg | 800+4d100sp | 481 |
| 37-42 | 34-42 | 40-51 | Educational AR Book | 4.4kg | Variable, see description text | 482 |
| 43-49 | 43-51 | 52-57 | Entertainment AR Projector | 6+1d6 kg | 600+3d100sp | 482 |
| 50-61 | 52-59 | 58-63 | Floating Menu | 4+1d4 kg | 200+1d100sp | 483 |
| 62-69 | 60-72 | 64-70 | Interactive Non-Human Adult Companions Catalog | 57kg | 1000+1d1000sp | 483 |
| 70-78 | 73-81 | 71-76 | Light Guided Pathway Pole | 3+1d3kg each | 200+1d100sp each pole | 483 |
| 79-84 | 82-86 | 77-84 | Personal ID and Data Record Tag | 45g | 50+1d30 | 483 |
| 85-91 | 87-93 | 85-92 | Traffic Sign | 6+2d6kg | 600+3d100sp | 484 |
| 92-00 | 94-00 | 93-00 | Virtual Furniture Demo Projector | 3kg | 400+2d100sp | 484 |

## Table XR-293 / Relic Vehicles, Set 2 (VR2)

| Low Rank | Mid Rank | High Rank | Relic Vehicle | Weight | Sale Value | Page |
|---|---|---|---|---|---|---|
| 01-67 | 01-50 | 01-27 | Combat Transport Vehicle | 2200kg | 15+2d10k sp | 485 |
| 68-88 | 51-68 | 28-44 | Armored Personnel Carrier | 8500kg | 50+3d10k sp | 485 |
| - | 69-71 | 45-59 | Standard Tank | 18 tonnes | 200+6d10k sp | 485 |
| 89-98 | 72-88 | 60-76 | Civilian Helicopter | 660kg | 16+2d8k sp | 486 |
| 99 | 89-94 | 77-85 | Combat Helicopter | 4100kg | 70+2d12k sp | 486 |
| 00 | 95-00 | 86-93 | Patrol Boat | 11 tonnes | 140+5d10k | 486 |
| - | - | 94-00 | Orbital Shuttle | 6 tonnes | 400+8d10k | 487 |

# Expanded Weapon Classification Tables

These updated Relic Weapon Classifications combine both those found in the TME Hub Rules and the TME Expansion Rules, and replace classifications WC-RC (Relic Concealed), WR-R (Relic) and WC-AR (Advanced Relic).

Items shown in italic type are found in the Hub Rules, with those weapons listed on page TME-100. All other listings have their stats listed on page XR-401 of this book.

| 1d100 | Relic Concealed (WC-RC) |
|---|---|
| 01-05 | *Switchblade knife* |
| 06-11 | *Pistol crossbow* |
| 12-15 | *.22 Cal pistol with 10+1d8 rounds* |
| 16-21 | *Auto pistol with 3d6 pistol rounds* |
| 22-25 | *Sub-machine gun with 4d6 pistol rounds* |
| 26-30 | *Pump shotgun with folding stock & 2d8 shells* |
| 31-35 | *1d4 Random grenades (see table TME-8-6, page 213, hub rules)* |
| 36-38 | *Dart gun with 1d4+2 type A, death poison darts* |
| 39-41 | *Dart gun with 1d4+2 type B, sleep poison darts* |
| 42-44 | *Stun pistol with 2d12 shots remaining* |
| 45-47 | *Laser scalpel, 2d100 rounds remaining* |
| 48-51 | *Pocket pistol, with 1d6 rounds in magazine* |
| 52-56 | *Survival rifle, with 1d10 rifle rounds in mag, folding stock* |
| 57-60 | *Stun stick, with 1d100 rounds remaining* |
| 61-63 | *Wrist laser, with 1d8+8 shots remaining* |
| 64-69 | *Wrist gun, with 1 loaded and 3d6 pistol rounds in pouch* |
| 70,71 | *Laser pistol, with 3d10 shots left* |
| 72-75 | *Sling shot, wrist-lock* |
| 76-80 | *Shotgun pistol, 2 loaded, 2d6 shells in pouch* |
| 81,82 | *Mini laser, with 1d20 shots left* |
| 83,84 | Revolver .357, with 1d6 .357 cartridges |
| 85 | Revolver .44, loaded with 1d6 .44 cal rounds |
| 86-89 | Tactical tomahawk |
| 90-93 | Flare gun, loaded with emergency flare, plus 1d6 spare |
| 94,95 | Nerve disruptor baton, with 4+1d6 charges left in battery |
| 96 | Rocket pistol, with 1d6 chase rockets loaded (chase rockets described on page XR-419) |
| 97 | Advanced laser pistol MK I, with 50% charge in battery (see variable power use options on page XR-408). |
| 98-00 | Electro-glove, 2d10 successful shocks worth of power remaining. |

## 1d100   Relic (WC-R)

| | |
|---|---|
| 01-05 | Compound bow, with 3d6 arrows |
| 06-08 | Compound crossbow, with 3d6 quarrels |
| 09,10 | Sniper rifle with 1+d6 HC rifle rounds |
| 11-15 | Assault rifle with 2d20 rifle rounds |
| 16-18 | Spring-spike |
| 19-25 | Pump shotgun with 2d6 shells |
| 26-28 | 1d3 Fragmentation grenades |
| 29-32 | Survival rifle, full clip and d10 rifle rounds |
| 33-34 | .22 cal Sporting rifle, with d20+5 rounds |
| 35,36 | Discsaw with 2d100 rounds remaining |
| 37-39 | Chainsaw with 2d100 rounds remaining |
| 40-44 | .22 Cal Semi-auto, 30 rnd mag with 3d10 rnds |
| 45-47 | Laser torch 4d20 rounds left |
| 48 | Razor sword |
| 49-53 | Harpoon gun and 2d6 harpoons |
| 54-56 | Assault shotgun with 2d12 shells |
| 57-63 | Sub-machine gun with 3d20 pistol rounds |
| 64-66 | Chem-sprayer, with 2d10 sprays of random chemical, see 1d8 random list on page XR-404. |
| 67-70 | Chainsword, with 40+1d100 rounds of power left in twin power cells. |
| 71-73 | BB rifle, with 100+1d00 BBs |
| 74-78 | Pellet rifle, with 20+1d30 pellets |
| 79-82 | Advanced harpoon gun, with 2d6 steel harpoons |
| 83-85 | Heavy assault rifle, with 3d10 high caliber rounds in magazine |
| 86,87 | Rocket carbine, loaded with 7+1d10 Chase rockets in magazine (chase Rockets described on page XR-419). |
| 88,89 | Mk2 laser carbine, with 10+1d12 shots remaining in power cell. |
| 90-92 | Stun rifle, with 3d10 shots in power cell |
| 93,94 | Heavy stun emitter, with 1d8 shots left in power cell |
| 95-97 | 8 gauge shotgun, with 1d6+1 8 gauge shot shells in gun |
| 98-00 | Lightning emitter, with 2d6 shots left in power cell. |

## 1d100   Advanced Relic (WC-AR)

| | |
|---|---|
| 01-06 | Assault shotgun with 2d20 shells in drum |
| 07-11 | Grenade launcher with 2d6 frag. grenades |
| 12-15 | Rocket launcher with d6 battle rockets |
| 16-22 | Laser pistol with 3d10 shots remaining |
| 23-27 | Laser carbine with 3d6 shots remaining |
| 28-31 | Pulse rifle with 5+1d20 bursts left in power cell |
| 32-37 | Heavy laser carbine with 3d10 bursts |
| 38,39 | Tripod based light laser cannon, 3d10 shots |
| 40-43 | Chain gun, 2d100 rifle rounds, drum magazine |
| 44-46 | Heavy machine gun, 2d20 HCR rounds, drum |
| 47-49 | Flame unit with 2d10 rounds of fuel |
| 50,51 | Rocket launcher with 2d6 battle rockets |
| 52,53 | Laser sword with d100 rounds remaining |
| 54,55 | .50 Cal sniper rifle with d10 rounds |
| 56-58 | Heavy pulse rifle with 2d10 burst remaining |
| 59-61 | Pulse rifle with power pack, d100 burst |
| 62-64 | Chain gun, belt fed pack, 2d100 rifle rounds |
| 65-67 | Particle beam rifle, with 2d8 shots left in battery |
| 68-70 | EM emitter rifle, 2d6 shots remaining |
| 71-73 | Advanced sniper rifle, 2d12 high cal rifle round sin 24 shot mag. |
| 74-76 | Combo assault rifle, 1d30 rifle rounds/ half liter fuel left in cannister |
| 77,78 | Intruder rifle, loaded with 1d30 rifle rnds/ 1d12 shots left in power cell |
| 79,80 | Sonic immobilizer rifle, with 2d8 shots left in power cell |
| 81,82 | Energy spear, power cell drained to half. |
| 83,84 | Mk2 laser sword, with 300_3d1000 rounds of use left in charge |
| 85,86 | Mk3 laser carbine, with 2d12 shots left in power cell |
| 87,88 | Mk4 laser carbine, with 1d10 tiers left in charge |
| 89-90 | Laser sniper rifle, with 1d10 shots left in charge |
| 91,92 | Belly cannon, roll 1d6: 1-4. Loaded with power cell with 10+1d10 shots left, or 5,6. Power pack with 1d100 shots left in pack |
| 93,94 | 6 gauge shotgun, with 1d4+2, 6 gauge shotgun shells remaining |
| 95,96 | Micro-wave gun, with 1d10 shots left in power cell |
| 97-00 | Electro-net gun, 1d6 nets, and 2d6 charges left in power cell in gun |

# Appendices

## Appendix 1: Personality Determination for Characters

The following 100 personalities are best suited to adventure minded characters, although can be used to quickly generate a personality for an NPC of almost any profession. If a player doesn't feel that a randomly determined personalty is a good fit for their new character, the GM can have the player re-roll until a more appropriate one is established.

A much larger, 15 page downloadable PDF personalty matrix is available for free to Society of Excavators members in the SOE area at this link: https://www.outlandarts.com/membersonly/TME-SOE-personality-matrix. htm . This online table uses a 1d1000 roll and has separate columns for people of many differed castes.

### Table XR-294 / Character Personality — Roll 1d100

| | | |
|---|---|---|
| 01. Abrasive | 35. Dynamic | 69. Paranoid |
| 02. Affectionate | 36. Eccentric | 70. Passionate |
| 03. Aggressive | 37. Erratic | 71. Pessimistic |
| 04. Ambitious | 38. Ethical | 72. Prankster |
| 05. Antisocial | 39. Fanatical | 73. Proud |
| 06. Anxious | 40. Fearless | 74. Quirky |
| 07. Arrogant | 41. Fiery | 75. Reckless |
| 08. Assertive | 42. Greedy | 76. Relentless |
| 09. Belligerent | 43. Grim | 77. Rigid |
| 10. Bloodthirsty | 44. Grouchy | 78. Roguish |
| 11. Bold | 45. Gutsy | 79. Rowdy |
| 12. Bragger | 46. Helpful | 80. Ruthless |
| 13. Brave | 47. Heroic | 81. Secretive |
| 14. Brazen | 48. Honorable | 82. Shady |
| 15. Brutal | 49. Humane | 83. Shameless |
| 16. Calm | 50. Humble | 84. Show-Off |
| 17. Careful | 51. Icy | 85. Skeptical |
| 18. Cautious | 52. Idealistic | 86. Sly |
| 19. Cocky | 53. Immoral | 87. Sneaky |
| 20. Compassionate | 54. Impulsive | 88. Stern |
| 21. Compulsive | 55. Independent | 89. Stingy |
| 22. Confident | 56. Intense | 90. Suspicious |
| 23. Cruel | 57. Joker | 91. Talkative |
| 24. Curious | 58. Lawless | 92. Thrifty |
| 25. Daredevil | 59. Lewd | 93. Unforgiving |
| 26. Debased | 60. Loyal | 94. Valiant |
| 27. Deranged | 61. Lusty | 95. Vengeful |
| 28. Devious | 62. Mischievous | 96. Violent |
| 29. Devoted | 63. Modest | 97. Vulgar |
| 30. Diplomatic | 64. Morbid | 98. Willful |
| 31. Discreet | 65. Obsessive | 99. Wrathful |
| 32. Distrustful | 66. Optimistic | 100. Zealous |
| 33. Dramatic | 67. Ornery | |
| 34. Driven | 68. Outgoing | |

# Appendix 2: Character Old World Ethnicity

While there is no in-game need to know the racial make-up of a character, and often any evidence has been visibly erased because of mutations and other modifications, knowing the ethnicity can be helpful when describing a new character.

To determine the racial make-up of a character as far as his or her human ethnic lineage goes, the following random table has been added to this book. While useful in trying to visualize a pure stock human, or ghost mutant, the following list is also helpful to flesh out the appearance of mildly mutated deviants, cyborgs, rebuilt, and other character types. For synthetic humans, the racial type is whatever person the clone or bioreplica was based on, while androids would also have the outer sheathing appearance of this randomly determined race. Roll 1d6 times to establish a racial mix of the PC, combining all racial features into a general description of the character.

This list has a random 1d100 optional roll, but a player may select any ancient ethnicity, or one of the many we grouped together below. This list, and the dice results for random determination, are based on game play by RPG enthusiasts from the western world, and is by no means complete nor represents the anticipated ethnic population make-up of some far off, fictional world. Second, while The Mutant Epoch Era is happening globally, in this game universe, much of the source material takes place in and around the Crossroads Region, which sits upon the vast ruins of the former megalopolis of Los Angeles.

In short, consider this random list as merely an example of a table the game master should make themselves, especially if basing their game setting in a part of the Earth where one or more numerically more common races are likely to exist, even in the twenty-fourth century. If the author has forgotten a race, or the game master would like to add another, we have purposefully left two blank spaces at the bottom of the random list for the GM to fill in. In the case where they are not filled in, and the dice roll lands there, consider the character's ethnicity to be the same as the player of that character.

## Table XR-295 / Ancestral Ethnicity for Human Characters

*Roll 1d100* (roll 1d6 times to establish potential blended ethnicity)

**01-04.** African, North African (Morocco, Egypt, Libya, Tunisia, Algeria)
**05-14.** African, Sub-Saharan (Bantu, Zulu, Akana, Afar, Swazi, Somalis, etc.)
**15.** Afrikaner (South African 'Boers')
**16-20.** American Aboriginal (Sioux, Apache, Mohawk, Cree, Inuit, Amazonian, Inca, Aztec, etc.)
**21,22.** Arab
**23.** Armenian
**24,25.** Assyrian (Iraq, Iran, Syria, Turkey)
**26.** Australian Aborigine
**27,28.** Balochis (Pakistan, Iran, Afghanistan)
**29.** Burmese  (Myanmar)
**30-35.** Chinese (Han, Zhuang, Uyghur, Manchu, Hui, etc.)
**36-38.** Japanese
**39.** Javanese
**40-43.** Jewish (Ashkenazim, Mizrahim, Sephardim, Teimanim, Kochinim, Etiopim, etc.)
**44.** Kazakh (Kazakhstan)
**45,46.** Korean
**47.** Kurd (Kurdistan)
**48.** Laotian
**49-57.** Latin American (Mexican, Cuban, Brazilian, Colombian, etc.)
**58.** Mongolian
**59.** Nepali
**60,61.** Persian (Iran)
**62.** Polynesian
**63.** Sikh
**64-67.** Slavic (Eastern European, including Russians, Poles, Ukrainians, etc.)
**68-70.** South Asian (Hindustani, Gujarati, Bengali, Burmese, Tamils, etc.)
**71.** Thai (Thailand)
**72.** Tibetan
**73.** Turkic
**74.** Vietnamese
**75-96.** Western European (Scandinavian, Germanic, French, Italian, Greek, Spanish, Irish, Scottish, English, Dutch, Swiss, etc.)
**97,98.** _______________________________________
**99,00.** _______________________________________

# Appendix 3: Popsicle People

*by Danny Seedhouse*

Popsicle People are a completely new way to roll-up a character for The Mutant Epoch. These folks have freshly awoken in a strange new world, a world that is vastly different than the one they started in. The basic premise here is that your character went into suspended animation some time before the major changes that rocked the world as it entered the Epochian era. This PC generation system was originally built for a local gaming convention to introduce new players to The Mutant Epoch RPG. To use this system, start with step one and proceed through each step in turn.

This is a set random chart for rolling up a random background for someone just revived from cryogenic storage. Or this can be used for folks stepping through an inter-dimensional portal or any other circumstance where they suddenly find themselves in a post-apocalyptic new era.

## Step 1: Why

Why did you end up in a cryogenic tube sleeping past the end of the world?

**Table XR-296 / Why?     Roll 1d12**

**1. No clue:** You have no idea how or why you're where you are... but you have a new tattoo of the Infinity symbol on your left arm.
**2. Volunteer short term testing:** You were a volunteer for a short-term test of new technology. Obviously, something went wrong.
**3. Government Shelter:** You were on a list and took the chance you were given as everything collapsed around you.
**4. Emergency:** Well, it was either a cryo-tube or a nuclear bomb, or some other horrible city killing disaster, and the only way you could see to survive was in the cryogenic vaults. You get a 3 in 10 chance of having something happen to your character, roll 1d10 on 'The Weird' table, ignoring 3 and 4.
**5. Personal Choice:** You were done with the world, but not done with life, and wanted to see the glories of the future.
**6. Selected:** You were to be part of a bright new future and rebuild the world from the Stone Age, or whatever it had become after the coming apocalypse. Some of these re-builders were private individuals or personnel from a corporation, and everyone was given an orientation document and has a job to do when they wake up.
**7. Prisoner:** Caught and thrown in jail for crimes you may or may not have committed, you may even have just been in the wrong place at the wrong time. Once in, you were "recruited" or "volunteered" for experiments to reduce the time spent behind bars. Everyone here gets to roll on 'The Weird' table, next page.
**8. Volunteer:** You suffered from a terminal disease or condition, and when the opportunity presented itself, you volunteered for a cryogenic experiment hoping medical science would catch up with your condition. Congratulations, it "worked" and your condition has been cured. What was the nature of the experiments tried on you? **Roll 1d4.**
    **1.** Radical Gene splicing with non-human DNA has resulted in you becoming a Bestial Human. Determine the species with a 50% chance of a bestial from this book, on page XR-58, otherwise from those listed on page 24 of the Hub Rules book.
    **2.** Dubiously ethical genetic and chemical tinkering has led to radical mutations in your body. You're now a Severe Mutant (1d4+3 prime mutations, 1d3+2 minor mutations, and 1d2 flaw mutations).
    **3.** Induced mutations where more controlled and resulted in you becoming a typical mutant (1d3+2 prime mutations, 1d3+2 minor mutations, and a 65% chance of 1 flaw mutation).
    **4.** Radical genetic experiments have cured you and awakened your mental power. You now count as a ghost mutant. (see page TME-22).
**9. Physical Trauma:** Injured in an accident, you were cryogenically frozen as a last ditch effort to save your life. Eventually cybernetic technology caught up with your injuries and they were repaired with cybernetic implants, while you were still in a deep sleep. If you want, you can re-roll your original occupation, as a disproportionate number of options from this section come from a military background, **roll 1d10:**
    **1-6.** You come from a military background.
    **7.** From a criminal background.
    **8.** Security background.
    **9-10.** normal career.

Cybernetics for physical trauma repair are less random than those seen in Epochian era cyborgs. To find out what cyber package you have been given roll for what it was repairing and consult the following chart. Details for each package listed below. **Roll 1d6:**

**1.** Head trauma and face: cybernetic eyes and ears, reinforcement to the skull and facial reconstruction.

**2.** Upper body trauma: cybernetic reinforced or replaced ribs, spine, heart and various other internal organs.

**3.** Arms: Spine and shoulders reinforced to accommodate two cybernetic arms (military personnel have one weapon arm (Implants #50), with a regular arm attachment.

**4.** Legs: Reinforced hips and lower back mount two cyber legs.

**5.** Tissue damage: skin and muscle replaced 1d4 extremities replaced (hands and feet) and extensive surgical repair.

**6.** Combination of two injury types. Roll twice, but re-roll this result.

**Head trauma:** 50% chance you have a partially computerized brain with 2 input and output jacks. This gives you 2 extra hazards rolls to resist mental mutations that affect the brain. Also, you get two cyber eyes, (# 30) with zoom and night-vision, military personal get a roll 1d4. 1. Substance reader/ 2. Targeting Optics / 3. Pulse laser/ 4. Holographic projector. On top of these eyes is a Communication implant (#7) basic model, and Alloy plated skull (#3) with no Appearance penalty.

**Upper body trauma,** cybernetic re-enforced or replaced ribs and spine give the character -20 DV, -0.5 MV and 10+1d10 END. Artificial heart (#4), Iron Stomach (#23) and Oxygen Supply Unit (#31).

**Arms:** Spine and shoulders reinforced to accommodate two cybernetic arms. Reinforcements give a -8 DV, and 10+1d10 END. Cyberarms have a strength of 80, give a -5 DV and punch damage of 2d8. (Military personnel have one weapon arm #50 with choice of 1 attachment and are issued a detachable lower arm #10)

**Legs:** Re-enforced hips and lower back mount two cyber legs. Reinforcements and legs give a -15 DV and 5+1d10 END, adding +6 to base speed, 3 meters to jump height (activity a #9) kick at +16 SV for 3d6+6.

**Tissue damage:** Full body skin grafts, muscle damage regrown and most fingers and toes replaced and regrown. Skin acts as Armor Enhancement (#3) roll 1d4: 1. Ballistic undersheath/ 2. Flame proof tissue/ 3. Acid proof tissue/ 4. Reflective plating. Character gets 10+1d10 Endurance and Strength and 1d10 to Appearance and is insulated against heat and cold.

**10. Project Rebirth:** Selected and vetted to rebuild the world, you received training in Wilderness Survival, and 1 random technical skill to increase your odds of survival. **Roll 1d8** for technician skill, with 1d3 points in that area of expertise: **1.** Bio / **2.** Chemical/ **3.** Computer / **4.** Electrical / **5.** Mechanical / **6.** Robotics / **7.** Cybernetics/ **8.** Junk Doctor.

**11. Project Green Thumb:** Devoted to the regrowth of Mother Earth back into a preindustrial state of nature, not implicitly anti technology but biases against the more destructive applications. You received training in Wilderness Survival, and Botany (basically Bio-technician for plants, with agriculture thrown in).

**12. Project New Dawn:** Technology is the future, robotics and cybernetics are the way forward for humanity. New Dawn members are trained to restart human technology after the coming storm. Basic training is 1d3 skill points each as a robotics technician and a cybernetics technician. All are given the basic electronic sensors and attachments needed to become full fledged cyborgs.

# Step 2: The Weird

Unless you have already ended up changed by your previous rolls, there is a 1 in 10 chance that you end up here, anyway. If plantoid and vat-brain characters are not being used, roll **1d10+2**, otherwise **1d10**.



**1. Humanoid Plant:** You died in the tube and a humanoid plant grew from your corpse. You have vague memories of a dream-like past and keep the skills of your former body. You are a corpse inhabiting plantoid. See page 115, this book.

**2. Vat-Brain:** You wake up as a brain in a vat and go from there. See page 187 of this book.

**3. Replaced by an Android.** Your body is now that of a robotic human — and you have no clue yet about the changes. No idea if there is some secret code or override in your brain, yet, you're sure you're still you, though. Create a unique android as described on page 29 of this book.

**4. Grown in the Vat, clone:** You either look like someone famous or important from the old world (9% chance), or else nobody specific and exist to fill the endless ranks of laborers needed to rebuild the world. Your history is only vague recollections of a life, the skills are real though. Clone type, roll 1d10: 1,2. Comfort. / 3-7. Labor / 8-10. Military. Clones are described on pages 19 and 20 of the TME Hub Rules.

**5. Unstable Mutations:** Your genetics have been altered in unpredictable ways and have developed a variant of Monstrous Morph (no.56, on page TME-70), usable twice per day per rank, and lasting one battle. This form has 1d4+1 prime and 1d4 physical alterations, increases your strength and endurance by 10, and adds +2 meters to movement.

**6. Nothing Happened... just kidding** your mutations are delayed and you get one Prime mutation and one minor mutation at character rank 2. Then 1 Prime Mutation at ranks 5, 8 and 11, plus 1 minor mutation at ranks 4, 6, 8, and 10. Also, you have a 25% chance of developing a flaw at ranks 3 and 12.

**7. Radically altered:** You have become a Bestial Humanoid. This will require re-rolling some stats but only physical ones (Intelligence and Willpower stay the same). Roll d100 for source book of bestial 10-50 a bestial from this book, on page XR-58, or 51-00, from those listed on page 24 of the Hub Rules book.

**8. One Really Good Mutation:** You have one prime mutation that you count as being 5 ranks higher for all the level dependent variables. If power strength is rolled on a random chart or depends on a character stat, you move two rows higher on the chart for the improved effect.

**9. Gene spliced:** Someone tinkered with your genetics and you have 1d4 physical alterations (minor mutations from page 77 of the hub rules).

**10. Well, you got lucky,** and just got genetically upgraded and add 1d20 to all stats.

**11. Ghost mutant:** Something happened to you in the tank that awoke your mind's vast potential. You have become a ghost mutant as described on page 22 of the hub rules.

**12. Nothing obvious:** Everything looks the same until you get damaged. Character has Body Regeneration (prime mutation #18, page TME-62), Increased Cellular Activity (prime mutation #50, page TME-69) and Limb Regeneration (prime mutation #52, page TME-69) and Longevity (minor mutation #95, page TME-77).

# Step 3: Stat Generation

Roll stats as normal unless you are something other than human. Trait generation table found on page 8 of this book or page 10 in the Hub Rules. Also, roll for mutations at this point if you have any.

# Step 4: Pre-Freeze Occupation

This chart replaces the Pre-Game Caste Determination chart, and gives you your pre freeze occupation. As a note, almost everyone from the modern age is literate to a basic level, can do math and count as having relic knowledge appropriate to items from their original career.

## Table XR-298/ Pre-Freeze Occupation  1d20

**1. Nobody.** You are a blank slate; you remember nothing from before except the local language, you've got a 50% chance at literacy and math skill, you gain 2d10 intelligence and have 1d3 randomly determined, miscellaneous* skills that are instinctual (you can't explain them, you just do them. You absorb knowledge like a sponge though, and take 1/2 the time to learn all new skills from teaching and gain double the number of skill points for the first 1d3+1 ranks of character advancement.

**2. Completely normal person:** You get 1d3 random miscellaneous* skills, as well as 1d6 points added to 2 stats of your choice. You were unremarkable in employment and get one or more benefits from the following list, **roll 1d20:**

1. Well you know how to work a till and count cash (math).

2. The ability to run an espresso machine and make a good cup of bean juice.

3. Two skill points in driver.

4. Fast food cooking experience.

5. You speak 1d6 other languages. See page 509 of this book for a random list of languages).

6. Accounting and knowledge of a long dead tax system.

7. Homemaker skills.

8. Teaching (basic math skills, knowledge of old world history (Historian, Pre-Apocalypse) as seen on page 215 of this book).

9. You know how to run a small business.

10. An encyclopedic knowledge of an aspect of 20th century life, like music, movies, the complete works of Shakespeare or RPGs.

11-20. Roll 1d3 Mostly Useless Old World Skills from the table on page 506 of this book.

**3. Manual Laborer:** Increase Endurance and Strength by 1d10 each, get 1 point each in the climbing and brawling skills, and 1d3 miscellaneous* skills.

**4. Student:** Gain 1d4 educated skills and 1d3 Misc skills from the table on page XR-13. Plus, add +1d6 to Intelligence and 1d6 to a stat of player's choice (other than INT).

**5. Professional Criminal:** You spent your time on the wrong side of the law earning a living from crime. You get 1 miscellaneous* skill and a roll to figure out what type of criminal you were, **roll 1d10:**

1. A con-artist, 1d3+1 points in the Lying skill, plus 1d2 points in Negotiating and Barter, also 1d6 to INT, Will and APP.

2. Burglar, 1 point in the Climbing skill, 1d3+1 points in Pick Locks, and 1d2 in the Stealth skill. Also, add 1d8 to AG and ACC.

3. Pick Pocket, 1d3+1 points in Pick pocket, 1d2 points in Stealth skill and 1 point in Lying. Add 1d8 agility and perception traits.

4. Hacker, 1d3+1 points in the Computer Technician skill, 1d2 points in Electronics Technician skill, and 1 point in the Forgery skill. Also, gain 1d8 INT and Will.

5. Gambler, 1d3+1 skill points in gambling, 1d2 points in Lying and

1 point with the Pick Pockets skill, also, add 1d8 traits points to agility and perception.

6. Thug or Muscle, 1d3+1 points in the Brawling skill, 1d2 in Weapon Expert (of choice), and 1 skill point in grapple. Add 1d6 END, STR and ACC.

7. Killer, 1d3+1 points with either the Sniper or Gun slinger skill, 1d2 points in Killer and 1 in Brawling. Improve traits by +1d8 to AG and ACC.

8. Transporter, 1d3+1 points in either the Driver or Pilot skill (player picks), 1d2 points in Mechanical Technician skill and Navigate by Stars. Add 1d8 to AG and PER traits.

9. Drug lab, 1d3+1 points in the Chemistry skill, and 1d2 points in Junk Crafter and 1 in Barter. Also add 1d8 to INT and PER.

10. Prostitution, add the Erotic arts skill, plus 1d2+1points in Disguise Artist, 1 point each in Negotiating, Lying and Barter. Add 1d10 to APP, 1d6 to AG and 1d6 to PER.

**6. Trades:** You were a skilled tradesperson, focused mainly on one area of expertise but having other talents, too. This character gets 1d4 miscellaneous* skills, +1d6 END, +1d6 INT and basic medic abilities (equivalent to Erotic Arts on the Medic Procedures Table, page TME-46). Roll 1d10 once on the following table for your main focus.

1. Driver 2 skill points (skp), mechanical technician 1 skp.

2. Mechanical technician 3 skill points

3. Computer technician 3 skill points

4. Electrical technician 3 skill points

5. Robotics technician 3 skill points

6. Gun smithing 3 skill points

7. Pilot 2 skill points and mechanical technician 1 skp

8. Maintenance worker 3 skill points in junk crafting.

9. Cybernetics expert, 3 skill points in cybernetics technician.

10. General Expert: 1 skill point in each technician area: bio, chemical, computer, electrical, mechanical, robotics and cybernetics.

**7. Prepper:** You were pretty sure the end of the world was close. By day you were a regular white-collar worker or semi skilled professional. At night and on the weekends, however, you trained to survive the collapse of society. You get the skills Wilderness Survival, 1d3 skill points in different weapon expert skills, 1 skill point in Brawling, and basic first aid skill (equivalent to Erotic Arts on the Medic Procedures Table, page TME-46) and 1d2 miscellaneous* skills. Stats increases: +1d4 to END, STR, PER and Willpower.

**8. Scientist:** You had an advanced degree and were practicing in your field when things collapsed. This character get +3d10 to INT and 4 skill points in a Technical Skill of your choice, plus 1d4 educated skills and 1d2 Misc Skills from table XR-7 / Starting Skill Set Rolls, on page 13 of this book.

**9. Athlete:** You where a professional athlete and gain +1d6 to Endurance, Strength, Agility, Accuracy and Willpower. Also, add 1d3 miscellaneous* skills and a specialty, **roll 1d8:**

1. Climber, 3 skill points in Climbing.

2. Swimmer, max out Swimming skill (pg 20 this book) and add 1d4 meters to swim speed.

3. Acrobatics, 3 skill points in Acrobatics skill, as seen on page 201 of this book.

4. Target Sports, 3 skill points in Weapon Expert with one of the following (player picks) Javelin, Rifle, Pistol, or Bow.

5. Running,. +1d6 meters movement, +1d8 to Endurance and a 1 point bonus in chases (chase rules on page 112 of the Hub Rules).

6. Wrestling, 3 skill points in grapple, +1d8 to both END and STR.

7. Boxing, 3 skill points in Brawling, plus add +1d6 to STR and Agility.

8. Combat sports, 2 skill points in Martial Arts and 1 skill point in Grappling.

*Roll on table XR-7 / Starting Skill Set Rolls, on page 13 of this book, and use the miscellaneous skills column, or whatever other column is called for.*

**10. Professional Bureaucrat:** You were part of the apparatus of government or a corporation, handling the day-to-day operation of your organization. You gain 1d8 to intelligence and willpower, 1 skill point in negotiations, an extra language (random language table on page 509 of this book) and advanced math, as well as 1d3 educated skills and 1 miscellaneous* skill.

**11. Backyard Inventor:** You were a tinker and a dreamer, building amazing and sometimes useful things. You made enough money to keep the cycle going. Add +2d8 to intelligence, 4 skill points in junk crafter, 1d4 skill points in technical skills, and 1d4 skill points in miscellaneous* skills.

**12. Celebrity:** You were famous for something. Well, almost famous or close enough to make a living at it. Be it music, acting, or any other occupation in the spotlight, you get +1d6 to WILL, INT and APP. 1 skill point in Disguise Artist, 1 skill point in Lying and 2 skill points in Performer (found on page 221, this book) and a choice of Erotic Arts or an extra skill point in Disguise, Lying or Performer, and 1 miscellaneous* skill. There is, at the GMs discretion, a slight chance that someone with knowledge of history, or your particular brand of entertainment, recognizes you from old videos, movies or musical recordings.

**13. Expert:** Pick one skill and get 1d3+3 skill points in that skill, plus roll for 1d3 educated skills, 1 miscellaneous* skill and +1d10 to the stat involved in skill, or if 2 stats then apply +1d8, or if 3 stats, +1d6 per stat. Variants on this include doctors who have 1d3+3 skill points in Medic.

**14. Security:** You were a member of the security apparatus, be they public police or private security. You get 1 skill point in brawling, 1d2 miscellaneous* skills, +1d6 endurance, +1d6 STR, 1d6 PER and basic first aid (equivalent to Erotic Arts on the Medic Procedures Table, page TME-46). Also a specialty, roll **1d4:**

1. Site security, 1 skill point each in grapple and weapon expert: club, and reduce the hazard check letter code to notice folks using stealth by one (or increase difficulty of stealth checks by those trying to sneak near this character by one tier of hazard).

2. Patrol officer, 1 skill point each in Driver, Negotiating and Weapon Expert: pistol.

3. Personal Protection, 1 skill point each in Disguise Artist, Driver and Gunslinger.

4. Tactical Response Unit. Player picks either 1 skill point each in Weapon Expert: rifles, pistols and shotguns, or 2 skill points in Sniper and 1 skill point in climbing.

**15. Revolutionary:** Rebel, terrorist, revolutionary, freedom fighter, radical — it all depends on who you asked, but somewhere along the line, violence became a part of your struggle. Training was unconventional and you're lucky if you had any professional training. As a dedicated member of your cause, you gain 1d10 Willpower and 1d3 miscellaneous* skill rolls. What you did for the revolution, **roll 1d4:**

1. Foot soldier, +1d6 Endurance, +1d4 warrior skill rolls, +1d2 criminal skill rolls.

2. Sniper, +1d6 to Agility and Accuracy, 1d3 skill points in sniper and 1d2 criminal skill rolls.

3. Agitator, +1d4 to Intelligence and Perception, 1d4 skill points in Lying, 1d4 skill points in Negotiating and 1d2 miscellaneous* skill rolls.

4. Infiltration, +1d10 to Agility, 1d4 skill points in Stealth and 1d4 skill points in Disguise Artist, and 1 skill point in knife fighting.

**16. Outdoors:** This covers professional hunters, guides, adventure tourists and anyone else who spent most their life outdoors in the wilderness. This character gets the following skills: Wilderness Survival, Navigate by Stars, 1d2 miscellaneous* skills, and +1d6 to Endurance, Accuracy and Willpower. What type of focus did your character have, **roll 1d4:**

1. Hunter, 2 skill points in tracking and 2 in Archery and 1 in Stealth, or, 2 in Sniper and 1 skill point in Weapon Expert: Rifle.

2. Guide, 3 skill points in Tracking and skill at Cooking and basic first aid (equivalent to Erotic Arts on the Medic Procedures Table, page TME-46).

3. Photographer, 2 skill points in Tracking, 1 skp in climbing and 1 skp in Electrical Technician.

4. Adventurer, 2 skill points in Climbing, +2 tiers to your swim ability, 1 skill point (skp) in Junk Crafting, plus you know 2 extra languages (see random list of languages on page 509 of this book).

**17. Military, Army:** You are a professionally trained member of a branch of your nation's military, in this case, the Army. You completed basic training and gets +1d10 to both your Endurance and Strength, 1 skill point each in Brawling, Climbing, Weapon Expert: Rifle, and basic first aid (equivalent to erotic arts on the first aid skill chart, page TME-46). You also receive a specialization, **roll 1d10:**

1. Infantry, gaining the skill of Wilderness Survival, and 2 skill points in Weapon Expert: Rifle.

2. Armor, 1 skill point each in Driver, Mechanical Technician and Weapon Expert: Gunnery (covers HMGs and vehicle mounted weapons).

3. Artillery, 2 skill points in Weapon Expert: Artillery and 1 skp in Navigate by Stars.

4. Aviation, 1 skill point each in Pilot, Mechanical and Electronics Technician.

5. Engineering, 2 skill points in Mechanical Technician, and 1 skp in Robotics.

6. Intelligence, 1 skill point each in Computer and Electronics Technician, and Communications, plus you know 1d3 extra languages (random list page 509, this book).

7. Medical, 3 skill points in the medic skill.

8. Support, 1 skill points each in Mechanical Technician, Gun Smithing and Junk Crafter.

9. Sniper, 3 skill points in the Sniper skill.

10. Recon, 1 point each in Wilderness Survival, Stealth and Navigate by Stars skills.

**18. Military, Navy:** You joined the Navy and have received basic training and a specialization. You get +1d10 trait points to Endurance, +1d6 Intelligence and +2 to swim ability. You've also gained a talent for firefighting and water rescue (unofficial and unwritten skills) plus, 1 skill point each in Brawling, Seamanship, Weapon Expert: pistol, and basic first aid (equivalent to erotic arts on the first aid skill chart). Specializations are as fallows, **roll 1d8:**

1. Naval infantry, 2 skill points in Brawling and 1 skp in Weapon Expert: rifle.

2. Aviation, 3 skill points in the Pilot skill, plus Navigate by Stars.

3. Small Boats, 2 skill points in Seamanship, 1 skill point in Mechanical Technician.

4. Engineering, 1 skill points each in Mechanical, Computer and Electrical Technician.

5. Medical, 3 skill points Medic.

6. Intelligence, 1 skill point in Communications, Computer and Electronics Technician and 1d3 you know extra languages (see page 509, this book for random list).

7. Surface Navy, 1 skill point each in Seamanship, Electronics and Computers Technician.

8. Support, 1 skill point in Mechanical Technician, Gun Smithing and Junk Crafter.

**19. Military, Air-force:** You were in the Air Force and received basic training and a specialty. Basic training gives you +1d10 to Endurance and 1d6 to Intelligence, 1 skill point each in Brawling, Climbing, Weapon Expert: Pistol and basic first aid (equivalent to Erotic Arts on the Medic Procedures Table, page TME-46). You then received specialized training, **roll 1d6:**

1. Support, 1 skill point each in Electronics and Mechanical Technician, plus 1 skp in Pilot.

2. Combat pilot, 3 skill points in Pilot and 1 rank in Weapon Expert: Aviation (this applies to weapons mounted on Aircraft).

3. Gunnery, Weapon Expert Machine Guns 1 skp, Weapon Expert: Missiles 1 skp, and 1 skill point in Pilot.

4. Paratrooper, skill with parachuting, fall training (take 4 meters off fall distance before calculating damage), 2 skill points in Weapon Expert: Rifles and 1 skill point in brawling.

*Roll on table XR-7 / Starting Skill Set Rolls, on page 13 of this book, and use the miscellaneous skills column, or whatever other column is called for.*

5. Medic, 3 skill points in Medic.

6. Space Force, 3 skill points in Pilot and familiarity with Zero G operations; PC is familiar with orbital shuttles, pg. 486.

**20. Military, Special Operations:** You where a member of your country's elite military such as Navy S.E.A.L or the SAS, etc. First pick a branch of military you came from the above three (Army, Navy or Air Force) and get all those benefits, then add +1d6 END, +1d4 to STR, Accuracy and Willpower, and 2 skill points in Weapon expert with a chosen firearm, 2 skill points in Martial Arts, 1skp in Stealth and 1 in Climbing. You are also trained in using parachutes and +1 to your swim ability.

**Roll on table XR-7 / Starting Skill Set Rolls, on page 13 of this book, and use the miscellaneous skills column, or whatever other column is called for.*

# Step 5: Starting Gear

There are 2 choices for equipment charts. The two charts cover a random list of items that were worn or put into the popsicle person's cryo tank at the time of hibernation. Those found in unprepared cryo-tanks include those who were frozen for reasons 1 to 7 on Table XR-296/ Why?, back on page 501. Those in Prepared cryo-tanks include those preserved for reasons 8 to 12. Your GM has final say, also backyard inventors always roll on prepared tanks chart.

## Table XR-299/ Unprepared Cryo-Tanks Roll 1d12

**1.** Nothing but dust. Basic pants and shirt only.

**2.** You find a pack of gum in one of your pockets.

**3.** At least you still have your watch on. Also, it works, tells time, temperature and direction like a compass.

**4.** Swiss Army knife in your pockets and very nice pants, that provide a -2 DV bonus.

**5.** Sun glasses, watch, and a pack of cigarettes, and 2d6 wooden matches.

**6.** Relic switchblade knife.

**7.** Concealed .22 caliber pistol in a holster with 1 full 18 shot magazine and one extra with 3d6 rounds loaded in it.

**8.** Mini laser with one full battery.

**9.** Armored survival suit reinforced for adverse conditions. This suit gives the wearer DV -4 add +1 to unarmed damage attacks, includes a first aid kit.

**10.** Basic survival kit. This kit includes a survival blanket, a fire starting tool, 16m of cord, a 1 liter canteen, 3 Days MREs (6 total, see details on page 436 of this book), pen and paper, a knife and a basic first aid kit. This is all packed in a backpack.

**11.** Basic survival kit, as described in roll 10, above, plus one relic from WC-RC (hub rules page 207).

**12.** Armored survival suit (From roll 9), basic survival kit (from roll 10) and an auto pistol with 2 full 20 shot mags.

## Table XR-300 / Prepared Cryo-Tanks   Roll 1d20

**1.** Junk, useless trash is piled in and around your tank. If you are a junk crafter you can make 1d4 items from this unexpected bonanza.

**2.** Nothing but basic clothing, pants, shirt and basic underwear. No footwear at all (this clothing gives basic environmental protection and pockets).

**3.** Basic clothing and a really good pair of boots. Smart fit, +0.25 meters of speed, and a -2 DV bonus.

**4.** Jumpsuit, better insulation with shoes and gloves. It's tough and gives a -2 DV bonus to the wearer.

**5.** Jumpsuit with a smartphone with a full charge, no signal and one number pre programmed in it. See smartphones on page 449 of this book.

**6.** Basic survival kit. This kit includes a survival blanket, a fire starting tool, 16m cord, a 1L canteen, 3 Days MREs (6 total, details on flavor page 436), pen and paper, a knife and a basic first aid kit. This is all packed in a backpack. You also have basic clothes and shoes.

**7.** Survival Bag. As basic survival kit, from roll 6, above, but add a flashlight (hand crank to charge), water purification kit, 20m of rope. Also included is $100 in relic cash, and a rather inaccurate local map.

**8.** Go Bag, survival kit as in roll 6, above, plus a set of warm clothes, 2 pairs of extra socks, a hand cranked radio, a whistle and a one person tent.

**9.** Go Bag, survival kit as in roll 6, above, with field medical kit (pg. TME-199).

**10.** Armed Go Bag. This is a survival kit as in roll 6, above, with an auto pistol, 2 full 20 round mags and a holster.

**11.** Archery Bag. Basic survival kit from roll 6 above, a compound bow and 20 arrows.

**12.** Hunter's Bag. Basic survival kit from roll 6, and a survival rifle with a sling and 2 full, 10 round mags.

**13.** Angry Go bag. As armed go bag from roll 10, above, but with 1d4 fragmentation, 1d4 tear gas and 1d4 smoke grenades.

**14.** Shotgun Go bag. As armed go bag from roll 10, with 1 pump shotgun and 20 shells in a bandoleer.

**15.** Bag of Blades. Basic survival kit, as in roll 6, but add 1d10 knives, 1d10 throwing knives, 1d6 machetes or short swords and 1d4 swords (pick long swords, sabers or rapiers) also sheaths for each blade and a sharpening kit.

**16.** Go bag, from roll 6, and a loyal pocket robot (Hub Rules page 180) keyed to your DNA.

**17.** Bag of random melee weapons. 1d6 weapons from WC-SS, WC-LA and WC-SM (page 206 Hub Rules).

**18.** Riot Armor Bag. Full suit of riot armor with helmet and a stun stick with full charge and a pair of handcuffs.

**19.** Armed go bag, as in roll 10, above, with an army helmet, ballistic vest and one relic from WC-R (page 207 hub rules).

**20.** Go bag, from roll 6, with scrap relic armor and one roll on TME-1-66 (fully armed PC relic, page TME-97) and a combat knife.

# Step 6: Finishing Touches and Notes

Here, you will calculate things like SV and DV

Popsicle people are survivors and refugees from a forgotten age. As such, the new state of the world will be confusing and frightening to them, and they're proverbial fish out of water. This will make them targets for some, especially opportunistic folks who will want to know about the old world for good or ill, such as the locations of old weapons and secrets of technology that the cryo-hibernator may or may not know about.

Also, there is the issue of disease and an immune system unused to ravages of The Mutant Epoch. After this PC's first exposure to a group of Epochian natives of 1 to 4 (1d4) days into extended contact, have the popsicle person make a Willpower based, Type E hazard check to avoid the flu (HUB rules, page 126). Of course, feel free to ignore this bit. *DS*

# Appendix 4: Mostly Useless Old World Occupations

These have no combat applications, but depending on the campaign, and where this character travels to, might be much appreciated, especially in one of the growing slum cities of the Epochian era. Oftentimes, characters brought out of cryo-sleep and who once existed in the old world will have two or more of these skills. Roll 1d100:

## Table XR-301/ Mostly Useless Old World Skills — Roll 1d100

**01.** 3d Miniature Sculptor and 3d printing specialist
**02.** Accountant
**03.** Administrative Assistant
**04.** Adoption Caseworker
**05.** Android Detection Specialist
**06.** AI Human Advocate
**07.** Art Therapist
**08.** Bank Teller
**09.** Call Center Representative
**10.** Cashier
**11.** Chauffeur
**12.** Coffee Roaster
**13.** Makeup Artist
**14.** Coffee Shop Barista
**15.** Community Association Manager
**16.** Compensations and Benefits Manager
**17.** Corporate Lobbyist
**18.** Cryogenic Chamber Maintenance Worker
**19.** Custodian of Safe Injection Site
**20.** Customer Service Representative
**21.** Day Care Worker
**22.** Deep Fake videographer
**23.** Delivery Truck Driver
**24.** Dental Hygienist
**25.** Digital Marketer
**26.** Drug and Alcohol Addiction Councilor
**27.** Editor
**28.** Educational Conformity Officer
**29.** Elder Caregiver
**30.** Environmental Sustainability Manager
**31.** Event Planner
**32.** Fast Food Worker
**33.** Feng Shui Consultant
**34.** Film Director
**35.** Financial Adviser
**36.** Flight Attendant
**37.** Food Bank Administrator
**38.** Fundraising Manager
**39.** Game Designer: Roll 1d10: 1-8. Computer and Phone Games / 9. Tabletop RPGs / 10. Tabletop Boardgames
**40.** General Office Clerk
**41.** Golf Caddy
**42.** Government Clerk
**43.** Graphic Designer
**44.** Hairstylist
**45.** Home Environmental Compliance Officer
**46.** Homeless Outreach Agent
**47.** Hospice and Euthanization Attendant
**48.** Housekeeper
**49.** Human to Mutant Liaison Coordinator
**50.** Human Resources Manager
**51.** Hydroponic Agricultural Worker
**52.** Interior Designer
**53.** Janitorial Engineer
**54.** Laser Hair Removal Technician
**55.** Lawyer
**56.** Librarian
**57.** Loan Officer
**58.** Marketing Manager
**59.** Massage Therapist
**60.** Nail Technician
**61.** News Caster
**62.** Pacifism and Civil Disarmament Advocate
**63.** Paralegal
**64.** Parking Bylaw Officer
**65.** Personal Shopper
**66.** Pet Store Salesperson
**67.** Photo Editor
**68.** Photographer
**69.** Poet
**70.** Political Aide
**71.** Politician
**72.** Postsecondary Education Administrator
**73.** Printing Press Operator
**74.** Public Relations (PR) Professional
**75.** Real Estate Agent
**76.** Retail Store Greeter
**77.** Ride-Hailing Driver
**78.** Secretary
**79.** Sewage Treatment Specialist
**80.** Social Conformity Camera Operator
**81.** Social Conformity Compliance Officer
**82.** Social Justice and Equity Liaison
**83.** Social Media Manager
**84.** Social Worker
**85.** Speech Pathologist
**86.** Stock Broker
**87.** Stock Market Investor
**88.** Tax Department Agent
**89.** Taxi Driver
**90.** Tour Guide
**91.** Travel Agent
**92.** Urban and Regional Planner
**93.** Vaccine Adoption Enforcement Officer
**94.** Waiter/Waitress
**95.** Wardrobe Consultant
**96.** Warehouse Worker
**97.** Website Designer
**98.** Wedding Coordinator
**99.** Yoga Instructor
**100.** Youth Counselor

# Appendix 5: Property and Estates
*by Timothy Berriault*

As players rapidly accumulate ranks and wealth through successful relic discoveries in the chrome caves and ruins of the old world, there comes a point when they can't easily dispense with the fortunes of their labors. Many of these grave diggers look towards property acquisition as a means to fulfill some reward for their many efforts, perhaps even building their own town as a means to grow a legacy that could surpass their wild adventures.

Publications used in this production are as follows:
- The Mutant Epoch hub rules
- The Crossroads Region Gazetteer

## Acquiring Property

The Crossroads Region has several prime locations that present their own strengths and weaknesses with accompanying plot hooks and adventure potential for a GM who aspires to breathe more life into their setting than an average random table can provide. For the sake of brevity, this document will focus on one settlement in the Crossroads Region, Sandbarra, for acquiring land and building a fortified homestead.

As detailed on page 67 of The Crossroads Region, a piece of property on the Barter River of 100x100m sells for 2000 silver pieces with a 40sp yearly property tax to the city. Each 100sqm area will yield 1 cash or produce crop, supplying the growing settlement with funds or food to ensure its healthy growth and profitability. It takes 4 of these small territories to be sufficient in feeding a family of 4 and yield some profit, or to support 8 individuals and yield no profit.

The land must be supplied with a fortified homestead capable of housing 4 families. This fortification is patrolled by Freehold Rangers with quarters set aside for their use with the sponsoring family responsible for their reasonable feeding, accommodation and to provide chores such as clothing mending, laundering and conversation that are otherwise unavailable to these rangers while they're on patrol.

## Produce, Profit and Production

For a piece of land to be productive, it must be sewn with a profitable crop and that crop being sell-able in the local market that is not consumed by the farmers themselves. Each household estate has an Agriculture Skill, similar to player skills to perform different tasks and represented by the chart below. A random family has 2d6 -1 skill at agriculture, any player with the pre-game caste of 'Farmer' or the skill of 'Homesteader' has 2d6 -1 skill points.

Add Intelligence + Willpower + Strength, divided by 3 for Agriculture Skill trait. Average Farmer has a Trait of 30.

| Agriculture Skill Points | Fertile Soil | Rocky Soil | Unproductive Soil | Ruins | Irradiated Soil |
|---|---|---|---|---|---|
| Nil | D | F | F | H | K |
| 1 | C | E | E | G | J |
| 2 | B | D | D | F | I |
| 3 | A | C | C | E | H |
| 4 | A* | B | B | D | G |
| 5 | A** | A | A | C | F |

* Can Re-roll
** Can Re-roll twice

Failure on this chart represents a poor harvest without profit. The player must roll again to determine if enough produce was collected to provide for the families themselves. Failing a second time indicates a crop collapse and without supplied goods from the outside, a family will starve to death. If starvation occurs roll 1d4 -1 (0 to 3) for each family, the resulting number is how many members die of starvation. A possible score of 0 represents the family finding just enough through hunting and foraging to survive to the next month. A productive 100x100m plot of land yields 1d100sp a month while it is worked. This amount can be adjusted by the use of the Barter Skill.

A single family of 4 can only ever work 4 100x100m plots at a time for them to be productive. Players who are employing sharecroppers receive only 75% of any profit made from any land they own, the rest going to the family working the land. Utilizing slaves and forced labor, while despicable, will allow an extra 100x100m area to be farmed per month per unwilling worker.

## Fortifications and Protection of Estates

Fortified homesteads are a common site in The Mutant Epoch, each being close enough to a settlement's protective walls to retreat towards in the event of a large siege but capable of holding their own against the dangerous wildlife and minor raids of primitive tribals. In addition, these homesteads act as secure checkpoints for weary soldiers of the Freehold Rangers, each homestead required to provide reasonable accommodations for any passing soldier who in return removes animal or sapient threats from the immediate territory. Farmers are armed using Weapon Code WC-FA, found below.

### 1d10 Farmer* WC-FA
1. Club
2. Hatchet
3. Shovel
4. Pitch Fork
5. Pickax
6. Sickle
7. Scythe
8. Staff
9. Crossbow with 1d20 bolts
10. Musket with 1d20 shots

*Plus Knife*

### Farmer Encounter Table

| Human Type | Farmer Man | Farmer Woman | Farmer Teen | Farmer Child | Farm Dog |
|---|---|---|---|---|---|
| DV | -3 | -3 | -7 | 0 | -8 |
| Armor Worn | Furs/Skins | Furs/Skins | Furs/Skin | None | None |
| End | 20+1d20 | 15+1d20 | 10+1d20 | 2d6 | 5+1d6 |
| MV | 5.75 | 5.75 | 5.75 | 6 | 11 |
| SV | 01-50 | 50 | 43 | 30 | 50 |
| Weapon Code | WC-FA | WC-FA | WC-FA | 60% Knife | Bite 1d6 |
| Valuables | VP | VP | VP | Nil | Nil |
| EF | 15 | 13 | 10 | 3 | 10 |
| Morale | Average | Average | Poor | Poor | Average |
| Note | Nil | Nil | Nil | Nil | Pg. 152 TME |

A typical Fortified Homestead style 'estate' is constructed of scrap material, felled timber, field stone, simple earth works and palisade. The palisade, constructed of timbers, is stout enough to repel animals and most would-be vagabonds, though is susceptible to fire and not designed to repulse a committed assault. The earthworks channel an attack into a sudden depression and hinged vertical swinging gate, which requires anyone entering the assistance of a rest pole to prevent the several hundred kilograms of solid wood from crashing down on them. Anyone on the inside has a raised position and, with the aid of a sharpened stick, can easily fend off an unprepared foe attempting to force their way within. The swinging gate can be lifted off its hinges from within easily enough and stowed during the day when no attack is imminent, making coming and going from the interior easy enough. This swinging gate is not typical of most homesteads and is a byproduct of the constant reptilius raids Sandbarra is subject to.

Peasants are not accustomed to the privacy afforded to more civilized folk, and the living spaces and dining accommodations in a fortified homestead are often communal. A centrally located dining hall is abutted to a kitchen with 2 to 4 clay ovens. If the building has multiple floors, the living quarters are often just above the kitchens. If not, they are as closely packed around them for the warmth they provide during the short but cold southern winter. Less affluent homesteads will usually only have an exterior privy and barn for labor animals while the rest of the arable ground within is taken over with herb gardens for the kitchens and medicinal remedies, with the rest being clawed over by chickens or children.

More affluent homesteads might have a central gazebo for recreation and sermonizing and even open ground for hosting larger parties of guests or a mustering ground for visiting patrols of Rangers, these Homesteads being the favored stops for most Freehold troops as they are more like small forts and offer considerable protection.

A small homestead can expect to have a stout palisade of felled timber, where available, or scrap material salvaged from ancient roadways and buildings. In the absence of either field stone, adobe is common in the Pacific southwest. Larger homesteads will attempt to build a redoubt with the assistance of Freehold Rangers to increase their defensive capabilities, equipping these with elevated firing positions that double as a scout's platform and signaling post.

Besides a palisade, a homestead is much improved with earthworks of 2-3 meters in elevation surrounding the fortification and raising the palisade itself up several more meters. This doubles as an improved anchor for the palisades sturdiness as well as an additional obstacle that can be further complicated, with sharpened stakes facing outward from the earthwork wall breaking up concentrated charges of massed bodies.

These constructions are not a simple undertaking and the expansion of any fortified position is the labor of a community who wishes to extend their available farming and defensive capabilities. The maintenance of such a position itself can distract from the near constant attention farming requires, though its daily upkeep is paramount to inform the eyes of potential raiders who designate their targets by the softness of their defenses and disorganization of its inhabitants. GMs can weave this into a narrative when describing reptilius raids or when designing an adventure with a fortified homestead or estate in mind as an adventure location. *TB*

# Appendix 6: Standards of Beauty in an Ugly Age

*by Graeme Hallett*

In The Mutant Epoch, characters have an appearance score used to determine how attractive they are to members of the opposite sex. The scale of beauty is based on the beauty of pure-strain humans. Mutations often reduce this score. This means that the best looking characters in the game tend to be those with few or no mutations. Everyone is attracted to pure-strains, and repelled by mutants, even the mutants themselves. In this article, we will examine why this is so; why don't mutants find other mutants attractive? We will also look at the effects of beauty to society in The Mutant Epoch setting.

Why are mutants not attracted to other mutants? It is a well-known fact that the human standards of beauty are extremely flexible. Some cultures find enormous noses sexy, some are attracted to short limbs, some to long, and some find any woman below 120 kg to be far too skinny. People are attracted to those who resemble the people they grew up around. A Caucasian child adopted by a Black family might find Black people more attractive than Caucasian people, and vice versa. So, if you grow up in a society where all the best looking girls weigh 200kg, this becomes your standard of beauty. Why does this not apply to mutants?

The mutants in The Mutant Epoch are still mentally human; their bodies are warped, but their minds function in exactly the same way as a pure-strain human's. They should acquire their standard of beauty by imprinting on the people around them, just like pure-strain humans do. If all the people in your family and neighborhood have eyes on stalks and giant pincers, it is reasonable to speculate that, given the imprintable nature of beauty, you would find long eye-stalks and polished pincers incredibly sexy.

This isn't the way it works, however, because though the human beauty template is flexible, it isn't infinitely flexible. Imagine that you were raised by Chimpanzees. Could you find them attractive, if it was all you had ever seen? I think it is just barely possible. What about wolves? Ravens? Lobsters? As one gets further and further away from human, the possibility of imprinting a standard of beauty from the creatures surrounding you gets slimmer. If we imprinted indiscriminately on objects in our environment, humans would have all sort of trouble, falling in love with trees and cardboard boxes. There must be a point at which the beings around you don't count as human enough to find attractive.

This is what happens in The Mutant Epoch. Nobody imprints a mutant standard of beauty because mutations break the instinctual definition of "human".

There is a second force at work here that makes mutants physically repellent. Some of the universal beauty markers are indicators of health, or lack of disease: clear skin, good teeth, thick hair, body odor, etc. Your brain is hard-wired to find these things attractive because they indicate a healthy, disease-free person.

Likewise, humans are repelled by signs of sickness, and this repulsion is powerful. Take zits for example. People find them unattractive because they resemble the pustules from diseases like smallpox and the plague. They are harmless, and we know they are harmless, but our repulsion-from-disease brain system is so powerful that it forces us to find them ugly, despite the fact that we know they can't hurt us. The brain-wiring that repels us from the diseased and the unhealthy is indiscriminate. When you ponder the damage that diseases like the black plague can do, it makes sense that evolution would set you up to want to get as far away from sick people as possible.

Many mutations resemble sickness closely enough that anything with a human mind finds them repellent, including the mutants themselves. Even though some mutations are useful and even powerful, the mind still interprets them as defects, and reacts accordingly.

Every person in The Mutant Epoch is attracted to pure-strain humans. Pure-strain human female slaves fetch unbelievably high prices in any slave market, and this has a serious effect on the way that societies in The Mutant Epoch conduct themselves. Slavers and raiders are always looking for opportunities to take slaves from pure-strain settlements. The high price of these slaves means that they can afford to spend money, manpower, and equipment pursuing them, so attacks on pure-strain settlements are usually far worse than those on mutant settlements. Pure-strain families that can afford it always hire a bodyguard for their children. Those that cannot often disguise their children as mutants, either with makeup and prosthetics. In extreme cases, pure-strain children are mutilated to make them unattractive. One small town, unable to defend itself from the constant raids, condition its citizens to suicide if they were captured, as a way of deterring slavers.

An attractive pure-strain woman without serious protection should be very, very worried.

The aggression of slavers towards pure-strain communities is part of what creates animosity and violence between mutant and pure-strain. It polarizes the two halves of humanity. Worse still, it gives propaganda material to human supremacists. Slavers represent a small proportion of mutant-kind, but their actions give human-supremacists a tool to inspire hate for mutants.

In The Mutant Epoch, beauty is reserved for the genetically privileged. The market forces created by the rarity of beauty drive the slave trade, and cause misery, hate, murder, and genocide. *GH*

# Appendix 7: Languages

The Common language spoken by a character, and the human NPCs in an area, is pretty much the same as whatever was spoken in that region prior to the final civilizational collapse. Of course, new forms of slang, cuss words, and terminology have arisen to describe the twisted environment, creatures, and mutant abilities which Epochian era people see about them, and for any bunker dweller or space inhabiting human accustomed to the old manner of speaking, these occupants of the mutated new earth might be hard to understand.

Many humanoids and intelligent animals, such as bipedal rats or reptilius, speak their own crude language which almost no human can speak — for often the sounds these creatures make are themselves impossible to pronounce without the facial and vocal capabilities of these evolving species. Beings who evolved from humans, such as skullocks, warmorts, skinners, garnocks and countless other varieties of sub-humans, did once speak the local human language. Over time, and through both isolation and a desire to form their own cultural and linguistic identity, these humanoids actively developed their own language — although to the trained ear, this new language is simply a highly contorted, jargon rich, and typically simplified variant of the old world language.

Still, many nomadic traders, savages and those who lived among or near such humanoids, these humanoid languages are occasionally learned, and a starting character or NPC might possess enough of the sub-human tongue to adequately speak it. Of course, most humanoids are often perplexed to encounter humanoids — especially excavators — who have among them somebody who speaks their language, and instead of the immediate impulse to violence, any dialog with the barbaric strains of humanoids can lead to negotiations, trade deals, pacts and even alliances, although more often than not, the simple exchange of gifts of booze and rare foods stuffs from human travelers can earn them free passage, a crude map, or invaluable intelligence on the part of the humanoids.

Certain strains of sub humans, particularly skullocks, are prone to being swayed away from fighting when faced with somebody who can speak 'skullish' and will usually opt to trade instead of fight, unless the interlopers are within the tribal stronghold or blood has already been shed between the two sides. Other humanoids, like skinners, garnocks, and warmorts, are exceptionally hard to deal with even if one can speak with them, with these mutant strains sometimes offended by the fact that their manner of speaking has been 'stolen' by an old kind trespasser.

Old world languages, of which there are some 7139 or more, are spoken as the common language in an area, however sometimes a family or tribe came from another part of the world, often generations before during the great migrations of desperate refugees, troop deployments, invasions, and displacements of people from every corner of the earth. In many households or settlements people grew up speaking a traditional language handed down to them by previous generations, although they also speak the common local language. For this purpose, a random list of the more common old world languages has been supplied here.

New characters, as well as NPCs when a GM needs to establish if a person the player character's meet speaks another language, can use the list below. Based on the caste of the character, determine what, if any other languages the character knows. For each other language known, roll a d6 for the degree of expertise in the language, with 1 being only a rudimentary knowledge and a 6 being an exert knowledge. Any score of 4 to 6 means the character can also read and write that language — although no humanoid race mentioned above has a written version of their speech.

When determining a second language, if one is rolled that is already the common language in an area, such as English in the Crossroads Region over old Los Angeles) then re-roll another language on the same list (humanoid, common, or less common).

## Table XR-302 // Languages Spoken

| Character's Pre-Game Caste | No Other Languages* | Knows Another language | Knows 2 or more other languages (1+1d6) |
|---|---|---|---|
| **Hub Rules Castes** | | | |
| Slave, Laborer | 01-89 | 90-99 | 00 |
| Slave, Kitchen Hand | 01-85 | 86-98 | 99,00 |
| Slave, Personal Servant | 01-72 | 73-96 | 97-00 |
| Slave, Whore | 01-87 | 88-98 | 99,00 |
| Slave, Court Attendant | 01-38 | 39-63 | 64-00 |
| Slave, Gladiator | 01–91 | 92-99 | 00 |
| Fisher | 01-88 | 89-98 | 99,00 |
| Hunter | 01-89 | 90-98 | 99,00 |
| Miner | 01-87 | 88-97 | 98-00 |
| Logger | 01-88 | 89-98 | 99,00 |
| Farmer | 01-86 | 87-97 | 98-00 |
| Nomad | 01-69 | 70-93 | 94-00 |
| Trader | 01-27 | 28-82 | 83-00 |
| Crafts person | 01-83 | 84-95 | 96-00 |
| Student | 01-36 | 37-88 | 89-00 |
| Scribe | 01-04 | 05-26 | 27-00 |
| Technician | 01-42 | 43-79 | 80-00 |
| Street Urchin | 01-87 | 88-99 | 00 |
| Street Thug | 01-86 | 87-98 | 99,00 |
| Raider | 01-85 | 86-97 | 98-00 |
| Pirate | 01-81 | 82-95 | 96-00 |
| Thief | 01-86 | 87-97 | 98-00 |
| Assassin | 01-84 | 85-96 | 97-00 |
| Draftee | 01-87 | 88-98 | 99,00 |
| Militia Soldier | 01-86 | 87-98 | 99,00 |
| Watchman | 01-85 | 86-97 | 98-00 |
| Infantry | 01-87 | 88-98 | 99,00 |
| Calvary | 01-85 | 86-97 | 98-00 |
| Mercenary | 01-58 | 59-85 | 86-00 |
| Elite Soldier | 01-43 | 44-78 | 79-00 |
| **Expansion Rules Castes** | | | |
| Aeronaut | 01-34 | 36-73 | 74-00 |
| Animal Herder | 01-61 | 62-94 | 95-00 |
| Blacksmith | 01-72 | 73-96 | 97-00 |
| Bounty Hunter | 01-39 | 40-95 | 96-00 |
| Bunker Dweller | 01-12 | 13-77 | 78-00 |
| Caravaneer | 01-24 | 25-83 | 84-00 |
| Carpenter | 01-86 | 87-98 | 99,00 |
| Cultist | 01-73 | 74-96 | 97-00 |
| Fuel Keeper | 01-76 | 77-93 | 94-00 |
| Healer | 01-68 | 69-94 | 95-00 |
| Hooch Brewer | 01-63 | 64-94 | 95-00 |
| Hooker | 01-78 | 79-93 | 94-00 |
| Junk-Doctor | 01-19 | 20-79 | 80-00 |
| Repairer | 01-57 | 58-92 | 93-00 |
| Scavenger | 01-48 | 49-89 | 90,00 |
| Teacher | 01-08 | 09-66 | 67-00 |
| Technician, Cybernetic | 01-23 | 24-73 | 74-00 |
| Wastelander | 01-61 | 62-87 | 88-00 |
| Wastrel | 01-85 | 86-98 | 99,00 |
| Water Keeper | 01-83 | 84-97 | 98-00 |

*The character only knows their own local language.

## Table XR-303 / Language Spoken
### Roll 1d100

| | |
|---|---|
| 01-06. | Humanoid, see table XR 304. |
| 07-88. | Common Old World (100 million or more speakers on 2021). See table XR-305. |
| 89-00. | Rare Old World (Under 100 million speakers). See table XR-306. |

## Table XR-304 / Humanoid Languages and Slang Dialects   Roll 1d100

| | |
|---|---|
| 01-44. | Skullock (Skullish) |
| 45-54. | Garnock |
| 55-58. | Warmort |
| 59-61. | Skinner |
| 62-66. | Moaner |
| 67-71. | Underfoot |
| 72-75. | Bipedal Rat Chatter |
| 76-80. | Reptilius Hissing |
| 81-83. | Abhorra Speak |
| 84,85. | Deepkin |
| 86.87. | Krenth |
| 88,89. | Oinker Snorts |
| 90,91. | Wolfur (Dogboy Speak) |
| 92,93. | Nubinz Nonsense |
| 94.95. | Piffer |
| 96,97. | Rubble Imp |
| 98-00. | Skayl |

## Table XR-305 / Common Old World Languages   Roll 1d100

| | |
|---|---|
| 01-05. | Bengali |
| 06-14. | Chinese, Mandarin |
| 15,16. | Chinese, Wu (China) |
| 17,18. | Chinese, Yue (China) |
| 19-24. | English |
| 25-27. | French |
| 28-30. | German |
| 31-36. | Hindi (India) |
| 37-40. | Japanese |
| 41-43. | Javanese (Indonesia, Java, Bali) |
| 44-46. | Korean |
| 47-49. | Italian |
| 50-52. | Marathi (India) |
| 53-58. | Portuguese |
| 59-61. | Polish |
| 62-66. | Russian |
| 67-75. | Spanish |
| 76-79. | Tamil (India) |
| 80-83. | Telugu (India) |
| 84-89. | Turkish |
| 90-92. | Ukrainian |
| 93-96. | Urdu (Pakistan) |
| 97-00. | Vietnamese |

## Table XR-306 / Rare Old World Languages
### Roll 1d100

| | |
|---|---|
| 01. | Amharic (Ethiopia) |
| 02. | Arabic, Algerian Spoken |
| 03,04. | Arabic, Egyptian Spoken |
| 05. | Arabic, Mesopotamian Spoken (Iraq) |
| 06. | Arabic, Moroccan Spoken |
| 07. | Arabic, Najdi Spoken (Saudi Arabia) |
| 08. | Arabic, North Levantine Spoken (Syria) |
| 09. | Arabic, Saidi Spoken (Egypt) |
| 10. | Arabic, Sanaani Spoken (Yemen) |
| 11. | Arabic, Sudanese Spoken |
| 12. | Arabic, Tunisian Spoken |
| 13. | Assamese (India) |
| 14. | Awadhi (India) |
| 15. | Azerbaijani, North (Azerbaijan) |
| 16. | Azerbaijani, South (Iran) |
| 17. | Belarusan (Belarus) |
| 18. | Bhojpuri (India) |
| 19. | Bulgarian (Bulgaria) |
| 20. | Burmese (Myanmar) |
| 21. | Cebuano (Philippines) |
| 22. | Chhattisgarhi (India) |
| 23. | Chinese, Gan |
| 24,25. | Chinese, Hakka |
| 26,27. | Chinese, Jinyu |
| 28. | Chinese, Min Bei |
| 29,30. | Chinese, Min Nan |
| 31. | Chinese, Xiang |
| 32. | Chittagonian (Bangladesh) |
| 33. | Czech |
| 34. | Deccan (India) |
| 35. | Dutch (Netherlands) |
| 36,37. | Farsi, Western (Iran) |
| 38. | Fulfulde, Nigerian (Nigeria) |
| 39,40. | Greek (Greece) |
| 41,42. | Gujarati (India) |
| 43. | Haitian Creole French (Haiti) |
| 44. | Haryanvi (India) |
| 45. | Hausa (Nigeria) |
| 46. | Hungarian (Hungary) |
| 47,48. | Igbo (Nigeria) |
| 49. | Ilocano (Philippines) |
| 50,51. | Indonesian (Indonesia) |
| 52,53. | Kannada (India) |
| 54. | Kazakh (Kazakhstan) |
| 55. | Lombard (Italy) |
| 56. | Madura (Indonesia, Java, Bali) |
| 57. | Magahi (India) |
| 58. | Maithili (India) |
| 59. | Malagasy (Madagascar) |
| 60,61. | Malay (Malaysia, Peninsular) |
| 62,63. | Malayalam (India) |
| 64. | Marwari (India) |
| 65,66. | Nepali (Nepal) |
| 67,68. | Oriya (India) |
| 69. | Oromo, West-Central (Ethiopia) |
| 70,71. | Panjabi, Eastern (India) |
| 72,73. | Panjabi, Western (Pakistan) |
| 74. | Pashto, Northern (Pakistan) |
| 75. | Pashto, Southern (Afghanistan) |
| 76,77. | Romanian (Romania) |
| 78. | Rwanda (Rwanda) |
| 79. | Saraiki (Pakistan) |
| 80,81. | Serbo-Croatian (Yugoslavia) |
| 82. | Sindhi (Pakistan) |
| 83,84. | Sinhala (Sri Lanka) |
| 85. | Somali (Somalia) |
| 86,87. | Sunda (Indonesia) |
| 88. | Swedish (Sweden) |
| 89,90. | Tagalog (Philippines) |
| 91. | Tatar (Russia) |
| 92-94. | Thai (Thailand) |
| 95. | Uyghur (China) |
| 96. | Uzbek, Northern (Uzbekistan) |
| 97,98. | Yoruba (Nigeria) |
| 99. | Zhuang, Northern (China) |
| 00. | Zulu (South Africa) |

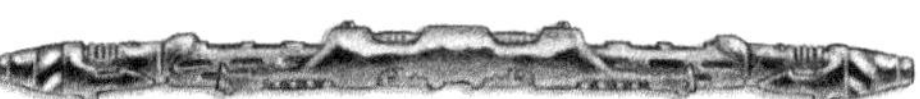

# Appendix 8: Expanded Character Sheets

# The Mutant Epoch™
*Role Playing Game*

Character Name

Player:
Game Master:
**Character Type:**

Date Rolled:
Generation System:
Pre-Play Caste:

Experience Factors:
**Rank:**
PC's Faction:

*Healing Rate*

Endurance

Strength — DMG Mod: — Range Mod: — %

Agility — MV Mod:

Accuracy — SV Mod:

Intelligence

Willpower

Perception — Initiative:

Appearance

**Base Strike Value:**

| Protection | DV | Move | Type |
|---|---|---|---|
| Agility Mod: | | | |
| Armor Worn: | | | |
| Helmet Worn: | | | |
| Shield Used: | | | |
| Dodge Skill: | | | |
| Other: | | | |
| Other: | | | |

**Defense Value:**

*Portrait or Insignia*

**Movement Rate**: Base:     Armored:     Other:

| Attack Mode | SV | Rate | Range | Damage | Ammo or Uses | Skill pts. | Skill Adds SV Mod. | DMG |
|---|---|---|---|---|---|---|---|---|
| | | | | | | | | |
| | | | | | | | | |
| | | | | | | | | |
| | | | | | | | | |
| | | | | | | | | |
| | | | | | | | | |
| | | | | | | | | |

## Mutations, Implants & Skills

Personality:

Gender: — Sexual Orientation:

Age: — Birthday:

Weight: — kg — Height: — cm

Skin Color: — Hair: — Eye:

Other Features:

Handed:

Swimming Ability:

Read & Write?:

Do Math?:

Religion:

Languages Spoken:

Diseases or Parasites?:

Cancer?:

Radiation Exposure:

**Equipment** — *Starting Pack Code:*

Days Rations: — Liters Water:

Bounty on PC's Head?:

Debts:

Valuables Carried:

Outland Arts .com™

# The Mutant Epoch™ Role Playing Game — Abomination

Player:     Game Master:     Name     Pre-Play Caste:

Date Rolled:     Generation System:     PC's Faction:

Experience Factors:     Rank:

**Endurance** /

**Strength**   DMG Mod:   Range Mod:   %

**Agility**   MV Mod:

**Accuracy**   SV Mod:

**Intelligence**

**Willpower**

**Perception**   Initiative:

**Appearance**

Base Strike Value:

Healing Rate

| Protection | DV | Move | Type |
|---|---|---|---|
| Agility Mod: | | | |
| Armor Worn: | | | |
| Helmet Worn: | | | |
| Shield Used: | | | |
| Dodge Skill: | | | |
| Other: | | | |
| Other: | | | |

Defense Value:

Portrait or Insignia

Movement Rate: Base:   Armored:   Other:

| Attack Mode | SV | Rate | Range | Damage | Ammo or Uses | Skill pts. | Skill Adds SV Mod. | DMG |
|---|---|---|---|---|---|---|---|---|
| Human-Like Arm | | | | | | | | |
| | | | | | | | | |
| | | | | | | | | |
| | | | | | | | | |
| | | | | | | | | |
| | | | | | | | | |

## Abomination Features

Body Structure:

Locomotion:

Optical:

Auditory:

Olfactory:

Mouth & Taste:

Touch:

Appendages:

Additional Details:

## Mutations, Skills and More

---

Personality:   Sexual Orientation:

Gender:   Reproduction:

Age:   Birthday:

Weight:   kg   Height:   cm

Skin Color:   Hair:   Eye:

Other Features:

Handed:

Swimming Ability:

Read & Write?:

Do Math?:

Religion:

Languages Spoken:

Diseases or Parasites?:

Cancer?:

Radiation Exposure:

**Equipment**   Starting Pack Code:

Days Rations:   Liters Water:

Origin Story:

Bounty on PC's Head?:

Debts:

Valuables Carried:

Outland Arts.com

# The Mutant Epoch™ Android
### Role Playing Game

Player:

Date Rolled:

Experience Factors:

Game Master:

Generation System:

Rank:

Name

**Original Purpose:**

**Pre-Play Caste:**

PC's Team /Faction:

*Portrait or Insignia*

Endurance          /

Strength          DMG Mod:          Range Mod:          %

Agility          MV Mod:

Accuracy          SV Mod:

Intelligence

Willpower

Perception

Appearance

Initiative:

| Protection | DV | Move | Type |
|---|---|---|---|
| Agility Mod: | | | |
| Armor Worn: | | | |
| Helmet Worn: | | | |
| Shield Used: | | | |
| Dodge Skill: | | | |
| Other: | | | |
| Other: | | | |

**Defense Value:**

**Base Strike Value:**

**Movement Rate:** *Base:*          *Armored:*          *Other:*

| Attack Mode | SV | Rate | Range | Damage | Ammo or Uses | Skill pts. | Skill Adds SV Mod. | DMG |
|---|---|---|---|---|---|---|---|---|
| | | | | | | | | |
| | | | | | | | | |
| | | | | | | | | |
| | | | | | | | | |
| | | | | | | | | |

## Android Features

Skeletal Structure:

Tissue Sheathing:

Healing Mode:

Power Source:          Continuous Operation:

Hibernation:          Activation Time:

Sight:

Eye Appearance:

Auditory:          Vocal:          Touch:

Olfactory:          Taste:

Non-Typical Sense:

**CPU in Head**

CPU Type:

INT Bonus:          WIL Bonus:

Processor Trait (PRO):

Firewall (FW):

Data Points (DT):     /

Special Features:

## Skills

Personality:

Gender Pattern:          Amatory Functional? ☐ Yes ☐ No

Manufacturing Date:          Age Appearance:

Weight:          kg   Height:          cm  Skin Color:

Hair:          Hair Type:          Hair Color:

Handed:          Swimming Ability:

Languages Spoken:

Radiation Exposure:

## Equipment          *Starting Pack Code:*

Bounty on PC's Head?:

Debts:

Valuables Carried:



Outland Arts.com

# The Mutant Epoch™
*Role Playing Game*

## Bestial Human

Name

Player:  
Game Master:  
Pre-Play Caste:  

Date Rolled:  
Generation System:  
PC's Faction:  

**Experience Factors:**  **Rank:**

Endurance

Strength — DMG Mod: — Range Mod: %

Agility — MV Mod:

Accuracy — SV Mod:

Intelligence

Willpower

Perception — Initiative:

Appearance

**Base Strike Value:**

*Healing Rate*

| Protection | DV | Move | Type |
|---|---|---|---|
| Agility Mod: | | | |
| Armor Worn: | | | |
| Helmet Worn: | | | |
| Shield Used: | | | |
| Dodge Skill: | | | |
| Other: | | | |
| Other: | | | |

**Defense Value:**

*Portrait or Insignia*

**Movement Rate:** *Base:*  *Armored:*  *Other:*

| Attack Mode | SV | Rate | Range | Damage | Ammo or Uses | Skill pts. | Skill Adds SV Mod. | DMG |
|---|---|---|---|---|---|---|---|---|
| | | | | | | | | |
| | | | | | | | | |
| | | | | | | | | |
| | | | | | | | | |
| | | | | | | | | |
| | | | | | | | | |

## Bestial Details | Skills | Skills or Mutations and Implants

**Personality:**  
**Gender:**  Sexual Orientation:  
**Age:**  Birthday:  
**Weight:** kg **Height:** cm  
**Skin Color:**  Hair:  Eye:  
**Other Features:**

**Handed:**  
**Swimming Ability:**  
**Read & Write?:**  
**Do Math?:**  
**Religion:**  
**Languages Spoken:**

**Diseases or Parasites?:**  
**Cancer?:**  
**Radiation Exposure:**

**Equipment**  *Starting Pack Code:*

Days Rations:  Liters Water:  
Bounty on PC's Head?:  
Debts:  
Valuables Carried:

Outland Arts.com™

# The Mutant Epoch™ CYBORG
*Role Playing Game*

Name

Player:  Game Master:  Pre-Play Caste:

Date Rolled:  Generation System:  PC's Faction:

**Experience Factors:**  **Rank:**

*Healing Rate*

**Endurance**

**Strength**  DMG Mod:  Range Mod:  %

**Agility**  MV Mod:

**Accuracy**  SV Mod:

**Intelligence**

**Willpower**

**Perception**  Initiative:

**Appearance**

**Base Strike Value:**

| Protection | DV | Move | Type |
|---|---|---|---|
| Agility Mod: | | | |
| Armor Worn: | | | |
| Helmet Worn: | | | |
| Shield Used: | | | |
| Dodge Skill: | | | |
| Other: | | | |
| Other: | | | |

**Defense Value:**

*Portrait or Insignia*

**Movement Rate:** *Base:*  *Armored:*  *Other:*

| Attack Mode | SV | Rate | Range | Damage | Ammo or Uses | Skill pts. | Skill Adds SV Mod. | DMG |
|---|---|---|---|---|---|---|---|---|
| | | | | | | | | |

## Implants

## Skills

Personality:
Gender:  Sexual Orientation:
Age:  Birthday:
Weight:  kg  Height:  cm
Skin Color:  Hair:  Eye:
Other Features:

Handed:
Swimming Ability:
Read & Write?:
Do Math?:
Religion:
Languages Spoken:

Diseases or Parasites?:
Cancer?:
Radiation Exposure:

**Equipment**  *Starting Pack Code:*

Days Rations:  Liters Water:
Bounty on PC's Head?:
Debts:
Valuables Carried:



Outland Arts™ .com

# The Mutant Epoch™ — Digital-Being

*Role Playing Game*

**Player:**    **Game Master:**    **Digital Being Type:**    **Name**

**Date Rolled:**    **Generation System:**    **Chosen Pre-Play Caste:**

**Experience Factors:**    **Rank:**    **PC's Team /Faction:**

**Data** *DT*    /

**Data points recover at a rate of 1 per hour, per rank, unless digital-being was reduced to zero or less DT*

**Processor** *PRO*    Hacking HK Mod:

**Shielding** *SH*    FW Mod:  → **Firewall** *FW:*

**Transfer** *TRA*

**Intelligence** *INT*

**Willpower** *WIL*

**Perception** *PER*    **Initiative:**

**Appearance** *APP*

### Persona:

Random Flashback*: (no.____)

Sex in Past Life*:
Current Gender ID*:
Life Recalled?*:
Personality:
Current Container or Body**:

**If Applicable*
*** It's best to record this on a separate sheet of paper or appropriate character sheet as this DB is likely to 'upgrade' to a new vessel during extended game play.*

*Portrait or Insignia*

| Physical Attack Modes | SV | Rate | Range | Damage | Ammo or Uses | Skill pts. | Skill Adds SV Mod. | DMG |
|---|---|---|---|---|---|---|---|---|
| **Shock Generation** | (Base 01-70) | 1 | (3m per rank) | (base 1d10 DMG, +1 per rank) | (3 shocks per day per rank) | | (Weapon Expert Skill Eligible!) | |

| Digital Attack Modes | Hack (HK) | Rate | Range | Damage | Ammo or Uses |
|---|---|---|---|---|---|
| **Hacking** | (Base 01-50) | 1 | (Usually contact) | (1d10 DT pts DMG inflicted/rank) | (1 hack attempt per day per rank) |

## Applications      Skills

## Additional Notes about this Digital Being or Current Container or Body



Outland Arts.com

# The Mutant Epoch™ Grafter
*Role Playing Game*

Name

| | | |
|---|---|---|
| Player: | Game Master: | Pre-Play Caste: |
| Date Rolled: | Generation System: | PC's Faction: |

Experience Factors:    Rank:

Endurance

Strength    DMG Mod:    Range Mod:    %

Agility    MV Mod:

Accuracy    SV Mod:

Intelligence

Willpower

Perception    Initiative:

Appearance

Healing Rate

| Protection | DV | Move | Type |
|---|---|---|---|
| Agility Mod: | | | |
| Armor Worn: | | | |
| Helmet Worn: | | | |
| Shield Used: | | | |
| Dodge Skill: | | | |
| Other: | | | |
| Other: | | | |

Defense Value:

*Portrait or Insignia*

Base Strike Value:

Movement Rate: *Base:*    *Armored:*    *Other:*

| Attack Mode | SV | Rate | Range | Damage | Ammo or Uses | Skill pts. | Skill Adds SV Mod. | DMG |
|---|---|---|---|---|---|---|---|---|
| | | | | | | | | |
| | | | | | | | | |
| | | | | | | | | |
| | | | | | | | | |
| | | | | | | | | |

## Grafter Parts

## Skills, Mutations and Implants

Personality:

Gender:    Sexual Orientation:

Age:    Birthday:

Weight:    kg    Height:    cm

Skin Color:    Hair:    Eye:

Other Features:

Handed:

Swimming Ability:

Read & Write?:

Do Math?:

Religion:

Languages Spoken:

Diseases or Parasites?:

Cancer?:

Radiation Exposure:

Equipment    *Starting Pack Code:*

Days Rations:    Liters Water:

Bounty on PC's Head?:

Debts:

Valuables Carried:



Official character sheet TME-Grafter-1a    *Character's history, non-carried possessions, property, henchmen, pets, list of vanquished foes, etc. on back....*

Outland Arts.com

# The Mutant Epoch™
## Role Playing Game

## Mutorg

Name

| Player: | Game Master: | Pre-Play Caste: |
|---|---|---|
| Date Rolled: | Generation System: | PC's Faction: |

**Experience Factors:**

**Rank:**

Endurance

*Healing Rate*

| Strength | DMG Mod: | Range Mod: | % |
|---|---|---|---|
| Agility | MV Mod: | | |
| Accuracy | SV Mod: | | |

Intelligence

Willpower

Perception

Appearance

**Initiative:**

| Protection | DV | Move | Type |
|---|---|---|---|
| Agility Mod: | | | |
| Armor Worn: | | | |
| Helmet Worn: | | | |
| Shield Used: | | | |
| Dodge Skill: | | | |
| Other: | | | |
| Other: | | | |

**Defense Value:**

*Portrait or Insignia*

**Base Strike Value:**

**Movement Rate:** *Base:*    *Armored:*    *Other:*

| Attack Mode | SV | Rate | Range | Damage | Ammo or Uses | Skill pts. | Skill Adds SV Mod. | DMG |
|---|---|---|---|---|---|---|---|---|
| | | | | | | | | |
| | | | | | | | | |
| | | | | | | | | |
| | | | | | | | | |
| | | | | | | | | |
| | | | | | | | | |

## Mutations          Cybernetic Implants          Skills

**Personality:**

| Gender: | Sexual Orientation: |
|---|---|
| Age: | Birthday: |
| Weight:  kg | Height:  cm |
| Skin Color: | Hair:  Eye: |

Other Features:

Handed:

Swimming Ability:

Read & Write?:

Do Math?:

Religion:

Languages Spoken:

Diseases or Parasites?:

Cancer?:

Radiation Exposure:

**Equipment**    *Starting Pack Code:*

Days Rations:    Liters Water:

Bounty on PC's Head?:

Debts:

Valuables Carried:



Outland Arts™ .com

# The Mutant Epoch™ Nanoborg
*Role Playing Game*

Name

Player:  Game Master:  Pre-Play Caste:

Date Rolled:  Generation System:  PC's Faction:

**Experience Factors:**  **Rank:**

**Endurance**

Healing Rate

**Strength** — DMG Mod:  Range Mod:  %

**Agility** — MV Mod:

**Accuracy** — SV Mod:

**Intelligence**

**Willpower**

**Perception**  Initiative:

**Appearance**

**Base Strike Value:**

| Protection | DV | Move | Type |
|---|---|---|---|
| Agility Mod: | | | |
| Armor Worn: | | | |
| Helmet Worn: | | | |
| Shield Used: | | | |
| Dodge Skill: | | | |
| Other: | | | |
| Other: | | | |

**Defense Value:**

*Portrait or Insignia*

**Movement Rate**: *Base:*  *Armored:*  *Other:*

| Attack Mode | SV | Rate | Range | Damage | Ammo or Uses | Skill pts. | Skill Adds SV Mod. | DMG |
|---|---|---|---|---|---|---|---|---|
| | | | | | | | | |
| | | | | | | | | |
| | | | | | | | | |
| | | | | | | | | |
| | | | | | | | | |
| | | | | | | | | |

## Nanoborg Skills

## Standard Skills

Personality:

Gender:  Sexual Orientation:

Age:  Birthday:

Weight:  kg  Height:  cm

Skin Color:  Hair:  Eye:

Other Features:

Handed:

Swimming Ability:

Read & Write?:

Do Math?:

Religion:

Languages Spoken:

Diseases or Parasites?:

Cancer?:

Radiation Exposure:

**Equipment**  *Starting Pack Code:*

Days Rations:  Liters Water:

Bounty on PC's Head?:

Debts:

Valuables Carried:

# The Mutant Epoch™ Parasite
*Role Playing Game*

Player: ___  Game Master: ___

Name

Date Rolled: ___  Generation System: ___  Current Host Body: ___

Experience Factors: ___  Rank: ___  Pre-Play Caste: ___  PC's Faction: ___

Healing Rate

Endurance ___

Strength ___  DMG Mod: ___  Range Mod: ___ %

Agility ___  MV Mod: ___

Accuracy ___  SV Mod: ___

Intelligence ___

Willpower ___

Perception ___  Initiative: ___

Appearance ___

Base Strike Value: ___

| Protection | DV | Move | Type |
|---|---|---|---|
| Agility Mod: | | | |
| Armor Worn: | | | |
| Helmet Worn: | | | |
| Shield Used: | | | |
| Dodge Skill: | | | |
| Other: | | | |
| Other: | | | |

Defense Value: ___

*Portrait or Insignia*

Movement Rate: *Base:* ___  *Armored:* ___  *Other:* ___

| Attack Mode | SV | Rate | Range | Damage | Ammo or Uses | Skill pts. | Skill Adds SV Mod. | DMG |
|---|---|---|---|---|---|---|---|---|
| | | | | | | | | |
| | | | | | | | | |
| | | | | | | | | |
| | | | | | | | | |
| | | | | | | | | |

## Parasite Properties

Size: ___  kg added: ___  Apparel: ___

Adhesion to Host Type: ___  Concealment HC Mod.: ___

Neurological Tendrils: Digestive and Waste Tubes: ___

Detached Locomotion: ___

Extra Appendages: ___

## Mutations

## Skills

Personality: ___  Sexual Orientation: ___

Gender: ___  Reproductive Capacity: ___

Age: ___  Birthday: ___

Weight: ___ kg  Height: ___ cm

Skin Color: ___  Hair: ___  Eye: ___

Other Features: ___

Handed: ___

Swimming Ability: ___

Read & Write?: ___

Do Math?: ___

Religion: ___

Languages Spoken: ___

Diseases or Parasites?: ___

Cancer?: ___

Radiation Exposure: ___

## Equipment

Days Rations: ___  Liters Water: ___

Bounty on PC's Head?: ___

Debts: ___

Valuables Carried: ___

Outland Arts .com

# The Mutant Epoch™ Plantoid
### Role Playing Game

Player: ______________________  Game Master: ______________________

**Name**

**Plantoid Type:** ______________________

Date Rolled: ______________________  Generation System: ______________________

**Base Plant (if known):** ______________________

**Pre-Play Caste:** ______________________

**PC's Faction:** ______________________

**Experience Factors:** ______________________  **Rank:** ______________________

*Healing Rate*

**Endurance** ______________ / ______________

| | | | | | |
|---|---|---|---|---|---|
| **Strength** | *DMG Mod:* | *Range Mod:* % | **Protection** | **DV** | **Move** | **Type** |

**Strength** — *DMG Mod:* — *Range Mod:* %

**Agility** — *MV Mod:*

**Accuracy** — *SV Mod:*

**Intelligence**

**Willpower**

**Perception** — Initiative:

**Appearance**

| Protection | DV | Move | Type |
|---|---|---|---|
| Agility Mod: | | | |
| Armor Worn: | | | |
| Helmet Worn: | | | |
| Shield Used: | | | |
| Dodge Skill: | | | |
| Other: | | | |
| Other: | | | |

**Defense Value:**

**Base Strike Value:**

*Portrait or Insignia*

**Movement Rate:** *Base:* ______________  *Armored:* ______________  *Other:* ______________

| Attack Mode | SV | Rate | Range | Damage | Ammo or Uses | Skill pts. | Skill Adds SV Mod. | DMG |
|---|---|---|---|---|---|---|---|---|
| *Manipulator Limbs* | | | | | | | | |
| | | | | | | | | |
| | | | | | | | | |
| | | | | | | | | |
| | | | | | | | | |
| | | | | | | | | |
| | | | | | | | | |

## Plantoid Mutations

## Skills, Implants, and Miscellaneous

NOTE: +4 Skill points in Conceal Self, and +2 Concealed Movement when hidden among simialar vegeation.

**Personality:**

Gender: ______________  Plantoid Reproduction: ______________

Age: ______  Lifespan: ______  Birthday: ______

Yearly Growth: + ____ cm  + ____ kg  Max Height: ____ cm

Weight: ______ kg  Height: ______ cm

Skin Color: ______  Hair: ______  Eye: ______

Other Features: ______________

Handed: ______________

Swimming Ability: ______________

Read & Write?: ______  Do Math?: ______

Religion: ______________

Languages Spoken: ______________

Diseases or Parasites?: ______________

Cancer?: ______________

Radiation Exposure: ______________

**Equipment**  *Starting Pack Code:* ______

Days Rations: ______  Liters Water: ______

Origin Story: ______________

Bounty on PC's Head?: ______________

Debts: ______________

Valuables Carried: ______________

www.mutantepoch.com

Outland Arts.com



Official character sheet TME-Plantoid-1a   *Character's history, non-carried possessions, property, henchmen, pets, list of vanquished foes, etc. on back....*

# The Mutant Epoch™ Role Playing Game — Rebuilt

Name:

Player: | Game Master: | Pre-Play Caste:

Date Rolled: | Generation System: | PC's Faction:

**Experience Factors:** | **Rank:**

| | | | | | Healing Rate |

**Endurance** /

**Strength** — DMG Mod: — Range Mod: %

**Agility** — MV Mod:

**Accuracy** — SV Mod:

**Intelligence**

**Willpower**

**Perception** — Initiative:

**Appearance**

**Base Strike Value:**

| Protection | DV | Move | Type |
|---|---|---|---|
| Agility Mod: | | | |
| Armor Worn: | | | |
| Helmet Worn: | | | |
| Shield Used: | | | |
| Dodge Skill: | | | |
| Other: | | | |
| Other: | | | |

**Defense Value:**

*Portrait or Insignia*

**Movement Rate:** *Base:* — *Armored:* — *Other:*

| Attack Mode | SV | Rate | Range | Damage | Ammo or Uses | Skill pts. | Skill Adds SV Mod. | DMG |
|---|---|---|---|---|---|---|---|---|
| | | | | | | | | |
| | | | | | | | | |
| | | | | | | | | |
| | | | | | | | | |
| | | | | | | | | |

## Rebuilt Features | Skills | Possible Mutations & Extras

PC's Demise:

Who assembled PC?:

PC's Suffering:

Vision Mode:

Speech Mode:

Auditory Mode:

Reproductive Capacity:

Additional Features:

Left Leg:

Right leg:

Rebuilt Arms:

Personality:

Gender: | Sexual Orientation:

Age: | Birthday:

Weight: kg | Height: cm

Skin Color: | Hair: | Eye:

Other Features:

Handed: | Swimming Ability:

Read & Write?: | Do Math?:

Religion:

Languages Spoken:

Diseases or Parasites?:

Cancer?: | Radiation Exposure:

**Equipment** — Starting Pack Code:

Days Rations: | Liters Water:

Bounty on PC's Head?:

Debts: | Valuables Carried:

# The Mutant Epoch™ — *Unique Robot*

Role Playing Game

Player:                          Game Master:
Date Rolled:            Generation System:            Chosen Pre-Play Caste:
Experience Factors:            Rank:            PC's Team /Faction:

Name

*Portrait or Insignia*

**Endurance**            /

| | | | | |
|---|---|---|---|---|
| **Strength** — DMG Mod: — Range Mod: % | **Protection** | **DV** | **Move** | **Type** |
| **Agility** — MV Mod: → | Agility Mod: | | | |
| **Accuracy** — SV Mod: | Armor Worn: | | | |
| **Intelligence** | Helmet Worn: | | | |
| **Willpower** | Shield Used: | | | |
| **Perception** | Dodge Skill: | | | |
| **Appearance** | Other: | | | |
| | Other: | | | |

Initiative:

Defense Value:

**Base Strike Value:**

**Movement Rate**: Base:            Armored:            Other:

| Attack Mode | SV | Rate | Range | Damage | Ammo or Uses | Skill pts. | Skill Adds SV Mod. | DMG |
|---|---|---|---|---|---|---|---|---|
| **Human-like Arm** | | | | | | | | |
| | | | | | | | | |
| | | | | | | | | |
| | | | | | | | | |
| | | | | | | | | |
| | | | | | | | | |
| | | | | | | | | |

## Robot Features

Chassis/Torso:

Cladding:

Primary Human-like Robotic Arm:

Secondary Robotic Arm:

Locomotion Mode:

Power Source:            Continuous Operation:
Hibernation:            Activation Time:
Primary Optics:
Other Optics:

Comms:
Voice:
Hearing:
Olfactory:
Other Senses:

## Head and CPU

**Head**

**Head Type**:
(DV      / END mod.
Details:
Can wear helmet? ☐ Yes ☐ No

**CPU**

**CPU Type**:
Processor Trait (PRO):
Firewall (FW):
Data Points (DT):   /

### Additional Parts and any Cybernetic Parts

## Skills

### Special Programs

---

Personality:            Gender ID (if any):
Who made this robot?:
Weight:            kg      Height:            cm
Handed:            Swimming Ability:
Languages Spoken:

Bounty on PC's Head?:            Debts:
Valuables Carried:

Radiation Exposure:

**Equipment**      *Starting Pack Code:*

Outland Arts™ .com

# The Mutant Epoch™ Vat-Brain
*Role Playing Game*

Player:    Game Master:    Character Name    Pre-Play Caste:

Date Rolled:    Generation System:    PC's Faction:

**Brain Experience Factors:**    **Brain Rank:**    **Chassis or Body Experience Factors:**    **Chassis or Body Rank:**

**Chassis/Body Endurance**
**Vat Endurance**

*Healing Rate*

**Strength***    DMG Mod:    Range Mod:    %

**Agility**    MV Mod:

**Accuracy**    SV Mod:

**Intelligence**

**Willpower**

**Perception**    **Initiative:**

**Appearance**

**Base Strength is ½ all limbs combined*

**Base Strike Value:**

| Protection | DV | Move | Type |
|---|---|---|---|
| Agility Mod: | | | |
| Armor Worn: | | | |
| Helmet Worn: | | | |
| Shield Used: | | | |
| Dodge Skill: | | | |
| Other: | | | |
| Other: | | | |

**Defense Value**:**

*Portrait or Insignia*

**Movement Rate:** Base:    Armored:    Other:

*** Chassis or Body DV, as all attacks are assumed to be against the PC's torso or vehicle.*

| Attack Mode | SV | Rate | Range | Damage | Ammo or Uses | Skill pts. | Skill Adds SV Mod. | DMG |
|---|---|---|---|---|---|---|---|---|
| | | | | | | | | |
| | | | | | | | | |
| | | | | | | | | |
| | | | | | | | | |
| | | | | | | | | |

## Vat-Brain Features

Brain Type:    Brain Endurance:    Brain Stat Bonuses: INT___ WIL___ PER___

Can Turn Head? ☐ Yes ☐ No    Vat Type:    Vat DV:    Vat END: /

Vat Weight:   *kg* Vat Height:   *cm* Vat Fluid Color:

Vat Power Supply:    Duration:    Cable? ☐ Yes ☐ No

Power Details:

Vat Special Defenses?:

**Vat's Sensory Parts**

Visual 1:

Visual 2:

Auditory Sensor:

Olfactory Sensor:

Taste Sensor:

Mask or Facial Focus?:

Vat's Additional Organic Parts:

Vat Unique Features:

## Chassis/Body Details, Skills and any Implants or Mutations

Vat's Chassis or Donor Body:

Weight:    Height:    Age:

Endurance:

Strength: ___ Agility ___ Appearance (of body) ___

Defense Value:    Movement:

Other Details:

Personality:    Sexual Orientation:

Gender:    Reproduction:

Age:    Birthday:

Total Weight:   *kg* Total Height:   *cm*

Skin Color:    Hair:    Eye:

Handed:    Swimming Ability:

Read & Write?:    Do Math?:

Religion:

Languages Spoken:

Diseases or Parasites?:    Cancer?:

Radiation Exposure:

**Equipment**    *Starting Pack Code:*

Origin Story:

Days Rations:    Liters Water:

Bounty on PC's Head?:   Debts:

Valuables Carried:

**Outland Arts**.com

# Index

Also Available are Pay What You Want PDFs
One Day Digs and Wasteland Treasure Tables
PAY WHAT YOU WANT
3 d100 Tables: General Loot, Humanoids and Old War Zone discoveries
Wasteland Treasures: 1
By William McAusland
One Day Digs 1 & 2
TWO INTRO PDF ADVENTURES ONE GREAT PRICE!
Blood for Bellridge
By Brandon Goeringer
DOUBLE F
Feast of Freaks
By Brandon Goeringer
One Day Digs 3 & 4
TWO INTRO PDF ADVENTURES ONE GREAT PRICE!
PAY WHAT YOU WANT
Beneath the Spire
By Brandon Goeringer
DOUBLE
Tunnels & Skulls
By Brandon Goeringer
PRICE: PAY WHAT YOU WANT
One Day Dig: 7
The Ascent
By Timothy Berriault
PAY WHAT YOU WANT
PRICE: PAY WHAT YOU WANT
One Day Dig: 6
Hunt in the Dark
By Giulio Iannarella
PRICE: PAY WHAT YOU WANT
One Day Dig: 5
Lilac Towers
By Danny Seedhouse
PAY WHAT YOU WANT
One Day Dig: 8
Baby Bupu
By Tim Schuster
PAY WHAT YOU WANT
One Day Dig: 9
Wizard OF THE Wastes
By Rey Rodriguez
PAY WHAT YOU WANT
For use with
THE MUTANT EPOCH
TABLETOP ADVENTURE ROLE-PLAYING GAME
For use with
THE MUTANT EPOCH
TABLETOP ADVENTURE ROLE-PLAYING GAME
OUTLAND SYSTEM
PDF

www.ingramcontent.com/pod-product-compliance
Lightning Source LLC
Chambersburg PA
CBHW081323090726
47907CB00010B/2348